This Rough Magic

This Rough Magic

Mercedes Lackey
Eric Flint
Dave Freer

THIS ROUGH MAGIC

Copyright © 2003 by Mercedes Lackey, Eric Flint & Dave Freer

A Baen Books Original

Baen Publishing Enterprises
P.O. Box 1403
Riverdale, NY 10471
www.baen.com

ISBN: 0-7434-7149-0

Cover art by Larry Dixon

First printing, December 2003

Library of Congress Cataloging-in-Publication Data

Lackey, Mercedes.
 This rough magic / Mercedes Lackey, Eric Flint, Dave Freer.
   p. cm.
"A Baen Books original."
 ISBN 0-7434-7149-0
 1. Venice (Italy)--Fiction. I. Flint, Eric. II. Freer, Dave. III. Title.

PS3562.A246T47 2003
813'.54--dc22

2003019966

Distributed by Simon & Schuster
1230 Avenue of the Americas
New York, NY 10020

Production by Windhaven Press, Auburn, NH
Printed in the United States of America

10   9   8   7   6   5   4   3   2   1

**To Bishop Bartolomé de las Casas
(1474–1566 A.D.)**

Corfu

Berm

North
Postern

Little
Arsenal

S
p
i
a
n
a
d
a

The
Causeway

South
Postern

Castel a Te

itadel

Where The Galleys
Beached

Mud
Shingle

orando's
ouse

Cliffs

Castel
a Mar

Umberto &
& Maria's
Home

Cliff

t. Agatha's
Chapel

Poplar

Cave
Entrance

Goddess Temple
Cave

Benito's
Climb

Prologue
Autumn, 1538 A.D.

ROME

Eneko Lopez was not the sort of man to let mere discomfort of the body come between him and his God. Or between him and the work he believed God intended him to do. The Basque ignored exhaustion and hunger. He existed on inner fires anyway, and the fires of his spirit burned hot and bright. Some of that showed in the eagle eyes looking intently at the chalice on the altar. The low-burned candles and the fact that several of the other priests had fainted from exhaustion, cold or hunger, bore mute testimony to the fact that the ceremony had gone on for many hours. Without looking away from the chalice upon which their energies were focused, Eneko could pick up the voices of his companions, still joined in prayer. There was Diego's baritone; Father Pierre's deeper bass; Francis's gravelly Frankish; the voices of a brotherhood united in faith against the darkness.

At last the wine in the chalice stirred. The surface became misty, and an image began to form. Craggy-edged, foam-fringed. A mountain . . .

The air in the chapel became scented with myrtle and lemon-blossom. Then came a sound, the wistful, ethereal notes of panpipes. There was something inhuman about that playing, although Eneko could not precisely put his finger on it. It was a melancholy tune, poignant, *old*; music of rocks and streams, music that seemed as old as the mountains themselves.

There was a thump. Yet another priest in the invocation circle had fallen, and the circle was broken again.

So was the vision. Eneko sighed, and began to lead the others in the dismissal of the wards.

"My knees are numb," said Father Francis, rubbing them. "The floors in Roman chapels are somehow harder than the ones in Aquitaine ever were."

"Or Venetian floors," said Pierre, shaking his head. "Only your knees numb? I think I am without blood or warmth from the chest down."

3

"We came close," Eneko said glumly. "I still have no idea where the vision is pointing to, though."

Father Pierre rubbed his cold hands. "You are certain this is where Chernobog is turning his attentions next?"

"Certain as can be, under the circumstances. Chernobog—or some other demonic creature. Great magical forces leave such traces."

"But where is it?" asked Diego, rubbing his back wearily. "Somewhere in the Mediterranean, an island, that much is clear. Probably in the vicinity of Greece or the Balkans. But *which*? There are a multitude."

Eneko shrugged. "I don't know. But it is an old place, full of crude and elemental powers, a repository of great strength, and . . ."

"And what?"

"And it does not love us," Eneko said, with a kind of grim certainty.

"It did not feel evil," commented Francis. "I would have thought an ally of Chernobog must be corrupted and polluted by the blackness."

"Francis, the enemy of my enemy is not always my friend, even if we have common cause."

"We should ally, Eneko," said Francis firmly. "Or at least not waste our strength against each other. After all, we face a common enemy."

Eneko shrugged again. "Perhaps. But it is not always that simple or that wise. Well, let us talk to the Grand Metropolitan and tell him what little we know."

VILNA

Count Kazimierz Mindaug, chief adviser and counselor to Grand Duke Jagiellon of Lithuania, scratched himself. Lice were one of the smaller hazards and discomforts of his position. To be honest, he scarcely noticed them. The Grand Duke tended to make other problems pale into insignificance.

"If a direct attack on Venice is out of the question now, given our recent defeat there," he said, calmly, "then why don't we just hamstring them? We can paralyze their trade. The Mediterranean can still be ours. We can still draw the enemy into a war on a second front."

The terrible scar on Jagiellon's forehead pulsed; it looked like an ugly, purple worm half-embedded in his skin. A throbbing worm. "The Holy Roman Emperor looks for our hand in everything now, since the disaster in Venice. Charles Fredrik would ally openly with the accursed Venetians. Their combined fleets would crush our own, even in the Black Sea."

Count Mindaug nodded his head. "True. But what if our hand was not shown? What if those who at least appear to oppose us, took action against Venice and her interests?"

The Grand Duke's inhuman eyes glowed for just a moment, as the idea caught his interest. Then he shook his head. "The Emperor will still see our hand in anything."

Count Mindaug smiled, revealing filed teeth. "Of course he will. But he cannot act against his allies. He cannot be seen to be partisan, not in a matter that appears to be a mere squabble between Venice and her commercial rivals, especially when those rivals are parties with whom the Empire has either a treaty or a very uneasy relationship."

Jagiellon raised his heavy brows. "Ah. Aquitaine," he said. "I have hopes of the Norse; my plans move apace there. But it will take a little while before their fleets ravage the north. But Aquitaine, even with Genoa's assistance, cannot bottle up the Venetian fleet."

Mindaug flashed those filed teeth again. "But they could blockade the pillars of Hercules. And if the Aragonese join them, and perhaps the Barbary pirates too . . . they will easily prevent the Venetian Atlantic fleet from returning. And let us not forget that you now hold Byzantium's emperor in thrall."

Jagiellon shook his head. "It is not thralldom yet. Let us just say we know of certain vices which even the Greeks will not tolerate. We wield a certain amount of influence, yes."

"Enough to send him to attempt to regain some of his lost territory?" asked Mindaug, shrewdly.

After a moment, Jagiellon nodded. "Probably. The Golden Horn or Negroponte?"

Mindaug smiled, shark-like. "Neither, my Lord. Well, not directly. If Byzantium reduces the ability of the Venetian fleet to extract vengeance on Constantinople, and on their shipping, then the Golden Horn, Negroponte, and even Zante are theirs for the taking.

Even the jewel, Crete. But while the Venetians have the freedom of the Mediterranean, Alexius dares not seize Venetian property. And one island is the key to the Adriatic. To bottling the Venetians into a little corner. Corfu. The Byzantines attack and capture Corfu in alliance with Emeric of Hungary. Corfu is the key to the Adriatic. With it captured . . . Venice's traders die."

The scar on Jagiellon's head pulsed again. "Corfu," he mused, speaking the syllables slowly. "But Emeric is not a thrall of mine, not yet. He seeks to challenge me. I will devour him, in time."

Jagiellon's metal eyes looked pointedly at the count. "And anyone else who tries to become my rival, rather than my ally."

Cold sweat beaded under Count Mindaug's heavy robes. Of course he had ambitions. To be part of this court you had to have them. It was a dog-eat-dog environment. But he knew just how well Grand Duke Jagiellon defended his position. He knew—or at least he thought he knew—just what Jagiellon had ventured into, and what had happened to him.

Kazimierz Mindaug was no mean sorcerer himself. You had to be to survive in the quest for power in Lithuania. He had experimented with dangerous rites—very dangerous—but there were some things he had held back from. Jagiellon, he guessed, had not. A demon now lurked behind those metallic, all-black eyes. The arrogant prince who had thought to summon and use Chernobog was now the demon's slave. The prey had swallowed the predator.

The Count cleared his throat, trying to ease the nervousness. "Our spies have reported that Emeric has been on secret expeditions down in the southern Balkans, beginning in the spring. It is a certainty that he must be looking at expansion there. A judicious hint or two to the Byzantines, and he would not even smell our hand. Corfu would offer him a safe staging post for attacks on the hinterland."

The Count smiled nastily. "After all, the Balkans can distract Charles Fredrik as well as that mess of principalities called Italy. He would be obliged to stop Emeric of Hungary. And if the Hungarians clash with the Holy Roman Empire over Corfu . . . both of our enemies may be weakened, while we remain strong."

Jagiellon smiled. It was not a pleasant sight. There were several rotten stumps in among the huge Lithuanian's teeth. "And Valdosta may be sent there. The younger one if not the elder. I do not allow a quest for vengeance to impede my plans; only a fool concentrates on a personal vendetta when larger affairs are unresolved. But this time I could perhaps combine both. Good. I will send my new errand-boy to Constantinople."

He clapped his meaty hands. A frightened-looking slave appeared almost instantly. "Have the new man sent to me. See that horses are made ready. Captain Tcherklas must also be called. He is to accompany my servant to Odessa. The servant will need five hundred ducats, and will require suitable clothes for the imperial court in Constantinople."

The slave bowed and left at a run. He could not answer. He had no tongue any more. Jagiellon allowed his servants to retain only those portions of themselves as were useful.

"Corfu. It was a powerful place of an old faith, once," said Jagiellon speculatively.

The Count said nothing. That was wisdom. His own plotting was subtle, and the less he even thought about it . . .

The demon Chernobog could pick up thoughts. And if he was correct, then what the Black Brain knew, Jagiellon knew also. And vice versa, of course. There was a chance that events might favor his progress and his ambitions, but if they did not, he needed to keep his hands clean.

Relatively.

"Still, those days are long gone now." Jagiellon nodded to the count. "We will take these steps. We will find old shrines. The stones will have some power. We will rededicate them to our ends."

The slave returned, escorting a blond and once handsome man. Now Caesare Aldanto was gaunt. His fine golden hair hung limp about his face, matted with filth and vomit. He had plainly, by the smell, soiled himself, not just once, but often. And, by those empty eyes, this matter was of no concern to him.

Jagiellon did not seem to notice the smell, as he gave detailed, precise instructions. Caesare was to take himself to Constantinople. Letters of introduction and certain tokens of the emperor's latest pastime, were to be presented to the Emperor Alexius VI. The tokens fetched by the tongueless servant were of such a nature as to make even Mindaug blanch for a moment. Caesare did not even look discomfited when he was told to participate if the emperor so desired. He didn't even blink.

"And you'd better have him cleaned up," said Count Mindaug,

when Jagiellon had finished. "He'll be noticed, else, and I doubt he'd get as far as the Greek emperor's flunkies in the condition he's in now, much less the emperor himself. He stinks."

The solid black eyes that now filled Jagiellon's sockets stared at the count. "He does?"

Jagiellon turned to Caesare. "You will see to that also, then."

Caesare nodded. Like his walk, his nod had a slightly jerky, controlled-puppet air about it. But just for a moment a madness showed in those blank eyes, a desperate, sad madness. Then that, too, was gone.

Jagiellon waved dismissively. "Go. See that Emperor Alexius engages in talks on military action with Emeric. Corfu must fall." He turned to the tongueless slave. "Has my new shaman arrived?"

The slave shook his head, fearfully. He was very efficient. Well-educated. Once he had been a prince.

"Very well," Jagiellon rumbled, only a little displeased. "Bring him to me when he appears. And see to this one. Make him fit for an emperor's company."

Count Mindaug scratched again as the servant nodded and hurried out. Lice were a small price to pay for power.

ROME

"I've gotten word from the Grand Metropolitan," the Emperor began abruptly, the moment Baron Trolliger sat down in Charles Fredrik's small audience chamber. The chamber was even smaller than the one the Holy Roman Emperor preferred in his palace in Mainz. Here in Rome, which he was visiting incognito, the Emperor had rented a minor and secluded mansion for the duration of his stay.

The servant had ushered Trolliger to a comfortable divan positioned at an angle to the Emperor's own chair. A goblet of wine had been poured for the baron, and was resting on a small table next to him. The Emperor had a goblet in hand already, but Trolliger saw that it was as yet untouched.

"Something is stirring in the Greek isles, or the Balkans," Charles Fredrik continued. "Something dark and foul. So, at least, he's being told by Eneko Lopez. By itself, the Metropolitan might think that was simply Lopez's well-known zeal at work—but his own scryers seem to agree."

"Jagiellon?"

The Emperor's heavy shoulders moved in a shrug. "Impossible to tell. Jagiellon is a likelihood, of course. Any time something dark and foul begins to move, the Grand Duke of Lithuania is probably involved. But he'll be licking his wounds still, I'd think, after the hammering he took in Venice recently—and there's always the King of Hungary to consider."

Baron Trolliger took a sip of his wine; then, rubbed his lips with the back of his hand. When the hand moved away, a slight sneer remained.

"Young Emeric? He's a puppy. A vile and vicious one, to be sure, but a puppy nonetheless. The kind of arrogant too-smart-for-his-own-good king who'll always make overly complex plans that come apart at the seams. And then his subordinates will be blamed for it, which allows the twit to come up with a new grandiose scheme."

"Get blamed—and pay the price," agreed Charles Fredrik. "Still, I think you're dismissing Emeric too lightly. Don't forget that he's got his aunt lurking in the shadows."

Trolliger's sneer shifted into a dark scowl. "'Aunt'? I think she's his great-great-aunt, actually. If she's that young. There is something purely unnatural about that woman's lifespan—and her youthful beauty, if all reports are to be believed."

"That's my point. Elizabeth, Countess Bartholdy, traffics with very dark powers. Perhaps even the darkest. Do not underestimate her, Hans."

Trolliger inclined his head. "True enough. Still, Your Majesty, I don't see what we can do at the moment. Not with such vague information to go on."

"Neither do I. I simply wanted to alert you, because . . ."

His voice trailed off, and Trolliger winced.

"Venice again," he muttered. "I'd hoped to return with you to Mainz."

Charles Fredrik smiled sympathetically. "The Italians aren't *that* bad, Hans." A bit hastily—before the baron could respond with the inevitable: *yes, they are!*—the Emperor added: "The wine's excellent, and so is the climate, as long as you stay out of the malarial areas. And I think you'd do better to set up in Ferrara, anyway."

That mollified Trolliger, a bit. "Ferrara. Ah. Well, yes. Enrico Dell'este is almost as level-headed as a German, so long as he leaves aside any insane Italian vendettas."

The Emperor shrugged. "How many vendettas could he still be nursing? Now that he's handed Sforza the worst defeat in his career, and has his two grandsons back?"

"True enough. And I agree that Ferrara would make a better place from which I could observe whatever developments take place. Venice! That city is a conspirator's madhouse. At least the Duke of Ferrara will see to it that my identity remains a secret."

Trolliger made a last attempt to evade the prospect of miserable months spent in Italy. "Still, perhaps Manfred—"

But the Emperor was already shaking his head, smiling at the baron's effort. "Not a chance, Hans. You know I need to send Manfred and Erik off to deal with this Swedish mess. Besides, what I need here in Italy, for the moment, is an *observer.*"

The baron grimaced. He could hardly argue the point, after all. The notion that rambunctious young Prince Manfred—even restrained by his keeper Erik Hakkonsen—would ever simply act as an "observer" was . . .

Ludicrous.

"I hate Italy," he muttered. "I'd hate it even if it wasn't inhabited by Italians."

KINGDOM OF HUNGARY, NEAR THE CARPATHIAN MOUNTAINS

Elizabeth, Countess Bartholdy, laughed musically. She looked like a woman who would have a musical laugh; in fact, she looked like a woman who never did, or had, anything without grace, charm, and beauty. Yet somehow, underneath all that beauty, there was . . . something else. Something old, something hungry, something that occasionally looked out of her eyes, and when it did, whoever was facing its regard generally was not seen again.

"My dear Crocell! Jagiellon, or to give it its true name, Chernobog, is an expansionist. And, compared to the power into whose territory I will inveigle him, a young upstart." She smiled, wisely, a little slyly. "Corfu is one of the old magic places. Very old, very wise, very—other."

The man standing next to her took his eyes away from the thing in the glass jar. "A risky game you're playing, Elizabeth. Chernobog is mighty, and the powers on Corfu are, as you say, very old." His middle-aged face creased into a slight smile. "'Very old' often means 'weary'—even for such as me. Those ancient powers may not be enough to snare him. The demon's power is nothing to sneer at. And then what?"

She dimpled, exactly like a maiden who had just been given a lapdog puppy. "Corfu is a terrible place for any *foreigner* to try to practice magic."

Crocell's gaze came back to the thing moving restlessly in the jar. "Hence . . . this. Yes, I can see the logic. It must have been quite a struggle, to get two disparate elementals to breed."

"Indeed it was." She grimaced at the memory, as well as the thing in the jar. "Nor is their offspring here any great pleasure to have around. But when the time comes, it will serve the purpose."

Crocell gave a nod with just enough bow in it to satisfactorily acknowledge her skill. "You will use your nephew as the tool, I assume."

"Emeric is made for the purpose. My great-great-nephew is such a smart boy—and such a careless one."

Crocell shook his head, smiling again, and began walking with a stiff-legged gait toward the entry to the bathhouse. "I leave you to your machinations, Elizabeth. If nothing else, it's always a pleasure for us to watch you at work."

Countess Bartholdy followed. "Are any of you betting in my favor yet?"

Crocell's laugh was low and harsh. "Of course not. Though I will say the odds are improving. Still . . ." He paused at the entryway and looked back, examining her. "No one has ever succeeded in cheating him out of a soul, Elizabeth. Not once, in millennia, though many have tried."

Her dimples appeared again. "I will do it. Watch and see."

Crocell shrugged. "No, you will not. But it hardly matters to me, after all. And now, Countess, if I may be of service?"

He stepped aside and allowed the countess to precede him into the bathhouse.

"Yes, Crocell—and I do thank you again for offering your assistance. I'm having a bit of trouble extracting all of the blood. The veins and arteries empty well enough, but I think . . ."

Her face tight with concentration, Elizabeth studied the corpse of the virgin suspended over the bath. The bath was now half-full with red liquid. A few drops of blood were still dripping off the chin, oozing there from the great gash in the young girl's throat. "I think there's still quite a bit more resting in the internal organs. The liver, especially."

Hearing a sharp sound, she swiveled her head. "Do be a bit careful, would you? Those tiles are expensive."

"Sorry," murmured Crocell, staring down at the flooring he'd cracked. His flesh was denser and heavier than iron, and he always walked clumsily, wearing boots that might look, on close inspection, to be just a bit odd in shape. They were—more so on the inside than the outside. The feet in those boots were not human.

Crocell was helpful, as he always was dealing with such matters. He was the greatest apothecary and alchemist among the Servants, and always enjoyed the intellectual challenge of practicing his craft.

He left, then, laughing when Elizabeth offered to share the bath.

His expression did not match the laugh, however, nor the words that followed. "I have no need for it, Countess, as you well know. I am already immortal."

The last words were said a bit sadly. Long ago, Crocell had paid the price Elizabeth Bartholdy hoped to avoid.

After her bath, the countess retired to her study, with a bowl of the blood—waste not, want not, she always said. There was still another use for it, after all, a use that the bath would actually facilitate. The blood was now as much Elizabeth's as the former owner's, thanks to the magical law of contagion.

She poured it into a flat, shallow basin of black glass, and carefully added the dark liquid from two vials she removed from a rank of others on the shelves. Then she held her hands, palms down, outstretched over the surface of the basin. What she whispered would be familiar to any other magician, so long as he (or she) was not from some tradition outside of the Western Empire.

All except for the last name, which would have sent some screaming for her head.

Rather insular of them, she thought.

A mist spread over the surface of the dark liquid. It rose from nothing, but swiftly sank into the surface of the blood. The liquid began to glow from within with a sullen red light. And there, after a moment, came the image of her conspirator.

Count Mindaug's face was creased with worry. "This is dangerous, Elizabeth."

The countess laughed at him. "Don't be silly. Jagiellon is practically a deaf-mute in such matters; he acknowledges no power but his own except as something to devour. He won't overhear us. Besides, I'll be brief. I received a letter from my nephew yesterday. He's clearly decided to launch his project."

Mindaug shook his head. "The idiot."

"Well, yes." Elizabeth's laugh, as always, was silvery. "What else is family good for?"

Mindaug grunted. He was hardly the one to argue the point, since his own fortune had come largely from his two brothers and three sisters. None of whom had lived more than two months after coming into their inheritance.

"He's still an idiot. I'd no more venture onto Corfu than I would . . . well." Politely, he refrained from naming the place where the Hungarian countess would most likely be making her permanent domicile, sooner or later. Elizabeth appreciated the delicacy, although she would dispute the conclusion. "However, it's good for us. I'll keep steering Jagiellon as best I can."

"Splendid. All we have to do for the moment, then, is allow others to stumble forward." Politely, she refrained from commenting on the way Mindaug was scratching himself.

THE ALBANIAN COAST

It was a bitter morning. The wind whipped small flurries of snow around the hooves of the magnificent black horse. The rider seemed unaware of the chill, his entire attention focused instead on the distant prospect. From up here, he could see the dark Ionian gulf and the narrow strip of water that separated the green island from the bleak Balkan mountains. Over here, winter was arriving. Over there, it would still be a good few more weeks before the first signs of it began to show.

The rider's eyes narrowed as he studied the crescent of island, taking in every detail from Mount Pantocrator to Corfu Bay.

The shepherd-guide looked warily up at the rider. The rider was paying a lot of money for the shepherd's services. The shepherd was still wondering if he was going to live to collect.

Abruptly the tall rider turned on his guide. "When your tribes raid across there, which way do they follow?"

The shepherd held up his hands. "Lord, we are only poor shepherds, peaceful people."

"Don't lie to me," said the rider.

The shepherd looked uneasily across at the sleeping island. Memories, unpleasant memories, of certain reprisals came back to him. Of a woman he'd once thought to possess . . .

"It is true, Lord. It is not wise to attack the Corfiotes. There are many witches. And their men fight. The Venetians, too, come and burn our villages."

"Fight!" the tall rider snorted. "If things develop as I expect they will in Venice, they'll have to learn to fight or be crushed. Well, I have seen what I have come to see. And now, you will take me to Iskander Beg."

The shepherd shied, his swarthy face paling. "I do not know who you are talking about, lord."

"I have warned you once, do not lie to me. I warn you again. I will not warn you a third time." It was said with a grim certainty. "Take me to Iskander Beg."

The shepherd looked down at the stony earth. At the dry grass where he knew his body might rest in a few moments. "No, King Emeric. *You* can only kill me. Iskander Beg . . ." He left the sentence hanging. "I will not take you to the Lord of the Mountains. He knows you are here. If he wants to see you, he will see you."

The King of Hungary showed no surprise that the shepherd had known who he was secretly escorting. After all, the thin-browed, broken-nosed face was well known—and feared. Yes, he was a murderous killer. That in itself was nothing unusual in these mountains. But Emeric was also rumored to be a man-witch. That was why this guide had agreed to lead him, Emeric was sure, not simply the money. Emeric would leave these mountains alive.

The King of Hungary turned his horse. "He can choose. He will see me soon enough anyway. He can see me now, or see me later, on my terms."

The shepherd shrugged. "I can show you the way back now."

CORFU

Across, on the green island, in a rugged glen, the stream cascaded laughingly amid the mossy rocks. In front of the grotto's opening, the piper played a melody on the simple shepherd's pipe. It was a tune as old as the mountain, and only just a little younger than the sea. Poignant and bittersweet, it echoed among the rocks and around the tiny glade between the trees. The sweet young grass was bruised by the dancing of many feet. And among the tufts were sharp-cut little hoof-marks, alongside the barefoot human prints.

Far below a shepherd whistled for his dogs. The piper did not pause in her playing to draw the hood of her cloak over the small horns set among the dark ringlets. This was a holy place. Holy, ancient and enchanted. Neither the shepherd nor his dogs would come up here. Here the old religion and old powers still held sway. The power here was like the olive roots in the mountain groves: just because they were gnarled and ancient did not mean they were weak.

Or friendly.

PART I
Autumn, 1538 A.D.

Chapter 1

Benito Valdosta, latterly a gentleman of the *Case Vecchie* of Venice, walked along a narrow alleyway in the most dubious part of Cannaregio, quite a long time after midnight. Benito sauntered in the shadows, just hoping someone would make his day. Women! Women, as every man on earth knew, were the source of all the damned trouble in the world. And then some extra, he thought bitterly.

No one obliged him. Even in the clothes of the *Case Vecchie*, walking where no sane *Case Vecchie* gentleman would go, the watchers—he could feel them, if not see them—knew who he was. These days he had a reputation, totally out of keeping with his age or size. Well, he would find a tavern. Not Barducci's. Too many memories there.

And then, in the shape of two sailors, some relief came in sight. They were, in their clumsy fashion, trying to box him in.

He let them.

The one with the cudgel tossed it from hand to hand. A mistake, Benito knew. It meant, as Caesare had taught him, in what seemed a different world, that for a few instants you were not actually holding the weapon. The cudgel-wielder obviously hadn't been taught this. He was amazingly stupid, part of Benito's mind thought. When he spoke to his companion with the knife, he actually looked away from the victim!

"Well, Spiro. Venice takes away . . . and she gives back to us. With interest." He laughed coarsely.

Benito judged that the one with the knife was the more

dangerous of the two, if the smaller. He showed signs of a recent beating-up, sporting a black eye and torn cloak. "Yeah. I suppose so. Give us your money, rich kid. Hand it over, and you won't get hurt."

Amateurs, thought Benito, wryly. Came in on the last tide. Got drunk. Maybe got rolled. Maybe just ran out of money and got thrown out of some tavern. Still at least half-drunk. Benito cringed, stepping back, to make sure neither could get behind him. "Please sirs, you're not going hurt me?"

"Just give us your money," repeated the knife-man, "and get out of here. This is no part of town for—what do they call noblemen around here?—yeah, a *Case Vecchie.*"

"I think I might just take that lucco, too," said the cudgel wielder. He was big man. An oarsman by the looks of his muscles.

"If . . . if I give you all my money, and my lucco too, will you let me go?" whined Benito, letting a quaver into his voice, still cringing.

"Yeah," said the knife-man, relaxing, dropping the point slightly.

Cudgel smiled viciously. "Well, I think you need a few bruises to take home to mummy, and maybe a cut on that pretty face." As he said this, cudgel-man had stepped in closer, still tossing the cudgel hand-to-hand and now getting in the knife-wielder's way.

From behind the cudgel-wielder, Benito heard the knifeman say: "Brusco, he's only a kid. Take his money and leave him alone." Brusco wasn't listening.

Cringing means your limbs are bent. You're into a fighter's crouch with a moment's change of attitude. Benito didn't bother to aim. He just hit the arm of the hand that was about to catch the cudgel. Grabbing cloth, as the cudgel went flying harmlessly, Benito pushed the sailor over his outstretched foot. As the former-cudgel-wielder fell, Benito stepped forward, planting a boot firmly in the thug's solar plexus. His rapier was suddenly in his right hand, and the *main gauche* in his left. Finest Ferrara steel gleamed in the gray dawn-light. Fierce exultation leapt inside him, as he moved in for the kill. Already the moves, long practiced, were in mind. Engage. Thrust. He had the reach. Turn and kill the other one before he could get to his feet.

And then, as he saw the look of terror on the sailor's face, the battle-joy went away. Her words came back to him. "I won't marry a wolf."

He settled for hitting the knife, hard, just at the base of the blade, with the rapier. It did precisely what cheap knives will do, given that, to save metal, the tang into the hilt is usually much thinner than the blade. It snapped.

The sailor looked briefly at the hilt in his hand, and prepared himself to die. "I didn't plan to hurt you," he said, hoarsely, his eyes now fixed on the two unwavering blades facing him.

Benito flicked a glance at the other man, who was up on one elbow, feeling for his cudgel. Safety, prudence and Caesare said: "Kill them both, fast. Dead men are no threat. Desperate men are." Her words came back to him again: "Are you the son of the wolf or the fox?"

"I know you weren't," said Benito. "That's why you're still alive. But if your friend moves a muscle, that's going to change."

The sailor looked at his companion. "Then you'd better kill me, milord," he sighed. "That Brusco has no brains at all. He got us into this mess in the first place."

Benito stepped over to where the brainless Brusco was busy proving his lack of intelligence, by trying to get to his feet. A slash of the rapier severed the man's belt. By the piggy squeal Benito's judgement must have been a touch off.

"Stay down, Brusco," said the other sailor, urgently. "The *Case Vecchie*'ll kill you. Milord, he's still half-drunk. We . . . our ship left us. Winter's coming and berths are few now. We thought . . . some eating money . . ."

Benito snorted in exasperation, feeling as if he were fifty instead of seventeen. "Come on. Both of you. Up on your feet, you. Use both hands to keep those trousers up . . . Brusco. Now. In front of me. Quick march. You're no more than a pair of damned virgins in a brothel, in this part of town! You're not cut out for a life of crime, either of you. You're not local or you'd never have been so stupid. Where are you from?"

"Liapádhes. Kérkira . . . Corfu," the former knifeman said. He jerked a thumb at his companion, who was staggering along, holding up his trousers. "Brusco's from Bari. Down south."

Benito prodded the former cudgel-wielder with his rapier. "They must breed them big and dumb down there."

"I'm bleeding," said Brusco, sulkily.

They'd arrived at the canalside by this time. Benito flicked the complaining Brusco's shoulder with his rapier so the man turned around. So did his companion.

"Bleeding. Ha. You're lucky, Brusco, that I didn't cut your damn-fool balls off before you sired any dumb kids. Now listen to me, sailor from Bari. You get yourself out of Venice and don't come back. If you do, you'll be lucky if the canalers cut your throat before I find you. Swim or sell your shirt. But get onto the mainland and don't come back. Go." They both turned. Benito put out his rapier and halted the smaller man, the one with the black eye, who had once bought a cheap knife. "Stay."

The man looked wary, glancing at the canal.

Benito shook his head. "Don't be as much of a fool as the idiot from Bari. If I'd wanted to kill you, I'd have done it back there. Anyway, a couple of mouthfuls of that water is more likely to kill you than any sword-stroke.

"Here." Benito reached into his pouch, took out some silver pennies, and handed them to the would-be thief. "Get yourself some breakfast. Go that way along the fondamenta, and you're in a better part of town. And then get yourself along to the Dorma shipyards. Tell Alberto on the gate that Benito sent you. Tell him you're looking for a berth and that I said you'd do."

The Corfiote seaman looked at the money in his palm. Then he shook his head, unbelieving. "Why are you doing this?" he asked quietly. "I thought you'd hand us over to the nightwatch. I was looking for a chance to run."

"I needed a fight," said Benito, shrugging. "And I needed to sort out some things in my head. You obliged. I owe you. Now, I've got to find a gondola. You've straightened out my mind a bit, and there's a girl I've got say good-bye to. I was going to go drinking, if I couldn't find a fight."

The sailor shook his head again, and then smiled. "If it's all the same to you, milord, next time you're in need of a fight, I'm not going to be around. I thought I was going to be killed back there. One minute you were a scared kid. Then—you were somebody else. When I looked in your eyes . . . for a minute I thought I was dead."

Benito took a deep breath. "You very nearly were," he said quietly.

The sailor nodded. "A risk a thief takes. It's not something I've tried before, or I'm in a hurry to try again. And your girl should be very sorry you're leaving. Any chance I'd be shipping out with you, Milord?"

To his surprise Benito realized the man wanted him to be on the vessel. That was admiration in his voice. "I'm not shipping out." He waved at a dark, sleek gondola out on the Grand Canal. "She is. And as far as I can see she's not a bit sorry," he added, bitterly.

The gondolier had responded to his wave, and the vessel was just about at the canalside. Benito vaulted down into it, with athletic ease. "Bacino San Marco," he said, taking his seat.

"Morning, Valdosta. Or are you too important to greet us these days?"

Benito looked up. "Oh, hell. Sorry, Theobaldo. My mind was somewhere else."

The gondolier shrugged. "It's too late, boy. She's married and he's a fine man. Besides, she is one of us and you're one of them. It would never have worked."

Benito was not in the least surprised that the canaler knew all about his private life. He'd lived next to these canals himself for far too long not to know that the real lifeblood of Venice was not the water in her canals or the trade of her far-flung colonies, but gossip. When you and your brother are real, romantic heroes, nobles hidden in slums, who come into their own while saving the city in its hour of need . . . When your patron is the new Doge . . .

Well, suddenly everyone knows you. To be fair, on the canals, most of them had known his brother Marco anyway. Marco was pretty well regarded as the local saint, for his work in healing the poor and sick of the canals. He, Benito, had a fairly well-deserved reputation for being a thief and trouble, and a pack follower of the assassin Caesare Aldanto, until almost the last. He'd redeemed himself in the fighting, to be sure. Fighting was one of the few things he was good at, thanks in part to the treacherous Caesare, and thanks in part to his father's blood—neither of which most people regarded as good things.

Benito sighed. His skills: fighting, carousing and climbing buildings. None of the three seemed to fit him for the aristocratic mold Petro Dorma wanted to cram him into.

His half-brother Marco, on the other hand, was a gentleman born. Fitting into the *Case Vecchie* mold was easy enough for him, so long as he could go on with his beloved medical studies and seeing Katerina Montescue. Besides, ever since Benito's brother and the Lion of Venice had shared a body, Marco was . . . different. He was still the brother Benito knew and loved. But he'd always been the thinker. Benito was a doer, not a thinker. Marco was no longer unsure of himself, and now it was Benito's turn to be. It was something Benito had never been before.

"I know, Theobaldo. I messed up good, huh? But I grew up as a bridge-brat. I'm still learning this *Case Vecchie* stuff, and, to tell the truth, I don't like it much."

The gondolier sculled easily, moving the boat along the limpid water of the canal, under the Rialto bridge. A few bankers' clerks were already setting up their masters' stalls. "We always reckoned you were born to be hanged," he said. "That brother of yours is too good for this world, but you! Anyway, you're not going to make trouble for Maria and Umberto, are you? Because if you are, I'm going to pitch you into the canal here. You and that fancy sword of yours."

Benito knew he was good with that fancy sword, so long as he was on dry land. He also knew what Maria had taught him: Never mess with a boatman in his own boat. The gondolier had spent forty years staying on his feet in this vessel. Benito was a landsman, even if he'd grown up canalside.

Besides, Benito had no intention of causing trouble. Umberto *was* a fine man, even if he was twenty-five years older than Maria. And never mind the gondolieri—Maria would pitch him into the water herself if he tried anything. She was certainly strong enough and quite capable of doing it.

"I'm just going to say 'good-bye,'" he said quietly. "And good luck. She deserves some."

He withdrew into a brown study, thinking back to that time of poverty he'd spent living with Maria and Caesare, when both of them, in their different ways—Maria as Caesare's lover and he as Caesare's young protégé—had thought Caesare Aldanto was some kind of demigod on earth. Until, in one night and day, Aldanto's evil nature had surfaced and Benito and Maria had wound up becoming lovers themselves. A night which was still, for all the horror of it, Benito's most precious memory.

Benito realized now with crystal clarity, looking back, how he'd been shaped by those times. His blood, if you were shaped by blood, was terrifying enough. His mother was an undutiful daughter of Duke Enrico Dell'este. The Old Fox, they called him. Lord of Ferrara, Modena, Este, Regio nell' Emilia, and, since Milan and Verona's defeat a month back, of several more Po valley towns. Dell'este was supposed to be the leading strategist of the age. A man feared and respected. A nobleman.

But Benito's father was worse. Carlo Sforza, the Wolf of the North. A man feared. The most powerful and deadly soldier-of-fortune of the day, Italy's most notorious *condottiere*. Undefeated, until the debacle at the Palatine forts on the Po during the battle for Venice last month, when the Old Fox had bloodied the Wolf. Bloodied the Wolf, but not killed him. Benito still had his father's broken sword in the cupboard at the *Casa* Dorma.

They all expected him to be like one or the other of these men. And maybe, in time he might be. But he knew very little of either of them, or of their very different worlds. He'd learned how to live, and how to behave, mostly from two women street-thieves, until he and Marco had tied up with Caesare. Like it or not, Benito had to admit he'd modeled himself on Caesare Aldanto. The man had been something of a hero to both of them. Caesare and Maria had been the center of their world for some very crucial years.

Maria. If there was ever going to be a reason why Benito didn't turn out as much of a *pizza da merde* as Caesare had turned out to be, she would probably be it. Deep inside him it ached. Her values were hard, clear, loyal and true. And she'd turned him down to marry a caulker. Here he was, protégé of the man who was the new Doge . . . hurting because some canal-woman had spurned his offer of marriage.

Deep down, he was also worried that she was dead right to have done so. He'd nearly killed those two stupid sailors, just because he was in a foul mood and looking for excitement to distract him. Caesare would have done the same, but would not have stopped short. So, according to rumor, would Carlo Sforza. As for the Old Fox—well, stories painted him as a good friend and a bad enemy, but a cautious and wily man. A cautious and wily man might well have done as Benito had.

Or perhaps, not.

But the Old Fox, Maria—or a younger, less arrogant Benito—would never have gotten into that position in the first place. He sighed. Maybe part of it was that he was so short. One of the other things he owed to growing up a thief, living under bridges and in secret in other people's attics. With no money, but lots of enthusiasm. More enthusiasm and conviction that things would come right, than food, sometimes. Food had been hard to come by for a few years. He was growing broader now. But he'd never be as tall as his brother. Marco had done his basic growing before hard times hit the two of them. Besides, the Dell'este were not tall. The tall willowy shape was that of the Valdosta family.

"You going to sit there all day?" asked the gondolier, interrupting his musing. "Or are you going to get out?"

Startled, Benito stood up and reached for the mooring-pole.

"You can pay me, Valdosta," said Theodoro, dryly.

Flushing, Benito did. Generously. After all, money was the one thing he had plenty of now.

Benito was not surprised to find Katerina Montescue on the quay-side. And if Kat was going to be there, his brother was almost inevitably going to be, too.

Marco and Kat eyed him with considerable wariness as he came up. "You shouldn't be here!" hissed Kat.

Benito held up his hands, pacifically. "I'm not going to cause any trouble."

"You *should* have caused trouble," said Kat crossly, "before she did this. It's too late now."

Benito nodded, and swallowed to clear the lump in his throat. "I know. Now all I can do is . . . not make trouble. So I'm just going to say good-bye to an old friend."

The spitting-tabby glow in Kat's eyes died. She patted his arm, awkwardly. "Maybe it is for the best. I mean, she seems happy enough."

Benito looked over to where Maria Garavelli—no, not Garavelli any more; Verrier, now—was talking to two older women. She seemed, if not happy, at least to be her usual abrasive self.

"Don't be crazy!" she was saying. "The boat's worth twice that. Put it up on blocks in Tomaso's yard if you won't use it."

Benito missed half of the reply. Something about " . . . when you come back."

Maria shook her head emphatically. "I'm not coming back."

Benito winced at that certainty.

Maria caught sight of him, then. Immediately, she turned and strode over to him, her dark eyes flashing.

"What are you doing here, 'Nito?" There was challenge in her voice, challenge, and deep down, anger. If there was anything else there, he didn't want to know about it.

Benito shrugged. "I heard an old friend was leaving Venice. She did a lot toward raising me. I came to say good-bye, good luck, and a safe journey. And I hope—I mean, I *really* hope—she's happy."

For a moment she said nothing. Then: "Good-bye, Benito." It was said very quietly, with just a flicker of pain. She turned her back on him and walked away.

Benito had spent his life knowing exactly what to do next. For once, he didn't. So he walked blindly off into the piazza, leaving Maria to embark with her new husband on the ship outbound for Istria.

Chapter 2

The roll of the ship on its way to Istria was comforting, something familiar in an increasingly unfamiliar world. Maria needed that comfort now, as she lay sleepless. For the first time in her life she wasn't going to be living in a city. That worried her, more than she liked to admit, but it worried her a lot less than the life stirring inside her did.

Beside her, Umberto snored. She'd get used to that, she supposed, eventually. At least the snoring made him different from Caesare. And Benito, for that matter.

Benito had upset her; the baby had kicked just when he'd said good-bye. She'd swear it was his—it was so damned restless, just like him. But it would be a long time before she forgot the look on his face, there on the quay-side. Not for the first time, Maria wondered if she'd made a mistake. Still, she'd made her decisions, made her bed, as the old ones said, and now she must lie in it. Benito just reminded her too much of Caesare. Caesare had hurt her, worse than she'd ever been hurt in her life, and in ways she was probably never going to get over.

Whatever else, she wasn't going to have that happen to her again. Umberto wasn't an exciting man, true, and hadn't been even in his youth. But Maria had known him since she was a little girl. Umberto Verrier was as decent as they came and as reliable as the seasons.

She sighed. It was good fortune that Umberto had gotten this post as chief forester for a district in Istria. The post usually went to one of the master-carpenters from the Arsenal, which the caulkers technically were, but normally it went to one of the more prestigious guilds, not to the poor-relation caulkers. She suspected the hand of Petro Dorma in that appointment. His family had huge estates in Istria, and besides, the Doge had influence everywhere in Venice. But she was grateful, even if all it meant was that the Doge was trying to get Benito Valdosta, of the *Casa Vecchie* Valdosta, away from the canals and a certain boat-girl who might try to exercise a hold over him. It would take her away from Venice before her pregnancy began to show.

Now all she had to do was bear with the interminable voyage, an alien new life, and try to love the husband she had bound herself to. He was a good man, Umberto. He deserved at least that she try, try as hard as she ever had in all her life.

The voyage wound up not being as long or as uncomfortable as she had feared it would be. But once the tarette had dropped them at the tiny harbor at Rovini, the enormity of the change in her life really struck her. She had not been on the dock for more than a minute before she was aware, deep in her gut, that Venetian-held Istria was . . . different.

All her life had been formed around the bustle of Venice, around an existence that centered on people and water. She stood on the dock with a bundle of her personal belongings beside her, as Umberto looked for the forester who was to meet them, and fought down a sudden surge of fear.

Fortunately, the forester was also looking for them, and his arrival pushed the fear aside in favor of more immediate and practical concerns. There was the usual confused comedy over boxes and chests. Eventually, Umberto and the other man got it sorted out while Maria stood by, trying not to feel impatient because *she* would have had it dealt with in two minutes. The effort to control her often-brusque temperament steadied Maria—the brusque temperament itself, even more so. Whatever else Maria had to worry about in the future, her own practical competence was not one of them.

The foresters had arranged for a small caretta to transport the new chief forester and his bride up to his home in the forests and the hills. Bouncing up the muddy track beyond the olives and the bare fields, they moved into the fringes of forested land. For the first time in her life, Maria found herself out of sight or scent of the sea.

The forest smelled. A damp, rich, mushroomy smell, that probably, under other circumstances, would have been pleasant. At least it wasn't the sewage-stink of the canals in high summer. But it wasn't familiar, either, it wasn't anything she was expecting, and it was strong. That, or pregnancy, or just the bouncing of the cart, made her feel sick.

But when they got to the house Maria was so astounded that she forgot her nausea.

It was made of *wood*, like a rich man's home! Wood was saved for things that could float, and bring you profit, not used for houses. And it was big. Set apart from the cluster of foresters' huts, it was a real *house*. She could not imagine how they could afford it.

The house was new, so it must have been built by the man Umberto was replacing. "How did he afford such a place?"

Umberto looked sour. "The admirals at the Arsenal discovered three weeks back that he, and five of the foresters, were in a very convenient arrangement with the *Lazzari*, the timber buyers from Trieste. That is why the post was vacant—and probably why I got it. They didn't want anyone who might still have a hand in the arrangement to come in and start it up all over again, which meant delving deep into the guild to find a replacement. As deep as the caulkers, even."

He sighed. "The nice part is that the house comes with the post. But I will have a mountain of paperwork to do and I doubt if the oxcart with our clothes and furnishings will be here until dusk. I'm sorry, Maria. I'll have to get stuck in straight away. Even when the oxcart gets here, the house will have to wait until I have time to arrange things. We have bedding at least, Rossi assures me, but the house is otherwise bare inside."

It was a crisp, and for a miracle, dry autumn day. The hills with their leaf-bare stands of oak and larch called to her. The thought of getting off of this carriage and onto her feet called even more. She'd walk up to the ridge where the dark pines stood like the raised hackles of some huge cat.

"I'll explore around," she said, not caring a pin whether or not there was a chair to sit on or plates to eat off. Hadn't she done without those things before? Well, she could again. "I need to walk. To get some air."

"Very well. But please don't go out of sight of the house. These wild places are dangerous. Rossi has been telling of bears and boar . . ." He trailed off, looking miserably at the house.

Personally, Maria thought Rossi's tales improbable even for the wilds of the fabled east. The half-Slovene was having fun seeing how many stories he could get his new boss to swallow, most likely. But she nodded, since she wouldn't contradict him in front of Rossi. Bad thing, for a boss to be shown up in front of his underlings by a girl-wife, before he'd even met most of those underlings.

Umberto wasn't quite finished. "Just remember, you're, um . . ." He flushed. "In a delicate condition."

Maria nodded again. Poor Umberto. She'd been brutally frank before accepting his proposal: She'd told him straight out that she was pregnant. He'd gone puce, but he'd also managed to say that it wouldn't matter to him. That was quite something from any-one.

Still, Umberto struggled to talk about the pregnancy. It had begun to dawn on Maria that it wasn't the mysterious father so much as the fact that, so far as Umberto was concerned, this was an area men didn't refer to. Ever. Babies just happened, and he would much prefer that things stayed that way, thank you.

Maria walked out past the house, looking about her with wonder. She had never in her life seen trees so tall or so—untamed. Beneath her feet, the springy turf felt very different from dockside boards and stone quays, and the cool air was dry. Wondrously dry. In Venice, the air was thick enough to wring out like a dishrag. The loneliness out here was compelling, and pulled her farther under the trees. In short order, she'd very rapidly broken the injunction about going out of sight of the houses. Rossi's stories and Umberto's concern aside, the hills seemed as unthreatening as a kitten.

And she was in a phase of pregnancy where she just seemed to have too much energy. She was over most of the morning sickness now, and although she'd been told she would become heavy and uncomfortable soon, she still felt strong, not needing to be pampered and cosseted.

Still . . . there was maybe less room in her lungs than there used to be. She sat herself down on a pile of leaves with a neat rock backrest just short of the ridge. The rock was sun-warmed, and she'd walked a long way. A canaler's strength, she realized after a moment, really didn't lie in the legs. She'd just rest a while. Just a little in the sun, the warm sun . . .

She woke with a start—though, out of habit, not moving, not even to open her eyes. Voices, strange voices; near, but not near enough to see her, obviously. She recognized the one: Rossi, the forester who had brought the caretta to collect them.

"—see any problems. The old man they've sent up doesn't look like he'll understand what is going on, Torfini." Rossi chuckled. "I reckon after the wolf, bear and boar stories I told the man and that young woman of his, the two of them will stay barricaded in the house for the next two years, never mind the next two months."

"Even so. I'm sure it was Rudolpho and Marco who somehow got word to the admirals at the Arsenal. I don't want those two to hook onto the fact that we still have timber to move out. Oak that well curved is much in demand."

"So who is buying ship ribs now? Constantinople?"

The other man snorted. "For heaven's sake! I don't care. It's all money."

"Good money, and I want mine, Torfini." There was a threat in that voice that made Maria press herself into the rock.

"You'll get it, all right. Just keep everyone away from the Mello ridges for a couple of weeks."

"I'll find you if I don't get it."

"You'll get yours."

Maria waited a good long while after they'd left; the last thing she wanted was for either of those two *pizza de merde* to guess she'd overheard them. In fact her descent was more alarming than she'd anticipated, for darkness had come on much quicker than she'd expected. It was twilight when she got down to the cottages, which were already twinkling with firelight.

Umberto was standing outside their house, with the door wide open, beside himself. "Where have you been? I have been so worried! I've got the men out looking for you. There are saw pits . . ."

She patted his cheek, and tried to make him really *look* at her. "I'm fine. I just walked farther than I meant to. Then I stopped for a rest, and fell asleep. But Umberto, never mind all that now! I found out something very important."

He wasn't listening. "You must be more careful, Maria! This isn't the canals of Venice. It is dangerous out here. You hear me? Dangerous! Rossi told me that before the Old Chief Forester left—"

She tried mightily to keep from snapping at him. She wasn't a child! This wasn't about a new flower or a wild hare she'd seen!

"Umberto, Rossi is a *liar*. He was trying to keep us indoors. And if the old Chief Forester's name was Torfini, then he hasn't gone far. He was up on that ridge over there talking to Rossi. I *heard* them."

He wasn't even listening. He led her indoors, patting her. "You're in a . . . a delicate condition, Maria. You must rest. I'll get someone to look after you."

Suddenly she was too tired to fight for him anymore. Maybe if a man told him what was going on, he might actually listen to it. "Very well. I'll rest. If you go out and get two of your men in here, Rudolpho and Marco."

"You really must be more careful Maria . . ."

In this, at least, she would be firm. "Rudolpho and Marco, Umberto. Now. And then I'll rest and be good."

Chapter 3

Grand Duke Jagiellon looked at his new shaman with a strange glow in his inhuman eyes. Count Mindaug was sure he understood the thoughts moving in that now-demonic brain: This particular shaman's skin would offer more eating than the last. It was very wrinkled, and the tattoos would give it an interesting color and flavor.

The face, especially, was heavily tattooed. The shaman wore a coat of reindeer hide, the shoulders of which were covered in feathers and the back with small brass bells. He carried a *quodba*, a magic drum, so large that it seemed to dwarf the wrinkled old man; the drumhead had also been tattooed. There was no expression on the old face. Only the eyes, narrow and slightly up-tilted, showed any signs of trepidation. They darted about, taking in details, faintly shadowed with unnamed and secret thoughts.

Count Mindaug detected the battle of wills going on between the huge, meaty Grand Duke and the scrawny old man. Not a word was said, but the air itself shivered as if with heat.

Eventually the old shoulders slumped. "The *haltija* is too strong." He bowed to the Grand Duke. "Master."

"Remember that," Jagiellon said coldly. "But you are stronger than my last shamans."

The shaman said nothing. He waited.

Jagiellon turned to Count Mindaug. "This one is not Karelian. Why has he come?"

Pacifically, Mindaug held out his hands with their perfectly manicured and sharpened nails. "I sent emissaries into the north seeking out their most powerful. Your new shaman, the one from Karelen, killed himself some days back. This one is from Kandalaksha."

The shaman nodded. "I am master of many words of power. Many sea words. Many water words. Some forest words. I kill small Karelian. He challenged my power, but I too strong for him." His Lithuanian was good, if accented.

This was talk Jagiellon understood. "You will give me that strength. All of it. And you will only kill at my express command." The dark eyes flared. "There will be plenty of opportunity."

"Who do I go kill?"

The big hands carved a shape in the air. A vision appeared, of a tall, willowy boy. "This one. Marco Valdosta is his name. See him. Taste his magic. He is weak in skill but deep in power."

The shaman's drum seemed to shiver. But other than the faint throbbing that came from it there was no sound or movement for some time. Eventually the shaman shook his head. "Not one. Is two. One human, very strong but no skill. And one big but not human. You no kill this one."

This did not, to Mindaug's surprise, anger his master. Not visibly, anyway. The purple scar on Jagiellon's forehead pulsed briefly. "The nonhuman one is limited to a place. If the human comes out of that, you can kill him."

The shaman nodded. "Eat his *haltija*. He strong, but not skilled yet."

"Good." A gesture and the vision was dispelled. "Now, this one." Again a shape formed in the air. Reddish hair. An aquiline nose, a single line of eyebrow, and eyes that burned. "Eneko Lopez, this one's name."

The drum-skin shivered. And then, with a sound like tearing cloth, split.

The shaman averted his face, making a warning-sign. "Make it go, master!" he said urgently. "He will see us, too."

The vision disappeared. The shaman shook himself, like a dog ridding water. "Too skilled, master. Not so strong as the last two, but very skilled. And much *haltija*. Much strength to that soul! More than the skill or power."

Jagiellon nodded. "Then we will work through intermediaries. There are powers in the shadow-world that are mighty—at least within their geographical area. And we can misdirect. He must be watched. Watched from a distance."

"Yes, master." The shaman bowed. "I have two watchers at my call. Birds can see a great distance."

"They are not magical creatures?" asked Jagiellon. "He will be aware of magical watchers."

The shaman flicked his fingers against the drum, scowling and muttering. The skin began to knit itself. As soon as it was entire, he began to drum a steady, demanding beat. Count Mindaug could see his lips moving, but despite listening intently he could not make out the words.

Two birds battered at the window. Jagiellon motioned to the Count to open it. The Count pulled open the window and then had to duck as two enormous goshawks streaked past his head to land on the shaman's now outstretched arms. Beneath his reindeer-hide robe the shaman wore heavy leather vambraces of what could only be the thickest bullhide. And well he did so—those power-ful talons would have pierced anything less right through.

Like most nobles, Mindaug had flown falcons. There was some-thing wrong with these birds. Those eyes were red insanity. Gos-hawks were always a little mad, but these two . . .

It was said that a goshawk with a threatened nest would attack anything short of an elephant. Mindaug had the distinct impres-sion that these two would not hesitate at the elephant, with or without a nest under threat. Most birds of prey killed only enough to feed on; goshawks and their kin sometimes went into killing frenzies if the opportunity presented itself. Mindaug sensed that this pair would create the opportunity if one didn't already exist.

"Feel them, master. Feel them with your power."

Jagiellon looked hard at the birds. "Hmm. It is there. But very, very light. Just a hold."

"Just their names, master. But I can see through their eyes."

Jagiellon turned to the count. "You served me well with this one, Mindaug. I am pleased."

The Count bowed, his fingernails digging into his palms. The shaman was a very valuable tool to give up to his master. But the Count had one thing that the Grand Duke did not have.

He had the shaman's own name of power.

Mindaug wasn't too sure how he'd use that, yet. But treachery was, after all, the core value of his world. His researches into magical creatures had stretched a wide net away from the Polish-Lithuanian power base that was his master's realm. He'd looked far, far back. What he'd found was this old one. The shaman was not entirely human any more himself.

But then, in the Ionian islands was something far, far older; quiescent, but far from dead. Jagiellon knew it had been a powerful place once, but actually he knew very little that was verifiable about the island once referred to as Nausicaa, an island which was settled before Etruscans came to the Venetian lagoon. Mindaug wondered if this was, at long last, the moment that the Grand Duke had overreached himself.

Chapter 4

It was bitterly cold down here in the water chapel below St. Raphaella. Marco felt it, even through the thick coat and fur collar. Brother Mascoli still wore his simple light-colored habit. The fringe of gray hair about his ears was, if anything, thinner than it had been when Marco first met him. Old people were usually touched more by the cold than the young, but the priest's faith seemed to keep him warm.

Warmer than Marco, anyway. He shivered.

"You are afraid, Marco," said the Hypatian Sibling gently. "Don't be. God's will is God's will."

"I know. But I still question the rightness of what I am doing. I do it for someone I love especially and dearly. This is not just a deed done out of love for my fellow man, or to serve a greater cause." Marco shook his head. "Kat and her grandfather must have been praying for the return of her father for years, and if it is God's will that he not return, so be it. All I want to do is find out where he is. If at least they *knew* what had happened to him, and where he is—or was—it might give them . . . not comfort, exactly, but . . ."

He groped after the concept that he wanted, but he might have known that a Sibling would know very well what he was getting at.

"I understand," Brother Mascoli said, soothingly. "Remember, Marco, there is nothing *un*Christian about asking creatures that are not human for their help, just as it is not unChristian to help them when they come to us for healing." He smiled. "Of course,

38

no evil creature would ever approach us for help; their very natures would prevent them coming anywhere near here. And since you helped to heal one undine, all of the unhuman creatures are kindly inclined to you."

Mascoli put a hand on Marco's shoulder. "If a stranger had asked this of you, you would have tried?"

Marco nodded.

Mascoli smiled. "It is not right to deny the same help to those one loves dearly. That, too, would be a sin. He who judges these things knows the intents of the innermost heart, and He is not fooled by the shallow and their pretences. In the presence of men it may sometimes be wise not to show favor to an especially loved one. In the presence of God . . . well, He knows already. And since He is Love incarnate, He will always look kindly upon a deed done out of unselfish love."

It didn't seem quite so cold down here any more. Marco took a deep breath, and began to ask the blessing of the four great archangels.

The warded corners glowed. Heaven would forfend any attempt to venture evil here. Remembering Brother Mascoli's instructions, he intoned, "*In nomine Patri, et Filii, et Spiritus Sancti, fiat pace.*"

Standing now within the veil of light lying weightlessly on the chapel walls, Marco dipped the wine cup into the cold, murky canal water. Discipline and concentration were called for, here. Marco held the wine cup until the water was mirror-still.

He began scrying, building up an image in his mind, calling by their true names, the triton Androcles and his mate Althea.

The images and response came quickly. *Wait. We come.*

An image of winter waves curling and foam-lines danced across the wine cup . . .

And a brief moment of a circular suckerlike mouth full of long needle-sharp teeth. And a terrible roaring.

The wards flared to an incandescent brightness, briefly, and there was a sense that *something* had impacted against them. Hard.

The tall candles were now merely burning wicks in a dripping pool of wax.

Marco nearly dropped the wine cup. He turned to Brother

Mascoli. "What happened?" he asked, afraid and angry at the same time. "What was *that*?"

The Hypatian Sibling was already kneeling, ignoring the fact that the stones were wet. "Join me," he said hastily. "We need to strengthen the wards. *Now.*"

One thing Marco had learned: when a magician said "now" in *that* tone of voice, it was no time to ask questions.

"What happened? Are Androcles and Althea all right?" Marco asked as soon as Brother Mascoli had finished leading the invocation. Marco's heart was in his mouth.

"Describe exactly what you saw," the Sibling said, his usual calm considerably thinner.

Marco did.

Brother Mascoli nodded. "Yes." He let out a gusty sigh. "In my opinion, your merfolk are probably all right. In fact, they're probably completely unaware that anything happened. *They* were not the target of what you encountered."

He blinked. "They weren't?"

Brother Mascoli shook his head, and looked very grave indeed. "It is clear to me, Marco, that we need to work on your focus, and your defenses. You are very vulnerable when you are scrying like that, and I fear that this time only your bond with the Lion saved you. Part of you was outside the wards—and your ability stretches the window of vision. It is rare that one person can do that sort of scrying alone and unaided. As a consequence, you can see much more than, say, I can. Unfortunately, it also means you are then visible to anything lurking, waiting for the sign of your magic. You are at your most vulnerable under such circumstances."

"And something attacked me."

The information that he, and not the merfolk, had been the object of an attack made him feel a moment of relief. At least he had not been the cause of two innocents getting in harm's way.

Brother Mascoli made the sign of the cross. "Something is definitely out there," he said quietly. "Something that dares not venture within the ancient boundaries of our current Venice, but knows what Marco Valdosta's mage-work feels like. Something that is so evil that the wards were called on to guard your very soul."

Marco's relief evaporated, and he felt as if he had been doused in iced water. And now that he came to think about it . . .

There'd been something very recognizable about that image, a feeling that he'd met it when they'd fought Chernobog's minions. He could almost *taste* the magic, foul beyond measure and polluted, yet with an edge of seductive sweetness—seductive, at least, if you were not aware that it was the sweetness of corruption.

"But . . . I thought the Lion had defeated the evil that attacked Venice?" he whispered.

Brother Mascoli was the gentlest and kindest of all the men that Marco knew. Right now he did not look gentle. "We have won *a* battle," he said quietly, sighing. "A battle, not the war. We need to go on being vigilant. And we need to remember that in this war it is love and care that are our weapons, as much as swords or magics. Our foe can match us sword for sword, magic for magic. But love and care are ours and ours alone. Our enemy cannot give those. They would destroy him if he tried."

It was Marco's turn to sigh; he had given so much already, and now that things were settling down for him, he had hoped for a respite. "I'm just so sick of fighting. I thought . . . I thought we could give peace a try."

The Sibling shook his head. "I am not a man of arms. But it is no use simply calling for peace when our foe takes our desire for it to be an opportunity to conquer brutally without meeting any resistance. We need swords, aye, and magic, beside the love and care. You and I and the Hypatian Order want to serve the latter. But we need the former, also. We need to support them."

The still canal water, greenish in the pale light, was suddenly ringed. The mermaid and the triton popped up.

The triton's voice boomed in the brick-walled water-chapel. "Greetings, Mage Marco. We had a sudden squall there. Very strange."

"You are unhurt?"

Marco's anxiety plainly struck the two of them as very funny. "Storms are to us what a fresh breeze is to you humans," said Androcles.

"That was no natural squall," said Brother Mascoli, quietly. "Marco is right to be anxious about you. That was caused by some magic."

"Weather magic is hard and expensive on the user," said Althea, her mercurial expression going from mischievous to somber in an instant.

Mascoli looked grim. "The squall was little more than an accidental slap of some great force's tail. Be careful, beloved ones. It was magic of the blackest, and powerful."

The two looked doubtful, and their tails beat the water behind them, in slow, measured waves of their fins. "Well," said the triton Androcles, "it wasn't trying to stop us reaching you with the news you asked us for, Marco. The truth is: We have next to none. If this friend's father is dead . . . he lies on land. But we will widen our search, and there are friends of fresh water, like the undines, that we can call upon the wide world over."

The mermaid, whose aquamarine eyes sparkled with mischief again, had wrapped her long, wet blond hair several times around her upper torso, creating an effective "garment" to cover her unclothed breasts. Her companion, the triton, blond-bearded and long-haired, looked exactly like the creatures that adorned the borders of tapestries and the basins of fountains all over Venice. Like the mermaid he had a fish's tail; unlike her, he also had a fish's dorsal fin adorning his backbone.

"Faugh! Magus Marco, how you humans can live among such filthy waters I cannot imagine!" The triton somehow managed to grin and grimace at the same time.

"Because we aren't very bright?" Marco replied, cautiously. That seemed to be the correct answer, for Althea joined in the triton's chuckles.

"Well, I cannot fault you overmuch for doing what we ourselves do," Androcles admitted. "You know, I have a friend Antonio, a netman. He drinks nothing but *grappa* and I asked him why he rotted his gut with the stuff. And do you know what he said?"

Marco shook his head.

"He said: 'What am I to drink? *Water?* After what *you* people and every fish in the sea *do* in it?'" The triton roared with laughter, which echoed in the brick-walled water-chapel and drowned out every other sound.

"If he is there, in the sea, we will find him eventually," said the mermaid, smiling with confidence. Her teeth, unlike those of undines, were white, pearly, and exactly like human teeth. Althea was very pretty indeed; Marco wondered idly if at some point his artist-friend Rafael de Tomaso would be interested in having her pose for him.

"We can follow the source of a single drop of blood in the water for leagues; it will take time, a year perhaps, but we will find him. And when we do find him? What would you have us do?"

Marco thought about the horror of Kat being presented with a body half-eaten by fish and crabs, or a skeleton—but then thought of the value of having *something* to weep over, *something* to bury, even if it wasn't much.

"Please," he said. "Can you bring him home?"

"We will, if he lies under the sea," the triton promised. Then, with a flick of tails, they were gone.

After they'd left, Marco and Brother Mascoli found themselves standing and gazing into the water. Marco wasn't certain what to think; perhaps at some level he had been so certain that Kat's father was dead and drowned that he had anticipated a quick answer to the question he had posed to the merfolk some weeks earlier.

At length Mascoli shook himself. "Come, Marco. Let us go upstairs and get a little warmer. No news is good news, I suppose."

Marco shook his head slowly. "It may be. But he could be dead on land. Or he could be a prisoner somewhere, or ill, or somehow lost his memory. It's the not knowing that is so terrible for Kat."

"Well, perhaps. But where there is life there is also hope, young man." Brother Mascoli seemed to regain his calm; he took Marco by the elbow and led him upstairs. "And I must find someone who is more skilled in combative magic to instruct you in how to ward yourself. It is a shame that Eneko Lopez is not still here in Venice. He is a harsh man, but he is on his way to becoming one of the greatest of Christian mages."

Brother Mascoli smiled wryly. "He has a belief in shared strength. That the brethren of Christ should unite, giving the powers of light a strength as of an army—while evil power stands as a tower alone, relying only on itself. Yet many of the Strega rituals are those of a bonding of power, so perhaps Father Lopez is mistaken in his ideas."

Marco pursed his lips. Sharing himself with the Lion had broadened his outlook somewhat from the one which he'd held once. "Maybe the Strega are not evil."

Mascoli laughed softly. "I might believe you. And truly, that is the opinion of most Hypatians. But you should always keep in mind when dealing with him that Eneko Lopez is not always as flexible in his ideas."

Chapter 5

Looking out from the palace on the summit of the terraced plateau of Buda, Emeric could see all the way to the Danube. He preferred the nearer view, however. Just outside the palace he had two new pole-ornaments. The one on the left writhed slightly; the chill air of late autumn had the interesting property of prolonging the futile struggle for life—in high summer heat and winter's cold his ornaments had a tendency to expire much too quickly.

The King of Hungary would not tolerate nationalism, or too much in the way of religious fervor. His kingdom's people were a mixture of Slovenes, Croats, Slavs, Magyar, Slovaks, Walachs and a half a dozen other minorities, not to mention several different religions. That didn't matter. They were, first and foremost, *his*. Impalement of those who sought to undermine that, in the interest of their insular little people, was an effective message.

His kingdom stretched from the edge of Istria to the Carpathians. Now he wanted the southern Balkans. To the west, was the Holy Roman Empire. To the east, the Ilkhan Mongols. To the north, the Grand Duke of Lithuania. Only the south offered softness, but unfortunately there were the hill-tribes between him and the Byzantines.

He wished that one of those pole-ornaments could be the infamous Iskander Beg. The Illyrian would pay that price one of these days, if Emeric could winkle him out of those mountains. The Hungarian heavy cavalry were at a disadvantage there, in the broken, steep country. Emeric hated the mountains. If he could flatten all the damned mountains in the world he could ride all of his enemies down, from the Holy Roman Emperor to the Grand Duke.

And now those idiots in Constantinople were going to give him his target on a platter; help him to bypass Iskander Beg and his hill-tribes. He smiled grimly, sat back on the golden throne, amid the tapestry-hung splendor of his reception room—he loved this display of wealth and grandeur—and let his eyes linger on the two victims outside the huge mullioned windows.

That view might unbalance the greasy Byzantine.

The servant was still waiting for orders, too used to his master's little ways to turn so much as a hair at the display outside the windows. Emeric raised a finger, and the servant snapped to attention. "Send the Byzantine emissary, Count Dimetos, up to me. Those accompanying him, also."

The servant bowed, and whisked himself out the door.

The Byzantine had been left to kick his heels for several hours. That did no harm, but little good either. He'd be used to that. Emissaries were often left in cold or overheated antechambers for hours, or even days at a time. A couple of would-be traitors on display on the top of sharpened poles would be somewhat more effective at impressing him.

"Count Dimetos, Imperial Emissary of Alexius VI," announced the majordomo from the arched doorway, "and his advisors."

Normally, Emeric discarded the hangers-on to any supplicant who came to seek a royal audience. They tended to bolster the confidence of the supplicant, an undesirable state of affairs. But the Byzantine Count had been nearly imperturbable last time, and very hard to read. Perhaps Emeric would get more from the escort's expressions.

They filed in. The effects of seeing the impaled men just outside of the windows were most satisfactory. On three of the five, anyway. Count Dimetos calmly looked away. The fifth man, the blond one— unusual, that hair color, in a Byzantine—didn't even blink or give the dying men a second glance. He bowed, along with the Count. Two of the others forgot to bow and had to be prodded to it.

Emeric's curiosity and caution were aroused immediately by the indifferent one. There was something very odd about that blond man. It made Emeric suspicious.

But he had no intention of revealing anything. Instead, Emeric nodded slightly, barely acknowledging the respectful bows.

"Well. Count Dimetos, you have taken some time to get back to me."

The emissary held out his palms. "My apologies, King Emeric. Travel is slow at this time of year. But for a few small details, about which I am sure we can reach a speedy agreement, I bring happy news."

Emeric was careful to look unimpressed. "I'm not some Turkish-bazaar merchant, Count. I do not bargain."

Actually, Emeric *was* impressed. The counterdemands he'd made a few months earlier when the Byzantines had first approached him with an offer for a secret alliance against Venice had been extreme:

Forty galleys, full crews, thirty carracks capable of carrying at least two hundred men each, and five hundred thousand ducats to cover the cost of the campaign. *And* Zante and Crete. Nothing less, and all that in exchange for simply seizing Corfu from the Venetians—which the Hungarians would keep, not the Greeks—so that the Byzantine Empire could finally be rid of the untaxed and commercially aggressive Venetian enclave in Constantinople.

To call it an "unequal exchange" would be like calling an elephant a mouse. Yet, to Emeric's surprise, the Byzantines were apparently willing to settle on his terms.

It all seemed opportune, much too opportune. If Alexius came up with the money, Emeric would know that it was indeed too good to be true. There was only one place Alexius could still raise that kind of money: by making a secret alliance with Lithuania.

Emeric suppressed a vicious smile. If Grand Duke Jagiellon wanted to give him money and ships to do exactly what he had already intended to do, so be it. Emeric couldn't see Jagiellon's exact plan yet, but his target was plainly the Venetian Republic. That was also fine. Emeric wanted Venice and its holdings, too, eventually, but he would take things one step at a time. Corfu, first. That would cripple the Venetians and allow him to turn on the Byzantines. Before that weak fool Alexius knew what was happening, Emeric would have Negroponte, and then . . .

The hell with merely holding the Golden Horn as the Venetians did. Constantinople itself would do. And Alexius himself— Jagiellon also, it seemed—would provide him with the wherewithal to do so.

Now he did smile, but pleasantly, and his voice was smooth and urbane. "However, please continue, Count Dimetos. I do not object to some small adjustment of the terms. Not necessarily."

"Just details to be arranged, not really adjustments," said the emissary, fluttering his hands. "The agreement we spoke of the last time was not entirely complete."

He's nervous, thought Emeric, incredulously. *The Greek is* nervous.

What did it take to make someone like Dimetos nervous? Dimetos's quick flicker of a glance at the expressionless blond man answered that question.

Emeric leaned forward. "Introduce me to your companions, Count."

The Count bowed. He indicated the tallest man of his party. "Your Majesty, this is Admiral Lord Nikomos of Volos. He is our naval expert. This is General Alexiou. He is, as you might gather, a military man. Mavilis here has come to support me with any financial . . . details."

Emeric raised his eyebrows. "That is one detail about which there will be no discussion." He pointed to the blond man, who looked back at him with dead eyes. "And who is this?"

"Ah . . . An advisor to the emperor," the emissary stated uncomfortably. *Decidedly* uncomfortably. "Milord Aldanto, is his name."

Emeric nodded with feigned disinterest, and yawned, his voice at variance to the curiosity sparked by Dimetos's reaction. "An Italian name. Interesting. Where are you from, Aldanto?"

"Milano." There was a toneless quality to the voice that matched the man's stony expression. Toneless? *Rather say, lifeless.*

Emeric simply raised his eyebrows again, and turned back to the emissary. "Well, Count. Perhaps you should explain these little details that you believe require—what did you call it?—'completion,' I believe."

There was a slight beading of sweat on the Count's face. "Well. The galleys—"

The admiral interrupted. "We just don't have that many ships to spare, King Emeric. It would leave us with too few for—"

"If I had wished you to speak, Admiral, I would have told you so," Emeric said curtly. "I need those vessels. Mine are not a sea-going people. I have enlisted what I can, but we are talking of blockades, escorts and transports. I can move men overland as far as the mouth of the Narenta. The rest will have to be achieved by sea. If you don't provide those transports, then the assault is a waste of time. The Narenta pirates have been brought into my fold for this task. Backed up by the galleys of Byzantium, you should be able to deal with any Venetian vessels. Provided we time this right, that's the key."

He studied the pole ornaments for a moment. The one on the left had now apparently died also. Pity. Emeric had hoped, idly, that he wouldn't be too preoccupied to observe the last moments.

"We must allow the Eastern and Western convoys to pass," he continued, looking back at the Byzantine envoys. "The commander of the Corfu garrison will send a request for replacement stores by coaster afterward. At that point we attack. If we fail to take the fortress and the island, we will have some months to lay siege before the Venetian ships can return."

"The emperor Alexius has arranged that neither fleet will be returning," said the blond-haired man expressionlessly.

Emeric had not asked for *him* to speak, either, but he let that pass. Instead, he snorted. "The last time that was tried it failed."

"This time it will not fail." The man made that statement with the same certainty with which he might have said, *The sun will rise tomorrow.* Which was . . . also interesting.

Emeric shook his head. "I don't gamble on my campaigns. Certainly not based on empty promises." His tone made clear his opinion of the spendthrift and debauched young Alexius.

"We do not make empty promises." There was such a cold certainty in that voice! Who *was* this fellow, that he could make such pledges on behalf of Alexius?

Emeric dismissed that with a wave. "We will calculate as if you are not that sure. First, let us settle the important question: money."

An unpleasant conviction was growing in his mind about this blond man. He would have to check with the Countess Elizabeth Bartholdy, his principal advisor in magical matters. Despite his reputation, fiercely cultivated, Emeric was little more than a hedge-wizard compared to her.

He was now almost sure that the money was coming from Jagiellon. That did not worry him. Money was not a potential threat, nor a potential spy. Gold had no loyalty, and was never a traitor or an assassin.

What he hadn't expected, and didn't like at all, was dealing with

Jagiellon almost face-to-face, as it were. He suspected the blond man was little more than a talking puppet. The name Aldanto rang a bell. He would have to investigate the matter further. Emeric didn't want this—*thing*—in his kingdom for one moment longer, if it was what he thought it was. Talking puppets could become doorways.

"The emperor wants to negotiate-er-payment in tranches," the little money-man stuttered. "P-part as and when the work is f-finished. So to speak."

Emeric shook his head. Alexius thought he had best put a brake on the Hungarian advance, did he? Withhold the money if the Hungarians moved into Epirus . . .

Ha! "No. I can't see the vessels up front. So I'll see the money. Otherwise I might find myself caught like a rat in a trap, without your ships."

"But . . ."

The blond man interrupted. "You will have the money within the month."

Emeric's eyes narrowed. He was fairly certain now he was right. So this was the face of the enemy across the northern Carpathians.

Odd, in a way. He knew this kind of possession was possible, but it took demonic power. And that demonic power too often ended up devouring the user. Emeric himself dealt with a power below . . .

But very, very cautiously. Well, he would need magicians for this project anyway. He would consult with Elizabeth; she had a long memory, and longer experience. She even frightened him a little. How could a woman that old look as if she were barely twenty?

She was truly beautiful, too, with the sort of allure that literally held men enthralled. And she used that beauty like the weapon that it was; ruthlessly and accurately. It was, fortunately for Emeric, the kind of beauty that he could close his mind to.

In the craggy and cliff-hung little valleys on the north end of the enchanted island, the night-wind was full of the clatter-clatter of little goaty feet on the limestone and the hollow trilling of reed pipes. The shepherd huddled down under his sheepskins in his little lean-to. It was a full moon out there. This was when all good men stayed indoors.

Kallikazori still walked on the high, barren hillsides on these holy nights. And a man might turn over to find his wife was not beside him. If he was a wise man, he went back to sleep and said nothing at all about it to her in the morning. If he was a fool, he might beat her for being half-asleep the next day. But a man who wanted children, fertile fields and fertile flocks would keep his tongue and hands still. A wise man knew that here on Corfu, the old ones still walked and still wielded their powers.

A wiser man stilled his mind to the fact, prayed to the saints, and pretended he saw and heard nothing.

The wisest of all . . .

The wisest of all found a way to pray to the saints by day—and something else by night. After all, the Holy Word said, *Thou shalt not have other gods* before *Me.* It said nothing at all about having other gods in reserve.

PART II
Winter, 1538 A.D.

Chapter 6

Eberhard of Brunswick waited patiently in the antechamber. He looked upwards and across toward the tall, narrow windows of the throne room, and then back at the empty throne. Weak winter sunlight patterned down through the windows and onto the mosaic-tiled floor of the throne room. The mosaic, a religious scene showing Christ feeding the multitudes, had been commissioned by the present Emperor's father, at tremendous expense. Personally, Eberhard thought the byzantine splendor did not fit well with the Gothic style of Mainz. The workers had been recruited—also at great expense—by the Venetians, all the way from Constantinople. Charles Fredrik's father, nearing the end of his life, had been convinced that the pious work would help to ease his path to heaven.

If God had the taste of a Byzantine, maybe it had. Eberhard grimaced. He had been close to the old Emperor. If Emperor Walther had lived to see the work finished, Eberhard had a feeling that the old flagstones might just have been put down again, on top of the mosaic.

He sighed. Charles Fredrik would be here, no doubt, shortly. In the meanwhile it would have been nice to have something other than these damn tiles to look at. It was damnably cold for an old man. He paced, to warm himself and distract his attention from the mosaic.

When Charles Fredrik finally arrived, with his aide Baron Trolliger, Eberhard of Brunswick began to wonder if he would be arranging for more Byzantine craftsmen to smooth this Emperor's path to heaven. Charles Fredrik looked tired. He looked more than tired: he looked worn. And he looked worried.

Still, his expression lightened when he saw Eberhard. He raised the old counselor up. "I see they have not even brought you a glass of wine to fight off the chill." He shook his head disapprovingly and gestured to one of the footmen. "Hippocras, for my Lord of Brunswick, and for us."

A few minutes later the three of them were seated in a small, warm side-parlor. An apple-wood fire burned merrily in the grate. That, and a goblet of rich, spiced hippocras had helped fight off Eberhard's chill and had lightened the Emperor's expression, even given some color to his cheeks. Charles Fredrik still looked twenty years older and much closer to the grave than he should. Eberhard knew that the wounds he had received in a youthful campaign still troubled one of the Emperor's lungs. Winters were always hard for him.

"Still no news from my nephew Manfred," said Charles Fredrik heavily.

"The roads and passes are snowed closed," said Baron Trolliger. "There is no reason to get too worried, Your Majesty. The Norse are honorable about their oaths."

Charles Fredrik shook his head. "I trust those petty pagan kinglets not at all, the so-called Christian ones not much more. I've sent a messenger through to Francesca in Copenhagen."

Baron Trolliger touched his head. "That woman . . ."

"Has secured us more cooperation with the Danes in two months than you did in five years, Hans Trolliger," said Charles Fredrik, almost snapping the words. "If I had twenty more like her, I could afford to die without worrying about the succession. As it is—well, at least Hakkonsen is with Manfred. Between Erik and Mam'zelle de Chevreuse, they keep one of my heirs on a reasonably even keel."

Baron Trolliger nearly choked. "That affair in Venice nearly had him killed! I still say we should have hanged every last one of those damned Servants of the Trinity."

Charles Fredrik smiled grimly. "If we'd hanged as much as one, the entire Pauline church would have been in an uproar. Instead *they've* excommunicated a few obvious bad eggs and we must put up with and isolate the rest. As for Francesca and Erik, I still say they kept Manfred on a reasonably even keel in very dangerous waters. Without either of them, he would have definitely been killed. Erik has made a warrior out of him, and Francesca has done even more. She's made him think. She might have led him by his testicles to that point, but she actually made him *think*. To my certain knowledge, that's something no one else ever succeeded at doing. The Venetian affair has done a great deal for one of my heirs. Besides, I enjoyed my visit to Venice and to Rome, even if you didn't, Hans."

Baron Trolliger looked as if he might choke. "The visit was bad enough. The months you made me stay there afterward . . ."

Eberhard of Brunswick chuckled. "Well, Your Majesty, at least Prince Conrad hasn't caused you as much trouble, even if he hasn't provided you with as much entertainment. What is Manfred doing in Norway, anyway? Winter in Scandinavia is not something I'd ever want go through again. I did it with your father in Småland back in '22, when we went in to bail the Danes out. Far as I was concerned, the pagans deserved the place."

To an extent, Charles Fredrik agreed with his advisor, though it was hardly politic to say so.

"In winter, it can be bleak. Nice enough in summer," said the Emperor, mildly. Eberhard of Brunswick had been one of his father's closest friends and the old *Ritter* was now one of Charles Fredrik's most trusted emissaries. He'd spent the better part of the last year in Ireland, with the Celtic Ard Ri, representing the States General and the Holy Roman Emperor to the League of Armagh.

Now he was home. Charles Fredrik knew the old man had delighted in the thought of seeing his grandchildren again. The *Ritter* had dropped some hints in his correspondence that he'd like to retire to his estates.

The Emperor bit his lip. The old man deserved retirement, had more than earned it, but men of his caliber were rare. Very rare. In point of fact, there was no one skilled and canny enough to replace him.

He'd have to send the silver-haired warrior out again. But not somewhere cold and wet this time; that was the least he could do.

"It's still part and parcel of the same business, Eberhard. Well, the aftermath of it. The Danes are content to hold the coastal lands, but the chapters of Knights of the Holy Trinity that my father established there after the '22 campaign are still pushing deeper into pagan lands. They stir things up, and the pagan tribes tend to take it out on the Danish settlers. The Knights are building little empires out there. At this point, they're a law unto themselves."

Eberhard snorted. "Rein them in, Emperor. Rein them in hard. We need the coast to keep the pagan bastards from raiding our shipping on the Baltic, but the hinterland . . . not worth the price in blood the Empire will pay for some bar-sinister *Ritter* to get himself an estate."

The Emperor nodded. "That's what Manfred had gone to do. Last I heard it was in hand, but then this business in Norway cropped up, and he went off to sort that out. We haven't heard from him in over a month."

"It is near midwinter, Your Majesty," pointed out Baron Trolliger.

"I know. That treaty is supposed to be ratified on midwinter's eve. He'd have sent me word . . ."

The Emperor rubbed his eyes, tiredly. "I know, Hans, the passes in Norway are closed. But I've had the Servants of the Trinity try to contact him by magical means, also. Nothing."

To Eberhard, he said in explanation: "He's gone to Telemark. One of those little kingdoms on the Norwegian side of the Skagerrak. Dirt poor, rotten with raiders and pirates because the land can't feed all of them. We concluded a treaty with King Olaf two years ago. He's dead, and his son Vortenbras has taken the throne, and so the treaty needs to be ratified again. Since Vortenbras is pagan, the oath must be sworn in the temple on Odin's ring at the midwinter festival. Only the ring's been stolen. Manfred and Erik and two of our best diviners have gone to see if they can find it. No word from them. All I can find out is that it's snowing heavily in the north."

The old *Ritter* looked as if even the thought of a trip into snowy Scandinavia was enough to make him break out in chilblains. Nevertheless, he said calmly, "Do you want me to go, Your Majesty?"

The Emperor leaned over and patted the age-spotted, sinewy hand. "No. I've sent a message to a woman who will see to it. The same Francesca de Chevreuse of whom"—here he gave Trolliger a sly glance—"Hans disapproves. But no matter what Hans thinks of her capability, I have confidence in her over any other possible agent in this case."

Trolliger shuddered. "She's capable enough. Her methods . . ."

"Work," said the Emperor. "Even you find her attractive, Hans. Men will tell an attractive, intelligent woman things they won't tell us; they'll *do* things for her they would not consider doing for us for any amount of money. They'll go to great lengths to help her."

"They reduce us to the level of Aquitaine, Your Majesty," said the baron, sulkily.

The Emperor pulled a wry face. "Which is why our officials fail so dismally when we have to deal with the Aquitaine. I'm almost tempted to send you to Francesca for lessons, Hans."

Charles Fredrik saw the look of trepidation on the old *Ritter*'s face. He smiled reassuringly at the older man. "Not you, Eberhard. You would enjoy her intellect and company, though, I can assure you of that. Baron Trolliger here finds her physically threatening— or her breasts, anyway. He fears they will cast a fascination over him and, like Samson, leave him helpless to resist the lady's whims."

Eberhard of Brunswick shook his head. "It is not the company of an intelligent woman that I fear, Your Majesty. It is rather that I am concerned that you'll send me to Aquitaine. I was hoping to spend some time in Swabia with my family." He touched his silver hair. "I'm not getting any younger, Your Majesty. Especially for Aquitaine, you need younger men. "

The Emperor gave a small snort of wry laughter. "The last thing I need in Aquitaine is *younger* men, Eberhard. But relax, I am not going to send you there. However, I'm afraid I can't let you go home to pasture either. Men like you are too few on the ground. The Holy Roman Empire still needs you. *I* still need you."

The older *Ritter* shrugged. " Well, I just hope it's somewhere warm this time, Your Majesty. This winter seems colder than last winter. Or maybe I'm just older. At least Mainz is not as damp as Ireland was."

Charles Fredrik allowed the corners of his mouth to ease into a smile. "Would the Holy Land be warm enough and dry enough for you?"

"A pilgrimage for my soul has always been one my desires," said the old *Ritter* quietly. Eberhard of Brunswick was one of the best and most reliable of officials in the States General. He was an adept politician and diplomat, but at the core, he was a pious man. His soul might need cleansing of what he'd done for the Empire, but not for himself, Charles Fredrik knew.

"It's more for my soul than yours, old friend," the Emperor said equally quietly. "I don't know how many more of these winters I can take, either." He smiled wryly. "No mosaics this time though, Eberhard. Perhaps some churches in places that need them. I haven't lived your life and I have a feeling I'll need a good many prayers to get me away from hellfire, as well as a pilgrimage to Jerusalem. But I can't go; you will have to go for me."

He lifted a heavy eyebrow. "Of course there are some small tasks you can do for the Holy Roman Empire while you're there. And along the way."

Eberhard nodded. He understood politics thoroughly enough to know precisely whom, in that part of the world, a "small task" might be directed towards. "The Ilkhan?"

Charles Fredrik nodded. "We've had tentative feelers from them. Baron Trolliger had a long discussion with a visiting Jew from Damascus, during the months he remained behind in Italy. The man was there strictly on family business, of course, but—as they often do—the Mongols were using the Jewish merchant as an informal emissary."

The Ilkhan Mongol Empire stretched from Egypt to the Black Sea and no one really knew just how far into the Asian hinterland. The Ilkhan were themselves pagan, but had no qualms about their subject peoples worshiping gods of their choice. Christians, Muslims, Jews—many religions—all prospered in the Mongol realm. They enforced a degree of tolerance that the fiery Christian Metropolitan of Alexandria might find irksome, but it did make things peaceful in their dominions.

Eberhard's eyes narrowed. "They won't like that in Alexandria."

The Emperor shrugged. "Politics and war make for strange bedfellows, Eberhard. And it all comes down to Grand Duke Jagiellon trying to flank me, or force me to fight on two fronts, and the Holy Roman Empire trying to flank him. The Grand Duke is building up quite a fleet in Odessa. Then, too, there's this: The news Hans brings back from his long stay in Italy leaves me concerned that the Hungarians are up to no good, either."

The *Ritter* nodded. "The Ilkhan could at least bottle them up in the Black Sea. But surely Emperor Alexius VI can do that just as well from Constantinople?"

Baron Trolliger coughed. "We have a treaty with him, yes. But we've had word that a few ships—which are definitely *not* from

Odessa—have been discharging visitors, who have gone on to visit the Imperial palace."

The old *Ritter* nodded slowly. "I see. That would indeed leave our flank wide open. Very well, Your Majesty, when do I leave?"

"Not until spring, Eberhard," said the Emperor. "Even if you left today, getting passage to Acre or Ascalon before spring would be impossible. You can have a few winter months to spend cooped up with your grandchildren. By the time spring comes, even the muddy road will probably look appealing."

Eberhard smiled. "There is some merit in what you say, Your Majesty. The last time I was home my daughter's youngest was teething. Yes, by spring it may even be good to be on the road without children."

Charles Fredrik coughed. "Well. Not strictly without. He's a bit old to be called a child, these days. But he is one of my heirs."

A look of horror came across the old statesman's face. "Not Manfred? Sire, I'm an old man!"

The Emperor nodded, ruefully. "It's a symbol of great trust, Eberhard of Brunswick. I am feeling my age, and my wound troubles me. I may not survive another winter and such a trip will take the boy a long way from the intriguers of court. If I die, the succession must be a simple matter of Conrad being the only candidate at hand. Not that I have the least fears about Manfred wanting the throne, but that has never stopped factions in the past. On the other hand, if by any evil chance Conrad and I are killed— as happened to the Emperor Maximilian and his son—I want Manfred safe and ready, where no one can get to him easily. Besides, you're the leading statesman of my Empire. I want him to learn from you. If there is time I'll send the boy to Ferrara to Duke Enrico Dell'este to see if he can learn strategy and tactics from the Old Fox, but statecraft needs to come first. And you'll find he's improved a great deal. Circumstances, Erik and Francesca have made him grow up a great deal."

But all the old man said was "Manfred!" with a face full of woe.

The messenger bearing dispatches from the Emperor to Francesca de Chevreuse only took ten days, and that was by spending imperial gold like water. A brief thaw and then a vicious freeze had made the roads full of iron-hard ridges and ruts . . . which was still better than fetlock-deep mud.

Francesca looked at the imperial seal—and the scrawl. Well, the Imperial tutors probably hadn't beaten him for untidiness.

She grimaced. One had to wonder what vagaries of imperial policy had stemmed from some terrified official doing his best to interpret this handwriting. It really was difficult. Looking carefully, though, she could see that was in part due to a definite tremor in the hand of the writer. Perhaps the rumors about the Emperor's health had some substance after all.

Francesca looked out over Copenhagen and the Sound. The water was gray, bleak, wind-chopped. She'd been out earlier, wearing her beautiful sable coat and muff. Her new venture into vertical diplomacy instead of the horizontal kind still required appearances. Even though, as the prince's leman, she was strictly off-limits, men could be just as foolish when flirting as they could in bed. More so, sometimes; in bed, they weren't trying to impress a woman with their brains.

So she needed to look as good, if not more so, than she had as one of the most sought-after courtesans in Venice. That, alas, meant keeping up with her rigorous exercise regime. The air had been biting cold and full of the dusty smell of coming snow.

Just the time for a little venture into the Norse wilderness. Ah, well. What the Emperor wanted . . .

The Emperor would get. Besides, she was a little worried herself about the lack of communication from Manfred.

She sat down at her writing desk and sharpened her quill. Then, in a hand that was both beautiful and legible, penned several letters. She shook the sand off them, and tinkled a delicate glass-and-silver bell. Poor little Heinrich could go out in the cold and deliver these.

Chapter 7

Winter in the Republic of Venice was not as bleak as winter in the Holy Roman Empire. It was still wet and cold, which made repair work a little more difficult than at other times.

This fact was relevant. The *Casa* Montescue was busy getting a facelift. True, the great house of Montescue was technically bankrupt twice over, but that was a good reason to do it now. "If we don't do it," said Lodovico Montescue calmly to his grand-daughter Katerina, "everyone will think we are down to our last ducat."

Kat shook her head at him, smiling. "But Grandpapa, we *are* down to our last ducat!" She couldn't bring herself to be hugely worried about it. Come financial ruin or any other disaster, she had Marco. And it seemed, now that the feud between Valdosta and Montescue was finally healed, that Lodovico Montescue, once the *Colleganza*-genius of Venice, had found his verve once again.

He chucked her chin. "*Cara mia*, if we have the place looking too shabby, then we'll have our creditors on our necks. Watch. We start spending money, they'll back off. We've got political connections, even if not business. Something will turn up."

She shook her head and sighed at him, but without the despair that had plagued her, waking and sleeping, for so many years. "All that worries me is where the money to pay for this lot is going to come from."

"If need be, we'll borrow it," he said, making Kat raise her eyes. "But watch. Things will begin to right themselves." He stretched out his big, liver-spotted hands and looked at the slightly bulbous knuckles. "Marco has not come yet?"

"He said he'd be here by the terce bell." Kat felt the warmth of knowing this lift her.

"Good." Lodovico nodded his satisfaction. "I want him to work on these old hands again. I'll swear that boy of yours has magic in his fingers, never mind his skills as a doctor."

"He is going to be great physician!" said Kat defensively, trying very hard not to think about the *other* things that he was. Magician, for one. Vehicle for—something else—for another.

Lodovico chuckled. "I don't disagree with you, girl. I'm becoming very fond of the boy myself. How is the annulment of that marriage of his going?"

Kat made a face; this was the one shadow on her days, for she and Marco could not wed until he had been rid of the wife-in-name-only he had taken out of a misplaced sense of honor and obligation to his benefactor, his wife's brother Petro Dorma. "Slowly. That Angelina! One moment it's a nunnery, and becoming a saint . . ."

Lodovico snorted with laughter. "Saint Puttana. I'll believe all the girls in the House of the Red Cat turned Siblings first."

Kat grinned, in spite of herself. "You shouldn't use language like that in front of me, Grandpapa. Anyway, one minute she's all set on being a saint and a martyr. The next she's screaming at poor Petro that he wants to lock her away."

"And if you didn't hate her guts you might almost feel sorry for her," said her grandfather, still amused.

Kat shook her head at him. "She was, and is, a spoiled, selfish brat. And stupid on top of it. She got herself pregnant and got poor Marco to claim it was his to save her face, and *then* tried to run away with her lover anyway! And she's still trying to manipulate things in her own favor, no matter what that does to people around her. And yes, I sometimes hate her. But at least I haven't taken out an assassination contract on her head."

Lodovico acknowledged the hit with a wry smile. "I was wrong that time. And Marco and Benito lived through it. Besides, if she delays any more with this annulment I wouldn't bet on you not doing just the same."

They were in a small salon just off the front hall, and thus the pounding of the great Lion-headed knocker was easily audible.

Lodovico chuckled. "He's eager, this young man of yours. Early, too."

A faint frown creased Kat's brow. That was a very forceful knocking. She'd come down to wait for Marco often enough to know he used the knocker tentatively. Maybe . . . bad news. Or good news, finally, about the annulment of his marriage to Angelina. She hastened out into the hallway.

White-haired old Giuseppe had not announced the visitor, because he was gaping at the two of them. They were . . . enormous. They loomed over Giuseppe in the way that the Church of Saint Hypatia Hagia Sophia loomed over the square outside it. Giuseppe and Kat would have been terrified, had the two blond giants not looked like two very lost little boys, crushing fur hats in their hands, hoping for a welcome.

"Pardon," said one, in Italian so atrocious that only familiarity with Erik Hakkonsen's accent enabled Kat to understand him. "But is this the dwelling of the family Montescue?"

"It is," said Kat, blinking at him. It wasn't just the accents of these—boys?—that was outlandish. It was every inch of them, clad as they were in garments like nothing she had ever seen before. Oh, in part, they resembled some sort of Norselander or Icelander; Venice saw enough of those coming in and out of their ports. But not all their garments were fur and homespun woolen. They also rejoiced in leather leggings with fringes of a kind that no Icelander had ever boasted, and there were beads and feathers braided into their hair, which was shaven on the sides, but long everywhere else. And in sheathes at their sides, each of them wore a weapon that Kat recognized. Erik Hakkonsen favored that kind of little axe or hatchet—a *tomahawk,* it was called.

"Ah, good." The speaker's face cleared. "And is the clan chieftain here? Chief-Lodi-Ludo—"

"Blessed Jesu, boy, don't mangle my name further!" Lodovico growled, as he limped into the hallway. "I am Lodovico Montescue, of *Casa* Montescue. Who the devil are you?"

Both boys drew themselves up with immense dignity.

"Gulta and Bjarni Thordarson, at your service," the speaker said, and both bowed. "Sent we were, by Clan Thordarson, a trade alliance to make. From Vinland we come, for that purpose." A corded oiled-sailcloth bundle was at the man's feet, and he used the hatchet to slice open the flax cords binding it. It opened, spilling out fine woven cloth, dyed in rich hues. Not wool; something finer, Kat thought. The weaving was done in geometric patterns like nothing she had ever seen, and when the boy bent down and pulled up a corner and handed it to her, she stroked it. And the touch—

"Grandpapa!" she cried involuntarily. "It is as soft as silk, but silk made into wool!"

"It is alpaca," said the one who had not yet spoken, diffidently. "And this is cotton."

He bent and pulled out a snowy white piece and held it to her for her inspection. She touched it as well—cotton she knew. The Egyptian and Indian cloth was shockingly expensive, so much so that only the wealthy could afford the gauzes and cambrics made from it. This was certainly cotton.

"We have these, and other things. Furs, spices. We wish a trade alliance with Clan Montescue to make," the first boy said proudly. "Carlo had said—"

At first, Kat wasn't sure she heard him correctly. "Pardon—*who*?" she managed.

The boy knitted his brows in puzzlement. "You know him not? Carlo, of Clan Montescue? Is he not here? But he had said—"

And that was when all hell broke loose.

Marco walked in at just that moment, which complicated matters further. Kat was weeping, Lodovico shaking the poor Vinlander boy in a way that would have made his teeth rattle had he not been as big as he was, and yelling at the top of his lungs, while the other boy looked utterly bewildered. Somehow Marco managed to separate Lodovico from his victim, get them all herded into a quiet room, and (relatively) calmed down.

With Marco's prompting—while Kat clung numbly to his hand— the boys managed to piece together part, at least, of what had happened to her father.

His vessel had been taken by pirates, who had, in turn, sold him to some strange Vinlander tribe in the south of the continent. He had escaped, or been rescued, by some other tribe—the boys were rather vague as to which, or how it had happened—and they in their turn had traded him up the coast until he came into the hands of the Thordarsons.

Now, they had had to pay a great deal for Carlo Montescue, and by their custom and law, he apparently discovered that he couldn't just find a ship and come home. No, he had to earn his freedom; until then, he was what they called a "thrall." Not exactly a slave, but certainly not free, and branded as such by the iron ring around his neck. The boys were very matter-of-fact about it, and although Kat could have wept even harder with vexation, the part of her that was a Venetian trader to the core could see their point.

At any rate, it soon was proved that Carlo was going to earn his freedom in record time, for exactly that reason. Records. Record-keeping and accounting, at which, apparently, the Vinlanders were shockingly bad.

Lodovico grunted at that. "So not all that cursing I did when he was a boy was entirely wasted."

Evidently not. "Our clan-folk have holdings down on the valley of the Mother of Rivers, as well as trading posts at Where-Waters-Meet upon the eastern coast," the first boy—Gulta, that was—said proudly. "Carlo made our profits to rise like a swan in flight! It was he who said that a trading mission to Europe and Venice and perhaps the silk houses of Constantinople might pay a very rich dividend. And we sent him home to await us and prepare the way, while we gathered goods and chose who to go."

"But he never arrived." The loss in her grandfather's face made Kat gulp down her own tears. If she began crying, he might not be able to hold himself together.

It was a crumb of comfort that the boys looked stricken, too. "We sent him home!" Gulta half-protested, as if he thought they doubted him.

Lodovico managed to reach out and pat the boy on the hand. "We believe you, lad," he replied, his voice cracking a little. "But a great deal can happen between Vinland and Venice."

They were all thinking it. *Including shipwreck.*

All but Marco, it seemed, who stuck out his chin stubbornly. "Not shipwreck," he said firmly. "I can promise you that. Whatever has delayed him, it isn't that. And until I hear otherwise, I will be sure it is only that—delay."

It wasn't sane, it wasn't rational, but Kat took heart from his surety—and so did her grandfather, who sat up straighter and nodded.

"By Saint Raphaella, Valdosta, you shame me," he said. "If you, a stranger to our family, can have such faith, how am I to doubt?

Right enough. My son has survived so much else, how can he *not* return home to us?"

"Exactly so, sir," Marco agreed, giving Kat's hand a squeeze.

Now Lodovico turned to the Vinlanders. "And that being so, young sirs, please: Let us hear your plans, and how *Casa* Montescue means to figure into them."

To anyone but a Venetian, that statement would have seemed callous in the extreme. Here, Lodovico's son had literally been raised from the dead, only to vanish again, and he was discussing trade alliances?

But Kat knew, and Marco surely knew, that this was perhaps the bravest thing that her grandfather could have done. There was nothing, or next to nothing, any of them could do to help Carlo, wherever he was. And this trade agreement was her father's hard-won legacy to the House of Montescue. Should they now throw it away because he had vanished again? That would be like taking gold he had sacrificed to send them, and flinging it into the canals and starving, setting his sacrifice at naught because he was not there himself.

No! She and her grandfather would trust to God and her father's eminent good sense and cleverness, and fight to preserve what he had given them.

Lying in bed, late that night, Kat realized her father's ambitions were going to cost a great deal. Yes, the profits from trade in Vinland goods, particularly this cotton, could be very, very lucrative. Egyptian and Indian cottons were only for the very rich. Cotton was as expensive, or more so, than silk, because picking the seeds out was such a laborious process. Either the Vinlanders had some process to remove the seeds or labor must be dirt cheap over there. Still, however it was done their prices would bring the fabric within reach of the merely well-to-do. But it would require offices and warehouses in either Flanders or Denmark or Ireland to meet up with the Norse-Celtic Atlantic trade ships. The family her father had tied in with were of Icelandic stock. The Icelanders tended to run a Denmark-Vinland journey. It was not a good route for serious volumes of merchandise. It was too slow, with too many overland expenses and tolls and tariffs. Yes, from a port somewhere on the Atlantic coast, they could and would sell to northern Europe. But the east and markets on the Mediterranean would be best served by meeting the Venetian Atlantic trading convoy and selling out of Venice. But that meant warehouses. Local agents. And money. Lots of money.

Are we in the fire, still? she wondered, before she drifted off to sleep, *or have we at least climbed back into the frying pan?*

Chapter 8

Svanhild Thordardatter was not a maiden easily intimidated; she had faced, in her time, bears, catamounts, blizzards that piled snow to the rooftree, drunken and aggressive *skraelings* who had gotten more *aqavit* than they should have, and *skraeling* war-bands. She could make a wilderness camp, milk a cow, goat, or sheep, cook a meal without a single implement but a knife, and read an Icelandic saga like a *skald*. She could hunt, fish, and ride as well as her brothers, besides having all of the usual skills of a well-bred maiden. She had, during the rough crossing, climbed into the rigging in her leather *skraeling* trews to help alongside her brothers.

She had not only been willing to go with them, she had been eager. Valkyrie-like she might well be, but like the storied Brunnhilde, she had her soft side. She wanted a husband, children, and a home of her own. But the only way she was going to get one was to find a husband who *wasn't* somehow related to her.

Impossible in Vinland. Well, perhaps not *impossible*, but difficult. The only unmarried men who were not somehow tied into the Thordarson clan were thralls (her mother would have died), *skraelings* (actually, not unacceptable, but she didn't really want to set up housekeeping in a bark lodge or a skin tent), or trolls. Trolls, at least, so far as she was concerned. Nasty, fat, obnoxious, hairy, smelly, uncouth, elderly *trolls.*

So for both Svanhild and her mother, this trade expedition was heaven-sent. For her mother, it would be an opportunity for Gulta and Bjarni to find their sister a fine, unattached nobleman, and if this furthered their trade alliances, all the better. For Svanhild, well, if unattached young men were so thick on the ground as all that back in the Mother Countries, *she* would make sure that any noblemen that the boys presented to her were young and handsome. Or at the least, not trolls.

She had strode confidently off the ship once it reached the harbor in Venice—and then, for the first time in her life, discovered something that intimidated her as bears, catamounts, and blizzards had never been able to do.

The women of Venice.

In the Piazza San Marco she encountered the women of Venice, and, though Gulta and Bjarni were deaf and dumb to such nuances, knew that although she might be considered to be one of the prettiest maidens in Vinland, here she was . . .

A troll.

The women of Venice were tiny, dainty, slim-waisted and small-breasted. Their perfumed hair was either dark as a raven's wing, or a becoming honey-colored shade. They did not stride, they glided. They did not wear leather and fur and homespun in tunics and trews, nor aprons and plain dresses; they wore elegant gowns of silk and brocade, velvet and linen, embroidered and trimmed with laces and ribbons. Their hands were soft and white; their complexions pale and faintly blushed. Svanhild towered over them; with her sun-browned face and brassy-gold hair, she looked like a huge, cheap trinket among a box full of dainty, gold-set jewels. Or a cow among a herd of deer, a goose swimming with swans. And she knew it, and *they* knew it; she saw it in their eyes, in the amused side-glances they bestowed on her.

No young man, noble or otherwise, would look at *her* with anything other than amused contempt.

In the time it took to walk from the ship to the lodgings her brothers had arranged for her, she had read this lesson in a thousand eyes, a thousand veiled smirks, a thousand smothered laughs behind their backs. Gulta and Bjarni were indeed oblivious to it all, excited as children at Christmastide by the newness and the bustle. So she put up a good front for them, marching with head high and cheeks burning with shame, pretending that she did not notice what was going on, either.

But she did, and it didn't stop at the door of the lodging, either. Even the servants here looked at her in that scornful way, until she was afraid to leave her room, lest she meet with their sneers and arch glances. And it quickly became clear that Venice had more people in a single one of its many districts than there were in entire cities in Vinland . . . so finding Carlo and Clan Montescue was *not* going to be the simple matter of appearing on the docks and calling out the name.

While Bjarni and Gulta searched the city for someone who could take them to Clan Montescue, she hid in her room, took comfort in what luxuries the boys found for her—food, primarily, which was of *immense* comfort, since food did not have sneers or scornful eyes—and felt despair creeping over her. And wondered if—just perhaps—Carlo Montescue, plausible fellow that he was, had somehow tricked them. That his clan was not the leader of trade that he had said. That he did not even *have* a clan. That she and Gulta and Bjarni had come here on a fool's errand, and she the most foolish of all . . .

Then her brothers finally returned after days of searching, with the news that Clan Montescue had been found, that it *was* as great as Carlo had claimed, that although Carlo had unaccountably vanished between Vinland and Venice, the ancient Clan Chief Lodovico had welcomed them and their plans with every bit of warmth and enthusiasm they could have hoped for. Which was all the more gratifying, since the resurrection and second banishment of the old man's son had been a heavy blow to him.

But then came a heavy and horrid blow to Svanhild, delivered lovingly out of the mouths of her own dear brothers.

"And we are to come to dinner with them, this night, and sit in honor at their table!" crowed Bjarni. "*Now* we will be sought for, and taken seriously! In fact, we are to come to their table most nights, and feast with them, and they will introduce us to all of the great clan chiefs of the city!"

"This will be your chance, Sister," Gulta said, in a kindly voice, as she felt the blood draining from her face. "For surely there will be many young men there. Ah, but I must warn you, do not cast those blue eyes upon the one called Marco Valdosta, for he is spoken for by the daughter of Clan Montescue."

"The daughter is clever as well," Bjarni tossed off, casually. "Well read, and canny, and of an age with you. You must cultivate her; the old one dotes upon her, and it is clear that she has great influence upon him."

The bare thought made her stomach turn over.

Oblivious as ever, the boys tramped off noisily with more of the samples of the trade goods that they had brought. In a sick panic, Svanhild looked over her best gowns, then sat down, and ate an entire basket of pastries. And in food, found what little comfort there was to be had.

If she ate like this all the time, marveled Kat, the svelte Svanhild would be the size of a barn by the time she was fifty. Unless she was one of those people who just never got fat. Looking sidelong out of her eyes at the Vinlander, Kat decided this probably wasn't the case. Svanhild had a perfect northern complexion, creamy-white with blossoming roses in her cheeks, but there was already a hint of a second chin. Well, thought Kat, uncharitably and just a touch enviously, most men would be far too distracted by the magnificent and well-exposed frontage to notice that.

Kat wondered what conversational gambit to try next. Her grandfather was deep in animated conversation about hunting with their male guests, Svanhild's brothers Gulta and Bjarni. They were as blond as their sister, and considerably larger, not that Svanhild was any midget. They were partners in her father's enterprise. It behooved her, as a good Venetian hostess, to talk to the women-folk. Only . . .

What did one say to someone who answered your comments with "Ja" or "Nu" and continued to eat as if there were a famine coming?

"Do you like Venetian food?" asked Kat, watching Svanhild mopping the last droplets of *mostarda di cremona* on her platter with a slab of *ciabatta*. The piece of *prosciutto*-stuffed capon breast was long gone.

Svanhild smiled. "Nu."

Kat was about to give up when Svanhild at last volunteered something: "I like more cream, ja."

"Oh. We don't use cream much in Venice. There are not many cows on the islands."

Svanhild swallowed the last mouthful. "Not many young men either, nu?"

Kat couldn't tell if that was relief or if the beautiful Svanhild was upset by the lack. "Well, a lot of the young *Case Vecchie* usually go off to the trading posts of the Republic. They say Venice lives on the patience of her women. A lot of the men are at sea or away sometimes for years. Even those who are married."

"I am supposed to make a marriage. Mama sent me with my brothers to Europe for that purpose."

It was said so blandly that Kat still had no idea whether she was in favor of the idea or not. "Er. Any suitors?"

Svanhild shrugged. "None that are noble enough for Mama, ja. Mama wants a nobleman for me."

"Do you like any of them?

"Nu." A pause. "Are there desserts?"

Chapter 9

Manfred and his fellow-confrere Erik Hakkonsen made as much noise invading Francesca's *boudoir* (or what passed for a *boudoir,* here in the frozen and barbaric Northlands) as a small army.

Then again, between the two of them, they *were* a small army. The Danish escort who had been cooling their heels here every day, awaiting their return, looked quite alarmed at their appearance, and Francesca didn't think that was entirely because of how battered they were.

She was pleased to see them, though. Charles Fredrik would be even more pleased.

The one thing that this room had was privacy, even if it was cold enough that she could see her breath except when she was right on top of the fire. And a lot of furs. Most of which were piled on top and around her in a kind of luxurious nest that Francesca was loath to leave—which was why she hadn't leapt to her feet to greet the Emperor's secondary heir as she probably should have.

Still, Manfred was not the kind to stand on ceremony. Neither was Erik.

Instead, Francesca looked up tolerantly at the two men, who were very much worse for wear than they had been when she last saw them. Then wrinkled her fine-boned nose. "You stink. And that's a thick lip and pair of black eyes you have there, Erik. How did you get those?"

They were unshaven and filthy, and she shuddered to think of how many fleas Manfred alone was providing a haven for. She was not exaggerating when she told them that they stank. In fact, they reeked: of sweat, of rancid grease, and something musky and animal. Clearly, they had come straight here the moment they arrived within the walls of the fortress-*cum*-palace complex.

Whatever had detained them had been physically hazardous, it seemed. She could well believe it. The Norwegian town of Telemark was some considerable distance inland from the sea. The countryside was steep, cold, snowy—which was to say, so far as Francesca was concerned, barbarous in all respects. She'd been born and raised in the Aquitaine and spent most of her adult life on the sunny coasts of the Mediterranean.

Erik looked balefully at her. "I'd rather not talk about it."

Manfred guffawed. "I'll tell you . . . for a consideration, darling."

"No, you won't," said Erik immediately.

Somehow, Francesca doubted she'd be getting that story. "Well, I've brought a fair number of sleighs here at your royal uncle's command." She gestured at the well-armed but nervous looking Danes. "The Emperor wants you back in Mainz immediately. Is your business here done?"

Manfred grimaced. "It is, although we had to agree to slightly modified terms. Give us a few moments to bid a farewell to Queen Borgny and her—ah—consort, and we can get the hell out of Norway. It's a nice country. For bears."

"They're welcome to it," said Erik, feeling his nose gingerly.

Francesca nodded. "I saw some of the Norsemen dragging a bear carcass, earlier. A big brute."

Both knights laughed, and she wondered why. Did it have anything to do with Erik's black eyes? Or something else?

"You can say that again," said Manfred. "Where do you think we'll find the queen and that Turk of hers, Erik?"

Erik gestured at the hall behind them. "Back in her rooms in the palace by now, I should think," he said.

Francesca stuck an enquiring nose out of her sables. "I thought this kingdom was ruled by a King Vortenbras?" She didn't just *think* that. It had been—but apparently *had* was the operative term. Getting to the bottom of this was imperative enough to tempt her out of her furs.

Erik laughed. "Not any more. You might say that's what we've been involved in, although most of the time it just felt like we were trying to stay alive. Come on, Manfred. We'll not introduce

Francesca to the queen. There are enough clever women in this world without getting two of them together. And the knights will be as glad to go as we are. Time they got back to Sweden, anyway."

Francesca snuggled her toes down against the still-warm brick at her feet. "From that I conclude, the knights feel even one clever woman is too many." But she had no real desire herself to emerge from her warm cocoon to meet this other clever woman. The Norse hall might be warm, but going there would mean moving out of this nest.

Still.

Before we leave, anyway. Nothing official. But if she's clever, she'll already know about me.

Just what did go on up there, anyway?

She couldn't help but notice that neither Manfred nor the icy Erik showed any signs of romantic attachment to this woman. That was a bit of a relief, since that would be a complication they didn't need. She wondered, briefly, just what a Turk was doing here, with a Norse queen.

But there'd be time for the story, somewhere warmer. Say . . . Italy. Or even . . . as she'd been thinking lately, Alexandria. She'd had several very interesting discussions with a Danish scholar about that city. And that fit in very nicely with the Emperor's plans.

After all, she was, first and foremost, the Emperor's servant, and she never, ever, forgot it. She couldn't afford to. And neither, if he was wise, could Manfred.

"Jerusalem!" Manfred nearly fell off the bed in shock. It was, especially for these parts, a very luxurious bed. It was certainly one he was very glad to be in, after all he'd been through, especially since it contained Francesca. "You're not serious, dear!"

"Do go on with your massage, Manfred," said Francesca languorously, turning slightly, and giving him a view of her magnificent breasts. He felt his blood heating up a little more; just as well, considering how cold he'd been over the past several weeks. He'd been wondering if he would *ever* feel warm again.

"I will say that the one good thing about all that drilling and training that Erik insists on is that it gives you very strong hands. You're the only man I have ever met with strong enough hands to give me a really relaxing massage." She twinkled at him. "And you do want me relaxed, don't you, dear? It gives me such a lot of energy."

Manfred went back to his task, but his mind was not distracted from her comment. "What's this about my going to Jerusalem for Charles Fredrik?"

Francesca ran a hand down his hairy, naked thigh. Nerves he'd thought frozen numb for the duration became most delightfully alive again. "Forget that I said it, darling. It just slipped out."

Manfred raised his eyes to heaven. But like a terrier onto a rat, he stuck to his questions. Rather admirably, he thought, considering the distractions. "Why Jerusalem, Francesca? I mean, it has got to be an improvement on Norway at this time of year, but—well, I thought I'd be involved in setting the Knots to rights. I'm only a confrere for another year and there's still a lot to do."

"I think you've started the ball rolling," she said playfully . . . nearly distracting the terrier. Not quite, but nearly. "Never make the mistake of thinking others cannot do the job, if not quite as you would, possibly just as well."

He grinned. "They don't have my hands, darling, or Erik to make theirs as strong. Now tell: There's more to this isn't there? Politics?"

Francesca gave him a look of deepest innocence, from under half-lowered lashes, spoiled only by a throaty chuckle. "How could you suspect that! The Emperor is an old man. He feels his age. He would like, for the sake of his soul, to undertake a pilgrimage to Jerusalem himself. But the Emperor's health . . ."

"Besides his dislike of leaving Mainz."

"Tch. Don't interrupt while I am betraying confidences, Manfred dear." She tapped his lips with one long finger. "His health and the running of an empire do not allow him to take the six months or a year necessary to go to Jerusalem. But as age creeps up on him he would like to prepare his soul for the inevitable. As would any man above a certain age."

Manfred snorted. "The Ilkhan do keep a substantial presence in Jerusalem," he stated, and was rewarded by her sly little grin, which told him he had struck dead in the black.

Well. Politics, then. Not his favorite task, but *he* wouldn't be the one engaged in it. He wasn't nearly crafty enough to deal with the Mongols. The Swedes and Danes were about at his level; if he hadn't had Francesca, the Italians would have had him raw, on toast. Even with her help, they nearly had, anyway.

"Who is going to accompany me? Trolliger? Or Brunswick?"

Francesca rolled over, exposing a front draped only in the sheerest bits of lace and silk, certainly not designed to conceal. "Eberhard of Brunswick. But I do believe your uncle *does* want to make his peace with God, and that he *is* feeling his age. And let's not talk boring business *right* now . . . unless you want to, of course?" She cocked her head slightly, lowering her long lashes, and ran an elegant finger down his torso. Reviving still more nerves.

"Argh!" He sighed, as a gloomy thought occurred to him. "I don't want to leave you for a year, Francesca."

Not that there wouldn't be plenty of distractions in the sophisticated and ancient (as well as holy) city of Jerusalem, not to mention the other delightful metropolises along the way. But they wouldn't be Francesca.

She pulled him closer and began to do very distracting things indeed. "Who said anything about leaving me behind?"

"You want to come with me?" He was startled enough to be distracted from her distraction. "But—"

Why had he thought she'd want to be left behind? Why had he thought that his uncle would *allow* her to remain behind? She was, after all, first and foremost, the Emperor's trusted servant, and he would be wise never to forget that.

Still. She was also Francesca. "That's wonderful!"

"Well, it is warmer there, is it not?"

It was only later, much later, on the verge of sleep, that it occurred to Manfred that Francesca did not betray confidences, and she didn't let things slip out. He'd been very skillfully manipulated. Very skillfully indeed.

Well, it had been more fun than being told. And even if he doubted that Charles Fredrik really needed any praying for another ten years, Jerusalem would still be interesting—and much more pleasant to visit with Francesca for company.

And if she was the Emperor's trusted servant, well, so was he. She was wise enough to remember that, even when he was distracted. Wise enough for both of them.

The thought gave him immense comfort.

Chapter 10

"Kat says I should have a talk with you," said Marco, plainly uncomfortable.

Benito put his hands on his hips. He could read the signs. *Big brother time*, he thought silently.

He wished Marco would pick some other time for it. He wasn't exactly hung-over . . . just . . . blurry.

"What is it?" he snarled. Marco frowned, ever so faintly.

All right, so it was a sulky tone. He didn't need lectures from Marco, and even less from Kat. Butter wouldn't melt in her mouth these days—but she'd been a night-bird, a smuggler, once, moving very gray cargoes of magical supplies. And, unless Benito misread the signs, by the *vacant-space-to-let* smile his brother wore these days, she hadn't waited for the marriage banns to share Marco's bed.

Right now, Marco was not going to listen to a litany of Kat's past sins. "Kat's worried about you, Benito. And so am I."

Benito could tell by the set of Marco's shoulders that his older brother wasn't enjoying this. He also knew Marco well enough to know that when Marco had decided that something must be done, it would be done. Still, Benito didn't enjoy this sort of thing either, and he was damned if he'd make it too easy for Marco.

"Well, stop worrying, Marco. I'm grown up enough to look after myself. I'm the one who usually ends up looking after you, remember. Or do I need to remind you of your little escapade with the love letters to Angelina, that got you into such a mess in the Jesolo marshes?"

Marco winced. "That was then. I'm older and wiser now."

Benito cocked an ear. Upstairs somewhere he could hear Angelina's shrill voice, berating a servant for something. Despite the fact that she was supposedly staying in one of the Dorma villas on the mainland, Angelina was forever finding some excuse to come back to Venice, to the *Casa* Dorma. "And heaven knows you've paid for it, Marco. What news on the annulment?" Perhaps he could head Marco off the lecture on his way of life.

Marco looked gloomy. "She's balking about which convent and which Order again. I really don't think she wants to go to one. I feel sorry for her. She's not really suited to a contemplative life." But Marco was obviously determined not to lose track. "But I want to talk about you, not my troubles. You can't go on like this, Benito."

Privately Benito thought Angelina would be better suited to a brothel than a cloister, but saying that would offend Marco. Marco was a sympathetic soul; Benito didn't like to offend him unnecessarily. He was very fond of his brother.

It would also probably also offend Petro Dorma, who was the Doge and their protector as well as Angelina's brother. Petro was not a sympathetic soul, or wise to offend, although these days Benito was often tempted. Anything to get out of here. "Like what, Brother?"

Marco shrugged helplessly. "The parties. The women. The drunkenness. The fights."

Benito shrugged in return. "The way I live my life is no concern of yours, Marco. Or of Kat's. Leave me alone."

Marco responded by putting an arm over Benito's shoulders. "You've got to get over her, Brother. She had a right to make her own choices. Maria wasn't ever the kind of person you could force to do anything."

Benito shrugged off the arm. "She's just a woman. Like all other women."

Marco stepped back, and this time he had more than a mere suggestion of a frown. "Benito, that's got to be about the dumbest thing you have ever said, and you've said some really . . ."

"Ahem." The servant at the doorway coughed. "Milor'. Milord Dorma wants to see you in his office. Immediately."

He left the two brothers, still glaring at each other. "Who did he mean?" said Benito finally.

"Probably you," said Marco curtly. "Kat and I are not the only ones to hear about your stupid escapades. Especially last night's stunt. Well, I'd better come along and put in a good word for you."

Benito tried to remember the details of last night. Truth to tell, he couldn't. He wondered what the hell he had done; he certainly wasn't prepared to ask Marco!

"I don't need your help," he said, sullenly, setting off up the passage. When Petro issued this sort of summons, nobody, but nobody, actually dawdled. It was a bit of a mystery to Benito. The head of the *Casa* Dorma was plumpish, balding and good-natured, so how come everybody jumped when he said "frog"?

"I'm coming anyway," said Marco, his long strides easily catching up with his shorter brother. "We Valdosta stick together. Besides, he may want me, not you."

"Ha." But it was mildly said. The Valdosta brothers did stick together; for many years they'd had no one and nothing else. Marco's loyalty touched him as nothing else, and when they walked into Petro Dorma's office, and Benito saw Angelina already there, looking ready for a five-star tantrum, he realized his brother might actually be the one who needed help, this time. Petro had been calling for Marco after all.

The Doge looked at him with a mixture of irritation and surprise. "What are you doing here, Benito? Aren't you are supposed to be at dancing classes or something?"

Best to dodge that one. He was in fact supposed to be at an elocution and poetry class that Dorma's mother insisted he take "to get rid of that working-class accent." Neither poetry nor dandified dottori from the Accademia, nor a desire to speak like the *Case Vecchie* motivated him. Besides, he'd been sleeping off last night.

"Came to support Marco," he said stoutly. "He's my brother, after all, and Grandfather said I was to look after him."

That was true enough, and when your grandfather was Duke Enrico Dell'este, one of Venice's greatest allies . . . it carried influence. Even if Benito had not spent much time with the old man since he'd been eight years old.

"Humph. Stay then. Even though this really has nothing to do with you." Dorma tapped the inlaid desk in front of him. "This is a document of the annulment of your marriage from the Grand Metropolitan in Rome. You will both sign it now. Angelina, I have arranged for you to take up the novitiate in the Carmelite sister-hood with the Cloister of Santa Lucia Della Monte outside Verona. Your escort will leave with you before Terce bell."

He said it like he meant it. He said it in a way that Petro Dorma, Angelina's indulgent brother, had never spoken before. Benito blinked.

"What!" squawked Angelina, rage flying banners in her cheeks. "I won't!"

"You agreed to," said Petro, calmly but implacably.

I'd keep my mouth shut if I were you, Angelina, Benito thought warily. *Or he might send you to some Pauline sisterhood in Sweden.*

Angelina pinched her lips. "I've changed my mind. I don't want to be a nun. And certainly not in the backcountry!"

"I don't want Angelina to do something that she doesn't want to, either," said Marco, though his eyes spoke volumes of despair.

Benito raised his eyes. That idiot brother of his! His own marriage and happiness in the balance, and he worried about this selfish, spoiled brat.

Petro turned to face Marco and Benito. "Marco, this is no longer a matter of what you or Angelina want; it is a matter of pledges and honor, the honor of the Dormas and the honor of the Dell'este. I have promised your grandfather that I will see you married, with all due pomp and ceremony, in the Doge's palace, within three months. This is not an option—not for you, not for Angelina."

Marco blinked, and Petro turned to Benito. "Benito, see that he signs that paper. You invoked your grandfather's name. See that his will is done."

"He can sign anything he pleases," snapped Angelina. "I'm not going to. I'd rather stay in town as the Doge's sister. Marco might be worth absolutely nothing as a husband, but he's *mine*. I've decided."

Petro stood up. He was not very tall. He was definitely plump. He still dominated the room.

He picked up a scroll of parchment from the desk, and handed it to her. "Sworn affidavits about your participation in the black lotos trade."

Angelina's blossoming cheeks went white. "It's . . . it's not true!" She tried to tear the parchment in two. The vellum resisted.

"The *Signori di Notte* and the Council of Ten also have copies."

Petro said grimly. He picked up a second scroll. "This is a warrant for your arrest."

Benito, watching his brother, saw Marco take a deep breath. With deliberate intent Benito stamped on his brother's toes. Hard. Having got Marco's attention he shook his head, fiercely.

Angelina began to produce the beginnings of tears. She wept, as Benito had reason to know, very prettily. There was an artful hint of a sob in her voice. "You wouldn't dare let them do this to me. You control the *Signori di Notte* and the Council. Besides, mother won't let you."

Petro Dorma shook his head. "I would prefer you to go to a convent, far from here. Verona is not as far off as I'd like, the truth to tell. I have been considering Spain, but I cannot be seen to be partisan. The people of Venice will accept your exile or your imprisonment and nod and forgive me as a slightly foolish brother; they won't accept my condoning your actions. And you forget, our mother was addicted to that same drug."

Marco was not going to listen to Benito. "Petro . . ."

The head of the house Dorma turned on him. "Stay out of this, Valdosta. She's my sister, and only your wife by my insistence, to give the baby legitimacy. Besides, I have agreed with Duke Enrico to send you off to Ferrara, today, under armed guard, if you don't do this my way. Now, Angelina, sign this."

Tears abandoned as a weapon that no longer served, cheeks white with anger, Angelina Valdosta stepped forward, snatched up a quill, and signed.

"Good," said Petro. "You have until terce. I suggest you spend the time saying farewell to our mother. I'd say you should spend it with your child, but I know you have not been into her nursery since you arrived in Venice three days ago."

"I didn't *want* her!" snapped the beauty.

Petro Dorma smiled wryly. "We do. So we will keep her. Goodbye, Angelina." He stepped out from behind his desk, his arms beginning to reach for her.

She evaded them. "I hate you."

Marco stepped forward too. "Angelina . . ."

"And you too! You're so boring!" She turned on her heel and stormed out.

Marco turned to follow, but Benito grabbed his sleeve. Petro took the other. "I'm sorry, Marco," said the head of *Casa* Dorma, with more sympathy than Benito had expected. He had to wonder if Petro wished he'd had Marco as a brother rather than Angelina as a sister. "Stay. There are still things I need to say, and I need your signature on that document before Angelina can go to that convent."

"I don't think I should sign," said Marco, seriously. "I made my promises."

Petro shook his head. Benito noticed that there was a tear trickling down the man's face. "I love her very much, Marco. She'll always be my little sister. We spoiled her after Papa's death, Mother and I, and perhaps that is why things turned out this way. But there are two reasons, both compelling, why this is the best thing for her. First, she has been experimenting with black lotos herself. She's been spending time over at the estate of a sister of Count Badoero. The Council of Ten have spies watching it. The Badoero house suffered what should have been punitive financial losses when their attack on Venice failed, yet there is money and lavish entertainment at Contessa Mirafioro's estate again. Badoero himself is dead, but the trade he set up in that narcotic continues, and my sister is in the thick of it."

Marco's mouth opened, then closed again. He looked as if he'd like to deny it; he also looked as though he knew that he couldn't.

Petro rubbed his eyes with a weary hand. "Angelina was drawn into the wild set the contessa cultivates. She is implicated in bringing some of the drug here, to Venice. We both know how addictive lotos is; the sisters are healers, and specifically are skilled in the rehabilitation of addicts. It really is the best thing we can do for her. Besides, there is a large force of Schiopettieri going to raid the Mirafioro estate soon. I really don't want her taken, or possibly injured. There's only so much that even I can keep quiet."

Marco bit his lip. "I can't believe she'd use the stuff—after your mother, and the difficulty we've had weaning her off it. I should think anyone with two eyes in her head would know better."

Petro shook his head. "It does seem insane, doesn't it? But Angelina always believed she was special, different from other people. Superior, maybe, and immune to their problems—despite her pregnancy proving that there was one thing she wasn't immune to. Besides, it is a popular myth among those who buy and sell the stuff that the addictiveness is totally exaggerated, and she was always readier to believe the people she wished to emulate than she was to believe people who love her."

He turned to his desk again and picked up another document. "There is another reason. Angelina has her ear to the network of gossips and rumor. I wanted her away in isolation before news of this one reached her ears."

The document bore the seal of Ferrara. "Word from your grandfather. Caesare Aldanto has been seen in Constantinople."

Benito went cold, and quite sober. *Trust the devil to save his own.* "I'm going to Constantinople, then," said Benito. "I've got unfinished business there."

Petro shook his head, and once again, it was in that implacable manner that warned of dire and inescapable consequences if his will was ignored.

"You are not, and for two reasons. First, after Caesare had seen the Emperor Alexius, he reembarked on a ship. Bound, most likely, for Odessa. So he is no longer in Constantinople for you to find. And for a second reason, both the Council of Ten and your grandfather have placed considerable prices on his head. We have more competent assassins in our pay than you would be. And in this case we will not hesitate to use them."

Benito looked mulish. "I know his ways. How he operates. They don't."

"That may be true," said Petro calmly. "But he is not where you can find him now, and what is more, even if you could, there is no reason to believe that he is not . . . contaminated. *Think*, Benito. There are only two sorts of power that could have saved him from his fate—and of the two, it was not likely the angels. Furthermore, where he has gone to, you are at a huge disadvantage. The Grand Duchy of Lithuania would eat you alive, Benito."

"What has this got to do with Angelina?" asked Marco.

Petro raised his eyebrows. "We know how Aldanto works. How he uses women and . . ." he looked pointedly at the two boys, "intermediaries. Angelina still claims he was wrongfully accused, and refuses to accept he was in any way responsible for the attack on the Republic. Just by being part of *Casa* Dorma, she is privy to a great deal of information that the enemies of Venice would appreciate. I love my sister, and no matter what she is and has become, I will continue to love her, but I know her weaknesses now. And I love and have a duty to the People and the Republic of Venice, too. What I am doing here is the best for both of them."

Marco bit his lip. And then he stepped up to the desk, took up the quill, dabbed it in the ink and signed. "I'll go up and try to see her now. I still feel she's getting a very poor choice in all of this," he said, sadness tingeing his voice.

Benito raised his eyes to heaven again. He loved Marco dearly, but . . . Here Marco had just received the freedom to marry the girl of his dreams, had his mistakes corrected, and he was worrying about the cause of those troubles. No doubt he'd be worrying about Aldanto next.

Well, if Caesare Aldanto ever came within Benito's reach, Benito would make sure his former idol was very dead. They'd been used, and the worst was they'd been grateful to be used by the traitor and murderer. And he owed Aldanto for Maria's account too. He turned to follow his brother.

Petro put a heavy hand on his shoulder. "I want to talk to you, too, Benito. Seeing as you're here."

He led Benito to the mullioned windows of his study. They could see out along the quays, busy with canal boats and lighters, to the forest of masts of the ships at anchor in the Bacino San Marco. Benito knew it was the merchant-prince's favorite view. But instead Petro pointed to the quay-side, to a solitary man lying in squalor against a bollard. "I know that man. He used to be good boatswain. Made a pretty penny or two out of various *Colleganzas*. He should be comfortable, well-off and happy."

"So?" Benito replied, though he had a good idea what was coming. "Sir," he added belatedly.

Petro sighed. "He can't find a job, even when ships are desperate for crew. If he doesn't drink, he shakes and hallucinates. He'll do absolutely anything for another glass of wine. He doesn't care how bad the wine is. Just so long as it is wine. We don't like to admit it, but too much wine can be as bad as black lotos. It just takes a bit longer. Are you going to turn out like that old soak? Because it can happen to you too. Like my sister, you are not immune. You're behaving just like her at the moment."

Nothing Petro could have chosen to say would have made more of an impression than that last line. For the second time that day, Benito felt something hit him with a distinct sense of shock, hit him in a way that made him grow very cold for a moment. Finally Benito shook his head.

Petro patted the shoulder. "Good. Because I don't think you'd fit into a monastery any better than Angelina is going to enjoy that convent."

"I'd drive 'em all mad. Sir."

Dorma managed a smile. "I'm far more inclined to send you out to factor in one of Dorma's trading posts Outremer, now that spring is coming, than keep you here or send you to a monastery. I've told mother that I'm wasting my time trying to make you into a *Case Vecchie* gentleman. Besides, I think the Valdosta and the *Casa* Dorma would lose something of value if they tried to cut and polish you. It's like trying to make a stiletto out of a perfectly good battleaxe."

"More like a rapier out of a cabbage," said Benito gloomily. "But the truth to tell, Petro, I really want to get out of here. I don't care where to, but out of Venice. And out of this 'education.' It doesn't suit me and I don't suit it."

Petro sat himself down again. "Very well. After your brother's wedding. And only if you learn to pull in your horns a bit. I've no objection to some wild oats, but it was only your status as my ward, and something of a hero in the last attack on Venice, that kept you out of jail last night. And you know Venice; there's only so long that you can trade on that before they start treating you exactly as you deserve."

Benito nodded. He really had to find out just what he'd done last night. "I've always had a fancy for Negroponte."

Petro gave a snort of laughter. "Benito, you are to subtle maneuvering what a randy stallion is to subtle seduction. If you asked for Golden Horn, Petro might smell a rat, eh? But Negroponte . . . is close enough to Constantinople? Not a chance, Benito. Not a chance."

Benito grinned, in spite of feeling somewhere in the bottom of his stomach that his world was not right, and probably never would be again. "It works on other people, Petro."

The head of the *Casa* Dorma smiled back. He looked younger. Nicer. Less like the Doge.

"But not on me. Now go and try to stay out of trouble. And pretend to be learning to be a good young *Case Vecchie* for my mother's sake. She has enough to bear with Angelina being taken away. You can speak like a gentleman when you wish to. Do so."

PART III
February, 1539 A.D.

Chapter 11

The forests of Istria were dripping and bleak. The mists seemed to hang heavy and cold around the trees. That matched Maria's mood fairly well. She was big bellied and uncomfortable. What she really wanted was someone to have a good fight with. A good fling-plates-and-break-things fight. In that respect her husband Umberto was hopeless. For starters he was always off marking trees or accompanying the foresters. The life out here didn't suit him, but he was a fiercely conscientious man. He'd far rather have been in the dockyards in the Arsenal back in Venice. This however, was where he had been sent. And after the affair with the previous chief forester he did his best to keep going out with the tree patrols.

At least he had listened to her—or if he hadn't done so consciously, some of her insistence that he look into the peccadilloes of those under him had unearthed the culprits still running the timber-scam.

She tried not to be too irritated with him, even so. He insisted on thinking of it purely in terms of "timber being sent away from Venice" rather than "timber being sold to the enemies of Venice." Sometimes, his focus was so narrow, so parochial, it made her want to scream. And never mind that not all that long ago, her focus had been entirely on running her cargoes and not enquiring too closely about where they were from, or where they were going, on being dazzled by a pair of blue eyes and not asking what was going on in the head that housed them.

Well, that had changed. If only Umberto had learned the same lesson.

At least he was on to the cheaters now, and he was off every day, trying to match his city strides with the long paces that the foresters took, and sneezing a lot.

She envied him, envied his long hikes through the forest, envied that *he* got out of the house every day, into the open, beyond the four confining walls. To her surprise she'd found that the openness, space and silences felt welcoming. Umberto complained of missing the people and the sounds of the city. She enjoyed their absence.

In the first day here, she had learned all that, despite the fact that things had been quite chaotic. To get out, under those old, quiet trees, had been a pleasure she would never have anticipated. So far as *she* was concerned, all that had happened was that she'd had a lovely walk and solved half the timber problems—and, yes, gotten a little lost and gotten home a little late, but that was hardly anything to worry about.

Umberto'd almost had the baby for her, to judge by the performance he had given when she came back at last. And unfortunately, she was no longer the sole arbiter of what she did; she was a wife now, and half of a couple, and it behooved her not to send her husband into a state of panic. The result—with her "delicate condition" in mind, was being confined to the house and yard with an elderly forester's widow as a combination between house-servant and guard.

Not that she was in any real sense a prisoner. No, she was just confined by chains of care and Umberto's ideas of how it all should be, and the proper arrangement of the universe. Women had their place. It was a pampered and protected one—well, as pampered as a caulker's wife ever got, anyway. It didn't include being out on the canals at midnight, running gray-cargo, nor traipsing about the woods like a forester.

It all chafed at Maria's soul. She was used to her independence. She was used to defining for herself what she would and wouldn't do. And if her mother had plied her own boat until the very day of Maria's own birth, why should she now be stuck within four walls, tending to the housework as if she hadn't a care except that the floor be clean enough?

For that matter, her world was *so* much wider now! The last year—no one who had lived through what she had could be unchanged. She'd come up against challenges she would never have dreamed of, and beaten them, and if she'd chosen to marry rather than try to raise a baby on her own, well, it was for the baby's sake.

She certainly wouldn't have done it for her own. So she'd taken the husband that she thought would best love her baby, no matter who the father was. And now, she found herself powerless to fight the trammels of Umberto's gentle care. She didn't even know how to start dealing with his hurt expressions when she didn't fit in with his expectations.

How did you fight this? She really could use a good screaming fight.

Issie, the black-clad forester's widow who was supposed to help her, tugged at her arm. "Why don't you sit down, dearie, and rest your feet. You'll get little enough rest when the baby is born."

Maria looked out into the black, bare trees, ignoring Issie. Umberto was out there now, trying to select good timbers for masts and keels, when what he knew about was cladding. The caulkers back in Venice were undoubtedly going to be grateful for the improvement in the quality of deck planking. Maria was, however, sure that he'd be getting more letters of complaint from the masters of the carpenters' guild. At least he got regular letters from Venice. It was more than she ever did.

She sighed. It wasn't as if reading came that easily. True, she'd spent more time working on it since they arrived here. But there weren't many people back home who could write in the first place. She only ever seemed to get letters from Kat. Letters full of Marco. Letters from a life she'd chosen to leave behind, to try to forget. Benito was always carefully not mentioned.

The second reason Maria found it difficult to pick a good fight with Umberto was straight guilt. He'd married her, loved her enough to take what fellow Venetians would have called "spoiled goods." She had taken his offer, not because she felt any deep affection for the balding, slightly worried looking gray-haired man, but because she needed a father for the child. She had grown up without that social protection, and she would not inflict it on her baby. Lately, she'd come to realize that Umberto's affections had been transferred to her from his love of her mother.

Her mother! Well, she should have expected that. Even as a tiny child, she had known that Umberto followed her mother with his eyes every single time she was anywhere around the docks where the caulkers worked. The older man had plainly been crazy about her. He had even called Maria by her name a couple of times by accident. How could she start a good fight with someone who was still in love with her dead mother?

At least she wasn't in love with Umberto herself. If this was hard, trying to rival the memory of her dead mother and win over someone *she* loved would be even harder.

Maria sighed again. She leaned heavily on the broom, and some of the birch twigs cracked. Outside the chief forester's house the rain fell in heavy sheets. Once upon a time all she'd wanted was a house that was warm and dry. Now she was almost tempted to go out in the rain. It hadn't melted her in all those years of sculling her gondola through the wet winter canals of Venice.

Housekeeping, cooking and preparing baby clothes did not fill up the day, let alone her mind. True, being warm was good and so was being well fed. But being cooped up, being a good wife, even a good pregnant wife, was going to drive her crazy, even if the final stages of this pregnancy were beginning to leave her feeling permanently exhausted.

"Really, why don't you have a little rest, dear," clucked Issie again.

Maria swept irritably. She'd been just about ready to do that. Now she wouldn't.

The jingle of a horse's harness was a welcome distraction. Ignoring the rain, ignoring Issie's squawks of alarm, Maria ran out to the messenger, who was wearing wet Venetian Republic livery. It must be something important to bring the man out here in this weather. The messengers of the Republic were supposed to conduct their business with the utmost dispatch, true. But out here, this far from the authorities in Venice, that meant "when it wasn't raining." The forests of Istria were vital to the shipbuilding in the Arsenal, but they were also a long way from the messengers' *capi* back in Venice.

She was drenched the moment she stepped foot outside the door, of course, and she didn't give a damn, of course. This wasn't the canal; she wasn't the same Maria who hadn't but two dry skirts to her name. There were several warm outfits inside that house that she could change right back into when she got inside. Issie could spread this one on chairs in front of the fire—it would give the old cow something to do.

Maria struggled with the buckle on the wet leather pouch,

ignoring the shivering messenger who was trying to tether his horse with numb fingers. "Can you help me?" he asked finally.

Maria looked up from her task with annoyance. "Take yourself and your horse into the stable, you fool. Are you not bright enough to get in out of the rain?"

A smothered snort from the messenger suddenly drew her attention to the fact that *she* was apparently not bright enough to get in out of the rain.

She got the pouch off the saddle, and retreated into the house.

Issie, clucking like a wet hen, handed her a rough towel. Maria had no time for it now. The fussing about while she was trying to get to the message in the pouch would drive her insane. "Go get the messenger a drink," she snapped. "He's wet through. I'm just a little damp."

Issie sniffed irritably. "He's not pregnant." But she went anyway. The pouch buckle finally surrendered to a superior will. There was only one wax-sealed missive inside. The seal was that of the House Dorma, the Doge's house, and not the familiar crest of the Montescue. It was addressed to her . . . and not to the chief forester of Istria.

Oh blessed Jesu—

Maria tore at it with trembling fingers.

No one would send a special messenger to the wife of a forester unless it was horrible news. The worst of all possible news.

No one from Dorma would send me news by a special messenger. It must be from Marco. It could only mean Benito had been killed. . . . Why hadn't she . . .

Inside was Kat's familiar handwriting. It started with the words: *Glad news!*

Maria sat down with a thump on a hard oak settle, and composed herself with a deep breath. She patted her bulging stomach to still the flutters just under the skin. "If Katerina only knew how close she came to causing your premature birth, child," she muttered, blinking to clear her eyes before reading further.

I've got Marco to use the Dorma seal so this will get to you as soon as possible, wrote Kat. *Fantastic, wonderful things have happened!*

That seal could indeed achieve great things. It had nearly achieved an early baby, thought Maria wryly. She read on, learning of the Vinlanders who would restore the fortunes of Montescue, of the annulment of Marco's marriage to Angelina, and Angelina's hasty internment in the Cloister at Santa Lucia Della Monte outside Verona. It seemed that this had been a very busy week.

She tried not to think how busy *she* would have been, had she been there, how in the thick of it all. She'd be poling Kat about, of course, and maybe helping her a little with the Vinlanders. And she wouldn't be getting the news of the wedding plans at second-hand like this.

Petro Dorma insists it is to be a great state function. Marco and I have had to agree. On conditions: First, I want you to come and support me on that day. Second, Francesca de Chevreuse will be returning to Venice. She is to be my other matron of honor. Dorma says he will make arrangements for you and Umberto to return to Venice for the occasion. She had to read that twice, and then a third time, before it began to make sense.

And when it did, Maria could only laugh helplessly. The flower of the House Montescue and the heir of the House Valdosta, grandson of the Duke of Ferrara . . . with a caulker's wife and one of Venice's most famous courtesans as her attendants to the altar.

Well, she could hardly refuse. Kat, after all, had come to her low-key caulker's wedding in the same role. But it would mean returning to Venice. Returning—she looked at the date of the wedding—returning with a three-week-old baby, if everything ran to time.

The back door banged, and her head came up. If it was Issie—

A sneeze. Not Issie; Umberto. He came through to the front parlor. Maria took in the wet-plastered gray hair and the faint bluish tinge to her man's lips. He smiled caressingly at her, and a wave of affection swept through her. Her man might have his faults and his rigidities, but he was a good one. People might become exasperated with Umberto Verrier, but you couldn't really dislike him; he was too mild a soul to engender anything so active as dislike. And he was such a good husband. A conscientious one, at least.

He was shivering slightly, and she beckoned to him, smiling. "Umberto! Come over to the fire, before ice forms on your poor nose."

He did, holding his thin hands out to crackling flames. "There is a message from Venice? One of the foresters said he saw a messenger in the Doge's livery coming across."

She'd pulled a chair up for him by this time, handed him the towel Issie had been trying to press on her. "It was for me, dear. A letter from Katerina Montescue, the lady who was my maid of honor at our wedding. She is to marry Marco Valdosta, you know, the Doge-elect's ward, in a great state ceremony in the early spring. It's all finally been sorted out, and settled at last."

Umberto looked at her wonderingly. "I have never understood how you came to know such a one. The *Casa* Montescue! She is a great lady."

I don't dare tell you how I know Kat, thought Maria. It was no tale to chance spreading about among all these foresters, especially as Issie had come in with a goblet of hot, spiced, honeyed wine, her lined face alive with curiosity. She'd have it all over Istria before tomorrow night. *The new chief forester's wife! Blessed Jesu, she's worse than we could have thought! A smuggler! Poling her own canal boat! And no better than she should be, no doubt!*

Well, the wine might be just an excuse to find out what was happening, but Maria was grateful. Umberto was in need of it. "There was more to it than just telling me that the wedding has been set, or she wouldn't have needed a messenger. She has asked that we—you and I—go back to Venice for the wedding. She has arranged with Petro Dorma to make it possible."

Umberto sipped some of the hot wine. "Well, it would be nice . . . I have been thinking how I would like to go to town. It would be very good to see people again, perhaps to ask if I might take a post closer to the city. But . . . what about the . . ." He hesitated, "the baby?"

Maria patted her stomach. "Baby should be born by then. It had better be. Katerina has asked me to be one of her matrons of honor."

The goblet crashed to the floor. Neither Issie nor Umberto seemed to notice.

Chapter 12

"You're not that old," protested Manfred for the fifth time.

The Emperor smiled wryly. "Thank you. Nevertheless, I still want you to do it. You will pray for my soul in Jerusalem. It needs it, believe me. And it wouldn't do you any harm to do some thinking about your own mortality."

Erik looked at the emperor's nephew. Manfred was trying to keep a straight face. He glanced at Charles Fredrik, and realized that the Emperor understood the humor in this too. Erik could see the similarity between the two men in the facial lines. Of course Manfred was bigger, and had a darker Celtic complexion, but the family likeness was definitely there—and went deeper than appearances. He could readily believe, looking at the Emperor, that there were some sins worth praying about.

Charles Fredrik shook his head ruefully. "When I was your age I didn't believe in my own mortality either. Just do it, Manfred. Humor me. I'm an old man. I know that both in Venice and now in Norway, the chances of you being killed or injured were remarkably good. Neither luck nor Erik is going to stop everything. So I'm putting in a formal request to the Abbot-General of the Knights of the Holy Trinity to furnish you with an escort of knights. He has already acceded to my 'request' that you go on a pilgrimage to the Holy Land for me, while you are still in the holy order. I don't think he will refuse this either. You will be invested, both of you, as knight-proctors and given discretionary command over the Knights assigned to accompany you. To assist you I'm sending my old friend and mentor, Eberhard of Brunswick, with you."

Manfred rolled his eyes. "To instruct me in statecraft no doubt, Uncle. This pilgrimage is going to be a real penance after all."

The Emperor covered a smile with his hand. "Yes. Poor Eberhard is expecting to find it that, for a certainty. Now, Francesca, stay with me a while. I would like to talk to you without that young idiot interrupting me. Go on, you two. I'll want to talk to you as well, Erik. But not tonight, I think."

Erik and Manfred had little choice but to leave. Francesca waved as she walked over to stand beside the Emperor.

"Did you see that!" said Manfred fuming. "One minute he's dying and wanting me to pray for his soul, the next he's stealing my girl!"

"She's scarcely a girl," said Erik, latching onto the one safe point in the entire argument.

The disapproving look brought a grin to Manfred. "Among the things I can promise you, she definitely isn't a boy. Or have you forgotten a certain night in a certain brothel? Francesca says you're the biggest stiff thing she's ever had between her legs. Your whole body was rigid . . . with shock."

Erik fumbled for something to say, and failed. The memory of the first time they'd met Francesca, fleeing from an ambush, still embarrassed him. They'd been ambushed in a brothel in which she was employed at the time, and she'd agreed to hide them—by using the expedient device of hiding them in plain sight, engaged in the sort of activity anyone would expect to see in a brothel. Erik himself, mortified, had faked his part of the thing. Manfred . . . had not.

Which was perhaps why Manfred reveled in the memory. "It's old age, that's your problem. Memory's going first. Never mind, I'll get Francesca to refresh the picture. Just some millefiori beads as I recall, all she was wearing."

"Manfred! You know that's not what I meant." Erik wondered just how he should deal with this. "Have you no morals at all? I meant she's a woman, not a girl."

Manfred snorted. "Only you Icelanders seem to worry about it."

"Vinlanders take it even more seriously. It's just not respectful!"

Manfred went off into a guffaw. "Well, that's something, considering her former profession."

Erik found himself blushing; as usual, confused by what his

response should be to the former whore, then courtesan, now a prince's mistress. His conservative upbringing said he should treat her with disdain. Yet . . .

Francesca, he knew from experience, lived by a rigid moral code too. It just had a totally different set of rules about sex.

He decided to take refuge in something he *was* familiar and comfortable with. "Come. You're getting fat, Manfred. Let's go down to the jousting yard."

"Erik, it's snowing out there. Besides, I know you just want to take it out on me."

There was some truth to that, even if, as the years went by, "taking it out" on Manfred was getting a great deal harder to do. But at the new rapier-work Erik still had the edge, and always would have. He was just faster than Manfred could ever be. "Then we will find a *salle* big enough for some more fencing practice. Come. I have the quilted jackets in my quarters."

"I'd rather go drinking," protested Manfred.

Erik threw him against the wall with a rolling hiplock.

Francesca looked severely at the Emperor. "Using me to tease your nephew is not kind."

Charles Fredrik smiled. "It's one of the few pleasures left to an old man." The smile widened. "And by now Erik will have talked him into some training and will administer some bruises, which his disrespect deserves."

"You are a very bad old man," she said, shaking her head at the most powerful man in Europe.

The first time she'd met the Emperor she'd been quaking inside. But when all was said and done, he was also a man. Men, she understood. This one, for all his power, was a good man. And behind the smiles she read genuine worry.

"He's turning out well, you know. But he is still very young."

"And very jealous. If I were twenty years younger he'd have reason to be. Now tell me, Francesca. What do you intend to do now? I am sending Manfred to Jerusalem. But I have a place for you here in Mainz. You've served me well in Denmark, much though Trolliger disapproves of your methods! Mind you, I don't think he realizes that your methods are—"

"More refined than in Venice. And not horizontal in the least." She smiled tolerantly. "Wait until his spies are done reporting to him—or until he finishes reading those reports he's already gotten. I believe he will be astonished that I have become a veritable pillar of respectability."

"Good," the Emperor replied, and sounded as if he meant it. "I gathered that already; unlike Trolliger, I read the entire reports from my spies—and his, by the way—not just the parts I deem are pertinent at the time."

"Well, I may not be Caesar's wife," she said thoughtfully, with a long look through her lashes at the Emperor, "but—"

"But you must still be above reproach, as my nephew's paramour," Charles Fredrik agreed with her. "Though a bit of banter between the two of us, in private, is harmless enough."

"And in public," she twinkled, "I find finance to be the most fascinating possible topic for discussion."

He chuckled, as she had known he would.

Francesca licked the corner her mouth. Slowly and catlike. "So, whatever could he find to disapprove of in finance?" she asked, innocently, looking at him through lowered lashes.

She was rewarded with the Emperor's laughter . . . which went off into coughing. It took a while to subside, and now he looked older. Gray and tired, though still able to muster a smile.

"Don't make me laugh, please!" he said breathlessly. "It's a pity. I find little to laugh at these days. No wonder the Danes were so willing to help you. You must have had them wrapped around your littlest finger. But what do you intend to do now? Because I would like to ask that you accompany Manfred. Not for the reasons *he'd* like, lucky young dog, but for my own interests. And yours, for that matter. I pay well, as you know."

Francesca chose her words carefully. She was aware just how dangerous these waters were. She knew she was tolerated as the *mistress* to the Emperor's second-in-line heir. But more than that? No.

"I was planning on accompanying Manfred. Not, I'm afraid, for the reasons he thinks. But the truth is that Mainz is not my sort of town. And I fancy seeing the east. Alexandria tempts me."

"Alexandria!" She was surprised by the enthusiasm in the Emperor's voice. "What a place! I went there, you know, as a young prince." He sighed. "A paradise of a town for a young man. But there is more to it. A place of intellect, too. More than anywhere else in the world, as I know it. I regret, in my old age, that I didn't explore that aspect more."

"I would wager you didn't regret it then!"

"True. But I'll have to tell you about it some other time. Right now I want to talk to you about Eberhard of Brunswick's mission."

"To the Ilkhan."

The Emperor shook his head. "If I didn't know you better, I'd have you burned for witchcraft."

She shrugged. "It is quite obvious."

The Emperor shook his head again. "I just hope that Grand Duke Jagiellon is not as intelligent and devious-minded as you are."

"If he isn't, he's bound to have someone who is," she said.

The Emperor looked thoughtful. "Not necessarily. The plots and machinations of Jagiellon are not constructed as you or I would construct them. You've given a lot of thought to western politics. Turn your mind now to the east. There is a factor at work there you must not forget: Power in the Grand Duchy of Lithuania is wrested by strength and cunning, not just by hereditary right or, as in Venice, by election."

He held up a hand. "Yes, I know. There are intrigues and schemes here, also. But this is the playing of puppies compared to the fight for pack-dominance there. Jagiellon dares not allow anyone into his trust. He must always act, to some extent, alone. Even his closest advisor, Count Mindaug, will pull him down if he can, and thus is not privy to the innermost workings and plans and secrets. That would require trust and a loyalty born of love, not fear. Those are as alien to Jagiellon as his kind of absolute enslavement is to us. He gains their loyalty by robbing them of their will and their self. Our most trusted people can betray us . . . his cannot. But his cannot think or act independently, either. Those Jagiellon allows free thought to must be kept weaker, and ignorant. We don't have that problem, although we do need to fear treachery. We must place our trust carefully."

Francesca looked at the Emperor in some surprise. "Maybe it really is a pity that you spent so much time in the pleasure-palaces in Alexandria."

The Emperor gave a small snort. "Not nearly as much as you might think. I learned a great deal about things that my tutors hadn't mentioned, while I was there. But a fool and his empire are soon parted. Alexius VI of Byzantium is busy proving that. And while I, or Conrad, or even Manfred might not be the best person for the job . . . as my father said to me, when I protested that I didn't really want to be Emperor, better those who have been trained for it but don't want it, than someone who just wants it. A man who wants this kind of power, does not want the responsibility that goes with it." He shrugged. "Nobody would."

Francesca's smile was small, tight, and sympathetic. "I think most of them would just choose to ignore the responsibilities. I think the Holy Roman Empire has been fortunate in its Emperor."

"To my sorrow, no. One of the reasons that I want Manfred to pray for my soul is that I know I have failed sometimes, Francesca. Too often," he said quietly, shaking his head. "And thanks be to the hard lessons I got from Erik's father that I can acknowledge this responsibility. You know, I once said something stupid and arrogant about some peasants. Hakkon explained that if they'd said the same about me, they'd have died. And, as I couldn't learn if I was dead, he'd simply made me wish I was dead. It gave me an insight the imperial heir had previously lacked."

He paused, lost in reflections. Francesca waited, patiently. "Now, to return to the Ilkhan. I think we can benefit each other. Of course Eberhard of Brunswick will be doing the actual negotiation but I would like you to be able to . . . shall we say, 'smooth things over' if there are difficulties." He smiled. "This means I will have to trust you, which Jagiellon would not."

Francesca shook her head. "So: You will have to trust me, which Jagiellon would not. But, Your Majesty, neither, by the sounds of it, would Emeric of Hungary trust me. He is, by all accounts, a man who would match your image of the Grand Duke. And he is closer, too. Why do you focus on the Grand Duke?"

Charles Fredrik sighed. "It is ill fortune to have two such men on the thrones of powerful neighboring lands. But Emeric is not threatening us at the moment." The Emperor smiled grimly. "I have reliable information that he is turning his attention to the southern Balkans. Being involved in a war down there would be, for him, what being involved in the wars of Italian principalities would be for us. There is an Illyrian chieftain down there who is giving him considerable pause."

"What!?" Manfred shook his head. "You want me to take a couple of hundred knights with me? That's an army, Uncle! That's ridiculous. *You* managed fine in Italy—with just Erik and me escorting you."

The Emperor shook his head. "I enjoyed that. But we were traveling incognito, Manfred. I am afraid that part of the point of this exercise is to travel in the full glare of public view. Even two hundred men-at-arms may not be enough."

Manfred thumped a meaty fist on the table. "When I went to Sweden I had seventy! And for all the use they were, I might as well have had none!"

The Emperor glared at him. "You were within my realms and supposedly protected by my hand. The fact that you went off into Norway, to Telemark, with just on half of that, when I had clearly and expressly told you to 'take a sufficient escort' just proves to me that I have to dictate how many men escort you. *And* I hear from the master of the chapter house at Lödöse that it was only on his insistence that you even took that many with you. Accept it, Manfred. I've heard the story from Erik. Your days of being the young, happy-go-lucky knight are over. Even in the Knights of the Holy Trinity, where you were supposedly anonymous and protected, you were a target. They tried to kill you, Manfred, as a way of getting at me. The day is fast approaching when they'll try to kill you just because of who *you* are. You won't always have Erik there. Besides, you need some command experience. The men I'm going to have sent with you are older, tough, solid veterans. You'll be younger than almost all of them. Less experienced. You'll spend half your life commanding men with the advantage over you of age and experience. Learn how to do it now, when you don't have to do it in combat."

Manfred groaned. "Bad enough that I've got to put up with old Eberhard's moralizing and carping. Now you're saddling me with a bunch of graybeards who are going to spend the entire journey, to and from Jerusalem, complaining about their rheumatism and grumbling how things aren't like they used to be when they were young."

The Emperor snorted. "You will treat Eberhard of Brunswick with respect, Manfred. Learn from him. He is a statesman and a truly skilled negotiator. One of the best. I've always thought that if he hadn't been born a noble he'd have been the richest horse-trader in the Empire. He's a valuable man, probably worth as much to the Empire as you are. If you don't treat him with respect I will curtail your personal allowance—which I imagine you and Francesca would find difficult. And as for the quality of the men I'm sending with you: I took Erik Hakkonsen's advice. I have asked the Knights of the Holy Trinity to send me a knight by the name of Von Gherens. Erik suggested I get him to select the men who will accompany you."

Manfred brightened. "Well, that's not so bad. Von Gherens can drink."

The Emperor shook his head and laughed. "Manfred! What are we going to do with you? I keep hoping Francesca and Erik have worked miracles and then you give me that sort of comment."

Manfred grinned. "Well, I have made some inroads in teaching Erik to drink! He still does it badly, though. And I've failed with Francesca entirely. Teaching her to drink properly, that is. I've had successes in other important areas, of course."

The Emperor shook his head again, helplessly.

"And I'm looking forward to visiting Venice again. Some fine red wines those Italians produce."

"I hope Erik beats you," grumbled the Emperor. "And I'm going to have a word with Francesca too."

"So long as you keep to talking," said Manfred, warily.

Chapter 13

Eneko Lopez stared impassively at the face of the Grand Metro-politan. He did not allow the thoughts roiling in his mind to show. He hoped not, anyway.

"You obviously made quite an impression on Emperor Charles Fredrik, Father Lopez," said the frail, pale—and powerful—man sitting on the throne before him. The Grand Metropolitan held up a scroll, almost as if it were a scepter.

The Grand Metropolitan had a reputation for vacillation; how-ever, he was still the most powerful figure in the Church. And Eneko was never certain how much of that vacillation was because of the Holy Father's nature, and how much was because, in the end, when one kept from making up one's mind, things tended to sort themselves out without forcing one to take a stand.

"I found the Holy Roman Emperor to be a pleasant enough companion on the road here," said Eneko dryly. "A not overly pious man, though."

The Grand Metropolitan gave a reedy chuckle. "It appears that he, on the other hand, did find you to be one. It is a signal honor of sorts. And, quite honestly, not a request easily denied."

"God is omnipresent," said Eneko stiffly. "He can be addressed as well from Mainz as from Jerusalem."

The Grand Metropolitan gave another reedy chuckle. "A view-point that I am sad that I will not be able to hear you express to the Metropolitan of Jerusalem. None the less, it is the express desire of the Emperor of the most powerful Christian state that you should go to Jerusalem to pray for his soul, as he, as the bastion stone of the Christian Empire, cannot leave his duty to millions of other Christian souls merely to indulge the desire of his old age."

Eneko stood in silence.

"He is a powerful friend of the Holy Church, Father Lopez," said the old man, mildly.

Eneko sighed. "I know. But, Your Holiness, I had hoped . . . The order I wish to found. The Emperor seemed quite well disposed to the idea."

The Grand Metropolitan scowled slightly. "More so than I have been. Your problem, Father Eneko, is that you have been a valuable tool for the church in your present role. I need an agent of your caliber. I am less sure that the church needs yet another religious order to create more schisms and infighting. But the Emperor is indeed well-disposed toward your scheme; he goes as far as to suggest a name. He seems to think a Petrine-based order devoted to holy magic in the active and combative sense would act as a counterweight to the Servants of the Holy Trinity. He also thinks that Father Eneko Lopez of the Basque country would be a good man to head such an order. I must read you his words."

The old man cleared his throat, unfurled the parchment and held the scroll at full arm's stretch. Then, began reading from it in a slight sing-song:

" 'I find myself in agreement with your proposal that the Hypatian order should open some chapter houses in Swabia, Brunswick and Prussia. Details may be thrashed out between our intermediaries, but I would be happy to see as many as twenty of these established in the Empire's central provinces. However, one does not use a shovel to do a sword's work and vice versa. I am of the opinion that the order of Saint Hypatia in particular and the Church in general have lost some of the militant purpose Chrysostom imbued it with. It has become very gentle, and as a result, we are seeing enemies springing up who do not scruple to use the darkest of magics against us. The Empire and the Holy Church need a force not lacking in some of the gentleness of the Hypatian Order, but with the steel to meet the spiritual and supernatural evils of the northern darkness which threaten the mother Church.' "

The Grand Metropolitan paused and peered at Eneko over the top of the parchment. "He then proposes you heading such an order. But I read further: 'However, I feel Father Lopez would still benefit from some broadening of his viewpoints before he takes up this challenge. Therefore my request that he undertakes this pilgrimage to Jerusalem can serve a double purpose. As one of the most pious men I have met, he can pray for my soul, which I fear stands in sore need of such intervention. Visiting the birthplace of our faith and then proceeding to the cradle of our learning, Alexandria, will also broaden his outlook. Besides, such an order as he envisages will need to consult the Great Library at Alexandria extensively, as it remains the greatest source and storehouse of arcane knowledge, both Christian and non-Christian, in Christendom. And if Alexandria cannot broaden his outlook, then nothing can. Even the brothels there are an education.'"

Eneko felt himself redden. The Grand Metropolitan was plainly amused by his embarrassment. "I think the Emperor's assessment is very acute," he said with a wry smile. "Both of your piety and your need for a broader perspective."

Eneko took a deep breath. "I have always wanted to undertake the pilgrimage to Jerusalem, Your Holiness," he said, seriously. "And the second pilgrimage to the heart and birthplace of the Order of Saint Hypatia. But the responsibility of another man's soul— any man's soul, never mind the Holy Roman Emperor's—is too much for me."

The Grand Metropolitan nodded. "Only Christ could carry such a weight," he said gently. "But all that is asked of us is to do as much we can and He has ever promised us that He will help us to bear the rest. You may choose some companions—say, three— to help you. I feel Emperor Charles Fredrik would agree that such broadening of the structure that you envisage will be better if it has a wider foundation, as it were. Now, my son. I have other interviews. Come, take my blessing and get along with you. You and your companions will travel as humble pilgrims to Jerusalem, and thence Alexandria. I have prayed on this and I feel you guided to this path." It was said with a quiet certainty and deep humility.

It was also a firm, unarguable dismissal.

"When you travel with a small army you have to behave as if you are traveling with a small army," muttered Manfred irritably. "We should break this lot up into ten parcels of twenty knights, and fit into inns rather than overflowing villages."

The grizzled and facially scarred Von Gherens smiled. "A good idea, eh, Falkenberg? We ride with the first twenty and Prince Manfred rides with the last twenty. Then *he* can apologize for all the damage and pay the peasants, and put up with short rations because we've eaten all the food, and drunk all the beer."

Falkenberg, who was riding on the other side of Manfred, was also a veteran, though younger than Von Gherens. And like Von Gherens, Manfred had discovered, able to drink his weight in ale without showing any sign of it. The Knights of the Holy Trinity—the "Knots" in popular slang—were supposed to be a religious order, sworn to abstinence from the worldly trappings of wealth. In practice, Manfred discovered, that meant they ate and drank well . . .

When someone else was paying.

Manfred was finding that being in an out-of-combat command—especially when you have a reputation as a tearaway yourself—was a lot more difficult than he'd thought. In a way a misery-guts like Sachs was almost called for. The presence of someone who'd put some fear and sobriety into this lot would keep the reckoning down. The Emperor had given Manfred what he had considered to be an ample supply of gold for the trip. At this rate they might—possibly—get to Ascalon. He'd have to sell them off as mercenaries to get back.

Falkenberg looked at Manfred with amusement. "Sounds very good. It would make a change from the way it is now."

The problem was that both of them had been in Venice with Manfred and Erik, when they had striven against Chernobog. The two of them, Von Gherens particularly, had been the catalysts who'd broken up the fight in San Zan Degola when Erik had refused to hand over the young woman who had claimed sanctuary there to Abbot Sachs. Von Gherens had been at the final destruction of Chernobog's Vessel and had been terribly burned there.

They both liked Manfred; he knew that. They were from northeastern frontier families, from the borderlands of the Empire where the battle between good and evil was stark and frequent. There was no doubting the toughness or the piety of either man. There was also no doubting their ability to soak up food and drink when it was available. They treated their young commander with a sort of jocular respect . . . and then did precisely what they intended to do. No doubt about it, in a fight they'd be what they were—

superb soldiers, disciplined and ordered. So how come they traveled at exactly the pace they intended to travel, despite Manfred's desire to pick the pace?

Manfred was left feeling he was being tested. He wished he could do with the troop what Erik did, in the daily drill session the Icelander put them through. They jumped when Erik Hakkonsen said "frog." There was always that sort of distance between Erik and the rest of the human race, and the barrier seemed to work in Erik's favor. No one, not even old Notke—who was fifty-five if he was a day—treated Erik as an equal.

That evening in the smoky room in one of the three crowded inns at Brixen, Manfred turned to Erik and Eberhard and sighed. "What the hell do I have to do to get the Knights moving? I wanted to be through to Bozen by now. At this rate, we're going to take twice as long as I'd intend to get through to Venice."

Eberhard looked at him with a frosty eye. "I was Knight of the Trinity with your grandfather. I had a commander like you once. Good fighter. Lousy commander when we weren't fighting."

Manfred had never really thought of the old man as a having once been a mere rank-and-file knight, but always as a prosy and disapproving important old man. "So, Milord of Brunswick," he said, in as serious a manner as he had ever donned. "What should I do? Lecture them on diplomacy?"

"Break a few heads," said Erik, looking up from his platter. "You are too young and too popular."

Eberhard shook his head. "That might work for you, Erik. You will lead troops. You already do that well. But Manfred is such a babe-in-arms, he still needs *them* to teach him. He will lead armies, not troops. And what he needs to learn is that you cannot lead armies on your own. You need to delegate."

Manfred stared at him in astonishment. *That* was a solution that didn't sound like a good idea. On the other hand, Eberhard . . . had experience. "Delegate to whom? I mean, wouldn't they just think I was trying to avoid responsibility?"

Eberhard gave his wintry smile. "This is statecraft, which your uncle wished me to instruct you in. I thought it was a waste of time but if you can see that there is a problem, well—perhaps you might learn something after all." He cleared his throat. "It is often a good idea to pick on the worst sources of your troubles—and make them responsible. If they fail, then you must display very clearly that you have not abrogated your responsibilities, by taking action against them, personally. But I don't suppose you'll have either the intelligence or maturity to take my advice."

Despite himself, Manfred knew that his face showed what he'd have been likely to do if the old man were not nearly seventy. Instead he clenched his fists and walked off.

"Francesca, he's going to drive me mad," said Manfred later in their chamber. "He treats me as if I were stupid and ten years old."

Francesca traced his deltoid with a delicate finger. "He's a very bad old man, to tease you so. But I think he wants to make sure he's got your attention."

"You think he's doing it on purpose?" demanded Manfred incredulously.

Francesca smiled catlike. "He is one of the leading diplomats and statesmen of the age, Manfred, dear. He's playing you like a lute."

Manfred did not like the idea of being manipulated by anyone, much less Eberhard. "The old bastard!"

Francesca shook her head in admonition. "I'm sure he's only doing it to oblige Charles Fredrik."

Manfred snorted. "Two can play his game. I won't rise to his bait. Tomorrow morning I'm going to call Falkenberg and Von Gherens. Make those two carry the can. Falkenberg can do the damned accounting. That'll stop him eating and drinking for a few minutes, which should save us a few pennies anyway."

"Good. Then maybe we can get moving a little faster. I had letters while I was in Mainz from Katerina. I said I would do my best to be there for her wedding, even if I cannot accede to her request to be a maid of honor." Francesca smiled wryly. "But I wouldn't mind being a trifle early to help with the organization."

"Von Gherens will have to make them trot," said Manfred languorously, leaning toward the caressing fingers.

Chapter 14

The woman didn't stop screaming. She'd gone beyond the edge of fear and into raw hysteria.

None of the three people in the room appeared to even notice, any more than slaughterhouse workers might notice a bellowing steer. Jagiellon simply continued to whet the cleaver.

Caesare Aldanto stood like a blond puppet that someone had propped against a wall. The position his arms were in was not quite natural and would have caused any normal man to alter it before more than a moment had passed. Aldanto stood as still as a log. His empty blue eyes stared unblinking at the altar. The shaman simply continued to rub the drum-skin, and walk in a widdershins circle, producing a low murmur of sound that seemed to slice through the screaming.

The cut, when it came, did not stop the screaming. That brutal chop was not intended to. This rite derived much of its power from the suffering of the victim. The *quodba* drum now was a fluttering, weakening, fast heartbeat, perfectly matching that of the woman. In the old face, the shaman's eyes burned with a fierce intensity. Sweat dripped from his forehead although the room was cold. Jagiellon showed no such signs of strain.

Neither did Caesare, who had come forward now to kneel, holding the stone-cut bowl into which the woman's femoral artery pumped.

Jagiellon scryed for his foes in a dark magic built on blood, pain, and defilement.

There was a price, a terrible price for this clear vision, and not just from the victim. But the Black Brain did not care. That part of Jagiellon was long dead anyway. And this was no new ritual being enacted for the first time.

In the blood that now pumped feebly into the bowl, Jagiellon saw Eneko Lopez, and a band of companions. Saw the canals of Venice, and a canal boat with what could only be a bridal couple. Abruptly that opaqued. Only a Leonine winged shadow remained.

The blood bowl cleared, showing a new vision. Eneko Lopez again, face uplifted, at peace, standing on the place which is called Golgotha.

There was a high, thin, sound that pierced the brain like a white-hot needle.

The bowl shattered. Blood erupted out of it, as if something had exploded within the depths of the bowl, splattering everything and everyone within the magic circle.

The woman's screams, which had grown weaker and weaker, were stilled. Cut off abruptly.

Silence, heavy and chill, hung over the scene for a moment. No one moved.

And then the shaman coughed, breaking the stasis.

Neither Caesare nor Jagiellon appeared concerned about being showered in fresh blood, but *something* had plainly affected them. There were sweat beads on both foreheads, mingling with the splattered blood. Caesare's eyes were wild and mad, not dead as they had been moments before.

"Very powerful place. Very powerful man," grunted the shaman, fastidiously cleaning his drum.

"I know where he is going," growled Jagiellon. "The forces of light marshal against us. A pilgrimage. And he intends to go via Venice. Somehow this ties with the wedding of the other one. Marco Valdosta. That joining must be stopped. Or at least I must stop Lopez reaching the marshes where the Lion holds sway."

The shaman nodded and rubbed his shoulder, wincing as he did so, as if the shoulder was deeply bruised. "Lion is very strong. Even if the young one is still unskilled, he is strong."

"I do not like failure. You will keep watch around the Lion's borderland." Jagiellon cleaned the cleaver on the victim's hair. "We will consult with Count Mindaug. He has been studying the magics of the West. He thinks I am unaware of this. Maybe he will know of some trap we can set."

The shaman nodded, and the Count was sent for, as servants cleared the mess away, moving with swift and fearful silence. As well they might: Any one of them might be next, if they drew attention to themselves. Until today, the dead woman had been a chambermaid.

The Count did indeed have an answer. A stray fact plucked out of a grimoire from the Ravenna region, from the southern margin of the sequence of lagoons and floodlands that had once stretched all the way from there to Grado in the north. Just off the southern margin of the ancient marshlands lay a grove of oak trees. The local people would go nowhere near the place. Local legend said a terrible rite had raised something there, something so evil that everyone for miles around found a reason to avoid the spot. It was a lonely and not very fertile area anyway, full of mosquitoes and malarial fevers. It lay not far from the causeway that led to Ravenna, and then onwards along the coast toward Venice.

"I will open the way," said Jagiellon. "Take a form to travel on land. See what, if anything, lies in this place."

The shaman nodded and stripped off his jacket with a tinkling of brass bells. The old body that lay underneath the leather was also tattooed. And considering the age of that lined face, the shaman's body was in remarkably good shape. Scrawny, yes; but sinewy tough under the tattoos.

The old man blurred into a feral-looking dog with yellow mangy fur, and yellow eyes, and yellower teeth. The dog slipped into the tunnel that Jagiellon had made.

Some hours later the shaman returned. "Some old beast of *kaos* make nest there. There are old magics which let it survive. It is very strong but nearly mindless. It exists just to feed, master."

Jagiellon's cold eyes seemed to glow. "Ideal."

"It cannot leave that place, master. It would die."

"No matter," said Jagiellon. "We will lead the priest and his companions to the beast, before they can reach the marshes. If it fails to kill them, it may at least drive them back. I want him away from Venice, and Marco Valdosta. There is something about that meeting that I do not like the feel of. Your birds will continue to watch and follow when Lopez moves."

First babies, the wise old midwives all said, were hard. Hard on the mother, hard on themselves. Issie evidently agreed with the wise old midwives of canalside, for the closer came the day that Maria was due, the more horrifying became the tales the old woman dragged out of her memory. Tales of birth-struggles that lasted for a week; of every possible complication; of girls that died and babies that died; of both that died together. And she had the unmitigated gall to bring in all the other foresters' wives to regale Maria with still more tales of birth-horrors, until Maria wondered why so many of them had gone through the ordeal not once, but six or eight times.

Maria had cause to thank all the saints together that Umberto was never around to listen to these stories, or if he was around when Issie began one of her tales, he was so used to ignoring her that he really didn't hear what she was saying.

As for Maria—well, Issie had been one of the people who had tried to frighten her with stories of ferocious wild beasts in the forest. The wild beasts had been no more ferocious than the occasional hare or deer, and by this time, Maria was disinclined to believe any of Issie's tales.

That didn't mean she wasn't prepared for a hard go; but her own mother had given birth and gone out to deliver a load the next day. Maria knew that *she* came of tough stock. She wasn't expecting much trouble, really.

She *still* wasn't expecting much trouble when the first pangs started, and the water broke—though *that* was a shock—and Issie chased Umberto out.

But then the real pains began. And after the first hour, Maria was vowing—between groans—that the next man who touched her with sex on his mind was going to draw back a bloody stump.

After the third hour, she knew that it wasn't going to be the stump of his *hand*.

After the fifth hour, when the pains were continuous, wave after wave after wave, and her throat was hoarse, she couldn't think of anything but the pain.

There were women milling about everywhere, praying out loud— what were *they* doing there? She hadn't asked them to come! The air was hot and stifling, her hair and bedgown were absolutely plastered to her with sweat, and someone was burning some vile herb in the fireplace. And all she could do was bite on the rope they'd given her, and tear at the bedclothes and it went on and on and on—

And that was when *she* swept into the room.

She was a tall shape in a dark, draped dress, and all the praying women fell silent as she raked the room with eyes that gleamed in the firelight.

"*Out*," she said. And the women, the horrible, useless women, fled before her like chickens before a falcon, cackling in panic.

She flung the windows wide, threw something on the fire that chased the stink out with the scent of fir and rosemary, and came to the side of the bed.

She leaned over Maria, and the silver pentacle gleaming at her throat told Maria everything she needed to know.

"*Strega*," she gasped. But in recognition, not condemnation. After all, none of those women and all of their calling on saints and angels had helped her.

"Exactly so." The woman smiled, and placed a hand on Maria's forehead; then, sketched a sign in the air and murmured some words.

Suddenly, Maria was . . . there, but not there. Detached from her body and all the pain and the mess. Floating within her own head, dreamily watching, as the Strega helped her out of the bed and got her to walk, then rest, then walk again, a little. She was *there*, but she did not care, except in the most detached possible way. Her body strained and hurt, but *she* did not.

Issie's friends all huddled fearfully at the door, and the Strega cast them glances of contempt from time to time, but said nothing. "I should have come to you before," she murmured in Maria's ear, "But I did not know your time was near. Did you think that we would leave one who was a friend to us alone with a flock of chattering monkeys in her time? No."

Then she made Maria squat on a peculiar stool, and there was a moment when Maria was *back* in herself, fully, and shouting, and then the baby dropped into the woman's hands in three, hard heaves.

Maria went back into the dreamy state, and the woman got her into bed again and put her little girl in her arms, and with an imperious gesture, allowed the silly chickens back in again. And *they* cleaned the room, and Maria, and made everything pretty so that poor Umberto would not be horrified, and she stayed awake only long enough to look into her daughter's eyes and fall in love—and smile vaguely at her husband in reassurance when he came in.

The last thing she saw was the Strega woman, whose name she never learned, sketching a sign of blessing in the air and leaving as mysteriously as she had come.

In the night, the cliffs loomed dark and threatening. The air was still cold, the wind blowing from Albania. Here, in the craggy folds of the mountains, winter still held firm. And threading her way through the darkness came a woman. She disappeared into the cliff. A little later a second woman came threading her way along the narrow path. Later a third. And then, two more. Deep within the caves the chanting began.

Georgio Steplakis was a hill shepherd. He had thirty sheep, and twenty-two goats, and a hut in the hills. He could hear the chanting. He had absolutely no inclination to leave his pallet. Rumor among the shepherds was that the women shed all their clothes for the dancing in the glades.

Georgio had reason to know the truth of this story. He'd been curious enough, and not superstitious enough, to try for a closer look when he was younger. You could be really stupid when you were sixteen or so. He hadn't believed in the naiads either. Well, he'd learned. The rite was as old as these hills and before people had chanted and danced, the nonhumans had.

And it was a women thing. Men who intruded would regret it. Georgio sighed in remembrance. Sometimes it was worth doing something you knew you would regret. She had been very beautiful.

Her hair was silvered and as fine as the finest silken threads. If she'd been standing, the tresses would have reached down to her knees. She lay in the glade, naked but for that hair. Her skin was very, very white, as white as almond-milk. It was also very, very old. The breasts were wrinkled and empty. They sprawled sideways across her chest. The chest did not move. Her eyes, wide open and sightless, stared at the sky. Half of a peeled almond was still clutched in her wrinkled hand.

When the women who had come to tend the altar found her thus, a low moan went up. There was sadness. And there was fear.

Who would take the half-almond from the worn stone altar when the winter came?

The cold lord must have his bride. There would be no fertility without it.

They buried her with honor and according to the ancient tradition, in a fetal position, half-almond still in the old hand. She was buried with the others, beneath the dancing glade.

Once the glade had been much lower than it was now, and the grass had grown less green.

Over the spot she was buried the grass would grow greener. The earth here lay many cubits deep. And it had all come from the same source. Many, many burials over long years.

Many brides.

PART IV
March, 1539 A.D.

Chapter 15

A shadow passed over the road in front of their mules; Lopez noticed that his mule flattened its ears at it. He looked up, and did not like what he saw. Those were blunt-winged hawks, not soarers.

Goshawks, he thought. What were goshawks doing here? In his former life, Eneko had flown hawks against game, as every young nobleman did. Goshawks were used in forested lands, not open plains, because they could not soar aloft on thermal currents as the long-winged falcons or broad-winged buzzards could. So why were those two up there, laboring away?

"Do you see those two hawks up there, Francis?

The priest squinted. "Well, I can see two birds, Eneko. They're very high. Could be hawks, I suppose."

Eneko frowned. "This is the third day I've noticed them. Sometimes one, sometimes both."

Francis shrugged. "Well, there are always birds up there. Why do you think they're the same ones? We've done a fair number of leagues every day, Eneko, since we left Rome. We're already nearing Venice."

Lopez had actually opened his mouth to explain, when abruptly, explanations became superfluous.

Darkness fell on them as if someone had just clapped a giant kettle over the road. Flames leapt and roared in the sudden darkness, blocking the road ahead of them. The mules were terrified, bucking and cavorting as if there were caltrops under their saddles and venomous snakes under their feet.

Only sheer determination had kept Eneko in the saddle. Father Diego had been less lucky; but Eneko had dragged him up across the saddlebow like a very ungainly sack of grain.

"It is an illusion," shouted Francis over the wheezing and braying of the mules, and the near-curses of the riders.

Father Francis had refused to ride anyway, so he had, perhaps, the advantage of not trying to control a mount. But as Eneko managed to get his beast under a little more control, he could see the flames, too. This was one of the most difficult kinds of sending, a kind of vision from afar. Thus, too, it was difficult to combat. The foe was not proximal. It was no use to attack the vision, they had to reach the sender.

And to make something of this magnitude required truly unearthly strength. Abruptly Eneko realized, as he struggled with the wild-eyed mule, that there could only be one purpose in this exercise: To delay and thwart them on this, the first leg of their pilgrimage. Something wanted to prevent them going on, or at least to hold them up. Perhaps whatever or whoever this was—and it reeked of Chernobog—wanted them to band together and try to pursue and find it. What it didn't want was for them to continue on their way. Ergo: they must.

"Francis!" he shouted. "A cloth!"

Francis might not care to ride, but he at least knew what Eneko was calling for and why. There was no reason to use magic to settle the mules. It would be a waste of effort and less effective than a scarf, anyway.

He unknotted and pulled off the sash he wore in place of a belt or a rope about his robes and whipped it over the head and eyes of the nearest mule, which happened to be Eneko's. Once the mule's eyes were covered, it stopped bucking, and stood, shivering all over. That gave Eneko the leisure to rummage in his pack and pull out the cloth that had lately been home to bread and cheese. Francis gave the next mule the same treatment, and the next, until all of them were blindfolded and no longer fighting to escape the illusory dangers.

The only inconvenience was that now they all had to dismount and lead their mounts, as well as the pack animals. And the mules were balky, obstinate about going forward when they could not see. Mulish, in a word. But they were no longer terrified, which meant that they were no longer an actual hazard to their riders.

The four pilgrims advanced slowly, leading their mounts. All four of them were chanting—not magic, as such, but prayers; which were probably just as effective as sacred magic in this situation. In Eneko's case, given their proximity to Venice, he elected to pray to Saint Mark.

Now they waded through sights and sounds that were nauseating, rather than frightening. Chernobog had plainly realized that it no longer served to terrify the mules. Instead, it flung alternate visions of sacrifice and torture at them. Then, when that failed, sybaritic scenes and succubi.

"Something together, perhaps, Eneko?" Francis muttered, as Eneko paused for a breath.

Eneko nodded, and led the pilgrims in the chanting of psalms. At last the way seemed to be clearing ahead. They were on a well-paved causeway across a swampland of slime-covered pools and reed patches. The relief almost beguiled them. But as Eneko was about to step forward, something whistled off to his left flank. An inhuman whistle; the kind that actually makes your eardrums vibrate.

Despite his resolve, Eneko looked—and saw an undine, rising half out of the water. She was wreathed in long green hair with magnificent bare breasts, much like the other temptations and apparitions.

Only . . . she was thumbing her nose at him. Sticking her tongue out. The gesture was so unlike the horror or the seduction of the other visions that had confronted them that Eneko realized immediately this was no illusion.

As if to reinforce the impression, the undine blew a raspberry at them. Then, beckoned. Eneko felt his brows draw together.

"Follow it," he commanded. And he stepped off the causeway into what appeared to be waist-deep water.

"We should stick to the path, Eneko," said Father Pierre worriedly. "Swamps are treacherous. And why do want to follow this illusion?"

For an answer Eneko pointed at his feet. "Because she isn't an illusion, Pierre. My feet are not wet."

"You look to be about waist deep!"

"It is the water that is an illusion. We are already lost. The horrors and visions were just a distraction while Chernobog or his minions tried to trap us more subtly. That undine is not an illusion. It is real."

"Nonhumans can be treacherous," Pierre warned.

Eneko stepped forward boldly. "Not more than Chernobog. And if I judge this correctly, she is the emissary of an ally of ours. An alliance of convenience, in which not much love is lost between the allies, but the common foe is worse."

There was, he thought, no point in mentioning that he thought this undine had come directly from Marco Valdosta, who had inherited his Strega predecessor's adherents. That would complicate matters altogether too much at the moment.

They walked slowly toward the undine, who smiled, showing altogether too many sharklike teeth. Father Diego glanced back, perhaps feeling doubtful, and yelped.

"My God!" he shouted, his voice rising a great deal. "Look!"

Eneko turned with the others to see what it was that had Diego so shocked. Behind them the illusion was dissolving. Ahead lay a far more dilapidated looking causeway. They were just on the edge of the reed-brake around some swampy pools. Behind them the ground was in fact higher. Higher and lashing with something that hissed unpleasantly, with distinctly reptilian tones.

The darkness lifted; the sun, long obscured, came out and cast reflections onto the still pools. And Eneko felt a warm breeze . . . and thought, perhaps, that he saw a reflection of something gold in the water.

"The Lion," said Pierre.

Eneko nodded. "Our guide has deserted us, but I think we no longer need her."

The breeze swayed the reed-brake. *Indeed*, it seemed to say.

Father Francis shook his head. "I feel we are in the presence of some powerful magic. You and Pierre seem to understand what is happening."

Eneko led his mule forward. "Chernobog made an effort to turn us before we could reach a place where he holds no sway. When the ruse failed . . . it tried to kill us, by luring us away from the safe paths and deeper into the swamp and the bogs, where something cruel and bloody lurks. But we are now in the lagoons and marshes of an ancient neutral power. One which is bound to a Christian soul."

"The Lion of Saint Mark," said Pierre. "The Winged Lion of Venice."

Father Francis looked troubled. "Why would one of the neutrals aid us?"

The undine stuck her head out of the water. "The Lion bids you a grudging welcome to his marshes. He sends messages to Eneko Lopez. By the inner flames that must be you, man. The Lion bids you come in haste. He needs you for a bonding. And he says that you should remember that although your God allows you free will, he too has plans. And that one such as he guides many threads."

The undine slipped back under the water. Then she popped her head up again. "Oh. Sorry about the nose-thumbing and the raspberry. But the Lion says the one thing Chernobog cannot understand nor feign is humor." She pointed. "The path is over there. Stick to it."

Lopez remained thoughtfully looking out at the horizon for a long time after she had gone. Francis, meanwhile, had taken the blinders off all the mules. Finally Pierre nudged him, and he started.

"What's wrong, Eneko?" the priest asked.

"It strikes me that this was a singularly ineffective attack, compared to what we have faced from Chernobog before this." Lopez turned to look into the faces of his companions.

"Well . . ." Pierre began, then nodded. "You know, you're right. But we did weaken him considerably, and this may be all he can mount."

"We weakened his instrument, Pierre," Francis pointed out. "We never touched Chernobog himself. He can always get new instruments."

"My thought exactly," Lopez replied, with a frown. "So why this halfhearted try at stopping us?"

"Because we aren't as important as we think we are?" Pierre replied.

"Your humility is appreciated, Pierre, but—" He thought a moment. "But Chernobog would assign an importance to us out of all proportion to how we actually rate in the Lord's grand scheme," Lopez said firmly. "We *hurt* him. We hurt his mortal vessel, physically, and we hurt his pride—and pride, as you well know, Brothers, is highly cherished among the dark ones. No, I think there must be another answer."

"He's dividing his attention?" Pierre hazarded into the silence.

Eneko nodded. "I think it must be. He is confined to a mortal vessel, and has limitations imposed by that confinement. At the moment, something is occupying his attention that is far more important to him than we are."

Francis snorted. "Well, I, for one, am going to consider that a blessing!" He turned and strode off up the road, leaving the rest to follow.

But it was Pierre who voiced precisely what was troubling Lopez, as he nudged his mule with his heels, and sent it after Francis.

"If there is something more important to Chernobog than we are, what *is* it?" he asked aloud. "Why haven't we heard anything about it, and why haven't the Grand Metropolitan's seers gotten any hint of it?"

"Why, indeed?" asked Lopez, and sent his mule after Pierre's. "Whatever it is, I fear it will come from a direction that none of us can anticipate."

Chapter 16

"She's beautiful! Oh, she's so cute!" Kat peered into the crib at the baby.

Maria yawned. "She's asleep. That is beautiful enough for me right now."

"She's so tiny! Oh, look at those little fingers."

Maria snorted, but fondly. "You should hear her yell. There's nothing tiny about her lungs. She yelled almost the whole way here to Venice, on the ship. Then I took her to see Umberto's sister to talk about the christening, and the baby screamed at her. You're lucky. Umberto's sister didn't seem to think much of being bellowed at. I thought she'd refuse to be a godmother, and Umberto particularly wanted her to be."

"*I* insist on being one of her godmothers," said Kat loyally. "And whether he likes it or not, Marco is being the godfather."

Maria smiled. "You're not losing any time putting your foot down, are you?"

Kat smiled back. "Start as you mean to go on. When and where will the ceremony be? At the Chapel at St. Hypatia di Hagia Sophia?"

"We haven't arranged it yet. Father Pasquari, the priest who married us, has died since. But we just need a small place. There'll only be a few friends."

"I'll talk to Marco," said Kat firmly. "We have a wedding to arrange. Let him arrange this. He's very good friends with Brother Mascoli of St. Raphaella."

Maria smiled. "That's a canalers' church. He's a good man, is old Mascoli."

The more she thought about it, the better she liked the idea. Small, intimate, and none of her friends would feel uncomfortable, as they might in St. Hypatia's.

"Marco will arrange it."

Petro Dorma blew across his steepled fingers.

"Of course a desire to please the Holy Roman Emperor must be a major factor. But . . . well. I'd have to clear a couple of great galleys. It's not just the entourage, Manfred, it's the horses, and at such short notice. The merchants are going to howl. The Republic of Venice is not like the Empire. The *Case Vecchie* are all engaged in the trade. I wish you were prepared to take carracks instead."

When Manfred and Erik and Eberhard had been admitted to the Doge's private working chambers earlier, he'd been delighted to see them. "You've arrived in Venice just in time for Marco and Kat's wedding!"

Now that they were asking to hire vessels to transport them to the Holy Land . . . he looked as if he'd just drunk a large draft of vinegar.

"The Outremer convoy leaves in less than three weeks. Even deck-space is bespoke."

From the corner of the room a stocky young man spoke up. "What about the four galleys that are in the Arsenal, Petro? The ones that are going to Cyprus? They should be finished by the end of March."

Manfred recognized the lad; it was the hooligan who had taken part in the raid on the *Casa* Dandelo slavers, which Manfred and Erik had participated in. The one who'd been in jail for supposedly killing the priest. Manfred had been properly introduced to young Benito Valdosta as Dorma's ward after Venice had been rescued, but now, suddenly, the connection made itself clear. Then he'd been dressed like a beggar-brat. Now he was dressed as a Venetian noble. But a twist of expression as he'd looked at Manfred had let him place the face.

Petro nodded. "It's an idea." He turned back to Manfred. "Would you consider remaining on in Venice for a week or two after the wedding? You would arrive in Ascalon just as quickly, as the vessels wouldn't accompany the convoy. The convoy stops for two or three days at each port to allow for trade. You'd be spared all of that, as well as all of the mess and confusion of herding pilgrims on and off again at each port. And with your two hundred men aboard, they'd be well-armed."

Manfred nodded. "That sounds fair. What do you say, Eberhard?"

The white-haired statesman looked thoughtful. "A personal convoy of brand-new ships will look as if the Empire and Venice enjoy a very cozy relationship. Rome may not like that. Constantinople may not either."

Manfred grinned. "We're expecting to have the Grand Metropolitan's very own delegation along, in the shape of Eneko Lopez and his companions, according to a letter I have from my uncle. And as for Alexius, well, let him worry. The news is he may be a shaky ally at best. A good idea to fill his mind with doubts. In fact—on the whole, I think it would not be a bad idea at all for Alexius to think the Empire and Venice are on better than mere speaking terms."

Eberhard looked speculatively at Manfred. "I detect Francesca de Chevreuse's hand here."

Manfred did his best to look affronted. "I can think of ideas too, you know."

The statesman shook his snowy head. "Explain to him, my Lord Dorma, that a wise politician always tells the truth. If one day it is necessary for you to lie, no one doubts your veracity."

Manfred snorted. "The truth seems pretty rare in politics, Eberhard."

"That," said Eberhard, grimly, "is because there are very, very few wise politicians. If you must play at politics, play by my rules."

But Petro had picked up on another point. "Francesca!" he said with unalloyed pleasure. "You have brought her with you?"

Manfred nodded, warily. There was a little too much enthusiasm in the way Petro had reacted to Francesca's name. And he began to remember a few things from their last sojourn here. How Francesca had made it very clear to him that their liaison was not going to be an exclusive one. That she had several clients. And once, to comfort him, she had said lightly that one of them was balding and big-nosed . . .

He found himself eyeing Petro Dorma's balding head and lumpy nose with new understanding. "Yes, we have," he said curtly, trying to keep hostility out of his tone. "But understand this: She is strictly off limits to anything but polite social calls, Dorma. Even if you are the Doge of Venice."

Petro smiled, not at all discomfited. "Ah, well. My loss is your gain. But Francesca's conversation is a jewel even more rare than her magnificent body."

Manfred coughed. "Hmm. Well, we are going to be staying at the Imperial embassy. Francesca's already gone to see Katerina Montescue. But she will be in this evening."

Petro bowed. "I will come and make a call. And I don't mind if Rome and Alexius of Byzantium see it as Venice wishing to cozy up to the Holy Roman Empire."

"I'll send you a messenger when she gets in," said Manfred. "No. Wait. A better idea. We'll take young Benito with us. Trusty native guide, y'know. Well. Native, anyway. And then I can send him back without exciting comments about a messenger running between the two of us."

Petro looked at Benito, who was grinning like a horse-collar. "Why do I feel this is a bad idea, Prince? Well, I can hardly refuse. Off you go, Benito."

Looking at Benito's eyes, alive with devilry, Manfred himself actually wondered briefly if this was a good idea. Then he dismissed the piece of caution with the contempt it deserved. What trouble could this young *Case Vecchie* cause that he, Manfred, hadn't had Erik rescue him from a dozen times already?

Surely none.

"Well, there is a font, yes," said Marco, thinking. "But it is a very small and very poor church."

"Maria likes the idea."

"I'll talk to Brother Mascoli, then. I don't think he'd mind, and his Hypatian ordination allows him to do this. I've hardly seen you for days with all this arranging. Come with me. Mascoli is a nice man."

So he and Kat went down to St. Raphaella, taking simple joy in just being in each other's company.

Brother Mascoli didn't mind. In fact, he was delighted. "Sometimes people seem to forget that St. Raphaella also does the work of an ordinary church. It will be a pleasure to christen this child."

His eyes moistened. "The child is healthy? Well? So many of those that I christen here . . . their mothers just wish to make sure

that at least their souls are safe, since we cannot help their bodies."

"Marco has been to see them," said Kat. "He says the child is
strong and healthy."

Mascoli smiled. "Well, that assessment is good enough for me.
We can do it whenever suits the parents."

"Brother, Mascoli—" Marco hesitated; then, as the little priest
cocked his head to the side, he went on. "Brother Mascoli, would
it be out of order to ask the water-people to come add a blessing of their own? Just in case, you know? Umberto's family doesn't
all approve of this marriage."

He decided he had better not say anything about the fact that
the baby had been, well, "early." Brother Mascoli knew the dates
of the wedding and the birth, and he was fully capable of adding for himself.

Brother Mascoli blinked. But to Marco's relief, he answered with
no hesitation. "I think that would be an excellent idea. Would you
care to ask, or shall I?"

"Would you?" he replied, with relief. "If I ask, they might feel,
well, obligated. If you do, and they'd rather not, there'll be no hard
feelings."

"Consider it done."

"What was all that about?" Kat asked, as they left the chapel
and stepped into her family's little gondola.

"Call it . . . a little something extra," he replied. "Maria's
always made her living on the water, and they're likely to be
in and out of boats all their lives. I just thought it would be
a good thing to get the baby a little extra blessing." He left it
at that, and Kat evidently forgot all about it, for she said
nothing else.

The next morning they gathered outside the church. Maria had
underestimated her popularity, and the grapevine among Venice's
waterways. There must have been at least thirty people. Brother
Mascoli, clad as usual in his faded, light-colored robes, but with
a special surplice for the occasion, smiled and let them all crowd
in.

"Your friends said they would be happy to help you, Marco,"
he whispered, as Marco and Kat took their places beside the
altar rail. And that was all he really had time to say, for the

crowd parted for Maria and Umberto to come to the fore at that moment.

The only person missing was Umberto's disapproving sister. They were already inside the chapel, voices upraised, when both Marco and Kat realized that Maria was looking around frantically for her.

"What's wrong?" whispered Marco.

"The other godmother," whispered Kat. "She isn't here. Can't you do something, Marco?"

Marco drew his breath in. And felt a deep roaring within him of anger and determination. Umberto's sister didn't have to take her disapproval of the marriage out on an innocent child!

He *almost* said something, when he suddenly knew that he wouldn't have to. It would be all right.

Brother Mascoli took the baby into his arms. The baby girl didn't scream at him. "She is a beautiful, healthy child, my daughter," he said. "Now, who is going to stand as the godparents to this child?"

"We are." Kat and Marco stepped forward. There was a hiss of approval from the crowd of canalers and Arsenalotti. Marco had treated enough of their children, many of them here in this very chapel, and they all knew that he and Kat had played very large roles in the salvation of Venice less than a year ago.

"And the other . . ."

The presence light on the altar flared, burning with a peculiar greenness. From behind the statue of Saint Raphaella a voice came. "*I do.*"

It wasn't, as many of the stunned audience concluded, the voice of the saint herself. Marco recognized it. That was the voice of the undine, Juliette.

She plainly had the ability to cast a glamour on her appearance. She came out from behind the statue. To Marco she looked her green-haired, green-toothed self. He could even see the line of the scar. But to the others in chapel, she obviously didn't look quite like that. Marco wondered if they could see the pool of water she stood in.

Brother Mascoli smiled. "She is a lucky little girl to have such godparents." He took the oil and anointed the baby's head, and the water, which Juliette contrived to touch. Marco was aware of the green glow to it.

Baby Alessia, in her delicate white shawl, was angelic

throughout the ceremony. Juliette took the baby into her arms. *"She will never drown. And if her mother is not there to care for her, she just has to touch running water to call me or my kin to help."* She spoke quietly, so that only those at the altar could hear her.

Maria sighed happily, when the ceremony was over and the crowd had left the chapel, looking at her daughter who had lapsed back into sleep. "Thank you both. I . . . I so desperately want Alessia to have what I didn't. I must find that other woman who stepped in for Umberto's sister and thank her, too. I really thought . . ."

Marco smiled reaching a finger to caress the baby's cheek. "You won't find her, Maria. But your daughter has a fairy-godmother."

"What?" Maria looked at him as if she thought he had gone mad.

"That was an undine," said Marco, calmly. "One of the water spirits of Venice."

"What!" Now her mouth dropped open with shock.

"She gave Alessia a powerful blessing too. Your little girl will never drown, and can call on the water-sprites for help."

"But . . . she looked just like an ordinary woman." Fortunately, Maria had far too much trafficking with the Strega in her past to be offended by the notion that a pagan creature, inhuman to boot, had just become the godmother of her child.

For an answer, Marco pointed to the pool of water on the floor, and the wet prints leading behind the statue of Saint Raphaella. "There's a water-door and a water-chapel through there. It is a consecrated place, too."

Maria shook her head and stared at the footprints. "I don't think I am going to tell Umberto about this."

Marco patted her shoulder "I don't think he'd understand and it would cause complications. Besides," he continued, feeling a laugh rising in his chest, "given the glamour that she used to make herself look human, I wonder if Umberto would believe you anyway. He'd probably think you'd just been seeing things!"

"Well, this is certainly an unexpected honor, Signor Lopez," said Petro Dorma, bowing. "You are the second great visitor I've had today."

"My companions and I are simple men of God, Milord Dorma," reproached Eneko.

"Traveling with a letter that bears the seal of the Grand Metropolitan in Rome? Not exactly 'simple,' I'd say. However that may be, you will do me the honor of staying here, I hope? Rooms will be made available for you."

"We'd be pleased to. But we do not intend to stay very long. We want to find a passage to the Holy Land."

Petro Dorma allowed himself a small smile. "Well, unlike Manfred of Brittany, you haven't walked in here and asked *me* to do so for you. He was here doing that not two hours ago. And—of course!—space for a couple of hundred knights, and—of course!—their horses. Emperor Charles Fredrik doesn't mind asking the impossible."

"The Emperor is here?"

Petro shook his head. "No, just Manfred, Erik, *Ritter* Eberhard of Brunswick—and an old friend, Francesca de Chevreuse. Oh, yes—and two hundred of those steel-clad Teutons. On their way to Jerusalem on a pilgrimage. Manfred needs one, I should think."

Eneko Lopez smiled. "I will talk to Prince Manfred. I suspect our journey is for the same purpose. Perhaps he'll have space for a few priests among his knights."

"He seemed to assume you would be joining them, in fact," said Petro. "Or, at least, he said so in our conversation. However, I'll pass on a message that you are desirous of seeing him, as I'll be seeing the fascinating Francesca this evening. And, speaking as the person who organized his ships, he does have space. Now, not to make too fine a point of it, Signor, but you and your companions appear to be generously splattered with marsh mud. I'm sure you'd all appreciate an opportunity to get clean, put on some fresh raiment, and then join us for our evening meal."

Father Pierre laughed. "You mean, Milord Dorma, we smell like a swamp, and you'd prefer us to come to dinner without the bouquet?"

"Well, I wouldn't have put it quite like that," said Petro Dorma, tinkling a small bell. "But . . . yes."

"We're lucky we just smell of swamp," said Father Francis, looking across the piazza to the column where the winged Lion of Saint Mark gleamed in the late afternoon sun.

A factotum arrived, bowed. "You called, milord?"

"Alberto, take these good men and see them to the rooms reserved for our guests. Arrange hot water, baths, and fresh clothes, and the cleaning of their present clothes. See them comfortable and happy, please."

The factotum bowed again. "If you will follow me, sirs."

Chapter 17

It was easier, Kat had learned, to say *yes* than to plan a wedding.

The momentous day when Marco's marriage was annulled and she had been able to actually say "yes" had been a wonderful one. The trouble then began immediately, although she had not realized it until the next day.

But the next day . . .

She awakened, remembered with a rush *everything* that had happened, but most importantly, that *she was going to marry Marco!* Accordingly, she had plotted her way through a wonderful bath, perfumed and luxurious, that Madelena set up for her before the fire, as soon as she had finished breaking her fast.

A small wedding, she had planned. *Just the grandfathers, Benito, Maria—perhaps a few guests. At St. Hypatia di Hagia Sophia. . . . Dare I ask Francesca?*

She would certainly ask Father Lopez to officiate.

As the day progressed Kat had gotten the sinking realization—sinking like a stone anchor at sea—that the "small private wedding" she'd been planning was going to be a matter of public—very public—celebration. And she would have very little to say in the matter.

There was no question of *where*—the basilica. The *Basilica di San Marco.* With the banquet to follow at the Doge's palace, of course. Nor any question of who would be invited—everyone. Those not important enough for a place inside would be crowding the *Piazza di San Marco.* She had stopped worrying about who would pay for all of this once she got to that point. This was no longer a wedding, it was a state occasion, and the state would absorb it. The state would also absorb the feast for the common folk, which she insisted on.

"My *friends* will be out there!" she had said stubbornly. "So unless you wish to have the ambassadors sharing their tables with Arsenalotti . . ."

Petro Dorma had gotten her point immediately. There would be a feast with enough to stuff every man, woman, and child in Venice until they were sick.

On one other thing she put her foot down. "My attendants will be Maria Garavelli, and Francesca de Chevreuse," she said to Dorma, flatly, when he presented her with a list of suitable bridal attendants. "*Just* Maria and Francesca. No one else."

She fixed him with her best glare, the one that had usually cowed her most dangerous customers back in the days she'd been smuggling in order to keep *Casa* Montescue financially afloat. *A canal-girl and a whore. But also the woman who got you the Arsenalotti and the woman who kept the Knots on your side.*

Dorma, caught in that glare, folded. "Maria Garavelli . . . Verrier," he agreed, swallowing. "That will please the Arsenalotti a great deal, certainly. And Francesca de Chevreuse has the good will of the Emperor Charles Fredrik."

He did not ask her if she could render up the canal-girl in an acceptable guise; he had wisely left her alone to deal with the piles and piles of paper this behemoth of a celebration had already begun to generate.

Benito, of course, would be one of Marco's attendants. She didn't know who the others would be, but it wouldn't surprise her to discover one would be his friend Rafael. Two more . . . interesting choices.

But at least this way, none of the Case Vecchi *can be offended, because we won't have chosen any of them. Or if they are offended, they can all be offended equally.*

There had never been any question of what dress she would wear. "Your grandmother's," her grandfather had said with pride and a tear in his eye. There was no choice, really. The dress would reflect *Casa* Montescue, and that dress was, perhaps, the only piece of clothing in the entire house that reflected the fortune that had been in possession of the *old* House of Montescue.

She had gone to the storeroom with no doubt in her mind that one thing, at least, would be as it had been in those happier times. After all, hadn't she rummaged out her mother's old gowns to remake for Francesca, and hadn't they been as sound as a bell? The gown she'd found to remake into Maria's attendant's dress had been a glory of scarlet brocade, still, despite all these years.

So the ruin that met her eyes when she opened the chest that contained her grandmother's wedding gown came as a total shock.

Silk had discolored, rotted in some places; the brocade was tarnished, the bullion dulled and blackened, the pearls—

She burst into tears, there on her knees beside the chest in the storehouse, and that was how Francesca had found her.

Francesca had taken one look at the contents of the chest and gathered her into her arms to let her sob, rocking her a little, and making hushing sounds while she stroked Kat's hair.

The last person to hold me like this was mother...

"Here, now," Francesca murmured. "This isn't as bad as you think."

"But it's *ruined!*" Kat wailed.

"Not . . . quite." Francesca took her chin in one hand and tilted her face to look up. "First, I don't think this is as bad as it looks. And second—" Her eyes twinkled, and Kat gulped down her sobs and sniffled "I've been casting about for a gift that you won't already have three dozen of. Unless you really, truly, desire *another* incomparably, grandiosely hideous silver saltcellar?"

Kat shuddered. "A twenty-third? None of which I dare have melted down?"

Francesca's silvery laugh startled a moth up out of the chest. "You clothed me—now allow me to clothe *you*. Madame Louise has, as you may have noticed, a very accomplished suite of seamstresses working for her. She still is very obliged to me."

"I had noticed," Kat said, a little embarrassed by the envy she felt for the wonderfully, flatteringly fashionable gown that Francesca wore—and for the air with which Francesca wore it. Next to the former courtesan, she felt as ungainly as a calf.

"Just close up the chest and we'll have it taken down to the gondola. I just came to thank you for the invitation to be your attendant, and to explain that it would be better for a certain party if I declined it."

Francesca's raised eyebrow and one finger tapping a ring with an elaborate crest gave Kat the hint.

"Oh. *Oh.*" She sighed. "Oh, bilgewater. I suppose it wouldn't be a good idea, would it? Your—friend—"

"Shouldn't be too publicly associated with me," Francesca agreed cheerfully. "Now, if you still want to name someone who will provide everything I can without the shock value..."

She shook her head.

"Never mind, then. Let's get this down to my gondola, and we'll salvage every scrap that we can from it—and what can't be salvaged, we'll replace. *We,*" she added, again with that significant tap on her ring, and Kat found herself having to stifle a slightly hysterical giggle at the idea that Manfred of Brittany was going to find himself paying for the dress of a lady he barely knew and had not the slightest chance of finagling into his bed.

It was the both of them, she and Marco together, who approached the last possibly difficult bit of the wedding plans that deviated from Petro Dorma's orchestrations.

Marco tapped on the door, at precisely the time of their carefully made appointment. One no longer sought the quarters of Eneko Lopez unannounced, not now that he was openly the Grand Metropolitan's representative and quartered in the palace of the Doge.

"Come in," came the harsh voice. "I assume it is you, Marco Valdosta."

Marco pushed open the door. Lopez sat at a desk where he had been writing. He pushed his work away, and raised an eyebrow when he saw that Kat was with him. "I had wondered if you felt the need of spiritual counsel," he said dryly.

"Actually, we had a favor to ask of you," Kat said, hesitantly. "The Patriarch is conducting the Nuptial Mass, of course, but..."

She couldn't get the words out; Marco squeezed her hand and supplied them. "We'd like you to be the officiating priest for the marriage."

Kat saw the imperturbable Eneko Lopez at a complete loss for words, at least for a moment or two.

"I... would be very pleased," he said at last. "In fact, quite honored. But *why*? Why me?"

"For a great many reasons," Kat said. "But it just seemed to us that—as a priest, as the kind of priest you are, you have to do so many things that are so difficult, so dangerous—and no one ever asks you to do anything that is, well, pleasant." She hesitated; corrected herself. "Joyful."

Then she added, very softly: "We don't think you have nearly enough joy in your life. And you can't do without it, you know. It reminds you *why* you have to face the bad parts."

For a moment, she wondered if she'd insulted him. Then amazingly, the grim, stern, rather frightening Eneko Lopez reached up and wiped the merest glitter of a tear from his eye.

"Thank you," he said simply. "I would be delighted."

The Church of St. Hypatia di Hagia Sophia was silent, that silence that speaks of emptiness. For a moment, Kat wondered if she'd come too early. Still, it was supposed to be the night before her wedding day. There would be much to do, if she did go ahead and marry Marco. Part of her, the part that was pragmatic, the part that most people saw, said that she was being ridiculous. At this point, the thing had a momentum of its own, and would carry her along whether or not she wanted it to. But as Patriarch Michael had said, humans were creatures of spirit as well as mundane flesh. And her spirit was troubled. It was always here that she came when she needed to sort that out.

Ah. Yes, there was a solitary Sibling in her white robes. Kat walked to the counseling booth, sat down and waited. A few moments later a female voice said: "Peace be with you, my child. How may I counsel you?"

Kat sighed. "By telling me I'm being stupid, probably. I am supposed to marry tomorrow."

The dress is ready. It fits like a second skin, and where Francesca found all the bits on no notice at all, I will never know. I look like a queen in it, and Maria looks like a princess in hers. The feasting has already begun, the Basilica is full of candles and flowers and priests. Everything is in place for tomorrow. Only I—only I am suddenly afraid!

"And? Do you love this man?"

"More than anything on earth."

"Is there any reason why you should not be married, daughter?

"No." Kat twisted her hands. "The Patriarch himself has sanctioned the marriage."

"I see. Does your husband-to-be abuse you?"

"*Marco?* He's the gentlest soul in Venice! The kindest, softest, bravest . . ."

"Then what *is* the problem, daughter? Is it sexual . . ." The woman hesitated, an element of doubt in her voice. The Siblings were all sworn to chastity and celibacy. Perhaps her counselor felt she might be out of her depth here.

"No. It's . . . It's nothing like that. It's spiritual, if anything."

"Ah. Marriage is a holy institution sanctified by our Lord himself. It is intended to be a union of bodies, minds and spirits."

Kat took a deep breath. "The man I am going to . . . supposed to . . . marry, is possessed. Sort of. Um. Part of him is a pagan magical creature. I am a Christian."

There was a silence. "I think, Katerina Montescue, that it would be easier if we went out into the church and I used those murals you sometimes sit and admire to advise you."

"You know who I am?"

There was a gentle snort of laughter from the other side of the scrim. "Katerina, all Venice knows who you are, now. But I have seen you come to this church for many years. I knew exactly who you were when I sat with Eneko Lopez and listened to you tell of your problems with the smuggling of supplies for the Strega. I listened with some amusement when you put him in his place with questions about Dottore Marina. Then, as now, I listened under the seal of counsel. I did not betray you then. I will not betray you now, just because I step outside of the booth."

Kat went out, to find the Sibling waiting for her. "Come. Let us go to the Chrysostom murals. They are not your favorites, but they make my point well."

They walked down until they stood below the first mural. The golden preacher was portrayed as a gaunt man with the eyes of a hawk. His painted gaze was unrelenting. They seemed to stare through her.

"He reminds me of Signor Lopez," said Kat, quietly.

The Sibling nodded. "I think they were cut of the same cloth. He was, like Eneko, a very intense man. And very charismatic. Not always right, however, nor always wise. Narrow-minded and even outright bigoted at times. Yet, with him our Hypatia formed one of the most influential alliances in the history of the Church. It was the meeting of those two great minds that set the course of the Christian Church from thenceforth, and put an end to—well, ameliorated, at least—what had become an increasingly entrenched tradition of schismatic dogmatism and heresy-hunting."

She paused for a moment. "I will not attempt, here and now, to explain the theological complexities of the matter. In the millennium that has gone by since, their tradition has become known as 'Petrine,' just as that of Saint Augustine has been called 'Pauline.' But, as is so often true, the names obscure as much as they reveal. Both creeds within the church are more like umbrellas than fences. Do not forget that if Sachs was a Pauline, so was the courageous young prince who broke the back of Chernobog's monster—and his companion Erik belongs to the Gaelic creed, which has its own history and doctrines altogether."

Her mouth grew a little tight. "Nor should you think for a moment that simply because a man calls himself a 'Petrine' that he is not capable of the vilest sins and crimes."

The Sibling pointed to the next panel, which showed the two, back-to-back. "There you see Hypatia writing, developing the philosophy, and Chrysostom, brilliant orator that he was, expounding it. He provided most of the driving force, she—when necessary, which it often was—provided the diplomacy. Because of that alliance, Hypatia and Chrysostom were able to formalize a doctrine of compassion and acceptance that emphasized wisdom and learning. But—"

She chuckled. "Not without a multitude of clashes, and even more in the way of compromises. And both of them left their own traditions, which are somewhat distinct. I represent one, Father Eneko Lopez another. The Church needs both, you know."

The Sibling turned away from her contemplation of murals. "All of this is the basis of the core tenet of the Hypatian order within the Petrine wing of the church. Which, since you choose to come to this church, I assume you are in sympathy with. Saint Hypatia gave to us that *all* men and women of good will, ultimately worship the same God, no matter what form they attempt to place on the unknowable. Whether they are Christian, Jew, Parsee or Hindu, Strega, Muslim, or even outright pagans."

"And what has this to do with my marrying Marco?"

"You would hardly say he was *not* a man of good will?"

"Of course not."

"And the Lion of Saint Mark? The Guardian of Venice? We of

the Hypatian order know it well. Would you agree that it is a creature of good will, of love?

Sudden tears filled Kat's eyes. "It loves this place, these marshes and its people . . . I see. Yes. Thank you. Thank you."

"It is a pleasure." The Sibling patted her gently. "I foresee yet another union, a meeting of minds and spirits."

Kat laughed, a slightly watery sound. "Marco can do the diplomacy."

In the end, the thing did have its own momentum, and Kat and Marco were carried, not along with it, but riding atop it.

It began with a pair of processions of gondolas that carried her and Maria from *Casa* Montescue, and Marco and Benito from *Casa* Dorma, to meet at the Piazza San Marco and disgorge their contents in front of the waiting crowds.

Kat, veiled from head to toe with the finest of silk gauze, saw everything through a sort of fog. The veil was white, but the overgown of her dress was as blue as the Med on a sunny day, and so stiff with bullion and pearls it could easily have stood by itself. The flower-crown that surmounted it surrounded her in a second mist of the perfume of roses and lily of the valley.

Kat had a sudden image of herself, from two years before, leaping into the canal to avoid a Schiopettieri sweep—wearing *this* outfit. She'd have gone down like an anchor! Not even quick-thinking Benito could have saved her.

The image almost caused her to burst into open laughter. As it was, she couldn't help but continue the procession with her face wearing a grin which, she suspected, was quite unsuitable for the solemnity of the occasion.

Fortunately, there were plenty of things to distract her. They were met by two sets of minstrels, who serenaded them with love songs as they made their way in twin processions to the basilica. And the mobs of Venice, who could be so unruly when they chose, parted like the Red Sea for them without a murmur—and kept their chatter and cheering down to where she could *hear* the minstrels telling her of the delights awaiting her.

Marco's procession arrived at the basilica first, of course. He was supposed to await her at the altar, so she took her time, trying to move like Francesca, with a willowy, gliding walk that would make her seem to slide along without having any feet. She was very conscious of the Lion on his pedestal as she passed him; *was* this something more than a statue? She thought she felt his golden gaze on her, warm and benevolent, as she passed by.

She had thought it would take forever to cross the piazza. It seemed to take no time at all. She had thought she would feel pressed in by all the people; instead, she felt as if she floated on their goodwill.

The minstrels left them at the porch of the basilica, and from within came the sweet voices of children, singing. She held up her head, and saw the path to Marco lying straight ahead of her, and if she did not fly up it, it was through no fault of hers.

She went through the Nuptial Mass as in a dream, hands that wanted to reach for his clasped demurely in front of her. But finally, finally, came the moment when Eneko Lopez stepped forward with his sober black robes enlivened by a blue stole, and she and Marco rose from their places, and he raised the veil with shaking hands and put it tenderly over her head and they knelt together, hands joined at last beneath Eneko Lopez's, for the blessing.

And it was at that moment, when she thought that her heart could not hold another drop of happiness, that a faintly glowing paw of golden mist placed itself atop the hand of the priest.

You will be happy, little sister. It was not a wish, it was a prophecy. And her heart rose, singing.

Chapter 18

Manfred whistled softly. "Holy Mother! See that blonde, Erik? The original paps of Anu, I swear."

Erik determinedly did not look up from the table. Ogling all the available—and, for that matter, all the unavailable—women of the world was Manfred's specialty, not his. "It is impolite to stare, Manfred. Women don't like it."

Manfred snorted. "Then why do they wear clothes like that? Anyway, Erik, you've got have a look. I'll swear she is one of those Viking Valkyries come to fetch you after all."

Despite all his best intentions, Erik did look.

And was trapped. There were occasional blond heads in Venice. A few Lombards, and travelers from further afield. But this woman was a true Scandinavian blonde, her great cascade of hair straight and fine and so pale as to be almost white. Her face, too, spoke of the northlands: the skin milk-white with blossomed cheeks, high cheekbones. And, as Manfred had pointed out, she had a magnificent figure. Despite himself Erik caught his breath and stared.

Manfred laughed coarsely. "It *is* impolite to stare at her tits, isn't it, Erik? You want me to organize a meeting for you? A quiet little alcove somewhere. I'll distract the bodyguards. And in this case, my friend, they really are *body*guards."

Erik realized that he'd been so taken up with looking at the Scandinavian woman that he hadn't noticed the two men accompanying her. Once he did, it was very clear to him why the blond woman was not being mobbed by cisebeos. Looking at the two of them, Erik was wary himself. They were as blond as the woman, even taller, and much wider. And they had beards, something she lacked.

Still . . . she was a magnificent, queenly figure. "Who is she?"

Manfred took a pull from his goblet. "I only know half the women in Venice, Erik. I'll have to find young Benito. He knows the other half."

Erik shrugged. "Wouldn't do me much good. See the furs she's wearing? And the jewelry, and the escorts. That is a very wealthy noblewoman."

"The wildest kind, believe me," said Manfred.

He stood up. "Anyway. Francesca asked that I come up to speak with the happy couple. She's scheming away for my uncle, I suspect. Wasting her time. Marco is a nice boy even if butter won't melt in his mouth, but there's steel in him that not all of Francesca's wiles will turn. Y'know one of my father's *duniwassals* back at Carnac caught me stealing arrows from the war-stores to go duck shooting with, when I was about eleven. I was the duke's son, and I wasn't really worried. He fetched me such a clip around my ear I thought it might come out of the other side of my head. I squalled blue murder, and threatened to go to my father about him."

Manfred pulled a wry face. "I still remember what he said: 'I don't care if you go and talk to the Ard Ri himself, boy. Siege stores are my duty. I keep them frae pilfering by anybody, even your father hisself. Now run along and tell him.' The old devil was as unlike young Marco as possible, but the two are cut from the same cloth in one way. They know what they believe is right and you can't turn them from that."

Erik nodded, his eyes still following the blond woman. "Besides, if what Francesca tells us is true—and after what happened here I have no reason to doubt it—he is at least in part possessed by the Lion of Saint Mark." Dryly: "That's quite a creature to try to talk into something."

Manfred snorted. "I don't think the Lion half is as easily distracted by Kat's figure." He turned and walked off.

Erik made no move to go with Manfred. After the prince was out of sight, he got up and found his way across to the three Scandinavians.

"*Goddag,*" he greeted.

He wasn't surprised at the Vinlander twang when one of the

men turned and greeted him in return. "Icelander! What are you doing here?"

He was the slightly larger of the two men, who were obviously brothers, as well as the older. A smile on his face—matching that on the other man and the woman, also—now displaced the wary reserve that Erik had seen characterizing the Vinlanders' response to the Venetian pomp.

Awkward questions first, dealt with as he had been instructed to do when he first took on Manfred as his charge. The role of the Hakkonsen family in imperial affairs was not something discussed. Few if any people in Iceland had any idea that Clann Harald, to which Erik's family belonged, did loyal service to the imperial house of the Holy Roman Empire. It was best so, Erik's father had always said.

"I am just passing through," said Erik calmly. "And yourselves? My name, by the way is Hakkonsen . . . Erik. Eirikur, actually, but I've grown accustomed to using the Danish version. These continentals have less trouble with it."

Hakkonsen was an honorable patronymic, as was Harald as a clan designation. Erik's own father was well known, in Iceland, and there were always some of the clan in the Althing. True, Clann Harald was not rich; in fact, wealth seemed to avoid them. His father's own holding at Bakkaflói was a place of stark beauty but little else. Still, it was a name that was well respected.

The Vinlander obviously recognized the name. The smile grew, considerably. "Bjarni Thordarson, at your service. This is my brother Gulta and our little sister Svanhild. We're setting up a trading house for Vinland goods. We have a Venetian factor and partner." The big Vinlander gestured. "This is his daughter's wedding."

"An honor to meet you all." Erik's smile might just have been a fraction brighter for Svanhild, but he thought he'd done well keeping it under control. "So, here you are invited to a Venetian function, and you don't know anyone, and your host is buried in having his daughter married. Uncomfortable."

"And it is quite an affair," said Gulta, looking at the laden tables, the richly dressed people. "As an Icelander you must find all of this ostentation odd."

Erik smiled, remembering his first Venetian banquet. The

ostentation had been overwhelming, yes, but it had been less so than the magical murder of the monk. "It was quite a shock, yes, but I've gotten used to it. Why don't we find a few glasses of wine and somewhere quiet to sit and talk? It has been five years since I went to Vinland. Where is your clan based?"

If he could find a quiet spot Manfred might actually not come and join them. Under the circumstances Erik thought he'd prefer that. Manfred had far more than his share of female attention anyway.

Something about what he'd said had made Svanhild smile upon him. Erik found himself hoping Manfred would stay away a *long* while. She was stunning.

Fortunately, her brothers seemed to approve. "The Thordarsons are a trading house," said Bjarni. "We have our headquarters at Cahokia in the Mississippi valley, deep in the interior, but we have factors on the coast also. And I agree. It has done us no harm to be seen at this gathering as guests of the Doge's ward's wedding, but I'm tired of all these people staring at my sister and none of them having the manners to come and speak to us."

Erik reflected silently that he'd nearly been amongst them.

"I don't mind," Svanhild said. But there was an undertone of faint unhappiness that told Erik that she minded a great deal. "After all, they don't know us, either. We must be odd to them."

We look like polar bears in a room full of lap-spaniels, said her tone.

"Well, if there isn't any business that you need to be doing, why don't we get out of the crush," Erik said, but said it to her. "I like these people, but I have to say that they must be the most obtuse lot I've ever seen. Nothing can be said or done directly, and they use occasions like this one to chatter around and around subjects they've already made their minds up about."

The older brother heaved a sigh of relief. "So I'm not the only one who thinks that!"

"I think I know where there will be a quiet room. Or quieter, anyway." Erik caught a passing page by the elbow, and gave him instructions. "Just follow me."

One thing that his previous visits had done was to give him a good grasp of the geography of the Doge's palace, and what was more, let him know what rooms were likely to be closed off to the general invitees. The little chamber off to the side of the council chamber, for instance. It was too small to be useful in a great gathering, and there was no comfortable furniture for assignations.

Not that something like that would stop Manfred . . . But, fortunately, Manfred wasn't there.

"Oh . . ." Svanhild said, as he closed the door behind the three Vinlanders. She looked around at the rather somber room with no hints of gilding or the usual Venetian opulence anywhere, only cold stone and dark wood and grim portraits of former Doges. "I thought all of the palace was red and gold."

"Not everywhere." Erik didn't tell her that this particular chamber was used for interviews with the spies—and sometimes, interrogations. At least they were interrogations that didn't require a trip to less salubrious quarters, the kind equipped with pincers and tongs and ropes and hot irons.

"Here." He purloined Petro's comfortable chair from behind the formidable desk for Svanhild, and offered the other, uncompromising pieces to her brothers. He sat on the desk, just as the page returned with wine and more refreshments.

"So, tell me why you're here, and about your clan holding in Vinland!" he said with enthusiasm. "It's been too long since I heard anyone speaking my own tongue."

Svanhild simply lit up at that invitation. If he was any judge, she was desperately homesick, and, if she'd been able, would have flung herself on the first ship going west. The brothers were full of enthusiasm for their mission and what they expected to accomplish in Venice, but Svanhild wanted to talk about home. About little things—how she missed being able to hunt, how horribly crowded this place felt to her.

"Just like a gigantic ship!" she said, which actually was an excellent observation, seeing how hemmed about Venice was by water. He asked her, in between declamations by her brothers, if she had seen much of the city, and she said "no" in a tone that suggested to him that she didn't want to. "There are so many people," she elaborated. "Too many. As many just in the inn in which we live as there are in all of our holding!"

Eventually, her brothers announced that they had stayed away from the celebration too long. There was, after all, *business* to be tended to.

"And the Venetians feel the same, you know." Erik escorted them out the door and back toward the party. "They discuss business everywhere, in church, even at funerals! I thought I would never get used to them, or their ways, but I can tell you that underneath it all, they're people who are no different from anywhere else. You'll find you've got plenty in common with them after all."

But Svanhild cast him a glance that told him that in this much, at least, she was in total disagreement with him.

Manfred sat down with thump next to Erik, who was sitting in an alcove staring at a wine goblet. "I never thought I'd see the day when I'd have to come looking for you, instead of the other way around," said Manfred cheerfully. "Two hours it's taken me to find you—at least! To think of what I could have gotten up to a few years back, if you'd been like this then."

Erik looked up, his eyes bleak. "Manfred, I think I'm in love."

The young prince grinned. "Don't worry. I'll get Von Gherens to give you some advice on how to do it. I think you'd prefer it from him rather than from me or Francesca."

Erik's voice was icy. "Shut up or I'll break your head. It's not like that."

Manfred was silent for a few moments. "Who?" he asked, in a quiet, serious voice. This wasn't like Erik; this could be serious. Erik usually shied away like a nervous horse from women. Francesca and Manfred had been discussing a hypothetical future partner for his mentor not a week back. What had she said? *When Erik falls he'll fall hard.*

That wasn't a problem. Manfred's opinion of what constituted a suitable girl for Erik, on the other hand, *was* a problem. She'd have to pass the Manfred test of approval. And for Erik, Manfred set very high standards.

"Svanhild Thordardottar." Erik sighed. "Such a beautiful name. And she moves like a swan too."

Manfred felt real alarm. He started looking around. He needed Francesca. "Who?"

"You're right. She is like a Valkyrie," said Erik, dreamily. "A true shield-maiden. Not one of those girls who needs ten servants just to get dressed in the morning. And such a sweet nature, too— getting stared at and snubbed, and not a complaint out of her about it."

Manfred stared at his friend, mentor and bodyguard. "You mean the one with the big pair of—of—bodyguards? The blond one?"

Erik nodded at him, scowling a bit. "You watch what you say about her."

"I wouldn't dream of uttering a wrong word," said Manfred, quite truthfully. Erik was ferocious enough on the training fields even when he wasn't mad about anything.

Erik sighed. "Not that it really matters. I think *I* must have said the wrong thing. We were getting on so well. She wanted to know all about Mainz. Next thing they got up and left. Polite, but . . . closing me out."

"Oh." Manfred tried hard to keep the relief out of his voice, because of the hurt in Erik's. "Well, I'm heading out of here. This affair is beginning to drag."

Erik stood up with a sigh. "Yes. I could use my bed, I suppose."

Manfred—given the circumstances—didn't point out that it hadn't been his bed he was seeking. Or at least, not his own. And right now Erik wasn't picking up the undercurrent of Manfred's words as he usually did. In fact, he actually wandered off to his own quarters without making sure that Manfred was coming with him, which suited Manfred right down to the bone.

Erik was welcome to a quiet night. Manfred had other plans; the hellion Benito would either be along presently, or Manfred would go find him.

Manfred snorted with amusement at that thought. It was a shock to find himself doing Erik's usual job of slowing a tearaway down. Francesca was waist deep smiling on, and politicking with, old admirers. Manfred found being around while she dealt with them set his teeth on edge. So the last set of plans he'd made with the rascal were that they were off to a place Benito had found—good Sicilian music and some dancers that, according to young Benito, could make the tassels on their boobs do amazing things.

Manfred finally got tired of waiting for Benito to find him, and traced Benito down at the wine-butts. "Let's go, tearaway. I find myself consumed with curiosity about these tassels."

The boy swayed gently as he stood up. He was already half-drunk. Manfred was mildly surprised. The last week Benito had escorted him to choice taverns and nightspots but the boy seemed to have some degree of caution about wine. What was it that he'd said? *"I don't want to end up as a lush."*

It had seemed to Manfred then that he was more inclined to

drink enough to get up to devilry and stop there, than to go on to the fall-down stage. Odd. Distinctly odd. But none of his business, when all was said and done.

"Time to find the girls," Benito said, and his speech was clear enough. "There's no one here worth bothering about."

Chapter 19

The evening was wearing on and Maria found herself exhausted. Now that the ceremony was over, and the banqueting begun, Maria had settled into having a tedious time. She'd been seated among the guests of honor, among the gilt and brightness, and had been very uncomfortable. And kept her mouth shut. Yes, she loved Kat, and she certainly had wanted to be with her for her wedding. Marco, the bridge-brat she'd seen grow up, had a special place in her heart, too.

But . . . That was Marco and Kat. Marco Valdosta and Katerina Montescue, in their magnificent finery, surrounded by *Case Vecchie*, were more like jeweled butterflies than real people. And, as with Caesare, she'd been painfully aware of her lower-class origins every time she opened her mouth.

Benito had been seated as far as possible from her and Umberto. He'd tried to catch her eye, once; she'd looked down. Umberto had also been plainly uncomfortable among all those people who ordinarily he would only see at a distance; and a far distance, at that. Now that the guests were mingling, he'd hastily gone off to join his fellow guildsmen. She looked across to where he stood with several men, all gray haired, and all at this stage very jovial. Umberto looked happy, for the first time in ages.

Maria decided she'd had enough. Out in the piazza there'd be real music and singing. Real talk, about things she knew, not her trying to keep her mouth shut. She got up; Alessia was in a room just off the banqueting hall with a dry nurse, and by the feel of it Alessia could use some feeding.

She walked across the crowded room to Umberto, moving carefully on the slippery marble, pausing every other step to keep from jostling someone who was probably important. It took an age to go thirty feet. He was laughing when she reached him, and greeted her with a smile that spoke of both care and happiness. "Ah, Maria! It is so good to be back in Venice again. Nice to be away from rude nature."

She smiled back. She couldn't exactly tell him that she was finding the smell of the canals hard to live with. "Yes. But I must go to the baby, husband." He'd like that, being called *husband* with respect in her voice, and showing herself a good wife and a dutiful mother. It would make him feel good, in front of the other masters.

"She must be fed, and then I think I'll take her to our lodgings. It has been a long day, and I confess I'm tired."

He took her arm. "I'll come along to assist you home. A woman needs an escort on a night like this."

Irritation flared. This being a good little wife was not something she did well. This was Venice. *Her* Venice! She'd sculled a vessel around it alone since she was fourteen.

She shook his arm off, but did it gently, so it didn't seem as if she was rejecting his help. "I still need to feed Alessia, and then probably to change her." That would put him off, quickly enough. "It will take a while. Then the nurse can accompany me. She can do something to earn the wage that Katerina has paid her, and we'll take a gondola. You stay, please. You're enjoying yourself, and I don't want to spoil that for you. You won't see the other masters for a long time again."

"You're sure?" He was plainly tempted, but he was dutiful. A solicitous hand touched her elbow.

"Absolutely. Enjoy yourself." She kissed him on the cheek and went to find Alessia.

She found the salon easily enough. By ear. Alessia was bellowing. The dry nurse was nowhere to be seen. There were, however, five or six empty goblets, one of which lay on its side in a pool of spilled wine. Wine stained the satin of the chair that had been provided for the nurse. And Alessia was demanding instant attention. Hastily Maria struggled with her lacing and quelled the bellows, rage building inside her that she had to tamp down, lest it affect Alessia's feeding.

She'd just fed, winded, and changed Alessia when the nurse returned with a goblet in her hand, slightly unsteady on her feet.

Maria put Alessia down. Carefully. Only then did she round on the slut who'd deserted her baby. "Where the hell have you been?" she demanded, anger putting an edge to her voice that only a drunk could have ignored.

The nurse, it seemed, was just such a drunk, and beamed at her. "Just went to get a glass of wine, dearie. The poppet was sleeping beautifully."

Fury passing all ability to use mere words seized Maria. She grabbed the woman and shook her like a rag doll. "You . . . you *puttana*," she hissed into the wine-laden breath. The woman swayed. "You're drunk. You left my baby, all alone. Anything could have happened. Anything!"

The nurse wrested herself away, clumsily, and looked down her nose at Maria, her face reddening with more than just wine. "You're nothing but a canaler, even dressed up like that. Why should I sit here with your misbegotten brat?" she spat. "You begrudge me a glass of wine . . ."

Maria stepped forward, pulled back her arm, and slapped the woman hard. And hard again. The nurse's head jerked back and her cheeks each had a scarlet handprint on them, but Maria wasn't done. She seized the woman by the front of her gown, and threw her at the seat. It cracked as the dry nurse fell onto it, her eyes wide, her mouth falling open with shock. It didn't break—quite— but Maria knew with satisfaction that it was damaged. The dry nurse was going to have to answer to one of the Doge's upper- servants for it.

"I might be a canaler," she hissed, "but I'm worth three of *you*. At least I always did what I was paid to do, honestly."

Maria snatched up Alessia and stormed out; out into the crowd, out past the crowd, too angry to even hear if anyone was trying to hail her. She was still so angry she wasn't really thinking, just walking, once she'd got past the revelers. But when she got out of the palace and past the fires in the piazza, the night air was cool. It helped to cool her temper and her anger, too. After a while she paused and took stock of where she was.

With a sense of surprise rather than shock, she saw that she was on one of the walkways bordering the canals, and must be more than halfway to their lodgings. She'd walked farther than she'd intended in this dress. The hem and the petticoat hems would need washing.

Her feet, crammed into shoes that were too narrow for her, complained. One of the disadvantages of marrying Umberto had been that she had to wear shoes all the time. His position, he said, demanded it. Well, her canaler feet demanded space. She kicked the shoes off, then struggled to pick them up, with Alessia fast asleep in one arm. She gritted her teeth, as she realized that the shoes were meant for dancing in ballrooms, not striding along canalside. The pretty doeskin would be ruined.

She sighed irritably; there was little point in spending money on a gondola now. Anyway, the gondolas would be as thick as flies down at the Piazza San Marco, and few and far between anywhere else. She might as well walk the rest of the way, cross the Rialto bridge and go to the apartment. Not more than a few hundred cubits now.

Besides, she'd been walking and poling for most of her life— her own two legs were good enough. She was just a canaler, after all; canal-born and canal-bred, and the day she couldn't make it anywhere in Venice on her own feet, they might as well start building her coffin. So she walked on quietly. With half of Venice already drunk on the Doge's wine, and the other half trying to get to that state, there probably wasn't a bullyboy or a pickpocket anywhere nearer than Naples. She'd be more than safe enough tonight.

The riot and rumpus met her just short of the Rialto bridge.

Schiopettieri. A lot of them. The professional soldiers who served Venice for a police force had two struggling figures in their midst, yelling and fighting like young bulls. Maria stepped up onto a mounting block, partly to avoid the press of Schiopettieri, partly to see what was going on.

She looked across the heads—and straight into Benito's eyes. As their eyes locked, he stopped, and a look of absolute horror transfigured his face.

That was the opportunity that the Schioppies needed. They piled onto him. Maria caught a brief glimpse of Benito, upended over someone's shoulder. He wasn't wearing any trousers. Or small-clothes.

Maria, with Alessia in her arms, stood transfixed, watching the tide of Schiopettieri bear Benito and his large companion away. The large companion seemed content to be restrained. All the fighting had obviously come from Benito.

The tide passed, and moved on, away from her, and Maria stepped down off the block, and walked on.

For a brief moment she'd nearly waded into that crowd of Schioppies to help Benito. Then Alessia had stirred against her, and how could she interfere in a drunken brawl with a baby in her arms? She couldn't exactly have put Alessia down. Benito had gotten himself into that trouble, whatever it was. Benito would just have to get himself out of it. It wasn't *her* job to rescue him anymore.

If it ever had been.

This close to midnight, even when there was a great wedding on at the Doge's palace, with feasting in the Piazza San Marco, the stall-lined wooden Rialto bridge ought to be quiet.

It wasn't. There were several groups of people, mostly local women, gossiping eagerly about what had just happened.

One of the women, her eyes bright with excitement in the lamplight that the Republic provided to make bridges and *sotoportegos* safer, turned to Maria as Maria tried to get past her. "Did you hear? Did you see? Isn't that younger Valdosta a scandal!" Her voice was full of glee.

Maria could not restrain her curiosity. "No, I wasn't there. I'd just come from the celebration. What happened? What did he do?"

She did restrain the "this time" she'd been about to add.

The woman pointed at one of the crossbeams that held chains that supported the center bridge section. "He was up there."

Well, Benito climbed things. He always had been like a little shaved ape. "What was he doing?" she asked warily.

The woman shook her head—then told her. "Scandalous! In a public place like that!"

Maria felt herself redden. "You mean he was . . ."

An older woman, looking out of her half-shuttered window, snorted. "Well, he was so drunk, that it'd be better to say he was *trying* to. Good thing for her the girl is a dancer."

"The Doge will have to make an example of him!" pronounced the first woman; half-primly and half-gleefully. "The last time—"

"And the other man?" asked Maria hastily.

"Oh, he was just singing some bawdy song and cheering. He

only got involved when the Schioppies got here. He's as strong as an ox."

Maria walked on. To think that that was Benito. Her Benito. No. Not hers. Never hers. And not her problem.

So she told herself. And maybe if she told herself often enough, she might believe it.

And pigs might fly.

Erik stared balefully at Manfred, and pointed a finger through the bars. "You are quite safe and I am going to leave you here. I have searched this stupid town for hours now. I thought you'd gone to bed, and suddenly I'm dragged out of my blankets and sent on a hunt that I should have known was going to end here." He glared, and an unrepentant Manfred glared back, then dropped his eyes and closed his hands around his head, looking very much the worse for wear. "I am going back to tell Francesca that waking me up was a waste of everybody's time, and that she should go back to sleep. I am going back to sleep. Back to my bed that I should never have left for a drunken oaf. I am going to leave you here, locked up like a common felon until this town goes back to normal business. After the wedding, that should maybe happen by Vespers bell."

Manfred held his head. "Don't shout, whatever you do. The jailor says I'll only be up for disturbing the peace and creating a nuisance. Just leave me some money for the fine and I'll get myself home. But find out what they've done with the kid, Erik. Dorma is unlikely to forgive me if I've let him get into serious trouble."

That was a change, Manfred thinking about someone else's woes rather than his own. Erik sighed and shook his head. "Just what did you do? Just what did *he* do? That boy must be the first person I've met who is worse than you are, Manfred."

"Uh. I don't think I'll tell you about all of it. But the first part involved some fellow bear-baiting. Benito took against the bear's master. The bear . . . Bears can swim, can't they?"

Erik put his hand over his eyes. "Why did I ask?"

"Well, when Benito set the bear after the Schiopettieri . . ." Manfred continued, and paused when Erik groaned.

"He set the bear—against the Schioppies! *Why* did he sent a bear against the Schioppies? Don't answer that," he added hastily, as Manfred opened his mouth. "It was a rhetorical question."

Manfred raised his eyebrows and managed a hurt expression. "It was very funny at the time, Erik. The tavern did get busted up a bit, but the girl seemed to like that . . ."

Oh, God. Erik shook his head. "I'll go and see Petro Dorma, and get it sorted out," he promised.

"Oh, good."

"But not immediately. In no small part because Benito is getting exactly what he was asking for. It will be after I have told Francesca that you are where you deserve to be."

Chapter 20

Manfred was more than a little nervous about this interview. The hangover had barely subsided. He had not even been back to the embassy to change—and after last night, these were not the clothes of a gentleman any more. Besides, he had a definite feeling that the Doge was not going to be very pleased to hear what Manfred had gotten up to with his young ward. Even if Manfred was here on an official imperial visit and was a noble of a great foreign power.

He was therefore both surprised and pleased to see that Petro was smiling, albeit slightly, when he entered the room. "Ah, Prince Manfred. I apologize for my people arresting you," said Petro urbanely. "They didn't realize who you were."

"And I didn't see fit to inform them." Manfred had the feeling that the more honest he was about all of this, the better off he'd be. "Less embarrassment all the way around. I've paid the fines. I'm afraid I gave your clerk a false name for his records."

"Wise," Dorma said, quite as if he had expected something of the sort. "But I still must apologize. Normally my agents would keep an eye on visiting dignitaries, and keep them out of trouble. Or at least out of jail."

"Should have left him there," grumbled Erik, glaring at Manfred. A glare like that should have qualified as an offensive weapon.

Manfred felt sheepish, and very much inclined to encourage just about any other thread of discussion, especially if it involved going home to bed. But there was the question of young Benito. "Um. About Benito . . ."

He was surprised to see the Doge go off into helpless laughter. Eventually, though, Petro stopped and shook his head.

"I am going to have the Justices come down on him like a ton of bricks, if only to stop every other damned young blade in Venice from doing the same thing—or trying, anyway. I doubt very much if they'd succeed. The boy has managed to make himself a legend, from the canals to the palace. The whole city is talking about it this morning, and there are bets on whether or not he actually did what he was trying to do. Just one thing I do want to know: Where on earth did he get a woman willing to go up there with him?"

Manfred felt his ears glowing as Erik stared at him. "She . . . uh . . . she's an acrobat at that place where they have the Alexandrine dancers. The stomach-dancers. Although there is a lot more to it than just the stomach," he amended weakly.

Petro put his head in his hands. His shoulders still shook. "And the bear?"

"We didn't really mean that to happen," he pled. "It just did. The poor thing really was being mistreated."

Petro sat back in his throne and closed his eyes for a moment, the corners of his mouth still twitching. "Prince Manfred. Erik. What do you think I should do with the boy?"

"Give him to me," growled Erik. "I'll take him away from Venice and sort him out. And right now I need someone to beat, besides Manfred."

Petro Dorma blinked, gave them both a penetrating look, and smiled broadly. "You know, I think I might just take you up on that. I was going to send him out to Corfu as my factor for a year or two, anyway. You two can take him along with you. If you don't mind that is, Prince Manfred?"

Manfred nodded. "Of course not." With a wry smile he asked. "How much trouble can one boy be?"

Petro snorted. "In the case of this one, plenty. I will arrange this with the chief Justice. He keeps a straight face better than I do. I, of course, am far too angry to even see him. He has damaged the reputation of our fair city and the *Casa* Dorma. *And* his brother. *And* he's quite spoiled the dignity of his brother's wedding."

"But hasn't he?" asked Erik, seeming rather puzzled by Dorma's good humor.

Dorma smiled. "Please, Erik! This is a port city. It's not quite as decadent as Aquitaine, but we are not Icelandic puritans here. The Venetians are shocked, yes, of course. Venetians *love* being shocked. It is a wonderful story and will grow into the most improbable legend. And Benito will acquire a reputation twice as large as it is already. I must send Benito out of town before he is forced, by a desire to live up to the legend, to do something even more crazy."

Erik shook his head. "You Venetians are *all* crazy."

Petro laughed, and shook his head. "There is something in what you say. Now tell me, Manfred, Benito's um, partner in crime. Do I have to get her out of prison too?"

"Who? Lolita? No, she took off like a scalded cat, Petro. Laughing like a mad thing." Manfred remembered that quite clearly. Her little bare rear was just as luscious as the front.

Petro raised an eyebrow, but said only: "Good. I would hate to think Benito had gotten someone other than himself into trouble."

Manfred snorted. "In this case your worry is wasted effort."

"Nevertheless," said the Doge, with an attempt at seriousness. "I feel I should investigate these dancers. It sounds like a lively spot."

"That young hellion would find a lively spot in a Shetland town," grumbled Erik. "And if he couldn't find one, he'd make one."

Benito was in trouble, and knew it. More trouble than he'd ever been in before.

He'd never been in this room before; this was where they took people who had done things that were just short of murder or robbery, a darkly somber room that left no doubt in the prisoner's mind that he had trespassed on at least five of the Ten Commandments. There was pretty little doubt that everybody was still nearly incandescently angry with him. The chief Justice had not so much as cracked a smile when the affair with the bear had been related to him by the bear's former owner. By the time it had got to the challenge on the Rialto bridge . . .

Well, he sounded like God Himself, thundering out the Law.

"The Rialto bridge is one of the most important landmarks of our fair city! Your drunken and licentious behavior has brought shame onto us. I gather only your drunkenness has saved you from the more serious charge of public fornication."

The chief Justice had eyes that could pierce a fellow like a pair of stilettos. "That you should do this on the occasion of your brother's matrimony!—and as a ward of our Doge!—simply makes your lewd behavior and other offences more heinous still."

The Justice paused. He seemed to be waiting for Benito to say something.

"Yes, milord," he said, faintly.

The floodgates opened again. "This is not the first time you have been in trouble in this court. I see the record indicates you have been fined for brawling here before. I therefore sentence you to a fine of one hundred ducats, and the owner of the bear is to be recompensed for the loss of his animal. And you, Benito Valdosta, are hereby given a choice. Remain imprisoned here for a year. Or be exiled from the City of Venice for a period of five years."

Benito swallowed; this was serious. Really serious, this time. One hundred ducats! That was a year's earnings for a gentleman-at-arms. More money than he had. Dorma had paid him an allowance, but he had a feeling that would not be available any more.

All right; he'd pawn everything he had. Somehow he'd take care of the fine. But he was damned if he'd turn tail and run away into exile; he'd messed up, he'd take it like a man. "I'll take the impri—"

But he was interrupted.

"Pardon, Milord Justice! If I might be permitted to speak?"

It was the one and only member of the public who hadn't just come to gawk at Venice's latest scandal: Marco. Benito wished like hell he hadn't come.

The chief Justice nodded approvingly. "Permission is granted, Milord Marco Valdosta."

"No!" protested Benito. *Damn it, Marco, you can't get me out of this one!*

The Justice looked sternly at him. "Silence. Or I will have you silenced, Benito Valdosta."

Marco cleared his throat. "Your Honor. As Benito, my brother, is the ward of the Doge, no special consideration can be shown to him."

The Justice nodded gravely. "Well said. Indeed, I have a message here from Petro Dorma, instructing me that Benito Valdosta is to be treated in the same way that any other citizen of Venice would be treated."

Marco nodded. "Nonetheless, I would like to appeal on the basis of his youth and the fact he grew up without the guidance of good parents, as an orphan, and that in the fight to save Venice last fall he fought and led with great courage. Many here can testify to that. Perhaps some part of this—ah, incident—is due to a nature that requires an outlet, and there has been nothing of the sort to purge him of his excess of spirits."

There was a murmur of approval. The Justice, however, was shaking his head. Marco hurried on. "I do not appeal for the sentence to be reduced. I just ask that the option of imprisonment be removed. Your Honor, many of Venice's wildest young blades have gone out to the outposts of our empire and served well, and faithfully, and returned as upright and respectable citizens. I do not think Benito would be improved by a year in the dungeons. I think he might learn if sent elsewhere."

Benito felt his mouth dropping open, and snapped it closed.

The Justice nodded, the look he bestowed on Marco the very image of benevolence. "I find this a reasonable plea, Marco Valdosta."

He turned back to Benito, and God On High was back. "Very well, Benito Valdosta, the option of imprisonment is withdrawn. You are exiled from Venice for five years. You will remain in custody until a passage is arranged for you out of the city."

Marco stepped forward. He tapped a pouch, which jingled. "Your honor, I have here monies to pay the reparations and the fines for Benito Valdosta.

The Justice pointed. "The clerk will see to it."

And Benito, his leg irons clanking, was led out. Marco did not even look at him.

On the whole, that was probably not a bad thing.

He did come down to the cell, later. "Petro would have added twenty lashes to the sentence," he said grimly, the first words out of his mouth. Not: *Are you all right,* or: *We were worried about you.*

Benito shrugged. "I'm sorry, Brother. The evening started in fun. It just got out of hand."

"Several people, including Prince Manfred, have said that you were simply looking for trouble," said Marco, who could have passed, at this moment, for one of the chief Justice's prize pupils.

He was doing a very good imitation of God on High, himself. "Petro's had some of his spies keeping an eye on you. You pitched one of them into the Rio San Felice. You're lucky that was not another charge you faced, by the way."

But then, suddenly, the whole stern image collapsed, as his brother added, plaintively, "Petro says you've been so much better the last while. And then this."

Benito shrugged his shoulders sulkily. He wasn't going to justify himself to Marco. He wasn't sure he could justify himself to himself. And he sure as hell wasn't going to let Marco know just how wretched he'd felt when he'd seen Maria with the baby in her arms, and she wouldn't even look at him.

Marco sighed. "I haven't even had a chance to tell you yet, but Kat and I stood as godparents to Maria's daughter."

Benito felt truly as if the wind had been kicked out of him. But he had to know—he was as starved for some word, any word, as a swampy was for a decent meal. "Is she all right? I mean with having the baby and all." In a very small voice: "She wouldn't even speak to me, Marco."

Marco looked at his younger brother with a compassion that hurt almost as much as Maria's silence. "So that was what it was all about, was it?"

Benito said nothing. What could he say? He couldn't deny it, but he sure as hell wasn't going to admit it.

Marco shook his head. "She's fine. Seems happy enough, Benito. The baby is fine, too." But then, he smiled, that purely Marco smile, with a touch of mischief. "She's got something unusual though. She has an undine as one of her godmothers."

That caught Benito off guard. "What?" he said, not sure he'd heard right.

"Umberto's sister was supposed to be one of the godmothers, only she didn't approve of Umberto's marriage. You know she always kept house for him. I suppose she must have thought that no one was good enough for him, but she absolutely hates Maria. So, at the last minute, she didn't show up. The Lion in me . . . I think the Lion must have guessed she might do something like that. I *asked* if the water-people would add their blessing, and the priest said he'd see about it. Well, I think the Lion sent an undine to take her place."

So that was the reason for the mischief. Benito could hardly believe it. Marco, doing something just for the reason of giving someone who deserved it their comeuppance!

"All things considered, since they're going to be around water all their lives, you could hardly ask for a more useful godmother," Marco pointed out with just a touch of glee. "That little girl will never drown."

Benito tried to imagine the scene, and failed. "I wish I could have been there."

Marco looked at him hard, and raised an eyebrow. "And who would that have pleased or helped, Benito? Nobody would ask you to be a godfather."

Benito shrugged. "I just feel . . . Oh, I don't know. I just feel I owe her some help." He sighed. "She saw me that night, you know."

"So I have heard," said Marco dryly. "She told Kat." He paused, as if he was considering something, then evidently made up his mind about it.

"They're shipping out for Corfu in a couple of hours. You'll have your chance to help her, if you can manage to stay out of trouble long enough to do anything useful. You're going there too. It's a small place. You'll probably see her every day."

Benito's mouth fell open in horror. And worst of all, the horror was so mixed with a thrill of delight that he couldn't tell where one started and the other ended.

"What?" he squawked. "I can't! I'd rather go to *prison*, Marco." He gripped the bars, pleading. "Go and talk to Petro. Tell him about this."

All right; he had to admit it. He *had* to. It was the only thing that might save him. "Seeing her is what sent me over the edge. Please, Marco! I'll go anywhere else, but I can't go there!"

Marco nodded. "I thought so. I'll ask him." He sighed. "But don't get your hopes up. He was pretty grim about this, and had made up his mind. And anyway, there aren't a lot of places you can go, now."

The Terce bell had rung before he returned. "I'm sorry, Benito. Petro says: 'If he can't learn to behave like a gentleman, then let him take the consequences. He'll have plenty of opportunity.' "

"No—" Benito whimpered. "You didn't tell him? Didn't you tell him about Maria?"

Marco sighed. "I told him everything, including how you felt about the christening, and how seeing Maria at the wedding just made you crazy. He said you'd have plenty of chances to help Maria in Corfu. He said you could offer to be a dry nurse, since the one Maria had was unsatisfactory."

Benito groaned, and dropped his head in his hands.

Chapter 21

The great carracks and the smaller tarettes in the Bacino San Marco twitched and jerked at anchor, responding to the winds, the short chop on the water and the loads being swung on board from the lighters. The fleet would proceed slowly to Outremer, hopping from Lissa, Corfu, Zante, Candia, Negroponte and points east as far as distant Trebizond. The loading would proceed for another week yet, but already many of the ships had to stay in deeper water. Weddings and celebrations were fine things in their way and at the proper time, but the ships must sail soon. So finery and jollification were best put in the past, to be talked about later. Now Venice hummed with industry. Spring was here, the time for trade was at hand, and the ships were outbound.

Over at the quay-side the great galleys bound for Flanders were at the point of final deck-cargo. They would not proceed slowly, navigating out through the Pillars of Hercules, and then across stormy Biscay; with such a voyage ahead, there was no spare time to waste. Their stops were few, but they would pause at Corfu—the last safe port for a final refit at the Little Arsenal there. The trip to Corfu was a good "sea-trial," revealing problems, especially with new ships.

And in Corfu, the ship would discharge a new assistant foreman for the Little Arsenal: Umberto Verrier.

Maria knew that the new posting was, in a way, her own fault. If she hadn't led to Umberto's men capturing Torfini and Rossi in those first few days . . . Well, Umberto wouldn't have acquired a reputation for sorting out problems, quickly and efficiently. The more senior guilds at the Arsenal were, on the whole, not pleased with his wood-selection abilities. On the other hand, they were satisfied that he could fix problems, and the Little Arsenal apparently had plenty. So, Umberto had his new posting. It was farther from Venice, but, as he said, it was in a real town. Maria wasn't as happy as he was about that part, but at least it would be back beside the sea.

It was one thing to be married to Umberto. It was quite another to be married to Umberto and feeling as if she was going to have to be responsible for his success, while at the same time allowing him to bask in the illusion that his success was due entirely to his own effort. And it was a third to do so while caring for a baby. . . .

Two babies. Umberto is as much a child as the little one.

But that was unfair. He was a *good* man. He cared for her.

He cares for what he thinks *you are.*

He loved the baby. And that insidious voice in her head could say nothing about that.

She had thought that she was going be able to settle down, and now they were moving again. On yet another ship, so Umberto would be ill again. Two babies to tend, in the close confines of a ship. Another set of new people to meet and deal with, another strange place to try to make into a home. Harder, this time. She could not count on a fortuitous accident to show her what she needed to know. And she already knew that although Umberto was good enough at dealing with honest men, he was lost when it came to those who were less than honest.

She had only traded one set of problems for another, in marrying the man. But he cared for her, and would do his best for her even if it killed him. It was up to her to see that it didn't. If she could not love him, she certainly owed him.

Maria stood on the quay, watching the corded trunks and canvas bundles being loaded, as little Alessia nestled into her arms and nuzzled. Maria looked down at her child, and sighed.

"To think a year ago I hadn't even been beyond the fringes of the lagoon . . ." she said, half to herself. "And now here you are, daughter, off to another distant place."

Beside her, Kat gazed at the ships, and her eyes were still luminous with happiness. Maria thought that she had never seen a more contented person, and yet she knew that Kat was not blind to Marco's faults. Nor, for that matter, was Marco blind to hers. They had both known exactly what they were getting into, and yet they were two of the happiest people Maria had ever known.

How very different, Maria thought forlornly, *from the way I felt after my wedding.*

"I wish you weren't going," Kat said with a sigh. "Or I wish we were going along with you. I'd like to visit Corfu." Alessia stirred and Kat reached for her. "Let me hold her a little. It may be years before I see her again."

Maria handed the baby over. She watched with some amusement at how awkwardly and carefully Kat took the child. Just on three weeks ago, she'd been just as tentative.

"When I left for Istria, I was never coming back, Kat. Never ever. Now here I am again. Things change. Who knows? Petro Dorma might get so sick of Marco that he'll ship you both off to Corfu."

Kat shook her head. "Marco is as much part of Venice now as the canals."

Involuntarily, Maria glanced across the thronged piazza behind them to the tall pillar where the bronze statue stood. "Or as the Lion of Saint Mark."

Kat nodded. "The Lion is Venice after all, and Marco is the Lion, too. He *can't* leave, Maria."

Alessia twitched, gave a tentative whimper, and then burst into full bellow. Kat rocked frantically, an expression of raw panic on her face. "What's wrong, my cherub? There, there . . . Help, Maria! What is wrong? I didn't do anything to her. What do I do now?"

Maria found laughter a welcome gift. "By the smell, I think she's probably done something to herself. Don't worry, that's not what's making her cry. It doesn't seem to worry her."

Kat hastily held out Alessia at full arm's stretch, as if she were a precious piece of porcelain suddenly found to harbor a poisonous spider. Maria did not reach for Alessia. "I'll show you what do about it," she said cheerfully.

Kat searched frantically for rescue. "Ah. Er . . . I see Papa's Vinlander partners are here. I'd—I'd better go and speak to them. I'll come back and see you in just a moment." She thrust the bellowing Alessia at her mother, and bolted.

Maria, familiar now with all the less pleasant aspects of babies, took Alessia off to change, glancing as she went at the tall, large, blond contingent that Kat was greeting. And there, hastening down the quay-side from the Doge's palace, was Marco. Probably been to see Benito. Benito's face, when he'd seen her, had been quite a study.

She scowled as she thought about it. If Umberto was one sort of child, Benito was another—a brat, a bridge-brat, destined to hang, no doubt. But Venice would not forget that latest exploit of his in a hurry. Being Venice, it would embrace it as quite a favorite story.

Eneko Lopez was on a high balcony of the Doge's palace, his eagle eyes looking out over the Jesolo marshes when Marco finally tracked him down. The stern visage cracked into a smile on seeing Marco. "And how is wedded bliss, Marco Valdosta?"

Marco felt himself blush. "Um. Blissful, thank you, señor."

This reply lightened the stern visage further. "It is intended to be, you know. That is why Christ sanctified the institution of marriage with his first miracle." He pointed out toward the sky. "Tell me: what is happening up there?"

Marco peered into the blue. "I'd say that a bird . . . or a pair of birds, rather, are being mobbed by seagulls. The gulls around here can be quite territorial, and there are thousands of them."

The part of him that was the Lion stirred. *And so am I,* it said within him. *They do not belong here.*

Of course, Eneko Lopez could not hear that voice, and Marco did not feel easy enough to explain. But he knew, now, why the gulls were attacking the hawks. The gulls were as much part of the lagoon as the water was, and the hawks were the eyes of the Lion's ancient enemy. The Lion would blind that enemy, if he could—and if he could not, he would at least deny him the use of those eyes over Venice.

Eneko nodded. "A pair of what I should guess were goshawks, although I am not an expert on birds. Are such things common over Venice?"

"Well, I've seen hawks in the reed-brakes and *barene* close to the fringes of the marsh, but not really out here," Marco temporized. "They don't belong here. The gulls will see them off."

The gulls will kill them if they can.

"I have seen two hawks in the sky rather often of late. They appear to be hawks, at least," said Eneko. "I have attempted to scry them. Birds are difficult to connect with, and raptors most particularly difficult. They think mostly of hunting and killing, and not a great deal else."

Well, this was the opening Marco had rather wondered how to make. "But if you were scrying and it turned out they were not hawks . . . wouldn't you be very vulnerable?" He took a deep breath. "Brother Mascoli said I should ask you for help with magical defenses for protection against evil."

He felt the eagle gaze again. "Mascoli is a good man. But he sees only good in everything. If he thought you should consult me on this, I must conclude that something particularly evil happened. Tell me about it."

So Marco explained.

Eneko Lopez's eyes narrowed when he came to the part about the undines and San Raphaella. "I was aware of this. I was also aware that the undines that live in the Lagoon have a great deal to do with the Strega mages. In particular with the late Luciano Marina." Something about the way he said it filled in the word "unlamented" before "late."

Marco nodded, but innate honesty forced him to defend Chiano. The Strega mage might have intended to kill him to save Venice— but . . . he'd also saved Marco's life before that. And been a friend when a terrified boy needed one.

And it was entirely possible—

Probable, chuckled the voice in his head.

—that the knife had been intended for some other purpose in the ceremony.

Bloodletting does not mean killing. Some ceremonies require the spilling of a token of blood, given freely. Ask your black-robed friend. He knows.

"Luciano was a good man, even if he was not a Christian," Marco said with more firmness. "And he helped the undines and they liked him, yes. Brother Mascoli said it was not wrong to aid nonhumans. No evil creature would come to the sanctified water, and no evil creature would ask help."

"We differ in levels of trust and points of theology," said Eneko, dryly. "But continue. I accept that *you* are a Christian soul, even if you are bonded to a creature about which I am less certain." He smiled. "And I do *not* mean your wife, whose Christianity I know well enough from the counseling booth of St. Hypatia. She gave me a lesson in honesty, once, when I was her counselor."

Marco took a deep breath. "Well, according to Brother Mascoli, it was only the strength of that 'other' that saved me. I got the fright of my life, señor. It was like being thistle-down slapped around by a maelstrom, just for an instant. The ward candles nearly burned up completely in that instant. Whatever it was, it was waiting out there for me when I went looking for the triton. It was . . . lying in ambush, so to speak, waiting to kill me."

Eneko pursed his lips. "The power of the Lion is very much tied to the area of the old marshes is it not?"

Marco nodded.

"And you were scrying outside of this area, and you were attacked."

Marco nodded again.

Eneko stood in thought, his heavy brows hooding his eyes. "I conclude that Chernobog still retains an interest in you. I cannot see why any other creature of power should take such a risk with a mage. You see, as much as you are vulnerable, so is your attacker. I should imagine that Chernobog uses an intermediary or a lesser servant, rather than direct intervention. Still, that servant is likely to be one who is himself—or herself—very powerful and danger-ous. There are defenses. The first one however, is 'stay home.' With-out you the Lion of Saint Mark would be somewhat less effective, am I correct?"

"Well, in times of crisis one of the four families must direct the Lion's power," agreed Marco.

"And if I am correct, all that remains are three Montescues and two Valdostas of the old blood?"

Marco bit his lip. "Well, Benito . . . He's my half-brother, Sir. We had different fathers."

Eneko nodded. "That is easy enough to guess without even seeing him, just to judge by his behavior. So: In fact it is only yourself and the three Montescues, one of whom is away, and one of whom is very elderly. This is a good reason to want you dead. And it is a good reason for you to keep scrying as the aspect of mage-practice you use only in dire emergency. However, I will teach you to attack when you are attacked, and how to best defend yourself—if you will agree to restrain your scrying to matters that are vital to your survival."

Marco nodded. "If you will extend that to 'what is vital to the survival of Venice,' then I will. You see, the Lion is Venice, in a way. So by defending it I defend myself, too."

"A fair caveat," agreed Eneko. He took Marco by the elbow and turned back to the chamber. "Come. Let us go inside. The gulls appear to have driven the hawks away. Gulls are less formidable than hawks, but gulls are certainly more numerous."

Marco watched with interest as Eneko Lopez laid out a few very simple objects. Four ward-candles, which he placed in each corner of the room, a silver mirror, and, of all odd things, a sharp needle stuck in a cork. With the mirror on a low table between them, Lopez invoked the four wards as Marco had learned to do, and set up the circle of protection around them. It was all done very quickly, neatly and efficiently.

"Now, your first and best protection when you attempt to scry when you do not know if something is watching for you, is to arrange so that you are not noticed."

"But how do I do that?" Marco asked.

"By finding some other thing that is in the area, and concealing 'yourself' within it. Those gulls, for instance. Scry for one of those gulls over the Lagoon just now."

Obediently, Marco bent over the mirror, and easily called one of the gulls into its silver surface, which was silver no longer, but reflected the blue sky and white clouds.

"Very good. Now move in closer," Eneko instructed.

In the mirror, and in his mind, the gull loomed nearer, nearer, until he was looking directly into its black, bright eye.

"Closer."

He couldn't imagine how he could do that, but then that familiar warmth inside him gave him a nudge—

And now, he looked down on the Lagoon, felt the wind in his feathers, adjusted the tilt of his wing for better lift in a thermal—

Good, said a voice from very far away, as he went very still and quiet. *Now, don't actually do anything. Just sit, and watch, and when another gull comes near, make that same jump to it.*

It wasn't long before a second gull joined the first, and the two locked gazes long enough for Marco to make that "jump."

Practice this for a while. Move from gull to gull. But don't try to interfere in what they do. Just observe.

It was a little—a very little—like being the Lion. The gulls didn't have much on their minds but food and flying. He made the jump into four more gulls, when Eneko's voice came back.

Now think about flying toward the piazza and landing on one of the piers.

But the gull didn't want to do that; he felt the resistance.

You could make him, but that would make you noticed. At the moment, unless a magician was aware that you were riding this particular gull, there is no way that you would be detected. This is how you can scry and not be seen. So, find another bird and see if you can jump to one that will do what you ask.

It took two more birds, not one, before he found one that felt that landing on the pier would be a good thing. This was a big, strong bird who often managed to snatch food from lesser gulls down there. With a tilt of its wings, it made a dizzying plunge down toward the water, skimmed along the surface, and made a graceful landing on the stone.

Good. Now reverse how you got to the first gull. Pull back. See the gull in the mirror—

And before the voice was done, Marco was looking into the eye of a fine, bright-eyed gull, then watching it strut nonchalantly along the stone walkway of the piazza. . . .

He was startled to see that Eneko Lopez had his left hand firmly in the grasp of Eneko's own, with the needle poised over it, as the mirror went to ordinary silver again.

"Excuse me, Father, but what are you doing?"

"A precaution," Eneko replied, immediately letting go of his hand. "In case you got lost in the gull's thoughts. A sharp reminder to your spirit that it still has a proper human body would swiftly recall you back."

"It would?" Marco was impressed by that; he could think of any number of ways that he could practice this trick with Kat's help, if this was the safeguard he needed to take.

"Oh, yes, indeed." Eneko smiled. "How are you feeling?"

"Um . . . tired." He was, suddenly. But he knew why, now; this leaping about from gull to gull was something that had all come out of his own reserves. "Can I draw on some other power to do this, next time?"

"Only at the risk of being noticed," Eneko warned. "You will make the gull look different to another mage if you start drawing on more power. Just as, if another mage was to try to scry the bird you were riding, he would notice you unless you take care to be very still and not draw attention to yourself."

"But could I scry, say, a bird over Cremona, and ride it?" he hazarded.

"Yes," Lopez said. "But if there was anything watching for you, it would find you. Your risk would be less, once you began riding the bird, but it would still be there."

Marco nodded. "But what about defending myself?" he asked, quietly.

"That will be the next lesson; I want you first to learn how to make yourself so inconspicuous when riding a bird or a beast that a mage will have to be very skilled to find you." Eneko softened his stern look with a little smile. "After all, the very best defense is not to need to defend yourself at all."

Chapter 22

The ships made their way, cautiously, under oars, the leadsman calling depths as ship by ship the first great spring fleet rowed around the sand-spit at the end of the Lido. In the deeper water of the Adriatic, something watched.

If the shaman had been in his own white sea he could have named many of the denizens of the cold deep and sunk all of the vessels above. Here the massive eellike creature that was his sea-form was restricted to watching. He was eighteen cubits long, but that was still not large enough to take on ships. As always his body-shape dictated his appetites. Ships were full of food that would be nice to suck dry.

He flicked his powerful tail, and began swimming southward. Best to see if the other fleet and army was well hidden.

This water was too warm. And the monk seals weren't worth eating.

The galley had a number of its berths taken by the Vinlanders that Kat had rushed over to see. Maria had watched them for a few days now, and she was fairly certain that the two men who looked like a pair of giant warriors were really nothing much more than boys, not much older than she was. They were very happy to be at sea, and she had the feeling that although they probably were quite fond of their sister, they were also just a little tired of having her fastened to them all the time. Back in Venice, no doubt, they'd been able to get out and about on their own, but here, they were forced into each others' company with no chance for privacy.

Maria came out to put the wicker crib on the deck. Other than the helmsman, the poop deck was empty except for the blond woman—who was dripping tears over the stern of the ship. It looked to Maria as if she might join them, to splash into the water amid the kitchen peelings the cook had just tossed there.

Maria bit her lip. She'd better go over and see what the matter was. After all, the Vinlanders were Kat's grandfather's business partners. And Alessia, looking like a particularly plump and pretty cherub, was fast asleep.

Maria walked over, quietly, moving easily with the rolling of the ship.

"What's wrong?" The Vinlander woman nearly fell overboard.

The woman sniffed, hastily scuffed a sleeve across her eyes, and turned to Maria with a fake smile plastered over a face that still had tear-streaks running down the cheeks. "Nothing. I thank you," she said. "I am well. Truly."

She looked as if she was going to dissolve into tears in the very next moment.

Fine. You and I are the only two women on this ship, young lady. And we're going to the same place. I think we had better be friends.

One thing she had noticed about the Vinlanders was that they seemed to be very direct, in a way that suited Maria's canaler sensibilities. So she decided to be direct, herself.

"No, you aren't well," She put an arm over the blonde's big shoulders. "I'm not blind," she continued, feeling a hundred years older than this poor young thing. "You can tell me what's wrong. I'm a friend of Kat's."

That earned her a look of puzzlement from the woman. "Katerina Montescue. I mean Katerina Valdosta."

"Ah. Ja." The girl sniffed again, and bit her lip—but a tear escaped anyway. "You were with the bride. In the beautiful crimson dress—you are the bride's friend, ja? Such a pretty girl, and such a fine husband. I did not recognize you in those clothes."

It was plain this meant a huge leap in status to the Vinlander, and thus in acceptability as a confidante. "You know them well, then?"

"Kat's my best friend," Maria said, and was a little surprised to realize that it was true. "And her husband is very, very good to my people in Venice." Any more would be too complicated to explain at one sitting. Maybe later.

"I know that your—" she searched her memory for the word that

Erik used "—your clan is going to be trading partners with Kat's family, and I know that Kat wouldn't want to see you so unhappy if there was anything she could do to help. So, can I help?"

"I cannot see how," the girl replied mournfully.

"Well, why don't you just *tell* me about it?" Maria said, reasonably. "That can't do any harm, and it's better than crying here all alone over the turnip peelings."

The girl's face worked for a moment, as if she was trying to hold herself back, but it all came out in a rush, anyway. "I am so unhappy!" she wailed softly, in tones of such anguish that they imparted a sense of heartbreak to the banal words. "I will never see him again!"

For one, sharp-edged moment, Maria was tempted to join her in her tears, for the words called Benito's stricken face up in her own memory. *I will never see him again—*

But she was older than this poor child—in experience, if not years—and she held onto her composure.

The moment passed. Maria patted the blond woman's arm awkwardly. What the hell did you say to a cry of pain like that? She settled for: "There, there . . ."

Even this provoked another flood of sobbing. "He was such a nice man. The nicest we have met here in all Europe. And so tall, too." How could something that sounded so silly also sound as if the girl had lost her first and only true love?

Tall? Well, that counted out Benito. "Didn't he, I mean, couldn't you . . . ?" Maria floundered. She really didn't know how to deal with this. "What happened? Why won't you see him again?"

"I did not want to go. But Bjarni said Mama would never allow it. I know Mama would not be happy. But his eyes are such a beautiful blue-gray. And his chin is so . . . so square-cut and manly." She sniffed; and then, obviously overcome by the vision she'd conjured up, began to cry again.

"I cannot sleep for thinking about him!" she sobbed.

From the tone of her voice, that was nothing less than the truth, and a great deal less than she felt.

"Why won't your mama approve?" Maria ventured, cautiously. "Is he married or something?"

The woman mournfully shook her head. "Erik is not married. But he is just a lowly bodyguard. *We* are the Thordarsons. We are one of the wealthiest families in Vinland. I cannot just marry a

Nithing. Mama wants me to marry a man of position. That would help the family. But . . . but he was so wonderful."

She began to hiccup, and Maria patted her back. *Good Lord. How long has she been crying like this? Hours? Days?*

She knew all too well what the girl felt like. She'd been there—before she learned just what a scum-bred bastard Caesare Aldanto was.

Cogs began to turn in Maria's head, though. And if this Erik was the Erik *she* knew, he certainly wasn't a scum-bred bastard. "Who was he guarding?" she asked.

The Vinlander girl shrugged, as if anyone other than Erik was of no importance at all, and pulled a handkerchief out of her sleeve. By the sodden look of it, she had been crying for hours. "I do not know. A guard is a guard."

Maria bit her lip again. "You don't know the rest of his name do you? Erik what?"

"Hakkonsen. It is a good family . . ."

Maria almost choked. *Just a bodyguard!* "Ah. Well. Have you heard of Prince Manfred?"

Svanhild nodded. "Of course. The heir to the Emperor. The son of the Duke of Brittany. He was at the wedding." Her tone turned bitter. "It is very good for business, these connections that Katerina brings to the Thordarsons, ja."

"Well, he's actually not *the* heir. That's his cousin, Conrad. Manfred's next in line after him. That makes him the third most important person in the Holy Roman Empire, which is the most powerful state in Europe. Maybe in the whole world."

"Ja," the girl said, indifferently. "And also the Duke of Brittany has great standing in the League of Armagh. He is a very important man. If only my Erik could have such friends—" She began to sob again.

Maria shook the woman's shoulders, just a little, although it was like trying to shake one of those Teutonic warriors that had come into Venice among the Knots. Mostly, she was trying not to laugh.

"Listen to me! Erik Hakkonsen is Prince Manfred of Brittany's personal bodyguard and master-at-arms. Only bodyguard is the wrong word to use to describe him. It's more like—"

She scrambled for some phrase that might describe what Erik did besides "keeper." Or maybe, "nursemaid." *And if Benito only had someone like that to knock some sense into him—*

"He's a sort of teacher, or companion, and—well, he keeps Manfred from getting into too much trouble. Being a bodyguard is just a small part of it. Kat's friend tells me they are really much more like friends. What he certainly *isn't* is a—" Again she searched her memory for what the girl had said. "—a *Nithing*. I suspect if you asked Manfred, he would say that Erik is very important to him."

The sobs stopped, abruptly, and the blond woman stood up from the stern rail, a look of fierce delight on her face. "Really?" she breathed, hope replacing the despair in her sea-blue eyes so quickly that Maria's breath caught.

Maria nodded firmly. "Really."

The blonde hugged Maria. "Svanhild Thordardottar is forever in your debt!" she said thickly. "I must now go and turn this ship."

Maria didn't try to tell her that you can't alter the course of a great galley in the Venetian Western convoy, not short of being the *Bora*-wind in person. But, by the looks of it, Svanhild would have a damned good try. Bless her heart, the girl had a good steel spine to her, when she wasn't sobbing in heartbreak!

Well, the captain had survived Alessia's bellows. He'd survive Svanhild.

The next day Svanhild and her two brothers sought Maria out, where she, Alessia and Umberto sat in the lee of the mound of deck-cargo. There was a bright, steely look in Svanhild's eye. "The captain says you and your husband are going to Corfu," she said.

Maria nodded.

"Do you know how often the ships sail back to Venice from this port?" demanded Svanhild. "And can you recommend to us a good vessel and captain? Not like this stupid captain! We even offered to buy his ship. He said it was the state's ship, not his to sell. What kind of captain doesn't own his own ship? At least, as a partner."

Umberto stared at them, openmouthed. Then he shook his head.

Maria was just as dumbfounded as he was. *Buy* a Venetian great galley? She couldn't even begin to guess how much that would take, even if one were for sale!

"We don't know Corfu," Umberto stammered.

"We've never been there," explained Maria, sitting Alessia up and rubbing her back. The baby rewarded her with a milky belch.

Svanhild deflated a little. "Oh. We thought . . ."

But some of Francesca's gossip had come back to Maria, and she'd been saving it for the next time she saw the girl. "But Svanhild, you don't *want* to go back to Venice! Erik and Prince Manfred are coming along somewhere behind us. They're going to the Holy Land."

One of Svanhild's brothers looked speculative and asked: "This ship will also stop in Corfu?"

Umberto nodded. "Almost all of our ships do."

The big Vinlander patted his sister. "There, Hildi—you see! It is good that we did not turn the ship! We can just wait for them."

"They won't be more than a few days behind us," Umberto offered helpfully. "A pair of weeks, at the very most."

"But—if they go to the Holy Land—" Svanhild began, desperately.

"Then maybe . . ." the boy replied, manfully, "maybe we need to see about the trade opportunities in the Holy Land too. Sven and Olaf can go to set up the warehouse in Bruges and then go back across to the family and tell them we will be delayed."

Svanhild burst into tears again, but they were tears of relief, as her brothers seemed to recognize. And she nodded, smiling around the tears. She had, Maria thought, a lovely smile. She only hoped that Erik was going to be receptive to it. Or, Manfred or no Manfred, Svanhild's brothers might just break him in half.

High on the hillside overlooking the sea, the King of Hungary watched, unmoving. Out on the white-flecked Adriatic, the Venetian convoy sailed past. He counted ships. Sixteen great galleys, carrying a small volume of valuable cargo. Pilgrims, too—rich ones. High quality furs from as far afield as Vinland. Bullion. Amber. Twenty-three round ships of varying size laden with salt, fish, timber. Strange that Venice should export timber, but really, Venice was just a clearing house. The produce of Europe was funneled through it. Half a dozen minor galliots, carrying anything from pilgrims to arms. A lot of Ferrara steel went to the east.

He would have loved to seize that convoy, just as he would have loved to seize the convoy of ships that had overwintered in Outremer. But it would not be wise to make the attempt, even with the help of Genoa or Aragon, or even the Barbary corsairs. The eastern fleet of the Republic was not a target to take lightly. Not at sea. Where land bombards and fortifications could be brought into play, as Alexius could manage in the Bosporus, it might be worthwhile.

The Atlantic fleet had been smaller, but it was all great galleys, so it had more men, and was far faster. Emeric had been in no hurry to tackle that either. Not even outbound for Flanders, laden with the rich goods of the east. He'd get it all, if he just waited. The Greek galleys were no match for this number of Venetian ships, but later, when traffic was down to occasional vessels, they and the Dalmatian pirates out of the Narenta could seize anything that came through the Straits of Otranto.

His bodyguards shivered in the bitter northeasterly wind. If it would quicken to a gale he might yet have some of the loot on those ships. But alas, the *Bora* was not forthcoming. He must look into weather-magic some day.

When the last ship had begun its upwind tack he turned to go. His bodyguards knew their master well enough not to utter a word. They rode over the ridgeline; below lay the huge sprawl of their camp. Nearly fifteen thousand men waited there, among them four thousand of his precious Magyar heavy cavalry.

It was a measure of the king's command that not one single fire burned. The Narenta pirates were too afraid of the Venetians to light a fire. The Hungarian forces, however, were more afraid of their king. From Croat light cavalry, to Slav pikemen, every last soul of them knew: *You freeze to death before you light a fire, if Emeric so commands.*

Three of his officers rode up to meet him, looking wary. The set of their shoulders altered, the king noticed, as he smiled his grim smile. He was pleased; a good general was valuable, but they must fear him. Good generals could become threats otherwise.

He nodded to their bows. "The Atlantic Fleet will have left Corfu. Another week, if our informants are correct, and the eastern fleet will be on its way. Then, within two days, I want us at sea. Nine days from now we must be on our way to Corfu. We need to strike fast and hard."

"My cavalry are ready, Your Majesty," said Count Ladislas.

"I'm still waiting on the siege cannon," said the artillery commander. "Even with double teams of oxen we keep getting stuck in the mountains, Your Majesty. The mud is over the axletrees in places."

Another thing Emeric's officers learned, and quickly, was not to lie to him. The man was scared but honest. Emeric knew the value of tolerating failure, up to a point. Besides, he'd come over those roads himself and wasn't surprised, nor did he blame the officer. This early in spring—which hadn't arrived in the mountains yet—the roads were just mud or still waist-deep in snow.

He waved dismissively. "If we have to move without them, we will. If we have to lay siege, then we'll have time to ship them in."

The relief on the officer's face was amusing, but best not to let it go too far. "Two weeks. *Mova ik,* or I'll have your head."

He noted that the Croat cavalry captain was looking even more tense.

He waited. The man simply couldn't take it after a minute's silence. "Your Majesty. The scouts you ordered sent out south . . . seven of them have not come back. One squad."

The king nodded. "Find them. You'll find their bodies or their mounts. Then, when you've found what became of them, find the nearest village and crucify all the men. Make the women watch."

Emeric raised a forefinger. "You have eight days."

PART V
April, 1539 A.D.

Chapter 23

Emeric erased the circle and the pentacle scratched in a section of his pavilion where he'd pulled back the carpets to expose the naked soil. Then he eliminated all other traces of the ritual he'd followed to reach the chief of his spies on Corfu, cleaned himself, and put the carpets back in place. The work had to be done carefully, since he was only guided by the light of a few candles. Night had long since fallen.

As always, Emeric was irritated by having to do such menial labor himself, instead of ordering a servant. But, he dared not do otherwise. Even the King of Hungary—even a king suspected by his subjects to be a man-witch—could not afford to have anyone observe him at such times. Not, at least, anyone knowledgeable in such matters, and it was always difficult to tell who might be.

Several features of those rituals were satanic in nature, not simple witchcraft. Hungary was, after all, a predominantly Christian country—and those portions that were not Christian were mostly Muslim. His polyglot subjects would tolerate a great deal, true, but not open trafficking with *that* prince.

Emeric didn't particularly fear rebellion, as such. His army was quite capable of crushing any combination of peasants or townsmen, as it had demonstrated several times over the past years. The problem lay with the army itself. None of Emeric's officers was burdened with any great moral sentiments. Still, the open use of satanic rituals would, if nothing else, give an ambitious general the handle to organize and lead a military overthrow of the Hungarian dynasty.

Emeric did not follow all of his aunt's advice. But he had never failed to observe Countess Bartholdy's strictures on this score: *Keep it secret, from all except those you trust. And trust only those you can control.*

Finally done, he soothed his irritation by ordering wine and cuffing the servant who brought it. He finished the goblet, ordered another, and cuffed the servant again.

Throughout, it never occurred to him—as it had never occurred to him before—to wonder why his aunt had given him those secrets in the first place, starting when he was a boy of six. To wonder why she had violated, seemingly, her own rule.

Like his master, Petros Fianelli erased all the symbols and signs of the ritual himself. In his case, not in the luxury of a king's pavilion but in the squalor of a basement owned by one who appeared to be a simple seller of secondhand goods in Kérkira, the chief town of Corfu. Which, indeed, Fianelli was—even if most of his income came from the criminal ring he operated on the island, as well as the subsidy he received from the King of Hungary.

There was only one way to perform these rituals on Corfu: to create the symbols in fire. Each one was created on a special platen made of obsidian, filled with oily cotton, fed from a reservoir of defiled holy oil. When the oil was lit, the symbol burned in the element that Corfu could not counter, the Devil's own. But the platens had to be carefully hidden when he was done. If anyone found them, it would be awkward. If anyone who understood what they were for ever found them, the consequences would be dire.

That done, he took the taper and mounted the stairs to the kitchen. It was a large kitchen, centered around a large table. Little cooking was actually done in the kitchen, these days, since Fianelli had quietly murdered his last woman a few months earlier after she'd become tiresome. Had her murdered, rather, by two of his three bully boys. Fianelli hadn't wanted to risk it himself, given his own short and pudgy stature. She'd been a large woman, full-hipped as well as big-breasted, with the shoulders of the Scuolo-born washerwoman she'd been before Fianelli made her his concubine.

No loss. She'd been a poor cook, and Fianelli preferred to dine in public eateries anyway. Besides, it made it easier to use the kitchen for its real purpose, which was to serve as the headquarters for his various criminal enterprises.

His three enforcers were already sitting at the table, lounging back in their chairs and enjoying the bottle of grappa he'd opened for them before going down to the basement.

"All right, it's on." He pulled out a chair and sat down himself. Zanari poured him a glass of grappa. "I just got the word."

None of the three enforcers asked him how he'd "gotten the word," or from whom. In truth, they didn't care. A large part of the reason they obeyed Fianelli, despite his unprepossessing appearance, was that they all considered him a veritable wizard when it came to knowing the right things and the right people.

Paulo Saluzzo grimaced. "Treason's a dangerous business."

"The more danger, the more profit," grunted Fianelli. "Besides, what do you care who rules Corfu?"

"I'm from Florence, by way of Naples. I could care less whether this island is run by Venetians or Greeks or Hungarians—or manticores or unicorns, for that matter. So long as we get our cut."

"We'll get it, and then some."

"What's next?" asked Zanari.

Fianelli considered, for a moment. "The Casarini bitch, I think. If you want to betray a town under siege, you've got to have an inside link with the big shots. She can get it, we can't."

The third enforcer, hitherto slouched in his chair, sat up straighter. Smiling slightly, he emitted a soft whistle. He'd seen Bianca Casarini in the streets, from time to time.

Fianelli scowled at him. "Forget her good looks, Papeti. Just *forget* it."

The enforcer frowned, obviously a bit puzzled. Fianelli normally didn't care in the least what his men did with women. He hadn't even cared, knowing full well that Papeti and Zanari would have raped his discarded woman before they cut her throat and sank her in the sea.

"Casarini's dangerous. Never mind the details. Just take my word for it. This is strictly business."

The enforcer shrugged. But since the gesture was one of acceptance, not indifference, Fianelli let it go. He wasn't planning on using Papeti as his intermediary with Bianca Casarini anyway. Casarini lived in one of the better parts of the Citadel. The Venetian elite wouldn't tolerate someone moving in their quarters who

looked like a thug, especially a Greek one. Of his three enforcers, Saluzzo was the only one who could carry off the needed pose
in that area. There were traces left of the Florentine bravo he'd
been, in an earlier life.

"This'll be your job, Paulo."

"I don't know where she lives. Only seen her in the streets and
cafés a few times."

"You don't need to know where she lives, for the moment. Just
approach her on the street tomorrow. She'll be passing by the
corner where the dock-road crosses the road to the inner wall gates;
you know—where Dendrago's old bake-house used to be."

"How do I know she'll be there?" There was a whining undertone in Saluzzo's voice. Like any such man, he hated to work—
and, for him, spending a day lounging about waiting for someone
to show up who might not constituted "work."

"Don't worry about it. She'll be there."

Fianelli spoke with confidence. He'd taken the time, after
receiving his instructions from Emeric, to use the magical symbols and rituals to speak to Casarini herself.

That very moment, Bianca Casarini finished the same—very
close, at least—satanic procedures. In her case, in the luxurious
room her aunt and uncle had provided for her in their house in
Kérkira after her arrival on the island the year before.

The face of her mistress appeared, hovering like a ghost above
the bowl.

"They have approached me, mistress, as you predicted."

Countess Bartholdy smiled cheerfully. "Surely you didn't doubt
me?"

This was dangerous territory. "Surely not, mistress," Bianca said
quickly.

"Do as they say, then," Elizabeth commanded. She cocked her
head a little, studying the woman who had become, over the past
few years, something very close to her slave. Bartholdy's quick mind
had detected the slight traces of discomfiture.

"Surely the fact that some of it will be unpleasant—even worse,
undignified—does not bother you?"

Again, dangerous territory. "Surely not, mistress."

The countess's beautiful face became just a bit taut; harsh, even,
insofar as that term could ever be applied to it. "Immortality has

its price, Bianca Casarini. Many prices, rather. Cavorting about with whomever I require you to cavort with and copulating with animals—even real ones—is one of the least. So do as they tell you. I need to remain informed at all times concerning the progress of their treachery, once the siege begins. My own plans require precise timing."

She did not explain what those plans were, and Bianca did not ask. Did not even think of asking, in fact. By now, she was well trained.

"Yes, mistress."

Bianca was able to say the last rather easily. Her own mind was quick as well, and she'd already realized that she could shift the worst of the work onto another's shoulders. Several others, in fact. In the year since she'd been living on Corfu, she'd ingratiated herself into the social circles of the Venetian aristocrats and the Greek Libri d'Oro. With the skills she'd learned from Countess Bartholdy, she'd been able to detect which of them possessed inner demons and vices. The ones which were most obvious, at least.

She'd start with Sophia Tomaselli, she decided, when the time came. The wife of the captain-general would be . . .

Easy. Like leading a pig to a trough.

After the image of Bartholdy vanished and she'd erased the symbols, Bianca laughed aloud. *Leading a slut to an orgy, more like.*

Casarini was beautiful herself, if not to the extent that Bartholdy was. But, unlike the countess, a sneer distorted her features badly. So, from long practice, she suppressed the expression. That was a bit difficult, thinking about the wife of Captain-General Tomaselli.

After a bit of practice, Sophia wouldn't care if her partners were pigs in a trough.

That sour thought was suppressed even more firmly than the sneer had been. The day would come, Bianca knew, when she'd have to undergo the rituals of bestialism herself. Immortality had its prices. But there was no reason to dwell on any of them before-hand.

The last work in erasing the traces of the rituals was on her, now. Bianca made no attempt to keep the distaste from showing on her face. A simple expression of distaste, unlike an outright sneer, was expected on the face of a noblewoman. Which she was not, in actual fact, but had long since mastered the art of appearing to be. She'd even successfully—and easily—fooled her "relatives" into thinking she was their niece.

She brought the bowl to her lips. It wasn't the taste that bothered her. Blood was blood. The problem was that there was so *much* of it that had to be drunk. She was normally a light eater, and drank little beyond an occasional glass of watered wine.

But it had to be done, so she got on with it. She comforted herself with the thought that at least she hadn't had to drink the niece's blood. There had been no rituals necessary, in that work. The silk scarf Bianca had used to strangle the girl had left no messy traces at all.

It was odd, really. Elizabeth Bartholdy discovered herself, these days, often coming to visit the monster in the glass jar. True, she'd created the thing, and she usually enjoyed studying her handiwork. But the unnatural elemental fetus she'd brought into being was unpleasant to look upon. Even worse, perhaps, was the aura of malevolence that emanated so strongly from the trapped monster as to permeate the entire chamber where she kept it.

Nonetheless, she came, almost every day. The creature was the blade she'd created for a masterstroke. And if the stroke succeeded . . .

Moved by a sudden thought, she left the chamber in the dungeons and made her way through the castle to her special bathing room. Once there, she studied the obsidian bathtub, gleaming with the sheen of oil in the light. It had taken a year to get it carved and polished, and she had gone through several craftsmen, not to mention blocks of volcanic glass, before one had managed to complete the task without shattering the tub. Now she regarded it as a carpenter might measure a cabinet.

I'll need a bigger one. Better order the work started on it now. This will be no dainty little virgin. Chernobog's blood will slop over in buckets, each drop worth more than diamonds.

Chapter 24

Maria looked around the whitewashed empty house. It was made mostly of stone, with plaster over the stone, and a floor of flagstones. The windows were small, but they had glass in them, in wooden frames that could be opened. It wasn't much, not compared to the wooden home in Istria. The few other houses here were crowded around like quizzy neighbors. It was, on a small scale, reminiscent of Cannaregio.

The house is a big improvement on Benito's little place in Cannaregio though, she thought, a smile tugging at her lips. You could be happy in all sorts of places, if you tried. Still, from what the porters had said, any house here on Corfu was a symbol of status. From what Maria could see, there wasn't much to build with except rock, and that had to be quarried from the main island itself. There were only a handful of houses up here between the two fortification-topped hills of the small island that formed the Citadel, Corfu's great fortress. The two hills were in a straight line running out to sea. Hence the fortress on the seaward side was called the Castel *a mar;* the one on the landward side, the Castel *a terra.*

The town of Kérkira itself—Corfu's largest—was on the main island, separated from the Citadel by a shallow channel perhaps sixty yards wide at its narrowest dimension. The town and the Citadel were connected by a causeway and a bridge. Most of the other staff of the outpost lived between the outer and inner curtain-walls of the Citadel, or in the barracks built into the walls of the fortifications. Only a few, most of them high officials and their families, lived in one of the castles on the hilltops.

193

She pushed open the shutters, looking out over the Citadel at the bright waters, across to the brown smudge they told her was Albania. The spring sunshine licked in at her, along with the tang of salt in the breeze off the sea. Awash with a sudden need for affection Maria turned to the wicker crib, and lifted Alessia into her arms and hugged her. Alessia was sleepy, full and warm. The baby made the small groaning sound that Maria had learned meant contentment and seemed to snuggle into her.

Maria stood there rocking her, loving her. "'Lessi. It's a home. And it's near the sea. It's peaceful . . . and you'll always have a mama."

Umberto came in and smiled at the Madonna-like scene when Maria turned at his footstep.

"How is the most beautiful, chubbiest baby on this island doing?" he asked cheerfully. Umberto's attitude toward babies, now that Alessia was born, was far more relaxed. He was as proud of the baby as any father could have been. Admittedly he still didn't look comfortable holding her, but he did delight in her.

Maria smiled at him, her good mood spilling over onto everything around her. "She's fine."

Umberto smiled back. "The house is good enough?" he asked, cautiously. "It is not as big as in Istria."

"It's wonderful." That was an exaggeration, but so what? At the moment it felt a minor one. "The whole place feels welcoming."

"Good." Umberto was plainly relieved. "They'll be bringing our boxes and things up from the ship presently. Can you come with me to be introduced to the captain-general? Then I must get down to the Little Arsenal." He shook his head. "It is in a sorry state. The old foreman is . . . well, old."

They walked along the narrow lane up to the gray stone fortress on the hilltop. It was cool here, inside the thick walls. A guard, a bit more sloppily dressed than any Venetian Schiopettieri or one of the Doge's Swiss mercenaries, led them up to the captain-general's office. The door was open, and the voices of those inside it were quite clear to anyone approaching.

"We don't have accommodation for visitors, Signorina," snapped a sharp voice from inside. "I can't help it if you think that Kérkira's taverns are too low-class for you. Rent a house."

"We have been trying to, ja."

Maria recognized Svanhild's distinctive voice and accent. She sounded tired.

"Everything decent they want a year's lease on. We should only be here for days," rumbled a deeper, similarly accented voice.

That must be one of Svanhild's brothers, thought Maria.

"Usually they hire for either the summer or winter, to fit in with the convoys," explained the sharp voice. Definitely a Venetian, probably the captain-general himself, thought Maria. *Oh, dear.* Umberto would have to work under him and he did not sound like an easy man. "You should be able to negotiate a six month lease."

"But we only want it for a few days until the eastbound convoy comes!" said the Svanhild voice, unhappily.

Maria peered into the room. It was Svanhild indeed, and both of her large brothers. And a comparatively small, dark man at a large untidy desk. The room was generously proportioned but it looked overfull of irritated Vinlanders.

The man at the desk sighed, snatched a piece of parchment from his desk, and scrawled something on it. "Here. Count Dentico has an estate outside of the town. He has a second villa some miles away. Perhaps he would be prepared to lease it to you for such a period. Perhaps there will be rooms enough for your escort. I do not know. Now please, I have business to attend to." He pointed to the door. "You can hire horses and a local guide at the *taverna* just across the Spianada. Good-bye."

Svanhild and her brothers emerged. The statuesque blonde blinked to see Maria and Umberto. "What are you doing here?" she asked, though her surprised tone made it very clear that she was not being rude.

"We have come to see the captain-general," said Maria. "My husband will be working here."

Svanhild sniffed and rubbed her hot forehead, leaving a little smudge. "He is not a very helpful man," she said unhappily, and walked off, following her brothers.

The military commander of Corfu stood up and limped across to the doorway. He looked at Umberto and Maria, and glared magnificently. "This is not an inn. Or an employment office."

Umberto looked more than a little terrified. "My name is Verrier. I have been sent from Venice. I am to be a foreman . . ."

The glaring eyes cleared. "Ah. You must the man they've sent to deal with the Little Arsenal. We've had some problems with the local labor and the guilds." The captain-general bowed to Maria. "This beautiful lady must be your wife. I am Captain-General Nico Tomaselli. For my sins the Council has stationed me here.

"Come in," he added, in a more pleasant tone of voice, as he walked back to his desk. "You must tell me how I can serve you. My people were supposed to see you in to your home and invite you to come up to see me. The Little Arsenal is the heart of this outpost of the empire."

Maria scowled at him, behind his back, then quickly smoothed her expression into something more pleasant. She was always wary with people who handed out the flattery too liberally, especially when she'd seen the same person ready to backhand those he disliked or looked down upon. But at least he was not letting his anger with Svanhild wash onto Umberto. Though poor Svanhild could hardly know that the conditions she had found in Venice would not hold in Corfu.

Umberto bowed. "Umberto Verrier. I am a master-craftsman in the Guild of Caulkers. I had heard there were problems, I mean, I had been told that there were some difficulties that needed smoothing out. Could you tell me more?"

The captain-general shrugged. "It's quite simple, really. The local men, whom we employ as laborers in the repair-yard, are an undisciplined bunch. They'll do any job. The journeymen complain they're encroaching. The locals say that as they can't be apprenticed, why should they obey 'prentice rules? They all drink too much and get into fights about it."

Umberto, who was a slight man, looked alarmed. "In the ship-yard? But guild rules . . ."

The captain-general blew out through his teeth. "We're a long way from the guild halls of Venice, signor. If you throw one of these guildsmen out, it may be six months before you can replace him. The Greek labor *should* be easy, but the honest truth is they don't much like working here. The Venetians say they're lazy. But the truth is that they're an independent lot, Greeks. Live on past glories and expect to be treated as if they were all sons of Ulysses. Or Odysseus, as they'll insist he should be called."

Tomaselli's practiced glare was back, this time aimed at the open window and the town beyond. "I can guarantee you won't be there for more than a week before you have at least one of the Greeks

calling you an uncivilized Italian upstart. There's always trouble.
We've got a fair number of Illyrians from the mainland as a result.
And they fight with the Greeks, too." He shrugged. "As I said:
There's always trouble. You'll need a firm hand. Part of the problem
is that they work frantically for about six weeks a year. The rest
of the time there really isn't enough work for half of them. But
to keep a skilled force we've got to employ them all year round."

Umberto had the look of man who, in the attempt to avoid a
dog turd, had stepped into a scorpion pit instead.

The town fanned out from the Citadel, on the main body of
the island. Maria crossed the causeway and walked south, toward
the quay-side. She had asked for directions to the market areas
and got several vague pointers in this direction. It made sense: This
was where the ships came in; this was where the traders would
congregate. As she got closer she realized she could have just
followed her nose.

The stalls along the pavements were full of things that were both
familiar and fascinatingly different. Barrows piled high with crocks
of olives, bunches of dried fish, boxes of filberts, trays of fried
cuttlefish, mounds of cheeses . . . jostled with racks of embroidered
jackets and starched white fichus. Next was what was plainly a
baker, with the enticing smells of fresh bread and a display of
strange, sticky-looking confectionary. Maria went into the narrow
little shop and up to the counter, where a little dark-eyed woman
studied her with undisguised curiosity. In a smallish town like this,
the shopkeepers probably knew most of their customers.

The little women bobbed. "And how may I help you, Kyria?"

"Kyria? What does that mean?" she asked, tilting her head to
one side.

The shopkeeper smiled at her curious and friendly tone. "You
are new to Corfu. It is a polite greeting. It means 'milady.' How
do you like our town? Are you just here with the fleet or do you
stay on in Corfu?"

A woman bustled in, wearing an elegant walking dress, with her
hair dressed up on combs in the height of last year's Venetian
fashion. She paused briefly beside Maria, waiting for her to cede
her place. Then, when Maria didn't move, shoved her aside. "Make
way for your betters, woman!" she snapped.

Maria had never taken very kindly to being pushed around, and this woman had bumped Alessia into wakefulness. Maria had broad shoulders and strong arms from sculling a gondola.

"I'll have three dozen of those—"

The woman found her orders cut off abruptly by a strong arm, pulling her backwards.

"I was here first. You can wait your turn."

The woman's jaw dropped. She caught it; pinched her lips, took a deep breath, and emitted a screeching: "*Do you know who I am? You—you—*" She looked at Maria's fairly plain, unfashionable garb. "You Corfiote *puttana!*"

Maria put Alessia down, carefully. "I don't care who you are. But if you like I can throw you into the harbor to cool off. With luck, your head will go underwater and spare me from having to stare anymore at what the elderly maiden aunts of the *Case Vecchie* were wearing last year."

The last part of the statement made the woman's eyes bulge. She looked uncommonly like one of those fancy poodles that had become the latest fashion among the *Case Vecchie* of Venice. Her eye-bulge was more fashionable than her hairstyle. "You—you— *How dare you?* I'll tell my husband of your insolence!"

"Do. Then I can toss him into the harbor, too," said Maria, advancing on the woman. "He's clearly not doing his duty in beating you often enough to curb that tongue of yours."

The woman retreated, tripping over her petticoats in her haste. "You haven't heard the last of this, you Corfiote cow!"

Maria turned back and retrieved Alessia, who was going into full wail. It took her a short while to soothe her down.

The little woman shook her head incredulously. "Kyria, do you know who that was?"

Maria shook her head, her temper cooling. "No. Who?"

"That is the wife of the captain-general! Sophia Tomaselli!"

Maria said something very indelicate.

The little woman just about fell apart laughing and trying to restrain herself. "They say that's what she was before the marriage."

Maria gritted her teeth. She'd better tell Umberto about this. It was not a very promising start to their stay in Corfu. She bought some fresh bread and headed back to the house.

Umberto's gloomy expression got deeper when she told him about it. "More troubles. I'm getting somewhere with the senior journeymen. I am not winning with the Corfiotes or the other masters. Oh, well. We must expect things to take time. There is a reception and dinner tonight for the new people sent out by the Senate. We will have to attend."

Maria had done certain small adaptations to the dress she had worn for Kat's wedding. She only had five dresses—though that was more than she would have ever dreamed of owning once, more than most ordinary women would ever own. This one, however, was special. Francesca with her impeccable eye had picked out the fabric from among all of the gowns that had once graced Kat's mother. Francesca's dressmaker had remade it, knowing it would adorn one of the ladies who would get an enormous amount of attention at the wedding.

The dressmaker had wanted to be absolutely certain of two things: First, that the dress would fill every aspirant of fashion in the *Case Vecchie* with a desire to own it. And, second, that the owner would love the dress so much that she would send all those who asked about it to Madame Therasé.

And, indeed, the dressmaker had succeeded beyond her expectations, even among the haut monde of Venice. By the standards that prevailed in little out-of-the-way Corfu . . .

The wine-red gown would excite envy to a fever pitch. The red velvet, with a pattern woven into it of high and low pile, was the sort of stuff that would never go out of style and was appallingly expensive. The low, square neckline and the flattened bosom were of the very latest style, as was the natural waistline, rather than the line that came just under the bosom. As was proper in a married woman, the undergown, of the finest linen, covered most of her exposed chest, right up to the collarbone, and it was pulled through the myriad small slashings in the sleeves, which were faced with scarlet silk.

The sleeves themselves were enormous, like a couple of hams. Maria often thought that she could probably smuggle most of what her old pole-boat used to carry in those sleeves. They ended in tight cuffs, though, which would make getting anything into them rather impractical. The beautiful pillow-lace that finished the sleeves of the undergown showed at the cuffs, and trimmed the edge of the undergown's neckline. The bodice of the overgown was sewn with tiny seed pearls in a latticework pattern, a pattern that was repeated on the sleeves.

The captain-general's wife had worn a gown with a high waist, and no slashings in the sleeves at all. And while her gown for this festivity would probably be of more opulent materials, Maria doubted that it would be of more recent date.

Jewelry . . . well, she only had two pieces. They'd not pass a jeweler's eye. But the three ropes of "pearls" of glass and fish-scale would stand up to any lesser scrutiny. Francesca had seen to that, and if anyone knew jewelry, it was a courtesan. And there were earrings to match.

Maria felt some pride when she looked at herself in the mirror. She gave a vixenish grin at the elegant woman with her dark, lustrous hair done up "a la didon" as Francesca had showed her. She was sorry that Caesare couldn't see her like this. Then she'd have been able to spit in his face and laugh at him. He'd always played her origins against her in a nasty game designed to keep her feeling at once utterly inferior to him and at the same time terribly grateful that he deigned to honor her with his attentions. She could see that now, with the benefit of looking back from a distance, and from the positively old age of nineteen.

She bit her lips to redden them, make them fuller, and used just a touch of belladonna around her eyes to make the pupils widen. Umberto's sharp intake of breath when he saw her brought a smile to her face.

She took his arm, and allowed him to reverently escort her to the reception, feeling a wave of warmth for her husband. Yes, granted, Umberto was unimaginative, often even stodgy—in bed as well as everywhere else—with not a trace of Caesare's golden charm or Benito's wit and bravura. And so what? He was conscientious, considerate, kindly; scrupulously responsible in his family duties; and, in his own sometimes fussy and always respectable way, he doted on her. That was its own treasure, after all, which she would repay in full with loyalty and affection.

Maria did not love Umberto, not really; but, slowly and steadily, she was growing very fond of the man.

The captain-general and his wife stood beside the elderly podesta and his wife to welcome the guests. Maria managed to keep an absolute deadpan face when she was introduced. Sophia Tomaselli did not. The captain general's wife saw the face first. And then . . . just as she was about to explode, took in the elegant hairstyling and the dress. Maria smiled vaguely at her as if she'd never seen the now ashen-faced woman in her life before.

It got worse. The podesta's wife was frail and white haired. She smiled at Maria with genuine warmth, instead of the *Case Vecchie*-greeting-the-lowly-Scuolo attitude that the captain-general and his wife adopted.

"My dear Maria! Welcome to Corfu. I have had a letter from the Doge's ward about you, begging my kindness to a dear friend. Marco tells me you are a close friend of his wife's, who was of the *Casa* Montescue."

The little white-haired woman twinkled at her husband, making light of a friendship between one of the Scuolo and a *Case Vecchie longi* house like Montescue. "My dear Alexio stole me away from that scamp Lodovico Montescue. Lodovico was a terrible tearaway when I was young. The scandal of the town! But very charming. I remember him with great fondness. Have you met him?"

"I . . . Yes, I know him, milady. He is a grand old man, gallant as anyone half his age. He can still be very charming."

The podesta's wife laughed and patted Maria's arm. "I am delighted to hear it. We must have a talk later. I can't wait to hear what that old rogue has been up to."

"I look forward to it, milady," said Maria with trepidation. How would she cope with *Case Vecchie* gossip? It was bad enough keeping her mouth shut, in case her tongue betrayed her origins in a crowd, where everyone simply said polite nothings. Back then—several lifetimes ago it seemed—she'd dreamed of being fine enough to be a *Case Vecchie* wife for the aristocratic Caesare. Well, a master-craftsman's wife stood far lower on the social scale, but it was still a long step from "canal-woman." A one-on-one conversation would be hell. But for Umberto's sake she'd had to try.

Maria couldn't help flicking a glance at the captain-general and his wife. Sophia Tomaselli's face was white under her makeup, and two red spots burned in her cheeks. Maria didn't need to look at her fulminating eyes to know that she'd acquired an enemy for life. Aside from their confrontation . . . now, thanks to Marco's well-meaning attempt to smooth her path, the woman also knew that Maria and Umberto had powerful political connections. If Maria knew anything about that kind of woman, the captain-general's wife wouldn't let that stop her. She'd just honey her spite in public—and plot, scheme and gossip in private. And doubtless nag that husband of hers. He, poor man, obviously knew his wife's expressions well. He was already looking nervous.

Then, Maria realized she'd done more than merely make the captain-general's wife look like she was wearing her mother's unaltered gown, which someone like Sophia Tomaselli would consider an insult of the first water.

Umberto smiled at her. "Phillipo here tells me you have quite stolen Signora Tomaselli's thunder, my dear. She is used to being the center of attention; everyone in our community considered her to be the most beautiful lady on the island. Tonight there are far more people looking at you. You cast her into the shade."

He meant it well, but Maria was hard-pressed not to groan. All it needed was that! She looked across the hall to where Sophia was saying something to two other women. They both suddenly glanced at her. And hastily looked away.

Chapter 25

She stood at the head of the stone breakwater, her long blond hair streaming like a banner in the wind. Farther back along the break-water, Maria could see the inevitable brothers were lounging against some crates, along with four or five of their Vinlander escort. To the north the galleys of the Outremer-bound Venetian convoy cut the bright water under full sail.

Maria suppressed a chuckle. Svanhild was making absolutely certain that the first thing that Erik saw was going to be her. The dockyard tarts were also on the quay-side, but Svanhild was making damn sure she got her hooks set before the island's hookers did.

But that wasn't really fair, Maria knew. She was thinking like a canaler. The Vinlander woman wouldn't see it that way; her heart might know what she was really doing, but her head would be telling her that she only wanted to get the first possible sight of the convoy and of Erik.

Maria left off watching the convoy coming in. They were still under sail; they'd have to drop their sails and come in to port under oars. Maria hoped Svanhild felt like a good long stand, because she was going to be on her feet there for a while.

But Maria couldn't wait about; she had food to prepare. The one thing that Corfu had going for it was the presence in the market of even better fish than were available in Venice. She'd bought some small octopus this morning. Umberto loved them, and he was having a rough enough time at work for Maria to wish to improve his day just a little. Umberto was used to working within the framework of rigid guild discipline, where a master-craftsman said something and was obeyed, instantly and precisely. Here, away from Venice . . . what was needed was a sharp clout from the Master before the 'prentices would stop their pretense of immobility.

The small house was redolent with the scent of *zuppa con popli*, and Umberto was still sitting with a glass of white wine, the frown-lines easing around his eyes and forehead, when someone knocked at the door.

Maria went to it, angry. "Can't you even leave the master to eat his meal in peace!" she yelled. The Little Arsenal would work day and night now until the fleet left, and she expected it to be yet another problem for Umberto's attention.

But, when she flung the door open, she saw it wasn't someone from the shipyard. Instead it was a very woebegone looking Svanhild and her brothers and their men. The narrow roadway seemed very full of large Vinlanders.

Maria was taken entirely aback. "Oh! I . . . I thought it was someone for my husband from the shipyard. I'm so sorry."

"Erik is not on the ships!" By the reddened eyes Svanhild had already been crying. The poor woman-child seemed to spend her life crying.

"Oh." That seemed a very inadequate thing to say. Maria knew the Vinlanders had almost certainly extended their stay in Europe for a whole season on the basis of what she'd told them about Erik's plans. The only reason they were here at all was because of what she'd said about the convoys stopping at Corfu.

"I know Prince Manfred is definitely going to the Holy Land," she protested. "Katerina told me herself! And she got that from . . . uh, from Mademoiselle de Chevreuse. She's, ah, a close friend of the prince."

"None of them are on the convoy," Svanhild repeated, half-wailing. "I've lost him!"

"I believe I can help you, my lady," said Umberto diffidently, from the table where he had hastily risen to his feet. "Prince Manfred and his Knights of the Holy Trinity are coming with four special great galleys that have been built for service off Cyprus. I heard from the admiral of the Outremer fleet that they were doing final outfitting in the Arsenal the day his fleet left. He says they should not be more than a week behind the Outremer convoy." Gloomily, he added: "The

Little Arsenal will be sore pressed to fix those vessels as well, if we haven't got the Outremer fleet out by then."

It was like the sun coming out on Svanhild's face again, and it looked as if she would gladly have flung herself at Umberto and kissed him, if it hadn't been so improper to do so. So Maria did just that for her. He was a good man.

Far enough away from the house not to be spotted in the darkness, two women studied the figure standing in the doorway talking to the enormous and crude Vinlanders. Sophia Tomaselli's expression was tight and pinched with anger; that of her friend Bianca Casarini, simply cool and calculating.

Maria Verrier's face was illuminated fairly well by the lamps inside her house. After a moment, Bianca turned away and began walking slowly toward the Castel *a terra*.

"I'll recognize her, Sophia, whenever I see her again. Let me give the matter some thought."

"You should have seen her earlier!" hissed Tomaselli. "The slut! She must have spread her legs for half the *Case Vecchie* to afford a dress like that—her, a *scuolo*'s wife!"

"Umberto Verrier is not exactly a *scuolo*," murmured Bianca. "Yes, he started as a simple guildsman, but he occupies a considerably more prestigious position these days."

She glanced at Sophia's face, which was momentarily well-lit by a lamp in a taverna they were walking past. "Be careful, Sophia," she said softly. "Whatever her past, Maria Verrier is well-connected now. Better than you are, to be honest, and—"

Her eyes slid down to Sophia's midriff. "Please take no offense, but she's also got a child."

As Bianca expected—the Tomaselli woman was *so* predictable—that drew an angry glare. But even Sophia had enough sense to understand the point. A married woman with a child, in provincial Corfu even more than in Venice, had a certain aura of respectability that a childless wife like Sophia didn't. Especially when the wife in question had now been married for several years, to a man as generally disliked as Captain-General Nico Tomaselli—and was herself detested by almost everyone except her cronies. Over time, quietly, snickering remarks had spread, speculating either on Sophia's frigidity or her husband Nico's impotence—neither of which enhanced her status at all.

They walked on in silence for a bit. Diffidently, Bianca cleared her throat. "Querini has been no help, I take it?"

Sophia's scowl was heavy enough to spot even in the sliver of moonlight. "That pig! Bad enough he ruts like one, but he doesn't even manage the job."

"Ah. His lovemaking does leave a lot to be desired, in the way of finesse. I admit I rather enjoy his energy myself. But then—" She issued a soft laugh. "I've been taking precautions to make sure I *don't* get pregnant. Unlike you, I have no convenient husband to assume he's the father."

Again, they walked on in silence for a time; and, again, Bianca cleared her throat. "I have another lover who might do the trick—two, actually—but . . ."

Hearing the pause, Sophia seemed to shrivel a bit. "You think it's me, Bianca? Tell me the truth."

Casarini kept the surge of triumph from showing. Hard, that. She truly enjoyed snaring her prey.

"I hate to say it, but . . . it could be, yes. Crude he may be, but Querini's certainly not impotent—and I know of at least two bastards he's sired."

Sophia Tomaselli seemed to shrivel still further. Bianca watched, sidelong, gauging the moment.

"I might be able to help, there," she added. "I know someone who's . . . well. A Strega mage, I think. Or . . . something else, but similar."

Sophia made a face. Bianca laughed softly again. "No, no, Sophia, not what you think. Ha! Aldo Morando's no shriveled up crone, that's for sure. Quite a handsome devil, actually. In fact, I've been considering . . . well. The point is, he's an accomplished apothecary and knows a number of magics."

"Have you . . ."

"I certainly wasn't trying to get pregnant! My problem was the opposite, actually. If Morando's as good at fertility as he was at abortion, you'll be fine."

They were now near the entrance to the Castel *a terra,* where the Tomasellis lived. Bianca drew to a halt. "So, do you want me to set you up with him?"

Sophia didn't hesitate. "Yes," she hissed. "If I could get that problem taken care of—" She glanced over her shoulder, back the way they'd come, her eyes narrow. "That bitch!"

Bianca issued her soft, friendly laugh again, and placed a hand on Tomaselli's shoulder. "One thing at a time, Sophia. I'll give some—*ha*." She broke off, as if struck by a sudden thought.

"What is it?"

"It just occurred to me that Morando might well be of help on that problem, also. Apothecaries and magic-workers—good ones, anyway, which he is—often know . . . You know. Poisons. Hexes. Curses."

The words seemed to fill Sophia Tomaselli's figure, removing any trace of hunched shoulders. "*Yes.* Set it up for me with this Morando, Bianca."

Bianca nodded and began to turn away, headed toward her own domicile in a less prestigious part of the Citadel. But Sophia stopped her with a sudden hug. "You're such a good friend!"

That was a bit startling. It was the first time Sophia had ever expressed any affection for Bianca beyond the gossipy and sniping camaraderie of two women of like temperament. Their friendship was close, after all these months that Bianca had spent cultivating it, but only in the sense that two spiteful conspirators were intimate with each other. There had never been any warmth in the thing before.

Immediately, Bianca returned the embrace. Rather fiercely, in fact. Partly, to maintain the pose—but mostly to disguise the sheer thrill from showing. She *loved* that moment when the trap was sprung.

"Well?" asked Morando, closing the door behind her and giving Bianca his well-practiced arching eyebrow. Morando, Bianca knew, thought the expression gave him a certain enticingly satanic air.

It did, in fact. Studying him for a moment, Bianca decided to let him finally seduce her. That would help snare him as well; all the more so because a man of Morando's type invariably thought of himself as the conqueror. Of all prey, predators were the easiest.

Besides, Bianca was tired of Querini's clumsy lovemaking herself. She'd only initiated the affair and continued it in order to tangle Sophia Tomaselli in her web. Morando would probably make a pleasant change. If nothing else, he'd be too suave to grunt.

"Well?" he repeated.

"It's done. She should be coming here before much longer."

Morando waved at the table where an open bottle waited. And two glasses. Not all *that* suave, alas.

So be it. Bianca had had worse, and would have much worse in the future. Gracefully, she slid into one of the chairs and allowed Morando to fill her a glass. Before it was half-finished, she'd accepted his invitation to tour his establishment.

It proved to be quite a bit more impressive than she'd expected. Later, after Morando fell asleep, she slid out of the bed and tip-toed into the hallway. There, she paused for a moment, listening carefully to be sure that she hadn't awakened Morando. Fortunately, he snored, though not as badly as Querini.

Yes, he was sleeping soundly. Bianca made her way to the flag-stone in the floor that was actually a trapdoor. Prying it up slowly and carefully, making sure to remain silent, she peered down into the darkness. All she could see in the dim light were a few steep wooden stairs.

She rose and padded, still nude, to the door to the bedroom. After listening for a moment longer to Morando's snores, she decided he was a heavy enough sleeper to risk further investigation. She went to the kitchen and picked up the oil lamp burning there. With it in hand, she returned to the trapdoor and went quickly down the steps. She left the flagstone pried up, rather than closing it behind her. That was a bit risky, perhaps, but less risky than finding herself unable to lift it when she wanted to emerge. The damn thing was *heavy*.

Once she was down in the cellar, she spent little time examin-ing what was obvious. Morando had already shown it to her, in the tour he'd given her earlier. She'd had a hard time to keep from laughing, then, and now found herself smiling sarcastically. Morando had been quite proud of his "secret magical lair," dropping a number of hints that he was even skirting the edges of satanic rituals. But to someone like Bianca Casarini, for whom those rituals were a reality and had been for several years, Morando's fakery was obvious. The man was a charlatan, pure and simple. Somewhere along the line—perhaps in Milan, in the days when Casarini had first met him as they each plied their separate swindles—he'd learned just enough of the trappings to be able to put on a reasonably good show. Good, at least, to anyone who didn't know the truth.

She wasn't interested in any of that. The only reason she examined the "satanic altar" at all was to check for a secret passageway. There was none, as she'd expected. That would be too obvious.

There *had* to be a bolthole somewhere. Morando would not overlook something that basic. The man might be a charlatan when it came to magic, but Aldo Morando was a genuine professional when it came to his real trade. Trades, rather, since Morando was many things: procurer, swindler, narcotics peddler, seller of information. Anything, really, that was outside the law and involved no muscular effort other than copulation. When Bianca had discovered him on the island a month or so after she arrived herself, she'd practically crowed with glee. He'd make the perfect instrument for her plans. Countess Elizabeth Bartholdy's plans, rather. Working through Morando, Bianca could manipulate both Sophia Tomaselli and King Emeric's agent on the island, Fianelli.

Eventually, she found the bolthole. It was hidden, not by cleverness, but by the crude expedient of size. An entire wall in a very small side chamber in the cellar could be swung aside. Not easily or quickly, though. At least Morando kept the hinges well oiled.

Bianca frowned. Morando was getting careless. He'd been on Corfu too long, two years longer than Casarini herself, and it was evident that he'd picked up some of the slack nature of Corfu's society. In Milan, he'd have made sure to have a bolthole he could get through in a hurry. Duke Visconti's agents were ferociously shrewd as well as ferociously brutal.

So be it. Bianca Casarini had no intention of finding herself trapped in that cellar, after all. She'd mainly wanted to find the secret escape route to see if she could get *in*, not out. The countess wanted the coming siege protracted long enough to force her nephew Emeric to come to her for help. Eventually, however, the Hungarians would overwhelm the city—Bianca's orders were to delay Emeric's victory, not prevent it. And when that day came, she wanted to be well out of the rapine and carnage that was sure to follow. It had occurred to her, when Morando gave her his tour earlier, that the cellar would make the ideal place to hide during the sack of Kérkira.

She'd have to make sure that Morando was out of the way by then, of course. But Bianca was not particularly concerned about that. Most likely, in the long months of the approaching siege, Morando would outsmart himself and get arrested by the island's Venetian authorities. If not, Bianca herself would see to his removal, when the time came.

After, with considerable effort, prying the wall open wide enough to slip through, Bianca used the oil lamp to guide her down the narrow passageway beyond. She had to stoop, bent almost double, to make her way through it. The tunnel—it could hardly be called a "corridor"—looked to be ancient in its construction. It had probably been built when the stone building was first erected, centuries earlier.

It wasn't long. Some twenty yards down, after a single sharp bend, Sophia found herself in front of a grating looking out onto an alley. The grating was old too, the iron coated in rust. From the outside, to anyone passing by in the narrow and—she had no doubt, though she couldn't really see it in the dim light thrown by the oil lamp—filthy, garbage-strewn alleyway, the grating would attract no notice at all. A town as old as Kérkira had a multitude of such architectural oddities.

Inspecting with her fingers, she discovered that, here also, Morando had taken care to oil the hinges on the inside of the grating. He hadn't grown *that* careless. When and if the time came, the grating could be opened—where most such would be rusted shut.

So. All that remained was to examine the latch. It was a simple bolt on the inside—her side—of the grating, tucked out of sight of anyone in the alley. She experimented a bit and satisfied herself that she could reach through the grating and pry it open, when the time came.

A good night's work. Now moving quickly, Bianca retraced her steps and, soon enough, was silently lowering the flagstone over the secret entrance to the cellar. She returned the oil lamp to the kitchen; then, made a quick inspection of her body to make sure there were no tell-tale traces of her activities. Beyond cleaning the soles of her feet and wiping her hands on a rag, there was nothing. Bianca, unlike Morando, had not grown careless with the passage of time.

She returned to the bedroom and eased her way back into the bed. Morando grunted faintly, as her weight depressed the mattress, but didn't wake up.

Bianca started to sneer, in the darkness. Sloppy oaf! But she removed the expression almost instantly. First, reminding herself that she had a powerful motive for always remaining careful which Morando lacked—her quest for immortality. And, secondly, reminding herself that too many sneers would eventually disfigure her face. Eternity was . . . forever.

Chapter 26

Benito was frog-marched onto the galley, still with leg irons on. The Justices were making absolutely sure he didn't escape, he thought grumpily.

As if he'd want to while he was still here in Venice! He'd spent a number of days in prison, any one of which was a day too many. It had brought home to him just how valuable being able to do things really was—especially being able to come and to go at times of your own choosing. Reluctantly, Benito came to acknowledge that maybe Marco knew him better than he knew himself. Staring at those walls for a solid year would indeed have driven him crazy. And if the food wasn't quite as bad as the swill the *Casa* Dandelo had fed their slaves, it was pretty close. Even the water was vile. Wine was a vain dream.

So: He kept his head down, he kept his mouth shut, and he behaved himself, irons and all.

It was only when he saw Erik Hakkonsen, with Manfred, staring down at him that he realized they'd played yet another trick on him.

Erik had the keys to his manacles. They dangled loosely, but obviously, from his left hand. "I have been given the duration of the voyage to Corfu to drill some sense into you," said Erik coldly. "I have nine days, perhaps, so we will start right now. You will address me as 'Sir.' You will speak only when you are spoken to. And if you aren't quick enough to do as you are told I will beat you."

"What the hell am I doing on board ship with you?" Bonito blurted, more in surprise than anger.

He got a sharp slap about the ear from Erik. "Have you already forgotten what I have told you? *Sir.* Speak when you are spoken to. Do everything as fast as your flesh will allow."

Benito found himself fiery mad clear through to the core. Why the hell should he put up with this? It wasn't as if he'd been alone in his carousing. Manfred had been there too. He stuck his chin out. "Make me."

In later years he would say that this proved the wise proposition that stupidity provides its own punishment. Erik proceeded, coldly and methodically, to prove that yes, he *could* make Benito do what he was told to do. Or, at least, regret that he had failed to do it.

As he lay against the bulkhead later, groaning, he looked up when Manfred leaned over. The prince's grin was cheerful, but sympathetic. "Best just do it, Benito-boy. Erik is mad with both of us for partying when he thought I was tucked up in my little bed. What's even worse, he's crossed in love. He's in the vilest temper I've ever seen him. Most of the knights are creeping around on tiptoes. Me too."

Benito heard Erik's ominous voice. "Manfred, I think it is time that you and I had a little more drill together."

Manfred's big shoulders shook with suppressed laughter. "Not again, Erik! You beat up Benito for a while, that should do. You've got all the way to Jerusalem to take it out on me. And my ribs are still sore from yesterday."

Erik's face loomed over him, his chill eyes back on Benito. "Up," he said. "You aren't nearly as damaged as you think you are. And once you've warmed up properly, most of your bruises will stop hurting."

Benito was engaged in Erik's idea of warming-up exercises, which he suspected would have him dead on the deck, when relief in the shape of Marco and Kat arrived to bid him farewell. And, to his surprise, Petro Dorma was with them.

Petro had brought with him Benito's rapier, *main gauche,* and also several porters with the rest of Benito's clothing. "You sail within the hour, and it may be some years, five perhaps, before I see you again. I have taken one liberty. I have given to your grandfather the broken sword that was in the armoire in your room. The duke requested it. He says he will have it reforged, since one day you may wish to give it back to Sforza. In which case, he says, it will be more useful if has a point with which you can drive it home. I will have it sent to you."

Somehow that polite civility made it all worse. "Thank you. And Petro . . ."

"Yes?"

"I'm really sorry I made all this trouble. It's just . . ."

Petro smiled. "That is behind us. You understand that as the Doge I have to be seen to be fair, dispensing justice, rewards and punishments, with an impartial hand. Even to my wards; perhaps *especially* to my wards. Now. Go well. Enjoy Corfu. Report to my senior factor there."

"Couldn't I go somewhere else?" begged Benito. *"Please?"*

"No." Petro shook his head emphatically. "You will just have to learn to live with her there, too. I suggest you go and see her, make your peace. If, after a year or two I hear good reports from my factor, you will be transferred elsewhere to learn more of how the Dorma business is conducted. Now, farewell, Godspeed, and try to stay out of trouble, boy."

Benito swallowed. "I'll do my best, Petro."

The farewell to Marco was harder. He wouldn't be seeing his brother for years. They'd never been apart for more than a month. Even when Marco was hiding out in the Jesolo marshes, at least Benito had always known where he could try to find him if he needed to. Now it would be a long time before they saw each other again. "Good-bye, Marco. I'm sorry I've been such a fool."

Marco was as gracious as Petro, and more understanding, perhaps. After all, he'd done stupid things for love, too. "We've both done that, Benito. Please take care. I know you usually ended up looking after me, but I won't be there to help. Remember to write to us."

"I will," said Benito gruffly. "Kat, I hope I didn't spoil your special day for you. You know . . . I wish you both to be very, very happy."

Kat smiled radiantly at him. "I don't think anyone could have spoiled the day for us, Benito. And we didn't even know about your adventure, anyway, until after lunch the next day." She blushed rosily and looked sidelong at Marco. "We didn't get out of bed until then."

Benito reevaluated his brother's enjoyment of premarital favors. "Beds are better than bridges," he said with perfect sincerity.

"Benito!" They shook their heads at him in tandem. His brother sighed and smiled. "You're impossible, Benito."

Kat grinned. "But if he wasn't . . . well, we might never have met properly, Marco. And he did sort out our misunderstanding, dearest. We'll have to forgive him."

Marco hugged his brother. "I'm going to miss you, Benito."

"Yeah. Likewise."

Kat hugged him too. "Listen. Try to be understanding about Maria? Give her and little Alessia my love when you see them."

"I will do. I promise."

The capitano of the galley came up and bowed respectfully to Marco. "We'll need to be getting underway, Milord Valdosta," he said.

So Kat and Marco went. The ship cast off, and the rowers began edging her out into the lagoon, toward the sea. Benito watched and waved.

And then Erik bellowed in his ear.

By the time Benito collapsed into sleep that night he was: first, sore in places he hadn't even known he had muscles; second, awake to the realization that Erik was possibly an even better swordsman than Caesare had been.

Benito was a lot of things, but a fool he was not. Not about learning combat skills anyway. Erik had had him in a quilted jacket, practicing with a blunt-edged, round-pointed rapier until he could barely keep the point up. Then Erik had pulled up a grizzled old knight, who was at least as broad as he was high. "Semmens's weapon of choice is the axe or the morningstar. He will drill you for an hour. You're not really big enough for those weapons, but knowing how they work will help you to stay alive when people armed with either are trying to kill you."

Then, when it seemed things could get no worse . . . Eneko Lopez came up on deck. "I have been asked by Petro Dorma to see to your spiritual welfare. This task is probably beyond me, but I will do my best."

He did, with an incisive tongue. When he finally left, Benito realized that having his brother's superb memory would have been more useful at this point than an ability to climb buildings. He also knew a great deal more than he had about Saint Hypatia, Saint Simon, and aspects of ecclesiastical magic he'd never even considered before. Magic was more complex and more frightening than he'd realized. He wished Marco wasn't involved in it.

Then more drill. Then Erik produced a stocky, bow-legged knight with the characteristic blue-speckled facial powder burns of a bombardier. The bombardier had a peculiarly high voice, totally out of keeping with his "pet": a small cannon, chased, ornate and heavy.

"Erik Hakkonsen has told me that the best way to your mind is to drub it into your hinder end with the flat of a sword. However I am prepared to give your mind a chance. If it fails, I will assist it with this cleansing rod. If you are lucky, I will only beat you with it."

By the time the day ended, Benito was only too glad to collapse into an exhausted sleep. To think he'd once dreamed of being one of these Knights!

The great eellike creature burrowed into the ooze and lay as still as if its physical movement could betray it to that which sailed above. The adversary's presence and magic burned like a balefire on an overcast moonless night to the shaman's perceptions. He lay still and tried not to even think. If he could sense the adversary ... then surely the mage could feel him?

For weeks now, his hawks had watched the roads away from the great marshes. He had driven them into it at first. He had nearly lost both birds doing that. Not only had the ancient lord of that place detected his hold, and sent his creatures to harry the hawks, but it had also attacked and somehow weakened the bonds that the shaman used to control them. The shaman found his creatures far less biddable now. They would turn and hunt, even when he commanded them to follow. And they would not go out over the open sea. It was contrary to their natures, but that had not stopped them obeying him before. They were becoming wilder, more their own, less his.

Above him the ships sailed on. At last he felt safe. As soon as he was sure this was the case he called: Master, open the way.

Not with his voice, of course; this shape didn't have a voice.

The answer came immediately; a kind of hole in the real world opened before him, with a shimmering green-black curtain across the mouth of it that kept off the seawater. Not a round hole, though;

more a kind of rift, an outline that changed constantly, warping and writhing like a living thing.

The great eel-shaped creature swam through the twisty contorted gap between the real and the spirit world. The passage, too, twisted and writhed from moment to moment. But the monster was well shaped for negotiating it.

He fell out of the passage onto the floor of the palace, where Jagiellon waited. The shaman shook himself back into a shape that could speak, taking care that the shape was prostrate on the floor before he tried to utter a word. One could not be too servile with Jagiellon.

He bowed his head right down onto the stone. "Master. The adversary is at sea. He sails south from Venice." Only when the report was given did he look up.

The black eyes glowed. "I fear he must somehow have gotten wind of my plans for Corfu. The old shrines there must be far more powerful places than I had realized. They must be found, and the rites of blood enacted there. And if possible we must destroy Eneko Lopez. Sink him beneath the waves before he gets to Corfu. Where are the Byzantines and Emeric?"

"Master, Emeric's galleys are already at sea. His army should be landing on Corfu by morning. The rest of his fleet is still to the north of the island."

"I am aware. My slave Aldanto is with them. Emeric plans to blockade the straits of Otranto. It will be difficult to do this effectively. But maybe his blockading fleet, and those that come with the rest of his troops, can be used to kill Eneko Lopez. That could be worth more than Corfu itself, in the long run."

Jagiellon's eyes flared. "You will return. Keep a watch over my adversary. I will use the slave Aldanto to direct forces against them. There are several of the galliots with the transport fleet of carracks. Between you and the slave they can be directed to contact the blockading galliots. We will direct them like a pincer on Eneko Lopez."

The priestess in the cave was old. The magics drew more from her each year. Soon she must find another acolyte to serve the great Goddess. Someone who could chant the ancient words, and who could instruct the women in the rites. It was no small responsibility.

And there must be a new bride for Him. Of course, ideally, the two should be one and the same. But that happened very rarely; not for many centuries now.

She sighed. Well, spring was here. And, though men might war and burn, the earth and the women of the island would bring forth new life.

Chapter 27

The outcomes of great ventures often hinge on small things. In this case it hinged on a southerly wind, and the price crates of cuttlefish were fetching at the fish-market at Kérkira. A few copper pennies increase in price had formed the basis of Taki Temperades' decision. The best time to catch cuttlefish, in these parts, was the twilight and the predawn, and the best place was the bay of Vlores some ninety miles north of Corfu.

The southerly wind had delayed Emeric's carracks. The galleys were forced to anchor in the bay of Vlores and wait.

Captain Taki left Corfu with four crewmen, some cheap wine, a lot of cuttlefish jigs and a sail-full of southerly wind in the late afternoon. The moon was full and the run simple. The wine was bad, but not that bad. The wind was dropping toward early morning. Taki was pleased by that. It meant it would swing to the north by dawn.

Taki's ratty little fishing boat rounded Cape Gjuhezes. The Corfiote skipper looked at the town of vessels lying there, in the sea-mist.

"Bloody Illyrian sons of bitches!" slurred the captain. He'd had quite a lot of that wine. "Stealing my fishing . . ." He shook his fist at the multitude of ships.

Spiro looked up from where he'd been busy with his horsehair lines. "Well, the cuttlefish must be as thick as flies on horseshit for so many vessels."

They sailed silently toward the ships, ghosting in on the last breaths of the wind. It had been dying and turning to westerly

anyway or there would have been no wind here at all. The moon
was nearly down. On one of the ships a horse snorted. Someone
said something to someone else. Across the water the voice carried clearly. It wasn't Greek. Or Italian Frankish.

"Turn, Taki. Turn now," whispered Spiro. His eyes were wide,
taking in the size of the vessels they were now nearly between.
"Those aren't fishing boats."

Taki didn't need telling. He swung the rudder hard across. The
sail flapped lazily. "Pull it down!" he whispered urgently. "I'll get
the others up. We start rowing, quietly." Taki wasn't drunk any
more. Just scared.

As quietly as they could, expecting yells behind them at any
moment, the fishermen eased themselves out past the cape, out
of direct sight. Taki slumped against the tiller. "Saint Spirodon
preserve us! That's the last time I drink that terrible *Kakotrigi* of
Yani's. We nearly sailed into them! Let's get that sail up and get
out of here!"

"Who the hell are they?" asked Kosti, the youngest of the fishermen, hauling on the coarse rope to pull the single patched sail
up again.

"Byzantine-style galleys," said Spiro, also hauling, for once not
being sarcastic.

"And Narenta galliots," added Taki, shortly. Like Spiro and most
of the islanders, Taki had done a stint or two as crew on Venetian ships. It was hard work, but the money was good, if you could
hang onto it. He knew a pirate galliot's looks from close up. That
was why he'd come home and become a fisherman. A fishing boat
was such a poor target, with so little loot, most pirates wouldn't
bother. Mostly, as a fisherman, you didn't go hungry, and the
wine—so long as you didn't set your standards too high—was
cheap on Corfu.

"But horses!" exclaimed Kosti! "And what did that person say?
It wasn't Greek."

"I don't know. I reckon it was trouble, though. And that's our
catch gone," said Taki, sourly.

Up on the headland a Serb guard stamped his feet in the cold.
The bay behind him was shrouded in sea-mist. But what was that
out there on the dark water? It could be a sail. He squinted at
it for a while and then went off to call the guard commander.

Make it that son of a bitch's decision whether to wake someone else.

Emeric stared at the shivering Serbs, guard and commander. "A small vessel. Why didn't you report it earlier? Where had it come from?"

"Y-Your Majesty." The guard pointed out of the tent mouth. "The mist. I just saw it. I called Micholovich . . ."

The man looked like he was going to soil himself. But what he'd said was true; no one could see far in this. And the man had at least reported it.

Most likely a coaster or a fishing boat, Emeric decided. As likely as not the mist had hidden the fleet, too. There was not much use in sending a galley. If the mist was this thick at sea they'd never find it. But it was a sign: Waiting would not do. Sooner or later vessels would find them, and he wanted to strike an unguarded target. One more day, and carracks or no carracks, they'd launch the attack.

By the next day when the story got home to Kérkira, it had grown somewhat. By afternoon, the story was all over the streets of the town. By sunset, the commander of the garrison had Captain Taki Temperades in his office.

Taki had a good memory—at least when fueled by fear. He remembered fairly closely the foreign words he'd heard, even if he hadn't understood them. And the garrison commander had been stationed in Istria. Commander Leopoldo knew a little Hungarian. Enough to recognize one swear-word.

The detachment on Corfu was a relatively small one, doing little more than policing work. Nine hundred men, some mercenaries, some Venetian marines. Fifty cavalrymen, nominally under the command of Captain-General Tomaselli. In practice, Leopoldo saw to the day-to-day running of most things, not just the garrison itself. This was Gino Leopoldo's first command post and he was determined to do well. Rumor had it that this could be Tomaselli's last command, and he might be able to replace him.

The commander had the *Capi* of the Cavalry in his office, before the sweating fisherman was going to be allowed to depart.

The cavalryman was skeptical. "I don't know, Captain. These Greeks exaggerate. Probably one vessel with a horse on her."

Taki wrung his hat. "Your honor. It was a lot of ships. I don't count too well, your honor. But Narenta galliots I know. And Greek imperial ships. My cousin Dimitri did service on one. I went to see him when he was stationed at Levkas. I saw them in Constantinople, too."

"And there is no way he makes up Hungarian blasphemy," said Leopoldo. "I want some men stationed on the slopes of Pantocrator. I don't know if this man was seeing things, I don't know if they're coming here, but I'm not taking a chance. We have to start preparing for siege."

He pulled a face. "I'll have to go and talk to the captain-general and the podesta. If people are going to be called into the Citadel, he has to authorize it."

"And stationing my men on the mountain? It's a waste of time. You should talk to Tomaselli about that."

The young commander looked at him in absolute silence. Eventually the *capi* said: "All right, then. It'll be done. But it is a waste of time."

Commander Leopoldo looked at Taki. "And you stay here before you chase the prices up in the market."

Taki leaned against the wall. "I think you're too late. The *capi* may not believe me, but the peasants do. You'll find the peasants are driving their flocks up into the hills, and sending their wives and children up, too."

The garrison commander snorted. "You stay in that corner."

The table, King Emeric thought, reflected his genius. There, molded in damp sand, was a reasonable scale model of Corfu and the Albanian coast. He'd studied the island from the Albanian shore. He'd assessed it from the sea-side nearly two months prior to that.

"It will be a three-pronged attack," said the king, pointing to his model. "Count Ladislas, you will disembark with your men, three hundred of your finest, here on the western side of the island directly in line with Corfu-town—Kérkira, as the Greeks call it. You will proceed with as much speed as you can overland. Seize a few locals for guides. Make sure that they give no warning. You should arrive at Kérkira about dawn. They have a habit of opening the gates at that time to allow inside the women of the town who work in the fortress. If possible you are simply to occupy the fortress. Admiral Volos, you will be in charge of the galley fleet coming around from the south. Should my flag be flying over the fortress, you will have a holiday."

There was polite laughter. "See that you enter the strait between the mainland and the island at dawn. Not before. If we have not taken the fortress, your men are to land and join the assault. The few cannon we have already will be landed with you." He turned on the chieftain of the Narenta pirates. "Chief Rappalli. You and yours will sail through the strait from the north. You are going to carry the Croats. Set them ashore to the north of the town. You will then take up the positions assigned to you in the North Channel. Sink any vessels attempting to flee the island. I warn you. If I find your men ashore, looting, while boats flee and spread the word . . ." Emeric drew his finger across his throat.

"Now. We are undermanned for this. The carracks with the bulk of our men have not yet been sighted. The forty-eight-pound siege cannon are still coming, behind them. If we need to put the island under siege . . . well, the men and the cannon will be here. But in this, speed and surprise are our allies. We still outnumber the garrison five to one. If my Magyar cavalry can strike at the fort as it opens at dawn . . . we're in."

Taki had sat quietly in the corner of Garrison Commander Leopoldo's office. It was a big, dim room. Officers and officials had come and gone. The scruffy Greek fisherman went on sitting in his corner. It was cool and comfortable. It was only when the garrison commander was finally ready to call it a night that Taki cleared his throat and asked, "Can I go home now?"

The commander had started in surprise. "I forgot you were here," he said gruffly. "Yes, get along with you. You've heard all sorts of things you shouldn't have. On the other hand, I don't suppose it makes much difference."

So Taki had found his way to his cottage on the western shore late, and, for a change, sober. He'd done a fair amount of thinking, sitting there in the corner. Early the next morning he'd gone around to the houses of his crew.

"I'm not going fishing anywhere," grumbled Kosti. "We might meet those galleys. I thought I'd go and visit some relations in the mountains."

"We're not going fishing," said Taki. "We're just making sure that we've got a boat to go fishing in, when all of this is over. Now get up. We'll need Spiro and my cousin Yani."

"Yani?" Kosti asked curiously stirring himself into an upright position. 'What do you want him for?"

"He's got a dingy," said Taki shortly. "We'll need it to get home."

Kosti pulled his shirt on. He pointed up the hill. "He's off burying his wine. I think it can only improve that last vintage."

Taki snorted. "I wouldn't bother putting it underground myself."

Kosti chuckled. "Spiro offered to drink it all for him. He reckoned it would end up in the ground that way, anyway."

Taki shook his head. "Spiro would drink anything."

Kosti laughed. "That's what he says about you, skipper."

"It is, is it? Well, I'll go and wake him up," said Taki. "I went to bed sober last night. I hope he's got a sore head on him this morning. You go and see if you can find Yani. Ask him to pick us up on the place we collect firewood from."

Together they sailed the old boat out to a little rocky islet off-shore. The current side of the islet was piled high with driftwood and debris from the winter storms. Taki made a habit of coming out here in the summer every year when it had dried out nicely, to load up with firewood.

"You reckon they're definitely coming?" Spiro asked, holding his head. "I don't feel like doing a whole lot of heavy labor for nothing. The last time I felt like this I was in Venice. I got beaten up and nearly killed by a *Case Vecchie* kid who turned out to be a lot tougher than he looked. This time it was just the wine."

Taki shrugged. "Where else could they be going? Once this is done I'm going to spend a few days up in the hills. Once they get over their looting and burning we can come back and get the old boat in the water again. They'll want fish, whoever wins."

Using some logs as rollers, they began to haul the fishing boat up onto the islet.

"Do you think the Venetians stand a chance?" asked Kosti.

Taki shrugged again. "What difference does it make to us? Or any fisherman or peasant?"

Spiro grimaced. "According to my grandfather, they're not the worst landlords."

"But they're not Greeks," said Kosti. "At least it would be a Greek island again."

Spiro grunted with effort, and the boat moved ⟨

"You should hear what sorts of taxes some of my m⟨

on Ithaca pay. So little they have to eat roots and ⟨

tend they're being starved."

"Uh-huh. Is that the people you said were no better⟨

"Shut up, Kosti!" said Taki, hastily. Young Kosti still ⟨...⟩t learned that it was all very well for a man to insult his own relatives, but you'd better not do it for him. Even if he had said it to you earlier. "Let's cover the old scow up with this driftwood. I want it to look like it's all part of it."

"That shouldn't be hard," said Kosti.

Taki gritted his teeth and set about stepping the mast. Kosti really had better learn to watch that mouth of his. Spiro was as sarcastic as a man could be, but somehow you always knew that he was joking.

Yani came along in his dingy at about midday. "Hurry up, Taki. I've still got some wine to move out."

With the four of them in the dingy, water had been slopping over the gunwales. Still, they made it back to the shore without throwing Kosti overboard. Then Yani and Taki loaded a few limestone boulders into the boat, took the dingy back out into the cove Taki launched out of. Having firmly anchored it with some rocks in a net-bag . . .

They sank it.

Yani knew his cousin well enough not to doubt what he'd seen off the Albanian coast. And Taki was ready to bet there were a good few carefully sunken boats around the island. A sunken boat couldn't be burned, smashed, or stolen. With a bit of patience and a few oxen—or even enough donkeys or just strong backs— it could be hauled out again.

Maria put the platter of grilled fish on the table in front of Umberto. "The prices in the marketplace today are just unbelievable. I wanted some chestnut-flour to make castagnaccio. Apparently, never mind chestnut-flour, there is no flour to be had at all. What's going on, Umberto?"

The gray-haired man rubbed his eyes tiredly. "There's a rumor about that there is a fleet of ships up the coast. Of course everyone believes they'll come here. It's probably nothing more than a bunch of pirates. They'll not trouble Venetian shipping or

Venetian possessions. Put off buying for a few days. The prices will come back down. And maybe I'll be able to get those idle fools in the boatyard to stop begging for news and doing some work instead," he finished irritably.

"There's no truth in it?" she asked, rocking Alessia's cradle with a foot.

He shook his head. "I doubt it. Some fisherman came in with the story. The man's a notorious drunkard, to hear the locals tell of it. You'd probably find the ships were pink and crewed by worms if anyone bothered to question him properly."

Maria nodded. And resolved to go and buy what she could. As a canaler, rather than a guildsman, she had a lot more faith in what fishermen claimed to have seen. She'd already bought basic household supplies in the first days, being pleasantly surprised by the low prices here, this far from Venice, of things like olive oil, honey and wine. She'd been unable to resist the bargain of a huge crock of olive oil. She had ample flour for a month . . . Salt fish had still been available . . . dried figs. They'd get used, eventually.

"I did think we might buy a goat. There is a pen in the back yard. And a chicken coop. I've never kept these things, but the goat would be useful for milk and cheese. Chickens lay eggs."

Umberto nodded. "So long as you don't spend too much on them."

"Very well. I'll see what I can find. Will you be back for lunch?"

Umberto shook his head. "No. I'll take something with me. There is a sea of paperwork to catch up on." He sighed. "This is not an easy task. The yard is an unhappy place, full of fighting. And the Greeks and the guildsmen are all as lazy as can be. My predecessor made up for lack of method by ordering huge stocks of everything. So: I have several years worth of stock of cladding timber, some keel and mast timbers we'll likely never use and enough pitch to caulk the entire Venetian fleet—but no brass nails, and barely a handful of tow."

When he had finished his breakfast and gone back to work, Maria took her largest basket and Alessia, and walked. There was no point in heading for the market, not when she was looking for living things instead of foodstuffs. But this was not such a big place that she couldn't reach a peasant cottage outside town.

After an hour's walk, Maria was less convinced she'd find what she was after. By the deserted status of the peasant houses, *they* certainly believed there was trouble coming. She was now away from the coast, and she could see the scallops of azure bay, and Kérkira, white in the morning sunshine. The air was already thick and warm and full of the scent of the fine-leaved shrubs by the roadside. Bees buzzed lazily while collecting their bounty from the flowers. Except for the empty cottages, stripped of everything moveable, it would have been hard to believe there was anything that could go wrong in this Eden.

Eventually she found a man and his wife struggling to remove an iron bedstead from a cottage. There were a couple of hens in the yard.

"Good day."

"Day to you too, kyria."

Maria was startled. *Kyria?* Lady? She'd dressed in an old dress, a relic of her days as a canaler. Then she realized that she spoke Venetian-accented Frankish, not Greek. The Venetians had been here for more than a hundred years and all the islanders she'd met could certainly understand the language. But Maria had rapidly gathered that there was a strong divide between even the lowliest Venetians and the local people. Among the women of the garrison this seemed to be even more of an issue. Greeks were servants! And one had to keep them in their place. You didn't speak to them. You gave them orders. Besides . . . she wore shoes. That set one apart from peasant women.

Maria set the basket and Alessia down, and took a hand with the bedstead. It was obviously the poor cottage's pride and joy, and the most treasured piece of furniture. A bed and the bedclothes were the one thing that the rent-collectors could not seize for debt, so they were usually the finest piece of furniture in the peasant houses, she'd been told.

The man and his wife nearly dropped it when Maria came to help. Their jaws certainly dropped.

The doorway had two broad buttresses outside. Inside, the door to the room that they were trying to take the bedstead out of was at such an angle that the bedstead just couldn't do the corner without hitting the strut. After a few moments of struggle Maria asked: "How did it get in?"

The man shrugged. "I do not know, lady. My grandfather put it in before I was born. There was only one room then."

Maria's patience was exhausted. Besides, she'd walked a long way carrying a baby on a hot morning. She took charge. There were some advantages to being a lordly foreigner. The peasant wouldn't have taken such instructions from his wife. "Put the end down. It'll have to stand on end to get it out."

At an angle, stood on end and scraping the white-washed clay, the bedstead came through.

The peasants grinned. "Lady, you are clever. And strong too," said the man admiringly. "Where do you come from?"

"Venice."

The peasant shook his head. "Can't be. Eh, Eleni? The women who come to the garrison and villas, they all are weak."

The wife nodded. "Anastasia is in service at Villa Foiri. She says the woman cannot even pick up a dish for herself."

Maria laughed. "They aren't weak, just lazy. Too lazy to do for themselves what they can pay someone else to do!"

This provoked laughter from both. "Why, lady, they say *we* are the lazy ones!"

Alessia stirred, and Maria went to her. The peasant wife looked longingly and adoringly at the baby. "She is so beautiful, lady."

Maria wondered why people always said babies were beautiful. She loved Alessia more than anything, but she wouldn't have called her baby "beautiful." Plump, yes. Soft and tiny, yes. Adorable, yes. "She is very lovely when she's asleep."

The peasant was plainly keeping out of this women's talk. "Eleni, why don't you bring us some of that young white wine and some food. It has been hot work, but now, thanks to the lady, the worst job is over."

Eleni nodded. "Sit, lady." She motioned to the bedstead. Her husband had already taken up the important task of supporting a tree, by sitting against it in the shade.

"I'll give you a hand," Maria offered. "I was brought up to know my way about a kitchen, never mind what the others do."

They went into the cool, dim cottage. The kitchen was around the back, actually a separate little room—the only light coming either from the hole in the roof or the door. The only "furnishing" was a hearth a few inches high, and a few small soot-blackened shelves. By comparison, Maria realized her little home was a palace.

The young peasant woman had plainly decided that such a person could be trusted with the innermost secrets of the heart. Questions about pregnancy and birthing followed as she took bread, olives and cheese, and a clay jug of wine from places in her kitchen and loaded these onto a board.

"I think I am pregnant," she confided in a whisper. "I have not . . . Yani and I have been married for three years and I have had no children. But this year I have been to the mountains. To the holy place for the dancing." She giggled. "It was very cold without my clothes on. But I will be blessed this year." She touched Alessia with a gentle hand.

She seemed to assume Maria knew what she was talking about.

They went outside, and woke her husband. The wine was cool and crisp, the bread crusty. The olives, wrinkled, tiny and black, were flavored with some rosemary. They ate in silence. Peasant table manners were simple: Talk and food did not go together. Maria smiled. Back in the days she'd been trying to learn to be more ladylike to please Caesare, one of the hardest things she'd had to try to master was the idea of eating and talking at the same time. It gave you indigestion. It was pleasant to slip back into the business of taking food seriously and talking later.

But when the eating was done, then it was time for talk and for business.

Maria found herself learning a great deal about the fleet that had been spotted at the bay of Vlores. She also found herself walking back to Corfu town leading a kid that did not wish to be led, and with a dozen fresh eggs, a crock of olives and some cheese. And with two disgruntled-looking brown chickens in her basket, their feet tied with twine and attached to the wicker.

Chapter 28

On the slopes of Mount Pantocrator, two bored mercenary cavalrymen were preparing a late dinner of a skinny fowl that some peasant was going to be very upset about in the morning. Spatchcocked and grilling over the flames, it had more of their attention than the sea-watch their not very impressed *capi* had ordered them to keep. They had every intent of finishing their chicken and some young wine, and sleeping beside the embers of the olive-wood fire. Gurnošec was a Slovene, and his companion from Lombardy. Their loyalty to the Venetian Republic was purely financial.

Still, when the one got up from the fire and wandered into the dark a bit to relieve himself of some of that young wine . . . he did glance at the moonlit sea. He nearly wet his boots.

"Chicken looks about done, Gurni," said his companion, from the fireside.

"Forget the sodding chicken! We'd better get to our horses." His tone of voice told his Lombard companion that this was no joke. The man stood up and came away from the fire.

"What is it?"

The Slovene pointed at the sea. "This wasn't the stupidest idea that Commander Leopoldo ever had after all."

The chicken, untended, burned. The cavalrymen riding through the dark olives had other things on their minds. Was a real war worth what they were being paid? And would it be possible to go somewhere healthier? Both of them now saw, with crystal clarity, the folly of taking service which involved being posted on an island.

The bells were ringing in Kérkira three hours later. The sound carried a long way. Up in the hills, other church bells took up the chime. The sound carried across the water.

Count Ladislas ground his teeth. "Well, so much for surprise," he said grimly.

His second in command patted his horse's flank. "They'll be expecting attack from the sea. If we can cross the causeway-bridge we'll still be in. We'll take them."

Count Ladislas said nothing. But that in itself was a condemnation.

They landed at a fishing harbor on the western coast—nothing more than a beach with a few boats pulled up. The island hills loomed dark beyond. The moon was down, and ripping a local or two out of their beds ought to have been easy. But Count Ladislas soon realized that they'd been watched. The doors were still swinging in some of the little whitewashed houses as they rode past. Finding a guide was not going to be that easy, after all.

However, there was a track leading inland. And it was a distance of not more than two or three leagues to the Venetian fortress on the other side of the island. The Magyar cavalry rode off on the heavy horses, up through the olive groves, vineyards and fields. It was very dark, and the track—for it could hardly be called a road—was quite indistinct.

Two or three leagues can be a very long way in the dark. Especially when She who watched over the island did not love invaders.

The hills and Mediterranean scrub on them were a good enough grazing place for goats. They'd found the goats, but not the goatherd. Just a dead-end valley. In the darkness, the scrub oak and myrtle bushes were sweet-scented. Pleasant for a ramble, the place was hell for an officer in a hurry. They found two peasant farms and huts, but no peasants. Dawn eventually found them on a hilltop a good league from the eastern shore, and a league too far to the north.

By the smoke puffs, the Croats had already entered the town of Kérkira and were now attempting to assault the fortified Citadel.

The Citadel was most definitely closed up and was most definitely returning fire on the Croats. The Venetian fortress, as Ladislas could now see, was going to be no pushover. It was on an islet just to seaward of the town. The wooden causeway he and his men had been intended to take by speed was reduced to a few smoking piles on the far shore.

So much for rushing it. The burning houses in the town, outside the walls, showed the Croats had been busy. It was unlikely they'd done much to the fortified Citadel though. All they'd achieved was to get shot at.

Count Ladislas sighed. King Emeric was not going to be pleased. He never was when his plans went awry, which they frequently did because he was inclined to excessively complex ones. The failure of his plans was always blamed on the errors of his officers when they went wrong, and attributed to his genius when they went right—despite the fact that success, as often as not, meant that some officer had disobeyed.

Still, they'd better get down there.

Taki leaned back against the big granite boulder and looked at the Hungarian cavalrymen. Saint Spirodon! Those horses were big! He and old Georgio had had quite a night up here with the devils. Of course they hadn't really been chasing after them or even Georgio's goats—as they discovered when they abandoned the goats. It had just seemed as if they were being followed.

They'd choose a place no sane man would go—if he wasn't chasing you—and the horsemen would come around the bend. They'd covered a good three leagues in the last few hours and these crazy soldiers must have ridden a lot more.

He watched in relief as the three hundred horsemen set off for the Viros road. Kérkira was burning down there. He looked gloomily at the scene, at the backs of the Hungarians, then at the black smoke from what had been a sweet taverna once. He wasn't surprised to see other Corfiote heads popping up from the underbrush of another hillside. They wouldn't be able to stay up here forever, but until the worst excesses were over, a lot of the peasantry would stay in the hills. It was still not summer, still cold at night, but at least it wasn't winter. And maybe She would provide. You never knew.

❀   ❀   ❀

There really was nothing worth destroying out here. The town of Kérkira outside the walls of the Venetian fortress was ruined or burning. Out of range of the arquebusiers on the walls, the Croats and Hungarians milled about ineffectually. By the screams, some of them had managed to find a woman. Or maybe not; a man with his privates blown off screamed like a woman, sometimes. Riderless horses roamed, wild-eyed. The air was full of gunpowder, smoke and shouts. Occasional cannon fire from the walls increased the carnage, and the invaders, without cannon, were unable to even return fire.

Count Ladislas knew by then that it was a complete fiasco. The fort and its cannon could defend the harbor very effectively. The buildings the Croats had been firing indiscriminately belonged not to the Venetians, but to the locals. They provided at least some rudimentary cover from the cannon fire . . . So the Croats were burning them. Wonderful.

True, the fortress was in reality designed to defend from attack by sea. The larger cannon would be there. But, no doubt, they could be moved. Ladislas couldn't really see how the situation could get any worse.

And then, looking back down the slope he realized it could— at least on a personal scale. That was one of the king's messengers. And by the way he was riding, His Majesty wanted someone in a hurry. With a terrible, sinking feeling in his gut, Count Ladislas realized that Emeric's messenger was looking for him.

Emeric of Hungary believed in personal comfort. He'd come close to the fighting, but not close enough to risk actual combat. Still, he'd been close enough on his hillside, outside his hastily erected palatial tent, to have seen Count Ladislas and his precious Magyar cavalry arrive too late. He watched them discharge their wheel-lock pistols ineffectually at the fortress wall across the empty kill-zone.

The narrow streets of Kérkira were no place for a cavalry charge. Emeric, instead of watching the victory he'd expected, had seen his plan totally unravel.

As Count Ladislas had known, someone was going to suffer for this and he had a feeling it would be himself. The king stood outside the tent. Count Ladislas dismounted and gave his great war-horse, seventeen hands at the shoulder and his pride and joy, a last pat. He hoped they'd find a good master for him.

He knelt before the king. There were little livid spots of fury on Emeric's sallow cheeks.

"You incompetent, bungling fool!" A quirt slashed at the count's face. He did his best not to flinch, as the blood began trickling down his cheek. "Where have your men been? Why did you come after the attack? Are you a coward, Ladislas? I don't tolerate cowards. Or incompetents!"

Count Ladislas knew the truth would serve him badly. "Sire. The peasant we took as a guide was there simply to betray us. He led us into an ambush the Venetian scum had prepared for us. Your heavy cavalry flattened them, Sire. But they knew we were coming. Someone must have betrayed us!"

The Count played on the king's passion for heavy cavalry and his belief that they could ride anything down. It was not a hard belief to feed. The Count believed in it himself. He also played on Emeric's belief that treachery lay everywhere.

For a brief moment, Count Ladislas thought it had been enough. Emeric's cruel eyes narrowed. Then he shook his head. "The peasant you found just happened to lead you into an ambush? Ha." The quirt lashed at the other cheek viciously. "Where is this peasant?"

No use looking to see how many of your troops the cannon were taking down when you charged. Straight ahead and devil take the hindmost. Scarred cheeks were a small price to pay for his life. "Sire. I ran him through myself. The village was deserted, except for this one man. He was hiding, but not well. He ran out of a building my men entered. He claimed he'd come down secretly after the others had left to steal some wine."

Emeric stared at him. Then shook his head. "Truth or not, I'll have to make an example. You love that horse, don't you?"

The Count had held back the cold sweat with difficulty. Now he felt the sweat pouring out. "Sire . . ." he croaked. "That horse is great bloodstock. Some of the finest bloodstock we've bred. Don't kill him, Sire. Kill me."

Emeric reached out his hands and put them on the count's shoulders. "I'm not going to kill your horse. It is far too valuable. You, on the other hand, Count Ladislas, are not. Your horse is going to kill you."

The king's brows flared satanically. "You've heard I am a man-witch? You've heard that I derive my strength from the pain of my victims?"

That wasn't all the Count had heard. "S-sire, please."

The king smiled, like a kill-mad weasel. Agony washed through the count, flowing from those hands. "It is true. All of it."

The Magyar officers stood in a silent circle. The corral that had been hastily knocked together contained their former commanding officer. And a horse he'd trained to follow him like a dog.

Count Ladislas had been a brutally efficient officer, but he'd loved that horse. Now, his eyes, fixed on the once beloved steed, were full of terror. The king reached out his hands and touched the horse. The animal screamed like a woman, reared and backed away. The king stepped out through the gate.

The horse was . . . shivering. Its eyes rolled, and its lips peeled back. It turned, then, its mad eyes suddenly fixed on the count. He tried to climb the corral, but the Magyar flung him back at the king's command. He scrambled to his feet in front of the advancing horse.

The horse lunged forward to bite and lash out with his iron-clad hooves. Ladislas dived, but the war-horse was faster. A hoof caught him and flung him into the rails. Blood flew. The Count was a tough and a strong man, though. He grabbed at his horse's mane and vaulted onto its back

The great horse went berserk. It dropped and rolled; kicking epileptically.

It took a while to kill the count. But eventually the horse stood, head hung low. And in a bloody ruin lay the remains of the Magyar commanding officer.

Emeric walked into the corral. The horse backed off. Emeric spat on the corpse and turned to the silent audience of Magyar cavalrymen. "Learn. If I order you to be at a place at a certain time— you will be there."

Towards midday King Emeric gathered his commanders on the hilltop overlooking Kérkira. Smoke and ruins surrounded the island fortress called the Citadel, but it was undamaged. "We have a handful of four-pounders. Not enough to make a dent on their walls. We have, however, an effective sea blockade in place. We have, even if the Greeks fail to stop the returning convoys, some months to reduce their defenses."

He pointed to a savagely scarred man. "You, General Krovoko, are going to remain here. You're in charge of the assault on the Citadel. You'll have cannon shortly, even if I have to go back to the Narenta mouth myself to find Dragorvich, the rest of troops, and the rest of my cannon. In which case, heads will roll."

He pointed to the Greek admiral and the chieftain who headed the fleet of Narenta pirate galliots. "You will arrange the blockade. I will have one ship captain's head for any vessel that escapes. On the other hand, the loot is yours—except for one fifth, which is mine. You will arrange how it is divided, Admiral. I leave it in your hands. Make me satisfied with the arrangements."

He turned to the second in command of the three hundred Magyar cavalry. "You are promoted into Count Ladislas' shoes. See that you fill them better than he did, Commander Hegedes. The cavalry will be of little use in this siege phase. See the locals are suitably cowed. Strip the Venetian estates. One fifth for Hungary. Two fifths for the besiegers . . . on success. Two fifths for the cavalry. When you've done that, let these Corfiotes know who their new masters are."

"Sire, it will be done to perfection," Hegedes stated crisply. "You'll be proud of us."

"I'd better be," said Emeric. "You've seen what happens to those who fail me."

As she held Alessia close, Maria listened to the thunder of the cannon. A pall of smoke hung over the city outside the walls, the fresh morning breeze bringing the smell of gunpowder and burning. War might sometimes be the stuff of song and full of dreams of glory for men. But a part of her knew without any telling that for women and children, wars were hell.

And sieges were usually worse.

She looked through opened shutters at the small walled courtyard. The goat-kid was eating the grass that straggled through the paving stones, ignoring the patch of grass farther back. The chickens were pecking about. Cannon fire hadn't put them off laying. It was still a pitifully small extra ration toward the siege she knew would come. It might be five or six months before some relief came to the fortress. Maybe longer.

The raiders had timed this well: The Venetian convoys were gone until autumn. Occasional vessels would have come past, little tarettes trading up the coast. But it could easily take two or three weeks before the news even got to Venice—if the invaders weren't sinking every vessel they could find. If they were, then it would take longer. Except . . . there were the vessels that Prince Manfred, Erik and the Knights were traveling to the Holy Land in. Great galleys, if she remembered rightly. They should get away, surely?

The thought of these vessels brought Svanhild to mind. Lord! She was out there somewhere, in an unprotected villa. Maria bit her lip. What could she do about it? A prayer maybe.

Smelling the smoke, Maria's thoughts turned to the peasants she'd been with only yesterday. Would they have managed to hide from the raiders?

A mangy, vicious-looking yellow dog hanging around the edges of the crowd snarled at a cavalryman who had made a move to kick it. The cavalryman picked up a stone and the dog slunk off into a gully. But the shaman had heard and seen enough. He walked away toward the water's edge to assume his other form. The sea attack on his Master's adversary needed orchestration. He was becoming quite casual about following the adversary-mage now. The mage did not seem to be able to detect him. That was very odd, but quite welcome. And foolish.

Chapter 29

"The other guild foremen and assistant-foremen have got to go and see the captain-general," said Umberto unhappily. "He has sent for us."

"I hope it isn't his wife complaining about the chickens," said Maria. "But you'd think he'd have other things on his mind."

"It is a great pity that you should have fought with her, Maria. She seems to wield a lot of influence here."

"I'm sorry, Umberto. It just happened. She's a vindictive bitch." Sophia Tomaselli had found small ways to needle at the Verrier family already.

"It's a shame she hasn't got any children to occupy her time," mused Umberto, looking at his wife rocking Alessia.

"They certainly occupy enough of it!" said Maria, dealing with a milky belch. "Wave good-bye, 'Lessi." Maria assisted a fat little hand. The baby gurgled and Umberto managed to leave with a smile.

He was back a little before the terce bell, frowning. "The commander wants to draft our men in as soldiers. He says the boatyard is sitting idle while the siege is on, and he hasn't enough men to guard his walls."

"It makes sense, I suppose," said Maria. "If the Citadel falls we'll all be in the soup. What happens to you, Umberto?"

The master-caulker shrugged. "He says he will brevet us as officers, but that's not the point, Maria. He simply can't do this. The guildsmen will refuse."

She blinked; she could remember all too clearly the fighting in the streets and canals of Venice, and calling out the Arsenalotti. Why wouldn't they help now? "But why not? I mean, if the Hungarians get in they'll butcher half of the people at least."

Umberto shook his head. "The Arsenalotti are already part of the military reserve—but of the Arsenal, not of Corfu. He is not our commander. We are part of the Militia, to do Militia duties when we are not at work. To assist local authorities at any time in dealing with fires, disasters, and in dealing with immediate military threat. It is very clearly stated in the deeds of the guilds. It is one of the oldest privileges. We are not soldiers under his control. And it is not within the right of the captain-general to terminate our employment. Even the podesta cannot do that. Such an order can only come from the full Senate in Venice."

Umberto pulled a wry face. "The guildsmen here are hazy about their duties. But their knowledge of their privileges is crystal clear. They're absolutely insistent on the maintenance of the same. I wish they felt the same way about their duties." He sighed. "I'm afraid their hardness of attitude has made the commander equally awkward. We'll be doing shifts of guard work, every night."

It was a peaceful and beautiful spot, if a little isolated, reflected Svanhild from where she sat on an outcrop just above the villa. The villa was perched above a little fertile valley of patchwork fields, olive groves and some salt-pans beside the bay. She sat plaiting sedge-stems and looking out across the sea. Of course the ships would not come from along the western coastline, but anyway. She reached for more sedges. She'd never been able to keep her hands still.

As she did this she noticed a column of white dust coming down the winding roadway that lead to the villa. Could it be news? Bjarni had ridden over to Corfu town earlier. The Greek servants had been full of some story the day before yesterday about an invasion. Then, yesterday, none of them had come to work. Today Bjarni had insisted on riding to the town, despite the fact that they'd offered the port officials handsome bribes to send them word if any ships were expected. And they'd been very reliable with the last fleet.

She got up and began walking down toward the villa. She could see the rider's blond head by now. Bjarni was flogging that poor horse. And it wasn't really up to his weight in the first place.

"To arms, all of you!" she heard him bellow.

By the time she got to the house, the Vinlanders were strapping on bucklers and breastplates.

"What is happening?" she demanded.

"Corfu town is under siege," he said, wrestling with a recalcitrant breastplate strap. "And there are bands of marauders out looting and burning the great houses."

"Who?" She tugged the strap through for him.

"How do I know? All these continentals look the same to me. All I know is that the one group I saw had red sashes on, and horsehair plumes on their helmets. There's a bunch of them not half a league hence and I think they saw me."

He turned to one of the men. "Olaf, go up onto that little knoll behind the house. Give Sven a wave if you see them coming. Gjuki, open that front door. There are not more than twenty of them. We'll give them a welcome. I want men with arquebuses hidden at the upper-story windows."

He pointed to the dark-haired Kari. Kari's mother had been an Osage tribeswoman, tall, strong, and handsome—no mean hand with a bow and a knife herself—and she'd raised her boys in many of the tribal ways. Kari and his brothers had been trouble all the way across to Europe, and through it. Now they would come into their own.

"Kari, you take your brothers out by the outside wall. I want this place looking open, deserted. Svanhild, you go back up to the knoll with Olaf."

Svanhild nodded. She also took a bow with her, and a belt-knife she hadn't worn since she'd left the holding on the Mississippi.

The marauding horsemen had indeed spotted Bjarni. They came on at a ground-eating canter, riding huge, magnificent horses. There were in fact only eighteen of them and they were loot and captive hungry. So far they'd met no resistance, and they needed to beat the Croats to as many more villas as they could find.

They yelled in delight and eagerness, seeing the villa with its open front door. It was plainly a wealthy nobleman's residence. The looting of Venetian villas had so far been a very profitable business indeed. Much wealth flowed into the Venetian Republic up the Adriatic, and not a little of it stayed here in this colony. Corfu was fertile, and had a good climate, and all the trade passed through it.

The doorway was fortunately too low or they might have ridden into the house itself. Instead they scrambled from their mounts in their haste for loot, yelling like banshees. The first eight were in through the door when Svanhild heard Bjarni yell: "Fire!"

There were six arquebusiers at the upper windows, all veterans of Vinland campaigns. All of them could shoot, and shoot well. Kari and his three brothers leapt over the wall and pulled down the only Magyar knight who hadn't dismounted or been shot. They attacked the last of the knights who was on foot outside, before hurtling into the fray inside the house.

From the knoll Svanhild could hear the boom of a wheel-lock pistol and clash of metal, mixed with screams.

She saw, briefly, someone emerge at a run from the front doorway and leap for a horse. It was a well-trained animal, and the rider was a great horseman. Almost flat on the horse's neck the rider clung, and spurred it to a gallop.

Svanhild took careful aim.

The horse ran on. But the rider lay dead, sprawled on the track, a feathered shaft between his shoulder blades.

Bjarni came striding out of the house. "Get the horse!" he bellowed.

Svanhild loosed. But neither aim nor heart was in it. She loved horses and this one was a beauty.

"God rot it, Hildi!" said Bjarni furiously. "Now they'll have a riderless horse coming back to tell them that someone is killing these useless *nithings*. Come back to the house. Hrolf has a cut that needs tending. And we need to gather food and gear. We can't stay here."

He brightened perceptibly, when she came up to him. "At least we have got some nice horseflesh out of it. And Gjuki hit one of them on the head—we can find out just what is going on here." Bjarni cracked his knuckles explosively. "He is going to be telling us. Or I'll pull his ears off and force-feed them to him."

It wouldn't be ears he'd be pulling off, if he left the work to Kari. The *skraelings* had some gruesome means of getting information out of captives.

"Where are we going to go, Bjarni?" asked Svanhild, hastily scrambling down to him.

The huge blond Vinlander shrugged his shoulders. "Let's see what the prisoner tells us. We can base our decision on that. But I suspect we'll have to hide out in the mountains to the north."

Unfortunately, the domicile from which Fianelli ran his operations had been built right against the fortifications. The walls of Fianelli's kitchen rattled every time the Citadel's cannons fired. So, at least, it seemed to Bianca.

"You get used to it," grunted Fianelli. He raised the bottle, offering her some more, but she declined with a little wave of her hand. Bianca Casarini didn't have a good head for wine, so she never drank more than a glass at a time. Half a glass, when she was in the presence of men such as Fianelli and his goons.

Fianelli set down the bottle, after refilling his own glass. "Been through it before," he said. "Twice."

Bianca frowned. Fianelli was only in his mid-forties. "Corfu hasn't been attacked in—"

"Not here. Someplace else."

He provided no details, and Bianca decided not to ask. She wasn't afraid of Fianelli, but she was cautious around him. A man like that . . . it didn't pay to press questions. Bianca didn't know what had happened to the woman he'd once been keeping as a bedmate. But she did know that the woman had disappeared a few weeks after she got bold enough to start nagging at Fianelli.

"Nagging," at least, as Fianelli would consider it. The criminal chief's definition had a pretty low entry bar.

So, best not to ask any questions not directly relevant to the work at hand. Bianca leaned forward in her chair a bit.

"I think I've got the man you want. And the way to trap him."

Fianelli cocked an eyebrow. "Can't be just some common soldier you're playing with."

Bianca suppressed a spike of anger. *I don't copulate with common soldiers, you—!*

But she suppressed the reaction. First, because while she didn't sleep with common soldiers—not lately, at least—she was in no position to be finicky about her bed partners. Second, because the moment was too delicate for anger to be muddling her. Third, because a part of her was enjoying the vengeful twist in the game. Querini really was an oaf.

"He's a cavalry captain. Querini's his name. Alfredo Querini."

One of the three men who were also lounging around the huge table grunted. Bianca thought his name was Zanari. "I know him. A bit, not well."

"What's the hook?" asked Fianelli.

"He likes to gamble. And he's not good at it, even in the best of times. Give it a few months—" Bianca let the rest of the sentence trail off. She'd been in a siege once herself, but saw no reason to let Fianelli know.

"Sieges get boring, true enough," mused Fianelli. "And since before too long everybody's on rations, there's always a lot of loose money around. Idle hands and idle money, so there always starts to be a lot of gambling."

He squinted a little, looking at Bianca. The expression was not exactly suspicious, but . . . close. "I don't run the kind of gambling establishments that a cavalry captain would frequent."

"No, but you can make contact with someone who does. Count Dentico and his sons."

Fianelli's suspicions rose closer to the surface. "Why not you? You're closer to those Libri d'Oro circles than I am."

This was the tricky moment. Fianelli was right, of course. In the year she'd been on Corfu, Casarini had made it a point to cultivate good relations with a number of the Greek aristocrats on the island. The "Libri d'Oro," they were called, after the "golden book" in which the Venetian masters of Corfu had recorded the names of those Corfiote families who were given preferential treatment.

The truth was that Bianca could easily introduce Querini to the Denticos. She knew all of them, after all. But Bianca was determined to keep herself at least one step removed from the treasonous links she was creating. Fianelli, like almost all criminals she'd ever known, tended to look at the world solely through his own eyes. He thought of what *he* would do, giving little more than cursory attention to what the authorities would do other than the obvious. Understandable enough, given the generally crude and sloppy methods of police work followed in most Italian or Greek cities.

Sloppy and crude when it came to simple *criminal* activity, that is. When it came to treason, those same authorities—given the history of Italy and the Greek territories—were far more energetic and astute. Bianca was pretty sure that Fianelli's activities in the past had steered clear of politics, though, so he wouldn't really understand the difference.

But she did. Sooner or later, there was a good chance the Venetian rulers of Corfu would detect treachery at work. They were almost bound to, even with a captain-general as incompetent as Nico Tomaselli. First, because anyone with any experience knew that treason was the single most acute danger to a fortress under siege, so they'd be looking for it. Second, because in this instance Bianca would also be undermining the traitors as well as the authorities. Her mistress Elizabeth Bartholdy wanted Corfu to fall to Emeric, true; but not quickly.

Fortunately, Bianca had prepared for the moment. She squirmed a bit in her chair, doing her best to let a trace of an embarrassed flush enter her skin. "I can't," she murmured. "Count Dentico— his son Flavio too, well . . . Let's just say we're not on good terms, any longer."

Fianelli smiled thinly. One of his thugs smiled broadly. Papeti, his name was. He had the annoying habit of openly ogling Bianca, she'd noticed. She was sure that her veiled suggestion that she'd had sexual relations with both the Count and his oldest son would make the man even more aggressive toward her in the future. Probably to the point of becoming a real problem, in fact.

But the future could take of itself. Bianca Casarini was not worried about her ability to handle a common thug. Countess Bartholdy was still withholding many secrets from her, but she'd given Bianca a great deal of other training.

Her ploy did the trick. Fianelli leaned back in his chair, visibly more relaxed. She was not surprised. Another characteristic of criminals was their ready willingness to believe the worst of people. "The worst," as they saw it—and they had a very limited imagination.

In point of fact, while Bianca knew the Denticos, she'd been careful to keep a distance from the family once she'd assessed them fully. Early on, she'd decided they would be the easiest among the Libri d'Oro to lure into treason, when the time came. For one thing, they were fairly open about their pro-Byzantine inclinations; for another, they were almost blatantly corrupt. But that had become apparent so quickly that she'd seen no reason to develop intimate relations with either the Count or his sons. She never lacked for bed partners, after all, and she wanted no obvious links between herself and those whom she was fairly sure would eventually be executed.

"All right," Fianelli said. He cocked his head a little, glancing to the man who seemed to be the chief of his little squad of enforcers. That was the Florentine, Saluzzo.

"See to it, Paulo. Since Zanari already knows Querini, he can start that side of it. Put on your best Italian manners and start cultivating the Denticos."

Saluzzo nodded. He murmured something in addition, but Bianca didn't catch the words. The kitchen was rattling again.

"I hate sieges," grumbled Fianelli, finishing his glass and reaching for the bottle. "Good for business, sure—but risky."

Bianca wondered what arrangements Fianelli had made with his master, King Emeric, to see to his own safety once the Hungarian troops finally breached the walls and poured into the Citadel. She was sure they were quite good arrangements. Fianelli was too experienced a criminal to be careless about something like that.

She was even more sure that Fianelli's arrangements would be meaningless, when the time came. Fianelli was accustomed to dealing with criminals and corrupt officials. He simply had no idea what the King of Hungary was like. Emeric took as much pleasure in betraying his own, once they were useless to him, as he did in betraying his enemies.

More, actually, Bianca suspected. She did herself, after all. Bartholdy had trained both of them well. The difference between Emeric and Bianca was that Emeric was too egotistical to realize that, sooner or later, his great-great-aunt would have the pleasure of betraying him. Bianca, on the other hand, had no illusions that eventually the countess would betray her as well.

Try to, rather. Bianca Casarini's skill and strength were growing constantly. Someday . . .

She shook her head slightly. The future was the future, and now was now. The kitchen walls seemed to be rattling again.

"I'm on duty tonight on the Vidos wall," apologized Umberto. "I've volunteered for the fourth vigil. If I take it, then none of my underlings can complain."

Maria wondered how many of the men doing militia duty had a small, restive child in their homes. But she said nothing. Just:

"Wake me. I'll prepare some frittata. Jemma and Rosa have been laying well."

"Those hens are a blessing. The goat, however—it has eaten one of my gloves," said Umberto crossly.

Maria shook her head. "I see why they are used as a symbol of Satan. The beast seems possessed by an eating-devil."

"Well, if she doesn't take care we'll dine on her," said Umberto.

Even if she does, we probably will, Maria thought, but did not say.

Chapter 30

"Up. Drill time."

Benito groaned, but after nine days of Erik's discipline he knew better than to argue. The wind had been blowing steadily from west-southwest since yesterday morning and they weren't making good speed. It looked like this purgatory would continue for at least two more days.

Oh, well. It was only purgatory, not hell. Besides, he'd realized the truth in what Manfred had said: Erik was savagely unhappy about some woman. Benito had exorcized his own demons in this respect with strong drink, wild antics, and occasional fights. Erik dealt with it by a regimen of training that would make mere war gods weak at the knees. He pushed Benito. He pushed Manfred. He pushed various of the Knights of the Holy Trinity. Most of all, Erik pushed himself.

Personally, Benito thought his own method of dealing with the decisions of those irrational creatures was easier, if not better. It wasn't something he was going to point out to the Icelander, however. Erik shared the inclination to an occasional fight, and Benito had realized by this time that you really, really, *really* didn't want to fight with Erik. Benito understood now how the Corfiote seaman who had tried to rob him must have felt when he had seen his intended victim turn, and realized that what he faced was an unleashed wolf.

Benito kept quiet, as quiet as ever he had in his life, maybe quieter. Manfred, however, was allowed to complain. So long as he actually did exactly what Erik demanded, of course.

Just now, it was dark, and Erik was toeing them both in the ribs.

"It's before dawn, you Icelandic madman," grumbled Manfred, in a voice like millstones grinding gravel. "This is a time for sleeping. For snuggling down next to a warm, cuddlesome woman. Just because you can't, don't take it out on me."

The fulminating look that Erik gave Manfred promised that in fact the Icelander would take it out on him, which suited Benito just fine. However, on this particular occasion both of them were saved from being Erik's frustration-release by a yell from the masthead.

"Sail ahead! Blessed Jesu—lots of sails!"

Within a few minutes, the knights were all awake and on deck. The capitano peered nervously forward from a perch on the bow. Erik joined him with Benito and Manfred in close attendance. "There's a lot of them," he said unhappily. "No reason for a fleet that size to be here, my lords, except for trouble. There'll be cannon on them too."

He shook his head. "We'll have to turn and run, my lords—"

"No. We won't," said Erik grimly, pointing to the northeast, behind them. Now that the gray dawn was breaking they could see a fan of other smaller vessels, under oars, stroking toward them.

The capitano turned, looked, and blanched. His lips moved silently as he counted. "Twenty-two galliots. No, twenty-three. Pirates, by the looks of them. That's the biggest fleet of galliots that I've heard of since my grandfather's day, when Admiral Gradineri broke their power off Otok Brac and burned their lairs on the Narenta."

"They don't seem to have stayed broken," said Manfred dryly.

The capitano shook his head. "They're like rats, milord. You can never find all the holes. What are we going to do? We're trapped between them."

"Run with the wind and fight our way out of whatever trouble catches us," said Manfred.

"No." Benito hadn't meant to say anything, but the words just came out of him without thinking. He couldn't believe that neither the capitano nor Manfred nor Erik could see it—but it was so obvious. Maybe it was all that time on the rooftops as a boy, but he could see the battle in his mind's eye as if on a map.

"Look at the pattern! The galliots are aiming to cut us off. Look at them! They're not rowing toward us at all. They're heading toward where we'll be if we turn and run. I'd guess we were spotted from the shore yesterday and this was planned between them. Those carracks there are bearing down on us with the wind. The galliots only have to burn our sails and stop the oarsmen from getting a good stroke with a peppering of arrows, and the carracks and their cannon will catch up with us. We need to drop the sails and bull straight into the wind."

Erik's eyes narrowed. "We'll evade those carracks. They can't quarter close enough to the wind for that. But the galliots are smaller, lighter and faster. They'll catch us."

Benito smiled savagely, seeing it all unfold in his mind. "They'll have to row a good dogleg to do it. And then they can face our cannon. We don't outgun all those round ships, but we do those little things." Then he looked at Erik and said, "Uh. Sir."

Erik snorted. "That was for training. Speak if you have sense to speak, and it certainly sounds to me like you do."

Someone clapped. It was Eberhard of Brunswick. "Well, he is speaking it now. That is the Old Fox's grandson talking. That is thinking. Real strategy."

Manfred nodded. "Give the orders, Captain. And make signal to the other vessels." He turned to the knights. "Right gentlemen. Below and arm yourselves! Into armor. They won't be expecting fifty knights on each of these ships."

Erik held up a restraining hand. "Wait. Those galliots—the rowers fight too?"

The capitano nodded. "Yes. One or two of them might have small cannon, but they rely on boarding vessels and hand-to-hand fighting."

"Good." Erik turned to Manfred. "I don't think we should have the knights don armor yet. If we give those galliots a long chase . . . They'll be good and exhausted by the time they do catch us." For the first time since he'd come aboard, Erik gave Benito an encouraging smile. "Or what do you say, young Benito?"

Benito nodded, looking inwards at the map in his mind. "Yes. If we can keep up the chase for long enough we can turn again and quarter on the wind. We'll be upwind of the carracks. The galliots will change course, to cut the corner . . . But that'll mean that they have to keep rowing while we can rest on the oars."

Manfred bellowed. "No armor, gentlemen. Not yet. You'll all be taking a turn at the oars."

The grumble at this order was stilled by Falkenberg, who swatted an already gauntleted hand against his breastplate. "You heard the prince! Those of you already in armor, strip it off."

"Falkenberg!" yelled Manfred.

"Sir!"

"I'll want a roster of what order the knights and squires will row in. I want them to spell the rowers but not exhaust themselves. Set it up for me."

In the meanwhile, the capitano had sailors on the rigging, with orders flying. A sailor on the poop deck was making signals to the other vessels. As the sails came down, four steersmen swung the great rudder hard over. Oars came out and the steady drumbeat began.

"The carracks are resetting their sails," said Erik, squinting across the water. The vessels were, Benito judged, still more than a league away.

"Won't matter. They can't sail close enough to the wind."

Eberhard of Brunswick looked thoughtfully at Benito. "Just how do you judge this? I know from speaking to your grandfather that you are not a sailor. You've never been outside of Venice before."

Benito shook his head. "I . . . I can *see* it, milord. In my head. I know how close to the wind the galliots can sail. We've done that for the last two days. The capitano said to Erik—yesterday—that he was lucky this wasn't a round ship. They cannot get enough points to the wind." Benito shrugged and held up his hands helplessly. "It's like a picture in my head from a high rooftop. I can see where people are going. I can see where they *can* go."

The *Ritter* nodded. "I knew your Grandfather well. I was based in Milano some twenty years back and he and I met on a number of occasions. Once, when he had delivered a crushing defeat against the odds to Phillipo Maria of Milano in some minor border dispute, I asked just how he did it. He described something similar. Only he spoke of it in chess terms."

Chess had been one of few things Benito had discovered in his life as *Case Vecchie* that was more enjoyable than the way he'd lived as a messenger and thief. "It is a great game, Milord."

Eberhard smiled wryly. "When this is over, you must give me a game. And if you desire a true challenge, that man is the master." He pointed to Eneko Lopez.

The cleric looked away from the sea, raising his eyebrows. "It is a challenging game. But the only man *I* know who sees a battle like a map is Carlo Sforza." He looked very penetratingly at Benito. Someone had obviously been telling family secrets.

Benito said nothing. So Eneko continued. "It is your birthright, boy. A God-given gift. See you use it wisely in his service." Eneko Lopez straightened up. "I will go below. Francis, Pierre, Diego and I will see if any protective magics may be worked."

"Better if you could blast them all to ash," grumbled Eberhard. "The pagans I fought in Småland had a magician who could do that, until someone put an arrow through his eye."

Eneko shook his head. "It is not fitting to destroy human souls, for thus is evil magic defined. In wars among Christian men, it is common for kings to claim God is on their side, but that is vainglory. God is on the side of those whose souls need him. God decides on rights and wrongs of a cause, not kings, and our magic will be as sand in the wind if we try to use it to attack. But evil magics—ah, now those *are* best countered by ecclesiastical power." He turned and went below decks.

Eberhard snorted. "He said much the same thing to the Emperor, can you believe it? He's a stiff-necked man, that one." He looked wryly at Benito. "I don't think you got much else from Carlo Sforza, boy. You should be grateful for that skill—from both your father and your mother's side. Yes, I know, too, Benito. Half the world does."

Benito felt his face grow hot as he flushed, and he thought of Maria, and what she had said. "They keep expecting me to be like one or the other of them. I'm not! I'm myself."

The elderly *Ritter* tugged at his white moustache. "Some of us struggle to live up to the reputation bequeathed to us by our blood. Others struggle to rise above that reputation. It can be done, boy. But we are shaped by it. It's whether we allow it to rule us or whether we direct it. That stiff-necked priest is right. You have a gift. Use it well. Use it as Benito Valdosta would use it, not the Wolf of the North—nor, even, the Duke of Ferrara."

Falkenberg came up to the deck and spared him having to answer. "Milord of Brunswick, here is the roster for the rowers. Prince Manfred asks that you control this matter. He says it will take true statesmanship."

The old *Ritter* smiled ruefully. "I detect Francesca's hand. I'm supposed to be training him and instead he's manipulating me."

He took the list. "Well, you don't have a monk's fist, Falkenberg. What's this? I see Manfred's name heads this list."

"Erik said it would set a good example, milord. He said all chieftains take a hand at portage, and therefore Manfred could do some rowing. Manfred swore at him."

The *Ritter* raised his eyes to heaven. "Well, I daresay if nothing else that will make it impossible for any other knight to claim rowing is beneath his dignity. Very well. Young Valdosta, I suggest you divest yourself of any extra clothing. Rowing is hot work, I've been told. You're also in the first shift."

Manfred had had Von Gherens assign places to all of the passengers. Von Gherens had arrived at "where to put everyone" by the simple expedient of counting an equal number into each cabin. Under their vow, all of the knights of the militant order were officially equal regardless of former station, or present rank. So knight-proctors had ended up in broom cupboards, while several squires had the third best stateroom.

Except, of course, for Manfred and Francesca's cabin. Francesca had smiled at Von Gherens. They had the very best stateroom.

Eneko, Diego, Francis and Pierre, on the other hand, had nothing but some floor space—if they all exhaled at the same time.

The others were waiting for Eneko. They'd plainly anticipated what he would try to do: Scry to see if this was some part of a larger evil. Eneko knew the dangers here at sea. The alignment of the consecrated area wouldn't stay aligned.

The candles were prepared. The incense was in the censer. Diego was taking a bottle of water out of his pack.

Weaving the sevenfold circle in this confined space took care. But one thing Eneko had learned: Magic required precision. There was no room for mistakes.

"*In nomine Patri, et Filii, et Spiritus Sancti, fiat lux.*"

Enclosed in the magical curtain of light the four joined hands and began the ritual of searching.

This was not simple scrying; in scrying, one knew where one wanted to look, but not necessarily what one wanted to look for. Here, they knew, not only where, but (in general), *what.* This might be nothing more than the ongoing battles of Venice against pirates, or pirates and some greater enemy—but Lopez did not think so. Here they had one of the possible heirs to the Emperor *and* one of Chernobog's great enemies—more than that, really, in the form of Erik Hakkonsen and the four priests. These fleets, this alliance, might be what the Black Brain had been focusing on when it had let them go so lightly, back in the Jesolo swamps. This, then, might well be what Lopez had feared. And if it was, then there would certainly be an agent of the Black Brain somewhere nearby.

That was what they were looking for.

Each of them undertook the invocation to one of the four archangels of the compass; this was no time for mere wards. But not without a moment of thought.

"You, Pierre, or me in the North?" he asked of the others. They all knew which creatures were the most likely to be under Chernobog's sway.

Pierre considered it. "Perhaps six months ago I was your superior in combative magic, Eneko," he said, soberly. "But I think you have surpassed me. I will take the East, though, which is—"

"Another source of trouble. Very well." This would mean that Pierre would begin the invocations, and Eneko would end. Pierre faced outward, raised his hands, and began to intone the prayer to request the presence of the Archangel Gabriel in their work.

The fact that, instead of a simple ward-pillar, they got something that was a towering blue flame, vaguely man-shaped, was not comforting. And yet, in a way, it was. They now knew, for certain, that this was what they had been expecting, dreading, waiting for. It had begun.

When it was Eneko's turn to invoke the Archangel Uriel, he had barely intoned the first sentence of the prayer when his ward roared up, in brilliant gold flame. Nevertheless, he completed the prayer, ending with a bow of thanks.

It was Francis, as the representative of the West, who blessed the chalice of wine that they would use as their mirror—though it was not the standard shape of a chalice, being more of a footed bowl to provide a satisfactory surface to use as a mirror.

They exchanged glances; Pierre looked fierce, Diego somber, Francis resigned. Eneko did not know what he looked like; his face just felt stiff. They focused their concentration on the chalice of blessed wine, and began the first careful probes for the taint of evil. Since there was no "earth" as such, and not much chance that even the Black Brain's creature could force a spirit of fire out over so much water, Eneko joined with Francis to search the waters, and Pedro with Pierre to survey the air.

They expected that the creature would be subtle. It wasn't.

Eneko felt the nausea, the icy chill, and the shock of encountering naked, unshielded Evil. The result was near instantaneous. The wine seethed and began to boil. The light curtain pulsed, as if sheet lightnings striated within it. And the North ward was filled with the sound of great angelic wings.

All four of them reeled; Eneko was the first to recover. Perhaps Pierre was right; perhaps he had grown in skill! But this was no time for pride, though the confidence that the fleeting realization gave him was a bulwark under his feet.

They were now no longer within the bowels of the ship. They, and their circle, wards and all, were . . . elsewhere. Not quite out of the world, but not in it, either. It was a place of swirling darkness, green and black flame, and sickly, polluted clouds.

Moving sinuously through it, looming over them, was— something. Serpentine, but it was no serpent. Black and green, with a mouth of needle-sharp, needle-thin teeth, long as stilettos and twice as lethal, piggy little eyes, and a strange, spiny crest. It confronted them.

No. It confronted Lopez. It focused on him, and drew back to strike.

"That which cannot abide the name of Christ, begone!"

Eneko Lopez drew strength from his companions, strength from his faith, and from the Archangel of the North to strike at the thing.

Perhaps it had not expected the blow, for it did not move out of the way. Perhaps it had expected that they would be paralyzed with fear. It neither dodged, nor did it invoke shields. The blow, a sharp lance of golden light modeled on the archangel's own weapon, pierced the thing's hide. It opened its maw in a silent scream.

Then, huge, slimy and vastly strong, the creature bled and fled, and they whirled away out of that not-world and were back in the belly of the ship. There was nothing left but the faintly glowing ward-circle, the overturned chalice, four thin Ward-candles, and a puddle of blood on the floor just outside the circle. The blood was black and stank.

"Well, now we know that it is more than just a conflict between commercial rivals," said Eneko, grimly. "The eel-thing smelled of the far north. That is confirmed by the Archangel of the North's intervention. I perceive the hand of Chernobog."

"But Eneko, there was more to it than that. It knew you—and feared you. The target of all these ships is nothing other than . . . you. We must pray and summon intercession," said Francis.

"And that was no eel," added Diego.

Eneko raised his eyebrow. "It was human, once. But it looked like an eel to me."

"It was a lamprey," said Diego, with certainty. "A hagfish."

"But it was enormous!" said Pierre

Diego shrugged. "It is very old. Fish don't stop growing as long as they are alive."

"Lampreys are parasites, aren't they?" Trust Pierre's basic curiosity to get him sidetracked.

"They can be. They like to feed off living flesh." And trust Diego to follow him down that diversion.

Francis cleared his throat. "In all of that . . . was I the only one to hear the panpipes? Further off but still distinctly."

"Panpipes?" mused Eneko. "As we heard in the scrying in Rome?"

"Yes."

Eneko shook his head. "No, I did not hear them, but I'd guess you were right. This is another attempt to either kill us or to lead us from the course again. And that course leads to the place where there is already some old power. Elemental, crude, and which does not love us. We know now where Chernobog and his minions focus their attention: Corfu.

"Brothers," Eneko said, carefully, "I believe that the Lord will not be averse to the judicious use of magic in the material plane. After all, if this galley is captured or sunk—"

Pierre grinned mirthlessly. "It will be, after all, purely in self-defense."

"Purely," Eneko assured him. The wards flared, as if in agreement.

Chapter 31

"Benito was right," said Erik, up on the poop deck after a spell at the oars. "The carracks will pass to leeward of our stern."

"They might be in cannon-shot for a short time," said the bombardier, "depending on what cannon they have on board."

"That would depend on who they are. Genovese most likely."

Erik squinted into the distance. "The pennant on that lead vessel is a black horse in flames."

Eberhard of Brunswick drew a breath between his teeth. "Emeric of Hungary! Our spies reported he was massing troops. But it was assumed that they were for his campaign against Iskander Beg. Where does he get a fleet from?"

"And where is he going with it?" asked Francesca, from where she stood under the canopy.

The old statesman narrowed his eyes and nodded. "A good point. Helmsman."

"Yes, milord."

"Do you see anything that gives you any idea whose ships those are?"

The helmsman, the sort of man who looked as if he'd been at sea on the very first hollowed log, and had only come ashore briefly since, nodded. "Aye. Not Genovese, Sir. Byzantine. You can tell by the way they rig the foresail."

The old *Ritter* turned a grim face to Francesca. "Alexius has allied himself with Emeric of Hungary."

Francesca frowned. "The only possible reason I can see for that is to attack Venetian properties."

"I can see that Alexius might want to do that, but he's too weak to go on military adventures against Venice. Also, it puts Emeric at his throat instead of Venice—which if anything is worse. I must admit I can't see why Emeric would attack Venice's colonies by sea, instead of Venetian holdings nearer home. To come overland through Fruili would make more sense."

Francesca nodded. "There will be a reason that is less than obvious. From what I've heard, the reason could be that Alexius is too weak-witted to see what he's doing."

Eberhard snorted. "I don't know if you're joking, Francesca. But you are being too accurate. And now I think it is time for a change of rowers. These men have nearly learned what they should be doing. Therefore it is time to change." He walked over to fore-rail and began calling the next group of knights and squires to oar-duty.

It was midmorning before the knights were actually called to leave the oars and don armor. The round ships were well astern, by then. They'd turned and were attempting to take a tack that would bring them closer. The galliots, having started in a tight group, were now trailing out in a long arc. The knights had made strong if inept rowers, although they'd been getting better with practice. However, what this had meant was that the great galleys had kept going under oars for nearly three hours now, and the actual rowers—the Venetians who were professional at it—were still reasonably fresh.

The enemy galliots were close now. The great galleys' sails were hoisted and they began to run with the wind. Now the galliot crews thought they would reach their prey, and their oarsmen began putting extra effort into their stroke.

Manfred came up on deck. "If we can keep this up for another half an hour, we won't even have to kill them. The beggars must be half-dead already."

Erik ascending the companionway behind him, smiled wolfishly. "And the fools have not had the sense to regroup."

The capitano shrugged. "They're pirates, Milord. They fight for loot. The best loot goes to the first ships."

Manfred felt the handle of his great sword. "So does the best dying. All right, Erik. You too, young Benito, seeing as you seem to have developed a genius for this sort of thing, how do we deal with them?"

Benito blushed and got up to leave. "I've only really been in the battle in Venice. And to tell you the truth that was all just hand-to-hand skirmishes. Our battle plan went to pieces after the first few heartbeats."

"He knows the difference between strategy and tactics anyway," said Erik dryly. "Stay and learn, youngster. You're not too bad when you're not out causing trouble." Erik pointed at the galliots. "They still outnumber us. If they want loot—let's give them some. Casks of wine will do for a start. Half empty ones so they'll float. Some of them will start on the jetsam. And that will break the followers up."

"Well, at least you want to start on the half-empty ones," grumbled Manfred. "And what else?"

"Tenderize them well with cannon when they get close. Keep the knights down until they're trying to board."

"And keep lots of casks and buckets of water on hand for the sails," said the capitano gloomily.

"Fine horse-flesh" grunted Bjarni. "Like to take them home."

Svanhild could only agree. She was having some difficulty riding, as the saddles were nasty, heavy things, and not the simple pads that the *skraelings* used and had taught her to use. But the horses themselves were magnificent. The horses at home had been bred, for the most part, from chunky little Icelandic ponies, with the occasional importation of something larger or more exotic, or the odd Spanish barb taken from the infrequent Spaniard expeditions come looking for gold and finding death. These, on the other hand, were bred for war, not packing. Steady, patient, big, and strong. And smarter than they looked. Rather like her brothers.

They rode northward along the high ground, keeping away from the smoke plumes, heading for the mountains.

They did see some local peasants doing the same. They scattered the moment they saw the horses, leaving their goods and fleeing. "Real fighters," said Gjuki, disdainfully. Svanhild kept her own council; the peasants they saw were armed with next to nothing, and certainly not mounted. How could they even hope to accomplish anything by standing and fighting? Except to get killed, of course.

"Why are they running away?" wondered Olaf, looking at the

disappearing backs. "We could use some guides and we mean them no harm."

"Don't be more stupid than you have to be," snapped Bjarni at the lanky *duniwassal.* "We're riding cavalry chargers, and we are plainly foreigners. How many blond heads have you seen here?"

"Oh. I hadn't thought of that."

"Your trouble is you seldom think."

"It's going to make finding shelter difficult."

Bjarni swore. "*Fandens osse!* I hadn't thought of that."

Svanhild bit her lip. Suddenly, that nasty little inn, overrun with bugs and rodents, where she'd have had to share a bed with six other women she didn't even know, didn't seem so bad. "We'll manage, Bjarni," she said, stoutly. "We'll find something."

The riderless horse joined up with another troop of Magyar cavalry. The officer in charge of this detachment of looters looked at it carefully. And felt his heart sink. It had once belonged to Hegedes—the commander who had promised King Emeric he'd be proud of the looting campaign. That everything would go well. It looked as if he had been wrong. It also looked as if he wouldn't be around to take the blame.

The cannon roared, kicking back against the restraining ropes. "Venetian gunners aren't worth shit," said the high-voiced Knight bombardier, with dispassionate professionalism. He moved in, shouting instructions, cuffing heads.

The next shot hit the second of the galliots.

The stern cannon, bearing now on the closest galliot, began firing.

The nearest galliots' crews rowed frantically, pulling hard to close, to get near to the galleys so that the cannons could not be depressed enough.

Some fifteen of the galliots were close enough to pose a threat. Others were so far back that either they would never catch up or they knew they would arrive far too late for the looting; their crews had already stopped trying.

The gunners were now working as fast as the Knight's bombardier could drive them. And that wasn't going to be fast enough. The first galliots were already too close. Already burning, pitch-soaked arrows were being fired at the sails. Sailors scrambled with buckets of water.

The arquebuses began firing in volley from the great galley. Despite this, there were wild-eyed men standing up on the bows of the first galliot, grappling irons in hand.

Then the pirates weren't there anymore. They might have been safe from ship's cannon, but the bombardier had his own little two-pound cannon loaded with fragments of steel and ready for them. To Benito it looked as if some giant blade had abruptly scythed through the crew of that galliot.

But the second vessel was already coming. Plainly they had decided to concentrate their attack on this ship. The bombardier could not reload in time for that one. One of the Venetian gunners grabbed a cutlass.

"Put that down you fool!" yelled the bombardier. "Reload! There are still other ships behind this one. You sink those and we only have this one to deal with."

The knights still waited silently behind the rampart of crates and boxes. The raiders targeted the bow—as far from the poop deck as possible. Grappling irons came along with a bunch of yelling, gleeful, loot-hungry boarders.

Then the knights stood up behind the rampart, and the yowl that went up from the mob of boarders was no longer one of glee. Even in the wilds of Dalmatia they knew the armor of the Knights of the Holy Trinity.

To get to the knights they'd have to mount the rampart. The Narenta pirates were unarmored. They had boarding axes, a miscellany of swords and knives, and occasional pistols. The steel-clad knights with their broadswords were backed up by Venetian sailors with pistols and arquebuses. Manfred had positioned two further sets of ramparts up on the poop deck.

Benito had elected himself an exposed but potentially death-dealing position. The great galley carried four grenadiers, and an ample supply of black powder grenades. Out on the end of a wildly swaying main-mast spar, with a bag of grenades and a slow-match, he could pick his targets. So long as he could cling to the spar with his legs, he could virtually drop grenades into the attacking vessels.

"You'll be partly hidden by the bell of the mainsail, Benito," Manfred had said seriously, when Benito had suggested taking this position. "But you'll also be a good target. The canvas and the spar are no protection at all against arrows or gunfire. Also, if they succeed in firing the mainsail, you'll be fried. You work to my orders. Don't draw attention to yourself. Wait until the melee starts. No one will be looking straight up while they're fighting. Then you see if you can drop something directly into the attackers' boats.

"But not before—have you got that?" Manfred demanded, jabbing a forefinger—to the first joint, it felt like—into his chest.

"Yes, sir."

Erik snorted. "You can quit that right now. I don't know how well you'll fight in actual combat. But I do know you can climb things."

Manfred grinned. "Yes. I've seen him do it. Don't take company up there, hear."

Benito held his tongue. He'd never live that one down. But he was still thinking about it, despite the coming battle, when he reached the spar end.

He had a bird's eye view of the boarders from up here. He also realized the one fault with his idea: The sway out here was wildly magnified. He clung, lit, and threw.

Only he hadn't factored in the roll. To his horror, he saw that the grenade was going to hit the great galley, not the galliot alongside. He gritted his teeth and restrained himself from closing his eyes.

It hit the rail, and bounced harmlessly into the water.

He lit again, as fighting raged below him. Waited for the roll . . . realized how short the fuse was and hastily flung the grenade as far as he could, not worrying about where he threw it, just wanting to get it *away*.

It exploded in the air between two galliots. Not if he'd tried for a twelvemonth could Benito have used a single grenade so effectively. The explosion sent steel shards flying at those who remained on both galliots.

Lighting the third grenade took immense determination. Especially as a couple of shots were now being directed at him. But he knew when on the roll to light and throw now. It landed in one of the galliots. A brief shower of sparks . . .

And it failed to go off. He waited on the roll to light another. A shot burned across his shoulder, sending the slow-match spiraling downwards. He was left with a newly lit grenade in one hand and another four in his bag.

He did something incredibly dumb, but the bullet graze had both frightened him and given him a rush of pure insane strength. He dropped the lit grenade into the bag; then, in a smooth movement, drew his *main gauche* and slashed the strap with the other hand.

He flung the entire bag. It splintered into the storm-decking on the prow of the latest galliot to join the fray; and, a moment later, erupted and blew a smoking hole in the bow at the waterline. The little vessel started to go down almost immediately.

Benito began edging his way backward along the mainsail spar. His shoulder was oozing blood and didn't seem to want to take any strain. Out here he'd get shot again for sure. And there wasn't anything more he could do up on the mainmast spar, anyway. Looking down he saw it was still going to be a vicious fight. They'd sunk some galliots and simply outrun others. But because all of the little vessels were concentrated on this one, the knights on board were badly outnumbered. They outclassed the pirates, to be sure. But sooner or later the mainsail would go down, more vessels would catch up, and eventually the carracks would get here.

As he thought all that, he saw a little sortie of pirates had indeed managed to get up to where the mainsail was tied. Benito saw one of the band slash at the port-side mainsail rope. As the saber struck the rope the man was thrown back in a great gout of sparks. The cable was undamaged but the pirates who had fought their way up to the sail were shrieking and diving over the side of the galley, not caring whether they hit water or their own ships.

Of course the shrieking wasn't in Frankish, but Benito was still sure he guessed what it was: "Witchcraft!" What had been a determined assault rapidly turned to a frantic attempt to reach their boats.

Clinging to the ratlines, Benito noticed the mast was actually thrumming, and the mainsail was now cracking with the strain. It was hard to say where the wind was coming from but it was certainly driving the galley forwards. The sail was glowing a bright royal purple. The other galliots, which had been closing, were now beginning to fall back. By the boom of the cannon they were back in cannon-range.

Benito just went on climbing down the mainmast rigging, struggling to do so with one arm not working properly. By the time he got low enough to jump down, the fight was turning into a rout, with pirates jumping into the sea rather than remain on board an accursed vessel.

Superstition can be a wonderful thing when it is someone else's problem.

Chapter 32

Manfred winced. "That's sore, you know."

"Why are men so brave about battles and so scared of having their wounds tended?" asked Francesca, calmly cleaning the bullet graze on Manfred's side. "I thought armor was supposed to protect you from this sort of thing?"

"Ow! It's less than perfect against firearms. Pretty fair against swords or magical efforts."

"And what is effective against firearms?" she asked, sprinkling on basilicum powder.

"Getting out of the way. Or a nice thick earth rampart. Even stone can be shattered by big enough cannon. But earth absorbs it."

"I'll get you to carry one, next time," she said, beginning to wrap a bandage around his ribs. "I would hate to have had to explain to your uncle what had happened to you, and if anyone's big enough and strong enough to carry around his own rampart, it's you."

The last was not said in an entirely admiring tone of voice. Francesca had spent a number of hours under that weight of bone and muscle—and Manfred did not always remember to support himself on his elbows.

She finished pinning the bandage with a cabochon-encrusted broach. "It's all I have in the way of pins, other than hair pins—which would certainly stab you." She kissed him. "There. You'll do. Now, tell me, where do we go from here?"

"Eneko Lopez says we go to Corfu. Some of the surviving pirates talked. They say Emeric of Hungary has invaded the island and

264

the Citadel is under siege. They also say we have no chance of getting back to Venice, or even across to Italy. There are some fifteen galleys between us and the mouth of the Narenta. And more galliots. Onward is a risky proposition, too. There is a fleet in the straits of Otranto."

"So: They intend to keep Venice bottled up?"

Manfred shook his head. "The capitano thinks that's a ridiculous idea. The Venetian convoys would punch holes through any other sea force trying to block the Adriatic."

Francesca was silent for a while. "I think I must go and talk to Eberhard. At sea, the Venetians have mastery of the Mediterranean. But Alexius controls the Bosporus and the Dardanelles. And if the Outremer convoy has already sailed for Trebizond, then he can prevent their return. If they hold Corfu—well, the straits of Otranto are only twenty-five leagues across. They can harry shipping even if they cannot stop it."

"Well, maybe." Manfred shrugged. And winced, for he'd momentarily forgotten his wound. "I'm no naval expert. But bickering between Venice and the Byzantines is nothing new. Venice's trading privileges and possessions, like Corfu, Zante and Negroponte have driven a succession of Byzantine emperors to try and redress matters. It doesn't happen. Imperial Greek naval power is no match for the Venetians. And the depth of the Byzantine Empire's money pouch is far shallower than Venice's. This time Alexius has gotten Hungary in to be his muscle. I suspect his muscle may end up eating him. But if it gets to that point the Empire will distract Emeric. We really don't want a powerful Hungarian empire all the way through the Balkans and Greece. We also don't involve ourselves in petty fights between our allies."

But Francesca had other news that she had not thought relevant until this moment. "I think it may be more complicated than that, not to mention nastier. According to Petro Dorma, Alexius VI has recently been entertaining a visitor, who possibly came from Odessa. An old friend of Erik's: Caesare Aldanto."

Manfred grinned, showing his square teeth. "The pretty blond who set him up to be arrested—or more likely killed—in the brothel? You'd better not tell Erik that or he'll want to go chasing straight to Constantinople."

"Aldanto already left there, a shade ahead of the Duke of Ferrara's best assassins, I gather." Francesca frowned and tapped an elegant finger against her lips as she tried to recall everything else the Doge had told her. "Dorma hinted that the Council of Ten has put an unprecedented price on Aldanto's head, too. But, Manfred, the reason I must talk to Eberhard is that this cooperation between Jagiellon, Alexius, and Emeric puts a very different slant on the Holy Roman Empire's desire to remain uninvolved. Alexius may want Venetian possessions. Emeric may want Byzantium. But Jagiellon wants only one thing—a route into the underbelly of the Empire."

Manfred grunted. "I guess we'll just have to stop him succeeding. Corfu is a large island, if I recall one of my more boring tutors. Surely there is more than one fortress?"

Francesca smiled in spite of herself. "You didn't pay attention, so you rely on the fact that I did. Of course." She waggled a finger at him. "You'd better start learning to pay attention! Someday you'll be somewhere where I'm not, and you'll curse yourself for not having the information when and where you need it."

He grinned sheepishly; she delivered a frown, then gave him what she knew. "There is only one real fortress. There are a number of small fortified towns, and villas, built to withstand attacks, but nothing that will stand up to modern siege weapons except the Citadel at Kérkira. The fortress there is on an islet, and the actual rock makes part of the ramparts. The Byzantines and then the Venetians have improved on what nature had already made fairly good."

Manfred assumed the impassive oxlike expression that Francesca had learned indicated deep thought. "I think we need to hold a council of war," he said eventually. "I don't know enough of Venice's affairs, their military strength on Corfu, the ability of the Venetians to withstand a serious siege or what our best course of action is. I have to think for the Holy Roman Empire, not Venice or Eneko Lopez. I think I will go and call Eberhard, Eneko, Erik, Benito— if they've finished with his wound—and Falkenberg. It's a pity Von Gherens is on the other vessel."

"I'd also ask the capitano to join you, if he's gotten over having a divine gale push his ship. He was still gibbering, according to Falkenberg."

"I'll ungibber him." Manfred cracked his knuckles. "He's been at sea in the service of the Venetian Republic for forty-five years, man and boy, as he has repeatedly informed me. A man of his experience shouldn't let a little of what Father Lopez assures us is ecclesiastically sanctified magic worry him."

Manfred looked regretfully at Francesca's lush form. "I know it seems a pity but maybe you'd better put some more clothes on." He looked appreciatively at the outfit. "I haven't seen that one before. Why were you wearing it when we were going to be attacked?"

"Practicality, dear."

He looked puzzled. "It doesn't look very practical . . . except for one thing, Francesca."

"My legs are not enveloped in clinging petticoats. And we fight with what we have. I know full well when men's bollocks start thinking, their brains stop. If I put on breeches and took up a sword, even one of these attackers little brother's could kill me. But if the best of warriors is intent on undoing his breeches . . . well, I have two knives. There are certain other features about this outfit that are less obvious than knives, too."

She did not add that, if the fight was lost, dressed in this fashion she'd almost certainly be booty for the captain. Manfred would possibly not understand that sometimes the things one did to survive were not pleasant. And she had a great deal of practice in that vein.

Manfred took a deep breath. "You'd probably get raped."

Ah, my dear, tell me something I don't know. Francesca gave a wry smile. "A nun's habit and a wimple wouldn't stop that, Manfred. Now, you go and get the others and I shall get changed."

He looked admiringly at the diaphanous outfit, which was intended to hint at, rather than reveal, what was underneath. "I admit the need, because I want your input at the council. But it does seem a waste of time."

"Dressing is never a waste of time, Manfred dear, because undressing someone again is part of the pleasure. I shall dress and contribute what I can to your councils. Then later you can help me undress and contribute something to me as well," she said, lowering her lashes.

"And now I'm supposed to concentrate on military matters," grumbled Manfred.

Eneko Lopez looked gray with exhaustion. The capitano looked as if his eyes were still about to start out of their sockets. He chose a position as far away from Eneko as possible. The others looked battered in various degrees, too, noted Eberhard—except for the old duke's grandson, Benito. Benito had a bandaged shoulder, but it didn't seem to have slowed him down much. He looked like one of those fused grenades he'd tossed so effectively. His eyes reminded Eberhard of a sparking and sputtering wick, as if he were alternating between wild excitement and exhaustion.

Eberhard was an old man and a politician now, but he'd been a soldier once: *This one loved danger.* You had to watch that kind. They took chances. And they took others with them into their danger.

Privately, Eberhard was pleased by the way Manfred had handled the battle. Manfred would serve the Holy Roman Empire well, with some more experience; very well indeed. Eberhard noted he was able to take advice. That was rare, especially when combined with an ability to act decisively and effectively, and even rarer when combined with the ability to lead. Advice seekers often wanted others to make decisions, not merely advise, or else they merely wanted their own opinions confirmed, and didn't listen when advice ran counter to it.

This meeting, too, showed a maturity that he'd not expected. Merely calling them together like this proved that he was thinking past the successful escape.

Of course, Eberhard wouldn't tell the young prince that. But Manfred had come a long way from the spoiled brat he'd had the displeasure of meeting when he'd been in Mainz some years before.

"I suppose the crucial issue is how well this Venetian fortress at Kérkira will withstand the siege. Basically it is the only fleet-size anchorage around."

The capitano made a wry face. "It could withstand nearly any siege . . . if it were well enough supplied, and had enough men, milord. But last time I was there the garrison commander was complaining bitterly about how few men he had."

"Commanders always complain about that," said Falkenberg. "The Venetians couldn't have taken and certainly couldn't hold the island without enough men."

But Francesca was already shaking her head. There was another one whose still waters ran deep, thought Eberhard. The old diplomat had a good idea that Manfred had learned as much at the white hands of Francesca as at the calloused ones of Erik Hakkonsen. Probably more, in fact.

"It wasn't *taken*," she said. "The Corfiotes invited the protection of the Venetian Empire, more than a hundred years ago, because they were having a lot of trouble with Illyrian raiders. The Venetians sorted that out with superior sea power very quickly and easily. They set up a feudal system of puppet local Greek aristocrats—the *Libri d'Oro*, as they're called. Things have gone a little less smoothly lately and—correct me if I am wrong, Capitano—the captain-general has little more than a policing force, to make sure taxes are paid and Venice's rules obeyed."

The capitano nodded. "They're mostly mercenaries. Dregs, signorina. I'd guess at less than a thousand on the whole island. The barracks are almost empty and several of the buildings haven't been used for some time. There are a couple of other castles—Vidos in Corfu bay, for instance. But a lot of the places have just got a local *capi* and a few men. All right for dealing with petty crime.

"And the mercenaries!" he spat. "Pah. They're not worth much as soldiers, ones who would take a job like that. There's no fighting, so there is no opportunity for extra profits, bonuses or loot. But you won't get killed either. Lazy and stupid—and maybe cowards."

"Locally recruited?" asked Erik.

"Not so as I'd noticed, milord," said the capitano. "If I remember right, I heard tell that the present Byzantine Emperor's father sent agents across to Corfu and stirred things up. Told them that they're Greeks, not Venetians; that Byzantium regards them as its own, and that they would be rewarded with Venetian-held positions and estates if they got rid of Venice. It's true the Corfiotes begged the Venetians to annex Corfu and protect it but . . . as is the way of things, the best jobs went to appointees of the Senate sent out from Venice. The Venetians have taken over a lot of estates. The local Greek nobility has a bit of an attitude about Venetians. As if they didn't want us in the first place! The Corfiotes are quick enough to take our money, though."

Francesca raised a perfect eyebrow. "And of course the Venetians are as innocent as lambs and do nothing to exacerbate the situation," she said dryly.

The capitano laughed coarsely. "Except treat the locals like shit. Sorry, signorina, pardon my language. Too much time at sea and not enough talking with ladies."

"I forgive you, Capitano." She looked at Manfred pointedly. "I'm used to occasional lapses."

Eneko Lopez yawned. "Forgive me too, but I am very, very weary. This discussion is all very well, but I must get to Corfu. If Chernobog seeks to prevent it . . . then there is a reason. Even if the Citadel stands or falls, I must get to the island."

He regarded all of them broodingly. "That fleet was sent with one end in mind: to sink us rather than to allow any of us to reach there. That may have been because of me and my brothers, or because of the large number of armed knights on this convoy, or because of—who we carry." He blinked, slowly. "However, I do know this much. Before we reached Venice a similar attempt was made to stop me and my brothers. I must conclude that this was no coincidence, and that Chernobog wishes to keep us, specifically, from reaching Corfu. I don't know why Chernobog is doing this, but there must be some far-reaching reason he has scryed. He does not play for small stakes. The Holy Roman Empire or even Christianity may be threatened. You can put Diego, Pierre, Francis and me off on a beach on the north end of the island."

Erik cleared his throat. "Aren't you forgetting something, Señor Lopez?"

Eneko blinked at him. "Quite possibly, Erik. The magic we worked was draining. I am exhausted and not thinking at my best. What is it?"

"They tracked you here. Chernobog tracked you previously, too. He can sense your movements, and now you tell me that you wish to land on an island occupied by his allies." Erik was not normally inclined to irony, but Eberhard sensed the tone now. "You are a great mage, señor. But an arrow or sword can kill you as well as it can kill me, especially if you are exhausted, as you are now. And unless you and your brothers have learned something new about turning invisible, I think this is not the wisest of plans."

"I've seen that on the northern frontier," rumbled Falkenberg. "Mages can fight great magics, but when all is said and done they need ordinary men and ordinary steel to guard them against purely physical threats. I've seen a pagan mage that could blast men to ash chopped down, unresisting, because knights with cold iron and the holy cross attacked while he dueled magically."

Eneko blinked again. "Still, I must go," he said tiredly. "Danger or no danger. Forgive me. I cannot even think now. But I see my duty clear."

Eberhard patted him on the shoulder. "Go and rest, Eneko Lopez.

You are no use to us or your duty when you're exhausted. Leave it to us ordinary soldiers to get you into the Citadel. You'll be protected there, and on Corfu. Will that do?"

Eneko stood up. "I believe it will. But we will pray for guidance."

"When you wake up," said Erik, with rough kindness. "Go and sleep now."

The cleric nodded and stumbled out, leaning a hand against the wall.

When he'd gone, Erik shook his head. "You may have just offered to do the impossible, *Ritter* Eberhard. Or volunteered us to do the impossible. We only have two hundred knights. Even with the ship crews and the squires, we muster perhaps twice that. Breaking the siege is more than we can achieve. Emeric must have at least . . . say ten thousand men there, and his siege cannon will prevent any access by water—even if we fought our way through his fleet."

"We lost two knights and five damn-fool glory-hungry squires, in that last effort. Some injuries, too. Gunpowder should never have been invented," grumbled Falkenberg.

Eberhard smiled dryly. "While the prince was being bandaged and you and Erik were seeing to the men, I saw to questioning one of the pirates. It helped that Knights of the Holy Trinity have something of an *un*holy reputation, and that he'd just seen some very terrifying magic. We didn't even have to resort to torture. The man was a mere sailor, but he had a very good notion of just how many ships were employed in the attack on Corfu. Most of them, most of the troops and most of the cannon, are still behind us: To wit, that fleet of carracks we avoided. So right now there are, at a guess, no more than three or four thousand troops investing the Citadel at Kérkira. Actually, there will be fewer than that, as many are out ravaging Corfu's countryside. If we can reenforce the Citadel, then it can hold until Venice and the Empire will send more forces to break the siege."

Manfred grunted. "We'd need to send word to get them here. Maybe send one of these vessels running for Bari, and send messengers overland to Venice?"

Eberhard was dubious. "The sailor seemed to think more vessels were on their way from Constantinople."

"Even so, it seems a fair idea," said Erik. "Split up. Squeeze all the knights onto one vessel. Land as much force as possible on the western coast of Corfu. Storm the besiegers and hope that someone has the brains to let us into the Citadel before Emeric's troops can regroup."

"Er," said Benito, tentatively. "Why don't we just sail up to the Citadel?"

Manfred made a face. "Siege cannon would smash the ships to kindling . . . Wait a bit. There are no siege cannon!"

"According to our pirate informant, anyway," said Eberhard.

"We'd hear and see the cannon duel from a good league off if it is happening. It'd be a risky enterprise, nonetheless. We'd have to sail into the strait between Corfu and the mainland at night. There are bound to be patrols."

"It might succeed for sheer audacity."

Benito had been looking thoughtful throughout all of this. "It is not as risky, milord, as all that. The moon is down from about three in the morning. We can come in under oars from the south. If we need to, we can turn and run with the wind. And it has to be the last thing they'd expect us to do."

"Aren't you forgetting something?" asked Erik. "Somehow, something is tracking Eneko Lopez."

Benito shrugged. "It still has to marshal its ground, or, in this case water, forces. Look at the trap we have just escaped. It's as likely to follow us at sea as to intercept us coming into Corfu."

Erik still wasn't convinced. "The other problem is that even if there are no siege cannon, the Venetians are as likely to sink us with their own cannon. In the dark they'll be watching for sneak attacks."

"We could unfurl the pennants," Benito countered. "They're unlikely to fire on the Lion of Saint Mark."

"Not in the dark," Erik pointed out.

Manfred brought his hand down. "Gentlemen. Francesca. We've got at least a day's sailing, before we have to decide. I suggest we eat and rest. I will think about the various ideas and reach a decision. But now I need to concentrate on the various contributions possible."

Eberhard wondered why Francesca smothered a smile.

Chapter 33

Manfred had had them bring four of the knight-proctors and the captain over from the *Dolphin, Swordfish* and *San Raphael* to the *San Nicolò*. The captain's cabin was rather crowded; Manfred wondered if he ought to ask them to breathe in shifts.

"Right. First, the bad news. We are being followed: Galliots under sail have been spotted from the masthead. That was why we changed course in the dark last night. A different sail was spotted this morning. They are spread out and looking for us. Second, more bad news. Corfu, our next port of call, is under siege, by the Byzantines and Emeric of Hungary. I have it from Eneko Lopez that making sure Corfu does not fall into the hands of these foes of Venice is vital to the future of the Church. Eberhard of Brunswick says it is also vital to the future of the Holy Roman Empire. Obviously, it's also vital to the Republic of Venice, a state with which we are on friendly terms if not formally allied."

Manfred looked at his audience, which wasn't difficult, since half of it was looming over him and the table, and the other half was crushed in against him. "So. We need to reinforce the garrison at Corfu. We also need to get a message back to Venice and to Emperor Charles Fredrik about what is happening here. We have four vessels, two hundred knights, and fair number of sailors. We need to achieve both of these objectives. We need to split into three parties: one ship to run on, one to attempt to dodge back—and two ships to attempt to relieve the Citadel at Corfu, or at least to add men to its garrison. We'll make landfall on one of the Diapondia islands. I will be taking the knights and what sailors

273

and food can be spared to Corfu. Capitanos Selvi, Bortaliscono, and Da Castres—of your vessels, one must come with us. It may be sunk, and I can't promise anything, not even safety. One of you must run for the open water of the Mediterranean and sail on to Rome."

His expression was grim. "You'll face interception, interference, and you won't be any safer than we are. If you get through, messengers can be dispatched from there to Venice and Mainz. Eneko Lopez will provide letters to the Grand Metropolitan of Rome. I will provide letters under the seal of the Empire for our embassy there. The other ship will attempt to return by sea to Venice. I'll do a note for Petro Dorma, but the captain can give the story best in his own words."

He cleared his throat. "All of these ventures are fraught with risk. There are vessels pursuing us. There are supposed to be Byzantine vessels on a blockade ahead."

"Prince Manfred, how do you intend to relieve the siege?" asked Captain Da Castres. "Surely the vessels with the knights on them can off-load you at some small fishing harbor or something. Then we can sail as a convoy. That will be a great deal safer."

Manfred smiled wryly. Captain Da Castres had an exaggerated notion of safety, if he thought four ships were going to be any safer than two. "The key to defending Corfu's citadel is actually getting the knights, and as many sailors as possible, *into* the Citadel. We—on horseback—could possibly take the besiegers by surprise. Hope that someone inside opens the gates and that the causeway bridge is intact. We and our squires, all mounted, could undertake that. If fortune favored us, if we took the enemy by complete surprise, if the cannon from the Citadel didn't simply fire on us . . . we could get maybe half of the knights into the Citadel. With no extra supplies and none of the crews of the ships. We could add maybe a hundred and fifty men to the defense."

He shrugged. "Not a great help, but some. However, we know the besiegers have several thousand men—but no cannon." Manfred pointed. "Benito Valdosta there . . . You all know the boy, you all know his bloodline."

Benito looked furiously at Manfred. Manfred knew why. For Benito, his bloodline—at least that on his father's side—was not something he boasted of. Manfred was *using* that reputation.

Manfred gave him a quelling look—*Damn right I am.* He would use anything he could get his hands on right now—and went right on. "He came up with the plan that got us out of the pirates' grip. Now he's come up with another idea, the only way I can see that will deliver an extra five hundred men to the citadel, as well as whatever supplies can be loaded into the vessels. When he put the idea forward, I thought he was mad. I've pondered on it all night. Talked to Capitano Douro here. We can indeed sail to the Citadel itself, by night. But once they're in, the ships won't be leaving."

"And assuming you succeed in the madness of sailing by night, through the fleet of the enemy, the guns in the Citadel will sink you," said the oldest of the captains, Selvi. "It has to be the most harebrained idea I have ever heard. Ah, Prince Manfred."

Manfred now knew which skipper to send onward. That one. He shared a look with Benito, who gave him a slight nod.

"Milord Valdosta. Do you think it will work?" asked Da Castres, ignoring the older man.

Benito nodded more vigorously. "I can't see a better way, Captain. There are some things in our favor. I have thought about it long and hard, believe me. We know from the interrogation of our prisoners that only eight or so vessels remain at anchor out of cannon-shot in the bay. The northern entry is guarded by Narenta galliots. The south is blockaded by some of these eight vessels. The rest of their fleet is out in the straits of Otranto. More ships are probably due from Constantinople, and if we're going to do anything, we need to do it before they get here."

He pointed at the sky. The low cabin deck, rather. "For a second thing, the moon is down from early morning. We can approach under muffled oars. Capitano Douro here has found a Corfiote serving among the oarsmen. This man swears he can navigate safely to Kérkira under those conditions. The enemy will have less confidence in unfamiliar waters, in the dark. Finally, the guns of the Citadel will not fire on the Lion of Saint Mark. Eneko Lopez and his companions say they can work a holy magic which blazons the banners as brightly as if in broad daylight. We'll never get a better chance to get more men and supplies into the Citadel with the fewest losses."

Manfred patted Benito's shoulder, proprietarily. "There you have it, Capitano Selvi. Besides, we'll have our trumpeters on the foredeck, sounding the battle hymn of the Knights of the Holy Trinity. There are few soldiers anywhere who would not recognize that. Finally, this is not a matter for discussion."

He hardened his tone, straightened his back, and tried to sound as much like his uncle as possible. "This is what I have decided. This is what will be done. All of the vessels will take the parts I assign to them. All I have called you together for is to finalize details. To decide which vessel will have the honor of joining in our attempt to assist the Citadel."

"I am captain of my ship," said Selvi stiffly, "and responsible to the Republic of Venice for her safety."

Von Gherens stood up and put his hand on his sword. "Captain, I am a soldier of Christ. I am sworn by a holy oath to serve the Church. *Señor* Lopez is a direct emissary of the Grand Metropolitan. I've been in combat with him. I have never met a man who serves Christ as well and with as much integrity as Eneko Lopez. He has said that the Church needs our aid. If I have to chop your head off and sail your boat myself to get there, I'll do it."

Benito looked at Von Gherens, and Manfred watched sudden realization dawning in his eyes. Well, not surprising; he hadn't lived with Von Gherens the way Manfred had. Benito had never really understood the bluff, hearty knight. There was a core of deep piety under that hard-drinking exterior. If Von Gherens truly believed in the rightness of his deeds, it would take a cannonball to stop him. That could be a problem, when his ideas were wrong—but when they were right, there was nothing short of an armored elephant that it would be better to have on your side.

The captain also plainly realized he'd misjudged. "It's a ship, not a b-boat," he stuttered. "I—of course, I'll do my best to assist. But—"

"I'll volunteer to take my ship to Corfu," said the plump Da Castres. He smiled, revealing skewed teeth, yellowed like a mule's. "I'm more afraid of that knight than I am of either the Senate or the enemy. Besides, my wife says I'm too fat. A siege will be just the thing. And if it lasts long enough, maybe absence will make her heart grow fonder."

"I'll explain that to her when I get back to Venice," said the lean, dapper Bortaliscono. "Are there any other little services you'd like me to render? While I'm there, you know."

Da Castres shook a fist at him, grinning.

Bortaliscono bowed mockingly to his fellow captain, and turned to Manfred. "I'll need those letters before this evening, Prince Manfred. As soon as it is dark we'll sheer off westward. The farther south we go, the more I'll have to beat back. I'll want to head for the Italian coastline, and creep up it."

Manfred nodded. "We'll need to bring the ships together, and transfer the knights, horses and food. I think we should be prepared to split up this evening. Selvi, it looks like you're going on to Rome."

"It's the course I should have chosen anyway, Prince Manfred," said the captain sourly . . . but not too loudly.

Manfred ignored him. "It will still be dangerous. But it could also be the crucial route. A message from there to Flanders could beat the Atlantic convoy. They'll have to return posthaste. I suspect the Outremer convoy will be out of contention, stuck in the Black Sea."

"And the enemy will know that," Da Castres pointed out. "They can count. If there are only two of our ships in the harbor—and you can be sure they have spies everywhere—then they'll know that the other two are running back for help."

He smiled nastily as Selvi looked a little green.

Manfred went below to write the letters.

Benito was left scowling, trying to think if there was any obvious hole in the plan that had now been laid squarely at his door. He was scowling, too, at Manfred's reference to his parentage.

"I think that went off rather well," said Francesca to him, smiling. "So why do you look so unhappy, Benito?"

As if he was going to tell her. "Oh. Nothing."

She looked quizzically at him. "It was that reference to your blood, wasn't it?"

"It's not exactly my favorite point of public knowledge," he said grumpily.

She patted him on the arm. "Benito, it *is* public knowledge. And Manfred needed to mention the fact that you are descended from not one, but *two* of the greatest strategists of the age to prevent any doubt."

"That doesn't mean I inherited anything from either of them," he pointed out, still irritated. But his irritation was fading fast. It was impossible to stay out-of-temper around Francesca, particularly when she was exerting herself to be charming. Maybe she was a little old for him, but . . . on the other hand, older women were . . . He forced his mind away from that line of thought.

Francesca nodded. "Benito, whether or not you have inherited your strategic sense, nevertheless, you *have* it—and if it's suggested that you inherited it from the Fox and the Wolf both, people will accept it as genius and be willing to act on it instead of thinking you're just an impudent boy."

Benito sighed. Well, that much, he could accept. "But Manfred's a commander—"

"Manfred is neither a seaman nor a Venetian. He isn't even Italian. Had this scheme been put forward as his idea, the seamen might have refused. They trust you and they trust that reputation."

"Von Gherens could have severed a few heads," said Benito, though he didn't really mean it. Well, maybe he did.

She shook her head. "Manfred, and especially Erik, are well aware that it would not have helped. You can threaten a weak-kneed captain that way, but not entire crews. Knights are not seamen. If the seamen thought what was being proposed was suicide—a hundred Von Gherens wouldn't have stopped them. Da Castres, Bortaliscono, and Douro are not cowards, even if Capitano Selvi is."

"I suppose so. But tell him I wish he hadn't done it."

Francesca dimpled. "He knows that. Just because Manfred is big, people think he doesn't notice things. Besides . . ." She pecked Benito on the cheek. "It wasn't his idea. I told him to do it. I apologize. I wouldn't have done it if I hadn't thought it necessary. But I think you let it worry you too much."

"Being illegitimate is not important, is it?" he asked sourly.

She raised an eyebrow. "Was it important when you were staying alive by your wits on the canals of Venice?"

He shrugged. "Not really, I suppose. Half the canal-side brats and bridge boys didn't know who their fathers were."

"So it was one of the *Case Vecchie* who mocked you about it?"

"Caesare did," admitted Benito. "Back after I went to live at *Casa Dorma.*"

Francesca gave a little snort of laughter. "And you are letting the opinion of such a one as *Caesare* worry you? A liar, a spy, a breaker of every oath he ever made, who was for sale to anyone who had the money? He was a bigger whore than ever I was—at least I always keep my promises."

Benito acknowledged a hit. "I hadn't thought of it that way."

She smiled. "It's all right, Benito. You may be of the bloodline of the strategists of the age, but I am a woman and therefore infinitely more perceptive. And now I'd better go and correct Manfred's spelling. For someone of royal blood he is near to illiterate. Mind, you should see his uncle Charles Fredrik's handwriting! The Emperor normally has a scribe, but anything he considers confidential or really important he insists on writing himself."

As she left, Eberhard of Brunswick came across from the other side of the table, and clapped him on the shoulder. "I hope this complicated plan of yours works, boy. I don't actually like complicated plans. Too much can go wrong when the actual fighting starts."

Benito nodded. "I don't like plans where things have to be well coordinated or rely on something else happening right or exactly on time either. Um. In my misspent youth, milord, I was involved with a thief who worked like that. It got him killed. Caesare Aldanto also liked multifaceted, multipronged plans." Benito cleared his throat. "I admired him, milord. I did understand that often his plans only worked because *he* was very good at what he was doing, and he changed his plans as he went along. He also didn't mind who else got killed or hurt, as long as he was all right."

The old man smiled wryly. "I've dealt with commanders like that when I was a soldier. I've dealt with kings and chieftains like that, as a statesman. If they must go down they'll pull everyone and everything down with them, but they'll sacrifice anyone and anything to keep from going down themselves."

"Well, yes. Except most complicated plans rely on other people. And if the word gets around they can't rely on you, your reputation is ruined. People need to know they can trust you to be where you said you'd be, and do what you said you'd do, before they'll even consider taking part in complicated plans."

"Which is why you wish to be seen as reliable?"

Benito blinked. "Actually, I hadn't thought of that. What I meant is: These people don't really know me. So this plan doesn't rely on other people. It might be crazy . . . but it is dead simple, really.

It doesn't rely on others having done something. It's just a simple sequence of events."

Eberhard laughed. "Events that just wouldn't occur to most commanders."

Benito smirked. "I've found plans work best when the enemy isn't expecting them."

Chapter 34

Swimming silent and deep and as far behind the ships as he dared,
while still keeping some kind of trace on them, the great hagfish
followed. The encounter with the adversary had been terrifying—
all the more so because the adversary had been not only supported
by his companions but linked to them, in a way that was as alien
to the shaman as mother-love. To link together thus was to open your
mind and will totally to your companions. The shaman would never
do that voluntarily. He could think of no one he would dare trust
like that.

He soon realized that the vessels above and ahead of him had
diverged. Hagfish can pick up blood and other scents in a part per
million. The darkness above was no cloak at all to the chemical-
sensitive barbels around his mouth.

For a moment he dithered, before deciding. Make it his master's
problem. His master's slave Aldanto had virtual control of all of the
Byzantine ships, and by virtue of exploiting ignorance, control over
the galliots. The captains of those little vessels were superstitiously
terrified of Aldanto. He could direct pursuit of the other ships. The
shaman could tell the master where they were heading.

A little later, after this was done, the shaman returned, determined
to follow and if possible arrange an attack on the two vessels head-
ing for Corfu. The adversary was in one of them.

Father Francis frowned, bracing himself against the bulkhead
while the vessel lurched. "Much of this plan relies on the enemy
not being forewarned. But, Eneko, if we are being followed by some

magical creature, and it was able to direct those fleets to attack, will it not warn the besiegers?"

Eneko nodded; he was tired, and he had rather not do this now—but there was certainly no time to wait. "So we shall have to try to drive it away."

Diego stretched. "Bah. So we have to deal with that *thing* again! You know, Eneko, I think I can still taste the slime. Well, soonest done, quickest mended. When will we try it?"

"Before the ships turn to make the tack back toward Corfu. It may conclude that we plan to make landfall. That is well and good. If it is in contact with the land-troops, let them patrol there while we attempt to reach the Citadel." He stood. "Brothers, let us cast the circle and call the wards. I believe that we will have much the same aid this time as the last. Perhaps, forewarned, we will make better use of it."

Perhaps, he thought, *This time the surprise will be on our side.*

Two hours later the shaman had retreated with desperate haste to deep water, and was begging the master to open up a passage. Jagiellon answered, with the same twisting passage through the spirit-world, but it seemed an eternity to the shaman. He fled up it, and was spewed out onto the stone floor in a heap, gracelessly.

The hagfish transformed into its human form, and the shaman started screaming. His wrinkled skin was blistered, with long, raised lash-marks. Even transposition could not heal them.

Jagiellon allowed him to scream for some few moments, before commanding: "Be still."

The shaman had little choice but to obey despite wanting to scream, and scream, and never stop screaming. It had not been a sword nor a lance that met him this time, but a great fiery form that had *dragged* him into some neutral part of the spirit-realm, and lashed him with a many-tailed whip while he frantically tried to crawl away. He had not gotten in a single blow of his own. He'd barely managed to escape.

"Eat skin," commanded Jagiellon. "Come. I go to eat some myself."

The shaman picked up his *quodba* drum with blistered fingers. He could not help noticing that the skin of his one-time foe, now the drumhead, was singing. Vibrating just faintly all by itself.

❀   ❀   ❀

Benito, a Corfiote seaman, Capitano Douro and Erik stood in the captain's cabin, peering at a chart of the island. "If they have patrols out, it will be here, milord," said the seaman, pointing. "Between Kavos and the mainland. It is only, oh, maybe three leagues across the strait there."

"They'll have lookouts on both sides, I presume?" asked Erik, studying the chart.

The seaman shook his head fiercely. "Not on the mainland! The Lord of the Mountains would never allow that."

"The Lord of the Mountains?"

"Iskander Beg. He is chief of the Illyrians over there. He is a very bad man." The Corfiote shuddered.

"So there will be a watch on the Corfiote shore," mused Erik. "But probably just a ship at anchor well off the other shore."

"Do ships sail this strait at night?" asked Benito.

The sailor managed to look shifty, evasive and shocked, all at the same time. "Oh, no! It is dangerous. It is not allowed. The podesta has ordered—strictly—that there is to be no shipping in the straits at night."

"But you just happen to know how to sail it," said Benito, dryly.

The sailor shrugged. "Fishermen do it. There are some fish best caught at night."

"Ah. Fish which would pay taxes if they were landed by daylight? You needn't worry my friend," chuckled Benito. "I'm not a tax collector. In fact a good friend, a very, very good friend of mine, used to be involved in smuggling stuff into Venice. Someone all of us here know, in fact, except maybe the capitano, and I wouldn't be too certain about that."

The sailor looked hastily at the Venetian captain, and said nothing.

Benito looked at the captain too. "Capitano Douro. Unless I'm a lot stupider than I think I am . . . you've got some goods you weren't planning to pay taxes on when the ship reached Ascalon?"

The captain looked startled. "Well . . ."

"I'm not planning on telling anyone," said Benito. "And this ship won't be getting to Ascalon. I just wish to reassure our guide."

The captain nodded. "A matter of some amber . . . just a few small, choice pieces."

The seaman looked at Benito, shook his head and chuckled.

"You're too sharp for one so young, milord. Yes. We'd bring cargo in and land it right on the wharf in Kérkira. I've been up the strait in the dark more times than I can count. There are a few places you need to avoid. This time of year the current runs strong. The worst piece will be the last bit. We need to approach close to the mole. Farther east, we'll rip her guts out. But as I said to the skipper: I can get us in."

The captain grunted. "Not as well as you could if we had a load of taxable cargo on board," he countered, but he did so with a smile.

The oars were bound in sacking. Men sharpened weapons. The gunners prepared the cannons, though they were not to be used, except as a last resort. Armor was readied but not donned. If they got through the screen of guard boats, then the armor would be hastily put on. Boarders and armor did not go together, and they might have to board a guard ship.

It was an awkward combination of circumstances. The moon, a hazy object often hidden behind gathering clouds, was slipping beneath the horizon. It was going to be as black as the inside of a cat out there. If they came upon a guard boat suddenly, the knights would act as boarders—no firearms, just swords and murderous haste. A single shot fired would mean retreat, and landfall elsewhere.

After that, if they were spotted they'd run for shore and try to beach the vessel. The knights had already planned to smash out the cladding timbers between the ship's ribs and swim their horses to shore. Once again armor was likely to drown both the knight and the horse. So, for that it would be helmets and shields only. But in the final attempt to reach the Citadel, they aimed to bring the ships to rest on the shingle just off the northern side of the islet. Sea access to this was between the islet and castle on Vidos and the Corfu Citadel itself.

The biggest difficulty was going to be keeping two silent, darkened vessels in touch with each other. They had one steersman, and two ships. A long line between the two helped. A man on the bow of the second ship kept a coil of this line in his hand, keeping the line tight without allowing it to pull. He had to feel whether it was pulling away to any direction or if the front vessel was slowing or speeding up. A second man in the bow of the second ship was ready to listen to softly made gull cries. One for port, two for starboard. Gulls shouldn't be calling in the small hours of the night, but Benito's ingenuity deserted him on this one. At least it wouldn't sound as unnatural as voices.

By the time they reached the southern channel it was so dark that all that could be seen was a shape of deeper darkness where the landmasses lay. Well . . . except for the cheerful lanterns that burned on the four equidistantly placed watch vessels.

How nice of them to show Benito where they were!

It was all Benito could do to stop himself laughing helplessly. They slipped through relatively close to the lantern-lit vessels, just in case the enemy had put unlit vessels between.

In the tense darkness, Manfred snorted. "We're past. Let's give a rousing cheer to celebrate."

"There are more hurdles," said Benito. "Listen. You can hear the cannon fire."

They could. A distant deadly rumble. The steersman pointed. "Those lights are Lefkimi. We're passing Lefkimi point now."

"How long is it going to take us to get to Kérkira?" whispered Erik.

The man looked at the sky. "If we get the sail up now, we should be within hailing distance just before dawn." Benito caught the flash of teeth. "Or within cannon shot. I hope those priests can come up with the magic they promised, milord, or the Venetians' own fort and Vidos castle will blow us apart."

"They're very powerful Christian mages, those priests," replied Erik stiffly.

The Corfiote didn't seem especially impressed. "I've no faith in priest's magic. On Corfu we have some real, old magics. Scary things, but powerful, sirs, maybe more powerful than anything you've ever seen."

"Eneko Lopez is one of the most scary men in the world. And he is not going to let us down." Benito spoke quietly, with a faith he hoped he felt.

"I reckon we'll get a chance to see if that is true. If he fails we're shit. Fish-shit, soon enough," said the steersman with morbid humor.

On the main deck the seamen were raising the carefully blackened mainsail. Under oars it had been tricky to keep the two vessels running in tandem. Under sail it would be virtually impossible.

The second vessel would just have to do its best with a helms-man following the dark patch that was the sail of the lead ves-sel. They still had a good few leagues to go before the final dash.

"There's a small vessel ahead! Also running without lanterns. Running away from us."

"Smuggler?"

"Must be. We've made someone shit themselves." The seaman grinned.

Manfred came up on deck. "What was that?"

"Smuggler-ship. Avoiding taxes," said Benito knowledgeably.

Manfred half-choked. "And just who is collecting taxes right now, Benito?"

"Oh, hell! Do you think it was a watch-boat? We'd better run for shore."

"No," said Erik decisively. "If it was a watch vessel, someone would have fired off a signal. What you saw there was a sign that things are pretty bad on the island. That 'smuggler' will have a human cargo. He's taking refugees away, not bringing illegal goods in."

"I've got three sisters and a brother in Achilleon," said their steersman, quietly. "I wonder what's happening to them."

"It's to be hoped that your brother was also involved with the *night fishing*, sailor," said the captain, dryly. "Emeric of Hungary has a vile reputation for how he allows his soldiers to treat con-quered citizens."

There was a chuckle. "Spiro is my older brother. That's how I came to be involved in the first place."

Chapter 35

There was just a hint of lightness in the sky. Dawn was still a little while off, but morning was definitely stirring in the bed of night. "You can see the Citadel against the sky. It seems pretty quiet now," said the Corfiote steersman.

"Well, maybe we can sneak in," said Benito. "I hope so. If we have to use the priests . . . The minute those banners are visible, the gunners on the ships that are sure to be lying just out of range will open fire on us."

"Uh-huh." Falkenberg grunted his agreement. "That's a sure sign that the Hungarians haven't gotten their cannon yet. When the cannon get here, they'll pound those walls night and day. But the Venetians in the Citadel will be watching for a sneak assault by sea. According to our captain there are places men could be landed outside the walls. If men could get inside the fortifications they could spike the cannon and nothing could hold off the assault."

"Er. Not from what I can gather," said Benito, diffidently. Falkenberg had, after all, been at a dozen sieges as opposed to his none—hard to believe in a man that relatively young, but still . . . Falkenberg was a veteran of the northeastern frontier of the Empire, where he'd been born and raised. "There are three walls. An outer curtain wall, the inner wall and then the two castles on the hilltops."

"A wonderful place for a holiday," said Falkenberg, dryly. "Great defenses are more than just three walls, Benito. They're enough men—with good morale—enough ammunition, and enough food and water. Perhaps most important of all, a loyal and determined

287

population supporting them, with no traitors. And even if you've got those, there's a lot to designing walls so that they work effectively. Making walls that can stand endless cannon fire is simply not possible. Entrenchments are more effective."

He went on to give Benito a concise study of siege-craft. "I've been years in the learning of this stuff, and before that, I had the best teacher in the world. It occurred to him that he should pass it on to me before I had to spend thirty years relearning it. I think maybe I'll start passing it on to you, just in case. You never know. You might be able to make some use of it."

Benito was sharp enough to understand the unsaid. Falkenberg thought most of them would die. And he approved of Benito Valdosta and wanted to pass his knowledge on.

It might be spring, but it was still bitterly cold here on the outer curtain wall in the small hours of the morning. Especially after crawling out of a warm bed, from beside a warm wife. True, the warm wife had gotten up as well, and had given him some food and a small flask of wine. Maria had her moments, but generally she was a gem.

Privately, Umberto acknowledged that his advancement was largely due to her, and her connections. He'd entered the marriage with a lot of qualms, but had come to treasure it more than anything he'd ever had in his life.

Still, Maria was back in that warm bed now, and he was out on this cold tower. By the grumbling from the other Arsenalotti, they were feeling equally miserable about the situation. While staying within the law—just barely—of Venice and guild alike, Captain-General Tomaselli was doing his best to make sure that they felt the misery of thwarting him.

Umberto stamped his feet. They were frozen already. He would dress more warmly next time.

He stared into the night. Just what would he do if a Hungarian or a Croat stuck his head up over the parapet right now? Panic, probably. He'd been a craftsman all his life, not a soldier, and had spent a lifetime holding tools in his hands rather than weapons . . . The arquebus felt as unfamiliar as the issue rapier.

Suddenly the darkness was lit by a bright golden blazon out on sea. And then a second. "Sound the Alarum!" yelled someone. "To the guns! To the guns!"

There was a boom and a flash from out in the dark strait. And, virtually a heartbeat later, an answering shot from the walls. Umberto ducked instinctively. He looked seaward again and saw clearly: The lateen foresail and the pennants of two vessels out there were glowing with a golden winged lion that outshone the darkness.

"Hold your fire!" he yelled. "Hold your fire! It's the Lion of Saint Mark!" His voice, he found, was being chorused by many others.

And then, echoing above the pitter-pitter of arquebus-fire from the shore—ineffective at this range—came the bright, glad sound of trumpets. It was the battle hymn of the Knights of the Holy Trinity, and it struck fear into the hearts of their foes. Umberto recognized it, and was deeply grateful he'd never faced it as a foe. Looking at the light from the glowing emblem of Venice he could see that it was gleaming off spiky helmets and armor. The captured shore was now a mass of hastily running figures. The enemy hadn't expected a night attack, and certainly not here, at the main point of their own assault.

"San Marco! San Marco!"

The men on the walls yelled and cheered. There was another flash as yet another one of the Byzantine or Dalmatian pirate ships fired a cannon. The ship was plainly in pursuit of the two galleys that were flying pennants with the strange glowing winged lions. The vessels looked like typical great galleys in the dim light from the pennants.

"Bring the guns to bear on those who follow!" Umberto shouted the words without thinking about whether or not he had the authority to give orders to the bombardiers. He might not be familiar with weapons—certainly not cannons—but he'd been a foreman by the time he was thirty. Commanding men in practical tasks was now second nature to him.

Already, he saw, there was cannon fire from Vidos.

"I hope to God they're firing on the pursuit!" The two galleys with their golden winged lion pennants streaming were now within cannon shot of both fortresses.

The Venetians' fire, seeking for targets in the darkness, might have been hampered by the lack of visibility—but luck, or the winged lion, was certainly with one of the gunners. Sudden fire flared out on the dark water behind the two galleys. Perhaps a ball had struck a banked stove and scattered embers into a smashed powder keg.

Whatever the cause, there was now a vessel on fire out on the water, and it wasn't either of the two flying the Lion. And the sky was definitely lighter. Umberto could see that the great-galley crews must be stroking as if their very lives depended on it. Which, in fact, they did. The blazoned winged lions, so clearly visible, made them easy targets. The cannon fire from the Citadel and Vidos would discourage pursuit, but they'd still be within cannon-shot of other vessels. But they were firing their own stern-cannon now. If they were in range, so, too, were their foes.

Along the shore, the trenches were flash-speckled with the muzzle-flash of arquebuses. If they planned to make landfall there, they'd do it in the face of stiff opposition. But it looked to Umberto as if the vessels were bearing down directly on the Citadel. The usual anchorage behind the berm-breakwater would be directly under small-arms fire from the shore.

Behind him, Umberto heard horsemen. The captain-general and the bulk of his cavalry were coming down at a hasty trot. Umberto saw that many of the troopers were still trying to buckle themselves into their breastplates. People, too, were streaming out of the houses behind the curtain-walls, heading for the wall.

"Direct your fire on the trenches! Keep the buggers' heads down!" bellowed an officer. "The galleys are going to make a landing here beneath the wall."

Umberto found himself holding his breath. There was a strip of shingly beach below the wall on this side of the berm. On the sea-side. The berm would provide some shelter and the ships would be at least three hundred and fifty yards from the enemy-held shore. That was well and good—but was the water deep enough, close in enough to allow the vessels to beach?

Umberto was a ship-builder. He doubted it. And moreover, the gate that had been used for workers to get access from the Citadel to the port was at least a hundred and fifty yards closer. The storehouses of the Little Arsenal lay just inside that gate.

He hastened over to Leopoldo, the garrison commander. "Milord. Permission to take some Arsenalotti down to the port gate. We can push some heavy balks of timber onto the beach for them to shelter behind."

Leopoldo peered at him. "Umberto Verrier. Go to it. Here, Sergeant. Go with him to provide my authority to the gate." He turned to one of his captains. "I'll want all the fire we can muster from the northeast tower. See to it, Domenico."

Umberto hurried down, calling to various people as he ran. He wasn't much of a fighter, maybe, but he could handle timber. And he loved ships—not sailing in them, the ships themselves. The thought of those ships ripping their bottoms out was not a pleasant one.

Maria had slipped back into sleep after Umberto left, but the sound of the cannons woke her.

It sounded serious; she got up, and listened harder.

It *was* serious. Had the Hungarian king got his cannons onto the island, then? Was this the moment they'd all been dreading for days? If so—

If so, then every able body would be needed on the walls!

There was no way she could leave Alessia, and she had a horrible feeling she might need both hands, so she tied the baby to her back in a large shawl. Then she took up the wheel-lock pistol that Kat had given her, when they'd gone out in search of Marco, in what seemed a lifetime ago. She also took the largest cleaver in her kitchen on her way to the door.

As soon as she was outside, she headed for the wall. She had no doubts as to what her fate would be, and that of Alessia, if the Hungarians breached the walls. If nothing else she could fling rocks. You didn't have to be a soldier to fling rocks down on those below.

She went pelting down the hill, along with several hundred others, all showing signs of hasty dressing and of seizing the first arms that came to hand: here a rolling pin, there an arquebus, or a boar-spear, or a bread-peel. Half the citizens of the Citadel seemed to be running to the outer curtain-wall.

Then, she heard the cheers. "*San Marco! San Marco!*"

That didn't sound as if things were going badly. In fact, it sounded more like a welcome than a call-to-arms. And it was coming, not from the landward side, but the seaward side. Her headlong run slowed slightly; she looked out into the darkness, peering at where the shouts were coming from. For a brief moment she thought she was seeing things. The Winged Lion of Venice was coming across the sea! And it was as golden as the sun itself.

Then she realized it was just an image of the winged lion

glowing from lateen sails and pennant flags. There must be a couple of vessels out there. Corfu wasn't being attacked, it was being reinforced! She went to join the throng on the wall, to join the cheering now, rather than the defense.

The two vessels, now easily visible in the growing light, looked as if they were racing each other for the shore. They were rowing toward the sheltered water of the L-shaped berm—except that they didn't seem intent on getting into it, which would have put them right up against the enemy-held shore. Instead, they were heading for the seaward side of the berm.

She saw the lead vessel shudder, and heard the snap of oars as the vessel hit some underwater obstruction. She could make out a stick-figure frantically waving at the other vessel from the poop. The other vessel bore hard to seaward. The first vessel was still edging forward—she was barely thirty yards from shore—but obviously leaking and sinking. The silence from the wall was now profound. People were hardly breathing. Cannon still roared from the landward wall, but here it was still.

The second ship passed over the obstacle and, with a sugary crunch they could hear from the wall, slid to a halt. It was still in the water, but not very deep water.

Men began pouring off it, jumping into the shallows on the eastern side of the vessel, with the ship between them and the firing from the trenches on the mainland of Corfu. Then part of the cladding timbers were smashed out of the side and knights, waist-deep, began hauling horses out of the hole in the hull of the ship.

By now, it was obvious the other vessel was not going to get much farther. Water was overhead deep, to judge by the men swimming ashore. To her shock, Maria recognized the stocky figure who emerged, dripping, from the sea.

Benito Valdosta yelled up at the watchers. "Hands to these ropes, all of you. Move!"

She was even more shocked when she recognized the emotion surging through her.

"Don't be stupid!" she snarled at herself, joining the little mob racing to help with the ropes.

Chapter 36

Benito was nearly thrown overboard when they struck the rock. He knew straight away they were in trouble. The galley had a draft of one and a half fathoms, when she was this heavily laden. They were relying on hitting the shore at speed to beach the vessel so that the men could emerge without swimming. Now they'd lost their momentum and she was holed. The ship would ride deeper than her one and a half fathoms. The sailors could easily manage the twenty yards to shore . . . if they could swim. The knights in heavy armor had not a chance.

"Get them to strip their armor!" yelled Benito.

"Takes too long!" bellowed Manfred, above the bedlam of screaming horses and shouting men.

"Get a rope to the shore!" commanded the captain.

Benito took the end of a light line. "Get the anchor rope on the other end!" he shouted, and dived overboard.

On the beach, he saw he'd arrived in the shallows just ahead of the Corfiote steersman who also had a rope.

"Hands to these ropes all of you. Move!" he commanded.

Maria saw how the port gate had opened farther up the shore toward the Hungarian trenches. Great balks of timber were being thrust out and now, in the shelter of these, hundreds of men and women from the Citadel were streaming to help.

Maria ran to join them. It was only when she was out on the shingle that it occurred to her that a woman with a baby on her back shouldn't do this. It was too late by then, though, so she ran on. By the time she got there, the men were hauling at the anchor ropes—twisted hempen lines as thick as her arm—of the galley still wallowing and sinking further out. They were using the second galley as a bulwark. And by the looks of it, the Arsenalotti who had pushed out the timber barrier were extending and raising it. Still, shots whistled overhead as, handspan by handspan, they hauled the other galley closer. Someone had unlimbered a small boat from the first galley and it was hastily paddled out the fifteen remaining yards or so, to begin bringing people in.

"Get men with shovels and start digging a trench, we need to unload!" shouted a voice Maria recognized. Erik Hakkonsen!

What a bitter irony. Svanhild was not in the Citadel but out there somewhere. Hopefully safe . . .

"What the hell are you doing out here, Maria?" Benito looked anything but pleased to see her. "And—Jesus wept!—with your baby! Get back! No, stay here! It's safer here."

"I've come to help you out of your mess!" she snapped back. "And my child goes with me. At her age she has to."

"*Merde!* Well, just stay behind the *Dolphin*. At this range they're not going to get a bullet right through her." He ran out, regardless of his own safety, getting into deeper water. "Come on! She's only neck deep on a short knight. Let's have what people we can off and then we'll haul her a bit further in. Another five yards and we'll get the horses out."

Maria saw Francesca and Eneko Lopez and some other clerics coming ashore in the small boat. She waved, but they didn't notice her. Well, there'd be time for greetings if they survived all this.

A group of very brave Magyar cavalrymen, or perhaps just very stupid ones, had swum their horses across the channel between the Citadel and Corfu Island. The cannon and gunfire from above had had a devastating effect on what had been perhaps four hundred men who had set out to cross the gap. Now the remainder had won the sand strip and were charging down it.

A handful of arquebusiers had taken up position behind the balks of timber. The gate swung hastily shut behind them . . . but there was timber in the way. It could not be closed. What had started out as a glorious rescue mission was fast turning into a fiasco.

And then Maria realized that Knights of the Holy Trinity were already swinging themselves into the saddle. Perhaps only thirty of them were ready to mount, but they were up and riding, broad-swords out, hurtling toward the oncoming Hungarians. When the Hungarians had begun their charge they'd outnumbered the Knights by five to one. By the time they clashed, however, those odds had been viciously reduced. The wall on their right was lined with people—some soldiers, firing, but the rest just men and women throwing whatever they had in their hands. Even cobble-stones.

The Knights were still outnumbered three to one. But these were the Knights of the Holy Trinity, perhaps Europe's finest. They hit the Hungarians on a narrow strip of beach, too narrow for either side to ride more than eight abreast. For the swim across, the Magyar knights had reduced the weight of their armor to breast-plates. They were very much at a disadvantage compared to the Knights in full armor.

Even as the first handful of Knights charged, more Knights were mounting, yelling and swearing at the Venetian sailors in their way. The sailors, too, were running to the timber-balk barrier with arquebuses, pistols and cutlasses.

If the Magyars could have carried their charge to the open gate, it would have been a different story. Speed had lent them some protection from those on the wall. But now, stopped and com-pletely defenseless against the attack from above, they were being annihilated. And the second galley was now discharging more wet, angry Knights.

"Let them handle that!" roared a bull-like voice. Manfred strode through the small waves, and grabbed the anchor rope. "Haul! On the count of three!"

Manfred had both the voice and the presence for command, so more men rushed to seize the ropes. The ship however was fill-ing up, settling, heavier. Much heavier. Maria, who was now hauling the water for their little house daily, knew just how much water weighed.

"One, two, three! *Heave.*"

The vessel moved sluggishly. It wallowed like a drunken cow.

"And again! One, two, *three.*"

Out beyond the ships, the Magyars were being reduced to bloody fragments. Maria promptly dismissed them from her mind, and went back to something she *could* do something about.

The rope snapped. Manfred's first heroic impression made on

the Corfu garrison was of himself sprawling on his backside in the shallows, legs in the air. The roar of general laughter was inevitable, if hardly kind to his dignity. Because only one rope was now hauling the boat it slewed sideways a bit, till the prow touched the stern of the other vessel. "I wouldn't have put my nose there!" said one wag.

Erik had returned to the scene. "Up, all of you. The ships must be unloaded." He, too, had the presence of command. Those who had been hauling on the first rope, if they could not find space on the second, fell into a line heaving bags and boxes and unidentifiable bits into the fortress.

Maria found herself sharing a burden, carrying in a grain bag with another garrison woman. The woman looked at her with the liveliest of curiosity. "You look terribly ordinary after the stories I'd heard."

"What stories?" asked Maria warily. "What have you heard from whom?"

"I had it from Rosalba Benelli, who heard it from her maid, whose sister is one of the poor girls who work for Sophia Tomaselli's friend Melina, that Milady Verrier had been seen in an alley in Kérkira with your dress up and two sailors." She snickered, clearly not in the least inclined to believe it—not now, at least.

Maria snorted. "She's talking about her own daydreams. I'm a respectable married woman. Besides, when would I have time? I do the work of my household myself, and thank you. I don't need twenty little girls to do it for me."

She felt slightly guilty saying that, since Alessia wasn't Umberto's child. But she owed it to Alessia—Umberto too, for that matter—to kill any such rumors.

The woman, slightly plump and with a distinct twinkle in her expressive eyes, clicked her tongue. "Tch! And there I was going to ask how you managed two." She rolled her eyes. "I can't even manage my Alberto. He keeps falling asleep, especially now they're doing these guard shifts."

Maria grinned. "I think we women should complain to the captain-general."

The woman at the other end of the sack snorted. "And have randy Tomaselli offer to help out? No, thank you very much!"

Maria's mouth twitched. "Maybe we should suggest to dear Sofia that he needs a little . . ."

The other woman began giggling. "What? That would be beneath her dignity. Besides it would spoil her makeup."

"Only she if she smiled, which seems unlikely," Maria said, thoughtfully, as they tramped over shingle that slipped and rattled under their feet. "Or maybe she doesn't just plaster her face . . . does she have to do the whole body?"

The plumpish woman looked as if she was going to fall over and drop the sack. "Oh, Lord and Saints! If she could hear you . . ."

She went off into shrieks of laughter. They reached the gate and the pile of food bags just as Maria was beginning to think the woman would kill herself laughing. They dumped the bag. And the woman hugged Maria. "You can't know how nice it is to hear someone being malicious about Milady Sophia Tomaselli for a change. My name is Stella Mavroukis. I don't care if we've been told by 'her ladyship' not to talk to you."

"Maria Verrier. I'm married to . . ."

Stella grinned wickedly. "We know *all* about Umberto. I even know what you send him for lunches. That's the trouble with Corfu. Small community. Not much to do but gossip. But it used to be fun back before 'her ladyship' got here. Come on, let's fetch another sack."

By the time they got back with the next sack, Maria knew the names, ages, childhood diseases and mischief of all five of Stella's brood, as well as several intimate details about her Alberto that Maria was sure would never allow her to meet Alberto without blushing, or at least laughing. She also knew that Alberto was a "Greek" Venetian, son of one of the many craftsmen that the Republic of Venice had seduced into her state with offers of citizenship, money and employment.

Also, of course, they'd torn Sophia Tomaselli's character, appearance and morals to shreds, very pleasurably.

Benito staggered under his load. Falkenberg in full armor was no lightweight. He was also not helping much.

They'd been up on the beach, where the battle-hardened knight had just gotten his precious horse to shore. He'd clapped Benito on the shoulder. "Well. We made it. Although this last bit has turned into a horse's—"

Then a stray ball hit him. It was one of those flukes that happened. It had hit his visor, which had shattered. The knight had fallen slowly . . . so slowly that Benito had been able to catch him.

Now they staggered toward the fortress. Benito no longer thought of strategy or tactics, just of getting the bleeding man to help, and off this beach. A Venetian came and took the other side of Falkenberg and together they staggered to the gate, while the firefight raged and the knights ripped the Magyar heavy cavalry to pieces. Falkenberg was now totally unconscious and lolling between them.

"What happened?" panted the Venetian. With a little sense of shock, Benito realized it was Umberto Verrier. The man who had married Maria.

"He was hit in the face by a ball." They were inside the gates by now.

"Let's put him down. See if we can stop the bleeding."

They laid Falkenberg down on the cobbles and Benito bent over his face, feeling sick. If only Marco was here!

"My God. What a mess." Fragments of steel had torn into the eye and right side of Falkenberg's face and head. The inside of the helmet was a mess of blood and flesh-shreds. It was still bleeding. "What the hell do we do?" he asked the older man.

For an answer, Umberto had already run over to two other men. He brought them over to the knight, with a couple of broad slats. "These men are from the hospital. They'll take him up there. The chirurgeons will help him."

"Will he live?" whispered Benito.

"Too early to tell," said one of the hospitalers critically. "But we'll have him on these planks and up there in two shakes of a lamb's tail. If you'll get out of the way, sir."

Hastily, Benito complied.

Meanwhile, Umberto called to two of the men who were struggling to push the timber further out so that the gate could be closed.

"The timber at the bottom is not going to move, Alberto! There's too much weight on it."

"So what do we do?" asked the other. "We need to be able to close this gate."

Umberto took a critical look. "They're still using it as a shelter. Let's move what we can on the top. It's only two or three of the lower balks that should be a problem. Maybe if we can get a lever of some sort to them."

Benito found himself manhandling huge pieces of keel and strut timber, when Maria came past. She was so busy talking to another woman that she didn't notice her husband, or Benito.

Working side-by-side with Verrier, Benito was finally coming to accept, not simply acknowledge, the truth of what everyone had always said about Umberto. He was a quiet, good man who loved his craft. And he was, by the looks of it, very good at it. Benito had met Umberto once or twice over the years, briefly, if not socially; a bridge-brat went everywhere and saw everything. He knew him to look at if not to talk to. But everybody always said the man was a solid fellow.

Working with him, Benito had to concede that they were right. He'd prepared himself to find reasons to dislike Umberto. Now he found that it was impossible.

And it stuck in his craw. And he hated that it stuck in his craw. Did life always have to be such a confusing mess?

Benito left organizing the off-loading of the galleys and the orderly retreat from the beach to Manfred. He concentrated instead on helping to lever the pile of timber a little further out, while Umberto organized ropes on each timber so that they could be snaked back over the wall. Umberto was a typical Venetian in that way. Not wasteful.

Benito was rewarded, when, a little while later, he saw Maria, still walking with her friend, still talking, stop abruptly and gawp at the two of them, working next to each other.

Chapter 37

"I can't deny I'm very glad to see reinforcements, Prince Manfred. I've been wishing I had some way of getting word to Venice."

Captain-General Tomaselli limped over to a cabinet on the wall, hauled out a metal flask and a tray of Venetian glassware, and limped back to his table. "Try this, gentlemen. I think we all need something a great deal stronger than wine. It's from the mainland. They distill it from plums, I believe." He poured the clear liquid into glasses and motioned that they should help themselves. He took one of the glasses.

"Is a lady permitted to try some too?" asked Francesca.

"Of course. Of course!" The flustered Venetian handed her a glass. "Unless you would prefer some wine? This stuff is frightfully strong."

Francesca lowered her lashes. "I think, milord, after the morning we've had, I'd better have some strong drink." She tossed it back without any sign of discomfort.

That was more than could be said for Erik. He choked and spluttered. Even Manfred went a little red. Benito sipped the clear liquid cautiously. It burned his throat and all the way down to his gut. Only Von Gherens managed to drink it with anything like Francesca's aplomb.

The captain-general stared at her with respect, for the first time seeing something beyond her cleavage. "Saints alive!" He shook his head. "I can't drink the stuff like that. Did you enjoy it?"

Francesca smiled and nodded her head.

The captain-general sat down, shaking his own. "Well. Back to the matter in hand. The podesta has offered the officers—and you, of course, Prince Manfred—quarters in the Castel *a mar*. Your escort also. We can quarter all your other men and horses here, at the Castel *a terra*." He sighed, softly. "Truth to tell, we could hold several hundred more men. There was no perceived threat here and we're badly undermanned. Four thousand men would be an optimum number for this fortress. I had twelve hundred under my command, but that is on the whole island. Only nine hundred and fifty odd are here."

"Where are the rest?" asked Manfred.

"About a hundred and seventy are on Vidos—that small islet out there. The rest were stationed in various towns and villages. Still, this siege can't hold. There are relatively few men out there, and they don't appear to have any siege pieces."

Manfred looked grim. "The guns and a lot more men are on their way, I'm afraid. You're in for the long haul. How are you for food and water?

"There are a couple of springs on the Citadel, and we have reservoirs here in the castle. The reservoirs are full, and this soon after winter, the springs are strong. As for food . . . we're not so well-off. Winter is over, but with the fleets coming and going, we're used to reprovisioning wheat, particularly on the autumn convoy. So we're about half way. Good for eight months at the very least. Arms are the one thing we have plenty of."

"Well, even rocks will do when it comes to defending walls," said Erik. "Rocks and enough people is what we need. And we have enough rocks, even if we could use more people."

"We brought you a good supply of knights and some extra citizens," said Von Gherens with a smile. "How are the Corfiotes outside the walls being treated?"

The captain-general blinked. "We've seen a lot of fires. Could be Venetian villas burning. Could be some peasant villages. We've seen some atrocities from the walls. Why, sir?"

"One of the things I've seen over and over again on the northeastern frontier: where the peasantry resent the hand of their overlords, we push forward easily enough. Emeric of Hungary is renowned to be a harsh man, a firm believer in the lash and the knout. I know my friend Falkenberg was involved in some fighting down in Bohemia—against Emeric's father—before the Emperor concluded the Peace of Brno. He said it was like a knife through butter. The peasants were fawning on the Prussians as if they were saints. Showed them all the Hungarian defenses, traps and so on. Found them food and fodder and guided them. And tore their former masters apart when they had the chance. It's different up in Sweden. There the tribesmen, even the Karls, resist us to the last man. Belike if your men out there stir up trouble it'll be more than Emeric can do to hold this island."

One of the captain-general's officers sniffed disdainfully. "I hardly think that will apply here. The Greeks are degenerate. Can't work, can't fight. All they can do is talk about ancient glory."

The plump captain of the *Dolphin* snorted. "I've had Corfiotes in my crew. They're good oarsmen. Better than Dalmatians, better than Venetians even. Seems to me you've got a local problem with them." He turned to Benito. "And how is *Ritter* Falkenberg, by the way, Milord Valdosta?"

"The chirurgeon says he will probably live. But he's lost an eye."

"I was across there, too," said Von Gherens, shaking his head. "His face is a mess, and he looks like he's been cupped fifteen times. But he's alive and has his wits. He said he got hit on the only soft spot in a head that's as solid as a rock. He also said the last thing he remembers is you lugging him in, boy."

"The landing wasn't the success I had hoped it would be," admitted Benito glumly.

"Hell's teeth, boy, it's a damn sight better than we'd have done any other way!" snapped Von Gherens. "We lost three men and we have three more with serious injuries. If we'd tried to charge our way in . . . we'd have considered ten times that light. War means casualties."

"Yes—but—"

Von Gherens slapped his breastplate with a mailed hand. "But me no buts! Our comrades get hurt. Our friends die. Falkenberg is a knight who swore an oath to serve the Church and to defend the weak. He'd be the first man to tell you to stop puling and start planning. Because what we are doing—at risk to ourselves— is what we have sworn to do. The West relies on us. It is a risk we take with pride. It is an oath we honor. Even when some soft southern burgher mutters about us, we know the reason he sleeps soft and comfortable, why his wife is able to complain about the price of cabbages as her most serious problem and why his children dare to throw dung and yell 'Knot' when we pass. It's because we are what we are. For all our faults we stand for law and light."

He smiled, and his tone softened. "A good plan is one that keeps our casualties light and costs our enemy dear. Keep making them, Benito Valdosta."

Manfred cleared his throat. "And that brings us to discussing the defenses of this place. With all respect, Captain-General, we have veterans of a dozen sieges here. We offer you our expertise as well as our arms."

"Your arms are appreciated," the captain-general said stiffly. "But this is a Venetian fortification, under Venetian command."

Manfred opened his mouth to speak and Francesca kicked him.

Von Gherens unfortunately wasn't in kicking range. He snorted. "You're undermanned, underprovisioned, and badly organized. You—"

"That will do, Von Gherens!" barked Eberhard, in a tone so stern it made even Manfred blink. "I apologize, Captain-General. The *Ritter* spoke out of turn."

"And we appreciate your hospitality and especially this drink," added Francesca throatily, holding out an empty glass. "But is it already being rationed?

The captain-general lost his train of angry thought and gawped, as she poured charm on him. "My apologies, signora! Of course not. Allow me." He poured out another.

After a moment's hesitation, Von Gherens put out his glass. "I spoke hastily there, Captain-General. Apologies."

"Accepted," said the captain-general stiffly. He limped forward and filled the knight's glass. "Anyone else?"

Benito watched Francesca calmly empty the glass into the purse hanging from her chatelaine, while the Venetian officer's attention was on Von Gherens.

"Perhaps later," she said, putting down the glass. "Right now I am dying to put off these salty clothes and have a wash." She fluttered her eyelashes at him.

Erik nodded. "Yes. The armor, especially the joints, must be cleaned and oiled. The salt water does it no good."

Von Gherens groaned. "That was the worst aspect of your plan, Benito."

The captain-general rang a bell. "I'll have one of my men show you to your chambers."

Francesca smiled at him. "Thank you, Captain-General Tomaselli. You are too kind."

"You may call me Nico, signora," he said bowing over her hand and kissing it.

Benito felt rather than heard the low rumble from Manfred. He also caught Francesca's wink to the prince, while the Venetian officer's head was down.

"Well, it's a nice bed," said Manfred, testing it. Naturally enough the bed complained. "But I don't know if it was worth you nearly seducing that Venetian ass for."

"A good bed is past price, darling," said Francesca, carefully emptying her purse. She looked at it sadly. "You will have to get me a new one, Manfred. I think the leather will be quite ruined by that vile drink."

"I thought you liked it?" said Manfred, with an evil grin. "You nodded when fancy-pants asked you. I saw you."

"I had to nod. I couldn't speak. I'm afraid the disgusting stuff may have ruined my vocal cords forever. Besides, if I had opened my mouth I might have been sick." She sniffed cautiously at the reticule. "*Bleh.* Even if it doesn't ruin the leather I refuse to live with the smell."

"And there I thought you'd finally learned to drink." Manfred shook his head sadly. "I'll admit the stuff was strong enough to make me pause. He might run a lousy garrison but he certainly has a drink that would put hair on your chest."

"I certainly hope not!" said Francesca. "But it was all part of the show, Manfred."

Manfred stood up and reached for her laces. "I better check about the hair," he teased. "What do you mean? 'Part of the show'? I hope you don't mean the hair . . ."

She lifted his hands aside, kissed them and said: "Later, when you don't smell of oil and old iron and fish and seaweed. What I mean by 'part of the show' was that it was our little captain-general's attempt to show how tough he was. Think of it. This is a backwater of Venetian defense. It's a major point in their resupply and trade routes, but for a commanding officer—well, it's not a place Venice expected to be attacked."

"A junior posting."

"More like a backwater posting. He's not so young."

She patted Manfred's broad shoulder. "Now, think. You are a given such a posting—a good trade spot but militarily a sign of being relegated to someplace where you can't do any damage. And suddenly—a siege! He hasn't done too badly, really. From what we've been told, had he been a totally arrogant ass like that fool who told us Greeks were no good, the fortress would have fallen to Emeric's sneak attack. Instead . . . someone did some preparation, saved the citadel, and saved a good many lives outside. It doesn't look as if he's doing too badly, so far, all things considered. Venice will be proud of him, that's what he's thinking. And then . . . in come a couple of hundred of the Empire's greatest knights, in the most dramatic style, poking a stick in the eye of the enemy. Led by a prince of the blood who offers to assist him in conducting the defenses."

Manfred swallowed. "It was well meant, Francesca."

"I know," she said, gently. "But then I'm not a thin-skinned minor noble with a dying military career. And I nearly ruined my toes kicking you. I wish I could have kicked Von Gherens too."

Manfred grinned. "He'd have asked why you were kicking him."

Chapter 38

Benito was assigned a room in the Castel *a mar*. After washing, he found himself in no state to sleep. So he set out to do what he had been told to on arriving in Corfu: reporting to the Dorma Factor.

Asking directions, Benito set out, got himself thoroughly lost and eventually found his way to the man's residence. He was not at home. So Benito left a message and walked across to the hospital to see how Falkenberg was doing.

"You can't see him," said the monk. "He's finally asleep. He's in pain, young man. Sleep, even assisted by laudanum, is the best thing for him."

"Tell him . . . I'll come back later. Is he going to be all right?"

The monk shrugged. "If he doesn't get secondary infections. We've prayed over him. We've used such skills as we have. We have used a fragment of the blessed Saint Landry's hand."

Benito wished, desperately, that his brother were here. But all he could do was thank the monk and leave.

He stood outside on the street, looked about, and bit his lip. Finally, with a feeling in his stomach as if he'd been kicked there by Von Gherens, asked a passerby: "Where can I find the home of Umberto Verrier?"

The man shrugged. "Never heard of him."

"He's a master caulker. Just come out from Venice."

"Try the store-yards down at the outer northeastern gate."

So Benito passed out through the inner curtain wall, and on down to the store-yard. Given the way his day had been going so far, he was not surprised to find that Umberto had taken a belated breakfast and was now back at home, which was inside the curtain wall.

"Look for the last house before the road to St. Agatha's. Between the hills. He's got a goat in his yard. You can usually hear it. It leans over the wall and bleats at passers by. They feed it. Only man I know with a watch-goat," said the Corfiote laborer, grinning. "It's got a weakness for Kourabiedies."

Benito knew exactly which house the man was talking about then. He'd passed it on his way to look for the Dorma factor, and again while walking to the hospital. He sighed. It had been that sort of day.

"What's wrong?" enquired the burly laborer.

"Nothing much. I've just walked down from virtually next door. Anyway, thanks."

The man grinned, showing missing teeth. "You're welcome. I saw you coming in from the ship this morning. And working with old Umberto. He's not a bad soul, for a Venetian."

So Benito walked back up. He found the house. The goat leaned over the wall and bleated at him. Taking a deep breath, he walked up to the door and knocked.

Maria opened the door, baby on arm. "Benito! What are you doing here?"

"You know this young fellow?" asked Umberto, smiling and getting up from the table. "He gave me a lot of help this morning. Come in, young man. We never got formally introduced. I know your face from Venice. This is my wife, Maria . . . but you already seem to know that?"

Benito bowed. "Maria was very good to me while I was growing up. I'm Benito Valdosta."

"Marco Valdosta's brother?" Umberto looked faintly awed. "The ward of the Doge?"

"And more trouble than he's worth," said Maria. It wasn't exactly welcoming . . . but at least she wasn't yelling at him.

Benito held out his hands pacifically. "I'm trying to reform. Really. Back when Maria met Marco and me, we were both bridge-brats and always in trouble."

Maria snorted. "You were. Marco wasn't. He was a trainee saint even then."

Benito grinned. "Even when he ran off into the Jesolo, after writing love-letters to Angelina Dorma?"

Maria shook her head, a reluctant shadow of a smile coming to her face. "He was a young idiot. He grew up."

"Oh, I agree. About the saint part *and* the idiot part, which he never grew out of. I still love him dearly." He sighed. "And if this wasn't such a hideous situation, I'd wish he was here now."

Maria smiled properly now. "He and Kat are both idiots—at least by your standards, Benito—but I also love both of them very dearly. They're our Alessia's godparents, you know."

"I know," said Benito. "She couldn't ask for better ones."

Umberto beamed on both of them. "Well, why don't you come in and have a glass of wine with us, you being by the way of things a sort of god-uncle to my daughter. Then you can tell us what we can do for you. You have a place to stay?"

Benito had to swallow hastily. He nodded, looking around.

Maria and Umberto's little home was small, Spartan, and lovingly tended, from the simple tablecloth to the little wicker cradle in the corner. Umberto certainly hadn't been able to smother Maria Garavelli in worldly goods. But he'd given her what she'd needed: a home, stability, and a reliable father for her baby. Someone who wouldn't go doing crazy things that might get him killed.

"I have a place to stay, thank you. I just came to pass on Kat's messages. She sends her love to you and to little Alessia. She said I must tell you to write. I also came to offer my help if there was anything useful I could do for you . . ." he finished lamely. It didn't seem like a very good reason for seeking someone out. He looked at the baby and Maria, standing Madonna-like. "She looks well-fed."

"At least you didn't say she looks beautiful like everyone else does," said Maria, tartly. "Here. Hold this well-fed baby while I get the wine." She passed the plump bundle over.

Benito found himself with a soft, milky-breathed baby in his arms. After the initial shock, it didn't feel too bad.

The habited woman on her knees tending the flowers outside the Hypatian Order chapel looked up as Eneko Lopez and Father Pierre approached. "And how can I help you, my sons?" she asked pleasantly.

"We're looking for a Sibling Eleni," explained Pierre.

The Sibling got up, dusting her knees. She had the ageless sort of face, ornamented by bright brown eyes, that Eneko tended to associate with Hypatian Siblings. There was something about the cloistered life that kept age at a distance.

"That is me. Actually, there is only me here. How may I help you?"

Eneko nodded. "It's rather a long story, Sibling, but we have here a letter from the Grand Metropolitan of Rome. We were on our way to Jerusalem, before our ship was diverted here."

The nun smiled. It was clear then, as fine lines appeared around her mouth and eyes, that she was, if not old, certainly no longer young. "If it is a long story, let us go into the chapel. God doesn't mind listening out here, but it is cooler for us there."

She nodded politely at Eneko. "Your reputation and description go before you, *Señor* Lopez. I'm afraid I don't know you," she said to the priest accompanying him.

"Father Pierre," he said simply, smiling.

"Ah." She said nothing else until they were within the tiny chapel, and seated on some stools she brought from the back of the building. "Well, now, how may the Hypatian Order on Corfu serve you? You've come to heathen parts, I'm afraid." She shook her head, but with more fondness than irritation. "The locals attend church faithfully, but I know for a certain fact that many of them continue their worship of a pagan deity. A bloodthirsty goddess of some sort, I suppose. That is, I suppose she is bloodthirsty, because the men seem to hold her in some fear. The women—well, they keep their secrets to themselves."

She sighed. "It's all nonsense, of course, but they are happy in their nonsense, and we try to educate them slowly. The island is simply stiff with such superstitions."

"You would not mind, Sibling, if we enact the ritual of the veil of divine privacy?" Eneko shook himself. "I've just seen two birds of prey high in the sky. I know there is a war on and the hawks and eagles come to feast . . . but I'll swear I've seen those birds following us since we left Rome."

The Sibling spread her hands wide. "You may do as you wish, Father Lopez. You know the Hypatian Order believes strongly in the appropriate use of Christian magic whenever needful."

The chapel was built with a careful alignment to the four cardinal directions. Statues of the archangels Michael, Gabriel, Raphael and Uriel stood on plinths in their corners. Eneko and Pierre set about raising the wards. Soon the distant sounds of the Citadel were shut off inside the veil. It was with a feeling of relief that they returned to their stools.

"We have had scryings both of great deeds and portents of magical conflict here, Sibling," Eneko said, certain now that nothing could overlook him. "Evil in the shape of Chernobog, and an ancient power that we could not identify."

The small Sibling started. "Here? Here on little Corfu? Oh, no, Father Eneko! Nothing ever happens here. The locals talk about magical Corfu, but it is small magics, if there are any at all. Superstitions and mutterings about the Goddess, but never have I seen a sign of great pagan power. There are a few Jews who may be involved. A Strega charm-seller or two. Virtually every hamlet has its so-called wise-woman, who might dabble in birthing spells . . . but that is it."

She shook her head emphatically. "Unless it is something the Hungarian invaders have brought with them, not something from here."

"Hmm. Might we try a scrying?" As an afterthought, Eneko added: "And also a contact spell. If there is any chance of contacting him, Brother Mascoli of St. Raphaella in Venice could pass word to the Venetians about the siege, and perhaps get it relieved."

"Of course, the chapel is yours, Father! I wish I could help you, but I fear that I myself am very unskilled in such matters." The Sibling smiled, but wistfully. "You know that the Order welcomes those with many skills—and there never seemed to be a need for a magician here, so they sent me. I'm better with small children and gardens than I am with great magic. A little magic to make my herbs grow, a soothing spell for a colicky child, that sort of thing. I do not believe these will be of service to you now."

"On the other hand, I could not soothe a child," Lopez felt impelled to tell her. "In fact, I rather think I would give it nightmares. The Lord welcomes all who serve, Sibling."

But a few minutes later, when concentrating on Brother Mascoli's image, Eneko Lopez discovered that now the greater magics were beyond him, too. It was a shock—like reaching for something you knew was there, only it wasn't. Or waking up to find that someone had amputated a hand.

"Look at the archangel Uriel," whispered Pierre, round-eyed.

Eneko turned, slowly, to look. What he was looking at . . . just wasn't there. The golden glow, haloing the statue, summoned by the invocation, was gone. There *was* no Ward of the North.

"We enacted the veil ritual without any difficulty."

"A power great enough to attack an archangel . . ." He took a deep breath and tried to steady himself. "No wonder our scrying didn't work!"

Pierre shook his head. "It's not so much 'attack,' as 'nullify.' It just isn't there."

Eneko Lopez stared at the statue of Uriel. "It can't be the creature of Chernobog; we sent that scuttling. And the archangels were potent enough against him, anyway. Why the keeper of the creatures of the Earth?"

Maria watched sidelong to see how Benito took Alessia, waiting to be amused at his awkwardness. To her surprise, there was none. He didn't, as Kat had, hold Alessia as if she was made of fragile porcelain. He didn't, as Umberto did, seem to have a problem knowing what to hold. He took and held her as if it was the most natural of things. He supported her head . . . without being told. And he looked oddly pleased. Not something most men looked when handed a baby.

Maria went into the kitchen, drew a jug of wine, and . . . sighed. At times like this, Benito—

She shook her head firmly, snatched up three wine cups and returned to the outer room.

Benito was rocking Alessia with a peculiar smile on his face. After Maria put down the wine and cups, Benito handed Alessia back to her mother.

"You know, that's the first time I've ever held a baby. They're heavier than they look." He sat down and took the cup of wine that Umberto poured out. "Thank you."

Maria smiled wryly. "And noisier, too. You know, Benito, there *is* something you could do for me. I've been trying to think how to get a message to him since I saw him this morning. Do you know Erik Hakkonsen? Prince Manfred of Brittany's companion? Sort of a bodyguard?"

Benito grinned wryly. "You might say so. He's beaten me, drilled me till I fell over, and made my life a misery for the last ten days or so."

"Oh," she said, sounding disappointed, but with a twinkle in her eye. "Well, then you're probably not the right person to tell him that a Vinlander girl called Svanhild, who was on the ship with us, has waited on Corfu to see him. Her and her two brothers. A whole crew of them, in fact."

Benito jumped to his feet, almost spilling the wine, grinning. "I'll go and find him right away. He's been like a bear with a sore tooth because of this woman—if it is the right woman. Svanhild, you say she's called? I'll go and ask. Where is she?"

Maria lost the twinkle, and sobered. "That's the bad part. She's outside the walls, somewhere on the island. I forget the name of the count whose villa they were staying in. Oh, wait—yes, Dentico, I think it is."

He stared at her in shock. "Out there? But why aren't they inside? I mean, I thought all the people would have been called into . . ."

Umberto shook his head. "Nobody was called in. See, some of the townspeople and Venetians who got wind of it just happened to be here. The call has to go out from the captain-general. The commander readied the citadel, but when he asked Tomaselli if the cavalry should go out and escort the people in, the captain-general refused permission."

Benito swallowed. "So they're out there—with the enemy burning, raping and looting. And you want me to tell Erik?"

She nodded.

Benito took a deep breath. "Well. I thought he was bad before. But I have a feeling that this is going to be worse. She definitely wanted to see Erik?"

The corners of her mouth went further down. "They waited here on Corfu, getting off the Atlantic convoy, just so that she could see him. She was on the breakwater-head waiting when the Outremer fleet came in because she thought he'd be on it."

"She was in tears because he wasn't on it," added Umberto.

"Oh. Like that, is it?" said Benito. "I got the impression that she'd given him the push."

Maria sighed. "It was a bit of a bit of a misunderstanding. Tell him to come and see me and I'll explain."

Benito swallowed the last of his wine. "In that case, I'd better see if I can find him. Today's been my day for not finding people easily. Thank you for the wine."

Umberto smiled. "It is our pleasure. Come again."

Benito gave a wary look at Maria. "I will . . . If I may?"

Maria snorted. "If you stay out of trouble. Which probably means 'no' in your case."

Benito grinned. "I'll do my best. But I think you've just landed me in it with Erik. Anyway, *ciao*. Good-bye, Alessia." He waved to the baby.

Benito walked out and set off in search of Erik, full of mixed feelings. Yes, it hurt seeing Maria, listening to her acerbic tongue. But still, he found himself curiously at peace. He had always regarded babies as good things for other people, something to be personally avoided at all costs. But his heart had gone out to Maria's child. He must think of ways to help her. To help Maria . . . and Umberto for that matter.

The search for Erik was like the rest of his day—a roundabout. Erik was not in his quarters. He was not with the knights who were assembling under Von Gherens's tongue lash. Von Gherens told Benito to try Manfred and Francesca's rooms. It was where, had Benito thought about it, he should have gone in the first place.

He knocked with some trepidation on the door. Manfred, Benito had noticed, was cavalier about the privacy of others, but protective of his own.

The door opened. Manfred grinned down at him. "Ah, Benito. So have you run to earth all the taverns in this place, and maybe some exotic dancers?"

Benito shook his head. "I can't run anything to earth in this place. Besides, I'm trying to stay out of trouble."

Manfred laughed and opened the door wider. "That'll be a shock to the world! A first time, I should think. Come in and have a drink. Francesca won't. She enjoyed the captain-general's liquor so much that she won't touch ordinary armor-polish like mine. And Erik is so crossed in love that I'm keeping him off the drink."

"Um. Is Erik here?"

Manfred nodded. "He is, indeed. In his personal cloud of gloom worrying about the Atlantic convoy and not this siege. Why? Are you in need of some drill?"

Benito hesitated, then realized that *not* telling Erik—

immediately—would put him in worse trouble than anything. "I need to talk to him," he said firmly.

"Talk to me, then," said Erik from the corner.

"I thought . . . a private word."

Erik sighed. "I haven't any advice to give you, Benito."

Erik plainly wasn't going to make this easy. "Well, I wasn't really looking for advice. I just heard about a girl called Svanhild—"

Erik crossed the room in a single lunge, picking Benito up by the shirt front. With one hand. "I have enough of this from Manfred. You leave her name out of it. You leave her out of it! Do you hear me?" He put Benito down with a thump against the wall, glaring at him.

"She's looking for you," said Benito, in a kind of undignified squeak. He had the satisfaction of seeing Erik totally rocked on his heels.

"What? Where?" demanded the Icelander. The look of hope in Erik's eyes took away the satisfaction.

Benito took a careful step away. "Erik . . . it's bad news. She's here on Corfu. But she's outside the walls."

Erik sat down. His blue-gray eyes bored into Benito.

But it was Manfred who spoke. "Where do you get this from, Benito? This no subject for your practical jokes." His voice, bantering earlier, was now deadly serious.

Benito held up his hands. "No joke, I swear, I got it straight from Maria and Umberto, who specifically told me to tell you. It's true. Someone called Svanhild from Vinland, who was on the Atlantic convoy, stopped here so that she could wait and see Erik. Specifically. Maria said she had two brothers with her and a number of other Vinlanders. Only they stayed in a villa outside town. Nobody warned them about the siege."

Erik's eyes were still boring into him. It was at times like this that Benito understood exactly why the Holy Roman Emperors relied on Clann Harald for their closest bodyguards. Erik Hakkonsen practically shrieked: *Deadly!*

"Maria, you know . . ." Benito half-babbled. "Er . . . Katerina's bridesmaid—at the wedding!—was on the ship with her. Svanhild, that is. She asked me—Maria, that is—to tell Erik, I swear it. And her husband Umberto confirmed it."

Erik got up, took a deep breath, and gave himself a little shake. "Benito, I owe you an apology."

Benito shrugged and grinned. And paid back the scores of an entire week of training. "It's nothing. No one expects logic of a man in love."

Then he lost his smile. "I'm sorry that I had to tell you she's out there. You can see fires up and down the length of the Island."

Erik swallowed. "Has she got her bodyguard, her brothers and their hearthmen, still with her?"

Benito shrugged again. "I don't know. I've told you literally all I've heard. Maria said you should come and talk to her about it."

The rangy Icelander put a hand on Benito's shoulder. "Will you take me to her? Please? Now?"

Benito nodded; he'd expected as much. Probably Maria had, too, if Svanhild had been as irrational about this as Erik was.

But if the girl had a pile of brothers and whatnot with her that were like Erik—well, maybe she, and they, were all right. In fact, maybe he was going to feel a little sorry for the invaders.

Manfred turned to Francesca. "I think we'd better tag along as well."

Francesca stood up. "Yes, I'd like to see Maria anyway. I never really got to know her." She raised an eyebrow at Benito. "This is 'your' Maria, isn't it? The one you got into trouble over?"

Benito reddened. "I've got over that now. Umberto Verrier is a very decent man. Gives her what I didn't."

Francesca smiled. "If you can come to terms with that, you've grown up more than most men ever do. Come, Manfred. Erik wants to go."

Manfred took her arm. "Do we need horses?"

Benito shook his head. Horses were one of the aspects of being "promoted" to the *Case Vecchie* that he really could do without. Living in Venice he'd not been on the back of one until he was fifteen. And then he hadn't stayed there for very long. "It's close. Five minutes' walk."

Francesca looked down at her little pearl-fringed Venetian leather shoes and grimaced. "Oh, well. I have ruined the purse that matched them already. Let's go."

Erik was already halfway down the hall, forgetting that it was Benito who would have to show them where to go. And as they walked, he was constantly having to check his long strides for the rest of them to catch up.

Benito didn't like this at all. It was fairly likely the Icelander's sweetheart had fallen prey to King Emeric of Hungary's forces. Erik was like a loose cannon with a lit wick on a crowded deck. When— if—he found out she'd been hurt or was dead, someone was going to pay in blood.

Probably Captain-General Nico Tomaselli.

Chapter 39

Maria decided that skirting Svanhild's reason for considering her true love ineligible was probably wise. Erik didn't seem to care anyway. All he wanted to do was to get out there and find out if she was all right.

"So you say her brothers and their party stayed with her?"

Maria nodded. "Two of them went on, saying they were going to return to Vinland. But the other fifteen or so stayed with her. Her two brothers included."

Erik shook his head, angrily. "I don't understand why she didn't stay here. The podesta has lots of space up at the Castel *a mar*. He told me that it is quite usual for important or high-ranking travelers to be their guests."

Maria made a face. "Um. She had a clash with the captain-general . . . and instead of sending them to see the podesta, he gave them directions to Count Dentico's villa. They had been trying to find place for a party of sixteen in the town. But Kérkira's tavernas, um, weren't good enough. Apparently."

"The Thordarsons are very wealthy. A powerful family in western trade," said Erik. "Svanhild would expect everything of the best. In a taverna, she would have to share a bed with other women, strangers."

Maria blinked. *Well, of course*, she almost said aloud. After all, what else? You put up in a taverna, you were going to have to share the accommodations with other travelers. That went without saying. Didn't it?

Erik seemed to read her thoughts; but, a bit to her surprise, he didn't react angrily or defensively. He simply shook his head, smiling a little.

"You're not telling me all of what she said, I'm sure, because you think I'd be offended at the thought she found me unsuitable until she learned about Manfred. But I understand her, Maria, and you don't. Well enough, anyway. Vinland's not really that different from Iceland. I lived there myself, you know, for three years."

Maria had forgotten that about him, if she'd ever known. But it explained Erik's skill with that peculiar Vinlander weapon called a *tomahawk,* and with the *skraeling* style of wrestling.

"She's from a very wealthy family," Erik explained softly, "but has no experience with towns and cities. Sent by her family, I'm sure, to find a proper husband. A girl who's known few strange men of any kind—and those, men whose customs she understands. Vinlanders or *skraelings,* who, at least in some ways, aren't all that different."

Manfred was staring at Erik oddly. "You understood all this about her? Then why . . ." He winced.

Erik shook his head. "Clann Harald is true to its oath to the imperial family. Always. I could explain nothing to her, even though it was obvious to me that—"

He waved his hand, curtly. "Ah, never mind. The point here, Maria, is that she's probably never shared a room, much less a bed, with any female she didn't know. She's never been away from home before, and I'm sure in all of the places she's stayed so far, they fell over themselves to give her a room to herself. Here, so crowded, not all the money even the Thordarsons have could buy a private room in a taverna."

He sighed. "And her brothers, naturally—you have no idea how protective such can be, in matters like this—would not have dreamed of asking her to do something so outlandish."

"Well, they did seem to have plenty of money. I suppose you look at things differently when you have that kind of money," Maria said.

Erik nodded, glumly. "She's as far above me as the earth is above the moon."

"Oh, nonsense!" muttered Manfred.

"Oh, nonsense!" Maria snapped the words, like a whip. "She was blubbering about you on the ship. The moment she found out your status was suitable—however those odd Vinlanders calculate such things—she stopped blubbering and tried to *buy* the damn ship to turn it around. I couldn't believe it! Then, when that didn't work, she got off here in order to wait for you. She was down on the dock, every day, watching for the galleys to come in. And her brothers didn't seem in the least unhappy about her interest, either!

"If that helps any," Maria ended, a bit lamely, her voice now less sure of itself. It had just dawned on her that, under the present circumstances, the girl might as well have been on the moon . . . if not further away.

The same realization seemed to have come to Erik as well. He was subdued, now, punctilious in thanks and farewells, but not really there.

Maria watched them go, feeling obscurely sorry for him. The last time she had seen anyone that mad for someone, it had been Kat for Marco . . . Or maybe Benito . . .

She pushed *that* thought away, firmly.

Poor Erik! She felt savage for a moment. And this was all Captain Tomaselli's fault!

Well, if—or when—Erik discovered Svanhild had been hurt, or worse—

Umberto would be getting a promotion again, probably. Could someone be promoted from the Arsenal into the captain-general's job? Eh, it probably wouldn't matter; if the captain-general was dead at the hands of Erik Hakkonsen, and the siege was still on, the captain-general would be whomever the governor said it was, and the governor and his wife both liked Umberto.

Maria closed her eyes, and recalled to herself those huge brothers, and equally huge followers. Maria had never seen Erik Hakkonsen fight herself, but both Kat and Benito had described to her the Icelander's ferocious ability in combat. If these Northlanders were all like that—

Maybe Umberto wouldn't be getting that promotion after all. She hoped so. In fact, she prayed so.

They trudged back up the hill. Now it was no effort to keep pace with the Icelander, which was a pity. An idea was brewing in Benito's head, but he wanted to talk to Manfred about it first.

When they got up to the Castel *a mar*, Erik finally obliged him. Manfred suggested a spot of rapier practice.

Erik shook his head. "I think I want to spend some time alone, Manfred. I've much to think about."

"I'll give you a bout, Manfred," said Benito, as Manfred stared open-mouthed at Erik.

Erik nodded. "You go and give the boy a lesson or two. I'll be in my room, if you need me."

He turned then to Benito. "I am in your debt. I have used you very hard over the last while. Forgive me."

"'S nothing. I understand," said Benito awkwardly. He'd rather have Erik chewing him out than being like this.

Erik nodded and went into his room.

"Well, let's get the quilted jackets and the buttoned rapiers," said Manfred, far too heartily. "They're with my gear."

When they got to Manfred's chambers, Francesca said, firmly, "Your swordplay will have to wait, Benito. I need to talk to Manfred."

Benito grinned. "So do I. And the truth to tell, all I feel like doing is falling asleep once I'm done talking. I didn't sleep at all last night. The last thing on my mind is rapier practice."

Manfred grimaced. "Except it is *never* the last thing on Erik's mind. I'm worried about him. Up till a couple of weeks ago I'd have thought he'd rather fence than make love to a woman. Cut line, Benito. Talk quickly. I need to discuss this with Francesca."

Benito cleared his throat. "Well . . . I thought . . . A siege, especially with that captain-general in charge, I'm not going to see a lot of action."

He looked pensively at Manfred. The prince had folded his arms across his massive chest, and was now looking at Benito in the totally expressionless, ox-dumb manner that Benito recognized, by now, as a sign of Manfred in deep thought.

"So I thought . . . Well, I can't do a lot of good here. Maybe I should go to where I can—out there. I'm pretty sure I could swim with the current, using a float of some kind, and come out clear of the troops tonight. I could probably even have them lower a small boat over the walls on the seaward side. Then I could do what Von Gherens was hinting at: raise the peasantry against the Hungarians. And I could also find out what has happened to Erik's girl. It's not likely to be anything good. But he's going to be torn up until he knows."

Manfred's eyes narrowed slightly. "I'll think about it. The captain-general won't approve."

Benito shrugged. "I don't think I really give a damn. But I do need your help to signal back what I find out about the girl."

"I'll think about it," said Manfred. "I'll come and talk to you later. Now go and get that sleep you need. I need to talk to Francesca."

Francesca pointed to a seat. "Actually, I think Benito had better stay. And *no*, Manfred, you are *not* going out there with Benito."

Manfred shook his head. "How the hell did you guess?" To Benito, plaintively: "The woman's a witch, I swear it."

Francesca smiled knowingly. "Your face doesn't give anything away. But I know just how your mind works. The minute you said you'd go and talk to Benito later, I knew just what you were planning. And quite simply: *No.* You can't do it. You, with your rank and the Knights at your command, are the only person who can effectively influence the defense of this Citadel. The captain-general will lose it to the enemy. He's done well enough so far, but he'll swiftly be out of his depth. You are the only one here who outranks him, and you, of everyone, are the only one here who can command the Knights to lock him in a room, if necessary, and take over command. Given how his own men have reacted to his commands, I do not think you will find a great deal of opposition if you are forced to that action."

She glanced at Benito. "And there is one thing that needs doing a lot more than raising the island's countryside—its rather *little* countryside—against the Hungarians. That is getting news to Venice. In time the news, garbled and distorted, will trickle over-land. But unless the two ships that did not take part in this landing manage to get to Rome or Venice—and I doubt they will, now that I've seen the effort Emeric's put into this—help will be many months in coming. It could take a month or two, if the block-ade is effective, before the Venetians even realize there *is* a blockade. We'll get you a small boat, a few seamen, and you should go across to Illyria."

"Forget it." Manfred shook his head. "Francesca, I'm barely a mouse to your elephant as far as your knowledge of politics is concerned. But I do have some military acumen, you know."

He grinned. "Even if Erik won't admit it. Look, assuming Benito got across all right, his chances of crossing the Balkans alive are nonexistent. Darling, why do you think a nonmaritime power like Hungary is transporting its troops and weapons by sea? The answer is pretty obvious even to the nonmilitary mind. Emeric is coming by sea because even with an army of tens of thousands he probably couldn't get through the Balkans. There's a fiercely independent Illyrian chief over there named Iskander Beg who is welding the tribes into a nation. And one thing that all those tribes do is kill people who try to pass through their territory. Do you imagine I'd have paid Dorma a fortune for the hire of these four vessels to transport horses if I could have sent them overland? We could have sailed in one vessel, and met them at Constantinople. However, crossing over the Adriatic and going via Rugosa down the old Roman Road to Constantinople is out of the question these days."

Francesca raised a perfect eyebrow. "What was it that Eberhard said to you the other day: 'If all politicians had to be soldiers first, they wouldn't ask soldiers to do the impossible.'"

Manfred shrugged. "He does make good points, occasionally."

Francesca laughed deliciously. "The poor old man. Every time he's getting to approve of you, you do the next rash thing, according to him. But as it happens I don't agree with him."

"Miracle of miracles." Manfred grinned. "Why not? For once he is simply making sense."

"Because it would make for monolithic thinking. All solutions would be militarily influenced, and military men don't always understand how civilians work, either. Anyway, forget Benito for a moment. You, too, Benito. Let's get back to what should be done for Erik."

Manfred, flopped into a chair, making it groan in protest. "I was all for Erik getting over her. Quite honestly, Benito, you and that ex-girlfriend of yours have stirred up something I had hoped would blow over."

Francesca had come to stand behind Manfred. She rubbed his shoulders. Benito couldn't help but notice how small her hands seemed on them. "I don't think it is going to happen quite as you'd like, Manfred dear," she said slowly. "He's a very intense man. A serious one. He is torn between his duty to you and his . . . shall we call it . . . infatuation, with this woman."

"He's stuck here. Fortunately, as far as I'm concerned! Can't we get him another girl to chase? I am not convinced *she's* good enough for *him*. I set high standards for Erik."

Francesca shook her head and smiled. "Manfred, you know as

well as I do that that might work for you, but it won't work for Erik. In your company, he has been trailed past more attractive ladies than most men would see in three lifetimes."

Manfred grunted. "And half them wanted that clean-cut face of his. And he didn't notice them at all. No, I suppose you're right, as usual, but the point is that he's still stuck here. She's probably dead by now, anyway."

Francesca patted him. "Too little sleep, that's what it is. Manfred, Erik is an Icelander. He probably has spent more time in small boats than he has on horseback. That means he's as capable of getting out of here as Benito. He is staying here out of loyalty to you and tearing himself apart in the process. Worst of all, for him, is the uncertainty. Erik is one of the most effective warriors alive. He's used to taking initiative. Right now loyalty means he can't."

Manfred flicked himself onto his feet. From reclining to standing in an instant. Benito realized again just how strong the prince was. Not simply strong, as an ox might be, but phenomenally athletic as well.

"Well. No point in that! I'm as safe here as a man can be with three thick walls and a moat around him. Well, sea channel and a small ocean—better yet. Erik should get out there, set his mind at rest and either bring this charmer home or bury her."

Francesca sighed. "For an example of why only ex-soldiers should take part in politics, you've just failed, Manfred. You regard this place as militarily secure?"

Manfred nodded, cheerfully. "It would do better with twice or three times the garrison. With six thousand men you'd be able to hold this place against virtually any force, as long as the food and water held out. But it is not too bad, actually. According to Captain-General Tomaselli, with his forces, our men, the ship crews and the militia we have maybe two thousand men. The food stocks should last that number a couple of years with rationing"

"And yet," said Francesca, "there are at least eleven thousand souls here in this Citadel. Aside from children, that is. Does something not strike you as odd?"

Manfred made a face. "Uh. These guys have four wives each? No wonder they look so dozy. How did you get this figure, Francesca?"

Francesca laughed. "Dozy indeed! I asked the podesta's secretary, Meletios Loukaris. He's a very efficient little Greek. The local eminences fled to the Citadel when the warning came on the night before the attack. Most of them are Corfiotes, the local gentry, people of the *Libri d'Oro* who live in town and have estates in the country. The Citadel refused to allow in arbitrary locals, but in addition to these, some people had chits signed by the podesta. There are nearly six thousand of them. The captain-general is not well pleased with this."

Benito blinked. "You mean he wanted to leave them outside? But . . . this is supposed to be a Venetian protectorate!"

"True," said Francesca, in an absolutely level voice that conveyed as much by its evenness as her normally expressive tones did. "Unfortunately, the Senate did not vote the captain-general a budget to allow siege provisions for the people of Kérkira. Or so my little Greek informant told me."

Manfred bit his knuckle. "Are you telling me this ass is planning not to feed them? They outnumber his troops, oh, nine to one, and he's not going to *feed* them?"

"Fortunately the podesta prevailed on him that this would be foolish. They'll be issued a ration. Smaller than the Venetians, of course. There is no love lost between the locally stationed Venetians and the Greeks."

Manfred shook his head. "How do you find all this out so quickly, Francesca? Here we are sitting on a powder keg waving slow-matches and I thought it was quite safe!"

She smiled demurely. "It is because I am just a woman, and not a soldier."

"You're not ever going to let me forget that, are you?" grumbled Manfred. Insofar as a man could grumble while grinning.

She chucked him under the chin. "No. But I am also not going to let you forget that many more fortresses fall by treachery than by strength of arms. And this fortress, with its divided populace, is probably in more danger than most."

Manfred's eyes narrowed. "It sounds like the captain-general is going to have to go. That could be difficult."

"It's difficult from more than one direction. The Corfiotes themselves reciprocate the feelings the Venetians have about them. They won't cooperate unless their lives are in direct danger." Francesca smiled gleefully. "To think I thought I would be bored during this siege! Manfred, between Eberhard and myself, we will manage the captain-general and keep an eye on the locals. The actual commander of the garrison is quite young, but a better soldier, apparently. Relax. Erik wouldn't be any good at this sort of thing anyway. He might as well go and look for his Svanhild."

She looked consideringly at Benito. "*You*, however, would probably be very useful here, because—"

She broke off, cocking her head a little. "What is happening out there?"

They went out, following the people who were streaming to see what the commotion was about.

The strait was full of sails. Emeric's cannon and the rest of his army had arrived.

Chapter 40

Capitano Da Castres pointed out something else, glumly, quietly: a hulk under tow. "My dapper friend Bortaliscono won't be going to comfort my wife after all."

Benito realized the implication of the burned and battered remains of the great galley. Those messages would not be getting back to Venice by sea. Of course, there was still a chance that the other vessel might have escaped and headed for Rome. But Benito had his doubts of Capitano Selvi, who, if he had managed to evade the blockade, was probably halfway to the Arabic emirates or the Khanates by now.

He turned to Manfred. "If Erik is going to go . . . this means he has to go tonight."

Manfred nodded. "True. By nightfall, Emeric's men will already be getting those cannon into action. By tomorrow night, they will keep up the bombardment. Sneaking out thereafter will be nigh impossible. I'll go and talk to him."

"Also, I think I'd better go with him."

Manfred shook his head. "Francesca wants you here."

Benito took a deep breath, and began his plea. He knew he would have a very limited time to convince Manfred of what he needed to do before it was too late to do it.

"I believe I can get a message back to Venice, Manfred. Francesca is capable of all of her schemes without a little guy like me. I'd rather stay and fight. I'd rather go out with Erik and organize guerillas. But I believe my duty to Venice, to Petro Dorma, is to get back to Venice. Magicians can send word to the fleets, warning them. Venice itself can prepare to relieve Corfu. I believe I've got an idea of how it could be done, without going through the Balkans."

Francesca nodded and smiled. "If you could do that, it would be worth more to us than your skills in fraternizing with lowlifes would be."

"Ha. How come I can't do the fraternizing with lowlifes while Erik is away?" protested Manfred, assuming an expression of hurt. "I've got years of experience!"

Francesca smiled. "Because as a leadership figure we need the people, all the people, to look up to you."

"Spoilsport!" muttered Manfred. "Mind you, Benito mentioned an option I hadn't even thought of: Eneko Lopez." Manfred grinned. "Maybe we can keep your low-life fraternizer here after all. If the clerics can send magical word, the taverns of the Citadel will not have to lose such a valued customer."

Eneko Lopez shook his head tiredly. "No. Magically we are hamstrung. We have tried, repeatedly, together and separately, to invoke the guardian archangels of the cardinal points. One simply does not respond. The angels did . . . once, for a minor magic. Since then we have failed."

Eneko sighed and rubbed his eyes. "I do not know what magical knowledge you have, but this is fundamental. We *must* operate behind our protections. As well for a knight to go into battle having forgotten to armor himself. Still, we ventured on a harmless minor spell to see what would happen. A blessing on the flowers around the church. Magic has a feel to it, Manfred. This was like wading through thigh-deep mud. There is something here, about this place . . . not so much opposition to us, as a simple resistance. In the end, the magic we worked was words. Merely words, nearly without substance."

"Chernobog?" asked Manfred, thinking of the terrible powers they had defeated in Venice. "Or something like that?"

Eneko shook his head, a puzzled frown on his face. "No. I have encountered various nonhuman powers. Chernobog . . . This is as unlike that as is possible. The Black Brain is a violent and malevolent force. It is unlike the Lion of Etruria, too. That has a personality, a shape. This seems amorphous, unfocused—almost as if it had lost its focus, somehow. But one thing is certain: It, too, is our enemy, if only because it does not love us at all." He sighed. "It must however have human agents. We'll try to find those. But I wish I could contact Rome. There are magic-workers in the service of the Grand Metropolitan who are as far beyond my brothers and me as we are beyond a charm-seller."

Benito had never been entirely at ease with the intense cleric, which, considering how they had met, was not surprising. "I'm thinking of trying to get a smuggler or a fishing boat to drop me across on the Italian shore, Father Eneko. I'll make my way overland to Venice. Do you want me to try and deliver any messages?"

Eneko's dour expression lifted. "I will prepare letters. Perhaps . . ."

"I don't think I want anything in writing," Benito interrupted. "I'm going to have to go as a fisherman or a common sailor. I don't want to get searched and have embarrassing things turn up. Dorma will believe me without such evidence."

Eneko nodded. "Yes. I quite see that." He exhaled through his teeth. "Unfortunately, the Grand Metropolitan might respond to something written in my fist, whereas a traveling youngster like yourself is just not going to get an interview with the Grand Metropolitan."

He smiled wryly. "It is difficult enough for high potentates to do so. I think the best possible thing would be for you to proceed straight to Venice. There you could speak to Siblings Mascoli of St. Raphaella or Evangelina of St. Hypatia di Hagia Sophia. Your brother can establish your credentials with the former and Katerina with the latter." Eneko raised the bar of eyebrow again. "I don't think they'd recognize you from your regular visits for counseling."

Manfred's shoulders shook. "If you want messages to the tapman at Barducci's . . . that's a priest and a chapel more likely to recognize him."

Eneko cracked a wan smile at this. "This is probably the case of the pot calling the kettle black, Prince."

Manfred shrugged. "Meaning no offense, but the way I see it the average barman has the experience of life to make him a better counselor than the average oblate who has grown into a cloistered monk. Anyway, what do you want Benito to tell these priests? I want him to get some rest before this next stunt of his."

Eneko nodded as Benito yawned copiously. "He should be at his sharpest for such a venture, and he doesn't look it."

"A couple of hours and I'll be fine." Benito yawned again. "I've just got to track down that Corfiote seaman that guided me onto a rock, coming in."

"I'll see to that," said Manfred firmly. "You are heading for bed. Alone, too. Get along with you."

When Manfred spoke like that, one went. So Benito went. Even the thought of the coming venture couldn't keep him awake.

Far above in the blue, two hawks circled.

Bjarni knocked Kari's arm up hastily. The shot ricocheted off the limestone rocks, and Svanhild winced. Thank goodness Bjarni had more sense than the rest of them, or they'd soon be fighting both the locals and the invaders. And the locals knew this area like the rabbits in the rocks did.

"What the hell do you think you are doing, you idiot!"

"But chief, he threw a rock at us!" protested the young Vinlander.

"Of course he threw a rock at us, you mindless fool! And now we'll be lucky if the locals don't shoot at us. You shoot at the Hungarians. They already shoot back. The kids throwing rocks we wave at and shout 'friend, friend!'"

"And when they throw more rocks?" growled Gulta, wiping the blood off his face. "The little devil hit me."

"Duck faster next time," Bjarni said flatly. "If a kid with a rock can hit you, you aren't paying near enough attention to what's going on. You can't hit anything with wheel-lock pistols anyway, more than a few paces off. And there's no way to use an arquebus on horseback."

But Bjarni's orders were unnecessary. Word must have run up the valleys ahead of them. Nobody threw rocks. And there was nobody they could shout "friend, friend" at either. Locals seeing them ran.

"Maybe we should ride one of them down," suggested Kari. "We could explain afterwards."

Bjarni snorted. "You should be thinking of this as if it were the plains around Cahokia and you were a foreigner chasing your mother's people. This is their place. Their rocks and paths. Ten to one they'd get away from you here. And if they did that, then the fat would really be in the fire. No, we'll find a spot to fort up and sit tight until things settle down. They'll come to us in time."

They rode on. Toward evening they came to a gorge. Kari pointed. "You won't let me shoot rock-throwers. Can I shoot us some dinner instead?"

Bjarni looked up. "Sure. I never was that fond of goats anyway."

Kari missed again. Twice. In the end, laughing, Svanhild used her bow to kill the goat.

Meanwhile, scouting ahead, Gulta had found them a cave. "They use part of it for penning goats. There's another section where we can sleep. It isn't luxury accommodation, but it is better than the houses in the burned-out villages we've passed. At least, the cave's still got a roof. There's a lot of cloud about, too. It looks like it could come on to rain."

"Is it defensible?" Svanhild asked. Other considerations no longer applied.

Bjarni shrugged. "Is anything?"

Manfred knocked on Erik's door. There was no reply. He knocked again, waited, and then was about to turn his heel and leave when Erik said: "Come in."

Erik was seated in a chair by the window staring out. He turned to see just who had come to disturb him, with a look that said it would be the worse for them. "Oh. Manfred. I thought it would be some servant or orderly or something. I've had a chambermaid and a page come looking for you, all in the last hour."

"I've come to talk to you about this Svanhild."

Erik sighed. "Yes. I'm sorry, Manfred. I've let myself be distracted from my task. It's just . . . I wish . . . Well, I can't. I'll try to put it aside. My oath comes first."

Manfred grinned, hiding emotions far from humor. "Besides, as a confrere Knight of the Holy Trinity you are supposed to be celibate and not think such things. Listen, I have talked it over with Francesca and young Benito." Manfred chose his words now with extreme care. "You are sworn by clan-oath to be my personal hearthman. To guard me and also prepare me for the possibility that I might become heir to the throne of Charles Fredrik. To keep me alive. To take appropriate long-term steps to make sure this happens."

Erik nodded, dully. It was a matter of note on his mental state that he did not snap that he knew all of this. "Yes. That is my duty."

"If my bodyguard—you, that is—arrived with a severe chill or was injured—I'd send him to bed until he was well enough to be effective. I'd use another bodyguard if he insisted." Manfred waited for a response.

"I would insist, if I was sick." Erik did not even look indignant.

"Who would you nominate?"

Erik shrugged. "Von Gherens, I suppose. Or Falkenberg, had he not been injured."

Manfred nodded. "I will have both of them. Falkenberg, if he recovers. Because you *are* sick. I'm sending you off to get cured. Benito, a Corfiote seaman and you are taking a small boat out tonight. You will go and see if this sweetheart of yours is alive. Come back when you're well."

Erik gaped at him. And then closed his mouth and shook his head. "I can't do that."

Manfred had come prepared for that. "Your responsibilities go beyond those of some simple day-to-day bodyguard, Erik. You're responsible for my long-term safety. How would you best ensure that?"

"Putting you in a padded cell and feeding you through the keyhole," said Erik, still staring at him.

"Be serious, will you? Besides, Uncle Charles Fredrik said I'm supposed to go to Jerusalem. How would I do that in a cell? The answer is breaking this siege. And the answer to that is getting word back to Venice. And that's exactly what I want Benito to do. But without you he'll probably fail."

Was Erik following all this? It was impossible to tell from that poleaxed look on his face. "Look, his plan relies on sneaking out of here in a small boat lowered from the seaward walls. But the rest of Emeric's troops and cannon have arrived. You can bet Emeric has shore patrols aplenty out now, especially after last night. The boy's a fighter, but he's not in your league. And he doesn't have your experience of small craft. He's Venetian, but a city-dwelling landsman, really."

Now, finally, he was getting a reaction out of Erik; the Icelander nodded, slightly. Manfred went in for the kill.

"But the crunch is that he's got to move overland by night to a fishing port, well away from here. The boy can move around a city like a ghost. But I don't think he's ever been outside a city. He'll get killed for sure if you don't go along with him. Once you've

got him safe—you can give your time to hunting for Svanhild."
Manfred paused. "But Erik . . . my friend, you do know what usually
happens to beautiful young women when an army invades."

Erik nodded. "Yes. She may be dead, or she may be raped and
enslaved. But . . . I have to know." He sighed. "I'm sorry. I can't
accept your logic. What you say about Benito and a message to
Venice makes excellent sense, even if you are using it as an excuse.
But I can't desert my post."

"Oh, for heaven's sake!" Manfred sat down on the bed. It complained. Beds generally complained when Manfred sat on them.
"I didn't want to do this. I've lugged this around since Venice."

Manfred hauled a letter out of his pouch. It was plainly much
traveled. He unfolded it. "Here. Come and have a look at this. Uncle
Charles Fredrik sent it to me when things started to unravel in
Venice."

Erik came over. The letter dangled half of the seal of the Holy
Roman Empire. The sprawling spidery handwriting was unmistakably that of the Holy Roman Emperor himself.

"Read from the top of this paragraph," commanded Manfred.
Erik did.

*Manfred, The most valuable coin the House of Hohenstauffen has
is loyalty. The house has no coin of a larger denomination than the
loyalty of Clann Harald. The reason is simple: they owe their loyalty not to the Empire, or the Emperor. They owe it to us. The
Hohenstauffen. The Clann have repaid their debt to the Hohenstauffen
many hundreds of times over. Yet they still answer the call. Why,
nephew? First, it is because they're raised and bred to it. They're a
very honorable house, even by the standards of a very honorable
society. But that is the lesser of the reasons. The reason is that they
are our friends—because we are as loyal to them as they are to us.
Always remember that. An Imperial house has very few true friends.
They are more valuable to us than to ordinary folk for that reason.
In every generation the time has always come when we, the Hohenstauffen, must put that friendship, that loyalty to our friends, above
all other obligations. Do not fail me in this, Manfred. When the time
comes, you will place Erik's interests above your own. I order this.
Do not fail me or our house.*

"I'm not going to fail him," said Manfred grimly. "You *will* be
on that boat this evening. This is not a matter of duty, Erik. It
is a matter of friendship. I won't see you dying by inches in front

of my eyes with your heart somewhere over those walls."

Erik stood up, came to stand before Manfred and put his hands on Manfred's shoulders. "Thank you," he said, gruffly. "I was . . . not happy when the summons came for me to come to Mainz to serve. Willing, because it is our sworn duty. But not happy. Our regard for the Empire isn't high in Iceland, or Vinland either for that matter. My father said something to me then that I didn't understand at the time. He said: *You will find it is not service.*"

Manfred felt those powerful long-fingered hands squeeze his shoulders. "I understand now. You have been a friend for some time now. I just hadn't understood. If I have sons . . . I will send them to learn this, too. The Clann Harald are loyal to their oath. They are also loyal to friends. *Linn gu Linn.*"

The emotion in that voice told Manfred that his uncle had been perfectly right. Manfred also knew that buying loyalty wasn't his reason for doing this.

Manfred stood up, and put an arm around Erik. He felt emotion thickening his throat and voice, and didn't try to stop it. "Wouldn't have mattered a bugger what Uncle Charles Fredrik said anyway. You need to go. You're going. I've made up my mind."

Erik took a deep breath. "Very well. Under certain conditions, which you will swear to me. First, Von Gherens will become your constant bodyguard. Second, you will not leave this fortress, unless I return or the siege is lifted. You will not make it a repetition of the affair of the Red Cat. You will *not* come after me. Promise me this."

Manfred was intensely grateful that Erik had not been there when Francesca had explained just how insecure the Citadel really was. "If there is a sally, I must lead the knights, Erik. You know that yourself. And this is a siege—God knows what will happen if Emeric breaks through. But within those limits . . . I'll swear. My Oath on it."

"If there is a sally. But don't stretch it." Erik took a deep breath. "Manfred, I didn't think you understood what it meant to be in love with someone. Thank you. Thank you from the bottom of my heart."

That didn't make Manfred feel much better about Svanhild. But all he said was: "Well, let's go and organize a small boat and see if we can find that Corfiote sailor who doesn't know the draft of a great galley."

Chapter 41

Sitting under a tasseled awning in front of his tented pavilion, King Emeric regarded the Citadel in the growing dusk. Oxen had proved more of a problem than he'd anticipated. The islanders seemed to rely heavily on donkeys. Unfortunately, the heavy forty-eight-pound bombards really needed teams of oxen to move them. And the cannon of the Citadel and the island of Vidos commanded the deep-water landings for some distance. The carracks had too deep a draft to bring them in the way that those bedamned galleys had run up the beach. The bigger guns were too heavy and too unwieldy to unload onto lighters and bring in. They needed a dock, a quay next to which the ships could tie up.

Unfortunately, the nearest spot they'd been able to find was the village of Patara, nearly a league away. Emeric had had his cavalry scouring the countryside for oxen, or even mules, to move the guns. And now to make matters worse, it looked like rain. He was scowling ferociously when the senior Byzantine captain of the seven carracks that had just come in from Constantinople arrived. The Greek saluted smartly.

"Well, Captain?"

"Sire, the Venetian Outremer Convoy had arrived in Negroponte before we left. They should be on their way to the Golden Horn by now, except for the vessels heading for the Holy Land."

"While that is good news, I wanted to know if you'd brought the supplies Alexius agreed to provide. And why you are late?"

The captain bowed. "Contrary winds, Sire. And this morning

we met, engaged and captured a Venetian great galley. I have her captain and most of her crew prisoner."

The captain cleared his throat. "They were carrying certain dispatches addressed to the Doge, the Grand Metropolitan and the Holy Roman Emperor. The captain, one Bernardo Selvi, pleaded for his life, saying he could give you valuable information. He has agreed to cooperate fully with us. I have promised him his life in return, Sire. He told me he was part of a charter for Prince Manfred of Brittany, and some two hundred Knights of the Holy Trinity, going to Jerusalem. They were on board their four vessels when they were attacked by a combined fleet of Dalmatian pirates and carracks bearing your banner. He said the others plan a night landing, perhaps at the very Citadel itself."

"Your news comes a little too late, Captain," Emeric said grimly. "Nonetheless I will see the prisoner and the letters he was transporting. Have them sent up to me."

The Byzantine saluted crisply again. "At once, Sire. And where and when shall I have my men land the food supplies?"

Emeric smiled his thin-lipped, crooked, and utterly humorless smile. "Vessels are discharging about a league away at a village called Patara. See the goods get handed over to my quartermaster there, see you don't get in the way of my cannon being off-loaded, and see I get the prisoner and his letters very, very fast."

"Sire!" The Byzantine saluted and left at a half-run.

Emeric, for the first time since the galleys had arrived that morning, felt something akin to pleasure. He enjoyed seeing Byzantines run. And the fact that the Holy Roman Empire's best troops were here purely by accident, caught up in this because they were on their way to Jerusalem, was excellent news. He must tell his spymasters to stop searching for the leak in his security.

Four men-at-arms from the Byzantine vessels and a prisoner, shackled neck-and-legs, arrived shortly thereafter. The prisoner was an elderly, slightly stooped man with a wattled chin. He fell on his knees before Emeric. "Spare me, Your Majesty. Spare me, I beg you," he wept.

Emeric stood up, put his hands on either side of the man's head, and forced him to look him in the eyes. He hardly needed to do anything; the Venetian was already crying with fear. Still, there was more to exerting his power than simply the need to cow.

"But of course, my dear chap. Provided you tell me what I need to know."

He blinked, and released a spell. A bolt of searing pain shook the captive. His back arched and he fell over backwards. The Venetian captain lay there on the ground gibbering, whimpering and crying. Emeric ignored him and held out his hand to the escorts. "The letters."

Hastily one of the men fumbled open a leather message pouch and handed the king the three letters. Two were sealed with the Imperial seal of the Holy Roman Empire, and addressed to Emperor Charles Fredrik and Doge Petro Dorma, respectively. The other was addressed to the Grand Metropolitan in Rome. Emeric walked to his desk, a particularly fine ivory-inlaid escritoire, pulled a stiletto out of a drawer and carefully cut the seal away. He walked closer to a multi-wicked lamp and read the letter, his smile growing more feral all the while. A prince of the Empire, no less—now, within Hungary's fist.

The king turned back to the Venetian captain still kneeling on the floor. "You will explain the purpose of this voyage. You will also tell me about this prince, or I will give you more pain. If you do well, I will reward you with my mercy."

When Selvi had done, Emeric called to his guards. "Take him out there and crucify him next to that fool who brought me news of the lost troop."

"You promised me mercy!" screamed the captain.

Emeric shrugged. "I lied."

Sophia Tomaselli looked nervously about. Despite the hooded cloak and the lateness of the hour, she really didn't want to be found here. The address, given to her in the strictest confidence by Bianca Casarini, was not a part of the Citadel she'd ever visited before. The poorer houses down inside the outer curtain wall were not in a place she would have admitted knowing even existed.

But she'd try anything. Now, especially, with her husband Nico's status likely to rise because of the siege.

Anything. She'd already tried at least twenty potions. All that they had done was to make her sick. She'd tried everything from saints' bones to amulets that made her clothing smell faintly of dead rat. She'd even, on Bianca's advice, tried a different man. She snorted at the thought. The young cavalry commander Querini thought he was the world's greatest lover. His breath smelled of onions. Then there'd been the long, nervous wait, to find her courses ran as normally as ever. And now she had to put up with a stream of lewd suggestions from the fool Querini.

She knocked on the dingy door, glancing hastily around to see if there was anyone in sight. The street was deserted, as far as she could see anyway. She knocked again, slightly harder.

The door swung open. At first glance the man standing there was not very impressive. She'd expected robes, not ordinary clothes. He was tall and stooped, and framed against the light his hair was sleeked and perfectly ordered. The most occult thing about him was a rather neat beard. "S . . . signor Morando?"

He nodded, cocked his head inquiringly, and said in a voice which was just faintly sibilant. "You have the advantage of me. Who are you and why have you come here?"

"S . . . signorina Casarini said you might be able to help . . ."

Bianca Casarini's name acted like a magical talisman. The man beamed. "Come in, signora." He ushered her forward respectfully, closed the door behind her. "And how may I help you, signora? Potions to draw a lover? To inflame passions? Perhaps to deal with some unfortunate consequences?" He rubbed his long hands.

"I want something to assist fertility. Not quack potions."

He looked at her thoughtfully, but didn't say anything.

"Please!" she said. "I'm desperate. I can pay well."

"There are certain rituals. You understand, they are frowned on by the Church?"

She laughed bitterly. "The Church hasn't exactly helped me so far. And they're a lot richer for not helping."

He nodded slowly. "Very well. Wait here. There are certain preparations I must make."

By the time he returned he looked far more like her idea of a practitioner of the black arts, right down to the robe. His eyebrows flared satanically and his beard and mustachios were now waxed to sharp points.

"Come," he said. "The sacrificial chamber is prepared. You must now be prepared. I must blindfold you."

Part of Sophia filled with fear at the idea of "sacrifice." But there was a guilty fascination too.

❁　　❁　　❁

Stepping out into the cold street, Sophia wasn't too sure what time it was. Her head was still mazed from the liquid in that chalice—or perhaps from the smoke in that room. She would have to wash her hair to get rid of the smell of it. Next time . . . and she felt the compulsion to admit there would be a next time—she must make sure she was dressed in something easier to remove. She would have to undress herself until the symbols he'd painted on her washed off. She could feel them. They seemed to have a heat of their own.

She stumbled. It was very dark, and a fine rain had begun to fall. She put out a hand to keep in contact with the wall. She heard the sound of footsteps. A number of people. She shrank back against the buildings, until they passed. At least six men. One, even in the darkness, loomed huge. They were carrying something between them, and they didn't notice her.

After they were well gone, Sophia continued hastily on her way home. Whatever those men were up to it was bound to be no good. But there was no way she could report it, without implicating herself. Thank heavens for Bianca's wild ways. She had told Sophia which guards were susceptible to bribes.

Sitting back in a comfortable chair, the black robes thankfully tossed off, and a glass of ouzo in hand, Aldo Morando grinned sharkishly. He'd hooked a big one tonight. A very big one. Did the wife of the captain-general think, honestly think, he wouldn't recognize her? Even if his accomplice Bianca Casarini hadn't told him she'd be coming, he'd have recognized Sophia Tomaselli.

Morando had been many things in a long and varied career. Pimp. Spy. Procurer. Seller of "saints" relics. Seller of shares in *Colleganzas* that were remarkably lacking in substance. And latterly . . . magician.

He would never have believed the number of wealthy idiots just dying to pay over good money for some wicked thrills. Particularly women with too much money and too much time on their hands. With husbands who had long sought mistresses, or were much away. Of course things could get a bit hot with the Church, and with injured husbands, from time to time, which was why he had been obliged to leave the Italian mainland. Corfu, he had been sure, would be far enough away. He'd been dismayed, at first, seeing Bianca Casarini here, but she was proving to be a remarkably good accomplice for him.

He put down his glass and gazed cheerfully at the stack of ducats on the table. Besides that, Sophia Tomaselli would be a mine of information. Very valuable information in the right hands, and he knew where to find those hands. To think he'd been angry about the siege. Well, he was now sure that he wouldn't go hungry, and the opportunity for pleasure as well as profit—she wanted to get pregnant, after all, and she wasn't bad-looking—was considerable.

A tall graveyard poplar grew flush against the cliff that was topped by the old Byzantine fortress. The cliff beside it was too high and too steep to make the tree any threat to the integrity of the fortress. The tree itself was, in the fashion of the plant, densely packed with small branches. Attempting to climb it would have been folly, anyway: The thin branches would cascade the climber down again.

About twenty-five cubits up, the branches masked a narrow gash of an opening into the cliffs. If you ascended the ladder, and then walked back along it, the cave widened considerably into a labyrinth of passages. Once, many years ago, these would have acted as one of the defenses of this place. Now you just had to follow the most worn path in the stone. It had taken the passage of many feet over many long years to wear away the stone, to round and smooth the steps. The sacred chamber was lit by a small oil lamp. Right now all was silent except for the steady slow trickle and splash of the fountain that fed the holy pool between the two altars, the great Goddess's altar and the smaller, darker one.

The white half-almond lay on the black stone. Waiting, for someone to come and take it up, and all that it represented. Behind the larger altar, half-hidden in the shadows, was the image of the Goddess Herself. It towered over the altar and it was old, old— older, some said, than the island itself. It did not look anything like the graceful statues of the great Grecian sculptors from the island's glory days. It was not even anything like those earlier images, stiff and rigid, with fixed, staring eyes and jutting breasts like twin mountain peaks. No, this was more like a pile of boulders, round-headed and faceless, with the merest suggestion of hair and of arms and legs, and enormous, sagging breasts and belly, the hallmark of fertility and plenty. And there was, if you looked at Her long enough, the suggestion of a faint haze of gold about her, and the feeling that She was looking back at you, out of her eyeless face.

The two women came in, one sweeping the old, dried leaves before her, the other strewing the new leaves. When the chamber was prepared, the two acolytes went to lower the ladder. Few would come tonight, for it was raining so hard that it would be difficult to come and go undetected. Here, in the middle of the Venetians, there were few devotees anyway. But this was the second oldest temple on the island, a place where the life-flame had been kindled many thousands of years ago. The temple had always had at least a holy mother and three or four devotees.

The priestess had not expected a group larger than three or four. But as she stepped out of the shadows she saw that tonight, despite the rain, there was an unfamiliar face, a comfortably middle-aged woman.

The priestess saw with a twinge of disappointment that the newcomer was beyond child-bearing age, unfortunately. Months had passed, and there was still no one willing to take up the almond. The rains had come, the crops—if the invaders left anything of them—would be no worse than usual, but this could not last forever.

Not for the first time, the priestess wondered how much of this was because of the Christians and their priests. For centuries, She and they had lived, if not in harmony, at least not in conflict. But just after the death of the last bride, the priestess had sensed that there was something inimical to the Goddess that was searching for the source of Her power.

Shortly after that, the attacks began. And shortly after *that* the four stranger-priests had arrived, and the two hawks that were the eyes for the hostile power. Was it coincidence? It hardly seemed possible, and that was especially so once the priestess had learned that these four priests, and their leader in particular, were closely linked with the Grand Metropolitan of Rome.

True, they had close ties to the Hypatian Order, which, unlike the Servants of the Trinity, were not known for the persecution of those who were pagan. In fact, it had been the Hypatian Siblings that had dwelled here quietly for so very long. But this particular priest had a reputation for militancy that was not typical of the Order. And directly after arriving here, he had attempted to work magic.

She had put a stop to that, needless to say. No one worked magic upon this island without Her approval. But how long could that hold? Great and evil powers were being bent against Her, to usurp Her Power, and without a bride, the Cold God could not defend Her.

The priestess drew her thoughts back to the ceremony, and the new woman who had come. After purification and the rituals she must speak with her. But now the withered bay leaves swept up from the floor must be fed to the life-flame.

The women repeated the old, old words. "Out of death there is new life."

It was, as the priestess suspected, someone from outside the walls. She had known this would come; to an extent, she was only surprised that it had taken this long. The captain-general was not, by nature, a cruel man, but he was a foolish one to think that he could demand the labor and allegiance of the populace and not assume the responsibility for them.

And attempting to close the gates against those who deserved shelter here was nothing but an exercise in futility, as the presence of this woman showed.

"My brother is with the boatyard. The sea took my Yani three years ago. My daughters are married. My sons are at sea," the woman said, simply. "My brother is here. The captain-general refused to allow the men to bring their families. But the men brought us in anyway, by the boatyard gate. There are several of the timber-sheds that are not in use, and now that the Hungarians are outside the walls there is nothing happening in the Little Arsenal anyway. It is crowded, but it is safer than outside." She sighed. "Why does the Goddess allow these *Xenos* to trample our soil?"

"Men's business, my daughter. We do not make war, and they do not make children. Invaders come and go, but the Goddess remains."

She did not speak aloud the question that was in her own mind. *. . . for how long?*

Caesare Aldanto walked past the man who had been crucified upside-down outside King Emeric's tent as if he wasn't there.

Emeric was sprawled in his gilded and gemstone-encrusted throne. Aldanto bowed mechanically. "You wished to see me?"

Emeric stared at the blond man. He stood up, and put his hands on Aldanto's throat. "You interfered with the admiral of my carracks and sent them north in pursuit of four vessels. You interfered and used my name to direct the Dalmatians in an attack on the same vessels. We lost a number of the galliots. According to my admiral you have only captured one of the Venetian vessels. Why should I allow you to live?"

Emeric allowed the pain to flow from his hands into his intended victim. But Caesare Aldanto didn't scream and writhe. He didn't even blink. He answered in the same calm voice that he'd used earlier.

"Because I had credible information that they were coming to the relief of Corfu. The ships had Knights of the Holy Trinity on board, including, according to our captives, Prince Manfred of Brittany. I considered that you would wish them sunk rather than at large on Corfu. There were also a number of powerful and dangerous magicians on board. We were not aware of that. That is why three of the ships escaped."

Emeric was somewhat shaken by the lack of response from the blond Milanese man; it took him aback, and left him thinking madly down directions he had rather not have gone. There could be little doubt now—Aldanto was indeed a puppet-man. He stepped back. Always before, he'd known his power stood between him and any threat of a knife-wielding assassin. With this man . . . he was potentially in his enemy's grasp. He had no doubt at all that Grand Duke Jagiellon was indeed his enemy, even if their purposes ran in the same direction for now.

Or could this be a trap?

Then logic reasserted itself. Jagiellon's man would hardly have risked his position and Emeric's displeasure if Jagiellon did not desperately wish the Knights to be sunk at sea.

"I was not told about the prisoners," said Emeric, moderating his tone by a degree or two. "Why have they not been brought to me?"

Aldanto shrugged. "Ask your admiral. But in truth only a handful of seamen were captured. The captain elected to remain with his vessel and blow her magazine up when she was boarded. The captives were taken from one of her small boats. The charges failed to sink her, but there were considerable losses among our boarders."

PART VI
May, 1539 A.D.

Chapter 42

"It strikes me very much as a conspiracy," said Eberhard. "I agree with your assessment, Francesca, but of course it is still likely to place us in very bad favor with the governor—the podesta, as they call him—and the captain-general, if and when the messages get through."

Manfred shrugged. "What they don't know, their hearts won't grieve over. Besides, Francesca has already cleared it with the governor."

Francesca looked innocent. Too innocent, Benito thought. "He's an old dear, but quite ineffectual. The conduct of war or siege is officially the military's business. However, I did ask him if the prince might be allowed to send messages to the Emperor. He said it was hardly something he could refuse permission for, but that it was of course impossible at the moment. I smiled and thanked him."

"Well, I suppose if the messenger happened to go via Venice, you could hardly blame him for telling the authorities about the situation here," said Eberhard with a perfectly straight face. "How are your preparations going, by the way?"

Manfred grimaced a little. "Well, the early morning detail guarding the outer wall was easy enough to organize. Our men are tired but still wish to do their part in the defense of the Citadel. The boat . . . well, that's the reason I suggested to Francesca we might have to go to the captain-general. I've tried to find one to buy, without making a great to-do about it. But this isn't Venice, you know. Most of the boats in the Citadel belong to the shipyard.

Of course there were lots of fishing boats out in the town. But they're rather far out of reach."

Francesca tilted her head to the side. "And I said, you and Benito should perhaps go and talk to Maria and her husband."

Benito shook his head. "Maria would give us a shipyard vessel in the blink of an eye. But Umberto—well, he's a good fellow, but he's a rules and regulations sort of man."

"He might still know someone with a boat to sell." She looked consideringly at Erik and Benito. "I think we need to think about your appearances, also. You can't go like that."

Benito caught on immediately. "I look as if I could possibly be a local. But Erik wouldn't pass in the dark. We'll need hair dye and old clothes."

"Something to stain Erik's skin too," said Francesca, looking pointedly at both hair and skin.

"I'm not planning to go passing as a local," said Erik, a little stiffly. "I'll stick to the hills and forest patches. These Hungarians won't even see me. I might blacken my face for the night-work. . . ."

Francesca smiled. "She'll still love you even if you're dark-haired, Erik. And never mind the Hungarians. It's the locals who will run from a blond-haired man, and you will need them if you are to find her, I suspect. We've got a map of how to get to Count Dentico's villa, but they might easily have moved out. You'll have to get directions from the locals. It won't help that you can't speak Greek and will frighten every local silly."

Erik shook his head. "How do you cope with her always being right, Manfred? I have a little classical Greek, but the language has changed."

"Get used to it," said Manfred with a grin. "It's usually easier to say they are right even if they're patently wrong." He ducked hastily.

Francesca just raised an eyebrow.

"That is a real danger signal," said Manfred. "It means it's being saved up. I'm just trying to further his education, Francesca."

"I'll just save that up, too," she said, with a thin smile. "Now, let's go down and talk to Umberto and Maria. There will be people selling things here in the Citadel, and Maria will know where."

Von Gherens looked speculatively at Benito. "The other thing you'll need to get him is a knife. He can't carry a Ferrara *main gauche* that would cost a fisherman five years' earnings, and a rapier's right out."

Benito gritted his teeth. Changing out of *Case Vecchie* clothes was something he was actually looking forward to, although he knew his feet would find being shoeless a painful experience. Going without his rapier and his beautifully balanced dagger would be a lot harder. He didn't feel dressed without at least the *main gauche.* But Von Gherens was right; he knew that from his time as a bridge-brat. One look at his *main gauche,* and even an idiot would know he wasn't what he was supposed to be.

Erik grinned. "And I suppose you'd like me to leave my new hatchet behind too? It's not a patch on my Vinland one, but the swordsmith at Mainz didn't seem to understand me clearly enough."

The scar-faced old Prussian *Ritter* sniffed "I think he probably thought you wanted it for chopping firewood, not having seen you use that barbaric thing. The Hungarians probably won't recognize it either. Until it's too late."

Erik nodded. "I can relieve them of anything else I need. And I think I've got a knife for you, Benito, in with my gear. It's better than any cheap local blade, anyway. I'll dig it out for you. It's a Shetland islander's knife. It's very plain. Could pass for a fisherman's tool, but it's good steel and well balanced."

"I'd have to get permission before selling you a boat," said Umberto, worriedly.

"Do you know of anyone who has one to sell?" asked Erik delicately.

Umberto shook his head. Then put up a finger. "It's not strictly a boat . . . but one of the Corfiotes who does some work for the Little Arsenal has his coracle stored down at the shipyard. He'd probably sell, right now. I don't see him using it for a while."

Maria, however, seemed enthusiastic about the project. "And clothes and dye for Erik's hair . . . Well, there is Fianelli. He sells secondhand goods. I wouldn't look too hard at where they came from, 'Nito, but that won't be any shock to you. He's got some quack medicines and stuff too. I wouldn't be surprised to find some dye there. I'll go along if you like. And green walnuts will do for skin color."

She looked at Benito. "You came to wish me farewell and

Godspeed. You're doing the kind of mad thing you like doing best. I'll wish you the same. At least you're doing it for a good cause and not your usual damnfool reasons."

Benito grinned. "And you and Umberto take care too, especially of my god-niece."

Maria scowled fiercely at him.

Fianelli had what Benito was looking for. After he left, Benito muttered to himself: "Good thing Erik didn't come along with me. That man practically stinks of foulness. If he knew an obvious nonislander was trying to leave the Citadel, he'd try to sell the information. Me, he just thinks I'm seeking a disguise for an assignation."

That was, in fact, exactly what Fianelli thought. It never occurred to him to warn his master Emeric that an escape was being planned from the Citadel. Within a day, he'd forgotten all about the sale. Fianelli sold a lot of stuff.

Unfortunately, it didn't occur to Benito to warn anyone about Fianelli, either. Benito had run into a lot of foul men in his short life, after all. And while he'd learned a lot about sieges from Falkenberg, he really hadn't fully absorbed yet one of Francesca's lessons: *More fortresses fall by treachery than by strength of arms.*

By midnight it had started to rain. A scruffy, tousle-haired, barefoot young man and a tall, dark-haired, plain-clad, and very dark-faced man were standing in front of Francesca for inspection. "Your hair's too clean, Benito. Remember you've got Manfred's seal there."

Manfred grinned. "He's the scruffiest personal letter I ever sent."

Benito grinned in reply. "You had to drop the sealing-wax on my ear, didn't you? Black wax is hotter than red."

Francesca had a close look at the tangle of black curls around Benito's ear. "It certainly isn't easy to find. Won't Count Von Stemitz be a trifle surprised? Give him my best regards by the way, when you see him."

Hiding coin had been a bigger problem. Benito had some ten ducats in smallish change. Too much would attract suspicion. Too little and he wouldn't be able to afford to live, never mind travel. He had a battered pin in his scarf, which might possibly once have been silver, and looked like plated brass from which the plating was rubbing off. No one would look too hard at such a tawdry thing. Except . . . The cheap stones that had been in it had been replaced with two good rubies, mounted in so hard you would have to break the thing to get them out, and had a liberal coating of dirt reapplied. It looked like rubbish. Benito wouldn't have bothered to steal it himself when he'd been a bridge-brat. The stones, cleaned up, would fetch a good thirty ducats each, even from a fence.

Benito was barefoot. In a ragged waist-sash, he carried a plain knife with a small brass guard and a cord-bound handle.

In all, Benito looked the part. Erik didn't. His face shape was just wrong. Too angular; his hair was too straight and too fine; and his eye color was a sure giveaway.

Francesca shook her head. "I think this is a lost cause. Maybe we could curl his hair . . ."

"I could break his nose for him," offered Von Gherens, feeling his own skew organ set in his burn-scarred face. "Always makes a man look different, that."

"Thank you," said Erik, putting his hand protectively over his threatened nose. "You are well suited to bodyguarding Manfred."

"I think you should just wear this woolen hat," said Francesca decisively. "And keep away from people if you can. Claim a passing sailor got you on your mother. That could account for the looks."

Erik smiled. Now that he was actually going to look for Svanhild, he seemed imperturbable; strangely at peace and at ease. "Why, thank you, too, Francesca."

Manfred grunted. "It's barely a cockleshell, Erik. If the wind comes up you'll be swamped in moments."

Benito agreed with Manfred, but they'd had some trouble finding a boat, quietly.

Erik didn't seem perturbed, however. At the moment nothing seemed to perturb Erik. The Corfiote seaman had refused, even for a considerable bribe, to guide them out. His first experience of being under fire, and the new troops arriving in the carracks, had frightened the bravado out of him. When he'd refused, Erik had just shrugged, asked a few questions, and proceeded as planned. The arrival of several more ships from the south at sundown hadn't worried him. Even the skin and withy coracle, normally used to hold a caulker working around a larger vessel, was fine by him.

"It's light enough to lower down the wall, Manfred. And the sea out there is not the Atlantic."

"Still looks like a cockleshell. And I wish you had your armor on."

Erik chuckled. "Von Gherens, this is what you'll have to deal with. One minute, I'm going to capsize. The next I should wear armor so I can drown when I do capsize. Stop worrying, Manfred. Next thing you'll want me to take a horse in the cockleshell, and wood for the signal fires."

"He's just jealous because he doesn't want to sit inside a fortress under siege while you're out there," said the older *Ritter*. "And don't worry, Hakkonsen. We'll keep him here."

"You're not savvy enough to be let out on your own," grumbled Manfred.

Erik smiled, a flash of teeth in the darkness. "I'm not dealing with the political infighting in Mainz, or tavern or brothel brawls, Manfred. I'll be fine out there. There's a lot of wild country; I cut my teeth in wilderness like this. You worry about Benito. He doesn't know how to move in it. Now let us go. I want to get moving while we still have a chance to get out without detection."

The rock wall was wet with the rain, feeling greasy underfoot. Manfred, along with several knights who were on guard on the outer wall, lowered Benito down first. From their daytime scouting Benito knew there was a little sill down there, just before the water. He felt for it on the rain-slick rock with his feet. Once he was down, Benito whistled up, and freed the rope. The ledge was less than a cubit wide. It sloped toward the sea and it was rounded. Benito was used to the pan-tiles of Venice, but this was even slipperier; it was like being on icy roof-tiles.

Erik nearly landed in the water as a result. His feet scrabbled for a purchase, and Benito put a steadying hand on his arm. "You're supposed to be looking after me," he hissed, as Erik cursed softly. "Anyway the rain should make it easy enough to paddle out of here."

The coracle came down next and it nearly had both of them off the ledge. And of course it was farther to the water than they'd realized from above. You couldn't just jump into a hide-and-wicker boat, either. Still, with care and patience they managed to board; each of them took a paddle, and they set off onto the dark water.

Maria stood back in the shadows, rain dripping from an eave above her. She didn't really know why she'd slipped out so late at night. She couldn't absolutely guarantee that Alessia would stay asleep—although she'd timed her feeds very carefully for this. Umberto wouldn't wake for anything short of the last trump. She'd wanted to say "good-bye, good luck, and don't be an idiot" to Benito, but there wasn't an opportunity. All she could do was watch him and the dark shape that was Erik go over the wall.

He hadn't even known she was there. She turned and walked back into the dark, feeling a little frightened, and very depressed. This might be the last time she ever saw him, and she hadn't really seen him at all. She wanted to let him know—

—*what?*

Maybe it was better this way. She had Umberto, who was good for her, and good to her, and she hoped she was being good to him. Benito could never be other than what he was, and it would do no good for him to know what she still felt.

She must have gotten a bit lost in the streets as she was lost in her own thoughts, for when she looked up she realized that she was not where she thought she was.

She took her bearings by the bulk of nearby buildings. There was St. Agatha, the Hypatian chapel, and she knew then that she had gone a little too far. Just as she was about to turn back, she caught sight of a flicker of light.

Someone was coming.

She leaned back against the wall, feeling a shock of apprehension, the kind of thing she used to feel back in Venice when she prowled the canals at night, waiting to be caught in her smuggling by the Schioppies.

But it was only two women talking quietly in Greek. Maria's Greek was still limited. The only word she could catch sounded like "Goddess." It was an odd time to be out, and an odd coincidence to see people. Well, less of a coincidence than all that. If anyone was going to go down to the houses inside the outer curtain wall this was the only road they could follow. Perhaps these were the wives of Arsenal workers or militia, or even guards, back from bringing them something to eat. After the women had gone by

Maria proceeded back on her way, crept into the house, and bolted the door quietly. She slipped out of her wet things, rubbed her hair dry and left the wet clothes in the kitchen. Then, crept quietly up the stairs. She stopped and checked on Alessia, and slid into bed next to Umberto.

But sleep was a long time coming.

Chapter 43

Out on the sea in the darkness, Benito was getting a first-hand lesson in the difference between paying a gondolier to transport you, or telling sailors where you wanted to go, and rowing yourself.

The first pointed difference was that you actually had to paddle. He was a lot less experienced than Erik, and the coracle was round, which meant they were spending a lot of time spinning slowly. The second difference was that in his previous experience Benito had simply told those in control of the boat his destination, and made finding it their problem. Now it was his and Erik's problem.

The rain obscured them from enemy watchers, which was a good thing. The trouble was it obscured everything, including possible landmarks.

At this rate, thought Benito, *we might just end up in Albania after all.*

And they hadn't guessed about the wind or the current or even the chop on the water either. They might just end up *swimming* to Albania . . . if they didn't end up swimming round and round in circles.

"I think we're going south," whispered Erik.

"I thought we planning on going north?"

Erik grunted. "In this thing we just go where the sea takes us. Bail for a bit."

So Benito bailed; it made more sense than having him try to paddle. It seemed the sea outside the coracle was keen to get into it as fast as possible. It came aboard in enthusiastic splashes that soon had Benito wet to the skin. Here he was, cheek-by-jowl in a giant bowl with Erik Hakkonsen, and he might as well have been alone on the water. Erik was as silent as a dead man, he couldn't see anything, and Benito was so cold he couldn't feel anything either.

The whisper came out of the dark again, at his ear, and he jumped. "There's a headland, I think. Help me paddle."

Gradually the headland loomed up out of the rain. Benito's feet were now ankle-deep in the water in the bottom of the coracle.

It proved to be an islet. They hauled up on it anyway. But they could vaguely make out a white building off across the water. "I think this must be Mouse Islet," said Benito quietly. "We could see it from the wall. There are some buildings on it."

"Dawn can't be that far off, Benito. Is that building we can see over there another island?"

"No. It's a monastery, I think. Just off the mainland jutting into the sea. We could go there, but there's a big inlet ahead. If we go ashore here, we'll be forced to go virtually back into Kérkira."

Erik sighed. "We'll be forced back into this bedamned tub instead, then. Come on. Let's get on with it."

They did. But it became rapidly obvious that the coracle had suffered during the landing on Mouse Islet. The water was calm here, but Benito had to keep bailing. By the time they got within sight of the further shore, it was a race between water coming in and the bailing and paddling. Of course, the more water there was in the vessel the heavier it was to row, and the slower they went, too. Benito started preparing himself to swim.

It proved unnecessary. Just.

Mind you, Benito thought, *my clothes are so wet by now that I can't really get any wetter.* Despite the exercise, Benito was shivering almost uncontrollably. At least the rain had stopped, but there was still a cold wind blowing.

"I don't think it is worth hiding that . . . bathtub," said Erik. "We won't be using it to get back, so we might as well just get away from here."

The darkness was still thick as they blundered off into it. Even Benito, used to "seeing" his way around by feel in the darkness of Venice's nighttime rooftops, found the going difficult. Man-made structures had the decency to be at predictable angles! Then his nose picked up something. A hint of wood-smoke.

"There's a fire ahead," whispered Benito.

Erik snorted. "I know. I've been trying to stalk it, with something stumbling along just behind me that makes more noise than a pair of bull-seals having a territory fight in the middle of a Venetian glass-shop. If it's local peasants, we need to ask them some directions. And if it's Hungarian soldiers, we need to avoid them if we can."

Benito shivered. "Right now I'd be happy to go and ask them if I could borrow their fire for a bit."

"Well, come along. But try to keep it quiet! If it is soldiery, we are staying out of a fight. You're too keen on fighting."

But when they got closer, and Erik worked out just what the two Croats were doing, it was he, not Benito, who rushed in to the kill. The two Croats weren't well positioned to resist.

By the time Benito got there with his Shetlander dagger in hand, Erik was already kneeling next to the woman, untying her; and a moment later, he was undoing the gag.

Her first response was to scream.

"Hush!" hissed Erik.

He might as well have tried to stop a storm with his hands. She had a proper breath now for the next hysterical scream. It was understandable. Besides being raped, she was covered in her erstwhile rapist's blood. When someone's head is more or less summarily removed by a hatchet, they bleed. A lot.

But understandable as it might be, she was probably telling everyone within a mile that there was a woman here. Even the Croats' horses were shifting nervously. Benito shoved Erik aside, hauled her up by what was left of her blouse, and slapped her. "Shut up!" he hissed. "We're rescuing you. You want others to come?"

She shut up. Erik cut her hands free. "Now we'd better run. Someone must have heard that scream."

"What about taking their horses?" asked Benito. "They're tied over there." He pointed with his chin.

Erik looked. "Good. That's the first bit of luck we've had."

The horses still had their tack on. It was plain that the two soldiers had slipped off from somewhere else for a little private pleasure. "You're lighter than I am. You take her," said Erik, pushing the staggering woman toward Benito.

"Uh. I don't ride so well, Erik."

"Oh, hell. She'd better come with me, then. Help her up behind me."

Benito did. She clung to Erik like ivy. It was just light enough now for Benito to see her huge, terrified eyes. He was then left with the difficulty of getting onto the horse himself. It kept moving every time he put a foot in the stirrup. Finally, in desperation, he jumped. He nearly went clear over the other side, but did manage to cling to the saddle. He pulled himself upright into it. He managed to find one stirrup. It was too long. This was a whole continent away from the *Haute Ecole Equestrienne* Petro Dorma had sent him to. There, he'd been surrounded by respectful grooms, docile mounts and mounting blocks.

But he had to try. Erik was already out of sight. The horse plainly knew it had a total amateur in the saddle. It was being as balky as only a horse can be, when it knows it has mastery of the rider.

There was a clatter of hooves behind him. Benito prepared to jump. Only his foot was now stuck in this damned stirrup. If he jumped he'd drag . . . He hunched in the saddle and struggled with his foot.

"Get a move on, Benito," snapped Erik. The clatter had come from him, returning to see what had happened to Benito. He slapped the rump of Benito's horse and the vile animal took off as if someone had shoved something red-hot in an unmentionable spot. With Benito swearing and clinging to the saddle, they headed upward into the rougher terrain. At least his horse was following Erik's now.

By the time they reached the ridgeline, the sun was just burning its way through the clouds. Benito had long since abandoned any pretense of "riding." He was just trying to stay on the Godforsaken animal. It took all his finely honed burglar's acrobatic skills to do so, and all his strength, too. He'd managed to get his foot free of the stirrup, at last. That meant when he fell off—not if, but when—he could try to fall clear.

When they got up to some pines on the ridge, Erik called a halt. More precisely, he pulled his horse to a halt, and Benito's horse stopped also.

Very abruptly. Benito continued for a few yards without it.

He got to his feet, to find the Icelander looking at him, his shoulders shaking with laughter. "Why didn't you say you couldn't ride at all, you crazy kid!"

"Uh. I *have* been to classes. *Case Vecchie* can all ride, but, well, I was a bridge-brat, Erik." Defensively: "I've only ridden a horse about five or six times before this, you know."

Erik snorted. "Well, you can't count this as another time. I've seen a sack of meal do a better job of it. And those things hanging down are stirrups. You are supposed to put your feet in them."

"I couldn't reach them."

Erik shook his head. "We'll shorten them now. Help this poor woman down, Benito."

Benito did. She almost fell off the horse—and then pushed away from him. "Who are you?" she asked warily, her eyes darting looking for a place to run. There was naked fear in that voice.

Benito waved his hands at her, trying to look helpful and harmless at the same time. "We're Venetians." It was easier than trying to explain. "You're safe now."

The young woman crumpled and began to cry. Then she started speaking Greek. At speed.

"Whoa." Benito squatted down beside her; it seemed it was up to him to try to calm her down. Well, he was smaller than Erik; maybe that made him look less threatening. "We don't speak Greek," he said gently. "I can't help you if I don't understand."

"They killed Georgio!" she wailed—but softly, hardly more than a whisper. "They—they—" she dissolved into tears, and Benito patted her shoulder, thinking that trying to hold her would probably be a bad idea at this point.

She got herself under control, a lot faster than he would have thought. "What happened?" he asked. "Why did you come down out of the hills?"

She gulped for air. "See, some of the goats were missing. He thought they'd gone home. So he went down to the house. And when he didn't come back I went down to look for him. He was . . ."

Her eyes were round with the memory of things Benito didn't want to think about. "They were torturing him. Burning him to get him to tell them where he'd hidden the money." She shuddered, then said, plaintively, "We don't *have* any money. Just a few pennies. We've only been married for two months."

She began to cry again; great heaving sobs, wringing her hands together so hard that her knuckles were bone-white. Then she caught her breath. She seemed determined to tell them; to get the vileness out. "I ran in to try and help him. The one . . . the one who . . . he said: 'Here's the bitch. We'll get it out of her instead.' They cut Georgio's throat. They cut my man's throat like you would butcher a hog."

"Here." Erik had produced a small, squat bottle. "Manfred gave me some of his armor polish. Give her a drink, Benito."

Benito did. She choked, but then drank some more. The woman looked at Erik. "At least you killed them."

Erik looked decidedly uncomfortable. "Look. Is there anyone we can take you to? Somewhere safe where they'll look after you?"

She laughed bitterly. It was a horrible, tragic sound. "Safe! Safe like you Venetians sitting in your fortress. There is nowhere safe for the poor peasants. We must hide in the hills."

"So . . . there is no one we can take you to?" Erik persisted, but without much hope.

She shrugged. "I have a brother on a galley at sea. Georgio's parents are somewhere in the hills." She looked at both of them with resignation, as if she was perfectly prepared for them to abandon her.

Erik cleared his throat, and looked worriedly back down the hill. "Look. We have to get on. I've got to get to Count Dentico's villa. My . . . my . . . a lady . . . I must go and see if she's all right. But we can't just leave you here."

"I have nowhere to go," she repeated tonelessly.

Erik cocked a wary ear toward the slope. "Then you'd better come with us until we find a place for you. Benito, let's shorten those stirrups. And try holding on with your knees."

Benito shook his head. "Erik, the only thing I wasn't holding on with were my teeth. And that was only because the mane kept bouncing around when I tried to bite it."

The Greek peasant woman managed a tremulous laugh. "I can ride. My uncle was a groom for Count Di Valva. The Count wasn't there very often. Where is this place you wish to find? I can probably get you in the right direction, at least." Underneath her shock and her grief, she was recovering some hope, and only because they had not offered to abandon her.

Erik nodded. "You ride, then. Benito can cling on like a tick behind you. The estate is somewhere near a place called Giannades. Do you have any idea where that is?"

She nodded. "I haven't been there. But it is to the west of Kérkira."

She went over to the horse and shortened the stirrups quickly and efficiently; clearly she knew what she was doing. Then she hitched up her skirts in a most unladylike but very practical way, and mounted with an ease that Benito envied.

"It's best that she does something," Erik said, quietly. "She's ready to go to pieces, Benito. She's like a glass that's cracked to bits; one touch, and she'll shatter."

"I'm not surprised."

Erik sighed worriedly. "That could be what happened to my Svanhild. Come on, let's go. If you look over at Kérkira, you'll see Emeric has troops coming in by the column. That's a good few thousand men down there. We should move before they get too organized, never mind before they notice a couple of missing Croats."

Caesare Aldanto's body slept. Long, long ago Chernobog had learned this was a necessity. They died quickly if you did not allow them to rest.

Caesare lay on a cot in the tent that had been allocated to him, and twitched occasionally, as a dog might when dreaming.

Chernobog's other dog, yellow and feral, prowled the hills. The shaman had been told to look for holy places, to sniff them out so they could be rededicated.

It should have been easy. It was proving impossible. The smell of magic was easy enough to find. The trouble was . . . everywhere reeked of it. Up in the wind-tumbled sky his two aerial eyes flew hither and yon, looking for groves. Or temples. Or even standing stones.

So far, all he'd seen through their infinite detail-seeing eyes were churches. The shaman-dog shivered, thinking about those. His master could and no doubt would rededicate some of those to his purpose, but it was a dangerous process, and there was that about them which struck at him. He could, of course, strike back . . . but that could easily draw the attention of the master's adversary. And the shaman was not ready for that.

The shaman-dog stumbled and sneezed. Pollen. It seemed as if every plant on this accursed island was flowering. Like the magic of this place, the pollen was in the air everywhere.

He left the roadway in haste. Horses, and a double-span of donkeys

*struggling to drag a heavy cannon, were coming along it. Horses took
a great aversion to this body-form. They would smell him out and
chase and kick him if they could. This road was busy with troops
and cannons coming along it. By evening at least a third of the guns
would be in place. Already the pounding thunder was beginning. The
shaman wrinkled his nose in distaste. He didn't like the smell of
gunpowder either. It was a new thing. The shaman hated new things.*

Chapter 44

"It's not that serious, Hildi!" Bjarni's voice was gruff, but underneath the impatience was affection, she could tell. "Just a few fragments of rock knocked off by a bullet. Head wounds always bleed like mad. Don't fuss about it. Just bandage it up so that when Kari or Gulta come back with a way out of here for us we can go. We might have to leave the horses."

"But they are such beautiful horses!" Svanhild protested, wrapping a torn section of her petticoat around her brother's head and ear. Now she was glad she had some of those travesties of Venetian gowns that her brothers had insisted she have made up. The masses of petticoats made excellent bandages. "If we leave them behind—those Magyars—"

"They won't be hurt. It's us they're after, not the horses." Bjarni managed a strained chuckle. "Actually, those brutes treat their horses better than they treat their wives. The horses will probably be better off with them."

Gulta and Kari scrambled down into the cave mouth. "There's only one other way out, like I said, Bjarni. And they've got people up there. Rolled a rock down on us."

"But there are a good few caves up there," said Gulta. "Looks like one of them is used. We could hide Svanhild up there."

Svanhild raised herself up. "I can shoot better than most of the men. And I will stand with my clan, not hide up in some other cave. We cannot get out of this valley? Well, so what? They cannot get in, either. We have food and water. Let them sit out there."

She did not add that if her brothers and hearthmen died, and

361

she were hiding in a cave, her best option would be to fling herself off the side of the mountain.

"And tonight we'll slip out and cut a few throats," said Kari evilly.

Bjarni regarded him with a jaundiced eye. "Well, if they can get to shoot into the cave mouth the ricochets will kill us."

"Without being able to shoot around corners they'll hard pressed to do that," pointed out Hrolf. "From the lip over there we can target anyone who comes into the valley. They can't even roll rocks onto us. And there is not enough growing here to burn properly."

Bjarni sniffed. "They don't have to. They'll smoke us out."

The villa was still standing as Erik and Benito rode toward it. Not torched, as most of the others they'd seen so far. The presence of Thalia, the peasant girl they'd rescued, had a very beneficial effect. They'd been forced to the back paths and side roads by patrols. She had actually managed to draw the hastily hiding or fleeing peasants back to them to get some directions. They would have struggled to find their way, otherwise.

Erik kicked his horse into a gallop when the villa Dentico came in sight, and rode straight up to it, as hard and as fast as he could make the horse gallop.

Benito, clinging to Thalia as she followed Erik, knew from Erik's own lectures that this was plain foolishness. He also knew stopping Erik would be beyond his ability.

Besides, Thalia was the one in control of this four-hoofed bollock-cruncher, not him. He was just trying to stay on.

Erik dismounted in a leap, and ran into the house calling "Svanhild! Svanhild!" at the top of his lungs. Alerting every single enemy within hearing distance, or lying in wait in the villa, that there was someone up here. Benito winced; he had expected nothing less.

Erik did at least have that tomahawk in his hand.

Benito dismounted with as much skill as he could muster, and pelted after Erik. "Catch his horse. And stay out here!" he shouted to Thalia. What he expected to find in there would be no sight for her. He raced into the villa with the Shetlander knife in his hand, wishing desperately for his rapier.

However, what Benito found was merely Erik, examining some bloodstains in the hallway. The blood had long since dried and gone a reddish brown, but a fair amount of it was splattered onto the whitewashed walls in various spots. There had been a lot of killing done here.

Benito swallowed. "Erik. I'm sorry."

But to his astonishment, Erik smiled at him. "It wasn't their blood. Or at least, not all their blood."

He ventured closer, and peered at the bloodstains as Erik was doing. He couldn't see how Erik could tell anything from them. "Vinlander blood is a different color?" ventured Benito.

Erik swatted his ear. From past comparative experience, Benito knew he was doing it gently. "No, you young idiot. There are no bodies. Somebody took the bodies away. I don't see that being the Hungarians, not if the bodies were Svanhild and her people. And with that many men and this much blood splashed about . . . I don't see that they'd have just captured everyone."

Well, it made sense when Erik pointed it out, if you accepted the idea that the Hungarians wouldn't take away the bodies of their victims. "So what happened?"

Erik shrugged. "How would I know? But at least they made a fight of it. They weren't caught unawares because there are no bloodstains anywhere except here."

Presumably Erik had already been everywhere but there. "So where do we go now?"

"We try to track them," said Erik, heading for the front door. "Ask anyone we can find, I suppose. It isn't going to be easy. Actually, I should say *I* try to track them. You should get up to the north coast and see if you can find a fisherman willing to transport you."

"The siege isn't going anywhere," he pointed out. "I can help you find them."

Erik shook his head. "With the numbers of men and guns that Emeric is moving in, this is going to be no light siege. And no besieged castle is that secure anyway. Days can count, Benito. Days mean lives. Lives of people like Thalia. I am a knight sworn to defend them. That doesn't mean I can let you waste time. Duty is not a narrow thing; you have yours, and I have mine. Mine is to find Svanhild if I can, then get back to Manfred with all possible speed. Yours is to make all possible speed to Venice, or at least to someone who can get help from Venice."

"I suppose so, Erik. But . . ." he began.

"Just make all possible speed to Venice. Do it, Benito."

They were outside in the courtyard by now. And Benito realized that Thalia wasn't. He tensed, heart suddenly racing . . . But there were the horses, tied up carefully.

Thalia was outside the wall, talking to a very nervous boy of twelve or thirteen. "He says the people who were staying here went north, on the horses of the raiders. He says they killed those who attacked, all of them. He says the soldiers came two days ago, and took the bodies. They've been looking for people to question. There are some of the soldiers in the next valley."

"Ask him if there was a woman with the people who got away. A woman with long blond hair."

The boy nodded. He made an unmistakable gesture with his hands. Benito had to stifle a laugh. Manfred had said she was top-heavy. "It looks like we go north together after all, Erik."

Erik nodded, and Benito had the satisfaction of seeing that it was not with reluctance. "As long as our paths run together, yes. Let us go now, before those soldiers come back. "

They rode out, heading for the mountainous north of the island. "Do you have any idea where we're going?" Benito asked Thalia, as they headed up toward the ridge through the olive grove.

"North. Up there. I have never been up there. They say it is very different." Thalia spoke as if she was referring to a different continent instead of a few miles off. She pointed to Mount Pantocrator. "There is a very holy place up there. There is another one near Paleokastritsa where my Aunt Eleni went when she was young."

She shivered suddenly, for no apparent reason. "But that is not men's business."

More to distract her from whatever thought this had been, Benito asked: "But haven't you been up to the north? I need to find a fishing harbor to find a boat that will take me over to Italy."

She shook her head. "I have been to Kérkira. Twice!"

That made her a well-traveled woman, in her opinion. After all, Corfu-town was at least a league away. Corfiote men traveled; women didn't.

Well, war had the effect of changing things. By now Corfiote women were doing all manner of things they'd never done before.

Benito was exhausted. It hadn't been possible to ride all day, as the heroes in the stories had. For starters, it looked like Emeric's commanders were finally starting to get themselves organized. There were patrols to dodge. And they'd spotted several guard posts being set up on hilltops. Fortunately, it appeared that Erik's combat experience against the Vinland tribes and with clan feuds on Iceland had involved a great deal of just this sort of warfare.

They were moving steadily north, at least. Benito's clothes were dry, which was something he was grateful for. His belly button was meeting his backbone, his stomach was that empty, but he kept reminding himself that he'd been this hungry and more before, and hadn't died of it. And Thalia was drooping in the saddle. Maybe she hadn't paddled a leaky coracle out of a besieged fortress, but she'd had the worst day of her life.

And it wasn't showing any signs of being over; Erik was driving them relentlessly. According to several peasants he'd found and questioned, with Thalia's assistance, the northern villages had closed their gates and were holding off the marauding bands. Not that this would do them any good when the Hungarians stopped being marauding bands and started being segments of an army; but for now, they were holding their own. None of the peasants had seen the Vinlanders, but that was hardly surprising. The sound of horses' hooves was enough to send the peasantry diving for cover.

At the last guard post, Erik had left the two of them and gone on a lone sortie. He'd returned, cleaning his tomahawk fastidiously. And smiling.

"They haven't found them yet, anyway. The guard told me about what happened at Dentico villa. The Magyars are furious, but they think they're after a bunch of Venetians. They have been trying to track them for days. They've gone to the northwest. There are several villages up there that are walled and resisting."

"There is one near the coast at Paleokastritsa, where many of the women go to the shrine," volunteered Thalia.

Benito sighed. "Do you think this shrine-place is serving dinner?"

Erik reached into his sling-bag. "The guard up there had some bread that he won't be needing any more." He pulled out a flat country loaf. "He had some wine, too, but I knew you wouldn't want that."

Benito glared at him. "Erik! I'll kill you!"

Erik hauled out a clay flask, miraculously unbroken. "It killed him," he said grimly. "Fortunately there isn't enough left to kill you. I hope."

Erik had also helped himself to the guard's pike and his arque-bus. The latter was filthy enough to give Erik the mutters. Still, with wine and bread in them, pressing on seemed easier. At last they saw a patch of lights.

"A town that isn't deserted. It must be one of the ones that is holding out." Erik peered through the dusk at them. "They can't last long."

"Could be a Hungarian camp," Benito observed, wearily.

"True," Erik sounded positively cheerful. "But we'll have to sneak a closer look to tell. Probably have more fleas than people in it, though."

Benito groaned. "If it is a town, and so long as it don't fall tonight, and they've got a place for us to sleep, I'll be pleased to meet the fleas."

"Our chances of getting in tonight are nonexistent," said Erik, urging his tired horse forward. "Unless it is a Hungarian camp, of course. In which case we won't get out. It's far more likely to be a Hungarian camp."

He was wrong about the Hungarian camp. He was also wrong about the town letting them in. Refugees had been coming up the steep narrow track for a week now, most of them by night.

Benito, Thalia and Erik found themselves with several others, requesting entry to Paleokastritsa. Benito found no trouble in understanding just why it hadn't been sacked. It didn't look large enough to be worth the huge effort it would take.

"Stand against the wall. Now take all your weapons off. Once that is done you can come forward one at a time. Remember, any false moves and you'll be shot from up here."

Paleokastritsa was crowded. A place to sleep . . . well, eventually they joined some thirty others, sleeping on the church floor.

Erik was right about the fleas, though.

Chapter 45

Benito woke to the certain knowledge that he was getting soft. Sleeping on a cold stone floor might once have been luxury. After all, he was dry, and the other sleepers kept the place relatively warm. But the stone was a lot harder than what he had become used to. Erik and Thalia were already up. So he assumed, at any rate, because they weren't lying on the stone next to him.

Benito got himself up, rubbed the sleep from his eyes, bowed to the altar, and walked off to find either the others or the town fountain. He hadn't slept that deeply for many years, and he knew that if he was going to keep alive out here, he was going to have to go back to the habits of his days as an unwanted and uninvited secret tenant in people's attics. He'd have to learn to sleep with his senses keyed again, where the slightest sound would wake him. Only, he had been so tired when they first arrived, he knew he couldn't have slept lightly. Now he was just so hungry, he couldn't have slept at all.

The first familiar face he saw, also at the town's fountain, belonged to neither Erik nor Thalia. The Corfiote sailor no longer had his black eye. The sailor looked at Benito. Blinked. Looked again.

Benito hoped that this wouldn't get unpleasant. He was fairly sure he could deal with the man's inept knife-skills. What he didn't want was the trouble that would inevitably follow. He also didn't want his identity nosed about. It might not cause trouble—but there could be ears out here in the street that it shouldn't come to. Benito glanced about. There was no one in earshot, at least.

The sailor shook his head. "I'll be damned! Just what are you doing here, *Case Vecchie*?"

He didn't say it too loudly, or with any malice. Benito decided to chance friendliness. If he remembered rightly, the sailor from Bari had called him "Spiro."

"Trying not to give away that I am a *Case Vecchie*, Spiro. Do me a favor. Don't shout or call any attention to it or I might have to remind you how we last met. And I don't want to do that; I've got plenty of trouble as it is."

The man didn't really seem to have heard. Instead he was studying Benito intently. "You are him!" he said unbelievingly. "You really are him!"

"I *really* don't want everyone to know, Spiro," Benito repeated, fixing him with a stare.

The sailor grinned widely. "Safe enough with me, milord. I owe you."

Benito noticed that a couple of people were staring at them. He clapped Spiro on the shoulder, and turned the gesture into an arm around the sailor's shoulders, as if they were old friends. Which, at the moment, Benito really hoped was the case. "Let's go and find some wine. I was going to drink some of the water, but I've decided that I'm really not that thirsty."

Spiro looked skeptical. "Right now, wine in Paleokastritsa is damn near as expensive as wine in Venice. And I'm afraid I'm broke again, milord, even if I owe you a drink or two."

"For heaven's sake, call me Benito. Forget the 'milord.' And the wine is on me, and something to eat, if you can forget that fact. Venetian *Case Vecchie* are not popular right now. Out there, the Hungarians want to kill us for protecting the island. From what I can work out, the Corfiotes in here want to kill us for not protecting the island."

Spiro shrugged. "As you're buying the wine, I wouldn't dream of killing you, m . . . Benito."

"Afterwards is a different story," said Benito wryly.

Spiro chuckled. "After a few glasses of wine even the stupidest idea can sound like a good one. But I did learn that that was a really, really insanely stupid one. So what are you doing here, m . . . Benito?"

"I'll tell you about it over that cup of wine. Where do we find one?"

Spiro pointed across the square at dark doorway. "Papavanakis'.

His taverna is dirty, it smells, his wife's face would curdle milk and I think he waters his wine."

Benito grinned. "So why are we drinking there?"

Spiro shrugged and grinned back. "At least what he's putting in the wine is water. And he is less of a thief than most of them."

They strolled over and went into the dim coolness out of the already bright day. Benito blinked, adjusting his eyes to the lack of direct sunlight. The taverna was clean and smelled of food and wine. Fresh bread and meaty smells, and the wine wasn't slightly used by prior customers. The pretty young woman behind the counter scowled at them. "Not you again, Spiro! Go away. Not another cup will I give you until you pay."

Spiro nodded to Benito. "See what I mean," he said mournfully. "Curdle milk, that face would."

She snorted and pretended to throw a wine cup at him. It was obviously an old joke. "Go away, Spiro. Papas will kill me if I give you any more credit."

Spiro gestured expansively. "It's all right, Anna. Beni here is paying."

The woman raised her eyebrows. "With the same coin as you pay? Or real money?"

Benito produced a silver penny.

"You shouldn't show her that much!" said Spiro. "She'll faint and we'll never see any wine. Or that food you promised me. It's been a while since I ate."

The taverna's keeper clicked her tongue. "He's impossible. How did he talk you into wasting good money on him?" She said it with perfect amiability, while filling two wine cups.

Benito realized that Spiro had addressed her in Italian Frankish . . . and that she'd replied in the same way. Plainly, by her accent and rapidity of speech, it was her mother-tongue. He'd been keeping his own mouth shut to play down his origins but it now seemed safe enough. "He borrowed money from me. He's had it for a year. So now he says I owe him interest," said Benito, earnestly.

The young woman snorted with laughter and handed them the wine. "And you'll keep owing him interest until the day he dies." She pointed to the tables. "Sit. I'll go and find you some food."

They sat. Spiro took a pull at his wine cup. "More water than wine."

It tasted pretty good to Benito. "So, what are you doing here, Spiro. Is this home?"

The Corfiote gestured expansively. "This dump? Ha. Liapádhes is a great metropolis. Broad streets, wonderful tavernas. Wine like a young lion. As far from this place as the sun is from the earth."

Benito was beginning to get the hang of Spiro by now. "So it is just like this, is it?"

Spiro gave him a conspiratorial wink and took another pull of his wine. "Two peas in a pod, really, except this has got a good defensive position. It's about a mile and half south."

"How did you get home from Venice?"

Spiro raised his cup. "A Dorma ship, thanks to you. I was with her all the way to Constantinople. I'd have stayed with her too, but when I got back to Corfu, on the return trip, there was a bit of family business I had to settle. A fellow had taken some liberties with my sister." He swallowed half the contents of his cup at a go. "So after I had thanked him very politely, I went back to Kérkira, but the ship had left. I couldn't come back to Liapádhes for a while. So I took a job with a fisherman. Taki drinks too much but he's a good skipper. Then this lot blew up. So I thought I'd come home. Only home seemed to be full of Hungarians. And you, Benito?"

Benito's ears had pricked up with the mention of the fisherman. "Got sent out here to be a factor for Dorma. And then this war blew up. Look, this fisherman friend of yours. He wouldn't like to earn a bit of money? I really want out of here back to the Italian mainland."

At this point, Anna the taverna keeper arrived with two earthenware platters, fragrant steam curling up from them. "I had some of last night's *stifado* still. I've just made it hot. That one," she pointed an elbow at Spiro, "didn't eat last night. So I thought he might as well eat this morning, and you looked hungry."

Spiro looked suspiciously at the plate of pearl onion-laced stew that she put in front of him. "It hasn't got quinces in it again, has it? You know I hate quinces."

She shook her head as she wiped her hands on her apron. Then she held out a hand to Benito. "And that's why he ate three helpings."

Benito handed over the silver. She looked at it very carefully. She was polite enough not to bite it in front of him. "It seems real enough. You want more wine with that?"

Spiro drained his cup. "Seems like a good idea. I'm not likely to get this lucky again in a hurry, and I don't see us fishing for a while yet. Which answers your question, Benito. The Dalmatian pirates sink any boat they can find. Even fishing boats."

Benito waited for the taverna keeper to walk off. "Even for a good bit of coin? Working at night?"

Spiro shrugged. "I'll ask around. My old skipper Taki would be your best bet. He's up in the hills with his cousin Georgio. He's probably so sick of the old man and his goats that he'd be ready to try anything by now. I could get word to him. Some of the boys who go out with the goats would do anything for a few coppers."

Wordlessly, Benito dug out a few copper coins and a silver penny. He held back the silver penny. "That one is for finding somebody else. A whole bunch of them. Big guys with blond hair and a blond woman with them."

Spiro stuck his hand out. "I'll have the silver too, thanks. Easiest money I've ever earned. They're in a cave in a gorge about a mile and a half east of here."

"What!" Benito started. "Are you sure?"

Spiro grinned. "Well, I was fairly sober when I heard about them. That's the trouble with being broke, you know. Do you want them alive or dead?" he asked around a mouthful of stew, still holding his hand out.

"Alive! Definitely alive!"

"Then you'd better get a move on. They stole some of Cheretis's goats and he's got all the men going out this morning. They're planning to burn them out."

Benito knocked over the chair in his haste to get up. "Come on! We must find Erik!" He hauled Spiro out of his seat.

"But I haven't finished eating! And the wine is still coming!"

"You want gold, not silver, you'll come and show us the way to this place as fast as possible." Benito hustled him along, try-ing to think where he'd be most likely to find Erik. The stables perhaps?

"Where are you going?" yelled the taverna keeper. "Here is your wine and your change. You haven't eaten your food!"

"We'll be back. Emergency!" yelled Benito.

Sure enough, Erik and Thalia were in the stable. Erik looked up as he and Spiro panted in. "So nice of you to bother to come and help. Finished in the taverna I saw you going into?"

"Get the tack on those horses! We've got to move, now!"

Erik didn't waste time asking questions, before starting to do that. Neither did the suddenly wide-eyed Thalia. But as he worked, Erik asked what was up.

"Your precious Svanhild is about to get roasted for goat-stealing," said Benito. "Spiro here knows where they are."

Erik didn't waste time on talk. But he worked at a pace that made lightning look as if it moved at a comparatively glacial speed. "Up." He hauled the one-time sailor onto the horse, behind him. Thalia was up and Benito struggled and scrambled behind her as they clattered for the gate. Erik nearly rode the stableman down. Benito almost fell off as the man used a pitchfork to make the horse decide to stop abruptly. "You owe—"

Benito frantically dug out some money and flung it at him. "We'll be back!" And then Thalia set off after Erik. Benito just hoped they'd catch up.

They did. The town gate was closed. "Let us out!" yelled Erik.

"Not likely. Let's see who you're running from first, foreigner," said the guard, clutching his spear.

Spiro saved the man's life. "Open up, Adoni! They're not running from anyone. They're trying to get to someone in hurry."

The guard peered. "Oh. It's you, Spiro Volagatis. Well, I guess if it gets you out of the town it's a good thing." He unbarred the gate, and they rode off down the steep, winding trail.

"Where now?" Benito heard Erik yell as they reached the foot of the trail. Benito missed the reply but they did manage to follow Erik off to the west. Then he spotted the trickle of smoke. By the way Erik was urging the horse into a gallop he'd seen it too.

The Corfiote men and boys, armed with a motley array of old arquebuses, pitchforks, spears and slings, were piling brushwood right across the mouth of the narrow gorge. Already someone had lit one edge. Benito arrived into what certainly sounded like a full-scale riot.

By the three men on the ground some of the locals had been foolish enough to try and stop Erik kicking the fire apart. But now he was under the noses of a dozen arquebuses, and there was a full-scale shouting match going on.

Thalia quelled it with a shriek and a stream of what could only be Greek vituperation. Hastily the locals began to pull the burning branches away and beat at the fire with branches of green leaves. "What did you say to them?" asked Benito.

"This is a sacred place! The holy mother is in the temple cave up there. This valley ends in some cliffs. There is no other way out."

"But they've stolen our goats!" bellowed one of the men at Erik. "They're bandits! They've been shooting goat-boys. And who the hell are you, foreigner? You knocked down my brother. I've a good mind to knock you down."

"When I come back," said Erik grimly, hauling brushwood out of the way, "you're welcome to try."

But the fire already had its teeth into the dry brush. Benito, beating at flames, got the feeling that he should somehow have gotten Erik there sooner. Already the heat was pushing at their faces and a river of smoke was funneling up the gorge.

And then there was a rumble.

Even the wet rag wrapped around her mouth couldn't stop Svanhild coughing as she tried, desperately, to calm the horses. Their eyes were wild and rolling and the animals were whickering and stamping. There was little likelihood that anyone could ride them now. The horses were already on the edge of panic.

"We'll have to leave them, Hildi," said Bjarni. "We'll have to get to the cliff and try and climb out."

"We can't! They'll die."

"If we stay much longer, we'll die."

There was a rumble and it grew darker, almost by the moment. "Look at the stream!"

From atop the high rock Benito reached down and hauled Erik back by the collar. As the Icelander struggled to turn and throw Benito's hand off, the water flumed through, hitting Erik at about knee-height. It knocked his feet out from under him anyway. Benito clung to Erik as if he were a roof-beam four stories from the ground. If he hadn't hauled Erik back, the water-wall would have stuck the Icelander at least belly-button height. Another strong pair of hands came and grabbed Erik's arms. Between Spiro and Benito they hauled him up.

The sudden rain hissed down like arrows. A glance showed the local heroes running for shelter, bedraggled figures pelting away from the scene.

"Thanks," said Erik, as they hastened to a rock lip that offered some vague shelter. Looking at the torrent and the already decreasing rain, Erik shook his head. "What caused *that*?"

Thalia shrugged. "I told you it was a holy place. The priestesses command the magic here."

Erik shook his head again. "Whatever it was, it certainly wasn't natural. It was a clear morning a few minutes ago. Anyway, let me see if I can get up there."

Thalia took him by the arm. "I tied the horses just back there. You can probably ride up the valley now."

Erik smiled at her. "You're the practical one, Thalia. Seeing to the horses, doing all the things we forget."

The peasant woman looked serious. "Somebody has to."

But Erik had already left at a run.

Benito looked out. The rain was slacking off. It would be gone in a minute or two. The stream was already dropping. And on the blackened, burned brush a green creeper was already twining, growing as he watched.

The intervention had been magical, of that Benito was certain. He was less certain that he liked it.

Chapter 46

Svanhild peered over her brothers' shoulders as they watched by the little protruding ridge of limestone, arquebuses at the ready. The stream, which had been no more than a bare trickle so recently, was now making so much noise that they were forced to shout. But at least the smoke was gone. The rain, too, was nearly over.

"Give it a little while longer and I'll go and scout. That was the luckiest rainstorm in history," said Kari.

Bjarni raised an eyebrow. "Maybe so. But why did the stream flood *before* the rain fell?"

"It must have rained higher up in the catchment, Bjarni."

The oldest Thordarson brother shook his head. "This damned trickle hasn't got a catchment worth talking about, Kari. There is something funny going on here. I hope things haven't just got worse."

"There is someone coming up the gorge!" shouted the hearthman on guard up on the slope.

They all took cover, including Svanhild. "Pick your marks!" commanded Bjarni. "Don't open fire until I say so."

Svanhild peered anxiously toward the mouth of the gorge. Bright sunlight was shivering into scatterings of brief rainbows through the last veils of rain. The rider came in sight around the corner. His dark hair was wet and plastered about his face, but Svanhild knew those facial planes instantly. Her heart hammered, and she found herself abruptly breathless.

"Svanhild!" he called, his voice echoing off the cliffs.

A shot boomed. The bullet kicked a white spurt of dust from the limestone next to the rider's head. Erik Hakkonsen whirled his horse in the direction of the firing and shook an empty fist. "You stupid Vinlander bastard! I've come to rescue you!"

Svanhild stopped only long enough to lay down her bow, and then was out and running down the slope. "Erik! Erik!"

A huge smile nearly split Erik's face in half. As she skidded to a halt on the slippery rock beside his stirrup, his face went from angry and anxious to—well . . .

Foolish. "Er. Good morning, Svanhild Thordardottar."

She stood there smiling up at him, feeling equally foolish and desperately wishing she could think of something to say. He vaulted down from the dun he was riding. She could see, though it was no help, that he too was fumbling for words. All the long and carefully thought-out speeches had gone from her head, as if she had never even considered making them. But she had to help get something started, or they would both stand there, looking, not touching, not saying anything.

"Why is your hair dark now?" was all she could think of to say.

He ran his fingers through his hair as if he had not known it was dark. "I was trying to pass as one of the locals."

Svanhild looked at him, branding his appearance into her memory, in case—well, in case. He was tall, lean and athletic; she had known that, of course, but now she was *aware* of it. His face had a hewn masculinity to it, planar and strong, and nothing detracted from the way he looked in her eyes, not even the soot on his face and the water dripping from his hair.

Then a thin sliver of reality intruded. With the high cheekbones and the straight hair, even with his skin and hair darkened, Erik looked as much like a local as a wolf looks like a bison. She had to laugh. And Erik began laughing with her. By the time that her brothers and their hearthmen joined them, they were virtually leaning on each other, helpless with laughter.

Benito heard the shot, and decided he'd come running. He was wise enough about his own horsemanship to approach on foot. He also kept his head down. Still, by the time he got to where he could see them, the Vinlanders, Erik and his sweetheart were all standing around beaming at each other.

"Well, they look really miserable."

Benito turned to see both Spiro and Thalia had followed him. Spiro was being his usual quirky self.

"Good," said Benito. "Let's go and make them more miserable and tell them they have got to get out of here. Before the villagers come back and roast them again, or roll rocks on them."

Thalia shook her head. "Not likely. The men will be hiding under their beds and hoping their wives don't find out where they decided to make a fire."

"I wouldn't tell these foreigners that in case they decide to have a roast goat to celebrate," said Spiro. "People are very touchy about their goats around Paleokastritsa. More touchy about their goats than their wives, which, if you look at the wives, makes sense. Not like the women in Liapádhes, of course."

Thalia looked at him with her mouth open, as if she wasn't entirely certain whether or not Spiro was mad.

Spiro winked at her. "Of course the goats around Liapádhes are prettier than those in Paleokastritsa, too. They have to be."

Benito walked out to the Vinlanders rather than find out any more about the local goats and goat-herds.

"Ah, Benito," Erik greeted him. "Friends, this young gentleman is the reason I'm here."

"And will be the reason we're getting out of here, Erik." Benito was getting increasingly anxious to break up the happy reunion. "The locals might come back, and besides, that fire will have told every Hungarian trooper in the area that something is going on here."

"But where will we go?" asked Svanhild, her face passing from joyful to desperate in a single moment. "Everyone is trying to kill us."

"We'll go back to Paleokastritsa," Benito said firmly, as Spiro and Thalia picked their way toward the group. "You'll have to do some explaining about their goats. And pay for them."

The biggest of Vinlanders snorted. "Of course we will pay for their goats! We would have paid in the first place, if anyone had been willing not to run away from us. What were we supposed to do? Starve?"

"You'd better pay up generously and say you are very sorry," said Spiro. "I'll handle it for you. For a fee, of course."

One of the huge Vinlanders—they all looked alike to Benito—looked nearly apoplectic. "Apologize? But they nearly killed us. They nearly killed my sister!"

"And you did kill their goats, no 'nearly' about it," Benito retorted. Then, couldn't resist adding: "And according to Spiro, goats are a lot more appreciated around here than sisters. Come on, let's go and see if they'll let us back into Paleokastritsa. I left my breakfast and a glass of wine behind to come and rescue you from the goat-avengers. Erik is not so bad-tempered, because he was only currying horses and he was looking for you anyway."

"He was?" Svanhild gazed upon Erik with blue eyes so bright they seemed to have stars in them.

Benito smiled slyly at Erik. "Oh, yes! When he heard from Maria Verrier that you were out here, he did not even let an entire besieging army stand in his way. He left the citadel by night, over the walls with a leaking boat, braving enemy patrols and the wild sea in the torrential rain, staying neither to sleep nor rest, riding *vent a terre* until he reached the villa Dentico. All that was in his mind was the safety of his golden-haired Svanhild."

"Shut up, Benito," growled Erik, glowing dully. Under the dye, that pale skin produced a truly vibrant red color. Benito decided that the next time they were cold, he'd embarrass the Icelander; you could warm a family of five by the heat he gave off.

"But it is true!" insisted Thalia. "He saved me from the raping Croats, kyria. He killed two of them, just like that. And the sentry on the hill. He is a great fighter. He pulled at the burning wood with his bare hands and he beat back the men of Paleokastritsa and—"

"*And* let's get out of here! Please," begged Erik. "Either the Hungarians will arrive, or the locals are bound to come back."

"Or both," agreed one of the Vinlanders. "Don't want to be in the middle of that."

Soon the entire party was riding to Paleokastritsa.

The yellow dog almost howled in triumph. At last the shaman had a trace of magic that rose above the general reeking miasma of this place. He ran through the olive groves, pine forests and the macchia. He ran on past sentries and past hiding peasants. He had many miles to go.

But it had been a piece of intense and powerful sorcery, not finely crafted and precise as the names of power he used, not demon-bludgeon strong as Jagiellon used. Precisely, he thought, what Jagiellon was looking for. This magic was raw and primal, elemental—big, in the way an earthquake or a thunderstorm was big.

Dangerous, too, but that was not his problem. His problem was to find it, Jagiellon's to tame it.

He sent his hawks winging north, a part of him seeing through their eyes, eyes that could see a field mouse twitch the grass at five hundred feet. It took him quite some time to realize that the hawks were being subtly pushed away. The thermals slid them off to the west, the winds seeming to buffet against them whenever they tried to fly to one corner of the island. The hawks were becoming exhausted. Worse, they were becoming recalcitrant. Ever since he had tried to use them above Venice, the shaman had noticed that his control over the two hawks was not as it should be.

He was both angry and astonished. It was not possible! He had their true names, which made them his. His absolutely. Yet . . . he could not ignore the fact that they were rebelling. Not in great things but in small ways, in a slow and steady erosion of his control. It must be this vile place's magic.

Well, where they could not go was as good an indication of where he had to go as them actually seeing something. The yellow dog ran on, allowing the hawks to go to roost.

It was midafternoon before he reached the place. He looked at the few burned branches and the evidence of the recently flooded stream and smelled raw magic.

He tried to take a step forward, and stumbled. Grass had grown around his feet, the thin strands intertwining and binding. He kicked his way loose, then moved forward, sniffing. A dog's nose is a wondrous instrument. He could smell the horses as individuals; he could smell the people, the peasants and the others, and know who had wandered where. He could smell the women among them, two of them. He could smell . . .

Achoo! He erupted in a volley of sneezes.

All the flowers suddenly seemed intent on smothering him in their scents. He flicked his ears. A horsefly buzzed about them; then another. One bit him just below the tail on the exposed flesh. The shaman turned and snapped angrily at it, cracking it in his yellow teeth. Another bit his ear as he did so. Several more came buzzing up. One affixed itself to his nose. The shaman pawed furiously at it.

The shaman was one of the greatest and most powerful of magicians. He was proofed against many great magics.

Horseflies made him flee.

Horseflies in those numbers could make anything flee. They seemed immune to his protective spells.

Still, he knew the area in which the magics were being worked now. The master could send Aldanto. It would do the blond puppet good to be bitten by few horseflies.

"Go away or we'll shoot you," said one of the pair of guards on the wall. He brandished his arquebus in a manner that was more awkward than fierce. "You're not wanted here!"

One of the Vinlanders, the one who seemed to do all of the talking, contrived to look sheepish and apologetic. "It was a misunderstanding, truly. We were running from the invaders, and we were starving. We have money! We want to pay for the animals."

There was a hasty consultation between the sentries. "We'll get someone to call old Cheretis. It was his goats."

The other guard peered at them more closely. "Oh. It's you again, Spiro. I thought we'd gotten rid of you. I see you're in bad company, as usual."

"But I haven't been anywhere near your sister, Adoni," said Spiro with a grin.

The guard glared at him. The other guard nearly fell over the crenellations laughing.

The goat owner, when he arrived, reminded Benito more of a sullen, bad-tempered porker than a goat. Like the ones a few people over on Guidecca had kept on the scraps in those big market-gardens over there. He had the same sparse, bristly beard and pronounced jowls.

But he was as obstinate as a goat, even if he didn't look like one. "They must be punished! Even if they pay for the goats, they must be punished!" He pleaded with the guards, in a squeaky voice. "After all, if you shoot them, I get paid for my beasts from the money they have with them. And you get the rest."

Spiro shook his head. "Don't be dafter than you have to be, you old *Malakas*. They were strangers visiting our beautiful island when the Hungarians attacked. Where is our famous Corfiote hospitality? Why are you fussing over a few miserable, scrawny goats?"

"Scrawny goats! They killed my best milker! She was the most beautiful goat on the island, hair like silk, an udder as soft as a baby's face and milk, so much milk you'd have thought she was a cow. And as for hospitality: what sort of guests kill your live-stock?"

Spiro turned to the Vinlanders, Benito, Erik and Thalia. "See? I told you how they felt about their goats in Paleokastritsa!"

The laughter might have infuriated the goat-owner, but it decided the two guards that they were obviously no threat. "Have you got the money to pay the old bastard?" asked one guard.

"In gold," said Bjarni, curtly.

Not much gold came to Paleokastritsa. Even the goat-owner looked less sour. "Such fine goats as mine are worth a great amount of gold."

"Let us in and we can argue about it," grumbled Benito, "before some Hungarian troopers come along because of all that smoke. And *they* take all the gold instead."

Benito reached into his own small pouch and hauled out a silver penny. "Here, Spiro. I owe you this for information. I promised him a ducat from you, Erik."

Erik dug in his pouch. "Here are two." He handed them over with a flourish carefully visible to the gate. "I'm in your debt for finding and helping my friends."

Guards and goat-owner had developed eyes like saucers; the goat-owner's were full of greed.

Spiro looked at the coins, beaming. "I'm rich!" He walked over to the gate and pounded on it. "Let me in. I need a drink."

"You'll have to leave your swords and guns in the gatehouse," said one of the guards. "And you owe me a cup of wine, Spiro."

Spiro grinned. "I'm buying, so you might as well get yours before the money's all drunk up."

"After you send some goat-boys to look for that friend of yours," said Benito. "The fisherman."

Spiro nodded. "Sure. But I intend to be already hung over and broke before Taki Temperades gets here." Then he elbowed Benito in the ribs. "Trying to rob you was the smartest dumb thing I ever did, eh?"

At the moment, Benito was inclined to agree.

Chapter 47

In the darkness, up on the landward wall of the inner curtain, Manfred paced. Von Gherens, as a bodyguard should, paced along-side him.

"It was a mistake. I should never have let him go." Manfred stared over the cannon-flash in the darkness. Emeric's heavy guns were being maneuvered into place and the first of the forty-eight-pound bombards were already in action.

"It's early days yet," said Von Gherens. "Erik won't be easily caught. And even if the boat sank, he swims like a fish." He looked pensive. "You know, there's something very wrong about that. A good knight should have the decency to avoid learning how to swim. After all, if you're in the water with armor on, what is the point?"

Manfred ignored him. He gnawed on a knuckle, and welcomed the pain when he bit a little too deep. "He and Benito were too valuable to risk like that. What the hell was I thinking of?"

Von Gherens didn't reply. Perhaps he realized that Manfred didn't really want an answer. Presently Francesca came up to the battlement, and took him by the elbow as he stared off into the hills. Reluctantly, he turned to face her. "It's time to come down, Manfred. Perhaps tomorrow night . . ."

"Look. Look, Manfred!" Von Gherens pointed. Manfred whirled and followed the direction of his finger.

On the far hills a bonfire had blossomed, a tiny pinpoint of yellow and red. Now another. Then a third.

"You're hurting me, Manfred," said Francesca quietly.

Hastily, Manfred let go of her shoulder. "Sorry, dear." He took a deep breath, then let out a long sigh of relief. He should have known; and he should have trusted that those damned Vinlanders were as hard to kill as his Icelander. "And he's even found the girl! Come on, Francesca. Now, I really will sleep. Not even Emeric's damned guns will keep me awake."

"About time, too," grumbled Von Gherens. "Keep him under lock and key, Francesca. I'm going across to the hospital to see how Falkenberg does."

Manfred smiled. "I'm too tired and, to be honest, too relieved to gallivant tonight, Fritz. How is Falkenberg, by the way?"

"He had some fever and infection. But Father Francis, one of Eneko Lopez's companions, has been treating him. It looks like he might mend, Manfred. He swore at me this morning, at least. That was a relief after all the 'I-am-about-to-die' piety when I visited him the time before. He must think he has more time to make his peace with the Lord."

"Well, we can use another knight-proctor. I must go over and see him tomorrow morning, and get him used to the idea."

"Oh, no." Von Gherens shook his head. "When he's up, he's coming to run alternate bodyguard shifts with me. Erik ordered it. And now that we know the mad Icelander is alive out there, do you really think any of us are going to take a chance on him coming back and finding out we didn't do exactly what he said?"

Taki looked at the boy. Looked at the silver on the battered table. Looked back at the boy.

He could easily be one of Taki's usual crew. Curly black hair, olive skin, old clothes, bare feet. Short, but broad of shoulder. Taki looked at the silver again. There was quite a lot of it, but Taki could count a table-full of coins with a single glance.

Finally, deciding, he nodded and reached for it.

The youngster put his hand over the coins. "Not so fast, Captain. One quarter when I get to your boat. One quarter when I get over there. And one half when you give Erik a note I write for you when I'm safe."

Taki eyed the man called Erik. A scary one, that. Nothing would get past him—and nothing would stop him if he felt the need to do something. Except maybe death, and Taki wouldn't bet on that. "How do I know he will give me the money?"

Spiro chuckled. "Taki, take it from me, the *Case Vecchie* isn't trying to cheat you. He just doesn't trust your ugly face."

Taki did his best to look affronted. "Me? You can trust me. Ask anyone!" he bellowed, gesturing theatrically.

"Except about the freshness of his fish," said one of men in the tavern with a gap-toothed grin.

The tavern's occupants laughed.

Taki scowled and waved a fist vaguely. "You want to lose some more teeth, Adoni?"

Spiro shook his head. "He's all right, Benito. One of the best skippers on the island. Even if his fish . . ." He ducked.

Benito grinned. "I'm not that fond of fish anyway."

"Ah, but do you like cheap wine?" grinned the gap-toothed one.

"I only know one person who is fonder of it," snorted Erik. He shook his head, dubiously, studying Taki and his crew. "I think I should ration all of you. Between the lot of you, you'll end up sailing off to Vinland instead of across the Strait of Otranto."

"I sail best when I'm drunk!" insisted Taki, belligerently.

"At least he thinks he does," said Kosti.

"Has he ever tried it any other way?" asked Benito. This fishingboat's crew were beginning to give him a pleasant feeling of nostalgia for his days as a rooftop thief. They were as crazy as Valentina and Claudia had been in the early days.

Kosti shook his head. "Not so as anyone has ever noticed. But to be fair, he hasn't sunk us yet."

"Let's hope he can keep that up." Benito put the silver back in his pouch. "When and where do I see you, Captain?"

"Tomorrow night. We'll have to go and fetch the old boat, and get her round here. But there's a cove a couple of miles beyond Paleokastritsa we can lie up in. If you don't know the coast, it doesn't look like it's there at all. We should be there sometime before tomorrow, and we'll sail on the windrise after dark. Spiro can get one of the local kids to guide you over there. We've got a fishing boat to get off an island."

"And we've got to get over to the islet," said Kosti, suddenly glum. "Yani's boat is still underwater, I suppose."

The captain grinned evilly and slapped him on the back. "And guess who is going to be swimming out there."

❁   ❁   ❁

Trudging up the hill carrying Alessia, Maria felt ill at ease about her destination. In the background she could hear Emeric of Hungary's cannon pounding away at the outer wall, reminding her that things weren't normal. But that wasn't what was making her nervous. She was going to the governor's palace in the Castel *a mar*. The Castel *a mar* was not nearly as grandiose as the Doge's palace in Venice, but it was somehow more intimidating. As imposing as it was, the Doge's palace in Venice had been the property of the people of Venice by sheer familiarity.

The guards at the gates also thought she didn't belong here.

They barred her way with their pikes. "You can't go in here, woman. His Excellency only has public audiences on Wednesdays. Come back then." The guard who spoke looked at her without much interest, his tone of voice more bored than anything else.

"I don't want to see his Excellency. I want to speak to Prince Manfred. He will see me."

The guard snorted. "And no doubt you've brought his baby with you! Go on with you, get lost."

"Maybe she's a Teutonic knight in disguise," said the other, chuckling at his own wit.

She reined in her temper, and remained polite. "Can't you send a message to him? Tell him Maria Verrier would like to see him. Please?" She hated her own voice, so subservient—but angering them wouldn't get her anywhere.

"Hark at her!" One of the guards jerked a disdainful thumb at Maria. "'Please!' Listen, dearie. We don't run a messenger service for Scuolo women to have chats with princes. He'll send for you if he wants you."

Maria flushed with anger, and was just considering whether it would be worth the consequences of pushing her dagger through his ear when the guards suddenly jerked themselves out of the slouch and came to attention. The frail, white-haired podesta's wife was coming down.

For all the attention that Contessa Renate De Belmondo paid the guards they might as well have been statues, except one does not nod to statues. She did, however, greet Maria with every sign of pleasure.

"Maria Verrier, is it not? Have you come for our little chat? I am so sorry! I have to go across to the garrison in the Castel *a terra* right now. Would you mind coming in and waiting for me?"

Maria realized that Marco's efforts on her behalf had borne fruit after all. She did her best to curtsey, which, as she'd never been taught and she had a baby in her arms, was not a success. But Lady Renate was real quality, certainly as far as Maria was concerned, and ignored the awkwardness. Such things were only important to *Case Vecchie curti,* new money that still had to try to establish how important they were. For the Lady Renates of the world, it wasn't important how you looked—money could buy looks—it was what you were.

Lady Renate smiled. "I see you've brought your baby up, too. I wish I could see my own grandchildren. Or Lodovico Montescue trying to be a good great-grandfather, ha! Mind you, hooligans usually turn out to be very strict with their offspring . . . but it is impossible to think that he might be a great-grandfather soon."

She touched Alessia's cheek gently. "So soft! I love them when they're this age." She smiled again. "What I love most, of course, is that you can give them back when they cry!"

"Actually, milady, I came up to see Prince Manfred, about a friend. To be honest, I hadn't come to see you at all."

Lady Renate pulled a severe face, with just trace of a betraying dimple in her lined cheek. "And why not me, Hmm? Young men have, as a rule, no liking for babies. They don't know how to hold them."

Maria blushed. "I was . . . embarrassed to come and see you, milady. I'm just a *Scuolo* wife."

Lady Renate shook a finger at her. "And a friend of my old flame's granddaughter! Close enough a friend to have stood as her maid of honor at her wedding. That is an honor for anyone, for it means the *Casa* Montescue holds you in very high esteem. As ancient a house as there is in Venice. And if Lodovico thought I was good enough for him, then you must be good enough to keep me company. Come up and see me—and soon. What about Wednesday just after Terce?"

Maria settled for a half-bow rather than trying to curtsey again. "Thank you, milady. I will come."

Lady Renate laughed. "You'd better! I look forward to it. And now I must run. The women from Kérkira have come in a delegation to see the captain-general. I shall go and prevent bloodshed." She waved and walked out.

"No escort," said the one guard disapprovingly. "And not riding."

The other shrugged. "There isn't a person in Corfu who would dare hurt her, and riding makes her sore these days." He nodded to Maria. "I made a mistake. Come on, I'll take you up to the prince's quarters myself. You won't report us, will you?"

Maria tempered the sharpness of her retort with just enough amusement to let them know that she wasn't really joking. "Not this time. But next time I'll pull your bottom lip over your ears. And don't tempt me to show you how it is done. You came that close." She showed a gnat-sized gap with her fingers.

The guard chuckled. "If they had women in the army you'd make a good sergeant major. Sorry, Signora Verrier. I'll pass the word around so you don't end up stretching too many lips around here."

"You tell them to watch cheeking the *Scoulo* people," she warned him. "We've got short tempers and long memories."

The guard led her up through the castle, around enough passages and up and down enough staircases that she was thoroughly lost, before finally knocking on an ornate door.

"Who is it?" asked a woman's voice.

Maria knew that voice well enough to answer before the guard could. "It's me, Francesca. Maria."

The door opened immediately, and the guard ushered Maria and Alessia into a sybaritically appointed chamber, vanishing prudently and closing the door behind them as soon as they were well inside. Manfred was sprawled on a heavy oaken settle, grinning cheerfully.

"We don't know a whole lot," he said, without waiting for the question. "I was going to come and tell you later that Erik signaled that he was ashore and he had found his Svanhild. I imagine Benito is all right."

"He was born to be hanged," said Maria, trying to hide her relief.

Maria must have squeezed Alessia. The baby woke and objected to being treated like a bundle. Maria had the interesting experience of seeing the normally imperturbable Aquitainian woman look decidedly alarmed, as an indignant squall arose from the wrappings. "Is something wrong with her?" Francesca asked uneasily.

Maria rocked and bounced; Alessia made a few more pointed remarks about her cavalier treatment. "She's fine."

"Good." Francesca shook her head. "I'm not really maternal. I don't like babies much, I'm afraid."

Manfred grinned. "They're not infectious, Francesca." He pointed at Maria. "Come on, Maria. Advance on her. Let's see if Francesca will retreat into the bedroom to escape. I've been trying to tempt her back there all morning. I never thought of herding her."

Francesca was recovering her composure, possibly because Alessia hiccupped and decided that she had registered enough complaints for the moment. "Manfred! Babies hold no interest for me, for excellent reasons."

She began counting off on elegant fingers. "You cannot have an intelligent conversation with them. They are utterly and selfishly demanding of all of your time and energy, regardless of war, peace, or any other considerations. You—ah, never mind." She shrugged. "Not all women love babies, legends notwithstanding. I'm one of the ones who doesn't."

Manfred stood up. "I won't hold it against you. I must admit I'm not too keen on them myself. Maybe one day. But certainly not yet."

Francesca chucked him under the chin. "I can't tell you how relieved this makes me."

Maria said nothing. She knew that talking to people who didn't have children about the subject was a waste of their time and her effort. Besides, it was hardly her business to go around urging parenthood on people. She certainly couldn't see Francesca with children. And truth to tell, at one time she'd thought she would not like to have any herself.

Instead, she decided to bring up something else that had been nagging away under the worry about Benito. She'd heard about it from Umberto and now had it refreshed by Lady De Belmondo. The food rations, even though they were barely into the siege, were already causing unrest.

"I met the podesta's wife at the gate. A delegation of women from the town is going to see the captain-general. She said she was going to keep the peace." Maria looked sidelong at Francesca. "From what Kat told me, you collect information. Maybe you already know all about this, but there is a problem about food."

Francesca smiled. "I trade in gossip, yes. I did know about the food. I didn't know about the podesta's wife. There is something of distance between me and 'respectable' women. They don't like to be seen talking to me. But tell me more. I'd like a female handle on what is happening out there."

"Lady De Belmondo is . . . different. She talks to anyone, and everyone talks to her; the guards at the gate said she can go anywhere without fear. And Lodovico Montescue was one of her suitors when she was young."

"The old dog probably made up to half the women in Venice," said Manfred lazily. "If the stories I've heard are anything to judge by, he was worse than I was." He raised an eyebrow at Maria. "Worse even than Benito. Anyway, I'll leave you women to chatter. I'm going across to see Falkenberg. And then I'll go and look at what Emeric is doing in the way of siege preparations. I need to keep an eye on that."

"Not without Von Gherens," said Francesca sternly. "I promised him I wouldn't let you go out without him, and I won't let you break my promises."

Manfred grunted. "All right, I'll collect my baby-sitter. He'll be pacing the hallway anyway." He went out, blowing a kiss to Francesca.

When the door latch had clicked closed behind him, Francesca turned again to Maria. "I'm glad you brought this up. I had wanted to come and talk to you about it anyway."

She paused for a moment as if gathering her thoughts. "I need to set up a network of contacts. Manfred and the Knights worry about what Emeric's army is doing out there. I worry about what is going on in here. In the few days since the siege began, I've established that the Citadel is overripe for internal troubles, which I think are more dangerous than the external army. This food story is just one aspect. I wanted to ask for your help. This place has limits as far as access is concerned."

Maria laughed, a little bitterly. "You have no idea! You might not be considered 'respectable' by the ranking women, but there isn't a man in this place who would dare to stop you from going anywhere you wanted to. Getting in here for me was quite difficult. I scarcely dare think how the ordinary Corfiote would be treated."

"Yes. And the problems in the Citadel, I think, will mostly come from the Corfiote citizens who are excluded." Francesca frowned, then focused intently on Maria. "I need people out there who can tell me what is going on. I need a place for them to meet me, that won't attract attention. I've some gold, and some favors to offer to them."

Maria looked at her thoughtfully. "Can you get out of here without drawing attention? Because if you can, I must introduce you to my friend Stella Mavroukis." Maria smiled. "She can talk the hind legs off two donkeys, but she knows everyone. She's been here for years, and she speaks Greek."

Francesca's eyes brightened with interest. "She sounds ideal. When can you organize this?"

"Tomorrow afternoon?" Alessia stirred in Maria's arms. "But now, I must go. Or you will get an experience of babies you won't enjoy."

Francesca was quick about showing her to the door.

Chapter 48

The rocks, in the paling predawn, were just visible by the lacing of foam around them. The wind was blowing spray off the water, leaving the descent greasy. The stony surface compared well to mossy pantiles in the rain, but it was steeper than any self-respecting roof would be. Benito decided the young shepherd guiding him had a great future in housebreaking, if he should need it.

Coming closer, Benito could now see that the rocks were twisted, shattered and sharp-edged, even in this poor light. That anyone would bring even a dingy in here, let alone a thirty-five-foot lateen-rigged fishing boat, seemed like insanity. Yet, there she was, snugged up beside a huge boulder. Someone was busy attaching a bush to her mast, the only bit that stuck out above the rock.

Benito whistled. Kosti nearly ended up in the cove. He dropped the bush. "Now, see what you made me do," he said grumpily.

"How do I get across?"

"There's a ledge of rocks over there. Time it right and you won't get too wet."

Benito paid off the guide, rolled his trousers up, and walked into the surge. The water was cold, and the mussels underfoot were sharp. He walked forward cautiously, his city-born imagination putting sharks and giant octopi in the dark water. Encountering seaweed nearly had him into the deeper water with a shriek. However, he reached the fishing smack's mooring without any ncidents. He pulled up onto the rock, and stepped into her. The smell nearly knocked him back ashore.

"Where is the skipper?"

"Where I'll be in a minute," said Kosti, finishing tying the bush to the masthead, just as the first rays of sunlight hit the mountain above them. "Under the sail. Asleep."

The sail had been made into a crude tent, and through the long, hot spring day, the crew slept. After an hour or so, Benito grew tired of the heat and the flies and waded back onto the shore and slept under a pine tree. He could see the open sea from here; and, waking during the day, he saw several patrolling Dalmatian galliots. But they didn't come close enough to the dangerous-looking rocks to spot the fishing boat. Even a land patrol would have to come very close to the edge of the near-vertical vegetation and crumbling limestone cliff to see her. The tough part was going to be avoiding being seen that night, once they were at sea.

The two men were overly well dressed for Paleokastritsa. They approached the table in the taverna diffidently. "Milord. We've heard a rumor that you came out of the Citadel."

Erik looked them over cautiously. The clothes, on closer inspection, had once been fine but showed signs of very hard wearing. Erik doubted that the Hungarians would have gotten around to using spies or informers . . . yet. "Why do you ask?"

The older of the two, the one with the neatly trimmed beard with hints of salt and pepper in the blackness, said grimly: "Milord, we're both Venetians who have estates here. Or, I should say, used to have. Our families have been killed and our homes burned. We want to know what is happening. We want the Republic's armies to sweep these Hungarian bastards into the sea. We've scouted along the ridgelines . . . all we can see is that the Citadel is under siege. There aren't that many men attacking."

"I just want to kill the bastards," said the younger one, morosely, his pudgy, neat hands forming themselves into fists.

Erik pushed his chair back. "What I can tell you is that Emeric has landed many more men. As for when the Venetian Republic's relief forces will be here—"

He shrugged. "That is anyone's guess. I believe word has been sent, but whether it got through or not, I can't tell you. Of course, Emeric's Dalmatian pirates will try to stop the messages. So it may take a long time. Months at the very least."

The younger man said: "I told you so, Ambrosino. I'm going back out to kill a few of the bastards."

In Erik's assessment, the young man would probably die the first time he encountered a real soldier.

The older man patted him on the shoulder. "Forgive him, milord. He lost his wife and their newborn son. Pardon us for intruding on you."

Erik took a deep breath. If he was going to organize resistance to Hungarians, he had to start somewhere. This unlikely looking material was as good as any. The younger man was going to get himself killed anyway in his fury and grief. Let him at least put them to some use.

"Sit down." It was a command, not a request.

Both men looked at him in some surprise. So did the Vinlanders. But the two sat.

"If you go out there, you may kill a Croat or a Hungarian or two. However, if you really wish to hurt Emeric and his troops, you're going to have to be more methodical about it. Emeric has plenty more Croat troopers. But if you destroy his cannons or burn his supply dumps, then not only will you hurt him far more badly, you will save the lives of others."

The young man shook his head stubbornly. "I just want to kill the bastards."

"You'll only die quickly without achieving anything." Erik gave him a measuring look, and allowed a touch of scorn to come into it. The young man detected that scorn, and reddened. "You aren't a fighter. You aren't a soldier. You certainly aren't a mercenary, who by nature is the toughest and cruelest sort of soldier. Your fancy dueling-master won't have taught you a single thing that will work in a fight against these bastards, and what you don't know will get you killed the first time you run up against one. Is that what you want? Or would you rather make Emeric pay fifty-fold for what he's done?"

The young man was scarlet by now, but he raised his chin defiantly. "I want him to pay a hundredfold, never mind fifty-fold. But I'm not scared of dying."

"Then either learn to be," said Erik grimly, "or go somewhere else. I have no space in my troop for foolhardy men."

"Your troop?"

Erik nodded. "I came out here for three purposes." He saw no reason to blather in public about his feelings for Svanhild, and certainly not Benito's secret mission. "Never mind the first two. The third, acting on Prince Manfred's behalf, was to recruit men and engage Emeric of Hungary's forces in . . . call it 'irregular warfare.' The kind of fighting we do in Vinland. I want to bleed Emeric white—draw off some of his forces from their attack on the Citadel, and make keeping the Citadel under siege a battle on two fronts. I want to make it as expensive as possible for him to be here, but I can't do that without men who are as interested in keeping their own skins intact as they are in killing Emeric's men. I don't need heroes, I need men who can be as cunning as foxes and hard to catch as weasels. Are you with me?"

"I am," said a firm voice from an unexpected quarter. Thalia spoke quietly but clearly. "I am. If I can save one other life, that's enough. If hurting this king will avenge my Georgio . . . then even if I am a woman I will fight. What kind of men will not?"

The plumper young man nodded, looking at Thalia in some surprise. Suddenly, with no warning, he began to cry. Deep, bitter sobs.

"He's upset," said the older man. "But he'll be an asset, milord. Giuliano's father was a master-at-arms. When he retired here, he married a local girl and they had one chick. Flavio Lozza gave his son one-on-one training from the day he could hold a sword." He smiled. "I think Flavio was secretly disappointed that the boy only wanted to grow olives and play the lute."

Lozza's son? Erik reflected that appearances could deceive. Flavio Lozza had been Giuliano Dell'Arta's instructor. Giuliano had taught both Manfred and him when they'd been in Venice with the Knights of the Holy Trinity's ill-fated tour with the Woden-casket. He had regarded Lozza as the father of rapier-work. Flavio, it would seem, had named his son for his old protégé—and this was certainly the last place Erik would have expected to see the son of Flavio Lozza.

Almost, he regretted what he'd said about "fancy sword-masters." But not quite. It was one thing to be a master of rapier-work; it was quite another to face mercenaries and Magyar horse-barbarians whose interest was in killing you quickly, not stylishly. Perhaps the plump boy wouldn't be killed that quickly. But there was a large difference between even the best-trained amateur and a battle-hardened professional soldier. "And you, signor? Have you got surprises for me too?"

The older man shrugged. "Not really. I hunt. I can ride. I know the island well."

"And you speak Greek?"

The older man shrugged. "Not as well as Giuliano. He got it from his mother, and then his wife was a local."

"And of course we will help, too," said Bjarni, slapping him on the back.

"To be direct, you are going to watch over Svanhild," said Erik, feeling uncomfortable. "Not go running around the Corfu hills in the dark. If possible I'd like to get you all a passage across to Italy or even Greece. This is not your war."

"We stand by our kin," said Bjarni, stiffly.

Erik grinned. "I'm not exactly that . . . yet."

The big Vinlander grinned back. "You haven't a chance, Erik. Hildi's made up her mind. Even if she has to chase you with a baby she'll get you."

"Bjarni!" said Svanhild, blushing. "It's a good thing Mama can't hear you." But she didn't deny it. In fact, she gave him a sidelong glance that had speculation in it.

"Maybe you can just lend Erik three or four of us. Like me," said Kari, looking eager.

"Maybe I can just pay him to take you away," growled Gulta.

They hugged the coast with great care, creeping southwards. No one who didn't know these waters intimately was going to come this close in the darkness. It was an alarming place to be sailing at some speed.

"It's coming up for a blow," said Taki ominously.

"So what do we do?"

Benito saw a flash of teeth in the darkness. "We set our nets. Then we haul them and then we run with the wind. We're fishermen from Levkas who've been blown off course. Fishermen have fish in their boats. So we're going to get ourselves some."

So, for the next two hours Benito learned to set nets. "Taki is making an extra profit out of your labor," said Spiro. "Demand wages. Or a share in the catch."

"You'd better hope it is a bad one," said Kosti. "Or we'll be here all night."

When the nets came in, twitching with silver, and Benito saw how Taki beamed in the moonlight, Benito began to realize Kosti might not have been joking.

With wooden crates full of fish they headed away from Corfu on a following wind. By that time, they all looked and smelled like fishermen, even Benito. He was no stranger to hard work, not after the way that Erik had been drilling him, but this required a whole new set of muscles and calluses. His hands were raw and cut up, and his arms and shoulders ached by the time it was over.

Taki rubbed his hands and produced the wine, passing it around to the rest of the crew. "Never let it be said nothing good comes out of a war. I've wanted to fish old Scathos' bank for years, but never dared."

"I kept wondering whether the old bastard would still come out and shoot at us," said Kosti.

Spiro took a pull at the wine. "What? Shoot at your handsome face? Scathos' daughters would kill him."

Kosti pulled the jug away from him and handed it to Benito. "I hear that's the reason he wants to kill *you*."

"Me? I'm shocked."

"Well, you or any other passing fellow. Those are wild girls of his."

"Time to shift those sails!" Taki yelled.

The boat went about and they sailed on, but the direction troubled Benito. It felt wrong. "Just where are we going?" he asked Taki eventually. "You're supposed to be running me across to the Italian shore."

Taki belched contentedly. "And I am. But we'd not get across the Straits of Otranto in the dark. Not with this wind. So we're taking a longer cut at it. Have some more wine."

He frowned. "I don't want to be drunk if we have trouble."

The captain chuckled. "What are you going to do if we do have trouble? Fight a galley's worth of men? Try and outrun them? This is a fishing boat, not a galley. There is nothing much you can do except try and look like a drunken bum of a fisherman. So have some more wine. The more like us you look and sound, the safer you are."

The day was still very young, and Antipaxos some miles to the north of them, but still in sight, when they were intercepted.

It was a Byzantine galley. Benito realized, as it raced closer, just how futile trying to run would have been. Briefly, he thought the galley was simply going to run them down. But it drew up beside them. The officer on the bow bellowed something in rapid Greek.

Benito had the unpleasant realization that his life was in the hands of a bunch of poor people he didn't know very well, who would be well rewarded for selling him out and who would be killed if they were caught harboring him. Worst of all, he didn't understand what they were saying. He resolved to learn Greek, if he got out of here alive.

With his heart pounding, his mouth dry, Spiro heard the Greek officer yell: "What are you doing out here?"

"We're fishermen," said Taki. "What do you think? We're on our way back home to Levkas. We got caught up in the blow last night and came too far north."

"Stand by to be boarded."

A dozen or so marines boarded the boat. The *Case Vecchie* did his best "I-am-a-poor-scared-fisherman" look. It wasn't hard to do the scared bit, Spiro realized. But he rapidly realized what a genius Taki had been to insist on catching fish last night. The fish, under damped sacks, were still cool and fresh—the most convincing evidence possible that this was, indeed, nothing more than a fishing boat.

The officer with the marines looked about—obviously searching for refugees, or maybe arms, supplies, valuables. There were few places anyone could hide, so it was a very cursory look. The nets, the boxes of fish, the small crew all said *fishing boat*.

"Why did you come so far north?" he demanded. "Orders went to all the villages that no one was to fish within sight of Antipaxos."

Taki cringed. "My lord. In the dark we drifted too far. We didn't mean to . . ."

The Byzantine officer hit him, sending him sprawling across the fish. "Fool. By the smell of you, I think you drank too much to celebrate the catch. It wasn't the wind that got you here, it was the wine. If we find you this far north again, we'll sink you. Do you understand?"

Taki, on his knees now, nodded furiously. "Yes, milord! It won't happen again." His voice quavered.

"It had better not." The officer pointed to two of the marines. "Here, you two. Take one of these boxes. We could use some fresh fish."

"Milord, my fish," protested Taki.

"Consider it a fine for breaking the law," said the officer. "And think how lucky you are not to have your filthy little vessel sunk."

Taki did the grovel magnificently. "Thank you, milord. But . . . can I at least have my box back? I'm a poor fisherman, milord . . ."

The officer laughed. "No."

The galley receded. The apparently hard-working crew of the fishing boat started to laugh. And laugh.

"Prissy-assed *malákas*." Taki blew a raspberry at the departing ship and then grinned at Benito. "You're my witness, *Case Vecchie*. They boarded my ship in the Venetian Republic's waters, stole my fish and—worst of all!—stole Venetian property."

Benito looked suitably mystified. "Venetian property?"

"The fish box. It belongs to the fish market in Kérkira. It is the property of the Republic of Venice—which is what that prim little official at the fish market tells me every time I come in. Property of Venice! And he took it!"

The crew started to laugh again.

"Piracy! That's what it was," said Spiro, trying to keep a straight face, passing over a jug of wine.

Benito took a swig and nodded sagely. "We'll swear out a charge against them in front of the podesta, and let him have the ambassador summoned, for a severe reprimand and a demand for reparations."

"Especially for the valuable catch," said Kosti. "The idiots chose a box of trash fish."

"So when do we turn and run across the straits to Bari or Brindisi?" asked Benito.

Taki raised an eyebrow. "We're not going to run across the strait. There they have twenty-five lousy little leagues to patrol. But they can't patrol the whole Ionian Sea. You're in for a haul, boy. I hope you don't get seasick easily."

Emeric looked with satisfaction at the bluish haze of gunpowder smoke blowing gently across the channel. The forty-eight-pound bombards took a huge amount of powder and a long time to load, but they were his second choice for reducing and penetrating the walls of a besieged fortress. Evening was drawing in, but the bombardment would not stop for that.

His first choice was treachery. Months before the assault on Corfu, he had begun to prepare the ground for it. Far better than the captain-general, he already knew the number of Corfiote refugees within the walls of the Citadel. He knew how much food there was in their garrison's storehouse, and he was already getting daily reports from Fianelli. He knew a great deal about the likes and weaknesses of the various officers, too.

One of the things that had made Emeric so sure Corfu would be an easy conquest was the past history of the captain-general. True enough, the man was not corrupt, but he was a vain and incompetent fool. His handling of the insurrection in the Venetian enclave in Trebizond had been so bad that it had gotten him sent to a station where there would never again be a need for military action. He was a bungler, but a bungler with political connections. In the Venetian Republic, a bungler whose godfather is the Doge could go far. Unfortunately for Captain-General Tomaselli, there was a new Doge.

The garrison commander, on the other hand, was a disaster from Emeric's point of view. Commander Leopoldo would have to die. Emeric had bought several of the soldiers within the forces at the commander's disposal. Most of the troops serving the Venetian Republic were mercenaries, for sale to the highest bidder. It was just unfortunate that they did not have a mercenary commanding officer. So: Commander Leopoldo would have to be assassinated. When he was engaged in some firefight—best to do it unobtrusively.

Emeric went back into his tent and drew the circle. Scratched the pentacle and began the ritual that would allow him to speak to the chief of his spies within the Citadel. At this time of day, Fianelli would be in his cellar waiting.

PART VII
June, 1539 A.D.

Chapter 49

Francesca shook her head. "To be honest with you, Eberhard, this place is positively Venetian with intrigue. There is a strong pro-Byzantine faction, of long standing, among the Libri d'Oro. Not surprising of course, since Corfu's local aristocracy are Greeks themselves. Fortunately, they distrust Emeric of Hungary. But they long for Venice to lose power and for their own stars to be ascendant under Alexius."

Eberhard snorted. "That wastrel would be more likely to sell their precious island to pay off some of his debts. Or just to have more money to spend on his vices."

"Precisely," Francesca agreed, nodding. "But not having the knowledge that you do, *Ritter,* the pro-Byzantines here entertain some very unrealistic ideas. So far as they know, Alexius is cut from the same cloth as his father, which would make them Byzantine allies rather than vassals. And, most importantly, would put Corfiotes—or at least Greeks—back in the seats of power here. They resent the way the Venetian overlords here on the island often treat them. It's the sneering, really, not anything material. But noblemen—especially sorry, idle ones like most of these wretched Libri d'Oro—take offense easily."

"And how well placed are they to act on those unrealistic ideas?" asked Manfred, looking concerned. "I've known people to be prepared to die for some really stupid things."

"I am still compiling a list, Manfred. But so far, they have some bodyguards and some interesting working positions."

Manfred nodded, frowning. "One thing in our favor is that the

403

Hungarians are present in such force. Nobody, not even the most self-deceiving pro-Byzantine Libri d'Oro, can believe that Emeric is going to give up this prize so easily."

Eberhard shook his head. "Self-deception is the greatest strength of such people, Manfred. Petty noblemen with neither work nor war to keep them occupied will often spend all their time wallowing in perceived insults and fantasies of retribution."

"True," said Francesca. "But Emeric's vicious reputation does work against him. So long as it does not appear that Alexius is allied with him in this venture, we may be able to keep the faction quiet. Quieter, anyway."

Manfred poured another cup of wine. "I never thought I'd be pleased to hear that Emeric was such a murderous, treacherous son of a bitch. So who else do we have stacked against us? A pro-Hungarian faction?"

"Fortunately, Emeric's reputation works for him there, too—or rather, works for us. There is, however, a Montagnard faction, that believes *you* have come to take over the island under the pretext of this war, and are very much in favor of the notion." Francesca dimpled. "Of course there are a few who also think it is true, but are opposed to the idea. And I have found evidence that someone is buying information. That suggests Emeric has some spies here in the Citadel."

Eberhard had been staring at her with more and more astonishment as she spoke, and now his mouth was actually agape. "How do you find all this out, Francesca?" he asked in disbelief.

"Among other things, Maria introduced me to the main artery of gossip in the Citadel. Sooner or later everything gets told to Stella." Francesca's smile faded, and turned to a frown. "She also told me another thing I must discuss with Eneko Lopez. She says there is a cabal of true magicians here, and they are not Christian."

Manfred chuckled. "Sleepy little seaside town, eh?"

In the living quarters which Sibling Eleni had provided for them adjoining the chapel, Eneko Lopez was scowling. "There, Francis— again. Did you sense it? And you, Diego?"

Both men nodded. "Someone is using Satanic magic in this Citadel," muttered Diego. "That was fairly close, although I couldn't sense the direction."

"And *that* one! A sending ritual requires blood."

"Most Satanic rituals do, Francis." Eneko shook his head. "At least that one doesn't require human blood."

"That's not my point, Eneko. We're under siege. Soon enough, finding a goat or chicken to slaughter isn't going to be so easy."

Lopez thought about it, for a moment. "True. We should speak to Francesca. Unless I miss my guess, she'll be running the counter-espionage work here before much longer. The podesta is an old man and the captain-general is . . . well. Not competent."

"So charitable, Eneko!" chuckled Francis. "I would have used a stronger expression."

Lopez smiled thinly. "Well, charity *is* a Christian virtue."

Diego didn't seem to share in the humor. "Finding a stray goat or a chicken will be getting hard. But with thousands of people packed into this place, finding a human to slaughter won't."

Eneko and Francis stared at him. Diego shrugged. "I would remind you that charity is not a Satanic virtue."

"We'd best talk to Francesca about that as well," murmured Francis. "Although . . ."

Gloomily, Lopez finished the thought. "How do you keep track of people to see if any are disappearing—when half the people in this Citadel are here illegally to begin with? Thanks to that jackass Tomaselli!"

"Charity, Eneko, charity," cautioned Francis.

"I *am* being charitable," grumbled Lopez.

"Not to jackasses."

Through the open door of the taverna in Paleokastritsa, Erik could see that the sky across the straits of Otranto was traced with clouds the color of salmon-flesh. The closer view was even more distracting to him. Neither Svanhild's profile nor the memory of salmon in the ice-fed rivers of home were helping Erik with the matter in hand: planning an irregular campaign against Emeric's forces.

"Essentially, we need two things. We need information, and we need safe bases."

"What's wrong with Paleokastritsa?"

Erik shook his head. "Its defenses are good, but not that good. It'll fall eventually, either to a determined assault or more likely to siege. There is no second way out of the town. And we think like foxes now. Foxes always need a second or third exit to their lairs. We'll rely on friendly towns and peasants for food and information—but never from the same one twice in a row, and we'll never stay in any of the settlements. If we bring the wrath of the Hungarians down on any Corfiote town, not only will we have betrayed them, we will have betrayed ourselves. We'll get no more help from the peasants."

He looked at the faces around the table; no one disagreed. "You all know what the Hungarians are going to do, every time we strike: they'll destroy the nearest village, if it shows any signs of our presence. The peasants are in hiding now, but they'll have to return to their holdings soon. Farms and crops don't wait. We need the countryside sympathetic to us and hostile to the Hungarians."

Ambrosino nodded. "It makes sense. Well, there is a spot I used to use when I was hunting. Not a village for three miles. You've got an excellent view of the surrounding countryside, there is water in the cave, and there are two ravines leading away. There'll be a bit of grazing down in the ravines, too. I thought of building a hunting-box up there, but it was just too expensive to get the materials up. There are wild boar and bears up there. Good hunting. And I've eaten worse than bear."

"We'll check it out tomorrow," said Erik. "We also need to organize proper scouting of Emeric's forces."

"We'll put you in at that fishing village," said Taki, pointing to the Italian shore. "The locals are at sea, by the looks of it, so we won't have to try and explain that we're not stealing their fish."

"As if we would," said Spiro, virtuously.

"Unless we got half the chance," snorted Kosti. "I thought we might visit a decent-size harbor and taste the local girls and meet the local wine."

"You mean meet the girls and taste the wine," corrected Taki. Kosti shook his head, grinning. "I prefer it my way around."

Benito realized he was going to miss these fishermen. He was going to miss being at sea, where all the responsibility devolved on Taki. Now he'd have to manage for himself, and it was a long way home to Venice. He had written up the prearranged message for Erik. It would pass as a bill of fishmarket landings. The Bonito on the listing would tell Erik to hand over the money.

Benito now felt guilty. He'd done his dangerous bit. But Taki,

Spiro and Kosti would have to get back through the cordon before they saw the paltry bit of silver. The only trouble was, short of the jewels—all he had was paltry bits of silver himself.

"Likely if we go to one of the big ports there'll be questions asked. We'd end up having to pay port fees!" Taki sounded as if he'd rather have his teeth drawn.

The idea seemed to horrify the others too. Spiro shook his head. "Besides, Kosti, we need to get home. There is a war over there and we've got people to look out for. Your mother. My sister—and you watch your mouth about my sister."

"Wouldn't say a word. Not while you're listening, anyway."

Spiro took a swing at him on general principles.

So Benito climbed off the boat and onto the Italian shore with no more than his clothes and the three fishermen's good wishes in his ears. After several days at sea, the ground seemed to be moving up and down.

He turned and waved. Taki's ratty old boat was already moving out to sea at a fair clip.

Benito turned his face to the shore and his more immediate problems. He was now faced with the problem of where, exactly, to go. It was midmorning, and he was outside a tiny little white-washed fishing village near the toe of the boot that is Italy.

Originally someone, maybe Erik, had said he should ride up the coast to Venice. That was before Erik had seen him ride. Also . . .

Well, it seemed very easy when discussing it with people like Erik, who knew how to do this sort of thing. "Get to Italy and ride to Venice." The first question, in a spot like this, would be: *Ride? On what?* By the looks of the fishing settlement even a donkey would be wildly optimistic.

Maybe he should follow the course of the cowardly Capitano Selvi, and head for the Tyrrhenian sea; then, travel up the west coat of Italy. The immediate question was: Should he cut across the Calabrian Apennines—or remain along the coastline?

The mountains looked threatening. Unfamiliar. In the distance up there he could see a hilltop village—other than that, the area was forested, with the forest only being interrupted by patches of what could be vines and white rock. A lot of white rock. It all looked very big and daunting.

He saw an urchin from the fishing hamlet—calling five tiny

houses a village was gross flattery—approaching cautiously. Ready to run, curiosity overwhelming obvious fear. He looked at Benito as if he expected him to sprout wings and horns or at very least large teeth.

Maybe thirty yards back were three others of still younger age, all peering, big-eyed, nervous but fascinated by this strange apparition. It didn't look like the village saw a lot of strangers. Benito waved at the kid, who was, at the outside, six years old. The older boys would be at sea, he supposed. *"Ciao,"* he said.

The kid backed off two steps; then realized Benito wasn't following and that *"Ciao"* was not really a threat. He said *"Ciao"* back, and was rewarded with a smile from Benito. And then the kid let go with such a rapid fire of local patois that Benito managed to understand one word in ten. Some of the words sounded like Greek. Spiro had said there were a fair number of Greek settlers here.

"Whoa." Benito spoke slowly and pronounced his words with care. "I want to buy food. I want to ask directions."

He still had to say it twice.

The fishwife in her peasant blacks was a little more intelligible. Slightly. She was just as curious. Benito didn't see the point in too much secrecy. "There is a blockade on the straits of Otranto. I'm from up north and I want to go home. So I scrounged a voyage over here. Where is the nearest big town? And can you spare some food for me? I can pay."

He pulled out a copper penny, guessing that even these didn't arrive too often in a place like this. The smile and the haste with which she produced some rosso wine, cipudazzi—little red onions pickled in olive oil and vinegar—and tiny spiky artichokes, told him he was dead right. She bustled off to bring him some fresh bread and some maccu, a broad bean and fennel purée; also some fresh figs. It was a repast he was sure would have been the family's main meal. Benito hoped the husband would bring home a good catch.

The peasant woman, with the children peering around her skirts, was less useful about the nearest town. "Catanzaro. It is great city! It has more than this many streets!" She held up a hand of work-calloused fingers. "But it is far. Perhaps thirty miles away, up a ravine. We go there with the dried fish every autumn for the festival of Saint Gamina. Or there is Reggio di Calabria, in the straits of Messina, but that is a huge place and so far I have never been there. My man once went there to sell fish, but he was cheated and never went back."

A town that had a reputation for cheating rural fisherman sounded good to Benito. He might at least be able to find a ship and also be able to sell a jewel in such a place—neither of which, he knew, he'd be able to do in a small rural hamlet.

"How far is this place?"

"Oh! It must be seventy miles, Your Honor."

A vast distance, almost unthinkable. Once, confined to Venice, it would have seemed so to Benito himself.

After his meal Benito set off, walking. It was slower than riding, but it seemed to be the only real option. By midafternoon he was very aware of just how soft his feet had become. He cut himself a sturdy stick, which didn't seem to help a great deal.

Leaving the fishing hamlet he'd struck a trail. It seemed unpopulated, and determined to take him away from the coastline. Eventually another track joined it, but it was equally lacking in traffic. He was beginning to wonder where he could sleep that night, when he caught sight of the hind end of a donkey, disappearing around the next bend.

Circumstances, thought Benito wryly as he hurried to catch up with the donkey, change your perspective. He'd never ever have thought he'd be glad to see the tail end of a donkey. The donkey was part of a string of seven, laden with gurgling, oil-sheen-gleaming ticklike skin-bottles. It was being led by a fellow who looked more than a little like a donkey himself. The oilman produced a thing that was somewhere between a knife and a sword, and well-supplied with rust.

"What do you want?" he demanded suspiciously. Benito repeated his story. It didn't seem to convince the oilman at all. "You stay behind me. I'm not having you tell bandits I'm coming."

"Saints! Look, any self-respecting bandit would kill you in about ten seconds. All I want is some information. And I'm not moving at less than donkey speed just to oblige you."

"Stay back or I'll make you into sliced salami!" The oil seller waved his knife about at Benito's nose.

"Look, I can pay." Benito pulled out what he'd thought was a copper. "I'm happy to pay . . ."

The oilman's eyes lit up. "Give it to me." He waved the knife at Benito.

Benito looked at his hand and realized he had silver, and not copper there. "I'll give you a copper penny for your help. I need this."

The oilman lunged. Benito used the stout stick he'd cut to hit the man's elbow. Hard. The clumsy knife went flying. Benito grabbed him. A nasty short scuffle ensued, ending with the oilman pinioned under Benito and shrieking: *"Help! Bandits! Murder!"*

Benito swatted the oilman's ear, reflecting as he did so that Erik had taught him very well even in such a short timespan. "Shut up. You tried to rob me, you idiot. Now get up and stop yowling. I dropped my silver penny because of you. If you don't find it for me I'll kick your ass through your teeth. Now get up."

"I can't. You're sitting on me."

Benito stood up. The oilman, on his knees, looked for the silver. Fortunately it was easy to find; nervously, the oilman handed it over.

"Pick up that cheese-cutter of yours." The oilman gaped at Benito but picked up his knife.

"Now—I need know where I can sleep tonight. And does this track lead back to the coast? I want to get to Reggio di Calabria."

The oilman bowed. "Your Honor, no one goes down to the coast. Well, only a few very poor fishermen. The Barbary Coast pirates raid it, and it is full of malaria. But this track joins another track which leads to Cantonia, maybe a mile away. There is road from there you can follow on to Reggio di Calabria."

"Right. Well, I think we go on together. Otherwise you'll come to this Cantonia place claiming I've robbed you."

The oilman did his best not to look as oily as his wares. "Your Honor, I would never do that! I'm an honest man."

"The sight of my only piece of silver seemed to change that," said Benito grimly.

They walked on at donkey pace. At length they came to the walled town. The oilman held out his hand. "Give me the copper you owe me for guiding you."

"Where are the two coppers you promised me for helping you with the donkeys?" demanded Benito very loudly, for the benefit of at least a dozen local residents. "Give it to me or I will swear out a charge against you with the podesta."

"I never promised you—"

"Yes, you did! Cheat! Thief!"

The oilman gaped. "But you—?"

Benito turned to the interested locals. "This man promised me money! I have worked and now he wants to cheat me!"

One of the women sniggered. "The podesta is in Montaforte. And if you can get money out of that old skinflint without a knife against his throat, you will have managed something no one else can do." She eyed Benito speculatively. "Though there is no knowing what a handsome man could do."

"Especially with you, Bella," said one of the onlookers. She snorted and flounced her hips for Benito's benefit.

Benito threw up his hands. "I'm a peaceful man. And I was coming this way anyway. Is there a taverna where I could buy a glass of wine to get the smell of donkeys out of my nostrils?"

"I can show you the taverna," said Bella archly.

Benito shook his head ruefully, looking at her swaying walk. Certain kinds of trouble you can get rid of. Others follow you around. He'd be leaving very, very early the next morning.

Predawn found him heading, very quietly, off down the trail for Reggio di Calabria. Evening found him there. As cities went it was a small one. After the back-country Benito found it busy, bustling, and comfortingly familiar.

"And so we came to Corfu." Maria took a sip of some of the finest wine she'd ever tasted. The white-haired Contessa Renate De Belmondo, wife of the Podesta of Corfu, smiled. She was one of those people who smiled to their eyes, and the fine creases in her skin bore testimony to the fact that she smiled often.

On the lace cloth between them, on a silver salver, lay some delicate almond biscotti. Maria marveled at them. Marveled at where she was. Marveled at the fact that she had just finished telling a *Case Vecchie* lady—a *Case Vecchie Longi* lady, born, bred and raised—more about her life than she'd ever told anyone.

There was something motherly about this woman. Maria's mother hadn't been "motherly." She'd been a working woman who'd done her best to look after her daughter, but she hadn't had any time to spare for cuddling and comforting. Their lives had been hard, Maria's as well as her mother's. Maria suspected that her mother had made the decision to ensure that her daughter learned early that life was hard, and would always be.

Francesca had helped and advised Maria, but she wouldn't choose the word "motherly" to describe her either. Maria smiled to herself. Francesca ferreted out information; she manipulated, charmed, sometimes lied through her teeth, but she showed no signs of being "motherly." But the contessa . . . got you to volunteer it. If Francesca could get her, as well as Stella, to provide information . . .

There would be very little in the entire confined world that was Corfu, great and small, that she couldn't find out. But somehow Maria knew that Renate De Belmondo was the perfect listener because she wouldn't ever tell anyone what she'd heard. Most people used conversation to talk about themselves. Renate De Belmondo volunteered little; she just listened.

The conversation shifted to babies. And here the contessa did offer something about herself. "My children were all born here on Corfu. I tried earlier in Venice, oh, I tried and I tried, but it was only here that I finally got pregnant." She smiled mysteriously. "It's a very fertile place, Corfu."

Chapter 50

From the shelter of the pines high up on the slope, Erik's small force watched and waited. Erik now had seventeen men. Some Venetian settlers, some locals with grudges, and Kari and his two brothers. They were about a mile and half south of the Citadel, above the oil-store that Emeric's men had taken over as their storage depot. The huge forty-eight-pound bombards took a lot of powder and it had to be stored somewhere a safe distance from the battlefront. There were some forty Serb pikemen doing guard-shifts and ten Croat light cavalry riding patrols.

The worst of Emeric's forces, Erik suspected. Probably a punishment duty for the Croats, as most of their comrades were still looting among properties that had not yet been picked over. The cavalry patrols consisted of going to a nearby village and sifting through the ruins for anything that even looked like loot, or sleeping. The guards at the gunpowder magazine looked unseasoned, and already looked bored. They were certainly lackadaisical about the patrols around their new palisade.

Erik and Kari had crept within twenty yards. From here Erik could see facial expressions and, if he'd been able to speak Serbian, could have eavesdropped. Erik studied the guards, their positions and their camp. Then they leopard-crawled back to the pines.

Giuliano had a surprise for them there. A shepherd boy who had come upon the group had been hastily seized and persuaded they weren't going to kill him. In fact he could profit by telling them about the Hungarian magazine.

"He says there is a place at the back where the stones prevented

413

them from digging the logs in. There are some small gaps. He has crawled in and stolen some things."

Erik sighed. "Now Kari will have to moan about how this crawling is ruining his breeches again. We'd better go and have a look-see."

Kari snorted and examined his knees, rubbing the material. "I wouldn't say no to a decent set of buckskins. These weren't meant for this work. This is almost too easy, Erik. We go in this hole, cut a few throats, and set fire to it."

Erik shook his head. "When that lot blows . . . well, I want to be at least a half-mile away and traveling. We might go in that way but we're going to have to get out fast. That means by the gate and onto a horse as quickly as possible."

King Emeric had been modeling things again. He pointed now to the model of the Citadel of Corfu; to the channel between it and the mainland. "How is the progress with the moles going, Count Dragorvich?"

The stocky count, Emeric's chief siegemaster, rubbed his chin reflectively. "If we worked on one at a time I could have one done in three weeks. But the two-pronged approach means progress is slower. Maybe five weeks? The channel is quite deep and we're under heavy bombardment. The mine is not going to work for now, Your Majesty. Water comes in as fast as we can take it out with a bucket-chain, and the diggers are not even at sea level yet. The ground is still saturated from the winter rains. Summer's only begun."

"I'll get the guns to focus on the south and north towers," said Emeric. "That's where their guns are firing onto the moles from. We'll leave off pounding the gate and the rest of the walls for a while."

An officer came hastily out of the dark and into the king's pavilion. Once there, he stood rigidly before the king. Emeric acknowledged the Magyar cavalry commander with a curt nod. "Ah. Colonel. How go things with sacking of the Venetian estates? Any resistance?"

The colonel sneered. "These Venetians are soft, Sire. There have been a few minor bits of fighting, but we've barely lost men. A couple of Croats who were where they weren't supposed to be. A checkpoint guard. But other than that, nothing much."

"You've taken appropriate retribution for these incidents, I trust?"

"Sire, the problem is: On whom? The peasants have hidden out in the hills. We've caught some, of course, but most of them just aren't there, and the men haven't left those they've caught in one piece. As for the Venetians . . . most of them have been killed anyway. So, Sire, the problem is there is no one to extract retribution from. There are few walled towns we haven't bothered with, but anything we can get to has been dealt with hard already."

Emeric pursed his lips, looking thoughtful. "I think it is time to stop using the sword on peasants, Colonel. It's time for the knout, instead. We need someone to work the land here. Pass the instruction to your men. Hunt the maquis. Round them up, put them to work. There is no need to be gentle, however. And any resistance still gets the sword. Or make an example of one of them on a sharpened stake."

"Yes, Sire."

In the darkness Erik sucked in his breath and squeezed his body forward through the gap. A ten-year-old shepherd might fit through it easily enough. A hundred-and-ninety-pound Icelander was a different matter altogether. He pushed forward.

Someone grabbed him by the hair.

"Got you, you thieving bastard," said the grabber. "Hey, boys, I've got him!"

Erik was in an awkward situation. One arm was still trapped in the gap between the two logs. His tomahawk and knife were on the wrong side of the barrier. Clawing upwards with one hand he managed to grab his assailant by the shirt front and hauled.

"Let go!"

Something smashed against Erik's ear. Suddenly the hand grasping his hair went slack. The man Erik was holding by the shirtfront flopped toward him. Pulling himself forward and rolling over, Erik saw Kari jump off the palisade, land in front of him and retrieve his knife from the man's back . . . And a guard came running up.

The guard saw Kari, his fallen companion, but not Erik. Erik snagged the newcomer's ankle as he rushed at Kari with a spear thrust that would have spitted the young Vinlander like a pigeon. The result of Erik's intervention was that he pole-vaulted on the spear to land in a crumpled heap at Kari's feet. The Vinlander leaned over and hit the guard with calculated force on the back of the head.

Erik had by this stage struggled free. "Wait!" he whispered to the others just through the hole. Grabbing a victim each, Kari and he hastily dragged them into the deep shadows.

No more guards came. So, after waiting perhaps a hundred heartbeats, Erik called the rest through.

Thalia came first. "You were supposed to stay with the horses!"

"There is work to be done," she said with a grim intensity, hands on her hips, but still holding a knife. "On Corfu, women work. I am here to do it. I've cut a pig's throat, and I don't see the difference between this filth and a pig, except that pigs are better."

Erik saw no point in a stand-up argument. Besides, as he'd learned on the Vinland frontier, a determined woman can be a lot more deadly than a reluctant male warrior.

"What happened?" whispered the plump Giuliano, after they'd popped him out of the hole like a cork from a bottle of petillant wine.

"That young shepherd wasn't as undetected as he thought," Erik whispered grimly. "The guards had set a trap for him. Fortunately they were expecting a small young thief and not for Kari to pop over the top of the palisade. Anyway, move out. They still outnumber us."

Shortly, they no longer did. It was brutal, murderous work. But, as Erik reflected, their enemies' choices were stark. Die quickly at the hands of the Corfiote guerillas, die when this magazine blew, or die slowly at Emeric's hands for failing him. The Corfiote guerillas couldn't keep prisoners, and the alternative to killing the enemy was to fail in their objective.

Erik didn't plan to fail. After this, Emeric's forces would be wary, and successes would be much more hard-won. They had to start big, because if they'd started with raids on outposts, they'd never have gotten to a big target like this.

But he didn't like killing sleeping guards either. It was too much like butchery.

The trickiest phase was the last one. The magazine was not a place anyone would want to strike a lucifer in, and they had no access to wicks. Before Erik set the long powder-trail, they took sixteen small casks of powder, one per horse, and loaded them up.

Then all but Erik left quietly. There was the barrack encampment not two hundred yards off, with sleeping Croats, and the rest of the guard detachment. One galloping horse could not be avoided, but at least there didn't have to be seventeen of them.

The gate was arranged with a spike holding the bar up, and a stout cord that could be tossed over the top of the gate. Erik could pull it when he was outside and drop the bar. Even if someone heard the horse gallop past and came to investigate the palisade, they would have to climb it to get in. Hopefully, by that time the powder trail would have burned to the open cask.

Erik laid the trail of black gunpowder carefully, wishing he had a better sense of how fast the stuff burned. He was experienced enough with firearms, but this kind of work really needed a bombardier who knew exactly what he was doing.

He laid it right to the gate. Lit it. It fizzed briefly and went out. He took a deep breath, forcing himself to be calm, then went back and laid a second, more generous trail. Lit it again . . .

It burned, burned fast—fizzing and racing toward the dark buildings. After an instant's horrified pause, a voice within him shrieked: *Go—go—go!*

The Icelander stepped out, closed the gate, his fingers shaking a little as he tugged the bar into place and pulled his horse's halter loose. Erik flung himself into the saddle and urged the horse to a gallop. He might break the horse's knees doing such a reckless thing—he might break his own neck—but this was still a lesser risk than staying around.

He heard a shout and a shot in the darkness. He just kept his head down and applied the spurs.

And then he didn't have to anymore. He just had to stay on the horse.

He certainly couldn't have heard any commands to stop.

Manfred and Von Gherens were up on the battlements of the inner curtain wall, looking out at the muzzle-flashes and camp-fires on the Kérkira side of the Citadel. So, for the first time since his injury, was Falkenberg.

"Two moles." Falkenberg shook his head disapprovingly. "This is Emeric interfering with his commanders again. He has the notion that he is a military genius."

"Thank God for a small mercy," said Von Gherens. "We could have someone who didn't sit on his brains out there, and then we'd be between the hammer and the anvil."

Manfred snorted. "Instead we have a commander in here who sits on his brains."

"The commander of the garrison is not too bad," said Falkenberg. "A likeable young fellow, if not very experienced. The captain-general . . ."

"That's who I was referring to," interrupted Manfred, sourly. "Do you know what he wanted to do this morning?"

"Hush," said Von Gherens, nudging Manfred.

Captain-General Tomaselli had just come up onto the battlements. He bowed to Manfred. "Prince Manfred. The guard told me you were up here." The tone was suspicious.

Manfred waved a hand in greeting. "We were having a look at the disposition of the enemy's cannon and their camps," he said pacifically, pointing out at the muzzle flashes in the darkness.

The captain-general didn't even give it a glance. "There is not much we can do about the position of the enemy's cannon, or their camps. It seems a poor reason to be out in the night air so late. Would you like to come and take a glass of wine with my wife and me instead?"

Manfred stood on Von Gherens's foot. He wished Erik were here to stand on Falkenberg's. Besides missing Erik's company, Manfred had come to realize that the blunt-spoken Icelander was a marvel of tact compared to either of the two Prussians who guarded him now.

He was spared Falkenberg's comments by an interruption. Off to the south of the Citadel, the sky was suddenly lit up. Moments later the flash was followed by a thunderous boom that seemed to keep rolling over them.

"Holy mother of God! What was that?" The captain-general's eyes were wide.

"I think that used to be their magazine," said Von Gherens.

"Hakkonsen's work or I'm a castrato Sicilian," said Falkenberg, grinning in the moonlight. "That's no accident. That is that mad Icelander of yours, Prince Manfred."

Manfred slapped his two bodyguards on the back. "I hope you're right. Typical Erik. He's got his girl, and now he's done more to hurt Emeric's siege cannon than ten cavalry charges could achieve. I just hope he didn't blow himself to glory. Saints! That was a huge explosion."

"You know what is happening out there?" Tomaselli looked totally nonplussed.

"We've got a knight out there raising native resistance to

Emeric," said Falkenberg with obvious satisfaction. "That'll be his work."

Tomaselli shook his head. "But . . . but you did not ask my permission to do so! *I* am in charge of military operations on this possession of the Republic of Venice. You cannot take these steps without advising me, Prince Manfred!"

Under his breath, Manfred swore at himself for easing his vigilance over his tongue in front of this insecure ass. His happiness at seeing signs of Erik's handiwork had made him forget himself.

He stood on Von Gherens's foot again. "Unfortunately, the knight was landed before we were able to consult with you, Captain-General. Actually, it would have been impossible to keep him here—he has a woman out there—so we just ensured he got out as safely as he could. To tell you the truth, I thought he'd probably be still hunting her—but evidently she was somewhere safe, and now he has nothing else to occupy him."

Manfred shook his head, as if he regretted what he had to say. In reality, he was doing it to hide the shaking of his shoulders with repressed laughter. "He's a headstrong fellow, with a very powerful idea of his duty, which includes doing all in his power to oppose Emeric. I'm afraid he's taken the bit in his teeth—independent action, which I certainly didn't order—and since there is no way to get beyond the walls now, I'm unfortunately not able to communicate with him."

"What was this about a woman?"

Trust the fool to concentrate on the single irrelevant piece of information!

"He had an attachment to a Vinlander lass that was here on Corfu. We landed him early to see if he could find her."

"I think we should go back to our quarters now," grumbled Von Gherens. "I don't think you should go and drink the captain-general's wine. You've had enough already. You keep standing on my toes."

From up here, they could see all the way to the gulf, and even beyond to Epirus. The thin bronzed scythe-blade of moon rose from somewhere over mainland Greece, as Erik sat with Svanhild looking out into the star-salted heavens. Their fingers barely touched, but Erik was intensely conscious of the warmth of those fingers.

The tintinnabulation in his ears could still be from the explosion, he supposed. Then Svanhild turned her head, and smiled at him, the stars overhead reflected in her eyes, and he knew that it wasn't. It was the sound of his own heart.

Francesca cocked her head sideways. "So why are two moles not better than one? It would seem logical to me. Does one never use more than one mole? I seem to recall that more than one mole was used in the siege of Acre, yes?"

Falkenberg assumed an oratorical stance. "It does depend heavily on the position, the number of forces at your disposal, and the ability of the defenders and the attackers to provide sufficient artillery cover. For instance, if the defenders cannot split their resources and you have plenty of munitions and manpower, the more moles the better. But a mole is no small task under fire. Emeric no doubt thinks he will pincer any attempt to sally from the main gate and attack or destroy his moles. Here, however— well, there are sally ports on the northern and southern sides and Emeric has relatively few men for such a siege. Making concerted use of both moles would be difficult. Once his forces are on this side of the channel they're directly below the walls. Either they must get inside those walls, fast, or they're going to be killed, easily, from the wall tops. Emeric will need to provide his troops with heavy covering fire just to get them across the mole. And for that he needs more cannon than he's got—and lighter cannon. Those forty-eight-pound bombards are so inaccurate they're as likely to kill his own men if he tries to use them for that purpose."

Falkenberg was now pacing back and forth slowly, like a lecturer. "We've been counting his lighter field pieces. He hasn't got what I would judge was enough for a worthwhile two-pronged assault. Which means he's going to have to rely on arquebus fire; which, in turn, means he'll have to build forward revetments or trenches on the Spianada—that open area in front of the fortress— and those will be under the Citadel's guns. That, in turn, will take a substantial number of his men out of the attack force, which, in turn—"

"Stop, stop!" said Francesca laughingly. "Enough. I'll never dare question Falkenberg's military assessment again."

"Even if he's wrong," said Von Gherens, sitting and rubbing his foot, "it is easier to go ahead, do it his way, and die if need be rather than listen to him explain it all to you."

He swiveled his head, transferring the sour gaze onto Manfred. "Prince, I've met lighter carthorses than you. I understand, since you explained it me, that you want me to keep my mouth shut when you stand on my toes. But my toes would certainly prefer it if you just said 'Shut up, Von Gherens.'"

"I'll cough," said Manfred. "Or can I stand on Falkenberg's toes for you, my love?"

"He seems to have stopped, anyway."

Falkenberg rubbed the scars above the empty eye socket. "I was just getting into my stride," he grumbled. "I wish young Benito was back here. That boy had a positive talent for understanding siege-craft. Reminds me of me. I started younger than he was, you know."

"I think you were born in armor, which must have made it damned uncomfortable on your mother," Manfred replied. "He's riding for Venice by now, to make this siege a thing of the past."

"I hope so," said Francesca, grimly. "I think this fortress is far more likely to fall from within than from the effects of one, two or even three moles."

Chapter 51

Sophia started, when she saw the back of Nico's head above the chair. Usually her husband was in bed by now, not sitting in the salon. They slept in well-separated rooms, and he was seldom in hers, these days.

Fortunately, she'd already removed her cloak, so she quietly dropped it on the floor behind a settle—it would be difficult to explain why she'd been outside at this hour—then gave herself a quick inspection. The dress she wore was unremarkable enough. What was under it wasn't, but then she had no intent of letting him or anyone else see that. Her maids had been dismissed already. She was getting quite good at undressing without them.

"Good evening, my dear," she said casually.

The captain-general swiveled his head, looking equally surprised to see her. He had obviously been so deep in thought he had not even heard her entering the room.

Probably been thinking of something really complicated, like what he'd had for supper. Sophia had no high opinion of Nico's brain-power. But then, what woman wants an intelligent husband any-way? A husband with money, power, prestige and prospects was more important.

Lately, she'd begun to realize that he had less of all of them than she'd thought.

He smiled rather abstractedly at her. "What are you doing up at this time of night, Sophia?"

"I might just ask you the same question, husband," she said archly, gliding toward him.

He yawned. "I've given orders that the guard are to call me when this prince goes wandering about. I don't trust him. He's undermining my authority among the men."

That won't be hard, Sophia thought sarcastically. Her trafficking with the guards who let her in and out of the fortress, unofficially and for small bribes, had given her an insight into his real prestige.

But all she said was: "And?" with an enquiring tilt of the head.

"I was called to say he was up on the inner battlements." He looked furious, in the petty way of a child. "The fellow *just happened* to be there when a huge explosion went off behind enemy lines. And he says he knew nothing about what his man there was planning. Ha!"

He rose, came over, and put his arm around her. "So what *are* you doing up, Sophia?"

Dangerous moment. The truth—

I sneaked out of the fortress to see a Satanist with whom I sacrificed a black cockerel, and then he painted fertility sigils around my nipples and vagina, before I performed certain acts on him with my mouth and then later on myself with a polished piece of vineroot in a pentacle pointed with black candles.

—was not going to be well received.

"I heard the explosion." She hadn't noticed it, but he plainly had. "I was worried, so I dressed and came looking for you."

"It's fine, dear," he said, patting her reassuringly. "Just some saboteurs attacking the Hungarians."

Best to distract him. "It's so comforting that you're in control," she murmured, leaning into him. "You're so manly!"

She felt his chest swell under her hands. "Yes, there's nothing for you to worry about." His own hands were starting to wander.

Sophia stroked his chest, calculating for a moment. Her cloak was dropped just in front of the cabinet in which the brandy decanter stood. She certainly didn't want him going that way for a nightcap!

No help for it, then. She successfully managed to lead him to her bedroom. She blew out the candles in the fancy girandole, making everything dark, since there was no way to remove the insignia now.

The painted sigils felt hot, and so did she. For the first time in at least two years, she actually enjoyed sex with her husband.

Not the sex itself—Nico was as clumsy and oafish in bed as the cavalry captain Querini—but what surrounded it. The knowledge of her duplicity, her sin, inflamed her.

Afterwards, as they lay in the warm darkness, she realized she could take further advantage of the now-rare moment.

"So why are you so suspicious of this prince? He could further your career."

Her husband snorted. "He seeks to ruin it, more likely! He is close friends with Petro Dorma. You know my father was a close friend of the late Doge, and also with Ricardo Brunelli, who was seen as the Doge-in-waiting. *Casa* Dorma's ascension has been a severe blow to us. The prince controls a sizable cavalry force, but the Knights will not take orders from anyone but him. He's refused to hand them over to me."

"Refused?"

"In the politest way. But refused nonetheless. And he's meddling in the defense of the Citadel." He patted her derriere. "Anyway. Why am I boring you with all this politics, eh? Some things it is best a woman doesn't know."

"You don't trust me," she pouted, tracing patterns on his chest. The sigil Ogerda, which Master Morando had told her was the sign for control. He'd also asked her for inside news on the siege. She was determined to find out something for him.

"Of course I trust you dear, but it is quite confidential."

"You're teasing me." She started teasing him, quite a bit more physically.

"Don't stop." His voice sounded somewhat breathless.

"Only if you stop keeping all these secrets from me!"

"Very well. If you go on . . . Well, you remember the prince's bodyguard?"

"Erik Hakkonsen. Handsome, blond, worried-looking."

"As handsome as me?"

"Of course not! Go on." To encourage him, she began applying some of the new skills Morando was teaching her. Her husband gasped a little, then:

"The prince lied to me about the Icelander being landed before they came here. I remember him. And now, he has somehow left the Citadel and started a campaign in the countryside, trying to rally some of the peasants. Silly business! War should be left to regular soldiers, not mules pretending to be men. But what's even worse is that"—Tomaselli's voice grew heavy with indignation as well as passion—" he sneaked out of here without my permission. Didn't even consult me! He's out there with that snotty Vinlander woman who tried to come and stay here in the Citadel."

"Really? This Erik broke out after the siege started? A likely story. He must be in league with the Hungarians. I wouldn't be in the least surprised to find this prince in league with them too, the way he openly consorts with that woman of his. Rumor has it she was a *cortegiana*. No morals at all."

By now, her husband's mind was addled enough by what Sophia was doing not to find anything amiss in the utterly illogical conclusions his wife was advancing. Sophia filled her mouth again just to keep from laughing. Addling Nico Tomaselli's mind was not much of a challenge.

"Yes, mistress, I think all is going well."

The image of Countess Bartholdy floating over the blood-bowl frowned a little. "Make sure it doesn't go *too* well, Bianca. I want this siege to drag on and on. It'll take months of frustration before Emeric will finally be willing to come to me for help."

"I understand, mistress." Casarini hesitated. Then, decided that risking Bartholdy's immediate displeasure was less dangerous than risking eventual failure. "But it would help me—considerably— if I had some better idea of what you are specifically seeking."

The frown on the countess's face deepened. Bianca grew tense. Elizabeth Bartholdy was less concerned than Bianca herself with the way in which grimaces could, over centuries and millennia, permanently distort her face. But she was not oblivious to the problem. To see such a frown on her face was . . . frightening, to anyone who really knew her.

Thankfully, the frown eased, replaced by that silvery little laugh. "Very well. I suppose I have kept you a bit too much in the dark. You needn't concern yourself with my final goal, Bianca, but . . . Let's just say that I need to inveigle my great-great-nephew to release some magics on the island which will advance my purposes. In order for that to happen, however, he will need to leave the siege and come visit me in my castle near the Carpathians."

Immediately, Bianca understood the point. Emeric of Hungary was one of those kings who insisted on meddling with the military details of his campaigns—much to his officers' despair and, often enough, grisly punishment. It would not be easy to get him to leave the siege in order to make the long journey from Corfu to the Carpathians.

A *long* siege, then, stretching through the summer and autumn and well into the winter.

Bianca had no control, of course, over the military side of the matter. Although—

"At a certain point, mistress, it may be necessary to have Captain-General Tomaselli removed. He's such an incompetent commander that, with him in charge—constantly interfering, rather—it may be impossible to prevent Emeric from simply taking the Citadel by force, before winter comes. The defense would be far stronger if it was fully in the hands of the garrison commander, Leopoldo—especially with Prince Manfred and his Knights here. They seem to get along well with Commander Leopoldo."

Elizabeth pondered her words, for a moment. "True. But keep in mind the opposite risk. I *do* also want Corfu to fall to my great-great-nephew, eventually." She cocked her head slightly. "You understand that if the military defense is capable enough, everything will eventually depend on treachery. Well . . . treachery combined with what I will unleash on Corfu. I will provide the magics—but will you be able, when the time comes, to provide the treason?"

This was no time for hesitation. Bianca nodded firmly. "Yes, mistress. I will."

"See to it, then." The image of the countess began to fade. Within seconds, it was gone.

For the next hour or so, after cleaning up all signs of the ritual, Bianca sat in her room simply thinking. She'd gambled, making her claim to the countess, and now she had to make good on it.

By the end, she'd reached two conclusions. One pleasant, one not.

She'd already reached the tentative conclusion anyway, once the siege began, that she'd have to have her "uncle and aunt" killed sooner or later. It was already cumbersome, the way she had to sneak around and keep her activities a secret from them. Over time, the needs of her work would be impossible to hide from people living in the same house—especially the assignations she'd have to begin with one of Fianelli's men.

That was the pleasant conclusion. Betraying those who had given you their trust was always enjoyable to Bianca—not to mention spiritually profitable. Casarini, like her mistress, hoped to cheat Satan out of her soul. But doing so required emulating the Great One in all respects. She was already doing quite well in that regard, she thought. Killing her "relatives" would enhance her progress further.

She began considering the ways to accomplish that. But then, guided by years of rigorous self-discipline, put the matter aside in order to ponder the other conclusion.

Not pleasant, that one. For some years now, sex had stopped being anything for Bianca Casarini other than a means to an end. Still . . .

Eventually, she was going to have to betray Fianelli also. And the surest way to do that was to form a liaison with one of Fianelli's three chief goons. Between the pleasures of her body and the lure of taking his boss's place, Bianca was confident she could manage it.

Paulo Saluzzo, she decided. *That won't be so bad. At least he's Florentine and takes a bath more than once a week.*

The next day, Bianca began both projects. At midday, by wearing a rather provocative gown when she went to meet Paulo Saluzzo in order to pass on further information to his boss Fianelli. Bianca was normally careful to wear nothing but modest attire whenever she met Fianelli or any of his goons.

Saluzzo noticed—immediately—but was suave enough to do nothing more than give her a fairly subtle ogle, and a leer that could charitably be called a friendly smile.

Bianca did not return the smile. Moving too quickly would make Saluzzo suspicious. He *was* Florentine, after all. This needed some finesse. In any event, Bianca was in no hurry.

"And make sure you stress to Fianelli that we need to start setting up a sacrificial lamb," she said sternly. "That whore of the prince's—the one who calls herself 'de Chevreuse'—she's a canny one. My informants tell me she's already more or less running the Citadel's countertreason work. There's no way she won't spot something, sooner or later. When that time comes, we need to have made sure that someone else's head goes on the block."

Saluzzo grunted. The sound was mildly sarcastic. "Don't teach double-dealing to double-dealers, Signorina Casarini. Fianelli's already got the man picked out, and Zanari's starting to work on him. Nachelli's his name. He's a small-time loan shark and rent collector. Too greedy for his own good. We'll cut him in on just enough to make him visible, without letting him know enough to lead anyone to us."

Bianca had her doubts. How could you "cut someone in" *without* the man knowing your own identity? But . . .

Fianelli was direct, after all, and not squeamish in the least. Presumably, when the time came, he would see to it that the Venetian authorities would be trying to interrogate a corpse.

She'd leave that to Fianelli and his thugs. Bianca had her own plans for getting rid of them, when the time came. They'd be her sacrificial lambs, just as this Nachelli would be theirs.

She left the hidden alley where her meetings with Saluzzo took place. They couldn't afford to be spotted, so the meetings were always very brief. On her way past him, she felt Saluzzo's fingers brushing her hip. But it was a tentative thing, more in the way of an automatic reflex to the gown and what it suggested than anything serious. Saluzzo was not actually stupid, and he would understand as well as she did that there was no safe place for them to pursue any affair. They might be able to find a place hidden from public eyes, to be sure. But they'd also have to keep it hidden from Fianelli—and that would be a lot more difficult.

The knowledge would frustrate Saluzzo, and for weeks to come. *Good.* After she arranged the killing of her "relatives," Saluzzo would be that much more eager to pursue Bianca, now that she had a house of her own in which to meet him.

When she'd arrived on Corfu, the year before, Bianca had brought several large pieces of luggage with her. There were secret compartments in two of those valises, where she kept her grimoires hidden along with her magical tools and ingredients. After pleading a headache to her "aunt" and "uncle," she spent the afternoon in her room studying the texts. By nightfall, she'd decided on the method she would use.

It required the blood of innocents, of course—and no mere animal blood. Not for that ritual.

Bianca rose and put away the grimoires. Then, moved to the window in her room. Looking down, she could see the narrow street of the Citadel which her room overlooked. As always, these days—even in this relatively prosperous area of the fortress, set aside for Venetians—the street swarmed with people. Children, many of them, and most of those beggars.

A little boy, perhaps five years old, looked up at her window and gave her a big smile. It was a beggar's smile, seeking aid from the fine lady.

Not all *that* innocent, to be sure, not with that trace of calculation which had no business on the face of a five-year-old. But . . .

He'd do. Bianca smiled back, very sweetly. Tomorrow, she'd start giving him food. Quite a bit, in fact. That ritual required fat as well as blood.

Chapter 52

First things first, Benito decided, when he arrived in Reggio di Calabria. He still had two silver pennies—he'd told that rogue of an oil trader he only had one to avoid trouble. He'd need money, but right now, immediately if not sooner, he needed food.

He found a very respectable-looking taverna next to the quay, plainly not a seaman's place, but aimed at the clerks and minor merchants who worked down there. It was a bit above his present guise, but . . . the bouquet drifting out of the doorway was pure temptation.

Benito had never been very good at resisting that kind of temptation. Or most any other, for that matter. He went in, looked around the crowded room for a seat, and finally took his place at the end of one of the benches. The clerkly type next to him gave him an opaque glance, but at least he didn't pull in the skirts of his coat.

The waiter looked rather doubtfully at Benito. "You have money?" he asked. The tone was carefully neutral. As likely as not, given the proximity to the quay, occasional sailors fresh off a ship and with their pockets full came this way.

Benito nodded. The waiter took a quick glance toward the kitchens, and then whispered to Benito: "I shouldn't say this, but my brother's a seafaring man. The prices here are sky-high. The food's good, so long as you don't touch the pork. But there is a cheaper place down the quay. The food is lousy but it's cheap."

Benito grinned at the fellow, and winked. "Well, this time I'll go with the good food with sky-high prices. Will two silver cover it and a jug of wine?" It was foolishness to spend down to the reserves, but Benito felt in need of a bit of foolishness. Finding a fence in a strange seaport was going to be a challenge.

The waiter nodded. "*Si*. I'll see you get the best," and he was scurrying off to the kitchen.

Benito had timed his arrival well. He hadn't been sitting for more than a few minutes when the locals came in. Mostly, Benito noted, middle-aged or elderly men who took the needs of the stomach seriously, by the looks of them.

The waiter appeared from the smoky kitchen sooner than Benito had expected, not that his empty stomach was going to complain. The man seemed bent on proving that, besides being a waiter in a sky-high–priced taverna, he had all the skills of a juggler. He carried a carafe of wine, a bowl of bread-rings, a platter of chargrilled baby octopus redolent of thyme and garlic with just a hint of bay leaf, a jug of extra sauce, and some olive oil and vinegar. He brought a plate of Melanzane alla finitese next, the crumbed aubergine slices bursting with hot melted cheese.

"Eat up. The cook gets upset if you aren't ready for the swordfish the minute it arrives. And do you need more wine?"

The fish, when it came, was worth suffering a fussy cook for. The succulent flesh, scented with bergamot, capers and oregano, was the kind of dish whereby gastronomes set their standards. Somehow, outside of this meal, the thoughts of finding a fence seemed far less threatening. Maybe it was the carafe of wine from the local Greco di Bianco grapes. They were a great improvement on the stuff he had drunk with Taki, Spiro and Kosti.

Feeling full, and almost somnolent, Benito parted with his silver and, as a well-deserved tip for the waiter, the rest of his coppers. He then went out looking for an alley in which to get mugged.

It seemed like a good idea at the time it had occurred to him. If he wanted to find a fence . . . ask a thief. Finding a thief just took some bait. Benito hoped he would get a solitary operator, and that he was able to avoid getting hurt first and robbed after, not that the mugger was going to be very pleased with the state of Benito's pouch. Well, that made two of them. Benito wasn't very comfortable about its flatness himself.

A little later, someone did oblige him. Very professionally. The thief stepped out of the shadows, put an arm around Benito's neck and a knife against his kidneys. "Don't try and turn around. Just give us the pouch and you'll stay alive."

With a calm that belied his racing heart, Benito untied the pouch and held it out.

"Drop it."

"You might want to look in it before I do that."

"Why?" asked the mugger suspiciously. "What's in it?"

"Absolutely nothing. Not even a copper penny."

"Damn liar." The mugger swung him around. "You're loaded. You ate at old Forno's. Give the money belt."

Benito lifted his shirt to show skin. "There isn't one. I spent it all. Every last penny."

The mugger gaped. "Wha—"

He never got any further than that. He found he'd been neatly disarmed and now faced his own knife and Benito's Shetland blade. Benito shook his head. "Never let yourself get distracted, my friend."

The mugger showed both courage and a sense of humor. "Well, I haven't got any money either." His eyes darted, looking for escape.

Benito flipped the mugger's knife over, and held it out, hilt first, to the man. "You can have it back. I'm not interested in your money. All I want is some information. If you wanted to sell something, ah . . . with ownership claims other than yours, where would you go? Who is buying?"

The mugger took the knife warily, not sheathing it. "Di Scala. He's the only big-time buyer in town. Follow the quay to the end. There's an alley there. It's up the stairs in the third last house."

"Thanks."

The mugger shook his head. "Watch him, laddie. He's bent." Which was about the worst thing a thief could ever say about a fence.

Di Scala looked like an underfed vulture. The fence shaded his hooded eyes with a skeletally thin hand.

"It's a fake," he pronounced, shaking his head. "A good fake, but a fake. I'll give you a florin for it." He took a golden coin from his desk and pushed it toward Benito.

"It's no sale," said Benito, grimly. The ruby was worth at the very least thirty ducats, a coin whose greater purity made it more valuable than the florin.

The fence tapped his long fingers. "The sale is not up for negotiation."

The faintest of sounds made Benito realize that they were no longer alone. That finger-tapping on the desk had been more than just a mannerism.

He glanced back. The two men who had come in behind him had that heavy-set look of brutality common to all enforcers. Between the two of them, there was enough flesh to make three of Benito, with a fourth not being that far off.

One of them cracked his knuckles. "You called, boss."

The fence nodded. "This fellow will be leaving. Now. With or without his money, but without this." He held up the ruby.

Benito considered his options, which weren't good. The sleazy little room offered him no space to maneuver. And the rent-a-thugs coming to grab his elbows were distinctly better than average.

Right now, he reminded himself, his primary task was to get to Venice as fast as he possibly could. "I'll take my money," he whined, cringing. Out of the corner of his eye he saw the bully boys relaxing. Not unready to hurt and possibly maim, but not expecting any resistance. He could take them . . .

Resolutely he put the thought aside and reached gingerly for the florin. "It's not fair," he complained, hangdog, looking at the coin.

Di Scala laughed sardonically. "And how you came by the loot was, of course."

Benito hunched his shoulders still more. "It was my grand-mother's."

"Yes. Very likely. Now get lost."

"I won't bring you any more stuff."

"I will sob myself to sleep tonight," sniffed Di Scala. "You aren't from round here anyway. That's enough money for you to waste on wine and whores. You're lucky I don't let the boys just drop you over the wharf with a couple of weights on your feet—and if you don't get out of here, that's just what I will do. *Get.*"

Benito got. "There's no need to push," he snarled at the thugs on the rickety stair. He was rewarded by a buffet and them grabbing his pouch. They took the florin reposed there, kicked him out to sprawl in an alley, and threw his empty pouch after him. The alley was narrow, slippery and reeking with ordure. He got up and staggered away, theatrically waving a fist at the laughing pair.

They'd have laughed less if they'd seen him round the corner and then grease up a drainage pipe. Before they were back inside, Benito was lying in the shelter of a chimney pot just behind the shady lip of an eave of a house beyond.

Watching. Without money he wasn't going anywhere anyway. He'd allowed himself to get careless. Rusty. Overconfident. He still had one jewel, but if he sold it anywhere in this town news was bound to get out, and they'd be looking for him.

Besides, he'd discovered that he had an extreme dislike of being robbed. It occurred to him, with somewhat wry amusement, that some of his own victims over the years might have felt just as angry. There was a kind of justice in it, he supposed, but he needed money to get to Venice. Corfu needed help. Maria needed that help. So did that kid of hers.

He waited and watched. A fence's busiest hours would be toward early morning—this rogue wasn't going anywhere. As the night wore on, he'd just get more careful.

Benito had no money and nothing else to do, after all. He steeled himself—as he'd done often enough above the canals of Venice, in years past—to ignore hunger, cold and tiredness. At least this time, hunger wasn't part of the equation; that excellent meal was still enough with him that his stomach was happy, but not so much as to slow him down.

Eventually, Di Scala and his two thugs appeared on the street. Moving surely and silently across the roofs, Benito trailed the fence back to Di Scala's own house. That was where the fence would keep his stash, he was sure.

The two thugs followed Di Scala into the house; then, a few minutes later, they emerged and headed off to wherever they slept themselves. As soon as they were gone, Benito came out of hiding and swung into position. Hanging like a bat from the eaves, he watched the fence through a shutter-crack in his bedroom. The man unlocked his cassone, opened up a cunningly disguised compartment in its lid and secreted some coin into it, and an item of what was probably jewelry.

Smiling to himself, Benito found a rooftop corner, rolled himself into a ball and slept. By midday he was back at his post. He watched the fence leave. As soon as darkness provided cover, Benito began slipping tiles from the roof, as quietly as possible. Then, he eased planks from the ceiling with the Shetland knife. It was proving a good, strong tool. Not exactly a Ferrara *main gauche*, but a workingman's ideal knife.

Lightly, Benito dropped into the fence's bedroom. He made no attempt to force the lock on the cassone—it would be a good one.

Besides, the hidden compartment probably had a booby trap. Instead he set to work with the knife on the board making up the back edge, being careful not to move the cassone itself. That might have unpleasant consequences. There'd been a case like that back in Venice. The thief had lost his hands, his sight, and, because he was caught in the screaming aftermath, his life.

Benito was not planning to chance imitating him. He cut a neat slot through the solid wood, and then tipped the cassone. It wasn't the most effective way of getting money out, but Benito was rewarded by a succession of coins and bits and pieces. He put them all hastily into his pouch, before leaving the way he'd come. As neat a job as he'd ever done, and as well-deserved a one as he'd ever pulled, thought Benito, quietly slipping out onto the roof.

But, as Valentina had taught him—in what seemed a lifetime away—the job wasn't done until you were clean away. Benito had done his homework. Two boats carrying fresh produce for the market in Messina left long before first light from Reggio di Calabria to have the crisp wares unloaded and in the market by dawn. This morning they took an uninvited fresh thief as well as their fresh vegetables. He had the grace to get off quietly on the Messina quay-side, carry a load of carrots to the waiting wagon, and even to steal only one carrot.

It was fairly woody, but, munching at the purple root as he went in search of a taverna, Benito found it remarkably pleasant. Sweet and tasty, even. His nose led him to a panetteria where stevedores were already buying hot ciabatta, before going on to a stall where a butcher was selling liver and tripe ragout from a steaming pot, at a copper a dip of the loaf. Benito felt in his pouch. He hadn't really investigated what his loot was yet.

What his fingers encountered was round—but not money. He stepped into a noisome alley to check it out.

He had to laugh. What he'd assumed was money was valuable all right. It just wasn't currency or saleable, except by priests. He had acquired some fifteen golden Hypatian medals. Four pilgrim medals, also golden, struck in Jerusalem, engraved with the pilgrim's name, some twenty-three pieces of silver of some foreign origin— a coin he'd never seen before—and . . . a ruby.

His ruby. Well, there was *some* justice in the world.

Chapter 53

Despite his hunger and tiredness, Benito set off in search of a Hypatian chapel. He would just drop the medals in the poor box or leave them in the font or something.

He found the chapel all right. This time luck wasn't with him. He slipped in quietly, only to have a Sibling emerge from the counseling booth as he approached the font.

"Can I help you, my son?" she asked gently. "Are you in need of counseling?

Benito took in the small, round, serious face of the woman in the pale Hypatian robe, liked the quiet calm in her eyes, and decided to chance honesty. "I've brought something that was stolen from the Church, back to it." He pulled out the golden Hypatian medals.

The Sibling looked, looked again, her eyes widening, then took a deep breath. "God be thanked! We have prayed for their return. May God forgive you for stealing them. I am so glad your conscience has made you bring them back to us."

A reasonable conclusion for her to have come to, but he decided he wasn't going to let it go. "Actually, I came upon them by accident."

The little Sibling looked sternly at him. "We are not going to prosecute you, young man. There is no need to lie to us. God knows the truth anyway."

He snorted. "Well, then, he knows I am telling he truth. I have just come over from Reggio di Calabria on the vegetable boats. I've never been here in my life before."

She looked doubtful, but there was a crack in the doubt. After all, he didn't have the local accent.

He laughed, which put another crack in her doubt. "I'll swear to it, my hand on the Bible. Or believe what you please." He shrugged. "I suppose I did steal them, but not from the Church. I took them from a fence in Reggio di Calabria, after he'd robbed me of my own property. I got my own back, and I got these as well."

Then it occurred to him that he had yet another card to play. "And I got some other things I'd like to see go to their rightful owners. They were headed for being melted down, I guess."

He produced the Jerusalem pilgrim medals. "They're worth," he felt the weight, "oh, maybe four ducats in raw gold. But they were really important to some people. They're named, but the names don't mean much to me. Except for this one, of course."

It was engraved: *Carlo Sforza*. Benito's father. Benito had been astonished when he found it among the others.

At a guess . . . after his defeat at the hands of Duke Enrico Dell'este, the Wolf of the North must have undertaken a pilgrimage to Jerusalem. Someone had robbed his baggage. For the thief's sake, Benito hoped Sforza had never caught up with him.

The little Sibling gaped at the medals, at the name, at the scruffy young man holding them out to her.

"He'll have traveled incognito. I'd like his medal, and the others, to get back to their owners. I can offer some silver to see that it does."

Benito emptied out his pouch again, only keeping back the ruby. "All of this is stolen. All of it is too hot to handle, I suspect, because it was hidden with the medals. I've no idea who it belonged to. But I get the feeling it would be best used for the support of those who'll carry these to their owners. All I ever wanted was to get my own property back from that—" he killed the obscenity before it got to his tongue "—worm, who cheated me."

The Sibling shook her head in amazement. "God moves in mysterious ways," she said faintly.

Benito sighed. "Good lady, you've no idea just how mysteriously. And this time I can only assume He intervened directly. And now I am broke, hungry and tired. You'll excuse me, but I need to go and do something about all of these things."

The Sibling smiled; whatever doubts she'd had, they'd

disappeared the moment that he turned out his pockets. "Well, it seems only right that seeing as you have brought our property back to us, we provide breakfast and a place to sleep." She raised an eyebrow with faint amusement. "The order has also offered a reward for the return of our property."

Benito's spirits lifted. "I don't suppose it's cash?"

"Well, no." The small round face dimpled. "You must know our order is sworn to poverty. But a medal, blessed by the holy Michael, our bishop, is worth having in its own right. He will be very pleased at the return of the medals. We use the sale of them to fund our charitable work. And we are sending a delegation to Rome in five months time. There is to be a convocation of the order, to discuss the new chapter houses and cloisters in Germany. We can use that opportunity to deliver the pilgrim medals to others of the order who will convey them onward to the owners."

She looked shyly at Benito. "Could I know who God's instrument was?"

Benito grinned. "Tell Sforza it comes back to him with the compliments of Benito. I think he'll know which Benito, if he thinks hard about it."

A thought occurred to him. "Sibling, I ended up retrieving your stolen property because when I wanted to change a jewel into cash, I was assumed to be a professional thief." Benito hoped he looked suitably horrified at the very idea. He stared very pointedly at her. "Actually, I have had the same reaction from other people."

The Sibling had the grace to look embarrassed. "You can speak like a nobleman born . . . but at first you sounded . . . and you look . . ."

"Scruffy. I have my reasons, Sister. They're honest enough for Father Eneko Lopez. You have heard of him?"

"Who has not? He is already famous in the order. A stern man," she added, a bit doubtfully.

"He's that, all right. But he is also a good man. A pious man, certainly. My journey has his blessing."

It was best not to say too much, he decided. The Hypatian Sibling might be closed-mouthed and as good as one of the choir of angels—but she might say something inadvertently to the wrong person. Venice was not popular with the Kingdom of Naples. Benito didn't need to spend time in a dungeon because he'd had too loose a tongue.

"But to get a passage on a ship I need money." She looked faintly alarmed. "For safety and security I have carried my funds in the shape of jewels. They're easily hidden. And they're easily turned into money." He smiled disarmingly. "Except when you look like a thief."

The Sibling looked rather nonplussed by all of this. "I suppose you are a messenger of some sort. A carrier of secrets . . ." She also didn't look as if she entirely approved.

"I am something of the sort, yes. But just because something is secret, doesn't mean it has to be evil, Sister. This isn't. I'll swear that on your Hypatian medal if need be. It is just politics. And I need to sell a ruby. Is it possible that the Siblings could sell it for me? After all, your order must get gifts you need to dispose of sometimes."

She looked sternly at him. "I know this seems ungrateful, but I must ask. Is this jewel truly yours to dispose of?"

Benito nodded. "Yes. I swear it, as God is my witness."

She held out a hand. "Give it to me. I will give it to Brother Marteno. He was once a jeweler, before he renounced worldly things and devoted himself to serve Christ."

Against his nature, but trusting his instincts, Benito handed over the ruby. He still had one more, after all.

The food in the Hypatian refectory was not exactly hot murseddu and steaming ciabatta—but bread, olive oil and sharp goats-milk cheese at least filled the hole where Benito had once kept his stomach. And the cell in the monastery was dry and cool, letting him sleep deep into the afternoon.

It was also not exactly where an irate fence would be sending his hirelings looking for a thief. But Benito found the bells no aid to sleep.

He was awakened by someone coming into the monk's cell they'd assigned him. For most of his life, Benito had slept lightly—a thief living on his wits in other peoples' property couldn't afford to do otherwise. It was better to sleep lightly and uneasily than to snore like a hog and be slaughtered like one. Since he'd left the Citadel, Benito's senses seemed to have honed themselves even more. But this time they'd woken him for something harmless. It was a small, large-nosed monk, bearing a chinking bag. "That was an exceptionally good stone, young man. I have some seventy-three ducats for you."

Benito reflected there were some advantages in not selling to a fence. The one disadvantage was the embarrassment of riches.

The little man cleared his throat. "Sister Genina has explained to me that you obviously don't want publicity, but we have this medal for you. It was offered as a reward, and it seems fair that you should get it."

He produced a small silver medallion. "It is supposed to have a strand of Saint Arsenius's hair in it, and it is blessed by the bishop. We cannot claim there is any miraculous great virtue attached to it, though. It may be of help to a seafarer and will protect and glow if you are exposed to evil magic."

The little man looked more than a little uncomfortable. "She, um, Sister Genina, led me to understand you'd recovered our medals in the course of getting your own property back. I realize you may not be able to do this but, well, there are certain church vessels missing too, and another four of those medals. You couldn't perhaps tell us where to look?"

Benito's youthful experience said: Betray someone to the law? Not likely.

On the other hand, the fence had already played foul, by the thieves' code. Besides, any piece of excrement that was low enough to take holy medals deserved whatever he got.

"A fence in Reggio di Calabria. His name is Di Scala. His home is up on the hill. Big place, walls with coppo tiles on top of them. He trades from upstairs on the third last house in the alley at the end of the quay. His small—ah, dubious stuff is kept in a secret compartment in the cassone in his room. I suggest you have whomever you send take an axe to open it. Those things have booby traps nine times out of ten. And I suggest the order send someone very large and well-armed. Actually, I suggest you send several someones like that. The fence has a couple of big bullies working for him, and I doubt, all things considered, that they'd respect the cloth."

The slight monk smiled. "I think not for long. Down here in the south the order is held in high esteem. The people will not allow us to be hurt."

Benito shrugged. "Make sure there are a lot of witnesses around, then. I got the feeling that this man has no respect for the Church, either."

❀   ❀   ❀

Benito left without fanfare that afternoon and went to a respectable dealer in secondhand clothing. By the time he walked down to the Messina quay-side to hunt a dockside tavern for a passage north, he'd changed from a shag-rag sailor into a minor, but respectable trader, with a plain but serviceable rapier and the Shetland knife riding where a *main gauche* would.

The weight of the rapier was comfortingly familiar. The boots were not comforting or comfortable on feet that had gotten used to being bare again—and before that to having boots cut by the finest cobblers in Venice—but Benito had little choice but to wear them. No scruffy seaman would pay for a passage. And right now, if it meant paying for the whole vessel, he'd do it. He felt time pressing on him. He wanted to get through to Venice, and back to Corfu.

Chapter 54

It only took three cups of wine to find a caique heading up the coast in the morning as far as Livorno. And another cup and five ducats had him installed in a cabin on her. It wasn't a big cabin, but it had a hammock and a small window.

Benito was resting in the hammock, enjoying having his new boots off, with the spicy warm evening breeze blowing off the straits and in through the window. He was slept-out, so he passed the time sharpening the Shetland knife and despairing of getting a good edge on the rapier. It wasn't a bad weapon, really. It just wasn't Ferrara steel. He examined the edge in the candlelight.

Suddenly, the door to the cabin was opened so violently it was nearly thrown off its hinges. In came the cadaverous Di Scala and his two thugs. There was very little doubt they'd come with murder in mind.

Benito rolled out of the hammock, landing on his feet, catlike, with the rapier in his right and the Shetland knife in his left. The cabin was narrow and quite full of hammock. This did mean that the three were in each other's way.

"You thought you'd got away with it, didn't you, you little *pizza da merde!*" hissed the fence, closing the door behind him. "Nobody does that to me! I'm going to make an example of you. Cut your *cazzo* off and shove it down your throat, spill your guts and leave you to die slowly. Take him, boys."

Benito grabbed the hammock with a forefinger and slashed the hanging rope with the Shetland knife. The rope raveled, parted, as Di Scala's two pieces of muscle pushed their way forward, slightly cautious. They'd plainly expected him to have a knife at best, and to be the cringing little thief they'd bullied. The rapier was unexpected.

But they weren't going to let it stop them. They were professionals, after all.

Benito flung the hammock at them. It was spread by two hardwood batons and therefore the net stayed open. The two thugs both had the same hand-and-a-half guardless knives that the rascally oil merchant had had. Perhaps they were popular here in the south. The hammock tangled one of them, so Benito neatly dealt with the other.

Terminally. There was no space for a swing here, but a rapier lunge was quite as effective. The extra reach made the thug's knife an ineffectual defense.

The other freed himself of the hammock, and pulled the spreader-baton from it. It still wasn't rapier-long, but it gave him something to fend off rapier cuts and thrusts with. Benito balanced on the balls of his feet, aware that Di Scala was fumblingly trying to prime a wheel-lock pistol.

Lunge. Twist. A slash of the *main gauche*.

The remaining thug's hand-and-a-half blade skittered across the floor. Blood pulsed from the man's wrist.

Benito kicked the knife into the corner behind him, nicking his toes. The thug, his eyes huge in the candlelight, dodged back, crashing into his master.

"*Testa di cazzo!*" snarled the fence, nearly dropping the gun. He pushed the man roughly away, back toward Benito.

The wolf was at the surface now. Both of them were going to die.

And then Benito paused. The medallion he'd been given was hot against his flesh . . .

He settled for neatly flicking the baton out of the hand of the surviving tough and kicking his legs out from under him. Di Scala was trying to aim the pistol, his hands now shaking so badly he could barely hold the weapon. Benito looked scornfully at him. Here was one who hired his dirty work done. Even the dead thug was worth two of him.

He jumped forward, planting both feet in the fallen thug's solar plexus. The man struggled weakly for breath.

The fence pressed against the door he'd closed, pointing the quivering pistol at Benito.

"I can put this knife through your eye," said Benito coldly. "You, on the other hand, haven't primed that thing properly. You'll be lucky if it goes off at all. It's rusty, too, so it's as likely to kill you as me. Besides, you couldn't hit a barn door from inside shaking like that."

Now the boot was truly on the other foot, and the fence knew it. "Just let me go! Please. I'll give you money."

"I've every intention of letting you go. You and your carrion. You're taking both the living and the dead one with you. But first I need to tell you something."

With a bare foot, he prodded the thug who was struggling to sit up. "This idiot, too. You may decide that being dead is easier. First, I returned those stolen Hypatian medals you had to the Church and I told them exactly where, and from whom, I got them. They want your guts for garters."

The thug looked accusingly at his master. His face was an unhealthy white and he was still struggling for breath, but he managed to gasp: "You bought 'ose?" His tone was one of unadulterated shock.

"They're just gold, you superstitious fool," snarled the fence.

The moment the fence looked at the thug, Benito stepped forward and knocked the pistol out of his hand. He used the flat of the rapier, but a couple of Di Scala's fingers were probably broken. Di Scala shrieked.

Benito held the rapier ready for the thrust. "I imagine you made sure we wouldn't be interrupted. You'd better hope we aren't, because if we are I'll kill you. Now, the other reason I wanted to speak to you was to advise a pilgrimage. Because the only place you might be safe is kneeling in the Church of the Holy Sepulcher, praying for forgiveness. I've already sent word, and his pilgrim's medal, to Carlo Sforza. I should imagine that he is going to send agents looking for you. You really don't want them to find you anywhere else, because compared to Sforza, I'm a gentle and kindly man."

"*Sforza?*" The fence stared at him as if he was mad.

"One of those medals that you bought for their gold value was stolen from the Wolf of the North." Benito grinned mirthlessly at the way all of the blood drained from the fence's face. The scum might not be afraid of the Church, but he was properly terrified now. "I think I'll leave you with the thought that gold is really worth far less than other things. Now, you'll take this dead man between you, and precede me onto the deck. I've foregone killing you, but I'm going to enjoy kicking you off this boat. I hope you can swim."

He marched them up on deck, dragging the corpse between them. "Drop that over the side."

They did. Benito's keen eyes noticed movement among the boxes and barrels on the quay-side. It could be helpers, or, more likely it could be those who'd been told to get out or get hurt. He'd give them a show, whoever it was.

He remembered what the Sibling had said, and decided, maliciously, to make life as difficult as possible for the fence from this moment on. He'd studied drama enough with Valentina to know how to declaim at volume. He filled his lungs, and began an oration for the benefit of the hidden audience.

"DI SCALA, YOU CUR! You came here TO KILL ME, but I have defeated you WITH GOD'S HELP! And you and I know that you also bought golden medallions STOLEN FROM THE CHURCH! Stolen from the Hypatian Siblings who would have used the money raised to care for the poor, to do Christ's work! See what sort of ILL-FORTUNE follows SUCH WICKEDNESS!"

Not bad, he though. Benito flicked his rapier forward, cutting the fence's pouch free. He stabbed it as it fell. And then, using thumb and forefinger from his rapier hand, he held it, ripped it open, and showered coin into the dark water.

"My money!" squalled the fence.

Benito clucked his tongue. "Sinner. Some things are worth much more than money."

With that, he applied his foot to the skinny fence's little pot-belly, sending him over the stern-rail. The thug didn't wait. He jumped.

Benito watched them flounder to the shore. No one came out of the darkness to help them scramble, dripping, up the rocks of the quay. No one followed them as they left.

Benito looked out at the quay for a while. Then he sheathed his sword and the Shetland knife. "All right," he said, "you can come out now."

Shamefacedly, the seven-man crew came out from behind the

stacked cargo where they'd been hiding, led by their captain. Benito noticed another couple of people sneaking away. It would be all over the tavernas by morning, thought Benito, knowing how these things worked.

So much for keeping his passage quiet. Still, with any luck he hadn't betrayed who he was or where he was from—or even where he was headed.

"Well, how much did he pay you?" Benito said grimly to the captain. "I should have smelled a rat. It was too easy. You weren't planning on going to Livorno, were you?"

The captain shook his head. "We only go to Naples, signor. Never been further. But word was out to agree to take you wherever you wanted to go."

Benito smiled wryly. "I'm getting old and getting soft. Well, Captain. Just how soon do we sail? Because these parts are going to be very unhealthy for a while. You might be wanted for questioning, about why you allowed a man with the Church's blessing on him to be attacked on your ship."

The captain looked about nervously. "We're not supposed to sail at night."

Benito just looked at him. Then looked at the water. You couldn't actually see a corpse there.

"However there's a good breeze," said the captain hastily. "Stilo. Cast us off, boy!"

"But, Captain . . ."

"*Don't argue, Stilo.*"

The seaman did as he was told. When he jumped back on board he asked Benito: "Is it true about the medals?"

Benito nodded. "The Siblings were going over this afternoon to fetch home the rest."

The seaman took a deep breath. "Di Scala is a big man, and he's got connections. But this time he's gone too far. You don't mess around with the Hypatians here. The people, especially the women, won't stand for it. He'd know that, if he could get a woman without paying double for her." Then he snickered. "Actually, after this, he couldn't get the worst puttana in town for the price of a prince's courtesan."

Benito pulled a face. "Besides, no matter how big a man you are . . . someone else is always bigger. There were some Jerusalem pilgrim medals, too. One of them belonged to a fellow with a reputation big enough to make even princes nervous. And when *he* finds out . . ."

He sighed. Having Carlo Sforza for a father had been the kind of thing that had made a boy wonder about himself, sometimes. He was finding that to be just as true, now that he was a young man.

"I think, Captain, you'd be very wise to stay away a long time. At least as long as the trip to Livorno is going to take you."

Chapter 55

Aldo Morando approached the secondhand merchant Fianelli with a smile. "I believe I've got some information that might be of interest to you."

"I deal in old clothing and cheap medicines," said Fianelli, disinterestedly. "Not information."

Morando wasn't fooled. Fianelli didn't want it known that he was the kingpin. His underlings did the legwork, bought and brought in the information, delivered it to the drop point, and collected their money from the same. But Fianelli was less professional than he thought he was. Morando had been a spy for Phillipo Maria once, in Milan. Now *there* was a son of a bitch who really understood underhand dealing. Fianelli was a provincial amateur by comparison.

Aldo Morando knew how the money worked, too. A lake at the top; a stream to the next tier; and drops to the actual sources. Well, that wasn't how it was going to work here. He was going straight to the lake.

"The details of who blew up the magazine out there might just be worth buying. But they'd be expensive."

"I don't know what you're talking about."

Morando raised his eyebrows. "I have a source to the captain-general's innermost secrets. For a price I can let you into them. It's as simple as that."

Fianelli shrugged. "And why would I want to know his secrets? Now do you want to buy, or just talk rubbish?"

"I'm not buying. I'm selling." Morando turned and walked out. The next move would be Fianelli's.

It wasn't long in coming.

❈   ❈   ❈

Petros Nachelli wasn't a man whom Aldo Morando would have chosen for a go-between. A short, fat, glib little man who oozed greasiness and dishonesty in equal proportions. The Greek was a rent collector for the landed gentry of Corfu's Libri d'Oro. Cockroaches came higher on the social scale of things. Spying was a big step up for Petros.

He knocked on Aldo's door with a smile of false bonhomie on his podgy face. "Ah, my friend Morando. I received a message that you had some . . . merchandise you wished to sell. You can entrust me with it. I'll see you get the best possible price."

"I deal directly or not all, Nachelli. You can tell him that."

The smile fell away from the pudgy face. "I was informed that you were either to sell or I was to take it." He twitched his head over his shoulder, in what he apparently intended for a menacing gesture. Across the road, two of Nachelli's men were loitering. Rent collection sometimes required a beating or two.

Morando gave them no more than a glance. Fianelli's three goons were, in their own way, fairly impressive fellows. Genuine professional thugs. Nachelli's "enforcers," on the other hand, were about what you'd expect from such a lowlife. From the looks of the two scrawny fellows, they were just some relatives of the rent collector pressed into service here. Reluctant service, from the expressions on their faces. They'd be accustomed to bullying long-suffering peasants, not someone like Morando who had a somewhat scary reputation of his own. Aldo suspected that a loud *Boo!* would send them both packing.

"I think not," Morando sneered. "I have taken precautions, Nachelli. His name—Fianelli's—and the names of his three errand boys. Due to go to the podesta, the captain-general, the garrison commander and this newly arrived imperial prince, if I disappear. So go away and tell the boss I don't deal with intermediaries."

Morando smiled nastily, before closing the door. "And remember that your name is on the list now, also."

Aldo Morando was in fact delighted by one aspect of Fianelli's choice. The use of Nachelli fingered several of the Libri d'Oro families who'd been enriched by the feudal system the Venetians had imposed on the island—and were now conspiring against the Republic. A potential source of much income, for a blackmailer.

❈   ❈   ❈

Fianelli came to see him after sundown. When he left, Morando went to the flagstone that served as a trapdoor to the "satanic cellar" and lifted it up. Bianca Casarini emerged from the stairs.

"I *still* don't understand why you didn't pass the information on to him yourself," he grumbled. "This is a bit dangerous for me, Bianca. Nachelli's just a toad, but Fianelli—crude as he may be— is something else again."

Bianca gave Morando her most seductive smile and chucked him under the chin.

"Surely you're not afraid of him? *Aldo Morando?* A veteran of *Milanese* skullduggery? Quaking at the thought of a criminal— ah, not exactly mastermind—on a dinky little island in the middle of nowhere?"

Irritably, though not forcefully, he brushed her hand aside and stumped over to the table in the kitchen. "Save the silly 'manly' stuff for someone stupid enough to fall for it, Bianca." He lowered himself into one of the chairs. "I survived Milan by not being foolhardy. So please answer the question."

Bianca came over and slid into a chair next to him. She took her time about it, to consider her answer. Morando was a charlatan, true, but it wouldn't pay to forget that he was also considerably brighter than any of the other men she was dealing with on Corfu.

She decided the truth—most of it, at least—would serve best.

"I can't afford to become too closely associated with Fianelli myself. Even more important, I can't afford to let *him* start getting the notion that I've become indispensable to him."

Morando arched a quizzical eyebrow. From long habit, he did so in a vaguely satanic manner. "Satanic," at least, as he—a charlatan and a faker—thought of the term. Bianca, as it happened, had once gotten a glimpse of the Great One, in her dealings with Countess Bartholdy. So she knew Morando's affectation was silly.

The real Satan had no eyebrows, nor could he. They would have been instantly burnt to a crisp, so close to those . . .

Not eyes. Whatever they were, they were not eyes.

She shuddered a little, remembering.

Morando misinterpreted the shiver. "Fianelli's not as bad as all *that*, Bianca." He chuckled. "I would have thought you'd want to be indispensable to him."

She shook her head. "You're misreading him. No, he's not that bad—but he is that sullen. Fianelli is the kind of man who hates anyone having a hold on him, especially a woman. If he gets sullen enough, he'll cut off his nose to spite his face. The nose, in this instance, being me."

Morando looked away, thinking for a moment. "Probably true," he mused. "He does remind me a bit of those crazy Montagnards in Milan, even if he hasn't got a speck of political loyalties. But . . . yes, he's got that somewhat maniacal feel about him."

"I don't think he's entirely sane." Confident now that she had Morando diverted down a safe track, Bianca pushed ahead. "He murdered that woman of his, you know—had her murdered, anyway—and for what? She was docile as you could ask for, and so dumb she posed no threat to him whatsoever. Didn't matter. At a certain point, she irked him a bit. Why? Who knows? Probably asked him to wipe the mud off his feet before entering the kitchen she'd just cleaned."

Morando grunted. "All right. What you intend, then, is to make sure that the information we feed him comes from both of us. You feed him stuff from the Libri d'Oro, I feed him stuff from the Venetians. And stuff which jibes with each other. That way he'll think he can play one of us off against the other. That'll please his fancy—enough, you think, that he won't start thinking of either of us as a threat to him."

"Exactly."

Again, he gave her that false-satanic eyebrow. It wasn't all fakery, though. Bianca reminded herself sharply that Morando hadn't survived Milan without being willing to shed blood himself, on occasion.

"Just make sure it isn't true, Bianca." The menace in Morando's voice was barely under the surface. "If I start thinking that you're playing me . . ."

"Don't be silly! Why would I do that?" She didn't try for offended innocence—Morando wouldn't believe that for an instant—but simple cold calculation. "This partnership is proving profitable for both of us. Besides, sooner or later—we're doing our best to make sure it happens, after all—the Hungarians are going to pour into this place. When that happens, I have every intention of being on the best possible terms with you."

She glanced at the flagstone. Morando, following her eyes, smiled. "It will make a nice hideout, won't it, until the Hungarians have sated their bloodlust?"

His eyes moved back to her, lingering for an instant on her body. "Simple lust, too, for such as you. Mind you, Bianca, I *will* expect to be entertained while we're waiting in the cellar."

She laughed huskily. "And have I ever given you grounds for complaint on that score?" Her hand reached out and began stroking his arm. "Now that you bring it up, in fact . . ."

Regretfully, he shook his head. "Can't, sorry. Not tonight. The Tomaselli slut is coming over later and she's supposed to bring a friend of hers with her." He rolled his eyes. "I need to save my energy. And other stuff."

Bianca laughed again. "What are you complaining about? Two women, naked, squirming all over you—most men would think they'd died and gone to Heaven."

Morando's face was sour. "Most men have never copulated with Sophia Tomaselli in a rut, with paint and ointments smeared all over her body and with her groaning what she thinks are words of passion. I'm coming to detest the woman." The face grew more sour still. "God only knows what her friend is like."

Discreetly, Bianca said nothing. She knew what the friend was like, as it happened, having been the one who steered her to Sophia in the first place. Like Sophia, Ursula Monteleone had all the vices and the unpleasant personality of a *Case Vecchie* woman moldering in a provincial backwater; unlike Sophia, who was at least physically rather attractive, Ursula was almost obese and had bad breath.

"Some other time, then," she murmured seductively. That was a waste of time, with Morando. But Bianca liked to stay in practice.

At midnight, Bianca communicated with Countess Bartholdy. Unbeknownst to her, not five minutes later, Fianelli used almost exactly the same magical methods to communicate with Emeric.

Both mistress and master were pleased at the reports.

Others were not.

Eneko Lopez glared out the window of the lodgings he shared with his fellow priests. There was nothing to see, in the middle of the night, except the occasional flashes of cannon fire.

Hearing footsteps enter the room, he glanced over his shoulder. It was Diego and Pierre, not to his surprise. Of the four of them, Francis was the least sensitive to evil auras.

"Yes, Diego and Pierre, I felt it also. It woke me up. Twice—
and with a different flavor to each. They're using the same rituals but following slightly different procedures. We've got *two*
Satanists, or packs of them, working in this place."

"Yes. But why two, I wonder? One of them will be Emeric's agent,
for a certainty. Who is the other working for? It wouldn't be
Chernobog. For his own reasons, the demon avoids satanic rituals as carefully as we do."

Lopez shrugged. "Hard to say. The Dark One penetrates everywhere, in this wicked world." He slapped the windowsill with
exasperation. "This cursed island!"

"It does not really smell like an evil place to me, Eneko. And
I am—you may recall—a rather accomplished witch-smeller."

Eneko sighed. "Yes, I know. But whether it's evil or not, there's
something on Corfu that impedes all of our own magic." He
clenched his fist, slowly, as a man might crush a lemon. "Were that
not true, we could deal with these Satanists easily. I could sense
that they are skilled enough—one, especially—but not powerful."

Diego cleared his throat. "Two things, then. The first is that we
should let Francesca know what we know."

Eneko's lips quirked a bit. He could guess what the second thing
was. "I agree to the first, not that I think she'll have any more
success than we're having. I will not agree to the second. Not yet,
at any rate."

He could hear Pierre's sigh. "So stubborn! Eneko, this island—
whatever lurks on it, rather—is *not* evil. Not friendly to us either,
no. But not evil. So why *not* try to form an alliance with . . ."

"With what?" Eneko demanded. "A formless, faceless something?
About which we know nothing, really, except that it seems able
to absorb all our magic like a sponge absorbs spilled water?"

Pierre cleared his throat again. For the first time since he and
Diego had entered the chamber they all used as a common room,
Eneko turned to face both of them squarely. The Basque priest's
eyes were perhaps a little wider.

"Ah. You're right, actually. We *do* know something about it. It
impedes earth magic, in particular."

"In particular? Perhaps—exclusively." Pierre stepped forward to
join Eneko at the window. Looking out into the darkness, he
frowned thoughtfully. "I admit, it's hard to prove, one way or the
other. None of us can fly and—"

Cannon fire illuminated the night. "—going out on a boat is probably not a practical idea, these days."

The next evening, the prevailing northwest wind—the *maestro*, it was called—was blowing hard enough to make the poles of Emeric's great pavilion tent creak, despite their heavy burden. The assembled officers carefully did not look at the two corpses swinging from them. One of those corpses was that of a purported rebel. But the other was that of a former officer in Emeric's army, the man who'd been in charge of the magazine that had been sabotaged—and there were still vacancies on the other four poles.

"His name is Hakkonsen. Erik Hakkonsen," said Emeric coolly. His men had been running around like chickens with their heads cut off since the destruction of the magazine, trying to find out who had blown it up. It gave him great satisfaction to show them that he could do what they could not.

"He's an Icelander, a Knight of the Holy Trinity. He's Prince Manfred of Brittany's personal bodyguard, so you can assume he's an excellent swordsman. He stands about six foot two, he is lean and athletic, broad-shouldered. He had fine, blond, straight hair, but it is now probably dyed black. He's wearing a short, dark Mungo cotte, a gray homespun shirt, and tawny woolen breeches. One of my agents actually sold him the clothes. He is possibly in the company of a blond woman. I want either of them. The woman will do for bait. Him, I want his head."

A guard came running in. "Sire! Sire! The camp at Patara is on fire. I can see it burning."

Emeric and his officers rushed out. In the darkness, the arc of leaping wind-driven flames stood out clearly. Some of the flames were easily thirty feet high. In their ruddy light, even from here Emeric could see the tents and the tiny stick figures of soldiers, fighting the fire.

"Get down there!" shouted the king. "That's the new shipment. That is the horses' hay!"

Cavalry commanders, particularly, left at a sprint.

Chapter 56

The remount guards had their attention on the blaze across the inlet. Stalking them was ludicrously easy, thought Erik, even in the bright moonlight. Would have been, at least, except for the horses. Horses are a lot more wary than men. Still, if the herd guards had noticed, then they put those whickers and ear flattening down to the fire-smoke.

Erik's five arquebusiers, their fire all directed on the guard tower, cut loose a moment too early.

The rest had to rush the last few yards, but surprise was still on their side. Erik didn't waste time on finesse. He ran one of the sentries through as the man was attempting to bring his pike to bear. A second blow felled another man. He half-turned to see how the rest were getting on.

In horror, he saw it was not going so well. One of the men was down. Thalia, thrusting wildly at another sentry, was nearly skewered. The guard had knocked her legs out from under her, even if he'd missed his pike stroke. Erik knew he'd never get there in time.

Panting, Giuliano did—but there were three sentries, all with pikes, facing a single pudgy swordsman.

And Erik was treated to a virtuoso display of bladesmanship.

Erik had been worried about Giuliano. Kari told him that he'd hesitated to cut throats in the magazine-guard barracks raid. Now, however, Giuliano had suddenly become transformed from a plump youth into a whiplash-fast razor. The three, prepared, ready and with a far greater reach, proved no match at all.

Guiliano administered his last coup de grace, and gently offered Thalia a hand up, as if he was at some court function.

Meanwhile, the guard tower had fallen. Erik's men were hastily opening the sheep pens that Emeric's forces had been using for their spare horses.

"Come on!" yelled Kari, already mounted, cracking a stockman's whip he'd found somewhere. "Let's move out. Let the Hungarians chase their own horses through the maquis instead of chasing us."

It had been one thing to talk, and to hate. But Giuliano had stuck to farming olives, wine and no livestock at all because he hated the thought of killing so much as a mouse. The magazine raid had been a moment of truth for him. When the fellow opened his eyes, so terrified . . .

It was perhaps fortunate that Kari had been there. Giuliano found himself replaying the blood and the horror, on top of the blood and the horror of finding his gentle doe-eyed Eleni raped and murdered. He hadn't slept much since then, without a lot of wine. Before this evening he'd been seriously considering taking a pistol and ending it all. In fact it had only been their unthinking assumption that he would go along on this expedition that had had him here at all.

He didn't know how to tell them he didn't want any more of this . . . this killing.

And then she'd fallen. He'd been close enough to hear her scream. He'd heard what she'd been through from Hakkonsen. Obviously, it was still raw in her, too. Her voice was remarkably like Eleni's.

Something inside him had snapped. He hadn't even thought about what he was doing. Years of papa's training reasserted themselves.

When he helped her to her feet she staggered. He caught her and she leaned on him briefly. He could feel her trembling and her heartbeat against him, racing, then she pushed away. "I'm sorry, master," she said, peasant-to-landowner relationships reasserting themselves. "I was just so scared."

"So was I," he said quietly.

"We'd better ride."

Most of the others had already mounted. Other guards would be coming; there was indeed no time to be feeling sorry for himself.

She must have seen the helpless look on his face. "Follow me. I used to live near here."

Giuliano, riding just behind her, wondered how a peasant girl learned to master a horse like that. There were few cavalrymen in the same league.

Up in the dark maquis near a stubby, wind-twisted Aleppo pine, she stopped and dismounted.

"What is it?"

"I just wanted to collect something. This is where Georgio and I were hiding." Her voice cracked slightly.

Giuliano decided he'd better dismount too. There was a narrow crack at the foot of the pine, that she'd slipped into. Giuliano tied his horse and, with some difficulty, squeezed in after her.

She lit a rush dip, and Giuliano could see that her eyes were brimming with tears. But she walked resolutely past the bed made up so neatly on the cave floor, past the ashes of the tiny fire. Past the two cook pots, and the oil crock. She took down a bundle of spidery net that hung from a crossbar that someone had rigged. Giuliano saw she was holding her lip between her teeth and determinedly not looking left or right. Her chin quivered slightly. She came back to the crack that was the door, turned briefly, looked at the bed, and let out a single, strangled sob. Then she put the rush dip out, and without waiting or even seeming to see Giuliano, scrambled out.

He was left alone in the darkness. He swallowed and pushed into the crack and out into the night.

She was struggling to mount with the bundle. "Can I hold that for you?" he asked, quietly.

The peasant girl seemed to see him again for the first time. "Please, master. Hold it here in the middle."

It was a fibrous bundle and surprisingly heavy. "What is it?" he asked, as he handed it up to her.

"My bird-net," she replied as he mounted.

He'd seen the peasant women casting their nets into the air to catch wild birds before. A fowling-piece of any sort was simply beyond the means of the peasantry, but with nimble fingers and a few weights they could catch feathered bounty. "What for? We have money for food."

She shrugged. "I can't fight men. I could cut their throats like animals when they were asleep. But I nearly died tonight, because I don't know how to fight. But I think a man in a net will not fight well. Then I can deal with him."

He took a deep breath. "I'll teach you. I should have taught Eleni."

"Who?"

"My wife. My beautiful, gentle wife. They killed her." It seemed very necessary to tell all of it. "They raped her first. They killed my son. My baby boy. I was away at my uncle Ambrosino's estate. Eleni doesn't," he swallowed, "didn't like him. So she and little Flavio stayed home. One of the family retainers brought me word. We rode as quickly as we could but . . ."

"Georgio and I never had a child." She paused. "You Libri d'Oro joke about the peasants always trying to save money with the priest being able to do the wedding and the christening at the same time."

Giuliano felt himself redden. He'd made the comment himself. Pregnant brides were almost the norm among the peasantry on his Ropa valley estate. "Yes. But I'm not one of the Libri d'Oro. My uncle is in the Golden Book, though."

They rode in silence, heading for the rendezvous. "But you are a landowner?"

"Yes. But my father did not approve of the Golden Book."

"And you lived on the estate and not in town. Very strange." She sounded slightly more at ease. "But you Libri d'Oro don't understand. A bride must be pregnant to prove that she can be fertile. Georgio loved me enough to marry me even though I . . . didn't fall pregnant. I had very little dowry, because my father died at sea. He married me anyway. I wanted a child. I wanted one so badly for my man. But now I am glad I didn't ever have one. This is no world for a child."

There seemed to be no reply to that. Peasant marriages, indeed even most noble marriages, had at least an element of commerce about them. It had been one of the things that had made him acceptable to Eleni's family. Thalia's must have been a rare marriage.

He decided, firmly, that by the next time this young woman went out seeking repayment for what their enemy had done, she'd be very capable of getting it. Hakkonsen had said he wanted two quick, immediate successes to draw recruits—and then they'd go to ground for a few weeks, and train properly. The Hungarians would be expecting them after this. The cavalry would recapture many of the horses—those that didn't come home by themselves, anyway—but they would be hunting horses for a while. Besides, more horse-tracks would muddle tracking operations. There would be time to train her. Maybe time enough, and recruits enough, that he would be valuable again, as a trainer, even if he couldn't slit throats.

Chapter 57

Emeric tinkled a little crystal bell. An officer appeared hastily. "I want to talk to the blond-haired one. Aldanto. Have him sent to me."

The officer of the royal guard bowed and left at a brisk run.

He was back very quickly. Alone. "Sire, he has gone out. The guards saw him walk out just after dawn. He went northwards."

"Hmm. Alone? Or with one of these Byzantine rats he is supposed to be with?"

The young officer hesitated. "Sire, he had no man with him. No woman, either. But the guards tell me he was accompanied by a yellow dog. The guard said it looked more like an overgrown jackal than a dog. An ugly yellow-toothed mangy thing. His horse tried to kill it, and Aldanto stopped him."

A yellow dog . . . The puppet-man would not have a pet. His master wouldn't allow it.

"Have the guards told about this creature. If it is seen again, have them shoot it."

After the officer left, Emeric's eyes narrowed thoughtfully. He was slowly—reluctantly—coming to the conclusion that before too long he would need to go back to Hungary and talk to his great-great-aunt, the Countess Bartoldy. His plans for Corfu were not working out as well as they should have, due to the incompetence of too many of his officers. And, what was worse, due to the delay it was becoming clear that magic would be playing more of a role in the campaign than he'd foreseen. Or wanted, even though he was a skilled sorcerer in his own right.

The problem with sorcery was that it was, ultimately, something that had no greater respect for monarchs than anyone else. That made it a risky business for someone with the name of "Emeric, King of Hungary." He hated to be beholden to his great-great-aunt any more than he needed to be, but it was just a fact that this sort of thing was Elizabeth Bartholdy's field of expertise, far more than his.

Traveling with the shaman, Aldanto was obliged to walk. No horse would tolerate the shaman within sight, and even the scent of him seemed to make them uneasy.

Being forced to walk was hard on Aldanto. It meant that muscles that had been torn by torture and forced to heal, laced with scarring, were forced into more work than they really should have had to do. He had not walked much in years before Jagiellon captured him, either. In Venice, he had traveled almost exclusively by the canals, and he had relied on someone else's muscles to propel him. His legs screamed with agony that he was not permitted to show.

Nobody was listening to his internal suffering. The puppeteer did not really understand life's prerequisites. Nor did he care. He worked his tools ruthlessly and sometimes they broke. So, driven by his master, Caesare walked on. The yellow dog walked on beside him. The shaman knew enough not to wish to go back to the place the horseflies had driven him from, and it would be Caesare who faced whatever guarded it this time.

They walked beneath the tall lianolia olives starred with tiny white flowers, past bee-busy masses of yellow broom by the dusty roadsides. Caesare trod on delicate orchid blossoms, thrust through myrtle bushes.

"The place stinks," said the shaman-dog, sneezing.

"We should be there by now, surely?"

"I would have thought so. It didn't take me that long to get back to the camp, master." The shaman looked at his paws. "We have been heading northwest for much time."

Caesare turned and looked up at the sun. He did not shield his eyes the way a normal man would. The sun was plainly heading toward rest, in the heavy hazy golden afternoon. "If this place is to the northwest, then why is the sun now on my back?"

The shaman blinked. "But . . . we have walked as straight as it is possible! I will look through the eyes of my hawks." He bent his will, using true names, names of power.

His eyes did indeed see through theirs. The ground hurtled toward him at terrific speed. The yellow dog lost its footing and sprawled—and the hawk struck the hare cleanly.

Aldanto, having stopped for the first time in many hours, fell over like a pole-axed steer.

The yellow dog staggered to its feet, calling desperately for the master to take him away. Away from the magic.

Barely five hundred yards away, Erik and Svanhild were lost in the magic. Their fingers entwined, they walked in the dell where anemones bloomed. The cicada song rose to its summer crescendo, and then as they walked closer to the holm-oaks, was stilled. An enormous orange-yellow butterfly suddenly skittered into hasty flight from the flowers in front of them.

Instinctively, Erik tensed. A tortoise stuck its head around the flower clump, regarding these invaders to its realm with a suspicious, unblinking yellow eye. Then, having correctly labeled them as moonstruck, it put its beaky face down and mumbled up a wild strawberry.

Erik found laughter and happiness, pure, easy and as sweet as the warm breeze, bubbling up within him. He picked up Svanhild in his arms and spun her round, her long golden hair flying. Round and around laughing like children together, until they fell together dizzy and still laughing, into the flowers, frightening the tortoise off his late afternoon snack. The tortoise lumbered away.

Erik held her gently now. Touched her cheek. "I love you, Svan. Will you marry me?"

For an answer, she pulled him closer.

The shaman shook himself. Spat. He behaved, for all Count Mindaug could see, just like a dog who had too closely encountered a skunk and was now trying at all costs to rid himself of even the memory, by any means.

"It too strong, master. Too strong and too . . . spread out. It has killed the slave." The shaman trickled his fingers across his drum, bringing a whisper of sound from it. It was almost as if the tattooed drum-skin sighed.

Jagiellon shook his head. "The slave just lost consciousness. I have been forgetful about feeding it."

"But master, that place." The shaman shuddered. "It eats me. I hate it. It has a dangerous magic there."

Jagiellon paused. And Mindaug hardly dared breathe. If the Grand Duke started really *thinking* about the shaman's experience, instead of being consumed by his lust for possessing Corfu's power . . .

But the dangerous moment passed. The Grand Duke shrugged heavily and said: "Yes, it is stronger than I had anticipated. Still, it seems purely defensive. And a crude sort of magic, too. Big sweeps of clumsy enchantment. Not blade-strokes of true power. We will find its cores, find them and break them to our use."

He turned to the count. "Well, Mindaug. The magic of the West is your study. What do you know of the magic of this place?"

Mindaug bowed. "Relatively little, Grand Duke. There is a mention in Angenous Pothericus of 'the rough magic of sea-girt Corcyra.' He says the place is a poor place for spell-craft. But I will search further."

"Do that."

Erik had drilled them all since early morning. He'd worked on simple, basic things: fitness, strength, how to fall. Thalia rubbed her arm reflexively. She'd always thought falling was something you could do without any lessons. But Erik believed "fall" was just the first part of "get up, fast, and unhurt." The Icelander was . . . odd.

Like all peasant women, Thalia had worked since she could walk. She'd been privately disappointed when Erik had said he was "going to get them fit first" before he taught them to fight. Getting fit was what the young master from the Ropa valley estate needed. The recruits called him *Loukoúmia*—slightly more warily, though, now that some of them had seen him use a sword.

He needed this fitness; she only needed to know which end of a sword cut, how to hold it, how to use it.

Well, Giuliano had struggled in this "fitness" regime; he was red-faced and panting. But so, to her surprise, was she. Peasants work, but they don't do so at the run. They don't waste strength. They conserve it so that they can work all day. Thalia found out that according to the Icelander's standards, she and Giuliano were equally unfit.

When he finally let them rest, Thalia sought out a patch of shade, and flopped down in it, too tired to think.

To her surprise the plump young man came over to where she lay in the shade of the myrtle bushes. He had two daggers in his hand. "I promised to teach you blade-craft," he said.

He was still red-faced and sweating. His fine linen shirt was so wet it stuck to him. And here he was wanting to teach her how to use a knife. A knife, not a sword. A knife was a tool you cut up food with. She didn't need to be taught how to use that! She shook her head. "You need to rest and I need to rest. You can show me later."

He took her arm and pulled her up. "Now. While you are tired. What you learn to do now you will do best, with least wasted effort. Trust me. My father used to do it this way, and he was the best swordmaster in Venice."

She felt the knife edge. It was razor keen. "But . . . these are sharp. Dangerous."

"Right. And those who are going to try to kill you are not going to use blunt knives. Now. Try to stab me. Not like that! Hold it like this. Now. Try again."

He was a very good and patient teacher. And, she had to acknowledge, a knife did not just have to be a tool you cut up food with. This *Loukoúmia* was plump, but he wasn't just sweet.

Erik walked across to the stream where he'd arranged to meet Svanhild. It ran through a glade quite unlike the rocky harshness where he was training the recruits of his guerrilla unit. This small oasis of fertility was green and soft and cool under the relentless sun and limitless blue skies of the Ionian islands. Svan was, as usual when she was waiting for him, plaiting things. Her long fingers moved steadily, gracefully, almost magically.

Often as not, when they were in camp, or almost anywhere else, she plaited practical things—bowstrings, the kind of twine that Thalia would knot into bird-nets, even rope. Here, she always plaited flowers.

At the moment she was making a chaplet of daisies. Not the mere simple twist that had satisfied lovers for time immemorial, but a complex thing. When she saw him she dropped it and ran to him. His arms were full of the softness and roundness of her. He led her back to where she'd been sitting, and picked up the daisy confection. "Come, darling Svan. Finish it for me."

"I'd rather hold your hand."

He smiled. For some reason, whenever he was here, all the urgency to get things done ran out of him. Well, for an hour or two—why not? "That's a persuasive argument. But I don't want to see something less than perfect on your golden hair."

She dimpled at him, finished it off with a few deft twists and presented it to him. "There."

He set it gently on her head and leaned in close to kiss her cheek. She pulled him closer, and changed what had been planned as a chaste kiss into something far more volcanic.

"I . . . ah, think we'd better stop. One of the recruits might come up this way."

She giggled. "I'm sure they're all too tired to move. Isn't that what you intended?"

Erik blushed. "Tactics," he mumbled.

From the shadows of a Judas tree, a satyr watched approvingly. This was what this place was intended for, after all.

PART VIII
July, 1539 A.D.

Chapter 58

Benito entered the city gates of Ferrara unobtrusively. Fourteen days of riding had improved his skill at staying in the saddle, if not his liking for horses.

The mare he'd bought in Livorno had been guaranteed as "quiet." The horse-seller had omitted words like "old" and "destined for glue-making, very soon." Benito, being fairly ignorant of horses, realized he'd probably been gulled. The horse-seller said the mare was very even-paced. That sounded good to Benito. He'd discovered it meant "moves at one speed—a slow walk." Still, it did carry him without his ending in a ditch. But he was very glad to abandon the beast at a hostelry near the gate and proceed on foot.

He made his way toward the castle, thinking how best to get access to his grandfather. He could simply go and ask, announcing his name. That should be enough to get him an audience at least. But for some reason he was reluctant to spread his identity around.

He was deep in thought when someone took him gently by the arm and began leading him into a shop. Benito was, by nature and background, wary. He hadn't even seen this fellow approach. The man was the definition of nondescript. Middle-aged, mousy and plainly dressed. "Good day, Milord Benito Valdosta. Step this way, will you. Come and admire the knives on display here."

Benito tensed. This man knew him. An enemy? The Milanese and Montagnard cause had been severely dented when the assault on Venice last year failed, but they were still a power. They could be resurging. And heaven knew, they wanted Benito Valdosta's head. "Who are you?" Benito asked, forcing himself to remain calm.

"One of your grandfather's emissaries. He's away right now, by the way. In Verona. A matter of a treaty."

"With the Scaligers? But they're our enemies."

The man shrugged. Benito recognized the gesture. He had indeed seen this man before, but until he'd seen that shrug, he'd been less than certain about it. "In the politics of princes, expediency is the key. At the moment, Verona leans away from Milan—and in uncertain times like these we need allies, even unsavory ones like the Scaligers."

Benito made a show of examining a blade. "What's uncertain? I thought things had stabilized nicely after the Holy Roman Emperor let it be known that Venice was his friend in the region, if not formally an ally. Or isn't this true any more, Signor Bartelozzi?" He said it in a tone that would suggest the merits of a so-so blade being discussed.

Antimo Bartelozzi allowed him a flicker of a smile. "Not since the Holy Roman Emperor fell suddenly and very seriously ill. A problem with his heart, they say. Now, I think we will part ways and you will go to a nearby inn, just up the road a ways. The Mandoril, it's called. The food's good, and your follower can be dealt with. I'll be there to talk to you later."

Walking to the inn near the gate, Benito looked for followers. Now that he was aware of it, he spotted the fellow fairly easily. He was good to a Caesare-fit sort of level. It took him some time to spot the second one, Bartelozzi's man, who was even better at it.

Knowing Bartelozzi's reputation, Benito made no attempt to shake them off. That problem would soon be solved. He went to the Mandoril, asked for a room and some dinner. After washing up, he went down to the tavern's main room and enjoyed a solitary supper of *risotto con finocchi* and a bottle of Venegazzù from Treviso. He reveled in the pleasure of familiar, simple, northern food again.

When he returned to his room, Antimo Bartelozzi was sitting there, waiting.

"The fellow marking you is following someone out on the road to Venice. He won't be returning," said the spymaster with grim certitude. "Now. What brings you to Ferrara, Milord Benito Valdosta? Your grandfather believes you to be in Corfu."

Antimo Bartelozzi was, Benito knew, the operative his grandfather used for family business. The best and most trusted; an exemplary assassin, too.

"I'm here *because* of Corfu. The island has been invaded. I've just come from there—via Sicily and the west coast of Italy—because the Byzantines and Dalmatian pirates are blockading the Adriatic."

Although Bartelozzi was not likely to let fall any expressions that might betray his feelings or his thoughts, his eyes did narrow, just a trifle. "Byzantium has attacked Venetian possessions? Alexius must be further gone into debauchery than we had thought. But he has been having dealing with emissaries out of Odessa."

"He's allied himself with Emeric of Hungary."

Bartelozzi showed no surprise. "We have had reports of emissaries going to and fro. But we assumed that it was for mutual cooperation against Iskander Beg. The mountain chief controls quite some part of Epirus that Alexius lays nominal claim to." Bartelozzi's voice grew very dry. "The duke said that if Alexius was fool enough to prefer Emeric for a neighbor to Iskander Beg he deserved what he would undoubtedly get. Giving Emeric a foothold on Corfu is sheer insanity. But we have suspected for some time that Alexius is unwell in the head."

"Well, Emeric is there all right. You can see his pavilion from the Citadel. All gold and crimson. His Magyar are pretty recognizable too." Benito sucked his teeth. "I've been instructed to relay this to the Imperial embassy in Venice. But if there is someone I could speak to here, it might save days."

"Unfortunately *Ritter* Von Augsberg has gone with the duke to Verona. All of Italy north of Naples has been in something of a turmoil since word came that the Emperor has fallen gravely ill. For all that many people disliked him—his policies, if not the man himself—the truth is that Charles Fredrik has been a pillar of stability in Europe for decades. If he dies . . ."

Bartelozzi shook his head. "I will of course prepare a full report for your grandfather, but I think the best would be for you to proceed with all speed to Venice. In the last two weeks, Doge Dorma and the Imperial embassy appear to have had a cooling of their former warm relations. The news of Charles Fredrik's failing health has allowed all sorts of rumors to spread. We are in for some turbulent times, and the Montagnards of Milan are sensing the change. That was one of their men who followed you. I think you should travel onward to Venice somewhat more circumspectly."

Benito swallowed a sense of urgency. "I don't care how I travel, so long as it is not by horse. I was thinking of a passage on one of the Po barges. Would that be circumspect enough?"

"Passengers will be watched. But as one of the crew of a cargo vessel, excellent. You may leave it to me, milor'."

Antimo took a long bundle out from under the bed. "The duke wanted to give this to you himself. But, I think he will forgive me for doing so. He has always said that expediency is more important than sentiment, in politics." He handed Benito the bundle. "It is your father's sword. Your grandfather had Marco De Viacastan repair it. Of course, being De Viacastan, he did a bit more than that."

Of all the swordsmiths in Ferrara, the Spaniard was rated the best, by far. His blades were for generals, princes and kings—and wealthy ones, at that. "I'm honored."

Antimo smiled in his wintry fashion. "It was one of his weapons in the first place. I know your grandfather wanted to reforge it himself, but he did not let sentiment stand in the way of practicality. He gave it to the man who could do the best job of it. But he took a hand in the work, so that any virtue in the Dell'este tradition might pass to this blade. You may need it. The Wolf of the North has been south lately, to the Kingdom of Naples."

Benito savored a moment of knowing more than a man who was plainly a master of his trade. "Actually, he's been further. He went to Jerusalem. I crossed his path, in a manner of speaking." And he related the story of the pilgrim medal.

An unholy glint lit up in the spymaster's eyes. "Not for a moment will he believe you were not stalking his footsteps. Interesting. This may prove useful to us."

Benito unwrapped the hilt first. It had been refurbished with tassels of Ferrara crimson.

Antimo saw Benito fondle them. "At your grandfather's express order. When you carry this blade openly . . . he wants everyone to know you are under his hand."

The tassels were worth a great deal more than mere silk to Benito. "The Fox's colors . . . on the Wolf's sword . . ." he mused. "I've had my birth thrown at me here, Antimo."

The spymaster's smile grew more wintry still. "This sword will throw it at your enemies instead. Reputation is a weapon, and wars are won and lost on reputations. Let them see that. Let them know fear."

Benito nodded, and continued to peel away the swaddling to reveal the sheathed blade. He drew it out. The steel trapped and shivered the candlelight into the myriad oyster-shell folds in the steel. "Saints! It's beautiful."

Bartelozzi nodded, his eyes glinting with appreciation. "And deadly. There is more than just fine craftsmanship in that blade, however. It has been a-journeying on its own, you see. Your grandfather took it to Rome. He said it was time the sword of the Wolf was rededicated to more wholesome purposes. I know only that it was thrice blessed."

Benito looked at the sword, so graceful, so deadly, almost hypnotized by it. It was no dress-sword with gilt and filigree. From the sharkskin hilt to the tip, it was a weapon. Benito picked it up. The balance was perfect. It felt like an extension of his arm.

"A killer's weapon."

Antimo shrugged. "A tool. A spade can be a killer's weapon too. A sword used for ill is an evil thing, a thing of oppression. But always remember there are also evil things that need killing."

Benito grinned. "You know, Eneko Lopez said something of the sort. Why is it that people are always preaching to me? Is it something about my face?"

Antimo Bartelozzi looked long and hard at him, as unblinkingly as a cat. Eventually he nodded. "Yes."

By morning, Benito was a deck-hand on a downstream-heading barge, piled full of hides. The smell was quite enough to discourage anyone examining its crew too closely. It could have been worse, though. They passed downwind of one laden with onions.

Benito Valdosta returned to Venice without pomp or ceremony, but with a great deal of bouquet. Some of the hides were definitely not well cured. Normally one got used to a smell, and stopped noticing it, but it had been hot and the bright Italian sun had ripened this one past ignoring. Even the familiar canal reek seemed positively perfumelike after that. And the sight of Venice stirred him. How grand! How . . .

Small.

That came as a shock. He stared, calculated, examined, trying to work out what had happened. The buildings were no smaller. Nor the canals. Benito realized abruptly that what had changed was himself. He felt a pang for the old Venice. The Venice that had been his whole world.

Hopping off the barge at the Fondamenta Zattere Ponto Lungo, Benito looked about for a familiar face, especially among the gondoliers. He didn't want to waste time.

He spotted someone. Carlo Zenetti was not a man Benito knew that well, but at least he knew him. He climbed down into the gondola.

Zenetti nearly dropped his oar. "Valdosta! Benito Valdosta! Saints! What are you doing here? We all thought you'd been sent to Corfu." It was plain that however well his disguise might have worked elsewhere, here among the *popula minuti* of Venice they knew the face of their prodigal.

Benito put down the small hide roll he'd used to camouflage the sword. Doing so gave him a moment to think. The last thing he wanted to do was start a panic on the canals of Venice. And he knew the speed at which gossip ran on those canals. It wouldn't do to have the news of Corfu's invasion arrive with a clamor of people in the Piazza San Marco before he'd even gotten to see Petro.

"I'm traveling on the quiet, Carlo. Let's get out of here before someone else recognizes me. Please."

"Sure." The gondolier cast loose. "But I reckon you're chasing a lost cause," he said with a grin. "I'm sure before Vespers tonight, good men will already be locking their daughters up. Where can I take you to?"

"The Doge's palace, I suppose."

Afterwards, Benito came to regret that decision. But at the time it seemed like a sensible one. After all, he had urgent matters to attend to there. Best discharge his duty as soon as possible, before he went looking for Marco.

"So how are things in Venice?" he asked idly. Might as well pick up on the news before he was having his news demanded of him. Perhaps his war tidings had already gotten here.

It appeared not, by the gondolier's reply. "Trade's a bit slow.

Plenty still coming in from the north. But nothing much recently from the Adriatic side."

Well, that was hardly surprising. He fished further. "No wars to speak of? Is the Philippo Maria of Milan finally getting to accept that the Venetian Republic is here to stay?"

"I reckon the Milanese might start one soon," said Carlo, grimly. "They're used to being dominant."

"They'll *try* again," said Benito with a grin. "And get the same again."

Benito climbed ashore at the Piazza San Marco. The great winged lion of Venice gazed sternly down from its pedestal. Benito gave the statue a fond wave, and turned to the palace with its Swiss mercenary guards.

Benito's chest swelled a bit. It had been a tough task, but he'd done it, and here he was, alive and undetected. Emeric would pay for his sneak attack on Venice. He walked up the shallow steps to the guard commander. "I need to see Doge Dorma on a matter of extreme urgency."

The guard commander was not one of the *populi minuta* of Venice. He was from a small village in the Alps. He plainly did not know this scruffy barefoot youth with a dirty face and an impudent grin. "And then you want to see the Grand Metropolitan, I suppose. Go on. Get off the stairs before I have my men throw you off. The Doge doesn't see common sailors. Not even on matters of *extreme urgency*."

Benito sighed. "I'm in disguise, you ass. I'm Benito Valdosta. The Doge's ward."

Never call an officer an ass in front of his men, even if he is one. The man swung the butt of his pike in an arc designed to bring it into contact with Benito's crotch. Benito jumped back. Unfortunately the hide-roll under his arm slipped in the process. The contents fell to the steps.

"A concealed weapon! Seize him, boys!"

Benito found himself again in a position he was all-too-familiar with: being sat on by a number of large representatives of the forces of law and order. Knowing that resistance—normally the only enjoyable part of the exercise—would only make things worse, Benito did his best not to. Very shortly he was being led down to the cells, his Shetland knife and the reforged sword of the Wolf of the North seized for evidence.

According to the charge list, he'd been clumsily attempting to assassinate the Doge before being arrested by alert guards.

"Look. Can I just get a message either to Marco Valdosta or Petro Dorma?" pleaded Benito. "This is a misunderstanding. Corfu has been invaded."

Snorts of laughter came from the guards and jailers. "It's not a dungeon that this one will end up in. He's for the madhouse." The jailors were new, both of them. No one recognized him.

Benito realized it was hopeless. Well, he'd be hauled up in front of the Justices shortly. Then they'd laugh on the other side of their faces.

By late that afternoon, he realized that "shortly" was a word that applied to the cases of the *Case Vecchie*. For a common—and mad—felon, the period before being charged and sentenced could be a long one.

It was at the changing of the guard at nightfall that Benito thought his luck had finally changed. The new guard coming on duty took one look at him and swore. "Lord and Saint Mark! What are you doing here, Valdosta?"

Benito recognized the man as one of those who'd overseen his previous stay in the dungeons. "Thank goodness somebody recognizes me. Please tell them who I am and get me the hell out of here. I've rushed to get news here—only to find myself put in jail by these . . . people."

The day-warder looked at his relief and at the prisoner. And then back at the relief. "You know this young man?" he asked his coworker, warily.

The night-warder nodded. "He's Benito Valdosta. We had him in here just after the big Valdosta-Montescue wedding."

The day-warder took a deep breath. "You mean the one who . . . on the Rialto Bridge?"

The night-warder chuckled. "That's him. What's he up for this time?"

"Attempted assassination of the Doge. Assaulting members of the Swiss Guard."

"Saints!" The warder shook his head in amazement. "Couldn't you just have stuck to public indecency, young Valdosta?"

Benito sighed. "It's a complete misunderstanding. I asked to be taken to see the Doge, as I have important news for him. I've been traveling in disguise from Corfu. The matter is urgent so I came straight here still dressed as a seaman. And then that *testa di cazzo* of a guard commander decided I was an assassin. As if I'm going to march up to the Swiss Guards on the steps and demand to be taken to the guy I want to kill! The 'concealed weapon' they're going on about is a rapier as you might see on the hip of any *Casa Vecchie* gentleman walking into the Doge's Palace. It's my father's sword, sent by the Doge to be repaired in Ferrara. I picked it up there."

"But, signor. You claimed to have come from Corfu."

"I *did*. I came around Italy and across the Apennines, because the Adriatic is blockaded. I came through Ferrara as a result, and tried to see my grandfather. I didn't, because he is in Verona, but I got my sword. I couldn't put it on my hip, as I would normally, because a sailor wandering around with a sword would be picked up by the Schiopettieri. So instead I got thrown in jail by some officious idiots who won't even believe who I am. Now can you get me out of here?"

The warders looked at each other. And then at Benito. At last the day-warder said: "No, Signor. But we can take you to one of the Justices. He can order you freed."

Benito sighed at the bureaucratic pettiness of it all. "Well, let's do that."

"But Milord Valdosta . . . they have all gone home."

Benito closed his eyes, begging for patience. "Then get one of them back here. Please. Or at the very least send for my brother Marco. We need to start preparing to break the siege on Corfu, and every day more people will die. The Citadel is secure, but the Hungarians are raping the country."

The night-warder pulled a face. "But, signor. Your brother Marco . . . has gone to Verona."

Benito felt like pulling his hair out. "And I suppose his wife has gone too?

The jailor nodded.

"Well, can you get me one of the Justices? Please. I know. They've gone home. But this is urgent."

The night-warder nodded. "I will go and ask the chief night-warder."

He returned a little while later. "I am very sorry, signor. The chief says no. It is not in the rules."

"*Testa di cazzo!* Rules! I'll have his guts for a skipping-rope, when

I get out of here," said Benito savagely. He shook the bars in frustration. And had an inspiration. "Listen. Can I at least see a priest?"

The warder nodded. "Brother Umbriel comes to see the prisoners every evening anyway."

"I need to see someone specific. Either Brother Mascoli of St. Raphaella or Sister Evangelina of St. Hypatia di Hagia Sophia."

The night-warder looked thoughtful. "You could ask Brother Umbriel. He is Hypatian."

And Benito had to content himself with that.

Brother Umbriel, when he came, proved to be willing to help. "Benito Valdosta needing to see Evangelina or Mascoli . . . on a matter of some urgency concerning Eneko Lopez." He smiled. "You certainly know how to inflame a poor Sibling's curiosity, don't you? Very well, my son. I will interrupt my work and go to old Mascoli now."

Brother Mascoli came a few minutes later. "Ah. Benito Valdosta. You are very unlike your brother! You wish to see me in connection with Eneko Lopez. I'm afraid Eneko has gone to Holy Jerusalem . . ."

"He's on Corfu. I'm afraid Brother Umbriel got the wrong end of the stick. I have messages from Eneko Lopez, too. For the Grand Metropolitan—and you."

Mascoli raised his eyebrows. "Which are?"

"What Eneko wanted me to tell you is that they have hit magical problems on Corfu, where they are besieged. He says that the archangel Uriel, the guardian of the creatures of the earth, cannot be raised. They are unable to raise wards. There appears to be some malign force preventing them from contact by scrying with other sacred magicians. He wants help from the Church. He wants help from Rome."

Mascoli gnawed his knuckle thoughtfully. "Well, these things can be confirmed. I will go now to Sister Evangelina. The Siblings will attempt to contact Eneko magically. And should we fail, we will try Rome. There are magical ways of establishing authenticity."

"Great. At least I will have succeeded in part of my mission," said Benito.

Mascoli looked at the bars. "I'm afraid I don't know if I can get you out of here, my son. I'll talk to Evangelina, and perhaps we can approach the Patriarch Michael . . ."

Benito yawned. "Don't worry about it. The Justices can spring me in the morning. I suppose there is not much that could be done tonight anyway."

Chapter 59

Odd. Unsettled. That was how Katerina would have described this meeting in Verona. Petro had insisted that Marco come with him, along with part of the Venetian Council of Ten. Marco had not wanted to go, but had been persuaded against his better judgment because of all of the strange and contradictory rumors that were now spreading about the likely intentions of the Holy Roman Emperor should Charles Fredrik die. More of these were coming out now that the meeting was in full session—and it occurred to her that if their Great Enemy wanted to eliminate most of the thorns in his side in one swoop, he would have had only to arrange for a human agent to pack the cellar of the palace in which they were meeting with gunpowder...

Which might explain who was spreading all these rumors, and why.

Fortunately, that seemed to have occurred to more than one of their allies as well; you couldn't move without bumping into a very alert-looking guard.

She couldn't make heads or tails of it. Some rumors had it that Prince Manfred had open designs on Corfu, and after that outpost, presumably Venice as well. Others claimed that he had quarreled with his uncle the Emperor over the *Emperor's* designs on Venice. Some said Manfred had quarreled with his cousin Conrad, the heir presumptive, over the same thing—with half the rumors ascribing evil designs on Venice to Manfred; the other half, to Conrad. Still others swore that nothing of the sort had happened, that, in fact, Manfred had never left Corfu and that so far as intelligence *out* of Corfu was concerned, there wasn't any.

Certainly ships were not coming from that direction, which was . . . odd.

"Tension" was not even close to describing what the atmosphere in this room was like.

And Marco was in knots. He'd told Kat yesterday that he knew there was something terribly, horribly wrong, but he was too far from the Lion to tell what it was, and too far from the Lion's protection to dare try to scry for it, either. Finally he'd gone out last night in search of the largest Hypatian establishment in Verona to ask them to find out what they could for him.

But if anything, this morning he was in worse case. Even the Old Fox had been forced to take notice.

"What's wrong? You look like you've been drinking the water out of your own canals." The tension underlying his words made the attempted jest fall flat.

Marco shook his head. "There's something wrong about all this— these rumors aren't spreading accidentally—and there's still more wrong back home—"

At just that moment, there was a commotion at the door. A burly man who looked more warrior than Hypatian Sibling shoved his way inside.

"Brother Ancetti!" Marco called, recognition and welcome in his voice, forestalling the guards who were going to shove the Sibling back outside again.

The Sibling bowed, in a curt manner. "Marco Valdosta, I have that word from Venice that you asked me for, and your instincts were correct," he said grimly. "Only this morning I have news from Sibling Mascoli, and from the Grand Metropolitan as well, and I believe it is something that everyone at this council needs to hear."

The Sibling proceeded to relate a tale that, had it not been vouched for by the most powerful Christian magician in Verona and, by his word, verified by the Grand Metropolitan's own magicians in Rome, would have sounded more incredible than any of the tales of Manfred of Brittany's supposed treachery.

Stunned silence greeted most of it, until the priest came to the end—and the fact that Benito Valdosta was at that very moment on trial for treason, and possibly worse.

Three men rose from the table at an instant, all three roaring the same incredulous word.

"*What?*"

It was Marco who recovered first. "Horses," he said decisively, looking at Petro. "Fast ones."

"Can't you—"

Marco shook his head. "The Lion's powers only hold within the boundaries of Venice. Once I reach the boundaries—then I can call on him, but not before."

Petro nodded, though it was clear to Kat that the Old Fox was utterly baffled. "Right, then. You and that hideous bodyguard of yours, on my bay and Giovanni's roan. We'll come behind you as fast as our horses can manage."

Marco didn't waste a word, and spared not more than a glance at Kat—not that she was going to complain, not when Benito might find himself facing execution before the sun set! He ran out the door, calling to his scarred shadow, Bespi, that strange, silent man with the haunted eyes.

And it was left to Petro and her to explain, as well as they could, what that abbreviated conversation had been about.

But *they* did it on the trot, because it was altogether possible that even Marco and the Lion would not be enough to do more than delay things until the Doge himself arrived.

Having his identity known did move Benito's case up the slate to head the morning list. Which was something positive . . . Benito thought. For the first moment. Until he saw the facial expression of the Justice assigned to the case. It would have curdled vinegar, never mind milk.

"What are the charges?"

"It's a misunderstanding," said Benito.

The Justice turned grimly to look at him. "Speak when you're permitted to. The clerk will now read the charges."

The clerk did so. Benito had in the meantime been struggling to place the sour face in front of him. When he did, he realized that his troubles almost certainly weren't over. The man was a Capuletti. A cousin of the man he was supposed to have murdered. A house that had fallen from grace along with Ricardo Brunelli. A man, by the looks of him, who held grudges.

The Justice turned to stare at Benito. "Are you Benito Valdosta?"

Benito nodded. "Yes."

The Justice looked at his clerk. "You may prefix that list with the breaking of exile. It is a charge which carries the maximum penalty."

"But I came to bring warning . . ."

"*Silence!*" thundered the Justice. He beckoned to the two Schiopettieri. "If the prisoner speaks without my express orders again, you will silence him. And Valdosta, if you speak out of turn again, I'll have you gagged. Is that clear?"

Benito said nothing. He knew if he did he'd explode. Fury was building up in him. And, because the jailors had been convinced by now that this was all a mistake . . . they hadn't shackled him when they'd sent him up.

"I said: Is that clear?"

Benito said nothing.

"The prisoner will answer or be held in contempt of the court. Is this clear?"

Benito leaned forward, gauging the distance to the door. "If I say something you'll gag me. If I don't say anything you'll hold me in contempt. This is a farce."

"Add contempt of court to the charge list. Now. We have the prisoner's own admission that he is Benito Valdosta, a person proscribed from the city and environs of Venice. The second charge relates to an attempt to carry a concealed weapon into the Doge's palace. Is that the weapon in question?"

"It is, Your Honor," said the reedy-voiced clerk. He drew the rapier from the scabbard and placed it on the desk. "It was hidden inside a roll of cowhide, your honor."

"Doubtless he wanted to avenge himself for being banished. And now to the assault charges. Call the first witne—"

Benito jumped up onto the rails of the dock that held him, and then feinted as if to leap for the doorway. Instead he sprang out into the room, knocked aside the little clerk and seized the rapier.

And Justice Capuletti. The man gave a terrified squeak as the blade touched his throat.

"Back off or I'll kill him," said Benito to the two Schiopettieri assigned to the court.

They looked doubtfully at each other. The Swiss mercenary guard commander who had been about to be first witness intervened. "Do what he says. That man is a professional, boys. He'll kill the

Justice and chop you into dogmeat if you try and rush him. And if you try to shoot him you'll as likely kill the Justice."

"Listen to the man. This sword—you all see it? It's the sword of my father, The Wolf of the North. Do you want me to prove I can use it just as well as he could? If you do, just push me. I've come a few hundred leagues, by sea, foot, and bedamned horse, and nearly been drowned, caught or killed a couple of times to bring word about the attack on Corfu. I'm not going to be stopped by some small-minded petty bureaucrat. Now, if you do things my way, we can clear up this little misunderstanding and no one needs to get hurt. Isn't that so, Justice?"

The man squirmed. "Yes. Just do what he says. You can go free Valdosta. I . . . I meant no harm. Just let me go."

"And I mean no harm either. I'll let you go just as soon as I've had my say. Now someone can go and fetch Petro Dorma. Then if it's all the same to you I'll go back into exile. I've discovered just how much I hate the pettifogging bureaucracy of this place."

One of the Schiopettieri cleared his throat nervously. "Signor Valdosta. The Doge has gone to Verona."

Benito sighed and raised his eyes briefly to heaven. Very briefly. "Why don't we just move the whole town there? Very well . . . Is Lodovico Montescue in Venice?"

The two Schiopettieri hastily consulted. "We think so, signor. We have not heard anything about him going."

Benito grinned. Lodovico Montescue might be old, but he'd do just fine. He was influential enough to get things moving. And he and Benito saw eye to eye.

"Have him fetched. You." He pointed to one of the Schiopettieri. "Go. And don't even think of bringing anyone but Montescue back here. If you let me talk to Lodovico, no one gets hurt. If you bring a bunch of Schioppies charging in here, I'll cut this Capuletti's throat first, and then see how many more of you the sword can bring down before I die. "

Wide-eyed, the Schiopettieri nodded. And went with a degree of speed Benito was sure his plump body hadn't managed for many a year.

"Now," said Benito, looking at the tableaux of waxworklike people in the chamber, "the Swiss gentleman with common sense, if you wouldn't mind bolting that door. I've come a long way to bring this story to Venice, and I'd hate to be interrupted while I'm telling it. Also, if something goes wrong and I get killed I'd hate to have failed to bring this warning after all this. Clerk, you will write all of this down."

The small clerk nodded hastily.

"Right. I won't bother with things you already know about, such as when we left Venice. As our ships were approaching Corfu, we were attacked by two fleets of vessels, Narenta galliots and Byzantine carracks . . ."

He led them through a brief synopsis of the landing in besieged Corfu and his escape from the citadel and his adventures on the way here.

At the end he prodded Justice Capuletti in the ribs. "I have done my best to serve the interest of the Republic. Yes, I have broken my banishment to do this. Once my warning has been heard I am willing for the Chief Justice of the Republic to pass appropriate sentence. I just wonder whether this man's actions were prompted by malice and a desire for revenge against the *Casa* Valdosta, or whether he is an agent of King Emeric's attempting to silence me. I'll leave that for the court to decide, too."

The Swiss mercenary cleared his throat. "It's something of my fault you're here, milord. I made an error of judgment. Apologies."

Benito grinned wryly. "We all make mistakes, soldier. Some of us have the balls to admit it. No hard feelings. I was fairly stupid in my approach."

The mercenary looked at the door and scratched his chin. "In my professional opinion, Signor Valdosta, we ought to put a few of these benches across the door, and you should move across to that corner, away from the direct line of fire. If you don't mind, I'll ask these lads to give me a hand." He jerked a thumb at the Schiopettieri and the clerk.

The Schiopettieri nodded. "Good idea, signor."

The clerk stood up nervously. "Signor Valdosta . . . couldn't we just end all of this now? Now that Justice Capuletti has heard the reasons he understands what you were doing and why. I certainly think we could end this unpleasantness now."

Benito turned the Justice's head by his forelock. "Well, Capuletti?"

"Ah . . . yes. Of course. Just let me go."

Benito shrugged. "Very well." He let go of the Justice's pinioned arm. The Justice staggered forward.

And ran for the door. The clerk attempted to stop him and was floored by a flailing fist. But the Schiopettieri stepped in front of the door, his weapon in hand.

"Shoot him! I'm free now! Shoot him!" shrieked the Justice.

The Schiopettieri raised his piece . . . and knocked the Justice to the floor with it.

"You better come and grab him, Signor Valdosta," said the Schiopettieri, hauling the bloody-faced Justice to his feet. "Here. Hold him in front of you. They're battering at the door."

Benito held the half-limp Justice in front of him.

At this point the upper half of the door broke.

"Back. Back off or he gets it," yelled Benito.

"Just what in the name of heaven is going on here?"

The voice was old, cracking slightly on the upper registers. But Lodovico Montescue's voice was still strong enough to stop everyone in their tracks.

Lodovico stumped forward. Reached over the gap and opened the latch. "Well, Benito Valdosta. What is going on around here? What are you doing in those clothes? Did you pawn your boots for drink?"

It was like olive oil on wind-riffled water.

"I've just brought news that Corfu is under siege. It's blockaded, so I had to travel in disguise. And I'd kill for a bottle of good Veneto Soave, never mind pawn my boots."

"Siege, eh. Who?"

"Emeric of Hungary, together with the Byzantines."

"The bastards!" He turned to the Schiopettieri officer accompanying him. "The Marangona must be rung. So must the Campanile of San Marco's bells. We're at war. Have some of your men summon all of the Council of Ten that have not accompanied the Doge to Verona. And call in the Senate."

The old man took a look at the Justice. "Well, no one's allowed to even give you a cup of Soave for killing Venetian Justices, much though some of them might like to. So you might as well let him go."

"With pleasure. All I wanted to do was tell the Republic that we are at war. This one—who is either a traitor or a fool—wanted to stop me. I haven't harmed him."

Lodovico looked at the clerk on the floor. "And that one?"

The clerk sat up, looking embarrassed. "I just thought I'd stay on the floor for a while, milord."

Lodovico snorted. "Probably a good idea with all these guns. Let's uncock those weapons, gentlemen. And Benito . . . *are* you going to let him go?"

"Certainly." Benito pushed him away.

Justice Capuletti staggered free. "Shoot him!" he shouted.

"Have you lost your mind, Justice?" snapped Lodovico, interspersing his powerful old body between Benito and the Schiopettieri. "Go and get that cut cleaned up, and have a glass of wine. You're overwrought. You'd better hope you're overwrought. If you're not, what you keep trying to do is treasonous."

He turned around calmly to face Benito, presenting his back to several half-raised firearms in a show of the bravura that had once made him the talk of Venice. "Do you mind sheathing your sword, young Benito? It causes unease."

The bells of the Campanile of San Marco began to peal, calling the people to the piazza. Benito knew that whatever happened to him now—and despite Lodovico's calm, Benito knew he was still in deep trouble—he had succeeded. Venice would go to the rescue of Corfu and Prince Manfred. He took a deep breath, allowing some of the tension to ease from his shoulders. And Maria and baby Alessia would not have to face the danger and privations of a siege. He calmly nicked his forearm—the blade must be blooded before it was put up—and put the blade back into its sheath. Then, hung that on the sash he had for a belt.

Chapter 60

Only seven of the Doge's Council of Ten were in Venice and only five were in the Doge's palace. On their way to the great chamber where the Senate met, they were accosted by a functionary, who quietly escorted them into a small salon. Council membership was secret and anonymous; it rotated every three years with different members of the *Case Vecchie* selected through a complex process to serve. Benito was not surprised to see that the five assembled were wearing carnival masks. After all, their anonymity had to be guarded.

The military questions were terse, pointed and incisive.

"Tell us what force attacks the Citadel."

"We estimate at between ten and fifteen thousand. Croat light cavalry, Magyar heavy cavalry, Slav pikemen mostly. From what we could see."

"What cannon did they have?"

Benito scratched his chin. "Well, most of the enemy cannon were not ashore and deployed when I escaped. That was how we were able to effect a landing the previous day."

"How do you assess the Citadel's state of readiness for siege?"

"Sir, it is both good and bad. Provisions seemed adequate by what the captain-general said. But the fortresses were under-manned. The Citadel has nine hundred and fifty and the fortress on Vidos a further hundred and ninety. There were very few cavalry. In the region of fifty, perhaps. Of course, we added to that a bit."

"Well, that tallies with the known facts anyway," said one of the men. A portly one, that Benito was almost sure was Lodovico's friend Admiral Dourso under that mask.

"This will still have to be thoroughly investigated," said another sourly. "And now, thanks to the furor you've stirred up, Montescue, investigated in the full Senate and not in private. They're clamoring for news in the piazza and in the great hall."

Lodovico smiled wryly. "I've never really approved of the secrecy of the Council of Ten's doings anyway. Best to have this out in the open. I think there is less room for deception there. Come, boy. Let us go and face them."

The huge hall was crowded. Benito found himself looking at a number of expectant, worried faces. The Venice rumor mill was already working.

"Why are the bells being rung?" demanded one elegant *Case Vecchie* gentleman in the foreground. "Are we at war?" The hubbub of questions coming from the hundred and twenty members of the Senate—who, with all the other functionaries of state, had multiplied amazingly—was overwhelming. This many despite the short time? It was frightening. There must have been at least three hundred people there. Benito took a deep breath. It would probably be the great Council of a thousand five hundred members next . . .

A very badly played trumpet blast stilled the crowd.

"*Quiet!*" Lodovico returned the trumpet to an indignant young herald. "Valdosta can't be heard above this racket. First he will speak. Then I will allow questions. At *my* discretion."

Benito cleared his throat in the hush. "First, I am here to bring news. A Venetian possession, the Island of Corfu, has been invaded. The Straits of Otranto have been blockaded by Byzantine and Dalmatian vessels."

"That explains the paucity of trade," muttered one of the senators. "We haven't had a vessel in for weeks. There's normally a trickle of coasters at least."

"Invading our territory—"

Lodovico snatched the trumpet again and blew it discordantly. It was a sound to make brave men quail. Even being quiet was easier than listening to it again.

Benito went on. "The Citadel of Corfu is under siege. Emeric of Hungary is conducting the siege in person."

A senator at the front of the press of people raised a long arm. "Lodovico, I need to ask a question."

"Ask away, Enrico. That's the gist of Benito Valdosta's news, isn't it Benito?"

"Have Byzantines also attacked other Venetian territory? And what is the proportion of Emeric's forces as opposed to troops of the Holy Roman Empire?"

Benito was almost sure that this had been one of those questioning him a few minutes before. "I don't know about other Venetian possessions, milord. I was sent from Corfu to bring word. I traveled disguised as a fisherman—which is why I am dressed as I am now. We were intercepted by a Byzantine galley but were lucky enough to talk our way out of it. We had attempted to send two great galleys following different routes with the news, but I think we may assume that the blockade vessels captured them, as you had not heard the news from Corfu. As for troops of the Holy Roman Empire as opposed to Emeric's forces . . . Well, we think Emeric has between ten and fifteen thousand men—and he may be bringing more. We managed to land some two hundred Knights of the Holy Trinity under Prince Manfred of Brittany to add to the Citadel's garrison."

"Are you trying to tell us that Manfred of Brittany is *inside* the Corfu Citadel?"

Benito nodded, puzzled. "Yes. I traveled south with his convoy of galleys. We managed to effect a landing the day before Emeric's carracks arrived with his cannon."

The tall man raised himself up to his full height. "Valdosta. I cannot think what you thought you'd achieve with this—this—" He fumbled for words. "This complete farrago of lies!" He turned to the other senators. "My fellow Venetians. I must tell you that well-substantiated reports—"

"They're nothing but rumors, you fool!" shouted another, but the speaker plowed on:

"—have Manfred of Brittany—having left Corfu for Canea— stating how much he would like to make it a possession of the Holy Roman Empire."

It was Benito's opportunity to fumble for words "But . . . that's impossible. There is no way he could have gotten out of the siege."

The tall man looked at Benito with cold hauteur. "It has been carefully verified."

"What nonsense!" That came from the same senator who had tried to interrupt earlier. He began pushing his way to the front of the crowd. "Rumors, that's all! And there are hundreds of them, flying all over Italy ever since word came of the Emperor's illness!"

The crowd in the huge hall started buzzing with jabber. Then, at the back of the hall, someone cleared his throat. "If I may speak?"

It was an elderly voice, but carried well. The assembled crowd turned to look at the elderly Patriarch of Venice. He came forward through the crowd, slowly. He plainly had no intention of speaking from where he was. All the time he was slowly walking down to the front of the hall Benito's mind was in ferment. This tall lord . . . he thought his name might be Enrico Licosa—a *Case Vecchie* who had served in Spain, and also in Naples—was he a traitor? Had the attempt by Justice Capuletti to sentence him to death really been nothing more than bureaucratic maliciousness? Benito started looking for ways out.

The elderly Patriarch reached the front of the hall where Benito and Lodovico stood. He was old, stooped, white-haired and white-bearded. No danger, surely.

He advanced on Benito, determinedly. Benito began to wonder if he was right about the danger. Did you kick the head of the Church in Venice in the crotch if he tried to seize you?

The old man reached out both skinny arms for Benito.

And then embraced him, and placed a blessing hand on his head. "This is a specific instruction from the Grand Metropolitan in Rome himself," he said, loudly, for the benefit of the audience.

Well, thought Benito. *This reduces my chances of being lynched. I'm not sure what it's all about, but it's welcome.*

The Patriarch continued. "Know all of you that as far as we have been able to determine the island of Corfu is under siege with great magical forces concentrated on it. The practitioners of sacred magic in Rome have detected demonism at work here."

He turned to the now-gaping Enrico Licosa. "I suggest this entire story of Prince Manfred reeks of the snares and deceits of the Evil One."

The Senate was in a hubble-bubble of frightened whispers now. Benito heard shreds of *"the Devil himself . . ."*

Then another man stood up. This one Benito recognized: Andrea Recchia. His son and Benito had had a small affray consisting largely of Benito giving the handsome scion of the house a black eye and a broken nose, and ending in considerable trouble with the law for the Recchia boy. By the look on his face Benito could tell he thought this was payback time.

"If you ask me, fellow senators, you need look no further for the Devil's helpers than the *Casa* Valdosta. That man"—pointing at Benito—"has only this very morning assaulted the core of our republic. He viciously attacked and held hostage one of our Justices. He was banished from our fair city, to the relief of all respectable citizens. He has broken his exile—a clear breach of our ancient laws! He is using this tissue of lies to benefit himself. He hasn't come from Corfu. He has just come from the deceivers in Ferrara. I have witnesses to prove this! No doubt now he will come up with some plan to have the Imperials 'liberate' Corfu."

"Recchia," said Lodovico Montescue, "is your son out of jail yet for the bearing of false testimony under oath? Against the *Casa* Valdosta, if I recall correctly. My fellow senators, it is normally said 'Like father, like son.' This time it appears to be 'like son, like father,' eh? The *Casa* Valdosta is one of the *Case Vecchie Longi*. One of the oldest houses, and loyal and true to the Republic. The *Casa* Montescue once was entrapped into doubting them, to our cost. Let us trust to those who have stood by us in our hour of need. Benito here fought on the barricades during the Badoero and Milanese attacks. His brother was prepared to even offer his life for our great republic. Their names are both entered on the lists of volunteers who enlisted for our defense."

The old man glared at his opponent, even shook his fist. "And where were *you*, Recchia? Where is *your* name?" To the rest of the crowd, Lodovico perorated: "Young Valdosta here was banished for the sort of wild foolishness of youth that most of you, and myself, engaged in. I could tell stories about half of you that you'd rather have forgotten, so don't tempt me. Benito went too far, and it was decided that he needed tempering that would enable him to learn the deportment and responsibilities of a man. It was for that reason he was banished, not because he is a threat to the state. But when danger threatened our Republic, the *Casa* Valdosta was again the first to answer the call. Like Ferrara. Let us not forget who our true friends are."

Recchia ignored the cheers. "That's as may be. But I have witnesses—reliable witnesses!—who saw Valdosta disembark from a Ferrarese barge yesterday. Ferrara, I remind you all—you especially, Montescue, as senility is obviously catching up on you—is to the north. And what took him from yesterday morning till now to bring this 'urgent news'?"

Benito put a hand on Lodovico's shoulder. It looked like the old man was likely to go and run Recchia through. "May I answer this? The Adriatic is blockaded. *Block-a-ded*. Think now, those of you engaged in trade: Have any ships come up from as far as the Straits of Otranto in the last three weeks? No. I was smuggled out of Corfu by fishing boat to Italy. Southern Italy. A nasty little fishing village on the coast of Southern Italy, and I was dead glad to get there at all. From Southern Italy I came up the west coast, across the Ligurian sea. I then crossed the Apennines by the best route. Which leaves me approaching the city from the north. But short of growing wings, how else was I to travel? And as for not bringing the news yesterday—that is, if you please, what I was attempting to do *when I was arrested*. And I would have been still effectively silenced, if I had not resorted to extreme means."

Benito drew his rapier. "And if necessary to get the Republic stirred to action I'll do it again. And you've offered insult to my friend Lodovico. The Valdosta stand by Venice and by our friends. Do you want to name your seconds, sir?"

Well, that put the bull in the glass-shop. The hall erupted into a bedlam.

Or—started to.

The room was suddenly hushed by the slamming open of the great doors at the far end of the hall.

Except that "slamming" was far too mild a description for what happened.

The doors exploded inward, with the sound of a thousand bombards. Benito looked up to see a familiar figure standing there. His heart leapt to see Marco. But his soft, kindly and gentle brother could scarcely quell this lot—

But this was not his soft, gentle, kindly brother. In fact, it wasn't entirely his brother at all.

Oh, Marco was there, all right. But he was completely overshadowed by a great, hazy golden figure with wide-spread wings that overfilled the doorway.

And it spoke in a roar, a roar that was also words that reverberated in the chest and actually caused some of the *Case Vecchie* to drop to their knees. *"What fools are you, who threaten my City?"*

The windows and walls trembled from the force of those words.

Marco strode to the front of the Senate, and with each step he took, the shape of the Lion shrank in around him until he wore the golden aura like a garment. And in nowise was that lessening of apparent size a lessening of the very real *power.*

Marco turned when he reached Benito's side, placed one hand on Benito's shoulder, and faced the gathering. The windows still shivered slightly with the force of his words.

"I have come in haste from Verona, sent by Doge Dorma as soon as we received word from our ally, Duke Enrico Dell'este, of the invasion of Corfu. We are at war and have work to do, gentlemen. You are the leaders of our Republic. Get out there and lead. The people need you."

Only Recchia stood his ground. Benito could not imagine how he could. *He* wanted to drop to his knees in front of his brother. Was the man too utterly blind and stupid to see nothing but what he wanted to see?

"The charges against Benito . . ."

"*SILENCE!*" Marco roared, and Recchia, at last, seemed to realize that he was in the presence of something that really did not give a damn about petty bureaucrats and petty feuds.

Marco—or the Lion—moderated his tone. Slightly. "These *charges* will be answered in a court of law and not in an open assembly. And your part in this will be questioned too, Recchia, be sure of it. *Now go!*"

It was an order, given with such force that even Benito felt compelled to obey.

Marco put an arm over his shoulder, holding him in place. As the *Case Vecchie* fled from the room, the gold aura began to fade, until it was only Marco again.

"Not you, Benito. And do you think you could put that sword away?"

Chapter 61

Marco handed Lodovico and Benito each a goblet of wine. "Bespi and my horses will be along from the border shortly. Petro, Kat and Grandfather are coming as soon as they can get to horse—and I expect that the treaty negotiations will be completed, if not within hours of my leaving, possibly in the saddle. We couldn't all leave without breaking the whole thing up, and we'd come a long way toward concluding a treaty. But when the word came about you—the siege—I knew I had to get here before someone managed to silence Benito. Or worse. Make him disappear, maybe. The moment I crossed the border and I could invoke the Lion, I did so, and I left my horses in Bespi's hands. I'm afraid—or perhaps I should say, I am glad—flying as the Lion in broad daylight is something that no one can silence; everyone in Venice knows that when the Lion flies, Venice is in danger, so besides getting here faster, it let everyone in the city know that *something* horrible has happened."

"Um," Benito said. He felt odd. Humbled. To be the center of *that*—

Marco smiled. "To be honest, all of this uncertainty since the Emperor's illness, and all of the conflicting rumors and reports, could have served us a backhanded good turn. Ferrara and Venice would have been a lot less obliging and conciliatory if they hadn't been spooked. As it is, it looks to me as if we'll get a good deal, which will improve security, benefit trade, and sideline Milan a bit further."

"Sounds good, Brother," Benito replied, trying to regain a bit of his composure. "But when I've finished drinking this, I need to get along to the Imperial embassy and show the ambassador my head."

Marco blinked. "Your head?"

Benito chuckled. "Come along and see."

Count Von Stemitz at the embassy was a very urbane and unflappable man, as a rule. But he looked a little taken aback at being told to feel in the hair behind the grubby, scruffy-looking young man's left ear. "There should be a lump there," said Benito.

"Er. Yes," said the Count rather gingerly. He'd met Benito before, briefly. Now, vouched for by Marco, whom he knew well, and Lodovico Montescue, who was a long-time friend, Von Stemitz was prepared to accept that this tousle-headed sailor was in fact the *Case Vecchie* tearaway, and normally attired somewhat differently. He was even prepared to grant that this bizarre ritual might have some deeper purpose.

Might. Benito's reputation preceded him.

"Cut it out, please," asked Benito unable to refrain from grinning. "I hope you have a sharp knife."

The grin plainly worried the count. "This is not one of your practical jokes is it, Signor Valdosta?"

"It's not my joke. If it's anyone's, it's Prince Manfred's."

Now that he was near to the end of this, Benito was beginning to feel all of it catching up to him. He was going to eat his way down the banquet table, and then sleep for a week. "And being funny is not its purpose. Believe me, I'm going to be glad not to have that lump there. A girl in Calabria tried to run her fingers through my hair and nearly pulled it out by the— Ow! You should sharpen that thing."

Count Von Stemitz stood examining the Imperial seal of the Hohenstauffen Dynasty. "I presume you are going to explain this. It is not used in jests," he said dryly.

"Oh, its purpose is earnest enough. Manfred just said I was the scruffiest personal letter he'd ever sent. We were in a situation where actually carrying a letter would be dangerous, given the possibility of a search. So this seal is to authenticate that I have come from the prince. I must tell you that he and his men are under siege in the Citadel on Corfu. Both King Emeric of Hungary and the Byzantines are laying siege to the fortress. The prince conveys his respects to his uncle, and asks for whatever assistance might be brought to their rescue."

Lodovico chuckled. "A talking letter. These modern advances! What will they think of next, eh, Hendrik?"

The Count had to smile too. "It's a very serious matter . . . but maybe cleaner envelopes? Well, if you will excuse me, gentlemen. A letter, slightly more conventional in form perhaps, must be dispatched to Mainz with the fastest messengers. I have a fit young *Ritter* here. I am going to dispatch him, with a covering letter, to see the Emperor—or, if the Emperor is too ill, at least the Privy Council and the States General."

"Good," said Lodovico. "Because I think the biggest problem with a relief force will be ships to transport them. Venice's fleets are away. We'll need ships from further afield. Few of the other Mediterranean powers are likely to wish to help us. Perhaps they will oblige the Emperor."

Benito hadn't thought of that. And ten to one, neither had Manfred.

The Count nodded, sighing. "We will surely find that Emeric has tried to prevent others coming to your rescue. I imagine part of the Hungarian's strategy is to get Alexius VI to trap the eastern fleet in the Black Sea. The western fleet is another question. Do you think the Barbary pirates may be involved?"

Benito bit his lip. "I don't know, milord. But this I will tell you: Eneko Lopez believes Grand Duke Jagiellon is also involved in all this. And that means Lithuania and its allies. And now, if you'll excuse us, Count. You have letters to write. And we have the Arsenal to visit. They'll be working night and day until another fleet is ready."

The situation at the Arsenal, Benito had to admit, was worse than he had hoped. Doge Giorgio Foscari had let the old policy of keeping a number of spare vessels in readiness, just needing to be rigged, lapse. The Senate had recently passed a new appropriation to restart the program, but it was still in its infancy. Only two extra new keels had been laid. The work had of course been proceeding on seven new great galleys to replace existing but elderly vessels, but the Arsenal simply didn't have a new fleet ready to sail. At least twenty great galleys would be needed, and three times that number of smaller galleys.

"How long?" asked Benito.

The representative of the Admiral of the Arsenal shrugged. "Six to eight months, milord. We'll start launching the smaller vessels within two, but it all takes time. We can't just throw money and resources at the problem: The limit is skilled manpower. You can't make shipwrights overnight, and they've got to sleep sometimes."

It was not what Benito had wanted to hear.

After two days Benito was rested, his saddle sores almost entirely recovered, and his appearance returned to that of a *Case Vecchie* gentleman.

By then, apparently shortly after Benito had fallen into a bed, Kat had returned from Verona, as part of the retinue of Petro Dorma. The Duke Dell'este was expected the following day.

Marco was watching Benito devour his second breakfast of the day, when Kat appeared. She melted into her husband's arms with a sigh of deep contentment, holding him as if she never wanted to part from him, even though Benito knew she couldn't have been away from him more than an hour or two.

Marco always just looked somehow more complete and at ease with Kat at his side, Benito decided. She was never waspish with him either, as she used to be with Benito. Still, she even kissed the prodigal fondly before taking a seat next to Marco.

"I supposed it's to be expected that you would find a unique reason to break your exile," she said, with a wink. "How is Maria?"

"She and Baby Alessia were fine when I last saw them. Mind you that was more than a month ago, and they're in a fortress under siege. But Umberto is looking after them." He paused. "That's a good man she married, Kat."

Now Katerina scowled at him, looking far more like the Kat that Benito remembered than the joyous Madonna-like person who was married to his brother. "You were a fool, Benito."

He grinned, though to be fair his heart wasn't in it. "I still am, Kat. But at least she's happy. Be honest, he gives her the kind of stability I can't."

She sniffed. "Stability is all very well. But you could have settled down a bit if you'd tried. Anyway. There is nothing you can do about it now. I'm supposed to tell you the Doge and your grandfather want to see you as soon as possible. They're in council with the Patriarch, Sister Evangelina, Brother Mascoli, and several other clerics that I don't know. They wanted to talk to Marco, too.

"I'm coming along," she added militantly, "just to see that they don't talk you into doing something dangerous, Marco."

"Flying with the Lion isn't really dangerous, Katerina. And we had to get someone down to Venice quickly when we heard about Benito's predicament from the Hypatians."

"Perhaps flying with the Lion is not entirely dangerous," she said sharply. "But you know very well what happened to Bespi once you left him! And if it hadn't been that you moved so fast, it might have been you who encountered that ambush, off Venetian soil where the Lion couldn't help you—"

Marco winced; Benito gaped at him, then demanded, "*What* ambush? What happened?"

"Oh," Marco replied, "Bespi ran into some—trouble."

"*Trouble?*" Kat's voice dripped sarcasm. "He was ambushed, Benito. And the only reason he's alive now is because Marco wasn't with him." She glared at him. "And the fact, I suppose, that they couldn't actually set up a good ambush, since they were expecting to catch you before you got on Venetian territory."

Bit by bit, Benito pulled it out of them. It happened right after Marco left Bespi on the road with their two horses, when he broke through a group of mercenaries who had set up an ambush on the road that showed every evidence of having been hastily set up. Wisely, rather than try to fight, he spurred his horse through them. But he hadn't gotten away without adding more scars to his considerable collection, and it was Bespi's opinion that the only reason the ambushers had broken off was that they had been confused, seeing only one man, and that man looking nothing like Marco Valdosta. He was recovering, but since the mercenaries were aided by something that Bespi had refused to describe, except as "black magic," there was no doubt that Jagiellon was involved.

"And if you had been outside the border of Venice, what then?" Kat repeated.

Benito shared Kat's distrust of these magical doings. Perhaps Marco understood and was in control of these forces, but they left Benito feeling like a weak swimmer in an undertow.

They walked across to the Doge's palace together, where the Swiss guards saluted very respectfully. It was amazing what a difference the clothes one wore made. No one even glanced at the scabbarded sword at Benito's side now. Ha! So much for the fuss about "concealed weapons." The same weapon could be carried openly without any comment by the *Case Vecchie.*

A footman led them up to a large, airy salon where Petro Dorma was in animated discussion with a number of other parts of the state machinery, and several clerics. The Doge broke off his argument to greet them. "Well, Benito. I thought I told you to stay away from trouble?" As it was said with a broad smile and general laughter, Benito knew that at least he wasn't still in Petro's bad books.

"Nonetheless, you have given us something of a legal conundrum," said the one hawk-nosed secretary. Benito recognized the voice from the Council of Ten interview. "You are still legally banished. And there are a small group saying no matter who you are and what you have done, or whatever the reason, holding a Venetian Justice hostage at sword's point is unacceptable."

"I'll face my trial and accept my sentence," said Benito stiffly, feeling irritated. "I did what had to be done, and I was the right person to do it."

"And Venice and the Church are conscious of their debt to you," said Petro. "But the form of the law must be observed."

"It's a pity you couldn't have put off arriving until tomorrow," said the secretary with a wry smile. "Your pardon was on the agenda for the Senate meeting."

Benito found this more than a little odd. He'd hardly been gone from Venice a couple of months and they wanted him back? Not very likely. "You were going to pardon me?"

Petro waved a hand, dismissively. "For reasons of state that no longer apply, since the rumors about Prince Manfred's schemes to seize Corfu proved to be untrue."

The hawk-nosed secretary cleared his throat. "Still, the item is on the agenda and must be debated. I think it would sit very ill with the commons if Benito were not pardoned now."

Dorma shrugged. "Very well. Leave it scheduled. It may help our case. Just try to stay out of trouble this time, Benito. We have scheduled the case for nine tomorrow morning, with a full bench of Justices. I'm afraid that will include Capuletti. I can't influence or be perceived to have influenced the case at all."

Benito snorted. "I did what I thought had to be done, Petro. If they want to be petty about the matter—well, so be it."

The Patriarch shook his head. "The church will certainly appeal strongly for clemency. Magical contacts have been made—considering the gravity of the situation and the involvement of the Ancient Enemy, the expenditure of magical power was reckoned worthwhile. The Hypatians in Messina give you a glowing character reference. And you have alerted the mother church to a terrible evil. Our sacred magicians are gathering to take the war to the enemy."

"Anyway," said Petro, "that is for tomorrow. Today we just want to extract as much information from you as possible. Wring you out so that a court-case will seem a minor thing." He sighed. "It will take time to relieve the Citadel. I wish we had a fleet at hand, but this attack was carefully planned to catch us when our ships were away."

"I have a feeling they've made plans to keep our fleets away," said Benito. "This wasn't a spur-of-the-moment attack, Petro."

"No," the Doge agreed grimly. "It wasn't."

Chapter 62

The court hearing was somewhat different from Benito's previous appearances. For starters, there were many more people there. For a second, Benito's sword was not even in the same building.

Petro had insisted on that. He'd also insisted that Benito swear out a charge against Justice Capuletti for treason.

"I'm sure it was just pettiness," demurred Benito, uncomfortable at the idea. "Revenge on the Valdosta."

Petro Dorma shook his head. "You're probably right. We probably won't make the charges themselves stick. But—and this is the point of it, Benito; you're still a political innocent—the *mud* will stick."

Petro Dorma's own legal counsel stood for Benito. He started by reading the synopsis of Benito's travels as told to the clerk. "Your Honors, it was necessary to have someone who could travel disguised as a commoner, yet whose testimony would be accepted at the highest level. Someone who was also skilled with weapons and subterfuge. With respect, your honors, there wasn't much of a choice. I think you will grant that he plays the part of a scruffy common sailor to perfection, and his skills with weapons and—ah—subterfuge cannot be gainsaid."

The Justices laughed; so did the audience. Benito tried not to squirm in his seat.

"He's a troublesome young blade," confessed the counsel. "And yet, to those of us who know him, he is utterly reliable. So reliable that Prince Manfred of Brittany chose to make him his personal messenger—and that Eneko Lopez, a churchman whose moral integrity is a byword, also trusted him to bring further vital information to the Hypatians, and thus, the Grand Metropolitan."

The chief Justice nodded. "You have made your point. Continue, signor."

Counsel turned to Benito. "We have now read the synopsis of your journey as transcribed by the Clerk, Michael Di Coulo. Benito Valdosta, you have had an opportunity to hear it. Is this a faithful and accurate account of your travels and your efforts to bring word to Venice?"

Benito nodded. "Pretty much."

"You do not mention your dealings with the Hypatian church in Messina, other than to say you overnighted there."

Benito shrugged. "I accidentally recovered their property and returned it to them. It didn't seem to have much bearing on either Corfu or Venice."

Rather dramatically, the counsel brandished a sheet of paper. "Nonetheless I have here a letter from the Patriarch, thanking you for your efforts for the Church, and stating that the Church would be glad to provide witnesses proving you were of great service to them." He paused. "Your Honors, we have here a young man who has served the Republic well, and the Church also. His banishment was for acts not of treason, but simply youthful folly. The banishment was due to be considered by the Senate on this very day. It seems likely that it will be rescinded, in any event. This case, with respect, must be considered on its merits. I appeal to you to consider any transgression in the light of the service performed."

The chief Justice steepled his fingers. "Does the prisoner have anything to add to this?"

Benito shook his head. "Except to say that if there had been anyone available who could have done what I did, or have done it better, they'd have been sent. We didn't have much time to make up our minds before the cannon were emplaced. And it is my intention to return to Corfu as soon as I can. I may not be able to get back into the Citadel, but I can join the irregular forces who are harrying King Emeric's rear. I've only stayed on here to show my respect for the law of the Republic and for the Doge. I came to give warning. I'll leave as soon as I am permitted to go. Unless there is need to warn or need to stand by the Republic I won't be back."

He allowed a trace of hurt to enter his voice. "I know when my presence is unwelcome. But the Valdosta honor their responsibilities, their promises, and their debts. We owe a great deal to Doge Dorma and to Venice."

The chief Justice scratched his chin. "Benito Valdosta, it is not that this court is unaware that the Republic owes the *Casa* Valdosta and you in particular a debt of honor, or that we do not understand why you undertook this mission. It is not even that Venice does not want you back, despite the fact that, as your eloquent defender put it, you're a troublesome young blade. The problem that this court faces is that despite the best of intentions your actions breached the law. And Venetian law is not arbitrary. It applies to everyone, regardless. What we wish to see is how we can combine Venetian law with Venetian justice. The court can grant clemency for your breaking of your banishment, under the circumstances. What is difficult is your conduct within the court. We cannot allow anyone to assault a Justice within his own court and get away with it."

Admiral Dourso rose to his feet. "Your Honor, may I offer the court a piece of information. The Justice to whom you refer is not on the bench today. The reason for his absence is that he is in fact in custody of the *Signori di Notte*, charged with treason and conspiring to aid an enemy of the Republic."

The Schiopettieri had to sound their rattles to restore order.

"Nevertheless . . . Yes, what is it, Signor Di Coulo?"

The little clerk who had written out Benito's story had advanced to address the Justices. "Your Honors. To prosecute Benito Valdosta for threatening Justice Capuletti you will need witnesses. I have to tell Your Honors, there are none. I will however testify that Justice Capuletti gave me this black eye when he assaulted me on that day. Schiopettieri de Felts will also testify that he inflicted an injury on the Justice, who appeared to be in a violent and disturbed state. The Justice was plainly not in his right mind that day, your Honors."

The chief Justice looked severely at the little clerk. "As a clerk of this court, you must be aware that you and these others are thwarting the law."

The little man didn't quaver. "We are aiding justice, Your Honors."

At this point a messenger entered the courtroom with a note, which he took to the chief Justice. The latter peered at it. "Ah. It appears that the first charge of breaking your banishment no longer stands. The Senate has decided to lift your banishment, and override the court for what is described as reasons of state." There was disapproval written on every line of the chief Justice's face. "And they have made this retroactive from the sixth of June of this year. So this charge is thereby struck from the roll. And as it appears we have no witnesses for—"

Benito stood up. "Your Honor. I appreciate the gesture of Senate. I also appreciate the fact that the people of Venice have shown their love for the *Casa* Valdosta in their testimony . . . or lack thereof. But *I* cannot accept it. The truth is—I did return when I was banished. I must admit that I didn't even give it a thought. My period of exile is both fair and right. I came to give warning because that was more important. I'll leave as soon as I can. I transgressed the letter of the law. If you like you can put me in prison, or, as is common in times of war, put me into the military. I'm volunteering anyway. My name is already on the list on the pillar of the Winged Lion of Saint Mark. Why not put me into a military encampment—like the Arsenal—until I leave for Corfu, and my banishment can continue? As for Justice Capuletti, I admit I did threaten him with a naked blade in his own courtroom. If need be I'd have cut his throat for the people of Corfu's sake. You need no witnesses. I admit guilt. Now the Court can decide what it is going to do about it."

In the silence that followed, only one person spoke. Lodovico Montescue. "Valdosta honor!" he said, almost shouting.

Then, with satisfaction and pride: "Now, Justices of Venice, the Valdosta have challenged your honor. What is more important? The spirit of justice and the honor of the Republic for a loyal son— or the dry letter of the law?"

The Justices looked to the chief Justice. He sat with his fingers steepled looking at Benito.

One of the younger Justices suddenly spoke. "I would like to recuse myself. I cannot give impartial judgment."

The other young one—young being a relative term, thought Benito, the fellow must be about sixty—cleared his throat. "I, too, am going to recuse myself."

The chief Justice looked more than a little taken aback. "Spinosa! You cannot just abandon the law when it suits you."

"We who administer the law tend to begin to think it sacred," Justice Spinosa said, stoutly. "It isn't. Justice is. And we forget that the law we administer is by grace of the Republic, and the Republic stands by the *vox populi*. Anyone who believes the law can stand without the people and without justice, is deceiving themselves."

"Thank you for reminding me of our status *quamdiu se bene gesserit*," said the chief Justice, dourly. "It is something that few have the courage to do. Nonetheless I will continue to act as both the law and my conscience dictate."

The younger Justice shrugged. "That is what I am doing. The Law must find him guilty and sentence him."

"I think you should not stand down until we have decided what verdict we reach . . . and what sentence we will impose."

Spinosa shook his head. "I cannot do so afterwards. Thus I will do so before."

The chief Justice shrugged. "Very well. Can the rest of us withdraw?"

The remaining three judges did. And they returned very rapidly.

"Benito Valdosta," said the chief Justice. "We find you guilty by your own admission of the charge of threatened assault with a deadly weapon on an officer of this court. However, as circumstances must alter cases, we feel that under the circumstances your actions were justified. You are free to go."

Benito looked uncharacteristically grim, especially for someone who had essentially beaten the legal system to its knees. "I'm still going to confine myself to the Arsenal. Get myself involved in getting vessels ready. The Arsenalotti have already agreed to work double shifts."

"We rather thought you would come and stay with us," said Kat.

Benito shook his head. "To be honest, it suits me to be busy. What would I do in Venice, waiting around for an expedition to Corfu? Get drunk, chase women and get into more trouble? Best to follow Erik's regimen. Go to sleep so tired I can't stand."

"Well, grandfather wants to see you," said Marco. "He's with Lodovico, so I have no doubt you'll do some of that drinking. We'll visit you, Brother. Right now, though, the Hypatians seem to need us to make another attempt to contact Father Lopez." He didn't look very happy about it.

❀   ❀   ❀

"Lodovico can call it Valdosta honor. But you're a Dell'este by blood," said the Old Fox.

Benito grinned wryly at both of the old men. "I'm a product of place, companions and blood. I'm a Valdosta by rearing, Grandfather."

"It's a fine house, even if that brother of yours is sometimes too good for this world," said Lodovico.

The Old Fox said nothing for a while. And then sighed. "You've come out very well, considering the likes of Aldanto and the part he had in your rearing."

Benito shrugged. "The bad I learned there got canceled out by my saintly brother and Maria, not to mention that granddaughter of Lodovico's."

"What happened to this Maria?" asked the Old Fox, casually. That casualness would have fooled most people.

"She's in the Citadel on Corfu now," said Benito quickly. "Married. And with a fine daughter."

Lodovico chuckled. "She's quite a young termagant, that woman. Between my granddaughter and her they were a pair to frighten any young man into the paths of righteousness. Not that it seems to have worked on you," he added, frowning fiercely at Benito.

"Well, I've still got some time in exile to go and to learn it." Benito was determined to get Maria out of the conversation, and quickly. "I want to lean on Petro to let me go back to Corfu as soon as possible. If I can let the defenders know somehow that Venice is coming, it'll do a lot for morale."

"True. But this blockade of theirs . . ." the Old Fox said, eyeing him with speculation. "It seems too good to be natural, boy."

Benito pulled a face. "Well, maybe we also need some unnatural help. I know Marco has had some traffic with undines and tritons. I'll talk to him. But I wanted to ask your advice, grandfather, on strategies. Erik Hakkonsen is conducting the campaign using the locals. I'm going to join him if I can. Talk to me. Tell me what works."

Chapter 63

The water trickled steadily into the rock bowl. Not in all the thousands of years that the faithful had tended the shrine here in the caves in the cliff, had that spring run dry. The holy pool remained full and still and drifted with the offering of flower petals.

Tonight there were more devotees than ever. The priestess looked around. The women from the Little Arsenal, smuggled in and hidden, were here in numbers. She was not surprised. The cult was mainly Greek, these days, although—as she proved herself—it did not make objection to foreign worshipers. The great Mother considered them to be women first; nationality was a secondary and unimportant thing. In troubled times, the Goddess knew that women came back to the old religion.

The priestess noticed that the devotees were looking thin and pinched—not starving, yet, but starvation was not going to be far away. She sighed. The women and children were always the first to suffer in sieges. And the women hiding away would be, if anything, worse victims than those who were legitimately within the walls. After the rite she would move to speak to them, to see if anything could be done.

The rite soothed her, and even seemed to give some comfort and courage to the other women. Enough so that when the priestess drew one aside as the rest left, she did not even get a token resistance to her questions.

"There are two of the guards," the woman said wearily. "They found where we women were hidden and now they demand some of the men's rations and money to keep their silence. They are selling food to those who have money. They were demanding sex, too, but some of the men said they would kill them, even if it meant discovery."

The priestess frowned. "We will see what can be done. Do you know the names of these two?"

The women nodded.

On the small black altar the half almond lay, unwithered, still waiting. The priestess looked at it and sighed again. There was power there. But it was not hers. It was not anyone's . . . without a price.

Stella had come over principally to gossip, but officially to see if Maria would sell her a few eggs. They were sitting in the kitchen because it seemed the place where Stella's smaller two could do the least damage. Maria looked on Stella's younger children—who were now engaged in an exercise in seeing how far they could try everybody's patience—as an experience that would put most women off motherhood. They were both little boys, and Stella let them get away with the kind of mayhem she plainly didn't tolerate in her older daughters.

There was a furious bleating from the goat, followed by a polite knock at the door. Maria went to it. Stella peered curiously around her shoulder—and gasped to see who the visitor was.

Contessa Renate De Belmondo did turn up on her charitable missions at any place she chose. Still, she was the first lady of the island, and this was a tiny Scuolo house—not where you would expect to find her.

She smiled as brightly as if this was a *Case Vecchie* mansion, while Stella made big eyes and backed up. "Maria, my dear, may I come in?"

Maria was more than a little flustered too, but she had her pride. With Stella watching, she had little option but to behave as coolly as she could, as if she entertained the governor's wife in her kitchen every day. She made her best attempt at a curtsey. "Certainly, milady. I am very glad to see you again."

Renate De Belmondo smiled and came in. "My dear, what a gorgeous rug. Where did you find it?"

Maria felt herself glow. The woolen rug was one of the few luxuries she had bought for Umberto and herself during their stay in the forestry region of Istria. It glowed with bright peasant colors, but was also beautifully woven. "I bought it at a fair in Istria. It comes from Dalmatia somewhere. The Illyrian women make them."

"It's a beautiful piece. We get some southern Illyrian goods here, but nothing nearly so fine." The contessa allowed herself to become aware of Stella, and the two children peering around her skirts. "Good morning. Signora Mavroukis, is it not?"

Stella did her best to curtsey with two clinging children. "Milady! Do you know everybody on Corfu?"

The contessa shrugged and laughed. "No. But I try. Signora, I hate to interrupt, but I need to talk to Maria. Can you spare her to me for a little while?"

Stella was plainly dying of curiosity, but could hardly say "I'll stay and eavesdrop." So she made as polite an exit as possible while, the moment that Renate De Belmondo turned her head away, miming to Maria: *I'll talk to you later. I want to hear all about it.*

When the door was firmly shut, and Maria's curiosity also fully aflame, she still felt she had to go through the niceties. "I have some of the local spoon-sweets, milady."

"Thank you. That would be delicious. And perhaps a glass of water?" Lady De Belmondo fanned herself with her hand; somehow, it was not an affected gesture. "I'm not getting any younger, and it is so hot already for walking. By August the full heat will be with us, and I'm really not looking forward to that at all. The first rains of autumn are always such a blessing."

So Maria fetched out the spoon-sweets and cool water from the earthenware ewer in the shade around the back of the house. They talked polite nothings while the contessa sampled the Sultanína glykó. "Ah. I love the flavor the *arbaróriza*—the rose geranium— gives to the grapes. Delicate yet definite."

"You speak Greek, Milady?"

"Fluently." She nodded her head gravely. "You really have to learn it, if you are going to live here. It's one of the greatest mistakes so many of the Venetians make. If you can't talk to people you can't get along with them, or really understand them."

"I am determined to learn," Maria said decisively.

The contessa smiled. "You will find the local people happy to teach."

Finally Maria could restrain herself no longer. "Milady, why have you come to see me?"

The contessa half hid a small smile behind her hand. "Because

I need your help. Your husband is fairly senior in the Little Arsenal, and I hope less set in his ways than old Grisini. I want, through you, to enlist his aid."

"I can try," said Maria doubtfully. "But the truth is, milady, Umberto is not the most flexible man in the world either. He's a good man, but he's a senior guildsman, and you don't get to be a senior guildsman without being very set in their traditions and ways."

The contessa nodded with understanding. "I have something of a problem with the wives and children of the Greek workers."

Maria made a face. "They're out there," she said, waving her hand vaguely in the direction of the rest of the island. "Their husbands must be distraught. Why did the men come in to the fortress when the siege threatened? They could have run away like the peasants did. They would have at least been together and a little safer."

Renate De Belmondo looked speculatively at Maria. And then said calmly: "They did one better. They brought the women in here. They're hiding in the sheds at the back of the Little Arsenal. There are more than sixty women and an uncertain number of children there, at least double that number. They're living on the men's rations, and a couple of the guards have found them and are exploiting the situation. According to my informant the men think the Illyrians must have informed on them. They're ready to kill the guards . . . which would be trouble. And the Illyrian workers too."

"Which would be more trouble," said Maria, grimly. "Those Illyrians are keen on using their knives, according to Umberto." She sighed. "The trouble between the Illyrians and the Corfiotes goes way back, he says, and both sides hold a grudge. The Corfiotes complain the Illyrians are stealing their work, the Illyrians say the Corfiotes are stealing their places."

"Oh, it goes back a lot further than that," chuckled the contessa dryly. "Further than you may think. Corfu has had waves of settlers for many thousands of years, but the original people of the region came here when there was no channel between here and the mainland, just a broad marshy valley and big bay. Then the invaders came; they were not the Illyrians . . . or even the Illyrians' forefathers, but they came from the same general direction: Thrace. The Illyrians are merely the inheritors of that hatred. Anyway, the point is that the hatred goes back so far that there is no counting the years. So far that there is a peasant belief among the women, that a desperate priestess of the Earth mother gave herself to be the bride of the lord of the under-earth to save her child. It's one of those things about the magic of Corfu I was telling you about. He moved the earth to drown the armies and forever put the sea between the invaders and this place."

Maria stared in puzzlement at the contessa. One minute she was telling Maria about a mess that could end in rioting—the next telling her about some ancient myth.

"How do you know all this, milady?"

The contessa shrugged. "It's a very old story. Or do you mean about the Greek workers' wives? People tell me things. I don't betray confidences, but I do sometimes act. This time I think I shall have to act. They can't remain a secret, but if the guild supports us in this . . . Well, it will be very difficult for the captain-general to make a fuss. I know Nico Tomaselli. He is likely to try to expel them, and certainly won't feed them. Now, the guild is in control of those sheds, and the Arsenalotti are not an inconsiderable force. Any attempt to throw the women out could cause a riot or even a breaching of the walls, if the Arsenalotti get involved."

"Besides, they're our own," said Maria resolutely. "You leave this with me, milady. I'll talk to Umberto."

The Contessa smiled. She took a small crystal bottle out of the pouch hanging from her chatelaine. "You may find this helps with your . . . talk." She laughed. "Sometimes men need to be distracted before they'll listen. I find a dab of this behind my ears even these days has the power to obtain my husband's full attention."

Maria blushed. "Milady. It is not necessary."

The contessa stood up. "I know. But I think you will enjoy it."

Another thought occurred to Maria. "Milady. I . . . am friends with Francesca de Chevreuse."

Maria expected disapproval. Instead she got another little laugh. "She has all the respectable matrons of this town in a terrible state! Mostly self-righteousness tinted with envy, I think. Do tell her that her attempts at information gathering have been reported to my husband."

That was more than a little alarming. But Maria persisted. "I could get her to ask the Knights to help."

The contessa shook her head. "This really is our own affair, Maria. We should handle it."

❀   ❀   ❀

The contessa was scarcely around the corner when Stella reappeared.

"All right," she said with a terrier look on face. "Tell all. What has she got you to do?"

Maria hadn't thought of a good story yet. "Ah. Well she wanted to ah . . . ask me to get Umberto to organize something down at the Little Arsenal. Nothing important, but she did ask me to keep it a secret. And Stella, I can't tell you and keep anything a secret. It'll be a nice surprise for her husband." Maria thought that was a good touch. The podesta was a renowned naturalist, collecting everything from butterflies to eggs. Surely Stella would assume it was a special cabinet or something.

Stella snorted. "It must be those Corfiote women hidden down in the Arsenal."

Maria gaped at her. "How—?"

Stella shrugged. "The contessa is forever helping women. So it had to be a women's problem, and if it involves Umberto and the Little Arsenal, then that must be it."

"But how did you know about it?"

"I have my sources."

Maria scowled at her. "I need to know."

Stella looked mischievous. "If you must know, Alberto found them. He went up to the top sheds to look for some missing tools a few days ago. They've got lookouts, and they hide if someone goes to the timber-stores. But Alberto took a shortcut up the wall. He's lazy, and it saved him a walk. So he came up to the upper gate very suddenly. A couple of the big porters tried to head him off, but you know Alberto, he's like pig after truffles when he gets onto something. And he speaks Greek so he gets on with the boys. So . . . because he was a friend of theirs, they put off hitting him over the head until it was too late. There was a bit of a scuffle, but my Alberto is quite solid."

He was indeed. A very large, amiable man. "And what happened then?"

"Well, you know what Alberto's like. Soft as goose grease with children. Of course he promised he wouldn't tell a soul." Stella smirked. "I had it out of him in two shakes. He's like you, Maria. A terrible liar."

"And so? Does the whole town know?"

"Not from me. It's all very well saying they shouldn't be there, but what kind of person would leave them outside the walls? The Croats and Hungarians—" She shuddered. "They're like wolves with two legs, Maria. But somebody else has found out about them. I've heard two juicy rumors about it already, as I said to Francesca."

Well, then. "I think you should take me down there to meet them. The contessa's right. This is going to blow wide open soon, and I'll need to work on Umberto about this. The *scuolo* need to stand by them."

"Most of the guildsmen don't like the Corfiotes much," said Stella doubtfully.

"But they like the *Case Vecchie* trespassing on their areas even less," Maria pointed out. "The *scuolo* are touchy about their rights and privileges. The porters and laborers at the Little Arsenal are ours. And if I can convince Umberto of this, and you get Alberto to back him up, we'll be able to sway the rest of them."

Stella pulled a wry face. "Especially if that idiot Tomaselli puts all their backs up like he usually manages to do." Her eyes lit up. "The latest malicious gossip is about Sophia, believe it or not. She's been slipping out of the fortress to come and see a lover down in the old town!"

Maria snorted. "I didn't think anyone was that desperate."

Stella giggled in a worldly-wise fashion. "Honey, there are some men that would make love to a hole in the wall. And others, like Alberto, who would just fall asleep. I'm going to ration his wine soon."

"If you take me down to meet the women hiding out in the wood-store, I'll give you a drop of this perfume to put behind your ears." Maria showed her the bottle. "It was given to me by the contessa. She guaranteed it would even wake her old man up."

Stella chuckled throatily. "If it can wake that old man up, it should be called resurrection juice, not perfume. You're on, sister."

When Maria went down to the wood-store with Stella, she was shocked by the thinness of the women, and by their obvious desperation.

"We can't go on like this, kyria," said one young girl—barely sixteen and trying to nurse a pair of twins. "I just don't have milk for them any more."

Maria took a deep breath. "We're going to sort this out. By tomorrow. Nobody should have to starve like this."

"We expected the siege to be over in a few weeks at most. When will help come from Venice?" asked an older woman bitterly. "Are we only worth keeping as expendable serfs, and not worth protecting?"

Maria looked her straight in the eye. "Venice had to be told before they could mount a rescue. And the Island is blockaded. You know that. I can tell you this much—a messenger has gone over to Italy, taking word to Venice, a clever messenger, who can get past anything."

She wondered just where Benito was, and uttered a silent prayer for his well-being. "The Republic won't fail you. And the *scuolo* won't fail you either. Your men work for us. It's up to us to care for you."

She was surprised by the hastily hushed cheers.

That evening Umberto arrived home a little late and looking worried. He didn't even notice Maria's belladonna-widened eyes at first. He was just looking gray and stooped. He took the cup of wine gratefully from her hand, then swallowed a long, appreciative draft. And then blinked at his wife. "You're looking beautiful tonight, dear. And your hair is done up in that way I like so." His nose twitched. He smiled tiredly. "I'm a lucky man. And I don't appreciate you enough. And how is our little girl tonight?"

Maria felt truly guilty. Like a complete slut. "She's fine, asleep now," she said gruffly. She decided that directness and honesty suited her better than feminine wiles. She was better at those than seduction anyway. "Umberto. I need to talk to you about the wives of the Corfiote laborers."

"They're hiding in the back sheds at the Little Arsenal," he replied conversationally.

She didn't need the belladonna to widen her eyes. Had everyone known except her?

"I'm sorry dear," he said apologetically. "That's what kept me. There was a fight between one of the Illyrians and a Corfiote—something to do with the women. I'm afraid both of them are with the hospitalers. I had to see to it."

"Oh, hell!" she said in dismay. "Will this mean fighting between the Illyrians and Corfiotes?"

He actually laughed. "Not unless they both don't recover from being hit by me with a cladding plank."

She stared, seeing a man she hadn't known hiding in Umberto's very ordinary frame.

"I had to do something," he said, uncomfortably. "The Corfiote accused the Illyrian of betraying the women to the guards. But Guildmaster Grisini asked the guard to organize more food, quietly."

"Two guards called Oliviolo and Nona."

It was Umberto's turn to gape at her. "How did you know—?"

"Because far from organizing more food, the pair of bastards have been extorting money and food from the Corfiotes," she told him with savage satisfaction. "The Corfiotes blame the Illyrians, which is where your knife-fight came from."

Umberto shook his head. "I don't understand them. They're our people. Why didn't they come to us? The *scuolo* looks after its own."

Looking at him with a mixture of pride and love, Maria realized that the perfume probably wasn't wasted after all. And she realized that—just as old women always said—you didn't have to be *in* love with the man you married to learn to love him. "Can I get you some supper?" she asked, rubbing his shoulders.

He looked at her. Speculatively, with a shy smile. "Maybe . . . later."

Chapter 64

The end came faster and more abruptly than any of the conspirators had anticipated. And it came at a damned awkward moment for Maria.

She'd gone up to the governor's palace the day before and missed seeing the contessa. Not wishing to make herself too obvious, she'd waited until this morning. Umberto had told her last night that the two guards had been transferred on to another duty, so something must be happening.

Renate De Belmondo had been organizing. Among the things she'd organized, Maria found, when she got up to the palace, was a huge basket of foodstuffs. Maria had the muscle in her back and shoulders from years of working heavy loads in a small boat—this basket she could hardly carry. "It's too heavy, milady."

Renate De Belmondo smiled. "You'll manage. There is considerable stage-management to be done before we can bring them out of there. Those women and children need food. And there are a lot of them."

So Maria had staggered down to the sheds. They were a good place to hide, actually; their men had chosen well. Although the sheds were within the compound, they were well away from the rest of the yard—up a steep bank, where there was a winch for loading materials from the street and a chute for sending timbers down to the workshops or the ship-gate. They were used when ships were in port and kept securely locked when they weren't. At the moment there just wasn't the call for cladding or masts. Getting up there unnoticed was considerably more difficult, but as Umberto's wife she could at least get into the shipyard.

She was distributing the contents of the contessa's basket when a hoarse whisper came up the bank. "Hide!"

Maria found herself dragged hastily into a long cavity roofed with masts and stacks of timber. It was dark, hot and airless.

And also a vain effort. Captain-General Tomaselli's men knew exactly where to look; somebody had plainly told them where to go. The women, Maria included, were hauled, blinking, into the bright July sunlight.

Maria knew that the one thing she must not do was to reveal who she was. At the moment the *scuolo* could still claim injured innocence; if they found *her* here, the cat would be out of the bag. Alessia was safely with Stella, but any baby would do for camouflage; almost all of them were awakened by the rough handling and almost all of them were crying. The poor mites were mostly hungry. She "borrowed" one, hastily. If there was one thing she'd learned since Alessia's birth it was that very few men will look directly at a breast-feeding woman that is not their own. It was as near as she could come to disappearing. She also realized that the moment was more serious even than she'd thought. There were some seventy of the captain-general's soldiers—quite enough to deal with frightened women and a gaggle of children.

What the captain-general hadn't taken into account was that there were some hundred or so Corfiote porters and laborers in the Arsenal. And they weren't about to watch their wives and children being herded away without a fight. Even if they weren't soldiers, they were men in a shipyard full of edged tools.

And more than just tools. Within less than a minute, a dozen angrily shouting laborers were standing on the walls around the compound holding, one between each two of them, pots of boiling pitch.

There was something very persuasive about that boiling pitch. A few of the troopers had been behaving with a fair amount of roughness to the captives. They suddenly became positively respectful.

"What do you men think you're doing?" demanded the captain-general.

"You tell them to leave our women and children alone and no one will get hurt!"

It was a very nasty situation. On one hand, the troops were armed, and armored. They had the women and children as virtual hostages. On the other hand, armor is no defense against hot pitch. And the Corfiotes were between them and the way out of the shipyard. Something else ominous was happening beyond the Corfiotes too. The *scuolo*, being Venetian guildsmen, were all part of the Militia. So they were in the habit of bringing their weapons and breastplates to work for duties afterward—and now they were arriving, armed, in dribs and drabs. They were positioned behind the Corfiotes with their pitch and crowbars, their felling axes and knives.

One of the guildsmen pushed forward. "Don't try to stop this, Master Grisini," said the big Corfiote. "We're desperate men."

The elderly guildmaster sniffed irritably. "We've no intention of stopping you. But I warn you, Dopappas. You get one drop of that pitch on my deck-planking and I'll shove that cauldron up your ass." Maria risked a quick peep to see that her Umberto was backing old Grisini up, coming up the ramp to where the soldiers stood with their prisoners. The master wasn't a big man. The Corfiote laborer he was threatening was enormous.

But the Corfiote nodded respectfully. "Yes, Master Grisini. But they want to take our women."

Grisini sighed gustily. "I'm old. I'm tired. But I'm also aware of the *scuolo*'s rights and responsibilities."

The Corfiote blinked.

The old man walked on through the Corfiotes, Umberto following behind him.

Maria saw that some more entrants had arrived for the affair. The Contessa De Belmondo and her husband, the governor. And, peering nervously through the gate: Stella, with Alessia and several of her own children. She'd plainly gotten a message to the contessa.

"Good morning. And what is happening here?" De Belmondo enquired with gentle curiosity.

"We've found these illegal entrants hiding here, Your Excellency," said the captain-general. "These men seem set on daring to rebel against legally constituted military authority in a war zone. The penalty for that is death, as you might like to remind them."

Old Grisini bowed respectfully to the governor. "Morning, Your Excellency. We seem to have a problem here about authority. Would you please explain to the captain-general that the Little Arsenal is part of the Arsenal of *Venice*—not part of the military of Corfu.

He has no authority here. We explained that to him when he tried to draft us, but he doesn't seem to understand it."

The captain-general looked frigidly at him. "In this case food and shelter intended for the island's people are being wasted on these women."

De Belmondo blinked. "Are these women and children from some other island then?"

"No, but they're not Venetian! They're locals." Tomaselli's tone added the unsaid words: *and thus beneath contempt.*

"I do not recall—as governor of this Venetian possession— anything which abrogates our responsibility for 'locals,' as you put it." The governor's voice was decidedly frosty. "In fact, I wasn't even aware of any such official category of people."

"But they're here illegally!" sputtered the captain-general.

Old Grisini snorted. "Not to make too fine a point of it—so are *you*, Tomaselli. They are in *our* building. They're the wives and children of *our* employees. We'll see to them. We'll see to their appropriate treatment."

The captain-general played his trump card. "Not with the food from the Citadel's stores. They must be put out!"

De Belmondo shook his head. "I cannot allow you to do that. And I don't think your men would be prepared to do something that would have them forever labeled as murderers of women and children. The Senate of the Republic would have my head, and yours."

This plainly hadn't struck Nico Tomaselli. "But we can't just allow them to freeload on the Citadel's stores!"

Umberto cleared his throat. "Excuse me, milords. I have an idea. If we put these women to work for the Republic, they would be entitled to a place as these men are."

The captain-general sneered. "You haven't even got work for yourselves! Besides, what can they do?"

Umberto answered instantly. "Weave sailcloth. We have flax, but the stores of sailcloth are very low."

"And what do we do with sailcloth in a siege?" grumbled Tomaselli, but you could see he was weakening.

"There is life after siege, we hope," said De Belmondo. "And if there isn't . . . well, we shall have no use for anything—never mind sailcloth."

❁   ❁   ❁

There was no help for it. Maria came and had her name—Elena Commena, she decided—scribed in the book with the other workers' wives. Umberto nearly dropped his quill.

"But why sailcloth? The flax is intended for ropes, Umberto. It's too coarse for good sailcloth," said old Grisini. He'd virtually collapsed when the tension and need went—he was in his late seventies, and it was hard on him.

Umberto paused. Bit his lip trying to think how best to put this to the old man. "Because, master, the captain-general is right. We don't have work for ourselves. That's really the main reason there's fighting and dissatisfaction. So I have been thinking ever since the Teutonic knights arrived here under fire, that we need to be able to strike at the enemy ships. We have everything we need, except brass nails and sailcloth, to build ships ourselves."

The old man blinked at him, confused. "We can't launch ships. And without nails we can't even build them."

Umberto shrugged. "We've got iron nails by the bushel, master. And we can lower smallish craft directly over the walls."

"But what good will that do?" asked Master Grisini, tiredly. "The enemy has some huge carracks out there. And iron nails will just rust."

"If the boats are on fire they can burn craft thirty times their size. And they won't have time for the nails to rust."

"It's a good idea," conceded the old master shipbuilder, after thinking about it for a few moments. "But how are we to convince the military of that? The captain-general would not exactly thank us for military help."

Umberto shrugged. "We will deal with that, like we did with this. When the time comes. In the meanwhile we can give the men work to do. It'll cut down on the fights."

Sophia Tomaselli lay wakeful, trapped in her husband's bed by the sleeping man's leg. She wanted out of here. Out of this boring man's bed, and away from his clumsy and drunken rutting. And "rutting" was the right word, too. She knew perfectly well he was only taking out his frustration with the world by mounting her.

As soon as she could get out of here, Sophia would make her way through the dark streets to her new interest. Now *there* was a man who could teach this husband of hers a thing or two about lovemaking. She felt herself aroused by the very thought of the shameful, exciting lust, the thrill of forbidden pleasuring. And she had some information about the plans for repulsing any attack on the inner wall. He always rewarded her well for these little snippets.

Bianca closed the lid of the chest in her room, after finishing the needed rituals to prevent decay. Fortunately, she didn't need a large chest, nor had the rituals taken much time—in both cases, because the body of the beggar boy was so small.

The corpse would keep, for the moment, under the linens. There'd be no tell-tale traces of putrefaction coming from the chest for at least a month. By then, Bianca would have Saluzzo under her control and would have him dispose of the body in some more permanent manner.

She put that problem out of her mind. Right now, she needed to concentrate on finishing the materials needed for the ritual she'd use to have her "relatives" removed. The beggar boy's blood needed to be mixed properly with the fat she had carved from his internal organs. The very little fat, unfortunately—the beggar boy hadn't been emaciated, exactly, but he'd been scrawny. There had been a little around the liver, the intestines; not as much as she had hoped. She might have to extend it with some of her other unguents, and hope that the principles of contact and similarity would make good the deficiencies.

Gingerly, she fingered her forearm where the boy had punched her, at the end. She thought there'd be a bruise there, by the morning. Little bastard. He'd put up more of a fight than she'd expected, once he realized the arm she'd wrapped around his throat was intended to kill him rather than to hug him.

True, it hadn't been much of contest. Bianca had not yet dared begin the rituals that would eventually provide her with the superhuman strength of her mistress, Countess Bartholdy. But she was still a full-grown woman, well-fed and in good health. Against her murderous resolve, a malnourished five-year-old boy had had no chance at all. She just wished that he had been a little fatter.

She lit the brazier under the bowl containing the blood and fat, and picked up the special instruments carved from human bones. With her right hand, she began stirring slowly; while, with her left, sprinkling into the mix the other ingredients required. All the while, softly chanting the needed phrases and intonations. Some of the words had never been meant to be formed by a human mouth.

As the mixture cooked down, she saw that there was no help for it; she would have to add precious defiled and deconsecrated oils to the recipe, or there would not be enough of it for her purpose. She reached for the vials and added them carefully, drop by drop, watching for some change that would warn her that this addition had "soured" the mix.

But it didn't. In fact, as she added the precious fluids, so difficult to come by and so very expensive, she felt the sullen power in the bowl increasing, and her lips stretched in a little smile of surprise. Well, well, well!

Last of all, she added the ingredients that had been the most difficult of all to obtain; the powdered hair of her "aunt" and "uncle," and allowed the fire to die away beneath the bowl. Finally the mixture ceased to bubble, and she now had, for all of her effort, a little puddle of a thick, black, tarry substance in the bottom of the bowl—black as tar, but not sticky. No, this stuff would be smooth and creamy to the touch, and would swiftly vanish into whatever it was combined with or rubbed on, leaving no outward trace.

And the power contained within it made her laugh aloud.

"We *must* find this monster," hissed Eneko. His hand came up and stroked a brow gone suddenly pale. "I have not sensed such a shriek of pure evil since . . ."

Diego, if anything, looked even more shaken. "At least we finally know the creature's sex. It's got to be a woman. That ritual—done that way, with a child—"

Francis and Pierre were frowning. Neither of them had the depth of knowledge regarding the Black Arts that Eneko and Diego possessed. Francis was a healer, essentially, and while Pierre's talents as a witch-smeller were superb, that was by its nature an applied rather than theoretical skill. They'd sensed the sudden blast of evil magic that had seemed, for a moment, to shake the entire island. But they'd been unable to discern the details.

"A woman?" queried Pierre. "Are you sure?"

Eneko shook his head. "Say a 'female,' rather. That *thing* is no longer human, in any sense of the term that matters."

Chapter 65

Commander Leopoldo had chosen to come and see Manfred while the knights were at morning drill, because he could do so while remaining unobtrusive. A party of men—and an officer—would come to do a stock-count at the magazine every Wednesday anyway. Leopoldo did this duty himself sometimes, so his presence while they were drilling in the courtyard was unremarkable. When the knights broke for a rest, it was simplicity itself to walk the few hundred feet under the arcade to the shade where Manfred sat with his watchdogs, and squat down so that he was virtually invisible. He was not a man given to peacocky clothes like Captain-General Tomaselli.

"Milords. I'm looking for some quiet advice. I've little siege experience and some things are worrying me."

Falkenberg grunted. "Not half as much as they worry me. And I have plenty of siege experience."

Manfred grinned at the young Venetian. "What can we help you with, Commander? Be warned. You give Falkenberg here the opening for a word on sieges and he'll give you ten thousand. And redesign your fortress. He's done so at least five times since we got here."

Gino Leopoldo smiled back, a little nervously. "The captain-general has expressly forbidden me to fraternize with you, Milord Prince. So if you don't mind keeping this quiet. . . I want to ask about those moles."

Manfred nodded. "They're creeping closer. Erik destroying the magazine out there stopped the covering fire for nearly twelve days.

But ten or twelve more days should see the south one complete. Another day, the north. And Emeric's siegemaster has men on a bucket chain on the south side of the Spianada. You can bet he has a tunnel project going. What are the plans to deal with this lot? The captain-general has decided to keep us in the dark."

The stocky young man grabbed a hank of his hair and tugged at it. He sighed. "We're planning on a sortie from the main gate. With footmen."

"I see," said Manfred, putting a restraining hand on Falkenberg. "Tell me more. Are these pikemen? Or arquebusiers? Or both?

"Arquebusiers. In a tercio. Only . . . the shingle is very narrow. No room for a tercio."

Manfred put another hand on Von Gherens's shoulder. "I see. But there are two moles. How are they to face both?"

"The first tercio will go south. The second north."

"The captain-general is certainly rewriting the science of war," said Manfred, so calmly that he thought Francesca would have been proud of him.

Falkenberg could take it no more. "No preemptive strike to destroy the moles?!"

The young Venetian shook his head.

"No flanking from the posterns?!"

Leopoldo shook his head again.

Von Gherens exploded. "Foot soldiers! Is the man insane? The minute those clumsy tercios try and get out of the gate the Magyar are going to charge from both sides. Without pikemen to allow the arquebusiers to reload they'll annihilate them! And the front gate'll be so packed with fleeing men they'll never close it!"

"Er. Yes. I know."

Manfred's eyes narrowed. "So where are the cavalry supposed to be in all this? Where are *we* supposed to be?"

Leopoldo looked, if possible, even more uncomfortable. "The captain-general wants to prove you're unnecessary. And my cavalry—and I don't have much, to begin with—is going to be kept in reserve for any street-fighting."

He shook his head ruefully at the gaping knights. "I am in charge of the Citadel garrison. But he is in charge of me. There is not a lot I can do."

Falkenberg took a deep breath. "Then I guess it is up to us."

Manfred shook his head. "Let's just remember what Erik and

you two have drummed into my head: The minute the first shot is fired the best battle plan in the world comes apart. And then, of course, commanders must act on their own initiative. What can you do?"

The commander shrugged. "All I'd thought of was the cannon. The captain-general has said they're irrelevant because the fighting will be below the walls. I've got about two hundred pikemen he seems to have forgotten in his plans. . . ."

Aldo Morando sat sipping his wine, waiting for Fianelli to come. He had a few interesting snippets, for which Emeric's agent would pay well. These rich, spoiled women—especially Sophia Tomaselli—were proving very effective spies. And now that he'd convinced Sophia that she should try to seduce Prince Manfred . . .

True, Aldo would be surprised if she actually managed the feat. Sophia was attractive enough, but nothing compared to the prince's leman, Francesca de Chevreuse. Still, who knew? Some men—Morando was one of them, himself—enjoyed variety. It was worth a try. If she succeeded, Aldo would possibly gain access to information hitherto locked away. To this point, he'd been able to discover nothing about the inner workings of the Imperial contingent in the Citadel.

There was hardly any risk, after all; to Morando, at least. If Sophia was publicly rebuffed or got caught in the course of success, the whole thing would just be ascribed to her sexual appetites—which were already fairly notorious in the Citadel, even if her dimwitted husband knew nothing about it.

Morando yawned. And success would have the added advantage of distracting Sophia from *him*. Ye gods, the woman was demanding! She came to him so often that he'd finally been forced to show her the secret entrance, or else she would have surely been spotted. Truth be told, Morando preferred his sexual liaisons to be with someone like Bianca Casarini. Casual, relaxed, basically distant despite the physical intimacy.

Speaking of whom . . .

He should start considering, with Bianca, the best ways to get out of here when the place fell. They couldn't hide in the cellar forever, after all, and there was no point in being rich and dead. He knew she was no more trustful than he was of King Emeric's final intentions toward his spies and agents on Corfu. She'd proven to be an excellent partner, and he thought she might be willing to continue the partnership somewhere else.

The Aquitaine, perhaps. Bianca would like the Aquitaine.

Sophia watched until Francesca went out into the town behind the second wall. She'd gone beyond being nervous about it. After all, men were just creatures of lust, easy to manipulate. And the thought of copulating with royalty, once Morando got her to think about it seriously, was . . . exciting.

She made her way across from her suitable vantage point where she had been apparently painting a picture of the battle scene, down to the prince's chambers. She was about to knock, when the door opened. Sophia took one horrified look at the profile of the woman turning to speak to the prince and fled.

Maria Verrier was not whom she'd expected to find there, beating her to her quarry.

"She should be back soon. You must literally have missed her at the gate," said Manfred. "Anything important?"

"No. Well. It's just odd. You know, Umberto's been doing night-watches. All of the men from the Little Arsenal have. Well, he told me that they've all been taken off duties on the north wall and at the tower that guards the postern at the Little Arsenal."

"Hmm. So who's taken over?"

Maria shrugged. "And how would I know, Prince Manfred?"

She opened the door to leave. As she did so, Manfred said, "If you hear—from your side—just who is on that shift, let me know as soon as possible."

She turned back and nodded. "I will." Who was that who had turned and ran when she saw her?

Sophia's face was contorted with fury. "I want her womb to shrivel and her breasts to turn to wrinkled dried-out dugs. I want her marriage blighted. I want her baby to scream. I want her dead. She's a thorn in my flesh. You promised me the curses. Give them to me."

Aldo Morando didn't entirely follow the logic of the woman, but then, if she'd been logical she'd have been useless to him. It seemed such a slight thing. But Sophia Tomaselli was unused to even the slightest check on her. He lifted an eyebrow, as he had practiced so long in the mirror. It made him look, he thought, particularly satanic. It had the desired effect on her, anyway.

"Please, master." She petted and fawned now.

"Remember that power has a price." He meant it in money.

She didn't. "Oh, yes. Whatever you like, master."

Morando considered the problem, for a moment, before deciding to accede to Sophia's wishes. She was an attractive enough woman, after all. And if she was now willing to do anything Morando told her to . . .

That could give better returns—as good, at least—as her spying. Leaving aside her own charms, such as they were, there were plenty of men in the Citadel who would pay handsomely for spreading this one's legs—just to cuckold her husband.

To think she'd originally come to him to help with fertility! She'd lost interest in that now. He'd certainly entrapped her well. This was what real Satanists were supposed to do. Typically, those who were crazy enough to deal with the Devil were not as good at it as he was, who did what he did for a sensible god: money.

He nodded. "Very well. Come tonight at midnight. Some things like this cannot be achieved under the sun. Bring gloves."

When she'd left, Morando reflectively scratched his beard. The belief in curses and cantrips was a strain on his imagination. A good curse token had to have one dominant feature: It had to convince the user. So Morando used some of the popularly recognized symbols. Deadly nightshade. Henbane. Pigweed. A rat skull. Some blood. And to ensure it smelled rightly vile—a sprig of parsley dipped in the privy. All tied together with entrails and a strip of parchment with a lot of garbage scrawled on it in red ink. The thing should cause a disease just by being in the house, thought Morando, inspecting the concoction with satisfaction. If the recipient found it—well, belike they would think themselves bewitched. That was usually enough to make a spell seem to work.

At midnight, with the inner room suitably lit with seven green candles, he handed it to her from under his cloak.

"You must hold it with a glove only. And you must burn the glove afterwards, saying the words *Rotas Astor Sotar Sator Araso*, seven times." He repeated the words twice, carefully, as if they really meant something. "It should be placed under the victim's bed or within the hearth ashes."

She reached a gloved hand eagerly for the bunch. "What is in it?"

"Some things which you are not ready to learn the powers of. But don't shake it. It has grave-mold from the tomb of an unbaptized infant mixed with the blood from the menses of a virgin sacrifice." He managed to say the last sentence with a completely solemn expression on his face. A bit difficult, that was.

She took it eagerly, but carefully, holding it as one might fragile porcelain, her face a candlelight-shadowed study in nastiness. Morando knew a brief inward shudder. From what he could work out the victim's main "crime" was a lack of respect for Sophia. Morando knew that he was dealing with a sick mind here. But business was business, after all.

Besides . . .

Morando had the psychological shrewdness of any successful swindler and procurer. Bianca Casarini was by nature an independent sort of creature. She might very well decide to go her separate way, after the Citadel fell and they made their escape to the mainland. If so, it would be wise to make sure that Sophia was still with him. She knew the secret entrance and would come to the cellar herself when it looked like the fortress was finally falling. He'd already, somewhat reluctantly, made the arrangements with her.

Now, thinking back, he was glad he'd done so. Sophia would have no choice but to abandon her past life and place herself under Aldo's wing. She was an attractive woman, and still young enough. The one thing about the future that was sure and certain was that a pimp could always get by.

Chapter 66

Maria habitually took Umberto something to eat and a small jug of watered wine at about Vespers bell, now that the Little Arsenal was working so late. It was amazing how purpose had transformed that place. Everyone but a few of the Illyrians seemed to be getting on fairly well.

She walked out carrying Alessia and a basket, closing the door behind her. Few people owned locks here. Maria and Umberto weren't among them. There was little enough to steal and besides the goat was turning into a terror. All she wanted was food, but then, would a thief be aware of this? The thief might of course want to steal her. . . . With each passing day the taste of meat became more of a memory.

There was of course food, even meat, to be bought. Some of it legitimately and on the open market: the produce of a few gardens; or hoarded by the wise before the event; a few fish caught over the walls that went down into the sea. Some—undoubtedly stolen from the Citadel's stores—on the black market that flourished for those who had real money. Maria and Umberto didn't number among them.

She was deep in these thoughts when the bleating of Goat— she'd never acquired a name, despite Umberto wanting to call her "Satan"—penetrated her brown study. She turned back to the house. The door was closed. But it sounded as if the goat was inside.

There was no telling what the creature would do if she'd got into the house. Maria turned and ran back as fast as a baby and a basket would allow. She unlatched the door and burst into the small living room.

Goat had someone cornered by the hearth. A cloaked woman who was thrashing away at her with a bunch of something. Maria had a moment's delay, to put the baby down, and then she sprang forward. She didn't think the intruder dangerous—half her mind was on restraining Goat.

She abruptly changed her mind. The intruder was all manic, scratching strength. Only the fact that the woman wore gloves saved Maria's eyes. Maria swung the basket. It and the strange bunch of stuff in the woman's hands landed just short of the grate. The woman grabbed desperately for the bunch. Maria lunged for her. The woman's gloved hand and forearm ended up in the hot ash as they wrestled.

The intruder might be manic, but Maria had both the weight and upper-body strength advantage on her opponent. Maria pressed her opponent's arm down against the fire grate. Was rewarded by a terrible scream, and a savage bite on her shoulder. Then, as the woman broke free, grabbing a poker, someone called: "Maria? Maria are you all right?"

Maria used the moment's distraction to grab the poker-wielding left hand, as well as the other arm. There was a frantic moment's struggle as old Mrs. Grisini—whom, to Maria, seemed half-absent from her own mind most of the time—peered at them. Then the strange hooded and masked woman wriggled her hand from the glove and tore free, bolting for the open back door.

Maria ran after, but she slipped on the spilled wine from her basket and fell, winding herself. By the time she got up, gasping, Mrs. Grisini had picked up and was comforting Alessia.

"She reminds me of my own babes. I lost all of them, you know," said the old woman in a dreamy voice, as if she had not just witnessed a savage fight.

The old lady's minder, a young Corfiote girl, hurried in. "Kyria, kyria? Where are you?" She saw the old lady with considerable relief. "Oh, thank heavens . . ."

Then she took in the rest of the scene. "What happened . . ." She looked at the bunch of strange stuff on the hearth that Goat was sniffing, screamed and pointed.

Maria nearly had her breath back now. She weakly shooed Goat off. Then, took a closer look at what had made the young Corfiote girl scream. It was pretty unappetizing, whatever it was. There was a rat skull and some hair. And some plants. Maria had grown up in Venice. She wouldn't have recognized many food plants before they'd gone to stay in Istria. But there old Issie had at least showed her some of those that were dangerous—including the deadly nightshade which she recognized in the bundle.

"A curse!" The girl crossed herself hastily. So did Maria. Old Mrs. Grisini just looked dreamily at Alessia.

Maria reached for the revolting bunch of nastiness to toss it into the hot ashes. "Don't touch," squeaked the girl. "Don't touch, kyria!"

Maria looked at the glove she was still clutching. "Makes sense. So what do I do with the damned thing, then?"

"You must take it to the Papas . . . the priests, kyria," said the girl fearfully.

Maria shook herself. "I suppose so. But how?" She didn't have so many pots that she wanted to sully any of them with the horrid bundle. Then she had an inspiration. The pot beneath the bed. It was only clay and could use replacing anyway.

The curse bunch fitted into the pot. The pot fitted into the basket. She tossed the glove in too. Poor Umberto would just have to wait for his dinner. Most of it was in the ashes anyway, and Maria didn't know what she'd find to give him instead. There wasn't too much to spare in the cupboard.

She went to old Mrs. Grisini, who reluctantly parted with Alessia and allowed the young Corfiote girl to lead her home. Maria set out once again.

She was heading for the church, at first, but then she changed her mind and headed for the small Hypatian chapel. If there was one person who knew all about magic and witchcraft it was that terrifying Eneko Lopez who was now staying in the monks' cells behind the chapel with his companions.

If they were there, of course. They seemed very busy these days trying to wander around the Citadel looking innocent . . . and failing completely. They were up to something, Maria was sure.

Fortune favored her, this time. They weren't in their rooms, but they were at prayer in the chapel along with the nun whose gardens were a byword in the town.

Not knowing how to disturb them, she waited. One, the tall dark one, noticed her. "Can we help you, signorina?"

Eneko Lopez's heavy line of dark brow drew together as he

looked at her. He nodded. "Maria Verrier. The friend and maid of honor to Katerina Montescue. Are you looking for us?"

Maria nodded. "Father. Uh, yes. You are an expert on witch-craft, I think?"

Lopez smiled wryly. The others chuckled. "I have had to deal with various forms of pagan magic. Whether that qualifies me as an expert, I don't know. But how may I help you?"

She opened her basket and, to everyone's surprise, took out the very recognizable pot and pointed into it. "I interrupted some-one leaving this in my house."

Looking up and seeing the bemusement on the faces of the monks, she realized the possible confusion. "Uh. I just used this pot to carry it in. I didn't want to touch it. I think it is a curse."

The priests came up and peered into the pot. "Come. Put it in front of the altar. Let us exorcize it anyway," said Eneko Lopez, taking it from her. "And this other thing in here?"

"It's a glove. The woman who was putting it in my house lost it in the struggle. She was using gloves to carry the thing."

Eneko's line of eyebrow raised. He went and placed the pot in front of the altar. He and the others arranged four candles very precisely around it, and then began to sprinkle salt, and then water, and burn incense as they chanted a psalm while walking around the pot.

Maria tried very earnestly to pray. Not for herself, so much, but for Alessia. Children were very vulnerable to disease. She wasn't sure, but she thought they might be especially vulnerable to black magic also.

When they'd finished, one of the priests went and fetched a pair of fine tongs—simple black iron things, but surprisingly delicate. They blessed the tongs and asked for protection on them, and then they began examining the bunch of plants and other fragments carefully. After a few minutes Eneko came over to where Maria still knelt.

"Maria." He spoke gently, and in a way she'd not expected from such a man. With understanding. "I know this is very frighten-ing, but I have some good news for you. That revolting thing is as magical as a brick. It was someone playing a very unpleasant and particularly nasty trick. It's a complete fraud."

One of the other priests had come up too. "A fraud by a per-son who knew more than is good for them about black magic and its symbols, but a fraud nonetheless. The words on the strip that bind the bunch together are indeed some demon names. But two of them are misspelled and there are no words of summoning. And one of those is the demon associated with senile dementia and the others are of little relevance, either."

"But the smell . . ."

The other monks had come up by this time. "I think you put it in the right place," said one of them. "It has been dipped in night soil. Unpleasant and smelly, certainly, but quite unmagical. Of that we are certain."

"A pity," said the other. "I really thought, Diego, that at last we had a lead on these devil-worshipers."

The short dark saturnine one shook his head. "I'm afraid not."

Eneko patted Maria, reassuringly. "Although you're disappointed, I don't think Maria is."

Maria shuddered. "No. Not at all. But . . . are you sure it is harmless?"

"Absolutely certain. There is not even a trace of magic about this thing."

"The woman I interrupted didn't think so. She fought me like a mad thing. She obviously believed in it."

Eneko walked back to the pot. "You say this was her glove? A wealthy enemy, this one of yours."

Maria had come over to it, too. She looked at the glove. It was made of the finest blemish-free kid with small pearl studs. Yes. Someone wealthy beyond Maria's dreams of avarice. Someone who could afford to spend on a pair of gloves the kind of money that Maria didn't spend on clothes in a year.

She shook her head. "But who? I don't really have any enemies— not that hate me that much, surely? And I know hardly any wealthy people. Here on Corfu, at least."

"Hmm. Do you want this pot back right away? We might try divining on it if we fail in this project we're currently busy with," said Eneko. "It may not lead us any closer to the devil-worshipers we seek, but it may be a good idea to root out whatever fraud is preying on people and letting their worst natures lead them into this."

Maria looked at the pot and shuddered again. "I certainly don't want it back. Ever."

Chapter 67

Emeric smiled rapaciously, looking at the assembled cavalry. When the details of the planned sorties had reached him, he'd been unable to believe the naiveté of them. But Fianelli assured him that the information was absolutely rock solid. It came from the best of sources. Emeric had told Count Dragorvich, his siegemaster. The Count had simply stared at him and then begun laughing.

"Why not just give us the keys to the gate, Your Majesty? We're finishing the south first, so they'll face the south. Well, Sire, you wanted to use the heavy cavalry. If this is really their battle plan, here is the opportunity."

Emeric nodded. "Light skirmishers and a testudo-covered ram on foot, as the sacrificial troops. Not too many. Use some of those Slovenes. And when the gates are full of arquebusiers—a two-prong charge. And tell the gunners not to aim for the gate any more. We want it to be able to open nicely and easily."

The moles had been basically complete since the previous day. Emeric made no effort to push troops across them yet, but kept the men working on them, widening and improving them; even clearing the sheltering mole walls, making the moles into causeways, under heavy Venetian fire. Then, in the morning, the first skirmishers began pushing across, using leather shields to protect them as best as possible. With them came the testudo and ram on its clumsy wooden wheels.

Watching from the southern postern, Falkenberg scowled. "Something's wrong, Prince. Even the captain-general can't believe that in an age of black powder and cannon, someone is going to sit and pound the gate down with a ram. They're waiting for a sortie. That's why there are so few of them. They are supposed to be able to get out of the way of the heavy cavalry, when it comes."

"We just happen to be wandering around with a hundred knights in full armor near the gate. We know nothing about this," said Manfred.

"And neither does that ass. Hark! There they go."

The trumpet sounded the sortie.

"Give it three hundred heart-beats before the first volley, and ten before the charge," said Falkenberg professionally.

He might have been off by two heartbeats when a horn blew on the Spianada.

"Here come the Magyars!"

Even from half a mile across the water they could hear the thunder.

"All right," said Manfred. "Out lances, *Ritters!*"

Commander Leopoldo, on foot among his arquebusiers, watched as it began going wrong. They'd burst out of the gate, the press of men behind him. The captain-general, perched on a showy gray, rapier in hand, attempted to organize them. The few Slovenes had fled, abandoning the testudo and diving into the water. "Reloa—"

The yells and thunder of heavy cavalry, massed and waiting between Emeric's earth cannon-ramparts, drowned the rest. Coming in a thick mass, ten abreast, Hungary's finest streamed onto the mole causeways.

Leopoldo gritted his teeth . . . waiting.

Emeric's cannon were not firing—too much chance of hitting his own troops, or possibly preventing the sortie. So, until that moment had Leopoldo's gunners been holding their fire also. Now all the Citadel's guns that it was possible to bring to bear on the causeways fired in unison. Leopoldo had had help from the blue-scarred Knot bombardier in ranging, and even in the choice of ball in those cannon.

The chainshot—intended to bring down masts, sails and rigging—hit the two Hungarian charges like sudden brick walls. One minute the Hungarians had been unstoppable.

The next . . . stopped. But the Knights had been right about their foe, Leopoldo saw. Not even that would stop them, and now the cannon would have to reload.

The pikemen on the walls poured the pitch and even managed to fling a few barrels to burst and shatter on the shingle just short of the north and south bastions.

"What are they doing!?" screamed the captain-general furiously. He waved his sword wildly at them. "Wait until they get to you, you idiots!"

But they were obviously too far off to hear that. Panicking, too. Some had even thrown a few faggots into the sticky mess. And in their panic, obviously everything else on hand—including caltrops and a number of burning brands. Leopoldo knew a moment's heart-stop when the naphtha and faggots on the south didn't catch. Pitch always was the devil to light. Then some brave soul tossed a grenade into it.

Between two fires, but still with half his men inside the gate, the captain-general yelled, "Charge!" His horse reared, and he waved his sword—a heroic figure.

And then he fell off his horse.

It's one of those things that will happen, even to the finest horseman—if a trusted sergeant has undone the belly cinch. But Leopold had no time to watch. He had a battle to deal with. He began bellowing orders.

Which did *not* include "Charge!"

The Knights of the Holy Trinity charged instead, sortieing from the northern and southern posterns. Hitting the flanks of the Magyars, they trapped some between the wall, the fire and themselves. Others they flung back onto the causeway. The Magyars had lost most of their impetus, the sheer weight of their charge that made them so unstoppable, in the cannon barrage. And then they'd had to gallop onto the thin strip of pebbles in front of the walls, and then the burning beach.

Horses—even well-trained war-horses—do not like fire. And the arquebusiers on the other side of the flames were making a very orderly retreat. Fire a rank. Step back. Within the gates, the officers had pushed the tercio apart and sent the men up onto the walls above.

The Knights of the Holy Trinity had the full two hundred and fifty yards to build their impetus. And on the narrow strip of land, superior numbers were no advantage. The Knights didn't like challengers to their position as the foremost heavy cavalry in Europe, and they inflicted a sharp lesson.

And once the causeway was packed with men dying, men fleeing, horses leaping into the water . . . they retreated at a sharp trumpet call. The near-rout was just being turning into a rally and second assault, when the reloaded cannon fired a second time. This time the targets were packed as tightly as possible. The carnage was terrible. The second charge of the Knights of the Holy Trinity was not so fast or fierce . . . but the resistance of the foe was gone.

The pride of Hungary were streaming from the causeways, and now the rout was unstoppable, even with Emeric's savage discipline.

The hastily following Venetian sappers, running up with kegs of black powder, whirling slow-matches and a prayer, had a good while in which to work, before one of Emeric's generals had the sense to push foot soldiers and Croats forward. Emeric himself had been too preoccupied shrieking threats at his cavalrymen.

The southern mole was blown apart, and only a narrow ridge remained of the northern one.

And someone had been kind enough to drag the captain-general inside.

Emeric seethed with rage, once he realized he'd stumbled into a trap. *I will crush them. I will crack them like lice. Every man, woman and child in that citadel will die.*

Despite his fury, a calm and calculating part of him was finally accepting the truth. The Citadel would not fall—not quickly enough, anyway—simply through military means. And while it might fall to treachery, treason was in the nature of things a slippery weapon.

I'll have to go back to Hungary and ask for help, damn her eyes.

"Ah . . . Your Majesty." Count Dragorvich, a clever man who always made sure that the king made all the crucial decisions— and took the credit for them, naturally—was without words this time. He just pointed.

The ricks of hay for the cavalry were on fire. Someone had obviously made the best of the distraction offered by the assault to attack their rear. Again.

"Get me the blond," Emeric hissed. *"Now."*

❀   ❀   ❀

"You're supposed to be an advisor to the Emperor Alexius VI of Constantinople. Why are you still here?" asked Emeric, looking at the blond man.

There was a pause. "I am here to see to my master's interests."

An interesting reply, thought Emeric. *Which master?*

However, all he said was: "It is very much in your master's interests to see us win here, and win decisively and soon. So I have a task for you. There is one of these Venetians—or rather an Imperial—on the loose. He and his men are attacking our rear. Our supplies, our materiel, even our men."

King Emeric leaned forward in his throne. "I've checked on your background, Aldanto. I know who you are, my Milanese traitor and sell-sword. This is the right sort of task for you, I think. Find Erik Hakkonsen—or his woman. Find them and bring them in. Hakkonsen I will have dead, happily. If you only get the woman . . . see that she survives. If not quite as she was, but in a good enough state to be bait. In the meantime, I'm returning to Hungary to fetch more troops and enlist some very powerful support. When I come back, I want to see Hakkonsen's head."

The blond man paused and then nodded jerkily. "Hakkonsen. Yes."

"Good," said Emeric. Nastily: "That'll keep you and that yellow dog of yours busy."

Chernobog did understand long-standing hatreds, for such things were meat and drink to it—and it indulged in such things itself, from time to time. It also understood the elimination of threats. Hakkonsen was the one who had put that throbbing scar on his forehead. The puppet himself hated the Icelander, for that matter, insofar as the puppet was still able to feel anything.

As for Emeric, well, Emeric did not merely nurse his grudges, he nurtured and watered them with blood, something else that Chernobog understood. So the demon would cooperate. It did not do this for Emeric, or in fear of Emeric. It did this for itself.

Compared to hunting for this place's seats of power, hunting peasants around the maquis was as easy as breathing to the shaman. He sent the hawks up, spotted a peasant and his son, and hunted them down with Caesare and his Croat escort.

❀   ❀   ❀

"You will find these hill-fighters," said the scary-looking blond in charge of the soldiers. "You will ask other peasants until you find them. And then you will give the leader this note. You will tell him I am a Greek with the Imperial fleet—but that I am from Corfu. I am shocked by the devastation, and wish to strike back at the Hungarians. Your family has worked for mine for many years. If he comes . . . Your son is free. Do you understand?"

The boy was perhaps four years old. The Greek peasant nodded. "Yes." He paused; quavered: "Do you promise you will do nothing to hurt him?"

The blond blinked. "Of course."

The yellow dog made no promises.

"It seems worth looking into," said Erik. "It would hit Emeric where it hurts. Money and weapons we certainly need. But can we trust this Xerxes?"

"My family have worked for them for many years, sir," said the peasant, nervously wringing his hands.

Erik's heart went out to the man. To be loyal enough to go looking for people the Hungarians would kill. Still, it could be a trap. "I'll meet him. Go back to him and tell him there is a small mountain just north of Giannades. There's a shepherd's hut on the ridge. I'll meet him there at moonset. Alone. Anyone else and he'll die. You'd better come back as a hostage, too."

"Where will I find you, master?" asked the man. "I'm from down south. I don't know my way around these foreign parts."

The Corfiotes always managed to make their island sound six hundred miles long, not about forty. "Just come up this valley. Someone will see you and bring you to me."

The man nodded resignedly.

"You must let me see my little one before I will go back. You must." There was an edge of hysteria and distrust in that voice.

The one named Aldanto shrugged. "See. But not touch or speak to. He's in the hut, guarded by the dog."

The peasant walked fearfully to the entrance of the hut. That yellow dog made him very nervous. Then, peeking inside, his face relaxed. He stared a while, then turned and reset his face into a grim determination. "Very well. But you hurt him and I will kill you."

The blond smiled at him. "Just do your part."

"You will let him go unhurt?"

"I will not touch a hair on the boy's head, if you do as you're told. I swear it. And I'll reward you with ten gold ducats."

"I don't want money. Just my child."

He turned and left.

High up in the clear blue sky, two hawks turned, too.

In the shepherd's hut, the shaman studied what was left of the boy: only a scrap of chewed bone on the bloody, but once lovingly embroidered, child's waistcoat. Just enough to conjure a good seeming from the magical principals of contagion and sympathy.

The dog's long red tongue licked the yellow teeth. Even the marrow in those dainty bones had been sweet.

"This is a bad place. Hawks keep chasing rabbits."

"Your control over them is weak."

"I have their names. They cannot do this," grumbled the shaman, muttering a string of words in Finno-Urgic.

The Caesare puppet shrugged. "Well, we have the general locality, we have a rendezvous. We need to plan everything carefully. It's not going to be easy. I've tried to ambush this one before once. It went badly."

Bianca was finally able to get rid of her "relatives" the day after the failed Hungarian assault. At her suggestion, her supposed uncle and aunt ventured outside with her the next morning, sharing in the general glee of the Citadel's inhabitants that another of Emeric's ploys had failed. They headed toward the walls, wanting to see the now-ruined moles.

Their path, as Bianca ushered them along, took them by an old stone-walled building that had suffered a fair amount of damage from cannon fire since the siege began. Some of the stones were now loose, held in place by wooden bracing. The night before, under cover of darkness, Bianca had smeared the stones and the wood supports with the special ointment she'd made up. Then, softly spoken the necessary incantations over them.

She accompanied her "uncle" and "aunt" on their promenade, chatting with them cheerfully. As they neared the wall of the old building, she stopped suddenly and went down on one knee.

"My shoe's got something in it. I'll catch up with you."

They continued on. When the moment was right, Bianca murmured the final words of the incantation.

It all worked very nicely. Following the principles of contagion and similarity, the wooden supports gave way and almost sailed toward her victims' heads. The loose stones followed, completing the work.

By the time Bianca's screams brought passersby to help her in her frantic attempts to remove the debris, her "relatives" were quite dead. The face and skull of her "aunt" were so badly crushed as to be unrecognizable.

Four priests, standing already at the fortress walls and inspecting the ruined moles, seemed to flinch as one man. Two of them raised hands to their heads, as if in sudden pain.

"And again!" hissed Eneko.

"Who *is* she?" wondered Diego, lowering his hands slowly and a bit shakily. "And where is she hiding?"

"I don't know. But we must start searching for her in earnest. This creature *must* be stopped."

Chapter 68

Something about the whole situation made Erik nervous. It just didn't feel right. "The rest of you stay back here. Deploy scouts on the ridge. Kari, Basil, Dimitris, let's go forward."

The hut appeared deserted. A low stone structure, a mere single room, it didn't appear to have many possible hiding places. And except for the long moon-lit shadows of the ridgeline they were advancing down, no close hiding places. Erik sniffed. It was a balmy night and warm air was full of the scents of wild thyme. So why could he now suddenly smell something totally out of place in the Ionian air?

Ice. Sea ice. And something he'd last smelled with Abbot Sachs and Chernobog's vessel. Like too sweet an incense. It made him want to sneeze.

It also made him very tense. The hilt of the tomahawk slid into his hand, and he walked forward alertly.

A shot rang out, from the hut ahead of them. Erik dove to the left. Basil screamed and fell. Kari's pistol boomed. The glamour used to hide the ambush wavered and was gone. Erik, yelling like a banshee and running for cover, threw the tomahawk. It hit the target dead center, splitting his skull. The arquebus he'd been aiming at Erik went off. A flurry of other shots followed.

There was more fire from the ridge where the rest had waited. But Kari, Dimitris and Erik, saved by a premature shot, were back in the rocks.

"Basil?"

"He was shot in the stomach." The Corfiote pointed. "Look down there, Erik!"

The last of the moonlight shone on at least fifty steel helmets coming up the valley.

"We'll go over the top, past the hut. They're coming down to look for us now. Just stay put."

"Fan out!" shouted an enemy officer, now so close Erik could have almost cut his throat.

"They'll be running down the hill," Erik whispered. "They might try to come back up when they see the squad down there."

A few hundred tense heartbeats later and the pursuit was heading off down the hill. At a loping dog-trot the three went upward. Erik had a chance to see young Basil. Someone had cut his throat in passing. Erik could only be glad. He'd have had to give the youth battle-mercy himself otherwise.

"Present for you," said Kari, handing him his hatchet. "Now let's get out of here. Dimitris is bleeding."

They ran on, finding it hard going in the dark. Fortunately, thought Erik, it must be as hard for the enemy . . . but it didn't seem to be.

"There's a dog or something with them," panted Dimitris. "It's following us. I heard it."

Pausing, Erik listened. He heard a baying howl, quite close, very clear. No other barks answered. And by crashing through the maquis, the dog was way ahead of its human support. "Kari, you go ahead with Dimitris. He needs help. I'll deal with this dog. We won't shake them while they've got the dog."

"You be all right?"

"It's only one dog. I'll see who follows it. Might be worth leading them astray a bit."

Soon Erik realized that the dog was definitely after him. And, just as he was turning to look for a good spot to deal with the beast, he ran into a neat ambush.

He nearly got three bullets in him—and would have if Thalia hadn't yelled "hold!"

"Erik!" It was some five of his own men, and Thalia. "Rearguard," said Giuliano. "The others are already ahead. We were just setting some booby traps to slow them down. Watch it. There is a cliff over there."

"Dog behind me," panted Erik.

And then it was onto them. Gaunt, pale in the starlight, yelping with hunting bloodlust. Erik saw the bullet hit it . . . but it did not stop. It sprang straight for his throat. Erik barely had time to grab the creature's paws, and stop it.

It was incredibly strong, and almost slimy. Hot, carrion-scented breath washed over him as it snapped furiously. Another shot rang out, with no obvious effect. The creature turned to bite at his hands. Erik dropped and, putting both his feet into its gut, gave the pale hound the full benefit of a flying mare. The dog hit a limestone boulder on the edge of cliff with a sickening crack.

And it got up in a single bound.

Thalia threw her bird-net. The creature tumbled in a tangle of meshes, snapping and yowling as if in pain. "Quick! Over the edge!" yelled Giuliano, grabbing one side of the net. He and Erik heaved and the net bag flew over the edge. Erik heard it bouncing and yowling on its way downward. He hoped it was a long, long way.

"Let's get out of here. We can set booby traps further on."

They hadn't gone more than a hundred yards when Kari hailed them. "Deal with the dog all right?" he asked cheerfully.

They'd taken every precaution to lose the scent, even if that demon-dog survived the fall. Down to the coast they'd gone, and walked in the water; then, come out into a stream, which they'd eventually left by way of an overhanging tree and then up onto some rocks.

Erik's feet were still very wet. And he was grim. He'd lost two men. Basil, who had been with him, and Luco, who had fallen in the skirmish with the rest of the group. And Dimitris's wound would keep him out of combat for weeks. What was more, he knew very well that they'd gotten clear by luck. The enemy were becoming more cunning.

Back in the forward camp, Erik found their peasant hostage— with a bump on his head and tied very securely. "He tried to make a bolt for it," explained Theo.

"Not surprising, that," said Kari, taking out his knife. "He's not going to have another chance."

The peasant's eyes widened with horror. Not at the sight of the knife. He didn't even seem to notice that. At the sight of Erik.

Erik looked back at him, dispassionately. "We'll have to move. But first we'll have to deal with this traitor. Show that no kind of money is worth this."

"I did not do it for money. I would not touch their filthy money. But they have my son, lord. They said they would kill him if I didn't bring you."

Erik's eyes narrowed. "Where do they have your son?"

"Please, lord. He is only a little boy. Four years old. Don't blame or hurt him."

"We do not make war on children," snapped Thalia. "Traitor."

His eyes blazed at her. "What could I do? They held my boy. They still hold him," he said bitterly. "They'll kill him. They'll think I betrayed them."

Erik saw a way to snatch a victory out this debacle. "Where is this child being held? We'll get him out."

The peasant prisoner gaped at him. Stammered. "But . . . but . . . I . . ." Words deserted him.

"Where is their base?"

"Kanakades."

"While they hunt us, we'll visit them," said Erik, with a savage smile. "They won't be in a hurry to trust peasants again, because they'll think you betrayed them. And they'll be a lot more wary. When you have to leave guards everywhere you have fewer men to fight with. Cut him loose, Theo."

"But Erik . . ."

"I can outrun him anyway. If we go along the other side of the Ropa, we should manage to avoid them."

The peasant made no attempt to run when they cut him loose. "I can show you where their patrols are." He paused. "If you save my son . . . well. I understand. My life is yours. But not my boy's. He is innocent."

"You've cost us two good men. And a good bird-net. And you've put some demon-dog onto our trail. As Thalia said: We don't make war on children. Or on peasants. But we'll expect blood-price from you for each of them."

"It was a very good net," said Thalia, quietly. "The priest blessed it. It fed us well."

Erik suspected it was not the knotted cords that had troubled the dog. The thing had not been worried by the bullets after all. It had been those blessings.

"It was an excellent net," Erik told her. "And one of the best throws I've seen. We must find you another one, since that's what stopped that creature. Although next time we'll try prayer, too."

❀   ❀   ❀

Having someone who knew where the patrols were made getting to the Croat encampment very easy and very fast. They could see their pursuit beating the bushes across the valley, but there were only two men in this camp: the cook and the remount escort. They weren't prepared for trouble.

The peasant sprinted for the ruined house on the corner, calling "Spiro!"

There was a moment's silence. And then a scream. A terrible cry.

Erik and several of the others ran toward him.

The peasant was on his knees, clutching at a piece of torn, embroidered cloth. There were a few bone fragments scattered around him. A partially gnawed femur lay in front of the man.

Erik closed his eyes. "God have mercy on his soul," he said hoarsely.

Eventually, the man stood up, his face a deathly gray. "He gave my son to the dog." He looked at the bones; looked at the remains of the little waistcoat. "The bloodstains are dry already." His voice began to rise. "My boy has been dead since I left. I swear before God and all the saints that I will kill that blond man. I will spill his life for the life of my son. *I will kill him!*" he shrieked.

"No." Thalia spoke. Her voice was flat. "You will pay back the blood-debt first."

She picked up the gnawed thigh-bone and pushed it into the hand still holding the scrap of the waistcoat. "Go. Go find your kin. Your brothers. Your cousins. Your friends. Hunt them through the maquis. Find them and show them these two things. Show them the tooth-marks on his bone. Tell them what you did, and how the Hungarians repaid you. And then bury these remains of your son. Bury them in the churchyard with honor, because he died with honor. You have not lived with it."

He looked at her for a long, silent moment. Then nodded and turned away.

"You are just going to let him go?" asked Ambrosino. "He betrayed us, after all. We can't have peasants thinking they can do that and get away with it."

Erik looked at the Venetian. Of all of the recruits, this one had fitted in least well. Ambrosino kept himself to himself. "He's suffered enough. Under the circumstances I might have done the same," said Erik shortly.

"And I reckon within two weeks the story will have spread to every peasant on Corfu, Uncle," said Giuliano, somberly. "You don't understand what it feels like. But I do. That man will suffer until he dies."

"And most important of all," Thalia said grimly, "no Corfiote peasant will aid them again. Not for fear or for money. You Venetians don't really understand us. The Hungarians can stay here a hundred years after that story gets told, and it won't matter. They will never crush us, and in the end, we will kill them all."

"All right. Let's turn these horses loose and get out of here," said Kari. "I'm not enjoying this like I thought I would."

PART IX
August, 1539 A.D.

Chapter 69

"You're a fool, Emeric." Even in such a gorgeous voice there was only one Hungarian in the entire kingdom who would have dared to say that. The speaker was petite, curvaceous and almost edibly beautiful. She was perfection itself from her musical laugh to her cascade of lightly curled, fine dark hair. Her skin had that bloom to it that spoke of youth.

Emeric of Hungary would have found a nest of angry vipers more attractive. His great-great-aunt habitually chastised him. She also never failed to assist him in his schemes. She had, she had admitted once, a fondness for him because he was the only one of her blood in which magical skill had manifested itself.

He waited. There was no point in rising to her bait.

"You should have come to me for assistance first. I would have advised you to stay away from Corfu."

"Jagiellon seemed to think it would be an easy conquest, by the money and materiel he arranged. He is not aware that, far from being his cat's-paw, I have had intentions to begin conquests to the south for some time."

Elizabeth, Countess Bartoldy, laughed musically. "My dear boy. The fertility rituals on Corfu go back to prehuman times. Something that ancient, which keeps its base of believers, has a power reservoir the size of the ocean to draw on."

"I haven't seen any signs of great magic yet."

She dimpled. "Corfu's is a passive kind of magic, tied to the earth of that place. Very difficult for invaders to deal with. I do have something that will work, however—because it is not in contact with the earth. Wait."

She returned sometime later carrying a glass jar. A large jar, a cubit in height. She carried it with a negligent ease that betrayed her great strength. Emeric peered into the cloudy fluid within, and then wished he hadn't.

"An experiment of mine," said the Countess. "I constrained a fire and an air elemental to mate. It is not a natural occurrence. This is their offspring, somewhat prematurely removed. I have placed certain magical constraints on the creature, as well as enhancing its power."

Emeric looked warily at it. "Just what does it do?"

The countess smiled "It is a bringer of fires. And, of course, winds. Sickness, too, is one of its aspects. But the core of its ability lies in dryness. An island—surrounded by water to contain it—should be the ideal place to release the thing."

Benito yawned, crackingly. "Sorry, Marco. It's not your company, honest. It's just . . . well, I have been working like a dog, and I haven't had much sleep lately."

Marco patted his shoulder. He noticed it was rocklike, stretching at the shirt. "You're working too hard. Everyone from the admiral to my father-in-law says so. Benito, one man, doing the work of a common laborer because he doesn't have the skills to build ships or clad them, isn't what Venice needs. She has plenty of good men working hard, but we need your brains."

Benito yawned again. "Why? Are we out of cannonballs?" He grinned and raised a hand pacifyingly to his brother. "Seriously, Marco. I have a problem here. Everyone expects me to lead like a *Case Vecchie* born. Giving orders, seeing that things are done. And I don't know how. I might be a direct blood relation of men who are great leaders of men, but I grew up among the canal people as a thief. The only way I know to lead is by example. So: I want these ships built. I don't shout at people. I challenge them to keep up with me. And when the carpenters say: 'That's caulker's work,' and sit back and say 'we can do nothing until they've done,' I pick up another balk of timber and ask, "Do you think this is *Casa Vecchie* work?' "

Marco grinned at him. "And the result is that you need new shirts. You've put an inch on your shoulders since you started here."

Benito pulled a rueful face and felt the tight seams on the shirt. "Yeah. I'm getting a bit heavy and bulky for the old upper-story work, Marco. Not so good for squirming in tight little holes. So, tell me, what's the news from the outside world? Any news from Mainz?"

Marco shook his head. "This kind of heart condition is not something that changes from day to day, Benito. Apparently the Emperor's physicians say he seems to be recovering a little. Of course he is struggling to breathe and his chest gives him a great deal of pain. But this may ease, and if there are no further recurrences . . . he may yet leave his bed again one day. But commonly, I'm afraid, when these problems start, they do recur. We can only pray for him."

Benito knew there were millions of people throughout the Empire doing just that. And there were very few indeed who would be privy to the detail Marco had just given him. Most of the citizens of the Empire would only have heard rumors that the Emperor was not well. But the Holy Roman Empire felt the tremors of an uncertain future run through it—as did all of Europe and much of the world beyond.

Benito scowled. "And on other fronts? How are your attempts to contact Eneko Lopez coming?"

Marco sighed. "Not so well. We can't raise him, for reasons that aren't clear at all. Anyway, what I came to talk to you about was what you'd said to me about the undines and the tritons."

"Get anywhere?"

It was Marco's turn to shrug. "They're not like humans, Benito. They . . . well, they only live partly in the same world as us and they don't see things the same way. But Juliette wants to meet you. That's a step."

Benito smiled. "Sure. I'll sweep her off her tail with my charm. When do we do this thing?"

"Well, full tide is a good time," said Marco. "That's in about an hour."

"Sure. Where? At San Raphaella?"

Marco nodded. "We can take a walk up together. Or take a gondola."

Benito shook his head. "I'm supposed to be confined to this place."

"Only by your own decision."

"Yeah. But I'll pretend to abide by it," said Benito, suddenly looking an impish five years younger. "The roofs of Venice miss me. And I might as well enjoy them while I still can."

Benito found the undine's gaze quite disconcerting. He'd been forewarned about the bare breasts, and if he ignored the color, they were quite attractive. One might say, pert. And besides, he'd seen a few more than Marco, anyway. But her unblinking stare he found . . . scary. Those golden eyes actually seemed to be looking inside him, at something just below the skin.

Eventually she spoke. "*Mage Marco, you are sure this one is your brother? His flames, and the fire in this one are strange. Powerful. There is an echo of you about him . . . but you are water. Cool, healing waters. This one frightens me.*"

Benito snorted. "Well, if it's all the same to you, green-hair, you make me nervous, too, just by the way you look at me."

Marco smiled and put an arm around Benito's shoulders. "Yes, Juliette. He is my brother. My half-brother, anyway. But he's been as close to me as a twin. And though at times he's as wild as fire, you can trust him to the ends of the earth."

Juliette didn't look entirely convinced. "*Spill a drop of your blood on the water then,*" she said to Benito.

Benito shrugged, took out the Shetland dagger and tried to prick his thumb. Hard work had calloused it, and besides, sticking a knife into yourself was never that easy.

"Do it for me, Marco."

Marco did, with all of a chirurgeon's practiced ease.

Benito squeezed the thumb. A red drop formed and splashed into the greenish chapel water. Juliette scooped some of it up in a long-fingered hand. Sniffed it. Tasted it. Looked penetratingly at him again.

Her next question startled Benito. "*Do you know the child Alessia?*"

Benito nodded. "She's on Corfu with her mother. It's where we wanted help to get back to."

Juliette regarded him keenly. "*Corfu! You mean Corcyra? Aieee!*" The golden eyes narrowed, still unblinking. "*Do you care for this child? Do you love her?*"

Benito blinked. "I . . . I don't really know her. I do care very deeply about her mother."

The look was now stern. "*I ask you again. Do you love this child? Will you guard her and care for her, if she needs it?*"

Benito had found the gaze of the Republic's chief Justice less disconcerting, less searching. Alessia was a baby, for heaven's sake. He'd hardly even touched one before her.

He remembered, suddenly and vividly, the warmth of her, the smell of her. She was Maria's kid. Of course he would love her. "Yes," he said, calmly.

Juliette continued to stare at him, but that flat golden stare seemed wary now. Benito noticed she'd edged away a little. *"The flame burns steady,"* she said at last. *"But it burns very, very hot. You must see to the child's welfare. I charge you with this. It is your responsibility."*

"And will you help us?" asked Benito, a little tired of the orders, the inquisition, the mysterious questions and references.

She nodded. *"I must. I will speak with the tritons."*

And then she slipped away into the water with scarcely a ripple.

"Well," said Francesca, with a small, satisfied smile. "I have finally found the link between several of the trouble spots. It's so simple that I am disgusted with myself that I didn't think of it earlier. It's the local black market. The factions all buy extra supplies out of the Venetian storehouses from two men. A nice little link of bribery and blackmail for spies."

Manfred almost fell off the chair he'd been endangering by rocking on. "What? How much of this is going on?"

"I'm really not sure of the extent of it, Manfred," said Francesca. "But from what I can work out most of the Corfiote Libri d'Oro families are involved."

Von Gherens looked grim. "Hang the lot of them. It's treason."

Francesca blinked at the knight. "It's buying food on the black market. Hardly a capital crime."

Falkenberg rubbed the scars above his eye. "What you don't seem to grasp, Francesca"—he'd finally gotten to calling her Francesca—"is that it undermines the military capability of the Citadel to resist. You see it as a chain of blackmail that spies and traitors can use. We see it far more directly as shortening the period a fortress can withstand siege."

"Both apply," said Manfred grimly. "And it has to be stopped. And it is no use just cutting off the supply. Von Gherens is right. We need to make it clear that the buying, too, is a crime."

Francesca made a face. "I see what you mean. But the biggest problem is finding someone in the Libri d'Oro who *isn't* buying."

"And we're going to have to find out what this corruption has done to the supplies."

"You are going to have to do so quietly, without causing panic," pointed out Eberhard.

"It'll also upset the Libri d'Oro. Make the fomenting of treachery easier for someone," said Francesca.

"Without food, Francesca, there won't be any need for treachery to bring this place down. We've got water until the winter rains at least. I thought we had good rations for a year. It depends now on how far this stupid greed has undermined the capacity of the Citadel to resist. We've got a lot of people here, you know."

"I know. I pointed it out to you," said Francesca dryly.

"Emeric is on his way back to Corfu." The words coming from Elizabeth's image had, as always, a faintly echoing air about them. "My plans are starting to come together nicely. So it is time for you to begin seriously undermining the Citadel. You have traitors in place by now, I assume?"

"Yes, mistress. I've managed to stall them, so far, although it's been difficult. They're mostly local noblemen. Corfiotes—the Libri d'Oro, they like to call themselves. Headstrong and amazingly stupid."

Elizabeth laughed gaily. "My dear Bianca, *all* petty noblemen are headstrong and amazingly stupid. If you think your Corfiotes are bad, wait until you meet the piglets who live in my part of Europe."

Bianca wondered if that was a promise. She'd visited the countess in her castle before, twice, but only for the brief periods of time needed to advance aspects of her training. At some point, though, it would be necessary for Bianca to take up residence with Bartholdy for an extended period. That would be a time that would be simultaneously exhilarating and extremely dangerous. Acolytes of Elizabeth, Countess Bartholdy, did not typically enjoy a long lifespan. But Bianca was determined—and confident—that she would be one of the few exceptions. Ultimately, the only exception.

The laughter having faded away, Bartholdy looked thoughtful. "I would have thought you'd be concentrating on the Venetians, though. The Libri d'Oro, when all is said and done, are simply parasites on Corfu. The real power is with their Venetian over-lords."

"I have infiltrated the Venetians also, mistress," said Bianca hurriedly. "In fact, the wife of the captain-general is now my creature, and through her—if and when the time comes—I can subvert him. But that poses certain obvious risks, which I don't think we need to take at the moment."

She hoped Elizabeth would let pass the fact that the "we" in the last sentence really meant "Bianca Casarini." Elizabeth was hundreds of miles away, after all. If Bianca's schemes and manipulations backfired, she'd be the one to pay the price, not the countess.

But Elizabeth seemed in a good mood. "Oh, yes, I can understand that. Very well. Try your Corfiotes first. There's actually no great hurry, Bianca. I simply wanted to alert you, not have you start rushing about frantically. If your Corfiotes fail, you'll have time to develop your plots with the Venetians."

After the image faded away, and Bianca finished cleaning up the signs of the ritual, she examined the man lying naked on her bed. Paulo Saluzzo's face was locked in the same expression of stuporous satisfaction that she'd placed him in before she began the ritual. Although his eyes had been open the entire time, staring bliss-fully at the ceiling, he'd been oblivious to the satanic practices she'd undertaken in the very same room.

He was completely under her control, now. Bianca didn't usu-ally bother to exercise that degree of magical control over her bedmates. She certainly hadn't bothered to do so with Aldo Morando. There was no need, as a rule. Sex itself, with most men, was enough to disarm them. But since Saluzzo needed to spend considerable time in her own house, unlike Morando or any of the Libri d'Oro with whom she'd copulated, Bianca had taken the time and effort to exercise the needed rituals on the man.

Besides, although those rituals were draining, they saved effort on the other end. She hadn't actually copulated with Fianelli's thug since the first few days after she'd murdered her "aunt" and "uncle" and seduced him. Saluzzo just *thought* she had. Indeed, he had the most vivid memories of wild and fantastic sexual activities, none of which had actually happened.

She laughed, softly. Deceiving Saluzzo was a small thing, of course. Once Saluzzo disposed of Fianelli for her, when the time came, she'd dispose of Saluzzo himself soon enough thereafter. And before too long, she knew, Bianca would have almost forgotten him entirely. Given the lifespan she intended to enjoy—eternity—she'd eventually forget him altogether. Still, she was discovering that she took increasing pleasure even in such small manipulations, deceptions and betrayals. Murdering the beggar boy had been almost ecstatically thrilling.

Such was the nature of her training and ambitions. She was very confident that she'd survive Elizabeth Bartholdy's regimen. Indeed, she intended to survive the countess herself.

Now, *that* would be a betrayal to cherish. Bianca even took the time, for a moment, to consider the ways she might use Elizabeth's corpse profitably. There had to be *something* immensely valuable to be squeezed out of that flesh.

Again, she laughed. No point bathing in the blood, of course. The one thing Elizabeth Bartholdy was not, was a virgin. Not in any sense of the term.

Chapter 70

Maria had taken to joining the Corfiote women in the weaving. After the incident in which she'd been arrested and hidden among them, she was accepted. And, she had to admit, now that Alessia was slightly older and sleeping through the night, staying indoors and being the good *scuolo* wife, shopping, gossiping, cleaning house, caring for the child . . . was far less active than she liked. It wasn't as if the house took much cleaning. Yes, Alessia did take a lot of time, and generate mountains of washing, but with Umberto working all hours and Alessia being a relatively easy baby—by comparison to Stella's children, who didn't sleep through the night until they were about four—Maria found herself wanting to be out, doing something.

Doing something to fight back. Weaving sailcloth would do.

Besides, she got on well with the Corfiote women. Most of the colonial Venetian women, even the *scuolo* wives, employed one or even several Corfiote girls in their homes. It was the largest difference in the way a Venetian *scuolo* wife lived in Venice and here. It also kept a gap between them and the local people. Working with them, Maria found she was absorbing the language in equal proportion to their respect. Here she wasn't a canal-girl who'd married a *scuolo* husband and gone up in the world. Here she was someone who they looked up to and who had earned their respect.

One of the women tickled Alessia. She gurgled. "She is a lovely child, Maria," said the woman wistfully. "I lost my first baby. The fever took him. I go to the temple to hope for another. But it may be better to only be blessed after this siege is over."

Maria lifted an eyebrow. "I think keeping your Spiro sober would be more worthwhile than the church."

The woman laughed. "Church, yes. But not the temple."

Maria was slightly puzzled. She'd seen them all at the chapel, at the Sunday communion. But she said no more.

"I accept that what you say is true, signorina," said Commander Leopoldo, a wry smile plucking at his lips. "But while it is true that a single young man like myself would seek you out and flirt with you . . . most people would assume that the prince would not take kindly to it."

Francesca lowered her lashes, smiling slightly. "Which is why you are cautious about it. Meeting me only occasionally and then keeping a safe physical distance, and well in sight of multiple witnesses. Believe me, I know men well. Not one of those watching will think anything more of these meetings than that you are brave philanderer."

The commander raised his eyes heavenward. "A stupid philanderer, more likely. Anyway. Just what does the prince want to tell me about?"

"The storekeeper. And a small coterie of clerks and guards. At first I thought it was just two of the guards, but we've pinpointed six now. They're running a black-market ring, selling extra rations to the Libri d'Oro families. Keep walking. You're supposed to be flirting with me."

His face was pleasant, but his voice was grim. "It's a hanging offense. I need names, Francesca."

"You need to go into this like a bull at a gate as much as a tavern keeper needs to give a drunkard a spare key to his cellar," she said sharply. "Eberhard pointed this out to us: If there is one thing we need even less than a shortage in the supplies, it's panic. Emeric has spies inside the Citadel, too. We don't need him to know, either. We want this quietly and efficiently done."

The young commander blinked. "I see I am in the hands of true professionals here. That sort of intrigue is not my forte, to put it charitably. All right. What do you want done? And can you walk a little slower? This hill is playing hell with my knee."

"Very well." She laughed—a musical sound, one that she had, admittedly, practiced. "This is my daily exercise too, Commander. In my former line of work, I could not afford to get fat and unfit.

I probably still can't, for that matter! But even if I could, I've developed certain ingrained habits. One of them is walking a lot, and the other is walking fast. I apologize."

Again, the commander blinked. Like many people, she thought, Leopoldo found Francesca's bluntness about her former status as a courtesan—even a whore—more than a little disconcerting. Especially coming from a woman with such a close personal relationship with an imperial prince. But—also like many people—that same straightforwardness produced a certain level of trust and confidence.

She smiled faintly, watching the quick interplay of expressions on his face. "Now, today at about Vespers a cart will be taking extra food to various buyers. It will be going to Count Dentico's lodging—among others. The Count is the head of the pro-Byzantine faction of the Libri d'Oro. Among other things, his 'volunteers' have been making their way onto the guard on the north postern, by the Little Arsenal gates. No, we don't think it is a problem yet. But it would be a good idea if they were unobtrusively split up. Anyway, that's another matter. For now I think you want to work on catching the count's staff, and the troopers, redhanded. If you play things right you should be able to get the clerks, too. I doubt very much if that will net the real traitors—these things usually have layers within layers, like an onion—but at least it'll put a stop to one immediate and major problem."

She paused. "Falkenberg wants to know why you haven't established a curfew, and night patrols. I agree with him about this one. It makes dark doings much more difficult, if not impossible."

The commander took a deep breath. "I tried. The captain-general said they were unnecessary. However, while he is on the back foot with this, we'll institute them."

"That's a good boy. Let me have passwords and chits or whatever system you use, please. And I think you'd better leave the Knights as above challenge except for a password. When they're in full armor, that is, since it will be rather difficult to counterfeit or steal *that* armor. I think Falkenberg wants a patrol or two of them. He's worried about mines. And now, farewell, my admirer. That same sergeant will bring you word when I need my exercise disturbed again."

"They're going to be cracking down soon on the black-marketeering, I hope you understand," Bianca said to Saluzzo, stroking his chin. "And there's never any guarantee that treason will work."

The Florentine thug, lying next to her in the bed, smiled lazily. The feline smile had a very self-satisfied air about it. Saluzzo was firmly convinced that he'd just enjoyed an hour of sweaty, energetic and very enjoyable sex.

"Don't worry your pretty head about it, Bianca. Fianelli's about as charming a guy to work for as a slug, but there's a good brain under that ugly exterior. He's had it set for quite a while that if the black-market business goes sour, somebody else will take the blame. Nachelli and his two little cousins have been the go-between with the greedy Libri d'Oro, instead of us directly. Besides, not even Nachelli's dumb enough to get caught in a black-market sweep. He'll still be around afterward, to take the blame if the betrayal of the north postern doesn't work."

She frowned slightly, still stroking his chin. "What's to keep them from fingering you, if they're caught? Us, I should say."

Saluzzo's smile shifted from lazy to something equally feline, but far more savage. For a moment, Bianca felt the muscles in his arms and chest moving. The Florentine was quite a powerful man.

"Like I said, don't worry about it. I'll take care of the problem. Might have Papeti give me a hand. Won't take more than that, not dealing with Nachelli. The rent collector and his two goons-in-name-only won't be talking to anyone, trust me."

"Still . . ." Her hand moved down, beginning to stroke his chest. "There's Fianelli himself. I really don't trust him, Paulo—and neither do you, don't try to pretend."

The Florentine's eyes rolled sideways, to examine her face. The look in his eyes was not suspicious, so much as simply cautious.

"Ambition's a dangerous beast, woman. If I learned nothing else in Florence and Naples, I learned that much. That's why I'm living here, on this misbegotten little island in the middle of nowhere."

She chuckled throatily. "It's not *that* misbegotten, Paulo. Lots of potential here, actually—especially once the Byzantines or Hungarians are running the place. Their notions of accounting are a lot sloppier than Venetian ones, to put it mildly. In the right hands, run by somebody less narrow-minded than Fianelli . . ."

"It is a both a civil and a military matter, your honors," said Commander Leopoldo. "Which is why I asked if both of you could come. I am sorry to summon you so late and so urgently, but it is I think of importance that this be dealt with quickly—and as quietly as possible."

"You can't do this!" protested a stout, florid-faced man. "I am one of the Libri d'Oro! Governor, this man"—Count Dentico pointed an accusing finger at Commander Leopoldo—"charged his troopers into my home and seized me. All for some imaginary infringement about some goods my staff—without my knowledge—bought in good faith."

The commander's face was bleak. "We have a cartload of grain from the Republic's granaries. In bags labeled 'property of the Republic of Venice.' We have seven ducats in gold seized in the act of changing hands between Count Dentico's steward and the soldiers from the granary. The steward confessed to doing this on the count's express orders—and, besides, such amounts of money can only have come from Dentico himself. Pursuant to these findings, my men took trooper Dorte at gunpoint and drove the empty cart back to the granary. Storemaster *Capi* Tapani demanded the money. We have arrested him, too. My men have seized the records and are examining the stores of grain and other foodstuffs. As a preventative measure, we have kept all the *capi*'s staff in custody."

He looked at the captain-general and the governor. "This is treason. Both buyer and seller endanger the fortress. But we don't want to create panic."

Captain-General Tomaselli looked excessively uncomfortable. Count Dentico was something of a friend of his. "These soldiers need to be dealt with harshly, according to military law. But the Count . . . well, my dear Commander. He's a nobleman and a loyal friend of Venice. One of the Libri d'Oro, as he says. We simply can't hold him accountable for the actions of his servants. Nor can you trust their testimony."

"He was feeding his horses and his hogs on it!" snapped the commander angrily. "Food that was meant to keep us safe from starvation during this siege turned into pig-shit."

The old governor sighed. "He's right, Tomaselli. If we let him off . . . if word gets out, and word will . . ."

"How?" the captain-general said, in disbelief.

The governor looked at him as if he had failed to be able to write his own name. "The commander has used men, not waxwork dolls, to arrest these criminals. So when the word gets out, the commoners who have been battling along on the siege-ration will riot, for certain. As likely as not, even the troops would join in. Then we have riots within and war without. The Citadel's fall is certain." He gave Tomaselli a weary look. "Besides, as the Count is a civilian, I believe I have the final say. I will examine the evidence, and question the steward and the servants of the Count's household."

He turned to the commander. "Do you have them in custody? Good. If the evidence is as compelling as it seems, we have little option but to apply the ultimate sanction to all the guilty parties, equally."

Chapter 71

Emeric leaned back on the cushions of his traveling throne. "And so. How goes the siege in my absence? How is the situation in general?"

Dragorvich had not survived as Emeric's siegemaster without developing a fine understanding of his master's moods. The king was in a suppressed good humor. Plainly he had got what he was looking for. Dragorvich knew he'd been heading for the Carpathians—a long journey with only one possible destination: the Countess Elizabeth Bartholdy. The most beautiful—and some said the most influential—woman in Hungary. Emeric had brought more cavalry, and more men with him. But Dragorvich knew his master well enough to suspect that was not all he'd brought back.

He also knew Emeric well enough to know the king wanted triumph for himself.

"Not as well as when Your Majesty was here. However, pursuant to your instructions, we have now started three more tunnels. My engineers calculate that all four are now beneath the walls of the Citadel."

He cleared his throat. "Pursuant to your instructions, we've halted repairing the moles. But a few weeks should see them repaired. We simply await Your Majesty's orders on that. As for the rest, we've kept up cannon fire on the western outer curtain wall. It shows some signs of damage, but it is still far from being ready to fall. Night-firing from the ships has been kept up, more for the nuisance value than anything else. The Venetian gunners have range and elevation on the ship's cannon, so we cannot really use them for pounding the walls. Also, with the fortress on Vidos covering that flank, we cannot bring guns to bear on the northern side."

"That fortress must go."

The Count nodded. "It would assist us to have it taken."

"I'll think about it. Now tell me, Aldanto, have you caught Hakkonsen and his saboteurs yet?"

"We caught and killed two of them," said the blond man, flatly. "The hunt will continue."

"It had better."

He turned to the Byzantine admiral. "And the blockade?"

The Byzantine snapped his fingers. A lieutenant hurried forward with a pouch. "These letters were taken from a vessel we intercepted some days after Your Majesty took the fleet back to the Narenta. They indicate that Doge Dorma has no idea that the island has been invaded. He is, however, taking steps for the reinforcement of it." The admiral smiled. "Or he was going to. One of the steps he commands is recalling Captain-General Tomaselli and promoting the commander of the garrison, Leopoldo, into his place. No surprise there, of course. If Tomaselli hadn't been well connected with the previous Doge, he'd have been recalled long since."

Emeric gave a little crow of laughter. "I want those letters. We shall have to see to a way of getting them into the captain-general's hands. He may wish to change sides." He rubbed his hands gleefully. "Any news out of Constantinople?"

"The Golden Horn enclave still holds out. Vessels are not expected back from Trebizond yet, Your Majesty. The Greek emperor is nonetheless pleased with some of the prizes he has taken from the ships sailing from Acre."

The king muttered something about Emperor Alexius. It could have been "Useless ass." Then he turned to the Croats and Magyar. "And the peasants? Are they getting back to the land? I want yields as well as loot."

The Croat nodded. "I had to hang a few men to get the message home. But there are more of them working their fields."

The Magyar captain cleared his throat. "There are some of the Corfiote nobility we've caught—what the Venetians call the 'Libri d'Oro.' Most of them are inside the Citadel, but some were still loose in the countryside. They're not worth ransom, but I thought we might make them into collaborators, Your Majesty. They can find and drive the peasants for us."

The king nodded. "An excellent idea. See to it."

"Your Majesty . . . there are several towns, too. Fortified ones in the north. We have them under watch but they're not besieged yet. When the Citadel falls, of course, they will be easy to take. But in the meanwhile . . ."

"Offer them terms. Once we're inside the walls, we can change our minds, can't we?"

All the officers standing about laughed heartily. They knew Emeric well enough to know the king admired his own sense of humor—and frowned on those who didn't.

Emeric had chosen a bare hilltop overlooking the Citadel from the southeast for the ritual he had to enact in strict accordance to the instruction from Countess Elizabeth. Initially, he had been pleased at extracting help from her; now, in retrospect, he was no longer as pleased as he had been.

Elizabeth Bartholdy had a way of bringing the kings of Hungary under her control. Emeric had watched the effect on his own father, over the years. By the time his father died, he had been no more than a shadow of the man Emeric remembered as a boy.

He wondered just how many strings were attached to this particular "gift." Elizabeth never did anything that was not to her advantage. And, yes, he made use of the darker powers himself, but not to the extent that she did. Nor did he meddle with the powers that she dared to.

But . . .

He had the damned thing, after all, so he might as well make use of it.

He went out to his picked site in a grim state of mind. He ensured that his men would cooperate by stationing guards around a perimeter that was far enough away that no one would be able to see what he was doing except for his special assistants. Those assistants had been provided for him by Elizabeth, also. The ritual that needed to be enacted here could not be done by one person alone.

The weather had decided to cooperate, at least. Storm clouds gathered and built around Pantocrator. The wind whipped angry flurries of dust from where the assistants had been assiduously clearing every scrap of living matter, even lichen and tiny rock plants, until there was nothing but sterile, barren rock. Another was sharpening the bronze knife.

The patterns and sigils Emeric would do himself; he trusted such things to no assistant, even ones trained by Bartholdy. The fact that he kept such iron control over important matters, delegating them to no one else, was one of the things he thought his great-great-aunt respected about him. The brushes and pens for that work he kept in a special case—an ancient thing she'd given him many years before. It was made of hide and bone. The hide was curiously dark and iridescent, the bone . . . jet black. Neither part came from any earthly creature, and neither did the fangs, which served as a sort of semi-living lock and guardian. They opened only on certain words, treacherously closing on the hand if a mere intonation were wrong.

Of course, the king needed a suitable supply of ink. That was what the knife was being sharpened for. These rituals were designed to constrain the nonhuman and to protect him from it. They had to affect the homunculus he was about to release. Elizabeth had supplied the nonhuman blood from her captive stock. And Emeric and his assistants would have to give of their own to protect themselves.

So, when the knife had been honed to an edge that would wound the wind, each of them carefully slashed his forearm in turn, beginning with Emeric. Each of them funneled the scarlet blood that ran from the slash into the bottle that Elizabeth had prepared, while Emeric recited the guttural phrases Elizabeth had provided him. The sky darkened and the wind whirled around the hilltop, shrilling in their ears. There were two bottles now, one of red "ink," and one of black. Taking the first brush, Emeric began to paint the body and face of his first assistant with an intricate interweaving of sigils and symbols. The first went to build a fire in the center of the cleared place—only the fuel was bone, human and unhuman. When he was done with the last of them, and only then, did his most trusted assistant take the brush and complete the job on his master, Emeric. Then Emeric took up the knife and cut the first of thirteen protective circles into the bare earth.

At length, when the summer storm had formed into a huge dark tumbling mass, with Pantocrator shrouded in rain and distant thunder growling and cracking closer, they were ready. Stripped to the waist and painted—only their eyes showing in the masks of lines of alternating black and red—the nine began their chanting. The bone-fire was lit, the fungus that Emeric had piled atop it burning with a greenish flame.

Lightning lashed the earth, as if it was trying to strike them, but inside their protective circles it could not touch them. The assistants were made of stern stuff; though the very earth outside their hilltop smoked with the strikes, and the thunder threatened to shatter their eardrums, they did not even falter for a moment in their chanting.

Then, when the winds began to roar and the flames were near horizontal and the first heavy drops were splashing down onto the sun-dried earth, Emeric picked up the glass jar and threw the container into the flames. By the time the jar left his hands, the creature inside was fully aroused. The King of Hungary could sense the malevolent rage emanating from it.

The jar shattered. The liquid ran out of the fire in little coruscating, hissing rivulets.

The earth shook, angrily. If Emeric and his assistants had not been warned of the effect and braced for it, they would have been knocked to the ground.

And then the screaming began.

The scream seemed to go on and on; it pierced the very brain. It was full of rage, and pain. And for one, terrible moment, even Emeric wondered if he had let something loose that should never have seen the light of day.

The mighty cloud above them was lit with sheet lightnings. And the rain, advancing moments before, slacked off. The scream thinned and faded, receding into the distance, leaving a strange taste in the back of the mouth, and somehow, in the mind.

Well. Whatever had been turned loose was no longer his problem.

Emeric stood triumphant, smiling toothily in the flickering firelight. The truth be told, high magics were something he followed by rote. He enjoyed the powers conferred on him, the use of which required no effort on his part, but he was always nervous about these tasks.

Suddenly the earth itself trembled. He was flung from his feet.

The rock beneath the fire burst explosively, scattering flames and ash over them. The ground shook beneath them, again and again.

The ground shook like a dog, flea-bitten. "What was that?" Svanhild clung to Erik. *First the storm and now this!* She wished for Cahokia.

Erik patted her comfortingly. "Its just an Earth-tremor, dear. We have had them up at Bakkaflói, especially when the volcano at Surtsey has been active. In my grandfather's time, one knocked down half of Reykjavik. Either it is not a very big one or we are far from its center."

"Are we safe?"

"We should probably get out of this cave."

"But it is raining out there."

"It seems to be stopping now."

Manfred picked himself up from the battlements. "Who in the hell needs cannons? Another one like that and the walls will just fall down. Does this part of the world often get earthquakes?"

The captain-general nodded, staying sitting down. "They have been heard of before, yes." Manfred had been trying for tact, especially when listening to the captain-general's version of the destruction of the moles. He'd been struggling with a volcano of laughter. Instead he got an earthquake.

"Well, it is a lot less welcome than that storm will be, if it comes here off the mountain. I thought I was going to boil in my armor today."

Eneko Lopez and his companions came breathlessly up the stairs.

"Did you hear it?" demanded Eneko. "Or see anything unusual?"

"No. But I felt it," said Von Gherens. "Knocked me off my feet."

"Not the earth tremor. Just before that. The scream. The agony and the rage and hatred."

Manfred shook his head. "It wasn't from out here. We were watching the coming storm and then we had the 'quake. The storm seems to be breaking up."

Eneko took a deep breath. "Something very magical, and very, very evil has come to this island. Something that should not ever have been created. I fear for this place."

✿ ✿ ✿

Count Dragorvich cursed. Then he swore. Then he kicked a rock. His adjutant kept well back. He had run to call the siegemaster, only to find the man striding to the mines already.

"All four, Tiepostich?"

The adjutant nodded. "Yes. We got two men out of the northern one. In the others we lost all of the sappers and we lost most of the bucket chain."

"Damn! Labor is scarce enough without this. And the king is not going to be pleased that we have to dig the tunnels again. We need to wait a few days before we restart too. There are always aftershocks."

Tiepostich knew that when the king was not pleased, one of Dragorvich's men was usually going to be heading for a slow death. He wondered if, this time, it would be him.

In the cave beneath the Citadel the rock moved, though not so much as a stalactite fell. But the priestess watched in horror as the sacred pool cracked across, and the water drained away into the rock.

She looked at the small altar with the half almond. Without a bride he would not help. The Goddess would defend, but this . . . this called for *him*. For the actual wielding of power.

But who would pay such a price?

Chapter 72

Francesca, Manfred thought, looked sour. She sighed. "I thought—as you wouldn't let me corrupt the black market for my own ends, as I wanted to—that we'd be better off getting rid of Count Dentico as the most dangerous of the lot. It appears I misjudged the nasty piece of work. He was such a pompous ass that he was thwarting, rather than aiding, the conspirators."

He eyed her uncertainly. Francesca was really in a rather foul mood, which was unusual for her. He needed to tread carefully here.

"That black-market ring had to go, Francesca. There were supposed to be siege rations for at least ten thousand souls for a year. Those stupid bastards were using the stuff like there was no tomorrow. Seven, eight times the ration per person. Wastage you wouldn't believe. Feeding animals on it. At a full ration now, the supplies will all be gone by December. Even on the slow cutback in rations that not causing panic demands, we're going to be eating boiled boots by March."

Francesca scowled. "Damned soldiers and their straight-ahead view of things." She gave him a look which was not entirely admiring. "Manfred, I *still* worry more about treachery tomorrow than starvation by next March. It's now blindingly obvious—to me, at least, if not you and Von Gherens and Falkenberg and—"

She waved her hand irritably, encompassing in the little gesture all of the world's *damned soldiers*. "Count Dentico and that crowd of Libri d'Oro were just tools, being manipulated by someone else. Or, more likely, *several* 'someone else's.' There will be manipulators manipulating the manipulators, be sure of it, each layer of them better hidden than the next. And they'll have a more fertile ground than ever to do their work now, since the Libri d'Oro families have gone from a diet not far removed from the presiege one to a siege ration."

"Nine tenths of a siege ration, actually," corrected Falkenberg. "Do their souls good to fast a bit."

"It probably would," said Francesca. "Unfortunately, what it has done instead is to have made most of them angry and some of them desperate. They're blaming the Venetian authorities for their hardship, rather than themselves. There is still some black-market stock out there but the price has gone up sevenfold. And that's just making the people more bitter and revolt-ripe. I'm beginning to think we should have followed through on Falkenberg's ideas and hanged the lot."

The one-eyed knight grinned. "My old mentor had been through six sieges on the inside, and five major ones on the outside. You look at the bottom of all the usual suspects for why a fortress falls to siege, supply is usually the driving factor behind it."

"I'm worried that real trouble will break out now. I know there have been a whole rash of secret meetings among the Libri d'Oro families." Francesca sighed. "For that matter, the occasional exception like Leopoldo aside—the podesta is all right, too, if it weren't for his age—the Venetian upper crust in the Citadel doesn't fill me with great confidence either. Whenever you have someone like Tomaselli in a position of power in a small and isolated region like this, things get very rotten, very quickly. Venice should never have given him the post of captain-general in the first place, and, having done it, should have recalled him at least a year ago."

The soldiers in the room said nothing. What was there to say? On this subject, they all agreed with her.

Francesca never stayed in a bad mood for very long, fortunately. That wasn't so much because she had a naturally sunny disposition, Manfred thought, as the product of her long and rigorous self-discipline. The time he'd spent in Francesca's company—almost two years now, most of it in very close company—had made a number of things clear to Manfred about the once-whore, once-courtesan. Perhaps the clearest was that Francesca was the most formidable and capable woman he'd ever met in his life. Out of bed, even more than in it.

"Well," Francesca said, visibly forcing a little smile, "thank goodness young Leopoldo altered the duty rosters or I'd say the north postern was very insecure. But still, Manfred dear, I think we ought to consider extra patrols of Knights. Hefty patrols, not just a pair here and there. And I'm sure Leopoldo will listen to you if you suggest a few extra checkpoints."

Manfred nodded immediately. So did Von Gherens and Falkenberg. Whatever private opinion the two devout Knights of the Holy Trinity might have regarding Francesca's past, they had no more doubt than Manfred of her present competence.

Querini had a weakness for dice. And the cavalry captain's head was a lot less strong than he thought it was. The grappa had thoroughly fuddled it.

When he looked at the total of his losses he sobered up fast. "Ah . . . you'll give me time, surely?" If the siege went badly he might just die. That would be out from under this, at least. He'd lost several months salary, and was habitually in debt anyway.

The younger Dentico, now Count in his father's shoes, shook his head regretfully. "Can't do, I'm afraid. Since . . . the unfortunate happenings, we're having to watch things with the Army. You know my father was really killed because Tomaselli had borrowed heavily from him. It was a totally put-up job. We thought," said the young man, bitterly, "that Tomaselli was a friend of father's. So: no carried debts."

The cavalry captain was sweating now. "I . . ."

"Of course, if you could help us out on another matter that's been irritating us, we could let it go by for a while. We'd know we could trust you."

"Of course! Only too pleased to help. You know I organized those duty transfers you and the other fellows wanted so you could all be together . . ." Querini's voice trickled off.

"As it happens, Captain, it was about that that I wanted the favor. Some idiot's gone and shifted us around again."

Querini winced. "Commander Leopoldo has taken all the duty posting under his control. I can't do that again."

"Oh, there'll be no need to. I've got the June roster here. We'll just . . . cross out June and put in September. It's all in your writing anyway. And signed by the commander."

The sweat beaded on the cavalry officer's face again. "If Leopoldo finds out he'd ... he'd ... He doesn't like me anyway. I can't do it."

The young Dentico sighed and tapped the pile of chits. "Look, Leopoldo doesn't check every day, does he? The boys and I—well, I'll tell you the truth. It's Desarso's daughter. She's available and she likes a bunch. You know, some women just can't get enough. It's Adriano's birthday, and we thought we'd have a little party for him. But several of the fellows' fathers are real sticky about them being out, especially with this damned curfew. I mean, we understand why it's got to apply to the commoners, but it is ridiculous for us. So if you just slip this onto the duty board for the sergeants the day after tomorrow ... we could forget this." He tapped the pile of chits again.

"It's done," said Saluzzo cheerfully, as he slipped through the back door of Bianca Casarini's house. "Within a fortnight, I'd say, maybe sooner. Hard to know, dealing with those idiot Greeks. But Fianelli tells me that Nachelli's cousin reported that the young Dentico handled Querini perfectly. He was there, watching, the fool. If it goes sour, the Greeks will finger him instead of us; through him, Nachelli—and me and Zanari will make sure that Nachelli can't finger anybody."

He laughed coarsely, pulling her to him and lifting her onto the table by the door. The Florentine's hands were already forcing up her skirt. "*If* it goes sour. It might very well not. Best thing the Venetians did, executing the old count. His son's smart enough to do the work right, and dumb enough to do it in the first place."

She responded to his lustful embrace with feigned enthusiasm. That was just a bit difficult, since Saluzzo was obviously in a rutting mood. He wouldn't, this night, give her the time to prepare the rituals that usually allowed her to leave him to his own fantasies.

So be it. It was a minor inconvenience, after all, and she could use the opportunity to advance another scheme. "That still leaves Fianelli himself," she gasped, spreading her legs. "I'd feel a lot better—*oh, Paulo!*"

The Emperor's hands shook as he held the parchment. He screwed up his eyes in effort, and then handed it to Baron Trolliger. "Read it for me, Hans. Damn this ailment. I want that boy safe, and I am too weak to see to it properly myself."

Trolliger read the agent's report aloud. The Emperor pursed his lips. They were slightly blue, Trolliger noted.

"Two things," said the Emperor, tiredly, but breathing slightly easier on the new medication. "One. I want an attack on Emeric's borders with the Empire. Give him a reason to come home. Second. Dispatch to Spain. If my commanders there can spare the Venetian Atlantic fleet as many extra men as the ships can carry. Rations too. These generals. So literal."

The Emperor closed his eyes. "I hope Francesca is all right. Sieges are hell on horses. And worse for women and children."

"Sieges are hell for everyone," said Trolliger quietly. He'd lost his younger brother, two sisters, his mother and his dog in a siege that had spawned disease. It had taken half his family, that plague. Except for the dog. They'd eaten that. The baron still gagged every time he thought of it.

"We've already got six light galleys ready for sea, Doge Dorma," said the Admiral of the Arsenal. "Mostly," he scowled at Benito, "because of that menace you have put in our midst."

Benito sipped his Soave, and smiled beatifically. "The admiral and I are the best of friends, really, Petro," he said innocently. "I've solved so many problems for him."

"Broken so many *scuolo* rules that the older masters want to murder him and the youngsters think it is a fine thing to do," growled the admiral. "I will say that this building program has been the better for it, though. Of course in the long term we'll regret it. You can't put the wine back into a grape when you want to."

Petro Dorma smiled and waved a hand pacifyingly. "Well, Admiral, how about if I took him off your hands? Of course, we'd want you to keep up the same rate of building, or we'll send him back."

The admiral scowled again. "We'll need an extra four laborers for the heavy lifting, but think of the tranquility! I don't think you'd need to send him back, Your Grace. The Arsenalotti are caught up in the patriotism of this young ward of yours now. I don't think I could slow them down. But what are you going to do with him? I can recommend a flea-ridden village a few miles from Eraclea. I have a grudge against the place."

"We want to send him back to Corfu, if we can. With three of those light galleys, some men, money and weapons."

Benito bounced to his feet, spilling wine. "I'm out of here! When do we sail, Petro?"

"Within the next two days. Your brother wants you to come and see him about 'special guidance,' Benito. As soon as possible. He said you could even walk, ride or come by gondola." The Doge raised his eyebrows. "I was not aware that you could get to him any other way."

Benito grinned. "You learn something new every day, Petro."

The blond-bearded triton Androcles was, as far as Benito was concerned, far less alarming than the undine had been. For starters, the look in those aquamarine eyes told Benito that the triton would probably delight in just the sort of practical joke that would appeal to Benito. And for a second thing, if the nonhuman's eyes looked into his inner being, Androcles wasn't as deeply interested in what he saw there.

"Whoever advised you, advised you well. There is indeed something out there. Something to be avoided. A monster of slime and teeth. A parasite that likes to eat its victims alive. And it is working with the ships above, sometimes."

"Can you help us avoid it?"

The triton grinned. "I can. But will I?"

Benito shook his head mournfully. "Questions, questions. That's a hard one . . . as the camerata singer said to the bishop."

Androcles' shoulders twitched. He smiled and nodded. "He'll do, Juliette. The Lion seems to think that your efforts might get rid of this menace. And the truth be told, we don't like the thing. It stinks and befouls water even worse than humans do."

"Two days' time?"

The triton nodded. "We'll go and range the deeps in the meanwhile. We can taste the creature from a good many miles off, now that we have learned what it is."

Chapter 73

Dragorvich had been prepared for Emeric's fury at the loss of his mines in the earthquake. So he'd been relieved to find his master taking it all in relatively good humor.

"They may be unnecessary after all, Dragorvich. My agent within the fortress has widened a good chink in the enemy's armor. In the meantime, see if you can make the north causeway at least passable by footmen, and light cavalry at a pinch."

Dragorvich nodded, too relieved to ask many questions. "I've had men on the dark nights sneaking as far as they can and then swimming across, to clear caltrops. A few have been shot, but they paint themselves with mud first. They're difficult to see. The shingle should be safe for cavalry from that point of view, anyway. The causeway . . . give me a week, Sire, two at the most. It'll be good enough. We can make a covered way with green cowhides on top and some sandbags. It won't stop all the fire but it should make it possible for us to push a number of men across."

"That sounds excellent, Dragorvich. Don't make your preparations too obvious."

"Very well, Sire." He hesitated a moment. "I have a request. I know the policy is to get these peasants back onto the land, but I am desperately short of labor. If there is any trouble, can I have some of the troublemakers? We'll put them in leg irons and use them up at the front. They're likely to die, but rather them than my sappers."

"An excellent idea. I'll let Ionlovich know. Don't spare them. They're not in that short a supply."

❈   ❈   ❈

That had been ten days ago. Dragorvich had gotten his peasant-prisoners and had achieved all he'd promised. In the darkness his men had been readying the causeway to take a push of several thousand footmen, mostly Slav pikemen, and a number of Croat light cavalry units, who had been forming up since dusk. Dragorvich wished he knew exactly what the king had planned. It was plainly treachery from within the Citadel, and plainly on the northern side, presumably with someone on the postern there.

In the meantime, the new mines had been started anyway. He had reluctant Corfiote slaves to do that work now. And the cannons still kept up their volleys against the walls. The walls—so far—hadn't crumbled much. The trouble with bombarding Corfu's Citadel was that so much of the fortress was made of natural rock. You could eventually pound a breach in it, but it was harder than mortised stone.

Sergeant Boldo looked up at the duty rosters above him. The current roster had been made out by that ass, Captain Querini again, he noticed. Lazy bastard just crossed out the month. Oh, well.

"My name is there, Sergeant," said the young Libri d'Oro buck languidly. "See."

Sergeant Boldo shrugged, and handed the young man a curfew pass. "Password for tonight is 'nightingale.'"

This new system of Commander Leopoldo's was a pain in the bollocks. Still, orders were orders, and the man was reasonable. After the chaos of the first week, the commander had given week-passes instead of daily ones for those who worked nights, whom he—and some mysterious other—approved. The recipients had to learn the week's worth of passwords and two of the Arsenalotti masters had ended up in the brig for the rest of the night because they'd forgotten them. The sergeant had expected them to kick up a stink the way the *scuolo* usually did when they thought their territory was being infringed, but they'd been sour but reasonable about it.

Umberto got up for the midnight-to-dawn guard shift when Alberto Mavroukis tapped gently on the window. Alberto was one of those rare individuals who could fall asleep at the blink of an eye—at any opportunity—and yet had an internal clock that could wake him when he needed to. Alberto and Umberto were two of the ten masters from the Little Arsenal who were recipients of week-passes for this new curfew system. Though its purpose was to allow them to work late, it also meant he could sleep at home if he was on guard with Alberto. Sleeping next to a warm, soft-skinned Maria was infinitely preferable to sleeping in the north wall guard barracks.

The two walked down the dark cobbles. As luck would have it they ran into a bored, small-minded guard, who refused to accept their week-passes and insisted on taking them to his guard commander at gunpoint. The guard commander was in the throes of waking the next shift, and it took a great deal of Umberto's patience to get them, late, heading for the guard barracks on the north curtain-wall. The bells were already chiming for midnight before they were halfway down there.

"That bastard of a guard commander will probably make us sleep there next time," panted Alberto.

"He'll just chew us out," said Umberto, and saved his breath for running. The two arrived at the guard barracks.

Both realized immediately that something was very, very wrong.

The guard barracks was silent. It should have been full of people getting their gear off and lying down to rest, earlier watches griping about the noise.

Umberto looked at Alberto. Then he took the issue rapier out of its scabbard and walked forward into the lamplight.

The guard commander wasn't going to chew anyone out. Or make them sleep in the barracks. He lay in a pool of his own blood.

"*Merde!*" said big Alberto, in a very small voice. "What the hell do we do now?"

"Raise the alarm!" Umberto took a deep breath.

"Keep quiet or I'll shoot," said a voice from the shadows.

Umberto yelled. "*ALARU . . .*"

He felt rather than heard the shot.

As he fell he saw in a sort of strange slow way how the big caulker had grabbed someone with a pistol. He saw Alberto fling the willowy, elegantly dressed young man at a second man. And Alberto was bellowing at the top of his vast lungs.

❀   ❀   ❀

Knight-Proctor Von Desdel and his patrol of ten knights were within a hundred yards of the guard barracks when they heard the shout, the shot and the yelling.

"That's inside the wall!" He was already urging his charger forward. "Sound that trumpet!"

Over on the Spianada, the Croats had heard the midnight bells without getting restive. The plan allowed the guards on the western outer walls to be changed and settle down before the northern postern would be seized. The biggest danger was the bastion on the northwestern corner. The king's artillery and the arquebusiers in the trenches were due to start a barrage on that when the charge started. The occasional cannon fire with its loading lulls allowed the sounds from the sleeping Citadel to carry well in the silent times.

They heard the trumpet. And the answer. And the bells begin to ring.

"Into those saddles!" yelled their captain. There was no time now to swing this whole thing into planned action. Now they must seize the moment—if it was there to be seized at all.

The Croats were some of the finest light cavalry in the world, with only the Ilkhan Mongols in serious contention in their portion of Eurasia. In many ways the Croats had the advantage over the Magyar—in speed, as scouts, and in tactical flexibility. The Croats had the first hundred and twenty men across the mole causeway before the Venetian cannon and arquebus fire began to make crossing it without heavy losses impossible. By the sounds above them, there was fighting on the north wall. But the traitors had at least prevented the barrage from above falling onto the galloping Croats.

And the gate was open! There were battle sounds from the watchtowers but they'd done it! If the Croats could get inside, they'd hold those towers, keep the gate open somehow, until the huge mass of Serb and Slav infantry who were waiting got in past the Venetian guns.

Yelling, the Croats spurred desperately forward, galloping horses spread out in a long race along the shingle. Then the first were in, under the raised portcullis, into the narrow roadway that led up into the Citadel.

And hurtling down on them, horses virtually shoulder to

shoulder, were the famous Knights of the Holy Trinity. The sound of the metal shoes of those heavy horses on the cobbles was like thunder in the confined space.

In the moonlight and house-shadow-darkness, in the narrow lane, the Croats didn't know there were only ten.

There are places and times when light cavalry is superior to heavy cavalry—when maneuverability and rough terrain are factors, for instance. But one advantage that heavy cavalry always has is momentum. And armor—which adds to the momentum. In the narrow lane, neither terrain nor maneuverability offered any advantage to the Croats.

The Knights of the Holy Trinity hit them like a ten-pound hammer hitting a pin. Literally smashed the Croats back through the gate, riding down those that could not turn. The Knights wheeled and rode back in, preparing for another charge. A few of the later arrivals and some of the better horsemen who'd turned their mounts followed in on their heels, showing the advantages of the Croats' speed and maneuverability.

The portcullis crashed down behind them. The great gates were still open, but the heavy metal grid now had some thirty Croats trapped inside. Men were running out of alleyways, hacking at them, hacking at their unprotected mounts as they tried to fight the Knights. And more Knights had suddenly arrived at the fray. Some half-armored . . . but too many.

The Croat captain knew the moment had slipped away. He never even saw that the great gates were closing. He did hear his lieutenant outside the gates yelling for a retreat. Inside the walls they'd die, he knew. But then, very few would live through the retreat either.

Umberto awoke to a blurry vision. At first he thought maybe he was dead and that Maria's mother . . . God, he'd loved her . . . was there, waiting for him. But would Heaven have so much pain?

Then he realized it was in fact Maria. Maria as he had never seen her. Maria with tears on her face, holding his hand as if she never wanted to let it go, with something so warm shining in her eyes that she looked like an angel. She'd looked at the baby like that; never at him. Until now.

"Maria?"

"Thank God!" He felt the pressure of her hand on his. "Umberto, don't you dare die on me."

"Try . . ." Things slipped away again.

It was some hours later that he awoke enough to make sense of his surroundings. He was in the hospital tended by the monks of Saint John, up on the hill.

"Did we beat them off?" he asked, wishing his head would stop spinning. "Alberto . . ."

"We did. We lost nearly fifty people, though. Alberto is fine, other than a broken finger. You two raised the alarm—because you slept at home. I am going to keep you there," said Maria, fiercely.

The seven surviving Libri d'Oro plotters attempted to look defiant when they were hauled before the captain-general and the governor. Only Flavio Dentico really succeeded.

"Kill us, then. You will get nothing out of us!"

The captain-general scowled. "We have torturers of sufficient skill to get the entire story out of you."

The old governor cleared his throat and turned to Eberhard of Brunswick. "Perhaps you would like to explain to them?"

The *Ritter* nodded. "Your families and the families of the dead we have identified have been taken into custody. You may be fools and decide to wait for torture. But if you wish to save your families further pain . . . well, we need to know just who the spy is. Who in here has contact outside? This plot was orchestrated. I'm afraid we need to know this. And I'm afraid you *will* talk."

There was something really terrifying about the urbane, calm way he said it.

"What are you going to do with our families?" asked one of the younger men. It was plain that this effect of their actions had not been considered.

"They're in the dungeons below the fortress."

"They knew nothing of this!"

Eberhard raised his eyebrows. "Then suppose you tell us who did know of your treason. Singly, so we can check your stories against each other. At the moment the real reason for holding your families is to keep them alive. The people out there know who betrayed them. They're baying for Libri d'Oro blood right now."

❀   ❀   ❀

Piece by piece the details of the plot appeared. A scant hour later troops were scouring the Citadel for Petros Nachelli, the glib, greasy former rent collector.

They found him, and the two cousins who served him as enforcers. But they weren't going to talk, not even under torture. Not without necromancy.

Captain Querini was tied to the chair. Commander Leopoldo was still half dressed, his face bloody, his tunic-jacket torn. He'd led the assault that had retaken the tower that held the portcullis levers, and he was furious about the loss of some of his finest men. He held the roster up to the cavalry captain's face and shook it furiously.

"You *testa di cazzo*! If it wasn't for a couple of *scuolo* sleep-at-homes who didn't come in to find they weren't on duty, we'd have lost the Citadel. As it is, I lost twenty-three men because of this!" He shook the piece of paper again. "You—!"

The captain gave a low moan. "I never knew. I was in my bed! I wouldn't have been in my bed if I known. I never meant any harm. . . . They tricked me. They lied to me. It was Dentico."

"You'll still hang."

Maria hadn't realized just how much the fireboat project had come to mean to Umberto until she'd sat with him the day after he'd been shot. Umberto was not a great communicator. His job and his home life—except when things were really boiling over and he would tell her—were two separate worlds. She'd followed progress in the yard more by snippets than anything else.

Now, weak and slipping into fever, he talked of little else but this. Maria passed an anxious day and an anxious, sleepless night listening to it. He was much the same the next day. She still dared not leave. Stella had come up to take Alessia for a few hours. Old Mrs. Grisini's Corfiote girl had come up with some food. A group of the Corfiote laborers' wives came with a small pot of sour cherry spoon-sweets. They were quiet—as befitted a hospital with a sick man—but each came and embraced her.

Maria sat there, biting her lip. She had never been hugged by this many people. They plainly thought he was going to die. The small pot of spoon-sweets sat there on the table beside her. She stared at it, eyes blurred with tears. She knew just how little they had, what sort of a sacrifice this was. She'd married Umberto to give Alessia a father. Now . . . she was going to lose him, too. For days he clung there, growing paler, growing weaker. Maria prayed. She prayed as she'd never ever prayed for herself.

It was late evening four days later, with Umberto tossing and mumbling, when two of the Corfiote women came in to the hospital. "You must come with us, Maria."

"I can't. I can't leave Umberto."

"If you don't, you will leave him at the graveside," said one of the women, brutally. "We have heard from Anastasia—the girl who works for Mrs. Grisini—that your house has been cursed."

"But what about Alessia?"

"The priestess said to bring her."

It was only when she got outside and well down the hill, that she came to realize that it was well after sundown. She was, she realized, dazed with exhaustion. "What about the curfew?"

The older of the two women shrugged. "We know where they patrol. And there are ways to pass. But it is difficult."

Maria was too tired to try to make sense of it all. She followed them to the cliff with the tall Italian poplar beside it. Ascended the ladder. Walked the winding cave trail into the inner chamber with its two altars, one white, one black. Looked at the cracked dry rock-cut pool where the water from the tiny waterfall now fell into a clay bowl drifted with flower-petals. At the huge, eminently female statue, terrible in its primitive beauty. Looked at the priestess in her simple white robe, with her long white hair in great waves around her. Looked into the compassionate eyes of . . .

Renate De Belmondo, the wife of the Podesta.

"Welcome, Daughter. The Peace of the Mother, the great Goddess be with you."

And the strange thing was that she'd felt just that. The hurt, the anger, the sadness had all receded, just as in her distant childhood memories, they had on those rare occasions when she'd turned to her own mother's arms.

The rest of the ritual, the soft refrains had not meant much to her. Except the priestess—who was also Renate De Belmondo in another life—had done her best with curse-exorcism.

"It may be best if you could move house, dear. There is lingering evil around you. Someone hates you very much, enough to spend a great deal of time cursing you. She is no witch, I think—but there is a great deal of magic here, and magic—"

She shrugged. "It is a tool. It often comes to the hand of those who do not know how to use it, yet succeed in doing *something* with it even in their ignorance."

Maria sighed. "Right now I'm living up at the hospital anyway. If Umberto lives . . . well, I'll try. I don't know how possible it will be."

"For your sake, your husband's sake, and for the sake of that lovely daughter of yours, you should."

When they returned to the small building on the north slope that was the monks' hospital, Maria fearfully hastened to Umberto's side.

He was still.

Maria felt as if her heart would stop. She put a trembling hand to his forehead. When she'd left it had been fire-hot.

It was cool.

Not deathly cold. Just . . . unfevered.

Maria didn't know how to thank the Mother. But she did it with all her heart anyway.

Umberto might have turned the corner, but to start him climbing the steep stair required a sickbed visit from Alberto, with his index finger strapped.

"How do you use a hammer with that?" asked Umberto weakly.

"Um. Haven't much, lately."

"What about the fireboats?"

"Old Grisini had another relapse and he's gone home. And well, Balfo, he's senior master after you, he said he couldn't see the sense of it. We'd never use them."

"*What?*" Umberto was struggling to sit. "I need to get down there! I'll tear his ears off, I'll—"

"You'll lie down!" said Maria crossly. "I'll tear any ears that need tearing."

"Maria, I've got to get down there! If we can deal with the enemy's fleet while they over-winter here . . . Most of them will have to be here, in the bay of Corfu."

"As soon as you are well enough to even sit on your own, I'll bring some of the lads up from the Little Arsenal to carry you down," promised Alberto. "Then we can carry you home."

Two days later they carried him down the hill. It started off with three big journeymen and Alberto, simply picking up the bed and carrying it out of the door. As they came out of the hospital, Maria realized that nearly every one of the Arsenalotti were there, from the masters to the Corfiote labor. And they weren't content to just carry Umberto. He had to travel shoulder high. Across the channel, across the Spianada, the Hungarians must have wondered just what the besieged had to cheer about.

Umberto didn't even have to tear ears. The issue was simply never raised and the Little Arsenal went back to hammering, sawing and working. In theory, Umberto was in charge of it. In practice he was still too weak and too tired. Maria was his eyes and ears, relaying orders, dealing with problems. The *scuolo*, as conservative as could be, would never have just taken orders from a woman. But Umberto's orders, relayed and made a lot more caustic by his wife—a different matter.

The only trouble was that Maria was not always inclined to just give Umberto's orders. Nor after the first few times did she say "Master Verrier says." She just told anyone from master to laborer to do it. And as they didn't know whether it came from Umberto or not, the Arsenalotti did it. Before two weeks were up, taking orders from Maria was so normal no one even thought about it. She was good at giving them.

For those first two weeks, Maria had had them knock up a space in one of the work sheds for Umberto. He was certainly not going to get home—or back—without carrying, and he was determined to be at the Little Arsenal. Maria did a trip to fetch Goat and the hens. One hen had disappeared, but the goat found more to eat in the shipyard than she had in Maria's own yard or than Maria had been able to scavenge for her.

PART X
September, 1539 A.D.

Chapter 74

The three light galleys Venice was sending to the aid of Corfu left without fanfare or fuss or any of the normal send-off. They left directly from the Arsenal sometime after midnight, with extremely select crews, a large supply of weaponry—and gold. Some fifteen thousand ducats worth, which would have made the small vessels a tempting target in any pirate's book. Led by the merfolk, the three ships slipped along the Dalmatian coast by night, pulling up, stepping masts and hiding on small islands by day. They laid up for two days with the mosquitoes in a swampy river mouth just north of the bay of Vlores, waiting for the merfolk to return with news of a safe route. The clouds rolled in, along with the triton, eventually.

"The water is clear of ships on this course," said Androcles, "because it's raining fit to raise the ocean level. You could sail within thirty yards of one of the carracks without anyone being the wiser. The galliots are all pulled up on the beaches. You humans don't seem to like getting wet."

They rowed on through worsening seas and squalls of rain. The light galleys had no real shelter for the rowers, and Benito found himself shivering. "Well, at least in this we should be able to land on the island during daylight," said Benito to the triton, who was pacing the vessel in the rolling gray sea.

Androcles shook his head. "No. The rain stops short of Corfu. Any lookout will see you. You'll have to wait for nightfall." He looked up at Benito and chuckled. "The seas are getting heavier. Looks as if you aren't wet enough already, you might just join us soon."

Never was Benito so glad to see landfall as in the lee of that unnamed cape. The Venetian relief force was cold, wet, and bedraggled.

And on Corfu—undetected.

The hundred and fifty men who had landed there were hand-picked as good seamen, with some knowledge of Greek—easy enough, as many Venetians spent time in the Greek possessions. They were all reasonably skilled horsemen, and were all combat veterans. What they weren't . . . was too sure where they were, where the enemy was, and just where they should go. Benito blessed the fact that at least it wasn't raining here.

He went down to the water's edge to bid farewell to the merpeople. Only Androcles had come inshore. "My thanks. We're in your debt."

Androcles grinned, his teeth pearly in the moonlight. "We'll keep it in mind." He looked at the three galleys. "What do you do with the ships now?"

Benito scowled. "I busted my ass building them and now we'll scupper them, rather than let the Byzantines have them."

Androcles shrugged. "Why not put them in the sea caves? There are some along the edge of the cape. You can only get in dry at low tide. If you take the masts down you should fit them. You will have to swim out of the cave, though."

Benito sighed. "I'm just about dry."

Most of the gear was off-loaded and skeleton crews of strong swimmers set out for the caves. They nudged their way forward into the darkness of the sea-hollowed limestone. "This is where we leave you," said Androcles. "Corcyra is another's territory, and this is too close already."

It was dark. They had to feel their way in, inch by inch.

"Trouble with sea caves like this, is that they cave in," said one of Benito's companion's cheerfully. "I went into one near Capri on my first voyage. They said it used to be a bigger one but it caved in."

"I needed to know that," grumbled Benito. "Reckon we can strike a light now? We're well into this thing and we've curved away from the sea. They shouldn't be able to see it from outside, and we need to work out how to anchor safely."

"It's as black as pitch in here. We'll need to chance it."

Someone struck a lucifer. A lamp wick caught.

Benito looked at the five Greek fishing-boats that were in there already. And at the people on them and on the shore-ledges. There were an awful lot of arquebuses, pistols, arrows and just plain rocks all ready to come their way.

Benito was extremely glad to recognize at least one of the vessels.

"Captain Taki! Spiro! Kosti! It's me! Benito!"

It was as near to inevitable that the caveful of fishing boats should have its own taverna, with a supply of the wine that Benito recalled so well.

"Why is this stuff so vile?" He demanded, eyeing the cup of russet-colored liquid. "And why do you all drink it?"

Spiro drew himself up in affront. "If you don't like our *kakotrigi*, don't drink it! I'll relieve you of the burden." He reached for Benito's cup. "It is a wine of the Corfiote character, and like us, it is hard to harvest. The grape clings to the stalk like we cling to our soil."

Benito held his cup out of reach. "I'm paying for this round. You snatch my drink when you're paying."

"Which will probably mean the end of the world is at hand, so you might as well drink it anyway," said Kosti.

"You're paying? I'd have had the *mavrodáphne* then," said Spiro with his wry grin. "*Kakotrigi* is cheap crap. But you get used to it. Even get to like it, if you drink enough."

And for a few cups they could have shelter for their ships, and advice on where the Hungarian troops were. It struck Benito as a bargain.

"How did you make it back? Did you have any problems?"

Taki laughed and waved his arms expansively. "I told you I was the finest seaman around. We sailed rings around them."

"We came back in a patch of bad weather. We nearly missed the island," said Kosti.

"I hate to ask this. But just where the hell are we?"

Spiro rolled his eyes. "Great sailors, these Venetians. Masters of the Mediterranean. You're about a league and a half away from Paleokastritsa. And your dangerous friend is about four leagues away. Together with his blonde with the . . ." Spiro crooked his arms in front of him.

Benito grinned. This was going to be easier than he'd thought.

He looked speculatively at the Corfiote sailors. "How are things going with Erik's private little war?"

Taki laughed shortly. "He doesn't have to do much anymore. The peasants are killing and sabotaging whenever they get the chance. Those Hungarians can't make up their minds what to do. One day it's reprisals and the next it's being nice to peasants. But the story is they ate a child from one of the villages down south. The father cooperated with them because they had his son hostage. And while he did that they ate the boy, like those Vinlanders did to old Cheretis' favorite goat. And fed the bones to their dog. There's this big yellow dog that goes about with 'em sometimes. People say it's no natural dog. Say it can be shot without being killed."

"That was Georgio's story," said Kosti. "Georgio once had a wild pig get drunk on fermented windfall apples in his master's orchard . . . and he tried to shoot it when it was sleeping it off. From about three feet away! He still missed it."

"Well, yes," admitted Taki. "But Serakis says he saw the boy's waistcoat and the thigh bone. Tooth marks right into it."

Benito scratched his chin, thoughtfully. "Doesn't sound like they're popular. So how do you think you lads and the other fishermen would feel about helping the Venetians do a bit of quiet raiding? Sink a few of those patrol vessels?"

"With our fishing boats? Are you crazy?"

"With the galleys. You spot them from shore. Dark nights we run out and sink 'em."

They eyed him with interest. Kosti's grin was feral. "Should make night-fishing around here safer," said Taki with a nod.

Even with a guide from the fishermen it was Erik's men who spotted them first. He plainly had scouts out. And any Hungarian patrol was going to have to deal with an ambush.

Erik himself came out to greet them. The Icelander was, Benito thought, looking as happy as he'd ever seen him. Obviously things were going exceptionally well for him with his Vinlander girl.

"Well, Benito!" He clapped Benito on the shoulder and grinned as he looked at the hundred and fifty men in the valley. "Is this all you bring me? And I had to part with perfectly good silver for your trip over!" Then he gave Benito an unexpected bear hug. Benito had never seen any real signs of emotional display from Erik. Perhaps this, too, was Svanhild. "Well done, boy."

Benito felt considerably taller. "I brought back the principal and interest on the silver. In gold. We've got arms for five hundred. We've got a secure hidden port and three light galleys we can use to raid the blockade ships. And there are more men coming, as soon as we have the ships. And now, let me introduce you to Captain Di Negri."

Benito pointed to the broad, curly-haired, swarthy man who was at the head of the column. The man stepped forward. "Knight-Proctor Hakkonsen? I am Fabio Di Negri." The two shook hands, sizing each other up. "I have orders from the Doge and the Senate to put myself under your command."

Erik raised his eyebrows. "That's good. And surprising, to be honest."

"I had to talk long and hard to get them to agree to it," said Benito, with a wry smile. "Fortunately Petro and, indeed, Venice know you."

"Well, Captain, you are going to be on your own anyway, a lot of the time," said Erik, comfortingly. "We've found the countryside won't really hide more than twenty in one group. I've three separate units working now already. With your men and the recruits we can bring in we should make the north virtually free of Hungary. We'll seriously affect them in the south too, I think." He turned back to Benito. "And you, Benito? Have they very sensibly made you have to take my orders too?"

Benito shook his head. "Actually, the Council of Ten has given me another assignment. Petro was opposed to it, but . . ." He shrugged. "I wanted to do it."

"What?"

"Trying to get the news back into the Citadel."

Erik winced. "Benito, things have tightened up a great deal since you and I came out. Largely, I am afraid, because of what we've been doing out here. It's nearly impossible to get within two miles of the Citadel. Emeric must have as many men patrolling around there as he has in the siege trenches."

"I'll have to go and have a look to see what I can think of."

Erik shook his head. "Something crazy, no doubt."

"Probably," said Benito with a yawn. "Meanwhile, can we get out of the sun and get a drink of water? I drank too much *kakotrogi* last night."

Erik laughed wryly. "Haven't you noticed how dry it is, Benito?

The stream in this little valley has dried up. We're maybe half a mile from the nearest spring that's still flowing. The Corfiotes say it should be raining, now that we're into September. The rains started . . . and then stopped. We haven't had a drop since the day we had the earthquake."

Benito scouted, with Erik. And then with Thalia, pretending to be a peasant with onions to sell.

He watched for hours, trying to find the obvious chinks in Emeric's armor. He had to admit that the organization was slick. Still . . .

"What is that compound over there?"

"Corfiotes. Slave labor. They are taken from villages where they suspect we have sympathizers." Thalia grimaced. "Mostly they get it wrong."

"They're not very well guarded. And they're marched up to the front lines every day."

"They have leg chains. The ones who are not working have a long chain threaded through all of the leg irons."

"Ah. I see. Do we know of a good blacksmith?"

Thalia turned to Giuliano. "Who is best? There are three making arrowheads and spear-blades for us."

"Gigantes, I think." The once-plump young son of an armsman smiled. "He used to make my plows. He was always coming up with new ideas that I didn't want."

"Do you think he could make me a set of manacles? And while I'm about it, provide me with some metal-cutting files."

"If you have the gold, yes. Files are precious."

"It's a mad plan!" snapped Erik.

Benito shrugged. "Of course it is. Do you think a sane plan would succeed?"

"No. But that's not the point. A breakout of those prisoners would certainly enhance our popularity even more. It's a good idea even if I don't like the way you want to do it. But look at the rest of it. It has one big flaw: Castles and fortifications are built not to be climbed. Trust me. I know about fortification."

Benito shook his head. "Erik, I don't try to tell you about hand-to-hand combat. Please don't tell me what I can or can't climb. I promise you that there are at least seven places where an upper-story man could get into the Citadel with ease. Of course they've got guards and I've got to get there. That's why I am going as one of the prisoners."

"It won't work. Look, after moon-down is the time they'll have their sappers sneaking over. The guards on the walls will shoot at anything that moves—or worse, if you're climbing, drop boiling pitch or oil on you."

"I know. Falkenberg told me. That's why I'm going in on the seaward side, near where we came down. I should be safe enough in the water."

"I forbid it," said Erik. "You're throwing away your life, Benito."

"I'm afraid, Erik, you can't forbid me to do anything," said Benito firmly. "Knowing for certain that relief is on its way will give the those inside the kind of fortitude that is worth an extra five hundred men. Those are my orders from the Doge."

He didn't tell Erik that what Petro had actually said was: *if you can let them know without killing yourself.* He wasn't planning on killing himself. If he died it would definitely be by someone else's hand. "What you can do for me is keep this sword. I don't think I can manage to hide it."

Erik looked at the rapier. It was plain he recognized the hilt. He'd been there the day it had been broken, and to someone like Erik weapons were as distinct as snowflakes. "That's quite an honor. What do you want me to do with it?"

Benito shrugged again. "Marco wouldn't appreciate it much. If I don't come back, have it for a wedding present that you can give to your firstborn son." He grinned at Erik's look of embarrassment. "If I do get away with this, you and Svan'll have to put up with a silver saltcellar or something instead."

Erik squeezed his shoulder. "It's a true Viking gift," he said thickly. "And our first. But I think—much as I envy this blade— I'd rather have the saltcellar."

"I'll do my best to see you get it."

Chapter 75

Benito had stripped down to match the slaves. The poor devils had nothing more than breeches, which mean that the Shetland knife, the three files, spare knives, and the manacle key had to be strapped to his legs. His body, face and the breeches were suitably covered in mud. His medal from the Hypatians he attached to the belt-line.

"If you're due a saltcellar, I'll have Manfred fly the Knots banner from the inner wall, north tower," whispered Benito in parting.

And then he was on his own. In what, he reluctantly admitted, were still his two favorite elements: darkness and danger.

Moving along the backs of the tent lines, once he'd dodged the initial sentries, was tricky. There were guy-ropes, and, on one occasion a soldier relieving himself. He moved silently, manacles bundled in sackcloth and on his back, closer and closer to his target.

At last he only had the palisade between him and the slaves. He lay there, trying not to shiver, and watched and waited, studying the movements of the guards. When he was satisfied at last, he took the moment and went up and over the eight-foot palisade like a chimney-rat under whom the fire has just been lit. Then he dropped, gently, from his full arms' stretch. This was the worrying part. There might be stakes or anything there.

He landed on something bony that swore at him in Greek. It was the one thing he'd learned reasonably well from Taki, Spiro and Kosti. As Spiro had explained, it wasn't that fishermen were crudely spoken. It was the fish. Fish don't understand otherwise.

"Shut up!" he hissed, in his now-passable Greek. "I've come to help you get out of here." Which was true, up to a point.

Sometime later, firmly manacled into the line, Benito lay among the huddled-together-for-warmth prisoners and pondered what he now knew. The prisoners had no idea which place they'd be working in next. There were, in toto, seven strings of twenty. The guards came and took chainfuls at a time. There were several strings out now. The prisoners—naturally—had wanted to escape immediately. Another day or night working meant a very real chance of dying. Benito had his work cut out to persuade them to let him chance getting to the Citadel wall.

His bait, however, was irresistible.

"Look—just running, you've got maybe one chance in a hundred. But the resistance fighters out there, the *klepthes*"—which meant bandits, but to the Greeks the two were remarkably close— "they'll be waiting for my signal from inside the fort. The night they get it, they'll do two things. First, they want to raid one of the outposts to the south. Second there'll be some, with horses and donkeys, near the ridge with the holm-oaks. You get up there, yell 'Kalimera,' and they'll try to get you away."

In the meanwhile, they took turns filing their manacle chains the better part of the way through. The new-cut metal would be plastered with dust and urine. If the opportunity arose, they'd probably be able to force them.

Morning came. Benito found himself sent to be part of a bucket-chain, passing earth out of one of the mines. His one worry now was that he was just that much stronger, better fed and less exhausted than his Corfiote companions. He hoped the bored, brutal guards wouldn't notice.

During that long, hot session one of the slaves died. The guards took him out of the chain by the simple expedient of chopping his foot off. "At least he was dead," whispered the man next to him. "Zikos was alive when they did it." And the mines were considered a lucky option.

That afternoon, Benito quietly swapped chains. "They've been in all day. They're bound to go out tonight to work on the causeway."

They did. The wrong one. He had to wait until the next night.

Benito no longer had to fake looking exhausted, hauling rocks and broken masonry to make walls for the troops to advance behind. They had hide shields to work behind, but these were poor protection against even arquebus fire. The guards stayed well back behind some sandbags. It was simplicity itself to slip his manacle and lie down when cannon fire made the guards pull their heads down. Then it was merely a quick wriggle and squirm through a gap and a scraping slide into the water. All too easy.

The water wasn't. It wasn't that cold, but it was still something of a shock. Benito began to ease his way, swimming very quietly next to the edge of the mole, so that his head, if anyone saw it, might be thought part of the stone fallen from it. The siege engineers had been using broken masonry from the town and there were any number of odd-shaped bits in the water.

Then, flipping onto his back, he began swimming away from the mole down the channel toward the sea. Oh, to be one of the merpeople! That thought put another into his mind: the creature that the merpeople said had been haunting the Adriatic. Benito decided maybe it would be a good idea to swim with his knife in hand. After all, it was dark and still here in the water.

When Benito's legs touched something moving in the water, he very nearly screamed. He would have if he hadn't swallowed water in his fright. Trying not to cough, he touched it again. It was a rope. A moving rope. Moving slowly toward the Citadel shore. Benito realized it sloped gently down. Someone was hauling something across—something quite heavy.

It almost certainly meant no good.

Benito swam in toward the Citadel, angling away from the rope. The rope was actually dragging something around to the south side. The shingle strip was very narrow here, and the original rock made up part of the corner tower. Benito eased out of the water, with that feeling in the middle of his back that he was in some arquebusier's sights.

The Citadel's builders had chopped and polished at the rock here so that the lower section was smooth. It did overhang slightly, though, and this brought Benito to where the load was being hauled. It wasn't a cave so much as another small overhang, also part of the original rock. Two men were straining to slowly pull something out of the shallows. It was plainly heavy. There was no way past, and besides, Benito had a feeling it might be more important than the mere news that Venice was on her way.

He waited, knife in hand, and watched. The moon was down and there was little light to see it all by. Just enough to see that the men were taking strain pulling the heavy weight up the beach.

The wind was cold and biting on his wet skin and wet breeches. Starting to shiver, Benito knew it was now or never. Two to one . . . and they might have swords or guns.

The first man was so intent on pulling he died without even knowing Benito was there. The second turned and managed to grab Benito's hand and draw his own blade. Benito had to seize his arm with his left. In the dark beneath the wall they wrestled desperately in absolute silence. The fellow was as strong as an ox. He was good eight inches taller and seventy pounds heavier than Benito. By sheer weight he was pushing Benito over.

What was it that Erik had said? "Use their strength. Get them off balance." Benito tried to foot-sweep the man. It was a dismal failure. Instead, Benito was thrown to the shingle and cobbles, and lost the knife. The Hungarian came diving in for the kill. Benito rolled and hit the fellow just behind the ear with a cobblestone-sized rock.

He hit him twice more. And then put some of the rope to good use, as well as the man's trousers as a gag.

Then he felt around and found the Shetland knife. Now to see what they'd been doing.

It was barrels! There were already five in the back of the overhang and they'd plainly been surreptitiously drilling into the limestone. Benito was no engineer. Would the explosion have damaged the wall? He had no idea. But the barrels were a great deal easier to roll than to drag. He rolled them out toward where the latest one lay. All but one. That he pried at with the Hungarian's knife. He wasn't breaking his own! He liked that knife.

The barrel was full of powder. Black gunpowder, by the smell of it. Benito wished he had some way of striking a light—once he was a bit further away. He then had the bright idea of searching his captive and found a flint and steel. Now all he needed was a gunpowder trail and he'd have fireworks to celebrate his return home. Taking double handfuls of the stuff he crept along the wall strewing it. He made a line out to the barrels and put a pile of it against them. The only trouble was, of course, that he couldn't see what he'd done.

Still, he decided he'd used enough. Then it was lug the

semiconscious prisoner—well, drag the prisoner—close to the postern. Benito looked longingly at it. It would be so nice and so easy just to go and knock on it now. But they'd probably shoot him first.

In the shadow of wall just short of the postern, Benito struck sparks into the powder trail he'd laid. It burned. It burned damned *fast*. Benito threw caution to the wind, dropped the striker and ran, jinking, farther away from the Hungarian lines, running eastward along the beach parallel to the wall. Running, there was a good chance the sentries on the wall would see him. If they saw him, they'd shoot at him first and ask questions later. On the other hand if he continued his slow progress, he'd either be blown up by his own sabotage, or spotted and shot in the aftermath of the excitement the explosion would cause. The shingle stopped, if he recalled right, and the cliff took over just beyond that.

There was a yell and a shot from above. Benito tried very hard to be small, and dove into the water. Water wasn't a wall or a sandbag but it deflected bullets. He was going to stay underwater as long as possible, and swim as far and as deep as possible, and not spend more time on the surface than he had to.

He came up in time to hear an explosion, but not the huge one he'd been expecting.

He risked a look. He could see men with brands, running down the length of the wall; running back in the direction he'd come from. He trod water, watching. Even from here he could see the barrels were still on the beach. They'd failed to explode. His powder trail hadn't worked. The explosion must have been the barrel he'd opened . . . obviously there'd been a powder trail to that too! That accidental powder trail had worked. Well, there was nothing for it now but to swim on. They'd not expect someone to go on swimming away from the Hungarian lines.

By the time Benito got to the ledge, swimming was just about too much of an effort. Once he'd hauled himself out of the water and onto it, his strength was gone. He was exhausted. Too tired to contemplate a sixty-foot climb on greasy limestone with anything but dread.

But it had to be done. It seemed like an awfully long way. Benito hugged himself, and danced up and down on the ledge trying to get warm. He wasn't succeeding well. But the sky was definitely paling—he wanted to be up this corner and over the wall before dawn or he was going to have a long wait on this ledge for nightfall. And he might be visible in daylight from the tower windows.

He began bridging his way up, one foot and one hand on either side of the corner, balancing between them. Fortunately it was a very nonstrenuous technique. A trick of balance, merely. Benito edged his way upwards toward the faint dark edge of the wall-top. He paused just below it, listening, although all he wanted to do was to get over that edge and rest. But there was no point in dying just yet. Not for the sake of a few dozen heartbeats.

Never had the top of even the most difficult building felt quite this satisfying to reach. Benito didn't walk away. He crawled to the stair . . . down it . . . To the deep shadows beside a building. He lay there for some time, trying to breathe quietly and gather himself up.

He was in, and almost home. Less likely to be shot, anyway. But he didn't want to end up in jail again, either.

So: Where did he go? Getting into the governor's palace like this was not going to be easy. Tiredly, his mind turned automatically to Maria. She wouldn't mind if he turned up half dead on her doorstep. And then . . . well, maybe that husband of hers—or a note to Manfred. Or Francesca . . . or . . .

He was too tired to think coherently. He stumbled through the narrow lanes, the dawn bell competing with the Hungarian cannon. He passed a few soldiers, coming off duty, yawning. One of them made a comment, but Benito simply wandered on. He obviously looked mad or drunk, but harmless, because they didn't follow after him.

He got there. The door was closed—a drift of sand across the doorsill. The shutters were still tight, closed although the other houses were now coming to life. He knocked.

There was no reply.

He peered down the narrow passage that led to the back yard. That goat of hers had harassed passers-by from here. There was no goat, today. The place had that "nobody-lives-here" look.

Benito sat down on the steps. The doorknob was unpolished. The steps were full of wind-blown debris. Maria would never have allowed them to look like that.

A gray-haired old woman peered at him. "Who are you?"

"Uh. Benito. I'm looking for Maria and . . . and Umberto." Here he was, without even a shirt, in salt-stained breeches, his body and face muddy. He wished he'd thought to wash when he'd been in the sea. Some of it obviously had washed away, but he'd chosen that fine-grained clay that needed hard rubbing. She'd think he was some kind of lunatic. However, looking at the old woman, he could see she really didn't seem to be all there herself. She'd made up half her face. The effect was a little odd, especially when added to the unfocused-looking eyes.

She sniffed, looking about to cry. "They've gone. The young man was shot. They've gone with that gorgeous baby. Like my baby. Babies always go . . ." She wandered off, seemingly having forgotten all about him.

Benito took a deep breath and pulled himself together. First things first. He needed to get off the street. He'd been plain lucky so far, but that couldn't last. Besides, the old woman's rambling had worried him. Upset him even more than finding the person he'd always relied on, known would be there as a last resort, wasn't. Could Maria and the baby Alessia be . . . dead? He swallowed and vaulted the gate into the tiny yard.

Definitely no one had been here for a while.

Benito sat on the back step and formulated plans as best he could. The worry had pushed back exhaustion. If there was no Maria he'd have to turn to his other friend.

The roofs.

Francesca got up early. In a relative sense, anyway. When she'd had the misfortune to have to survive life in the Red Cat she'd thought she got up early. Then along had come Manfred, and with him, Erik, and she'd finally understood that all things are relative. "Early" to a hooker meant before noon. To a knight in training it meant before dawn.

With Erik away she'd thought Manfred might ease back on the predawn training. But he seemed to treat it as an act of faith.

Now, with the sun peeping through the shutters in long golden streamers, was a far better time. She swung the shutters open. And screamed.

It was a perfectly natural reaction to seeing someone dropping from the eaves and into her bedroom. It took her a moment of hasty retreat to recognize the dirty, half-naked stocky man, who simply sat down on the floor.

"Benito!"

"Yep. Why do you get up so late? I've been waiting for you to open up for hours."

"Why didn't you knock?"

"And get shot through the shutters? I tried calling quietly but you obviously didn't hear. Where's Prince Manfred?"

"Over at the exercise yard. I'll send someone for him. No, I'll go myself. Is Erik—?"

"Fine." Benito yawned. "Got any food?"

"In the next room. Look, help yourself. I'm going to fetch Manfred. I haven't even done my hair!"

She left at a run. Francesca never ran.

Benito got wearily to his feet, went into the next room, and found a bottle of wine and a small loaf. He didn't bother to try any further. Just flopped down in a chair in the far corner and drank wine straight from the bottle with a few hunks of bread to keep it company.

"He just dropped in through the window," said Francesca, unlocking the door. "I nearly died of fright."

Manfred grinned. "Made your hair stand on end, did he?"

She looked dangerously at him. "I came straight out to call you without even thinking of brushing it, Manfred."

"You're beautiful even with all your hair standing on end, Francesca. Now where is the boy?"

"I left him here . . . oh."

She'd spotted Benito, fast asleep, curled into the seat.

Manfred surveyed the boy. Mud. Bruises, scratches. And a pair of tired breeches. A three-quarters-full wine bottle still clutched and half of a dropped loaf on the floor beside him.

"I suppose he had to choose one of the good bottles," said Manfred, looking at it wryly. "The kid must be all in. He normally sleeps like a cat."

"Should we let him sleep?"

Manfred shook his head. "I'm afraid not. He can sleep once he's told us what is happening." He stepped over to the chair and began shaking Benito. The boy's skin was clammy to the touch. He was shivering faintly. "Here, Francesca. Get him a shirt and one of my cottes."

Benito woke with a start. An eyes-unfocused start, reaching for a knife. "It's all right, Benito," said Falkenberg, beaming at him. "You're with us."

Benito shook his head, obviously trying to clear it. "Sorry. Wine on an empty stomach. And I was a bit tired. Thanks." The latter was addressed to Francesca, who handed him a shirt and cotte.

He stood up. Manfred noticed he was swaying. "Come on, Falkenberg, let's get him into those and he can sit down again."

"I can dress myself."

"Shut up," said Manfred, his big fingers struggling with buttons. "Or rather, tell us news. Francesca said you said Erik was all right?"

Benito nodded. "Yeah. Fine. He's looking like the cat that ate the cream. He's got his Vinlander, and he's got his insurgents, and he's making the Hungarians bleed."

"We've seen some of it from the walls, but I'm damned glad to hear it for certain." Manfred sat Benito down. "You've grown, boy. But my clothes are still a little big for you." That was something of an understatement. But at least he should be warmer. For an autumn day, it was warm. Benito wasn't.

"So: What happened to the plans for getting you over to Italy? Is the blockade just too tight? Or are there just no fishing boats?"

"I've been there and back. I came back with a hundred and fifty men to help Erik and news that the Arsenal is building a new fleet. As soon as they have the ships, Dorma will put to sea. There's a new war levy. They're recruiting mercenaries and calling for volunteers. The Old Fox himself has put up a thousand men."

Manfred blinked. "There and back . . . and back inside?" He looked at the wine standing on the floor. "And to think I begrudged you that. You deserve the entire bottle! In fact, make it a hogshead."

"I'd rather have some brandy. Listen—do you know what happened to Maria? My . . . my friend who told Erik. I went there first. It's all shut up."

Francesca smiled knowingly. "She's fine, Benito. She's down at the Little Arsenal. Her husband got himself shot by the Libri d'Oro traitors. But he's recovering slowly. Look . . . is there anything else you really must ask him immediately, Manfred? Is there anything you really have to tell us, Benito?"

Benito shook his head. "Just was told to bring the news that relief was coming. It might be four, five more months though. And

I left a prisoner at the southern postern. Oh. And to ask that you hoist the Knots banner at the inner wall north tower at sundown. Tell Erik he's getting a saltcellar after all." Benito stood up on this cryptic utterance. "I'm going to the Little Arsenal."

"Sit down. You need to rest," said Francesca firmly. "I'll go down and tell her."

Benito shook his head. "You'd frighten her silly. Besides," he added, grinning in a pale shadow of his usual impishness, "I've got to tell her that Kat wants to know why she hasn't written. And I have to check on the baby for her god-mama. Heh. If you'd met the god-mama, you'd know I don't dare delay."

Francesca shook her head disapprovingly, "I know men well enough to know I'd be wasting my time arguing. But Manfred, I think he needs an escort."

Manfred nodded. "And his own clothes. Everyone would think a fair had come to town, otherwise."

"I'm going *now*." There was a determined tilt to that chin and a feverish glint in Benito's eyes.

"Fine, fine," said Falkenberg soothingly. "We'll just get you a horse."

Benito closed his eyes momentarily. "Not a horse. Please!"

"Well, at least wash your face!"

Chapter 76

Maria was working on the looms on the upper tier, keeping a weather eye on the carpenters working on the next level down. The gates opened. Maria blinked at the sunlight on armor, then rubbed her eyes unbelievingly.

She got up slowly and deliberately, took Alessia from her crib in the shade, and walked down the stairs—being very careful not to stumble. Her knees felt a little weak.

Benito was grinning at Umberto, trying not to show his shock. The master-caulker had never been a big man. Now he looked as if a puff of wind would blow him away. He was gaunt and pale, and he looked at least twenty years older. "I hear you got in the way of a bullet, Umberto."

"The master is a hero!" said one of the other *scuolo*, affronted by this familiarity. "He saved the Citadel!"

Umberto's eyes narrowed, focusing on Benito. "Signor Valdosta?"

Benito nodded. "Just Benito Valdosta. Or as your wife would have it, just trouble."

"You got out? Maria told me you had been successful in getting out, that someone had signaled from the main island. Raftopo," he pointed to Benito, "this is the young man who bought your coracle, remember?"

The fellow nodded. "*Si.* I remember. Umberto wouldn't say what you wanted it for."

"We went over the wall to the island," said Benito. "How's Maria, Umberto?"

The former coracle-owner shook his head. A stolid oxlike thinker, he plainly ground everything to its finest. "If you got out, how come you're here?"

Manfred patted Benito on the shoulder. "Because he came back, of course. After he went all the way to Venice."

"In my coracle? Ha." The former owner looked as if people had all too often tried to put one over him.

"Hell, no—that sank about a mile away," said Benito. "Fishing boat to Italy. Small trader up the west coast and then a damned horse over the Apennines to Ferrara. Barge to Venice."

The *scuolo* wrestled with the implications of this. "You mean . . ."

"Back again, I see," said Maria. "You know, Benito, you're the original bad penny." But she was smiling broadly as she said it, and her eyes seemed a little moist.

He was looking like . . . Benito. At first she thought he had shrunk. The she realized it was just outsize clothes. Good clothes but enormous. The cotte hung like a dress on him, which was maybe just as well. The breeches he wore were muddy and salt-stained. His feet were bare and filthy. And his face . . .

She looked at it, remembering. It had lost a little of the youthfulness, and he was as pale as a nocturnal *Case Vecchie* gentleman. He was smiling at her, very oddly. "How's Alessia?" he asked. "Her godmother wanted me to ask."

She put a hand on his forehead. It was clammy but hot. "You can find out when you get out of the hospital, you idiot! He's feverish, Prince. Take him there before he falls over on us."

Benito obliged her by doing just that.

Manfred walked over to the commander's offices after they'd deposited Benito in the care of the monks. There were times for subtlety and quiet contact. This wasn't one of them.

"Commander Leopoldo's over at the south wall, sir. There's a bit of a situation there. We had explosions there early this morning."

Manfred laughed. *Benito!* "I'll go and see him there."

He went by horse, with Von Gherens, having had a sudden thought. He dispatched Falkenberg to go and keep a watch over Benito. The boy could easily be the target of whoever the spies in the Citadel were. The morale boost to the Citadel of having news from Venice was huge. That was why Manfred had told the men at the Little Arsenal what Benito had done. It would run like wildfire around the fortress. It would get to whoever was spying, too. Emeric wouldn't enjoy hearing that news.

"We think he may be some sort of trap," said Leopoldo, pointing to the man at the foot of the tower. "He's alive. We've seen him move. So why is he tied up? Who is he? And there are those barrels of what is probably gunpowder over there."

Manfred looked at the bound, trouserless man, and at the shingle strip with four haphazardly lying barrels on the beach. "Nope," he said with a grin and in a good carrying voice. "That's Benito's work. You can go out and collect the prisoner. I'll go out and fetch him if you like."

"That's a lot of black powder. If there is shrapnel in it and it goes off, Prince, you'll be mincemeat."

"I told you, Commander. My agent, Benito Valdosta, caught that saboteur last night, when my man was coming in from the Venetian forces. You should come up to the hospital and hear all the details."

"*Venetian* forces?"

"Hadn't I told you yet? The scouts for the Venetian relief force have arrived."

If the black powder in the barrels on the shingle had suddenly gone off, it could scarcely have caused a bigger explosion.

Hidden in some Aleppo pines in a rocky little defile, Erik surveyed the Citadel gloomily. It was still defiant, bathed in the last of the evening light, but he didn't see what he hoped to see. On the first day after the young tearaway left, he actually expected to see the banner of the Knights in that corner tower. When it wasn't hoisted, he'd given orders to move from all the localities Benito knew. Torture got information out of anyone. So did black magic. And Emeric used both.

The next day he still hoped. Tonight was merely a duty. The youngster was either a prisoner or dead, and most likely the latter. Erik thought about the sword Benito had left in his keeping, and sighed. He'd love to own it, but he'd part with it in a heartbeat if it could have spared the boy. He was so caught up in these morbid thoughts that he didn't realize that, flying above the north tower of the inner wall, was the famous treble cross of the Knights of the Holy Trinity.

"It'll be the most welcome saltcellar a bridal couple ever got," he said to himself, laughing in relief. "He must be down to two of his nine lives."

The slave breakout that night brought Erik sixty-two fanatical new recruits. But Erik's first priority was to feed the poor devils up a bit.

The Magyar officer shook his head. "They seem to have forgotten the meaning of trust. They won't even parley, Sire, let alone agree to terms. Early days—back in June—all they did when they saw our men was make sure the gates were shut and watch us. But now . . . Feeling has hardened, Sire. They're shooting on sight. Both Paleokastritsa and Kassiopi are still holding out. I've put men on watch, and they're in a sort of siege, but without cannon and a lot more men I don't see reducing either."

Emeric considered. "We'll play a waiting game, then. I don't want to take men off the siege here."

"Getting the heavy cannon to either of those two towns would be very difficult anyway, Sire. There is no road, just a donkey-track. It could be done, but it would take a lot of men and a lot of effort. Easier to starve them out. When the Citadel falls, they'll be forced to surrender."

Emeric nodded. "I see the peasants are coming back onto the land."

"The men and the older women are, Sire. You don't see a child except running away. Basically, hunger forced them out, but the lack of rain is worrying them."

Emeric snorted wryly. "I can only have it one way. The rain must stay away from the Venetians, too. So: What did you find out about the murder of those two Libri d'Oro collaborators?"

The Magyar officer scowled. "The peasants did it, Sire. But they swear it was some *klepthes*—bandits from the hills in the north. We really do have a problem with that. Our troops can't move singly. I have to send them everywhere in squads. I've tried torture. I've tried beatings. I've executed a few in front of their families. No one talks. So I tried a different tactic in Gastouri, with that second murder. We're twenty miles away from where I'd tried the last time. This time I pretended it hadn't happened. I told my men to go easy. To buy the locals drinks. To convince them we were simply taking over from Venice and that they'd find us far better masters. The peasants won't drink with us unless you hold a knife to their throats. I finally asked one old bastard why. He said we eat babies and feed our dogs their bones. I told him this was rubbish, but he insisted he'd been shown the gnawed bones."

"I don't want to go back there, Umberto," Maria said, knowing she couldn't tell him the real reason—that she was certain Sophia Tomaselli had put some kind of ill-wishing on the house and on him. For that matter, she wouldn't put it past the woman to try to get someone to poison them at this point. Living there just made her feel too exposed.

But none of those things would have made any sense to Umberto. "I know, it's getting colder down here. We'd benefit from living in a proper house again, but I'm scared. I won't take you there. I won't take Alessia there."

Umberto smiled. "Well. It makes a suggestion I have to make easier, Maria. I have here a letter from Master Grisini. He's not well. The honest truth is he's concerned for his wife's future if he should die. The captain-general would then reallocate his home. His wife should go back to Venice—in the normal course of events. Of course that can't happen right now because of the siege. Grisini is deeply worried that the captain-general will take a rather spiteful and petty vengeance by moving the old lady out. He could do it, too. However, the house is a very large one, and what Grisini proposes is that we—you and me and Alessia—move into the lower section. It's still bigger than our old house. The move doesn't have to be approved by anyone except Commander Leopoldo, and he's a reasonable man. If Master Grisini dies, we'll be 'sitting tenants,' the captain-general won't be able to evict us, and we can give house-room to old Mrs. Grisini until the siege is lifted and she goes back to Venice. The house is a lovely one, and Grisini is afraid if the *scuolo* lose tenancy of it we'll never get anything nearly as good again. He suggests we move four of the Illyrians into our old house, to stop fights with the Corfiotes down here."

Maria shrugged. "Umberto, old Mrs. Grisini isn't really in this world anyway. But if it means I don't have to take you and Alessia back to that house, fine."

❀　　❀　　❀

"*Your* agent? You dared to do this without my permission?"

Eberhard cleared his throat. "Captain-General Tomaselli, while this place is a Venetian possession—Prince Manfred is *not* a Venetian subject. To be a bit blunt, he doesn't need permission to get his men to do anything. And he did, in fact, obtain *carte blanche* from the governor to get a message out. Signor Valdosta here was delivering a message to the Emperor of the Holy Roman Empire from the prince. That was his primary task, which he achieved. It was done on the prince's orders and with the prince's money. The fact that young Benito is a good citizen of your Republic and did his civic duty by reporting the matter to the relevant authorities there also, and returned with ships and men, was a bonus for Venice."

He paused. "I know you see this as an attack on the Venetian Republic. But please understand: To us it is a danger to the man who is second in line for the throne of the Holy Roman Empire. By comparison, the Emperor holds Corfu or even the Venetian Republic—though staunch friends—to be of lesser value. The reason that huge imperial efforts are going into relieving this siege is the prince. Our secrecy has nothing to do with a lack of faith in you personally, it was just that this matter was purely about Prince Manfred."

It spoke volumes for the influence that the older statesman had been able to exert over the captain-general that Tomaselli did calm down. "I hadn't thought of it like that. But nonetheless I should have been consulted! The security of this fortress is my responsibility. And any route this man followed could be followed by hundreds of enemy troops. The way must be blocked!"

Benito laughed. That made him cough. When the paroxysm finished he said, "I swam the better part of a mile in two sections, I climbed a sixty-foot cliff on the seaward side of the Citadel in the dark. Next thing the Magyar will be doing it on horseback and in full armor."

Eberhard patted Benito soothingly. "He's not well, Captain-General. I'm sure he'll show your men the spot when he's up. But it would not be easy for anyone else."

"I'll take you down it personally, Captain-General Tomaselli. I wouldn't dream of letting someone else assess the security." Benito went off into coughing again.

"He's fevered. I think we must leave him to rest. Come,

Captain-General." Eberhard showed Tomaselli out and on the way shook his fist at Benito, behind the captain-general's back.

Manfred and Benito restrained themselves from sending Benito off into a coughing fit again, until the captain-general had mounted his horse and was clopping away.

"It is a good thing I insisted on Von Gherens staying outside," said Manfred, his shoulders still shaking.

Benito looked at Manfred. "It's an equally good thing I didn't tell him that Petro Dorma has decided to relieve the pompous ass of his post and promote Commander Leopoldo in his place."

"What! That would solve a hell of a lot of problems."

Benito raised his eyebrows. "Really? Do you think he'd believe me? It's not as if I can prove it. Captain Di Negri has a set of orders signed by the Doge with the seal of the Republic on them ... but I didn't see swimming in with them."

"I hadn't thought of that."

Chapter 77

Maria went to the door to answer the knock. It wasn't Anastasia, the young Corfiote girl who looked after old Mrs. Grisini. She always knocked firmly, and in a recognizable pattern. A pity; she'd have loved to ask her to mind Umberto and maybe even Alessia, if the old lady was asleep. She really had to go up to the temple again. Umberto was up—and then down—and she didn't know who else to turn to. But this was a very quiet knock. Tentative.

She opened the door to see Benito standing there. "What are you doing out of bed?"

"No one's asked me into one," he said with his old impish grin. "Even the monks have chased me out."

His face became earnest. "Maria, before I left Venice for the first time, Petro said I should come and see you and offer to baby-sit. Before I left Venice this time an undine called Juliette charged me with seeing to Alessia's welfare. I'm better. But I'm still forbidden drill or to do too much exercise. So I came to do what Petro and Juliette said I must. I've come to baby-sit."

Maria gaped at him. "You can't be serious!"

Benito shrugged. "As much as I ever am. Petro Dorma's no fool, as I learned eventually. And I sort of made a bargain with Juliette. So: Lead me to it. Tell me what to do, and you go out and get some time off."

Maria held her head and shook it, as if to check that it was still attached to her shoulders. "Holy Mother! I don't believe this. Look, Umberto's not so good today, either. I've promised him I'd look in at the Little Arsenal, see how thing are going. I've, um, got another visit I really need to make. 'Lessi's asleep now. But would you stay with her and Umberto? If you mean it, that is?"

He smiled. For once, it was a smile with no overtones, no sense of anything hidden, and nothing of his mad recklessness in it. "I mean it. Like I said, lead me to it."

When Maria came back, guiltily, knowing that she'd been away for longer than she'd meant to be, she heard laughter from inside her new home. She found Benito had Umberto sitting up against the cushions in the bedroom, while he was executing intricate Venetian dance steps with Alessia in his arms.

"She's a better dancer than you are," said Maria, trying not to join in the laughter.

"She couldn't be worse!" Benito grinned. "I absolutely hated the dancing instructions that Dorma's mother made me suffer through. Marco now, he makes it look easy. Here, Maria. I think she's getting hungry."

"He even changed her, Maria," said Umberto wonderingly. "He's a braver man than I."

Maria thought Umberto was looking a great deal better than when she'd left.

Benito wrinkled his nose. "You've just got to switch your senses off, sort of. Make it just a job to be gotten through. It's no worse than a lot of other things I've done, and better than no few."

Maria shook her head at him. "Just when I think I know how your mind works, Benito, you go and surprise me again. I never thought you'd be any good with children."

Benito looked like mischief incarnate. "It's because they trust me. Nobody else does."

Maria snorted. "And that's no surprise!"

"Now Maria," said Umberto gently. "He's made me laugh. I'll say I feel better for it."

Maria gave Benito a reluctant smile. "Oh, he's not all bad. Just half bad. Now, I'm going to feed Alessia. Excuse me."

Benito gave her a little bow. "I'll take my leave, too, Umberto, Maria. I'll take a look in down at the Little Arsenal, Umberto. I want to see those boats."

"Come back and tell me what you think."

Maria walked him to the door. Bit her lip, looking at him. "Thanks," she said quietly.

He shrugged. "It's nothing. I'll come again, if you like. Umberto kind of surprised me. He's got interesting ideas about those fireboats."

That had surprised her too. "He looks better for the visit. But next time let me show you how to fold a napkin." It was a tacit admission that she wouldn't object to a next time, she thought, as she patted Alessia's derriere. "This is a mess."

"So was what I found there, believe me. I'll see you."

He probably wouldn't, she thought. He'd be off on his next madcap stunt, which would be far more interesting than looking after a sick man and a baby.

"And where have you been, young feller-me-lad?" asked Manfred, with a buffet that would have made Benito's ears ring for a good while if he hadn't ducked. "Enjoying the adulation of the admiring young women of the Citadel? Francesca tells me you're a very sought-after young bachelor."

Benito grinned. "It's hard being popular. If only you weren't seven sizes too big you could try it." He ducked again. "Listen, seriously, do you know about the project they've been busy with at the Little Arsenal? The fireboats?"

Manfred shook his head. "No. And whose project is this?"

"That's just it: The Arsenalotti have been at odds with the captain-general. So they've been doing it on their own. They've got nearly thirty of these things built. They reckon they've materials for twice that. They're smallish boats—long and slim and designed for speed. Umberto—Maria Verrier's husband—designed the things. I've just been down to have a look. The guy is good, Manfred. Those things, with a good following wind, will be like arrows."

"And just how are we supposed to launch these arrows?" asked Falkenberg, curiously. "Hold the beach while they're carried outside?"

"They've been built to be lowered over the wall into the water. He got the idea from Erik and me and our coracle stunt. Except they're making davits and winches. One of the men down at the Little Arsenal was showing me."

"And you say they've kept this in the dark?"

"Not deliberately. They were just looking for an opportunity to bring it up."

"With Tomaselli in charge, that won't happen," said Falkenberg.

"Not that it isn't a good idea. Might be, at least. Take me down for a look in sometime, Benito."

Count Mindaug was scowling fiercely. Given the slight distortion always present in the summoned image above the blood-bowl, the expression made him look even uglier than ever.

"I hadn't thought he'd be this cautious, Elizabeth," Mindaug admitted. "By now, I'd expected Jagiellon to have intervened directly."

The countess decided that her silvery laugh would irritate Mindaug too much, at the moment. So she kept her expression simply serene. "Keep in mind, Kazimierz, that *Chernobog* is ancient, even if the shell he inhabits—that thing that used to be the prince Jagiellon—is still a relatively young man. For demons, 'ancient' and 'prudent' are almost synonyms. Even for a demon with a savage temper like his."

"True enough. Still—"

"Give it time. Which we have, by the way. Months yet, probably. The attempted treason failed, and my agent in the fortress informs me that any further attempts will take considerable time to organize. Unfortunately—or perhaps fortunately, given Chernobog's hesitancy—the woman who is running the Citadel's counterespionage work is extremely astute."

Mindaug's eyebrows rose. "A *woman?* Since when do Venetians—"

"She's not Venetian. She's one of the Imperials. Prince Manfred's leman, to boot, so she has plenty of influence. Her name is Francesca de Chevreuse. The name she goes by, I should say, since I doubt very much it's her real one."

Now, the Count was shaking his head. For a moment, the tips of his sharp-filed teeth showed. "What is the world coming to? In the old days—yourself excepted, of course—women handled the gossip, not the statecraft."

Since Mindaug's mood seemed to be improving, Elizabeth issued her silvery laugh. "Don't be silly. Even in Lithuania, that's not true. Or have you already forgotten Grand Duchess Imenilda?"

"That was almost a century ago. Besides, she was Ruthenian. The Ruthenians have always been a peculiar lot. Meaning no offense." Elizabeth Bartholdy had quite a bit of Ruthenian blood in her own ancestry.

"None taken, I assure you. To get back to the point, Kazimierz, I really think you're worrying too much."

Count Mindaug studied her for a moment. Then said abruptly: "That may be, Elizabeth. But the fact remains that I now need to consider, seriously, the consequences of failure. If this trap of yours doesn't work—even if only because Jagiellon avoids it—I will be the one to face the immediate repercussions. Not you." He raised his hand and eyed it. "Granted, it's not the finest skin in the world, but it's the only one I've got. I'd just as soon avoid having it served up for one of the monster's meals."

He lowered the hand and brought his eyes back to hers. "I'll need to run, Elizabeth—which means I'll need a place to run *to.*"

The countess ran a delicate fingertip across her lower lip, thinking. She was not surprised, of course, that the issue had finally come up. She'd already given it quite a bit of thought herself, in fact.

"You understand that I do not share your interest in territorial and material matters?"

Mindaug's pointed teeth showed again. "You're not *that* indifferent to them, Elizabeth. Or do you really think you'd be able to pursue your own interests—if you were a peasant woman?"

She laughed. "Point taken. Nevertheless—"

He was shaking his head. "I'm well aware that your ambitions and mine are different. All the more reason, it seems to me, that there needn't be any clash between us. Even if . . . how to say it? Even if—"

"Even if you were residing in the Carpathians instead of Vilna— and trying to subvert my great-great-nephew and assume the throne of Hungary, instead of Jagiellon's."

"That's putting it bluntly. But . . . yes."

He waited, his face impassive.

Elizabeth thought a moment further, then shrugged. "I can't say I have any particular attachment to Emeric. He's easier to manipulate than you would be, but on the other hand . . ."

Mindaug finished the thought for her. "I'm smarter than he is. Which means I'd cause fewer messes for you to have to manipulate me out of." He left unspoken the obvious final clause: *assuming you could.*

But Elizabeth was not worried about that. And the more she thought about it, the more she could see a number of advantages to having Mindaug—if necessary, which she still didn't think it would be—taking asylum and refuge with her.

"Done, then. That *assumes,* of course, that our plans fail."

"Needless to say. I assure you, Elizabeth, that I'd much prefer to remain in Vilna, if at all possible. If nothing else, I'm too old to take any pleasure at the thought of a frantic race to get out of Lithuania ahead of Jagiellon's wrath."

"*Chernobog*'s wrath, Kazimierz. Don't ever forget who you're really dealing with."

For the first time, he laughed himself. "No chance of that, Elizabeth! It's why I approached you in the first place. A mere Grand Duke, even one as capable and vicious as Jagiellon, I would have been confident of handling on my own."

He glanced aside, as if looking over his shoulder. "I simply prefer to avoid the name, that's all. The Black Brain is near to me, and it never pays to do anything to tingle its attention. Speaking of which . . ." His hands began moving. "I think it's time to end this discussion."

Within seconds, his image had faded away.

PART XI
October, 1539 A.D.

Chapter 78

Diego sighed. "It is fairly certain that whoever the Satanist is—whoever *they* are, I should say, since there's certainly more than one—he or she is aware that we are hunting for them. This is the third place where we have found their foul traces, but never anything more. And they've been very cautious never to leave material we can trace to a physical place or person."

Francis nodded. "And venturing beyond the physical, here, where we are denied the protection of one of the wards, is nearly impossible."

Eneko Lopez went to a cupboard in the back of the chapel. "So. I think we should investigate this." He produced the dried-out bundle of herbs and other unpleasantness that someone had once tried to use as a curse on Maria Verrier.

"But it is a fake," protested Diego.

"I know," said Eneko. "But let us consider the very nature of Satan-worship. Its essence is to recruit more souls. Unlike demons who are content to devour, devils accumulate—and use their acolytes to accumulate. And whoever did this is ripe for accumulation. They—or parts of their coven—may already be drawn into this." He held up the bundle, a bit gingerly. "Here, we have physical traces. With some risks, we can use these to divine where they came from. And once we have that, we may catch some trace of our other tormentor. Or tormentors."

By the time that the afternoon sun was sinking, the priests knew more about the "curse." One of the things they knew was that the maker knew absolutely nothing about how to stop themselves being traced by magic. The priests, patiently, set a watch on the suspected house. Curfew or no curfew.

It was after the midnight bell that they saw the various "visitors" arrive. Then the priests calmly went down the street and waited for the Knights' patrol.

"Just what are you doing out here, Father Lopez?" asked *Ritter* Wellmann. "It is after curfew, you know."

"We need some Venetian soldiers, too, *Ritter*. Please fetch some for us."

"To do what?" asked Wellmann.

"God's work, Brother."

"I'm supposed to be on patrol, not on missionary work."

Eneko Lopez was not amused. "You are Knights of God. Your oath is to serve Him first, *Ritter*. Send two of your men to fetch a detachment of troops and their officer here. *Now*."

Ten minutes later, an alarmed-looking lieutenant and some twenty pikemen arrived at a run. "I sent a message up to the fortress," said the lieutenant. "What is it? A mine?"

"Spiritually speaking, yes," said Eneko. "Follow me. The house must be surrounded and we must move in quickly. Wellmann, take the door down with your axe."

Ritter Wellmann was an artist with an axe.

Business, thought Morando, was booming. He always tried to think of other things at this stage. It required detachment. The carefully soundproofed inner sanctum he'd created in the cellar of this unobtrusive house had no less than five of the Citadel's leading social lights in it. And they were dressed exquisitely for the occasion, thought the confidence trickster, forcing down a snicker. Bianca Casarini was a true gem of a recruiter. The trade in information he sold Fianelli was even more profitable than the money he got directly from the women.

Since the curse incident—which had apparently even worked, to Morando's astonishment—Sophia was his to command. The one problem with her, and the other women she'd brought around, was that all of them seemed to derive more from the "sinfulness" of the ritual he'd invented than they did from the actual deeds. It was trying his imagination, not to mention at times his spine.

The other problem was getting the paraphernalia. Black candles had to be made; and he'd had to resort to stealing chickens to dye black. He had a fortune hidden under a paving stone in this room, but he still had to steal chickens, because they just weren't for sale any more. Tonight he'd used a cat. They seemed to like that, even if he'd felt rather sorry for the poor creature.

His supply of hashish was running dangerously low, too. He couldn't see replacing that until the siege was lifted or lost.

Still, the cellar was well hidden, and he had stores of food and water. He'd sit out the orgy of killing and looting that he knew would happen if the Hungarians won, with Bianca and Sophia to keep him company and provide him with pleasure. If the Venetians won . . . well, he'd farm Sophia and her friends a little longer and then it would be time to shave his beard and leave with a convoy heading to Outremer, to enjoy a rich retirement in Constantinople. Bianca had already agreed to come with him.

By the moaning and panting, he would soon be called on to chant some gibberish again. Morando had even made an effort with a grimoire he'd obtained years earlier to garner some real words and phrases.

"Grimoire" so-called, at least. Morando suspected the thing was probably a fake. Which was fine with him, when all was said and done. Playing with Satanism served his purposes, well enough, and Morando wanted no part of the genuine article.

And then Aldo Morando discovered the real fault with good soundproofing and a cellar whose only secret escape route took considerable time to open.

They stormed in. Lieutenant Agra made sure he was the very first in through the door.

The room was a grave disappointment. It had a very ordinary table, a straight-backed chair, and a simple oil lamp, the flame wavering in the sudden disturbance. There was no one there. Nor in the single bedroom or the kitchen. But the priests seemed unperturbed, if in a hurry. They joined hands and chanted. As they did a misty trail of footprints appeared on the floor, ending at what appeared to be just another flagstone in the floor.

"Break it," commanded the short, slight priest with the eagle gaze. "Quickly. There is bound to be another way out."

The knight with the axe tried to put the edge of his axe into the crack. With a growl of impatience the priest took the axe from him and smashed it into the flagstone.

It split. The stone was set into a wooden frame full of lambswool. The knight took the handle of the axe and hauled and ripped the hidden trapdoor right out. Agra was down those smoke-shrouded stairs so fast he nearly broke his neck on them. At the foot of them, amid the screaming, despite the press at his back, he stopped.

He'd expected nearly anything but this.

The room reeked of smells, that of hashish prominent among them. Naked masked women, their breasts, groins and in at least one case buttocks painted with strange bloody patterns, clung to a man wearing a long cloak of black-and-red velvet, black boots, and nothing else. Not all of the women had the sort of bodies that the lieutenant would have paid to see naked. Even the smoky room lit with black candles could only do so much. It was the black altar and the headless cat lying with its neck in a bowl, though, that really got him.

At least, until the women went berserk. The lieutenant then discovered how well frightened and desperate women can scratch and bite.

Benito sat drinking some wine with Maria and Umberto in their small bedroom. Umberto sat against the pillows and Maria on the foot of the bed. Benito was sitting on the chair from the living room. Alessia was attempting to suck her toes on a rug at their feet.

Benito had been back every day to sit a while with Umberto and Alessia. Maria's initial surprise had given way to acceptance. But today she hadn't taken advantage of it to go out. Today she wanted to know what was happening. She was worried, and not without reason.

Benito grimaced at the wine. "I suppose the one thing we can be grateful for is that we've still got enough wine for a full ration. If it was good wine, we wouldn't have. The Libri d'Oro didn't want to buy it because it was so lousy. So even though the granary is down to an eighth full and the upper wells are running dry, we've got wine. If you can call it that."

Maria shook her head at him in irritation. "Benito, stop burbling about wine, and tell us what happened. You were there. You should know. The rumors in the lower town today are amazing!

A coven of witches sacrificing babies and having orgies with demons and blasting priests and buildings to ashes—a high-class brothel—a cabal of female thieves. God knows what. People are claiming all sorts of things. I've even given in to curiosity and been to have a look, not that there was much point. There's a guard and a smashed-in door but you can't see anything else."

"Manfred says it's like a traveling players' version of a mixture between hell and a brothel down below in the cellar. They took him to see it. It's pretty tawdry in daylight, apparently, but the lieutenant who was testifying is thinking about becoming a monk after last night." Benito chuckled. "Apparently he saw a great deal more of a number of mostly unattractive women than he really wanted to. Anyway, it seems that some bored *Case Vecchie* women had initially gone to Morando because of his reputation as an astrologer and chemist and—ah—sexual physician. Apparently, no matter what else he can do, he's quite a lover, or at least, they think he is. And they, finding—at last!—a lover who wanted to hear gossip as much as they wanted to indulge in it, came in droves. Well. I guess five women isn't really a 'drove.'"

Maria snorted. "They're saying Sophia Tomaselli was right on the top of the heap."

"The captain-general is trying desperately to hush it all up," said Benito, nodding. "She's his wife, after all."

Both her eyebrows went up. "And the wife of the Salt Minister and of the largest oil exporter on the island. Come on, Benito! Everybody already knows all that. He might as well try to hush the sea. People are getting very restive about it. The *scuolo* are all for burning the Castel *a terra*."

Benito was silent for a moment. Then he said wryly: "Fortunately, they jailed the man and the women separately, because all the women came out singing one tune: It was a complete fraud, a put-up job by the Knights to discredit their husbands and allow the prince to take over. They'd been kidnapped, stripped, abused, and locked in the cellar. They wanted the Knights punished for the degradation by being thrown out of the sanctuary that Venice had kindly offered them—and the cowardly mercenaries who'd sold out to them shot."

"What!" Umberto had started upright. Alessia stopped playing with her toes. "You can't be serious!"

"Dead serious. And Tomaselli was ready to make it stick. Heh.

It was pretty exciting, what with Lieutenant Agra having to be restrained and calling the captain-general's wife a whore and witch."

"Well, he was dead right!"

"Yes, well, as it pans out . . . half right. Morando lent her some of his occult books—those were fakes, too, Eneko says—and apparently she tried to cast curses on—ah—people she considered to be her enemies." He interrupted himself before he said the name, but Maria saw the guilty look in his eyes, and she knew who he was going to say. And although she had suspected it, having the evidence in front of her was enough to send her simmering temper into full boil. So that was, indeed, where the ill-wishing had come from!

But Benito was continuing. "Fortunately, old man De Belmondo was sick and we had the assistant podesta of Corfu standing in. He's one of the Libri d'Oro, but he did his law in Padua University and takes it pretty seriously. He pointed out that since it was the captain-general's wife accused, Tomaselli couldn't take part in the hearings. And he sent the guard off to fetch the other Justices, even De Belmondo from his sickbed. And, as I say, it was fortunate that they'd kept the man separate. He's from the north of Italy, originally. Milan, in fact—Pauline country. They burn witches up there on suspicion. His name—the one he goes by here, anyway, is Aldo Morando. He was so keen to prove he wasn't a man-witch or a Satanist, that he was spilling the beans as fast as he could. He was selling information and black lotos, and acting as a glorified pimp for that gaggle of rich women. They followed up several of his confessions, and found them all true. Then they had the brains, finally, to split the women up and question them individually. Then they came apart. Their stories didn't tally. Eventually, the truth became obvious."

Umberto shook his head, confused. "What? That he really was training witches in our midst, practicing black magic?"

"Well, no," Benito said. "That he was casting horoscopes, telling fortunes, dabbling in the occult mostly as window dressing for his real interest—getting information from one set of stupid, bored, sexually unsatisfied women to sell to whoever might be interested in it. The Justices called Eneko Lopez. And he said, although they'd hoped to catch real practitioners of black arts, that this lot were simply nasty, spoiled, bored, rich women."

"And what happened then?"

"Well, to make a long story short, Eneko had cut the legs out from under the Justices. It's not an offence to prance around naked in a cellar done up to look like a cheap whorehouse with astrological trimmings. And, while selling the stuff is illegal, simply using black lotos is also not a crime. As for participating in orgies and gossiping to your lover, well, the outcome of that is mostly up to the husbands, not the courts."

"What! You mean they've got away with this? The *scuolo* will—" Umberto was struggling to stand up.

Benito flicked up out of the chair and pushed him down, gently. "Relax! For starters, selling information to enemy agents is a serious matter. So is pimping. Morando is the one who's really to blame here, and they have him dead to rights. They even got him for chicken theft! And two of the ladies of Corfu high society are up for ... prostitution. It appears that Morando was selling their favors for certain services he rendered—including Tomaselli's Sophia. But the cream of it is that Lieutenant Agra—the one who got so upset about being called a cowardly sell-out mercenary—has slapped a civil suit for defamation against them."

"So what's happening to them now?"

"Morando will rot in jail until trial in Venice. The treason part will probably have him executed. The others ... well, they've been bailed. Released into the custody of their spouses. Except for the wife of the Salt Minister. She asked to remain in jail for her own safety, since he threatened to kill her." Benito shook his head, ruefully. "Not that I think, under the circumstances, those other women will find their husbands very, ah, 'protective.' Probably beat them to a pulp."

"So you mean that Tomaselli bitch is out there, free?" demanded Maria furiously.

"Calm down, Maria."

"*I will not calm down. I'll—*"

"You're upsetting Alessia." Benito had picked the baby up and was soothing her.

Maria pursed her lips and took a deep breath. "I am going out," she said between clenched teeth.

"Maria!" said Umberto, anxiously. "Promise me you won't do anything stupid. Please."

Benito had moved between her and the door. "Think of Alessia,

Maria. You hurt Sophia, you're the one who will end up being punished. And by doing that you'll be punishing your baby. She'd rather have a mother at home."

"Get out of my way, Benito Valdosta. I'm not going to kill anybody unless it's you, for not moving. I'm going to talk to someone. A friend."

"I'm your friend."

"I need to talk to a woman. A man wouldn't understand. Now give me Alessia."

"I'll stay and take care of her. Just promise us you won't do anything crazy."

She laughed bitterly. "That's rich, Benito, coming from you. Just let me go, see. I'll be back once I've got this out of me."

Renate De Belmondo handed Maria a cup of steaming, fragrant liquid. "This tisane is a kind of magic too," she said with a gentle smile. "There are more and deeper magics than Eneko Lopez and his kind understand. There is magic in things they consider inert. There is power in people that they cannot detect. There are magics in love and hatred, too. Especially here."

Maria sipped the brew. It was soothing, there was no doubt about it.

"Vervain and a little heartsease. There are times and places for the picking of both. And it can only be done by one who has the great Goddess's hand about her." Renate looked sternly at her. "You must learn, Maria, to control and direct that anger of yours. Otherwise you'll hurt those closest to you."

Maria bit her lip. There was some truth in that, she had to acknowledge. Especially this afternoon. She knew that the source of the "curse" on her house was Sophia Tomaselli, even if she couldn't prove it. She'd heard some of what Benito had not told her—just what Sophia had said, to the Justices, to the curious gathered around as she and the other women were taken away. Vitriolic, to say the least, and Sophia placed all of the blame on being caught on Maria. And though of course it was not in the least logical, if you believed Sophia, it was Maria who had somehow *forced* her into the spy's service.

"It's . . . it's just the injustice of it all. It's not *right!*"

The older woman looked at her thoughtfully. "A sense of justice is a part of what makes us what we are. Some of us are willing to suffer ourselves to make sure there is retribution . . . even if it costs us. You are one like that."

Maria thought back to her single-handed vendetta against the *Casa* Dandelo, when Caesare wouldn't help—and Benito, the scamp, did. "Yes. I suppose so."

"But are you prepared to extract the cost of your retribution from others? From innocent parties. From your friends?"

Just the intonation said to Maria that this was a very important question. A question far wider than just the issues she'd run to Renate with. She paused to think. Maria thought of what Benito had said about Alessia. And of what she'd decided to do.

She shook her head. "No."

Renate smiled. Maria noticed that small lines eased from around her eyes. "The Goddess and her followers do not practice retribution."

"I don't think I can forgive that woman for what she tried to do."

Renate shook her head. "Neither could I. But our justice is based on restitution. And restitution finds no gain in mere retribution. Sophia Tomaselli was looking for retribution. She was quite content to hurt innocent parties in her quest to get it."

Maria sighed. "Yes. But . . . well, it was such a small thing. I mean she set out to attack everything—my life, my loved ones' lives, for something so small. So unimportant. Who on earth *cares* if some people think I'm more attractive than she is? Why would it make any difference to me? It's not as if I'm competing with her for anything! It's not fair."

Renate curled her lip. "Of course it is not fair. Such a person is an island of their own self-importance. The fact that their retribution is totally out of proportion, will not benefit them, and will hurt others, is irrelevant. You dared to slight the most important person in her universe. Anything is acceptable to punish you."

Maria paused for a while sipping the tea. This might all be true. But it didn't apply directly to her problem right now . . . did it?

"So what do I do about her, Priestess? I'm not having that woman on the loose to endanger my man or my child again. She might try anything. Poison. Thugs. Planting evidence to make us look like traitors."

Renate smiled. "I am only the priestess when I let down my hair and don the robes." She pursed her lips. "Of course, a charge of attempted murder should stick. I suggest tomorrow you swear one out. The fact that she used a weapon that she did not know wouldn't work, does not alter the fact that she tried. After all, if a man tries to shoot another and the weapon fails to fire, it is still an attempt at murder. She would be confined again in that case." The older woman took a deep breath. "Other than that, you must come to me every day now. I must teach you certain magics and certain rituals that will protect you and yours. I must teach you, too, how to control that temper of yours. How to break it to harness."

"Me? I can't do magic!"

The priestess stood up and put her hands on either side of Maria's head. "You already do magic. Magic that Eneko Lopez does not understand exists. Magic more powerful than he understands. An old, rough and elemental kind of magic, but strong."

She took her hands away and tugged at a sidelock of her white hair, a gesture indicating thought in the priestess who was also the governor's wife. "You know, I know a great deal about Sophia Tomaselli. In some ways we are very alike."

Maria shook her head vehemently. "You couldn't be more un-alike!

Renate twinkled. "I think that's a compliment. But there are some similarities that Eneko Lopez would see. For example: We are both aristocrats at the apogee of our social setting. We both turned to other sources of comfort after we arrived here. We both, I believe, did so for the same reasons: We both wanted to get pregnant. I know Sophia has tried all sorts of 'treatments' and diets and consulted churchmen at some length. She fell in with a trickster. I . . . fell in with one of my maids. She was a Corfiote and felt sorry for me. There, but for fortune, went I."

Maria shook her head again, vehement. "No. Sophia cares for nobody but herself. It's a blessing she's never had a child. You care for everybody. I don't believe you'd have done something like trying to curse me and mine. That's not like you."

"I don't think I would have done what she did, no. And caring is what the sisterhood looks for: sisterhood. And that was why I was taken to the temple. That is why you were. And that is why she wasn't."

"The two things are not alike at all," said Maria, stubbornly sticking to her earlier contention. "The Mother is gentle—not sick!"

Renate shrugged ruefully. "Stella is inclined to sensationalize news, but still, yes, those women were seeking perversion. Probably some of it came out of their mothers telling them that the natural urges and pleasures of their bodies were bad, wrong, and evil. Therefore they came to conclude that evil gave pleasure. Possibly only because they were bored and their husbands were under the impression that if *they* were pleasured and pleased, it didn't matter if their wives were." She sighed. "I don't want to deceive you, Maria. The great Goddess . . . well, there is one aspect that does call for a willing sacrifice. And the spring ritual dance is conducted in the nude. But no men are part of it. It is done for a reason."

She stood up again. "Now, I think you're all safe enough tonight. Here." She took from her reticule a sprig of green holly. "Prickly thing. And full of the heart of green-ness. Put it above the door lintel. Not with cold iron. If it turns black—come running, and bring your child. And go barefoot if you can. Touching the earth, it will be difficult for any other magic to affect you."

Now she looked mischievous. "Don't tell Eneko Lopez that's why his spells don't work well here. Contact with the earth of Corcyra. The earth here drinks magic. The more they use, the less well it works. And the magic is reborn in other forms within the Earth. We use it."

"I want to learn."

"Very well. You must come to me, here. This hilltop was a temple before it was a fort. One of the entries to the inner temple is still here."

Chapter 79

He looked as though he might very possibly throttle her, thought Sophia. He hadn't said a word all the way back to their chambers in the east wing of the fortress. Now, with the heavy door closed behind them, he turned on her in fury.

"How could you, you bitch! How could you! I'm the laughingstock of the Citadel. I'll be the laughingstock of all Venice when the siege is over. I'll never hold another position of authority you—you— My mother was right! I should never have married you!"

She drew herself up. "Nico, I did this for you. I went to this man to try and see if there was something—anything—I could do to have the heir you needed."

He snorted disdainfully. "Ha. Yes. By turning yourself into a *puttana*! By sleeping with half my officers! Grand. You give me an heir that isn't even *mine*."

She looked down her nose at him. "Those are absolutely trumped-up lies, Nico Tomaselli! As if I would ever desire another man but you." She sniffed. "I thought it was a fertility rite. Harmless. And they . . . they made out we were having orgies and . . . and all I wanted was a baby for you." She burst into calculated tears. They had never failed her before.

But they did this time. He folded his arms, and not around her. "Even if it were true, it's not what people are going to say. Venice takes a dim view of these things. That new Doge, Dorma, is very straightlaced. Why, he even exiled his own ward for his antics and they were nothing like being paraded through half the streets of

634

the Citadel, screaming and fighting, stark naked. I don't know how
I will ever hold up my head in Venice again!"

"Then don't."

"What choice do I have, Sophia?" he demanded. "What choice
have you left me?" His weak man's rage was beginning to build
again.

Sophia had one last card left to pay. One last token from
Morando, which she'd been trying to think of a way to use for
weeks. It had come, magically transported, her lover had said. He'd
suggested she make a lever out of it. She'd hesitated, but . . .

Now she had no choice.

"I have to show you something. In my bedroom."

"I'm not interested right now."

"You will be. Come." She simply walked up to her room.

By the time he got there, she'd taken out the folded letter. "Here."
She handed it to him.

He looked at the address. The seal. "Who opened a letter to me
from the Doge?" he demanded.

"I did. Because I love you and look after you. Open it. See how
well Venice rewards you for your loyal service after all these years!"

He opened the letter. She watched as his ruddy face turned pale.
He looked as if he were about to burst into tears. "Who cares what
they think of you in Venice?" she demanded. "Let us go where they
will appreciate us!"

He bit his knuckle. "Damn Dorma. Damn him to hell. Leopoldo
in my place! After all I've done here!"

It was entirely typical of her husband, Sophia thought contemp-
tuously, that he never thought to ask her how she'd obtained the
letter. But, not for the first time, she was glad he was a fundamentally stupid man. She was in desperate straits herself, now—
with outright treason as her only option.

"Damn, drat, and blast the man for an interfering busybody!"
said Francesca furiously. "I've had a watch on Fianelli for *weeks*—
and now, thanks to Lopez's meddling, I've lost him. He was gone
before the soldiers got to his shop. Who cares about Morando?
He was just a minor player, working for Fianelli."

Manfred patted her soothingly. "There, dear. Look at it this
way—you'll have a splendid time finding him again."

If looks could kill, Manfred would have been ripe for burial.

"It's not a game, Manfred!" she said, in such a tone that even he sat up straight. "Morando by himself was nothing. Fianelli was *dangerous*. He still may be. *Somehow* he was getting information out—Fianelli, *not* Morando—in a way that none of your clever men suspected, and that nothing you did uncovered. If he was getting information out, what did he get *in*? What *could* he get in?"

Von Gherens looked puzzled. "If you knew who he was weeks ago, why didn't you let us deal with him then?"

Francesca eyed him darkly. "Von Gherens, you are to intrigue what deportment lessons are to a brothel."

The *Ritter* thought about this one for a while. "Useful, you mean? So why didn't we deal with this spy weeks ago, Francesca? I don't get it, like the deportment lessons."

"I'd guess she was planning to start feeding him wrong information," said Manfred, yawning. "She'd have had Morando arrested quietly, and blackmailed him into turning on his former allies."

Francesca smiled on him. "You're proof it is possible for someone to learn even if carrying all that armor starves the brain of blood. That's one reason. The other was I wanted the final link. I wanted to know how he was getting the information out to Emeric."

Von Gherens rubbed his broken nose. "You should have talked to Eneko Lopez earlier, then. You could have helped each other. Each of you had what the other needed."

"What do you mean?"

Von Gherens crossed himself. "I mean Fianelli was the Satanist Eneko was actually looking for. He was using demonic magic to send the information. Eneko and his friends had detected him sending it, but couldn't find him. You found him, but couldn't work out how he sent it. You two should talk."

Francesca gritted her teeth. "I should have. And I will."

Captain-General Tomaselli was not the most effective soldier or administrator. Privately, he knew that. But he'd tried. He had been loyal to Venice. That they should promote that—that—*upstart* Leopoldo into his place was unbearable. It was unfair! And thinking of that unfairness, Tomaselli dwelled more and more on the unthinkable.

He could ask for a great deal, if he switched his allegiance to the Hungarians. He wouldn't have to soldier or administrate any more, things which he was not really good at. And Sophia would be out of jail. He'd been horrified when apologetic soldiers had come to fetch her again. Those damned disrespectful *scuolo* sluts! How dare that woman swear out a charge against Sophia? He'd taken small, but satisfying steps to have some of her family's ration reduced. After all, her husband wasn't working.

Now all he needed was a way to contact Emeric to make a deal.

He would talk to Sophia. She might have some idea how he could do it. She was the only one he could trust. It was clear to him now that the charges against her were all false; she'd been betrayed as surely as he had. And he could take her some decent food and wine again. He went as often as three times a day, anyway. Her trial . . . He'd have to reach a deal before then. They'd conspired against her thus far. The trial would be a mockery, of course, magnifying her small digressions into vast things as a way of getting at *him*. That was what was behind the whole thing, he now understood.

Well, he'd show them.

"What are you *doing* here?" hissed the man who opened the door for Fianelli. The secretary for the podesta glanced over his shoulder nervously, looking to see if there was anyone in the corridor behind him.

Fianelli shouldered his way past him. "Close the door, you idiot, instead of gawping at me."

Hastily, Meletios Loukaris closed the back door, which served as the delivery entrance for Governor De Belmondo's palace. That done, the podesta's secretary started hissing another protest. But Fianelli silenced him by the simple expedient of clamping a hand over his mouth.

Fianelli was not a big man, and fat besides, but the secretary was smaller still—and slightly-built. He had no chance of resisting Fianelli with sheer muscle. So be it. In a former life, in Constantinople, Loukaris had carried out several assassinations. Despite his initial nervous reaction at seeing Fianelli, the secretary knew that he was alone in the rear portions of the palace. He could kill Fianelli, then dispose of the body by—

But, as his hand slid into his cloak and closed over the hilt of the special blade he kept hidden there, he felt Fianelli's other hand clamping onto his wrist. The criminal boss was stronger than he looked.

"Don't even *think* of trying to use that needle on me, Loukaris.

Forget those silly Byzantine political games. I'm a lot tougher than you'll ever be."

To emphasize the point, Fianelli hauled the secretary's hand out of the cloak and slammed his knuckles against the wall. The little needle-shaped stiletto clattered onto the tiles. Then, for good measure, Fianelli pounded Loukaris's head against the wall also. Twice, and hard enough to daze him.

When his senses cleared—and to his surprise—Loukaris saw that Fianelli was extending the stiletto to him. Hilt first.

"Here, take it back. You might need it later." Fianelli gave him a piercing look. "*We* might need it. We're still in business, Loukaris. The only thing that's changed is that you'll be hiding me, from now on."

Loukaris took the stiletto. He considered trying to kill Fianelli with it, for just an instant, but discarded the idea as if it were a hot coal in his bare hand. True, Meletios Loukaris had killed before. But his victims had all been aristocratic elderly men, and one woman, none of whom had Fianelli's criminal history and skills. The secretary had no doubt at all that Fianelli would overcome him—and then shove the stiletto into his own throat.

Quickly, he slipped the stiletto back into its special pouch. "This is *dangerous* for me. If anyone spots you—the alarm's out all over the fortress—"

Fianelli was faster that he looked, too. His fat, heavy hand cracked across Loukaris's cheek. "Shut up. You'll hide me in your own chambers. Nobody ever goes in there except you, do they?"

"The maid," complained Loukaris, rubbing his cheek. Fianelli's slap had been hard enough to really *hurt*.

The criminal boss grunted. "We'll figure something out."

A horrid thought came to the secretary. "What about your men? I can't—"

Fianelli waved his hand. "Don't worry about them. It'll just be me. They've made their own arrangements, whatever they are." He grunted. "Not that I care. If they get caught, they have no idea where I am since I never told them about you."

He jerked a thumb forward. "Now show me the way to your chambers."

By the time they got there, moving carefully through the corridors of the palace, Loukaris had already figured out the solution.

"She only comes in once a day. Always in the early afternoon." Sullenly, he went over to a very large freestanding dresser and swung the doors open. The dresser was full of clothes, since the secretary to the governor fancied himself something of a dandy. "You can hide behind the cloaks and stuff. There's room in the back, and the lazy slattern never looks in here anyway."

"Good enough." Slowly, Fianelli's eyes scanned the room. By the end, he had a crooked smile on his face. "You'll have to share the bed. Unless *you* want to sleep on the divan. No way I'm going to."

The secretary grimaced. The bed wasn't really that big, but . . . He'd already more or less resigned himself to the inevitable.

By the end of the evening, his resignation had become complete.

Fianelli forced him to watch the ritual he used to conjure up the image of their mutual master, King Emeric of Hungary. Loukaris had never known that Fianelli was a sorcerer, in addition to everything else.

"Still in business, like I said." Fianelli seemed very satisfied. He'd also forced Loukaris to clean up the traces of the ritual. "I get the wall side of the bed."

"You can have all of it." Loukaris almost gagged on the words. It had only been chicken blood, but he felt like he might vomit. "I think I'll sleep on the divan."

"Smart man," murmured Fianelli. The squat criminal boss gave the podesta's secretary a look that combined menace and complacency. And well he might. To Loukaris, he looked like the King of the Frog Demons—contemplating a fly.

Chapter 80

"The Barbary corsairs and the Genovese are uneasy allies, Grand Duke," said Count Mindaug. "They're traditional enemies. Of course, both sides hate the Venetians like poison but still . . . It is a fragile alliance. Alexius may be a weak reed, but he is being a very effective stopper to the Dardanelles."

"And what news have you from the Holy Roman Emperor, Mindaug?"

It didn't surprise Mindaug at all that Jagiellon knew of his secret messenger from Germany. His communications with Hungary were far more carefully orchestrated. "The Emperor is worse. He took the news that his nephew is trapped on Corfu by Emeric's men as reason to find more energy, to organize things. But now he is sliding again. His campaign against Emeric is a measure of the man."

"Why? It seems quite a small campaign."

"It is meant to be. The Emperor knows he is dying. He doesn't want his heir to take over with a huge war on his hands. A conquest of Hungary would be an immense war, even for the Empire. This one is designed to cost Emeric a great deal—but it will do so only if he doesn't react to it. The Emperor knows that Emeric simply cannot leave such an incursion alone, when it becomes clear what ignoring it will cost him. Frankly, in my opinion, because Emeric believes himself the greatest commander alive, he would be unable to ignore any challenge, however insignificant, that threatened what he holds. The effort, I should guess, is to get him to withdraw from Corfu to protect assets closer to home."

Jagiellon's black eyes stared into nothingness. Then he turned to Mindaug again. "And have you progressed at all with your researches into the magic of Corfu?"

"In one respect, yes. I have been investigating the works of one Trigomenses Commensus. He has recorded various nonhuman interviews, attempting by virtue of their long lives to piece together early history. It appears that, back when Corfu was part of the mainland, it was the center of a fertility cult, long before the area was overrun by invaders—perhaps the Dorians. The nonhumans he questioned—dryads, undines and satyrs—regarded the place as sacred, too. It is an old place."

"I know that it is an old place, once regarded as being of great power. I can feel no trace of any great power there now, myself, though. Yet my slave and the shaman are not succeeding in their quest there. They are being magically hampered, but I do not know by what or exactly how. It is like wrestling smoke! I need to find the source of this and know if it can be harnessed. This began as an exercise in attempting to flank the Holy Roman Empire. It has become a search for whatever it is that can even thwart the magic of the shaman. He is an adept of great strength."

"I was coming to that, Grand Duke. Commensus' interviewees all agree: Power there requires a connection to the earth."

"You mean I would have to physically go there?"

"At least in spirit, my lord."

Mindaug held his breath, doing everything in his power to keep his mind blank. This was the moment for which he and Elizabeth Bartholdy had schemed for so long.

"Yes," grunted Jagiellon. It was all Mindaug could do not to let his breath explode in a gust. There had not been a trace of suspicion in the sound.

"Yes," Jagiellon. "I think you're right. Risky, but—worth it, to shackle that power and bend it to my will."

"It's *infuriating,* mistress," snarled Bianca Casarini. "And I don't have any choice—I *have* to hide Fianelli's men from the Venetians, even if it's in my own house."

Elizabeth laughed. "Having three louts lounging about your house would try the patience of a saint. Which you are certainly not." The countess cocked her head sideways. "I assume you've taken steps to bring them under control."

The last words served to ease some of Casarini's foul temper. "Oh, yes. One of them—Papeti's his name—has been lusting after me for some time. So now he thinks he's succeeded—and the one whom I did seduce is furious about it. The right two words from me, and they'll cut each other up."

"And the third?"

Bianca shrugged. "He's just a slug. Seems interested in nothing much beyond sleeping, drinking and eating. I haven't bothered with him, since I need to keep my magics to a minimum. I have to be careful here, mistress, sharing a small island with Eneko Lopez and his damned priests. They can't do much because they're afraid to work without their wards. But they're still accomplished adepts, especially Lopez."

"Yes, I understand. Well, that should be enough. My plans look to be coming to fruition. For the moment, just stay out of sight."

Before she'd even had time to finish erasing the traces of the ritual, Bianca heard a ruckus erupting in the rooms downstairs. A brief one, but very loud, ending in a cut-off scream.

"Those *idiots*," she hissed, hurrying from her bedroom. "They'll make the neighbors curious."

When she reached the bottom of the stairs, Bianca saw that her "two words" wouldn't be necessary after all. Papeti's body was lying on the floor, bleeding all over the tiles. Saluzzo, red-faced, was crouched over the corpse cleaning his knife on Papeti's blouse.

He hadn't even heard Bianca arrive. The Florentine's eyes were fixed on Zanari, the third of Fianelli's thugs. Zanari was standing in a nearby archway, with a very nervous look on his face.

"She's *my* woman," Saluzzo growled. "Don't forget it, or—" Angrily, and despite having already cleaned the blade, Saluzzo drove the knife into Papeti's ribcage again. The corpse jerked under the impact.

Saluzzo spotted Bianca then. Leaving the knife stuck in the body, he rose and took two strides toward her.

"Paulo, what—"

Saluzzo was a powerful man. His slap sent her sprawling on the steps. The next slap, on the back of her head, dazed her.

Fortunately, perhaps, since the pain when he seized her by the hair and began dragging her up the stairs would have been considerably more agonizing otherwise.

"*Bitch.* I'll teach you!"

By the time they reached her bedroom and Saluzzo flung her onto the bed, Bianca had recovered her senses. Furiously, she began muttering the words that would destroy the man. Saluzzo didn't even hear them, he was so consumed with anger combined with lust.

Before she finished the incantation, though, Bianca had suppressed her anger. The situation, she realized, was ideal for a different use of magic. Someday, she might well have to flee her house in a hurry—a task that would be made considerably easier if Saluzzo remained behind to attack her pursuers with demonic fury.

That, of course, would require turning him into a demon—the shape of one, at least—which could be done, under the right circumstances.

These were the right circumstances. Rage and lust, combined, were the key raw ingredients.

"I'll teach you to fool around with anyone else," Saluzzo snarled. He'd already hoisted her skirts and forced her legs apart. Now, he slapped her again and started untying his breeches.

"Paulo, please!"

Another slap. "Time for your lesson, slut."

The period that followed was unpleasant. Even painful, toward the end, as Bianca's murmured incantations began effecting the first transformations of Saluzzo's form. But Bianca had been through worse in the past, and would face still worse in the future. Immortality, as the countess often remarked, had its price. Many prices, in fact.

Fortunately, Saluzzo was raping her on the bed—still better, on a bed in the upper floor of her house, almost twenty feet above the soil of Corfu. Had he been assaulting Bianca on the ground itself, her magics would have drained away. The more so, since the sort of transformation she was carrying out on him was closely connected to earth magic. It was not quite the same as making a golem, but close.

"What's the matter, Eneko?" asked Francesca, leaning forward in her chair. "You look suddenly ill."

"You cannot sense it?" The priest's voice was brittle; his temples held in both hands.

Puzzled, Francesca shook her head. "Sense what?"

"The magic. That is a hideous spell being used. The one who uses it—it's the female, this time, not Fianelli—is reckless beyond belief. I'd never dare use a spell that powerful here on Corfu, without wards—not that I'd ever use that spell anyway— because . . ."

He croaked. Surprised, Francesca realized it was the sound of strained laughter.

"Of course, I imagine she's not concerned with the danger of attracting demons. Since she's one herself, in all that matters."

Magic was something Francesca knew very little about. So she focused on what, to her, was the key point. "You're sure it's a woman? Not Fianelli?"

Eneko raised his head slowly, staring at her through eyes that were nothing much more than slits. "Oh, yes. There's a succubus—of sorts—loose in this fortress, Francesca. And she's even more danger-ous than Fianelli. More powerful, at least, when it comes to magic."

Francesca leaned back in the chair, her lips pursed. "A woman. Could it be Sophia Tomaselli?"

Before Lopez could respond, Francesca raised her hand. "Yes, Eneko, I know the fetish she placed in Maria Verrier's house was a fake. But perhaps that was just a subterfuge—a way to protect her from charges of practicing *real* witchcraft, in case she ever got caught." Francesca chuckled, throatily. "It's the sort of thing I'd have thought up."

Eneko's smile was thin. "At a rough estimate, Francesca, you are eighty times more intelligent than Sophia Tomaselli. But it doesn't matter. You forget that Pierre went to see her in her cell, after she was arrested. The Savoyard's the best witch-smeller I've ever met. He says, quite firmly, that while the Tomaselli woman is evil enough, in a multitude of small and petty ways, she's got no more demonic power than a carrot."

Francesca must have looked a bit dubious. Lopez's smile became still thinner. "Please, Francesca. I have learned not to second-guess you when it comes to intrigue and espionage. Please don't try to second-guess me when it comes to magic. Whoever the female is, it is not Sophia Tomaselli."

Francesca spread her fingers in a gesture that, subtly, indicated assent. More precisely, that she was beating a demure but hasty retreat.

"I wouldn't dream of questioning you, Eneko!"

The two of them laughed, abruptly.

"Still," Francesca continued, "I think we should start with Sophia Tomaselli. We should question Morando again also, of course, but I doubt he'd say anything. If this mysterious woman—"

"*Female*, Francesca—not 'woman.' Trust me. The distinction, if you understood it, would be even more important to you than to me."

"'Female,' then. If this female is an accomplice of his, at this point he'd never tell us. Even that she exists, much less her identity."

"Why? He seems eager enough to tell us everything else."

"Because Morando is expecting he'll be executed, when he's returned to Venice. A traitor's death, too, his legs broken first." For a moment, she glared. "Thanks to those idiot men! That includes you, Eneko! A lesson: *Never* tell a man you're going to execute him, if there's any chance he might still have information you want. You just eliminated any motive for him to keep talking."

Eneko scowled. "He was guilty of—"

"*Who cares?*" Francesca slapped the armrests of her chair with exasperation. "Why does a whore have to keep reminding priests and devout knights that justice belongs to the Lord? Ours is the province of practicality, damnation!"

Eneko's lips quirked. "I believe it's 'vengeance' that belongs to the Lord, Francesca, though I understand the point. Nor, by the way, have I ever called you a 'whore.'"

She shrugged. "It's just a word. Means nothing to me, to be blunt. And to get back to the point, Morando won't tell us anything because perhaps the only hope he has left—however faint it may be—is that his accomplice, if she remains at large, might somehow rescue him from his predicament. Yes, yes, it's a very faint hope—criminal associates are hardly noted for their personal loyalties and devotion. But, who knows? There might be some deep tie between them. And, even if there isn't, a man expecting a noose will hope for anything."

"Ah. That's why you think Tomaselli would know—"

Francesca shook her head. "We should question her also, but I doubt we'll get anything useful. The problem in *her* case being somewhat the opposite. Too much talk instead of too little. That woman is driven by spite more than anything else. At one point in her interrogation, you may recall, she named half the women in the fortress as being witches participating in regular Black Sabbaths. She had Maria Verrier copulating with Satan himself, while the podesta's wife—" She threw up her hands. "Ah, never mind! But you see my point. How reliable is the information given to us by a woman who'd insist that Renate De Belmondo—at her age!—was . . . well. You remember. You were there."

Lopez grimaced. He'd been present for most of Tomaselli's interrogation. Sophia, hysterically, had swung from protesting complete innocence at one moment to claiming, in the next, that she was the least guilty of several thousand women in the Citadel. The accusations she'd made regarding Maria Verrier and the podesta's wife had been particularly grotesque.

"I see your point. But, that being true, what do you mean by suggesting we start with Tomaselli?"

"We need to start tracing Sophia's associations. Not by asking *her,* but others. I'll have Mouse start working on that."

"Mouse" was the nickname Francesca had given to the best agent she'd started employing, since she arrived on Corfu. Eneko had met the man three times, but could never quite remember what he looked like afterward. When he'd commented to Francesca to that effect, she'd simply looked very smug.

"I'll tell Mouse to start with Stella Mavroukis, Maria's friend," Francesca mused. "That woman knows all the gossip there is to know about this island. Kérkira and the Citadel, anyway."

"What would you like me to do?"

"Eneko, would you be able to recall—precisely—when each instance of this 'female magic' took place?"

Slowly, Lopez nodded. "Yes, I think so. Diego sensed it, too—and sometimes Francis and Pierre—so we can compare our memories. Yes. I should be able to reconstruct it. What good will that do?"

"Maybe none," replied Francesca, shrugging. "But you never know. This sort of work is like trying to piece together a broken tile. The more pieces you have, the more likely it is that you will succeed."

Prince Manfred came into the room, at that point. His cheerful smile vanished like the dew under Francesca's glare.

"And *you*! If I succeed in piecing this all together—I *will* expect you to exercise your power and offer Morando a pardon. A commutation, at least. So that he can confirm whatever my suspicions are."

"What are you talking about? Piece what together?"

"*Manfred!*"

"Yes, darling. Certainly."

Eneko laughed. "These are the times when I know celibacy is a blessing."

"*Eneko!*"

"Sorry, Francesca. It's true."

His lust satiated, Saluzzo's anger had faded also. He sprawled across her limply.

"Paulo, he *forced* me," Bianca said, in a pleading tone. "He held a knife to my throat."

Saluzzo grunted. The sound was skeptical, but Bianca could sense there was no longer any danger that he would strike her again.

That was good. She was having a hard enough time as it was, restraining her fury. The bastard was *heavy.*

Her hands began stroking his back. Saluzzo would think she was still trying to placate him. In actuality, she was trying to determine if her incantations had succeeded.

Yes. She could feel the small nubs of the wings, just under the shoulder blades. They'd remain vestigial, until she spoke the words of power.

Double-checking, her left hand stroked his brow. Yes, she could feel the slight nubs there also.

Unfortunately, her apparent caresses were stimulating Saluzzo again. His own hands began moving. Bianca resigned herself to another unpleasant few minutes. There was no way, in the circumstances, to do the rituals needed to allow Saluzzo to wallow in his own sexual fantasies.

So be it. Immortality had its prices. At least he wouldn't be as rough this time.

Although—

"*Ow!* Paulo, you have *got* to start trimming your fingernails."

A bit puzzled, he raised his head and glanced at his fingernails. "How did they get so long?" he wondered.

"You're careless, that's how." She took the sting from the reproach by nuzzling him. "Just keep them trimmed, will you?"

She decided it would be best not to comment on his toenails.

Those would be getting shorter soon, anyway. Shorter, wider, and much thicker, as his feet began to change. In fact, she'd have to take steps to slow down the transformation. Even a thug—and this one was Florentine, after all—would start wondering why he was walking around on hooves.

PART XII
November, 1539 A.D.

Chapter 81

"And how are you doing at fending off the pursuit of the young ladies of Corfu, young man?" asked the governor's white-haired wife as they talked in a break during the soiree that was Corfu Citadel's attempt at maintaining a facade of normalcy in spite of the siege. The attempts were pitiful, looked at from one angle; but, after being under siege for half a year, the defenders needed them.

Benito decided he liked Renate De Belmondo, even if he'd rather have been having a glass of wine down with the Arsenalotti. "Oh, I'm not trying too hard."

That was true enough. He simply wasn't interested. Other than their physical charms, the "young ladies of Corfu" lacked salt. If he'd said the moon was green, they'd have agreed with him.

It had amused Benito at first to be considered a prize. But it had come as a shock to realize that more than one of the delicately bred young damsels of Corfu's high society, never previously in a man's company without a duenna, would happily lift her skirts on the floor of her parlor for the mantle of his name, his position with the Doge and his reputation as hero. As an actual person he was unimportant. He could have been a hunchback or a pygmy able to speak in short grunts only. It was his position that made him valuable—grandson of the Old Fox, second son of Valdosta, friend to the Doge, brother to the Young Lion, confidant of Prince Manfred. Political power, a coin he held as debased to the point of worthlessness, was the true gold to them.

Then there were the real hero-worshipers. They were almost worse.

"He was complaining about the lack of spice here only yesterday, Contessa," said Manfred, grinning at Benito.

She waved her fan. "Well. If it's 'spice' you're after, I would think you'd want to consort with the ladies of our little covey of degenerates and try one of their Romanesque orgies. Except that they seem to be keeping a very low profile, these days. They used to be the glitter of these little affairs."

Benito snorted. "I think I want a girl to chew me out, not chew me up."

The contessa smiled. "The best kind, those. They probably remind you of your mother."

He shook his head. "You obviously didn't know my mother, Contessa."

Before this conversation could go into details about his mother, Benito was glad to see Von Gherens bumping through the butterfly crowd, like a steel bumblebee. "Prince Manfred," he said without bothering to excuse himself for interrupting. "Emeric's doing an inspection of his troops. It looks like he's planning something. You'd better come and have a look."

"Very well," said Manfred. "You'll excuse me, milady."

"You coming, Benito?" asked Von Gherens. "There is someone I want you to see."

So Benito went along, tagging behind Falkenberg, who had been doing an uncomfortable job of bodyguarding. He knew it was a put-up job that Manfred had organized to save himself from sitting through a second hour of a hard seat and bad music. Well, Benito didn't mind being out of there either.

"As it happens, Emeric really is out and about," said Von Gherens to Benito, "and we really do want you to look at one of his companions. We think we last saw him in Venice. We'll go down to the main gatehouse. You get the best view from there."

The late autumn air was cool and dry, and that dryness lent great clarity. The enemy trenches and earthworks across on the Spianada were so visible it was possible to see the rough mortaring between the stones. Von Gherens looked to a knight staring across from the battlements. "Are they still there, Klaus?"

The knight nodded. "Yes. They're just at that end of the rampart. They should move across soon."

They waited. And, sure enough, men moved from one earthwork to the next. It was a pity that accuracy on the cannons was so imprecise, and that the king and his generals were out of range of arquebusiers. "There."

The blond head stood out clearly against the dark background. Benito squinted. If only it were closer! He gritted his teeth. "It could be Aldanto. Damn his soul to Hell. It could be."

"Klaus here is long-sighted. He saw him in Venice, during the troubles there. He says it is him. By the walk."

"If Erik was here, I'd say we'd have to stop him going out to look," said Manfred. He glanced at Benito. "No, Benito. *No.*"

"I'm not doing anything useful here. Besides sitting with Umberto and 'Lessi."

"No, Benito. No," repeated Manfred firmly.

Benito shrugged his shoulders. "I'll see you later. I want to go and look for something in among my gear."

"So," said Emeric, glaring at the Citadel, which, after all these months, still refused to fall. "We've lost four ships. All at night. All in the north. And at last count—"

His voice was rising dangerously. "—over two hundred horses. And more than seventy men." He pointed an accusing finger at Caesare. "You said you'd catch Hakkonsen. You and that yellow dog of yours. As far as I can work out, the situation has simply gotten worse. So, my involuntary and so-far-useless ally. *Where is he?*"

Caesare looked at Emeric with empty eyes. "We have a traitor at last. We will have either him or his woman soon. And given the kind of man he is, we will have him if we take her."

Emeric looked at him with narrowed eyes. "Where did you find a traitor? The peasants are terrified of the idea. They'd rather die. We've tried."

"Word has spread that the Libri d'Oro we captured are being reestablished on their lands."

"Ah. That policy has played handsome dividends. It is always easier to corrupt the leadership than the people. And it achieves more."

If Benito had remembered he had it, in the early days after Caesare turned out to be as false a hero as possible, he would have burned it. But it had stayed tucked away somewhere in his gear at the *Casa* Dorma. He certainly wouldn't have brought it along to Corfu. But, as he'd been sitting in jail, some anonymous servant had packed it along with just about anything he owned that was reasonably presentable. So, it had come into the governor's palace in the Citadel, along with a corded bag of other clothes and bags of grain and spare weaponry and whatever else he could carry easily. He'd seen it while looking for spare stuff Maria could cut up to make winter clothes for Alessia. The fabrics that the *Casa Dorma* had clad the younger Valdosta ward in were the absolute finest. Finer than Maria could dream of buying. And, damn her pride, she wouldn't take money.

When he'd found the silk scarf, he'd decided that he wouldn't give that to Alessia. Some residual trace of Aldanto might cling to it. Maria might just recognize it, too. She noticed clothes. And if she wouldn't take money from Benito . . . she certainly would have nothing to do with Caesare, in any shape or form.

But Benito remembered how Luciano Marina had used Maria's scarf to give them some idea whether she was alive or dead. Perhaps Eneko Lopez could do the same. With the scarf in a pocket, Benito went in search of the Basque priest.

He wasn't at the Hypatian chapel. In fact, it took Benito some time to track him down. He spotted Father Francis first. He was trying to be unobtrusive, but definitely up to something. Benito didn't disturb him in whatever it was. He walked on, and ran into another of the tight-knit group; this time it was Diego. And around the third corner, Lopez.

"Father Lopez, you don't do this well," said Benito calmly, as he walked past.

Eneko Lopez was a man of deep faith and great patience. So he didn't swear at Benito. He did turn around and let his breath hiss between his teeth. He gave Benito a look that would have turned many a man's wavering footsteps back to the paths of righteousness.

"Valdosta! This is difficult—and we're trying to be unobtrusive."

Benito looked about calmly, and pretended to catch sight of something on one of the rooftops. He leaned back casually against the wall and stared at it, while speaking very quietly out of the corner of his mouth. "Well, Father Eneko, it looks like I'd better teach you how to do that. It's something bad men do well. Good men, by the looks of it, do it badly. I was taught by one of the worst. I think you all need lessons and I'd be glad to help."

Eneko Lopez sighed. "Let me get the others, Benito. We may as well go back to the chapel. You may have a point. And what we're hunting is not just bad, but evil to the core."

"I'll see you there."

Back at the Hypatian chapel Benito explained. "If you look like you belong, no one looks twice at you. If you look like you're doing something perfectly ordinary, for a reason anyone can figure out without even thinking about it, no one is interested. On the other hand, if you skulk, all in the same habits, and look at a building furtively while muttering, you stand out like a bunch of daisies in a coal scuttle. At least one of you needs to move out of these clothes. Become a seller of something. Beads perhaps."

They all looked dubious. He sighed. "Let's work this out. How long does this—whatever it is that you're doing—take you?"

Francis answered immediately. "About three hundred heart-beats, to detect sorcerers. Perhaps a little less, in the case of the female one we're after. She's powerful and skilled, but careless."

"The night-soil cart."

All four of them blinked at him in confusion. "What?" asked Eneko, after a moment. "Can you explain that rather remarkable statement?"

"It trundles along all the streets, stops, people load their buckets, and it trundles on. Easy to stop it in the right spot. It stinks, so no one stays near it longer than they have to. It's the perfect cover for anything one of you wants to do. As for the other two of you— one of you should get a shill and argue religion with him. Stop and argue at whatever point you need to stop. The shill can argue, loudly, drawing as much attention to himself as possible. You do your ritual, while you just nod and frown."

"And the third?" Eneko asked.

"Ah, the third one can stop and preach at passersby; say something a little bizarre, or preach about the end of the world coming soon. Then he can do a few moments in prayer. He'll look like any other religious lunatic, and no one ever pays any notice of them."

"It appears Aldanto taught you well," said Eneko, dryly.

"Yeah. Well, he was using us for his work, or he wouldn't have. He was like that. Look, that's what I wanted to talk to you about." He pulled the scarf out of his pocket. "Can you tell me if the owner of this is on the island?"

Eneko Lopez looked at the scarf. "It is possible. It requires the same spells we use to trace anything that was once the property of someone else. Why? Who does it belong to?"

"Caesare Aldanto." His voice was flat.

Lopez looked askance at Benito. "I thought he had drowned, young man."

"He's been reliably reported as alive. In fact, I *think* I recognized him myself, today, at a distance. He was also reported heading back to Odessa. I want to know if he's really here. If he is here, Manfred, Francesca and Eberhard will want to know for the implications that it will have on the situation."

"Odessa!"

Father Francis looked at the piece of bright cloth. "It would explain the Chernobog traces, Eneko. Perhaps he is an emissary."

"I thought he was just an opportunist and a traitor," said Eneko, slowly. "I thought we'd dealt directly with all of the demon's vessels. Why do you think he's here?"

"We think we saw him from the battlements. Hard to tell . . . but the way he walked, the posture, the head-color, and the fact that he was seen in Constantinople some months before all this blew up." Benito shrugged. "That's why I'm asking."

Eneko took up the scarf. "This could be exceptionally dangerous. We're deprived of some of our usual protections. Still . . . we know that we have come here to confront him. Let us try this thing, taking courage in faith."

Benito watched as they prepared. The scarf was placed over a chalice of holy water. The wards placed . . . Uriel too. Even if the archangel did not respond, he would still be there. Then, all of the priests placed a hand on the cloth.

Benito's Latin did not extend to much beyond "Deus," so he didn't recognize anything they were chanting.

Suddenly, the scarf burst into flames. Not ordinary flames, either; these were greenish, and altogether nasty-looking.

The only sign of alarm was in the widening of their eyes. The priests fell back a step, and began chanting something different; it *sounded* different, too, harsher, and confrontational— Benito got the impression of swords being drawn, though no weapon was in sight. The water in the chalice vaporized with a violent hiss, as the flame changed color, this time to a dark, glowing purple. At this point, a horrible scalp-crawling howl arose from the flame itself, a howl that cut right through Benito's head.

The chalice melted in part, and the burning shred abruptly gathered itself into a ball. Then it started moving; it bounced off the table and rolled rapidly out of the door.

"Stop it!" yelled Eneko.

As soon as it was outside, the flames gathered new life, and the ball doubled in size in the blink of an eye. Without thinking, simply obeying the priest, Benito did one of the most stupid things he'd done in a lifetime of doing stupid things. He stamped on it, grinding it into the earth.

The Saint Arsenius medal on his chest grew hot, briefly. Then Benito stepped back from the ash fragments. The dead ash fragments.

Eneko grabbed him with one hand, holding up a relic in the other. *"Let that which cannot abide the name of Christ depart!"* he commanded.

"It has already gone, Eneko," said Diego. He looked wonderingly at Benito. "You are both a very crazy and a very lucky young man. You just *stood* on a demonic emissary of Chernobog."

"It must have been weakened and limited by the holy place, by the holy water and the blessed vessel," said Francis in a shaky voice.

Benito examined the soles of his footwear and shrugged. "Well, my holy medal got hot, but I can't say it even scorched my boots."

Eneko held out a hand. "Let's see this medal," he said grimly.

Benito took it out from next to his skin. Eneko examined it as did the others.

"It is an old one . . . and undoubtedly genuine," said Eneko, thoughtfully. "How did you get a real Saint's relic, Benito?"

He raised his eyebrows. "It was given to me by the Hypatian monks in Messina, after I did them that little favor."

"I don't think they realized what a valuable gift they gave you," said Diego, "or what a powerful one."

"Or how well it would serve the church," said Eneko, exhaling a little sigh of relief. "Forgive me, Benito. 'Stop it' was meant for my comrades, not for you."

Benito shrugged. *He* was quite certain that the Hypatians of Messina knew exactly what they had given him; after all, it was meant to reward someone—even a thief—for returning some rather valuable property. And just perhaps, because you never knew with the Hypatian magicians, they might have gotten an inkling that he would be going into spiritual and magical danger. "It worked. And I'm the one who got you to try this in the first place."

"Well, you have your answer. Caesare Aldanto is here, indeed. And he is possessed by the Black Brain, Chernobog."

The priest sighed. "This calls for more than we four can do. This calls for the Knights of the Holy Trinity. Perhaps true steel and faith can destroy this thing as magic cannot."

Benito took a sideways glance at the man. He appeared in earnest. There were times when Benito wondered whether the intense Basque cleric was in the real world or not. "There is a siege out there, Eneko. A whole army between Aldanto and the Knights."

"If he is destroyed, Chernobog will be one factor removed from the siege." Lopez sounded earnest—but also resigned. After all, how was even a single Knight going to slip out unnoticed?

Benito shook his head. "I wouldn't mind doing it, Eneko. But it is a question of how."

"If it means going outside the wall, then it must be done," said Lopez.

"Fine. You tell Manfred to let me go. He's already forbidden me to try. I haven't said I am going to listen, though." He paused. "You know, there *is* one Knight out there already. Erik Hakkonsen. And if *he* knew Aldanto was alive, and worse, a minion of Chernobog—"

He let that percolate into Lopez's mind. "Still, you have to talk Manfred into letting me go over the wall or I can't tell him."

Eneko sighed. "I will. If in that brief encounter I divined it right, then he is seeking something in countryside. Erik could perhaps deal with him. Ideally, I should like to be there. While this is a perilous foe—like all slaves, it would lack most of the strength of Chernobog. It would still be very dangerous. Certain relics could limit it. That medal of yours, for instance."

Benito looked down. "And to think I nearly didn't tie it to my belt when I was disguising myself as a slave."

"It is a sailor's talisman. It might just be what kept you afloat," said Francis.

Mindaug noticed that the Grand Duke was distinctly short of breath. And that his jowls beneath the mask were almost gray. He hardly seemed to hear the news that the Venetian Atlantic fleet had been forced to retreat from the pillars of Hercules.

He wondered what had just happened, but knew that he would never learn. Jagiellon would never, ever tell a subordinate about anything that had given him so much as a moment of weakness.

Manfred rubbed his chin. "Getting out there . . . Well, Eneko. You have a spy—no, two, you say—with some ability at black magic to catch. Who is more important? And can your companions do it without you?"

Eneko Lopez pursed his lips and thought a while.

"Chernobog is a great threat. On the other hand . . . the cunning of these magicians, whoever they are—is almost worse. I suppose this fight is against Emeric and his minions first. And we need four for the cardinal points. But . . ."

"But me no buts, man of God," said Manfred, firmly. "I'll have Klaus on watch. If we get a chance again like today where we can maybe get Emeric and Aldanto . . . we'll sally. Speed and steel. We can get away with it at the moment. The captain-general isn't playing the role he was since his wife got herself into trouble."

Being a fugitive hampered Fianelli's movements, thought Emeric, studying again the latest reports his agent had sent through. But the man was capable and had found a safe hideout. So. It was time to destabilize the military structure of the enemy from within. Fianelli had mercenaries still on his payroll.

The commander must die. And so should this Benito Valdosta. He'd become an icon in the Citadel. A symbol. Well, he'd be a dead symbol, proving how long Emeric's arm was.

Chapter 82

Only a flicker of movement in the window saved Benito. He rolled just in time. The crossbow bolt was buried to the flight-feathers in the bed. Benito stared at the bolt. Felt his neck; looked at the broken glass; got up and went over to the mirror. His neck had a fine cut from the touch of the barb.

A crossbow was slow to reload. By the time the bastard in that tree reloaded, Benito was going to be shoving his rapier right up the place the would-be assassin deserved it.

But by the time he got there . . .

There was no one in the tree. No one anywhere around. In fact, there might just as well never have been anyone there at all. Except for that crossbow bolt in the pillow.

Ten minutes later, Benito, crossbow bolt in hand, was in Manfred and Francesca's chamber.

"Manfred. I worked with him for years. This," he held up the bolt, "stinks of something Caesare would organize, if he didn't do it himself. He can't fly, so this must be something a hireling did. But I'll bet it was at his orders. He and his master know we found them. Now they're out to kill me, personally. Well, I won't sit still while they do it. And I don't care what you say about it."

"You could be right," said Francesca. "Indirectly, at least. It would have been Fianelli who gave the actual order, though, not Caesare. He's still somewhere in the Citadel, and his three goons have evaded capture also."

She turned to Manfred. "My dear, you are going back to living

660

in a Koboldwerk shirt, now that they seem to be turning to crude assassination. You're a target, too."

Manfred rubbed his jaw thoughtfully. "Look, Benito, I understand what you're getting at. But . . ."

"But this fortress is flue-full of conspirators, spies, and traitors. I don't know who, or what, to trust—sweet Jesu, man, what can I do if I can't even be safe in my own bed?"

Manfred winced. Benito kept going while he had momentum. "Aside from anything else, out there, they seem to have sorted out the treachery problem. I'm safer running with Erik than I am here. Besides, if we get the chance I want Aldanto's head." He knew what his voice sounded like, and he moderated it before Manfred decreed he was too emotionally involved to go safely. "Look, it might not be Aldanto, but all the signs point that way, and I agree with Eneko. Get rid of this assassin, this agent of Chernobog—whoever, or whatever he is—-and we'll get rid of half the menace."

"*Will* you let me finish?" asked Manfred irritably. "What I was trying to say is the story of your exploits getting in and out of this place is now common property. You can bet your last penny that Emeric has had a full report. You can bet you're being watched. You can also bet that Emeric has done his damnedest to make sure you don't use those ways again. We've seen the beach patrols. The small-craft screen. It's a lot harder. The chance of you making it into the slave encampment, never mind out again, has vanished."

Benito shrugged. "I'll have to think of something else then."

"What I was going to suggest is that we do this the old-fashioned way. Von Gherens and I were just saying we are letting the enemy have too much leisure to do what they feel like. Those causeways are basically both repaired. We're going to lose what advantage the water gives us when they are able to attack in large numbers at will. We thought we might use one of these misty mornings we've been having to damage their little causeway, and make Emeric concentrate on defending his siege camp more. From this side, as well as Erik's side."

Manfred grinned. "So what do you say, young fellow? Get you on a good horse and have a little gallop. I won't promise to take you to the other edge of Emeric's camp, but in the chaos, mist, and few nice little fires . . . We'll dress you up as a Croat horseman and you should get yourself to the far side and out easily enough. It'll beat this swimming or sailing, eh?"

Benito groaned.

"It sounded like a good plan to me," said Manfred, a little defensively. "Given the mist and the fact that there hasn't been a sally except in response to an attack, they won't be expecting it. Von Gherens was just saying their entrenchments on the Spianada are too central. Emeric wanted the space to marshal his cavalry, no doubt, but it'll work in our favor."

"It's the horse part I was groaning about. I fall off the damn things."

Manfred chuckled. "There had to be something you weren't much good at."

"I can't dance. And Marco says I can't cook, either."

Francesca gave a little snort of laughter. "But a little bird told me you can change diapers," she said mischievously.

Manfred stared incredulously at Benito and then burst into laughter.

Maria listened to Benito in silence. Her expression grew more severe as he talked.

Then she stood in silence, looking at him for a while. Finally she said: "I don't suppose anything I say will stop you."

"No. I just stopped by to say good-bye, and to see Alessia and Umberto. I had to stop and see my favorite baby."

Maria shook her head. "Have you ever even touched another one?" She sighed. "Wait here. I want you to take something with you."

She came back a few minutes later with a wheel-lock pistol. "Kat gave it to me. You take it with you. And promise me this. If you get close to Caesare, blow his guts out before he gets too close. Remember, he'll mislead you with his talk. Don't give him a chance. And don't miss."

Clinging to the saddle, Benito cursed all horses. There had to be a better way to travel fast overland. Had to be!

Chariots. Or cutting canals everywhere. Or . . . *anything.* Trained giant serpents such as there were reputed to be in far-off Africa. Or dragons, as in far-off Qin. Or flying carpets. *Anything* but an idiot animal that went up and down in order to go forward.

True, the gallop hadn't been as bad as he'd expected. True, too, a grinning *Ritter* had had to haul him back upright when he'd started that slide down the side of the horse during the charge. But—like the raid on the Hungarian camp—it had been pretty successful.

The Hungarians were totally unprepared for those inside the Citadel to take the offensive. The men had settled into the hum-drum of siege. Cannon fire every now and again. Daytime arquebus fire to slow down any signs of repair work on the walls. Otherwise sit around. Sleep if you could. Play dice. Eat. Keep a weather eye behind for an officer. The assault would come, when they had to go in and face enemy fire, but for now . . . the worst you had to fear was a work party or being part of the outer perimeter guards and patrols. That was dangerous. This was just military routine.

Sleep while you could. Even in the front trenches, a good two thirds had been in dreamland. The night workers on the cause-way were already pulled back. The sea-mist was blowing and swirling. It would burn off in an hour or two, having given the cracked, dry earth no relief.

The mist swallowed sound quite well. The Knights' scouts had advanced cautiously, on foot, with their trumpets in hand. Seventy or so yards back, the Knights, a hundred of them, had come forward at a walk. They'd been able to get right onto the causeway—and the scouts off the far side—before the trumpet had called them to charge.

Yes, it had all gone well. Benito hoped the retreat had gone just as well. He hadn't stayed around to find out.

Instead he'd discovered the two drawbacks to Manfred's plan. The one was that he was still very close to the Hungarian camp and it was now full daylight and the horse was a lot more in control than he was. The other drawback was trotting. Now all he had to do was find Erik without the two downsides killing him.

He decided the best thing for it was to abandon the horse. He must be at least a couple of miles from the camp now.

A shot boomed from a nearby hillside.

Benito abandoned the horse by falling off into the dry broom. Up the hill he saw two Corfiotes scrambling for cover. Lying there, trying to catch his breath, Benito decided that the Croat's head-gear had to be the next to go, before he was killed by own side.

Falkenberg came running in. "Leopoldo's been shot! A cross-bow again."

Manfred's chair fell over as he sprang to his feet. "Damn! We should have expected this." He started heading for the door.

Von Gherens blocked his way. "Not without plate armor. And that Koboldwerk mail shirt. And Francesca, he's to stay away from all windows until we find this crossbow man. Leopoldo may live. Benito was lucky. Next time we may not be so lucky."

Francesca nodded and steered the prince back to a chair. "It's left a power vacuum, Manfred. The captain-general hasn't been near his office for two weeks. He's just abandoned things. Commander Leopoldo has been running the defense of the Citadel since then."

"And much better run it has been," Manfred said grimly. "You say he's not dead?"

"Well, not yet. He's being taken to the hospital."

"Is he conscious?"

"He was a short time ago. Cursing ferociously, in fact."

"Go there, Von Gherens. Get him to appoint a successor, if he's *compos* to do so. One of his junior officers will fill the post on seniority otherwise. And that may be a poor idea right now."

Von Gherens came back a little later. "The opium seems to be making him think clearly," he said with a wry smile. "He's just nominated Falkenberg to fill his shoes."

"But Falkenberg isn't part of the Venetian forces," protested Francesca. "The captain-general is bound to kick up a fuss."

Eberhard of Brunswick cleared his throat. "You could second him to the service of Commander Leopoldo, Prince. That would be completely legal."

The one-eyed Falkenberg grunted. "If this means I have to take orders from Tomaselli, forget it."

Eberhard smiled. "Well, technically you'd be taking orders from Leopoldo, as you would have to be seconded directly to his service. And Leopoldo would be taking orders from Tomaselli. We could persuade him to be too ill to pass them on. Of course this does presuppose Leopoldo staying alive. If he dies, it is another matter."

"You really could have trusted me with the sword, Benito," said Erik. "I would have given it back to you. I think."

Benito blinked. Svanhild was definitely giving Erik a sense of humor. Which was strange, as Benito didn't think she had had much of one to share. Perhaps it was just that the Icelander was so much happier.

"I needed it, Erik. Otherwise I'd have trusted you. Truly. But there is someone I have to deliver the sharp end of it to."

"And who would that be?"

"A mutual friend who had a crossbow bolt delivered to my pillow a couple of days back. A blond fellow with excellent classical features that the girls all admired. At least, they used to. I'm not sure what he looks like after all he's been through."

Erik's head shot forward like a snapping turtle. "Aldanto! He's here?"

Benito nodded. "And he hasn't changed except for the worse, either. He's joined up with another old friend that you've met before. With your old tomahawk."

The look in Erik's eyes was something that gave Benito a shiver. "I want him."

But Benito was not about to back down this time. "You'll have to stand in line, Erik. I've got a claim on behalf of my mother, my brother's wife's family, and Maria. Not to mention myself. And this time I intend to get him. If I fail, he's yours."

Erik looked speculatively at Benito. "He doesn't play by the rules, you know."

"I know.

"So should we play tag with him?" asked Erik, with a foxlike look. "I'll find out where he is. Our network of informers is unbelievable, especially since your jailbreak." He grinned at Benito. "Your status on this island is at a level that'll never survive the reality!"

Chapter 83

The middle-aged man looked about nervously. "You're sure we can't be seen or overheard?"

Caesare Aldanto shook his head. "The dog would have detected anyone, Ambrosino. He can smell out the smallest trace of life over as much as two hundred yards. And we simply cannot be seen through the solid walls of the olive-press. You are satisfied with what you have heard from Count Quatrades?"

Giuliano Lozza's uncle nodded. "Yes. I was surprised, to tell the truth."

The empty-eyed blond shrugged. "Why? King Emeric wants an income off the lands he conquers. He'll need vassals who understand local conditions, local peasantry, and how to get the most out of them."

Ambrosino's eyes were wary. "I would have thought he would have given the land to his own nobles, Signor Aldanto."

"There is enough. And as you have seen, Count Quatrades is well treated." If Aldanto sounded indifferent, it was for a good reason. He was.

"And protected?" Ambrosino asked sharply. "The peasantry have become violent. If there is one thing these peasants should never have been allowed, it is encouragement to rebel. To take up arms. The Venetians have planted and nurtured a seed in this war that will be impossible to put back into the seed-pod. I've said as much but they don't want to listen to me."

The Magyar captain who had accompanied Aldanto laughed coarsely. "King Emeric has a way of dealing with that. There are always more peasants."

"Nonetheless. I want that estate in the Ropa valley, but I also want a full-time guard of least twenty men stationed there. And five thousand ducats." He raised his chin; clearly, he was not going to be bargained down.

Aldanto nodded. "We have brought the gold. The bags are behind you, on that press-shelf."

Greed overrode the man's nervousness. He looked into a number of the bags eagerly, spilling gold pieces.

"We have had engineers from the army repairing the villa on the estate," said Aldanto, smoothly. "You could go there now, if you can tell us where to find Hakkonsen. Or the girl."

Ambrosino snorted with contempt. "You'd need a lot of men to take Hakkonsen in that spot. It's got three ways out, and he has good lookouts. Hakkonsen is planning a raid on Trembolino in two nights. You could ambush him."

"And why is he going to attack Trembolino?" asked the Magyar captain suspiciously. "That's where we are based!"

"I believe," said the middle-aged man slyly, "that they wish to kill a certain blond man. A man they call Caesare Aldanto."

The empty eyes gazed at the Corfiote aristocrat. "Why?"

"It appears that they want to repay some old scores with you, milord," he said, picking up every loose ducat and carefully putting them back where he had gotten them.

"That is an aspect I had not considered," said Aldanto. "Are you privy to the detail of Hakkonsen's plans?"

The man closed up the bags. "No. I'm not part of this raid. My nephew Giuliano is. I could have asked him, but I thought it best not to excite comment. We've had a bit of a falling out. Milord, if you could try and spare him? He and I have argued about the way things are being done, but he is still my sister's son."

"Of course. Families do have their differences, but blood is still thicker than water." Aldanto spoke with the ease of one who does not care what he promises. "Would you be able to guide, say, five of my men in, while the bulk of Hakkonsen's troops are trying to find me? We could be waiting for them when they return, with all the advantage of surprise."

The man coughed politely. "Five men? You would need fifty, milord."

"The five will do to open the path. We will have a hundred men out of our camp without it appearing too deserted, Signor

Ambrosino; a hundred men, in blackened cuirasses. What's left will give them a fight, while we do our business."

Svanhild clung to him. "Couldn't someone else go, Erik? I worry so about you, my precious man."

Erik hugged her. "I worry about you, *elskling*. But I am going with that young rascal. He has the luck of the devil, so it should be fine."

She kissed him, but frowned, just a little. "I do not approve of Benito. He is not enough respectable for you, ja. And altogether too wild."

Erik patted her soothingly. "Never mind, love. When all this is over, my time of service to the Godar Hohenstauffen will be near an end, and we can go home and never see him again. He reminds me of Manfred a few years back, in many ways. And you don't disapprove of him, do you?"

"Oh, no. But he is a prince," she said, kissing him. The kiss turned into a longer kiss.

Outside the cave—which the Vinlanders had made unrecognizably comfortable, and Erik still felt terribly guilty about having to have Svan live in—someone cleared his throat. "Time to go, sir."

Erik recognized the apologetic voice. Lozza.

He had to smile to himself. Giuliano Lozza. Fat and unfit. Undisciplined and obsessed with revenge.

Then. He was now lean, athletic and tough as whip-leather. Also now Erik's chief arms instructor. What a difference six months could make.

The curious thing was that Lozza hated to kill. He was, Erik admitted, better with a rapier than Erik would ever be. His father, possibly the greatest master of Bravura style, had started training him when he barely breeched. Giuliano used the weapon like other men used their fingers. He had the reflexes, and he had the strength. He just didn't like to kill. Erik was terribly afraid that such a weakness would kill him one day.

It was why he always paired Giuliano with Thalia. For one thing, Giuliano *would* kill anyone who came near her. He was as protective as a mother hen about the peasant girl. And Thalia, with her new net—carefully blessed—and the knife-skills Giuliano instilled into her, did not hesitate. Ever.

A strange relationship. Erik had never seen either so much as touch each other. She still called him "Master Lozza."

He kissed Svan for a last time and parted from her.

"Take care," she called after him.

"Do my best."

They rode through the darkness; Benito, as usual, clinging to his horse and swearing. Horses, even the most docile-natured, like the one they'd mounted him on, seemed to know Benito was not a rider and that he was afraid of horses. They sensed his nervousness and that made them skittish . . . which made Benito worse.

"Doesn't it seem odd, Benito, that Caesare Aldanto is out here, instead of with the main army?"

"Damn this animal," said Benito, in his mildest comment so far. "He's probably out here up to no good, Erik. Someone to be murdered, or spied on, or stolen from."

"And who do you think that could be, my young friend?" asked Erik, dryly.

"You or me at a guess. Probably you. Of course, he probably doesn't know who he's hunting."

Erik cantered a few more yards in silence. "I'll grant him this. He was very good with a sword. And he's not afraid to use it."

"Good with a sword he was indeed," Benito acknowledged grimly. "And if I get a chance, Erik, I won't give him an opportunity to use it. He's a master of dirty fighting. And one of the things he taught me was to never try to be fair in a fight. Kill your opponent before he kills you."

He ground his teeth, angrily. "I intend to return the favor of that lesson."

Caesare Aldanto might have been far more successful at seizing control of the canals of Venice had he been able, then, to select men as he did now. But he had perceptions of their natures and ability now that he didn't have then. The men he'd brought along for this expedition were killers. The most effective he could cull from an army. He'd principally stuck with cavalry since moving fast would be of the essence.

The other four accompanying Ambrosino into the defile should all have been hanged long ago. In a proper army, with the discipline to take half-mad killers out of their ranks and dispose of them, they would have been. These four would not only cheerfully perform atrocities on the defeated and the peasantry of the defeated, they'd perform them on their own comrades if they got the chance.

They reached the first sentries. Ambrosino called the password.

"Who's that with you?" asked the sentry.

"New recruits. Good men all."

"We can use . . . ahh!"

And they moved on. The yellow dog pressed against his flank. They talked as minions of the same master did: without audible words. The shaman sniffed. *The net-woman, she has been here, curse her name.*

I'll deal with her. Or the troops will.

Erik looked at the fires, at the sentries, not quite lazy enough in the darkness, and peered through the gloom at the horse paddocks. Something prickled his awareness. He looked at the horse-paddocks again. It was like ice water running down his spine.

"There's something wrong here. That's half the number of horses reported."

Benito looked. "Caesare!" he took Erik by the sleeve. "Mount up now. Let's get out of here. This smells of Aldanto and ambush."

Erik nodded. "Tomorrow is another day. We've got him tagged now. The country-people will tell us where he goes. We'll choose the time, not him."

"Svan will be pleased to have us home, unbloody."

Somewhere in the distance a horn sounded. It didn't mean anything to them and it was a good distance away.

"The Vinlanders are in the cave to the south there." Ambrosino pointed. "The others use the caves lower down. The very bottom cave is water-filled. It's their water supply and something to be very careful of. The valley over there is where the horses are kept. It's another way out. They can also go over the back there, but only on foot."

"Guards on both?"

"Of course. Hakkonsen leaves nothing to chance."

"Except you." Aldanto turned. "Sylarovich. Bring the cavalry up to that point. Tell them that any man that even so much as allows a harness to clink is dead. You saw the exits. Split three units of twenty off the troop. When I sound the horn, they must ride as fast as possible for each exit. Kill any guards and seal them off from escapees. The other forty are to take the caves, especially the top one. And tell them about the lower cave. We should have at least an hour to clean this lot out before the rest come back from the camp, very pleased with themselves. We should surprise them nicely."

Full dark, and Erik's nerves were on edge. They rode into the narrow gully that Erik had designated sole entry to the camp. Erik, at the head of the file paused . . . waiting for the request for the password.

Silence. And then distantly, a scream. Arquebus and pistol shots.

"*Ride!*" yelled Erik. "Ride! All of you get out of here!" But he himself was spurring his horse frantically, riding into the defile. Kari and his brother took off after him as if their tails were on fire.

Benito turned to the rest. "You heard him. You—Alexander. Take some of the boys to the top way out. And *Gino*. The other half of you to the valley way."

Alexander hesitated, and his horse curveted and danced sideways. "We need to follow our captain."

Benito aimed a blow at him. "You need to obey his orders! Now *move!*"

"Alpha group will go with me," Giuliano said calmly. "Omega takes the bottom way, and Theta, you will ride around to see if survivors need help. If there is nobody there, dismount and set up an ambush. Lower the horse-barriers. They will not ride out of here." These were the groups used in raids. They were each twenty strong. They were used to working together and each had its section leaders.

Perhaps it was that, or Giuliano's calm that did it. The troop split fast. As soon as they were on their way Benito began kicking the horse, to get it to follow Erik and not the other horses. His will triumphed, to his surprise. Maybe the animal thought it was going to pasture down in the valley bottom. The stream had stopped flowing; but, thanks to the water-cave, they had water there and some grazing. Donkey loads of stolen Hungarian oats had added to that.

"Thalia, Georgio, Stephanos, Gigi, Marco. You will take the inner guard post. Stop any of them escaping and buy time for us if we need it to get out," said Giuliano Lozza, taking charge.

"Mikalos will go instead of me," said Thalia. "That calls for shooting. I can't shoot."

"Don't argue."

"Or what, master?" she said calmly.

"Please, Thalia." Giuliano wasn't quite begging.

"No."

Chapter 84

Svanhild had gone down to the horses, restless with a bright moon overhead. They were upset about something. She loved horses, and especially the steeds of the Magyar, which were superb. She'd talked with Erik about taking some home to the great plains beyond Cahokia. Apparently the Magyar steeds were bought from the Ilkhan and crossed with an old war-horse breed. She'd certainly never seen their like.

She walked among them in the moonlight, murmuring a bit of praise here, patting a neck or a flank there. Then she heard the thunder of galloping hooves. Erik must be back. So early? Something must have gone wrong. She gathered her skirts in order to run back toward the cave.

A group of cavalry thundered past her, heading for horse-paddocks she'd just come from. She ran for the cave and her brothers. She could see Bjarni, already out, sword in hand, running toward her, yelling and beckoning.

The main body of Caesare's cavalry had waited until the two blocking groups were past. Caesare mounted his horse. The yellow dog had gone ahead, scrambling up a steep limestone edge, claws scrabbling for a hold on the rock. It would attempt to deal with the guard on the upper footpath.

The shaman basically had to get out of the way. Horses tried to trample the shaman if they smelled or saw him. The iron horseshoes were painful. Lead bullets the creature found harmless, but cold iron he liked not at all.

Now Caesare pushed forward and saw in the moonlight how things hadn't waited to begin going wrong. Those idiots going down to valley floor had broken open the horse-corrals. And ridden straight past his target! Horses, panicky and confused, were running back toward the camp.

He could see her, blond hair streaming, running in the moonlight. She'd never get to the men pouring out of the cave. As they began to charge into the little valley, Caesare saw her turn and look back.

And stop. Even amid all the other noise he heard the whistle she gave. The twist of horses that the rush of cavalry had released . . . stopped too. And, as a group, they began galloping toward her. They had less than half the distance to cover that Caesare did. And they had no riders to weigh them down.

Caesare knew that this one would have no trouble riding bareback. She'd get away!

He called for the shaman. The shaman was closer! Sliding and scrabbling, half falling, the yellow dog came down the slope from nearly straight above her. He would end virtually at her feet.

As, in dust and flurry and snapping teeth, the yellow dog cascaded toward her . . . Caesare saw that the horse herd was nearly at the woman. And then he realized what he'd done.

"GO! Leave her! Stay away!"

But the steepness of the slope meant that for all the pale creature's snarling and scrabbling the shaman-dog still ended up actually hitting Svanhild. It half knocked her over. The lead stallion reared.

Chernobog, looking through his slave's eyes, didn't understand horror in human terms. But he felt the slave's horror nonetheless, when he saw the blond woman and the yellow dog fall beneath the flailing hooves. The horror of failure. The horror of knowing what his master would do to him, when the woman died. Which, with iron-shod hooves pounding her as they tried to reach the yellow cur, was an inevitability.

The yellow dog, yowling with pain, exploded out of the side of the horse-mass. Straight toward Caesare.

The Magyar cavalry's horses felt just the same way about the yellow dog as the Corfiote guerillas' horses. Horses and humans had been together a long, long time. There was a deep bond between them. Only the true dogs hate the betrayer more. More than half of the main body of the cavalry charge, including Caesare, were unseated as the Hungarian horses tried to kill the yellow dog.

Erik arrived at a scene of pandemonium. It was apparent that Caesare's raid had run into more resistance than he'd expected. Part of the problem was horses. There were riderless horses, at least forty, milling in the narrow valley.

Standing in the middle of the slope were three Vinlanders. They were defending something against a considerable force. Defending it well, by the rampart of bodies. As Erik galloped toward them one Vinlander fell. Screaming like a banshee, Erik struck the flank of the attackers. He was vaguely aware of Kari and his brother beside him.

There were a good fifteen or so Magyars attacking the remaining Vinlanders, but the sudden furious attack drove them off, just as the second to the last Vinlander collapsed. Only big Bjarni remained standing. And it was plain that it was only sheer force of will that kept him up. "Erik," he croaked, his breath bubbling. "Svan. Take her home . . ."

Erik was already kneeling beside the crumpled form on the ground, his heart swelling until he thought it would choke him. He took her up, tears pouring down his face as he felt her bones grating against one another, felt the pulpy flesh moving in ways it never should. Gently, he called her, holding her. "Svan! Svan!"

She stirred in his arms. The horse hooves had left her body bruised and broken, the skull half-shattered. Her long blond hair was soaked with blood, looking black in the moonlight. "Erik." It was barely a whisper. "You came. Love you. Stay with me . . ."

He could not see for tears. "I'll never leave you, Svan. Never."

When Benito and the others burst on the scene, Kari and his brother were desperately defending Erik, who was holding some- one. Svanhild, Benito guessed, seeing the long hair in the moon- light. Erik seemed oblivious of his own impending death. Then, just as the impetuous Kari fell, Erik put his burden down. Stood up, picking up a sword from the ground as he did so. Even from here, Benito heard his scream. It was both heartbreak and pure rage.

And with Bjarni's great sword in his hands—a weapon so long

it had had to be slung across the Vinlander's back—Erik went berserk.

Benito had heard of berserkers before. Now he realized that the magnitude of the truth defied the stories. In berserker rage Erik literally split a horse's head. Hewed two more attackers apart.

From downslope Benito heard Caesare yell: "We want him alive!"

Stupider things have been said, but not often. Benito didn't care. He was too busy fighting his way down the hill toward Caesare.

The thing that was Aldanto's puppet master saw through the puppet's eyes how one man could turn a battle. And that, far from being trappers, his troops were now surrounded, by men who knew the terrain. By men who were determined on vengeance, too. And in the middle of his Hungarians was a man seemingly possessed of superhuman strength, unstoppable, who was cutting down seasoned warriors like a scythe through cornstalks. Somehow this man had turned the situation from one where they outnumbered their surprised foes . . . into a developing rout.

He heard someone yell: "Just keep out of his way! He can't tell friend from foe."

The only trouble with this advice was that the newly arriving Corfiote irregulars were herding men toward their berserker. And fear—and the stupidity that it brings—was killing them fast.

It was time to intervene. The slave still had considerable skills, one of them being with the sword. And if need be, Chernobog could draw on reserves of strength that might kill the slave. Later.

Then there was someone in his way, between him and his target. Someone who had once been a nobleman, by the ragged finery, and the dark wavy hair, not showing the rough crop of the peasantry. He was clean shaven too, which in itself was unusual, among these spiky rebels.

The slave had many "duel" assassinations to his credit. This fool would be one more. Chernobog allowed the reflexes of the slave to take over.

And came within an eighth of an inch of losing the slave's life. An accident, surely? The slave's one real attribute had been that he was a truly great swordsman. Chernobog, seconds later, realized that it was no accident. The swordsman had looked like he'd be another provincial aristocrat—full of delusions about his swordsmanship, and short on real skill or practice. A quick kill. A soft man, despite being lean and sun-browned. Chernobog could see it in the eyes. Doe's eyes. He could see it in the face. The fine lines there were those of someone more accustomed to a lazy smile than to anger. The slave Caesare was a lion to such men.

Except . . . this time the prey was a lot better with a rapier than Caesare Aldanto ever had been, or could have been. The swordsman's movements seemed almost effortless, fluid. Yet the blade moved faster than Chernobog's slave physically could. Caesare was driven back, forced back down the hill toward the opening of the lowest cave, the water-cave, fencing with one who could kill him in a heartbeat.

It also took the Black Brain very few of the slave's heartbeats to realize something else: The master-swordsman didn't *want* to kill.

So he lowered the sword point. Took the blade itself in his left hand and held the hilt out to the man. "I surrender!" he called out.

As the master-swordsman stepped forward to take the sword, Caesare stabbed him with the stiletto shaken from his sleeve. It struck something hard and skittered, cutting—but not, as intended, piercing the heart.

As he did this Ambrosino, the traitor, shouted and rushed to him, and grabbed at him. "You promised you wouldn't kill him!"

Caesare hit the traitor with the butt, and pulled back the stiletto to stab again.

Something hit him so hard he sprawled yards away, the stiletto gone. He'd been hit by the lead weights of the bird-net that the yellow dog had so dreaded. The woman threw herself over the fallen swordsman, protecting him with her body. Caesare staggered to his feet, snatching up the rapier he had pretended to surrender, from where it had fallen conveniently near at hand. She was now trying to pick the swordsman up.

So be it. Two for the price of one.

Then, a voice like doom behind him.

"*Aldanto.*"

Caesare turned, slowly, and realized it was Erik Hakkonsen. Hakkonsen was at that final stage of berserk, when sanity returns— just before the berserker collapses.

Hakkonsen was bleeding from a dozen wounds and swaying with exhaustion. He was also intent on killing Caesare, even if it meant dying himself.

Hakkonsen, had he been in the peak of physical shape, would have been very evenly matched to the old Aldanto. Now his muscles were quivering with fatigue. And yet a will, a spirit harder than adamantine made Erik Hakkonsen drive Caesare back, back toward the water-cave.

One quick double twist-disengage, riposte, twist . . . and Erik's sword fell, clattered to the rocks.

"Die!" Caesare lunged forward. Somehow Erik managed to move so that the sword passed between his arm and ribs. He trapped the blade, holding Caesare's sleeve. The tomahawk came up.

The part of Caesare that was elsewhere used powers that could only be released in fleshy contact. A coup de grace of spirit world . . . only hampered by this place. Magical force, huge amounts of it flowed through from Chernobog, to the slave, and then into the Icelander. Coruscating rivers of power that should have burned and shattered the victim. Should have, but did not. Instead it seemed to flow through him and into the earth of Corfu. Nonetheless, Hakkonsen fell back as if flung by some great force. He lay sprawled on the ground like a puppet with severed strings. The dry grass he lay on smoked.

"There's still me, Caesare."

The tiny part of Caesare that remained Caesare saw Benito Valdosta. An older, broader but not taller person, yet a very different boy from the one who had once idolized him. Benito had plainly hurt his one arm, as it was tucked inside his shirt.

"See this sword, Caesare Aldanto? It's my father's. Carlo Sforza. The Wolf of the North. He'd eat five of you for breakfast. I'm going to cut your head off with it."

The boy-man stalked closer. "You think you're a great swordsman, Aldanto."

"What's wrong with your arm, Benito?"

"Cut the tendons back there. The fingers aren't working. But that's all right, because I only need one hand to fence with you. If I hadn't cut it, I'd tie it behind my back."

Sheer bravado, Caesare was sure. Benito had always been prone to that mistake. He had the mental edge on the boy.

The boy was close now. Barely three yards off and walking in. *Fool.*

Benito stopped, just about within reach of a lunge. "I thought I told you not to brag when you fought unless you had a reason," said Caesare.

"You did." Benito smiled mockingly. "But I didn't always listen. You also said this business of saluting your enemy before you fence with them was an opportunity to kill someone, while they're sticking to fencing etiquette. But I've got a salute to give you from Maria."

Benito raised his sword.

As Caesare began to lunge . . . something slammed into his chest with the force of a mule kick, driving him down. His rapier went flying.

Dazed, Caesare looked up to see Benito drawing a wheel-lock pistol from the shirt where he'd hidden it—holding it in his supposedly maimed hand. The boy had fired right through the fabric. Some part of Caesare felt an odd little pleasure, then, realizing how much he'd taught the boy in happier days.

"It's Maria's," grunted Benito, holding the pistol up. Smoke was still drifting from the barrel. "It seemed a nice touch to me, you swine."

The cave was just behind the puppet, Chernobog realized. The puppet's vision began to blur. It was dying. But if he could lure the boy close enough . . .

Benito stepped in, hefting the sword.

Chernobog's power built—

And fled, hastily, from the mind and soul of the slave. The sword itself was blessed! And there was something about the boy himself—some strange *virtue* that would not allow the magic to even touch him.

Benito wished he could just turn away. But Caesare had always taught him: *Finish it. Be sure.*

And then the dying man spoke. The voice sounded . . . ecstatically joyful.

"Benito. Thank God! Kill me. Kill me, please. Kill me before it can get to me again. Please. Please! If you ever loved me—"

Suddenly something huge, black and slimy with a barbel-fringed long-fanged mouth launched out of the water. Benito barely managed to dodge aside, cutting at it.

Caesare didn't dodge and it seized him. The water closed over the monster and the blond assassin.

There might be a battle going on, but Benito sat down. There wasn't much of a battle left anyway. Caesare had been lying with his "I surrender," but the Hungarians had been similarly fooled. Unfortunately for them, it had been a case of "No quarter," after Caesare's treacherous about-turn.

Chapter 85

Some time later—probably somewhere near midnight, Benito guessed by the height of the moon—they were taking stock. Erik lay wrapped in a blanket beside Svanhild. His wounds were bandaged and the stump of one finger cauterized. He lay as still as death, his breathing weak, bloody and bubbling, his pulse, which could only really be felt in his throat, tremulous and faint. The physical wounds, even the one to the lung, he might survive. The greatest physical danger was that he had nearly bled himself white. But everyone knew it was that final magical blow that left him in the coma from which Benito doubted he would ever wake.

He looked dead. Svanhild was. It had seemed right to put them beside each other.

The cost to the insurgent camp had been high. All but one of the guards had been killed. Of the fifteen men and three women left in the camp—besides the Vinlanders—one survived. Of the Vinlanders—only Bjarni and Kari and two of the *duniwassals* might yet live. The youngest of Kari's brothers had been one of those who'd been in camp as part of Svanhild's guard.

There were some dead and some injured among the raiding party too, but by comparison they'd suffered lightly. Erik's berserker attack had cost the Hungarians dear in sheer numbers and in panic—trapping them between a human threshing machine and guarded exits. The Vinlanders had cost the enemy at least thirty men.

It would take daylight and a collection of body parts to say just how many Erik had killed in his frenzy.

Of the hundred Magyar who'd galloped into this place, not one had escaped. Some thirteen were wounded. Some would die. A number had retreated into the store cave. They were still holed up there. The Corfiote irregulars were collecting firewood while they watched the cave mouth.

And there were three prisoners. Two who had surrendered to the guard on the upper way out. And Ambrosino.

Giuliano Lozza had bandages around his chest, but he'd very much taken charge of the camp. And now he came to his uncle.

"I always looked up to you. Trusted you, Uncle," said Giuliano quietly. "But my Eleni didn't. And neither did Thalia. They both tried to warn me in their ways. And both of them saved my life from the results of your treachery." He took a golden locket—a large one—perhaps three inches by two. There was a gouge through the gold-plate, revealing the harder metal underneath. The locket was so indented that it would never open again.

"One day I'll have her picture repainted. It was all I had left of her. There's a piece of my baby son's hair in there, too. You babbled on about family, about blood ties, about how important it is to support your own, no matter what. And then you betrayed us to the people who killed your kin."

"I . . . asked them to spare you. I tried to save you."

"And you killed our comrades. And now I am your judge, jury, and executioner. I find you guilty, guilty by all the gold in your pockets. Gold was worth more to you than blood. More than honor. I find you guilty of treason, of murder. Do you want to make your peace with God before I carry out the sentence?

Ambrosino looked disdainful. "You'll never kill me. You haven't got the guts. You don't even kill rabbits on the hunt. You'll get someone else to do your dirty work."

"I'll do it," said Thalia.

Ambrosino gave her a look that was full of more contempt than if he had spat on her. "Peasant slut."

Giuliano put a hand on Thalia's shoulder. "It is a pity in a way that I am going to execute you. Otherwise I would challenge you to a duel and cut you into doll rags for insulting a good woman. And you know I could do it. But I am going to execute you as the ranking officer of this unit of the Venetian Corfiote Army. I am giving you a last chance to pray."

This time, Ambrosino spat.

Giuliano Lozza drew his sword and ran him through.

Ambrosino's mouth gaped wide widened. "You did it! You bastard! You—"

He coughed blood; his eyes rolled up. Giuliano withdrew the blade and turned away from the dying man.

"May god have mercy on his soul. Throw his body with the other carrion." His voice was hard. "Our own we will bury with honor. This lot we will dump outside their camp."

"There are the wounded. And the ones in the cave," said Benito. "What are we going to do with them?"

"Kill the lot of them," said one of the peasant-recruits. "Cut the throats of the wounded and the prisoners. Best way of dealing with vermin."

"What do we want?" asked Benito calmly. "A few more dead Hungarians? Or a lot of frightened ones? If you ask me, scared ones will make them weaker than a few more dead bodies. They sent their best, with a traitor, to ambush us. They were outnumbered by a smaller group of men. I don't see them telling their commanding officers that, though! By the time they get back, there will be thousands of us in the hills. I reckon we offer them a choice. They can live, stripped bare-ass naked, or they can die and we'll strip their bodies."

"Strip them?"

Benito grinned nastily. "They all wear those stupid helmets and that sash over their cuirasses. I suppose we can be grateful this wasn't a full-armor mission—they'd have been harder to kill—and I don't think armor is easy for people who've never worn it. I need a group of men in those clothes. I want anyone who sees us to take us for Magyar. And if we do that once, is there any reason for the Hungarians to assume we won't do it again? Fairly good chance we'll get some of them to shoot at each other. And they'll never be sure that patrol they see over in the distance . . . is it really their men over there?"

Giuliano nodded. "It makes every kind of sense. We'll make them nervous about everything. There'll be accidents."

"Tell me about it!" said Benito. "I nearly got shot by our supporters for wearing a Croat hat."

Giuliano sighed. "Well. We must get to it. Get those uniforms, get out of here. We need to get this camp broken and moved before dawn. My traitor uncle might have told them how to find this place as well as just showing them, and they might come looking. Moving our wounded is going to be difficult."

He sighed again. "Most of them are going to die, I'm afraid. We lack medicines or surgeons and quite a few, like Erik, can't ride. We can't abandon him. He is our leader. And he's a symbol of some fear to Emeric, or he wouldn't have sent this Aldanto hunting."

Benito shook his head. "Giuliano, Erik is not ever going to get better. Neither are a good three of the others, in their case for simple medical reasons. But Erik . . . My brother is the physician, and I wish he was here now, but I'm sure that what is wrong with Erik is magical. There is only one person that I know of on this island who could treat that: Eneko Lopez, or his companion Francis. And they're inside the Citadel. Erik meant a lot to you men out here, didn't he?"

Giuliano nodded. "He is a legend. More now, I suppose. The peasants refer to him as the ice-and-fire man. Or the hand of God."

"Right. I want to break into the Citadel—again. I'm beginning to feel like a ball tossed between inside and outside! I'll need at least fifteen, maybe twenty volunteers who are prepared to do something insane to keep Erik and the other badly wounded alive."

"Signor Valdosta, you always do the insane," said Thalia, who had come up quietly behind them. "I will volunteer. I owe you and Erik my life. I was not sure if I was grateful at the time. But I have decided I am glad to be alive after all."

"I wish you'd call me Benito. Everyone else does."

"She insists on calling me 'master,'" said Giuliano. "No matter how often I have said that we're comrades-in-arms now. And of course, yes. I am with you too. I owe him my sanity, my life, and it was my blood-kin that betrayed him."

"The bad news is that I won't take either of you. You've got to take over here, Giuliano. Recruit to replace what we've lost. And you, Thalia, you've got keep him tough. He's too nice for this. But he is also too valuable to waste. He's a good man."

"I know," she said quietly. "You and Erik saved my life. But he gave me back myself. My dignity."

"I'm an olive-grower," said Giuliano irritably. "Not a saint or a soldier."

"You're also the best man for the job. And as Doge Dorma

was silly enough to invest me as a captain in the army of the Republic, I hereby give you a field-brevet to lieutenant. I'd do more, but as a captain I am limited to promoting you to below me. And I wish the two of you would stop wasting time and get a priest to marry you, as I don't think either of you will settle for anything less."

There was an uncomfortable silence.

Thalia looked down and wrung her hands. "It is too soon. Master Lozza will mourn his wife and child. I will mourn my man. Someday he will marry someone from his own order."

Giuliano looked Benito in the eyes. "I'll thank you to keep to your own business, Benito. Thalia . . . and I, both lost precious people."

Benito shrugged. "You both also nearly died tonight. And I'm not blind or stupid. This is a war. You could both still be killed while you fuss on about not hurting the other one's feelings. I don't think either of you didn't love your spouses. I just think you're hurting each other now. As for this difference in rank: Worry about it if you're still alive at the end of the war."

Giuliano put a hand gently onto Thalia's arm. "I don't wish to hurt you, Thalia. You were hurt enough."

"You are hurting me now," she said with a sniff. "You . . . all the other men in the camp. They make suggestions. Passes. You just taught me to fight. They mock you, too. They are scared to do so in the open because of your swordsmanship, master."

"If I married you, would you stop calling me master?"

She gave a watery sniff. "You don't want to do that."

"Actually, in among the ten thousand other things Erik's injury has forced on us, I want to do *that* most. But I don't want to hurt you more than you've been hurt. I don't expect much . . ."

"Would you two, hug, kiss, and get on with it," grumbled Benito. "I've got a crazy plan to go through with, and I need to find a wagon and something to hide the wounded in. And I've got some bodies and prisoners to strip, and some blacking to clean off the breastplates."

"Is that an order, sir?" asked Giuliano, putting his hands on her shoulders.

"Yes. And you, too, newly promoted sergeant. It is about time we had a few female sergeants. They're naturally good at telling men what to do."

"Yes, sir," said Giuliano, putting his arms around her. She folded into them as naturally as breathing. "You're good at managing people's lives, Benito."

"Yes. I wish I'd been as good at managing my own. Now, do you think anyone in that crowd speaks Hungarian?

Chapter 86

Late the next afternoon a wagon, escorted by a mounted patrol of Magyar, joined a number of other wagons heading into the camp. Erik's raids had forced Emeric's troops to dig earthworks and station guards, but a wagon with a Magyar driver and a military escort excited no comment. It didn't even get stopped. Benito reflected that Erik had missed some wonderful opportunities.

Benito put his earlier time within the Citadel to good use. He'd stood on the inner battlements making sure he'd get through the ruins of the town and the maze of tent-areas belonging to the different units of Emeric's army. Eberhard of Brunswick had stood up there with him while he watched, and had explained the interactions between the various tribes and nationalities in Emeric's kingdom. To the old statesman, those were potential danger areas of misunderstanding to be avoided.

To Benito they were something to be used. The Magyar, the elite of the army, Emeric's pets, weren't very popular, according to Eberhard. If you had to choose for least love lost between two groups, the levies from southern Carpathia detested the Magyars most. The Slovenes came a close second. And in the watching of detachments moving to and fro to the front, Benito knew where these two groups were encamped. They were on the southern end of the Spianada, behind a half-screen of buildings that the officers of both sets used for slightly more comfortable quarters—just out of cannon-shot. There was an open patch that both sets of troops used as a parade ground.

Benito took his set of "Magyar" there with the wagon and parked it on the edge of the parade ground. His men dismounted. Some played dice. Some just lounged against the wagon. It was covered with a tightly tied-down tarpaulin. Benito hoped the poor devils inside weren't roasting as the afternoon sun blazed down.

Nobody came over and talked to them, except for one Slovene officer. Benito didn't understand a word. However he could offer a pretty good guess.

Stephanos, with his few words of Hungarian, was posing as the group officer. Stephanos snapped one word—"orders"—with as much arrogance as he could muster and jerked his thumb at the ornate pavilion on the hill. Benito thought he could have done a better job, but then he had to give Stephanos credit for looking the part. The man had been a taverna owner at the start of the war. In younger days, however, he had spent some years in Rugosa as a clerk, working for a Venetian buyer—who couldn't operate there, and had needed a trusted man. Stephanos was a positive graybeard to Benito, but he had the posture and attitudes of someone who is used to being respected.

Stephanos's Hungarian, unlike his Illyrian, was limited, and certainly wouldn't fool a Magyar trooper for an instant. But it worked fine on the Slovene.

Benito got to drive the wagon, with Nico. Nobody seeing Benito ride would have believed him to be a Magyar cavalryman. Just after dark they set out for the northern causeway. It meant crossing the entire front—but the Croats were on that side. They had two fluent Croat-speakers from Istria, whom Benito had recruited from Captain Di Negri's Venetian volunteers.

One of the wounded from inside the covered wagon groaned. "Shut him up!" whispered Benito hoarsely.

They were approaching the two earthwork and masonry fortresses that had been constructed to deal with any sally. By the looks of it, a lot of work had gone into these since Benito had left.

They stopped the wagon just short of one of the forts. The two Croat speakers dismounted. Benito held the wheel-lock pistol between his legs. If things didn't work now . . . It would mean they'd failed to fool the guards. Then it would be whether they retreated, and tried to leave the Hungarian base in the morning—because there'd be no leaving now—or decided to rush the causeway forts.

Having looked at the causeway and the improved forts, Benito knew that one in ten of them might make it.

Halfway. Before the Venetians started shooting.

The two returned and said something in Stephanos's drilled-in Hungarian. The twenty fake Magyar dismounted, grumbling suitably, looking hangdog. A number of grinning Croats had turned out to take the horses and watch the Magyar's discomfort. The Magyar and the Croats had a healthy respect for each other. That didn't mean they didn't enjoy seeing the other lot suffer.

Really suffer. Proud Magyar having to do manual labor—off their precious horses—which had to be left with the Croats' flea-bitten nags, was a sight to be enjoyed.

Mocking cheers and jeers followed them struggling to haul the heavy wagon by hand along the causeway. Dragorvich's engineers had built a snaking set of ramparts along it, and the farm wagon had to be backed and hauled around these. Several of the engineers and a group of sappers actually gave them a hand.

Tch. What a degradation for the crème de la crème. It served them right for being stupid enough to be caught drunk on duty. They were lucky the punishment was so slight. If it had been the king who'd caught them, they wouldn't just have to take a load of gunpowder casks to the front for Count Dragorvich. The sappers might have wondered why they hadn't been told about this latest plan. But, in an army—especially Emeric's—nobody ever told common soldiers anything.

Since Manfred's sally, a forward post had been added to the defenses. By the looks of it, the Venetians had been pounding them. The wagon would certainly go no further.

The officer from the forward post emerged and snapped something caustic. Probably: "What the hell are you doing here, you idiots? Get that damn wagon out of here!"

The poor fellow wasn't expecting a blow to the head with a knife pommel. The Corfiotes and Venetians moved fast, into the forward post. Now there was no time for subterfuge. Just violence.

Benito and the eight cutters didn't wait to see how it went in there. He flung off the Magyar helmet and tore the sash off and joined in cutting the cords that held the cover, flipping it over so the carefully chalked inner lining of the canvas sprang onto its banner-support poles.

Benito just had to hope shots being fired in that forward post would be taken as normal around here. In the meantime he had a stretcher to carry. Erik and the other three couldn't run themselves.

They started running forward. Benito just hoped the shooting would only start in earnest after the wagon got to burning. The wagon was neatly jammed across the causeway, supporting a banner of the winged lion of Saint Mark.

Shots rang out from the walls. They'd been seen. "*SAN MARCO!*" yelled Benito, with what breath he could spare. The other runners were shouting too. He looked left, back at the causeway. The wagon was burning merrily. The chalked outline of the Lion of Saint Mark reflected back golden.

They were almost at the corner tower. And then round it. Now the Hungarian forces were firing too. "Press against the wall. *San Marco! San Marco! A rescue!*"

"Who in the hell is down there?" bellowed someone from the wall.

"Valdosta! Wounded men! Help!"

"Valdosta?"

"San Marco! Help us! We've got wounded men."

The north postern spilled light. Benito saw pikemen come hurrying—but wary, and with their pikes ready. "Valdosta?" yelled someone from their ranks.

"Here!" Benito waved a hand. "Help us."

"It's all right boys! It's him. It's the madman!" Benito recognized the voice of large Alberto, Umberto's Arsenalotti friend. The Citadel's pikemen surged forward, grabbing them, grabbing stretchers, shouting "Valdosta." Cheering. Even laughing.

Benito didn't feel like laughing. Only eighteen of his band of heroes were here to enjoy the cheering.

Jagiellon prepared his favorite dish for the shaman. There were properties about it that would help to heal the shape-changer, even if the skin was only that of a palace servant. In the meanwhile, the shaman huddled in a corner in his feather-and-bell-hung spirit cloak. He sat there shivering, making the bells tinkle, and flickering his fingers across the surface of the tattooed *Quodba*-drum.

The noise—which reverberated outside the mere physical plane— was an irritation, but Jagiellon ignored it. He had no choice if he wanted to retain the services of this very powerful shaman. The shaman was enacting a kind of self-healing and pain-stilling. He was, despite his formidable skills, still a primitive man. Or something near that anyway. Right now, Jagiellon could have killed him effortlessly. The shaman was in too much agony to care.

But Jagiellon needed to send him back. Whatever it was about Corfu that hampered his own magics was powerful, intensely so. Jagiellon could not afford to let it fall into Emeric's hands. He knew that Emeric was a cat's-paw for someone whose interest in mere geographical possessions was limited: the sorceress across the Carpathians.

Soon, therefore, the shaman must go back. The power of Corfu would be centered on a specific place. The shaman must be the first into that place. The slave was useless now. His wounding had been physical and dire, and Jagiellon was not sure if he was going to bother to repair him.

Chapter 87

"So I was thinking," said Marco, "maybe I could try to contact Benito."

Sister Evangelina shook her head. "Even our most powerful mages cannot contact Eneko Lopez. Corfu seems to have become an island in a magical sense also. Besides, Eneko Lopez advised you not to try scrying out of the confines of the Venetian lagoon, did he not?"

Brother Mascoli smiled gently. "According to my researches, Corfu has always been a magical island."

Marco looked stubborn. "Look. The danger with my scrying was that the focus of my vision was too wide, that evil can enter and attack me. I can defend myself now. I've been practicing, as you know. With Kat, whom I know and love, I can narrow that down. Eneko didn't say 'never,' he said only in a case of dire need. I think there is now need."

Mascoli nodded. "And blood connections are always stronger. There is a magical resonance between them. But still, Marco, even if you could narrow your search and only reach Benito, and protect yourself, Corfu cannot be reached."

"I grant there is need," said Evangelina, "but is it dire?"

"I believe so," said Marco quietly. "I believe Benito needs me."

"Is there anything that can be done for him?"

"God willing, yes." Eneko Lopez scowled. "Although here on Corfu . . . But we will do our best."

Manfred let one of his meaty hands rest on Erik's forehead—

692

a surprisingly gentle gesture for so big and powerful a man. "I owe you a debt I can't ever repay, Benito. May God forgive me for letting him go. Or I should have gone with him."

He shook his head. "What a mess, Benito. I always thought... other people died in combat. Since this siege started, I'm beginning to realize that 'other people' can be your closest friends."

"If Eneko succeeds then he's going to need close friends, Manfred. She's dead. Caesare's men, or at least their horses, killed her. I didn't know Erik like you did. But ... before this happened he was very much in love. He—they—were about as happy as a couple can be. When he got there, she was dying already. He went berserker. He killed half the Hungarians himself. Then Caesare nearly killed him with this magical blow."

"And what happened to Caesare Aldanto? I swear this world isn't big enough for both of us to live in." It was said with a calm assurance that was no less terrifying for its calmness. All the more so, coming from a prince of the Holy Roman Empire.

"I shot him. I think he's dead. Some monstrous eel thing took him down into the water."

"Chernobog's minion!" exclaimed Brother Francis. "The hagfish."

Manfred put a big arm around Benito. "You shot him? Well done! Are you sure you hit him?"

"Certain. I wasn't more than three yards off. I shot him in the gut. Liver and spine would have been hit too."

"How did you get so close? Melee?"

"I did what he taught me. Distracted him. Convinced him I was going to fence with him. And then I shot him when he thought I was dead meat."

"Well done!" repeated Manfred. "He never taught you anything better in his life. Now, you look exhausted." He managed a grin. "These jack-in-the-box visits to the Citadel are all very well, but they're not good for you. Go and rest. I'll sit with Erik."

"I'll just go to see Maria ... 'bout Caesare."

"You're swaying on your feet. She'll have the news by now or I know nothing about women. And I'll send Von Gherens down to tell her you're fine, but that you're in bed. Your own, alone, asleep."

Benito chuckled. "Not that she cares. But I suppose it will keep."

❧   ❧   ❧

Benito slept a full twenty hours. He hadn't realized just how exhausted he was. Now up, washed—in salt water, as fresh water in the Citadel was under severe rationing—and dressed, he carefully checked, unloaded and reloaded Maria's wheel-lock pistol. Then he set off to see her.

"It's the bad penny again, Umberto," said Maria.

"And it is good to see him. If we had ten bad pennies like this youngster, Emeric wouldn't have a siege!" Umberto waved to a chair. "Have you come to see my daughter again?" he asked, with an attempt at a stern look. "I tell you I want a respectable *scuolo* husband for her, Benito, not someone everyone calls 'the madman.'"

"Where is she?"

"Mrs. Grisini and her maid have taken her out for a walk. The old lady is a little crazy too. I've sat with her a few times when Anastasia has been sick. She . . . sees things. But she's harmless. And she adores 'Lessi. I don't normally let her alone with her, but Anastasia is very good with both of them."

"And where's the goat?"

There was an awkward pause. "We sold her. We just couldn't find enough food for her any more. I couldn't bear to kill her myself. She was a black-hearted menace, but she was twice the guard that a dog would have been. Have you heard that Sophia Tomaselli escaped? The guards claim it was witchcraft."

Maria sighed. "I suspect it was simply money. They've searched all over. Even searched the captain-general's apartments, at his invitation. Anyway, let's talk about something else. Is it just as dry out there?"

"Just about. You can still find water underground or in the bigger rivers. But even the olives are suffering." Benito took out the wheel-lock pistol. "Here. I'm returning it with thanks. It did exactly what it was supposed to do. I think he's dead, and if that woman is around she might get vindictive. You might need it. Careful. It's loaded and primed."

She took the pistol. "You killed Caesare?"

"Yes. I think so, anyway."

Maria nodded. Seeing her husband's frown, she shook her head. "Good riddance, I say! I'm sorry, Umberto, I'm just being honest. Caesare Aldanto was an evil man. He did terrible harm to me and Benito and Marco, and lots of other good Venetians. Best that he is dead. He'd only go on doing it to other people."

Umberto nodded. "I agree with you on this one, my dear. You told me how he deceived our Garavelli cousins. But he was supposed to be a great swordsman and a fighter. How did you . . . ?" He smiled apologetically at Maria. "It'll be a story to tell the other *scuolo* masters. Young Benito here is one of the favorite sources of stories. I must tell you, Benito, it has done my prestige and popularity no end of good with all the wild journeymen and apprentices, that I am Valdosta's friend."

Maria snorted. "That lot are as bad as he was."

Umberto smiled. "They are the ones who really believe in my fireboats. The masters mostly say the authorities will never use them. That they will say we wasted the materials." He sighed. "They would work. It is my dream to see that they get the chance to work. Well, tell us about this Caesare."

"I had Maria's pistol in my hand inside my shirt. I pretended the hand was injured. I boasted a lot about fencing. About the sword. And then when were close . . . he lunged."

Benito lunged himself, demonstrating.

The glass in the small window shattered. A black crossbow bolt sailed through the space Benito had just vacated and hit Umberto squarely in the chest.

Maria still had the pistol in her hand. She turned and, as you might point a finger, fired.

By the time the guards arrived, Umberto was dead in his wife's arms. His hand was still holding Benito's.

There was a blood trail outside, from next to the low wall where the killer had hidden.

"They found him," said Benito quietly. "He was hiding down in the ruined houses near the Kérkira side of the outer wall. Your shot shattered his right hand and hit him in the gut. He'll die. It's amazing he got that far. They've been questioning him, hard, as they reckon his time is short."

Maria held Alessia and rocked her. "Who was he? Why did he kill my husband?" Her voice was hard, bitter.

"His name is Zanari. A mercenary from Apulia who's been working for Fianelli."

Benito looked down, and bit his lip. "He shot Umberto by accident. His orders were to shoot me. Only I moved, imitating

Caesare. That bolt was meant for me. I'm sorry, Maria. I'm really sorry. All I ever seem to bring you is sadness."

Her eyes were luminous with tears. "No, Benito. I still believe this is that woman's hatred. I'm learning that here on Corfu, magic goes further than the chants and words and symbols that Eneko believes in." She closed her eyes briefly. "I'm scared for Alessia, 'Nito."

Benito patted her awkwardly. "We'll do what we can, Maria. Francesca is hunting. She always finds, eventually." He cleared his throat. "We, um, I've been down to the Little Arsenal, talking to the *scuolo* and the workers. They want to arrange the funeral. Your husband was a much-respected man, Maria."

Maria stood there, tears now pouring from her eyes. Slowly, as if her head was too heavy to move, she nodded. "He wasn't . . . like you. Bravura. Just solid. Good. Not clever, but wise; he used every little bit of intelligence he had, and used it like—like the artisan he was. And he was kind, so kind; you would never believe how kind. I wish . . . he could have seen his fireboats used. He put so much into that project."

Benito squeezed her shoulder. "He was a damn fine man. I started out intending to hate his guts. Only . . . well, I couldn't."

Maria nodded again. "His fussing used to drive me mad at first. I wasn't used to being a 'good little *scuolo* wife.'" She gave out a half-sob. "I guess I'm not any more."

"Well, there is a pension. And I know you won't take money from me, but for Alessia . . ."

She shook her head firmly. "No, Benito. Anyway, right now what we need is food—and all the money in Christendom can't buy much in the Citadel right now. Thanks to old Grisini, Alessia and I have a place to stay. It was a kindness that has repaid itself already, I suppose."

Alessia squirmed and grumbled in Maria's arms.

"Is something wrong?" asked Benito anxiously.

Maria shook her head. "According to Stella—who should know—she's starting with teething pains."

Alessia gave a niggly bellow. Maria rocked her to try and soothe. "Can I hel—"

Both Benito and Alessia cut off their vocal output on the instant. And both of them seemed to be staring right through Maria.

Then Benito shook himself, like a wet dog. "Weh! What an

experience!" He took a deep breath. "Marco and Kat send their love and their condolences, Maria."

"*What?!*"

"I've just had a magical communication with my brother," he said, absently. He looked—not dazed, exactly, but certainly deeply preoccupied. Obsessed, even; there was, of a sudden, a strange look in his eyes, a fire that was nothing like that crazy look he used to get whenever he was about to go off on some wild excursion.

A magical communication from his brother?

"But—" she began. "Benito, how—"

He shook his head violently. "Look Maria, I must go. I need to see Manfred and Eneko straight away. I'll be back later to see if there is anything you need. I'll come and baby-sit for a while, maybe, if you need to go out."

There was a furious knock at the door. It was a panting Alberto. "Maria. Come down to the workshops quickly! There's a fight between the Illyrians and the Corfiotes again."

"Me?"

"They listen to you, Maria. They're used to it. Oh, Jesu, Maria, if you don't come someone is going to get knifed!"

She swore a sailor's oath, halfway between anger and weeping. "Oh God's Teeth—I'll come! Go on, Benito."

Benito went. But he was privately certain that Maria would be spending a fair amount of her time at the Little Arsenal, even if Umberto was dead. And that would be no bad thing. She would need something to keep her mind off her grief for a while.

And maybe that would keep her from blaming *him* for Umberto's murder.

Chapter 88

"Rome must hear of this!" said Mascoli excitedly.

Evangelina shrugged. "The requirement is a powerful magician, with a nonhuman, demideity in support, who has a blood relation on Corfu. I don't think it will help Eneko much."

Marco blinked. "You know, the strangest thing was that I was talking not just to Benito, but to someone else as well. A sort of person."

"Human?"

"I think so . . . although its thoughts seemed somehow formless. It was sore, hurting; just an annoying ache. I soothed it."

Eneko Lopez stared intently at Benito. "A blood bond! And with such a one as Marco Valdosta. Powerful indeed."

"Yeah. And the news was pretty powerful too, even if none of it was good. The Atlantic fleet still being held outside the pillars. The fire in the Arsenal. The heavy snows in Bohemia, so the imperial forces have made poor headway into Slovenia and Hungary."

"To say nothing of the Church failing to prevail on either the magical defenses or the earthly authorities of Aragon and Genoa." Lopez shook his head. "We never did have much influence with Barbary."

"Anyway. What I wanted to say was—if crisis struck—or if we found out something, could I contact him?"

Eneko shrugged. "Magical ability tends to run in families. The Valdosta—given their long association with the Lion—are known for it. And with the working of metals . . . so are the Dell'este. Sforza? Well, not that I know of. But we could try, with us supporting you. It might be dangerous because of the warding problem. We could try. If the need was great."

"Signor Valdosta," said Alberto, diffidently. "It would mean a great deal to all of the *scuolo* from the Little Arsenal if you'd say a few words at the funeral. We . . . well, Umberto derived a great deal of pride and pleasure from having his family associated with the *Casa* Valdosta. It would be a mark of respect."

Benito found the last part of that statement compelling. He found the rest of it an alarming burden. "I don't think I've ever met a man I came to respect more than Umberto Verrier," he said quietly. "And I've met all sorts from priests to princes. But . . . well, me? Alberto, the honor of the *Casa* Valdosta belongs with my older brother. He got all the honor and I got all the wildness."

Alberto shrugged. "Everybody expects a young *Case Vecchie* to run amok," he said tolerantly. "But what counts with us is that when the real trouble came, you were there. We've heard from one of the Venetian sailors who fought their way back with you, how you worked in the Arsenal." He took Benito's hand, turned it over, looked at the calluses and smiled.

"That's not the hand of an idle nobleman, signor. We *scuolo*, we're guildsmen. We respect a man who labors, we respect the fact that you've been first in the fight for us, and we like it that you can work and drink just like us. We're proud that the *Casa* Valdosta chose to be the friend of one of the *scuolo*. It would be a good thing for his widow, too. It will do no harm that some people see the mantle of the Valdosta is there to protect her."

Benito raised his eyes to heaven. "It's a pretty thin mantle. And don't say that to Maria. She doesn't believe she needs any protecting. Tell you what, Alberto. I'll ask her."

"I'm sure she'll agree."

Benito was certain she wouldn't.

He was wrong. Maria nodded, when he said that they'd asked him to do a eulogy. "It would have meant a lot to him, 'Nito. He really liked you. He was very proud of you, you know." She sniffed. "He even asked me to be nicer to you."

Benito found his reply had got stuck behind the lump in his throat. But he nodded.

The little Hypatian chapel was full to the wall-bulging point. The Little Arsenal's *scuolo*, the Corfiotes, the Illyrians, men, women and children . . . Today there was no fighting among them. Today they'd come to pay their last respects, to commit to God and the earth one of their own. To show to his widow, whom they'd come to respect, and love too, how much they'd valued her man.

Sibling Eleni conducted the service, giving comfort with the old words. The air was full of incense. It was getting in his eyes. After the homily, Benito had to stand up and speak. Facing the court had been easier. He swallowed.

"Umberto Verrier . . . When I was asked give this eulogy, I struggled to get the words I wanted to say about this man. So: I came here last night. It's not a place I come to often enough. My head stayed empty. I knew what I wanted to say about Umberto, but not how to say it. And my eyes wandered to the icons. Then I saw a face that had something in it that reminded me of Umberto. I saw the same look as I have often seen on the face of the man I was proud to call my friend, in the face of the Holy Saint Peter. The face of man that you know is as solid and reliable as the rock beneath your feet.

"When I first met Umberto, we hauled baulks of timber together at the gate where our ships landed. It took me very little time to realize that here was a man who spoke not with his mouth but with his hands, and that those hands knew exactly what they were doing. Umberto wasn't a great talker. He was a man who did, instead. And like the rock, he was a man you could rely on and trust. Because he was what he was. As good and solid as a rock."

Benito had struggled to start speaking. Now the words came easily, painting a deep and full picture of Umberto, of the treasure that this husband had been to Maria. Benito had not realized what effect the quiet, small *scuolo* master craftsman had had on him. He was always just there when Maria was. Solid. You almost didn't notice him, until he wasn't there.

If Benito felt like this now, how then was Maria bearing it?

The pallbearers were all *scuolo*. Alberto had been polite but firm in his refusal of Benito's offer. "You can speak for him. But we carry our own."

They laid him in the grave and gave him into the embrace of the earth. And the world seemed a poorer place, full of dust and ashes.

Maria stood white-faced and weeping at the graveside. Work-roughened hands touched her, awkwardly, gently. Hands trying to say what the *scuolo*, the Corfiotes, the women and Illyrians could find no words for.

Benito did it himself. Words were too inadequate.

She turned to him. "Thank you," she said, quietly. "You said the right things about him."

"I wish that bolt had hit me instead," he said. "I'm worth less than he was. Maria, if you need anything, or need help with 'Lessi . . . I'll be there."

She nodded.

He was not too sure what she was agreeing with.

Erik opened his eyes at the end of what seemed like a long, long tunnel of grayness. He looked up into Manfred's face.

"Are you dead as well? Did I fail you, too?" The voice was a dry, cracked whisper.

"No. You're alive thanks to that mad scamp Benito. I must talk to Uncle about a barony for the boy, at the very least. Maybe on the border of Aquitaine. It'll do him and the Aquitaines good."

Erik blinked. "Where am I?"

"In the hospital, in the Citadel."

Then the despair washed over him. "She's dead, Manfred. She's dead. I promised I would never leave her. I must go to her."

A firm hand pushed him down onto the bed. "She's dead. You're alive and you're going to stay that way. Because you are my hearthman. I need you here. I order it."

Manfred knew the Icelander was still on the border between life and death . . . And the direction he took now was very uncertain. But he had never seen Erik cry. Tears welled up in those gray eyes, drowning them. Then Erik swallowed, tightened his jaw and said in a quiet voice:

"Very well. Duty remains, Manfred." He paused. "To every life there comes a season of happiness. I have had mine."

The baby wailed, and Maria tucked sweat-damp strands of hair behind her ears, then bounced Alessia in an attempt to soothe her. She might as well have tried to stop the tide; she got no more result than when she'd tried to feed the poor mite a moment ago.

Maria felt her own irritation building to an irrational anger, and did her best to control it.

"I know you're teething, child," she told the youngest member of the Verrier family wearily, "and I know your poor mouth is hurting. But you've been so good up to now, can't you suffer in silence?"

She heard a familiar step at the door. It was Benito. "I tried knocking but the competition was drowning it out," he said with a smile. "I was down at the Little Arsenal and Alberto's wife was there. She told me Alessia's teething and giving you a hard time."

Maria nodded tiredly. "I'm nearly at my wit's end with it."

Benito produced a jar from his pocket. "I came here via the monks at the hospital. Brother Selmi said this might help."

"What is it?"

Benito grinned. "I don't even look like Marco, Maria. It's no use asking me. I told him what it was for, I told him how old she was, and I told him that if it did her any harm I'd feed him his own cassock. He seemed a bit taken aback that I'd offer a man of the cloth violence."

Maria raised her eyes to heaven. "You're impossible, Benito."

"Well, he seemed to think his cassock was safe. Let's try it anyway. It's in a honey base and it has cloves in it, but that is all I know." He opened Alessia's mouth and rubbed a fingerful onto the sore gums. "I wish I had ice for her. But the nearest is over in Illyria."

"Which you are not to fetch!" He was quite capable of deciding to do that.

Benito chuckled. "Only if this doesn't work, which it seems to be." He held out his arms. "Alberto's wife said you've been trying to quiet her half the night. I'll be glad to take her for a bit until she falls asleep. Which probably won't be long; I bet she's tired herself out to nothing, with all that crying."

"She's tired me out, if nothing else," Maria admitted, letting Benito take the baby from her arms.

"It'll pass, according to the brother at the hospital. The truth to tell, I think he was glad of a teething baby problem that he could help with, rather than malnutrition and siege wounds he can't."

Maria watched as Benito moved with a sort of slow, catlike walk that Alessia always seemed to find comforting. She was still amazed at how good he was with the child, and how frequent and constant he'd been about visiting 'Lessi. He seemed to have no problems about the fact that she, Maria, was using him as a mere baby-sitter. His arrival usually signaled her departure. He wasn't just coming to see her.

The truth was she was uncomfortable about her feelings for Benito. Umberto's death was still recent and raw. She'd been troubled about it when Umberto was alive. Now . . . she was careful to keep her distance.

But he was very good with 'Lessi, seeming to derive a deep satisfaction from looking after her. She'd never have thought it of him, although there was a tender side to the younger Valdosta. He just tried not to ever let it show. Perhaps it was having to survive on the canals after his mother had been killed. He'd been very young.

She sighed. He still seemed completely oblivious to the fact that Alessia could easily be his child. Probably was, in fact. Had no one ever explained to him about how long a pregnancy was? Or had he just deliberately excluded the idea?

"She's out, poor lamb," said Benito quietly. "Shall I put her down in her crib?"

Maria nodded.

PART XIII
December, 1539 A.D.

Chapter 89

"Benito!" the panting Arsenalotti porter yelled. "You'd better get yourself back to Maria Verrier. You're needed there. Somebody's kidnapped her baby."

"Who?" he snapped, the chill grip of fear on his throat. "Who took her?"

The Corfiote porter shook his head. "Don't know, nobody knows. Some says it's more witchcraft, some reckon it is something to do with a Hungarian spy, some blame the captain-general's wife. It's every rumor you can think of going through the Citadel like a fire. No ransom note, no clues, no nothing. But there's guards and that Eneko Lopez, looking."

Benito felt stark horror. Eneko Lopez and the Satanists he was sniffing for! And a missing baby. It added up to things he didn't like to think about.

When he got there, out of breath, he found a crowd of Arsenalotti, an officer of the Citadel guard, Eneko, and Francesca, too.

"The baby vanished some time between when you left Signora Verrier and about half an hour ago," Eneko said curtly, raising his voice a little to be heard over the crowd of Arsenalotti. "You don't remember seeing anyone hanging around the outside when you left, do you?"

Benito shook his head.

"Whoever took her didn't leave a note, and hasn't tried to contact us," said the guard officer. "Unfortunately, that doesn't rule anyone out."

"They must have been around, watching," said Benito numbly, "If they took her that soon after I left."

The guard officer nodded. "We just don't know where to start, milord."

"Have you asked Anastasia?" Seeing the officer's blank look Benito explained. "The girl who looks after old Mrs. Grisini. In the upper floors of the house."

Maria shook her head. "She's up at the hospital, Benito. Just lack of food, I think. I found her passed out on the stairs the day before yesterday. The old lady was still pottering around and hadn't even noticed. The old lady is also up there, at the hospital. She has arthritic pains and it turns out she's been taking poppy-juice tablets to help her with it." Maria made a face. "It appears she's been taking too many of them. Washing them down with grappa on the quiet."

"Well, that leaves her out," mused Benito. "I'd wondered. She's always been potty about Alessia."

"About babies in general," said Maria. "She lost her own, from her first husband. Poor woman. I can't blame her entirely for her tablets and grappa. She's had a miserable life."

Benito shrugged. "Well, my sympathies, but I want to find Alessia. I'm just glad to have her excluded because I'd worry about what she might do to a child. She always seemed as mad as bedlam to me."

Maria pursed her lips. "She made some bad decisions. That first marriage of hers . . . poor, short but happy. Then she married Grisini. It was childless and—on her side anyway—more for sustenance than affection. The childlessness obsessed her a bit. But she'd never have hurt a baby. It can't be her, anyway. She was being looked after up at the hospital, the last I saw."

"If we knew roughly where Alessia had been taken to, we'd have a pretty easy time finding her," Benito said. "She's going to wake up in a strange place with her gums hurting, and she's going to start right in screaming. We'll set the Arsenalotti kids to listening for a baby where there shouldn't be one."

"If we knew roughly where she was." Francesca pondered that for a moment, while Benito turned away from the window and slumped down into another chair. "So who'd want a baby? Especially one that's likely to give them away?"

Benito thought about that for a moment.

"If I were some kind of agent, or someone wanting a baby for a ritual, the last thing I'd pick to kidnap would be a teething baby," Francesca persisted. "You can't reason with it, and you can't shut it up without hurting it. You can't even shut it up *by* hurting it. So what if this isn't a kidnapping, as Maria thinks it is? Who else would want a baby?"

"Who would want a baby—except a mother?" He looked up to see Maria nodding thoughtfully.

"Somebody who lost a baby already? And maybe can't have any more?" Francesca pursed her lips and sat up a little straighter. "And you've got a little china-doll right here, about as pretty as anybody'd ever want. All right, that makes sense. But who?"

"Remember, Benito, we are probably looking for someone who isn't entirely well balanced, but it's also probably someone too careful to give herself away by disappearing with it. Lord only knows why they took the baby—"

Benito felt a finger of ice trace the line of his spine. "You don't— you don't think they'd hurt her, do you?"

"Not if it was someone looking for a baby to care for. They'd try to look after her."

"Which leaves harming her by accident." His heart sank again. "Saints. If the baby starts fussing again, wakes up and starts crying—"

It was around dusk when the young Corfiote boy came panting in. "Down near the southern wall! There's a building that's been pretty well wrecked in the shelling, milord. No one living down there. But I heard a baby!"

Benito got to his feet. "Let's go."

Maria struggled to keep up.

Emeric's bombardment had turned from being largely focused on the front wall to working on the morale of the besieged by shelling the buildings inside the wall. The result was that the forequarter of the city, inside the southern curtain wall, was largely uninhabitable with many damaged buildings. It was to this part that the boy led them, into a small square.

"It was here I heard it, milord."

At precisely that moment, a baby cried. A fierce howl of pain and frustrated anger. Benito knew that it had come from directly overhead. He knew that cry, knew that baby-voice. It was his baby, his little girl—

Anger he'd been carrying around inside since the abduction exploded into a white rage.

He went up through the skeletal remains of the building without a thought to fragile masonry. But at the third floor level he was confronted by a piece of staircase that was plainly newly fallen. This stopped Maria, but it didn't stop him. Not for an instant. He climbed across on tiny stubs of masonry, willing them to be big enough to hold him.

He gained the landing. "Get someone with some planks!" he called back to Maria. He pushed open the door at the top.

The room here was virtually intact. And leaning over the cradle at the far side of the room was a woman they'd supposed safe in the hospital. Mrs. Grisini's hair was awry, gray straggling locks hanging about her face. Her eyes, looking up from Alessia and into his, were unfocused, the pupils wide. She saw him and screamed in competition with Alessia.

"It's all right," said Benito, trying for an air of reassurance. She looked mad enough to do anything and Alessia was right within her grasp. He walked slowly forward, making no hasty movements.

She screamed again, and snatched the infant from the cradle, holding it so tightly against her that the baby howled in protest at this mishandling.

Benito froze where he was. She edged away from him, step by step, until her back was against the outer door that had once led to another room. Before Benito could stop her, she kicked the door open and dashed out onto what was left of the structure.

Torches and lanterns lit her eerily from below. She looked like one of the condemned souls in the Holy Book. "Get away!" she cried, her eyes wild, waving her free hand at him. "Get away from me!"

Benito walked toward her, through the broken masonry, then out into the room one slow step at a time. "I won't hurt you, signora," he said, as quietly and calmly as he could and still be heard over the baby's screams. "I've just come for my little girl."

His heart pounded painfully in his chest, and his throat was too tight to swallow as she backed up another step. A cool, reasoning corner of his mind was calculating footing, the length of his own lunge, the amount of safe wood still behind her. The rest of him wanted to shriek and grab for his baby, now.

"You can't have her!" The woman said, shaking her head

violently. "She's mine, not yours, she was meant for me. I saw it in the dreams!"

"What dreams, signora?" Benito asked, edging another foot closer. The wood creaked dangerously underfoot, and the whole building swayed again. He made a drastic revision of his safety margins.

"The dreams, the holy dreams," the woman babbled, clutching her hand in her hair while the baby subsided to a frightened whimper, as if she somehow sensed the danger she was in. "She's mine, she was meant for me—"

He was almost within reach—

Suddenly she looked over his shoulder, as light poured from the door behind him, and her eyes widened still further. "Benito?" Maria called. There was a murmur of shocked and frightened voices, and someone stifled a cry of despair.

"Stay back!" he warned sharply, as the woman took another two steps backward onto wood that moaned under her weight.

"Signora," he said urgently, recapturing her attention. "Signora, the dreams. What about them? What did they tell you?"

She transferred her attention from whoever was behind him back to his face. "You don't care about the dreams," she said accusingly. "You just want my—"

The wood gave.

Benito made a desperate lunge as the woman shrieked and teetered on the brink of the gulf, one arm flailing wildly, the other still clutching the baby. He reached her—she fell, just as his hands brushed the cloth—

He grabbed for it and held, as he was falling himself.

A blow to his chest knocked breath and sense from him, but he had a handful of fine linen fabric, and he held onto it past all pain and sense. The universe spun, then came to rest again.

He was dangling face-down over the street, three floors down to the cobblestones. With one hand and both legs he held on to the timber-strut that had saved him. The other hand was clutched in the linen dress of the little girl-baby, who was likewise dangling head down over the empty darkness, howling at the top of her lungs.

He edged back until his chest was supported by the timber, then drew her up. Only when she was safely cradled against his chest did he breathe again.

And held her carefully, like the precious thing she was, murmuring her name over and over, hardly daring to believe he had her back safe. He might even have burst into tears of his own at that point, but suddenly the others were on him, hauling him to safety, praising him to the skies. Arsenalotti, Arsenalotti wives everywhere, pounding his back, touching his sleeve, crying over the baby. Maria, her face as white as fine porcelain held Alessia, and stared down at her, fierce tears in her eyes.

No one seemed to be thinking about old Mrs. Grisini. Benito tilted his head to look down; and then, wincing, looked away. The torchlight showed enough. The crazed old woman's body was a broken ruin.

In the crowd below, Bianca Casarini turned and began walking away. She was disgruntled, a bit, at the failure of the scheme—but not excessively so. It had been Fianelli's idea in the first place, not hers. Emeric's servant was now desperate to do *anything* that might placate his master, given that all the other attempts at treason and sabotage had failed. No matter how petty the attempt might be.

Under pressure, Bianca had agreed to inflict the dreams on the old woman. She hadn't wanted to, herself, because she could sense the net thrown by Eneko Lopez and Francesca de Chevreuse closing steadily around her. But Countess Bartholdy had insisted.

"I can't afford to have Emeric get suspicious, this close to success. Which he will, if Fianelli reports that you are suddenly balking. So do as Fianelli wants, Bianca."

"Yes, mistress."

Well, she'd made the attempt—and the attempt had failed. Now the net would be closing more tightly still. It was time for Bianca Casarini to prepare for her escape.

Chapter 90

"The entire point of the exercise is not to surrender," said Captain-General Tomaselli. "It is to waste time. We know Venice is coming to our rescue. We know they have been delayed."

Manfred was pleased to note that the captain-general seemed to have accepted the de facto situation that first Falkenberg and now Erik had simply assumed control of the military of the Citadel. Erik, especially Erik these days, was someone people tended not to question if they could avoid it. Besides, Erik had produced the letter from the Doge brought by Benito, putting him in overall command of "Any Forces in support of the Republic of Venice, who are still at large on the Island of Corfu."

Somebody might argue they weren't at large. But so far no one had been that stupid, not even Captain-General Tomaselli. Ever since his wife's escape from prison, Tomaselli had been a very subdued man. All the more subdued, Manfred thought, because he clearly had no idea what had happened to her. Francesca had Tomaselli under constant observation, and she was sure the captain-general had no contact with his wife.

Manfred knew that Francesca herself was puzzled by Sophia's ability to stay hidden, in such a relatively small place as the Citadel of Corfu, and was getting worried about it. Some of the possible implications were . . . disturbing.

Manfred shook off the thought. Erik was speaking.

"It is a possible idea," the Icelander agreed.

Falkenberg chuckled. "We'll send old Eberhard out. If there's anyone in the whole world who can turn 'please pass the salt' into a three month negotiation, it's him."

"We have to be wary whom we send," said Erik grimly. "Emeric's middle name should be 'treachery.'"

"Well, you're not going. He wants your head," said Manfred firmly.

"And you're not going either," said Von Gherens. "Too valuable as a hostage. Send Falkenberg or me. They don't know us, and we can observe the military layout on the ground."

"I think I should go," said the captain-general. "I am high-ranking but expendable."

Manfred blinked. That had been in his mind, but he'd kept his mouth shut about it. "Very well. I'll ask Eberhard. The old man has been feeling underutilized."

When the captain-general had left, Francesca stood up. "I must go and talk to Eberhard too. This has interesting possibilities for espionage."

"A parley?" Emeric smiled savagely. "Such a thing presents some opportunities. Yes. Raise a truce flag. We can use the time to move materials onto the causeway without hindering cannon fire."

"Sire." Dragorvich hesitated. "You don't think they're using this to buy a respite? This would be the first time for many months that the western half of the citadel will not be being fired on."

Emeric shrugged. "I think it worthwhile. Aside from anything else, we can see if their delegation is worth taking hostage."

Dragorvich kept silent, of course. But, not for the first time, he reflected that the king of Hungary was ultimately something of a fool. Emeric always thought rules were for other people, without ever once considering that his own behavior might bite him back. There was a good reason, after all, that civilized nations considered diplomatic envoys untouchable. The Mongols were utterly fanatical on the subject. They had, on three occasions that Dragorvich knew of, destroyed entire kingdoms for breaching that rule of war.

They were met by a delegation of Magyar officers. "His Majesty will not receive you with weapons. Weapons are to be left here."

Falkenberg, in full armor, creaked to Eberhard of Brunswick. "It is to be hoped that he doesn't want us mother-naked, as I hear these Magyar cavalry have to go now."

By the pinched lips and dull red faces, Falkenberg hadn't made any new friends. Eberhard of Brunswick smiled sweetly. "Now, *Ritter*. Accidents will happen when you are foolish enough to give Carlo Sforza's son trouble."

"The story will be a matter of interest to the brotherhood of Knights. I'm sure it will elevate the status of the Magyar no end," said Falkenberg, calmly putting down his sword. The Knight knew he was playing to the gallery watching from the walls. Plainly the Magyar knew it too. But by the looks of the bright eyes . . . it might not make any difference in a minute.

Fortunately, a factotum from Emeric turned up to escort them down the causeway to the king.

"Sire. This was given to one of the guards by the Venetian officer," said the factotum, handing Emeric a slip of parchment.

It read: *Contact me. Deal.*

Emeric smiled wolfishly. "Well. Captain-General Tomaselli. Maybe his wife did pass on that little letter to him."

"Additionally, the elderly imperial . . . who I accompanied when he went to relieve himself, asks that Your Majesty consider a private deal. The man said he has magical word from his master. The Emperor wants his nephew intact. For which he is prepared to pay a quarter of a million ducats and also Your Majesty's former territory of Ceská, and to withdraw from the districts of Soporon and Vas."

"What!" Emeric started forward. "What did he say?"

The Factotum repeated himself faithfully.

"Damn him! *Damn him.* He's letting me know what the Emperor is doing. Trying to draw me back to Hungary. Ha! Well, I'll play him at his game. The Citadel is so close to starvation I'll win soon enough anyway. Then I'll take back Soporon and Vas—and take Ceská in the bargain. "

"My principal fear about your plan, my dear," said Eberhard to Francesca, "is that it may backfire on us. I think we may just have told Emeric what a valuable card he has to play in Manfred."

Francesca shrugged. "Surely he's figured that out for himself by now, Eberhard."

The older statesman shook his head. "Emeric . . . I have serious doubts about his sanity, Francesca. He thinks himself vastly clever, and vastly superior. He has welded the fractious elements of the Hungarian kingdom into a unit. But his decisions are sometimes . . . odd. There is a theory that the Emperor has that someone else in Hungary is pulling his strings. It may well be true. I did very little time in Buda, and I've never been so glad to leave anywhere, not even the weather in Ireland. His capital is a pretty place—with a monster corrupting it."

"I can see I still need to stop thinking like an Aquitaine," said Francesca. "But I was sure we'd get an approach from his spies. Soon."

"We may," said Eberhard. "But first we'll get the attack. Emeric simply agreed to everything. You don't negotiate like that when you're in earnest. Trust me. Negotiations are one thing I've done so often that I know exactly how genuine ones feel. Erik is preparing for Emeric to break the truce."

Falkenberg yawned. "It was long, boring and windy and dusty." He grinned nastily. "The dust was getting to Emeric, too. Now, is there any wine? Eberhard rationed me on Emeric's. I wouldn't buy horses from that man."

"Who? Emeric? Erik never *bought* any of them." Benito had come, full of curiosity, to nose out what he might.

"No. Eberhard of Brunswick. He kept that dickering going all lifelong day, when we had no intention of surrendering—and Emeric has absolutely no intention of abiding by the terms he offered us. Man's a snake. Dresses like a pimp, too."

"Well, how long have we got before fighting resumes?" asked Manfred. "We've probably given the outer wall another two weeks' life with the work we've done to it today."

Falkenberg shrugged. "Eberhard insisted on until sunrise tomorrow to consult his principals. I suspect Emeric will try an all-out assault about an hour before the truce is over."

As events proved he was wrong. The assault came at midnight. It was overcast and as black as the inside of a cat out there, and Emeric obviously found the opportunity too good to miss.

Erik's men had also found the opportunity too good to miss. Since sunset, they had been outside the walls digging pits in the shingle and covering them with sailcloth and more shingle. The oil and pitch pots had been heating since dusk.

Sometimes a bad reputation is a serious impediment to treachery.

Chapter 91

Two days later, after the failed attack, the approaches Francesca had expected arrived. They arrived in a way she'd never expected, however—from someone she'd liked and trusted, who had given her a great deal of information: the little Greek secretary to the governor, Meletios Loukaris.

Francesca had put a lot of Manfred's money into watching. And she'd put a lot into the gossip grapevine. It had brought her a fair amount of information, but not the kingpin. Not yet. Now the gossip chain brought in another piece. The captain-general—having withdrawn from social life of any sort since his wife's arrest, and become almost entirely reclusive since her escape—was hosting a gathering. It couldn't really be counted as a party; the guest list was comprised of the worst bores among the *Case Vecchie* and Libri d'Oro. No women were invited. Francesca had a very good idea of the guest list for someone who hadn't seen it. An interesting group to choose for a party . . . and now on her watch-list.

"The awkward question," said Francesca, "is whether De Belmondo is involved, because his secretary is."

"Test him," said Von Gherens. "Tell De Belmondo we're going to arrest the man. And watch the secretary to see if he runs."

Francesca screwed up her face in disgust. "The thing I think I hate most about you military people is your crude attitude toward espionage. I was going to feed De Belmondo some information—confidential, and absolutely not to be repeated—and see if the Hungarians got it."

"And what were you going to tell him?" asked Manfred.

717

"I've been trying to think of something," said Francesca irritably.

"I think we should arrest this secretary and make him talk," stated Falkenberg.

Francesca shook her head. "The trouble with that, Falkenberg, is that some people will keep their tongues, even under torture. And you would make a feeble torturer, anyway."

Falkenberg tugged his moustache. "And why is that, milady?"

"Because there is a great deal you wouldn't do."

Falkenberg nodded. "True enough. But I've usually found that it's not what I would do, but what the ones being interrogated believe I am going to do."

Manfred sighed. "Look, Francesca, we'll do it your way—until tomorrow sundown. Then we do it Von Gherens' and Falkenberg's way. We'll tell the governor we're going to arrest the man at dawn. And arrive at midnight. If he's packing we know where we stand. If not, we put my one-eyed frightener on him. I just don't believe we can play around with this."

As it happened, they didn't need either step. Good fortune finally favored them.

De Belmondo came to see Manfred a little later, just after Francesca had left for her walk. The timing was too precise to be coincidental.

"Prince Manfred," said the old man, uneasily. "Forgive me intruding on you like this. But this morning one of the Libri d'Oro, a gentleman by the name of Alexander Konstantis, came to see me in secret." The old man looked embarrassed. "He and I share an interest in the collection of naturalistic curiosities. He is an avid collector of birds' eggs. Under this pretext he came to see me, privately, and not in the office. He, ah, has something of a reputation as a malcontent. I think he just likes to argue, but that is easily misconstrued. Alexander was invited to a gathering at the captain-general's rooms last night. Now, Signor Konstantis doesn't like Captain-General Tomaselli, and very nearly didn't go and only decided to do so to give the cloth-head—in his words—a good mocking. He found himself part of a group of very unlikely people. Either very wealthy landowners or people with a reputation—like himself—for being malcontents. His curiosity was pricked and he decided, instead of just enjoying himself, to find out why the captain-general wanted to mix the likes of him with those."

The old governor shook his head sadly. "The purpose of the gathering was treason, I'm afraid. Tomaselli sounded each of them out, and Alexander played along when it came to his turn. He is astute, and in his words Tomaselli is as subtle as a charging bull. He was invited to stay on after many of the others had gone home. Then it came down to open treason. Tomaselli pointed out that Venice had not only failed to protect their estates but also had armed the peasants. He gave details of water and food stocks. He argued that the Citadel must fall, and that all within would lose everything, even their lives. He offered—conditional to the surrender of the Citadel—that his allies would retain lands and privilege, under Emeric."

"I see," said Manfred.

De Belmondo smiled. "My nasty-tongued friend said he'd go along, that he had both the perfect plan and method, but that he wanted some guarantees first. In writing. And Tomaselli was much struck by the goodness of this idea!" De Belmondo snorted and shook his head. "As if Emeric would abide by a piece of paper! Anyway, they're due to meet again an hour after Vespers at the captain-general's rooms in the Castel *a terra*. Alexander thinks that action is imminent and so we need to take steps. Unfortunately, I don't know what parts of the army the captain-general may have suborned. But I was sure it wouldn't be the Knights, as you are outsiders."

"We'll be glad to assist," said Manfred. "I think we'll need some witnesses, Your Excellency. And I think that the only reason that the captain-general has resorted to civilians is that he has very little following in the army any longer. If he ever did."

De Belmondo looked around uneasily. "Very well. Now, Prince Manfred, I have a very awkward request. Do you mind not telling Francesca de Chevreuse about this?"

This sent ideas racing through Manfred's head. But he allowed no sign of his perturbation to show. "Certainly. But why?"

The governor pulled at his earlobes. "Well . . . someone has told me she may possibly be a spy."

"Interesting," said Manfred, keeping his urbane expression. Eberhard would have been proud to see how well he'd learned. So would Francesca. "And who told you this?"

"My secretary, Meletios Loukaris. De Chevreuse has been pumping him for information, and tried to use him to set up other informants."

Manfred couldn't keep a straight face any more. He grinned. "You're quite right, De Belmondo. She *is* a spy. Or at least an agent. She's been working for my uncle—and for me, of course—since we came here."

"Are you sure that is her true allegiance?" asked the old man doubtfully. "I mean, in this revolting world of double-dealing and treachery, it is possible for a person to serve two masters."

Manfred nodded "Indeed, it is. Which is why I want to show you these." Manfred produced the letter from Emeric, offering to Manfred safe conduct—and setting out the terms. "This was delivered this morning in response to a trap set by Francesca and Eberhard of Brunswick. I think you must agree that he is beyond suspicion? He has been one of the Emperor's finest and most trusted statesmen for many years."

De Belmondo sighed. "Treason and treachery all around us. Who brought this to you?"

Manfred looked steadily at the governor. "Your secretary, Loukaris. Who has been an agent of Francesca's and provided her with several other informants. This man didn't serve two masters. He served three."

It was, Eneko Lopez admitted, an effective way of being unobtrusive. And as he'd felt he could not ask any of the others to take the night-soil wagon duty, he at least got to sit down. This weather had been troubling the old wound, and that made walking and standing painful. Nothing that could not be borne, but it was still a relief to sit. And Benito had been right. No one stuck around the wagon, or paid it any more attention than they had to.

And then he had to leave the wagon in hurry. They'd found him—at last! Fianelli must have been laughing at their earlier efforts. Given where the demon-user had been hiding all this while.

"We have him. We have him absolutely pinpointed! The magic use was unmistakable!"

Erik Hakkonsen looked at the cleric skeptically. "And why have you come to me, Eneko? You are very capable of arranging for Satanists to be caught."

"Because this is within the Castel *a mar*. Inside the governor's wing."

"The governor himself no doubt," said Erik, dryly. "Or maybe his wife. Yes, Eneko, no doubt after the last performance, which I've heard all about, the governor's wife. Reputedly the kindest women on the Island. You're getting like Sachs, Eneko. Witches under every cobblestone."

Eneko Lopez's single line of eyebrow lowered fractionally, but he kept his even tone. "Actually, Erik, it is the governor's secretary we suspect. A man named Loukaris. Or rather, someone hiding in his chambers, as he wasn't there when the magic activity took place."

Erik made a face. "Hmm. Awkward. But better than the man's wife being a black magician, I suppose."

The stern lines on Eneko eased. He shook his head and smiled easily. "Saintliness shines out of her, Erik."

"He just dropped dead, Mam'zelle." The tail was one of the best Francesca had hired. Right now he was also one of the most distressed. He'd been following the Count Timeto, one of the guests at the captain-general's suspicious little gathering the night before. "Franco or I had him right under our eye almost every moment of the time. He went in to try to see Governor De Belmondo this morning. I was at the door when he spoke to the governor's secretary.

"And what did he say, Mouse?"

"He wanted an appointment with the governor. Now! He was very insistent. The secretary lied to him. Loukaris said he would check to if the governor was available. Franco followed him. He went into his own chambers and nowhere near Signor De Belmondo. And then he came back and told the Count that the governor was out."

Mouse took a deep breath. "I was following the count. Not too close, not too obvious. There was quite a crowd in the courtyard and it was easy. But when he got to the gates . . . There was no one near him and he just fell over. He was dead, signora. They took him to the hospital, but he was already dead. And no one killed him." The small spy crossed himself.

Francesca bit her lip. "Mouse, do you know where Benito is?"

The spy looked startled. "He was nowhere near, signora. He was on his way to the armory."

"I need to see him. Ask him to come here."

"*Si*. But why, signora?"

"A good spy like you should never ask questions like that." But she had a soft spot for the little nondescript man. He'd brought her so many interesting titbits. "My elders taught me how to play politics and manage spies. Benito's master taught him how kill people."

"He is a soldier, signora," said Mouse, looking doubtful. "The Count was killed by magic, I'm sure of it."

"Benito might be starting to become a soldier. But Caesare Aldanto was an assassin. And Benito learned a lot from him."

A few minutes later, Benito appeared. He looked wary. "What is it, Francesca? That's a thief you have running your errands, by the way."

"I know. Benito. If Caesare had wanted someone to die, without making it obvious, how could it be done in a hurry? Let me tell you what happened." And she explained.

Benito raised his eyebrows. "There are a couple of possibilities. But the most likely . . . Well, Caesare told me that if you push a very sharp, thin-bladed stiletto—actually, a sort of lethal pin—into the victim's heart, the bleeding is almost all internal. The strange thing is there is apparently no more than a momentary pain, especially if the victim is corseted up like a woman, or used to momentary aches and pains, like someone who's elderly or out-of-condition. The blade is pulled out, and the victim can continue walking for a good few heartbeats while the killer escapes. Get someone to examine the corpse, carefully."

One of the guards was suitably corruptible, and Mouse was sent on another errand. Francesca had to wait impatiently.

Benito was right. De Belmondo, at least, was in the clear. Why else would the Count have been murdered?

"It's a good thing not all De Belmondo's informants are so trusting that they'd talk to his secretary," said Manfred, when she told them the story. "Or Alexander Konstantis might be dead, too. And for once, just once, I know more than you do, dear. You see, De Belmondo really *was* out of his office. He was seeing me. While that wicked spy his secretary had told him about was away!"

Erik came in from the office of the garrison commander. "I have news for all of you. Eneko has found Fianelli."

❀   ❀   ❀

The actual arrest, coming after all those months of looking for Fianelli, was almost an anticlimax. Thanks to Alexander Konstantis's inspired meddling, those who had conspired with Captain-General Tomaselli were caught, red-handed, in possession of documents from Emeric, with their names on each. Eneko and the Knights burst in on the secretary's chambers at the same time, so that Loukaris could not get warning. They caught him and his master, Fianelli, who had been hiding like a boll weevil right in the middle of his hunters.

"Well, Francesca. You should be pleased with yourself," said Manfred, patting her on the back.

She looked at him, consideringly. "What I have found is a series of strings and levers pulled by an evil man. I can't call Emeric anything else. I'm just afraid of what else there is."

Eneko nodded. "This drought, for example. It is undoubtedly magical and undoubtedly the product of Emeric, although I had not realized him capable of such great magics. And the female Satanist is still at large, don't forget."

"So is Sophia Tomaselli," grumbled Manfred. "How can a woman that dimwitted have evaded us for so long?"

That evening, as she studied again the records she had slowly compiled, it was Francesca who felt herself to be dimwitted. Never more so than the moment she realized the truth.

"Of course!" she exclaimed, slapping the table with a combination of exasperation and triumph. "How could I have been so *stupid*? It's right there in Eneko's records—once I match it properly against every else! Especially the inheritance records! The creature inherited the house within days after her aunt and uncle were killed—and they were killed, according to those same records, at the same moment that Eneko and Diego remember a terrible burst of black magic."

Manfred raised his head from the pillow. He'd been lying on the bed, a bit disgruntled because—very common, lately—Francesca was working at her desk instead of being her usual seductive self.

"What are you talking about?"

Francesca ignored the question, too busy scrabbling furiously through the mass of papers piled on her desk. "Yes! And again! That little boy who disappeared—another burst of satanic magic— and he was known to beggar on the same street where she lives!"

More scrabbling. "Her name's everywhere in these records, now that I finally have my senses. *Everywhere.* Always seeming—taking each thing at a time—like a minor and insignificant figure. But—"

More scrabbling. A paper held up triumphantly. "Yes! She was known to be a friend and confidant of Sophia Tomaselli!" Scrabble; another paper; scrabble; yet another.

Francesca rose, a paper clutched in each hand. Her eyes were slitted. "*And* she was noticed, twice, in the company of one of Fianelli's thugs. *And* in the company of Aldo Morando, on one occasion. All small incidents, buried in the mass. But taken as a whole, it's obvious. I have been so *stupid.*"

Manfred was on his feet, now, reaching for his armor and weapons.

"You won't need those," Francesca muttered. "She's just a woman, Manfred, not a Magyar cavalryman. Besides, the Venetian authorities will do the arrest."

He shrugged, continuing what he was doing. "Eneko says she's a 'female,' not a woman. I've encountered a monster in the Basque priest's company, once—so I think I'll do it my way."

Impatiently—no moving Manfred, in a stubborn mood—Francesca waited till he was done. By the end, she was even in a good mood about it.

"Might be just as well. I need to get confirmation from Morando—and, for that, I'll need you to intimidate the Venetians into allowing me to offer him a commutation of his sentence." She patted Manfred fondly on the cheek—with only two fingers, that being the most she could get past the cheek guards. "You do look *so* impressive in full armor. You would even if you weren't a prince. Come, dear."

Morando had been half-asleep when his cell was suddenly invaded. He woke up instantly, however—as a prisoner condemned to death is bound to do when he finds his cell occupied by almost every major figure of authority in the area, several priests, three Knights of the Holy Trinity in full armor—and a beautiful woman.

Francesca de Chevreuse, in a dramatic gesture, drew forth several slips of paper from her gown. She handed one each to the podesta, the commander of the garrison, one of the priests, and the hugest of the Knights.

"I've written a name on those slips, Morando. The same name

on each one. If you can match that name—it's the identity of your accomplice, the one you've been keeping a secret from us—you'll live. If you can't—or won't—you'll be executed. Here. Today—not later in Venice. So forget about the possibility of being rescued if Emeric takes the Citadel. Not that he wouldn't kill you himself anyway."

She grinned at him mercilessly. "In honor of Venetian authority, we will use the traditional Venetian method of execution. It begins, I believe, by breaking the legs. Then—though I'm not sure about this, it's all too ghastly for a delicate woman to contemplate—they do something with your innards."

Morando swallowed. He *did* know the procedures used by Venetians when they executed someone who had truly and genuinely infuriated them. Traitors being right at the top of the list.

It was, indeed, too ghastly to contemplate.

"Bianca Casarini," he croaked.

Slips of paper were studied briefly. A moment later, the cell was empty again.

Chapter 92

Bianca detected the coming soldiers when they were still some distance away—and had sensed the presence of Eneko Lopez even sooner. She had, many weeks earlier, established a faint degree of mental control over the urchins who were always in the streets, and who served her as unwitting and unconscious human alarm signals.

"That's it, then," she murmured to herself. "It's time to hide."

The thought was neither hurried nor frantic. She'd prepared for this moment, and prepared well. Three weeks ago, working mindlessly under her control, Saluzzo had finished breaking a hole through the rear wall into an adjoining house. The residents of the house, an elderly couple, had never noticed a thing—being, also, under Bianca's compulsions.

She'd slide through the hole, pass through the house, and be out on another street and heading for Morando's hideout before Lopez and the soldiers could finish breaking down the front door.

She rose and took a small bag from the side table in her bedroom. She'd had the bag ready for days, with all of her essential instruments and ingredients in it. Moving quickly down the stairs, she smiled savagely.

Then they'll have Saluzzo to deal with. And the fools came at night, to boot! In the darkness, the mindless thing he becomes will be twice as dangerous.

Saluzzo was slumbering on a divan in the front room, as he usually was, these days. He spent most of his time lately doing nothing but eating and dozing, awash in the reveries Bianca provided him. He'd grown a bit fat and soft as a result, but that didn't concern Bianca. The transformation he was about to undergo would make "fat and soft" completely meaningless.

She strode over, placed her hand on his face, and sent a jolt of sheer agony blazing through his head. Then, stepped back quickly.

Sputtering and yowling, Saluzzo scrambled to his feet and stared at Bianca. He was simply confused, at the moment.

His confusion vanished, as Bianca slapped him across the cheek. Then, spit in his face.

Rage came instantly to a man like Saluzzo. His face contorted with fury, looking even uglier in the light cast by the single lamp in the room. He took a step toward her, his big fist raised.

Perfect. Rage was essential to a full transformation. All that was needed now were the words of power, words that had never been intended to be shaped by human lips, but which Bianca had long practice in uttering.

Again, Saluzzo yowled with pain. A yowl, this time, that went on and on and on—and, as it continued, started changing in timbre and tone, within seconds sounding more like the scream of a beast than a human being.

Bianca sped from the room. She had perhaps a minute to escape, while Saluzzo's body was paralyzed by the changes it was undergoing. By then, the semi-mindless demon-shaped beast he'd have become, tormented by the agony of muscles, nerves, and bone wrenched into new shapes and the unfettered, pain-charged anger she had invoked, would not be able to think at all, much less clearly. By then, also, the soldiers would have started breaking in the door and the Saluzzo-monster's rage would have a different target.

And what a shock they would have, when their steel and iron weapons and armor did not protect them.

Outside, on the street, Eneko Lopez fell to one knee. His hands clasped his head as if he'd been struck by a sudden and ferocious pain-lance straight into his brain.

The Venetian soldiers paused, as did Manfred and Erik. The arresting unit was still some twenty yards from the Casarini house. There was a full moon out, this night, so the house was clearly visible.

"What's wrong, Eneko?"

The priest seemed unable to speak. Manfred could see that his face was tight with pain. It also seemed pale as a sheet, although that could have been the effect of the moonlight.

Erik waved to the sergeant commanding the ten soldiers. "Go on. There's no time to waste."

The sergeant and his men continued forward, two of the soldiers hefting axes while four others held torches aloft. Erik knelt alongside Eneko. Manfred couldn't, because he was wearing full armor. His Icelander bodyguard, as he usually did given the choice, had opted to wear nothing more than half-armor for the occasion. Erik had learned to fight in Iceland and Vinland, and never was really comfortable in the heavy Teutonic armor favored by the Knights.

"Can we do anything, Eneko?" he asked.

The priest shook his head. Then, slowly, withdrew his hands from his temples. When his eyes caught sight of the soldiers—now standing before the door, raising their axes—they widened. And his face, impossibly, seemed to grow paler still.

"Oh, dear God—*no*. Erik, get them away from that door! They will be no match for—"

It was too late. The door shattered from within, not a second after the first axe landed. *Something* erupted out of it. Because of the darkness, it was difficult to see it clearly. Manfred could only discern a thing of scales and wings and horns and talons, with a face like a gargoyle's, shrieking fury.

The soldier holding the axe was smashed aside, by a taloned paw that shredded his throat in passing. A backhand blow from the same paw sent the other axe-wielding soldier sprawling, knocking down two other soldiers with him, their torches scattering.

The monster took a stride forward and crushed the sergeant's skull, its talons stripping away the helmet as if it were a mere skullcap. Then, to Manfred's horror, seized the sergeant by the shoulders as he collapsed and *bit* his head in half. The fangs sheered through the poor man's skull and brains like a knife through cheese.

The creature flung the sergeant's corpse aside and spit out the top part of his head, then spread its huge arms and bellowed with rage and a kind of hideous, triumphant glee.

Still, the moments the demon had taken to kill the sergeant had given the rest of the soldiers the time to back away. Back away *frantically.* Two of them dropped their weapons and simply ran. The remaining soldiers stood their ground, more or less, but they looked about as confident as five-year-boys facing a tiger in full fury.

Manfred felt calm settling over him, a calm so profound it was almost serenity.

"There's always adventures when you're around, Eneko," he said cheerfully, drawing his broadsword. "Erik, get that creature's attention for me, if you would."

Manfred stepped forward, holding his sword in both hands, the huge blade gleaming in the moonlight. From the corner of his eye, he could see that Erik was hesitating. Not surprising, of course—the Icelander was supposed to guard the prince from danger, after all, not draw the attention of monsters upon him.

"*Now*, Erik." Manfred's voice was soft, but the words came like iron. The commanding words of a prince, when all was said and done.

Erik stared at Manfred. And then, felt calmness coming over him as well.

He knew, finally, in that moment, what he had begun to suspect for some time. If Manfred survived his life—no telling *that*, of course—he would become one of Europe's great legends.

So be it. Erik Hakkonsen had been charged with guarding a prince, not just a man. He could hardly complain if, in the end, the man lived up to his station. A true prince was not simply an heir; he was also charged with protecting his people.

Erik drew his tomahawk, stepped forward and hurled it. Unerringly, the weapon flew toward the demon—unseen by it in the dark of night—and struck the creature between its horns.

Had Erik been using the proper Algonquin tomahawk he'd once had, that strike might well have felled the monster itself. As it was, the blade sank into the skull but didn't succeed in splitting the creature's brains. Not too surprising, of course. The thing's skull was considerably thicker than the little brain remaining within.

The demon screamed with pain and fury, its vaguely boarlike face swinging toward Erik and Manfred. Erik thought the eyes gleamed red; though it was difficult to be sure of color, in the dim moonlight.

Manfred took another step forward. *"Come to me, beast!"*

Still screaming, the demon sprang off the stoop and hurtled down the street toward Manfred. Its wings were spread fully now, and flapping. They were not sufficient to lift the great, heavy thing off the ground entirely, but they enabled it to race forward at an inhuman speed.

An instant later, the horrible creature was leaping in the air, sailing down upon Manfred like a hawk stooping on a chicken.

A very large and dangerous chicken. Manfred's great shoulders hunched and he swept the sword across, chest-high to the demon.

"*DIA A COIR!*"

It was an incredible sword-strike. The blade severed the monster in half. The upper half, still screaming, bounced off Manfred's lowered helmet and shoulders and spilled on the street behind him, almost at Eneko's feet. The lower half, gushing ichor and intestines, flopped backward.

Eneko Lopez stared at the thing writhing in front of him, the boar's face with its tusks still gnashing, the taloned paws scrabbling at the cobblestones.

He raised his crucifix. "That which cannot abide the name of—"

He never finished the sentence. *THUNK*. Manfred's sword removed the monster's head entirely, sending it rolling down the street like a loose cannonball. Erik hurried after it, muttering something about lost tomahawks.

THUNK. Manfred's sword, driven straight down with both hands, pierced the monster's spine and pinned the torso to the street itself. Whether by luck or simply the prince's great strength, the tip of the blade wedged itself between two cobblestones.

Meanwhile, working both fearfully and frantically, the soldiers were hacking the lower part of the demon's body into pieces. It was hideous work, if not particularly dangerous—though one soldier was knocked off his feet by a reflexive kick from one of the monster's flailing legs. Fortunately, the leg ended in a hoof instead of talons, so the soldier suffered nothing worse than a bad bruise.

The demon's torso was still twitching, but more feebly now. Eneko looked down the street the other way and saw that Erik was returning—his tomahawk in one hand and the demon's head held by one bat-shaped ear in the other. The head's maw was still gnashing, and, as the priest watched, made an attempt to bite Erik on the leg.

"Stupid," Manfred grunted.

Sure enough, Erik set the head down on a nearby stoop and proceeded to smash out all its fangs with the tomahawk. Three quick blows, delivered with all of Erik's skill with the weapon, and there really wasn't much left of the thing except blood and bone fragments, held together by strips of hide.

Not that Erik was probably planning to mount it as a trophy, anyway. Manfred glared down at his sword.

"Damnation," he growled. "It's going to take me *hours* to sharpen it properly. Eneko, sometimes I think you're more trouble than you're worth."

The priest rose to his feet, scowling. "We're not finished yet, Prince Manfred. This"—he pointed at the demon's carcass—"was just a tool. The real monster is still inside."

Eneko looked at the shattered door, feeling immensely frustrated. "Or not. Probably not, any longer. That's why the creature set this thing loose. I sensed the incantation—as horrible as any I've ever encountered—which is what sent me to my knees."

Manfred's bull-like strength was put to use again. Even for him, withdrawing the sword was a struggle. But, within a few seconds, he and Erik were pushing through the entrance into the house. Their weapons ready, with Eneko and his crucifix coming right behind.

And, as Eneko had foreseen, it was too late. Bianca Casarini was gone.

Within a minute, they'd found the escape route she'd taken. But the elderly couple living in the adjoining house seemed comatose, and their own rear entrance was wide open.

After looking down that street, Manfred stated the obvious. "It's nighttime. She could be anywhere, by now."

Chapter 93

As soon as she entered Morando's cellar from the secret entrance, and closed the wall behind her, Bianca felt a thrilling surge of triumph. Her plans were working—and working perfectly!

She'd be safe from discovery here. The Venetian authorities in the Citadel had, weeks earlier, sealed the front entrance to Morando's domicile. They'd had to, in order to put a stop to the constant stream of curious visitors. That meant no one would even think of reopening the cellar and looking in it again.

Only one danger remained, and she'd deal with that now. Bianca went directly to the altar, not bothering to look around. The altar was a fake, true enough, but put to Bianca's use instead of the charlatan Morando's, it would serve her purpose.

Quickly, using the tools and ingredients in the bag she'd brought with her, she performed the necessary ritual. Not like the much more difficult scrying in blood she needed to use to speak with her putative mistress, this was a simple thing—communication by fire. Nothing that the powers of Corfu would be able to touch or hinder.

She kindled the flame of a candle made of the rendered fat of an unbaptized baby; then bent over the flame, cupping her hands about it, and whispered a single name.

This was a mild incantation, not something she had any fear that the cursed Lopez would be able to detect. In and of itself, simply a communication—and with someone whom she'd prepared long ago for the purpose.

※　※　※

In his cell, Morando suddenly awoke, gasping for breath.

"Bianca?" he whispered. "Is that you?"

He saw the image of her beautiful face emerge, seeming like an apparition in midair. She was smiling gently.

"It's me, Aldo. But keep your voice down."

"Thank God!" Then, speaking softly: "Listen, they still don't know anything about you—and they say they'll commute my sentence to ten years on the galleys. So with your help—"

"*Nothing*, Aldo? They don't know about the secret entrance to the cellar?"

He shook his head. "No, I kept that from them. The only—"

He got no further. Bianca said some words he didn't catch and a sudden sharp pain stabbed through his chest. He gasped, clutching his chest with both hands.

Dimly, through the pain, he saw Bianca's smile widen. "Poor Aldo," she said. "That's the needle you're feeling. The one I implanted below your skin months ago while you were sleeping— and then numbed the nerves in the area, so you'd never sense it."

Her mouth worked, speaking more words. He knew it was an incantation of some kind, though he didn't understand the words themselves. "It's working its way into your heart now. Don't be concerned, though. I don't have time to enjoy this properly. It'll all be over within a minute."

The agony was now too intense for speech, or even screaming; the shock, even more so. He simply gaped at her, until he died.

In Casarini's abandoned house, Eneko Lopez broke off his part of the search they were conducting. His hands started to fly to his temples, again. But, this time, his frustration and anger was so great that he slammed them against a wall instead.

"*May the saints blast the monster! She's doing it again!*"

He leaned against the wall, shuddering. His face full of concern, Manfred took a step toward him.

Then, suddenly, the priest whole body grew rigid. "Wait," he murmured. "Something is happening . . ."

Perhaps a minute later, Eneko pushed away from the wall and turned toward Manfred. To the prince's astonishment, there was a smile on the priest face.

A very, very, very grim smile. "I shall have to do penance for this, of course," said the priest. "Vengeance is, indeed, the province of the Lord. Still, I can't help but treasure this moment."

As she turned away from the altar, smiling broadly with satisfaction—treachery was *so* sweet—Bianca was startled by a sudden motion in the darkness of the cellar.

Sophia Tomaselli's face loomed in front of her. Bianca barely recognized the woman. The once-fastidious *Case Vecchie* looked like a hag. Filthy, her hair disarrayed—and with a hag's contorted grimace.

"You bitch! This is *my* refuge!"

Too late, Bianca saw that Sophia held a heavy candlestick in one hand—and was raising it to strike.

She threw up her arm to block the blow, but her recent use of two powerful incantations had left her very fatigued. She couldn't get the arm up in time. The brass candlestick smashed into her forehead like a mallet, sending her dazed and half-conscious to the floor.

Consciousness returned perhaps thirty seconds later, pain leading the way.

She couldn't breathe!

Her hands flew to her throat. There was something—

It was a silk scarf, she realized. Digging deeply into her throat, cutting off all air and blood. Somewhere behind her, Sophia Tomaselli was holding the thing, strangling her as Bianca had once strangled a niece.

"You stinking slut! Aldo's mine, not yours!"

Tomaselli's words came in grunts, sounding more like something uttered by a peasant than a noblewoman. "Besides," Sophia hissed, "there's not . . . enough food. I'll share it . . . with Aldo . . . when he comes . . . but not *you*."

Bianca was frantic now. The situation was absurd. How could such a pathetic creature as *Sophia Tomaselli* possibly be a threat to her? But the fact remained that the hag was in such a frenzy that she'd kill Bianca if she weren't stopped.

Automatically, Bianca started to utter the incantations that would destroy the creature—only to realize, then, that whether Sophia understood what she was doing or not, strangling a sorceress is perhaps the safest way to kill her.

She couldn't speak a word! In fact, her mind was becoming so fuzzy from lack of air that she wasn't sure she could have remembered the words well enough to incant them properly, even if she had been able to speak.

Bianca went into a paroxysm of terror, writhing and twisting on the floor. But everywhere she went, Sophia stayed on top of her—like some hideous leech, sucking out her life.

Desperately, she planted her hands on what part of Sophia she could reach. Nothing more than her hips, unfortunately, which were protected by the woman's tattered but still richly thick garments. The pain touch worked much better on bare skin—especially skin with a lot of nerves close to the surface. Even if she could have clawed her way past the fabric to Sophia's buttocks, she'd only have been touching fatty flesh.

Still, Bianca used the last of her strength to send agony pouring into Sophia's body as best she could. And a great deal of agony it was, too, despite the handicaps. Bianca Casarini was fighting for her life, and the agony she summoned was driven by a will to live that had sent her into every foulness imaginable, for years.

It was perhaps the worst thing she could have done, not that she really had any options. Sophia's body arched like a suddenly drawn bow from the excruciating pain—but her hands, clenched by the same agony, never let go of the scarf. The silk that had been choking Casarini now collapsed her windpipe completely, crushing it into ruin.

Bianca spit out blood, feeling her life going with it.

I can't believe it! Sophia Tomaselli!
I WANTED TO LIVE FOREVER!

"She's dead," Eneko said grimly. "I felt the monster dying. I knew the moment she was gone."

He knelt and crossed himself, then kissed the crucifix, reverentially—and yet, Erik thought, with some other emotion as well. Guilt? Regret? Though Erik could not imagine what Eneko Lopez could possibly have to feel guilty about, at least in this instance.

"How did she die?" asked Erik.

After he rose to his feet, Lopez shrugged. "That, I couldn't tell you. I am not clairvoyant, you know. I could simply sense the monster's frantic attempts to use magic to forestall her death—somebody or something was killing her, that much I know, though I couldn't tell you who or what—and her eventual failure."

His expression was grimmer than Manfred had ever seen it—and Eneko was a man given to a grim view of the world. "'Vengeance is mine, sayeth the Lord,'" he heard the priest murmur. "Still . . . the beast died in great despair as well as fury. It was fitting."

And you shall *live forever, Bianca Casarini. Oh, yes, most certainly.*

Confused, Bianca opened her eyes. She was more confused, then, by what she saw.

First, because all the images seemed duplicated—no, multiplied, many times over.

Oh, you'll get accustomed to compound eyes soon enough. Perhaps unfortunately, from your point of view. Not mine, of course.

The strange voice seemed to be coming from all directions at once. Bianca's eyes moved over the . . . landscape?

Hard to tell. It just seemed like a world made of cables. A kind of enormous net of cables. Dirty-white in color, stretching to what seemed like infinity. She sensed that the effect was not simply caused by the weird multiplication of her vision.

A reddish glow somewhere to her left drew her gaze that way. Dully, she stared at it for a while. How long, she couldn't say. She seemed to have difficulty determining the passage of time.

The color of the glow changed, slowly; shading from red to yellow to, eventually, a particularly loathsome shade of yellow-green. The color of slime, if slime were as hot as lava.

Also the color she'd once seen, in a glimpse she'd gotten of the Great One. The eyes that weren't eyes at all, but something that had reminded her at the time of staring into bottomless, volcanic cesspools.

Welcome, Bianca Casarini! Welcome to eternity!

Realization finally came to her. She opened her mouth to scream.

Tried to, rather. She had no mouth. Looking down, all she could see was a proboscis of some kind, where she'd once had a nose.

Looking down still further, at her body, she saw that her lungs were now on the outside, red-veined and pulsing.

Oh, yes, that. I'm afraid that certain physical laws still apply here. On this level, at any rate. There are quite a bit more than nine, incidentally. How many? Hard to say. Depends on which mathematical formula you use.

She tried to scream again. The only effect was to make her proboscis grow more rigid—and cause the lungs to pulsate quicker.

Yes, yes, I'm afraid so. Volume to surface-area ratios, that sort of thing. All very tawdry, I'm afraid. It also means that discreet little spiracles won't do the trick at all. So I've had to modify your lungs a bit.

It does make you hideously ugly, true. But, then, that's now the least of your problems. I'm afraid Crocell lost his sexual appetites long ago—and wouldn't care in the least if you were still as comely as you were.

Paralysis was giving way to terror. Bianca's eyes now ranged down the rest of her body.

There were *way* too many legs, and she was quite sure that wasn't simply a function of her strange new vision. Skinny, weirdly jointed, *hairy* legs.

Six legs, to be precise. I'm something of a stickler when it comes to tradition. Very conservative, actually, despite my reputation as a rebel.

Ah. Here comes Crocell, now. Give him a nice run, would you, Bianca? I have to keep him well-exercised, for the rare occasions when I let him out.

She sensed the vibration first. Looking down, she saw that her feet—*feet? what were those horrid claw-like things?*—were planted on one such cable. The cable seemed to be undulating. As if some great weight had been placed upon it.

She twisted her body—awkwardly, since she was unaccustomed to its new shape—and saw that a monster was moving toward her along the cable. Like a great spider, except for the face.

It was the face that finally broke what was left of Bianca Casarini's self-control. For some reason, the sight of a middle-aged man's face on such a monster—except that he possessed mandibles as well as jaws—was more horrifying than anything else.

Worst of all, was the look of bleak despair in the man's eyes. Utter and complete despair, such as Bianca had never seen before—not even in the eyes of her own victims.

Crocell was a much *better cheater than you were, Bianca. Oh, much better. That's why he gets a privileged position here. So to speak.*

As I said, I even let him out now and then. A privilege which, I'm afraid, you'll not be enjoying.

Bianca fled down the cable, shrieking silently. She could feel the cable thrumming beneath her feet, under the treads of something much heavier than she.

Oh, please, Bianca! Have no fear—after he sucks out your juices, I'll replenish them again. It's agonizingly painful, of course, but not terminal in the least.

If only she could scream!

No, no, not in the least bit terminal. Even though you were planning to cheat me, I'm not at all vengeful. Despite what you may have heard.

If only she could scream!

You wanted eternal life, Bianca Casarini. And now you have it.

If only she could scream!

As food.

PART XIV
January, 1540 A.D.

Chapter 94

"They've landed on Vidos Island!"

Like everyone else, Benito scrambled out of bed and rushed for a viewpoint of the island off to the northeast of the Citadel. Benito eyed the beached vessels on the island with impotent fury. The castle's defenders were firing, but it was obviously too little and far too late.

Vidos Island had guarded the northern sea access to the Citadel. Now, with the island obviously under heavy attack, the people of the fortress realized that there would be no place that would be entirely free from cannon fire. There would be no respite. The cannon from Vidos would not be able to hit the Citadel, but the Byzantine fleet would now be able to sail into that area and shell the Citadel without coming under direct fire from both flanks.

Benito strode off in search of Manfred. He found him standing with Erik contemplating the situation grimly. "They're in the outer walls of the island already," said the Icelander. "The keep might hold out a while, but it won't be for too long."

"And they'll be able to harry the northeast too." Benito sighed. With Emeric's latest increase in bombardment on the city itself, rather than just the walls, much of the population had taken to at least sleeping over there. True, very few people had been killed by the cannon fire, but it was frightening and hurt morale. Knowing there was no place that they could truly get away from the possibility of a cannonball killing them—or, worse, their children—was going to dent morale even further. Emeric was slowly chipping away at the spirit of Citadel with starvation and fear.

741

"We need to strike back somehow."

"A sortie is out of the question," Manfred said. "You two have forced Emeric to invest more in defense than he has in attacking capability. The shingle out there is a set of death traps for horses."

"Then let's take it to the bastards by sea," urged Benito. "We've got the fireboats. If the keep on Vidos hasn't fallen by tonight, they'll have all their carracks bunched around the island, firing ship's cannon at the keep."

Manfred cocked his head at Erik. "You've looked at those cockle-shells. What do you think?"

Erik nodded. "Almost all of their larger cannon are on the carracks. The cannon on those carracks are what they've mostly been using to harass the Citadel from the sea with anyway. Burn them and you'll reduce their marine gunnery to a pitiful effort."

"But will it work?"

Erik shrugged. "Those little boats are works of shipbuilder's art, Manfred. They've got one weakness: they were built to run straight with the wind. If we can row them to a point where they're directly upwind, leave each of them with a slow-match and a dead bearing . . . well, it is going to be a question of how well we aim and how well we can judge the slow-match time. You'd be aim-ing a small boat at a small target a long way away. Most of them would miss. Still, it's worth trying. We're not going to get as many Byzantine ships so close together again. Get one of those little sailing bombs in among them and we'll likely see a fair number catch fire."

Benito compressed his lips. "We're *not* going to miss. Not if I have to ride those little ships all the way in myself. Call it Umberto's legacy. The Little Arsenal has about fifteen longboats. The Byzantines would either have to up anchor and out oars in the dark, or, with the light galleys beached at Vidos, launch. It's the better part of a mile . . . but with a start and twelve rowers we should do it."

"What are you suggesting, Benito?"

"We lower longboats. Give each team two fireboats to tow out. The enemy are going to be focused on Vidos. We should be able to get really close—they're firing and the muzzle-flash will be easy to see. Set the fireboats on their line, leave one man to each, have him jump overboard at the last moment. With luck, the longboats will recover the aimers."

"Why does someone need to stay with each fireboat?"

"Because they don't have steerage if they aren't moving quite fast." He saw the puzzled look on Manfred's face. "Just take it from me or Erik. That's how it works, Manfred."

Manfred looked at him with a strange expression. "You'll need men who are tired of life, Benito. The longboats won't be able to hang about looking for anyone."

"Manfred, we're starving. We're down to four cupfuls of water a day per man. You don't have to be tired of life to volunteer for this—you have to want, desperately, to live." He shook his head. "The people down at the Little Arsenal are furious about Umberto's murder. They're tired of being powerless to do anything. A lot of them—especially the caulkers—swim like fish. The caulkers have to, for when there's a sprung plank. There's only so much you can do to repair a ship from the inside, and if the ship's on the water it means diving with a rope around your waist and some wadding. I'll get volunteers all right." He sighed. "I'll get too many."

"You know I will not assist in the war of one Christian soldier against another," said Eneko Lopez. "Regardless of what vileness Emeric delves into or what Chernobog does, most of Emeric's troops and the Byzantine soldiers are of our faith."

Benito held up his hands pacifyingly. "I'm not proposing you do anything that kills anyone, Eneko. All I was hoping for was some way to save good men from drowning in the darkness. Like the glowing winged Lion on the sails of the great galleys."

Eneko Lopez looked at him with those penetrating eyes, and apparently decided in Benito's favor. "Tell me what you are planning. I suppose I should be grateful that a fiendish mind like yours is on the side opposing Chernobog and the Devil-worshipers."

Benito told him. Eneko Lopez shook his head. "And you have thirty men prepared to do this?"

"I think at last count even places on the longboats were double-subscribed." Benito looked at Eneko consideringly. "You know, Father Lopez—everybody always lectures or preaches to me. Antimo said it was my face. Now I'm going to do the same for you, seeing as you've also done it to me." He grinned wryly. "Fair's fair, after all. You priests, Justices—even princes—seem to think you have the monopoly on a sense of justice. It isn't like that at all. I promise you the scuolo, the boat-people, hell, even thieves, have a sense of justice. Of what is right. It may not always be what the priests and others think is right, but they believe in it. And they're prepared to pay a high price for what they believe in. The Arsenalotti are angry and frustrated about this siege, and about the murder. Umberto was a quiet fellow, but he was theirs. He'd stood by them, he'd bled for them. Maria too. The Corfiotes think more of her than they do of the governor, for instance. They're bitter about her loss. She's even won over the Illyrians. I've got men who can't swim volunteering. I had four times what I wanted for the fireboats. Now, are you going to help me keep these men alive or are you going to get sanctimonious with me?"

Eneko Lopez looked at him in silence. Then he drew a deep breath. "I stand humbled. You know, those of us who fight the battle for the human spirit do so because we believe in its potential. We are, after all, made in the image of God. But sometimes we spend so much time isolated and only dealing with the bad that we forget. Yes. Some luminescence can be magically contained in small bottles. It is not without cost, but I suppose if you fail and the Citadel falls . . . evil will have its day unchecked."

"I'll take the bottles with gratitude," said Benito. "But as for 'unchecked,' Eneko, short of clearing Corfu of people, Emeric is just going to meet unending resistance, whether we're here or not. Erik sowed the wind out there. Emeric is reaping the whirlwind."

The wind was to the southeast, blowing dust from Corfu's once green fields across the Citadel. "It's not natural," grumbled one of the Corfiotes. "It should be blowing northwesterly."

"And it should be raining, too," said his friend with a dry smile. "And then we could row twice as far and get wet from above with fresh water and below with salt. Stop complaining, Dimitros."

His companion continued blackening his face. "I need something to keep my mind busy. This is crazy!"

"Have your tot of grappa, and let's get on with it."

One by one, the small boats were lowered into the sea. In tense silence now, the little flotilla began running out toward the muzzle flashes around Vidos. The inner keep had no large cannon. The Byzantine vessels were perfectly safe.

But some good admiral had still deployed a couple of small galliots to patrol. Benito thought his heart would stop when one of them loomed up through the darkness.

"What ships?" called the watchman on the prow.

"Tell them we're some Greek name, we've sprung a leak and we're taking water," whispered Benito. "And then we row like hell. We have to board them."

Obviously, at least five of the longboats had had the same idea. The small galliot was a twenty-oar vessel—but she was quartering the wind and the oars were shipped. Abandoning all stealth the longboats closed fast.

Shots rang out . . . and then they were on board, desperate Venetians and Corfiotes, outnumbering the crew, boarding from several vessels. The silence they'd hoped for was a lost dream. Now all they could do was move fast.

Benito had volunteered for the fireboats. The *scuolo* liked him too much to tell him he was an inexperienced amateur seaman. Besides, he was lucky. And crazy. They needed that, too.

A caulker grabbed him by the shoulder. "Come, milord. The lads are getting the sails up. We'll deal with this ship. You get to yours. There'll be trouble coming."

Benito scrambled over the side of the galliot and onto the fireboat assigned to him. Someone handed down the slow-match. "Go Valdosta! Go!"

The darkness ahead was Vidos. With the fireboat's sixteen feet of oil-and-gunpowder-laden hull accelerating beneath the belling sail, Benito did what steering was possible. Then he put the rudder into the bracket. She'd run straight now, but any lookout attracted by the shooting out at the galliot could hardly miss her. Just as he thought that, Benito realized that the carracks at anchor were firing now, not at Vidos Castle keep, but at them. Salt spray flying, Benito touched the slow-match to the fuse. It sputtered and lit. Taking a deep breath, Benito dove overboard.

The water was chilly. As he came up the night sky was suddenly lit by an explosion and a plume of flames. One of the fireboats wasn't going to get to the fleet.

Benito tugged at the bottle tied to his waist. "Fiat lux!" he spluttered.

There was light. There were other lights in the water, mostly farther back toward the Citadel. And the oil from the cannon-hit fireboat was burning on the water—much too close for comfort. Benito took a desperate look around, wondered how long he could hold his breath and swim underwater, and resolved he'd drown before he burned.

Then a longboat with the boatswain calling stroke, as if this were a regular trip out to a carrack at anchor, came out of the darkness and hauled him inboard. "I might have known you'd be the closest to the enemy," said a wet Erik, grimly. "We've lost a good few men, and the galleys are going to be after us. Look."

Benito saw a galley silhouetted against the flames. Saw the muzzle flash. And laughed helplessly. "That's the one we captured, Erik. It looks like the boys are trying to take it home."

There was huge explosion and flash behind them. The men at the oars pulled. The little boat raced toward the Citadel. Vidos might fall, but, as Benito peered back at the pandemonium of fireboats exploding, he knew Umberto's idea made sure it hadn't been a cheap victory for King Emeric.

It was a fitting repayment.

It was morning before they could see just exactly what the damage had been. Benito already knew the cost. Four men had not been picked up. One, Dimitros, had ridden his fireboat right in, while his longboat team, rowing frantically behind, had screamed at him to jump. Only God knew what had been in his mind now; presumably he was explaining himself to the recording angel, trying to persuade him that it hadn't been suicide. In attacking the galliot, now beached on the northern shingle beside the *San Nicolo* and *Dolphin's* hulks, the Venetians and Corfiotes had suffered nine wounded and five killed.

They'd seen that some of the Byzantine fleet had burned last night. But now at first light every survivor (who wasn't in the hospital) of what was being called "Umberto's revenge" was on the northern wall looking out. Counting ships.

There was silence. "Lord and Saints," said someone awed. "If we could come along now with four great galleys we'd hold the sea!"

That might have been something of an exaggeration. But the carrack fleet was considerably reduced. The fire had taken—or made the skippers run up onto Vidos—at least fifteen carracks, the bulk of the cannon-bearing vessels.

But it was the flag on the outer walls of Vidos castle that brought a cheer that must have rung right across the bay between them. When the fireboats had struck, the besiegers must have run to the shore. The island's trees had also caught fire, and the galleys and smaller craft the enemy had landed with must have had to either be rescued or burn. And the surviving soldiers had used the opportunity to retake the outer walls. How long the small garrison could keep the winged lion flying there was another matter, as the gate must be smashed. But it was a heartwarming sight, nonetheless.

A gunner from the walls of Vidos celebrated first light with a round into a largely intact carrack.

But looking at the cheering men and women on the Citadel, Benito couldn't escape the fact that they were all gaunt. The siege had now lasted more than eight months. Starvation might beat them yet, even if they'd just singed Emeric's beard for him.

Chapter 95

"We still hold total military superiority here on the island. We've still got some several hundred men on Vidos, and the barricade the defenders have put up on the gate's ruins can't hold."

General Krovoko was trying to put the best face on the situation that he could, but he was going to have to tell all of the truth, and he knew it—as he knew of Emeric's propensity to kill the messenger. "But the Byzantines are whimpering. With the bad weather most of their fleet was here in the shelter, so, naturally, we used them for the attack on Vidos. It was a fiasco. They were anchored in close formation off the southern side of the islet. When they saw the fireboats, several captains tried to run."

Anger crept into his tone. "If they'd just stayed put we'd have lost half as many vessels. In the dark, in panic, they ran into each other, fired cannon into each other, ran aground or just plain ran. Three of the vessels ran all the way to the Albanian shore and one of them was wrecked. We had a ship, burning, make landfall at Kommeno point. The local people killed most of the crew before the cavalry arrived. We lost nineteen carracks, and three galleys, with fire damage to another four vessels. We're down to seven carracks. The blockade, with nothing more than the Narenta galliots and that handful, is worth little, Sire."

General Krovoko was done with his report. Now he waited, fatalistically, for the sky to fall on him. Emeric pushed himself back in his throne. "I know. But that's not really what concerns me. The Atlantic fleet hasn't come home and we know that the eastern fleet is still sitting in Trebizond after their attempt on the Dardanelles.

It's the steady trickle of losses here on the island that worries me, especially as the weather, and the lack of ships, limit my fetching more troops."

Krovoko shook his head. He was a little surprised to find himself still alive and discussing the matter. "Sire, the countryside is definitely hostile, the insurgents in the north must number in the hundreds, and although we've taken Kassiopi, Paleokastritsa still holds out. The place is inaccessible and the locals have managed to resupply when the insurgents have attacked the forces we have there."

"But the island grows drier. Lack of water must be affecting them."

General Krovoko nodded. "What we really is need a safe place to rest our men. This campaign of raids and ambushes . . . it's wearing them down, Sire."

Emeric looked thoughtful, but offered no comment.

The Magyar cavalryman pointed to the map. "We can land men here, on the mainland, near this lake. Make a base for accumulating supplies and let the troops rest. We have more men than we need for the siege, and less than we need to hold siege and subdue the island. They'll be safe from the Venetians or even Corfiotes."

The Narenta pirate captain muttered in his dialect. It was, by the tone, something derisive.

Emeric looked coldly at him. "What was that?"

The pirate captain looked uneasy, but stood his ground. "I said that would be escaping from an angry cat into the lion's den. That is Iskander Beg's land. The Lord of the Mountains will not like it."

Emeric pinched his lips into a harsh line. "He doesn't have to like it. I've tried to contact him, to reach an agreement with the bandit. Well, he doesn't wish to treat with me. I would have preferred to bring my men here by land, but the mountains have too many places where ambushes are easy. But the land next to the lake is gentle. With the lake behind us, the sea in front, this should be an easy strip to hold. I like the idea. See to it, General. It will act as one side to the pincer I want to work on the coastal strip. I'll leave the bandit chief to his mountains. We'll hold the lowlands from here to Montenegro in the next few years.

"Now onto other affairs. We must press the attack on the Citadel hard now. Let drought take the rest of the island."

"We've walled and entrenched the moles," said Dragorvich. "The troops can move forward protected. The front wall is crumbling. Give us another two weeks' cannonade, Sire. A determined push will take the first curtain wall."

"You can have a few weeks. I want them pounded into submission. At the end of February—or at the latest, early March—we must be in. The Venetians will doubtless make something of a push in the spring with whatever ships they have ready. We'll want at least three weeks to repair and reequip the Citadel against that attack."

"We're down to third-rations." It was so dry that Maria and the other horta gatherers were not finding much to gather. Winter was not the best time for wild greens anyway, but there had always been something. . . .

But with this many women, and a restricted area to hunt in, it was getting less easy by the day. The sound of the cannons was by now such a normal part of the background noise, that it was only its stopping that they would have noticed. The attack on the walls now was relentless. The Hungarians had so increased their forward positions and fortifications that they could sally and attack the walls repeatedly with relative impunity. Food ships and water carts arrived for them each day. Here inside it was relentless starvation and less in the water ration by the day. Maria's biggest worry was having milk for Alessia. Two of the other women's breasts had already dried up. Too little water. Too little food. Alessia now weighed less than she had two months ago.

Maria could not weep for Umberto anymore; she dared not waste the water on tears. What would she do if her milk dried up? It was a constant nagging fear.

"I know it's risky," said Benito, irritably. "But we're on our last legs here. If we actually knew when they were coming, it would make the world of difference. Come, Eneko. Please."

The cleric nodded, wearily. "Very well. We'll try again."

But there was no response.

Marco had an almost overpowering compulsion to make contact with his brother. But both Mascoli and the Strega sage Du Catres who sailed with them advised against it. They had, to be precise, forbidden it utterly. Marco had insisted on going on this voyage. "They'll need healers and food more than soldiers," he'd said. Finally Doge Dorma had given permission for him to go. Under conditions. The first was the shield of mages who accompanied him. The second was that Kat remained in Venice, at least until the siege was lifted. Dorma made it very clear that he would prefer it to be until Marco returned.

The priestess looked at the half-almond on the altar, and wondered. There was only one candidate. She had explained everything, as best she could. She had instructed, without demanding, without, as far as she could tell, even hinting. The candidate must choose of her own free will; that was the law. But would she? Would she even see the need?

She must. She must. Or they would all die here. Perhaps, even, the Goddess, and the Cold God.

Yes. Perhaps even them.

PART XV
March, 1540 A.D.

Chapter 96

"Back!" shouted Erik. "Back to the inner curtain-wall!"

Maria watched as the knights charged again, making space and time for the footmen and others to pull back without endangering the wall. Benito was out there, somewhere. Rearguard, setting explosives with the Knights' bombardier. She herself had only just gotten up here, having led the women up from the wall by the Little Arsenal. Toward the end, they'd been reduced to throwing cobbles and bricks at the enemy. The arquebusiers had shot out their powder. Blades were blunted and nicked. And yet there always seemed to be more foes.

Maria closed her eyes to pray, then opened them, looking at the scene below. Already the bulk of the Hungarian forces were pouring in through the breach in the outer wall. The inner wall, which enclosed the Castel *a mar* and the Castel *a terra*, was higher than the outer curtain wall—but it certainly wasn't thicker. And the wells in the upper part of Citadel were long dry. True, they'd all taken part in the filling of the huge cisterns up in the Castels . . . uphill all the way, carrying water ewers. But when that was gone, there would be no more.

According to Benito, the water available might last the ten thousand people inside the Citadel two weeks. The cisterns had been intended for the garrison only. On wet, verdant Corfu, the wells and the two springs in the inner citadel never ran dry.

Except now. There was an evil thing out there, as the high priestess had explained. A spirit of dryness, fire and death. A thing that caused green life to wither just by its existence.

Maria sighed. First her home. Then Umberto. And now this. They were being devoured slowly. She made her way through the crowded streets and to the hospital and the Hypatian chapel, where some women and the children who were too young to fling rocks had been sent when it was realized this was an assault that might actually succeed. Stella had taken Alessia and a number of other *scuolo* and Corfiote children so that the younger women could go to help on the walls.

She found Stella at the chapel, looking stunned and crying. "Alberto—he's missing! They tell me he was shot. He was with the rearguard. There was no one to bring him in. Dear God! Dear God!"

For once her children were silent. Big eyed. Scared, even the ones too young to fully understand.

Maria couldn't find words, so she simply hugged her, hard. The older woman clung to her. Maria swallowed. "Stella. You . . . you stood by me, when, when Umberto and I were new and friendless. You were there when there was that curse and others avoided me. You've stood by me. I'll help as much as I can."

Stella pulled away, despair warring with anger in her face. "God's Death, Maria, don't you understand? We're all going to die here. My man. My babies. All of us. We'll either die of thirst and starvation or the Hungarian monsters will get us."

Maria picked up Alessia. The little girl hung listlessly in her arms. "I'll do something. I have to."

She turned and walked out of the chapel. A horrible thought had just crossed her mind. If there had been no one to bring Alberto in . . . where was Benito? He was with the rearguard. Benito would always choose the hardest, the riskiest task. He would be in the front of the vanguard . . . and at the back of the rearguard. Maria went searching.

Eventually she found Erik and Manfred. The prince's armor was dented. His visor was now up and there was blood oozing from a small cut above his eye.

"Prince Manfred. I'm looking for Benito."

He looked a little annoyed that someone should trouble him at this stage. At the mention of Benito's name, though, the expression eased.

"Last I saw of him was when we were returning from that final sortie. He and a couple of others—a big fellow and another man—

were lighting the charges to the houses on the road. Have you seen him, Erik?"

Erik frowned. "No. And he's supposed to report to me. Check with the gate guards. Wait. I'll come with you. That'll get answers."

Very shortly, Maria knew the worst.

Seven of the rearguard hadn't reached the gate. Alberto and Benito were both among them.

Benito. Gone.

What little remained of the bottom of her world crumbled and fell away, leaving her hollow and utterly, utterly alone.

She turned blindly from Erik, not hearing what he said, and walked away. Alessia whimpered and nuzzled weakly, but Maria had no milk to give her. Maria's eyes remained dry. There were no tears to cry now. The time for weeping was over.

She'd lost Umberto . . . He'd not been her soulmate, perhaps, but he'd been someone she'd gone from liking to loving. And now she'd lost the man she'd truly loved, too. Benito was gone. She hadn't even had a chance to say good-bye to him, much less tell him—well, much of anything. Except that he was a fool. Which he was. And that his wildness was going to get him killed.

Which it had.

And very soon she'd lose her baby, too. Alessia was dying, slowly, of hunger; the worst of all possible deaths. Even being spitted on a Hungarian spear was better than this, dying by inches.

And that was when she knew what she had to do.

It came to her, all of a piece; not as a blinding flash of revelation, but settling over her like a blanket. Certainty. And perhaps it was folly equal to Benito's, or insanity, and perhaps her soul would be damned, or perhaps it just wouldn't work at all . . . but there was only one person here who could and would do what she was about to. Therefore, she would do it. She had nothing to lose, now. Except Alessia, and if she did not do this thing, Alessia was lost anyway.

There was only one way forward. Squaring her chin, Maria walked determinedly through the frightened crowds, onward and upward to the Castel *a mar*—

—to see the high priestess. To tell her that she was ready to become the bride of the master of the black altar.

The guards recognized her; let her pass unquestioned. It all happened very quickly.

Renate was waiting for her, her hair loose, her white robe on.

"If you had not come—" The priestess looked exhausted, and seemed twenty years older than when Maria had first come to the island.

"Well," she said. "I did."

They took the passage down from the Castel to the hidden temple.

"Merde! They've come up the side!"

Struggling with the weight of Alberto—he might no longer be fat, but he was still large—Benito took a side street. Alberto was plainly in shock, but was doing his best to hobble, supported by the smaller man. The road was unfamiliar to Benito, but the sound of hooves galloping up the street was not. He hauled Alberto over a low wall and they hid as a troop of Croats rode past. Lying in the shadows, Benito suddenly realized that he had in fact seen the house across there before. It was dilapidated-looking, with a smashed door that was now boarded over.

The last time he'd been there, there'd been a guard on it, to keep away the curious from the house of the "black magician," Aldo Morando. He'd been there to look at the fraud's cellar. It might do as a place to hide. Alberto needed his leg tended, needed to rest. The gates of the inner curtain wall were bound to be closed by now. They were stuck on the outside, and Benito had a feeling getting in might be next to impossible, even for him.

"Come. We must hide better before the footmen start searching for loot."

Alberto, wincing and trying not to cry out, struggled up, leaning on Benito. "God. I can't. Leave me, Valdosta."

"Can't do that. That gabby wife of yours told me to look after you, big man. Come on. There's a place just over there."

It didn't take Benito long to pry away the boards sealing the doorway. Inside, Benito found the place much as he remembered it. Even with Morando in prison people had been too superstitious, after the initial curiosity, to come here. The trapdoor, as he remembered, was in the passage. He hoped it wasn't too damaged to put back.

Only when he looked in the passage . . . the broken door wasn't there. He had to get down on hands and knees to find it. The knight's axe had split the thin stone, but someone had put it back together again and smeared dirt very carefully in the crack.

Benito used the faithful Shetland knife to lever it up. Someone had nailed the split wood together again also.

Who? And why?

The whole thing smelled of trouble. But could it be worse than the Hungarians?

He helped Alberto to the stairs. "I can crawl," said Alberto through gritted teeth. "You close it."

Benito did so, as Alberto edged his way downwards. It was as dark as Stygia in here. There was also a bad smell. Nothing very strong, just the trace of corruption that came from a putrefying corpse or carcass not buried deeply enough.

Suddenly, someone struck a light on the far side of the garish cellar. And Benito knew at last the answer to the mystery that had been plaguing Maria.

Sophia Tomaselli looked a lot more like a storybook witch now. Her once magnificent hair was wild and tangled. She wasn't wearing any clothes. She'd painted herself with something . . . black now, anyway. Some of the patterns were smeared.

She had a wheel-lock pistol. She was also swaying drunk—which was presumably why they'd made it this far.

She blinked owlishly at them. "Two of you. What's wrong with him?"

Benito really hadn't had time to look. He'd been just ahead, running for the gate when Alberto had gone down with a scream. He knew the man had been hit in the lower leg. He was in pain and bleeding. "I don't know. I'll have a look." He spoke in as level a voice as he could manage.

Sophia's eyes narrowed. "You! You're Valdosta. The wonderful hero." She snarled that out in such a way as to make it abundantly plain that whatever he was in her opinion, it was neither wonderful nor heroic.

"I need to see to his leg," said Benito calmly.

He might as well not have spoken. "Come over here. Come here or I'll shoot you." Her voice was ugly with triumph. "My prayers to the Devil have been answered. I saw how she looked at you, that *scuolo* puta . . . Baby-sit! Ha."

She stepped over to the altar and took up a knife. "Now we're going to have the true sacrifice." The little giggle that followed had a half-insane flavor to it. "The one that Morando was too scared to do. But I'm not afraid! I promised if he let me destroy her I would give him the old sacrifice. Killing you will do both. First I'm going to cut . . ." She gestured obscenely with the knife in her hand, for the first time pointing the pistol at the roof and not them.

Benito threw the Shetland knife. By now, the once-stocky boy had the shoulders and chest of a very powerful man. The blade went right through her thin chest, stopping only when the hilt slammed into the flesh. Sophia was flung backwards onto Morando's mock-altar.

Benito already had his rapier out, and was running forward. But . . .

She wasn't going to vent her spite on anyone ever again. From the amount of blood, the Shetland knife had split her heart.

"Holy mother of God! Let's get out of here!" Alberto was already trying to crawl up the stairs again.

Benito looked at the dead woman. Death had eased the lines of hatred, fear and misery from her face. "Stay there, Alberto. She was crazy and now she's dead."

"She said she prayed to the Devil to destroy Maria. That she promised human sacrifice . . ."

"And look what it got the poor silly bitch. Don't worry, Alberto. The best priest I know examined this place and said it was all a fake. A complete fraud. She was crazy and she believed in it, but it's nothing for us to worry about. Your leg and the Hungarians out there are a lot more serious." Benito tugged at his knife, struggling to free it from the bone.

"But you did come here. Here of all places."

Cleaning the knife on the piece of black velvet that Morando had used for his pseudo altar cloth, Benito shrugged. "Maria says this is Corfu. Magic here happens. And so do coincidences."

He took up the lamp and the knife and started toward Alberto. And then stopped, his eyes caught by something to the side. "Well, I'll be . . . No wonder she could hide out here! Morando must have been prepared to do just that. There's more water and food stashed in here than there is in the whole Citadel. This was a false wall."

Benito walked over to Alberto and started gently cutting the fabric away from the bloody mess. A bit of bone protruded from the jagged wound. Benito sucked breath between his teeth. "I wish I was my brother. I *really* wish he was here. I think you've got a open fracture of the fibula. I'll have to see what the hell I can find for a splint. And let's see if that woman left any of Morando's wine. I could use a cup myself, actually. Even *kakotrigi* would do."

Alberto managed a weak laugh. "*Kakotrigi* is like this place. You get used to it. Get to like it."

The hagfish had swum as close to the edge of the shingle as it dared. If anyone had looked down from the walls now, they would have seen the sinuous shape of it in the clear azure water. Fortunately, the fury of the attack—as seen through the eyes of the shaman's hawks—was on the front wall. The Hungarian forces had gained a foothold inside the broken wall, and men were starting to pour through the gap and up onto the walls. The shaman was able to change into the other form and lope ashore. Shaking the water clear of its fur, it ran to where the wall was pounded into steep rubble. Here, with no defenders, it gained entrance. With the fleeing towns-people, it ran through the inner curtain-wall gates.

It began searching. Tasting the air. Relishing the fear, hating the crowd.

On the slope behind Corfu town, Giuliano Lozza marshaled his men. He was de facto commander of the Corfiote irregular army, because he had the most soldiers by far. The Venetian captain had had the sense to recognize an unstoppable local force and go along with it. And across the island, so had everyone else. The story of the naked Magyar having to walk back to camp in the buff spread from village to peasant to fishermen. Greeks loved to laugh, and their sense of humor could be a bit rough.

This man Lozza was no foreigner, they'd decided. This was someone who spoke their language and knew more about olives than any Libri d'Oro they'd ever met. He'd even married one of their own, a peasant woman.

Once they'd called him *Loukoúmia*—fat little sweetmeat. No one did that any more. Not since he'd given a very pointed but non-lethal lesson in swordsmanship to one idiot who had dared put a hand on his wife.

"We beat neither our women nor our olive trees on Corfu," he'd said firmly and finally. It was a local peasant saying, too. That was the final and vital detail. Women asked their menfolk why they hadn't joined.

Giuliano had nearly three thousand men, men with everything from old boar-spears to new and recently acquired Hungarian arquebuses. And torches.

Waiting. Like the great banks of heavy cloud that hung seemingly just off shore. The rain never came. The Corfiotes were going to.

When the Hungarian units had begun pulling back three days ago, Giuliano had known this was to be the big assault. He'd begun sending out word, and the Corfiotes had come.

Giuliano was a master swordsman. He knew he was outnumbered and that the enemy had the edge in professionalism and equipment. But he also knew that it was not the strength of the swordsman that wins the day. It was the timing of the stroke. With the Hungarians sweeping into the outer Citadel, now was the time for the stroke. Loot, or the desire for it, made the Hungarian encampment virtually empty. The artillerymen were sitting around, disgruntled at not being able to join in the spree. The cannon would have to be moved now. All they got out of this was hard work.

And Giuliano Lozza.

Chapter 97

"The circle is unbroken. Out of life comes death, and out of death, life."

Maria looked at the point in the rock, engraved with a circle—the symbol of the mother—and surrounded by spirals so old that time was weathering them away. From the middle of that circle the water of the sacred spring had flowed—apparently unceasingly, for millennia. Now, as she watched, a tiny drop slowly formed and dripped down to the clay basin that stood in for the cracked holy pool.

Maria put Alessia down beside the cracked pool. The baby girl was too listless to go anywhere. Too listless to even cry. Maria turned with sad eyes to Renate. "You'll see her safe to Katerina, Holy Mother?"

Tears streaked the older woman's face. She nodded. "This can fix things, Maria. If you are willing."

Maria shrugged. "It is too late for me. Benito's dead. It'll be too late for Alessia soon. So what do I have to do?"

"Drink the water of the holy pool. Take up the almond. Offer yourself as a willing bride. I will do the rest."

Maria stared up at the figure of the Mother, the old, old figure cut out of the living rock. Legs like barrels, fat thighs that stood for the plenty She provided, the cleft of Her mystery, overhung with the great belly of fertility, the huge domes of pendulous breasts, the round ball of a head, featureless except for a hint of carving that might have been hair, a mouth. How old was She? Who had carved Her? Was there still any power in Her at all?

Maria tried to feel something from that figure; all she could feel was her own despair.

Well, even if nothing happened, there would be a few drops of water.

She went to the basin; raised it to her lips, and drank. With the taste of sweet water still on her tongue, she walked the two steps to the altar, and took up the half almond.

Her fingers touched it, with a shock.

Her hand closed involuntarily on it, and she whirled, to stare at the Mother.

Gathering about the shapeless form were tiny, dustlike sparks. Only they weren't dust, they were sparks of golden light, more and more of them with every moment, outlining the figure, then enshrouding it, enveloping it in a blanket, a haze of gold, the color of corn, the color of wheat, the color of life . . .

A sigh eased from her; she closed her eyes, and let the power lead her where she needed to go.

The yellow dog found the cliff entrance to the temple-cave by nose. There was only woman-scent coming from it. And, for the first time on this accursed island, also the strong, heady smell of powerful magics. Unless the other had sent a woman . . . he was here first. The only problem was that the cave mouth was up there, and the yellow dog form was not good for climbing trees. He wondered briefly if he should assume his human form, but decided against it. That was by far the most vulnerable.

He hesitated. By the intensity of the magics up there, time was not on his side. He changed into the hagfish form. This body did not like the dry, but it could climb like a snake.

He ignored the screams of people who saw the huge, oily-black monster twining its way up the graveyard poplar, and oozing into the cave mouth. Soon it would not matter.

It was dusty and dry and spiked with stalagmites here, so the shaman assumed the doglike form again. His nose led him, hastening, up the narrow labyrinthine passages, panting and slobbering a little.

Yes. This was what he had been sent to find. To the shaman's senses, the entire place pulsed with power; throbbing like a racing heart. The master's advisor, Mindaug, had said the master needed to be physically present to claim this. The shaman wished he knew how to do so himself.

He ran into the temple chamber yowling in triumph, ready to fight.

There were two humans there. An old woman with long white hair, unconscious and crumpled on the floor. And a baby—dying, by the smell of it.

He could feast later. The shaman's nose told him there had been three. He quested for that third, to rend, to kill, with the magical energies in this place growing around him. To his eyes the place was full of sheets of green light.

She wasn't here—yet she had not left.

The shaman gave a half-vulpine, half-canine sort of shrug and began the ritual to call his master's physical presence here.

It was as if all solid things had become shadows. Maria, with the almond in her hand, her firm chin up and heart hammering, walked down steps of light set into the shadow.

She could not have said how long she walked, but she came at length to a great hall. At the far end were two thrones. A tall man stood up from the left-hand throne and walked toward her, palms out. On his right hand rested the other half of the almond. A tall man, made of shadows, as the Mother had been made of light. Shadows, but not evil—the restful shadows of twilight, the dark before dawn. And yet, she sensed there was a great deal concealed by those shadows, and she willed them away.

"Greetings, bride." He seemed to be looking through to the inside of her. He did not seem to notice that his concealment was melting until he stood before her unveiled. "Your spirit is very beautiful."

He was black-haired and gray-eyed; lean, pale, grim-looking. She set her jaw. Just because she had agreed to this, did not mean she was going into it blindly. Oh, no. All right, the marriage with Umberto, not unlike this one, had worked out—but she'd known Umberto, hadn't she? This—*Person*—she knew nothing at all about. So before she took the last irrevocable step, she had to know. She would do it, yes, but she still had to know.

"Just exactly who are you?" she demanded. "Husband," she added, as an afterthought.

It took the man aback. In fact, he literally stepped back a pace.

"You are a willing bride?" The pale-visaged man showed both surprise and a hint of doubt.

Maria nodded, feeling completely out of her depth, and brusque with it. "Yes, of course I am. The priestess said that without a bride the Mother could only resist, passively. That without a bride you would not intercede. Look," she continued, in growing irritation, "my baby was dying. My friends are dead or dying. The man I loved, Benito Valdosta, is dead. I was too proud to tell him that I loved him, and now he's dead. The whole island is dying. Somebody had to do something, so I said I would do it. I knew I had to be willing and I had to be fertile, of childbearing age. I didn't know I had to know all about it."

Just like a man! Assuming, she supposed, that because things had always gone a particular way, they always would go that way! Just proving Gods could be as dense and intransient as humans.

"I'm a new acolyte, and somehow or other nobody got around to telling me what I'm supposed to be doing. The priestess assumed I knew everything already, I suppose, and I assumed she'd tell me sometime and never got around to asking. I knew that to take up the almond, to become the bride, meant I would die. But if that was what it took to get you to help, I was willing. You are going to help us, aren't you?"

Perhaps that last came out a bit aggressively, but—oh, *stupid* man-God! Why was He just standing there, as if none of this mattered to Him? Was He going to act, or not?

He seemed altogether startled, now. "It is not that I did not wish to help. It is just that I cannot. My only connection with the Mother is through her embodiments. You are the embodiment of the Mother. The things above the earth are hers only. I have no power there, but I can lend my strength. I always have willingly given my help to my Mother."

Maria was now more confused than she'd been before. "I don't understand," she repeated. "Just who are you?"

He blinked, slowly. "I am the Lord of the underworld. Aidoneus is the name I am sometimes given."

"The devil?" He didn't seem evil. Just distant.

He shook his head in violent negation, the first time he'd shown any sign of emotion. "No! Shaitan's realms are elsewhere, and I want none of his kind of darkness." He spread his hands, as if in apology. "The spirit world is a complex place. All things are possible here. And none."

Well, that was certainly unhelpful. It was like arguing with Eneko Lopez. "It all seems to be shadows," she said doubtfully.

He nodded, more certain. "This has been called Shadowkeep,

at times. And Hades, which is nothing like Hell. More often, simply the realm of the dead. Some of the dead leave here to go on to other realms, but all are here at least for a time. Time is meaningless to the dead. Of course, you are not dead, so you are not outside of time."

She wrinkled her forehead. She thought the point of this was that she died; this was getting more confusing by the moment. "So am I not dead?"

He shook his head. "No. Only a living one can be the living embodiment of life. One day you will die, but you are not destined to do so for many years. You will stay down here and be my wife. And the Mother Earth will be fertile and grow, because I can lend Her my strength."

Stay here and be his wife? Was that what all this bride business was about? To be a real—wife? To a God? Or something—

Well, she'd accepted dying. And you could get used to anything.

She shook herself all over, and one thing swam up out of her sea of confused thoughts. Alessia. What was going on out there? Or up there? Or wherever "there" was?

"Alessia—my baby?" Surely the Lord of the Dead would know if Alessia was dead? Or if the Hungarians had broken through . . . there'd be many dead, including Stella.

He looked past her, his face gone indifferent again. "Your child is lying beside the sacred pool in the temple of the great Goddess. There is an evil creature of darkness, a cursed one, sniffing at her." He sounded as if it all meant nothing to Him. Actually, it probably didn't.

But she reacted with outrage. "But—but you're supposed to help! Renate was supposed to take her away! Why didn't she? She's not going to kill my baby, is she?"

He looked into the middle distance. He was plainly seeing things in the shadowy places. "The priestess lies within the portals of the underworld. She has expended too much opening the way."

Outrage was no proper word for what she felt now. All the sense of betrayal, all the despair, all the anguish that had brought her here welled up inside her and spilled out.

"*You're supposed to help!* You—you cold fish, you're supposed to be stopping all of this! That's the bargain! That's why I came here!" Maria knew she was screaming, although in this strange place it didn't seem so. The sound was curiously deadened.

He looked at her as if she was a child to whom he had already explained the situation. "I need to be asked. And death and life need to be joined so the circle can be complete."

"Well, *I'm* asking you. Do something! Now!" She stamped her foot. This sound too was faint and thin. More like the memory of a sound.

For the first time a flicker of expression ran across that cold face. It was hard to say what it was. But his voice was somehow warmer, more interested. "You remind me of my first wife. Kore was from before the humans came. She brought fire and light into this place. We had some terrible fights, as I recall. She also had a quick temper like yours." He sounded nostalgic.

Maria felt her fury rage against the flatness of the man, and the place. "Listen, you! I'll make your life a misery for all that long life you've said I'd have, unless you do something now! About my baby. About the siege. About Renate. *NOW!*"

Her voice seemed louder somehow than it had when she'd shouted earlier. And edges to everything seemed sharper, clearer.

"You have a beautiful, strong spirit," he said, with what could almost be a smile. He reached toward her and she saw the hands were like Benito's brother's hands. Long and shapely. And the almond seemed to glow. "Come. Join me then, avatar of the great Goddess. Join me and then I can do this 'something' you demand."

She reached out her hand, opening it to reveal the almond. Her hands were work-calloused and rough compared to his. "Doing something is always better than doing nothing," she said firmly.

As their hands clasped, the two almond halves touched. She felt them draw toward each other.

Click . . .

The seed began to swell and then burst into growth. The roots were wriggling against their clasped hands and leafy shoots came questing upwards. And Maria found she could see things in the strange shadows of this place. People and places, myriads of them.

"It's a strong tree. The strongest I have seen in centuries," he said. His voice was definitely warmer now. And somehow he seemed less inhuman. "Let us plant it."

"It needs light, and earth and water," snapped Maria. "Not shadows. And I need to get on before it is too late for little 'Lessi."

The place was definitely lighter. "Then get on. Make earth and light and water for it." His voice was deeper, stronger and more powerful now. And there was definitely a gleam in those gray eyes.

It was a test of some sort, she knew. And she had no idea what to do. She looked into the strange shifting shadows, looking for a place for it.

Instead she saw Alessia, lying still and pale. Renate just beyond, fetal and breathing so faintly you could hardly see movement in that frail chest. And a great yellow-furred dog-creature. It was scratching symbols with undoglike precision on the stone floor of the temple. Drool hung down from its jaws.

She searched her memory of all the things the priestess had said, desperate for a clue. All she could think of was Renate saying calmly: "Use your anger. Channel it with your will."

She looked around at the pale, shadowy hall. Either she was getting used to it or it really was more substantial and more clearly defined than it had been. There was a dead piece of wood there, in the middle of the floor. She channeled her will at that place.

Let there be earth, rich fecund . . . earthy, steaming with the scents of morning, as she remembered it from the forests of Istria. That wonderful earth that could support a hundred thousand mighty trees, growing strong and tall and straight.

Let there be sunlight, as warm as a lover's caress, as golden as . . . as the morning sun on the wings of the Lion. Oh, she remembered that, too, that sunlight that was so full of life you could drink it like wine, light that touched hurt and left healing behind it.

Let there be water, cool and clean and refreshing as the water in the temple had been that first time she'd gone to pray for Umberto. Water, oh blessed Jesu, let there, of all things, be water!

She felt the power answer to her will; where it came from she did not know, but she launched it as she had launched a thousand rocks at the enemy, as she had launched herself into this voyage, as she had launched Alessia into life—

By the hotness of her anger at wrongness of all this, by the love she held for all of them, let them *BE*.

And . . . *they were*.

The earth-smell, that had been so strange to her when she first came to the forest, tickled her nose with its lush scent. Sunlight welled around the dead stick, coming from everywhere and nowhere. And there was a mist, curling, lush with water, around the remains of the last bride's tree. And suddenly, the hall seemed very small to contain such richness.

He actually laughed. "I'm grateful you left me some hall! Come, let us plant this tree, and see to your need."

They walked forward into the sunlight, off the cold flags and onto the loamy earth. Using their free hands they dug a hole into it, and then put the seedling into the soil. The rootlets actually started reaching through their fingers and pushed hungrily into the earth. It was growing, growing even as they formed the soil around it.

"It will be the finest tree I have had here in many millennia." There was respect there; interest, too. Still holding her hand, he turned to point earthy fingers at the shadows. The yellow dog was howling there. "Let us see what happens with the half-jackal first— the cursed one. In a way it is protected from me. It cannot die."

In the shadows Maria saw the creature now for what it was: No dog. One removed from the dog-line. A cross between gray wolf and golden jackal, a howling half-domesticated creature from the wet northern forests that *could* have been the father of humankind's four-footed loyal companion.

Could have been. It had once fawned and guarded, and pretended loyalty. And when the man and the woman had left it to guard their most precious thing, it had eaten the child. The one they had trusted was cursed, cursed to live until it had been forgiven for the betrayal that was now long forgotten by men. But the memory and the shame were with all dogs—whose ancestors were cousins to it—and man's other ally, the horse, forever. The hyena they would hunt and hurt as often as possible. They could hurt it, even if they couldn't kill it.

There was also a shadowy person in there. Someone who had taken the cursed creature's name. The shaman had taken the form and with it the curse. He thought not being able to die a good thing, and cared nothing for the rest.

"How do we deal with it?"

The lord of the dead shrugged. "We protect your babe, and that is all we need do, for now. The great Goddess is dealing with it already, as She does with all those who work magics here. This is the place of the great Goddess. You know what the earth of Corfu does to foreign magic. The greater the magic—the faster it will draw that power. The creature relies on magic for its being. It would have been dead millennia ago if nature were to have run its course. The magics it uses now would kill it—were it not unkillable for magical reasons. The more it does, the more the earth of Corfu will draw that power that sustains it."

She understood now. The Goddess was absorbing anything worth having from the creature, and the longer it remained, the more She would take. Even the curse that kept it alive would be affected.

It was diminishing itself.

Still—this was that passive defense again, and that was not enough. "Surely there is something I can do," she said, feeling her anger welling again.

The God shrugged, very much amused. "You are She. And my power is yours. Take it up, my bride."

And she did.

Chapter 98

The shaman paused, as a wave of weakness came over him. Just a few more lines and Jagiellon himself would arrive here. He could rest then. He started to scratch symbols again. He shook himself, trying to focus his tired old eyes.

And then it came to him. He did not ever *feel* tired. Not in this body. And as for the ill-effects of age... the curse that had been laid on the yellow wolf-jackal had stopped the creature knowing those.

At last the shaman understood the nature of Mindaug's trap, and Mindaug's treachery. The shimmering half-materialized form of the master felt it too. Now the shaman knew why he had found the stink of magic everywhere. This place was a fertility temple. A mumi-place. The whole damned island was that. And the shaman, who was old past the reckoning of most men, knew that new life was a cyclic thing. It needed death. Life and death were one big wheel. The very soil here was sucking him dry, rotting him away like decomposing leaves in winter, to fuel new birth. The more magic he used in trying to fight it, the faster it was happening. It was swallowing him, and it would have swallowed the master... because their own magic was the fuel used.

A trap! He could sense his master's shriek, and his own thoughts shrieked in answer. All of it—a trap. Laid by the traitor Mindaug to supplant Jagiellon, working with his ally the Hungarian witch-countess.

But Chernobog had not yet fully materialized. The demon could still—barely—withdraw from the closing jaws. The shaman felt him

772

fading away, leaving his servant behind. Behind, and alone, and sucked nearly dry of magic.

The arthritic, near-toothless, rheumy old wolf-jackal dragged and swayed his way to the cave mouth. It was a long way down, and the sight of the hagfish had brought people, and knights in armor and on horseback.

The wolf-jackal didn't care. Even pain was better than death. By the time it had dragged itself to the water, hounded over the wall and attacked afresh by the Croat horses, it was yowling and shrieking with agony.

The curse assured that the wolf-jackal wouldn't die, although the pain was not ameliorated. The magic of Corfu meant that each time his body repaired itself he was closer to the real death. Every spell, every twist of enchantment he controlled was drawing it out of him. He abandoned what magics he could. The shaman knew Jagiellon would not help. He must have suffered too, and wouldn't dare use magic to help the shaman.

Falling into the water and assuming the shape of the hagfish kept the shaman alive, but did nothing for the pain. And it was not the great beast it had been, oh no—it was a little, little thing, a wraith of the monster it had been, struggling feebly toward the deeper water—

—and two hawks hit the hagfish in the shallows, gouging at it beak and claw in their new-freed fury. Had they been creatures of the earth, not sky, the island of Corfu would have freed them long ago.

They were goshawks, torn from their native forests, forced to fly over water, stranded here. Their fury knew no bounds.

But behind that fury was Another, who lent speed to their wings and strength to their talons and beaks and when the shaman tried to strike them, knocked it back into the water, yet would not let it escape. The hawks savaged the hagfish with rage—the rage of goshawks protecting their young, for that Other told them, deep in their half-made hearts, that this *thing*—this *outrage*—had menaced young, had *eaten* young. They were going to avenge every young thing it had ever taken in its long, long life.

And so they did, as the Other hauled it back from the depths and protected them from its ever-more-feeble assaults. They tore at it and tore at it, until there was nothing left to tear. Nothing, but blood slicking the water like oil, and shreds of flesh, and the taste of its vileness in their mouths.

Then, that Other gave them some strength as their own began to fail. Lifted them, lofted them back to the land. And showed them a place—forest. Not like theirs, but like enough. And it soothed them with the promise of game to hunt and sweet water to drink and no one to disturb them, ever again.

Go. Build a nest. Raise young, and prosper.

And so they went, flapping heavily away through the hot, heavy air, bird-wise, and with the wisdom of birds, letting go of their rage and forgetting the thing that had bound them. Except not quite; keeping enough that they would never allow themselves, or their young, to be bound, ever again.

Maria took a deep breath, and flexed her hands, and the Lord of the Shadows now turned and pointed to a shadow that nearly made her sick. "There is the thing that is causing the Mother much pain."

It was hideous. Anger and pain radiated out from the little fetal-creature. It had wings, crumpled and twisted and deformed. It would never fly. But the small wings beat furiously, thrashing away the mere pressure of their gaze, that hurt, that burned it like acid. It was trapped by the magical confines of this place. It floated above the earth, a creature without weight—but still pinioned here, above Corfu. Pinioned with chains of blood—the nonhuman blood of its parents.

Her first reaction had been horror. Now she felt simply pity.

"It's just a baby!" she objected.

"Of sorts, yes." He waited—perhaps to see what she would do.

Not destroy it—blessed Jesu, it didn't know what it was doing! No, she had to—heal it? Help it? "What can I do for it? It's not on the earth of Corfu."

The Lord of the Underworld shrugged. "It's somewhere between death and life. That puts it in both of our realms. We can see it, and it can see us."

The anger, hurt and bitterness flowing from it were almost too much to bear. "Whoever did this must be a monster," said Maria, recognizing the unborn fetal thing for what it was.

"Elizabeth Bartholdy." There was a brief shadow moment of a

beautiful woman. Plainly the twisted, warped creature saw it, too, because it howled in frustrated rage.

"How do we help the poor creature?" she cried, feeling its pain deep inside herself. It was a baby—only a baby—forced to do what it was doing.

"Remove its bonds. Remove just one of the sigils in its parents' blood. Wash them away." In the shadow now she could see the spidery tracings on the rocks of a blood that had never been red.

"With what? There is no rain or water because of the poor thing. If it would let it rain . . ." Maria sniffed. Swallowed. "I won't cry," she choked. "This is no time to cry!" She had to do something, not dissolve in tears! Crying wouldn't help—

"Why not?" the Shadow Lord asked, quietly. "Tears will wash as well as rain. It won't live, you know. It only survives in this sort of half existence because of the magics worked on it."

"I won't cry because it's soft to cry." She paused, feeling a strange stillness come over her. Like that blanket of understanding that had settled over her, letting her understand what she needed to do, a new understanding stole quietly over her in the stillness. "Maybe it needs something soft."

"Yes?" the Shadow Lord said, a hint, just a hint, of encourage-ment in His voice.

"I don't think it's ever had care or any love." She thought of Alessia, how even so loved a baby as she had nearly driven her mother mad a time or two.

"This isn't its fault. It's just a baby. A baby doesn't mean to make you miserable when it's hurting. It just doesn't know how to do anything else. And it's hurting, it's hurting so much, from what that awful woman has done to it!"

This time, it was rage that followed the words, it was despair, for all the children that had died because of those horrible people out there, for this poor little thing that had suffered the tortures of the damned, been forced into birth. No baby ever *asked* to be born, but this one had been tormented into existence, and noth-ing would make it better except to be ushered out of life—

Maria wept for it, a mother's tears. The tears fell down and into the shadow.

And the silvery blood-writing boiled. There was a brief moment of movement, of wind and of fire.

And then there was a surcease of pain.

The rain began. The clouds, so long held back, swept in, swept over the hawks in their new forest, so that they held up their heads to the falling rain and drank in the sweet water that washed away the foulness on their tongues. It swept over the peasant women who set out jars and bowls to catch it. It soaked into the earth, that drank it with a million thirsty throats, and sent it down into the streams, into the unseen crevices of the rocks, with the sound of life renewing, at last.

"It is in my kingdom now," said her new husband. "I have put it where it belongs."

"What else must we do?" asked Maria tiredly.

He shrugged. "The Mother's place has rain at last, and will heal. *It* has got its people again, and they love it. It is in a magical place with those that perished giving birth to it. They blame it no more than you, and now they can cherish it. With that, it will heal."

"What about the siege?"

"Ah." Tall already, he seemed to grow taller. And grimmer. "War is death's kingdom. *Mine*, not Hers."

"Hah," Maria replied, feeling anger giving her back her strength. "Maybe so. But I'm going to help."

Chapter 99

Erik was on the battlements of the inner curtain wall, organizing and trying to prevent panic. Most of all, wishing silently that the inner walls had been built as the outer had: to withstand cannon. But the outer walls had been rebuilt not fifteen years back. This inner wall was probably a century old.

The outer wall had stood up to months of pounding. The inner wall would last weeks at best. Which was more time than they had water for, anyway.

A cannon across on the Spianada boomed. They must be mad! They should move them up first . . . a second, then a third cannon spoke. And Erik realized they were firing into the outer city. Into their own troops. Peering out to the enemy encampment on the other side of the Spianada, Erik's jaw dropped. For the first time since Svanhild's death he began to laugh. It was harsh sound, but it was laughter nonetheless.

The Hungarian camp was burning. Not as if from a little brave band in a small patch, but across a wide front. It must have taken thousands of men. And more and more of the Hungarian artillery fired into the Hungarian troops in the Citadel. If they spiked those guns before retreating . . . the inner citadel would last as long as its water held out.

Erik wondered whether this was Venice's forces at last. Like the rain, those had just never seemed to get here.

Manfred came up behind him, helmet under his arm and grinning like the cat that had eaten the cream. Von Gherens was just behind. "Well, Erik. What do you think? Half of them seem to be running back to camp. Are we going to sortie again?"

Erik shook his head. "The cannon-fire is doing it for us. As soon as it stops—"

A cold wet something hit him on the nose. Then another hit his cheek. "I don't believe it! It's raining!"

The rain came down in a gray, hissing curtain. So heavy that the view of the Spianada and then the section of the Citadel outside the inner curtain suddenly disappeared.

Manfred, Erik and Von Gherens stood there, rain driving in their faces, plastering their hair down, grinning at each other.

"Come on, you pair of loons," said Von Gherens. "Your armor's getting wet."

Behind them the Citadel was echoing—despite the rain—to cheers and cries of *"San Marco!"*

Erik was the last to leave the battlements.

He looked out at the rain, but he saw her face. And no one in the downpour could tell rain from tears anyway. He hadn't been able to weep, since that early moment in the hospital. Now, here, alone in the rain, where no one could see him, he could. Somehow it lifted a weight from his soul.

Giuliano saw the first heavy drops splash on the dusty earth. Like Erik he gaped. But he'd lived here all his life and he knew that when it rained here, it rained in earnest. "Sound the retreat," he said to the young Venetian with him.

"But sir, we still have some cannon to spike!"

"Believe me, Nico. They won't be using them for a while anyway. Look at that rain. This place is going to be fetlock deep in mud soon. And this rain will cover the retreat beautifully, eh, Thalia?"

She smiled at him, eyes like stars. "Good for the olives, too."

She was a jewel past price.

The cannonball must have hit the house, because even in the cellar they felt the impact of it. Flakes of black paint fell from the ceiling. Alberto looked owlishly at Benito. "I believe I'll have that second drink after all. No sense in dying sober."

In Benito's informed opinion, if the next cannonball came right through into the cellar in two heartbeats' time and hit Alberto . . . he still wouldn't die sober. Yet he'd suffered Benito's rough surgery stoically. The wine might have helped. They hadn't eaten much in the last while and a little wine went a long way.

"Air holes, but no view," grumbled Benito, passing the bottle over. "No wonder the woman went mad in here."

"You ask me she was mad to start with," said Alberto phlegmatically. Once he'd got over his shock the big man had rapidly reconciled himself to staying down here for a while.

Benito hadn't. He'd been pacing the cellar like a caged animal for the last while. Being pinned down would kill him as surely as bullets or swords, he decided.

"Alberto. I'm going to have a look outside."

In the temple cave, Alessia stirred. The rock beneath her moved slowly, slightly, readjusting from the terrible stresses that had been put on it and were now washed away. The crack that split the holy pool healed. Water, rising from a deep artesian flow, began to drip slightly faster. And, as the rains beat down outside, faster still. The drops became a trickle and the trickle became a stream. The clay bowl overflowed. The pool filled up.

The healing and the magic in this place affected other things, too. Alessia woke up. She got to her knees; then, waving her arms for balance, stood up. It was no great height. She took little swaying baby-steps forward.

And fell into the pool.

Another baby might have drowned. But this child was hemmed in by certain protections. She sat up, wet through, and screamed. And screamed. She wanted her mother.

She wanted her mother NOW.

And if her mother is not there to care for her—she just has to touch running water to call me or my kin to help.

So had the undine Juliette stated at her christening. Alessia hadn't understood the words at the time, of course. Nor would she have now. But in a pinch, the new baby-sitter would do. He was big and warm and smelled nice.

Not like Mother. But nice. Familiar.

Benito had eased the trapdoor up very cautiously, ears straining for the sounds of danger. Instead he heard a peculiar drumming noise. He couldn't place it at first. It was a long time since he'd heard rain on the roof.

"Hey, Alberto!"

"What?" asked the big *scuolo* man, warily. He'd bet Alberto had the late Sophia's wheel-lock at the ready.

"It's raining out there! Not just raining. Bucketing it down."

"No! After all this time!"

"I'm going out."

"You'll get wet," said Alberto with a laugh.

"Yeah. But so will anyone else. It's nearly as black as night out there."

"I'll stay here and look after the wine. I can't run and you'll probably need to."

Benito realized very shortly that "rain" was an understatement. It was as if the heavens were trying to catch up on the whole dry winter in one fell swoop. Even in a final assault on a beleaguered city, troops would be reduced to seeking shelter in this. He stalked up the narrow street, seeing no one. Benito felt he could hardly have seen someone across the narrow street, it was sheeting down so hard.

And then he realized he was seeing someone after all, walking toward him. As he turned to shrink back against a doorsill he realized this was a very strange someone. The woman wasn't wearing any clothes, except for a crown of water lilies. And even in this light, her hair was green. In spite of his attempt to hide she obviously knew where he was, and beckoned imperiously at him.

"You! Your daughter needs you. Come."

"Who are you?" he said warily.

"I am the Crenae of the spring within the hill. And your daughter wants either her mother or you. Our kin promised we would help if she was in need. Besides, she is nearly shaking the holy mount with her screaming. Nothing we can do will comfort her."

"Er, I'd help. But you've got the wrong person. I don't have any daughters."

The cold rain was soaking Benito. It didn't seem to perturb the nymph. "Yes you do," she said firmly. "Juliette examined your blood."

"Alessia?" The rain was getting in his eyes. "She's *my* daughter?"

"She certainly isn't your son!" snapped the nymph. "Now come.

We must go to the cliff on the side of the Castel *a mar*. She is in a cave there."

Benito's mind groped at the thought of Alessia as his daughter. He'd thought—Caesare—

Suddenly it all clicked into place for him. The timing—Maria's sudden determination to marry Umberto—

And, the truth was, the baby didn't look in the least bit like Aldanto. In fact, now that he thought about it . . .

He pushed it all aside for a later time. "Got a place I can climb the inner wall in this?"

"The gates are open. The people of the city have pushed back the attackers."

"What? I must go and tell Alberto!"

"Your daughter needs you, *now*. She is very young and very unhappy. I have left my sister with her, but she is screaming the place down."

Benito shrugged. "Let's go, then. I'll send someone for him."

On the way to the gates, the rain slackened off slightly. It looked to be a mere lull in between waves of heavier downpour, but Benito realized the Venetians were making the most of it. Troops were marching down to the outer wall, set on doing what repairs they could. Ordinary people were hastening to their homes and lodgings to see what the Hungarians had left. Benito was pushing against this tide when a wet-haired, red-eyed woman grabbed his arm. Benito hadn't even recognized Maria's friend Stella without her permanent smile.

"Signor Valdosta!" Her face was a map of misery. "My Alberto? You haven't seen him? Even, dear God, his body . . ."

He squeezed her shoulder. "He's fine. He's got a broken leg, that's all."

Stella simply dissolved on his shoulder, clinging to him. "Where is he? I'll murder him! I've been so worried. So unhappy—"

"I hid him. Now look, he doesn't know what's happened out here and he's scared and has a pistol. For God's sake, don't get yourself shot getting to him."

She nodded. Her smile was back in full-force. "I'll call. He'll recognize my yelling at him, for sure. Where is he?"

"You know the house that guy was using for his orgies with the *Case Vecchie* women? The fake magician, Morando? I know you went and had a look."

She nodded. "I even got a peek into the cellar, where they did . . . that stuff."

"Well, we hid out in that cellar. The trapdoor is closed and it has been mended. It's in the passage. And as I said, for heaven's sake, be careful. He's armed and scared."

She kissed him. "Bless you, Benito Valdosta! I will be careful." She started to hurry with the tide of people.

He grabbed her shoulder. "Uh. Stella."

"Yes," she turned.

"He's also a bit drunk."

"I'll break his other leg for him!" she said, with cheerful savageness. "And you'd better go and find Maria. She'll be worried sick by now."

"Will you come on?" said the nymph, tapping her foot impatiently. Benito realized, as he hadn't in his preoccupation, that no one else seemed to notice his strange escort. Well, Marco said that the undine Juliette had done much the same thing to the audience in the church at Alessia's christening.

She led him to the cliff. The hagfish had broken away part of the concealing tree, and Benito could see the cave. "I can go with water-flow. You will have to climb up there."

The limestone was wet. The handholds and footholds were tiny and rounded. It didn't matter a damn to Benito. He kicked off his boots, and began to climb. Reaching the cave, he wondered for a moment just where to go. The cave was dark. But then he realized that all he had to do was follow his ears.

A hundred heartbeats later he was holding and comforting a small, cold, wet child against his wet but exertion-warm body. "Why in hell didn't you dry her?" he snapped at the two nymphs.

"We don't know much about human babies."

"What sort of gratitude is this?" demanded the other crossly.

Benito sighed. "Look, I'm sorry. I thank both of you. Now I must dry her, warm her up, and find her mother. What was she doing here?"

"You'd better ask her," said one nymph, pointing to the curled body of Renate De Belmondo. "She's been starting to stir." And with that, they slipped away into water that Benito would have sworn could not hold a minnow.

Benito looked around the temple, and took the finely woven cloth off the altar-stone. He stripped off Alessia's wet clothes and, using the Shetland knife, cut the altar cloth into a sort of poncho for her. Cut a strip to make a nice belt. He took off his own soaking-wet shirt too, and tossed it onto the altar-stone. He'd be better off without it.

There was no food down here, and 'Lessi was undoubtedly hungry. The whole of the Citadel was. But she could at least drink. He took a tiny clay bowl from beside the altar and helped her to drink. It seemed to do her a great deal of good, and she'd warmed up nicely against him. She started settling down for sleep. Loved, cared for, and with not a worry in the world. Benito put her down carefully.

Then he took a double handful of water and splashed it on Renate De Belmondo's face. He did it several more times, adding more sacrilege to the large number of incidents he'd already managed.

She moaned. He tried shaking her. She opened her eyes. He sat her up. Then, remembering something Marco had said, put her head between her knees.

Chapter 100

Renate De Belmondo had been in the service of the great Goddess for nearly forty years. She came to the temple almost every day. The sounds here were as familiar as her husband's breathing. The fountain bubbling and the sounds of the tiny waterfall cascading into the sacred pool were like the voices of old friends. Even in her giddy and confused state they comforted and caressed. She tried to sit up. The someone who had been holding her head between her legs helped her to lean back against the wall. Then it came to her, as she tried to focus her eyes. The fountain had been reduced to oozing droplets, the cascade to accumulating drips falling slowly into the clay bowl instead of the rock pool. She blinked and then screwed her eyes up, willing them to focus. The pool swam into clarity.

It was brimful. And the glad cascade was running stronger than she'd ever seen it. She breathed a sigh of relief. At least their troubles were over.

Then, as a very angry male face leaned into hers, Renate De Belmondo realized that *her* troubles, on a personal front, might just be starting. And being nearly seventy and the high Priestess of the great Goddess weren't necessarily going to help.

"What was 'Lessi doing down here?" he demanded angrily. "And where the hell is Maria?"

It was a question she really didn't want to have to answer. She struggled to focus her mind, to draw on some of her powers. She looked at him. He was bare-chested, and muscled like a stevedore across that chest and those shoulders. When she'd first met Benito

Valdosta he'd looked like a mischievous imp of a young man. Now . . . he looked like some kind of dangerous wild beast.

"Men are not allowed in the Mother's temple. You will be curs—"

He shook her again. Respect for persons or places was not with him. "I want Maria! And as for your God-forsaken temple, I'm here because *you* left my daughter where she could drown. The nymphs from your private water supply—that you've been enjoying while the citadel's people went thirsty—called me because my daughter has an undine for a godmother."

She put her hands to her head. "Please don't shout. You must leave now. I understand why you came, but the great Mother Goddess's temple is forbidden to men. I see you have committed various sacrileges—I am sure unknowing, because you are still alive. But you must go and never return. Be assured there was no water here before the rite, and the baby was in no danger. Now go. You will leave Maria's child here. I have sworn by the great Mother that I will see that she is taken to Katerina Valdosta."

Benito took a deep breath. Renate De Belmondo saw deeper into people than most mortals, if not as deeply as the undine Juliette. She saw the wildfire in there. Wildfire accepts no limitations.

"She's my child, too. I always thought she was Caesare's baby. It doesn't matter to me anyway. Long before I knew, the undine asked me if I loved her. I do. She as good as told me I was the father then, but I didn't understand."

The words were tumbling out of him in no particular order, but Renate was used to hearing hysterical words tumbling out of distraught women, and managed to make sense of them, or at least, as much sense as *could* be made, since she had no idea of who, or what, most of the people he was talking about were.

"She told me it was my responsibility to look after Alessia. I accepted it then and I accept it now. I'll look after her if anyone but her mother is going to. Maria told me about Katerina and babies. Kat might be better when she has her own, but for now I'm keeping her. As for you: 'Lessi was cold, wet, and miserable and whether you admit it or not, in danger while you were supposed to be looking after her. I'm keeping her. Try if you can to stop me."

He stepped over to pick her up.

Reluctantly, Renate called on the power of the great Goddess to prevent it.

And realized that absolutely nothing was happening. Benito picked up the baby, and cradled her as naturally and easily as any mother.

"The great Goddess obviously feels the justice of your claim," said Renate, reluctantly. "But I did promise her mother. I must admit she thought you were dead."

"Where is she?" said Benito, in a calm voice that Renate could feel paper-thin skin over a volcano of emotion.

The priestess took a deep breath. There was no avoiding it. "She has gone to be the bride of Aidoneus."

Benito gave her a flat stare that said: *If you thought one man and an altar cloth were sacrilege—I haven't even started yet.*

"I'm more patient than Maria, but not that much. We're in the middle of a war. Maria only married Umberto for Alessia's sake. And now you come with a cock-and-bull story about Maria getting married—now—and just abandoning Alessia. *Merde.* I'm going to find her if I have to pull the Citadel and every person in it apart. I'll start right here if I have to."

Renate held herself in stillness, and acknowledged the justice of his words. If Maria had known he was still alive—she would never have gone. Renate had not tricked her, but . . . there it was.

"Maria went, as a willing sacrifice, to live in the underworld with Aidoneus, the Lord of the Dead. Believe me, she only did this because . . . because she believed you were dead, and that her baby was dying. She did this to save Alessia. To save the island."

"Sacrifice. You killed her."

It was not a statement. It was a death-sentence. Renate saw it in his eyes.

"She's alive. I did not touch her. I swear by the great Goddess, as Her high priestess." He looked at her without understanding. "She is alive; only a living bride can go to the Lord of Shadows. She will probably live a very long time; the last bride must have been nearly a hundred before she died in the body. It is magic, Benito. She has gone, living, into the Underworld."

She shook her head. "I'm sorry Benito. There is nothing you can do about it. She's alive. But there is no way back."

Benito looked at her with eyes of flame. "Hear me . . . Priestess," he spat the word out. "I want her back from wherever you've hidden her. Alive, unhurt, *now*. Or there won't be any priestesses, or any temple. I'll hunt down all of you. And I won't send you to any play-play Lord of the Dead. I won't be stopped. WON'T."

The baby wailed at his anger, interrupting his tirade—he suddenly had to turn his attention back to the child, which would have been comical, except that it wasn't. There was heartbreak for him. He just hadn't figured it out, yet. "There, Alessia. It's all right. I'll fix it."

"You aren't letting yourself understand, Benito Valdosta." Renate had gathered herself by now, and stood straight, looking him directly in the eyes. "The Lord of the Dead is as real as your brother's Lion, or Eneko Lopez's Saint Hypatia. His kingdom is just as real. The magic that allows a living bride to serve as the channel for his power is as real as that which allows your brother to serve as channel for the Lion, or Lopez as the channel for his angels. The choice was hers to make. She has gone to spend the rest of her life in the Kingdom of the Dead. The real dead. You can kill me. I won't even try to resist. You can kill every priestess on the island. You can destroy the temples of Mother, of the great Goddess. All it would take would be enough gunpowder."

Somehow, that was starting to get through to him. Perhaps it was her conviction and her steadiness. Perhaps it was the Mother, reaching him past his anger.

"You could be an inhuman monster to make Emeric look pleasant," she continued, sternly. "Massacre dozens of innocent women. It wouldn't make any difference to Maria. Believe me, I didn't want to make this happen; in fact, I didn't make it happen at all, it just did. The priestesses and devotees have been dreading it. We are a peaceful fertility cult, and we have never taken an unwilling woman to be the bride. But there has to be a bride, an opposite for the Lord of the Underworld, just as there has to be a male as well as a female for fertility. And it has to be a fertile woman. I love my husband dearly, and still, I would have gone rather than Maria. But I couldn't. There was only one among us who could, and did, at the crucial moment."

She took a deep breath. His anger was fading, but the bleakness that was taking its place was painful to see. "Accept it, Benito. Accept it as you have accepted your daughter. No one comes back from the Kingdom of Aidoneus. She is trapped there until her body is returned to be buried with honor in the sacred glade. I'm very, very sorry, Benito. There is really nothing you or I can do, other than accept it and honor her sacrifice."

There were tears in Benito's eyes. But his voice was rock steady.

"You can accept it. And the consequences. I'm not going to. I'll keep trying to find a way, if I have to study magic until the day I die." He pointed an accusing finger at her. "She wasn't due to die. You did this to her. I'm not finished with you—or this place—but I need to get Alessia out of your hell-hole. Besides, I want to mourn among decent people and not with a murderess. You can run if you like. But it won't help you."

Renate was a high priestess and not without pride. "I won't run. And I'm just as unhappy as you are."

"Ha."

"Benito, this was her choice; she was a willing sacrifice."

"Alessia and I aren't willing. And if I can't get her back, I'll at least see there are no more victims. I will clean up this rotten mess if it is the last thing I do."

He turned on his heel and walked away into the darkness, toward the cave-mouth, holding the baby in his arms.

He was scarcely out of sight when the two nymphs came sinuously out of the pool. "It had to be that one's lady-love, didn't it? You humans are such fools."

Now that Benito had gone, Renate allowed herself the weakness of tears. "She was willing, and she thought he was dead."

One of nymphs looked at her with disgust. The other stamped her foot. "And now he's going to blow up the sacred pools, dig up the glades, burn the groves."

"The great Goddess has always had the power to stop that. We endure."

One of the nymphs said dourly, "And who do you think the current embodiment of the great Goddess *is*? And how do you think she's going to respond to your requests for help, when she sees who you want help against? Especially if she thinks you deceived her about him being dead."

"I didn't know!"

One of the nymphs rolled her eyes. "You could have found out, though. Minor magic. And Aidoneus would have known. I've been through a fractious bride-period before. But that woman's lover was a fool and as ordinary as dung. This one . . . he's been on a knife-edge between good and evil—or, worse, what he's probably going to inflict on Corfu. The kind of narrow intolerant 'good' that's worse than evil, even."

"I don't see what you expect me to do."

"Nothing. As usual," said the one nymph cattishly.

Renate sighed. "If they could only talk. It's . . . it's all just a terrible misunderstanding. We all did it for the best."

"Well, let him talk. Let him go and see her."

Renate shook her head "Aidoneus can see out through the shadows and together they can affect all things living and dead, but short of being in the land of the dead they can't see each other. They can't talk."

"So let's send him there," said the one nymph, tugging at a tangle in her hair.

Renate drew herself up. "We don't kill."

The nymph clicked her tongue at her. "Oh, you don't have to be dead to go to Shadowkeep. That's the easy way. It's been done the hard way before a couple of times and by different ways, but you short-lifers have probably forgotten."

The one nymph turned to the other, cocking her head. "What do you think, Sister? Acheroussia?"

The first nodded. "If the limnaiad there is willing."

Renate sighed again. "Well, let me at least make sure the rituals of spring still happen this year."

"Very well. We'll ask Valdosta if he wants to visit the Lord of the Dead, and make arrangements with she of lake Acheroussia."

Chapter 101

"It's my opinion," said Benito stiffly, "that even the Paulines are too lenient with witchcraft and magic. It's time they were both eliminated. I'm sorry you don't see things my way, Eneko. But I'm not going to let that stop me."

"The Church believes we will achieve more by a degree of tolerance, Benito."

"Tolerance is well and fine, Eneko Lopez. But tolerance doesn't mean making doormats of ourselves. The price of our tolerance is that they practice their religion within the constraints of our law and our society. If they step outside it—and if human sacrifice isn't stepping outside it then the Church, law, and society need a wake-up—I'm not going to sit back and turn a blind eye, even if you are."

Eneko Lopez shook his head. "I think you're allowing personal unhappiness to affect your judgement, Benito. This is not exactly 'human sacrifice.' Of course, the Church frowns on it . . ."

Benito stood up. "You can continue to dance around this, Eneko. I'm not going to."

He walked out, down toward the sea. Part of him longed to simply fling himself off the walls and down into it. To make an end of sorts. But . . . well, there was Alessia. She depended on him. And, right now, he depended on her. And there was work to be done.

As he was passing a street fountain, now gurgling with water— the Citadel had water, if not food—he heard someone call. He turned to see the Crenae nymph he'd followed to Alessia's rescue beckoning to him. "Valdosta."

"Alessia? Is she all right?"

"There are less-well-guarded crown jewels," sniffed the nymph sarcastically. "Anyway, you're worrying about nothing. The priestess wouldn't hurt a child, not even for her own life's sake."

"A matter of opinion," said Benito angrily.

"Not really," said the nymph. "We see deeper into the spiritual side of you humans than you can. And our sister Juliette would not allow harm to come to Alessia. Since her mother sacrificed herself for the island, we of nonhuman kind feel repayment to her child is the great Goddess's justice."

"Good. Now, if you'll excuse me I have a poplar tree to fell. The first part of *my* justice."

The nymph plainly realized just which tree he was speaking about. She winced. "Retribution won't help, Benito. And you will hurt many of those who are trying to help the child. Our kind depend on the protection of the Mother Goddess. Maria is the living embodiment of that Goddess."

Benito shrugged. "That's what you say. As far as I can work out, De Belmondo at best helped Maria kill herself, deprived Alessia of her mother and me of my anchor. I don't look on what I am going to do as revenge. I'd call it prevention of this ever happening again. As for the nonhumans: You're long-lived. Don't tell me this hasn't happened before. Don't tell me it was always a case of siege and starvation. You let probably miserable women do this, time and again, leaving broken hearts and spirits in their wake—for your benefit. You were content to benefit from their misery. You just let it pass. You had your chance to do something. You didn't. Now you must suffer the consequences."

The Crenae-nymph wilted back somewhat from the sheer force of his bitterness. There was some justice in what he said. Most of Aidoneus' brides had gone to him deeply unhappy.

"If we arranged it so that you could speak to Maria . . . you could see that we and the priestess spoke the simple truth. Would that be acceptable to you? She isn't dead, Benito Valdosta. Just beyond the reach of mortals, creating life and light into the shadow world so that it may be reborn into ours."

Benito shook his head. "I only look stupid, nymph. I'm not gullible. You nonhumans are masters of illusions. I'd want to see, touch and be sure this was Maria, before I trusted. And then I'd bring her home."

The nymph bit her lip. "You could try. She—like you—doesn't belong in the Kingdom of the Dead. Aidoneus can do nothing to stop you. She is there by her choice. And while glamour may work on other people—we know it doesn't work on you. You can see us."

"Probably because you choose to be seen. The honest truth is that I don't trust you, I certainly don't trust that priestess of yours, and I don't trust this great Goddess cult. Show me and I might change my mind. It's not likely, though."

The nymph nodded. "Very well. We'll arrange it. You will need to take a boat to the Acheron and then go to Acheroussia, the lake of lamentation."

"You tell me where and when, and I'll be there," said Benito. "I'll have to break out of here, and I'll have to take a bit of care about that. I've got responsibilities now."

The nymph lifted a shoulder. "Then why don't you wait? The Venetian fleet is coming tomorrow and with it your brother, the mage Marco. You can give Alessia into his care."

"Very well. I'm going to go and read up on this Acheroussia and this Aidoneus. I never saw the sense in book-learning before. I'm beginning to understand its purpose. Your tree and your temples have a respite. But it is a temporary one. And I'm going to take steps to see that just killing me won't get your lot off the hook." His expression left no doubt about the reality of that threat.

In shrines across the island, women enacted the rites of spring, danced the star dances, to the sound of the reed-pipes. And this year the embodiment of the great Goddess, She who is fertility and new life, responded with a vigor not seen for many a century.

Renate had the satisfaction of knowing that the new avatar was the strongest for many years. The women who had gone as willing brides weren't usually of the caliber of Maria.

She also knew that Maria had brought a dark cloud to rest over the old religion's centuries of invulnerability. From time immemorial the great Goddess's place had been something immovable in the face of changing times.

Now it met a force that would not be stopped.

"I told you I would help," Maria said, stubbornly, but with no little pride.

He laughed; she was a little startled. She hadn't expected a laugh out of him. "So you did," he said. "So—you, whose magic is of the earth and life—what is it that you think you can do in war?"

Maria paused, and thought, and remembered a certain legend she'd heard, sung by a troubadour at Kat's wedding-feast. The man had run out of love songs, and, in desperation, was trotting out some wildly inappropriate ballads.

This one was about Saint Joseph of Arimathea, and his staff, and a thorn-tree.

"I'll show you," she said, taking a deep breath, and gathering in her power.

She began on land, for everywhere in Emeric's camp there was wood. Tent-poles, wagon-wheels, gun-carriages. Where the blessed rain fell on them, she reached with her power, woke up the wood, and reminded it that it had been alive once, and growing. She passed over the land with her power, and His, stretched out in a great shadow behind her. And where her shadow fell, whatever could grow, did. Whatever had once grown, grew again. On the plains of desolation, a carpet of flowers grew.

And trees. Many of them. Growing out of what had been Emeric's weapons of war. Which he would not be moving again any time soon, if at all—for out of life, comes death, and his mighty cannons were not faring well at all beneath her rains.

Now she turned her attention toward the siege on the water. True, water was not her province. But eventually, all ships come to land—or have earth aboard them, in the form of ballast. And where earth was, so was she . . .

Beside her, the Lord of Shadows laughed, and laughed, and laughed.

Emeric looked at the stream of muddy water creeping into his ornate gilded pavilion and swore. It had been raining now for five days. Sometimes it had slacked off to a drizzle. But mostly it had just poured. The homunculus Elizabeth had provided had plainly been destroyed. Emeric had to regard any magician who could do that with respect. The resultant rain was making the siege into a disaster. The Spianada was a quagmire. The accursed Venetians used the chaos ensuing when the Hungarian cannon were turned on Emeric's own men, and the burning of the camp by raiders, to retake the outer curtain wall.

They probably couldn't hold it . . . if the rain let up. But the rain was altering everything. The rain had flooded the mine; it had also flooded the gap between the moles, washing one away and making the other unstable. Emeric had insufficient tents for his men after the fire, and the mosquitoes had used the rain as a time to catch up on a winter's worth of breeding. The night-air hummed with them. Emeric could only hope the Venetians in the Citadel and the insurgents in the mountains were suffering just as much. But apparently the sea breezes gave the Citadel some relief, and the higher places were never as bad.

What was truly worrying were the reports of disease starting to break out in the crowded quarters. It appeared to be some sort of cyclic fever. What the locals called "malaria." It was apparently something they'd mostly lived through as children. Emeric's troops largely came from areas where it didn't occur. Without that childhood immunity, the soldiers who caught it often died.

A rider came galloping up through the rain. "Sire, the Venetian and Imperial troops have landed in Sidari. We think at least twenty thousand men."

Emeric closed his eyes. "Call the admiral."

"He is coming up the hill, Sire."

Emeric and the admiral looked at the hulls of the galleys. They wouldn't be sailing anywhere in those vessels.

The dead wood had started to sprout. Sprout? That was too mild a word for what was happening. It was growing before his very eyes. Roots were creeping down toward the earth. Shoots were edging out of the twisting wood toward where the sun would be if it stopped raining.

"If they were touching the shore, this is what happened. Even if they weren't touching the shore, this is happening in the holds, where the ballast is. With the fireboat attack and then this . . ."

The admiral shrugged. "I don't have a fleet any more. The galliots have almost all been pulled up and won't be sailing again. Unless you want to start building from scratch, that is. The timber is turning back into woodland. It's plainly magical."

Emeric snarled in frustration. "It is magic. Very powerful magic." He sighed. "Very well. We need to start ferrying my troops across to our camp over on the Illyrian shore." He already knew what would be happening to the wooden wheels of the gun-carriages.

Emeric saw defeat looming. It was time to snatch what he could and run.

Maria was learning how the shadows of this place intersected and related. They shifted and moved in something like a great, complex dance, but she had as yet to find exactly how the steps went or hear the music they moved to. She found she could see into places distant and remote, if not quite as Aidoneus did—at will—at least with increasing clarity.

Some of them led into this place, too. It was vast beyond all imagining. Here she could walk into the shadows, walk among the dead—even talk to them.

The intensity which they'd had in life was gone, and now they gave her great deference as the lady of the living and bride of the king. She discovered she could find people just by desiring to do so. They were considerably less frightening than she'd thought they would be. And somehow, no matter where she was, the almond tree remained in sight.

She'd expected to find Umberto, or Erik's Svanhild, but—

"Not here," the Lord of the Dead, said, divining her thought before she could speak it. "Not now; they came here, and passed on, to their own place. Your Christians all merely pass on, and the followers of Allah, and of other gods. Only those who believe that death will bring them here, to me, remain with me. Every man goes to his own afterlife, according to his beliefs. And every man sees me as his beliefs dictate."

He looked over his kingdom, musing, a little smile on his lips. "You would be surprised to hear what your Christians see me as."

That made her blink. "Saint Peter?" she hazarded.

"Sometimes. Sometimes." And he would say nothing more than that.

Time down here seemed to have little meaning, but Maria found there was one person she had not been able to find. She supposed Aidoneus might be keeping Benito aside. She was at first embarrassed to ask. He was dead, and she'd made her choices. But she wished she could just tell him . . .

She asked instead for help in choosing the right shadow to see Alessia. Aidoneus would be a patient lover, she thought—if he was going to be a lover at all, in that sense. He seemed to have infinite time to attend to her, to talk to her, to listen. He was, she decided, much like Umberto in some ways—except that he allowed her space, too. But now Aidoneus took her hand again, and directed her eyes into a pattern of shadows.

She could see Alessia as if she was leaning over her crib. But the place was unfamiliar. It was very grand. It must be Renate's apartments. She tried to move her view outwards to see the priestess, wishing she could thank her for her care.

Something resisted that change in focus.

Maria tried again.

The resistance held firm, but she recognized the person behind it now: Aidoneus.

She let go his hand, still staring into the shadow. It blurred, becoming one with a myriad of other shadows. She squinted at it, wrinkling her forehead in effort. It was like staring into the brightness of reflected sunlight on the water. But she saw now. Saw through it. Saw Benito pick his daughter up and hold her.

She turned away, after staring for a long, long time. She turned to Aidoneus. "You knew."

He nodded. "I number the living and the dead. I know each by their inner flames. Each and every one is different. I know the when of their passing if not the other details that the fates weave. Sometimes there is doubt. A place where the thread is thin. That one's thread is like a cable."

From a high vantage point, Iskander Beg watched. The Lord of the Mountains was waiting. Very few of the invaders would return to Hungary.

Jagiellon had known before he arrived in Count Mindaug's chambers that the treacherous advisor had fled. Still, there were ways of extracting information even from walls if one were as powerful as the Grand Duke was.

Mindaug had plainly planned it well. Every volume of his precious library was gone, too. Jagiellon set about the magics that would let him know where Mindaug had gone. Eventually a face appeared in the blood-filled bowl. A very beautiful woman's face.

Elizabeth Bartholdy.

So. Much was now clear to the demon who lurked within Jagiellon. The Grand Duke of Lithuania had a new enemy, it seemed. Not "new," exactly, for he'd always known that the

Hungarian sorceress was hostile. But he hadn't realized, till now, that she was such an active opponent; a player herself in the great contest, it seemed—and a major one.

Her motive was clear also, and it was not the normal drive for conquest. Elizabeth Bartholdy was, in her own way, more interested in the spirit than the flesh. She thought to tap the power of the one whom not even Chernobog would name, without paying the inescapable price. And might even have grown powerful enough to have done so, had she succeeded in trapping him. Bathing in the blood of virgins prolonged her life. Bathing in the blood of Chernobog... would have prolonged it for a very long time, if not perhaps eternally.

Grand Duke Jagiellon ordered servants to sterilize Mindaug's quarters, clean away every trace of the traitor. Then, when they were done, ordered his soldiery to sterilize the rooms still further, smearing the walls with the blood and brains and entrails of the servants. Then, when that was done, he ordered that wing of the palace burnt to the ground.

The bonfire produced a memorable stench. The flames, despite the feverish efforts of the soldiers, singed some other portions of the palace also. But Jagiellon was indifferent. A few charred timbers here and there were a small price to pay for power. He need no longer fear that Mindaug might have left some magical links behind.

Jagiellon's fury had ebbed by then, in any event. There was always this to look forward to: The skin of the beautiful Hungarian sorceress would make a memorable meal, someday in the future, with Mindaug's as the appetizer.

The triumphal fleet sailed into the anchorage off the Citadel of Corfu, led by three light galleys and a number of fishing vessels. It was a small gesture, but a significant one.

Amid the cheering, Marco was one of the first ashore, looking for Benito among the emaciated defenders. He found him, with a baby on his knee.

"Ah. Godfather," said Benito with a tired smile. "The man I need. Here. Have her."

"Er."

"Stella here will help you with practical details like feeding and cleaning," said Benito, putting a hand on her shoulder. "As for entertainment, Brother, you're on your own. She sleeps a lot, luckily for you. And she likes to dance. Even my dancing. Although she probably won't by the time I get back."

"But . . . where are you going? What happened to Maria, Benito?"

"I'm going to try and bring her back from the Kingdom of the Dead."

Marco grabbed Benito as he began to turn. "Maria was my friend too, 'Nito. Now tell me exactly what you're planning to do and what has happened."

Marco was unprepared for the tears streaming down Benito's face.

Chapter 102

"I'm going to Hades," said Benito grimly.

"Hades?"

"Apparently where this cult sent Maria to."

"You mean Hell?"

"They say it isn't the same at all. Just the Kingdom of the Dead. Except that she is alive in it. I want to bring her home."

"Are they telling you the truth?" Manfred asked doubtfully.

Benito shrugged. "It's a chance I'll take. I'll try anything. The nymphs seem quite earnest about it. The entry is on the Greek mainland. The Byzantines are nominally at least in control, but I can get a fishing boat to take me across without causing any upset, I reckon."

"I will accompany you," Erik said firmly. "For two reasons, Benito. One is that you've come with me, and been my spear carrier, and borne me away on my shield when I needed that. The other is that I also lost someone precious. I would give anything to see her again. Anything at all."

Benito took a deep breath. "I don't know, Erik. I don't know if they'll allow it. And even if you do find Svanhild . . . she is dead, my friend. Maria is somehow alive down there. They tricked her into this. I'm going to get her back if I can."

Erik smiled sadly and put a hand on Benito's shoulder. "I know this. But you must understand. Even if the chances are tiny, we must take them. Even if I can only speak to her, I will accept that. The loser must accept what terms he can get. And Svan . . . there were so many things I still wanted to say."

Manfred lumbered to his feet. "Well, I have to tell you this. This time, you're not—either of you—going off on this without me."

"I cannot permit it. It is too risky," said Erik, automatically.

Manfred squeezed his shoulder. "Erik, you are my bodyguard and my friend. But the dangers of the halls of the dead don't relate to the body. The dead don't touch the body. They can't. What they can damage and destroy is the mind and the heart. To be honest with you: Your mind and heart are a lot more fragile than mine."

"You don't have a mind to damage, above your belt," said Erik grumpily, a spark of his old self asserting itself. "But I cannot take that chance."

"I'm not actually giving you the choice, Erik," said Manfred with simple finality.

Benito realized, then, just what power rested in the House of Hohenstaffen. The Emperor ruled millions in the Holy Roman Empire . . . but it wasn't just because of being in line to the throne that Manfred could speak so. Erik had always seemed to order Manfred around. For his own safety and good, of course. But when he wanted to exercise it, ultimate authority rested with Manfred. It always would.

"We'll have to do this quietly," said Manfred. "Or I'll have to go through this pointless argument with everyone. Organize it, Benito."

"The Acheron? You want the *Nekromantio Arheas Efiras*?" asked Spiro. "Don't do it Beni," he said, for once in earnest. "That's a bad lot of fakes that. They prey on the fact that if you've lost someone—you're miserable. Easy victim. They're parasites, blood-sucking ticks. Once someone's time comes; they're gone." He put a hand on Benito's shoulder. "Come and have a drink with me and talk it out. I'm buying this time."

Benito was touched. Spiro's ability not to pay for wine was as legendary as the fact that he would never be serious. Now he offered to do both.

"Thanks, Spiro. Not this time. And I'm not going to the *Nekromantio*. Maria was taken before her time. I have talked to the nonhuman waterfolk. They say there is a way that I could go, on a lake called Acheroussia. And neither you nor anyone else can stop me. Apparently if it isn't my time, the Lord of the place can't touch me. Of course, he might not help either."

"Well, we'll take you. Land you quietly. The truth is the Byzantine officials aren't locals and the locals aren't about to tell them about a fishing boat from Corfu. A Venetian galley would be another matter."

Benito nodded knowingly. "Exactly what I thought. So: Can I hire a passage over?

Spiro nodded. "Taki will say yes."

Chapter 103

Manfred spent the trip over-polishing his armor. Polishing it to a mirror-gloss. Manfred was methodical about weapons and armor, without the fanaticism that characterized some Knights. This was excessive and unlike him.

Finally Erik asked why he was doing it.

"Cleanliness is next to godliness. And where we're supposed to be going to . . . I thought I could use a bit of help."

Erik snorted. "In your case, I think it is futile."

"My nurse used to tell me about the gray hosts when I was a gossoon," said Manfred. "Bright steel was supposed to banish 'em. I thought it might be useful."

From the hilltop, they could see the lake. Its dark waters were long and narrow, and a patch of cold mist clung to the middle. But it looked depressingly like a very ordinary lake.

They walked down to the edge where the limnaiad awaited them with a bag of old, old coins. She pointed at a seemingly ordinary boat rowing toward them. "Charon. You will need the obols for the ferryman. Don't expect the other side to be anything you recognize."

Erik shrugged. "I can see the other side from here. It looks very much the same as this side."

"There is more than one other side to the Acheroussia," said the limnaiad, in a cool voice. "You'll see."

Benito opened the bag and counted the coins. "Three is not enough," he said, sternly. "I want eight."

The limnaiad pouted. "They said you wouldn't know."

"The more foolish them, whoever they were."

"The Crenae."

"I wonder how well they do in dry fountains. I saw some ways of draining this lake, on the way here."

"Don't pay the ferryman until you get right across," said the limnaiad hastily.

The beach of black sand seemed to stretch to the far horizons. The only mark on it was the keel of the ferryman's boat. And looking back they could only see mist.

"You won't need the rest of that," grumbled the ferryman, as Benito put the purse away.

"Return fare."

The ferryman snorted. "I've never had one."

"We'd still hate to get back here and find you weren't going to take us because of it," said Manfred cheerfully.

They walked onward, in toward the gray gloom of the interior of Death's country. The way ahead was funneled by tall, glassy black cliffs. And then they came to an end point, a place where only three trails led on. One steep, rocky and draggled with straggly thorns, and seeming to peter out a few hundred yards on. The second, wide and well cobbled, went on into the middle distance. The third seemed to lead off into a valley winding up toward the cliff-top.

"Where now?" asked Benito, looking at the three trails.

Erik took one look. "The narrow one. The hardest one. Mortals are not supposed to pass."

"It would be," said Manfred with a groan. Climbing a steep path in armor was pure misery.

Upward and ever upward the trail wound. Eventually they came out at a misty gray plain.

"Do we have any idea where we're going next?" asked Manfred.

"To look for the dead, I suppose," said Benito.

"We're already among them," said Erik slowly.

Benito realized that the gray mist around them was full of shifting forms, almost seen . . .

Out of the corner of his eye he could see faces. He could also see the expression of eagerness on Erik's face.

Benito took out a small crock sealed with wax from the bag

he'd carried with him. He opened it and poured the contents into a dish.

"What's that?"

"Colyva. Taki insisted I bring it. He said it feeds the souls of the dead and they'd be more likely to leave us in peace." Taki had had no trouble in believing they were coming to visit the dead. The captain had stayed sober the whole trip and Benito had seen him crossing himself and fingering an amulet repeatedly.

"What is it?" Manfred looked curious and hungry enough to steal morsels off the plate set for the dead.

"Wheat, pine nuts, almonds and raisins. And pomegranate seeds. I had the merry devil getting hold of those. All soaked together in honey. Each part of it has some significance, but Taki was pretty vague about it. It's as old as Greece, he said."

"If the dead don't want it, I could use it," grumbled Manfred. But the dead did. Kin came first. And then friends.

Erik looked for Svanhild. But she wasn't there.

He peered forward, into the distance.

Manfred looked oddly at his friend. "Erik. You remember you said you'd never leave her?"

Erik nodded. "My vow. I wish . . . I wish I had not broken it. I will doubtless go to the place of oathbreakers."

Manfred shook his head. "No," he said solemnly. "You won't. She promised the same, didn't she?"

"I think so. In her dying breath."

Manfred took a deep breath. "I think you've been looking in the wrong place. I don't think she'd come here; this place is for the people that believe in it. She's gone somewhere else. And she's waiting for you. But I think—" he added, warningly: "That if you try to get there too soon, she's going to have some sharp words for you."

"The Lord of the Dead has sent me to fetch you into his presence," said one of the shades. "But only you may come into the presence of the living Embodiment of the great Goddess. She wishes to see you, and Aidoneus cannot refuse her."

"I want to see her, too. But what about Manfred and Erik?"

"They must remain here. No harm will come to them. No harm can."

❋   ❋   ❋

Benito walked through shadows. At length, he came to a great hall. In the middle of it, in a patch of sunlight, stood an almond tree in full blossom.

And standing in front of it were two people. Not the insubstantial shade-people of this place, but real people. One of them was Maria. Benito gave a glad cry and would have run forward, seeing her there. But something stopped him.

"I can put unimaginable distances between us should you even take one step further forward," said the stern-faced man at her side. "The avatar of the Mother, the great Goddess, She who is the earth of Corcyra wants to speak with you. Speech I will permit. Nothing more."

"I've come to fetch her. She doesn't belong here in this prison."

The Lord of the Dead shook his head. "She came willingly. She has to honor her bargain."

"Did you, Maria?" asked Benito calmly.

She nodded. "I thought you were dead, Benito. Alessia was dying. I thought I could save her and the island."

Benito grinned. "You told me I wasn't allowed to die without your permission. You think I'd dare disobey? Seriously, Maria. They tricked you into this on false pretenses. That's no bargain. A bargain takes honor on both sides, Lord of the Dead."

Maria turned to Aidoneus. "You knew he wasn't dead."

Aidoneus nodded reluctantly. "Yes. I told you: I number the living and the dead. I can see the ends of the threads of destiny. I can see his end and I can see yours. Yours is far. Further than earthly time would allow. You must be remaining here in the underworld. Our time passes differently, and does not wear out the flesh as fast."

Maria's eyes narrowed. "But when you asked if I was a willing bride, I told you that was why: Because Benito was dead. You deceived me. *You cheated!*"

Aidoneus was silent for a long time. Finally he spoke. "Yes. I do cheat, but only by allowing people to cheat themselves. I wanted you. Your spirit is bright and strong. Many of the brides who have come were barely able to sustain themselves, never mind sun and light and flourishing life."

"The compact is for a willing bride," said Maria. "You told me that. You asked me if I was willing. Twice! You knew that you were deceiving me. That's why you tried to stop me seeing Benito in the shadows."

The Lord of the Dead held up a hand. "You gave me three reasons for being willing." Aidoneus pointed to Benito. "He was dead. Your baby was dying. And the siege was killing your friends."

Benito's eyes narrowed. "You know that Maria is destined to live for many years. Just exactly when is Alessia's time?"

"It is some time into the future," said Aidoneus calmly. "I may not tell mortals the exact time or place of their dying. I also may not lie."

"So you cheated a second time," accused Benito.

Aidoneus nodded. "But the third reason would have been true. The weave of fates was altered by her coming here."

"So does one third of a compact make it valid?"

Maria pursed her lips. Then, rubbed her square chin. "I don't cheat, Benito. It makes it one third valid. Because I was willing for that reason."

Benito sighed. "Agreed. But that still makes you mine for one third, 'Lessi's for another. Doesn't that outweigh the other?"

Maria sat silent for a while. She looked from Benito to Aidoneus, biting her lip. "Benito. You've just come all the way to the Kingdom of the Dead for me. No one else could do something like that. But fair is fair. One third of my life is Aidoneus'. He—and Corfu—need me."

The Lord of the Dead looked at her with eyes of longing, and sadness. "I'll accept that," he said quietly. "I did cheat. But I also gave fair return."

Maria nodded. "You did. But can *you* accept it, Benito?"

He started to reply immediately. Always the quick-witted one, Benito was. But then—perhaps for the first time in his life—stopped to think first. *Really* think.

He thought for quite some time.

In the end, it was the quietly sad, longing face of Aidoneus that gave Benito his decision—and, perhaps most important, allowed him to accept it calmly. For all that the two didn't look at all similar, there was something about Aidoneus that reminded Benito of Umberto Verrier. Lonely men in middle age—insofar as that term could be applied to someone like Aidoneus—who always did their duty. Including, when the need arose, sheltering and caring for a woman that a younger and more flamboyant man had not been able to do. Or willing to do.

Benito still felt that he was responsible for Umberto's death. That aching guilt had never left him. Until now, when he made his decision. The first truly adult decision he thought he'd ever made in his life.

"Yes, I can accept it." Benito shrugged. "I'd be a damned liar to say I liked it, Maria. But I thought I'd lost you forever and completely. Two thirds is a sight better than none at all. I see Aidoneus' point. I'd take one third if that was what I could get. How about eight months with me . . . and four down here?"

Aidoneus actually looked nonplussed. "I thought you'd refuse. Very well. I accept also. Maria will spend the four months of winter with me, the rest of the year with you."

Maria looked at him with a curious expression. "You've grown, Benito. I'm still not sure if I want a man—even for eight months of the year—who doesn't know if he's a wolf or a fox."

"I'm neither, Maria. I'm me. And I'm yours if you want me. I'll have you under any terms. Take me or leave me."

Maria bit her lip again. Then, nodded. "I think I prefer Benito to wolves or foxes."

Aidoneus sighed. "Very well. A bargain is a bargain. But this is my kingdom. There is a last clause to our agreement. Go back to your friends now. Maria can follow you out. But if you look back before you reach the far shore you have lost her forever." Aidoneus' voice was full of grim certainty.

Benito looked at Maria. "It's a deal. But how do I know if Maria is following us out?"

"You can turn and have a look," said Aidoneus with a raised eyebrow. "Or believe. She cannot make any sounds out there, away from the tree."

"You're cheating again, of course."

Aidoneus smiled wryly. "Yes."

Benito shrugged. "My companions can't turn either, I suppose?"

"It doesn't mean as much to them as it does to you. It is possible for them. But no, they can't turn either."

Benito took a deep breath. "You're on."

"What happened?" demanded Manfred.

"She doesn't belong here, and he cheated to get her—on two

of three counts. But he did keep his side of the bargain on that third count. So Maria will spend four months of the year here. She can come out now, following us—but only if I don't look back to see if she is following. Not until I get out on the further shore. And you two can't turn around either."

"That's impossible," said Manfred.

Benito shrugged. "It's the terms I've got. It's better than no terms at all. But I have one request, Manfred."

"What?"

"Walk in front of me."

"If I walk behind you I can try and stop you turning."

Benito shook his head. "Manfred, you said you owed me for bringing Erik back. That I could ask for anything. Well, this is what I ask."

They marched. And marched. Even the final black beach sands seemed endless. The ferryman held out his hand. "Pay me."

Benito snorted. "You'll get our fares on the other side."

"Show me the money."

Holding the ancient coins firmly, Benito held up four obols.

"Isn't that one too many?"

"Play fair," said Benito boredly, and sat down. He did not even twitch his head.

The sunlight on his face was the sweetest thing Manfred had ever felt. The boat slid into the shallows . . . and Benito, still not turning around, held out the four obols.

"Can I keep the change?" asked the ferryman grimly.

"Play fair," said Benito, climbing onto the beach, without so much as a glance. Both feet firmly on the beach he turned, and took Maria into his arms, out of Charon's ferry.

He kissed his love slowly and long. Her lips were warm, as was her body pressed against his. They stood like that for a very long time.

Manfred leaned back against Taki's bulkhead and grinned at Benito and Maria. "I take my hat off to you, Benito. I'd have looked. I'd have had to."

Benito grinned. "I didn't need to look."

"You've got faith," said Erik seriously.

"Actually, Erik, what I had was Manfred walking ahead of me. You've got well-polished armor, Prince."

Manfred laughed until the ship shook. "The Fox's grandson, all right!"

Maria stuck her tongue out at him. "No. He's just Benito. My Benito."

Benito smiled at Maria, lovingly. "I could see you the whole time, Maria, dearest. All the way. I wished I could have told you not to look so worried. He cheated. I never said I wouldn't. For you I would do anything."

Epilogue
Spring, 1540 A.D.

Now that the relief effort was fully underway, the Citadel was allowed a day of celebration, of feasting, of laughter. The feast was of course entirely brought from the ships. It was not very good food, but there was enough.

"Governor De Belmondo is retiring, as soon as Venice sends a replacement," said Marco. "The doctors have told the old man to quit or die in harness, soon. The siege took a toll on him and he's nearing eighty. But he'll stay on in Corfu. He has a small estate in the south."

Benito snorted. "Him, I can deal with. But his wife I'd prefer to see back in Venice, if not Vinland."

Maria pinched his arm. "You're not being fair, Benito. I've told you."

Benito's expression hardened slightly. "I've heard you. I'm never going to entirely agree with you. But I agreed to let it be."

"You're impossible, Benito Valdosta," said Maria. It was plain that there'd still be some stormy exchanges on this one. But Marco noticed she still held his hand, firmly.

"So who will they send to govern us?" asked Alberto, plainly keen to move the subject away from this area.

Marco laughed. "He's come to talk to you, O new head of the Little Arsenal. I was in magical communication with Venice from the ships this morning. Benito has been nominated to be interim deputy governor by the Senate; and to repair the war ravages here, the Senate has voted a budget allocation of half a million ducats."

"Deputy Governor!" Benito gaped. "Me? Are they crazy?"

Marco shrugged. "The Senate was adamant, apparently. For the moment, given De Belmondo's age, they mostly want someone whom they trust to keep Corfu Venetian—and, despite your hair-raising reputation in some other respects, you now have a rather towering reputation as Venice's man-in-a-pinch."

Benito was still gaping. Marco smiled and patted him on the shoulder. "Don't worry, Benito. It's just temporary until the Senate can finish wrangling over who they want as a permanent governor to replace De Belmondo. If it makes you feel any better, Petro told the Senate they were out of their minds. He proposed you for temporary captain-general, instead. But the military types had fits over that idea."

That brought a grin to Benito's face. "And well they might! I'm never going to be their favorite in peacetime. But I've got the perfect candidate for the job: Giuliano Lozza."

"Now that the supply distribution is well in hand," said Manfred, "we'll be heading onward to Jerusalem. A part of the fleet is going east to Canea. There'll be other vessels there, and we can go on to Ascalon."

Manfred looked sad. "I've a need to do some praying for my uncle, who may well not live much longer. And the business of politics goes on. So: We'll be loving you and leaving you, Benito Valdosta. Unless you'd like to come along. I've always a space for you in my company."

Benito felt the earnestness behind those lightly spoken words. He thought back. Command and siege had made Manfred grow. He was no longer likely to challenge Erik's watch-keeping ability. "I'd enjoy it. But I think Venice and Maria would prefer me to stay put awhile. I'll be here when you come back. They also wanted me on the fleet that is set to deal with the Aragonese, Barbary corsairs and the Genovese, too. Strange, to be wanted—and not just by the Schiopettieri, for a change."

Everyone laughed. "Benito, I have to agree with Maria: You were born to be hanged," said Francesca.

Erik squeezed Benito's shoulder. "I really don't feel party-like, yet. I'll be back, to collect Bjarni and the other Vinlanders—except Kari, who insisted on coming with us—and to collect what remains of Svanhild's things. Honor demands I must return them to her kin in Vinland. You'll take care of them for me?"

Benito nodded. "They're managing to feed Bjarni, at least, Erik. If he comes out of it . . . I'll take care of him."

Erik mustered a smile. "I couldn't think of a better caretaker."

Benito assumed a look of injured virtue. "I'm respectable these days. I'd be a married man if the church would agree."

"I think the authorities are mistaken in that. Still. I think I have learned. Those who are truly joined, neither man's laws nor God nor death really put asunder. Words and rituals don't really seem to mean that much."

"Are you entirely mad?" demanded Giuliano, looking at Benito as if he had offered him a lifetime in purgatory instead of the highest military position on the island. "Who would look after my olives? No! Thalia and I," he put a possessive arm around her, "are going to grow good eating kalamatas, not little lineoleas. I've got a new vineyard in the planning, too."

"I could have told you that he wouldn't do it," said Eberhard quietly, when Giuliano had walked away. "Cincinnatus."

"What?"

"You'd benefit from some history lessons, young Benito," said Francesca. "Giuliano Lozza could be a great condottiere if he wanted to. He doesn't. All he wants is a few acres of olive trees, some vines and a wife to make plump with his spoiling. Give him a pack of noisy children, too, and he'd be happier than any king. There are some people who just don't want power, or adulation, or even too much money."

Benito laughed. "You know why?"

"No."

"Because it is his for the asking. So, if I can't have Giuliano, who do we make captain-general? Leopoldo will do for now, while he recovers, but he's good, and ambitious. Venice will move him on for sure. You're all off to the Holy Land. So who am I left with?"

"You can always do double duty while you look for someone else. And why don't you make Thalia the minister of agricultural reform? You'd get Giuliano that way. And if the island really needs him—Giuliano will be there."

"That should give the surviving Libri d'Oro the hissy-fits," said Benito, with a look of pleasure.

"When they discover what you're planning on doing about tenant farms," said Manfred cheerfully, "you might just *need* Lozza."

Benito grinned evilly. "No. We'll do it slowly. It's like cooking lobsters. If you start with cold water then they don't flap and snap like they do when you try to drop them into boiling water. But the system as it stands is a recipe for insurrection."

"As we saw during the siege," said Eberhard. "But you may find that loosening the bonds will lose Venice this island."

Benito shrugged. "The system as it is will definitely lose it. I plan to work on ties of trade and blood instead."

"You'll make a good deputy governor," said Manfred with a chuckle. "Keep the taverns in trade anyway."

"For four months of the year," said Maria sternly.

Benito looked at her. There was a sadness in his eyes, but acceptance, also. He put an arm around her. "It's not every husband—in all but name, anyway—who gets a four-month holiday."

Spiro came up with a Venetian glass of tawny liquid in hand. "Here you are Beni. *Kakotrigi.* You'd better get used to it, if you're going to be our governor."

"That's your third," said Maria, taking it herself.

Benito shook his head. "I should have said it is not every man who *needs* a four-month holiday. *Ow!* I was only joking, Maria! You'll get 'Lessi wet if you pour it over me."

Maria looked sternly at him. "I have walked among the dead and asked them secrets hidden from ordinary mortals, Benito Valdosta. And among them I found out your weakness. Tonight, I am going to tickle you."

The last part was said with a Maria smile, full of promise, full of loving. An older Maria, confident at last of herself. Of being loved enough. Of being someone who no longer felt insecure about her station, about being a canaler with a *Case Vecchie* man. She had something now that made her realize just how irrelevant these things were.

Maria pointed a finger at Spiro. "You. Fetch us two more glasses of this—this *kakotrigi.* I didn't like it much at first sip, but I'm finding it better and better."

"It grows on you," said Benito, putting his arm around her again. "Part of the magic of this place."

Eneko Lopez tasted the wine. "Rough magic," he said with a grimace.

"But good and strong," said Maria, laughing.

In the high valley in the shadow of Pantocrator, the faun played on his panpipes a part of the ancient dance that is love, life, death, joy, sorrow and Corfu.

CHARACTERS

Principal Characters

Aldanto, Caesare: Sellsword, spy, Milanese of aristocratic family; formerly a Montagnard agent, now enslaved by Jagiellon.

Bartholdy, Elizabeth: Hungarian Countess, great-great aunt of King Emeric of Hungary; a sorceress, appearing to be about twenty years old.

Casarini, Bianca: Florentine resident on Corfu; follower of Elizabeth Bartholdy.

De Belmondo, Renate: Wife of the Podesta, priestess of the Mother Goddess.

De Chevreuse, Francesca: Courtesan, formerly of Orleans.

Emeric: King of Hungary.

Hakkonsen, Erik: An Icelander, and bodyguard and mentor to Manfred.

Jagiellon: Grand Duke of Lithuania; possessed by the demon Chernobog.

Lopez, Eneko: A Basque cleric and ecclesiastical magician.

Manfred, Prince, Earl of Carnac, Marquis of Rennes, Baron of Ravensburg: nephew to the Holy Roman Emperor.

Mindaug, Kazimierz: Count, advisor to Jagiellon. A student of western magic.

Montescue, Katerina (Kat): Lodovico's granddaughter, married to Marco Valdosta.

Shaman of Kandalaksha: His name remains a closely guarded secret. He is the servant of Jagiellon.

Thordardottar, Svanhild: only daughter of a powerful Vinland trading house.

Tomaselli, Nico, Captain-General: Venetian Military commander of Corfu.

Tomaselli, Sophia: wife of the captain-general.

Valdosta, Benito: grandson of the Duke of Ferrara, illegitimate son of the *condottiere* Carlo Sforza; ward of Doge Dorma.

Valdosta, Marco: grandson of the Duke of Ferrara.

Verrier, Maria: former Venetian canaler, married to Umberto.

Verrier, Umberto: Master in the Caulker's Guild.

Verrier, Alessia: Daughter of Maria.

Minor characters

Bartelozzi, Antimo: Agent and advisor to Enrico Dell'este.

Beg, Iskander: Illyrian chieftain, know as the Lord of the Mountains.

Bespi, Fortunato: Former Montagnard assassin, now bodyguard for Marco Valdosta.

De Belmondo, Alexio: Podesta of Corfu.

Dell'este, Enrico, Duke of Ferrara: The Old Fox. One of Italy's leading military tacticians; grandfather to Benito and Marco.

Dorma, Petro: Doge of Venice. Head of the commercially powerful House of Dorma.

Dorma, Angelina: Petro Dorma's younger sister.

Evangelina, Sister: A Hypatian Sibling.

Falkenberg, Ritter: A Prussian Knight-Proctor. Master of siege-craft.

Fianelli, Marco: A Corfiote criminal; and a spy for King Emeric.

Hohenstauffen, Charles Fredrik: Holy Roman Emperor.

Kari: Half-Osage tribesman. Hearthman to the Thordarsons.

Kosti: Fisherman, crewman on Taki's boat.

Leopoldo, Commander: Commander of the garrison, Corfu Citadel.

Loukaris, Meletios: Secretary to Podesta De Belmondo.

Lozza, Giuliano: Son of Flavio Lozza, a legendary master-at-arms. A plump olive grower.

Mavroukis, Stella: Maria's gossipy friend.

Mavroukis, Alberto: Stella's husband; a Master in the Little Arsenal of Corfu.

Mascoli, Brother: Hypatian priest of St. Raphaella.

Montescue, Lodovico: Head of the formerly powerful House Montescue.

Morando, Aldo: Swindler, fake Satanist.

Nachelli, Petros: Rent-collector and go-between for spies.

Saluzzo, Paulo: A thug working for Fianelli.

Sforza, Carlo: The wolf of the North, Milan's chief *condottiere*. A military legend.

Spiro: Corfiote sailor, fisherman, crewman on Taki's boat, friend of Benito.

Taki: Skipper of a fishing boat.

Thalia: Peasant woman, first female sergeant in Venetian Corfiote forces.

Thordarson, Bjarni: oldest son of a powerful Vinland trading house.

Thordarson, Gulta: Third son of a powerful Vinland trading house.

Trolliger, Baron Hans: One of the Holy Roman Emperor's courtiers and advisors.

Von Gherens, Ritter: A Prussian Knight-Proctor.

GLOSSARY

Aquitaine: An independent kingdom in western Europe; it comprises parts of what in our universe would be called France and England.

Armagh, The League of: A loose alliance of Celtic/Nordic states.

Arsenalotti: The workers at the Arsenal, Venice's state shipyard.

Ascalon: A port in Palestine.

Bacino: Harbor basin.

Barducci's: A tavern well known for music.

Bretagne: Brittany. An independent Duchy, part of the league of Armagh.

Carnac: Capital of Celtic Brittany.

Capi: Roughly the equivalent of a lieutenant.

Carreta: A pony/horse trap.

Case Vecchie: Great houses; the Venetian aristocracy.

Cassone: A carved chest.

Chrysostom, John: Charismatic preacher associated with Saint Hypatia, at the breakpoint between this universe and ours; born 349 A.D.

Colleganza: A collective trading venture.

Cotte: A surplice-like garment, the predecessor of coat.

Curti: Literally, "short"—the Case Vecchie who had not been ennobled for many years.

Dalmatia: The eastern coast of the northern Adriatic Sea. Once the source of much of Venice's timber.

Ferrara: City-state in the Po valley in northern Italy; famous for steel-working, particularly swordsmiths.

Fruili: Region to the northeast of Venice.

Galliot: Small galley.

Golden Horn: Venetian trading enclave in Constantinople.

Hohenstauffen: The ruling house of the Holy Roman Empire.

Hypatia, Saint of Alexandria: Patron saint of the Hypatian order. Neoplatonist philosopher and librarian of the great library at Alexandra. Her saving of the Library from the mob instigated by Cyril the Patriarch of Alexandria is the breakpoint between this universe and ours.

Ilkhan Mongol: The Mongol khanate.

Istria: Peninsula to the south of Trieste. A Venetian possession.

Jesolo: The marshes to the east of Venice in the Venetian Lagoon.

Koboldwerk: Cunningly wrought chainmail made by dwarves.

Libri d'Oro: "Of the Golden book"; landowners; the Greek aristocracy of Corfu.

Longi: Literally, "long"—the Case Vecchie who had been ennobled for many generations.

Marangona: The bell which rang for half an hour from dawn to summon the Arsenalotti to work. Also rung for national emergencies.

Misericord: Thin dagger intended to penetrate joints in armor.

Narenta: Large river on the Dalmatian coast. A pirate lair.

Negroponte: Venetian trading outpost on the east coast of Greece.

Outremer: Originally "outré mer"—beyond the sea. Refers to the East, on the far side of the Mediterranean.

Paulines: The faction of Christianity taking its lead from the writings of Saint Paul. In this universe, the dominant religious faction in the north of Europe. More hierarchical and militant than the Petrine faction.

Petrine: The gentler, more tolerant southern faction of the Church.

Poignard: Dagger.

Podesta: Governor.

Ritters: Teutonic Knights.

Scaliger: The ruling house of Verona.

Schiopettieri: Mercenary soldiers under the control of the Lords of the Nightwatch (Signori di Notte); Venice's equivalent to a police force.

Scuolo: Guilds.

Surcoat: Loose sleeveless garment with insignia normally worn over armor.

Trebizond: Venetian trading outpost in the Black Sea.

Veneto: The region of northern Italy which includes Venice.
Veneze: People of Venice.
Vinland: North America.
Visconti: The ruling house of Milan.

FOOD

Kourabiedies: Almond cookies.
Stifado: Lamb or kid stew, on Corfu, commonly with quinces.
Loukoúmia: Turkish delight.
Sultanína glykó: Spoon-sweets (grape preserve flavored with rose geranium).
Melanzane alla finitese: Crumbed aubergine 'sandwich' of melted cheese.
Risotto con finocchi: Rice dish with fennel.
Kakotrigos: A grape variety which clings to the vine. Made into a tawny wine on Corfu called Kakotrigi.

Peace Process

WILLIAM B. QUANDT

Peace Process

AMERICAN DIPLOMACY AND
THE ARAB-ISRAELI CONFLICT
SINCE 1967

THE BROOKINGS INSTITUTION
Washington, D.C.

UNIVERSITY OF CALIFORNIA PRESS
Berkeley and Los Angeles

Library of Congress Cataloging-in-Publication data

Quandt, William B.
    Peace process : American diplomacy and the Arab-
Israeli conflict since 1967 / William B. Quandt.
     p. cm.
    Includes bibliographical references and index.
    ISBN 0-520-08388-1 (alk. paper)—
    ISBN 0-520-08390-3 (pbk. : alk. paper)
     1. Jewish-Arab relations—1967–1973. 2. Jewish-
Arab relations—1973– 3. United States—Foreign
relations—Middle East. 4. Middle East—Foreign
relations—United States. 5. United States—Foreign
relations—20th century. I. Title.
DS119.7.Q69 1993
327.73056—dc20   93-18804
                                    CIP

9 8 7 6 5 4 3 2 1

Foreword

Each of the past six presidents became deeply involved in the diplomacy surrounding the Arab-Israeli conflict. The same will doubtless be true of President Bill Clinton. The hopeful message of this book is that the United States, if it plays its role of mediator skillfully, can contribute to a resolution of the dispute between Israel and its Arab neighbors. Just as often, however, presidents and their advisers have misread the realities of the Middle East, have pursued flawed policies, and have contributed to a worsening of the conflict. They did so particularly when they viewed the Middle East through a cold war lens.

This study provides a detailed analytical account of American policy toward the Arab-Israeli conflict since the crisis that resulted in the June 1967 war. Each administration's initial approach to the problem of peacemaking is assessed, along with the evolution of policy as it confronted the stubborn realities of the region and the mine fields of domestic political controversy.

Given the complexity of the challenge, American policy has shown remarkable consistency and surprising successes. Egypt and Israel are at peace with each other and are both close friends of the United States. More recently, other Arab parties have begun to negotiate with Israel under American auspices. One point on which presidents of both political parties have agreed is that a U.S. role in support of Arab-Israeli peace is consistent with U.S. national interests.

William B. Quandt, a senior fellow in the Foreign Policy Studies program at Brookings, participated in the policymaking process as a member of the National Security Council staff in both the Nixon and the Carter administrations. He brings his direct experience to bear on the analysis of how decisions are made on a particularly sensitive foreign-policy issue.

In 1977 Quandt published a book called *Decade of Decisions: American Policy toward the Arab-Israeli Conflict, 1967–1976*. The University of California Press published that study. The current work is, in part, a revision and updating of *Decade of Decisions*, and Brookings is pleased to copublish it with the University of California Press.

In revising the early chapters on the Johnson, Nixon, and Ford administrations, Quandt was assisted by a number of former American officials, including Alfred L. Atherton, Jr., Lucius Battle, Richard Helms, Robert Oakley, Richard Parker, Harold Saunders, Joseph Sisco, Eugene Rostow, and Walt Rostow. Ephraim Evron was also especially helpful on the 1967 crisis.

For the Carter period, the author was assisted by Zbigniew Brzezinski, Jimmy Carter, Hermann Eilts, Samuel Lewis, Gary Sick, and Cyrus Vance. For the Reagan period, he benefited from discussions with Geoffrey Kemp, William Kirby, Daniel Kurtzer, Richard Murphy, and Nicholas Veliotes. Former secretary of state George Shultz generously shared an early draft of the Middle East chapters of his memoirs. On the Bush administration, the author was helped by Richard Haass, Aaron Miller, and Dennis Ross, among others. Throughout, Helena Cobban was a supportive critic and adviser.

The author also wishes to thank Elisa Barsoum for staff assistance; Marlin Dick, Susanne Lane, and Deborah Rivel for research support; Agnieska Paczynska for verification; Leila Rached for proofreading; Caroline Lalire for editing the manuscript; and L. Pilar Wyman for preparing the index. Professor L. Carl Brown, William Kirby, and John Steinbruner provided helpful reviews of the manuscript.

Brookings gratefully acknowledges the financial support of the John D. and Catherine T. MacArthur Foundation.

The views expressed in this book are those of the author and should not be ascribed to any of the persons whose assistance is acknowledged above, to the sources of funding support, or to the trustees, officers, or other staff members of the Brookings Institution.

Bruce K. MacLaury
President

March 1993
Washington, D.C.

Author's Note

In one way or another, I have been studying and writing about American policy toward the Arab-Israeli conflict since 1968. Mostly I have been an outsider, trying to figure out how policy is made by looking at the results, talking to those in positions to know, reading the records when they become available. Twice I have been close enough to events, as a member of the National Security Council staff in 1972–74 and in 1977–79, to observe the process up close and to play some part in it.

This book was designed to revise and bring up to date my earlier study, *Decade of Decisions: American Policy toward the Arab-Israeli Conflict, 1967–1976* (University of California Press, 1977). About one-half the material in the present book is new. Only chapters 4 through 9 are essentially unchanged from their counterparts in *Decade of Decisions*. Even there, however, I have incorporated any new material that has come to light, especially in the various memoirs of participants.

Chapter 1 is an essentially new introduction, although the analytical scheme is similar to that used in the earlier volume. I still find that an emphasis on the president and his inner circle is essential, although I now emphasize more than before the on-the-job learning that seems to take place and that produces a degree of convergence in the policies of administrations after they have encountered the realities of the Middle East region and of Washington.

The chapters on the 1967 war (2 and 3) are almost entirely new. In recent years the Lyndon Baines Johnson Library in Austin, Texas, has released a large quantity of material that helps to answer questions of how Johnson saw the crisis. As a result, my present interpretation of those important events is somewhat different from what it was when I published in 1977.

The three chapters on the Carter period (10, 11, and 12) are derived from previous writing I did on the subject, primarily my *Camp David: Peacemaking and Politics* (Brookings, 1986) and a chapter entitled "The American Strategy in the Camp David Negotiations," in S. Seikaly, R.

Baalbaki, P. Dodd, eds., *Quest for Understanding: Arabic and Islamic Studies in Memory of Malcolm H. Kerr* (American University of Beirut Press, 1991). Chapter 13, on the early Reagan years, is a heavily revised version of a chapter that appeared in a book I edited called *The Middle East: Ten Years after Camp David* (Brookings, 1988). Chapters 14, 15, and 16 are entirely new.

Inevitably the latter chapters of a book of this sort must be somewhat speculative. Less is known about how decisions were made in the Reagan and Bush administrations. In due course memoirs will be written and gaps will be filled. But for now, much of the narrative must be derived from publicly available sources. I recognize that this creates something of an imbalance between the in-depth treatment of the earlier periods and the less-detailed accounting of the later ones. But because much of the logic and the approaches to Arab-Israeli peacemaking were forged in the Johnson through Carter periods, I feel that the detailed accounts of those periods are warranted.

W.B.Q.

To Lorna

Contents

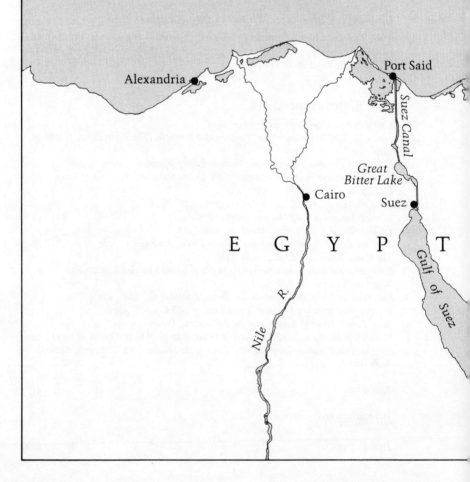

The Arab-Israeli Arena

Mediterranean Sea

Alexandria

Port Said

Suez Canal

Great Bitter Lake

Cairo

Suez

E G Y P T

Nile R.

Gulf of Suez

Peace Process

Page Process

CHAPTER ONE

Introduction

Sometime in the mid-1970s the term *peace process* began to be widely used to describe the American-led efforts to bring about a negotiated peace between Israel and its Arab neighbors. The phrase stuck, and ever since it has been synonymous with the gradual, step-by-step approach to resolving one of the world's most difficult conflicts.

In the years since 1967 the emphasis in Washington has shifted from the spelling out of the ingredients of "peace" to the "process" of getting there. This procedural bias, which frequently seems to characterize American diplomacy, reflects a practical, even legalistic side of American political culture. Procedures are also less controversial than substance, more susceptible to compromise, and thus easier for politicians to deal with. Much of U.S. constitutional theory focuses on how issues should be resolved—the process—rather than on substance—what should be done.

Whenever progress has been made toward Arab-Israeli peace through American mediation, there has always been a joining of substance and procedure. The United States has provided both a sense of direction and a mechanism. That, at its best, is what the "peace process" has been about. At worst, it has been little more than a slogan used to mask the marking of time.

THE PRE-1967 STALEMATE

The stage was set for the contemporary Arab-Israeli peace process by the 1967 Six-Day War. Until then, the conflict between Israel and the Arabs had seemed almost frozen, moving neither toward resolution nor toward war. The ostensible issues in dispute were still those left unresolved by the armistice agreements of 1949. At that time, it had been widely expected that those agreements would simply be a step toward final peace talks. But the issues in dispute were too complex for the many mediation efforts of the early 1950s, and by the mid-1950s the cold war rivalry between Moscow and Washington had left the Arab-Israeli conflict suspended somewhere between war and peace. For better or worse, the armistice agreements had provided a semblance of stability from 1949 to 1967.

During this long truce the Israelis had been preoccupied with questions of an existential nature. Would the Arabs ever accept the idea of a Jewish state in their midst? Would recognition be accompanied by security arrangements that could be relied on? Would the Arabs insist on the return of the hundreds of thousands of Palestinian refugees who had fled their homes in 1948–49, thereby threatening the Jewishness of the new state? And would the Arabs accept the 1949 armistice lines as recognized borders, or would they insist on an Israeli withdrawal to the indefensible lines of the 1947 United Nations partition agreement? As for tactics, would Israel be able to negotiate separately with each Arab regime, or would the Arabs insist on a comprehensive approach to peacemaking? Most Israelis felt certain that the Arabs would not provide reassuring answers to these questions, and therefore saw little prospect for successful negotiations, whether with the conservative monarchs or the new brand of nationalistic army officers.

From the Arab perspective, the conflict also seemed intractable, but the interests of existing regimes and the interests of the Palestinians, who had lost most from the creation of Israel, were by no means identical. The regimes struck the pose of defending the rights of the Palestinians to return to their homes or to be compensated for their losses. They withheld recognition from the Jewish state, periodically engaging in furious propaganda attacks against the "Zionist entity." The more militant Arabs sometimes coupled their harsh rhetoric with support for guerrilla attacks on Israel. But others, such as Jordan and Lebanon, were fairly content with the armistice arrangements and even maintained under-the-table contacts with the Israelis. "No war, no peace" suited them well.

The Palestinians, not surprisingly, used all their moral and political capital to prevent any Arab regime from recognizing the Jewish state, and by the mid-1950s they had found a champion for their cause in Egypt's president Gamal Abdel Nasser. From that point on, Arab nationalism and the demand for the restoration of Palestinian rights were Nasser's most potent weapons as he sought to unify the ranks of the Arab world. But Nasser also sought to steer a course between war and peace, at least until the momentous days of May 1967. Then, as tensions rose, Palestinian radicals, who had hoped to draw the Arab states into conflict with Israel on their behalf, rallied to Nasser's banner and helped to cut off any chance that he might retreat from the brink to which he had so quickly advanced.

THE 1967 WATERSHED

The 1967 war transformed the frozen landscape of the Arab-Israeli conflict in dramatic ways. Israel revealed itself to be a military power able to outmatch all its neighbors. By the end of the brief war, Israel was in control of the Sinai desert; the West Bank of the Jordan River, including all of East Jerusalem; Gaza, with its teeming refugee camps; and the strategically important Golan Heights. More than a million Palestinians came under the control of the Israeli military, creating an acute dilemma for Israel. None of the post-1921 British mandate of Palestine was now free of Israeli control. If Israel kept the newly conquered land and granted the people full political rights, Israel would become a binational state, which few Israelis wanted. If it kept the land but did not grant political rights to the Palestinians, it would come to resemble other colonial powers, with predictable results. Finally, if Israel relinquished the land, it would retain its Jewish character, but could it live in peace and security? These were the alternatives debated within the fractious, often boisterous Israeli democracy.

Given the magnitude of their victory in the 1967 war, some Israelis seemed to expect right afterwards that the Arabs would have no option but to sue for peace. But that did not happen. So, confident of its military superiority, and assured of American support, Israel decided to wait for the Arabs to change their position. But what would happen to the occupied territories while Israel waited? Would they be held in trust, to be traded for peace and security at some future date? Or would they gradually and selectively be incorporated into Israel, as the nationalists on the right demanded? Jerusalem, at least, would not be returned, and almost immediately Israel announced the unilateral expansion of the municipal boundaries and the annexation of the eastern parts of the city. Palestinians living there would have the right to become Israeli citizens, but few took up the offer. Apart from Jerusalem, Israel signaled its willingness to return most of the occupied territories, although the passage of time and changing circumstances gradually eroded that position.

The 1967 war was a shock to Arabs who had believed Nasser could end their sense of weakness and humiliation at the hands of the West. Indeed, although Nasser lived on for another three years after the war, his prestige was shattered. Arab nationalism of the sort he preached would never again be such a powerful force. Instead, regimes came to look more and more after their own narrow interests, and the Palestinians followed suit by organizing their own political movement, free of control by any Arab government. One of the few dynamic developments in the Arab world after the 1967 war was the emergence of a new generation of Palestinians leading the fight for their rights.

The Palestine Liberation Organization (PLO), originally supported by Arab regimes to keep the Palestinians under control, quickly became an independent actor in the region. It symbolized the hopes of many Palestinians and caused much concern among established Arab regimes, which were not used to seeing the Palestinians take matters into their own hands.

In theory, these changes in the Arab world might have opened the way for an easing of the Arab-Israeli conflict. A certain amount of self-criticism took place in Arab intellectual circles. Political realism began to challenge ideological sloganeering. But no one made any serious peace effort immediately after the 1967 war, and by September of that year the Arab parties had all agreed there would be no negotiations with Israel, no peace, and no recognition. Once again, "neither war nor peace" seemed to be a tolerable prospect for both Arabs and Israelis.

THE NEED FOR A MEDIATOR

With the parties to the conflict locked into mutually unacceptable positions, the chance for diplomatic movement seemed to depend on others, especially the United States. Because of the close U.S.-Israeli relationship, many Arabs looked to Washington to press Israel for concessions. The example of President Dwight D. Eisenhower, who had pressured Israel to relinquish its gains from the Suez war of 1956, was still a living memory. The two main areas of Arab concern were the return of territories seized in the 1967 war and some measure of justice for the Palestinians. In return, it was implied, something short of peace would be offered to Israel, perhaps an end to belligerency or strengthened armistice arrangements.

The Arab regimes were still reluctant to promise full peace and recognition for Israel unless and until the Palestinians were satisfied, and that would require more than Israeli withdrawal from occupied territories. As time went by, and the PLO gained in prestige, it became more and more difficult for the Arab states to pursue their narrowly defined interests with no regard for Palestinian claims. And the Arabs were reluctant to deal directly with Israel. If a deal was to be struck, it would be through the efforts of the two superpowers—the United States and the Soviet Union—and the United Nations.

By contrast, Israel was adamant that territory would not be returned for less than peace, recognition, and security. And the means for getting to a settlement would have to include direct negotiations by each Arab party with Israel. For most Israelis, the claims of the Palestinians were impossible to deal with. At best, Jordan could act as a stand-in for the Palestinians, who would have to be satisfied with some form of internationally supported rehabilitation and compensation scheme. Above all, Palestinians would not be allowed to return to their homes, except in very special circumstances of family reunions and in very small numbers.

AMERICAN AMBIVALENCE: POSITIONS AND POLICIES

Confronted with these almost contradictory positions, the United States was reluctant to get deeply involved in Arab-Israeli diplomacy. The Vietnam War was still raging in 1967, and the needs of the Middle East seemed less compelling than the daily demands of an ongoing war in Southeast Asia. Still, from the outset the United States staked out a position somewhere in between the views of Israelis and Arabs. Israel, it was believed, was entitled to more than a return to the old armistice arrangements. Some form of contractually binding end to the state of war should be achieved, and Israeli security concerns would have to be met. On the other hand, if the Arabs were prepared to meet those conditions, they should recover most, if not all, of the territory lost in 1967. These views were spelled out by President Lyndon Johnson soon after the war and became the basis for UN Resolution 242, of November 22, 1967, which thereafter provided the main reference point, with all its ambiguities, for peacemaking.

In the years from 1967 through 1992 every American president—Lyndon Johnson, Richard Nixon, Gerald Ford, Jimmy Carter, Ronald Reagan, and George Bush—was drawn into the intricacies of the Arab-Israeli conflict, often much more than he had intended to be. American mediation became essential to the diplomatic effort.

The basic American position adopted in 1967 has remained remarkably consistent. For example, each American president since 1967 has formally subscribed to the following points:

—Israel should not be required to relinquish territories captured in 1967 without a quid pro quo from the Arab parties involving peace, security, and recognition. This position, summarized in the formula "land for peace," and embodied in UN Resolution 242, applies to each front of the conflict.

—East Jerusalem is legally considered to be occupied territory whose status should eventually be settled in peace negotiations. Whatever its final political status, Jerusalem should not be physically redivided. Reflecting the legal American position on the city, the American embassy has remained in Tel Aviv, despite promises by many presidential candidates to move the embassy to Jerusalem.

—Israeli settlements beyond the 1967 armistice lines—the "green line"—are obstacles to peace. Until 1981 they were considered illegal under international law, but the Reagan administration reversed position and declared they were not illegal. But Reagan, and especially Bush, continued to oppose the creation of settlements. No American funds are to be used by Israel beyond the green line.

—However Palestinian rights may eventually be defined, they do not include the right of unrestricted return to homes within the 1967 lines, nor do they entail the automatic right of independence. All administrations have opposed the creation of a fully independent Palestinian state, preferring some form of association of the West Bank and Gaza with Jordan. Over time, however, the Jordan option—the idea that Jordan should speak for the Palestinians—has faded, and since 1988 the United States has agreed to deal directly with Palestinian representatives.

—Israel's military superiority, its technological edge, against any plausible coalition of Arab parties has been maintained through American military assistance. Each U.S. administration has tacitly accepted the existence of Israeli nuclear weapons, with the understanding that they will not be brandished and can be regarded only as an ultimate deterrent, not as a battlefield weapon. American conventional military aid is provided, in part, to ensure that Israel will not have to rely on its nuclear capability for anything other than deterrence.

With minor adjustments, every president from Lyndon Johnson to Bill Clinton has subscribed to each of these positions. They have been so fundamental that they are rarely even discussed. To change any one of these positions would entail costs, both domestic and international. These positions represent continuity and predictability. But they do not always determine policy. Policy, unlike these positions, is heavily influenced by tactical considerations, and here presidents and their advisers differ with one another, and sometimes with themselves from one moment to the next.

Policies involve judgments about what will work. How can a country be best influenced? What levers exist to influence a situation? Should aid be offered or withheld? Will reassurance or pressure—or both—be most effective? When is the optimal time to launch an initiative? Should it be done in public or private? How much prior consultation should take place, and with whom? On these matters, there is no accepted received wisdom. Each president and his top advisers must evaluate the realities of the Middle East, of the international environment, of the domestic front, and of human psychology before reaching a subjective judgment. While positions tend to be predictable, policies are not. They are the realm where leadership makes all the difference. And part of leadership is knowing when a policy has failed and should be replaced with another.

HOW POLICY IS MADE: ALTERNATIVE MODELS

More than any other regional conflict, the Arab-Israeli dispute has consistently competed for top priority on the American foreign-policy agenda. This study tries to account for the prominence of the Arab-Israeli peace process in American policy circles since 1967. It seeks to analyze the way in which perceived national interests have interacted with domestic political considerations to ensure that Arab-Israeli peacemaking has become the province of the president and his closest advisers.

Because presidents and secretaries of state—not faceless bureaucrats—usually set the guidelines for policy on the Arab-Israeli dispute, it is important to try to understand how they come to adopt the views that guide them through the labyrinthine complexities of Arab-Israeli diplomacy. Here several models compete for attention.

One model would have us believe that policies flow from a cool deliberation of national interest. This *strategic* model assumes that decisions are made by rational decisionmakers. Such a perspective implies that it does not much matter who occupies the Oval Office. The high degree of continuity in several aspects of the American stance toward the conflict since 1967 would serve as evidence that broad interests and rational policy processes provide the best explanation for policy.

But anyone who has spent time in government will testify that policymaking is anything but orderly and rational. As described by the *bureaucratic politics* model, different agencies compete with one another, fixed organizational procedures are hard to change, and reliable information is difficult to come by. This perspective places a premium on bureaucratic rivalries and the "game" of policymaking. Policy outcomes are much less predictable from this perspective. Instead, one needs to look at who is influencing whom. Microlevel analysis is needed, in contrast to the broad systemic approach favored by the strategic model. Much of the gossip of Washington is based on the premise that the insiders' political game is what counts in setting policy. Embassies try desperately to convince their governments back home that seemingly sinister policy outcomes are often simply the result of the normal give and take of everyday bureaucratic struggles, the compromises, the foul-ups, the trading of favors that are part of the Washington scene. If conspiracy theorists thrive on the strategic model—there must be a logical explanation for each action taken by the government—political cynics and comics have a field day with the bureaucratic politics model.[1]

A third model, one emphasizing the importance of *domestic politics*, is also injected into the study of American policy toward the Arab-Israeli conflict. Without a doubt Arab-Israeli policymaking in Washington does get tangled up in internal politics. Congress, where support for Israel is usually high, and where pro-Israeli lobbies tend to concentrate their efforts, can frequently exert influence over foreign policy, largely through its control over the budget.[2] While some senators and representatives no doubt do consider the national interest, for many others positions taken on the Arab-Israeli conflict are little more than part of their domestic reelection strategy. Some analysts have maintained that American Middle East policy is primarily an expression of either the pro-Israeli lobby or the oil lobby. Little evidence will be found here for such an extreme view, even though in some circumstances the lobbies can be influential.

Besides considering the role of Congress, one must also take into account the effect of the workings of the American political system, especially the four-year cycle of presidential elections. This cycle imposes some regular patterns on the policymaking process that have little to do with the world outside but a great deal to do with the way power is pursued and won through elections.[3] One should hardly be surprised to find that every four years the issue of moving the American embassy to Jerusalem reemerges, arms sales to Arab countries are deferred, and presidential contenders emphasize those parts of their program that are most congenial to the supporters of Israel. Nor should one be surprised to find that once the election is over, policy returns to a more evenhanded course.

THE MIND OF THE PRESIDENT

As much as each of these approaches—strategic-rational analysis, bureaucratic politics, and domestic politics—can illuminate aspects of how the United States has engaged in the Arab-Israeli peace process,[4] the most important factor, as this book argues, is the view of the conflict—the definition of the situation—held by the president and his closest advisers, usually including the secretary of state. The president is more than just the first among equals in a bureaucratic struggle or in domestic political debates. And he is certainly not a purely rational, strategic thinker.

More than anything else, an analyst studying American policy toward the Arab-Israeli conflict should want to know how the president—and the few key individuals to whom he listens—makes sense of the many arguments, the mountain of "facts," the competing claims he hears whenever his attention turns to the Arab-Israeli conflict. To a large degree he must impose order where none seems to exist; he must make sense out of something he may hardly understand; he must simplify when complexity becomes overwhelming; and he must decide to authorize others to act in his name if he is not interested enough, or competent enough, to formulate the main lines of policy.

What, then, do the president and his top advisers rely on if not generalized views that they bring with them into office? No senior policymaker in American history has ever come to power with a well-developed understanding of the nuances of the Arab-Israeli dispute, the intricacies of its history, or even much knowledge of the protagonists. At best policymakers have general ideas, notions, inclinations, biases, predispositions, fragments of knowledge. To some extent "ideology" plays a part, although there has never really been a neat liberal versus conservative, Democrat versus Republican divide over the Arab-Israeli conflict. Only when it came to dealing with the Soviet Union as a power in the Middle East region—up until 1990—did the cold war ideological divide between conservatives and liberals seem to make a difference, and even then the evidence is not conclusive.

Any account of policymaking would, however, be incomplete if it did nothing more than map the initial predispositions of key decisionmakers. As important as these are in setting the broad policy guidelines for an administration, they are not enough. Policy is not static, set once and forever after unchanged. Nor is policy reassessed every day. But over time views do change, learning takes place, and policies are adjusted. As a result, a process of convergence seems to take place, whereby the views of senior policymakers toward the Arab-Israeli conflict differ most with those of their predecessors when they first take office, and tend to resemble them by the end of their terms. Ford and Carter disagreed on Middle East policy in 1976–77 but were later to coauthor articles on what should be done to resolve the Arab-Israeli conflict. Even Reagan in his later years seemed closer to his predecessor's outlook than to his own initial approach to Arab-Israeli diplomacy.

It is this process of adjustment, modification, and adaptation to the realities of the Middle East and to the realities of Washington that allows each administration to deal with uncertainty and change. Without this on-the-job learning, American foreign policy would be at best a rigid, brittle affair.

What triggers a change in attitudes? Is the process of learning incremental, or do changes occur suddenly because of crises or the failure of previous policies? When change takes place, are core values called into account, or are tactics merely revised? The evidence presented here suggests that change rarely affects deeply held views. Presidents and their advisers seem reluctant to abandon central beliefs. Basic positions are adhered to with remarkable tenacity, accounting for the stability in the stated positions of the United States on the issues in dispute in the Arab-Israeli conflict. They represent a deep consensus. But politicians and diplomats have no trouble making small adjustments in their understanding of the Arab-Israeli conflict, and that is often enough to produce a substantial change in policy, if not in basic positions or in overall strategy. One simple change in judgment—that President Anwar Sadat of Egypt should be taken seriously—was enough to lead to a major reassessment of American policy in the midst of the October 1973 war.

Since most of the American-led peace process has been geared toward procedures, not substance, the ability of top decisionmakers to experiment with various approaches as they learn more about the conflict has imparted an almost experimental quality to American foreign policy in the Middle East. Almost every conceivable tactic is eventually considered, some are tried, and some even work. And if one administration does not get it right, within a matter of years another team will be in place, willing to try other approaches. Although American foreign policy is sometimes maddening in its lack of consistency and short attention span, this ability to abandon failed policies and move on has often been the hallmark of success.

Foreign-policy making seems to involve an interplay among the initial predispositions of top policymakers, information about the specific issues being considered, the pull of bureaucratic groupings, the weight of domestic political considerations, the management of transitions from one presidency to the next, and the impact of events in the region of concern. It is often in the midst of crises that new policies are devised, that the shortcomings of one approach are clearly seen, and that a new definition of the situation is imposed. And it is in the midst of crises that presidential powers are at their greatest.

Only rarely are crises anticipated and new polices adopted to ward them off. As a result, American policy often seems to run on automatic pilot until jolted out of its inertial course by an event beyond its control. Critics who find this pattern alarming need to appreciate how complex it is to balance the competing perspectives that vie for support in the Oval Office and how difficult it is to set a course that seems well designed to protect the multiple interests of a global power like the United States—and to do all this without risking one's political life.

NATIONAL INTERESTS

To get a sense of the difficulty, consider the nature of American interests in the Middle East, as seen from the perspective of the White House. An assessment of these interests almost always takes place at the outset of a new administration, or just after a crisis, in the belief, usually unjustified, that light will be shed on what should be done to advance the prospects of Arab-Israeli peace at the least risk to American interests.

Politicians and some analysts like to invoke the national interest because it seems to encompass tangible, hard-headed concerns as opposed to sentimental, emotional considerations. There is something imposing about cloaking a decision in the garb of national security interests, as if no further debate were needed.

In the real world of policymaking, interests are indeed discussed, but most officials understand that any definition of a national interest contains a strong subjective element. Except for limited areas of foreign affairs, such as trade policy, alternative courses of action cannot readily be tested against an objective yardstick to determine how well they serve the national interest.

In discussions of the Arab-Israeli conflict, several distinct, often competing, national interests confound the problem of relating interests to policy. For example, most policymakers until about 1990 would have said that a major American interest in the Middle East, and therefore related to the handling of Arab-Israeli diplomacy, was the *containment of Soviet influence* in the region. This interest derived from a broader strategy of containment that had been initially developed for Europe but was gradually universalized during the cold war.

In Europe the strategy of containment had led to the Marshall Plan and the North Atlantic Treaty Organization (NATO). But the attempt to replicate these mechanisms of containment in the Middle East had failed, in part because of the unresolved Arab-Israeli conflict. So, however much American policymakers might worry about the growth of Soviet influence in the region, they rarely knew what should be done about it. In the brief period of a few months in 1956–57, the United States opposed the Israeli-French-British attack on Egypt (the Suez war), announced the Eisenhower Doctrine of support to anticommunist regimes in the area, forced the Israelis to withdraw from Sinai, and criticized Nasser's Egypt for its intervention in the affairs of other Arab countries. How all that contributed coherently to the agreed-upon goal of limiting Soviet influence was never quite clear.

Over the years many policies toward the Arab-Israeli conflict have been justified, at least in part, by this concern about the Soviet Union. Arms sales have been made and denied in pursuit of this interest; and the Soviets have been excluded from, and included in, discussions on the region, all as part of the goal of trying to manage Soviet influence in the region.

One might think that a strategy of challenging the Soviets in the region would have led the United States to adopt belligerent, interventionist policies, as it did in Southeast Asia. But in the Middle East the concern about overt Soviet military intervention was high, especially from the mid-1960s on, and therefore any American intervention, it was felt, might face a comparable move by the Soviets. Indeed, on several occasions, in the June 1967 war, in 1970 in Jordan, during the October 1973 war, and to a lesser degree in 1982 in Lebanon, the United States feared a possible military confrontation with the Soviet Union. Thus, however ardently American officials might want to check Soviet advances, they wanted to do so without much risk of direct military confrontation with Moscow. In brief, the Soviet angle was never far from the minds of policymakers, but it did little to help clarify choices. With the collapse of the Soviet

Union in 1990–91, this interest suddenly disappeared, leaving oil and Israel as the two main American concerns in the Middle East.

Oil has always been a major reason for the United States to pay special attention to the Middle East, but its connection to the Arab-Israeli conflict has not always been apparent. American companies were active in developing the oil resources of the area, especially in Saudi Arabia; the industrialized West was heavily dependent on Middle East oil; and American import needs began to grow from the early 1970s on.[5]

The basic facts about oil in the region were easy to understand. Saudi Arabia, Iraq, and Iran, along with the small states of the Persian Gulf littoral, sat atop about two-thirds of the known reserves of oil in the world. The least expensive place to produce oil was also the Middle East. Production costs were remarkably low. Thus Middle East stability seemed to go hand in hand with access to relatively inexpensive supplies of oil.

Throughout most of the 1950s and 1960s Middle East oil was readily available for the reconstruction of Europe and Japan. American companies made good profits. And threatened disruptions of supply had little effect. A conscious effort to keep Persian Gulf affairs separate from the Arab-Israeli conflict seemed to work quite well.

But by the late 1960s the British had decided to withdraw their military presence from east of Suez. How, if at all, would that affect the security of Gulf oil supplies? Should the United States try to fill the vacuum with forces of its own, or should it try to build up regional powers, such as Iran and Saudi Arabia? If arms were sold to Saudi Arabia to help ensure access to oil supplies, how would the Israelis and the other Arab countries react? What would the Soviets do? In short, how could an interest, which everyone agreed was important, be translated into concrete policies?

American calculations about oil were further complicated by the fact that the United States is both a large producer of oil and a large importer. For those concerned with enhancing domestic supplies, the low production costs of Middle East oil are always a potential threat. Texas oil producers argue for quotas to protect them from "cheap" foreign oil. But consumers want cheap oil and will therefore resist gasoline taxes, tariffs, or quotas designed to prop up the domestic oil industry. No American president would know how to answer the question of the proper price of Middle East oil. If forced to give an answer, he would have to mumble something like "not too high and not too low." In practice, the stability and predictability of oil supplies have been seen as more important than a specific price. This perception has reinforced the view that the main American interest is in reliable access to Middle East oil, and therefore in regional stability. Still, price cannot be ignored. In the early 1990s the annual import bill for oil from the Middle East exceeded $10 billion, out of a total oil import bill of $35 billion. Each one dollar increase in the price of oil added more than $1 billion to the oil import bill.

The other main interest that has dominated discussion of the Arab-Israeli conflict is the *special American commitment to Israel.* The United States had been an early and enthusiastic supporter of the idea of a Jewish state in part of Palestine. That support was clearly rooted in a sense of moral commitment to the survivors of the holocaust, as well as in the intense attachment of American Jews to Israel. During the 1980s a "strategic" rationale was added to the traditional list of reasons for supporting Israel, although this view was never universally accepted.

Support for Israel was always tempered by a desire to maintain some interests in surrounding Arab countries, because of either oil or competition with the Soviet Union. As a result, through most of the years from 1949 until the mid-1960s, the United States provided few arms and only modest amounts of aid. As Eisenhower demonstrated in 1956, support for Israel did not mean offering a blank check.

Even though each of these perceived interests was readily accepted as important by successive administrations—and there was little argument over the list—what the implications for policy were of any one, to say nothing of all three, of these interests was not clear. To take the most difficult case, what should be done when one set of interests seemed to be at variance with another? Which should get more weight, the economic interest of oil, or the strategic interest of checking Soviet advances, or the moral interest of supporting Israel?

Without a common yardstick, the interests were literally incommensurate. How could arms for the Saudis or Jordanians be squared with support for Israel? How could Soviet inroads in a country like Egypt be checked? Was it better to oppose Nasser to teach him a lesson about the costs of relying on the Soviets, or should an effort be made to win him away from dependence on Moscow? And what would either of these approaches mean for relations with Israel and Saudi Arabia?

In brief, U.S. national interests were clearly involved in the Middle East and would be affected by every step of the Arab-Israeli peace process. But there was almost no agreement on what these interests meant in terms of concrete policies. Advocates of different perspectives, as will be seen, were equally adept at invoking national interests to support their preferred courses of action. Often policy preferences seemed to come first, and then the interests were found to justify the policy. Precisely because of these dilemmas, policymaking could not be left to bureaucrats. The stakes were too high, the judgments too political. Thus Arab-Israeli policy, with remarkable frequency, landed in the lap of the president or his secretary of state. More than for most issues of foreign policy, presidential leadership became crucial to the Arab-Israeli peace process.

Insofar as presidents and their advisers saw a way to resolve the potential conflict among American interests in the Middle East, it was by promoting the Arab-Israeli peace process. This policy is the closest equivalent to that of containment toward the Soviet Union—a policy with broad bipartisan support that promises to protect a range of important American interests. If Arab-Israeli peace could be achieved, it was thought, Soviet influence in the region would decline, Israeli security would be enhanced, and American relations with key Arab countries would improve. Regional stability would therefore be more easily achieved, and oil supplies would be less threatened. Obviously, other sources of trouble would still exist in the region, but few disagreed on the desirability of Arab-Israeli peace, or the need for American leadership to achieve it. The differences, and they were many, came over the feasibility of a peace settlement and over the appropriate tactics. In making these judgments, presidents made their most important contribution to the formulation of policy.

PRESIDENTIAL LEADERSHIP AND POLICYMAKING

In U.S. politics, there is a strong presumption that who is president matters. Huge sums are spent on electoral campaigns to select the president. That office receives immense respect and deference, and most writers of American political history assume that the man occupying the White House can shape events. Does this perspective merely reflect an individualism rooted in American culture, or does it contain a profound truth?

One can easily imagine situations in which it would be meaningless to explain a policy by looking at the individuals responsible for making the decisions. If no real margin for choice exists, individuals do not count for much. Other factors take precedence. For example, to predict the voting behavior of senators from New York on aid to Israel, one normally need not consider their identity. It is enough to know something about the constituency, the overwhelming support for Israel among New Yorkers, and the lack of countervailing pressures to be virtually certain about the policy choice of an individual senator.

If context can account for behavior, so can the nature of perceived interests or objectives. If we were studying Japan's policies toward the Arab-Israeli conflict, we would not be especially concerned with who was prime minister at any given moment. It would make more sense to look at the dependence of Japan on Arab oil and the lack of any significant cultural or economic ties to Israel to predict that Japan will adopt a generally pro-Arab policy. When interests easily converge on a single policy, individual choice can be relegated to the background.

Finally, if a nation has no capability to act in foreign policy, we will not be particularly interested in the views of its leaders. To ask why a small European country does not assume a more active role in promoting an Arab-Israeli settlement does not require us to examine who is in charge of policy. Instead, the lack of significant means to affect the behavior of Arabs and Israelis is about all we need to know. A country without important economic, military, or diplomatic assets has virtually no choices to make in foreign policy. Obviously none of these conditions hold for the United States in its approach to the Arab-Israeli conflict. Capabilities for action do exist. The nature of American interests, as generally understood by policymakers, does not predetermine a single course of action. And despite the obvious constraints imposed by the structure of the international system and domestic politics, choices do exist on most issues, even though at times the margin of choice may be narrow.

CONFRONTING COMPLEXITY AND UNCERTAINTY

Most political leaders, with no noteworthy alteration in personality or psychodynamics, are likely at some point to change positions on policy issues. Often such changes will be portrayed as opportunism or waffling. But they could instead be a reaction to a complicated situation, suggesting that people can learn as new information is acquired. Particularly when dealing with complex events and ambiguous choices, people may shift their positions quite suddenly, without altering the fundamental aspects of their approaches to policy. As Raymond Bauer said, "Policy problems are sufficiently complex that for the vast majority of individuals or organizations it is conceivable—given the objective features of the situation—to imagine them ending up on any side of the issue."[6]

Policymakers often find it difficult to recognize the difference between a good proposal and a bad proposal. In normal circumstances, bargaining and compromise may be rational courses for a politician to follow, but to do so assumes that issues have been defined according to some understood criteria. When such criteria are not obvious, what should one do?

On most issues of importance, policymakers operate in an environment in which uncertainty and complexity are dominant. Addressing an unknowable future with imperfect information about the past and present, policymakers must use guidelines and simplifications drawn from their own experience, the "lessons of history," or the consensus of their colleagues. The result is often a cautious style of decisionmaking that strives merely to make incremental changes in existing policies.[7] At times, however, very sudden shifts in policy may also take place. How can one account for both these outcomes?

Leadership is only rarely the task of selecting between good and bad policies. Instead, the anguish and challenge of leadership is to choose between equally plausible arguments about how best to achieve one's goals. For example, most presidents and their advisers have placed a very high value on achieving peace in the Middle East. But values do not easily translate into policy. Instead, several reasonable alternatives are likely to compete for presidential attention, such as the following:

—If Israel is to feel secure enough to make the territorial concessions necessary to gain Arab acceptance of the terms of a peace agreement, it must continue to receive large quantities of American military and economic aid.

—If Israel feels too strong and self-confident, it will not see the need for any change in the status quo. U.S. aid must therefore be used as a form of pressure.

Presidents Nixon, Ford, Carter, and Bush subscribed to both the foregoing views at different times.

Similarly, consider the following propositions, which were widely entertained by U.S. presidents until the breakup of the USSR:

—The Soviet Union has no interest in peace in the Middle East, because it would lose influence unless it could exploit tensions in the area. Hence the United States cannot expect cooperation from the Soviet Union in the search for a settlement.

—The Soviets, like ourselves, have mixed interests in the Middle East. They fear a confrontation and are therefore prepared to reach a settlement, provided they are allowed to participate in the diplomatic process. By leaving the Soviet Union out, the United States provides it with an incentive to sabotage the peacemaking effort. Therefore, U.S.-Soviet agreement will be essential to reaching peace in the Middle East.

Concerning the Arabs, one may also hear diverse opinions:

—Only when the Arabs have regained their self-respect and feel strong will they be prepared to make peace with Israel.

—When the Arabs feel that time is on their side, they increase their demands and become more extreme. Only a decisive military defeat will convince them that Israel is here to stay and that they must use political means to regain their territory.

Each of these propositions has been seriously entertained by recent American presidents and secretaries of state. One could almost say that all of them have been believed at various times by some individuals. The key element in selecting among these plausible interpretations of reality is not merely whether one is pro-Israeli or pro-Arab, or hard line or not so hard line on relations with Moscow. A more complex process is at work.

LESSONS OF HISTORY

In choosing among plausible, but imperfectly understood, courses of action, policymakers inevitably resort to simplifications. Guidelines emerge from recent experiences, historical analogies, wishful thinking, and group consensus.[8] Categorical inferences are thus made; confusing events are placed in comprehensible structures; reality is given a definition that allows purposive action to take place. Recent experience is a particularly potent source of guidance for the future. If a policy has worked in one setting, policymakers will want to try it in another context as well. Secretary of State Henry A. Kissinger, for example, apparently relied on his experiences in negotiating with the Chinese, Russians, and Vietnamese when he approached negotiations with the Arabs and Israelis in 1974–75. Step-by-step diplomacy was the result.

More general historical "lessons" may loom large in the thinking of policymakers as they confront new problems.[9] President Harry Truman was especially inclined to invoke historical analogies. He well understood that the essence of presidential leadership was the ability to make decisions in the face of uncertainty and to live with their consequences. By relying on history, he was able to reassure himself that his decisions were well founded.[10]

Several historical analogies have been notably effective in structuring

American views of reality. The lessons of Munich, for example, have been pointed to repeatedly over the years, principally that the appeasement of dictators serves only to whet their appetite for further conquest. Hence a firm, resolute opposition to aggression is required. The "domino theory" is a direct descendant of this perspective, as was the policy of containment.

A second set of guidelines for policy stems from President Woodrow Wilson's fourteen points after World War I, especially the emphasis on self-determination and opposition to spheres of influence. As embodied in the Atlantic Charter in 1941, these principles strongly influenced American policy during the Second World War.[11] Since the failure of U.S. policy in Southeast Asia, new "lessons" have been drawn, which warn against overinvolvement, commitments in marginal areas, excessive reliance on force, and risks of playing the role of world policeman. Whether these will prove as durable as the examples of Munich and Wilsonian idealism remains to be seen, but American policy continues to be discussed in terms of these historical analyses.

When recent experience and historical analogies fail to resolve dilemmas of choice, certain psychological mechanisms may come to the rescue. Wishful thinking is a particularly potent way to resolve uncertainty. When in doubt, choose the course that seems least painful, that fits best with one's hopes and expectations; perhaps it will turn out all right after all. In any event, one can almost always rationalize a choice after making it. Good reasons can be found even for bad policies, and often the ability to come up with a convincing rationale will help to overcome uncertainties.

Apart from such well-known but poorly understood aspects of individual psychology, the social dynamics of a situation often help to resolve uncertainty. If through discussion a group can reach consensus on the proper course of action, individuals are likely to suppress their private doubts. Above all, when a president participates in a group decision, a strong tendency toward consensus is likely. As some scholars have emphasized, presidents must go to considerable lengths to protect themselves from the stultifying effects of group conformity in their presence and the tendency to suppress divergent views.[12] Neither President Johnson's practice of inviting a large number of advisers to consult with him nor President Nixon's effort to use the National Security Council to channel alternatives to him are guarantees against the distortions of group consensus, in part because presidents value consensus as a way to resolve doubts.

At any given moment presidents and their key advisers tend to share fairly similar and stable definitions of reality. However such definitions emerge, whether through reference to experience or to history, through wishful thinking and rationalization, or through group consensus, they will provide guidelines for action in the face of uncertainty. Complexity will be simplified by reference to a few key criteria. In the Arab-Israeli setting, these will usually have to do with the saliency of issues, their amenability to solution, the role of the Soviet Union (up until late 1990), and the value of economic and military assistance to various parties.

CRISES AND THE REDEFINING OF ISSUES

Crises play an extremely important role in the development of these guidelines. By definition, crises involve surprise, threat, and increased uncertainty. Previous policies may well be exposed as flawed or bankrupt. Reality no longer accords with previous expectations. In such a situation a new structure of perceptions is likely to emerge, one that will reflect presidential perspectives to the degree the president becomes involved in handling the crisis. If the crisis is satisfactorily resolved, a new and often quite durable set of assumptions will guide policy for some time.

Often crises can produce significant policy changes without causing a sweeping reassessment of a decisionmaker's views. It may be only a greater sense of urgency that brings into play a new policy. Or it may be a slight shift in assumptions about the Soviet role, for example, or the advantages of pursuing a more conciliatory policy toward Egypt. Small adjustments in a person's perceptions, in the weight accorded to one issue as opposed to another, can lead to substantial shifts of emphasis, of nuance, and therefore of action. Again, policymakers do not change from being pro-Israeli to pro-Arab overnight, but crises may bring into focus new relations among issues or raise the importance of one interest, thus leading to changes in policy. Basic values will remain intact, but perceptions and understanding of relationships may quickly change.

In the case studies that follow, I explore the important role of crises in defining issues for presidents and their advisers. And I try to account for their views, to understand their reasoning, and to see situations from their standpoint. Between crises, as is noted, it is difficult to bring about changes in policies forged in the midst of crisis and having the stamp of presidential approval.

This approach shortchanges the role of Congress, public opinion, interest groups, the media, and the bureaucracy. All these are worthy subjects of study and undoubtedly have influenced American diplomacy toward the Arab-Israeli conflict. Nor do I discuss in this book why Arabs and Israelis took the decisions that they did. Only in passing do I deal with the protagonists in the conflict, describing their views but not subjecting them to the kind of analysis reserved for American policy.

Starting, then, with the key role of the president and his advisers in shaping policy, particularly in moments of crisis, when domestic and organizational constraints are least confining, the book examines how politics and bureaucratic habits affect both the formulation and implementation of policies in normal times. But at the center of the study are those rare moments when policymakers try to make sense out of the confusing flow of events, when they strive to relate action to purposes, for it is then that the promises and limitations of leadership are most apparent.

PART ONE

The Johnson Presidency

CHAPTER TWO

Yellow Light: Johnson and the Crisis of May–June 1967

Lyndon Baines Johnson brought to the presidency a remarkable array of political talents. An activist and a man of strong passions, Johnson seemed to enjoy exerting his power. As majority leader in the Senate, he had used the art of persuasion as few other leaders had; building consensus through artfully constructed compromises had been one of his strong suits. His political experience did not, however, extend to foreign-policy making, an area that demanded his attention, especially as American involvement in Vietnam grew in late 1964 and early 1965.

Fortunately for the new president, one part of the world that seemed comparatively quiet in the early 1960s was the Middle East. Long-standing disputes still simmered, but compared with the turbulent 1950s the situation appeared to be manageable. The U.S.-Israeli relationship had been strengthened by President Kennedy, and Johnson obviously was prepared to continue on this line, particularly with increases in military assistance. His personal sentiments toward Israel were warm and admiring. To all appearances he genuinely liked the Israelis he had dealt with, many of his closest advisers were well-known friends of Israel, and his own contacts with the American Jewish community had been close throughout his political career.[1]

Johnson's demonstrated fondness for Israel did not mean he was particularly hostile to Arabs, but it is fair to say that Johnson showed little sympathy for the radical brand of Arab nationalism expounded by Egypt's president Gamal Abdel Nasser. And he was sensitive to signs that the Soviet Union was exploiting Arab nationalism to weaken the influence of the West in the Middle East. Like other American policymakers before him, Johnson seemed to waver between a desire to try to come to terms with Nasser and a belief that Nasser's prestige and regional ambitions had to be trimmed. More important for policy than these predispositions, however, was the fact that Johnson, overwhelmingly preoccupied by Vietnam, treated Middle East issues as deserving only secondary priority.

U.S.-Egyptian relations had deteriorated steadily between 1964 and early 1967, in part because of the conflict in Yemen, in part because of quarrels over aid. By 1967, with Vietnam becoming a divisive domestic issue for Johnson, problems of the Middle East were left largely to the State Department. There the anxiety about increased tension between Israel and the surrounding Arab states was growing after the Israeli raid on the Jordanian town of Al-Samu' in November 1966 and especially after an April 1967 Israeli-Syrian air battle that resulted in the downing of six Syrian MiGs. Under Secretary of State Eugene Rostow was particularly concerned about the drift of events, suspecting as he did that the Soviets were seeking to take advantage in the Middle East of Washington's preoccupation with Vietnam.[2]

One indication of this mounting concern can be found in a report filed by the American ambassador in Cairo, Lucius Battle, after his last meeting with Nasser before returning to Washington to become the assistant secretary of state for Near Eastern affairs in the spring of 1967. He warned that Nasser was looking for some foreign-policy adventure to divert attention from his internal difficulties. Battle predicted that this would come in the form of heating up the Yemen crisis, trying to subvert the pro-Western regime in Libya, or, least likely, trying to heat up the Arab-Israeli conflict.[3] So great was the concern with the situation in Yemen that the National Security Council planned to hold a session on that crisis in late May. (As events unfolded, the meeting was held as scheduled on May 24, but by then the focus was on the mounting tension between Egypt and Israel.)

If the tensions on the Syrian-Israeli border provided the fuel for the early stages of the 1967 crisis, the spark that ignited the fuel came in the form of erroneous Soviet reports to Egypt on May 13 that Israel had mobilized some ten to thirteen brigades on the Syrian border. Against the backdrop of Israeli threats to take action to stop the guerrilla raids from Syria,[4] this disinformation apparently helped to convince Nasser the time had come for Egypt to take some action to deter any Israeli moves against Syria and to restore his own somewhat tarnished image in the Arab world.[5] The Soviets, he seemed to calculate, would provide firm backing for his position.

On May 14 Nasser made the first of his fateful moves. Egyptian troops were ostentatiously sent into Sinai, posing an unmistakable challenge to Israel, if not yet a serious military threat. President Johnson and his key advisers were quick to sense the danger in the new situation. Because of his well-known sympathy for Israel and his forceful personality, Johnson might have been expected to take a strong and unambiguous stand in support of Israel at the outset of the crisis, especially as such a stand might have helped to prevent Arab miscalculations. Moreover, reassurances to Israel would lessen the pressure on Prime Minister Levi Eshkol to resort to preemptive military action. Finally, a strong stand in the Middle East would signal the Soviet Union that it could not exploit tensions there without confronting the United States.

The reality of U. S. policy as the Middle East crisis unfolded in May was, however, quite different. American behavior was cautious, at times ambiguous, and ultimately unable to prevent a war that was clearly in the offing. Why was that the case? This is the central puzzle to solve in examining Johnson's reaction to the events leading up to the June 1967 war. Also, one must ask how hard Johnson really tried to restrain Israel. Some have alleged that, in fact, Johnson gave Israel a green light to attack, or in some way colluded with Israel to draw Nasser into a trap.[6] These charges need to be carefully assessed. And what role did domestic political considerations play in Johnson's thinking? Did the many pro-Israeli figures in Johnson's entourage influence his views? Finally, what is one to make of the specific allegations from anonymous sources that the United States sent a military team to Israel on the eve of the war which carried out reconnaissance missions on the Egyptian front after hostilities had begun?[7]

INITIAL REACTIONS TO THE CRISIS

Nasser's initial moves were interpreted in Washington primarily in political terms. Under attack by the conservative monarchies of Jordan and Saudi Arabia for being soft on Israel, Nasser was seen as attempting to regain prestige by appearing as the defender of the embattled and threatened radical regime in Syria. Middle East watchers in the State Department thought they recognized a familiar pattern. In February 1960 Nasser had sent troops into Sinai, postured for a while, claimed victory by deterring alleged Israeli aggressive designs, and then backed down.[8] All in all, a rather cheap victory, and not one that presented much of a danger to anyone. Consequently the initial American reaction to Nasser's dispatch of troops was restrained. Even the Israelis did not seem to be particularly alarmed.

On May 16, however, the crisis took on a more serious aspect as the Egyptians made their initial request for the removal of the United Nations

Emergency Force (UNEF).⁹ This prompted President Johnson to sound out the Israelis about their intentions and to consult with the British and French. On May 17 Johnson sent Eshkol the first of several letters exchanged during the crisis in which he urged restraint and specifically asked to be informed before Israel took any action. "I am sure you will understand that I cannot accept any responsibilities on behalf of the United States for situations which arise as the result of actions on which we are not consulted."¹⁰

From the outset, then, Johnson seemed to want to avoid war, to restrain the Israelis, and to gain allied support for any action that might be taken. Two possible alternative courses of action seem not to have been seriously considered at this point. One might have been to stand aside and let the Israelis act as they saw fit, even to the extent of going to war.¹¹ The danger, of course, was that Israel might get into trouble and turn to the United States for help. Johnson seemed to fear this possibility throughout the crisis, despite all the intelligence predictions that Israel would easily win a war against Egypt alone or against all the surrounding Arab countries.

The second alternative not considered at this point was bold unilateral American action opposing Nasser's effort to change the status quo. Here the problems were twofold. A quarrel with Egypt might inflame the situation and weaken American influence throughout the Arab world. The Suez precedent, and what it had done to British and French positions in the region, was very much in the minds of key American officials. Nasser was not noted for backing down when challenged. Moreover, U.S. military assets were deeply committed in Vietnam, so that a full-scale military confrontation with Egypt was ruled out. But even if American forces had been available, Congress was in no mood to countenance unilateral military action, even in support of Israel. Therefore, the initial United States effort was directed toward restraining Israel and building a multilateral context for any American action, whether diplomatic or military.

Eshkol's reply to Johnson's letter reached Washington the following day, May 18. The Israeli prime minister blamed Syria for the increase in tension and stated that Egypt must remove its troops from Sinai. Then, appealing directly to Johnson, Eshkol requested that the United States reaffirm its commitment to Israeli security and inform the Soviet Union in particular of this commitment. Johnson wrote to Premier Aleksei Kosygin the following day, affirming the American position of support for Israel as requested, but suggesting in addition a "joint initiative of the two powers to prevent the dispute between Israel and the UAR [United Arab Republic, or Egypt] and Syria from drifting into war."[12]

After Egypt's initial request for the withdrawal of the UNEF on May 16, there was danger that Nasser might overplay his hand by also closing the Strait of Tiran to the Israelis. The opening of the strait to Israeli shipping was the one tangible gain made by Israel in the 1956 war. American commitments concerning the international status of the strait were explicit. It was seen as an international waterway, open for the free passage of ships of all nations, including Israel. The Israelis had been promised that they could count on U.S. support to keep the strait open. According to a February 11, 1957, aide-memoire presented to Israel, the United States undertook to "exercise the right of free and innocent passage [in the Strait of Tiran] and to join with others to secure general recognition of this right." In subsequent clarifications of the American position, Secretary of State John Foster Dulles recognized Israel's right, under article 51 of the United Nations Charter, to use force to open the strait if it was ever closed to Israeli ships by force.[13]

The UNEF had stationed troops at Sharm al-Shaykh since 1957, and shipping had not been impeded. If the UNEF withdrew, however, Nasser would be under great pressure to return the situation to its pre-1956 status. Israel had long declared that such action would be considered a casus belli.

In light of these dangers, one might have expected some action by the United States after May 16 aimed at preventing the complete removal of the UNEF. But the record shows no sign of an urgent approach to UN Secretary General U Thant on this matter, and by the evening of May 18 U Thant had responded positively to the formal Egyptian government request that all UNEF troops leave Egyptian territory.

The strait still remained open, however, and a strong warning by Israel or the United States about the consequences of its closure might conceivably have influenced Nasser's next move. From May 19 until midday on May 22, Nasser took no action to close the strait, nor did he make any threat to do so. Presumably he was waiting to see how Israel and the United States, among others, would react to the UNEF's withdrawal. The United States made no direct approach to Nasser until May 22, the day Nasser finally announced the closure of the strait. It issued no public statements reaffirming the American view that the strait was an international waterway, nor did the reputedly pro-Israeli president respond to Eshkol's request for a public declaration of America's commitment to Israel's security.

Some Israelis had feared that Nasser might view the cautious U.S. stand in this initial period as an invitation to interfere with free passage in the strait.[14] At that point, however, the Israeli position itself was not particularly strong, as Eshkol's May 22 speech showed, and made a restrained American position easier to justify. Instead of spelling out its position on the UNEF and the threatened closure of the Strait of Tiran during the period between May 16 and May 22, the United States continued to warn Israel not to act unilaterally. A preference for working within a UN framework was conveyed to the Israelis, including a suggestion that the UNEF troops might be moved to the Israeli side of the armistice lines.[15]

The day before Nasser's May 22 speech at Bir Gifgafa announcing the closure of the strait to Israeli shipping, Johnson sent a second letter to Eshkol reassuring him that the Soviet Union understood the U.S. commitment to Israel. At the same time, however, Johnson sought to explain why he could not make a public statement on the consequences of a blockade of the Gulf of Aqaba. In particular, he noted that any statement by him on the strait might complicate the mission of U Thant, who was on his way to Cairo. Johnson did, however, refer to the need for suitable measures inside or outside the UN to deal with the crisis.[16] Israeli Foreign Minister Abba Eban felt that this letter did not reflect Johnson's real views and must have been drafted by a "frightened bureaucrat."[17]

On May 22 Johnson finally sent a letter to the Egyptian leader. The thrust of the message was to assure Nasser of the friendship of the United States while urging him to avoid any step that might lead to war. In addition, Johnson offered to send Vice President Hubert Humphrey to Cairo. Johnson ended the letter with words he had personally added: "I look forward to our working out a program that will be acceptable and constructive for our respective peoples." The message was not delivered by ambassador-designate Richard Nolte until the following day, by which time the strait had already been declared closed to Israeli shipping and strategic cargoes bound for Israel.[18]

Johnson informed Eshkol the same day that he was writing to the Egyptian and Syrian leaders warning them not to take actions that might lead to hostilities.[19] In addition, another message from Johnson to Kosygin was also sent on May 22. Reiterating his suggestion of joint action to calm the situation, Johnson went on to state, "The increasing harassment of Israel by elements based in Syria, with attendant reactions within Israel and within the Arab world, has brought the area close to major violence. Your and our ties to nations of the area could bring us into difficulties which I am confident neither of us seeks. It would appear a time for each of us to use our influence to the full in the course of moderation, including our influence over action by the United Nations."[20]

These messages, which might have helped to calm the situation earlier, were rendered meaningless by the next major escalation of the crisis.[21] The well-intentioned American initiative of May 21–22 was too little and too late. Shortly after midnight May 22–23, Nasser's speech announcing the closure of the strait was broadcast.

THE CRISIS OVER THE STRAIT

If Johnson had feared that Israel might resort to force unilaterally before May 23, the danger now became acutely real. Therefore he requested that Israel not make any military move for at least forty-eight hours.[22] During the day of May 23 arrangements were made for Foreign Minister Eban to visit Washington for talks prior to any unilateral action. Johnson also decided to accede to an Israeli request for military assistance worth about $70 million, but he rejected an Israeli request for a U.S. destroyer to visit the port of Eilat.[23]

American diplomacy went into high gear. Johnson issued a forceful public statement to the effect that "the United States considers the gulf to be an international waterway and feels that a blockade of Israeli shipping is illegal and potentially disastrous to the cause of peace. The right of free, innocent passage of the international waterway is a vital interest of the international community."[24]

In Tel Aviv, U.S. Ambassador Walworth Barbour repeated the request for a forty-eight-hour delay before any unilateral Israeli action and raised the possibility of pursuing a British idea of a multinational naval force to protect maritime rights in the event that UN action failed to resolve the crisis. Eban's trip to Washington was designed in part to explore the feasibility of this idea.

In Washington, Israeli Ambassador Avraham Harman and Minister Ephraim Evron met with Under Secretary Eugene Rostow and were told that "the United States had decided in favor of an appeal to the Security Council. . . . The object is to call for restoring the status quo as it was before . . . the blockade announcement. Rostow explained that the congressional reaction compels a president to take this course."[25] Rostow reportedly referred to the realities created by the Vietnam War in describing Johnson's approach to the blockade.

As U.S. policy began to move toward consideration of multilateral action to break the blockade of the Gulf of Aqaba, Johnson understandably was concerned about Congress. On May 23 Secretary Rusk briefed the members of the Senate Foreign Relations Committee and reported back to Johnson that Congress would support Israel but was opposed to unilateral U.S. action.[26] In an effort to build public support for the administration, the president contacted former president Eisenhower, who confirmed that in 1957 the United States had recognized that if force was used to close the strait, Israel would be within its rights under article 51 of the UN Charter to respond with force.[27] George Meany, president of the AFL-CIO, was also asked to issue a statement in support of administration policy.

The basic elements of Johnson's approach to the crisis as of May 23 were the following:

—Try to prevent war by restraining Israel and warning the Egyptians and Soviets.

—Build public and congressional support for the idea of an international effort to reopen the Strait of Tiran. (Unilateral U.S. action was ruled out without much consideration.)

—Make an effort through the UN Security Council to open the strait. If that fails, as is anticipated, a multilateral declaration in support of free shipping will be drawn up. This will be followed, as the British suggested, by a multinational naval force transiting the strait.

Noteworthy was the continuing reluctance either to consider unilateral American action or to "unleash Israel," as a second option came to be known. These alternatives had been ruled out virtually from the beginning, and even the closure of the strait did not lead to a reevaluation of the initial policy. Instead, the two key elements of policy dating from May 17 were merely embellished as conditions changed.

A complex multilateral plan was designed that would surely be supported by Congress and public opinion, but could it produce results rapidly enough to ensure the other element in the U.S. approach—restraint of Israel? A dilemma clearly existed. To keep Israel from acting on its own, as even the United States acknowledged it had a right to do in order to reopen the strait, an acceptable alternative had to be presented.

The stronger the stand of the United States and the firmer its commitment to action, the more likely it was that Israel could be restrained; by the same token, the less likely it was that Nasser would probe further. Yet a strong American stand was incompatible with the desire for multilateral action, which had to be tried, in Johnson's view, to ensure congressional and public support. Such support was essential at a time of controversy over the U.S. role in Vietnam.

Johnson was mindful of the furor over his handling of the Gulf of Tonkin incident in 1964. Then he had seized on a small incident to broaden his power, with full congressional approval, to act in Vietnam. Subsequently, however, he had been charged with duplicity, with misleading Congress concerning the event, and with abusing the authority he had received. In mid-1967 Johnson was not about to lead the United States into another venture that might entail the use of force unless he had full congressional and public backing. Consequently he insisted on trying the United Nations first, and only then seeking a multilateral maritime declaration and sending ships through the strait. By moving slowly, cautiously, and with full support at home, Johnson would minimize the domestic political risks to his position.

The goals of restraining Israel and pursuing a multilateral solution were not necessarily incompatible, if sufficient time was available. For time to be available, perhaps as much as two to three weeks, the situation on the ground could not be allowed to change radically, nor could the balance of forces within Israel shift toward those who favored war. At a minimum, then, Nasser had to sit tight, the Soviet Union had to remain on the sidelines, and Eshkol had to be given something with which to restrain his hawks. If any of these conditions could not be met, the assumptions of U.S. policy would be undermined and war would probably ensue.

At the National Security Council meeting held on May 24, Rusk reviewed the broad strategy that had been decided upon. He noted that the Senate was unanimous in believing the United States should work through the UN and multilaterally. "The President then said he would like to hear views on what we do if all these other measures fail. We should play out the UN and other multilateral efforts until they are exhausted. 'I want to play every card in the UN, but I've never relied on it to save me when I'm going down for the third time. I want to see Wilson and De Gaulle out there with their ships all lined up too.' But all of these things have a way of falling apart. He mentioned, for instance, early congressional support for his actions in Vietnam. Therefore, we have to figure out what we can do if all these other courses fail."[28]

EBAN'S VISIT TO WASHINGTON

The impending visit of Israel's foreign minister served as a catalyst for the further definition of an American plan of action for dealing with the closure of the Strait of Tiran. If Israel was to refrain from forceful action, it needed to be given a credible alternative to war. But the process of moving from general principles—restrain Israel, act within a multilateral context—to a more detailed proposal revealed inherent contradictions and ambiguities, as well as bureaucratically rooted differences of opinion. What had initially been a fairly widespread consensus among Johnson's top advisers on how to deal with the crisis began to fragment as the crisis grew more acute. When Johnson felt most in need of broad support for his cautious, restrained approach, the viability of that position came under question.

The key to Johnson's policy on the eve of Eban's visit was the British idea of a multinational naval force. On May 24 Eugene Rostow met with the British minister of state for foreign affairs, George Thomson, and an admiral of the Royal Navy to discuss the British proposal. They agreed to try for a public declaration on freedom of shipping through the Strait of Tiran, to be signed by as many countries as possible. A multinational naval force would then be set up, composed of ships from as many maritime countries as were prepared to act, and a flotilla, soon to be known as the Red Sea Regatta, would then pass through the strait.[29] Rostow talked to Johnson later in the day about the plan and found the president receptive toward it.

Johnson was scheduled to make a trip to Canada on May 25, and he used the occasion to seek Prime Minister Lester Pearson's support for the multinational-fleet idea.[30] Meanwhile the Pentagon was charged with coming up with a concrete plan for forming a naval force. At this point, consensus began to erode.[31] Although some Pentagon analysts reported that the United States was capable of managing a crisis involving possible military intervention in the Middle East as well as Vietnam, most believed that Israel could deal with the Arab threat perfectly well on its own and that there was no need for a costly American commitment of forces. In any event, it would take time to get the necessary forces in place to challenge Nasser's blockade. At one point in the crisis, for example, the chairman of the Joint Chiefs stated that antisubmarine capabilities would be required and that two weeks would be needed to bring the appropriate ships to the area.[32]

The idea of a token display of U.S. force to reopen the strait did not have many fans in the Pentagon. What would happen if the Egyptians fired on an American ship? Would the United States respond with force? Would Egyptian airfields be attacked? Would ground troops be required? If so, how many? If the Egyptians held their fire, but did not back down, the U.S. Navy might find itself in the awkward position of having to patrol the strait indefinitely, under the guns of the Egyptians. Nothing would be solved politically, and the United States would simply find itself stuck with another commitment that diverted forces from other essential theaters. Furthermore, what could the Navy do about the growing numbers of Egyptian ground troops deployed along Israel's borders?

On balance, the military was not in favor of the use of U.S. force. Bureaucratic self-interest and a professional attitude that dictated the use of force only when success was assured and when superior power was available lay at the root of the opposition. The multinational fleet was a military man's nightmare. It was not the way the military would plan such an operation. It was too political. Deeming it undesirable, the military did little to make it feasible. Almost imperceptibly, Johnson was being deprived of his principal policy instrument because of the Pentagon's skepticism.

The State Department, at least at the top levels, was, by contrast, enthusiastic about the idea. Secretary Rusk endorsed it, and Under Secretary Rostow became its chief advocate. From their point of view, the fact that it was a flawed military concept was less important than its politically attractive features. First, it would associate other nations with the United States in defense of an important principle—freedom of navigation—and in the upholding of a commitment to Israel. Second, it would deflate Nasser's prestige, which was once again on the rise, without putting him into an impossible position. If Nasser wanted to back down from confrontation with Israel, the fleet would provide him with an honorable excuse to do so. The State Department therefore set out to find cosigners of the maritime declaration and donors of ships for the fleet. This essentially political task was what State was best at performing; the planning of the fleet was the province of Defense. Unfortunately, little coordination went on between the two.

Foreign Minister Eban arrived in Washington on the afternoon of May 25. His first talks were held at the State Department at 5:00 p.m. The result was to sow confusion among U.S. policymakers, who had just adjusted to the crisis and thought they saw a way out of it. Eban, who had left Israel with instructions to discuss American plans to reopen the Strait of Tiran, arrived in the United States to find new instructions awaiting him.[33] No longer was he to emphasize the issue of the strait. A more urgent danger, that of imminent Egyptian attack, had overshadowed the blockade. Eban was instructed to inform the highest authorities of this new threat to peace and to request an official statement from the United States that an attack on Israel would be viewed as an attack on the United States.[34] Despite his own skepticism, Eban followed his instructions in his first meeting with Secretary Rusk, Under Secretary Rostow, and Assistant Secretary Battle.

Rusk quickly ended the meeting so that he could confer with Johnson about the new situation. The meeting with Eban resumed at 6:00 p.m. for a working dinner, at which Eugene Rostow, Lucius Battle, Joseph Sisco (assistant secretary for international affairs), and Leonard Meeker (legal adviser) were present among the American group. The Israelis were told that U.S. sources could not confirm an Egyptian plan to attack. Nonetheless, the Egyptians would be warned against the use of force, and Moscow would be asked to make a parallel demarche. Discussion then shifted to the British proposal, including the declaration of maritime powers, its endorsement by the United Nations, and the multinational fleet. Israel was once again warned not to preempt.[35] The opinion was put forward on the American side that Egypt would not resist the fleet when the time came. But first the declaration of maritime powers must be issued and the debate in the UN proceed; only then could the ships move. American public opinion, it was stressed, must be convinced that all avenues had been explored before using force.

The conversation must have had an unreal quality about it, the Israelis being preoccupied with reports of imminent Egyptian attack and the Americans talking about declarations, the United Nations, Congress, and hypothetical naval forces.[36] After the talks ended, Israeli Ambassador Harman returned to the State Department at about midnight to reemphasize Israel's need for a concrete and precise statement of U.S. intentions.[37] He also warned that Israel could not accept any plan in which the strait might be opened to all ships except those of Israel.

American intelligence experts spent the night of May 25–26 analyzing the Israeli claim that an Egyptian attack was imminent. Several specific items had been presented by the Israelis in making their case, and by the morning of May 26 the intelligence community had analyzed each of these charges and concluded that an attack was not pending.[38] The Israelis suffered a loss of credibility at an important moment, and Johnson seems to have become suspicious that he was being pressured to make commitments that he either could not make, such as a statement that he would view an attack on Israel as an attack on the United States, or did not want to make yet, such as a precise plan on the multinational fleet. According to those who worked with him during this period, Johnson did not want to be crowded, he disliked ultimatums and deadlines, and he resented the mounting pressure on him to adopt Israel's definition of the situation. After all, as president he had to worry about the Soviet Union, about Congress and public opinion, and even about U.S.-Arab relations; he did not want to be stampeded, to use the imagery of his native Texas.[39]

Johnson was obviously reluctant to see Eban on Friday, May 26. He knew it would be an important, perhaps crucial meeting. The Israeli cabinet was to meet on Sunday, and what he told Eban might make the difference between war and peace. The Israelis were pressing for a specific commitment, for a detailed plan, for promises to act, and for understanding in the event Israel took matters into its own hands. Faced with these pressures, Johnson tried to stall. Rusk called Harman early in the morning to find out whether Eban could stay in Washington through Saturday. This would allow Johnson to learn the results of U Thant's mission to Cairo. Eban, stressing the importance of the Sunday cabinet meeting, said he had to leave Friday evening for Israel.[40]

During the morning of Friday, May 26, Eban went to the Pentagon, where he met with Secretary of Defense Robert McNamara, Chairman of the Joint Chiefs Earle Wheeler, and CIA Director Richard Helms. There he was given the results of the intelligence review of the previous night.[41] No evidence could be found that Egypt was planning to attack. Moreover, Eban was told, both the CIA and the Pentagon were convinced that Israel would easily win if hostilities were to begin, no matter who struck first. The fighting would not last a week. This assumption was probably more reassuring to the American military, which did not want to be called on to intervene, than it was to the Israelis.[42]

Meanwhile Secretary Rusk and Under Secretary Eugene Rostow had prepared a policy memorandum for the president. A meeting was scheduled for noon to discuss it and to plan for the Eban meeting. Walt Rostow called Evron during the morning to request a delay in Eban's meeting with the president, claiming that Johnson was busy studying the 1957 documents on the American commitment concerning the strait.[43]

Rusk's memo to the president began with a review of his talk with Eban the previous evening, including the Israeli information that an Egyptian and Syrian attack was imminent and the request for a public statement of American support for Israel against such aggression. Eban, it was stated, would not press this point with Johnson, and the president's talk could concentrate on the British proposal. Rusk then outlined two basic options:

—"to let the Israelis decide how best to protect their own national interests, in the light of the advice we have given them: i.e., to 'unleash' them"; or

—"to take a positive position, but not a final commitment, on the British proposal."

Rusk recommended strongly against the first option. Noting that the British cabinet would meet on the multinational-fleet plan the following day, Rusk endorsed the second option, which he then reviewed in some detail. Included in his outline was the idea that a UN force should take a position along both sides of the Israeli-Egyptian frontier. If Egypt refused, Israel might accept.

Eban's need for a strong commitment from Johnson was made clear in the Rusk memorandum. Congressional views were reviewed, and the option of unilateral U.S. action was referred to with caution. A draft joint resolution of the Congress was being prepared to support international action on the strait. In closing, Rusk referred to the possibility of offering Israel economic and military aid to help offset the strains of continuing mobilization.[44]

On May 26, shortly after noon, President Johnson convened at the White House the most important full-scale meeting of his advisers held during the crisis. Present were Vice President Humphrey, Secretary Rusk, Secretary McNamara, National Security Adviser Walt Rostow, Under Secretary Eugene Rostow, Chairman of the Joint Chiefs of Staff Wheeler, CIA Director Helms, Deputy Secretary of Defense Cyrus Vance, Assistant Secretary Battle, Assistant Secretary Sisco, press secretary George Christian, and unofficial advisers Supreme Court Justice Abe Fortas, George Ball, and Clark Clifford. Wheeler began with a military briefing, which included the evidence available on each side's force postures. He expressed the judgment that Israel could stay at its present level of mobilization for two months without serious trouble. In a military sense, then, time did not seem to be running out. Rusk followed with a review of the diplomatic situation, especially his talks the previous night with Eban. Rusk told the group that he had cautioned Israel not to launch a preemptive strike. McNamara then spoke of his morning session with Eban in which the Israeli foreign minister had raised the issue of United States commitments made in 1957 as part of the negotiations that resulted in Israel's withdrawal from Sinai. These consisted of the aide-memoire of February 11, 1957, signed by Secretary Dulles, which stated that the United States considered the Strait of Tiran to be an international waterway. Eban was apparently trying to extend this and other statements made at the time into an American commitment to use force if necessary to reopen the strait. On the American side, the most that was acknowledged was that Dulles had said that the United States recognized Israel's right, under article 51 of the UN Charter, to use force to open the strait if it was closed by force.

One by one, each of Johnson's advisers then expressed his views to the president. Discussion turned to the idea of a multinational fleet, with McNamara stating his disapproval of the idea on military grounds.[45] Rusk then reported on U Thant's talks in Cairo, which had elicited from Nasser a promise not to take preemptive action and had led to some discussion of how the blockade might be modified. He then introduced a phrase that was to be repeated to the Israelis frequently in the coming two weeks: "Israel will not be alone unless it decides to go alone."[46] To Rusk, it clearly mattered who opened fire first.[47] Johnson, who seemed to be reassured by the judgment that the military situation would not deteriorate suddenly, spoke of the maritime effort approvingly, terming it his "hole card" for his talk with Eban. But he realized this might not be enough for Eban. He asked his advisers if they thought Eban would misinterpret this as a "cold shoulder." Johnson expressed his feeling that he could not make a clear commitment to use force, because of congressional sentiment.

Fortas joined the discussion, stating that the problem was to keep Israel from making a first strike. This required an American commitment that an Israeli ship would get through the strait. Fortas recommended that Johnson promise to use whatever force was necessary. Johnson said he was in no position to make such a promise. Eban was not going to get everything he wanted. Congress, he said, was unanimously against taking a stronger stand. He wondered out loud if he would regret on Monday not having given Eban more today. Then he left the meeting. The others talked on for a few minutes, with both McNamara and Rusk taking the strong stand that Israel would be on its own if it decided to strike first. Fortas countered by saying that Johnson could not credibly say to Israel that it would be alone. The president did not have a choice of standing on the sidelines.[48]

Thus were the two main schools of thought among Johnson's advisers presented. The president seemed to be taking his cues from McNamara and Rusk, but he no doubt was also attentive to what Fortas was saying. The drama of the next few days in American policy circles involved the gradual shift on Johnsons's part from supporting Rusk's "red light" views to siding with Fortas, who began to argue that Israel should be allowed to act on its own if the United States was unwilling or unable to use force to reopen the strait—the "yellow light" view.

By late afternoon the Israelis were becoming anxious to set a definite time for Eban's meeting with the president.[49] Minister Evron called Walt Rostow and was invited to come to the White House to talk. Johnson, he was told, did not want any leaks to the press from the meeting, and several details of the visit had to be discussed. While Evron was in his office, Rostow contacted Johnson, who, upon learning of Evron's presence, asked him in for an informal talk. Johnson knew and liked Evron, and presumably felt that it would be useful to convey his position through Evron before the more formal meeting with Eban. Johnson began by stressing that any American action would require congressional support of the president. He repeated this point several times. Talks in the UN, though not expected to produce anything, were an important part of the process of building support. On a more positive note, Johnson mentioned the multinational-fleet effort. He acknowledged that Israel, as a sovereign state, had the right to act alone, but in that case, the United States would feel no obligation for any consequences that might ensue.[50] He stated that he did not believe Israel would carry out such unilateral action. In closing, Johnson stressed that he was not a coward, that he did not renege on his promises, but that he would not be rushed into a course of action which might endanger the United States simply because Israel had set Sunday as a deadline.[51]

Eban arrived at the White House unannounced while Evron was with the president. After some confusion, their meeting began shortly after 7:00 p.m. The Americans present included Johnson, McNamara, Walt and Eugene Rostow, Joseph Sisco, and George Christian. In response to

Eban's appeal that the United States live up to its explicit commitments, Johnson emphasized that he had termed the blockade illegal and that he was working on a plan to reopen the strait. He noted that he did not have the authority to say that an attack on Israel would be considered an attack on the United States. He again stressed the two basic premises of American policy: any action must have congressional support, and it must be multilateral. He told Eban he was fully aware of what three past presidents had said, but their statements were "not worth five cents" if the people and Congress did not support the president.

Twice Johnson repeated the phrase that Rusk had coined: "Israel will not be alone unless it decides to go alone." He said he could not imagine Israel making a precipitate decision. In case Eban doubted his personal courage, Johnson stressed that he was "not a feeble mouse or a coward." Twice Eban asked the president if he could tell the cabinet that Johnson would do everything in his power to get the gulf open to all shipping, including that of Israel. Johnson replied "yes." [52] Eban was given an aide-memoire spelling out U.S. policy:

The United States has its own Constitutional processes which are basic to its action on matters involving war and peace. The Secretary-General has not yet reported to the UN Security Council and the Council has not yet demonstrated what it may or may not be able or willing to do, although the United States will press for prompt action in the UN.

I have already publicly stated this week our views on the safety of Israel and on the Strait of Tiran. Regarding the Strait, we plan to pursue vigorously the measures which can be taken by maritime nations to assure that the Strait and the Gulf remain open to free and innocent passage of the vessels of all nations.

I must emphasize the necessity for Israel not to make itself responsible for the initiation of hostilities. Israel will not be alone unless it decides to go alone. We cannot imagine that it will make this decision.

As Eban left the White House, Johnson turned to his advisers and stated: "I've failed. They'll go." [53]

PRELUDE TO THE JUNE 1967 WAR

Johnson obviously was aware of the awkwardness of the policy he was pursuing. The multinational-fleet effort would take time, and even then might fall through for any number of reasons. The alternative of unilateral American action was not seriously considered. Congress was obviously a major concern, and behind Congress lay the realities of the Vietnam conflict. Johnson understood that Israel was subject to a different set of pressures and might be forced to go to war. But if so, the United States, he had said, would not be committed to act. He apparently still wanted the Israelis to hold off on military action, but as time went by he seems to have become resigned to letting the Israelis take whatever action they felt was necessary. Above all, he was not prepared to give Israel the one thing that might have kept it from acting on its own—a firm guarantee to use force if necessary to reopen the strait. Eban had almost extracted such a promise, but in Johnson's mind it was clearly hedged by references to United States constitutional processes and "every means within my power."

What Johnson had asked for was time—time for the fleet idea to be explored, for passions to cool, for compromises to be explored. He had tried to pin the Israelis down with a commitment to give him two weeks, beginning about May 27. On that day the Soviets had told Johnson they had information that Israel was planning to attack. The president replied to Kosygin and sent a message to Eshkol, which reached him on May 28, repeating the information from Moscow and warning Israel against starting hostilities.[54] Meanwhile, the president decided to initiate further contacts with Nasser, and to that end Ambassador Charles Yost was sent to Cairo to assist ambassador-designate Nolte in his dealings with the Egyptians, and Robert Anderson, former secretary of the treasury, was requested to talk to Nasser privately to help set up an exchange of visits at the vice-presidential level.

Rusk followed up Johnson's message to Eshkol with one of his own to Ambassador Barbour, for transmittal to the Israelis:[55] "With the assurance of international determination to make every effort to keep the strait open to the flags of all nations, unilateral action on the part of Israel would be irresponsible and catastrophic." Rusk also paralleled Johnson's message to Kosygin, which had called for a U.S.-USSR effort to find a prompt solution to the Strait of Tiran issue, with a message to Foreign Minister Andrei Gromyko calling for a two-week moratorium on the Egyptian closure of the strait. The message to Eshkol had its intended effect. At its Sunday, May 28, meeting, the cabinet seemed evenly split on the issue of whether to go to war. Eshkol, reflecting on Johnson's letter and Eban's report of his talks, decided to accede to the president's request.

From this point on, many Washington officials began to act as if they had at least two weeks in which to work toward a solution. The critical period, it was felt, would begin after Sunday, June 11. Although there was reason to believe that the Israelis would stay their hand until that date, as Johnson had requested, clearly such a pledge would lose validity if the situation on the ground or within Israel changed substantially. And in the ensuing days, changes did indeed occur.

INFORMAL LINES OF COMMUNICATION

During this period, Justice Abe Fortas, presumably with Johnson's blessing, spoke frequently with Israel's respected ambassador, Avraham Harman.[56] Fortas and Harman were close personal friends, who met on a regular basis during late May and the first days of June. And with considerable regularity, Fortas talked to the president by telephone. The Israelis had every reason to assume they were dealing with one of Johnson's true confidants, although Harman reportedly did not view his talks with Fortas as constituting an alternative channel for dealing with the U.S. government. He and Evron, who also talked to Fortas, did know, of course, that they were dealing with someone who was close to Johnson and whose views deserved careful attention. They were also dealing with a man who was deeply committed to Israel and who seems to have been suspicious of the State Department and Dean Rusk in particular.[57] What they heard from Fortas would be one more piece of evidence they could use in trying to fathom Johnson's thinking.

Eban's report of Johnson's views was not universally credited in Israel. Some thought he had misunderstood the import of the phrase "Israel will not be alone unless its decides to go alone." It was not an absolute prohibition. In fact, Johnson had acknowledged that Israel had the right to act on its own. But he had urged them not to do so, at least not right away. And he had made it clear that he could not do much to help if they got into trouble. Over the next several days the Israelis mounted a major effort to check on exactly where Johnson stood and to signal that time was working against Israeli interests. Central to this effort was a visit by Meir Amit, the head of Israel's intelligence service (the Mossad), who traveled to Washington under an assumed name on May 31.

Just as the Israelis were setting out to determine Johnson's views with precision, he left town for a long weekend at his Texas ranch. None of his foreign policy advisers accompanied him, although they were able to stay in regular touch by telephone and cables. Much of his time over the Memorial Day weekend—which extended from Saturday, May 27, until his return to the White House very early Wednesday morning, May 31—was spent in the company of Arthur and Mathilde Krim, Mary Lasker, and Jake Jacobsen, a former legal adviser. All were involved in party politics, and the Krims and Mrs. Lasker were large contributors to the Democratic party. Johnson must have been thinking about the party that weekend, since he was scheduled to speak to a party fund-raising event on June 3. Arthur Krim was to preside that night, and the audience would certainly be keenly interested in what the president said about the Middle East and Israel. Robert Kennedy was also scheduled to be there, and Johnson may well have been concerned about Kennedy's efforts to win the party away from him.[58] In short, he had more than the Middle East and Vietnam on his mind as he raced around his ranch with his guests.[59]

Just before Amit's arrival in Washington, an extremely important change took place in the Middle East situation. Jordan's King Hussein, under great pressure to join the Arab-nationalist mainstream, had flown to Cairo and signed a mutual-defense pact with Nasser. He returned to Jordan with an Egyptian general in tow who would head the joint military command. Walt Rostow saw this as a major turning point, and underscored the military danger represented by the dispatch of Egyptian commandos to Jordan. From this point on, he believed, Arab actions were making war virtually inevitable. Unless the Arabs backed down, or unless enough time was available for American power to make itself felt, Israel was bound to take matters into its own hands.[60]

In Washington on May 30 and 31, mixed signals were being given precisely on this crucial issue of whether the United States had the means and the will, alone or with others, to break the blockade of the Strait of Tiran. A proposed joint declaration of maritime powers had been shown to the Israeli ambassador, but it made no mention of the use of force, if necessary, to break the blockade.[61]

Eshkol replied to Johnson's letter of May 28 on May 30, noting that American assurances to take "any and all measures to open the straits" had played a role in Israel's decisions not to go to war and to agree to wait for "a week or two."[62] Within that time frame, Eshkol urged, a naval escort must move through the strait. Apprised of this message on May 31, Johnson became angry, claiming he had not promised Israel that he would use "any and all measures," but rather had stressed that he would make every effort within his constitutional authority. Walt Rostow was told to contact Evron to ensure that there should be no misunderstanding on this point. Evron replied by warning of the implications of what seemed to be a weakening of the U.S. commitment.[63]

From Cairo, Yost reported on May 30 his impression that Nasser "cannot and will not retreat," that "he would probably welcome, but not seek, military showdown with Israel," and that any American effort to force the strait would "undermine, if not destroy, US position throughout Arab world."[64] The following day, Anderson met with Nasser and discussed the possibility that Egyptian Vice President Zakariyya Muhieddin would visit Washington on June 7.[65] Some officials in Washington suspected that Nasser might propose referring the dispute over the strait to the International Court of Justice. The United States might find such a proposal difficult to refuse; Israel would certainly find it impossible to accept.

Rumors began to circulate in Washington on May 31 that the United States was looking for possible compromises to end the crisis.[66] In fact, some consideration was being given in the State Department to such steps, and Rusk's consultations with Congress to this effect rapidly reached Israeli ears and caused alarm.[67] That same day the Israelis picked up a report that Rusk had told a journalist, "I don't think it is our business to restrain anyone," when asked if the United States was trying to restrain Israel.[68]

This was the atmosphere that Amit found when he filed his first report on his soundings in Washington. His advice was to wait a few more days, but he observed that the mood was beginning to change. In his opinion the fleet idea was increasingly seen as bankrupt. If Israel were to act on its own, and win decisively, no one in Washington would be upset. The source for these impressions, it is worth noting, was not the State Department or the president. Amit's talks on June 1 and the morning of June 2 were focused on the Pentagon, where he saw McNamara, and on the CIA, where he talked with Helms and James Angleton.[69]

On June 1 the simmering political crisis in Israel broke. Late in the day Moshe Dayan, hero of the 1956 Suez campaign, was brought into the cabinet as minister of defense. War now seemed likely in the near future. Some leaders in the Israeli military were eager to strike quickly. Eban, however, was mindful of the Suez experience, when Israel had gone to war without the blessing of the United States. He wanted Johnson's support, or at least acquiescence, if Israel took military action. And based on what he had heard on May 26 in the Oval Office, reinforced by Rusk's stern message of May 28, that support could not be taken for granted if Israel acted preemptively.

Then on June 1 Eban received a message that contributed to his change of position. It was an account of a meeting that Minister Evron had had with Fortas. Fortas reportedly said that "Eshkol and Eban did great

service to Israel by giving the U.S. a chance to explore options other
than Israeli force. If they had not done so, it would have been difficult
to secure the President's sympathy."[70] Eban concluded that this was as
near a green light as a president could safely give, and he then called on
Generals Yitzhak Rabin and Aharon Yariv to tell them that he no longer
saw any diplomatic necessity for further military restraint.[71]

June 2 was the last occasion for serious diplomatic efforts before Israel's
decision to fight. The Israeli ambassador was scheduled to leave for Israel
later that day, and another "fateful" cabinet meeting would be held on
June 4. At about 11:00 a.m. on June 2, Minister Evron, without
instructions from Jerusalem, called on Walt Rostow at the White House.
He wanted to make sure Johnson understood that time was very short
and that Israel might have to go to war. He was seeking further
confirmation of Amit's impression that the United States would not object
too strenuously if Israel acted on its own. Evron stressed that he was not
conveying an official communication from his government, but his points
were taken seriously. First he emphasized that time was working against
Israel and that the military cost of war with Egypt was rising every day.
He then asked what the American response would be if an Israeli ship
tried to break the blockade, drawing Egyptian fire, and then Israel
responded with an attack on Sharm al-Shaykh. Would the United States
see this as a case of Israel's asserting its legitimate right of self-defense?
What if the Soviet Union intervened?

Rostow said this scenario was very different from the one discussed
with Eban, but was an alternative that might be considered. He would
seek Johnson's views. He then asked Evron how much time remained, in
reply to which Evron referred to June 11, although he stressed that there
was nothing ironclad about that date.[72] Evron noted, and Rostow
confirmed, that intelligence reports indicated Nasser would probably not
fire on a U.S.-escorted probe of the strait.[73] Therefore, the issue of Israeli
access to the Gulf of Aqaba might be left hanging indefinitely.

Evron then mentioned the 1957 commitment, emphasizing that it had
two parts: an American commitment to assert the right of free passage in
the strait, and acknowledgment of Israel's right to act with force if the
strait was closed. It was this second track he was now exploring, the
former having been discussed with Eban. Among other things, he noted,
it would be better for U.S.-Arab and U.S.-Soviet relations if Israel acted
alone rather than relying on the United States to use force to open the
strait.[74] This was a point that several American ambassadors in Arab

countries had also made, and it was not lost on Rostow, who urged Johnson to "urgently consider" Evron's suggestion.

Johnson's reaction to Evron's ideas is unknown, although he reportedly discussed them with Rusk.[75] But the letter he sent to Eshkol the following day shows little hint of a new approach. Evron noted, however, that the letter did specifically refer to him and also contained the following sentence: "We have completely and fully exchanged views with General Amit."[76] Johnson, in fact, had inserted the sentence on Amit by himself after having received on June 2 a full memorandum from Helms of his talks with Amit, coupled with a warning that Israel was on the verge of striking.[77] Otherwise, the letter, a reply to Eshkol's message of May 30, largely repeated what Eban had already been told. The text of the aide-memoire was quoted in full. Johnson promised to "provide as effective American support as possible to preserve the peace and freedom of your nation and of the area." He again referred to the need for the backing of Congress and for working through the UN. After mentioning the maritime-powers' declaration and the naval escort, Johnson added, "Our leadership is unanimous that the United States should not move in isolation."[78]

Ambassador Harman had a last talk on June 2 with Secretary Rusk before departing for Israel. Rusk had little new to report. Efforts to gain adherents to the maritime declaration were continuing. The necessary multilateral context for action in the Gulf of Aqaba did not yet exist. The question of which side fired first would be extremely important, and Rusk cautioned Harman against Israeli action.[79]

That same caution, however, was not heard when Harman called on Fortas just before leaving for the airport. According to Fortas's law clerk, who overheard the comments, Fortas, who had spoken to the president earlier in the day, said to Harman: "Rusk will fiddle while Israel burns. If you are going to save yourselves, do it yourselves."[80]

The following day, June 3, it was announced in Cairo that Muhieddin would visit the United States for talks on June 7.[81] Rusk had informed Harman of the planned visit the day before. The Israelis were obviously irritated. Such a visit could only work to their disadvantage. In Israel, both Harman and Amit, who had returned together, reported to Eshkol that there was no chance of unilateral U.S. action or of successful multilateral action. The conclusion was inescapable: Israel was on its own. Amit judged that the United States could not object if Israel opened the blockade in its own way.[82] Sensing that time was running out, Rusk cabled ambassadors in the Arab world with the warning that Israel might act soon. He underscored the American commitment to the political independence and territorial integrity of all the nations of the area, reminded them of American commitments made to Israel in 1957 concerning the strait, and urged that they send in any ideas on how to avoid war.[83]

That same evening Johnson flew to New York for the Democratic party event that had apparently been much on his mind over the previous days. He referred to his "deep concern" about the situation in the Middle East but did not elaborate. While at dinner, seated between Mathilde Krim and Mary Lasker, Johnson was reportedly told that the Israelis had made the decision to go to war. Abe Feinberg, a prominent banker and fund-raiser for the Democratic party, leaned over and whispered in his ear: "Mr. President, it can't be held any longer. It's going to be within the next twenty-four hours."[84] Thus, it seems, the president learned war was imminent.

In the twenty-four hours, more or less, remaining before the Israeli attack, Johnson took no further action. He was not officially informed by the Israelis of their decision, but he had no reason to be surprised when he was awakened on the morning of June 5 with the news that war had begun. After all, he had taken steps to assure the Israelis that the "red light" of May 26 had turned yellow. Johnson, while far from instigating the Israelis to attack, seemed to feel he had nothing to offer them. The "yellow light," hinted at in his letter to Eshkol on June 3, and reiterated in remarks from Fortas and Goldberg, meant "be careful," and "don't count on the United States if you get into trouble." But, as for most motorists, the yellow light was tantamount to a green one.

The Middle East would never again be the same. A war that might have been avoided was soon to transform the politics and the map of the region. American policy toward the region was about to be radically overhauled. A conflict that Washington had tried to consign to the "icebox" for the past decade could no longer be so casually ignored.

CHAPTER THREE

War and Its Aftermath

The outbreak of war on June 5 created a profoundly changed situation for U.S. policymakers. The premises of the preceding three weeks were invalidated overnight, and new issues assumed priority. How would President Johnson cope with the urgent problems that now confronted him? Would he hold Israel responsible for preempting, or would he recognize there really was no alternative? Secretary of State Rusk had repeatedly told the Israelis that it would matter who opened fire, but Johnson had hinted that he did not share this view. What about the territorial integrity of all countries in the region, which the United States had pledged to uphold? Would that now apply to Arab countries that had lost land to Israel? Fundamentally, would U.S. policy aim for a return to something like the status quo ante, or would an effort be made to devise a different basis for Arab-Israeli relations in the future? In short, were the armistice agreements of 1949 now obsolete? And, if so, what would take their place?

Johnson never blamed the Israelis for starting the war, although he did express his "disappointment" that they had not taken his advice.[1] And in a meeting with his advisers on June 7, when Israeli success on the battlefield was clearly evident, Johnson expressed his pessimism about the war solving deep-seated problems of the region.[2] His national security adviser, Walt Rostow, who talked to the president more frequently than anyone else during the crisis, maintained years later that Johnson had firmly opposed the Israeli decision to go to war.[3]

If Johnson had genuinely had qualms about Israel's resort to force, why did he become such an ardent supporter of Israel once the fighting began? Was he responding to pressures from pro-Israeli opinion in the United States, or to his own sympathy for the Jewish state? Certainly his sympathies did play a part, as did the fact that he knew he had been unable to solve the crisis for the Israelis. Only an early American commitment to use force to reopen the Strait of Tiran could have stayed Israel's hand, and that was more than he had been prepared to contemplate.

Perhaps his own bitter experience with Vietnam made him skeptical that military solutions could be found to complex political problems. Johnson had not quite given the Israelis a green light, but he had removed a veto on their actions. He had signaled that there would be no repeat of Suez. But what would there be? Would the United States underwrite Israel's occupation of sizable pieces of Arab land indefinitely? Would it seek an early political settlement? If so, on what terms? All these issues would soon have to be tackled. But once it had become clear that Israel had won an overwhelming victory, "there was a great sense of relief," because the United States would not have to get involved militarily.[4]

The United States quickly turned its attention to obtaining a cease-fire and ensuring that the Soviet Union would not intervene. The question of how the war had begun, which excited some interest in the early hours, was quickly overtaken by events. (Israeli Foreign Minister Eban told U.S. Ambassador Barbour that Egypt had attacked first. By midday on June 5, when it was known for sure that Israel had struck the first blow, it no longer seemed to matter.)[5]

Johnson was anxious to convey the impression that the United States was not involved in the fighting. This might help to minimize the danger to U.S. interests in the Arab world, reduce the likelihood of Soviet intervention, and facilitate a cease-fire. Here again the memory of the Suez crisis seemed to play a part. The United States did not want to be perceived in the Arab world as a co-conspirator with Israel, as Britain and France had been in 1956. When the war began, the Marine Battalion Landing Team was instructed to remain on shore leave in Malta.[6] Two carriers were on station near Crete, but they were not moved closer to the area of conflict. Once hostilities were under way, the United States imposed an embargo on new arms agreements to all countries of the Middle East, including Israel. The embargo remained in force through the end of the year, despite Israeli urgent requests to lift it.

The first news of the fighting reached Johnson early on the morning of June 5. Three hours after the start of hostilities, Secretary Rusk, after consultations with the president, sent a message through normal channels to Moscow expressing surprise at the outbreak of war and calling for an early end to the fighting.[7] At 7:47 a.m. Premier Kosygin replied over the "hot line"—the first use of this channel of communication in a crisis. He referred to the dangerous situation and the need for U.S.-Soviet cooperation in bringing about a cease-fire. Johnson's answer, sent by the hot line at 8:47 a.m., stated that both superpowers should stay out of the conflict and encourage a cease-fire. In all, twenty messages were exchanged over the hot line during the crisis.

The American position quickly became one of support for a cease-fire, but there was ambiguity about whether it would be linked to a provision for return to the prehostilities borders. Restoration of the immediate status quo ante of June 4 was clearly ruled out, inasmuch as that would have kept the strait closed; but a withdrawal of Israeli forces in conjunction with a lifting of the blockade might have found support in Washington if the Soviets or the Arabs had pressed the issue on the first day.

By June 6, however, the United States had come out in favor of a simple cease-fire in place.[8] Kosygin had communicated with Johnson during the day on the need for a cease-fire coupled with Israeli withdrawal, but by the end of the day the Soviets had agreed to accept the American position. The Egyptians, however, rejected a cease-fire in place. By that time Johnson was not in a mood to help President Nasser, who that day had falsely accused the United States of directly participating in the air attacks against Egypt. The result of his charge was that six Arab states broke off diplomatic relations with Washington, all of which created considerable bitterness toward Nasser, even among the State Department Arabists.

Apart from denying Nasser's accusations and continuing to support a cease-fire, the United States did little on the next day of the war, June 7.[9] On the 8th, however, an American intelligence ship stationed off the Sinai coast, the USS *Liberty*, was attacked by unidentified aircraft, which proved later to be Israeli. When news of the attack was flashed to Washington, Secretary of Defense McNamara and Johnson both feared that the Soviet Union might be responsible, and dark predictions of "World War III" were briefly heard in the White House situation room. The identity of the attackers was soon clarified, and Johnson informed Moscow by the hot line of the incident and the dispatch of aircraft from the Sixth Fleet to the scene of the attack.[10]

The incident shows the extraordinary degree to which Johnson was attuned to Soviet behavior once the war began. If during the May crisis he had been prepared to see the conflict primarily in terms of Arabs and Israelis, once hostilities were under way the main focus of his attention was the Soviet Union. With Israel secure from defeat by the Arabs, only Soviet behavior could trigger a direct American military response. The regional dispute paled in significance before the danger of superpower confrontation. The risk of Soviet intervention appeared once again before an effective cease-fire on all fronts went into effect on the sixth day, June

10. On the Syrian front, where fighting was particularly intense on June 9 and 10, the Israelis seemed capable of threatening Damascus. Although American officials were sure that Israel was on the verge of agreeing to a cease-fire once the Golan Heights had been secured, the Soviets were apparently less sanguine. At about 8:48 a.m. on June 10, Washington time, Kosygin sent a hot-line message to Johnson warning that they would take necessary actions, "including military," if Israel did not stop its advance.[11] Johnson responded by assuring the Soviets that Israel was prepared to stop and by instructing McNamara to turn the Sixth Fleet toward the Syrian coast to make certain that the Soviet Union would not underestimate Johnson's determination to meet any Soviet military move with one of his own. CIA Director Richard Helms, who participated in the meeting in the White House Situation Room, recalled that the conversation during the first couple of hours was in the lowest voices he had ever heard in a meeting of that kind. The atmosphere was tense. As the morning wore on, everyone relaxed a bit as it became clear that the fighting was petering out and that the two nuclear superpowers were not, in fact, heading toward confrontation.[12]

By noon the crisis was nearly over, a cease-fire soon went into effect, and the Sixth Fleet stopped its eastward movement. The war was over. Once again, a new situation existed and new policies were called for.

WAS THERE U.S.-ISRAELI COLLUSION?

Johnson publicly maintained after the war that he had done everything in his power to prevent it. He further claimed that he had opposed Israel's decision to go to war. Rusk asserted that he was shocked and "angry as hell" that the Israelis had launched their surprise offensive just before the Egyptian vice-president was to arrive in Washington. He added, with a note of caution, "To my knowledge, Israel had no undercover encouragement from the United States to start the war."[13] Others, however, have challenged this interpretation, and the documentary record does raise serious questions about its accuracy.

The extreme case against the Johnson version argues that the United States actively colluded with Israel during the crisis in the hope of weakening, perhaps even toppling, the Nasser regime. In brief, the critics see the 1967 crisis as a rerun of Suez 1956, but with the United States in the role of Britain and France. Mohamed Heikal's entrapment theory, and Mahmoud Riad's less extreme version of the same, stand out as Egyptian interpretations from this perspective.[14]

Stephen Green has given greatest credence to the conspiracy theory by asserting that the United States sent reconnaissance aircraft to Israel a few days before the war and that they continued to fly during the hostilities. He maintains that at least three sources confirm this secret exercise, but none has allowed his name to be used and no documentation has been produced.[15] The Johnson Library claims to have searched its files and come up with nothing. Moreover, none of the senior American officials interviewed for this study—Helms, McNamara, Lucius Battle, Harold H. Saunders (member of the National Security Council staff)—had any knowledge of this supposed American involvement in the 1967 war. One might have thought that the secretary of defense and the director of the CIA would have known of these events even if lower-ranking officials might not have. Nor has any Israeli source ever hinted at such collusion.

What, then, to make of the story? Johnson did have some forewarning that Israel was about to go to war. He had expressed some concern that Israel might need help, and he had approved a military assistance package on May 23. A small reconnaissance unit might have been seen as a useful, nonintrusive way of assisting the Israelis. But whatever plausibility this story may have, it does not meet the normal standards of historical evidence. Barring further disclosures, it should be rejected as unproved.[16]

From a thorough examination of all available sources, and many interviews, I conclude that there was no collusion between the United States and Israel before the crisis. The "entrapment" theory does not hold up. If anyone was trying to provoke a crisis in the Middle East in mid-May 1967, it was the Soviets.[17] The United States had its hands full in Vietnam. Nasser did not have many friends in Washington, but he was not such a big problem that Johnson, or anyone else in a top position, was out to get him.

Once the crisis began, Johnson, and especially Secretary of State Rusk, initially tried to prevent war. This remained Rusk's position throughout.[18] There seems little doubt from the stream of messages to Israel from May 17 to May 28 that Johnson was serious in urging restraint and pleading for time. But the Israelis are also correct in sensing a change in tone, if not in substance, by the first of June. Johnson, after his long weekend at his Texas ranch, and after Jordan had thrown in its lot with Egypt, seems to have concluded that war could no longer be avoided. No purpose would be served by trying to hold Israel back. Israel was free to act, but on its own. This is not quite the same as a green light—but certainly it was not a red one either. Johnson made sure the Israelis understood that the light had turned to yellow.[19] There was no U.S.-Israeli collusion, but there was acquiescence in what Johnson had come to believe was an inevitable Israeli resort to force to solve a problem for which the United States could offer no solution of its own.

POSTWAR DIPLOMACY

Johnson and his advisers were mindful of how Eisenhower had dealt with the Israelis after the Suez War. They were determined not to adopt the same strategy of forcing Israel to withdraw from conquered territories in return for little in the way of Arab concessions.[20] This did not mean that the United States endorsed Israel's indefinite hold on the occupied territories, but rather that the territories should be exchanged for a genuine peace agreement, something that had been missing in the Middle East since Israel's creation. This would take time, obviously, but time seemed to be on Israel's side. And the Israelis had officially made it clear that they did not intend to enlarge their borders as a result of the war.[21] The need, as American officials saw it, was to establish such a framework for a peace settlement and then to allow time to pass until the Arabs were prepared to negotiate to recover their territories. Apart from helping to establish the diplomatic framework, the United States need only ensure that the military balance not shift against Israel. Such a change was not likely in the near future, however, because the Egyptian, Syrian, and Jordanian armed forces lay in ruins.

In brief, a major shift in U.S. policy took place in the days following the war. But there is no record that this change was accompanied by much debate or consideration of alternative courses of action. Instead, it was almost as if the president and his top aides just assumed that they could not go back to the old, failed policy. Quite possibly, the intensely pro-Israeli tone of public opinion, the views of Congress, the private lobbying of Johnson's many Jewish friends, and Nasser's unfounded accusations all played a part. Perhaps. But Johnson also had his own memories of Suez. He had opposed Eisenhower's policy of forcing Israel to withdraw from Suez without peace in return. He would not emulate Eisenhower now, not when Israel's moral and legal case seemed so much stronger than in 1956.

Johnson apparently did not believe the United States should launch a high-level, intensive peacemaking effort immediately. Either he considered that such a move could not succeed, given the minimal influence of the United States in Arab capitals, or he did not feel he could sustain such an effort at a time when Vietnam was demanding so much of his attention. In either event, the option never seems to have been seriously considered. Instead, Johnson suggested a general outline of a settlement in a major policy statement on June 19, on the eve of his meeting with Soviet Premier Kosygin at Glassboro, New Jersey.[22]

In his June 19 statement, drafted in large measure by his special adviser McGeorge Bundy, Johnson clearly placed the major responsibility for the war on Egypt, terming the closure of the Strait of Tiran an "act of folly." He then stated that the United States would not press Israel to withdraw in the absence of peace. Five principles essential to such a peace were spelled out: the recognized right to national life, justice for the refugees, innocent maritime passage, limits on the arms race, and political independence and territorial integrity for all. In brief, Johnson contemplated a full settlement of all the issues stemming from 1947–49 and 1967.

In the course of the next five months, American diplomatic efforts were aimed at achieving a UN Security Council resolution that would incorporate Johnson's five points. The main areas of disagreement between Israel and the Arabs, as well as between the United States and the Soviet Union, rapidly emerged. The Arabs insisted on full Israeli withdrawal from newly occupied territory prior to the end of belligerency. Israel, on the other hand, held out for direct negotiations and a "package settlement" in which withdrawal would occur only after the conclusion of a peace agreement. The Soviet Union generally backed the Arab position, whereas the United States agreed with Israel on the "package" approach, but was less insistent on direct negotiations.

As to the withdrawal of Israeli forces, the American position changed between June and November.[23] Initially the United States was prepared to support a Latin American draft resolution that called on Israel to "withdraw all its forces from all territories occupied by it as a result of the recent conflict." The resolution was defeated, as was a tentative joint U.S.-Soviet draft in mid-July that was never considered because of radical Arab objections to provisions calling for an end of war with Israel. In late August the Arab position hardened further at the Khartoum conference, where Nasser and King Hussein of Jordan, in return for subsidies from the oil-producing Arab countries, were obliged to subscribe to guidelines for a political settlement with Israel based on no recognition, no negotiations, no peace agreement, and no abandonment of Palestinian rights.[24]

When the UN debate resumed in late October, the United States position, in part because of Eban's persuasive efforts with Goldberg, had shifted to support for "withdrawal of armed forces from occupied territories." The ambiguity was intentional and represented the maximum that Israel was prepared to accept. Even with this change, however, the United States made it clear in an early October minute of understanding signed with the British that the text "referring to withdrawal must similarly be understood to mean withdrawal from occupied territories of the UAR, Jordan and Syria, the details to be worked out between the parties taking security into account."[25] Finally, on November 22, 1967, a British compromise, known as UN Resolution 242, was passed. (See appendix A.) It incorporated all of Johnson's five points, along with a deliberately balanced call for "withdrawal of Israeli armed forces from territories occupied in the recent conflict" and "termination of all claims of belligerency and respect for and acknowledgement of the sovereignty, territorial integrity, and political independence of every state in the area and their right to live in peace within secure and recognized boundaries free from threats or acts of force." As a sop to the Arabs, the preambular language emphasized "the inadmissability of the acquisition of territory by war." But in UN documents, preambular language has no binding effect, so Eban raised only perfunctory objections.

In brief, the resolution fell just short of calling on Israel to withdraw from all territories and on the Arabs to make "full peace" with Israel. Note that the Palestinians were nowhere referred to by name, an omission much remarked upon in later years. But the United States did maintain from the outset that 242 did not mean that Israel should gain any significant amount of territory beyond the 1967 lines once peace was established.[26] Much of the diplomacy of the subsequent years revolved around efforts to make more precise and binding this deliberately vague wording. The resolution called for a UN-appointed representative to work with the parties to find a solution, a task that fell to Gunnar Jarring, Sweden's ambassador to Moscow, whose only Middle East experience was as a Turkic language specialist who had lived in Kashgar in the 1930s—a long way from the vicissitudes of the Arab-Israeli conflict.

During most of 1968 the Johnson administration assumed a comparatively low profile in Arab-Israeli diplomacy, leaving the main task to Jarring. In private, American officials consistently told the Israelis that a peace settlement would have to be based on virtually complete Israeli withdrawal, but in public nothing was said to modify the language of Resolution 242. Johnson was clearly preoccupied with Vietnam, especially after the Tet offensive in February, and in late March he announced his intention not to seek the presidency for another term, a decision that set off an intense political campaign within his own party and, after Hubert Humphrey's nomination, between the two parties. In this atmosphere major initiatives for peace in the Middle East could not be expected. Instead, Johnson acted to ensure that the post-1967 status quo would not be disrupted by Soviet arms shipments to Syria and Egypt. With a war on his hands in Vietnam, he was not anxious to see a resumption of fighting in the Middle East. In January 1968 he ended the American embargo on new arms shipments to the region.[27] Both Jordan and Israel were the beneficiaries, though on quite different scales.[28]

Johnson met with Prime Minister Eshkol in January 1968 to discuss Israeli arms requests. Topping the Israeli list was the high performance F-4 Phantom jet. Before 1967 the United States had not been a primary supplier of military equipment to Israel. The Israeli air force was of French origin, but France, because of Charles de Gaulle's Arab policy, was no longer a reliable arms supplier; hence the need for American arms.

Johnson reportedly assured Eshkol that Phantoms would be provided, but left unspecified the terms, timing, and possible conditions.[29] Within the bureaucracy many officials felt the United States should link the furnishing of F-4s to some concessions from Israel. Two possibilities were considered. First, to reverse Israel's growing appetite for territory, some felt that Israel should be asked to agree to the principle of full withdrawal in the context of peace in exchange for the jets. Others, fearful of Israeli nuclear development, argued that Israel should be required to sign the Nuclear Nonproliferation Treaty (NPT) before receiving U.S. arms.

The NPT issue was discussed at length with Israeli representatives. The most the Israelis would say was that they would not be the first ones to "introduce" nuclear weapons into the Middle East. In trying to clarify what this meant, U.S. officials discovered that Israeli Ambassador Rabin understood it to mean that Israel would not be the first to "test" such weapons or to reveal their existence publicly. Paul Warnke, assistant secretary of defense, then sent a letter to Rabin spelling out the American understanding of what nonintroduction of nuclear weapons meant: no production of a nuclear device. Before the issue was ever resolved, Johnson ordered the bureaucracy to end the search for a quid pro quo on the F-4s. Pressure was mounting for an affirmative United States response to the Israeli request. Political candidates were all endorsing the Israeli position, and in July the Senate passed a resolution calling for the sale of F-4s to Israel. Finally, on October 9 Johnson publicly announced that Israel would be allowed to purchase the Phantoms.[30] The two countries signed a deal for fifty F-4s in late December, providing for delivery of sixteen aircraft late in 1969 and the rest in 1970.

Perhaps in the hope of offsetting negative Arab reactions to the Phantom deal, Secretary of State Rusk, on his own initiative, informed the Egyptians on November 2 that the United States favored full Israeli withdrawal from Sinai as part of a peace settlement.[31] A year later, this position was publicly disclosed in the Rogers Plan, but in fact it had consistently been part of the American official consensus on the terms of an Israeli-Egyptian agreement. It did little, however, to win the confidence of the Israelis, and the last months of the Johnson administration were marked by a perceptible chill between the two countries.

In December, with the administration of Richard Nixon on the verge of taking office, the Soviet Union sent the United States a diplomatic note urging a more active search for an Arab-Israeli settlement. Britain and France were also pushing for a role in any Middle East peace talks. But time had run out on the Johnson presidency, and these issues would be passed on to Nixon, against a background of escalating violence and mounting guerrilla activity on the part of the Palestinian fedayeen.

ANALYZING JOHNSON'S MIDDLE EAST POLICY

The development of American policy before, during, and after the June 1967 Arab-Israeli war highlights the importance of a few key assumptions held by top decisionmakers, especially the president, at each stage of the crisis. The situation in the Middle East in May and June 1967 was extraordinarily complex. To make sense of the flow of events, decisionmakers needed some guidelines, some simplifying assumptions. They found them, not surprisingly, among the "lessons of the past" and the categorical inferences that had served well in other circumstances. An element of wishful thinking also existed. Together, several key principles provided a gyroscope of sorts for the decisionmaking process; order was perceived where it might have otherwise been missing. Little real discussion took place on these core assumptions.

The basic principles from which policy flowed in each of the phases of the crisis can be summarized as follows:

—Pre-war imperatives: do not commit American forces unilaterally, primarily because of Congress.

—Wartime policy: deter Soviet intervention; seek a cease-fire (but not a return to the status quo ante, which had been dangerous and unstable).

—Postwar policy: try for "full peace"; do not consider a Suez-like return to the status quo ante; insist that occupied territory would ultimately be traded for peace; keep Israel strong through arms shipments.

Several things about the decisionmaking process during the crisis are noteworthy. First is the obvious preeminence of the president. Crises, by their nature, bring the president to the center of the policymaking arena. His perceptions tend to define the situation for others; his needs tend to dominate the process. In May and June 1967 that meant a great sensitivity to congressional views, a desire not to become involved in another war, and a hope that time could be found to pursue the more cumbersome, but politically preferable, multilateral alternative. When this policy began to lose credibility, Johnson signaled his acquiescence to Israel's taking action on its own. When war began on June 5, it was primarily the president again who defined the stakes in the new game, as he did once more after the cease-fire went into effect on June 10.

Although Johnson's advisers did not completely agree on policy during the crisis, they nonetheless showed a remarkable degree of consensus. No one made a case for unilateral United States action; only a few voices were raised on behalf of "unleashing Israel"; little debate occurred over policy on a cease-fire in place as opposed to a cease-fire plus withdrawal; nor did anyone challenge the "package settlement" approach that emerged almost imperceptibly after the war. When divergent perceptions did appear, they seem to have been more deeply rooted in bureaucratic rivalries than anything else. For example, on political-diplomatic grounds, both Secretary Rusk and Under Secretary Rostow strongly favored the multinational fleet. McNamara and the professional military men were skeptical of the fleet on military grounds and were doubtless not anxious to see forces diverted from Vietnam or NATO for use in the Middle East. Small, politically motivated uses of force are not what the Pentagon tends to favor.

Advisers did not split primarily along pro-Israeli or pro-Arab lines. In fact, it was hard to say what course of action might be most dangerous for American interests in the Arab world. Some American ambassadors in the Arab countries, sensing that war was inevitable, hoped that Israel would act quickly, but on a limited scale, to break the blockade without involving the United States. Such a view came close to being the "unleash Israel" option that the Israelis were seeking by late May. The State Department, however, normally thought to tilt toward the Arabs, did not favor this option, at least not at the policymaking level of Rusk and Rostow.

An important lesson of the crisis, and one often encountered in Middle Eastern policymaking, is that American policy choices rarely come to be seen in simple pro-Israeli or pro-Arab terms. Thus individuals, whatever their particular sympathies, may find themselves in support of policies that to the outside observer seem inconsistent with those sympathies. In a crisis, however, policy evolves in complex circumstances, is defined under presidential directive, and comes to be rationalized in terms of principles that are easily supported by high-level policymakers.

Outside the circle of the president's official advisers, however, there were people in his entourage who were very committed to Israel and very close to its leaders. Johnson spoke frequently with Justice Abe Fortas, quite possibly in the knowledge that he could convey Johnson's real views to the Israelis.[32] The Israelis knew they had many friends around Johnson—U.S. Ambassador to the UN Arthur Goldberg, Fortas, Vice President Humphrey, Eugene and Walt Rostow, Arthur and Mathilde Krim, Abe Feinberg, and White House aides Joseph Califano, Harry McPherson, and John Roche, to mention just a few.[33]

What seems to have been missing from the policymaking process during the crisis was an explicit effort to relate policies to outcomes, as the rational decisionmaker is supposed to do. To a limited degree, of course, outcomes were discussed. But no one seems to have thought through the full implications of Israel's going to war, especially the problems this might cause in the long run. The future is indeed unknowable, but policymakers can be expected to consider consequences. They do so, however, in fairly simple ways. For example, Johnson gave serious consideration to the extremely low-probability event of Israel's being militarily defeated by the Arabs, to the point where it became one of the chief reasons for his effort to restrain Israel. He acknowledged the more likely outcome, predicted by the intelligence community, of rapid Israeli victory, but did not think through its consequences in detail. No one asked what Israel would do with Sinai, the West Bank, and the

Golan Heights after the war was over. Would East Jerusalem ever be returned to Jordan once it had been conquered in war?[34] What would happen to the Palestinians on the West Bank? These were all important questions and came to be seen as such after 1967, but they paled in comparison with the overriding question of what would happen if Israel faced defeat.

Noteworthy by their unimportance during the crisis were the allegedly powerful pro-Israeli interest groups and the oil lobby. Johnson was sympathetic to Israel already and did not need to be reminded of the U.S. interest in supporting the Jewish state. He paid no attention to the formal pro-Israel lobby, but he was in constant touch with Americans who were friendly to Israel, some of whom were also key personalities in the Democratic party. His desire to keep the fund-raisers of the party in his camp, and not see them drift toward his nemesis, Robert Kennedy, may have had some impact on his thinking about the crisis. During the crucial days of late May he spent many more hours in the close company of the Krims, for example, than he did with any of his top advisers. And we know from the official records that Mathilde Krim regularly passed messages, documents, and suggestions to him. To say the least, she had a strong pro-Israeli point of view.

More important, however, than the pro-Israeli personalities that surrounded him was Congress. This was the institution in which Johnson had spent most of his political life. And Congress did not want another open-ended unilateral commitment of American troops. More than any other single political fact, that seemed to weigh on Johnson and helped to turn this normally energetic and aggressive personality into a cautious, reluctant leader in this crisis.

Once the war had begun, and especially in its aftermath, the extremely pro-Israeli tone of American public opinion, coupled with Nasser's hostility, probably did make it easier for Johnson to adopt a policy of unquestioning support for Israel. Lobbying, however, was not a significant factor.

Oil was of only marginal significance to the formulation of policy. It was clear to some policymakers that any increase in Nasser's prestige would weaken the positions of the pro-Western oil-rich Arab countries, such as Saudi Arabia and Libya. Some officials also recognized that unilateral American use of force to open the strait could damage U.S. interests in the oil-producing Arab countries. And some feared that an oil embargo as part of an Arab-Israeli war might have dangerous consequences for NATO allies and Japan. But, on balance, oil was very much a secondary factor in presidential policy considerations in 1967.[35]

Finally, an important lesson of the policymaking process can be learned from the 1967 Arab-Israeli crisis: the initial definition of a situation tends to endure unless subjected to overwhelming disconfirming evidence from external sources. Between May 16 and the end of the month, Johnson and his key aides maintained essentially the same basic perceptions, adding details to a framework created in the initial stages of the crisis but not fundamentally altering policy. The president seems to have changed his views during the long weekend at the ranch. At least the signals the Israelis began to receive started to change. But the evidence is not clear as to what, precisely, the president was thinking as the possibility of war became more and more real. The available record, however, is certainly consistent with the Israeli belief that the red light that had been switched on in mid-May had turned to yellow by early June.

When war did occur, a new definition was required and was quickly provided. Not surprisingly, the Soviet Union assumed a much greater salience once war had begun.[36] Then, with the cease-fire achieved, the third basic policy framework emerged, which emphasized the need to pursue a full peace agreement. This last policy was largely a reaction to the 1956–57 approach of pressing Israel for immediate withdrawal. The war of 1967 had shown that the Eisenhower decision had not brought peace; Johnson had opposed Eisenhower's pressure on Israel at the time, and now he had the chance to try an alternative approach. With little discussion and no apparent dissent, the United States found itself supporting Israel's hold on the newly conquered territories pending Arab willingness to make peace. Such is the power of the lessons of history that accumulate in the minds of presidents. "No repeat of Suez" may have seemed to President Johnson as plausible as "no more Munichs," but it would not be long before the dilemmas of the new policy would become evident.

PART TWO

The Nixon Presidency

CHAPTER FOUR

Cross-Purposes: Nixon, Rogers, and Kissinger, 1969–70

Richard M. Nixon was, to say the least, an unusual president. By the time he resigned from office in disgrace on August 9, 1974, his domestic support had virtually disappeared. The Watergate scandal, exposed in exquisite detail by the press, Congress, and the tapes of the president's conversations, revealed a suspicious man in the White House who lied, who was vindictive, and who appeared to be strangely indecisive and incoherent when it came to dealing with important policy issues. Many Americans, as well as foreigners, had difficulty reconciling this image with that of the Richard Nixon who was overwhelmingly reelected in 1972 to a second term in office, a man whose achievements in the realm of foreign policy won him the grudging support of many former opponents.

These two faces of President Nixon were no doubt part of the same complex, unhappy personality, but it is Nixon as foreign-policy strategist who is of primary concern here. Nixon viewed his experience in international affairs as one of his strongest assets and foreign relations as a particularly important arena for presidential action. As Eisenhower's vice-president for eight years, Nixon had been on the margins of key foreign-policy decisions of the 1950s. He had earned a reputation as a tough-minded anticommunist and an advocate of a strong international role for the United States.

During his period of exile from elective politics, from 1961 through 1968, Nixon had traveled widely and had met many heads of state. By chance, he was in Morocco at the time of the June 1967 war. His cable to Secretary of State Dean Rusk gives a glimpse of his views, uncluttered by those of subsequent advisers, at that defining moment:

I hope that with the outbreak of the Arab-Israel hostilities, our government will bring all possible influence to bear to have all major powers stand up to their responsibility for the maintenance of peace. Let us make it clear that the key to peace in the Middle East is now in Moscow and that peace efforts in the United Nations and multilaterally up to this time have been blocked by the Soviet Union. I hope, too, that in considering our actions in this situation, we remember that while all Arabs have strong feelings on the subject of Israel, many are not in agreement with Nasser and his ambitions for the UAR [United Arab Republic] and leadership of the Arab world.

My fear in the present circumstances is that unless we can demonstrate that our attachment to peace is impartial, we will have given the Soviet Union an unparalleled opportunity to extend its influence in the Arab world to the detriment of vastly important United States and free world interests.[1]

These trips to the Middle East must have made an impression on Nixon, for he spoke of them frequently in later years. In discussions of the region, he would refer to his talks with Israeli, Egyptian, and Saudi leaders, emphasizing his personal knowledge of key individuals and their countries. His experience in foreign affairs, such as it was, came largely through his own firsthand experience and discussions. He had little patience with academic studies or lengthy briefing materials. Nixon was very much a loner, rarely reaching out to others to discuss his views.

Unlike President Johnson, Nixon never betrayed a strong desire to immerse himself in the day-to-day flow of events and information. He prided himself instead on his detachment and his analytical ability to see problems in their broad strategic context. He admired strength and toughness, and firmly believed that foreign policy should be formulated in secret, with only minimal contributions from Congress and public opinion. And Nixon prided himself on not being beholden to the pro-Israeli lobby, since relatively few Jews had voted for him.[2]

THE NIXON TEAM

From the outset it was clear that President Nixon intended to make the basic decisions in foreign policy. To ensure his control of the vast foreign-policy bureaucracy—which he distrusted as being a bastion of the Democrats—he decided to reinvigorate the National Security Council system.[3] Nixon's NSC evolved substantially over the years, but at the beginning it was designed for two purposes: to provide the president with genuine policy alternatives, or options; and to educate the bureaucracy concerning the new themes in Nixon's foreign policy. Toward both these ends, Nixon requested an unprecedented number of policy studies in his first few months in office, mostly in the form of National Security Study Memoranda (NSSMs). These were to be discussed by a Senior Review Group (SRG),[4] then referred to the full NSC for decision, after which a National Security Decision Memorandum (NSDM) would be issued. Overseeing this elaborate system was a former Harvard professor, Henry A. Kissinger, Nixon's national security affairs adviser.

Kissinger was a well-known foreign-policy analyst. He first gained public recognition with the publication of an influential book in 1957, *Nuclear Weapons and Foreign Policy*. Subsequently he became a consultant to both the Kennedy and Johnson administrations, but his closest ties were with his earliest patron, Nelson Rockefeller. Kissinger's acceptance of the national security affairs position was as unexpected as Nixon's offer. The two men seemed fundamentally different in temperament and character, but they quickly recognized in each other a remarkable intellectual compatibility. Nixon was instinctual and decisive; Kissinger was analytical and subtle. Nevertheless, they held similar views of the international role of the United States, of the need for strength wedded to diplomacy, of the intimate links between domestic and foreign policy, and of the danger of nuclear war.

Within a short time, the Nixon-Kissinger team was working smoothly, and Kissinger had ascended from the obscurity of the White House basement to a well-appointed office on the first floor of the west wing.[5] Nixon and Kissinger both had a keen sense for the symbols as well as the realities of power. Nonetheless, Nixon deliberately kept Kissinger from dominating Middle East policy during the first year and one-half, at least in part because of his Jewish origins.[6]

For the position of secretary of state, Nixon named a close personal friend, William P. Rogers, a lawyer by profession who had served as attorney general in Eisenhower's cabinet. He was not particularly experienced in foreign policy, nor was his a strong, assertive personality. He did, however, have an affable, reassuring style and a dignified bearing. Given the modest role that Nixon envisaged for him, these were perhaps enough. Nonetheless, Nixon decided to entrust Rogers with the Middle East dossier, perhaps realizing that success there was unlikely and domestic controversy could be deflected toward the State Department rather than the White House.[7]

If Rogers seemed unlikely to be a particularly aggressive secretary of state, some of his subordinates in the department were men of considerable talent, energy, and ambition. Elliot Richardson, during his brief tenure as under secretary, played an important role in the running of the department and in keeping lines open to the White House. Unlike Rogers, Richardson quickly developed a close working relationship with Kissinger.

The new assistant secretary of state for the Near East and South Asia was a controversial figure. Joseph Sisco, formerly assistant secretary of state for international organizations, was a Democrat and had never served overseas in his long career in the State Department. His knowledge of the Middle East came from his years in Washington. He was a consummate bureaucratic politician; he knew the ins and the outs of the State Department; he was a man of drive, a skillful speaker, and a shrewd tactician. Working closely with him was Alfred L. Atherton, Jr., first as office director for Israel and Arab-Israeli affairs and later as deputy assistant secretary for the Near East. Atherton represented continuity, experience, professional expertise. He was cool when Sisco was hot. The two were a formidable pair in Middle East policymaking circles.[8]

NIXON'S FOREIGN POLICY

President Nixon, with the assistance of Henry Kissinger and some parts of the State Department, quickly established a set of priorities and guidelines for American foreign policy. Some represented new departures; others reflected continuities and standard responses to long-standing problems. Inevitably, Vietnam stood at the top of Nixon's agenda of foreign policy issues. Domestic dissent over Vietnam had destroyed Lyndon Johnson's chances for reelection and had produced a grave crisis of confidence and of conscience within the United States. Nixon was no doubt less tempted by the prospects of "victory" in Vietnam than Johnson had been, but at the same time he was strongly opposed to a sudden withdrawal of American forces.[9]

In private, Nixon and Kissinger expressed the fear that a precipitate withdrawal from Vietnam, followed by a communist victory, might provoke a right-wing McCarthyite backlash in the United States and would reinforce latent isolationist sentiments. The art of managing the Vietnam commitment was to disengage American troops in such a way that, domestically and internationally, the United States would still be able to conduct an effective foreign policy in other parts of the world, such as the Middle East, where important interests were at stake.

Apart from Vietnam, Nixon and Kissinger were primarily concerned with the other major powers, especially the Soviet Union. Both men were preoccupied with the dangers of nuclear war; both were intrigued by the possibility of establishing a new relationship with the Soviet Union that would help to ensure global stability and to minimize the risks of confrontation; both were prepared to transcend the ideological rivalry of the cold war and to establish ties with adversaries based on mutual interest.

Part of Nixon's strategy of restructuring the relations between the superpowers involved China. In October 1967 Nixon had published an article entitled "Asia after Viet Nam."[10] In it he wrote, "Any American policy toward Asia must come urgently to grips with the reality of China." Little public notice was taken of China during Nixon's first two years in office, but it is clear in retrospect that the president and Kissinger were already laying the groundwork for a dramatic opening to Peking. Apart from intrinsic benefits from restoring U.S.-Chinese relations after a generation of hostility, Nixon recognized that an American-Chinese connection could have a moderating effect on Soviet foreign policy. In addition, improved ties to Moscow and Peking might help bring about a Vietnam settlement and ensure that the post-Vietnam era in Asia would be comparatively free of conflict. Consequently, Vietnam, the Soviet Union, and China came to be linked as priority concerns to the Nixon administration. Significantly, each was managed almost exclusively from the White House, the president providing general guidance and Kissinger and his staff working on the details of the new policies and overseeing their implementation.

One priority area remained for the State Department to deal with: the Middle East. The Arab-Israeli conflict was generally seen as potentially dangerous, although hopelessly complex and perhaps less urgent than the other tasks facing the administration. Some momentum had already been established under Johnson, and around it a modified policy might be constructed. The State Department was anxious to play a leading role and was able to call on impressive expertise. Thus, with some skepticism about the likelihood of immediate results, Nixon authorized the State Department to develop and carry forward a new American policy toward the Arab-Israeli conflict. If it should succeed, there would be credit enough for everyone; if it were to fail, Nixon and Kissinger would be relatively free of blame.

Nixon's own views on the Middle East, as reflected in his cable to Rusk on the opening day of the June 1967 war, seemed to combine a strong dose of cold war assumptions about the role of the Soviets, along with an expressed belief that the United States could best compete with Moscow by being "impartial" in the Arab-Israeli conflict. The concern with the Soviets was similar to Kissinger's, but Nixon's "evenhandedness" was closer to the conventional State Department position. In short, Nixon embodied in his own mind the two competing paradigms for how best to tackle the Arab-Israeli conflict. What came to be seen as a great battle between Kissinger and Rogers was also, apparently, an unresolved debate within Nixon's own mind.[11]

By contrast, Kissinger had well-developed, if not well-informed, views on the Middle East. This was not a part of the world he knew well. His inclination was to look at issues in the Middle East in terms of the broader U.S.-Soviet rivalry. His views may have crystallized at the time of the Suez crisis, when he concluded that Eisenhower's policy of checking the British-French move against Nasser was misguided. One should not, he believed, weaken friends and help adversaries who depended on Soviet support.[12] In terms of the realities of 1969, this led Kissinger to advocate strong backing for Israel until such time as the Arabs decided to break with Moscow. The normal State Department instinct of launching initiatives was anathema to his way of thinking, and he did what he could to persuade Nixon of the correctness of his views. For the first year or so, he did not always get his way, but that did not stop him from trying to undermine State's preferred strategies.

Nixon's initial approach to foreign-policy issues did not center on the Middle East. His big themes were aimed at managing America's extrication from Vietnam without upsetting the global balance of power. To these ends, he spoke frequently of "linkage," a "structure of peace," "détente," and "negotiations," all against the backdrop of keeping the United States strong and restoring domestic consensus behind broad foreign policy goals.

A favorite Nixon-Kissinger concept was linkage. This meant that issues would not be negotiated with Moscow in isolation from one another. Rather, the United States in its talks with the Soviet Union would aim for a global settlement of issues. Progress should be made across the board on Vietnam, strategic-arms talks, and the Middle East. Simultaneous negotiations in each of these areas would mean that trade-offs could be made, thus adding flexibility and nuance to the negotiations. A Soviet concession on Vietnam might be reciprocated by an American move in the Middle East. As an intellectual construct, it made sense; in practice, it rarely worked. Nevertheless, throughout 1969, linkage was one of the key concepts of the Nixon foreign policy.

"Negotiations" became another theme of the Nixon diplomacy. Nixon and Kissinger shared the view that force and diplomacy must go hand in hand, which meant that negotiation with adversaries was not incompatible with threats or the actual use of military might. Kissinger in particular was fascinated by the process of negotiations and proved to be an astonishingly successful negotiator in his own right. Soon after Nixon took office, negotiations on a wide range of issues—the Middle East, Vietnam, China, and strategic arms—were begun or accelerated.

The objective of the negotiations was to create, in the Nixon-Kissinger jargon, a "structure of peace," the main components of which would be U.S.-Soviet "détente," arms limitations, and eventually a normalization of U.S.-Chinese relations. All this was to be accomplished without detriment to traditional allies—the NATO partners and Japan—and without much regard for the third world, where détente would serve to limit the dangers to global peace inherent in local conflicts.

To pursue such an ambitious foreign policy at a time of great popular disenchantment, President Nixon sought to meet the demand that America no longer play the role of world policeman, while at the same time avoiding the extreme of isolationism. This delicately balanced posture of restrained internationalism came to be known as the Nixon Doctrine, one manifestation of which was Vietnamization—the gradual disengagement of American combat troops from Vietnam, coupled with high levels of aid to the Saigon regime and an active search for a political settlement.[13]

Nixon's great hope during his first term was that he would be able to recreate a domestic consensus on behalf of his foreign-policy goals. The style and timing of each major foreign-policy step were chosen with an eye toward domestic public opinion. Vietnamization and the end of the draft helped to ease the divisions created by the war, and the prospect of a peace agreement in Vietnam during 1972 greatly enhanced Nixon's popularity. The spectacular opening to China, carried out in total secrecy and with high drama, also strengthened the Nixon-Kissinger team. Finally, the Strategic Arms Limitation Talks (SALT) agreement of May 1972 seemed to hold out the promise of an end to the nuclear arms race.

Nixon seemed to worry about the explosive potential of the Arab-Israeli conflict—he repeatedly used the pre–World War I Balkans analogy. Tempering Nixon's willingness to tackle the Arab-Israeli conflict, however, was the poisoned domestic political climate created by the Vietnam War. And Middle East diplomacy held little prospect of restoring the shattered domestic consensus. On the contrary. A serious effort to resolve the differences between Israel and its Arab neighbors was bound to be controversial. In addition, the president's key advisers were not in agreement on how to proceed. Public opinion was very pro-Israeli, still seeing the Jewish state as a heroic David facing a pro-Soviet, aggressive Arab Goliath. Nor was there a compelling strategic reason for tackling the Arab-Israeli conflict, since the oil issue was generally not seen as related, the Arabs were not believed to have a serious military option, and American interests therefore did not seem to be immediately at risk. With these perceptions in mind, it seems, Nixon was only prepared to allow State to test the waters of Arab-Israeli diplomacy, but was reluctant to throw the full weight of his office behind an activist policy.

THE DEBATE OVER INTERESTS

Two sets of concerns dominated the thinking of policymakers in early 1969 as the administration undertook its first review of the situation in the Middle East. The president and Kissinger seemed to be chiefly worried by the global ramifications of the Arab-Israeli conflict. Nixon repeatedly used highly colored and explosive imagery in describing the area. Again and again the theme of confrontation between the superpowers was mentioned in discussions of the Middle East. This, it was said, was what made the Arab-Israeli conflict even more dangerous than Vietnam.[14]

The State Department professionals tended to agree that the situation in the Middle East was dangerous, but their perceptions were more affected by the prospective threats to American interests arising from trends within the area. At State, one heard of the "erosion" of American influence, the "deterioration" of the American position, the "radicalization" of the Arab world, and "polarization." The region was viewed in stark, sometimes simplistic terms: the United States, with Israel and the "moderate" Arabs, aligned against the Soviet Union and the "radical" Arabs. It was widely believed that the continuation of the Arab-Israeli conflict would work to the advantage of the Soviet Union, resulting in the isolation of the United States and Israel in a sea of radical, anti-American Arabs. The rise of the militant Palestinian fedayeen movement during 1968 was a harbinger of things to come: increased violence and terrorism, direct threats to American lives and interests, mounting instability, and eventually another war.[15]

The White House and the Departments of State and Defense were all concerned with one other issue involving the Middle East: the possibility that Israel would develop, or possibly already had developed, nuclear weapons. This fear brought together those who worried about regional trends and those who were preoccupied by global, strategic issues. No one knew quite what to do about the Israeli nuclear option, but it added to the sense that the Middle East was too dangerous to ignore.[16]

The combination of these preoccupations led to several related policy guidelines that shaped the American approach to the Middle East from early 1969 until August 1970. Most important was the broad consensus, minus Kissinger, that the United States should adopt an active diplomatic role in promoting a political settlement based on the principles embodied in UN Resolution 242. The efforts of the Johnson administration were judged as having been too passive, those of UN Ambassador Gunnar Jarring as too cautious. The United States, in concert with the other major powers, and in particular the Soviet Union, should therefore seek to engage the regional parties in a negotiating process, the first step of which would be a refinement of the principles of a settlement to be worked out in talks between the two superpowers. The hoped-for result would be considerably less than an imposed settlement, which the administration rejected, but would be something other than the directly negotiated peace agreement that the Israelis desired.[17]

The State Department had long advocated an "evenhanded" approach to the Arab-Israeli conflict. In essence, this meant adopting a posture that was neither overtly pro-Arab nor openly pro-Israeli. With respect to arms deliveries to Israel, the evenhanded approach urged restraint, and on territorial withdrawal it favored a clear statement opposing Israeli acquisition of territory from the 1967 war. As to the quality of the peace agreement, the standards to be applied to Arab commitments were not too rigorous. From the Israeli perspective, an "evenhanded" American policy was tantamount to being pro-Arab. When President-elect Nixon's special emissary to the Middle East, Governor William Scranton, used the word *evenhanded* in December 1968, it set off shock waves in Israel.

Fortunately for the Israelis, Kissinger was skeptical of the virtues of evenhandedness, and at an early date the Israelis began to bypass Rogers in favor of direct dealing with the White House. Kissinger, unlike Rogers and Sisco, believed a diplomatic stalemate in which Israel was kept strong would ultimately persuade the Arabs that it was pointless to rely on Soviet support. Then they would turn to the United States for assistance, the price for which would be a break with Moscow. The Arabs, in Kissinger's view, should not be given the impression they could count on both superpowers to pressure Israel to make concessions unless they were prepared for very far reaching concessions of their own. Kissinger had little patience with the view that the Arabs would show more moderation if the United States took some distance from Israeli positions and acted with restraint on arms supplies to the Jewish state.[18]

The basic difference between State and Kissinger could be summed up fairly easily. State saw tensions in the Middle East as growing from regional conditions that the Soviets could exploit for their own advantage. To reduce Soviet options, State officials argued, the United States should try to resolve the underlying disputes. Kissinger was less sanguine about the prospects for resolving the regional conflicts, and in any case he believed it was Soviet involvement in the disputes that made them particularly dangerous. From his balance-of-power perspective, the first order of business was to reduce the Soviet role. Nixon, interestingly, seemed to agree with both schools of thought, depending on circumstances.

POLICYMAKING

In January 1969 President Nixon expressed the view that the Middle East situation was potentially explosive. His thinking was best reflected in his answers to questions posed during a press conference on January 27, 1969, just one week after he took office:

What I want to do is to see to it that we have strategic arms talks in a way and at a time that will promote, if possible, progress on outstanding political problems at the same time—for example, on the problem of the Mideast and on other outstanding problems in which the United States and the Soviet Union, acting together, can serve the cause of peace. . . . I believe we need new initiatives and new leadership on the part of the United States in order to cool off the situation in the Mideast. I consider it a powder keg, very explosive. It needs to be defused. I am open to any suggestions that may cool it off and reduce the possibility of another explosion, because the next explosion in the Mideast, I think, could involve very well a confrontation between the nuclear powers, which we want to avoid.[19]

On February 1 the National Security Council met for an exhaustive review of Middle East policy. Three basic alternatives, each discussed at length in NSSM 2, were considered:

—Leave the search for a settlement of the Arab-Israeli conflict to the parties and to Ambassador Jarring.

—Pursue a more active U.S. policy, involving U.S.-USSR talks.

—Assume that no settlement is possible and concentrate efforts on objectives short of a settlement.

The second alternative was decided on, the third remaining available as a fallback position in the event of failure. The NSC discussions identified several principles that should guide U.S. policy.

—The parties to the dispute must participate in the negotiations at some point in the process. Although the United States would not hesitate to move somewhat ahead of Israel, any final agreement would be reached only with Israel's participation and consent.

—The objective of a settlement would be a binding agreement, not necessarily in the form of a peace treaty, but involving some form of contractual commitments. The administration was concerned about the imbalance in the concessions to be sought from each side. The Israelis would give up territory; the Arabs would give promises to respect Israel's sovereignty.

—Withdrawal of Israeli forces should take place back to the international frontier between Israel and Egypt, with a special arrangement for Gaza. There should be Israeli evacuation of the West Bank of Jordan, with only minor border changes.

—Some critical areas should be demilitarized.

—Jordan should have a civilian and religious role within a unified city of Jerusalem.

—There should be a settlement of the refugee problem.

Issues of a guarantee to Israel and assurances of arms were also discussed. Then the NSC considered two possible diplomatic strategies. First, the United States could unilaterally present a peace plan. This was rejected. Second, the United States could follow a step-by-step approach whereby specific elements of a settlement would be gradually injected into the negotiations. It was recognized that withdrawal and the nature of the peace agreement would be the most critical issues. Primacy would be given to developing common ground in the U.S.-Soviet talks, with the aim of producing a joint document that could then be approved by the four powers and given to Jarring to present to the local parties.[20]

On February 4 Nixon again met with the NSC to discuss the Middle East. This time he asked for a study that would describe a peace settlement, assess its acceptability to the parties, and discuss the role of outside guarantees. He also asked what the links would be between the two-power and four-power talks. Finally, he asked what the United States should plan to do if a general settlement was impossible. The following day Nixon announced that the United States was preparing a new initiative in the Middle East on a multilateral basis to head off a "major war." For the rest of the year U.S. policy adhered closely to the guidelines laid down in February. The eventual result was the Rogers Plan.

LAUNCHING THE ROGERS PLAN

Several simultaneous rounds of negotiations were soon under way. U.S.-Israeli meetings were frequent, as the administration tried to allay the apprehensions of the Israeli government, now headed by Prime Minister

Golda Meir.[21] Once the U.S.-Soviet talks began in earnest, Israel was initially kept closely informed of the progress in the talks, although by the fall this pattern of consultations had weakened. Finally, the four-power talks proceeded simultaneously with the U.S.-Soviet ones.

The U.S.-Soviet talks, conducted primarily by Sisco and Soviet Ambassador Anatoly Dobrynin, quickly took center stage. Between March 18 and April 22, they met nine times. The American objective in this round was to determine whether there was sufficient agreement on general principles to justify trying to reach a joint proposal. During this phase the United States spelled out its basic position on a settlement in a document presented to the participants in the four-power talks on March 24. The main points of this document were the following:

—Final borders would be agreed upon by the parties. Minor adjustments in the 1967 lines were possible.

—There would be no imposed settlement.

—The four powers would work closely with and through Ambassador Jarring.

—A final agreement would take the form of a contract signed by all parties.

—Peace would be achieved as part of a package settlement.[22]

The last point, on the need for a package settlement, was of fundamental importance. It meant that there would be no Israeli withdrawal until all elements of a peace agreement on all fronts had been achieved. This stood in stark contrast to the insistence of the Soviets and the Arabs that Israel should withdraw first, after which an end to belligerency and other issues could be discussed.

During March and April the situation in the Middle East began to deteriorate significantly. Fighting broke out along the Suez Canal; fedayeen attacks mounted in severity, as did Israeli retaliation; and in early April Nasser announced the abrogation of the cease-fire, initiating what came to be known as the war of attrition.[23] In Lebanon a state of emergency was declared in April after clashes with the fedayeen, and for months Lebanon was virtually without a government.

Against this background the pace of diplomacy quickened. The four powers—the United States, the Soviet Union, Great Britain, and France—held their first meeting on April 3. These talks continued at regular intervals into June. Meanwhile the United States began to talk directly with two of the Arab parties to the conflict, Jordan and Egypt.

King Hussein met with Nixon and Rogers on April 8. The administration was sympathetic to Jordan but realized that the king was unable to move on a settlement without Nasser. To help Jordan, it would also be necessary to help Egypt. Hussein did bring with him a concession from Nasser that might smooth the path of U.S.-Egyptian relations. The king publicly declared that he was authorized to state that, as part of a settlement, there would be freedom of navigation in the Suez Canal for all nations.[24]

Several days later Nixon met with a top aide of Nasser, Mahmoud Fawzi, who confirmed this point and added privately that Egypt would not feel constrained by Syria's opposition to a political settlement. In short, Egypt and Jordan indicated they were prepared for a settlement, even if Syria was not. Kissinger, however, was not persuaded by Fawzi that Egypt was prepared for much real flexibility.[25]

To assess the results of this first phase of Middle East talks, Nixon held a meeting of the National Security Council on April 25. The major question to be discussed was whether the United States should put forward more specific proposals for a settlement. Secretary Rogers took the position that the talks had not yet reached the "cutting edge." He noted that Nasser was an "enigma" and that the Israelis were showing a growing tendency to define security in terms of territory. It was decided that Sisco should resume his talks with Dobrynin, introducing more specific proposals as appropriate.[26]

Between May 6 and May 12 Sisco conveyed the main points of the United States proposal on an Egyptian-Israeli settlement to Ambassador Dobrynin. The Soviet position had evolved somewhat, the most important change being acceptance of the idea of a package settlement.[27] In the American view it was now up to the Soviet Union to bring pressure to bear on the Egyptians to accept these points. In return, the United States would be prepared to use its influence with Israel to gain Israeli adherence to the basic principles agreed upon by the superpowers.

A crucial debate within the American administration concerned the role of the Soviet Union. Some at State felt that the Soviet Union, for global-strategy reasons, would be prepared to cooperate with the United States in the Middle East, even if that might cause Moscow some strain in its relations with Nasser. In fact, it was privately hoped that the Soviets might weaken their position in Egypt by trying to force Nasser to accept the U.S.-Soviet proposals. Kissinger doubted that the Soviets would be prepared to sacrifice regional interests for the sake of improved U.S.-Soviet relations. He argued that the Soviet Union had worked hard to build a position of influence in the Middle East; to maintain that position, it depended chiefly on providing arms to key clients; and if peace was established, these arms would no longer be needed in large quantities. The Soviets therefore had an interest in preventing a real peace agreement, preferring instead a state of "controlled tension." From this perspective, the U.S.-Soviet talks had one purpose, as seen by Moscow and Cairo: to get the United States to pressure Israel to withdraw from Arab territory in return for only minimal Arab concessions. Nixon appeared to be suspicious of the Soviets but felt they should be tested.

An early indication of Soviet intentions was provided by Soviet Foreign Minister Gromyko's trip to Cairo from June 10 to 13. After high-level talks in Moscow, which included Ambassador Dobrynin, the Soviets on June 17 made a formal counterproposal to the U.S. position presented to them in May by Sisco. Although the Soviet position was still not entirely compatible with the U.S. proposal, there was agreement on the need for a lasting peace agreement and on a package settlement. In addition, the Soviets reported that they had persuaded Nasser to accept informal direct talks with the Israelis, patterned on the Rhodes armistice negotiations in 1949.

The Soviet proposal was sufficiently encouraging to prompt further discussions. From July 14 to 17 Sisco met in Moscow with Soviet leaders, and on July 15 he presented a document to them that embodied the earlier United States proposals, which had been modified to correspond to the Soviet points of June 17.[28]

With the completion of Sisco's talks in Moscow, the positions of the two superpowers were fairly well defined. Each pleaded its inability to move further in the absence of concessions from the other side. In particular, the Soviet Union urged the United States to be more explicit on the final border between Egypt and Israel. Sisco had said in Moscow that a more concrete American position might be possible on the final border if the Soviets could be more specific on Egyptian commitments to peace and on direct negotiations. In particular, the United States insisted that the state of war should end with the signing of an agreement, not with the completion of Israeli withdrawal, and also was adamant that peace was incompatible with continued fedayeen activity.

For the rest of the summer the positions of the superpowers remained essentially frozen,[29] but the situation in the Middle East did not. Fighting along the canal intensified; Israel informally approached the United States in July with a request for an additional 100 A-4 Skyhawks and 25 F-4

Phantoms to make up for the Mirages that France was refusing to sell.[30] Then, on September 1, one of the most conservative and pro-Western of the Arab governments, that of King Idris of Libya, was overthrown in a surprise coup d'état led by young Nasserist army officers. Coupled with the "radical" coup in Sudan the previous May, this seemed to confirm the fears of those who saw a trend toward extremism and violence in the Arab world in the absence of progress toward a peace agreement.

Early in September, the first F-4 Phantom jets (the furnishing of which President Johnson had agreed to in late 1968) reached Israel. They soon became a potent symbol to the Arabs of American support for Israel, and an intensive campaign began in the Arab world to prevent further such agreements.

On September 11 another NSC meeting on the Middle East was held. Rogers argued that the time had come for the United States to move to its fallback position on Israeli withdrawal to the Israeli-Egyptian international frontier. According to Kissinger, "The advocates of further concessions argued that time was working against us; the longer the deadlock lasted, the more our position in the Arab world would deteriorate. I stressed that the opposite was true. A continuing deadlock was in our interest; it would persuade Egypt to face the reality that Soviet tutelage and a radical foreign policy were obstacles to progress and that only the United States could bring about a settlement; it would demonstrate Soviet impotence and in time might impel a fundamental reconstruction of Arab, and especially of Egyptian, foreign policies." Nixon, who had already been warned of the "domestic buzz saw" that awaited him if he backed Rogers on the 1967 borders issue, sided with Kissinger. Thus Rogers was not given authority to reveal the fallback position in his upcoming talks with Gromyko.[31]

Between September 22 and 30 Rogers and Sisco met with Gromyko and Dobrynin in New York at the United Nations. President Nixon, in his speech to the UN General Assembly on September 18, had emphasized the need for "binding, irrevocable commitments" as part of a peace agreement in the Middle East. The question now was whether the Soviets would be able or willing to elicit such commitments from Egypt.

Meanwhile Nixon met with Prime Minister Golda Meir on September 25. Meir treated Nixon as if he were a great friend of the Jewish people, and in return he indicated considerable sympathy for Israeli concerns. Meir requested additional arms, 25 more F-4 Phantoms and 100 A-4 Skyhawks, as well as $200 million a year to help pay for them.

Nixon's response was somewhat elliptical, suggesting that he would trade "hardware for software," which seemed to mean that arms supplies would be linked to political concessions.[32]

During Meir's visit Nixon also agreed that a direct channel of communications between the two leaders should be established, bypassing the State Department. Nixon was fond of using such back channels, and soon Henry Kissinger and Israel's ambassador, Yitzhak Rabin, were linked by a private phone line. Rabin used this improved access to the White House to argue forcefully that Israel should intensify its bombardments deep inside Egypt. Even if the State Department might be urging restraint, Rabin could argue that his sources were egging Israel on.[33]

Seemingly unaffected by Meir's visit, the State Department continued to press forward with its plan for reaching a common position on principles with the Soviet Union. Gromyko reported some progress in his talks with the Egyptians. They would apparently agree to Rhodes-style talks. But then on October 10 Egypt denied that it had agreed to any such thing. Meanwhile attacks on United States policy in the Middle East were mounting, especially in Lebanon, where serious fighting was going on and Syria seemed to be on the verge of intervention.

In this confusing setting Rogers asked for authority to go forward with the fallback position in talks with the Soviets. Nixon agreed, and on October 28 Sisco handed Dobrynin the final paragraph of a proposed joint document containing the United States fallback position on Israeli withdrawal. (See appendix B.) But, according to Kissinger, the president characteristically sought "to hedge his bets by asking John Mitchell and Leonard Garment—counselor to the President and adviser on Jewish affairs—to let Jewish community leaders know his doubts about State's diplomacy. Nixon implied strongly to them that he would see to it that nothing came of the very initiatives he was authorizing."[34]

THE ROGERS PLAN AND ITS RECEPTION

The Rogers Plan, as it came to be known, consisted of a short preamble calling for the conclusion of a "final and reciprocally binding accord" between Egypt and Israel, to be negotiated under the auspices of UN Ambassador Jarring following procedures used at Rhodes in 1949, and to be based on the following ten points:

1. As part of a package settlement, Egypt and Israel would "determine a timetable and procedures for withdrawal of Israeli armed forces from UAR territory occupied during the conflict of 1967."

2. The state of war between Egypt and Israel would end, and a formal state of peace would be established. Both sides would undertake to prevent all forms of aggressive actions from their territory against the people and armed forces of the other.

3. Both sides would agree on the location of secure and recognized borders between them. The agreement would include the establishment of demilitarized zones, the taking of effective measures in the Sharm al-Shaykh area to guarantee freedom of navigation in the Strait of Tiran, and arrangements for security and the final disposition of Gaza. Within this framework, "the former international boundary between Egypt and the mandated territory of Palestine would become the secure and recognized boundary between Israel and the UAR."

4. The two sides would work out agreement on zones to be demilitarized, measures to guarantee freedom of navigation through the Strait of Tiran, and effective security measures for and final disposition of Gaza.

5. The two sides would agree that the Strait of Tiran is an international waterway, and the principle of free navigation would apply to all states, including Israel.

6. In exercising sovereignty over the Suez Canal, Egypt would affirm the right of ships of all nations, including Israel, to pass freely through the canal without discrimination or interference.

7. The two sides would agree to abide by the terms of a just settlement of the refugee problem as agreed upon in the final accord between Jordan and Israel.

8. Egypt and Israel would mutually agree to respect and acknowledge each other's sovereignty, territorial integrity, and right to live in peace within secure and recognized borders.

9. The final agreement would be recorded in a document signed by the two sides and deposited with the UN. The final agreement would provide that "a material breach of that accord by one of the parties shall entitle the other to invoke the breach as a ground for suspending its performance in whole or in part."

10. The two sides would agree to submit the final agreement to the UN Security Council for ratification.

On November 10 both the United States and the Soviet Union presented the text of the plan to Egypt. Several days later, the Egyptian foreign minister sent a noncommittal reply to Rogers, noting some positive elements in the proposals, but holding off on a final commitment until an "integrated formula" for a comprehensive settlement was put forward.

In brief, Egypt was not prepared to consider a bilateral deal with Israel even if it stood to recover all its territory.[35] After nearly a month with no further reply from Egypt and no official reaction from the Soviet Union, Secretary Rogers, on December 9, outlined the basic elements of the plan in a public speech.[36] The following day Israel rejected Rogers's proposals; the NSC met on the Middle East, against the background of warnings of worsening trends in the area conveyed the previous day to Nixon by a group of prominent businessmen and former officials, David Rockefeller, John McCloy, and Robert Anderson.

On December 18 the United States presented a parallel plan for a Jordan-Israel settlement to the four powers.[37] It was hoped that this would strengthen King Hussein at the Arab summit meeting that was to open in Rabat the following day. The plan contained many of the same points as the October 28 document, adding or modifying a few points to fit the special circumstances on the Jordanian front.[38] The permanent border, for example, would "approximate" the armistice demarcation line existing before the 1967 war but would allow for modifications based on "administrative or economic convenience." In addition, point four of the December 18 document stressed that Israel and Jordan would settle the problem of Jerusalem, recognizing that the city would be unified, with both countries sharing the civic and economic responsibilities of city government. Point eight provided guidelines for a settlement of the refugee problem that would allow for repatriation or resettlement with compensation. An annual quota of refugees to be repatriated would be agreed upon between the parties.[39] King Hussein was reported to be pleased with the American proposal.

On December 22 the Israeli cabinet issued a statement saying that "Israel will not be sacrificed by any power or inter-power policy and will reject any attempt to impose a forced solution on her. . . . The proposal submitted by the USA cannot but be interpreted by the Arab rulers as an attempt to appease them at the expense of Israel."[40] As Rogers was deploring the Israeli use of the word "appease" the following day, the Soviets delivered an official note rejecting the Rogers proposals virtually in their entirety.[41]

The Israeli and Soviet rejections of the Rogers Plan, and Egypt's nonacceptance, put a sudden end to the first Middle East initiative of the Nixon Administration. With it died the hope that "linkage" diplomacy would help provide the key to peace in that area. Not for the first time, a basic reassessment of policy toward the Arab-Israeli conflict was undertaken. And although the Rogers proposals remained the most explicit statement of a preferred American peace settlement, they ceased to be the operational basis for American policy toward the Arab-Israeli conflict. Somewhat ironically, however, the eventual peace agreement between Egypt and Israel in March 1979 bore a remarkable resemblance to the principles of the Rogers Plan.

REASSESSMENT

When foreign policies have fallen short of expectations or have spectacularly failed, previously held images that buttressed those policies may be rapidly revised. New "definitions of the situation" are likely to emerge in short order, reflecting both the "lessons learned" from the preceding phase of policy formulation and the assessment of the new situation to be dealt with.

The Rogers initiative of 1969 had clearly failed, at least for the time being. Apart from Jordan there were simply no takers, and the Israeli reaction in particular was extremely hostile. What had gone wrong? Most policymakers agreed in retrospect that it had been naive to assume that the United States would be able to separate the Soviet Union from Egypt during the process of negotiations. The justification for the two-power talks had been that the United States and the Soviet Union would find it easier to reach agreement on principles than Israel and Egypt, and that they could both use their influence constructively to moderate the positions of their "clients." The concept fit nicely with Nixon's emphasis on "linkage," "détente," and "negotiations."

Even if the Soviets could have been persuaded to sign on to the Rogers Plan, it is not at all obvious that Israel could have been budged. Kissinger was actively opposing the plan, and he seems to have been signaling Rabin that Washington would welcome a more aggressive Israeli military campaign against Nasser. Unless Nixon had been prepared to back Rogers fully, and he apparently was not, the Israelis would not conceivably comply. The Rogers-Kissinger feud, and Nixon's own ambivalence, meant that the Rogers Plan really never had a chance of succeeding.

Domestic politics in the United States played a role. Kissinger and Nixon respected the strength of Israel's support in Congress and in public opinion generally. Kissinger also found it misguided and possibly dangerous for the United States to try to improve its relations with adversaries—the Soviet Union and Egypt—by pressuring its own friend, Israel. While such things might be done in the interest of achieving a genuine peace agreement, they should not become part of the standard American negotiating repertoire. The Soviets and Arabs should instead learn that U.S. influence with Israel was conditional on their restraint and moderation.

The lessons drawn from the failure of the Rogers Plan of 1969 were fairly obvious by early 1970. First, since it was impossible to separate the Soviet Union from Egypt, Washington would henceforth deal directly with Nasser when necessary rather than through Moscow. Second, since American concessions had not been reciprocated, the next move would have to come from the Soviets or Egyptians. No further unilateral U.S. concessions would be made. The United States and Israel could afford to sit tight until the "other side" had completed its own reassessment and concluded that a resumption of serious negotiations was needed. Third, any future American initiative would be less legalistic in tone, less public, and perhaps less ambitious. The package-settlement approach, though appealing in theory, was simply too complicated. Failure on one issue would prevent progress anywhere. More modest initiatives would henceforth be considered.

Two developments threatened this new consensus almost as rapidly as it emerged. First, the fighting in the Middle East escalated sharply during the spring of 1970, particularly with the introduction of Soviet SAM-3 surface-to-air missiles in Egypt, Israeli deep-penetration bombing attacks near Cairo, the dispatch of ten thousand or more Soviet advisers to Egypt, and the appearance of Soviet combat pilots flying air cover over the Egyptian heartland.[42] Second, the domestic pressures on the Nixon administration to abandon the Rogers Plan and to accede to an Israeli request for 100 A-4 and 25 F-4 jets mounted rapidly. With congressional elections on the horizon, members of both the House and Senate became particularly vocal in support of Israel.

The administration now faced two urgent problems in the Arab-Israeli dispute. One was to take some type of political initiative to end the fighting and to begin talks on a settlement. The other was to respond to Israeli arms requests, especially as Soviet involvement in the conflict grew. A dilemma, however, was acutely perceived by State Department officials. To pursue a credible political initiative aimed at Nasser, the United States would have to appear to be evenhanded. This was particularly difficult at a time when American-made Phantom jets were bombing the outskirts of Cairo with impunity and the Israelis were virtually declaring that their goal was to topple the Nasser regime. At the same time the United States could not indefinitely stand by and watch Soviet arms and personnel flow into Egypt without some response. This need to respond had as much to do with global politics as with the Middle East. Kissinger was especially insistent on this latter point, and his influence with Nixon was on the rise. The somewhat schizophrenic nature of U.S. policy during the next seven months was rooted in this bureaucratic and conceptual dualism.

RESUMPTION OF DIPLOMACY AND ARMS FOR ISRAEL

The first signs of a new tone in American Middle East policy after the abortive Rogers effort came in January 1970. President Nixon, in several public statements, tried to mend the U.S.-Israeli relationship and warn the Soviet Union about the consequences of its uncooperative policy in the area. For example, on January 25 the president sent a message to an emergency meeting of the conference of presidents of American Jewish organizations in which he reaffirmed his support for Arab-Israeli negotiations and stated that the United States was carefully watching the military balance. Then, in a press conference on January 30, Nixon surprised his staff and the Israelis by stating that he would announce his decision on Israel's pending arms requests within thirty days. The issue of arms to Israel had become particularly acute in the aftermath of the French decision to sell Libya more than 100 Mirage jets, some of which had originally been earmarked for Israel.

While Nixon was seeking to mend fences with the Israelis, President Nasser was seeking to accelerate the flow of arms and aid from the Soviet Union. Early in January the Israelis, finally taking the advice of their ambassador in Washington, had begun an intensified bombing campaign in Egypt's heartland, ostensibly designed to force Nasser to divert some of his forces from the sensitive canal area but also aimed at exposing his weakness to his own people.[43] In response, Nasser decided to make a secret visit to the Soviet capital. According to Egyptian sources, Nasser pleaded not only for an effective missile defense against the Israeli Phantoms but also for Soviet personnel and pilots to ensure that the system should operate effectively while Egyptians were being trained for the new equipment.[44] The Soviet reply was affirmative, and by March large quantities of arms and advisers were arriving in Egypt. In mid-April the first Soviet pilots were observed flying combat sorties in response to Israeli raids.

The stepped-up Soviet role in the conflict did not come as a total surprise in Washington. In a very frank letter to President Nixon dated January 31, Premier Kosygin had stated:

There is danger that in the immediate future the military actions may become wide scale. . . . We consider it our duty, however, to draw your attention, Mr. President, to the highly risky consequences the course chosen by the Israeli leaders may have both from the point of view of the situation in the Middle East and international relations as a whole. . . . We would like to tell you in all frankness that if Israel continues its adventurism, to bomb the territory of the UAR and other Arab states the Soviet Union will be forced to see to it that the Arab states have means at their disposal with the help of which due rebuff to the arrogant aggressor could be made.[45]

Kissinger forwarded Kosygin's letter to Nixon, with the notation that this was the first Soviet threat to the Nixon administration. Kissinger recommended a tough reply, which was forthcoming on February 4.[46] President Nixon rejected the Soviet effort to place the blame for the fighting on Israel alone and called for the prompt restoration of the cease-fire and an understanding on limitations of arms shipments into the area. In concluding, the president noted:

It is a matter of regret that Soviet unresponsiveness to these proposals [of October 28 and December 18, 1969] is holding up this process [of negotiations]; a more constructive Soviet reply is required if progress toward a settlement is to be made.

We note your desire to work with us in bringing peace to this area. We do not believe peace can come if either side seeks unilateral advantage.[47]

This last point was stated even more forcefully in the president's "State of the World" message, released on February 18:

This Administration has shown its readiness to work with the Soviet Union for peace and to work alongside the Soviet Union in cooperation with nations in the area in pursuit of peace. But the United States would view any effort by the Soviet Union to seek predominance in the Middle East as a matter of grave concern. . . . Any effort by an outside power to exploit local conflict for its own advantage or to seek a special position of its own would be contrary to that goal [the freedom of other nations to determine their own futures].

For these reasons, this Administration has not only pressed the efforts to restore observance of the cease-fire and to help begin the process of negotiating a genuine peace. It has also urged an agreement to limit the shipment of arms to the Middle East as a step which could help stabilize the situation in the absence of a settlement. In the meantime, however, I now reaffirm our stated intention to maintain careful watch on the balance of military forces and to provide arms to friendly states as the need arises.[48]

Here are to be seen the strands of American policy over the next months: a warning to the Soviets; a call for restoration of the cease-fire and for the beginning of negotiations; and an ambiguous policy on arms for Israel, refusing a posture of unilateral restraint and promising to watch military developments closely. A distinctly Kissingerian tone could now be heard.

On balance, Nixon seemed to be leaning toward an early and positive decision on Israel's arms requests. The rest of the bureaucracy was generally opposed to the supply of more Phantom jets, arguing that Israeli military superiority was still unquestioned and that Soviet arms shipments were a response to Israel's reckless campaign of deep penetration bombing using the Phantoms.[49]

The president's thirty-day self-imposed deadline for making a decision on the F-4s came and went with no announcement. Several factors seem to have dictated continued restraint. First, and perhaps most important, was Nixon's displeasure at the way in which the American Jewish community had treated French President Georges Pompidou during his visit in late February.[50] According to many sources, the president was so incensed at the demonstrations and discourtesies during the Pompidou visit that he ordered that routine messages to pro-Israeli groups be suspended. Second, the four-power talks were resumed in late February and the Soviets hinted at a more flexible posture. In a secret meeting with Rogers on March 11, Ambassador Dobrynin stated that the Soviet Union had managed to obtain political concessions from Nasser in return for the new arms shipments that were just beginning to reach Egypt.[51] Third, the situation in Jordan was unstable, and a U.S. decision on arms to Israel might further weaken the king.

Just as Rogers was meeting with Dobrynin, Kissinger met with Rabin to signal the impending decision to hold Israel's request for aircraft in abeyance. At the same time he told Rabin that new supplies of aircraft would be forthcoming in due course, but that deliveries should not be accompanied by so much fanfare. Rabin then met with Nixon, who reiterated these points, and left Rabin with the impression that Israel should consider attacking the newly deployed SAM-3 missiles.[52]

Finally, on March 23 Secretary Rogers announced that the president had decided to hold Israel's request for 100 A-4s and 25 F-4s in abeyance pending further developments in the area. As a consolation, economic credits of $100 million were offered.[53]

AN APPROACH TO EGYPT

In an effort to build on the limited credibility with the Arabs generated by the decision on the Phantoms, the administration decided to send Joseph Sisco to Cairo for direct talks with Nasser. The Soviets had said that Nasser was prepared to make concessions. The Americans would try to find out for themselves. During his stay in Cairo from April 10 to 14, Sisco essentially invited Nasser to try dealing with the United States as an honest broker.[54] Although Nasser had little reason to hope for much from the United States, he was experiencing great losses in the continuing fighting with Israel, his dependence on the Soviet Union was growing, and perhaps a positive approach to the Americans would prevent new shipments of Phantoms to Israel. Nasser's reply to Sisco came in his May 1 speech in which he invited the United States to take a new political initiative.[55]

The Sisco visit and the Nasser speech marked the turning point of one aspect of American diplomacy and led the State Department during the following three months to pursue an intensive effort to restore the cease-fire. A parallel, partly related, strand of policy involved both arms to Israel and the growing Soviet involvement in Egypt. The White House assumed control of this area. Nixon had denied that arms supply would be used as a form of leverage over Israel, but in the ensuing months that fiction was dropped.

The last half of April was a very important period in the Middle East and for American foreign policy generally. Within the region, riots in Jordan prevented Sisco from visiting Amman, and King Hussein requested the replacement of the American ambassador there. In Egypt, Soviet pilots were first noted flying combat patrols on April 18. Several days later President Nixon began planning for a bold, and very controversial, military move into Cambodia. The operation began on April 30; violence flared on university campuses; and several of Kissinger's closest aides resigned their positions. The atmosphere in Washington was extraordinarily tense. In the midst of it all, Nixon, long preoccupied by other issues, finally ordered a full investigation of the expanded Soviet role in Egypt. A policy of restraint and dialogue would clearly be difficult to maintain much longer. Besides incurring hostility to his Southeast Asia policy, the president was earning little support for his policy in the Middle East.

On May 21 President Nixon met with Israeli Foreign Minister Abba Eban. The president assured him that the flow of military equipment to Israel would be quietly resumed, but he urged that no publicity be given to this. He gave no specific commitment on the A-4s and F-4s but made it clear that the jets that remained to be delivered from the December 1968 agreement would be delivered without conditions.[56] In return, Nixon asked for a public Israeli statement that would indicate a degree of flexibility on terms of a settlement. This was forthcoming on May 26, when Prime Minister Meir formally announced that Israel continued to accept UN Resolution 242 as the basis for a settlement and would agree to something like the Rhodes formula for talks.[57]

The next move came from the Soviet Union. On June 2 Dobrynin met with Rogers and Sisco. The Soviet Union, he claimed, had won two important concessions from Nasser. First, Egypt would agree to control fedayeen activities from Egyptian territory if a cease-fire went into effect. Second, Egypt would agree that the state of war would end with the signing of an agreement.

The American response was to ignore the Soviet bid for a joint initiative and to press forward instead with its own unilateral call for a cease-fire and renewed talks. The National Security Council met on June 10 and 18 to discuss the Middle East.[58] The president authorized Rogers in NSDM 62 to request the parties to agree to a cease-fire of at least three months' duration and renewed talks under Ambassador Jarring's auspices. This was done on June 19.[59] Rogers publicly revealed the initiative on June 25.

Israel's immediate reaction was to reject the appeal. Ambassador Rabin, however, refused to deliver the note of official rejection, and during the next month the White House devoted considerable energy to persuading the Israelis to accept the new initiatives.[60]

The first step in the campaign was to reassure the Israelis on continuing arms deliveries. This was done in a letter from Nixon to Golda Meir dated June 20. Next, Henry Kissinger was quoted on June 26 as saying: "We are trying to get a settlement in such a way that the moderate regimes are strengthened, and not the radical regimes. We are trying to expel the Soviet military presence, not so much the advisers, but the combat pilots and the combat personnel, before they become so firmly established."[61]

In an interview on television on July 1, President Nixon spoke at length on the Middle East. Referring to Egypt and Syria as Israel's "aggressive neighbors," the president went on to state:

I think the Middle East now is terribly dangerous. It is like the Balkans before World War I—where the two superpowers, the United States and the Soviet Union, could be drawn into a confrontation that neither of them wants because of the differences there. . . . Now, what should U.S. policy be? I will summarize it in a word. One, our interest is peace and the integrity of every country in the area.

Two, we recognize that Israel is not desirous of driving any of the other countries into the sea. The other countries do want to drive Israel into the sea.

Three, then, once the balance of power shifts where Israel is weaker than its neighbors, there will be a war. . . . We will do what is necessary to maintain Israel's strength vis-à-vis its neighbors, not because we want Israel to be in a position to wage war—that is not it—but because that is what will deter its neighbors from attacking it.

And then we get to the diplomacy. The diplomacy is terribly difficult, because Israel's neighbors, of course, have to recognize Israel's right to exist. Israel must withdraw to borders, borders that are defensible. And when we consider all these factors and then put into the equation the fact that the Russians seem to have an interest in moving into the Mediterranean, it shows you why this subject is so complex and so difficult.[62]

Several days later, on July 4, the president authorized the shipment of electronic-counter-measure (ECM) equipment to be used against the SAMs in the canal zone.[63] Although still holding back on new commitments on aircraft, the administration was now prepared to help Israel attack the SAMs with new sophisticated equipment. On July 10 the president also ordered that the remaining A-4s and F-4s under the existing contract be shipped to Israel at an accelerated pace.[64]

President Nasser had left for Moscow on June 29, primarily for a health cure. While there, he discussed the American proposal with the Soviet leaders and reportedly informed them that he intended to accept it.[65] At a minimum, it would provide him a breathing space to complete the construction of the "missile wall." Accordingly, shortly after his return from Moscow, on July 22, Nasser accepted unconditionally the Rogers initiative of June 19.[66] On July 26 Jordan also accepted.[67]

The United States now had to bring about a positive Israeli response or risk the collapse of its Middle East diplomacy. President Nixon wrote to Prime Minister Meir on July 23, urging that Israel accept the proposal and making several important commitments. First, the United States would not insist that Israel agree to the Arab definition of UN Resolution 242. Second, Israel would not be forced to accept a refugee settlement that would fundamentally alter the Jewish character of the state or jeopardize its security. Third, and most important at the moment for the Israelis, Israel would not be asked to withdraw any of its troops from the occupied areas "until a binding contractual peace agreement satisfactory to you has been achieved." This was merely the standard American position on the "package settlement," but the Israelis apparently saw it as a significant step away from the Rogers plan of 1969.[68] In addition, Nixon promised to continue the supply of arms to Israel.

In reply, Prime Minister Meir sought assurances that Israel would be allowed to purchase Shrike missiles and Phantom jets, that the Rogers Plan would be withdrawn, and that the United States would veto any anti-Israeli resolutions in the United Nations.[69] Israel received a commitment only on arms, but that was apparently enough for Meir to accept, with clear reservations, the American initiative on July 31.[70] The previous day Israeli pilots had downed four Soviet MiG-21s over Egypt.

The formal Israeli written reply was not forthcoming until August 6, and included some changes in the language that Jarring was authorized to use in announcing the cease-fire. The United States ignored the Israeli changes, to Prime Minister Meir's great displeasure, and on August 7 a three-month cease-fire, with a provision for a complete military standstill in a zone fifty kilometers wide on each side of the Suez Canal, went into effect. In the State Department the mood was one of elation. It was not to last for long.[71]

CONCLUSIONS

Between January 1969 and August 1970 the Middle East policy of the Nixon administration passed through two stages. During the first year an apparent consensus existed that the State Department should take the lead in negotiating with the Soviet Union to produce a set of principles that would spell out in some detail the terms of an Arab-Israeli settlement. As part of this policy the administration adopted a restrained position on new arms agreements with Israel.

Two potentially divergent concepts underlay this policy. The first saw the Middle East as primarily an issue in global politics, and was characteristic of Nixon and Kissinger. This view underscored the danger of superpower confrontation and the desirability of U.S.-Soviet talks. The second perspective stressed regional trends more than global "linkages." It emphasized that the American position in the Middle East was eroding and that radicalization of the area was inevitable in the absence of a peace agreement. So long as the Soviets seemed cooperative and the regional conflict remained within manageable limits, these two approaches were compatible with a single policy. Nixon orchestrated an uneasy truce between the State Department and Kissinger that resulted in the Rogers Plan of October 28 and December 18. But almost as soon as these documents had been presented, Nixon, prodded by Kissinger, undercut his own policy by signaling to the Israelis that they were not to be taken seriously.

The second stage of policy toward the Middle East began with the failure of the Rogers Plan and the escalation of Soviet involvement in Egypt early in 1970. The shift in policy was the result both of developments in the Middle East and the growing influence on Middle East policy of Henry Kissinger, who all along had been critical of Rogers's handling of Middle East diplomacy. The growing Soviet role made the possibility of direct superpower confrontation increasingly real. This was what the White House wanted to avoid. One way of meeting the Soviet shipment of arms to Egypt, and of demonstrating that lack of Soviet restraint in the Middle East would not pass unnoticed, was to provide arms to Israel. This decision was made in principle during the spring and was set in motion on a large scale during the remainder of the year.

The intensified fighting along the canal and the increasingly important role of the Palestinian fedayeen in Jordan confirmed the worst fears of the State Department specialists. In their view the best way to reverse the trends was with a new diplomatic initiative, this time less ambitious in scope than the Rogers Plan and less dependent on Soviet cooperation. A simple "stop shooting, start talking" formulation was therefore proposed directly to each party on June 19.

These two perspectives risked collision on one issue, namely, arms to Israel. New U.S.-Israeli arms agreements might lead Nasser to reject the American initiative and might provide the "radical" Arabs with strong arguments to use against the United States. Nixon recognized the danger and therefore dealt with the arms issue circumspectly.[72] Above all, he tried to ensure that arms for Israel should be coupled with Israeli acceptance of the new American initiative.

On August 7, as the cease-fire went into effect, it seemed as if both the State Department and the president could feel satisfied that their preferred policies had produced a successful outcome. Within days, however, the provisions of the cease-fire were being violated and a new crisis was in the making. The tenuous, delicate balance between the State

Department and Kissinger, who opposed the cease-fire initiative, was also shattered.[73] By the time the next crisis was over, Kissinger had won Nixon to his side, and those in the State Department who had urged evenhandedness were virtually banished from center stage. The Jordan crisis of September 1970 was thus a fitting culmination of the first two stages of the Nixon diplomacy in the Middle East.

CHAPTER FIVE

The Jordan Crisis, September 1970

As the guns along the Suez Canal fell silent on August 7, 1970, a new phase of the Arab-Israeli conflict opened. A few optimists held out the hope that talks might soon begin that would lead to a resolution of at least some of the issues stemming from the 1967 war. Nasser had hinted that he was prepared to consider a political settlement. King Hussein, despite the erosion of his authority within Jordan, could be expected to play his part. The United States seemed anxious that the Jarring mission be resumed.

The cease-fire, however, unleashed forces that quickly undermined the prospects for peace talks and instead led to a crisis of unprecedented danger for the Nixon administration. Regional in its origin, the Jordan crisis at its peak had much more to do with U.S.-Soviet relations than with the Arab-Israeli conflict or the Palestinians. At any rate, that was the view in Washington.

To understand this dramatic episode in American policy, one must look beyond the ostensible issues in dispute between Israel, Egypt, Jordan, and the Palestinians. As the Jordan crisis erupted in September 1970, Nixon was approaching an important moment in his presidency, the congressional elections of November. His popularity had been hurt by the worsening crisis in Southeast Asia during the spring. His foreign policy was still more rhetoric than realization. U.S. relations with the Soviet Union were strained, the Vietnam War was continuing to take American lives, the strategic arms race went on unchecked, and the Arab-Israeli conflict had reached an extremely critical point. The State Department had labored to bring about a cease-fire between Egypt and Israel, which had gone into effect, but, almost immediately, threatened to collapse.

During August and September Nixon and his national security adviser, Henry Kissinger, were increasingly preoccupied with the crisis in the Middle East. They held a particularly stark view of Soviet intentions, and as they began to reshape American policy in the midst of the Jordan civil war, the U.S.-Soviet perspective dominated their thinking. The result was a new definition of issues in the Middle East and a revised understanding of the political dynamics of the region, in which the U.S.-Israeli relationship came to be seen as the key to combating Soviet influence in the Arab world and attaining stability.

From the standpoint of the Nixon administration, the Jordan crisis was successfully handled: King Hussein remained in power; the militant fedayeen were crushed; U.S.-Israeli relations were strengthened; and the Soviet Union was forced to back down, reining in its Syrian clients under U.S.-Israeli pressure. Finally, Nasser's death, just as the crisis was ending, seemed to open the door to a more moderate Egyptian foreign policy. This image proved to be flawed in many respects, but for nearly three years it served as justification for an American policy aimed primarily at reducing Soviet influence in Egypt, mainly through a generous provision of U.S. arms to Israel.

PRELUDE TO CRISIS: THE AUGUST CEASE-FIRE CONTROVERSY

The achievement of the cease-fire on August 7 created a breach in U.S.-Israeli confidence that continued to widen in subsequent weeks. Before Prime Minister Golda Meir had time to recover from her anger at the way in which the United States had ignored Israel's efforts to qualify the terms of the cease-fire, a new issue of dispute had arisen. Israeli sources maintained that Egypt was not adhering to the standstill provisions of the cease-fire agreement. Missiles were being moved into the canal zone, new sites were being prepared, and missiles were being rotated from active sites to previously inactive ones.

Unfortunately no one in Washington had thought about the problem of how to verify compliance with the agreement. Normal American intelligence activities did eventually detect major changes, but the issue now was whether Egypt had moved new equipment into the canal zone immediately after the cease-fire had gone into effect. A baseline measure was needed to establish what was allowed and what was not. Israel was not, however, willing to authorize U-2 flights along the canal as the cease-fire came into effect.[1] Satellite photographs had been taken the previous week but could not serve as a point of comparison, because a very rapid buildup on both sides of the canal had gone on in the days just before the cease-fire. It was not until August 10 that a U-2 finally flew over the canal, providing a reference point for judging any subsequent changes in military deployments.

Nixon and Kissinger were angry at the State Department and the CIA for not anticipating the problem of determining violations. The Israelis were producing evidence of Egyptian movement of missiles. State was dismissing it as inconclusive and was urging the Israelis to stop making such a fuss and to get on with the talks sponsored by UN Ambassador Jarring.[2] Israel's credibility at the White House was by now greater than State's.

On August 14, before American intelligence had confirmed Egyptian violations, Nixon authorized a $7 million arms package for Israel, consisting of military equipment that could be used against the missile sites along the canal in the event the cease-fire broke down. Deputy Secretary of Defense David Packard met with Israeli Ambassador Yitzhak Rabin to try to work out an understanding on how the arms might be used and to ensure total secrecy. Nixon still did not want to provoke Nasser needlessly, but Israel would receive sophisticated electronic equipment, Shrike missiles, and cluster-bomb units (CBUs) that could be used to attack missile sites.

Gradually the United States was able to piece together a picture of what had happened along the canal after August 7. On August 19 State acknowledged there had been some forward deployment of Egyptian missiles, but that hard evidence of numbers and locations was still difficult to obtain. Three days later Egypt and the Soviet Union were informed that the United States had "incontrovertible evidence of clear-cut violations" of the standstill cease-fire agreement.[3] Egypt replied on August 24, claiming the right to rotate missiles within the zone and denying that any new missiles had been introduced. Finally, on September 3 the United States made a strong demarche to Egypt and the Soviet Union concerning the violations, presenting evidence that at least fourteen missile sites had been modified during August. There was little evidence of completely new sites—these were constructed later in September—but a number of technical violations had been confirmed: incomplete sites had been finished; dummy sites had been activated, and some live sites had been abandoned; and a few new missiles appeared in the canal zone.[4]

The military significance of the violations was difficult to assess, but the political consequences were very important. At a minimum, they showed bad faith on Nasser's part and added weight to Israeli demands for compensation through new American arms deliveries. In retrospect, it does appear as if Nasser had accepted the cease-fire mainly to be able to complete construction of his missile defenses. But Nixon and Kissinger read an even more sinister design into the violations: Egypt was not acting alone. Those were Soviet missiles that were being installed, with the help of Soviet technicians. Therefore the Soviet Union was clearly aiding and abetting Nasser in violating the cease-fire agreement. Beyond that, it was trying to sabotage the Rogers initiative, which had aimed at getting talks started to settle the conflict. The Soviets, so it seemed, were afraid that peace in the Middle East would hurt their position; hence they were doing all they could to sabotage it.

One might have wondered what obligation the Soviet Union had to respect the terms of an American-arranged cease-fire to which it had not been a party. The Soviet bid for a cooperative approach had been rebuffed in early June, and the United States had proceeded unilaterally. Nixon and Kissinger, however, were unhappy with the Soviets for a host of reasons—Southeast Asia, arms talks, the Middle East.[5] They felt the time had come to stand up to Moscow. Events in the Middle East were about to provide an unexpected opportunity for just that.

Perhaps the Soviets thought Nixon was too preoccupied with Vietnam to act elsewhere; perhaps they misread the public reaction against the Cambodian invasion as a lack of will to use power; perhaps they misunderstood American restraint in arming Israel. If that was how the Soviets were thinking, Nixon seemed to believe, they would have to be taught otherwise. Equally important, the Chinese, with whom Nixon hoped to open a new relationship, must recognize that the United States had the will and the capability to resist aggressive Soviet actions. Otherwise Mao would see little reason to compromise his ideological purity by tacit alignment with the United States against the Soviet Union. Only a strong America would be of interest to the Peking leadership.

Nixon was also aware that his domestic base of support would be affected by any signs of weakness toward the Soviet Union. If détente was seen as appeasement, Nixon believed his foreign policy would be in trouble. Munich had not been forgotten, nor had the cold war. The running quarrel with Israel over arms had already taken its toll. Nixon had been prepared to put up with that if peace talks could begin. Now, however, Israel was in a morally justified position, for Egypt had violated the cease-fire agreement, with apparent Soviet connivance. Public and congressional support for Israel was strong. Evidently a new policy on arms supply was needed.

Throughout his first year and a half in office, Nixon had exercised considerable restraint in responding to Israeli arms requests. But he had failed to convince the Soviet Union that it should observe comparable limits, as its behavior from January to August 1970 had unmistakably shown. Nor had American restraint served its purpose with Nasser. He, like the Soviets, seemed to be taking advantage of the cease-fire at Israel's expense. Consequently, on September 1, 1970, Nixon met with Kissinger, Secretary of State Rogers, and Assistant Secretary Sisco in San Clemente to review Middle East policy.[6] The decision was made to sell Israel at least eighteen F-4 Phantom jets. Egypt would be told of the sale, and it would be explained in the context of the violations of the cease-fire agreement. On September 3, Nasser was so informed. Meanwhile, the previous day the Senate had approved a military authorization bill with an amendment sponsored by Senator Henry Jackson, giving Nixon virtually unlimited authority to provide arms to Israel with U.S. financing.

On September 6 Israel announced it was unable to participate in the Jarring talks so long as the Egyptian violations of the standstill cease-fire had not been rectified. That same day the Popular Front for the Liberation of Palestine (PFLP) astonished the world by hijacking three international airplanes, two of which were flown to a desert airstrip in Jordan, where their passengers were held as hostages, while the other was flown to Cairo, where it was blown up minutes after the passengers disembarked.[7] Suddenly the Jarring talks and the cease-fire violations along the canal were overshadowed by a new situation, one that soon provided Nixon and Kissinger with an opportunity to confront the Soviet Union.

THE HIJACKINGS

When Egypt, Jordan, and Israel agreed to a U.S.-sponsored cease-fire in late July 1970, a danger signal went out to the Palestinian fedayeen. From February 1970 on, the fedayeen had succeeded in undercutting King Hussein's authority to the point of virtually becoming a state within a state. Now their position was endangered, as President Nasser, their most prestigious backer, was apparently joining Hussein in a political settlement that could only be at their expense. Leaders of the Palestine Liberation Organization energetically opposed the Rogers initiative, with the result that Nasser suspended their right to use Radio Cairo.

The fedayeen movement had reached a decisive crossroads in late August 1970, when it convened an emergency session of the National Council in Amman.[8] Some of the more radical groups called for the overthrow of the Hashemite monarchy, but Fatah, the mainstream movement, led by Yasir Arafat, contrived to temporize. Before any consensus could emerge, however, the maverick PFLP, led by George Habash, carried out the hijackings on September 6. On September 9 another plane was hijacked and flown to Dawson Field in the Jordanian desert.[9] Altogether, the PFLP held nearly five hundred hostages, many of whom were Americans.

The PFLP's announced objective was to force Israel to release fedayeen prisoners held in Israel. Beyond that, the PFLP sought to upstage other Palestinian groups by appearing more militant than they were. Most dangerous of all, the PFLP sought to provoke a confrontation between Hussein and the fedayeen movement, with Iraq and Syria throwing their weight behind the Palestinians. Iraq had nearly twenty thousand troops in Jordan, and the Syrian army was just across the border within an easy two-day march of Amman.

The United States had been concerned about Hussein's weakened position for some time. The situation in Lebanon was also worrisome. These two moderate Arab states might well be taken over by radicals, just as Nasser seemed ready to move toward a settlement with Israel. On June 17 a National Security Council meeting was held to discuss contingencies for U.S. military intervention if Lebanon or Jordan should be threatened. According to Kissinger, Nixon spoke to these possibilities: "Let us suppose late in the summer we get a request from Lebanon or Jordan for assistance. . . . There comes a time when the US is going to be tested as to its credibility in the area. The real question will be, will we act? Our action has to be considered in that light. We must be ready. . . . Is the question really a military one or is it our credibility as a power in that area?"[10]

Several days later the Washington Special Action Group (WSAG) met to plan for these Middle East contingencies. The conclusions were somber: without access to bases in the eastern Mediterranean, the United States would find it difficult to send a sizable ground force into the area. The Sixth Fleet could provide some air support if it was on station, but otherwise American military capabilities were not impressive. If a serious military option was required, Israel was far better placed to provide both ground forces and air cover, particularly on short notice, but that issue, of course, was politically sensitive.

No Arab regime would want to be rescued by Israel if there was any alternative. Hussein was a realist, however, and had gone so far as to query the United States early in August on the full range of available options, including Israeli intervention, if Iraqi troops were to move against him. At the end of the month, on August 31, the king informed the American embassy in Amman that he might soon have to take drastic measures against the fedayeen and hoped he could count on the United States.

When faced with the hijacking challenge, Hussein militarily played for time. His choices were not very attractive. If he did nothing, the Jordanian army might move on its own against the fedayeen, thus destroying his authority. If he acted, Syria or Iraq might intervene. Hussein knew his army could handle the fedayeen alone, but what about their friends? Hussein was therefore forced to look for possible support against outside intervention, and that meant the United States and Israel.

The initial American response to the hijackings was cautious. Rogers felt that nothing much could be done. Nixon, by contrast, wanted to use the crisis as a pretext to crush the fedayeen, and apparently went so far as to order that Palestinian strongholds be bombed. Secretary of Defense Melvin Laird reported that the weather was not suitable for such attacks, and Nixon did not raise the issue again. But at the outset of the crisis Nixon was much more prepared to use American force than to countenance Israeli intervention.[11] At a minimum, it might prove necessary to evacuate the several hundred Americans in Amman. Perhaps an opportunity to rescue the hostages would present itself. Looking a bit further ahead, Nixon could see the need for a strong show of American force in the eastern Mediterranean as a deterrent to Soviet, Syrian, or Iraqi moves.

The Egyptians and Soviets were acting circumspectly and were not openly supporting the fedayeen in Jordan. On September 9 Nasser had gone out of his way to inform the United States that he was still interested in the American peace initiative. If that was true, perhaps the crisis in Jordan could be contained and resolved without igniting a broader conflict. Nixon was determined, however, that the crisis should not be settled on terms set by the fedayeen. He would not pressure the Israelis to release prisoners as the price of recovering the hostages, and he urged the British to adopt the same tough attitude. This was Nixon at his law-and-order, no-capitulation-to-blackmail best. Kissinger agreed, insisting that the United States should look implacable. But Kissinger disagreed with Nixon over the advisability of using U.S. troops. If military action was needed to help King Hussein, he preferred that Israel take the lead.[12]

Determined to take a tough stand, Nixon ordered a series of steadily escalating series of military moves as deliberate signals of intent and to provide a modest intervention capability if needed. On September 10 the

82d Airborne Division at Fort Bragg, North Carolina, was placed on semialert; six C-130 transport planes were also flown from Europe to Incirlik air base in Turkey, where they could be available for evacuation of Americans from Jordan. The following day units of the Sixth Fleet began to leave port as part of what the White House termed "routine precautions in such a situation for evacuation purposes." Four more C-130s, escorted by twenty-five F-4 jets, were flown to Turkey. That same day the fedayeen blew up the aircraft and moved the remaining fifty-four hostages in their hands, thirty-four of whom were Americans, to an undisclosed location.[13]

On September 15 King Hussein told the British, who then contacted the United States, that he was forming a military government with the intention of moving against the fedayeen. He indicated that he might need to call on the United States and others for help. When the news reached Washington, Kissinger quickly convened a meeting of the WSAG at 10:30 p.m. Further military moves were ordered. The aircraft carrier *Saratoga* would proceed to the eastern Mediterranean, where it would join the *Independence* off the Lebanese coast; airborne units in West Germany would be placed on semialert; additional C-130s would fly to Turkey. Despite these preparations, it was decided that the United States would not unilaterally try to rescue the hostages, but the administration was determined to try to preserve King Hussein in power.[14]

CIVIL WAR IN JORDAN

With the outbreak of heavy fighting in Jordan between the army and the fedayeen on September 16 and 17, the United States suddenly faced a new set of dangers in the Middle East. At one extreme, the conflict in Jordan might ignite an Arab-Israeli war if Israel intervened directly. Egypt and the Soviet Union could then be drawn in, which might lead to a U.S.-Soviet confrontation, the fear that all along had haunted Nixon and Kissinger. Almost as dangerous would be Hussein's overthrow. A close friend of the United States would have been defeated by radical forces armed with Soviet weapons. Even if the Soviet Union was not directly involved, the symbolism of a fedayeen victory would work to Moscow's advantage.

Nixon clearly wanted Hussein to crush the fedayeen, but he also wanted the conflict contained within Jordan. The American role, as he and Kissinger saw it, was to encourage Hussein to act while restraining the Israelis from precipitate military moves. At the same time an American and Israeli show of force might help to deter the Syrians, Iraqis, and Soviets. The balance between restraint and belligerence would be difficult to establish; too much of either on the part of the United States or Israel could be counterproductive. Timing and a close monitoring of events on the ground were essential, and a high degree of coordination among Jordan, the United States, and Israel would be vital.

Nixon's first moves were to warn against outside intervention. At Kansas State University on September 16, he gave a tough law-and-order speech in which he denounced the fedayeen. He then flew to Chicago, where he met with Kissinger and Sisco for an update on the crisis. There were conflicting views in the intelligence community on the likelihood of Syrian or Iraqi intervention. On the whole, it was discounted as a possibility.

Nixon thought otherwise, however, and on September 17 he met twice with editors of Chicago newspapers to discuss the crisis in Jordan. The *Sun-Times* rushed into print that evening with a story summarizing Nixon's views. The United States was reportedly "prepared to intervene directly in the Jordanian war should Syria and Iraq enter the conflict and tip the military balance against Government forces loyal to Hussein." [15] Hussein's survival was judged by Nixon to be essential to the American peace-settlement effort. Israeli intervention against the fedayeen would be dangerous, and if Syria or Iraq were to enter the battle, the United States would have to intervene. Nixon reportedly also told the editors that it would not be such a bad thing if the Soviets believed he was capable of irrational or reckless action. [16] This was vintage Nixon—be tough; keep your opponents off balance; remain mysterious and unpredictable. With luck, no one would then test to see if you were bluffing.

Returning to Washington the evening of September 17, Nixon met with his advisers again. A third aircraft carrier, the *John F. Kennedy*, was ordered to move from the Atlantic into the Mediterranean, and the *Guam*, a helicopter carrier with fifteen hundred marines on board, was ordered to proceed as rapidly as possible from Norfolk to the Mediterranean. Nixon also discussed the meeting he was scheduled to have with Prime Minister Meir the following day. The time had clearly come to mend U.S.-Israeli relations, because the two countries might have to work closely during this crisis. Nixon therefore authorized $500 million in military aid for Israel and agreed to accelerate the delivery of eighteen F-4s.

Nixon and Meir met on September 18 for what the *New York Times* termed the most important talks between the United States and Israel in twenty-two years. Relations were judged to be at an "extraordinary low ebb" because of the quarrel over the cease-fire and restraint in providing arms.[17] The reality actually was less stark. Nixon's promise to give Israel's aid requests his "sympathetic attention" helped to set the stage for a remarkable improvement in the ties between the two countries during the next few days. In view of subsequent developments it seems odd that Nixon apparently did not discuss the possibility of intervention in the Jordan civil war with Meir. That was left to Rogers, Sisco, and Kissinger, for it still seemed a remote contingency. The king seemed to be gaining the upper hand in Jordan, and the Soviets were behaving themselves.

It was not until Saturday, September 19, that the first reports of a Syrian armored probe into Jordan reached Washington.[18] The Soviet Union was quick to warn against outside intervention in Jordan and joined President Nasser in a call for a cease-fire. The Soviet chargé in Washington, Yuli Vorontsov, informed the State Department that the Soviets were urging restraint on the Syrians and were themselves in no way involved in the attack. Kissinger relayed this news to Nixon at Camp David. Nixon was unimpressed and skeptical. The Soviets, after all, had denied complicity in the standstill cease-fire violations along the Suez Canal. And now their client, Syria, was sending tanks into Jordan. Could this really be done without the Soviets at least giving their tacit blessing? More likely, Nixon believed, the Soviets were egging the Syrians on.[19] Whatever the truth, U.S. diplomatic and military moves would thenceforth be aimed at getting the Soviets to pressure the Syrians to withdraw their forces.

CRISIS MANAGEMENT

It was not until Sunday, September 20, that the Syrian intervention became ominous. While Secretary of Defense Laird was denying any need for U.S. intervention, Nixon was preparing for precisely that contingency. This was his crisis, not Laird's or Rogers's. Only Kissinger would be fully involved with the president's decisions.

Kissinger recommended, and Nixon approved, an enhanced alert status for some military units in West Germany, and the Sixth Fleet was ordered to move farther east.[20] Besides these signals to the Soviet Union, Sisco conveyed a strong warning to Vorontsov in the afternoon, stressing that Syria's action "could lead to the broadening of the present conflict."[21] Rogers publicly denounced the Syrian "invasion."[22]

Besides these developments, U.S. diplomacy was engaged in two other vital tasks that day. First came King Hussein's urgent request through his trusted aide, Zaid Rifai, to the American ambassador for American help against the Syrians. The situation in Amman was under control, but in the north it was very threatening. Late in the evening in Jordan, King Hussein ordered Rifai to send U.S. Ambassador L. Dean Brown a request by radio for intervention by air and land from any quarter against the Syrian tanks.[23]

In Washington, the WSAG met at 7:00 p.m. to consider the king's extraordinary appeal. According to Kissinger, "A quick review of the pros and cons of American military intervention strengthened our conviction that our forces were best employed in holding the ring against Soviet interference with Israeli operations. To be effective unilaterally we would have to commit our entire strategic reserve; we would then be stretched to near the breaking point in two widely separated theaters and naked in the face of any new contingency. Our forces would have to go in without heavy equipment and with air support only from carriers."[24]

Nixon called Kissinger from the meeting at 7:50 p.m. and invited the other senior members of the WSAG to his office at 8:00 p.m. Shortly thereafter Kissinger's deputy, Alexander M. Haig, Jr., received a call from the British ambassador with the news that the king was now requesting immediate air strikes. He also informed the WSAG that Irbid had fallen to Syrian troops.[25] Responding to these developments, the WSAG recommended placing the airborne brigade in Germany and the 82d Airborne on a higher-alert status and flying a reconnaissance plane from a carrier to Tel Aviv to pick up targeting information and to signal that American military action might be nearing.[26]

At about 9:30 p.m. Kissinger, joined by Sisco, went to see Nixon, who happened to be at the bowling alley of the Old Executive Office Building. Nixon approved the WSAG recommendations and agreed it was important to establish contact with Ambassador Rabin.

Golda Meir and Rabin were in New York at that moment at a fund-raising dinner. At 10:00 p.m. Kissinger managed to reach Rabin by phone. He told Rabin that the king had asked for assistance, but the United States urgently needed intelligence on Syrian positions before it could respond. Could Israel fly reconnaissance as soon as the sun was up? Rabin asked if the U.S. favored an Israeli air strike. Kissinger said he first wanted to see the results of the reconnaissance. At this point, according to Kissinger, a new message arrived from King Hussein and he broke off the conversation.[27]

The king's new message spoke of a rapidly deteriorating situation and an urgent need for air strikes. Ground troops might also be needed. Kissinger spoke with Rogers, and both decided to recommend to Nixon that the United States should endorse an Israeli air strike. Sisco and Kissinger returned to the bowling alley to seek the president's approval, which was forthcoming. Kissinger again called Rabin, this time informing him that the United States would look favorably on an Israeli air attack if Israeli reconnaissance confirmed that Syria was in control of Irbid with large armored forces.[28] Before midnight Rabin called back with Golda Meir's response. Israel would fly reconnaissance at daybreak. Air operations might not be sufficient, but Israel would take no further action without consultations.

Monday, September 21, was indeed a critical day in the Middle East. King Hussein had called for help but had made it clear that Jordan must have the final say on the kind of intervention. He preferred that the United States or Great Britain be involved, not just the Israelis.

Early on September 21 Rabin contacted the White House to say that Israel did not believe air strikes alone would suffice. Ground action might also be needed. Kissinger called Nixon, and, after a short period of deliberation, Nixon dictated a message to Rabin. According to Kissinger, he said: "I have decided it. Don't ask anybody else. Tell him 'go.'"[29] Kissinger then consulted with Rogers and Laird, who had reservations. Nixon reluctantly agreed to convene a full meeting of the NSC at 8:45 a.m. Present were Laird, Rogers, Packard, Thomas Moorer (chairman of the joint chiefs), and Kissinger. Moorer was opposed to U.S. ground intervention because the capability simply was not there. Hence if ground action was needed, Israel would have to act. Intelligence estimates from Israel claimed that 250 to 300 Syrian tanks were in the Irbid area.[30] Nixon finally decided that Sisco should tell Rabin that the United States agreed to Israeli ground action in principle, subject to determining the king's view and prior consultation.[31]

In the course of the day, as the situation on the ground changed, the king frequently modified his initial request. During the morning Rifai had indicated that the king preferred air strikes alone but that ground intervention would be acceptable without further approval if communications broke down. Later that afternoon Rifai requested an immediate air strike to check the advancing Syrian tanks. In the evening Hussein shifted position once again, urging Israeli ground action into Syria but ruling out Israeli armored intervention in Jordan.

In view of the critical situation in Jordan and the apparent need for Israeli action, Kissinger was made responsible for providing Israel with answers to a list of questions about American policy in the case of wider hostilities. No further decisions seemed immediately necessary, since Israel was proceeding with its mobilization in any case and the battle would not be joined again in Jordan until the next day.

As events unfolded, the Israelis developed a plan for sending 200 Israeli tanks toward Irbid, combined with air strikes. Israel would guarantee that its forces would be withdrawn from Jordan once the military operation was over. Kissinger and Sisco relayed to Rabin the king's preference for Israeli ground action inside Syria, not Jordan. Such action was considerably more risky for the Israelis and might provoke an Egyptian military response along the canal, or even Soviet threats to intervene. Rabin therefore sought an American commitment to prevent Soviet intervention against Israel, as well as a promise of aid if Egypt attacked.

By the end of the day Rabin conveyed to Kissinger the cabinet's decision to intervene if Syrian tanks continued to advance on Tuesday. The Israeli air force would attack first, but if this was insufficient, a tank force would also be sent into Jordan, and perhaps also into Syria. Rabin insisted, however, on an American "umbrella," a presidential commitment to use the force necessary to prevent a Soviet attack on Israel, as well as a promise of arms. Nixon readily approved the request for arms, and considerable discussion of the "umbrella" assurances took place, without formal agreement ever being reached.[32]

The next day, Tuesday, September 22, was decisive. Israel, with U.S. encouragement but no binding agreement, was poised to act. Hussein, with the assurance that Israel and the United States were behind him, finally ordered his own small air force to attack the Syrian tanks around Irbid, which it did with satisfactory results.[33] By afternoon Syrian tanks were beginning to withdraw from Jordan. The need for Israeli intervention was less urgent. The king, speaking in code, informed Ambassador Brown that Israeli intervention was all right "up high" but should be directed elsewhere "down below."[34] An Israeli air strike would still be welcome, but land intervention should be only against Syria. Israel did not wish to undertake ground action in Syria, and by the end of the day the prospects for Israeli or American intervention had virtually passed.[35]

Kissinger and Nixon had met several times that day. They were acutely aware of how difficult it would be for the United States to intervene.[36] Even with access to British bases in Cyprus, only 50 sorties daily over Jordan could be flown. Aircraft from the Sixth Fleet would be able to carry out an additional 200 sorties a day, but even that could not compare with what the Israelis were capable of providing. With considerable relief, the president learned that Syrian tanks were beginning to withdraw. Just to make sure the Soviet Union did not change its position, Kissinger went out of his way that evening to tell Vorontsov at an Egyptian reception that it was up to the Soviets to rein in their friends. "You and your client started it, and you have to end it."[37] The State Department had announced earlier that day that the Soviets were claiming to be restraining the Syrians, but Kissinger seemed to feel that a few added tough words could do no harm.

By Wednesday the acute phase of the Jordan crisis had passed. Shortly after noon Nixon met with Rogers and Kissinger in the Oval Office. While discussing the crisis, they received the news that all Syrian tanks had left Jordan. A statement was soon released from the White House welcoming the Syrian withdrawal, and Sisco was asked to contact Rabin to obtain his assurance that Israel would make no military move.[38] The Jordanians had the situation under control and no longer wanted outside intervention. For the United States and Israel, the crisis was over. Nixon celebrated on Thursday by playing golf at Burning Tree Country Club with Rogers, Attorney General John N. Mitchell, and AFL-CIO president George Meany. The following day a cease-fire was announced in Jordan.

Nixon was proud of the way he had handled the Jordan crisis. He compared his restrained, yet forceful, use of military power with John F. Kennedy's behavior in the Cuban missile crisis of October 1962. Many of the participants praised Kissinger's management of the WSAG. On the whole, everyone from Nixon on down was pleased with the way the crisis had been handled. In something of a "victory lap," Nixon flew to Rome on September 26, and from there to the aircraft carrier *Saratoga*, where he spent the night of September 27.

Meanwhile President Nasser of Egypt was trying to arrange a stable cease-fire and a new modus vivendi between Jordan and the PLO. Nasser had differed with the fedayeen in their opposition to the Rogers initiative and in their desire to bring down King Hussein, but he did not want to see the PLO crushed by Hussein's troops. He therefore summoned Hussein, Arafat, and other Arab leaders to Cairo to work out an agreement that would govern the PLO presence in Jordan and prevent further clashes. The agreement was signed on September 27. The following day, while seeing off his last guests at the airport, President Nasser fell ill. He returned home, where, several hours later, he died of a heart attack. With Nasser's death, an era in Arab politics came to an end. By chance, it coincided with the beginning of a new U.S.-Israeli strategic relationship.

THE AFTERMATH

The outcome of the Jordan crisis was widely considered a successful result of American policy. Certainly Nixon and Kissinger portrayed it as such, and in terms of declared American objectives the claim seemed justified. King Hussein was securely in power. The fedayeen had been badly weakened, and the hostages had all been rescued. The Syrian military intervention had been turned back by Jordan without Israeli or American involvement. The Soviet Union had refrained from direct intervention once the United States made a strong show of force. And U.S.-Israeli relations were stronger than ever. The outcome of the crisis being consistent with U.S. goals, few bothered to consider the extent to which American or Israeli actions were responsible for these developments, nor were the premises of American policy closely examined. Apparently successful policies are spared the type of critical scrutiny reserved for failures.

Nixon and Kissinger, with considerable justification, were therefore able to take credit for successfully handling a major international crisis. Jordan was the first in a series of foreign-policy spectaculars that boosted Nixon's prestige and popularity and made Kissinger's name a household word. After Jordan came the opening to China, the Strategic Arms Limitation Talks agreement, and the Vietnam negotiations. Each of these achievements looks a bit tattered from the perspective of two decades, but at the time they contributed immensely to the reelection of Richard Nixon in November 1972. The theses of his foreign policy—negotiations, détente, a new structure of peace based on a multipolar power balance—all appeared to take on substance in the period after the Jordan crisis.

U.S.-Israeli relations, which had reached a low point in mid-1970, were quickly brought to an unprecedented high level by the Jordan crisis. There had been a long-standing debate within the bureaucracy concerning policy toward Israel. The conventional wisdom, especially in the State Department, was that American support for Israel was an impediment to U.S.-Arab relations. By granting economic and military aid to the enemy of the Arabs, the United States was providing the Soviet Union with an opportunity to extend its influence in the Middle East. Although few questioned that Israel's existence should be defended by the United States in an extreme case, many felt that an "evenhanded" policy, whereby the United States would not always align itself with Israel and would not become its primary arms supplier, was the best guarantee of U.S. interests in the region. In this view Israel was more of an embarrassment for U.S. policy than a strategic asset. Even if Israel was an impressive military power, that power could be used only to defend Israel, not to advance American interests elsewhere in the region.

Israelis have generally resented the idea that American support is rooted primarily in domestic politics or in some vaguely felt moral commitment. They reject the reasoning of the proponents of "evenhandedness," who regard Israel as a burden on U.S. diplomacy in the Middle East. Particularly after the spectacular military victory of June 1967, Israelis began to argue that a strong Israel was in America's strategic interest.

The Israeli argument was less than fully convincing, especially to the seasoned Middle East specialists in the bureaucracy. Apart from appearing too self-serving, the argument did not fit the facts of the post–June 1967 situation. Soviet influence in the region did not decline; instead, it attained new levels, especially in Egypt, Syria, and Iraq. Radical forces in the Arab world gained strength, particularly with the rise of the fedayeen, the coup in Iraq in July 1968, and the overthrow of the conservative monarchy in Libya in September 1969. If King Faisal of Saudi Arabia was grateful to Israel for having checked Nasser's ambitions, he had a curious way of showing it. He was among the harshest critics of American support for Israel, arguing that such support played into the hands of radicals, communists, Zionists, and other dangerous elements. Even King Hussein, who, more than any other Arab leader, saw Israel as an important element in the regional balance of power, was angered by American aid to Israel and the continuing Israeli occupation of formerly Jordanian territory. He shared Faisal's view that Israel's 1967 military victory, and the subsequent American support for Israel, would polarize and radicalize the area. Only the Soviets and their friends would profit.

Nixon, however reluctantly, had been prepared to allow the State Department to pursue the logic of an evenhanded approach to the Arab-Israeli conflict up to a point, and this had led to the Rogers Plan and the August 1970 cease-fire. But both efforts had been flawed. The Soviet

Union had failed to cooperate; U.S.-Israeli relations had been badly strained, with little to show for it; and the Arabs had displayed little gratitude for U.S. restraint in providing arms to Israel.

As the Soviet dimensions of the Arab-Israeli conflict grew during the spring of 1970, Nixon began to accept Kissinger's argument that only a strong Israel could deal with the growing Soviet presence in Egypt. If the Soviet Union was allowed to succeed in helping Nasser recover Sinai by force of arms, Soviet aid would be sought throughout the region. Only by frustrating the Soviet-Egyptian scheme would American interests be protected. Arms to Israel would therefore serve an important global interest of the United States.

The August cease-fire violations created the necessary political climate for Nixon, encouraged by Kissinger, to turn to Israel as a strategic ally. The Soviets and Egyptians appeared to be double-dealing and were trying to exploit the American policy of restraint and to drive a wedge between Israel and the United States. Even without the Jordan crisis, Nixon would have agreed to new arms aid to Israel, but the crisis provided a convincing rationale for a policy based on arming Israel as a strategic asset for American policy in the Middle East. In an emergency Israeli forces had been prepared to protect King Hussein, a task that would have been much more difficult for U.S. forces.[39] By its mere presence, Israel had deterred the Syrian air force from entering the battle; Israeli armor massed in the Golan Heights must have helped convince the Syrians that they should withdraw. Then, too, by helping to force Syria to back down, Israel and the United States had further tarnished the Soviet image in the region while demonstrating that moderate Arab regimes could count on effective American support. The understandings, such as they were, worked out between Kissinger and Rabin on September 21, 1970, suggested the possibility of forging a far-reaching strategic relationship between the two countries.

For the next three years U.S.-Israeli relations flourished. Washington provided unusually high levels of aid. To both parties' satisfaction, the region remained comparatively calm, and Soviet influence seemed to be declining. When President Anwar al-Sadat suddenly expelled more than ten thousand Soviet military advisers from Egypt in July 1972, Nixon, Kissinger, Meir, and Rabin must all have congratulated themselves on the success of their joint policy.

The aftermath of the Jordan crisis did indeed constitute a momentary period of comparative stability. The cease-fire remained in force on all fronts. King Hussein successfully reestablished his authority in Jordan, from which the remnants of the fedayeen were expelled in July 1971. U.S.-Jordanian relations flourished, reaching substantial levels of economic and military aid. Jordan came to be treated as a regional partner of the United States. Jordan's special task on behalf of American interests, in King Hussein's view, would be to promote stability in the small oil-producing Arab states of the Gulf after the British departure at the end of 1971.[40] Nixon and Kissinger gave the king some encouragement and boosted aid to Jordan accordingly. In true Nixon-doctrine style, Israel, Jordan, and Iran were emerging in official Washington's view as regional peacekeepers. Aid and arms to these U.S. partners would serve as a substitute for a costly American military presence in the region or unpopular military intervention.

Elsewhere in the Middle East, post-Jordan-crisis trends also seemed favorable. In Syria the faction of the Baath party most closely associated with the intervention in Jordan was ousted by General Hafiz al-Asad in November 1970. Syria's new leaders were reportedly more moderate, or at least more cautious, than the former regime. Sadat was also viewed in Washington as a considerable improvement over Nasser. Sadat, at any rate, had less prestige in the Arab world than Nasser had possessed, and therefore less troublemaking potential. Perhaps he would turn to Egypt's domestic problems instead of promoting revolution elsewhere. This had long been the hope of American policymakers and had served as a major justification for aid programs to Egypt in the early 1960s.

In foreign policy Sadat was something of an enigma at first. His feelings toward the Soviet Union were unknown, but by the spring of 1971, after he successfully survived a coup attempt organized by Nasser's closest aides, Sadat's anti-Soviet colors became more evident. Even in Egypt, therefore, the trend seemed to be encouraging.

LESSONS LEARNED

The net effect of the regional developments growing out of the Jordan crisis was to breed a sense of complacency in Israel and the United States. The fears of radicalization, polarization, and confrontation that had haunted policymakers from 1967 to 1970 all but disappeared after September 1970. Now the region seemed to be relatively stable, and the key to this stability was a military balance that unquestionably favored Israel. The chief remaining threat came from the continuing Soviet military presence in Egypt and Syria. It thus became a prime objective of U.S.-Israeli policy to demonstrate to Sadat that the Soviet military presence in his country was an obstacle to his recovering Sinai. Soviet arms to Egypt would be matched by American arms to Israel, thus ruling out Sadat's military option. And so long as a Soviet military presence remained in Egypt, U.S. diplomacy would make only half-hearted attempts to promote a settlement.

The roots of this view, which dominated American policy during the next three years, can be traced to the Jordan crisis. Nixon and Kissinger had convinced themselves that Israel had played a vital role in helping to check the Soviet-inspired Syrian invasion of Jordan and might play a comparable role in thwarting Soviet designs in Egypt. Nixon and Kissinger, however, failed to grasp two critical dimensions of the Jordan crisis.

First, on the regional level, they misinterpreted the Syrian invasion, overemphasizing the Soviet role and minimizing the degree to which it grew out of internal Syrian politics. The difference was significant. If Syrian action was primarily rooted in domestic Syrian politics, a policy directed at the Soviet Union was unlikely to have much effect. Syrian withdrawal from Jordan may well have had little to do with Soviet pressure, and much more to do with the refusal of General Hafiz al-Asad to commit the Syrian air force to an adventure planned by his rival, Salah Jadid. Jordanian power, along with the obvious danger of Israeli intervention, was probably the key to the Syrian retreat, not Soviet demarches made in response to U.S. threats. In short, American policy in the crisis may well have had very little effect on the Syrian decision to withdraw its armor.

Second, Nixon and Kissinger exaggerated the global U.S.-Soviet dimension of the crisis. The Soviets had comparatively little at stake in Jordan. They were not on particularly good terms with the PLO, which was criticizing their primary client in the area, President Nasser. Syria was receiving military aid but was refusing to follow the Soviet political line on a settlement. Moreover, Syria was faction-ridden and unstable, was quarreling with Egypt and Iraq, and was essentially unpredictable. Once Syrian units did enter Jordan in the September crisis, the Soviets adopted a cautious policy. They made no threats. Instead, they warned against all outside intervention in Jordan, called for a cease-fire, and pointedly took credit subsequently for making demarches in Damascus to bring the fighting to an end.[41]

If the Soviet stand had been primarily a function of the strong position taken by the United States, and if Soviet pressures had significantly influenced Syria's behavior in the crisis, Nixon and Kissinger might have rightly concluded that the combination of U.S. and Israeli threats to act had produced the desired outcome. But no evidence can be found that such was the case. This is not to say that Nixon and Kissinger were wrong to make a strong show of force in the Jordan crisis. Among other things, it might have been a useful signal to the Soviets and the Chinese. The error was to conclude that the outcome of the crisis was mainly due to U.S. action. That was at least a debatable proposition, but instead it became something of an axiom in subsequent policy debates.

Although Nixon and Kissinger were wrong in the significance they attributed to American behavior in the Jordan crisis, this does not imply that the U.S. role was unimportant. On at least two counts the American contribution may well have been essential to the regional outcome. First, King Hussein needed encouragement to draw fully on his own military resources. He seemed to be afraid of committing his own air force without assurances that outside help would be available if he got into trouble. His willingness to order the successful counterattack on September 22, which removed the need for U.S. or Israeli action, may well have been a result of the assurances he received from the United States.

Second, the United States coordinated the Israeli response. Left to their own devices, Israeli leaders might have responded to the Jordan crisis differently. By working closely with the United States, Israel made its power available on terms King Hussein was able to accept. Because direct communication between Israel and Jordan did not exist during the crisis, serious miscalculations could have resulted. The United States was in close and continuous contact with both parties, however, and could urge restraint on Israel at the beginning and end of the crisis, while ensuring that Israel was prepared to act at the critical moment on September 22. To play this role effectively, the United States had to consider placing its own forces on the line as a possible backup to the Israeli operation.

Seen in this light, U.S. action in the Jordan crisis still appears relatively successful. Hussein took the necessary risks on September 22 because he knew that assistance would be available if needed. He thereby succeeded in removing the need for U.S. or Israeli intervention. The lesson of the crisis, from this perspective, was that American diplomacy, through a mixture of subtlety and restraint combined with visible force, had helped to create a situation in which Jordan was able to cope with its own problems. It had been a close call, however, involving a number of imponderables, such as factional balances in Syria and King Hussein's shifting moods. It would be hard to repeat the Jordan experience elsewhere, especially in situations in which U.S. and Israeli interests might not overlap so clearly with that of any other Arab regime. Even in this crisis the United States and Israel had not seen eye to eye. Rabin had characterized the American response to his request for an "umbrella" as reflecting a "predicament," perhaps alluding to the problem of any president promising to use force on behalf of a foreign power without congressional approval.[42]

What guidelines could this crisis provide for dealing with the serious problems of the Egyptian-Israeli conflict or with broader issues of the Soviet presence in the Middle East? What was the lesson regarding the role of American threats to use force in the crisis? Had they really been effective? Against whom? After all, the Syrian intervention came after Nixon's widely publicized threat on September 17 and after the visible movement of American military forces to the eastern Mediterranean. Was it possible that the Syrians had not taken the threats seriously, or that they came to their senses only when confronted with Soviet pressure and Israel's might? These were legitimate questions, well worth asking, but it was much easier for Nixon and Kissinger to see American power and diplomacy as responsible for the favorable outcome. Israel was regarded as the helpful junior partner in the successful management of a grave global test of superpower wills.

The result of these perceptions was a U.S. policy in subsequent years that was narrowly focused on Israel, Jordan, and the Soviet Union. The military balance was seen as the key to stability, if not to peace. Arms to Israel and Jordan were of higher priority than new peace initiatives. Little attention was paid to political developments in the region, to the mounting frustrations in Egypt and Syria and among the Palestinians, and to the growing activism of the Arabs, who had begun to recognize the potential power they possessed because of their petroleum resources.

In short, American policy became a captive of the perceived success in handling the Jordan crisis. The global dimension of the conflict was virtually all that Nixon and Kissinger seemed to care about. By ignoring regional trends, they misjudged the very forces that would lead within three years to a much more dangerous outbreak of war. During the interval the State Department launched several ineffectual diplomatic efforts, but Nixon and Kissinger, having taken charge of Middle East policy during the Jordan crisis, were reluctant to relinquish authority to Rogers and Sisco. The result was a series of half-hearted State Department initiatives, lacking White House support, that simply raised the level of Arab frustrations while reinforcing the sense of complacency felt in Israel and in Washington.

Several important opportunities to pursue a political settlement of the conflict may have been missed during this period. Caught in a perceptual trap largely of their own making, Nixon and Kissinger failed to notice them. The period of "standstill diplomacy" from 1970 to 1973 will not go down in the annals of American foreign policy as one of the more enlightened. In many ways the success in Jordan in 1970 resulted in a series of failures in the succeeding years, culminating in the October 1973 war.

CHAPTER SIX

Kissinger's Standstill Diplomacy, 1971–73

With the continuation of a cease-fire along the Suez Canal, the restoration of King Hussein's authority in Jordan, and the death of Egypt's president Gamal Abdel Nasser, the situation in the Middle East appeared to American policymakers to be less dangerous and more manageable than at any time since the 1967 war. The danger of U.S.-Soviet confrontation had passed. U.S. interests had survived intact through a difficult period, and less urgency was now attached to new American diplomatic initiatives.

Before the Jordan crisis the State Department had been primarily responsible for the formulation and conduct of policy toward the Arab-Israeli conflict. Thereafter Nixon and Kissinger were to play a more important role, chiefly through their emphasis on the Soviet dimension of the regional conflict and their desire for a close relationship with Israel. Over the next three years the White House refrained from day-to-day involvement in Middle East diplomacy but kept a careful eye on the State Department to ensure against excessive activism. Ultimately Nixon and Kissinger succeeded in undermining State Department initiatives and in establishing almost complete control over policy toward the Middle East.

The State Department was understandably loath to surrender this last remaining area of substantive responsibility. Instead, for nearly a year Secretary Rogers and Assistant Secretary Sisco tried to revive American diplomatic efforts. Initially they emphasized a resumption of talks through Ambassador Jarring. As that effort faltered in February 1971, they began to explore a conceptually different approach based on the idea of an "interim settlement" between Egypt and Israel. By August 1971, this approach had also failed. For the next two years the Arab-Israeli conflict was absent from the headlines, American diplomats remained uncharacteristically quiet and passive, and Arab frustrations mounted in direct proportion to the warmth of the U.S.-Israeli relationship. Even President Sadat's bold move in expelling more than ten thousand Soviet advisers from Egypt in July 1972 was not enough to lead to a serious reassessment of American policy. Instead, U.S. diplomacy continued to aim at what Kissinger was later to term the "complete frustration" of the Arabs, a policy that he later admitted was shortsighted and may have contributed to the October 1973 war.

The period from 1971 to 1973 thus seems to have been one of lost opportunities to prevent war and move toward a settlement. With the advantage of hindsight, one might say the type of agreement arrived at between Israel and Egypt in January 1974 could have been reached three years earlier at much less cost. But this conclusion may be wrong, for it fails to take into account other concerns weighing on policymakers at the time. The context of decisions must be kept in focus when one looks back at what might have been.

To understand this uninspiring chapter in American diplomacy between the Jordan crisis and the October 1973 war, one must recall the administration's intense preoccupation with other parts of the world. It was with relief that policymakers turned away from the Middle East to areas of higher priority. The Vietnam War was still raging, but in May 1971 Kissinger began a series of secret talks with top-level North Vietnamese representatives to try to reach a negotiated settlement. In parallel to these important talks, Nixon and Kissinger were planning a momentous opening toward Peking, symbolized by Kissinger's secret trip to China in July 1971. Finally, serious negotiations with the Soviet Union on limiting strategic armaments were under way.

Each of those three areas was so handled that in 1972, the presidential election year, Nixon would be able to point to visible achievements—visits to Peking and Moscow, and, it was hoped, an end to the war in Vietnam. The same election-year imperatives dictated a very low profile in the Middle East.[1] In the absence of any chance for a negotiated agreement there, Nixon focused instead on maintaining the military balance in Israel's favor, thereby preventing an unwelcome outbreak of fighting and no doubt earning the gratitude of Israel's many supporters in the United States.

In many ways the period from 1971 to 1973 is rich in lessons. It demonstrates the way in which Middle East issues can be influenced by global developments and by American domestic politics. Particularly in noncrisis periods U.S. foreign policy tends to be insensitive to regional developments, responding instead to strategic concepts, bureaucratic rivalries, and electoral necessity. The vacillation that so often seems to characterize American policy, especially in the Middle East, is likely to be especially intense at such times. The president is less involved than during crisis periods, and the bureaucracy is therefore left to devise policies that may ultimately fail for lack of presidential support.

Only one new policy concept concerning the Arab-Israeli conflict emerged during this period. Responding to Israeli and Egyptian suggestions, the United States backed away from the "package settlement" approach and began to emphasize the desirability of partial agreements unlinked to a final peace plan. A serious, but flawed, initiative was launched in the spring of 1971; several months later it came to an inglorious end. However, the concept of "interim steps" was eventually revived in a new setting by Henry Kissinger, the very person who opposed the 1971 effort. And it was he who made step-by-step diplomacy famous. By then, of course, Rogers was no longer secretary of state, and Sisco, the architect of the 1971 initiative, was serving as Kissinger's under secretary of state and chief adviser on Middle East policy.

THE JARRING TALKS AND U.S.-ISRAELI RELATIONS

During the post-Jordan crisis policy reviews on the Middle East, American officials considered several alternative approaches, including one dealing more directly with the Palestinians, before deciding to resume the interrupted Rogers initiative of the preceding June.[2] This time, however, the U.S.-Israeli relationship would remain close. Kissinger, in particular, felt that if Israel was ever going to make concessions, it would be from a position of strength and self-confidence, not under American pressure. Consequently a two-stage policy was adopted: first, an understanding would be reached with Israel on the terms of reference for the Jarring talks and on U.S. military assistance; second, Ambassador Jarring would be encouraged to take a more active role than previously in seeking agreement on basic principles of a peace agreement. The United States would support Jarring's efforts through bilateral talks with Israel, Egypt, and Jordan. The State Department was anxious for Jarring to try to establish the principle that Israel would withdraw from the occupied territories in return for Arab commitments to peace. That, after all, had been the essence of the original Rogers Plan.

The first step in the new American initiative was to bring Israel back into the Jarring talks and to extend the cease-fire beyond its expiration in early November. On October 15 Nixon approved an arms package of $90 million for Israel, consisting of antitank weapons, reconnaissance aircraft, and other minor items.[3] In addition, the administration decided to seek a $500 million supplemental appropriation for Israel in the current fiscal year to cover arms expenditures.[4] Israel was particularly anxious to receive a guarantee of the supply of high-performance aircraft in 1971 and had requested 54 F-4s and 120 A-4s. The Israelis were also beginning to press for long-term military agreements that would prevent the periodic supply disruptions and quarrels that had marked the previous two years.

Despite the American decision to send substantial quantities of arms to Israel, Egypt's new president, Anwar al-Sadat, agreed to a three-month extension of the cease-fire in early November. During this period he expected the Jarring talks to resume and to produce results. Egypt and the Soviet Union also began to show interest in outside guarantees as part of a peace settlement. If the United States adopted the idea, it might be prepared to pressure Israel to abandon Arab territory in return for guarantees from the major powers. In any event, this was an idea that might appeal to the Americans.[5]

Nixon's immediate problem, however, was to get the Israelis to return to the Jarring talks. The memory of the August cease-fire violations and the American vacillation was strong in Israel, and Prime Minister Meir decided to exact a high price for resuming the Jarring talks. Israeli Foreign Minister Eban informed Rogers on November 7 that Israel might return to the Jarring talks in the near future, but that it first needed assurances from the United States.

On December 1 Prime Minister Meir wrote to Nixon, asking for explicit commitments on aircraft deliveries after the end of the year; on freedom for Israel from American pressure in future negotiations; on support for Israel against Soviet intervention in the Middle East; and on the use of the U.S. veto against any anti-Israeli resolutions introduced at the United Nations.[6] Two days later Nixon replied with general reassurances and a strong bid to Israel to return to the Jarring talks. Israel would not be allowed, said Nixon, to be put at a diplomatic or military disadvantage if talks were resumed.

Meir pressed for further clarifications. In particular, she wanted the United States to drop its support for the idea of full withdrawal on the Egyptian front and from all but "insubstantial" portions of the other captured territories.[7] Defense Minister Moshe Dayan, who arrived in Washington for talks in mid-December, raised the issue of long-term military commitments. In return, he was told that the United States was prepared to participate in a multilateral UN-sponsored peace-keeping force as part of a settlement.[8]

This new twist in American policy was hardly what the Israelis wanted to hear. On December 17 Nixon replied to the Israeli prime minister's plea for further clarifications. The United States could not make any formal promise to use the veto at the UN, but it could offer more general assurances that Israel's security would not be endangered. The United States also promised to deliver twelve F-4s and twenty A-4s during the first six months of 1971. Not inclined to let the Americans off quite so inexpensively, the prime minister termed this a "step backward," one of the "greatest blows" from the United States. Soon her emotions calmed, however, and on December 28 she announced that Israel would return to the Jarring talks.

According to Meir, the United States had made commitments to preserve the balance of power in the Middle East. Israel would be allowed to negotiate freely, without fear that the United States would be a party to any UN effort to determine borders or the terms of a refugee settlement. The United States, she claimed, upheld the principle that Israel should have defensible borders, that Israel should be strong, that Israel should not be forced to withdraw to the June 4, 1967, lines, and that Israel would not be obliged to accept the Arab version of a refugee settlement. Furthermore, the conflict must be ended by a binding, contractual commitment to peace. Until that was achieved, not a single Israeli soldier would be expected to withdraw from the cease-fire lines. And finally, Jarring's terms of reference should not be altered.[9]

If indeed this represented United States policy, it was hard to see why Meir had been so upset at Nixon's December 17 letter. Perhaps she sensed the impending crisis over the Jarring mission and the American bureaucracy's reluctance to offer a blank check on arms. Perhaps she also realized that her insistence on no Israeli withdrawal without peace was being undermined by her own defense minister, who had begun to hint as early as November that it might be wise for Israel and Egypt to thin out their forces along the canal, perhaps even to withdraw them to a certain distance and to allow the canal to reopen.[10]

THE EGYPTIAN REACTION

While Nixon's exchanges with the Israelis were going on, he and Rogers had been in contact with Sadat as well. Sadat had sent Nixon a letter dated November 23, which reached him on December 14, indicating Egypt's interest in the Jarring talks. Nixon had replied orally through Mahmoud Fawzi on December 22, and Sadat sent word two days later through Donald Bergus, the American minister in Cairo, that he was genuinely interested in peace. Sadat, who had originally been viewed as something of a lightweight by Washington officials, was beginning to be taken more seriously.[11]

On January 5, 1971, Jarring met at the UN with representatives of Israel, Jordan, and Egypt. The next day he left for the Middle East. The Israelis presented him with a statement of their position, emphasizing the need for explicit and binding commitments to peace. Jarring conveyed this to the Egyptians, who replied with their own draft on January 15.[12] As might have been expected, Egypt stressed the need for Israeli withdrawal from all territory captured in 1967. Jarring redrafted the Egyptian document somewhat and presented it to the Israelis on January 18. The Israelis responded with a new draft on January 27.

At this point the United States began to urge Jarring to take a more aggressive approach, abandoning his role as message carrier and putting forward ideas of his own. The Israelis were opposed to such a procedure, but the State Department strongly favored it, particularly as time seemed to be running out. Sadat had agreed in November to a three-month renewal of the cease-fire, which therefore would expire on February 7.

Rogers had been in contact with the Egyptian foreign minister, Mahmoud Riad, earlier in the month. The Egyptians were clearly more interested in knowing what role the United States was prepared to play and what type of settlement it envisaged than they were in receiving Israeli proposals through Jarring. They had long believed that Israel was little more than an extension of the United States, so that if Washington favored full Israeli withdrawal, Israel would have to comply.

On January 27 Rogers sent Riad an oral message through Bergus. He appealed for an extension of the cease-fire, promising that Israel would submit new "substantive ideas" for a peace settlement immediately thereafter. Rogers confirmed that the views he had expressed in his December 9, 1969, speech were still valid and that the United States was prepared to make an "all out effort to help the parties reach a settlement this year." He took credit for having got Israel to drop the demand for face-to-face talks and denied that Israel had a veto over U.S. policy.[13]

With these assurances in hand, Sadat announced on February 4 that he would agree to a one-month extension of the cease-fire. Although he castigated the United States for its "full alignment with Israel," Sadat nonetheless presented a "new Egyptian initiative, compliance with which we shall consider as a true yardstick of the desire to implement the UN Security Council resolution." He went on to say:

We demand that during the period when we refrain from opening fire that a partial withdrawal of the Israeli forces on the east bank of the Suez Canal be achieved as the first stage of a timetable which will be prepared later to implement the other provisions of the Security Council resolution. If this is achieved within this period, we shall be prepared to begin immediately to clear the Suez Canal and reopen it to international navigation to serve the world economy. We believe that by this initiative, we shall be turning envoy Jarring's efforts from ambiguous words into definite measures.[14]

In fact, Sadat's initiative was soon to supersede Jarring's mission, but not before Jarring had made one last effort. On February 8 Jarring presented a memorandum to Egypt and Israel in which he asked both parties for "parallel and simultaneous commitments." Israel was asked to agree in principle to withdraw to the former international boundary between Egypt and the British mandate of Palestine, subject to practical security arrangements and freedom of navigation in the Suez Canal and the Strait of Tiran. Egypt was asked to enter into a peace agreement with Israel, including an end to belligerency, respect for Israel's independence and right to live in peace within secure and recognized boundaries, and noninterference in Israel's domestic affairs.

On February 15 Egypt replied, accepting all of Jarring's points and adding a number of others. Israel's reply was not forthcoming until February 26. Israel welcomed Egypt's unprecedented expression of readiness to enter into a peace agreement with Israel, but on the crucial issue of withdrawal the reply was blunt: "Israel will not withdraw to the pre-June 5, 1967, lines." Instead, Israel offered to negotiate without prior conditions. Egypt, however, viewed Israel's refusal to accept the principle of full withdrawal as an unacceptable prior condition. Under these circumstances the Jarring talks came to an abrupt end.[15]

THE INTERIM CANAL-AGREEMENT INITIATIVE

As Jarring was making his last effort to get the parties to agree to the outlines of an overall settlement, an alternative approach based on a partial agreement involving the Suez Canal was gaining increasing attention. Thus the collapse of the Jarring talks did not leave the diplomatic field empty. In fact, the idea of an "interim agreement," which had been in the wings for some time, was now to move to center stage.

Defense Minister Dayan had publicly spoken in November 1970 of the possibility of a mutual Egyptian and Israeli thinning out of forces along the Suez Canal. In Dayan's view such a step would help to stabilize the situation along the canal and reinforce the cease-fire then in effect. If the canal was open and the cities along its banks were rebuilt, Sadat could obviously not resume hostilities without paying a high cost. Besides, such a small step might relieve Israel from the continuing international pressure to accept the principle of full withdrawal from Arab territory.

Within Israel, Dayan's ideas received a mixed reaction. The prime minister seemed unenthusiastic, and others were overtly hostile. The concept apparently did have some appeal, however, to the Egyptian leadership. Shortly after the resumption of the Jarring initiative, a high-ranking Egyptian official approached an American diplomat in Cairo, on January 11, 1971, and expressed interest in Dayan's idea of a mutual thinning out of forces and a reopening of the canal. Several days later, Assistant Secretary Sisco informed Israeli Ambassador Rabin of this communication. Then, on February 4 Sadat publicly announced his initiative: in return for a partial Israeli withdrawal from the canal, Egypt would begin to clear and then reopen it. No mention was made of a mutual thinning out of forces, nor were specifics about the line of Israeli withdrawal mentioned.

The Israelis were immediately urged by Washington to take Sadat's proposal seriously. Egypt was pressing for a rapid reply. On February 9 Golda Meir stated that Israel was prepared to consider the idea of reopening the canal but that Israeli troops would not withdraw from the existing cease-fire lines until an overall settlement had been reached. In passing, she criticized the Americans for emphasizing international guarantees, which she implied might be substitutes for peace.[16] Three days later Israel asked the United States to convey a message to Egypt reiterating Israel's interest in discussing the reopening of the canal. This message was sent on February 14, along with an expression of hope that Egypt would respond positively to Jarring's initiative, which was done the following day.[17]

Nixon's own views, as articulated by Kissinger, were spelled out in his report to the Congress on U.S. foreign policy on February 25, 1971. Nixon termed the Middle East the most dangerous region in the world, chiefly because of the potential for superpower confrontation. After describing earlier American peace initiatives in 1969 and 1970, the report called for negotiations among the parties to determine the shape of peace. The United States would not impose a settlement. No specific mention was made of the interim canal-settlement idea. Instead, a lengthy analysis of the "great-power contest" ensued. In a direct warning to the Soviet Union, Nixon declared: "Any effort by any major power to secure a dominant position [in the Middle East] could exacerbate local disputes, affect Europe's security, and increase the danger to world peace. We seek no such position; we cannot allow others to establish one." [18]

In contrast to Sadat's insistence on a major U.S. initiative and a partial agreement between Egypt and Israel, Nixon placed greater emphasis on the U.S.-Soviet relationship in the area and the responsibility of the local parties to negotiate their own terms of settlement within a comprehensive framework. Sadat was not discouraged, however, and continued to try to draw the United States toward his own views, suggesting at one point that it was up to the United States to "squeeze Israel." [19]

After a secret two-day trip to Moscow on March 1 and 2, Sadat sent Nixon a long letter, on March 5. In it he set forward his reasons for not renewing the cease-fire upon its expiration two days later. More important, he appealed to Nixon to launch an initiative to bring about an interim agreement along the lines of his February 4 speech. Nixon took Sadat's bid seriously, and the State Department was instructed to begin work on the interim canal-settlement idea.

Israel was not particularly pleased to see the signs of American activism. The Nixon report to Congress, with its emphasis on the Soviet presence in the Middle East, had been welcomed, but now the State Department was showing signs of vacillation. Israeli leaders were distrustful of Rogers, suspecting that he would be prepared to pressure Israel for concessions as a way of conciliating the Arabs. Whether Nixon and Kissinger would support such a move was an open question. After the close working relationship established with the White House during the Jordan crisis, the Israelis had reason to hope that Rogers was not reflecting Nixon's true feelings.

As the American initiative began to get under way, the Israelis complained that arms agreements were being delayed as a form of pressure. [20] Reacting to questions about Israel's peace map, Prime Minister Meir publicly stated on March 13 that Israel must retain Sharm al-Shaykh and an access road to it, that Sinai must be demilitarized, that the border around Eilat must be changed, that the Egyptians must not return to Gaza, that the Golan Heights would remain under Israeli control, that Jerusalem must remain united, and that border changes on the West Bank would be necessary. [21] In talks with Foreign Minister Eban a few days later, Rogers urged Israel to rely on guarantees instead of territory for security.

As these exchanges suggest, it was difficult to keep the diplomacy focused on a limited, partial agreement involving the Suez Canal and a thinning out of forces. Both sides wanted to know the other's position on broader issues, and when those were raised the gap was enormous, especially on the issue of territory.

Nonetheless, on March 31 Nixon wrote to Sadat, welcoming the canal proposal. This message led to an intensified exchange of positions, with Sadat conveying to the American minister in Cairo, Donald Bergus, his opinion of the terms for a final settlement on April 1. His frame of reference was Meir's statement of March 13. Sadat would not accept the complete demilitarization of Sinai, nor could Israel remain at Sharm al-Shaykh. Limited demilitarized zones would be acceptable only if they were on both sides of the frontier.[22]

In an effort to get the talks back to the issue of the Suez Canal and a partial agreement, the United States encouraged the Israelis to set forth their position in writing. As an inducement, it was announced on April 19 that twelve more F-4s would be sent to Israel.[23] That same day Israel offered a proposal containing the following terms:

—After the reopening of the canal, Israeli ships and cargoes should be allowed through.

—A cease-fire of unlimited duration should be part of any future agreement.

—Israel would retain control of the Bar Lev line along the canal.

—Egypt would thin out its forces to the west of the canal.

—The line of withdrawal established in the interim agreement would not be considered a final border.

In addition, Israel asked for full U.S. support for its position and a reaffirmation of the assurances contained in Nixon's letters of July 23, 1970, and December 3, 1970. Two days later Nixon conveyed the desired assurances but declined to offer full support. The Egyptians were told that an Israeli proposal had been received, but its content was not immediately disclosed.

Reacting to press reports of the Israeli proposal, Sadat met with Bergus and Michael Sterner, the Egyptian-desk officer from the State Department, on April 23. Egyptian forces, he said, must be allowed to cross the canal; Egypt must control the strategically important Mitla and Giddi passes; demilitarized zones could be established; and Israel could retain Sharm al-Shaykh in the first stage, but within six months a full settlement must be reached. If Israel was not prepared to give up the passes, said Sadat, the United States should end its initiative.

Sadat's statement, if taken literally, would have brought the American effort to a halt. Israel was obviously not prepared to accept these terms. The White House drew the conclusion that there was little chance of agreement, but State was not prepared to give up so easily. Instead, hoping that Sadat would moderate his position, Rogers decided to travel to the Middle East, the first secretary of state since 1953 to visit Egypt and Israel.

By the time Rogers reached Cairo on May 4, Sadat's domestic political situation was clearly somewhat shaky. Two days earlier he had dismissed the powerful secretary general of the Arab Socialist Union, Ali Sabri. Since Sabri had a reputation for being pro-Soviet, his removal was welcomed by the Americans, and in this atmosphere the talks with Sadat went well. Sadat was polite, charming, and apparently willing to be flexible. Rogers reportedly praised his moderation and implied that the United States had nothing more to ask of him—or so Sadat later said.[24]

Rogers encountered more difficulty in Israel. The Israelis were cool to Rogers personally and suspected him of being pro-Arab. Nonetheless, the discussions were detailed and quickly hit upon the key issues. How would an interim agreement be linked to an overall peace settlement? Israel wanted no linkage, whereas Sadat wanted a timetable for full Israeli withdrawal, of which the interim agreement would merely be the first step. How long would the cease-fire last? Israel wanted an indefinite extension, whereas Egypt preferred a short renewal. How far would Israel withdraw from the canal? A few kilometers, or halfway or more across Sinai? How would the agreement be supervised? Would Egyptian troops be allowed across the canal? Would Israel's ships be allowed to use the canal after its opening? On each of these points the parties were far apart. Defense Minister Dayan sensed the danger of deadlock, and in talks with Sisco he outlined some modifications of the Israeli position. Israel would be prepared to accept Egyptian civilians and technicians on the east bank of the canal, but no military forces. Once the canal was reopened, Israel would agree to talk about the withdrawal of its forces.[25] Sisco was authorized to return to Egypt to discuss these ideas with Sadat and to report on the talks in Israel.

In Cairo, Sisco offered a number of ideas that he hoped might bridge the gap between the two parties.[26] Sadat indicated a willingness to consider only a limited Egyptian force on the canal's east bank and promised to send his trusted aide, Mahmoud Fawzi, to Washington with a reply to Sisco's other suggestions. A few days later, having just deposed some of his key ministers for having plotted against him,[27] Sadat asked for clarification on the points raised by Sisco. Was it correct to assume that the Israelis might consider a line of withdrawal east of the passes? Sisco replied on May 18 that such a line was not precluded, that there was some flexibility in the Israeli position.

Rogers and Sisco must have realized they were in a very delicate position. With the Egyptians, they were trying to present Israeli proposals as more forthcoming than they actually were. With the Israelis, the Egyptian statements were recast in the best possible light. But instead of succeeding in convincing either party of the other's good intentions, Rogers and Sisco seemed instead to lose credibility, especially with the Israelis. With the Egyptians it took a bit longer, but ultimately the sense of deception was equally great. At the White House, meanwhile, support for Rogers and Sisco was quickly fading.[28]

On May 20 Foreign Minister Riad met with Bergus to present Egypt's reply to Sisco's points of May 9. Bergus was sure the Egyptian statement was so negative in tone that the diplomatic effort would collapse. Riad was known to be opposed to an interim settlement in any event, but perhaps Sadat would agree to a softer statement of the Egyptian position.[29] Bergus returned to see Riad's deputy three days later with a redraft of the foreign minister's paper, which he offered as a suggestion of how Egypt could present its position more positively. He emphasized that he had done the rewriting on his own initiative and that his government had not been informed. At the top of the paper Riad's deputy wrote in Arabic that these were points suggested unofficially by Donald Bergus.

Meanwhile Sadat was trying to consolidate his tenuous hold on power in the aftermath of the internal shake-ups of May. The Soviet Union was uneasy because of the disappearance of some of its friends from key positions. On May 25 Soviet President Nikolai Podgorny arrived in Cairo with a draft treaty in hand for Sadat's signature. After two days of talks Sadat agreed, and on May 27 an Egyptian-Soviet treaty of friendship, to last for fifteen years, was signed.

Sadat hastened to inform the Americans that the treaty changed nothing, and to demonstrate his continuing interest in an interim agreement, he met with Bergus on May 30 to discuss Egypt's terms for a settlement. He still insisted on obtaining the passes and on sending tanks across the canal. Then, on June 4 Sadat handed Bergus a formal Egyptian proposal that included these and other points and that was virtually identical to the paper Bergus had prepared on May 23.

Sadat must have expected an early and positive reply to his proposal. After all, it was very close to Bergus's paper, and Sadat presumably thought Bergus must have been reflecting official American thinking. Bergus carried Sadat's June 4 document to Rogers immediately. But there was no reaction.[30] A month passed with no American reply. Rogers had asked Nixon if he could relaunch his initiative, but Nixon had demurred. There simply did not appear to be grounds for an agreement. A quarrel with Israel at this time would serve no purpose, and it could only hurt the administration. Moreover, this was a time when Nixon needed all the support he could muster. Unknown to the general public, Kissinger had begun to hold secret talks with the North Vietnamese in Paris, and Nixon wanted to concentrate on big issues like Vietnam. He had one other surprise in store as well. On July 9 Kissinger secretly flew to Peking from Pakistan, and this opening to China was made public a few days later. Compared with those dramatic developments, the Middle East was a tiresome distraction.

Meeting in San Clemente for a review of foreign policy after Kissinger's China trip, Nixon, Rogers, and Sisco discussed the Middle East. Sadat was apparently still interested in a limited agreement, but his patience was wearing thin. Nixon agreed that Sisco should travel to Israel to learn whether the Israelis would drop their objection to a token Egyptian force on the east bank of the canal. He pointedly refused, however, to promise that he would exert pressure on Israel if Sisco encountered difficulty. In brief, Sisco was on his own. Sisco's talks in Israel dragged on from the end of July through the first week of August.[31] Israel would not budge, and Sisco could do nothing but admit defeat. He did not even stop in Cairo, so that it was left to Bergus to brief Mohamed Heikal on the talks.

To say the least, the Egyptians were disappointed. At worst, the Americans had played Sadat for a fool. He had announced that 1971 would be a "year of decision," either war or peace.[32] He had made unprecedented concessions in February and had again tried to meet American expectations in June. He had risked his relations with the Soviet Union by moving against its supporters and by helping to crush a communist coup in Sudan in July. Not only had he failed to win the Americans to his side, but the Americans were considering new arms agreements with Israel. Frustrated and humiliated, Sadat decided to abandon the interim-settlement idea. The result was a two-year diplomatic stalemate.

KISSINGER TAKES CHARGE

The failure of the interim canal settlement effectively ended the predominance of Rogers and Sisco as Middle East policymakers. If there were to be any new American initiatives, Nixon and Kissinger would be in charge.[33]

Kissinger was critical of the way the State Department had handled the Middle East from the beginning. He had little admiration for Secretary Rogers and was unenthusiastic about the plan that bore his name. His attitude toward Sisco was more complex. He genuinely admired the assistant secretary's energy and intelligence but felt he was too much of an activist, a tactician more than a strategist, and more interested in procedure than in substance. Perhaps Sisco's worst fault, however, was that he did not defer sufficiently to Kissinger's authority.

With respect to the interim-settlement effort, Kissinger drew a number of lessons that later guided his own diplomacy after the October 1973 war. The United States, he thought, had become involved too quickly in the substance of the negotiations. Once that happened, the role of impartial negotiator was in jeopardy. Only when the parties were near agreement was it appropriate for the United States to make substantive recommendations. Kissinger also felt Rogers and Sisco had not been fully candid with Egypt and Israel. Although they had tried to soften the real positions of the two sides, they had succeeded only in raising false hopes, especially on the part of Sadat.

Kissinger strongly believed negotiations, to be successful, had to be carried out in secret. To do so was always difficult with both the Arabs and the Israelis, but Rogers and Sisco had deliberately conducted too much of the negotiations in the glare of publicity. And when secrecy was maintained, as during Rogers's talks in Cairo, it was the White House that was kept in the dark! Kissinger never knew exactly what Rogers told Sadat, nor did he know of the Bergus memorandum until it was publicly revealed at the end of June.[34]

The idea of an interim agreement unlinked to the final terms of settlement very much appealed to Kissinger. He was particularly anxious for such an accord if it would ensure the departure of the Soviet military advisers from Egypt. In practice, however, the interim-agreement approach had quickly drifted back to the package-settlement concept, with the canal pullback as only the initial stage of a comprehensive accord. Therefore Kissinger's initial interest in the approach began to fade by April, and by summer he was prepared to see it die an ignominious death, even at some risk to U.S.-Egyptian relations.

Kissinger also disagreed with the State Department's contention that Israel could be persuaded to moderate its negotiating stance if arms were withheld. Kissinger argued that to do so would simply make the Israelis feel more insecure and therefore intransigent. It would raise the hopes of the Arabs, particularly since Soviet arms were being delivered to Egypt and Syria in large quantities. Only if Israel felt strong would it be reasonable in negotiations, and only if the Arabs saw that Soviet arms did not hold the promise of a military solution would they turn to diplomacy in a serious way. Finally, Kissinger felt that the Israelis were on firm ground in refusing to make concessions to Egypt while the Soviet military presence there remained so large. Let Sadat expel the Soviets; then peace talks could begin.[35]

Kissinger's hope that the Soviet position in the Middle East might be undercut had been strengthened since the Jordan civil war. First, Sadat had moved against his allegedly pro-Soviet advisers in May; then Jordan had eliminated the remnants of the PLO remaining in the country. Even more important, a communist coup d'état in Sudan in July had been reversed by the combined intervention of Egypt and Libya.

Offsetting these desirable developments, however, was the Egyptian-Soviet treaty and an increase in the flow of Soviet arms to Egypt and Syria. Sadat had, on several occasions, stated that the Soviet advisers in his country would leave after the first stage of Israeli withdrawal, but until then he was anxious to keep his military ties intact. Kissinger now hoped to convince Sadat that the removal of the Soviet advisers would have to precede the first stage of withdrawal.

Sadat soon realized it was not worth dealing with Rogers and Sisco any longer. After the talks between Rogers and Riad in September 1971, Sadat thereafter communicated with Kissinger or Nixon through intermediaries, including his adviser on national security, Hafiz Ismail.[36] This link, which bypassed the State Department by relying on each country's intelligence channels, was rarely used in the following months, but it was available when needed.

The State Department nonetheless continued to try to promote an Egyptian-Israeli agreement. On October 14, 1971, Rogers spoke at the United Nations, outlining six areas of disagreement between the two parties that had emerged in the interim-canal-settlement talks. Now Rogers proposed that Egypt and Israel send high-ranking officials to the United States to engage in "proximity talks," with Sisco acting as mediator and "catalyst."[37] Sadat accepted, apparently still hoping for some progress before the end of the "year of decision."

Israel was less enthusiastic about proximity talks. Before returning to such a forum, Israel wanted a basic understanding with the United States on arms supply and on the U.S. and Soviet roles in future negotiations. On November 1, 1971, the United States and Israel signed a significant memorandum of understanding regarding American aid to Israel to enhance its military self-sufficiency.[38] Israel was planning to build a jet fighter modeled on the French Mirage. A complete set of blueprints for the plane had been smuggled out through Switzerland.[39] Israel could not produce the engine, however; hence the United States agreed in principle to provide the missing components.

Since midyear the United States had refrained from signing any new arms agreements with Israel. It had done so out of a conviction that the military balance remained in Israel's favor and in the hope of gaining leverage over Israeli policy. Moreover, the State Department did not want to undercut Sadat's position during the interim canal negotiations.

Prime Minister Meir visited Washington in early December 1971 to discuss a new arms agreement with Nixon. She argued that Israel needed to be assured of a continuing flow of aircraft and other equipment well into the 1970s. The Soviets had no hesitation about helping their friends. Why did the Americans insist on punishing Israel by withholding arms? That only increased Arab intransigence. A long-term agreement would convince the Soviets and the Arabs that they could not separate the United States from Israel and that a military solution was impossible, and such an agreement would allow Israel to negotiate from strength.

Nixon and Kissinger basically agreed with Meir's points.[40] A long-term agreement would also help to avoid periodic squabbles over new arms agreements. Each time a new arms package was requested, the United States and Israel argued over the terms and the timing. The Arabs saw the quarrels as encouraging signs, but then felt disillusioned when the United States eventually provided the arms. In an election year especially, Nixon had no desire to confront Israel over arms. Should a diplomatic initiative prove to be possible after the 1972 presidential elections, it would not be marred by arguments over a new arms agreement if a multiyear deal could be concluded in late 1971. Consequently, on

December 31 it was announced that the United States had agreed in principle to resume shipments of F-4s to Israel.

Equally important, Nixon and Meir reached an understanding on strategy and tactics for future peace efforts. They would abandon the search for an overall agreement for the time being. The focus now would be on an interim Egyptian-Israeli agreement. Sisco would try to arrange for "proximity talks" between the parties, but, in Kissinger's words, "the real negotiations would be carried out between Israeli Ambassador Rabin and me, and also between Dobrynin and me."[41]

Much of January 1972 was spent in discussing the terms of the new arms deal with the Israelis. And Sisco and Rabin met frequently to establish the ground rules for proximity talks. The result was another memorandum of understanding on February 2, 1972, whereby the United States agreed to sell Israel forty-two F-4s and eighty-two A-4s over the coming years. In the proximity talks the Soviet Union would play no substantive role. Most significant, the United States would take no initiative in the talks that had not first been fully discussed with the Israelis. If the memorandum was taken literally, the United States had tied itself almost completely to the Israeli position.[42] Four days later the Israeli cabinet agreed to the idea of proximity talks, but Egypt now refused, and no further diplomatic progress was made.

U.S.-Israeli relations, however, were stronger than ever. Throughout 1972 Nixon was able to portray his administration as a firm supporter of Israel. All the old disputes were forgotten, and Ambassador Rabin came very close to endorsing Nixon's bid for the presidency against the Democratic contender.

During 1972 U.S. Middle East policy consisted of little more than open support for Israel. The White House explicitly told the State Department not to consider any new initiatives until after the elections. Meanwhile Nixon set out to reap the rewards of Kissinger's negotiations with the Chinese and the Soviets. A successful foreign policy was clearly going to be a major theme in his reelection campaign.

In his survey of foreign policy presented to Congress on February 9, 1972, Nixon highlighted the Soviet role in the Middle East. He quoted himself to the effect that U.S.-Soviet interests were "very diametrically opposed" in the Middle East, except for the desire to avoid a confrontation.[43] He then reviewed earlier U.S. initiatives, emphasizing the obstacles to an Arab-Israeli agreement. The shortcomings of both the package-agreement and the interim-settlement approaches were candidly discussed, but the main theme of his remarks was the need for great power restraint:

The Soviet Union's effort to use the Arab-Israeli conflict to perpetuate and expand its own military position in Egypt has been a matter of concern to the United States. The U.S.S.R. has taken advantage of Egypt's increasing dependence on Soviet military supply to gain the use of naval and air facilities in Egypt. This has serious implications for the stability of the balance of power locally, regionally in the Eastern Mediterranean, and globally. The Atlantic Alliance cannot ignore the possible implications of this move for the stability of the East-West relationship. . . .

We hope the Soviet Union understands that it can serve this interest [of avoiding a major conflict in the Middle East] best by restraint in its arms supply, refraining from the use of this dispute to enhance its own military position, and encouraging the negotiation of a peace.

Aside from urging the parties to begin serious negotiations, Nixon made no suggestions on how the conflict might be resolved. He did, however, add: "Injecting the global strategic rivalry into the region is incompatible with Middle East peace and with detente in U.S.-Soviet relations."[44]

SUMMITRY

Toward the end of February 1972 President Nixon traveled to Peking for talks with Chairman Mao Tse-tung and Prime Minister Chou En-lai. The occasion was not only historic for U.S.-Chinese relations but also carried broader significance. Nixon and Kissinger were attempting to alter relations among the major powers in the interests of stability and the avoidance of nuclear war. They assumed the Soviet Union would remain the principal adversary of the United States and the greatest threat to U.S. interests. To help induce restraint on the part of the Soviet Union, the United States was prepared to develop ties with Moscow's main rival, the leadership in Peking. This was a classic stroke of balance-of-power politics, and if successful it would lend substance to the policy of détente that Nixon and Kissinger had widely promoted. Peking was thus an important way station on the road to Moscow, where Nixon was expected in May.

Between the Peking and Moscow summits, developments in Vietnam took an alarming turn for the worse. The North Vietnamese sent troops across the demilitarized zone on March 30, and for several weeks the communist forces made impressive gains. The United States responded with intensified bombing, and with a major concession to the North Vietnamese during Kissinger's talks in Moscow in late April.[45] On May 8 Nixon made a controversial decision to resume the heavy bombing of North Vietnam and to mine the harbor of Haiphong, hoping by those actions to cut the flow of arms to Hanoi. He realized this might bring the United States into open conflict with both the Soviet Union and China. Many of his advisers were sure that Brezhnev would feel compelled to cancel the upcoming summit conference. Nixon held firm, however, and the Soviets swallowed their pride and received Nixon in Moscow on May 22.

One of the great hopes of the Nixon-Kissinger foreign policy had been that détente between the superpowers would have benefits for American policy elsewhere. The summits seemed to confirm their belief that neither the Chinese nor the Soviets would allow developments in Vietnam to stand in the way of their interests in dealing with the United States. Perhaps Moscow could also be persuaded to subordinate its Middle East policies to the requirements of détente. In any event, Nixon and Kissinger were prepared to explore the possibility as one means of reducing the chances of superpower confrontation in the Middle East and, they hoped, of undercutting Soviet influence in Egypt.

In essence, this was a return to the linkage concept that had guided the Rogers-Sisco initiative of 1969, but now there was more to build on in the U.S.-Soviet relationship, particularly with the achievement of a treaty limiting strategic nuclear arms. Equally important, from Kissinger's point of view, was the fact that he, not Rogers or Sisco, would handle the talks with the Russians on the Middle East.

Kissinger's ostensible goal was to reach agreement with the Soviet leadership on a set of principles that could serve as a framework for an Arab-Israeli peace settlement. Next he would enlist their support for beginning a step-by-step negotiating process based on those principles, but leaving key issues such as final borders to be negotiated by the parties themselves.

Unbeknownst to the State Department, Kissinger and Foreign Minister Andrei Gromyko reached a tentative working agreement on eight principles. The two superpowers were in accord on the following points:

—The agreement should be comprehensive, but could be implemented in steps.

—The agreement should contain provisions for the withdrawal of Israeli forces from Arab territories occupied in 1967.

—Any border changes should result from voluntary agreement among the parties.

—Security arrangements could include demilitarized zones, UN forces at Sharm al-Shaykh, and international guarantees with the participation of the United States and the Soviet Union.

—The agreement should lead to an end of the state of belligerency and to the establishment of peace.

—Freedom of navigation through the Strait of Tiran and the Suez Canal should be assured. This would be consistent with Egyptian sovereignty over the canal.

—The agreement must include recognition of the independence and sovereignty of all states in the Middle East, including Israel.

—The Soviets maintained that the Palestinian refugee problem should be solved on a just basis in accordance with appropriate UN decisions.

—The United States maintained that completion of the agreement should involve negotiations between the parties.[46]

Although this tentative agreement remained secret, the United States and the Soviet Union did announce agreement on a set of basic principles.[47] The two superpowers committed themselves to conducting their relations on the basis of peaceful coexistence (article 1) and to "preventing situations capable of causing a dangerous exacerbation of their relations. . . . They will always exercise restraint in their mutual relations, and will be prepared to negotiate and settle differences by peaceful means" (article 2). "The U.S.A. and the U.S.S.R. have a special responsibility . . . to do everything in their power so that conflicts or situations will not arise which would serve to increase international tensions" (article 3).

In the joint communiqué issued on May 29, the United States and the Soviet Union reaffirmed their support of UN Resolution 242 and of the Jarring mission. A settlement of the Arab-Israeli conflict "would open prospects for the normalization of the Middle East situation and would permit, in particular, consideration of further steps to bring about a military relaxation in that area."[48]

Read in Cairo, the basic principles and the joint communiqué seemed to confirm Sadat's worst fears. Both the United States and the Soviet Union had agreed to freeze the Middle East situation for fear of damaging their own relations. Under the guise of détente, the United States had persuaded the Soviets to reduce their support for the Arabs. This would explain the Soviet reluctance to provide advanced weaponry and the delays in deliveries that had been irritating Sadat for months.

Sadat was well aware that the Americans viewed the Soviet presence in Egypt as an obstacle to a peace settlement. Rogers had raised the issue in May. Now, with the results of the summit meeting available, it seemed clear to Sadat that the Soviets were not prepared to press his case with the Americans. Not only was their presence in Egypt of concern to the Americans and the Israelis, but his own officers were complaining about it. Then, in June, Saudi Arabia's minister of defense, Prince Sultan, reported on his conversations with Nixon and Kissinger. Until the Soviet presence in Egypt was eliminated, the Americans would not press Israel for concessions.[49]

Which of these factors was most compelling to Sadat is unknown, but in early July he decided to act. On July 8 Sadat informed the Soviet ambassador that he was requesting the departure of most of the Soviet advisers and technicians in Egypt. Sadat publicly announced his decision on July 18. More than ten thousand Soviet personnel would leave Egypt, precisely as Kissinger and the Israelis had hoped.

REACTION TO THE EXPULSION OF SOVIET ADVISERS

If Sadat's primary motivation in announcing the expulsion of the Soviet advisers in Egypt was to open the way for an active U.S. diplomatic role, he had chosen a curious time for such a momentous step.[50] Nixon was in the midst of an election campaign and was not prepared to jeopardize his substantial lead over Senator George McGovern by embarking on a controversial policy in the Middle East. He and Kissinger, however, did recognize the importance of Sadat's move, and through the "back channel" they informed the Egyptian president that after the American elections were over, a new initiative would be launched. This time it would be under White House control.

A reelected president would presumably be immune to the normal pressures of domestic politics. Nixon's prestige was at its zenith, Kissinger's reputation was growing, and perhaps they could together fashion a settlement in the Middle East.

In midsummer 1972 few could have anticipated that Nixon's ability to conduct foreign policy, and eventually even his tenure in office, would be greatly affected by a seemingly minor incident on June 17. On that day five men had been apprehended inside the offices of the Democratic headquarters in the Watergate complex in Washington, D.C. Investigation of the break-in revealed that the burglars had curious connections with the Central Intelligence Agency and with the Committee to Reelect the

President. Perhaps some zealous Republicans had broken the law, but no one suspected that the president himself might be involved. On June 23, 1972, however, in a conversation with his chief of staff, H. R. Haldeman, Nixon became enmeshed in the Watergate affair by ordering the CIA to block the FBI's investigation of the incident for political reasons. The conversation was recorded on the president's secret taping system. Its disclosure a little more than two years later proved fatal to Nixon's struggle to survive Watergate. For the moment, however, Nixon and his aides had little reason to fear that the Watergate affair would not be contained.

On the eve of his reelection Nixon took pains to speak of his plans for the Middle East. "The Middle East will have a very high priority because while the Mideast has been, over the past couple of years, in a period of uneasy truce or armistice or whatever you want to call it, it can explode at any time."[51] The message to Sadat was intended to be that he should remain patient a bit longer. It would soon be his turn, once Vietnam was settled.

Nixon was reelected overwhelmingly on November 7, winning 60.8 percent of the popular vote and 97 percent of the electoral vote. But the "peace at hand" in Vietnam remained elusive. It was only after an intensive bombing campaign against North Vietnam in December that negotiations resumed. At long last, on January 13, 1973, the Paris talks were successfully concluded; on January 27 the final agreement was signed.

THE KISSINGER STRATEGY

With the end of the fighting in Vietnam, Kissinger was ready to turn his attention to the Middle East. He had previously paid little attention to briefing materials prepared for him on that region; now he requested studies, perused long memoranda, and began to develop a detailed strategy of his own.

Kissinger wanted to avoid endless debates over the meaning of Resolution 242, the Rogers Plan, and the Jarring memorandum. A legalistic approach was bound to bog down rapidly. The key demands of both parties were phrased in totally incompatible terms. The Israelis wanted peace and recognition; the Arabs wanted territory and justice. Rather than try for initial agreement on these ultimate goals, Kissinger hoped to move quickly to practical agreements, but he realized the importance of some formulation that would address the end result of the negotiating process. The Jarring formulation of "peace" for "withdrawal" did not appeal to him. Instead, he preferred the formulation recommended by his aides of establishing a balance between "sovereignty" and "security." The virtue of such a formula was that it opened the door to a wide range of negotiating outcomes. For example, it might be possible to recognize Egypt's sovereignty over Sinai at an early date, while establishing special security arrangements that would allow the Israelis to maintain a presence in key areas during a lengthy transitional period. If agreement could be reached on such a general formulation, then negotiations could begin on concrete issues, such as those identified during the interim-canal-settlement negotiations.

Kissinger had the chance to try out his ideas in February. King Hussein arrived in Washington for talks with Nixon and Kissinger on February 6. He had proposed the previous spring an unpopular plan to establish a United Arab Kingdom consisting of the East and West Banks of the Jordan, subject to approval in a referendum among the Palestinians. Little support had been found for the idea in the Arab world, and both Egypt and Syria had reacted hostilely. Nevertheless, Hussein was still interested in recovering the West Bank and was anxious, as always, for American help. In addition, he was in need of substantial increases in economic and military assistance. Nixon was prepared to accommodate him, for he liked and admired the king.

Still, little could be done to advance a settlement between Jordan and Israel without taking Egypt into account. Kissinger's next visitor, Sadat's national security adviser, Hafiz Ismail, was therefore unusually important. Ismail was the first high-level Egyptian official to meet with Nixon in some time. The visit had been arranged through the "back channel." The State Department was not informed until the last moment. Nixon met with Hafiz Ismail on February 23 and appeared relaxed and self-confident. He outlined a strategy for negotiating on two levels: one would be handled in secret by Kissinger, as with Vietnam; the other would be public and would involve the State Department.[52] Nixon also mentioned the sovereignty and security formula.

Ismail's real purpose in coming to Washington, however, was to confer with Kissinger. During the next two days Hafiz Ismail and his aides Ihab Wahba and Ahmed Maher met with Kissinger, who was accompanied by National Security Council staffers Peter Rodman and Harold Saunders, at a private estate in Connecticut.[53] Kissinger argued for the necessity of accepting the idea of a settlement being implemented over a prolonged period. He implied that Egyptian sovereignty over Sinai could be acknowledged at an early date but that special security arrangements might be required for a long time. Ismail seemed interested, and the talks seemed to go well. He indicated that a normalization of relations with Israel might eventually be possible and that Jordan might have a role to play in solving the Palestinian issue, but he was adamant about full Israeli withdrawal from Sinai and Golan, hinting at some flexibility in the West Bank.[54]

They then discussed in detail the obligations that Egypt and Israel would undertake as part of a peace agreement, the relationship between an Egyptian-Israeli agreement and resolution of the Palestine problem, and concrete security arrangements for Israel in Sinai. Unable to resolve all these issues, Kissinger and Ismail agreed to meet again at an early date. Kissinger was in no rush. He told Ismail that little could be accomplished before the Israeli elections, scheduled for late October 1973.

Three days later, on February 28, Golda Meir arrived in Washington to meet with Nixon and Kissinger and was told of the talks with Hussein and Ismail. As usual, she pressed the case for more military assistance to Israel. A decision on a new arms package was at that moment pending. In a meeting on March 1 Nixon urged her to be more forthcoming with ideas for an agreement on the Egyptian front. Pressed by Meir for new arms, Nixon agreed in principle to a new schedule of aircraft deliveries but sought to keep the agreement secret.[55]

As Hafiz Ismail was returning from his trip to Washington, an article appeared in the press saying that the president had decided on new arms aid to Israel. The timing of the article seemed designed to embarrass Ismail and raised serious doubts in Cairo about U.S. intentions. Kissinger, somewhat disingenuously, hastened to inform Ismail that the article was inaccurate. Shortly thereafter, however, an accurate account appeared in the press confirming that a decision on new arms had been made.[56]

The diplomatic effort launched in February had as its goal the establishment of a "negotiating framework" between Egypt and Israel. Kissinger saw this as being complemented by a U.S.-Soviet agreement on principles of a settlement, based on those tentatively drawn up in Moscow the previous May. He realized it would take time for all the pieces to fall into place.

During the spring, however, several events occurred that diverted the attention of the policymakers from the Egyptian-Israeli front. First was the assassination of the American ambassador in Khartoum, Cleo Noel, and his deputy, George Moore. The CIA had received intelligence that Black September, the terrorist wing of Fatah, was responsible and that Arafat might have ordered the killings.[57] In the wake of the Munich atrocity the previous September, when eleven Israeli athletes at the Olympic Games had been killed during a Palestinian terrorist attack, and the assassination in November 1971 of Jordan's prime minister Wasfi Tal by Black September, the Khartoum murders created an intense preoccupation with Palestinian terrorism. This was hardly an ideal moment to take initiatives aimed at improving U.S.-Arab relations.

A second preoccupation was the "energy crisis" that was increasingly apparent on the horizon. The price of oil had been rising rapidly since 1971. U.S. production was stagnating, U.S. refinery capacity was insufficient to meet the demand, and shortages of gasoline and fuel oil might be felt by the end of the year. The oil companies were nervous. The president had no policy except to appear to be in control while he cast about for someone to take charge. Visitors to Saudi Arabia began to report that King Faisal, for the first time, was speaking of using the oil weapon to bring pressure on the United States unless Israel was forced to withdraw from Arab territory.

Against this background, tensions in the Middle East mounted sharply in mid-April. Lebanon was thrown into a crisis by an Israeli raid into downtown Beirut that killed three top PLO leaders. More dangerous still, toward the end of the month Egyptian war preparations along the Suez Canal took on an air of determination.[58] Intelligence reports were also received that Syria had completed a detailed war plan and was prepared to attack Israel on short notice. Israel took the signs seriously and ordered a partial mobilization; by mid-May the crisis atmosphere had passed.

Meanwhile the smoldering Watergate issue had flared up. On March 21 a young lawyer working for the White House, John Dean, had informed Nixon of the extent of high-level involvement in the Watergate cover-up. He warned Nixon of a "cancer" growing on the presidency. Within weeks of this conversation Dean was telling his story to the FBI investigators dealing with Watergate. Evidence was rapidly accumulating that implicated the president's closest associates—John Mitchell, Haldeman, and John Ehrlichman. Increasingly, Nixon was obliged to devote his time and energies to the Watergate crisis. On April 30 he accepted the resignations of Haldeman and Ehrlichman. Of his closest advisers, only Kissinger now remained.

Kissinger tried to keep Middle East policy on the track charted in February, but because Nixon's authority was being undermined, it was increasingly difficult. On May 3 Nixon's fourth "State of the World" message was sent to Congress. It spelled out clearly the Kissinger strategy. In a section entitled "The Situation Today," Nixon argued for serious negotiations between the local parties, insisting that an imposed settlement would not last. Sovereignty and security were identified as key issues. Nixon continued to develop the theme of negotiations:

A step-by-step approach still seems most practical, but we fully recognize that one step by itself cannot bring peace. First, there is a relationship between any initial step toward peace and steps which are to follow toward a broader settlement. We are open-minded on how that relationship might be established in a negotiating process, and on what role the United States might play. But the relationship cannot be ignored. Second, all important aspects of the Arab-Israeli conflict must be addressed at some stage, including the legitimate interests of the Palestinians. Implementation can occur in stages, and it should not be precluded that some issues and disputes could be resolved on a priority basis. But a comprehensive settlement must cover all the parties and all the major issues.

The issues are formidable, interlinked, and laden with emotion. The solutions cannot be found in general principles alone, but must be embodied in concrete negotiated arrangements. The parties will not be tricked into compromise positions by artful procedures. But there is room for accommodation and an overwhelming necessity to seek it.[59]

Kissinger began to think of how he might induce the Soviet Union to cooperate with his efforts to begin a negotiating process. He wanted Moscow to endorse publicly a set of principles that would serve as guidelines for a settlement. Perhaps the Soviet Union would be more cooperative if it could be persuaded that the status quo was not working to its advantage in the Middle East. The expulsion of Soviet advisers from Egypt in 1972 had been a welcome development. Kissinger toyed with the idea of trying to weaken the Soviets in Iraq and South Yemen as well, perhaps with the help of Iran and Saudi Arabia. In his view such anti-Soviet moves in the Middle East would not be incompatible with his objective of enlisting Soviet support for negotiations, provided U.S. involvement remained secret.

On May 4 Kissinger arrived in Moscow to prepare for the second Nixon-Brezhnev summit meeting. While there, he received a new document from Gromyko that set forth nine principles of an Arab-Israeli settlement. Gromyko's document, unlike that of the previous May, called for complete Israeli withdrawal to the June 4, 1967, lines. It also referred to the "legitimate rights" of the Palestinians. One new note was included: failure by either party to implement any part of the agreement would give the other party the right to refuse to fulfill its own obligations. On the whole, Kissinger much preferred the May 1972 document.[60]

The State Department was kept in the dark concerning these discussions, which added greatly to Secretary Rogers's frustration. Kissinger's domination of U.S. foreign policy was increasingly apparent as Nixon became engulfed in the Watergate crisis. His position did not go unchallenged, however. On May 15, 1973, Rogers proposed a new American initiative for settling the Arab-Israeli conflict. He suggested an "exploratory" effort by the United States, which might help to stabilize the region even if it did not immediately produce results. He proposed a two-track approach, one public and one secret. The public effort would focus on a canal agreement, as in 1971. The secret effort would aim at direct Egyptian-Israeli talks on broader issues. To break the impasse encountered earlier, he recommended that the United States try to persuade the parties to agree that Resolution 242 neither endorsed nor precluded return to the pre-June 1967 lines. Kissinger was unenthusiastic, and at his suggestion Nixon gave Rogers no encouragement.

Rogers's exasperation was further increased when he learned by accident that Kissinger was planning to meet again with Hafiz Ismail. This time he insisted that one of his own representatives be present, and when Kissinger and Ismail met secretly outside of Paris on May 20, Alfred Atherton, the deputy assistant secretary of state for Near Eastern affairs, was part of the U.S. team.

Ismail was less interested in substance during these talks than he had been in February. He concentrated his questions instead on the role the United States intended to play. What kind of White House involvement could Egypt expect? Why was the United States continuing to arm Israel so lavishly? How could Egyptian sovereignty in Sinai be made real, not just a symbol? The unresolved issues from February were discussed, but inconclusively. Ismail insisted that a final peace between Egypt and Israel was contingent on a solution to the Palestinian problem.

Kissinger described to Ismail his strategy of trying for a U.S.-Soviet agreement on principles, to be followed by secret negotiations between the parties. Kissinger spoke with Ismail privately for a few minutes and felt he was making some progress. He then suggested that further talks would be desirable. Ismail promised an early reply, but when it came on

June 3, it was guarded and unenthusiastic. Perhaps the Egyptians were beginning to have their doubts about Nixon's ability to produce results, given his crumbling domestic base. In any event, the promising tone of the February talks was missing in May.[61]

BREZHNEV'S VISIT

If U.S.-Egyptian relations seemed to be stagnating, the same could not be said for U.S.-Soviet ties. Kissinger had been treated with great courtesy and attention in May, and now, in June, General Secretary Leonid Brezhnev arrived for his first visit to the United States. Talks on the Middle East were focused on the May 1972 document, with some additions from Gromyko's more recent draft. The Soviet language on full withdrawal and the "rights" of the Palestinians, however, was not accepted by the United States.

Nixon and Brezhnev, along with Kissinger and Gromyko and their staffs, discussed the Middle East at length. Brezhnev warned that the Egyptians and Syrians were intent on going to war and that the Soviet Union could not stop them. Only a new American initiative and, in particular, pressure on Israel to withdraw could prevent war.[62] The joint communiqué issued on June 25, 1973, gave little idea of the content of the talks. The Soviets even refused to allow Resolution 242 to be mentioned unless Jarring's February 1971 document was also included. The final language therefore merely stated: "Both parties agreed to continue to exert their efforts to promote the quickest possible settlement in the Middle East. This settlement should be in accordance with the interests of all states in the area, be consistent with their independence and sovereignty, and should take into account the legitimate interests of the Palestinian people."[63]

Following the June summit talks, U.S. Middle East policy entered the summer doldrums. Nothing much could be done until after the Israeli elections in any case, according to Kissinger. The Arabs were clearly frustrated—Sadat called the United States the "world's biggest bully" on July 23—and King Faisal was publicly linking oil and the Arab-Israeli conflict.[64] Sadat also seemed intent on forcing the United States into an anti-Arab posture by calling for a UN debate on the Middle East crisis and then pressing for a vote on a resolution strongly condemning Israel. For the fifth time in its history, the United States cast a veto. The Arab world reacted angrily. Kissinger wondered why Sadat was seeking a confrontation. Was he merely trying to compel the United States to take a more active role?

During the third week of July 1973, Kissinger devoted considerable time to the Middle East, particularly to the question of Soviet involvement. He was concerned that the State Department's penchant for solving conflicts made the United States "lean on" its friends. His preference was to build on those friendships to look after American interests in the region.

Kissinger, speaking to the press on background and to his staff, developed this perspective with regard to the Arab-Israeli conflict. He called the highly publicized American peace initiatives in the Middle East "disastrous." When the United States had gone public with its views, it had been attacked by Israel, the Israeli lobby, and the Arabs, and was thus caught in the middle. In his view the United States lacked the kind of leverage in the Middle East that it had in Vietnam. Before moving publicly with a new initiative, it should have one side lined up "so we can move against the other." In that way the United States would not be attacked by both sides. In addition, it could not dissociate itself too greatly from Israel without displaying dangerous signals to the Soviet Union.

He thought of the Arab negotiating position as "impossible." The Arabs called for total Israeli withdrawal in return for an end to belligerency; then, according to the Egyptians, Israel would have to negotiate with the Palestinians for a final peace. Egypt's position on the difference between the end of belligerency and a final peace was very vague. The United States could not simply tell Israel to withdraw and then to talk to the Palestinians. Furthermore, Egypt was not clear on whether King Hussein could speak for the Palestinians.

Kissinger argued that Israel could not be forced to accept an overall solution all at once. It would be necessary to segment the negotiations into pieces that Israel could manage, after which the negotiations should proceed step by step. Egypt, he felt, was playing into the hands of the Israelis because Israel was primarily interested in wasting time. On the other hand, if a negotiating process could begin, history could work on the side of a settlement.

Kissinger continued to try to separate sovereignty and security. He knew Sadat saw this distinction as phony, but it was better for Egypt's interests than previous positions. He also thought that for the United States to adopt a more balanced policy might be self-defeating. The Arabs wanted the United States to strike poses, but that would serve no useful purpose. Instead, Kissinger wanted to preserve American influence with Israel until the time when taking a separate position could produce tangible results. The United States sought a balanced policy, but it needed a "fulcrum to move the situation." It could not support the maximum Arab position in negotiations, but once negotiations did start, Israel would begin to move back and a process would be under way. In Kissinger's view it would be easier to dislodge the Israelis from almost anywhere else in Sinai than it would be from the cease-fire lines.

These thoughts well summarize Kissinger's views on the Arab-Israeli conflict as of mid-1973. The importance of the U.S.-Israeli relationship and his preoccupation with the Soviet Union stand out. The Jordan-crisis lessons were still alive nearly three years later.

On August 22 Nixon made a surprise announcement that he was nominating Henry Kissinger as secretary of state to replace William Rogers. Kissinger would keep his position as adviser to the president for national security affairs as well. No longer would Kissinger have to worry about the secretary of state undercutting his strategy.

Three days after becoming secretary of state, on September 25, Kissinger met with most of the Arab ambassadors to the UN. He tried to establish his credentials as a credible mediator, joking about his own Jewish background.[65] He promised to work for a settlement but warned the ambassadors not to expect miracles. He would only promise what he could deliver, but he would deliver all that he promised. This became a common refrain in Kissinger's talks with the Arabs.

Over the next two weeks Kissinger spoke several times with the Arab and Israeli foreign ministers attending the UN General Assembly in New York. He proposed, and they seemed to agree, that serious talks between Egypt and Israel, with the United States as mediator, should begin in November. On October 5 he met with Foreign Minister Zayyat of Egypt to confirm these arrangements. On the whole, he was satisfied with the results of his first foray as secretary of state into Middle East diplomacy.

The next day, Yom Kippur, Egypt and Syria launched a combined military offensive against Israeli forces in the Golan Heights and Sinai. Kissinger's policy lay in ruins, overtaken by a war that he had occasionally worried about but had not really foreseen. At the core of his misreading of Arab intentions was his belief that war would be prevented by maintaining the military balance in Israel's favor. This view, forged in the midst of the Jordan crisis, had been dangerously misleading.

CONCLUSIONS

The period between the Jordan crisis in September 1970 and the October 1973 war was deceptively calm in the Middle East. In the absence of acute crises, American policymakers paid comparatively little attention to the area. The basic frame of reference, set by Nixon and Kissinger, emphasized the U.S.-Soviet rivalry and the need to maintain the balance of power in Israel's favor. Periodically the State Department tried to launch a new initiative—the Jarring talks, the interim canal settlement, proximity talks—but the White House was only mildly supportive at best, and on occasion was distinctly negative. Bureaucratic rivalries became personalized in the Rogers-Kissinger quarrel. On the whole, Nixon sided with Kissinger.[66] As a result, United States policy during this period was particularly ineffective and inconsistent.

During the interim canal-settlement talks, it was especially flawed; the Rogers-Sisco mediation and the Bergus memorandum left a bitter aftertaste in Israel, Egypt, and the White House. During this noncrisis period domestic politics also began to intrude on policymaking in noticeable ways. Because of election-year imperatives in 1972, no initiatives were undertaken, even in response to Sadat's expulsion of the Soviet advisers. Then, in 1973, Watergate began to divert the attention of the president from the region to which he had promised to devote highest priority in his foreign policy.

As Kissinger began to focus on the Middle East, he toyed with the idea of seeking U.S.-Soviet agreement on principles as one strand of his policy, while also talking to Egypt and Israel about both interim steps and principles for an overall settlement. Curiously, each of these approaches had been tried by Rogers and had failed. Kissinger was no more successful, but his larger purpose, in any case, seems to have been to frustrate the Arabs so that they would break with their Soviet patron and turn to the United States for help. But when Sadat began to move in this direction in 1972, Kissinger did not take him very seriously.

The most impressive shift in policy during this period concerned U.S.-Israeli relations. Despite occasional disagreements over arms, the United States and Israel entered an unusually cooperative phase in their often troubled relationship. This phase was very much the result of the Jordan crisis and Kissinger's view of Israel as a strategic asset. In fiscal years 1968, 1969, and 1970 Israel had received from the United States military credits worth $25 million, $85 million, and $30 million, respectively.

After the Jordan crisis, in fiscal years 1971, 1972, and 1973, Israel received military credits of $545 million, $300 million, and $307.5 million, respectively—nearly a tenfold increase in aid.

Yet the military balance proved not to be the key to regional stability and the prevention of war. Nor did détente prevent the Soviet Union from continuing to arm Egypt, Syria, and Iraq despite the mounting signs of Arab intentions to resume hostilities. Nixon and Kissinger remained insensitive to the regional trends leading to war and ignored the growing importance of Arab oil as an element in the regional equation. The concepts guiding their policies were simply too broad to incorporate these developments; nor was Kissinger convinced of the need for a major American initiative in the Middle East.[67] It required the October war to change U.S. policy and to engage Nixon and Kissinger fully in the search for an Arab-Israeli settlement.

CHAPTER SEVEN

War and Reassessment, October 1973

The Arab-Israeli war of October 1973 had all the elements of a severe international crisis. It caught most of the world, including the United States and Israel, by surprise; it did not fit anyone's preconceptions of how a war in the Middle East was likely to develop; it threatened core values of the countries directly involved as well as those of outside powers; and it ended with a near-confrontation between the two nuclear superpowers, the United States and the Soviet Union.

Crises, by their nature, expose prevailing assumptions about reality in particularly acute ways. Faced with surprise, danger, and uncertainty, decisionmakers act from previously formulated conceptions of reality. When reality no longer conforms to these images, and policymakers are under great pressure of time and events, they are likely to restructure their perceptions with extraordinary speed. Impending failure or danger, much like the prospect of a hanging, clears the mind. Pieces of the puzzle are quickly rearranged, and new policies are tried. If the crisis is resolved successfully, the revised or restructured image is likely to endure for some time; lessons will be drawn; and a new policy framework will emerge to guide action until the next failure or crisis. The October war is therefore doubly important as an object of study, for it revealed the underlying assumptions of American policy toward the Arab-Israeli conflict from 1970 to 1973 and produced a major revision of those assumptions within a very short period.

WHY THE SURPRISE?

Shortly after 6:00 a.m. Washington time on October 6, 1973, the White House situation room received a flash cable from the American embassy in Tel Aviv. Israel finally had conclusive evidence that the Egyptians and Syrians planned to attack by 6:00 p.m. Middle East time (noon in Washington). Prime Minister Golda Meir assured the United States that Israel did not intend to preempt and asked that American efforts be directed at preventing war. Kissinger received the message while in New

York; Nixon was in Key Biscayne, Florida, worrying about recent evidence of corruption by Vice President Spiro Agnew. Nixon was not immediately informed of the alarming new message. From the outset, this was to be Kissinger's crisis, not his.

In the less than two hours that remained before the war began, Kissinger took charge, calling the Israelis to warn against preemption, urging the Soviets to use their influence to prevent war, telephoning the Egyptian ambassador to the UN with the Israeli message that Israel would not preempt, and sending messages to King Hussein and King Faisal to enlist their help on the side of moderation. Kissinger's efforts were futile, and the first word of hostilities was received shortly after 8:00 a.m.

Why was Washington caught off balance? Surely there was ample evidence that Egypt and Syria were frustrated over the status quo, that they had sizable military capabilities, and that they intended to resort to force at some time to recover their territories lost in 1967.[1] Sadat had publicly stated on several occasions his intention to go to war, most explicitly in April 1973.[2] During the spring Egyptian military maneuvers had been unusually realistic and had prompted a genuine war scare. State Department intelligence analysts, reflecting on the spring crisis, had predicted on May 31 that the chance of Sadat's going to war by fall was "better than even" in the absence of a credible political initiative toward a settlement.[3] General Secretary Brezhnev, in his talks with President Nixon in San Clemente in June, had warned that the Arabs were planning for war and that this time they were determined. Only American pressure on Israel to make concessions would prevent hostilities.

Kissinger had been sufficiently alarmed by these signs of tension in the Middle East to ask that a new contingency plan on the Arab-Israeli conflict be drafted. What would happen if there was another war? What options would be available to the United States? The bureaucracy abhors contingency plans, so the task fell to a junior State Department official who thought the whole exercise was a waste of time. The Israelis were so powerful that the Arabs would never dare attack. When war broke out several months later, the contingency plan lay half-finished in his file drawer.

By fall several new signs of danger were available to anyone who cared to watch. Soviet military shipments to Egypt and Syria, especially to the latter, were going on at a high level. In mid-September Egypt, Syria, and Jordan patched up their differences, just as tension flared on the

Syrian-Israeli front.[4] Shortly thereafter Syria began to redeploy some of its forces from the Jordanian border to Golan and moved large numbers of surface-to-air missiles into the region between Damascus and the Israeli front. These movements were known in Washington and were interpreted as a reaction to the September 13 air battle in which Israel had shot down twelve Syrian planes and to the easing of tensions with Jordan. At about the same time Egypt began its fall maneuvers. On September 26 Kissinger was awakened with news that Egyptian forces had gone on a high stage of alert. In response, U.S. intelligence-collection activities in the Middle East were increased, and Kissinger requested that the CIA and the Bureau of Intelligence and Research (INR) prepare an estimate of the likelihood of an Arab-Israeli war. The flow of information was staggering, but it was also inconsistent. Along with one "reliable" report that Egypt and Syria were planning a combined military offensive in the near future came dozens of equally reliable reports painting a very different picture.

On October 5 a new element entered the equation. Soviet civilians were reportedly being evacuated from Syria and Egypt. Did the Soviets know something of which the Americans were ignorant? Or was the evacuation, as in July 1972, a sign of a crisis in Arab-Soviet relations?[5] Neither interpretation could be confirmed initially, but the CIA daily report on October 6 tentatively concluded that the latter explanation seemed more plausible, inasmuch as there were no clear signs of impending hostilities.[6]

Why was the American intelligence community wrong? Why was Kissinger caught by surprise?[7] Where were all the Middle East "experts"? Two basic conceptual biases led to the misperception of Egyptian-Syrian intentions. First, it was widely assumed that the "military balance" was the key to whether there would be another war in the Middle East. This had been a basic element in American policy since 1967. However strongly the Arabs might feel about the need to regain their territory, they would not go to war if they faced certain defeat. In view of Israel's qualitative advantages in the military realm, and the substantial flow of American arms after 1970, it would be an act of folly for the Arabs to initiate a war. Nor was it expected that Israel would feel the need to preempt.

A deliberate, rationally planned war was simply implausible in the light of military realities. An unintended war, caused by each side's reacting to defensive moves of the other, seemed more likely, but it would be difficult to anticipate or predict.[8] Finally, war as an irrational act might occur, but again could not be predicted with accuracy.

Second, war seemed to make sense for the Arabs only if a political alternative for recovering their territory was precluded. Although most of the U.S. bureaucracy remained uninformed, top officials were aware that Kissinger, in his talks with Israelis and Egyptians at the UN, had arranged for preliminary talks on a settlement to begin in November, after the Israeli elections. The continuation of Israeli military superiority and the option of a political alternative made an Arab-initiated war implausible. The maneuvers, threats, and warnings could all be explained away as part of a Soviet-Arab campaign to force the United States to lean on Israel to make concessions.

Perhaps as important as these conceptual errors was a sense that Israel had the greatest incentive and the best capabilities for determining whether war was likely or not.[9] After all, Israel, not the United States, would be the target of any Arab military threat, and Israeli intelligence had an excellent reputation, drawing on sources unavailable to the United States; therefore, if the Israelis were not too worried, why should Americans be? Repeated checks with Israeli sources showed a fairly relaxed attitude. Even on October 5, when Israel was close to putting the pieces together accurately, a message to Kissinger from Golda Meir included the assessment that neither Egypt nor Syria was planning to go to war. But just in case the Arabs feared Israel's intentions, Meir asked Kissinger to reassure them that Israel had no plans to attack.[10]

Despite all the technically accurate information available in Washington about Arab war preparations, Egypt and Syria did manage to observe high standards of secrecy and deception. Well-placed Israeli intelligence agents in Egypt had been captured early in 1973.[11] Presidents Anwar Sadat and Hafiz al-Asad confided in almost no one concerning the precise moment of the attack. Communications security in the days preceding the attack was unusually good, and deliberate deception tactics were used successfully. Even so, Israel had nearly ten hours' warning.[12] But there was not enough time to take any steps to prevent war, and very little could even be done to limit the damage of the initial Arab attack.

Some have argued that if Israel had launched a preemptive air strike, the course of the war would have been significantly different. And in some quarters the United States has been blamed for preventing Israel from preempting. It is true that Kissinger and Nixon had consistently warned Israel that it must not be responsible for initiating a Middle East war. Kissinger repeated this admonition immediately before the outbreak of hostilities, but by then Prime Minister Meir had already said that Israel would not preempt. The Israeli decision was not made in Washington, at least not on October 6.

For several hours after the outbreak of war, Washington did not know whether the Israelis or the Arabs had fired the first shots. During the rump session of the Washington Special Action Group (WSAG), convened at 9:00 a.m., the prevailing view was that Israel had probably struck first.[13] CIA Director William Colby judged that, in any event, neither side had premeditated military action, but rather that the war was the result of mutual fears of actions and reactions that had escalated to hostilities.[14] The United States, it was felt, should not make accusations against either side. A multiplicity of interests was at stake—U.S.-Soviet détente, U.S.-Israeli relations, American credibility with the Arabs, and the weakened authority of the president. The initial American reaction was therefore cautious.

It soon became clear that the Egyptians and Syrians had indeed begun the hostilities, but at no point during the next three weeks did any United States official make this an issue. The public record will be searched in vain for references to Arab "aggression."[15] Unlike President Johnson, who held Nasser responsible for the 1967 war despite Israel's opening fire on June 5, Nixon and Kissinger ignored the issue of who was at fault. Among the reasons for this "evenhanded" perspective was the feeling that U.S.-Arab relations were growing in importance because of oil and this was no time for a confrontation; that an Arab attack on Israeli forces in occupied Arab territory was not the same as an attack across recognized borders; and that the status quo prevailing before the war had, in fact, given the Arabs ample incentive to try to break the "no war, no peace" stalemate by engineering an international crisis. For several days it was widely considered that the Arab action had been foolish, but not that it had been immoral.

Toward the end of the first day of fighting, a second WSAG meeting was convened, this time under Kissinger's chairmanship. For all practical purposes, he, usually in consultation with Nixon directly or through Chief of Staff Alexander Haig, made policy during the next several weeks, with occasional inputs from Defense Secretary James Schlesinger. Kissinger's initial views are therefore of particular interest.

When Kissinger entered the situation room at 7:22 p.m., one cabinet member was calmly reading the comic strips in the local newspaper.

Other WSAG participants were bantering lightly about the crisis. With Kissinger's arrival the serious discussion began. He reported that he had just been on the telephone to Nixon, to the Soviet ambassador, Anatoly Dobrynin, and to the Israeli foreign minister, Abba Eban.[16] The president wanted the Sixth Fleet moved east and held near Crete as a visible sign of American power. One aircraft carrier was ordered to leave port in Athens; other moves would be considered later.

Kissinger was concerned about the Soviet Union. If the Arabs suffered a real debacle, he thought, the Soviets would have a hard time staying out of the fighting. U.S. military moves should be restrained so as not to give the wrong impressions to the Soviet Union. Reminded that future American military steps might require the use of the Azores base, Kissinger quipped that the Portuguese would be happy to grant permission, because he had just refused to see their foreign minister in New York!

Discussion ensued on the diplomatic contacts taken to date. In the UN the United States would try to work with the Soviet Union to reestablish the cease-fire on the basis of the status quo ante. Kissinger, expecting a reprise of June 1967, said the Arabs, in their "demented state," currently opposed that position, but they would beg for it once the Israeli counteroffensive got under way. The U.S. strategy would be to prevent the diplomatic debate from going to the UN General Assembly, where an automatic pro-Arab majority would be available. The Soviets, it was acknowledged, would have a problem accepting a cease-fire based on the status quo ante, for it would mean Arab forces would have to withdraw from Arab territory. A Soviet response would nonetheless be forthcoming the next day.

Israel would undoubtedly reject any cease-fire not based on a return to the status quo ante. Nixon did not want a situation in which Israel, the victim of the attack, would be condemned for rejecting a cease-fire appeal. The U.S. goal was to adopt a position that would remain consistent throughout the crisis. The war would quickly shift in Israel's favor, and what appeared to be a pro-Israel position of a cease-fire on the post-1967 lines would soon look pro-Arab. If Israel went beyond the previous lines, the United States would oppose that, thereby regaining some credit with the Arabs. Consequently the United States would propose a cease-fire status quo ante but would not push hard for it until the military realities made both parties want to accept it.

Everyone felt the crisis would be crucial for U.S.-Soviet relations. If collaboration worked, détente would take on real meaning; if it failed, the Soviets could "kiss MFN [most favored nation] goodbye."[17] Although the Soviets might have been duplicitous in helping the Arabs plan the war, some still held the hope of working with Moscow to end it. U.S.-Israeli relations were also on many minds. By sticking close to the Israelis during the war, the United States should be able to enhance the credibility of a future guarantee as part of a peace settlement. Eventually American and Israeli positions on a settlement would diverge, and the only way to get the Israelis to withdraw from Arab territory would be to offer some kind of formal U.S. guarantee. The president felt strongly about this issue. The Israelis must see the United States as a reliable partner during the crisis for the sake of postwar diplomacy. Arms and oil were briefly mentioned. Kissinger concluded with the thought that the worst outcome for the United States would be to appear crippled by the domestic crisis over Watergate. Kissinger then left for an evening meeting with Ambassador Dobrynin.

A basic strategy was already set. The United States, expecting a short war in which Israel would quickly prevail, hoped to be in a strong position vis-à-vis Israel and the Soviets for postwar diplomatic moves. In addition, Kissinger wanted to avoid a confrontation with the Arabs. For the moment, the United States would adopt a low profile, developing a position on a cease-fire that would soon be seen as balanced. The viability of this policy depended on a quick Israeli reversal of the military situation and Soviet restraint. For the next two days these conditions seemed to hold.

On Sunday, October 7, Kissinger kept in close touch with the Soviets, Egyptians, and Israelis. Nixon sent Brezhnev a letter urging mutual restraint and calling for a meeting of the Security Council. Brezhnev's reply was conciliatory and encouraging.[18] Together with the movement of Soviet ships away from the zone of combat, this was a promising sign.

Supplementing Kissinger's talks with Foreign Minister Zayyat, the Egyptians began to send messages through the back channel that had been established in 1972. Although rejecting the idea of a cease-fire that was not linked to Israeli withdrawal to the pre-1967 lines, Sadat, communicating through his adviser, Hafiz Ismail, made it clear he did not want a confrontation with the United States.[19]

The Israelis were in a grim mood, but in communications with the United States they still appeared confident of success. Anticipating Israeli requests for arms, Kissinger made arrangements for El Al aircraft to pick up some items—ammunition, high technology products, and Sidewinder missiles—at a naval base in Virginia. Ambassador Simcha Dinitz, just arrived from Israel, met with Kissinger in the evening and, as expected, presented a list of arms that Israel needed, but the sense of urgency was not particularly great, or at least so it seemed to Kissinger and Schlesinger.[20] A modest resupply effort soon began, but Kissinger was still hoping to keep any visible involvement with Israel's war effort at a minimum.

By the time the WSAG met shortly after 6:00 p.m. on October 7,[21] the best estimate of the CIA was that Israel would regain the initiative the following day and would go on to win the war by the end of the week. Initial concentration would be on the Syrian front, then on the Egyptian front. Kissinger voiced his perplexity about why the Arabs, if their situation was really so precarious, were refusing a cease-fire that would protect their initial gains.[22] Schlesinger felt they were being illogical; Kissinger replied that the Egyptian strategy would be to cross the canal and then sit tight. The Arabs, he thought, had attacked to upset the status quo, because they feared there would be no diplomatic movement unless there was a crisis.

After a brief discussion of oil, the possible evacuation of American citizens from Libya[23] and other Arab countries, and the Israeli request for arms, the meeting ended. Kissinger said he would ask the president, who was arriving at 10:00 p.m. from Florida, about further American military moves and Israeli requests for arms. For the moment, he felt, the United States was in a good position to come out of the crisis with its essential interests intact.

The following day, October 8, the UN Security Council was convened. John Scali, the American representative, mentioned in his speech that a cease-fire based on the status quo ante would be the "least damaging" solution to the crisis, but he did not formally propose a resolution for a vote.[24]

Israel was now beginning to encounter military difficulties on both fronts. In Golan the Syrian air-defense system was taking a high toll of Israeli Skyhawks and Phantoms. In Sinai an Israeli effort to break through Egyptian lines with armor had been thwarted. Demands for resupply of equipment from the United States mounted. Dinitz spoke to Kissinger several times and was told that Israeli losses would be replaced. When Dinitz complained about the slow American response, Kissinger blamed it on the Defense Department, a ploy he used repeatedly with the Israeli ambassador over the next several days.[25] In fact, the U.S. position was still based on the expectation of an early end to the fighting and a desire to maintain a low profile. The arms issue was therefore handled discreetly.

The WSAG met again at 5:30 p.m. on Monday, October 8, to review the day's events.[26] The CIA reported that Israel was making rapid progress and had virtually retaken the Golan Heights. One member offered the opinion that if the Soviets did not resupply the Arabs, perhaps the Americans should not resupply Israel. Kissinger again expressed puzzlement over why the Arabs were refusing a cease-fire. The Soviets, by contrast, were being very conciliatory. With their help, it was felt, a cease-fire could be achieved by Wednesday night. The Soviets would respond on Tuesday. Even if Israel crossed the canal, the United States would be in a good position by sticking to a call for a cease-fire based on the status quo ante. Military realities would shortly make the American proposal acceptable to Egypt, Syria, and the Soviet Union. When the meeting ended at 6:30 p.m., Kissinger immediately went to his White House office to confer with Dinitz. He then delivered a previously scheduled speech to the Pacem in Terris conference in Washington in which he alluded to the Middle East and the need for Soviet restraint there if détente was to survive.[27]

The basic U.S. policy, rooted in the initial assumptions of a short war with an Israeli victory, was still on the tracks, but it would not be for much longer. In the jargon of Washington it was about to be "overtaken by events."

THE CRISIS DEEPENS

From the perspective of Washington the war entered a new and acute phase on October 9. Reality was refusing to conform to the comparatively optimistic forecast upon which initial U.S. policy had been based. Between October 9 and October 12 the possibility of a swift and conclusive Israeli military victory on both fronts faded; Soviet restraint began to erode; and pressure began to build for an urgent military resupply of Israeli forces. The American response was to modify gradually two aspects of policy: the call for a cease-fire based on the status quo ante was replaced by an exploration of the idea of a cease-fire in place; and arms for Israel began to flow in modest quantities, not only aboard El Al aircraft, but increasingly with direct American involvement.

In one of the most controversial decisions of the war, Nixon and

Kissinger held back on a full-scale commitment of American resources to the resupply effort until the fate of the cease-fire-in-place initiative was clear and the scope of the Soviet resupply effort made further delay politically difficult. Under pressure on the ground, short of supplies, and without a guarantee of a full-scale American airlift of arms, the Israeli government reluctantly accepted a cease-fire in place on October 12. But early on October 13 President Sadat refused the cease-fire proposal, which led to a dramatic change in American policy.

This second stage of the crisis opened on Tuesday morning, October 9, with an urgent Israeli appeal for arms.[28] Dinitz informed Kissinger of heavy Israeli losses, especially of aircraft on the Syrian front, as well as some 500 tanks, mostly on the Egyptian front. At the end of the meeting Dinitz asked to talk with Kissinger alone to convey a request from Meir for a secret visit to Washington to plead the case for arms with Nixon. Kissinger refused to consider the proposal, later claiming that it reflected "hysteria or blackmail."[29]

Shortly thereafter Kissinger convened the WSAG principals for two emergency sessions before noon. Only Schlesinger, Thomas Moorer (chairman of the Joint Chiefs), Kenneth Rush (deputy secretary of state), William Colby (CIA director), and Brent Scowcroft (deputy national security adviser) met with Kissinger to consider the new Israeli request. To date, this was the most difficult moment of the war. The two recommendations that emerged from these sessions were presented to Nixon by Kissinger at 4:45 p.m. First, some arms must begin to reach Israel quickly, without violating the principle of maintaining a low American profile in the conflict. Second, over the next several days a new formula for a cease-fire would be explored. Nixon, deeply distracted by the impending resignation of his vice-president, agreed to meet most of Israel's requests.[30]

While these deliberations were going on, word began to reach Washington that Israel had launched a major counteroffensive on the Syrian front. On the ground, Israeli troops had recovered virtually all the territory lost during the first three days of fighting and in some areas were pushing beyond the former cease-fire line. Nonetheless, the fighting was still difficult. The Syrians were not breaking, and Iraqi reinforcements were on their way. In the air, the Israelis, thwarted in their efforts to use the air force for close support of ground troops, initiated a campaign of strategic bombing deep within Syria. The oil refinery at Homs was attacked; the defense ministry and air-force staff headquarters in Damascus were bombed; and, by mistake, the Soviet cultural center in Damascus was hit, causing at least one Soviet fatality.

As the Syrian front began to weaken, King Hussein of Jordan came under great pressure to enter the war, if not by opening a new front, then at least by sending some of his troops to Syria. Israel conveyed an extremely harsh message to Hussein on October 9, warning of the consequences of opening a front along the Jordan River. Kissinger also urged Hussein to stay out of the fighting, stressing that a diplomatic effort was under way that, it was hoped, would succeed in ending the war within a few days.

This diplomatic effort consisted of sounding out the Egyptians, Soviets, and Israelis on the possibility of a cease-fire in place. Dinitz was the first to convey his government's refusal, emphasizing the need for any cease-fire to be tied to the restoration of the status quo ante.[31] Egypt's position was equally negative. Any cease-fire must be directly linked to a concrete plan calling for full Israeli withdrawal from all territories captured in 1967. Kissinger had raised the issue of a cease-fire in place through his back channel to Hafiz Ismail on October 9, stressing that Egypt had "made its point." Ismail's reply, reportedly drafted by Sadat, reached him the following day:[32]

—There should be a cease-fire followed by a withdrawal within a specified period, under UN supervision, of all Israeli forces to the pre–June 5, 1967, lines.

—Freedom of navigation in the Strait of Tiran should be guaranteed by a UN presence at Sharm al-Shaykh for a specified period.

—Following the complete withdrawal of Israeli forces, the state of belligerency with Israel would be ended.

—Following the withdrawal of Israeli troops from Gaza, the area would be placed under UN supervision pending its self-determination.

—Within a specified period after the ending of the state of belligerency, a peace conference would be convened under UN auspices, to be attended by all interested parties, including the Palestinians, and all members of the Security Council. The conference would deal with all questions of sovereignty, security, and freedom of navigation.

Egypt also promised that once Israeli evacuation began, diplomatic relations with the United States would be resumed, and work on clearing the Suez Canal would start.

This proposal was hardly the simple cease-fire in place that Nixon and

Kissinger now envisaged. Under no circumstances were they prepared to link a cease-fire to the terms of a final settlement. Not only would the Israelis adamantly refuse such a linkage, but it also was entirely contrary to Nixon's and Kissinger's negotiating strategy. Sadat was aiming far too high. Either the Soviets or Israeli military successes would have to bring him to a more realistic sense of what was possible.

Fortunately for Kissinger's strategy, the Soviets now seemed to be supporting the idea of a cease-fire in place, and indicated in a message on October 10 that Egypt would most likely go along. The Soviets thought that both great powers should abstain on any Security Council Resolution calling for a cease-fire. Kissinger claims that his initial reaction was negative because he felt Israel needed more time to change things on the battlefield. In an effort to stall, he accepted the Soviet proposal "in principle" but urged the Soviets not to take any immediate action at the United Nations.[33]

THE CEASE-FIRE INITIATIVE

Offsetting this conciliatory gesture, however, was the first evidence that the Soviets were beginning an airlift of arms to the Middle East. On October 10 twenty-one AN-12s flew to Damascus with more than 200 tons of military equipment.[34] Late that day Washington learned that seven Soviet airborne divisions had been placed on a high state of alert. Obviously the Soviets were worried about the deteriorating situation on the Syrian front. Whether their solution to the danger posed to their interests would emphasize diplomacy or force was at the moment an unanswered question. Elements of both courses of action were visible.

Meanwhile the U.S. resupply of Israel was beginning on a modest scale. On October 9 Dinitz had been informed that a number of F-4 Phantoms would soon be on their way. In addition, El Al planes were being allowed to pick up preassembled cargoes at Oceana Naval Station near Norfolk, Virginia. The first of these resupplies had reached Israel by October 10, the same day on which the first Soviet resupplies by air reached Damascus.

The intensity of the fighting was such, however, that Israeli requests for arms could not be met simply by El Al flights. Consistent with the principle of avoiding direct official American involvement in the transport of arms to Israel, Kissinger and Schlesinger began on October 10 to explore the possibility of chartering civilian transports for that purpose. Ten to twenty flights a day were envisaged. That same day Kissinger spoke with Dinitz several times about arms, a possible Jordanian movement of troops to Syria, and Moscow's renewed interest in a cease-fire in place. Dinitz relayed the Soviet position to the prime minister, who still refused to consider it.[35]

At this point the American and Israeli positions began to diverge. The United States wanted an early cease-fire, at least within the next two days. Israel wanted arms in sufficient quantity to ensure a military victory. Over the next forty-eight hours the United States seemed to move slowly on sending arms to Israel, either, as Kissinger maintains, because of bureaucratic confusion, or, as others believe, as a form of pressure to induce the Israelis to accept a cease-fire in place and in the conviction that the fighting was nearly over in any case.

President Nixon, in one of his rare public remarks about the crisis while it was under way, summed up the American position on October 10 as follows: "The United States is trying its best to play a mediating role and bring the fighting to an end and then, beyond that, to help to build not just a temporary, but a lasting peace for the people in that very troubled section of the world."[36]

October 11 was a day of regrouping and consolidation. Nothing extraordinary happened on the battlefield or in Washington. Israel began to transfer troops from the Syrian to the Egyptian front in order to push Egyptian forces back to the canal. U.S. diplomacy aimed at restraining King Hussein, now under pressure from Asad, Sadat, and Faisal, from joining the war, and at reassuring the Israelis that the charter flights and F-4s would soon be on their way. Israel's refusal to consider a cease-fire in place was now beginning to weaken somewhat. Having made new gains on the Syrian front, Israel was prepared to consider a cease-fire coupled with a subsequent exchange of Israeli control over captured Syrian territory for a restoration of Israeli positions in Sinai.[37] Syria might see some merit in this plan, but Sadat would not; hence the United States continued to press for a simple cease-fire in place. On October 12 it seemed within grasp.

The day began with Israeli queries about the charter flights that had been promised but that had not yet begun. In an effort to retain credibility with the Israelis, Kissinger tried to accelerate the process. A message was sent at 11:09 a.m. to the Portuguese requesting the use of Lajes airbase in the Azores for chartered civilian aircraft flying military consumables to Israel. Ten to twenty flights, chartered by the Defense Department, would pass through Lajes each day. The flights were to begin that same evening. The Portuguese, no doubt resenting the fact that the United States seemed to take their acceptance for granted, delayed their response.

Meanwhile the Defense Department, having failed to arrange the charter of civilian transport, was exploring the possibility of using American military transports to carry equipment to Lajes, where it would then be transferred to Israeli transports. The United States was still reluctant to have its own military aircraft fly into Tel Aviv. Nixon, concerned with delays on resupplying the Israeli military, called Schlesinger in the afternoon to urge him to accelerate the effort, including the use of American military aircraft if necessary.[38]

According to Kissinger, during the morning he was informed that Israel was prepared to accept a cease-fire in place.[39] Apparently Golda Meir, in consultation with her top military leaders, but without a formal cabinet vote, had made the decision out of concern about both the costs of continued fighting and the pressure generated by the delay in the resupply effort.[40]

At a press conference called at 11:00 a.m., Kissinger tried to clarify the various, sometimes conflicting, strands of American policy as of October 12:

After hostilities broke out, the United States set itself two principal objectives. One, to end the hostilities as quickly as possible. Secondly, to end the hostilities in such a manner that they [sic] would contribute to the maximum extent possible to the promotion of a more permanent, more lasting solution in the Middle East. . . . We have not gratuitously sought opportunities for confrontations in public forums which might harden dividing lines. . . . [T]he Middle East may become in time what the Balkans were in Europe before 1914, that is to say, an area where local rivalries . . . have their own momentum that will draw in the great nuclear powers into a confrontation.

Kissinger went on to "urge, all the parties in the conduct of their diplomacy now to keep in mind that whatever momentary advantages might be achieved in this or that forum, our principal objective should be to maintain relationships that can move both the area and the world towards a more lasting peace."

Kissinger then referred to the "traditional friendship" of the United States for Israel and to the continuing military relationship with that country. He termed the Soviet airlift "moderate," "more than light. It's a fairly substantial airlift." Then, in something of a forewarning to the Arabs of the impending United States role in aiding Israel militarily, Kissinger stated: "We have made a very serious effort, in this crisis, to take seriously into account Arab concerns and Arab views. On the other hand, we have to pursue what we consider to be the right course; we will take the consequences in pursuing what we consider to be the right course." [41]

Kissinger was apprehensive that, in the absence of a rapid end to the war, the United States would have to increase the visibility of its role in rearming Israel; then the Arabs might react by embargoing oil and attacking American interests throughout the region. There was all the more reason, therefore, for one additional try at a cease-fire.

Prime Minister Meir's acceptance of the idea of a cease-fire in place was followed by a message from Dinitz that Israel would not object if the cease-fire idea was put to the UN immediately. Later in the evening of October 12 Dinitz came to the White House with an urgent personal appeal from Meir to President Nixon to order an immediate resupply of arms to Israel. She went so far as to raise the specter of an Israeli military defeat. [42]

Meanwhile the cease-fire initiative was running into trouble. Kissinger had urged the British to introduce the idea in the UN on October 13. During the evening of October 12 the British told Kissinger they would only introduce a resolution the following day if they were sure it would be accepted by the parties. From their information, they doubted that this would be the case. Kissinger assured them that they should proceed. But late in the morning of October 13 the British informed Kissinger that they had concluded that a cease-fire in place was a mirage. Britain insisted on getting Sadat's prior acquiescence. Meanwhile Kissinger began to explore the possibility that Australia might introduce a cease-fire resolution. But, inexplicably, the Soviets were cool to the idea. Finally, at 3:35 p.m. the British told Kissinger that Sadat rejected any variation of a cease-fire. The initiative had reached a dead end. [43]

THE AIRLIFT

President Nixon's role in shaping American policy during the October war is difficult to assess accurately. He was obviously preoccupied by his own domestic political difficulties and with the resignation in disgrace of his hand-picked vice-president, Spiro Agnew, on October 10. The president showed little interest in the details of policy, leaving the task of day-to-day diplomacy to Kissinger. Nixon did make key decisions, however, and it was his authority that could be invoked to influence other governments.

Early in the morning of October 13 Schlesinger became convinced that the only effective way to get arms to Israel would be in American military planes. Kissinger and Haig were opposed, still preferring to keep a low profile.[44] On the morning of October 13, having been briefed on Meir's urgent appeal for help and Schlesinger's recommendation, and without any positive indication that a cease-fire agreement was in sight, President Nixon took the responsibility of ordering a full-scale airlift of military equipment to Israel.[45]

The Portuguese, who had still not granted the United States permission to use Lajes, received a harsh note from Nixon, dispatched from Washington at 8:00 a.m. At this point, consideration was still being given to the plan to fly equipment to the Azores, where it would be picked up by the Israelis. Portuguese permission was finally received at 3:40 p.m.

Besides Nixon's decision to mount an American airlift, an SR-71 reconnaissance plane was ordered to photograph the battle area to provide an independent basis for judging losses on both sides. The continuation of the Soviet airlift, Israel's apparent trouble on the battlefield, and the collapse of the cease-fire effort were creating a concern in Washington that the war might now drag on. Good battlefield intelligence was needed. This was the first such flight during the hostilities.[46]

The main considerations underlying this stage of the Nixon-Kissinger strategy were to convince Sadat that a prolonged war of attrition, fueled by Soviet arms, would not succeed and to demonstrate to the Kremlin that the United States was capable of matching Soviet military deliveries to the Middle East. Above all, for the sake of the future American position globally and in the region, Soviet arms must not be allowed to dictate the outcome of the fighting. This did not mean that the United States now favored a total Israeli military victory, but it did mean that Israeli success on the battlefield had become an important factor in persuading the Arabs and the Soviets to bring the fighting to an end.[47]

Nixon and Kissinger were aware of the likelihood of adverse Arab reaction to the airlift of arms to Israel. Up to this point in the crisis there had been no confrontation between the United States and the Arab world. The "oil weapon" had not yet been brandished, as many had feared; American lives were not endangered in any Arab country, including Libya, which had been a source of early concern; no Arab country had broken diplomatic relations; and Sadat was in continuing contact with Nixon through the back channel. U.S. influence with King Hussein had helped keep Jordan out of the war, although a token Jordanian force was now being sent to Syria. All this might change as a result of the airlift, but Nixon and Kissinger were prepared to take the risk. The airlift, they would argue, was a response to prior Soviet intervention on the Arab side. Global political realities dictated that the United States respond. This was not an anti-Arab move, for it was not designed to ensure Israeli supremacy over the Arabs or to rob the Arabs of their recaptured dignity. Rather, it was a simple fact of international political life. In any event, the United States would use its influence with Israel, gained through the provision of arms, on behalf of an equitable peace settlement. This, at least, was how Nixon and Kissinger would explain the policy to the Arabs[48] and to the U.S. bureaucracy. In Washington there was little dissent, even from allegedly pro-Arab elements.

By 12:30 p.m. Washington time, on October 14 (6:30 p.m. in Israel), the first giant C-5 transport plane arrived at Lod airport. An air bridge capable of delivering nearly 1,000 tons a day was now in operation, consisting of four to five flights of C-5s and twelve to fifteen flights of C-141s. El Al planes also continued to carry military supplies to Israel. In addition, twelve C-130 transports were flown to Israel and were turned over to the Israeli air force.[49]

When it became clear that Sadat would reject a cease-fire, Kissinger had proposed going all-out with the American airlift of arms to Israel. No longer would the United States try to minimize its visibility by seeking charters. With the airlift in full swing, Washington was prepared to wait until the new realities on the battlefield led to a change of Egyptian and Soviet calculations.

In the meantime the United States began to plan for an anticipated Arab oil embargo. Only 12 percent of U.S. oil consumption, or 5 percent of total energy, consisted of crude oil and refined products received directly or indirectly from the Arab world. Through reduction of demand for oil and some redirection of imports, the overall impact of a selective Arab oil embargo against the United States would hardly be felt. If, however, an embargo was combined with severe cutbacks in production, then not only the United States but also Europe and Japan would feel the pinch. Consequently plans for the sharing of oil among allies, as well as a domestic energy plan, were required. At a minimum, the Middle East crisis might provide an incentive for Congress and public opinion to support a major energy project. Former governor John Love, energy coordinator for Nixon, his aide Charles Di Bona, and Deputy Secretary of the Treasury William Simon were given primary responsibility for working out a plan in the event of an embargo.

By the time the first C-5 had set down in Israel on the afternoon of October 14, the decisive battle of the war on the Egyptian front had been fought and won by Israel. An Egyptian offensive toward the Mitla and Giddi passes had failed, at a cost to Egypt of more than 200 tanks. It had been for the sake of this battle that Sadat had rejected the cease-fire in place offered by the British ambassador the previous day.[50] Now, with this victory behind them, the Israelis showed little interest in the cease-fire they had been prepared to accept two days earlier.[51] Instead, Israel, assured of continuing American supplies, decided to undertake a risky military operation to cross the Suez Canal. If successful, this action might result in the destruction of Egyptian missile fields, thereby exposing Egyptian ground troops to bombing by the Israeli air force. Also, Egyptian forces in Sinai ran the risk of being cut off from their lines of communication and surrounded by the Israelis. A critical moment was approaching. The Israeli operation was scheduled for the night of October 15–16.

Kissinger convened morning sessions of the WSAG on both October 14 and October 15. Besides discussing oil, the group assessed the evolving military and diplomatic situation. By October 15 the American airlift to Israel had been publicly acknowledged and widely reported. Kissinger was surprised at the moderation of the Arab response. Although he did not expect the Arab oil ministers' meeting in Kuwait the following day to cut off oil to the United States, he did feel that a plan for counterpressure on the Arabs was necessary if they did. An administration already weakened by its domestic political problems could not afford to appear susceptible to "blackmail" by Arab oil producers.

On the Soviet role in the conflict, Kissinger still reflected a certain ambivalence. The noted Washington columnist Joseph Alsop had published an article on the morning of October 15 accusing the Soviets of collusion in and extensive foreknowledge of the Arab war effort. Kissinger was suspicious, but at the same time he felt the Soviets were still interested in a diplomatic settlement. Perhaps because of the American airlift, or perhaps because of the outcome of the October 14 battle in Sinai, the Soviets early on October 15 had indicated that they were again actively trying to persuade the Arabs to accept a cease-fire. Premier Kosygin, the secretary was told, would go to Cairo the next day.

Kissinger planned to see Egyptian Foreign Minister Zayyat on October

16, and President Nixon would meet with four Arab foreign ministers on October 17. Diplomatic channels would thus remain open with both the Arabs and the Soviets despite the growing superpower involvement in the conflict.[52]

THE TIDE BEGINS TO TURN

October 16 was a crucial day for the war and the diplomacy. Both President Sadat and Prime Minister Meir gave important public speeches outlining their policies. Israeli forces had managed to cross the Suez Canal in small numbers and were moving into the missile fields, causing havoc among the Egyptian forces. Kosygin was en route to Cairo to try to persuade Sadat to stop fighting, and Kissinger had reason to feel that the U.S. strategy was working well. Sadat's speech was fairly moderate in tone and contained an "open message" to Nixon on Egypt's peace terms. Kosygin's mission had been foreshadowed in Soviet communications during the previous day. As yet, no Arab embargo of oil had been announced. And the Israeli military successes, although not specifically designed or intended by Washington, were consistent with Kissinger's view that Sadat had to be persuaded by battlefield developments to accept a cease-fire. It was of prime importance that the fighting should be ended at the moment when all parties could still emerge from the conflict with their vital interests and self-esteem intact.

At the WSAG meeting on Tuesday morning, October 16, Kissinger further elaborated on the objectives of the airlift. He minimized its importance in the context of the Arab-Israeli conflict. Rather, he stressed, the Soviets must see that the United States could deliver more than they could. Each day until a cease-fire the United States should send by air 25 percent more equipment than the Soviets did. The Soviets should be "run into the ground," "forced down." American arms in Israeli hands would outmatch Soviet arms in Arab hands.

As Kissinger was expounding on the U.S.-Soviet aspects of the crisis, the door to the situation room opened and a message was passed in. The time was 10:55 a.m. General Scowcroft read the message and passed it to Kissinger, who broke into an embarrassed laugh and then a proud grin. He had just received word that he would share the Nobel peace prize with North Vietnam's Le Duc Tho, his negotiating partner during the Paris talks.

Turning its attention again to the Middle East, the WSAG addressed the question of aid to Israel to finance the arms being sent. To some, it was time to get maximum credit with Israel, because during the subsequent diplomatic effort the U.S. and Israeli positions were bound to diverge. Kissinger therefore argued for a very large aid bill for Israel—as much as $3 billion—as well as another $500 million for Cambodia and other countries, thrown in for good measure. In his view the United States had already paid its price with the Arabs, and a massive aid bill for Israel would do little further damage.

By noon he may have had some second thoughts upon receiving a letter from King Faisal in response to his message on the airlift to Israel. The king was "pained" by the American action. The United States should stop sending arms and should call on Israel to withdraw. Otherwise U.S.-Saudi relations could become "lukewarm." (Nonetheless, the aid bill went forward, and on October 19 President Nixon formally requested $2.2 billion in aid for Israel. The following day King Faisal announced an embargo of oil to the United States as well as substantial production cuts. In retrospect Kissinger wondered whether he had pushed too hard on the Arabs with the $2.2 billion aid request just as the military situation was turning to Israel's advantage.)

The following day, October 17, was largely devoted to talks with the foreign ministers of Morocco, Algeria, Saudi Arabia, and Kuwait. Shortly after 10:00 a.m. Kissinger met with the four ministers in his White House office.[53] He listened while the Saudi foreign minister spelled out the Arabs' concerns: an immediate settlement of the conflict based on complete Israeli withdrawal from Arab territory seized in 1967 and restoration of Palestinian rights in accordance with UN Resolution 242. Kissinger then explained that the basic American policy was now to end the current fighting and to prevent its spread. After the war the United States would engage in a diplomatic effort for a just and lasting peace. U.S.-Arab relations should therefore remain as strong as possible. The Arabs had created a new reality in the Middle East, and the time had come for a diplomatic effort. The United States had initially expected the Arabs to be defeated, which was why the October 6 lines had been proposed for a cease-fire. Now a cease-fire would have to take into account new realities, but it would be a mistake to try to link a cease-fire to a total settlement. A better strategy would be to get a cease-fire quickly and then to launch a diplomatic effort. The guarantee that such an effort would be made resided in Arab strength. The United States had more influence with Israel, the Arab military and diplomatic positions had improved, and the time was therefore ripe for diplomacy. The United

States would not promise to do what it could not accomplish, but it would do everything it promised.

Kissinger concluded by remarking that he did not like big plans, but preferred quiet diplomacy. He recounted how his talks with the Chinese had progressed and urged the same step-by-step procedure on the Arabs. He warned that the Middle East should not become involved in the U.S.-Soviet global rivalry. Then he excused himself, remarking lightly that he was not used to dealing with "moderate Arabs" and that he needed to talk to the president for a few minutes before their appointment in the Oval Office.

At 11:10 a.m. President Nixon began his talks with the four Arab foreign ministers. Omar Saqqaf, the Saudi representative, again presented their collective position, emphasizing the American responsibility to force Israel to withdraw to the 1967 lines. He evoked the long history of Arab friendship for the United States and appealed to it to uphold the principle of the territorial integrity of all states in the area. Nixon replied by referring to his visits to the Middle East, his meetings with various Arab leaders, and his desire to travel again to the area once a peace settlement had been achieved. Echoing Kissinger's themes, he said the United States was now working for a cease-fire, after which it would engage in active diplomacy. He denied that domestic politics would influence U.S. Middle East policy and urged the Arabs to trust Kissinger despite his Jewish background. He concluded by promising to work for the "implementation of Resolution 242" after a cease-fire, but emphasized that he could not promise that Israel would withdraw to the 1967 lines.

After the talks Saqqaf spoke briefly with the president alone, and then proceeded to the Rose Garden to tell the press that the talks had been constructive and friendly. Kissinger then returned to the State Department with the ministers for further talks in the early afternoon.

On the whole Kissinger felt the meetings had gone well. At the afternoon WSAG meeting he stated that he no longer expected the Arabs to cut off oil to the United States. Ironically, just as he was drawing this optimistic conclusion, the Arab oil ministers meeting in Kuwait were announcing that oil production would be cut by 5 percent each month until Israel had withdrawn from all Arab territories. Three days later King Faisal pushed even further, calling for a 10 percent cut immediately and an embargo of shipments of oil to the United States and the Netherlands.

On the diplomatic front the only sign of progress from the Kosygin visit to Cairo was a Soviet request for the U.S. view of a cease-fire in place linked to Resolution 242.[54] The American response was positive, but asked for a concrete proposal. The Soviet position was conveyed to Ambassador Dinitz, who passed it to Israel, where Golda Meir found it unacceptable. Rather than link a cease-fire in place to Resolution 242, the Israelis favored a link to direct negotiations between the parties.[55] The next day brought little change. Sadat was still not ready to stop.

As Kissinger had expected, the diplomacy opened up on October 19, shortly after Kosygin's return to Moscow from Cairo.[56] During the morning a message from Brezhnev reached the White House requesting urgent consultations on the Middle East crisis. Kissinger should come to Moscow "in an urgent manner." Time was of the essence.[57] Kissinger now felt that a cease-fire could be achieved quickly. In talks with Dinitz he implied that by agreeing to go to Moscow, he would be able to gain Israel a few more days to complete its military operations.[58] Dinitz emphasized the need for a link between a cease-fire and negotiations.[59]

Later that afternoon the administration sent Congress its $2.2 billion aid request, which stated that the United States was trying to reach "a very swift and honorable conclusion, measured in days, not weeks." Then, shortly after midnight, having dined with the Chinese representative in Washington, Kissinger left for Moscow.[60] Before his departure he congratulated the WSAG members on "the best-run crisis ever."

THE MOSCOW TALKS

Whatever he had told Dinitz, Kissinger primarily went to Moscow not to gain time for Israel's battlefield success but to obtain Soviet and Arab agreement to a cease-fire resolution that could serve as the basis for a subsequent diplomatic effort. If the Soviet and Arab position remained locked into an unacceptable formulation, then Kissinger was prepared to wait, assuming that Israeli advances on the west bank of the canal would eventually bring about a change. On the other hand, if Brezhnev and Sadat were prepared for a simple cease-fire, then Kissinger would press for a quick end to hostilities. He had no interest in seeing Sadat humiliated, especially in view of the encouraging tone of U.S.-Egyptian exchanges over the past two weeks. Nor did he want to force the Soviets to choose between standing aside to watch their clients be defeated by Israel with American arms and intervening militarily on the Arab side, with the attendant risks of nuclear confrontation.

The trick would be to get a cease-fire at just the right moment. Until then, Israel should continue to advance on the ground, but, Kissinger felt, Israel must be prepared to stop once the superpowers reached agreement on a cease-fire. After all, the stakes were no longer confined to the Middle East; they were also global. If necessary, Kissinger was prepared to lean hard on the Israelis.

During his flight to Moscow Kissinger received two important messages. One informed him of the Saudi decision to embargo oil shipments to the United States. Another, from Nixon, was a message for Brezhnev in which Nixon made it clear that Kissinger had full authority to negotiate. Kissinger claims that he resented this unusual procedure, since it deprived him of the tactic of saying that he would have to refer to Washington for final decisions.[61] At the time Kissinger was unaware of the depth of the domestic crisis surrounding Nixon. The appeals court had ruled against Nixon on his bid to withhold nine Watergate tapes. The special prosecutor, Archibald Cox, was requesting tapes that Nixon did not want released, so he decided to fire Cox. However, Attorney General Elliot Richardson and his deputy, William Ruckelshaus, refused to carry out Nixon's orders to dismiss Cox, preferring instead to resign. All these events culminated in the "Saturday night massacre," just as Kissinger's first talks with Brezhnev were getting under way in the Kremlin.[62] Little wonder that Nixon had decided to leave the cease-fire negotiations to Kissinger.[63]

The crucial U.S.-Soviet talks began in Moscow on October 21 at about 11:00 a.m. and lasted only four hours. The Soviets, who had initially tried to link a cease-fire to some type of call for Israeli withdrawal from all Arab territory and to guarantees by the superpowers, were swift to change their negotiating position. Time was at a premium, and their client's position was in jeopardy. Ultimately Brezhnev agreed to a simple cease-fire in place, together with a call for the implementation of Security Council Resolution 242, and, at American insistence, also agreed to negotiations between the parties under appropriate auspices.[64] In addition, both sides agreed that they would serve as cochairmen of an eventual peace conference and that prisoners should be immediately exchanged by the parties after the cease-fire.

By noon, Washington time, on October 21 the United States and the Soviet Union had agreed upon the text of a cease-fire resolution. It was now up to Kissinger to persuade Israel to accept it. In mid-afternoon Alexander Haig, now serving as Nixon's chief of staff, telephoned Ambassador Dinitz with the proposed text of the resolution. Dinitz was told that time was short and that no changes could be made. The Security

Council would meet that evening. Dinitz was given a message from President Nixon to Prime Minister Meir asking that she immediately agree to the resolution. Arms would continue to flow to Israel. Dinitz immediately called Meir with the text of the resolution and Nixon's message. She was irritated that she had not been consulted in advance and was now being confronted with a fait accompli. At about 8:00 p.m., Washington time, Meir reportedly tried calling Nixon direct to seek a delay in the cease-fire, but she did not get through to him.[65] At 9:00 p.m., shortly before the UN Security Council was to convene, the Israeli cabinet decided to accept the cease-fire resolution. In her message informing Nixon of Israel's decision, Meir requested that Kissinger stop in Tel Aviv on his return from Moscow for consultations.

At 10:00 p.m. the Security Council met. Two hours and fifty minutes later, at 12:50 a.m. October 22, it adopted Resolution 338 (see appendix A). Within twelve hours the fighting was to stop on all fronts.

Kissinger left Moscow on the morning of October 22 for Tel Aviv,[66] where he arrived at 12:45 p.m., Middle East time (6:45 a.m., Washington time). The cease-fire was still not in effect, but in his talks with Meir, Kissinger was insistent that Israel move into defensive positions and not violate the cease-fire. He later claimed that he was very tough with the Israelis on this point, and that Prime Minister Meir, Defense Minister Dayan, and Foreign Minister Eban, if not the Israeli military, agreed that Israel had nothing further to gain from fighting.[67] Kissinger emphasized that the resolution called for the first time for negotiations between Israel and the Arabs. He also assured Meir that there were no secret U.S.-Soviet understandings. Resolution 242 remained as ambiguous as ever as a guideline for the subsequent diplomacy. Israel's bargaining position was not being undercut in advance. Arms would continue to be sent. Kissinger left Israel five hours after his arrival with a feeling that Israel would abide by the cease-fire.[68] One hour after his departure, at 6:50 p.m., Middle East time, the guns fell silent, but not for long.

TOWARD CONFRONTATION

With the achievement of the cease-fire on October 22, Nixon and Kissinger had reason to feel satisfied. A long and dangerous crisis had been brought to an end without a U.S.-Soviet military confrontation. The parties to the conflict had each made some gains to offset their heavy losses, so perhaps the prospects for peace negotiations would be good. Even the oil embargo seemed manageable, if irritating.

Soon after he reached his office on Tuesday morning, October 23, Kissinger was contacted by the Soviets with charges that Israel was violating the cease-fire.[69] Kissinger was worried. He had sensed the bitterness among the Israeli military at being deprived of victory. He had assured the Soviets that Israel would respect the cease-fire; hence when he called Dinitz to report the Soviet charges, he made it clear that Israel should not try to destroy the nearly surrounded Egyptian Third Army Corps.

From the onset of the crisis Kissinger had realized that American credibility with the Arabs might ultimately be tested in circumstances like these. If the United States were now to stand idly by and watch the Third Army Corps be destroyed with newly delivered American weapons, Kissinger's future role as peacemaker would be gravely jeopardized. It did not now matter which side was technically responsible for firing the first shot after the cease-fire was to have gone into effect. What was clear was that Israeli forces were advancing beyond the October 22 cease-fire lines. Despite his concern, however, Kissinger was not yet unduly alarmed.

During the afternoon of October 23 the UN Security Council passed Resolution 339, calling for immediate cessation of hostilities, a return to positions occupied on October 22 when the cease-fire went into effect, and the dispatch of UN observers to supervise the cease-fire on the Egyptian-Israeli front. Syria had still not accepted the cease-fire but finally did so later that evening.

Wednesday, October 24, began for Kissinger with a series of exchanges with the Egyptians, Israelis, and Soviets. Sadat was now in frequent communication with Nixon, even on small matters.[70] He asked for the president's help in getting the Israelis to allow medical and food supplies through to the nearly entrapped Third Army Corps. He requested that a U.S. military attaché from Tel Aviv proceed to the front lines to verify Israel's observance of the cease-fire. Kissinger was prepared to cooperate. He called Dinitz and requested that Israel respect the cease-fire and allow supplies through to the Third Army Corps.[71]

At 10:20 a.m. Kissinger met with the WSAG. He expressed his feeling that the United States was now in the "catbird seat. Everyone is looking to us." But he would not act under the threat of the Arab oil embargo. Egypt, he thought, understood this point and would be helpful. The next phase would involve direct Arab-Israeli negotiations under U.S.-Soviet auspices.

In mid-afternoon word reached Washington that President Sadat had publicly appealed to the United States and the Soviet Union to send forces to the Middle East to oversee the cease-fire. The White House immediately issued a statement rejecting the idea of forces from the superpowers being sent to the area. Shortly thereafter Kissinger met with Dobrynin at the State Department to discuss the convening of a peace conference. They agreed on Geneva as the site and considered other procedural matters. Dobrynin denied that the Soviets were interested in sending a joint U.S.-Soviet force to the Middle East in response to Sadat's appeal. The meeting ended on a cordial note, and there was no hint of impending crisis.[72]

Three hours later, at 7:05 p.m., Dobrynin called Kissinger to tell him that the Soviets would support the idea of a joint U.S.-Soviet peacekeeping force if the nonaligned members of the UN were to call for one, and shortly thereafter called again to say the Soviets were considering introducing such a resolution. These messages caused deep concern in Washington. Then, at 9:35 p.m. Dobrynin called Kissinger with a "very urgent" message from Brezhnev to Nixon. He slowly read the text over the telephone. It began by noting that Israel was continuing to violate the cease-fire, thus posing a challenge to both the United States and the Soviet Union. Brezhnev stressed the need to "implement" the cease-fire resolution and "invited" the United States to join Moscow "to compel observance of the cease-fire without delay." Then came the threat: "I will say it straight that if you find it impossible to act jointly with us in this matter, we should be faced with the necessity urgently to consider the question of taking appropriate steps unilaterally. We cannot allow arbitrariness on the part of Israel."[73] Kissinger quickly relayed the message to Haig for Nixon. The president's records show that he spoke to Haig for about twenty minutes around 10:30 p.m. That was his only communication with his advisers until the next morning. Nixon reportedly empowered Kissinger to take any necessary action, including calling a military alert.[74] Kissinger then convened an ad hoc session of the National Security Council, which at that point consisted only of himself and the secretary of defense as ex-officio members. In addition, Colby, Moorer, Haig, Scowcroft, and Jonathan Howe, Kissinger's military assistant, participated in the deliberations.

Unquestionably the situation was dangerous. No one knew what the Soviet Union intended to do, but Brezhnev's note unmistakably conveyed his determination not to let Israel destroy the Egyptian Third Army

Corps. Kissinger understood the difficulty of the situation for the Soviets and the pressures they would be under to act. Their prestige as a superpower was on the line. This was something with which Kissinger could empathize. But did the Soviets have the capability to intervene, whatever their intentions? The answer seemed definitely to be yes. The transport aircraft that had been flying arms to the Middle East had all returned to the Soviet Union and could be used as troop carriers. At least seven airborne divisions were on a high state of alert.[75] Two amphibious landing craft were in the eastern Mediterranean with the Soviet squadron.

Even though a massive Soviet intervention was still hard to imagine, even with this combination of motives and capabilities, Moscow might yet resort to impressive displays of military power that could have explosive political, and perhaps even military, consequences. For example, a small "peacekeeping" contingent might be sent to deliver supplies to the entrapped Third Army Corps. Would the Israelis fire on Soviet forces in such circumstances? If so, the Soviets might feel compelled to react on a larger scale. If not, Soviet prestige would have gained a significant boost, precisely at a critical moment in U.S.-Arab relations.

Kissinger and the other participants in the NSC meeting reached two conclusions. The Soviets, who had seemingly not taken seriously U.S. warnings about the introduction of their forces into the area, must be under no illusion that the United States did not have the will and the ability to react to any move they might make. To underline this ability, U.S. military forces would be placed on a Def Con 3 alert, which meant that leaves would be canceled and an enhanced state of readiness would be observed. The Strategic Air Command would be on a higher state of alert than the normal Def Con 4. No change would be needed for the Sixth Fleet, which was already on a stage 3 alert. Although considerably short of a decision to go on a war footing, these visible moves should convey to the Soviets the American determination to act if necessary. If the crisis was quickly resolved, it would be easy to change the alert status.[76]

As had been true earlier in the crisis, Kissinger was concerned that the Watergate scandal not appear to impede the conduct of American foreign policy. Intentional overreaction would be better than underreaction. To underscore the meaning of the alert, Kissinger sent a message to Brezhnev in Nixon's name saying that the sending of Soviet troops to the Middle East would be considered a violation of article 2 of the agreement on the prevention of nuclear war of June 22, 1973.

Before the Soviet threat of intervention, Kissinger and his colleagues had felt that Israel must stop its advances on the Egyptian front. The Israelis had been told in no uncertain terms that the United States would not permit the destruction of the Third Army Corps.[77] But the Soviet threat introduced a new element, and apparently Kissinger signaled to the Israelis that they should be prepared to move against the Third Army if Soviet troops tried to intervene.[78]

Around midnight the first orders for the alert were issued, and at 1:30 a.m. on October 25 its scope was widened. Nixon had not participated in the deliberations of the NSC, but he had reportedly given his approval for the alert in advance.[79] Now the United States would await the Soviet reaction.

During the morning of October 25, while most Americans were first learning of the alert and wondering about its meaning, Kissinger met with Nixon for a long talk.[80] Several new bits of information were now available. Further messages had been received from Sadat, denying that Egypt was violating the cease-fire and emphasizing again that U.S. and Soviet forces were needed to enforce the cease-fire. Moreover, several ships from the Soviet squadron, including the amphibious landing craft, were steaming toward Egypt. A fragmentary piece of intelligence had been received referring to the imminent arrival of Soviet troops in Cairo. In fact, these proved to be the seventy observers and their interpreters that the Soviets did send to Cairo, but at the time the number was unknown. All in all, the Soviets seemed to be moving toward a confrontation, and the Egyptians seemed to be encouraging it. The president ordered Kissinger to develop a plan for sending U.S. troops to the Middle East in case the Soviets did intervene. Doing so would, at a minimum, provide some leverage to get the Soviet troops out of the region after the crisis subsided. Nixon also told Kissinger to hold a press conference explaining the U.S. moves.

At 10:15 a.m. Kissinger convened the WSAG once again and explained the steps leading to the crisis and the president's latest instructions. Kissinger was worried by the behavior of the Soviets, who did not seem interested in finding a solution and were instead exploiting the situation. Schlesinger suggested that they might be genuinely fearful of a collapse on the Egyptian front and might even suspect American duplicity in urging the Israelis on. The meeting ended at 10:50, with Kissinger requesting a contingency plan for sending U.S. forces to the Middle East, including Arab countries if possible.

Shortly after noon Kissinger appeared before the press in the State Department auditorium. In a somber but restrained tone he described the various stages of the crisis and the evolution of U.S. policy. It was a brilliant performance, one of his most impressive.

After reviewing the diplomatic efforts of the first two weeks of the crisis, he spoke of the cease-fire and the alert. In the president's name he reiterated U.S. opposition to the sending of U.S.-Soviet forces to the Middle East. He was even more strongly opposed to a unilateral Soviet move into the area. He then reviewed the prospects for a peace settlement, which he termed "quite promising," and had conciliatory words for Israel, the Arabs, and even the Soviets. Afterward he took questions.

In response to several questions about U.S.-Soviet détente, Kissinger emphasized the complex adversarial nature of the relationship, but he refused to condemn the Soviets for violating the spirit of détente. Asked whether the alert had been called because of the American domestic crisis, Kissinger, more in sorrow than in anger, dismissed the idea, although he went on to say that the Soviets might have acted as boldly as they did because of the weakened position of the American president. "One cannot have crises of authority in a society for a period of months without paying a price somewhere along the line."

In his concluding remarks Kissinger spelled out the principles of a new American policy toward the Arab-Israeli conflict:

Our position is that . . . the conditions that produced this war were clearly intolerable to the Arab nations and that in the process of negotiations it will be necessary to make substantial concessions.

The problem will be to relate the Arab concern for the sovereignty over the territories to the Israeli concern for secure boundaries.

We believe that the process of negotiations between the parties is an essential component of this. And as the President has stated to the four Arab Foreign Ministers, and as we have stated repeatedly, we will make a major effort to bring about a solution that is considered just by all parties. But I think no purpose would be served by my trying to delimit the exact nature of all of these provisions.[81]

One hour later the UN Security Council passed Resolution 340, calling for an immediate and complete cease-fire, return to the October 22 lines, dispatch of an augmented UN observer force, creation of a UN Emergency Force composed of nonpermanent members of the Security Council, and implementation of Resolution 338. This time the cease-fire did take hold, and the fourth Arab-Israeli war finally ended. A new chapter in American diplomacy was about to open, with Kissinger as the star performer.

CONCLUSIONS

American policy toward the Arab-Israeli conflict was fundamentally affected by the events of the October 1973 war. Before the outbreak of hostilities it was widely believed in Washington that stability in the Middle East was ensured by Israeli military predominance; that Arab oil could not be effectively used to pressure the West; that Sadat was not seriously interested in a peace settlement with Israel; and that Soviet influence in the region had reached its limit. The situation in the area caused concern, but not anxiety. Diplomatic initiatives were contemplated, but not with a sense of urgency or with expectations of success.

It would be wrong to maintain that the United States shifted from a pro-Israeli to a pro-Arab policy as a result of the October war. The changes that did occur were more nuanced and multidimensional than the simple Arab-versus-Israel dichotomy suggests. The war did, however, challenge several basic assumptions of U.S. policymakers that had been central to prewar policy.

First, Israeli military power had not ensured stability, as had been expected after 1967. That "lesson," reinforced in the September 1970 crisis, was shattered on October 6. This did not mean, of course, that the military balance was seen as having no importance. The latter stages of the war clearly showed that military power counted for a great deal. Israeli strength alone, however, would not lead to a political settlement, as Johnson in 1967 had hoped it would.

Second, the October war undermined the belief that U.S.-Soviet détente would serve to minimize the danger of regional conflicts. Although Nixon, Kissinger, and Schlesinger all emphasized that détente had been helpful in resolving the crisis, they were acutely aware that the two superpowers had not been able to remain aloof from the Middle East conflict. Each side was too deeply committed to allow its friends to be sacrificed for the spirit of détente. Concrete local interests won out over global abstractions when put to the test. This meant not that détente was illusory or dangerous but rather that it was limited in scope. Superpower confrontation was still a possibility in the era of détente and negotiations, and this, above all, preoccupied the senior decisionmakers. The events of October 24–25 confirmed their worst fears.

Third, the war challenged the prevailing attitude of policymakers toward the Arab world. Despite the remarkable Israeli military achievements on both fronts, the Egyptians and Syrians had apparently fought quite well. They had also achieved surprise in the initial attack. Moreover, the degree of Arab solidarity was impressive; the use of the oil weapon was well coordinated with the diplomatic and military moves; and the tone of restraint in private and public communications was a welcome contrast to that of 1967. Sadat, in particular, was emphatic in his desire to work with Nixon and Kissinger for a post-hostilities diplomatic settlement. This was a very important new element in the picture.

Fourth, American officials, and Kissinger in particular, found themselves having to learn about petroleum economics as a part of international strategy. Kissinger had paid almost no attention to oil issues before the October crisis. He and others had a hard time distinguishing between the effects of the embargo, which was highly visible but not very important, and the curtailment of production, which sparked the dramatic price increases. Had Nixon and Kissinger been more sensitive to these issues, they might have been more discreet in their handling of the $2.2 billion aid package to Israel, announcing it after the war was over rather than in the midst of the battle. In any event, much of the subsequent diplomacy surrounding the Arab-Israeli conflict was played out under the shadow of the Arab oil weapon, which not only added a sense of urgency but also raised the specter of blackmail.

These changes in widely held beliefs did not all take place at once. Some came more readily than others. In particular, the reassessment of Egyptian policy began within three days after the outbreak of war. The initial call for a cease-fire based on the status quo ante, and the restraint in rearming Israel, were products of pre-war views—namely, that Israel would win a quick and fairly easy victory over incompetent Arab armies. Between October 9 and 13 these perceptions underwent steady modification, culminating in a revised position on both a cease-fire and arms for Israel. The new policies, which contributed to the cease-fire on October 22, resulted from a reordering of a few elements in the views of the decisionmakers, rather than from an entirely new appreciation of the situation. The Israelis were encountering more difficulties than anticipated; the Arabs were both more effective at arms and more skillful at diplomacy. These incremental changes in perception, combined with the reality of a prolonged and dangerous war, produced a shift in American policy that was both quantitative and qualitative.

The United States would henceforth devote much more attention to the Middle East. It would be a top-priority concern for Nixon and Kissinger. Moreover, the United States would consciously try to improve its relations with the principal Arab countries, especially Egypt. This effort would be a primary element in the new American diplomatic strategy, an element that had been conspicuously lacking before October 1973. Nixon and Kissinger felt they could court the Arabs without sacrificing the U.S.-Israeli relationship. In fact, as they saw it, it was the strength of the U.S.-Israeli tie, with the obvious influence this gave Washington over Israeli policy, that would impress the Arabs and convince them that the United States held most of the diplomatic cards once the fighting was over. The Soviets could provide arms; the United States could help regain territory, provided the Arabs were prepared to make appropriate concessions of their own in the context of peace negotiations.

The shift in policy brought about by the October war was at least as important as that produced by the Jordan crisis of 1970. The result of the earlier crisis had been an inactive, status quo–oriented policy; the result of the October 1973 crisis was a much more active approach aimed at bringing about substantial change. For the first time the United States committed its top diplomatic resources to a sustained search for a settlement of the Arab-Israeli conflict.

In view of the importance of the policy change during October 1973, one is tempted to seek explanations in domestic or bureaucratic politics, or in the psychological makeup of the individuals involved. After all, Watergate and the energy crisis were persistent themes throughout the crisis. And both Nixon and Kissinger had strong and unusual personalities.

Domestic politics is often linked in complex ways to foreign policy, and Nixon and Kissinger certainly took it into account as they considered policy choices. The key decisions of the crisis, however—the cease-fire proposals, the airlift to Israel, and the alert—were not responses to domestic politics. Pro-Israeli groups were not responsible for the decision to rearm Israel, largely because Kissinger skillfully persuaded the Israeli ambassador not to "unleash" Israel's supporters. Pro-Arab groups and oil companies played no role in Nixon's decision to press Israel to accept a cease-fire on October 12 or to save the Third Army Corps. Nor does Watergate explain the military alert of October 24–25.

Crisis periods, especially, tend to isolate policymakers from domestic pressures. Decisions are often made rapidly, before public opinion can be mobilized. Information is closely held, depriving interest groups of the means for effective action. The stakes are high, and the public tends to be deferential to presidential authority, even when that authority has been weakened, as Nixon's had been.

One theme did recur in Kissinger's comments: the rest of the world must not draw the conclusion that the Watergate crisis had weakened the president's ability to conduct foreign policy. The size of the U.S. airlift to Israel, once begun, the magnitude of the aid bill for arms to Israel, and the scope of the American military alert may have been partly related to this desire to appear strong and decisive. In each case, however, the basic decision was not rooted in the fear that Watergate had led other nations to underestimate the United States. Rather, the decisions were responses to external events that seemed to require urgent action. With or without the Watergate affair, the same course almost certainly would have been taken.

Other explanations of U.S. policy during the war have emphasized bureaucratic or personality factors. In some accounts Schlesinger and Deputy Defense Secretary William Clements are portrayed as opposing the airlift to Israel; in others, Kissinger is painted as responsible.[82] The reasons given may be institutional—military men resented seeing arms taken from active U.S. units and sent to Israel; they may be linked to economic interests—Clements had ties to the oil industry; or they may be traced to personality—Kissinger and Nixon had deluded themselves with the success of détente and therefore failed to appreciate the ways in which the Soviets were manipulating the situation to their advantage.

Those perspectives, however, do not account for the fact that individuals from widely different backgrounds agreed on each of the major decisions. Whatever their subsequent relationship, Kissinger and Schlesinger did not argue over basic policy in the October war. Whatever his personal feelings toward Israel, Clements helped organize a remarkably efficient airlift to Israel once the orders were given. Bureaucratic politics was barely in evidence, so tight was Kissinger's control over the policymaking machinery. Nor did the policy changes result from the replacement of individuals with one set of views by those of contrasting persuasions. The same officials were in place, with about the same relative power, before and after the war. The difference was that they now saw the situation differently.

The key to the consensus among top officials was the ability of Kissinger to draw on President Nixon's authority. On occasion Nixon directly gave orders, but even when he was not present, Kissinger was clearly speaking in his name. In the principal decisions the president was involved, although sometimes rather remotely. When Kissinger would say, "The president wants" or "The president has ordered," few of the other key officials were inclined to argue. Moreover, only Kissinger—and Haig, who often relayed Kissinger's views to the president and then reported back to his former boss—had direct, continuing access to the president.[83]

American policy during the October 1973 war demonstrated once again the centrality of the authority of the president in the conduct of foreign policy, particularly in crises. In this case, Kissinger must be considered an extension of the president, for he was given an unusual margin of responsibility. It was his tie to Nixon, however, not his position as secretary of state, that ensured the acceptance of his formulations. Perhaps if the policies had been less nuanced, less complex, there might have been some overt dissension within the bureaucracy. The Nixon-Kissinger policy, however, could be seen as pro-Israel, pro-Arab, pro-détente, or anti-Soviet, depending on what one was looking for. Those who disagreed with one element of policy were likely to support other aspects. This complexity left Kissinger in a commanding position.

As the crisis came to an end, the Middle East undoubtedly had top priority in American foreign policy. American relations with allies had been damaged by the crisis; détente was under attack; the energy crisis was likely to become more acute. Progress toward an Arab-Israeli settlement would not necessarily solve these problems, but failure to defuse the Middle East situation could only complicate them. Perhaps equally important, for the first time Nixon and Kissinger sensed the opportunity to make progress toward a settlement. The Arabs were looking to Washington now, not to Moscow. The Israelis were heavily dependent on American arms and financial support, which could be translated into influence in the proper diplomatic setting. Public opinion would be supportive of a major U.S. initiative provided it did not become anti-Israeli or appear to be responsive to the Arab oil embargo.

By the time the cease-fire had gone into effect, the United States was already preparing for a new diplomatic effort. It would not be like the Rogers Plan, formal, legalistic, and worked out in U.S.-Soviet negotiations. Instead, the Soviets would be kept out of the substance of the negotiations. Their record during the war had not inspired confidence that they were prepared to play an evenhanded role in settling the conflict. Nor did Sadat seem to want them involved. Furthermore, no American plan would be presented to the parties. Instead, the United States would try to play the role of mediator, eliciting propositions from the parties, trying then to modify them, and eventually pressing for a compromise. The process would move slowly, beginning with concrete issues of particular urgency and proceeding later to more fundamental problems, such as the nature of a final peace settlement. Above all, each step must remain independent of the next; otherwise the process would never get under way, as the United States had discovered in the interim-settlement effort of 1971.

As the war came to a close, Kissinger had already decided on his new strategy—step-by-step diplomacy. Now he merely needed to persuade Israel, the Arabs, the Soviets, Congress, and the American public to give him a chance to prove his success where others had failed. For the next six months Kissinger was accorded the opportunity to demonstrate both the strengths and limitations of his conception of how to solve the Arab-Israeli conflict.

CHAPTER EIGHT

Step by Step: Kissinger and the Disengagement Agreements, 1974

The eight months that followed the October 1973 war witnessed an un-precedented American involvement in the search for a settlement of the Arab-Israeli conflict. Henry Kissinger, before becoming secretary of state, had devoted little energy to the seemingly intractable issues dividing Israel and its Arab neighbors. Nor had he progressed far in his understanding of the "energy crisis" and the part played by Middle East oil in the international economy. Only the danger of confrontation between the superpowers growing out of tensions in the Middle East seemed capable of arousing in him a sustained interest in the affairs of the region. Now with the October war a vivid example of the volatility of the Arab-Israeli conflict, Kissinger, with Nixon's full backing, set out to become the peacemaker, orchestrator, mediator, and catalyst in a new diplomatic initiative that would take him repeatedly to countries he had never before visited to deal with statesmen he had previously not taken seriously.

Although President Nixon was eager for the United States to play an active part in resolving the Arab-Israeli conflict, he was also increasingly preoccupied with his crumbling domestic base of support as the Watergate scandal continued to unfold.[1] Kissinger was therefore allowed extraordi-nary latitude in shaping the details of American diplomacy, calling on Nixon to invoke presidential authority as necessary, keeping the president informed at each stage, and on occasion ignoring his directions.

Above all, Nixon wanted results. Internationally, he worried about the consequences of other nations concluding that the American domestic crisis had weakened the president's ability to act in foreign affairs. Domestically, he hoped that foreign-policy successes would help him through the crisis of confidence in his judgment and leadership stemming from his handling of Watergate.

SHAPING AN AMERICAN STRATEGY

During the October 1973 hostilities Kissinger and Nixon had both promised an active American diplomatic initiative aimed at "implementing

Resolution 242" after the war ended, but they steadfastly refused to promise any specific results, despite Sadat's pleas. The United States, they repeated, was committed to a process, not an outcome. The administration could guarantee that it would make a major effort, but it could not guarantee that Israel would withdraw from all Arab territory or that Palestinian rights would be restored. To do so would be to invite severe domestic criticism and to raise Arab hopes to an unrealistic level. Kissinger frequently mentioned that he feared the Arabs' "romanticism," their impatience, their desire for quick results.[2]

These initial perceptions, shaped by the October war, became the foundations of postwar policy. With the achievement of the shaky cease-fire of October 25, Nixon and Kissinger began to define what the contours of that policy would be. Two key elements quickly emerged. First, the United States would play an active role in trying to resolve the Arab-Israeli conflict. Unlike Johnson after 1967, and they themselves after 1970, Nixon and Kissinger now felt the situation in the Middle East was too threatening to American interests to be ignored; perhaps even more important, an opportunity for a successful American initiative existed.[3]

As Kissinger had sensed during the war, everyone was looking to the United States. He held the cards, or at least so the principal actors believed, which was what mattered. The Israelis, more isolated internationally than ever before, were in the awkward position of being heavily dependent on Washington for arms, economic aid, and diplomatic support. The Arabs, realizing the potential for U.S. influence with Israel, were anxious to turn that potential to their own advantage. As Kissinger and others had hinted, the Soviets could provide arms to the Arabs, but only the United States could produce Israeli territorial concessions through negotiations.[4]

Second, the new American strategy would try to avoid linking initial diplomatic steps with the nature of a final peace agreement. Kissinger had disliked the Rogers Plan of 1969 and was not even particularly keen on UN Resolution 242. Such public statements of principles might provide psychic gratification to one side or the other, but in his view they did little to advance the diplomatic process. Instead they allowed each side to focus on what it rejected in the abstract plan instead of concentrating on tangible issues in the present. If an active U.S. role in the diplomacy was meant as a signal to the Arabs of a more balanced American policy, Washington's refusal to link first steps with final outcomes was meant to reassure Israel that a settlement would not be imposed against its will.

To sustain an active and effective U.S. role in the evolving diplomacy of the Arab-Israeli conflict, Kissinger felt it necessary to mitigate the international pressures created by the October 1973 war. The Arab offensive had succeeded in mobilizing European, Japanese, and third world support for a rapid settlement on essentially Arab terms. The UN could be counted on to support Egypt, Syria, and the Palestinians. The Soviets were committed to the Arab position, even at some risk to détente and U.S.-Soviet relations. The Arab oil embargo was an added source of tension, as was the continuing danger that the cease-fire would break down.

Although he admired the way in which Sadat had succeeded in marshaling his forces, Kissinger was not prepared to act under these combined pressures. He would therefore try to persuade the American allies to leave him a free hand; he would isolate the Soviets from the substance of the negotiations; he would endeavor to get the oil embargo lifted; he would build support for "moderate" Arab positions at the expense of "radical" ones; he would try to avoid a public quarrel with Israel that might have serious domestic repercussions; and he would attempt to win over the U.S. Congress and press to support his role in the diplomacy. Much of Kissinger's tactical maneuvering in succeeding months was aimed at ensuring that the United States could act free of the multiple pressures, domestic and international, generated by the October war. On the whole, he was remarkably successful.

Kissinger felt previous administrations had erred in viewing their choices as being pro-Israel or pro-Arab. In his view it was precisely the special American relationship with Israel that obliged the Arabs to deal with the United States in the diplomatic arena. Power, not sentiment, was what counted. The difficulty, of course, was that to keep the Arabs looking toward the United States, the diplomatic process had to hold out more hope to them than would another round of war. If war was seen as the answer, the Soviet Union could always provide more than the United States. Consequently, progress toward a settlement was an absolute prerequisite for maintaining the confidence of the Arabs. At a minimum, this meant the return of territory, and eventually some move in the direction of addressing Palestinian grievances. For the United States, it meant that Israel would have to make concessions to keep the diplomacy alive. Where possible, the United States might try to extract comparable Arab concessions, but given the kind of issues, to do so would be difficult. An additional dimension of U.S. diplomacy would therefore be offers of aid to Israel—with the implied threat of withholding it if circumstances so dictated—and promises of assistance to Egypt, Syria, and Jordan to strengthen bilateral relations through other means than delivering Israeli concessions.

U.S.-Egyptian relations were seen as the linchpin of the new American policy in the Arab world, with Jordan and Saudi Arabia playing key supportive roles in favor of Arab "moderation."[5] Only gradually did Kissinger come to perceive Syria's importance; he was even more reluctant to acknowledge the Palestinians as participants in the settlement process. For the moment the new U.S.-Egyptian relationship, already in evidence during the war, was to receive most of Nixon's and Kissinger's attention.

The role of the Soviet Union in the Middle East had long preoccupied Nixon and Kissinger. Having at one time overrated Soviet influence in the Arab world, they were now inclined to minimize the Soviet role in the settlement process. Soviet behavior in the October war, though not viewed as totally contrary to the spirit of détente, was nonetheless not encouraging.[6] Nor had previous U.S.-Soviet efforts to reach agreement on the terms of settlement been successful. The two superpowers not only had different interests in the region but also had a different concept of what a peace settlement should entail. Perhaps most important of all, the key participants in the regional conflict were not anxious to see the Soviets deeply involved in the diplomacy. Certainly the Israelis were unenthusiastic, given Soviet hostility and the lack of diplomatic relations. Jordan was still prepared to work with the United States instead of with the Soviet Union. Sadat was also ready to play his American card, and Soviet-Egyptian relations suffered as a result. Even President Asad of Syria showed a willingness to let Kissinger try his hand, although his skepticism was considerably greater than Sadat's. Finally, there was enough of the cold warrior left in both Nixon and Kissinger to produce a sense of real pleasure in demonstrating the limits of Soviet influence in the Middle East.[7]

To maintain an effective American role in the resolution of the Arab-Israeli dispute, domestic public opinion would have to be mobilized. Most Americans were sympathetic to Israel, a sentiment that was particularly strong in Congress and in the press.[8] The Arab oil embargo was doing little to change this feeling; in fact, it seemed more likely that an anti-Arab backlash might result, making it difficult to pursue the policy of building the new ties to the Arab world that were central to the Nixon-Kissinger strategy. American policy could not appear to be dictated by Arab oil pressures. Domestically and internationally, that would be an untenable posture for the administration. Consequently the new diplomatic initiatives would have to be explained to the American public and to Congress in terms of the overall objective of seeking peace in the Middle East, of strengthening United States ties with the Arab world without sacrificing Israel, and of minimizing the ability of the Soviets to threaten Western interests, including oil. Broad support for these objectives could be expected, especially if aid to Israel continued to flow at high levels and if the oil embargo was lifted.

If an active United States diplomatic role in the search for an Arab-Israeli settlement was the first principle of the new American policy, the second was the pursuit of a settlement through a step-by-step process.[9] This method soon came to be the hallmark of the Kissinger diplomacy. Kissinger's negotiating experiences with the Chinese, the Vietnamese, and the Soviets had convinced him that the process of negotiation had a dynamic of its own.[10] It was important to create the proper balance of incentives first, and then to reach limited results at an early stage without making commitments to the final goal; eventually, when a mutuality of interests had emerged, more substantial areas of agreement would be possible. Kissinger was skeptical of the American penchant for the "quick fix," the technical solution to a political problem, of negotiations carried on in the blaze of publicity, of bureaucratic compromises, and of good will as a substitute for tangible concessions. Although he would later be charged with some of these mistakes in his own conduct of diplomacy, he was at least conscious of these pitfalls, the weakness of his own role as mediator, and the sizable gap that separated the parties. Unlike other negotiations he had engaged in, the Arab-Israeli arena was one in which the United States faced the challenge of persuading adversaries to make commitments to one another. It was not enough for the United States to develop its own policies; the key to success would be to induce the parties to modify their irreconcilable positions.

Timing would be an important element of the Kissinger step-by-step diplomacy. He envisaged negotiations probably going on for several years. The Arabs were pressing for immediate Israeli withdrawal; the Israelis were pleading for time. Kissinger was anxious to pace the negotiations so that some results could be produced at an early date, while still allowing time for all parties to adjust to a gradual, phased approach to a settlement. Most immediately, the Israelis had a national election scheduled for the end of December, and until then no serious negotiations could be expected. Somehow the Arabs would have to be persuaded to wait until early 1974 for the first Israeli withdrawals.

In the meantime it would be important to establish a negotiating framework, a forum that would provide the symbolic umbrella under which various diplomatic moves might be made. This forum would be a multilateral conference, with U.S. and Soviet participation, to be held at Geneva under UN auspices. Its primary value would be to legitimize the settlement process, give the Soviets enough of a sense of participation to prevent them from disrupting the peace effort, and provide a setting where agreements could be ratified, talks could be held, and delegations could meet. Kissinger fully expected, however, that progress toward agreements would not be made in such a cumbersome forum.

Instead of counting heavily on Geneva, Kissinger planned to deal with concrete issues through bilateral channels. Most urgent were the problems on the Egyptian-Israeli front. There the armies were entangled in a dangerous fashion, constantly tempting one side or the other to resume hostilities. The Egyptian Third Army Corps was nearly cut off from supplies, a situation that was intolerable for Sadat to accept. International pressure was building for Israel to pull back to the October 22 lines, which would release the Third Army. Prisoners of war had to be exchanged, an issue of very great sensitivity to the Israelis. The Egyptian semiblockade of Bab al-Mandab at the southern entrance of the Red Sea was preventing the movement of Israeli shipping to and from Aqaba. Taken together, these issues might be negotiated in a first step that would stabilize the cease-fire through a "disengagement" of military forces.

The conceptual underpinnings of the new American policy in the Middle East, initially forged in the midst of the October war, were quickly established. Nixon and Kissinger, with virtually no opposition from the bureaucracy, were committing the United States to an unprecedented active role in mediating the Arab-Israeli conflict, to a step-by-step diplomatic process, and to a disengagement of Egyptian-Israeli military forces at an early date.

SETTING THE STAGE

One result of the improved relationship between Cairo and Washington was President Sadat's frequent and urgent appeals to the United States to help the entrapped Third Army Corps. The Israelis, by contrast, were determined to use pressure on the corps to obtain the release of prisoners of war and the end of the naval blockade at Bab al-Mandab. The stalemate threatened to destroy the precarious cease-fire. Kissinger therefore quickly set two urgent goals: first, to stabilize the cease-fire; second, to bring about a separation of military forces. By October 27 the State Department was able to announce that Egyptian and Israeli representatives had agreed to meet to implement the cease-fire agreement. Even before the talks began on October 30, temporary arrangements had been made for the nonmilitary resupply of the Third Army Corps.

The Egyptian and Israeli positions on the terms of a cease-fire and on a military disengagement proved to be far apart. Ismail Fahmy, Egypt's new foreign minister, met with Kissinger on October 29.[11] Two days later he again met Kissinger, as well as President Nixon. Besides discussing the secretary's forthcoming trip to Egypt, Fahmy was authorized to present an eleven-point proposal. Most urgently, Egypt insisted that Israel withdraw unconditionally to the October 22 lines, as called for in UN Resolutions 339 and 340. Once that was done, Egypt would agree to release all prisoners of war. Then Israel should withdraw to a line inside Sinai that would lie east of the passes, and Egyptian forces would remain in place. UN forces would man a zone between Egyptian and Israeli forces. The blockade of Bab al-Mandab would be lifted once Israeli forces began to withdraw toward the disengagement zone, and the clearing of the Suez Canal would begin after this stage was completed. Within an agreed time period Israel would withdraw in one more step to the international frontier, at which point the state of belligerency would end. Similar steps should be planned for Syria, and a peace conference should be convened during the implementation of the disengagement phase. Finally, U.S.-Egyptian diplomatic relations would be restored at an early date.

Kissinger told Fahmy that the plan contained constructive ideas but that it seemed too ambitious at that stage. In discussions during the next two days, Kissinger raised the issue of the October 22 lines, emphasizing that it would be difficult to persuade Israel to withdraw to them and that a broader step as part of the disengagement of forces would make the October 22 lines irrelevant in any case.[12] Reflecting the new tone in U.S.-Egyptian relations, President Sadat, in a speech delivered on October 31, termed the American role "constructive."

Kissinger and Nixon then talked with Prime Minister Meir, who arrived in Washington on October 31. Kissinger met with her on the morning of November 1.[13] She was particularly concerned about the fate of Israeli prisoners in Egypt. Continued resupply of the Third Army

Corps, she argued, was conditional upon the return of wounded prisoners of war (POWs), a complete list of all prisoners, and Red Cross visits to them. Israel would agree to a permanent nonmilitary supply of the Third Army Corps once the prisoners were returned and the naval blockade was lifted. Only then would Israel agree to talk to Egypt about the October 22 lines. Kissinger was authorized to convey these terms to Sadat, with the understanding that the United States would not take a position on the location of the October 22 lines and would not pressure Israel on this issue, leaving it instead to negotiations between the two parties.

Shortly after noon, President Nixon met with Prime Minister Meir. Nixon offered the opinion that Sadat really wanted peace and then laid out the American strategy for the months ahead. He would try to break up the problems so they could be dealt with step by step. The United States would stand up to the Soviets, as it had done in the October war. It would try to improve its relations with Egypt and Syria, which would also help Israel. Nixon's goal would be to ensure "secure borders" for Israel. Meir was undemonstrative, emphasizing only that Israel did not want to be pressed on the October 22 lines. That evening Kissinger dined with Meir and a few others. The atmosphere was chilly, if not hostile. The Israeli prime minister barely spoke to Kissinger, and when she did, her tone was reserved. There was no expression of gratitude for U.S. aid, only anger at being deprived of victory by "friends." No toasts were drunk.

The following morning Kissinger convened a meeting of the WSAG. Still incensed over the previous day's talks with the Israelis, he implied that Israeli leaders had deliberately misled him on several occasions during the war. Now, Kissinger said, U.S. foreign policy would be determined by the United States, not Israel. By working for a moderate peace proposal, the United States would reduce Soviet influence and end the oil embargo. If this effort failed, the Arabs would be driven back to the Soviets, the oil crisis would worsen, and the United States and Israel would be isolated internationally. The Arabs must see that they would be better off dealing with the United States than with the Soviet Union. Kissinger expressed the view that Egypt's position on accepting a nonmilitary resupply of the Third Army Corps and an exchange of POWs once Israel returned to the October 22 lines was reasonable. If necessary, Israel would be forced to accept it. Eventually the tone of the discussion moderated, but Kissinger's anger at Israeli intransigence was genuine and would be displayed repeatedly in succeeding months.[14]

KILOMETER 101

With these initial talks behind him, Kissinger set off for the Middle East on November 5. His first stop, which also marked his first visit to an Arab country, was in Morocco, partly to symbolize the long tradition of friendly U.S.-Arab relations, and partly to open channels through King Hassan to Syria and the Palestinians.[15] Cairo, not Rabat, however, was the real goal of Kissinger's travels. There, on November 7, he met President Sadat for the first time. In private talks that day Kissinger began to develop a genuine admiration for the Egyptian leader.[16] The turning point came in discussing the issue of the October 22 lines. Kissinger was in an awkward position, for he knew the Israelis could not easily be pressured and yet he felt Sadat was right that Israeli forces should not be allowed to keep the Third Army Corps at their mercy. By the time Kissinger arrived in Cairo, the Israeli cabinet had approved the positions presented to Kissinger by Prime Minister Meir on November 3. He was thus able to tell Sadat that Israel would respect the cease-fire; that nonmilitary resupply of the Third Army Corps would be allowed, with UN and Israeli inspection of convoys; and that the town of Suez would receive food, water, and medicine. Concurrently with the agreement on nonmilitary supplies, POWs should be exchanged and the naval blockade lifted, and the October 22 lines could be discussed in the framework of the disengagement of forces. Israel had also said that in exchange for the POWs in Syria, Syrian civilians could return to areas controlled by Israel and two outposts on Mt. Hermon could be transferred to the United Nations.

Sadat was prepared to accept most of these points, although he was still anxious for Israel to pull back to the October 22 lines. Kissinger replied that if Egypt insisted, he would agree to try to persuade the Israelis. But he offered his opinion that it might be just as easy, although it might take more time, to work out a substantial disengagement of forces that would bypass the issue of the October 22 lines. Meanwhile arrangements could be made to resupply the Third Army Corps. To Kissinger's surprise Sadat agreed with this line of argument. He urged Kissinger to strive to obtain rapid agreement on the Israeli points. At the conclusion of the talks they agreed that diplomatic relations between Egypt and the United States would be restored "in principle" immediately.[17]

Kissinger promptly decided to send two of his aides, Joseph Sisco and Harold Saunders, to Israel to work out the details of an accord. Upon learning that Sadat had agreed to drop the issue of the October 22 lines, the prime minister termed this a "fantastic achievement," but she quickly found fault with the Egyptian position. Sadat did not want Israel to control the road used to supply the Third Army Corps, nor was he prepared to acknowledge publicly that Egypt would lift the naval blockade. After several rounds of discussion on these two points, Israel agreed to accept United States assurances that the blockade would be ended. On November 9 agreement on a cease-fire plan and the exchange of POWs was announced, and two days later a six-point agreement modeled on the original Israeli proposal was signed by Israeli and Egyptian military representatives at a point along the Cairo to Suez road known as Kilometer 101.[18] The settlement process was off to a start, albeit a shaky one.

Meanwhile Kissinger flew to Jordan to talk with King Hussein, and encouraged the king to participate in the peace negotiations. Without making firm commitments, he expressed sympathy with the king's opposition to a West Bank Palestinian state dominated by the Palestine Liberation Organization. For the moment, however, Kissinger was still concentrating on the Egyptian-Israeli front. Jordan and the Palestinians would be left for later.

In Saudi Arabia Kissinger appealed to King Faisal for support of his diplomatic effort, referring to the oil embargo as an obstacle to the American efforts.[19] He argued the logic of the step-by-step approach and appealed to Faisal for help in opening channels of communication with the Syrians.[20] Faisal gave Kissinger his standard rendition of the Zionist-communist conspiracy but also promised some help, including an easing of the oil embargo once progress began on Israeli withdrawal.[21]

On balance, Kissinger felt pleased with the results of his first trip. He had established a personal relationship with Sadat, and U.S.-Egyptian relations seemed off to a good start. The cease-fire had been stabilized. An important agreement had been signed by Israel and Egypt, with American help. Faisal had promised to relax the oil embargo. Now it was necessary to develop the broad negotiating framework at Geneva as a prelude to disengagement talks. Kissinger was in no rush, being still committed to a gradual pace under close U.S. control.

THE GENEVA CONFERENCE

The first Egyptian and Israeli prisoners were exchanged on November 15. The next day General Aharon Yariv of Israel and General Abd al-Ghany Gamasy of Egypt began talks at Kilometer 101 aimed at implementing the six-point agreement, particularly its second point, concerning "return to October 22 lines in the framework of agreement on the disengagement and separation of forces." On November 18 Kissinger reminded Foreign Minister Fahmy that disengagement should be the first order of business at the upcoming Geneva peace conference, but it could not become a precondition for the convening of the conference. Nor could the issue of Palestinian participation in the peace conference be settled at this stage. Only at the peace conference would the United States be able to use its full influence. In short, Kissinger was trying to build up Geneva as an important step in the process of negotiations and to keep the U.S. role central to substantive progress.

Meanwhile Israeli and Egyptian positions were being discussed at Kilometer 101. Israel initially proposed that both sides should pull back from territory gained in the October war and that UN forces should take over those areas. The Egyptian reply was to insist that Egyptian forces would stay in place and that Israeli forces should withdraw to a line running from Al-Arish to Ras Muhammad in the southern tip of Sinai. Gamasy then proposed Israeli withdrawal in a more modest disengagement phase to the vicinity of the Mitla and Giddi passes, with designated zones for both the Egyptian and the Israeli main forces, lightly armed forces, and a UN buffer between them. On November 22 General Yariv replied that Israel would withdraw from the west bank of the canal provided Egyptian forces on the east bank were thinned out.[22]

Negotiations continued for several days, with Israel offering deeper withdrawals in return for a substantial reduction of Egyptian armored strength. On November 26 Yariv suggested that Israel would even withdraw east of the passes if Egypt would reduce its level of armor in Sinai to token strength. Egypt showed interest in the proposal but insisted on mutual force reductions; then on November 29 Gamasy discovered that Yariv had gone back to his original proposal that both sides should withdraw from territory gained in the war. This reversal of position angered the Egyptians and led to the breakdown of the talks.

Kissinger has been charged with responsibility for aborting this promising experiment in direct Egyptian-Israeli negotiations.[23] There is some truth in the charge. Kissinger felt the talks were proceeding too rapidly. He was beginning to think of the Syrian front, and feared that if Egypt and Israel reached a disengagement agreement before Geneva, Asad would insist on the same, which might mean an indefinite delay in convening the Geneva conference. Then, too, Kissinger wanted to demonstrate that a U.S. role was essential for sustained diplomatic progress. Perhaps Egypt and Israel could reach agreement without his help, but would the same be true when it came to Syria, the Palestinians, or even a second Egyptian step? He doubted it. If the oil embargo was to be lifted, which Nixon was very keen on, that would also be in return for American success in promoting agreement.[24] And if Soviet prestige was to remain low, the United States must remain in control of the negotiations. Kissinger therefore advised the Israelis to slow down at Kilometer 101 and to withhold their position on disengagement until Geneva. To some observers, the suggestion seemed cynical, but it fitted into Kissinger's broader diplomatic scheme. And it should be added that Israel did not resist this piece of advice, as it so often did on other occasions. In retrospect, it appears as if General Yariv was considerably ahead of the Israeli cabinet in his willingness to offer concessions in the disengagement stage.[25]

Kissinger now turned his attention to organizing the Geneva conference.[26] On December 6 he announced it was "extremely probable" that a conference would be convened at Geneva on December 18. But who would attend? Egypt would go, and Sadat had implied that Syria would go as well.[27] Jordan could be counted on, but since the Arab summit meeting in Algiers the previous month the PLO had been recognized by all Arab countries except Jordan as the sole legitimate representative of the Palestinian people. If the PLO attended the Geneva conference, Israel would not, nor would Israel sit with Syria unless a list of Israeli prisoners held in Syria was forthcoming.

To help overcome Israeli reluctance to attend the conference, Kissinger talked to Defense Minister Dayan in Washington on December 7. Dayan presented a long list of arms requests, and Kissinger implied that the United States would give it favorable consideration. In return, Dayan said disengagement need not await Israeli elections. He proposed a disengagement based on Israeli withdrawal to a line west of the passes, combined with substantial demilitarization of forward areas and an Egyptian commitment to reopen the Suez Canal. Once again, however,

Kissinger urged the Israelis not to move too quickly in negotiations. Israel should not look weak. The Arabs should believe it was difficult for the United States to influence Israel; otherwise their expectations would soar.

Kissinger set off on his second trip to the Middle East on December 12, stopping in London en route to deliver an important speech.[28] He proceeded to Algiers for talks with President Houari Boumedienne and was successful in gaining his support for the Geneva conference. Boumedienne would thereafter be kept well informed on the peace negotiations, for Kissinger believed Algeria's endorsement of his strategy would make it easier for both Sadat and Asad to resist radical Arab pressures.

During the next several days Kissinger traveled to Cairo, Riyadh, Damascus, and Tel Aviv. Only the talks with Sadat were devoid of difficulty. Sadat had already accepted a short delay in opening the Geneva conference, and he now agreed to postpone the substantive phase of disengagement negotiations until mid-January, after the Israeli elections.[29] With King Faisal the next day, December 14, Kissinger won Saudi endorsement for Sadat's approach and a promise that the oil embargo would be ended and production restored once agreement had been reached on the first stage of a settlement.

While Kissinger was lining up support for Geneva among key Arab countries, Israel was making its participation in a peace conference conditional on a number of important points. Israel opposed a strong role for the UN secretary general, it refused to discuss the issue of eventual Palestinian participation at the conference, as Sadat had proposed, and Israel's representatives would not sit in the same room with the Syrians until Syria complied with Israeli demands for a list of POWs and Red Cross visits to them. It began to appear that Israel might boycott Geneva.

At this point Nixon and Kissinger began to exert heavy pressure on Israel. At 6:45 p.m. on December 13 in Washington, Israeli Minister Mordechai Shalev was handed a letter from Nixon to Meir. She had objected to the draft of a joint U.S.-USSR letter to the UN secretary general on convening the Geneva conference. Nixon said he was disturbed by her attitude and denied that the UN secretary general would have more than a symbolic role. Regarding the Palestinians, Nixon argued that the mention of Palestinian participation in the conference did not prejudice the outcome and that, in any case, the participation of additional members of the conference would require the agreement of all the initial participants. In short, Israel would not be forced to negotiate with the

Palestinians. Nixon concluded his letter by warning the prime minister that the United States would not understand Israel's refusal to attend the conference and that he would no longer be able to justify support for Israel if Israel did not send its representatives to Geneva.[30]

The next day, on learning that the Israeli cabinet had not been able to reach a decision on attending Geneva, Nixon sent another message. The United States was prepared to delay the conference to December 21. Nixon referred to Israel's long-standing goal of negotiations with the Arabs, terming it inconceivable that Israel would not now take this step. In any event, the president had ordered Kissinger to attend the opening session of the Geneva conference whether Israel was present or not.[31]

While an effort was being made to obtain Israeli agreement to the Geneva conference through a combination of pressures and promises,[32] Kissinger set off for his first meeting with Syria's president, Hafiz al-Asad.[33] Kissinger found Asad to be intelligent, tough, personable, and possessed of a sense of humor. He was also the least conciliatory of all the Arab leaders Kissinger had met to date. Asad implied that he did not object to the convening of the Geneva conference on December 21 but that Syria would not attend unless a disengagement-of-forces agreement was reached first. And disengagement, he thought, should involve the entire Golan Heights. Nor was he prepared to yield to Kissinger's pleas to turn over a list of Israeli POWs. After six and one-half hours of talks with Asad, Kissinger left for Israel empty-handed.[34]

During the next two days, December 16 and 17, Kissinger used all his persuasive abilities to convince the Israelis they should attend the Geneva conference. He met with Golda Meir alone and with members of her cabinet, painting for them a grim picture of the consequences of a breakdown in the diplomatic process. Much more than the Middle East was at stake. Global stability, international economic order, the coherence of the NATO alliance, and virtually every other major issue in world politics was linked to Israel's decision. During a private dinner with most of the Israeli cabinet at Foreign Minister Eban's house on December 16, Kissinger was at his most persuasive.[35] The Israelis held out for one more change in the letter of invitation—no mention of the Palestinians by name—and, subject to that condition, the cabinet met late at night to approve of Israel's attending the Geneva conference on December 21.

Kissinger now made one last try to obtain Syrian attendance. In return for a list of POWs, Israel would allow Syrian villagers to return to their homes in Israeli-controlled areas. Egypt's foreign minister, Fahmy, discussed the proposal with Asad at Kissinger's request, and the American ambassador in Beirut traveled to Damascus to take up the matter again with the Syrian leader. On December 18 Kissinger received Asad's reply, to the effect that Syria would not attend this phase of the Geneva talks but might participate later.[36]

On December 21 the Geneva conference finally convened under the auspices of the UN secretary general, with the United States and the Soviet Union as cochairmen, and with the foreign ministers of Egypt, Jordan, and Israel in attendance. A table with Syria's nameplate on it remained unoccupied. Each foreign minister spoke, but largely for the public back home, not for one another. Kissinger tried to articulate his step-by-step strategy, stating that the goal of the conference was peace but that the urgent need was to strengthen the cease-fire by accomplishing a disengagement of forces as the "essential first step" on the path of implementing UN Resolution 242.

With these formal remarks the Geneva conference recessed, not to be convened in plenary session again for an indefinite period. A symbol now existed, however, a useful fiction perhaps, and a forum where working groups might discuss aspects of a settlement was available if needed. The endeavor had not all been in vain, but one might wonder if the results were commensurate with the effort.

EGYPTIAN-ISRAELI DISENGAGEMENT

Having successfully convened the Geneva conference, Kissinger now faced the challenge of producing early results on the Egyptian-Israeli front. Several related problems stood in his way. The Syrians were on a high level of military alert in late December, and a resumption of fighting seemed possible. The oil embargo was continuing, and, equally important, the Organization of Petroleum Exporting Countries (OPEC) had decided to double oil prices on December 23. The fact that the shah of Iran played the leading role in the price rise did not make it any more palatable. More than ever, the energy crisis hung over the Arab-Israeli negotiations.

Apart from difficulties with Syria and the frustration of the continuing oil embargo, Kissinger had to confront again the fact that the positions of Egypt and Israel on disengagement were still far apart. In Israel on December 17 he had discussed disengagement with Meir and her top aides. The Israeli position was that a small Egyptian force would be allowed to remain on the east bank of the canal up to a distance of ten kilometers. A lightly armed Israeli force would control the main north-south road beyond the Egyptian forces, and the Israeli main forces would be stationed east of the Mitla and Giddi passes, beyond Egyptian artillery range. Israel would not yield the passes in the disengagement phase. On other points there was less Israeli consensus. Some cabinet members felt Egypt should end the state of belligerency in return for the pullback of Israeli forces and should allow free passage for Israeli ships in the Suez Canal and at Bab al-Mandab. Some limits on Egyptian forces on both banks of the Suez Canal were also desired. Egypt should begin work on reopening the canal and rebuilding cities along it as a sign of peaceful intentions.

Egypt's position, as conveyed to Kissinger during his pre-Geneva talks in Cairo, began with the proposition that neither Egypt nor Israel should gain military advantage in the disengagement phase. In other words, any force limits would have to be mutual, as Gamasy had insisted at Kilometer 101 in November. Egypt would keep its forces east of the canal on existing lines in numbers not to exceed two divisions, a reduction of three divisions from current levels. No heavy artillery and no surface-to-air missiles would be placed across the canal. Israel would retain control of the eastern ends of the passes. A demilitarized zone would be established between the Egyptian and Israeli lines, to be patrolled by UN troops. Egypt would begin work on clearing the canal and would rebuild the cities once Israeli troops had withdrawn. Israeli cargoes would be allowed to pass through the canal after it reopened.

Two gaps separated the Egyptian and Israeli positions. Egypt wanted Israeli forces to withdraw east of the passes; Israel refused. Israel wanted only a token Egyptian force on the east bank; Sadat was thinking of two infantry divisions with 100 tanks each. It would be difficult for him publicly to accept substantial force limitations in territory returned to his control. Nonetheless, the conceptual underpinnings of the two sides' positions were not very far apart, and agreement seemed possible.

Israeli elections for the Knesset were held on December 31. The opposition to Prime Minister Meir's Labor Alignment coalition gained some strength, but not to the point of making a new cabinet and prime minister necessary. For the next six months, despite her own loss of popularity and the public disenchantment with her defense minister, Moshe Dayan, Meir carried the heavy burdens of government, fighting hard against American and domestic pressures in order to win agreements that protected Israel's vital interests. Kissinger found her to be tough and often emotional, and their talks were at times stormy, but the two nevertheless developed a genuine respect for each other during the difficult disengagement negotiations.

With Israeli elections out of the way, Dayan was sent to Washington for talks with Kissinger on January 4 and 5. He presented a five-zone concept for disengagement, in which each party would have two limited-force zones, separated by a UN buffer. He also specified the type of force limitations Israel could accept. Basically, each side's forces should be beyond the artillery range of the other side, and surface-to-air missiles should not be able to reach the other's aircraft. Also, the number of tanks in the limited zones should be kept very small.

During their talks Dayan urged Kissinger to return to the Middle East to aid in reaching an agreement. This idea proved to be acceptable to Sadat, and Kissinger left late on January 10. Kissinger originally expected to help establish the framework for an agreement, the details of which would be worked out by the parties at Geneva, but Sadat was anxious for results and asked Kissinger to stay in the region until an agreement was reached. Kissinger thus embarked on his first exercise in "shuttle diplomacy," flying between Egypt and Israel with proposals.

On January 13 the Israelis handed Kissinger a map of the proposed disengagement line and authorized him to show it to Sadat, which he did the next day. Sadat had already accepted, in his first talk with Kissinger, the idea of force limitations in three zones, and had promised to work for the end of the oil embargo once an agreement was reached. Now he also said he would accept Israeli forces west of the passes, but he had trouble with the extent of force limits.[37] To overcome Sadat's reservations, Kissinger suggested that the United States might take the responsibility for proposing the limitations on forces. Perhaps it would be easier for Sadat to accept an American plan than an Israeli one. And instead of publicly announcing the limits in the formal documents, these could be defined in letters exchanged by Sadat and Nixon. In addition, Sadat's private assurances on Israeli cargoes transiting the canal could be handled in a secret memo of understanding. Sadat agreed.

In Israel the next day, January 15, Prime Minister Meir dropped the demand for an end of belligerency as part of the disengagement agreement. A few changes in force levels and the line of disengagement were made, wherein Dayan played an especially constructive role. With a new map in hand Kissinger returned to Aswan to see Sadat on January 16, and Sadat agreed to scale down the Egyptian presence on the east bank to eight battalions and thirty tanks.[38] Kissinger then went back to Israel, and the next day, at 3:00 p.m., President Nixon announced that the two parties had reached an agreement on the disengagement of their military forces. The following day the chiefs of staff of Israel and Egypt signed the agreement at Kilometer 101.[39]

As part of the agreement, Israel and the United States signed a detailed ten-point memorandum of understanding.[40] The United States conveyed several Egyptian statements of intention concerning the Suez Canal and the demobilization of its armed forces. The United States promised that the completion of the disengagement agreement would take precedence over new steps at Geneva; that UN troops would not be withdrawn without the consent of both sides; that the United States regarded Bab al-Mandab as an international waterway; and that the United States would try to be responsive to Israel's defense needs on a continuing and long-term basis.

In letters exchanged with both Sadat and Meir, Nixon detailed the force limitations agreed upon. In the limited zones there would be no more than eight reinforced battalions with thirty tanks; no artillery above 122 mm would be allowed, and only six batteries of these weapons were permitted.[41] No weapons capable of interfering with reconnaissance flights over one's own zone were permitted; a maximum troop strength of seven thousand in the limited zone was set; and up to a distance of thirty kilometers from the Egyptian and Israeli lines, no weapons capable of reaching the other side would be allowed, nor would any surface-to-air missiles. Arrangements were specified whereby the United States would perform reconnaissance flights at regular intervals to monitor the agreement, and the results were to be made available to both sides.[42] Finally, a timetable for implementing the agreement was made part of the public text, and Sadat received a special guarantee from Nixon that the United States would use its influence to bring about the full implementation of Resolution 242.

With the signing of the disengagement agreement on January 18, Nixon and Kissinger had entered into important and unprecedented commitments for the United States. American prestige in the Arab world was on the rise, and more than ever the United States seemed to hold the key cards. The Israelis might complain of excessive pressure, but the agreement was not bad for Israel and U.S. aid was still flowing in large quantities. A mood of optimism, a rare occurrence, could be sensed in much of the Middle East.

INTERLUDE BETWEEN DISENGAGEMENTS

Kissinger's next task was to preserve this mood by translating it into new agreements that would help develop momentum toward a settlement. To do so, he set off immediately from Aswan for talks with King Hussein and President Asad. Meanwhile President Sadat, as promised, flew to Saudi Arabia to try to persuade King Faisal to take the lead in lifting the oil embargo against the United States, an act that Kissinger had termed "increasingly less appropriate" earlier in the month.[43]

Agreement on the Egyptian-Israeli front did little to dampen expectations or ease tensions elsewhere in the Middle East. Now Syria, Jordan, and perhaps even the PLO were ready to get in on the act. Israel, however, was hardly anxious to face a new set of negotiations, fearing that once more American pressure would be brought to bear to extract territorial concessions as the price of keeping diplomacy alive. Much as improved U.S.-Arab relations might be desirable in the abstract, Prime Minister Meir feared they would be purchased in Israeli coin. Timing of a second step was therefore bound to be a problem. Kissinger decided to use the unavoidable interval to consolidate the gains of the first round and to lay the basis for a next step between Syria and Israel.

Before returning to Washington after the signing of the Egyptian-Israeli disengagement agreement, Kissinger flew to Jordan for talks with Hussein. This was basically a holding action, since no movement on the Jordanian front was likely until after Syrian-Israeli disengagement. Kissinger told the king that Israel opposed the idea of territorial withdrawal from the Jordan River, preferring to allow Hussein to assume gradual administrative responsibility on the West Bank without immediate Israeli withdrawal. Kissinger posed the issue as one of reinstating the king's authority on the West Bank. Israel would deal either with Jordan now or with Arafat later. Despite Kissinger's efforts to convince Hussein of the merits of "administrative disengagement," the king insisted on recovering some territory, delineated clearly on a large map given to the American party before its departure. The Jordanian plan would have Israel withdraw to a line parallel to the Jordan River at a distance of approximately eight to ten kilometers.[44] Given the Israeli insistence on keeping control of the Jordan Valley, this plan seemed like a nonstarter, but at least an exchange of positions had begun. At this point Kissinger was not thinking so much of an early agreement as he was trying to devise a strategy for keeping the more radical PLO out of the picture for a bit longer. He would have problems enough in dealing with Asad, as he discovered the next day in Damascus.

In talks with President Asad on January 20, Kissinger managed to obtain a new Syrian disengagement proposal. In December Asad had spoken of Israeli withdrawal from all of the Golan Heights as part of a disengagement agreement. Now Syria was holding out for half of the territory conquered by Israel in 1967, as well as all of that gained in 1973, in a disengagement agreement. Asad also clung tenaciously to his one bargaining card—the Israeli prisoners. Kissinger left Damascus with the feeling that Asad did want an agreement and with a map showing two straight lines running north-south through the Golan Heights. These, presumably, would be the disengagement lines under the Syrian proposal.[45] Later that day Kissinger flew to Israel to brief the Israeli leadership on Asad's thinking, and then returned to Washington to explain the details of the Egyptian-Israeli agreement to a generally supportive Congress and public.

Kissinger next began to try to end the oil embargo, while simultaneously laying the groundwork for a Syrian-Israeli agreement. Nixon was anxious to be able to announce the end of the embargo in his State of the Union message to Congress at the end of the month, and the Egyptians and Saudis were bombarded with messages to that effect.[46] Kissinger also began to try out an idea he had tentatively discussed during his recent trip to Syria and Israel. If Syria would give the United States a list of Israeli POWs, Israel would agree to make a concrete proposal on disengagement. This vague procedure was conveyed to Sadat for his information and approval. Several days later, on February 3, King Faisal, who had just conferred with President Asad in Saudi Arabia, informed President Nixon that the oil embargo could not be lifted until a disengagement agreement had been reached on the Syrian-Israeli front. Nixon replied on February 6, saying that unless the embargo was lifted, the United States would not be able to continue its diplomatic efforts.

Nonetheless, the United States did propose a five-point plan to Asad on February 5. Syria would tell the United States the number of Israeli POWs, and the information would then be conveyed to Israel. Syria would give a list of POWs to the United States Interests Section in Damascus, and in exchange for the list Israel would make a concrete proposal. After Red Cross visits with the Israeli prisoners in Syria, Kissinger would transmit the Israeli proposal to Asad and would invite an Israeli delegation to Washington for further talks. Negotiations would then begin at Geneva in the context of the already existing Egyptian-Israeli military working group. On February 9 Asad accepted this procedure.

The following week Presidents Asad, Sadat, and Boumedienne, and King Faisal, met in Algiers for two days. They agreed not to lift the embargo until further progress toward Syrian-Israeli agreement had been made, and Foreign Ministers Fahmy and Saqqaf were sent to Washington to inform Kissinger. Nixon and Kissinger were angry but realized they could not go through with their threat to withdraw from the diplomacy. That would clearly link American policy to the oil embargo, and Kissinger was anxious to convince Asad and the American public that U.S. action in the Middle East was not primarily a function of oil interests. If the United States had reasons of its own to want peace in the Middle East, it would continue its efforts despite the embargo. On February 18 Nixon and Kissinger decided to drop the issue of the embargo for the time being. The next day Nixon announced that Kissinger would make another visit to the area, and on February 25 Kissinger departed on his fourth trip in as many months.

SHUTTLE DIPLOMACY

Kissinger met with Asad for four hours on the night of February 26 and again on the following morning. The discussions were complex but basically friendly, Asad showing flexibility on procedural issues and toughness on substance. As previously agreed, Kissinger was authorized to transmit to the Israelis the list of POWs, which he had actually been given before he left Washington.[47] Red Cross visits would begin, and Israel would be expected to make a concrete proposal on disengagement. Asad made it clear that if Israel offered nothing more than a pullback to the post-1967 cease-fire lines, he would break off the talks. Kissinger was inclined to think he was serious and so told the Israelis during his stop on February 27. He then left the Israelis to develop their proposal over the next twenty-four hours before his return visit.

Meanwhile Kissinger flew to Egypt for talks with Sadat. U.S.-Egyptian ties were developing well and rapidly, and full diplomatic relations were restored on February 28. Sadat extended an invitation to Nixon to visit Egypt. Bilateral issues, including aid and the long-term prospects for U.S. arms sales to Egypt, financed by Saudi Arabia, were also discussed. By that time Kissinger was relying heavily on Sadat's advice on how to deal with other Arab leaders. The Libyans wanted to purchase American radar. What was Sadat's opinion? Asad was insisting on Israeli withdrawal beyond the 1967 cease-fire lines. What were Sadat's views? When would the oil embargo be lifted? How could Soviet influence in Iraq be weakened? Kissinger and Sadat began to develop what amounted to a joint strategy in the Middle East.

As for the specific problem of disengagement on the Syrian front, Sadat argued for a line just west of the town of Quneitra. He offered to send his chief of staff to Syria before Kissinger's next visit, to press for an agreement based on such a line. If Asad refused, Sadat would nonetheless support it publicly and would continue to try to build Arab backing for a moderate disengagement agreement between Syria and Israel. Kissinger was pleased with his talks with Sadat and began to count heavily on Egypt's leadership in the Arab world. Having once erred by underestimating Sadat and Egypt, Kissinger now seemed on the verge of making the opposite mistake.

From Egypt Kissinger flew to Israel, where he received the Israeli proposal. Basically the Israeli plan was for disengagement to be modeled on the Egyptian-Israeli agreement of January, with three zones—one Israeli, one UN, and one Syrian—all within the territory captured by Israel in October 1973. Not only would Quneitra remain entirely under Israeli control, but also Israeli forces would remain well beyond the October 6 lines.

Kissinger feared that Asad would reject the proposal and that the talks would end then and there. Therefore, when in Damascus on the evening of March 1, Kissinger did not give Asad the details of the Israeli plan. Instead he concentrated on the concept of limited-force zones and a UN buffer. He also pinned down Syrian agreement to send a representative to Washington for talks later in the month, following a similar visit by an Israeli official. Kissinger left Damascus with little in the way of substantive progress, but did reach agreement on a further exchange of views over the next several weeks. Asad, not to be outdone by the more effusive Sadat, had embraced the secretary in Arab fashion for the first time. An improbable but genuine personal relationship was beginning to develop between these two very different men.

Kissinger's next stop was Saudi Arabia, his goal there being to urge again the removal of the oil embargo and to solicit support for a Syrian-Israeli disengagement. The secretary also discussed with the Saudis ways of strengthening bilateral economic and security relations. The idea of creating several joint commissions was put forward and eventually was implemented, symbolizing in a tangible way Kissinger's desire to use American technology and arms as complementary to his diplomatic efforts, with the aim of building a strong U.S. presence in key Arab countries.

On March 2 and 3 Kissinger met with King Hussein for lengthy strategy talks. Hussein was growing impatient. The Arab leaders who had met in Algiers in February had agreed on the need to create a Palestinian state headed by PLO leader Yasir Arafat. Pressures were building for the creation of a Palestinian government-in-exile. Hussein asked whether the United States would recognize such a government. Kissinger denied any such intention. The king went on to stress his need for a good agreement with Israel to justify his participation in future negotiations. Ultimately, he said, he would have to obtain all the West Bank of the Jordan and Arab Jerusalem. Anything less would expose him to charges of being a traitor. If Israel was not prepared to go that far, then perhaps Jordan should step aside and let the PLO try to negotiate a better deal than he was able to get. It would, of course, fail, which might bring the Israelis and Palestinians back to reason and open new possibilities for Jordan.

Kissinger urged the king to give the Israelis another chance to come up with a more meaningful proposal than "administrative disengagement." Meanwhile both Jordan and the United States should work to forestall the creation of a Palestinian government-in-exile. Hussein would be visiting Washington shortly; hence further talks would take place soon. Meanwhile Kissinger would contact Sadat on the Palestinian issue, and Jordan should try to learn whether Israel was prepared to make a serious offer. If not, Jordan should threaten to pull out of the negotiations.

As Kissinger flew back to Washington on March 4, the Egyptian-Israeli disengagement agreement was completed, with all parties in their new positions. Simultaneously, tensions increased on the Syrian front as Asad began to raise the danger of renewed hostilities. In the course of the next two months, negotiations on Syrian-Israeli disengagement were to be accompanied by heavy shelling and many casualties on the Syrian front. Asad was clearly going to be more difficult to deal with than Sadat had been, nor were the Israelis in a particularly conciliatory frame of mind.

Upon his return to Washington Kissinger consulted with Nixon on the results of his trip. By that time the president was deeply preoccupied with his Watergate defense. His closest aides had been indicted by a grand jury on March 1 for perjury, obstruction of justice, and illegal payments to suppress evidence. Tapes had come to light that seemed to suggest that Nixon himself had been involved in the payment of hush money to one of the Watergate burglars. Demands for the full transcripts of the tapes of presidential conversations were being made. With all these worries Nixon turned to foreign policy as a form of release and escape, but only to deal with the large issues. Details were still left to Kissinger.

One question requiring presidential decision concerned the terms on which Israel would receive the $2.2 billion in emergency assistance to cover the purchase of military equipment. Nixon was not averse to pressuring Israel; he was unhappy with the recent Israeli proposal on disengagement. He and Kissinger therefore agreed that for the moment all $2.2 billion would be extended as credit. The president would have the option until July 1 of waiving repayment of as much as $1.5 billion. If Israel was forthcoming, it could expect favorable presidential action. Meanwhile an aid package was being put together for fiscal year 1975 which would, for the first time in years, contain a substantial sum, $250 million, for Egypt, and an unprecedented $207.5 million for Jordan.[48] Only $350 million would be requested for Israel, in the knowledge that Congress would increase that sum significantly in any event. Aid was clearly going to be an important adjunct of the Nixon-Kissinger diplomacy.

Kissinger recognized that it would be difficult to reach an agreement between Israel and Syria on disengagement. The United States alone might be able to persuade Israel to make the necessary concessions, using a combination of pressure and positive inducements, but how could Syria be brought to a more workable position? Could Sadat and other Arab leaders play a role? What about the Soviets, who seemed so anxious to be involved in the negotiations? Would Asad be influenced by the offer of American aid? Kissinger needed time to explore each of these possibilities and to let each of the parties reconsider its opening stance on disengagement.

The first order of business was to end the oil embargo. Nixon referred to this again in a press conference on March 6. The Arab oil producers would soon be meeting in Tripoli. If the embargo was not then lifted, the American diplomatic effort would be undermined. After some delays most Arab oil producers announced on March 18 that the embargo against the United States was ended, at least provisionally. Privately, Faisal stressed the importance of achieving a Syrian-Israeli disengagement agreement within two months to avoid the reimposition of the embargo. Already Arab oil production was inching back up to pre-war levels, after a reduction of some 15 percent in December and January. OPEC had imposed a new price of about $10 per barrel, a quadrupling of pre-war levels, but further increases were no longer likely once production returned to normal levels.

Syria had opposed the lifting of the embargo. Kissinger was now anxious to bring inter-Arab pressure to bear on Asad to accept a disengagement agreement. Egypt, Saudi Arabia, and Algeria could all play a role. If Syria refused a reasonable offer, Kissinger wanted to make sure that Asad would be isolated rather than supported by a bloc of rejectionists. Only Iraq might be able to strengthen Asad's resolve to resist making concessions. Iraqi forces could help reinforce the Syrian front, as they had done in October. If fighting resumed, Asad might be obliged to turn to Iraq and the Soviets for more military help. But Iraq was becoming preoccupied with its border with Iran, where serious clashes had occurred in February, and with the Kurds, who had entered into armed opposition to the Baghdad regime in late February. Egypt, Israel, Iran, and the United States all played a part in orchestrating this operation to ensure that Iraq would not be able to go to Syria's help.

Kissinger now needed a reasonable Israeli offer to lure Asad toward an agreement. On March 15 and 19 Kissinger met with Foreign Minister Eban. He explained his strategy of trying to isolate Syria from the radical Arabs and stressed the need for continued movement in the diplomatic arena. Israel would have to pull back to the October 6 lines, if not farther, and would have to give up Quneitra. Israel should not, however, be expected to abandon any settlements on the Golan Heights at this stage. Dayan should bring an Israeli proposal based on this thinking when he visited Washington later in the month.

On March 24 Kissinger set off for the Soviet Union, where, among other things, he would try to keep the Soviets from obstructing his efforts at disengagement on the Syrian-Israeli front. During a three and one-half hour meeting on March 26, described as the "toughest and most unpleasant" he had ever had with Brezhnev and his top aides, Kissinger resisted Soviet pressure to return the negotiations to Geneva. General Secretary Brezhnev hotly accused Kissinger of violating agreements that the talks would be held under joint U.S.-USSR auspices, and referred to assurances given to Foreign Minister Gromyko in February that the negotiations would be conducted at Geneva. Kissinger defended his actions as being taken at the request of the regional parties. In any case, they were only paving the way for talks on a final settlement that would be held at Geneva.

Brezhnev referred to the good relations existing between Iraq and the Soviet Union, and also mentioned Asad's forthcoming visit to Moscow, observing that he would surely ask for more arms. Kissinger replied that he was sure Asad would ask the Soviet Union for arms, because he had just made such a request of the United States. Brezhnev noted that he was withholding arms from Egypt, and then returned to the discussion of Syria, asking Kissinger why the United States did not give Asad arms. Kissinger replied with a straight face that he did not want to fuel the arms race! Obviously irritated at the growing American involvement in the Arab world, Brezhnev accurately accused Kissinger of trying to keep the Soviet Union out of the substance of the negotiations. He argued that Syria wanted the Soviets to be present.

Kissinger quickly checked with Asad on whether he did in fact want the Soviets involved at this stage. Asad obliquely replied that the agreed procedure was for Dayan to go to Washington, followed by a Syrian representative. Then Kissinger would return to the Middle East, after which a military working group could conclude the details of an agreement in Geneva with the Soviets present.

Shortly after his return from Moscow, the secretary of state met with Dayan in Washington on March 29.[49] Dayan brought a large arms request—for 1,000 tanks, 4,000 armored personnel carriers, and much more—as well as an Israeli proposal for a disengagement line that would run east of the October 6 line. Israeli forces would emphatically remain in Quneitra. Kissinger was irritated by the Israeli proposal, whose only value, in his view, was the concept of a buffer zone flanked by two limited-force zones to the east and west. Kissinger warned the Israelis that Asad would not accept the line and termed their proposal inadequate, but he repeated that Israel should not give up any settlements at this stage. Against the background of intensified fighting on the Syrian-Israeli front, Brigadier General Hikmat Shihabi of Syria flew to Washington for talks with Kissinger on April 13. Shihabi brought with him a revised map showing a disengagement line running west of Quneitra. Though far from being Dayan's proposal, it was an improvement over the Syrian position of January. Kissinger showed Shihabi the line proposed by Dayan, terming it unacceptable but emphasizing the desirability of the three-zone concept. The secretary implied that he would try to persuade the Israelis to go back to the October 6 line and to leave Quneitra, but that would be the most that Syria could hope for at this stage. Two days later Kissinger passed the Syrian map to Israeli Ambassador Dinitz.

While Kissinger was trying to induce Israel and Syria to modify their respective proposals, Sadat spent the month of April in a strident press campaign against the Soviet Union. He publicly mentioned that he had nearly canceled the treaty between the two countries. On April 18 he declared his intention of ending his exclusive dependency on the Soviets for arms and said he would seek arms in the West, including the United States. His foreign minister, Ismail Fahmy, was at that moment talking to Nixon and Kissinger in Washington, presumably on the same topic. Surprisingly, a long-time ardent supporter of Israel, columnist Joseph Alsop, responded to Sadat's bid by calling on April 26 for an American policy of becoming the main arms supplier of Egypt. Such a policy would confirm the "complete reversal of alliances that President Sadat has been publicly talking about" and would constitute "the most dazzling feat of diplomacy in the 20th century."[50]

This tone in Sadat's speeches and in Alsop's column could scarcely be expected to put the Soviets in a conciliatory mood. Kissinger did, however, meet with Gromyko several times during April and seemed to succeed in at least neutralizing Soviet opposition to his diplomatic efforts with Syria and Israel. Having achieved enough during March and April to justify another round of shuttle diplomacy, Kissinger departed for the Middle East on April 28. Little did he realize at the time how long and difficult the negotiations would be.

SYRIAN-ISRAELI DISENGAGEMENT

It was clear to Kissinger and his colleagues that a disengagement agreement between Syria and Israel would be much more difficult to attain than the one between Egypt and Israel. In the latter case, both sides wanted an agreement and had come close to an accord on basic issues before Kissinger began his shuttle. In the Syrian-Israeli case, the positions of the two parties were far apart, the incentives for an agreement were lacking, and the objective situation on the ground lent itself less well to an agreement than did the situation in Sinai. Moreover, both Syria and Israel were governed by somewhat shaky coalitions. Neither could afford to appear soft in the negotiations.

If the local parties had less interest in an agreement, the United States had more of a stake than before. Among other things, it must protect the

Egyptian-Israeli agreement, and beyond that, the flourishing U.S.-Egyptian relationship. If Syria refused to reach a comparable disengagement agreement, Sadat's position would be threatened in the Arab world, and a radical, rejectionist bloc might gain influence. War might resume on the Syrian front, and Egypt might well be pulled in. Apart from the intrinsic danger of another war, that situation would provide the Soviet Union with new opportunities for reasserting its presence in the region. Finally, without an agreement there might be another troublesome oil embargo.

Kissinger realized he would have great problems with the Syrians and the Israelis. To deal with the former, he counted on building strong Arab support for his efforts. With the Israelis, he would, as usual, have to combine carrot and stick. Before Kissinger's departure for the Middle East, Nixon had waived repayment on $1 billion of the $2.2 billion in aid to cover arms purchases. In normal times that might have won Kissinger a cordial reception in Israel, but these were not normal times. Besides, the United States had just voted in the UN to condemn Israel for a retaliatory raid in southern Lebanon. Whatever credit Kissinger may once have had with the Israelis was rapidly being dissipated. Nixon's authority would have to be invoked when the going got rough, but that authority was itself in question. The day after Kissinger's departure Nixon released edited texts of a large number of taped conversations concerning Watergate. They did not make for edifying reading. Slowly but surely the judicial process seemed to be leading to Richard Nixon's impeachment. For this very reason Nixon seemed extremely anxious for Kissinger to succeed in his mission. During the ensuing weeks a severely weakened president repeatedly threw his weight behind his secretary of state, in what proved to be some of the bluntest exchanges with the Israeli leadership ever to take place.

Kissinger's itinerary took him first to Geneva, for talks with Gromyko, and then to Algeria and Egypt. Boumedienne and Sadat were key Arab leaders, whose support Kissinger sought. The Algerians had close relations with the Syrians and had good credentials as revolutionaries.[51] No one would accuse them of being stooges of the Americans. In Alexandria, the next day, Kissinger received Sadat's blessings and a prediction that "my friend, Dr. Henry" would succeed in his mission. With that, Kissinger braced himself for the arduous business of talking with the Israelis and Syrians.

Kissinger felt that Israel would have to make concessions on the line of disengagement and that the Syrians, who rejected any force limitations other than a narrow buffer zone, would have to back down as well. First he would try to win consensus on an acceptable line. Then, it might be hoped, the other elements of agreement would begin to fall into place.

His talks in Israel on May 2 did nothing to make Kissinger optimistic. The Israelis were angry at the United States for its UN vote and were obdurate about any alteration of the position Dayan had presented in late March. Why should Asad be rewarded for having gone to war against Israel and lost? Why now should he get a better offer than the more reasonable Sadat? Was it good for U.S. interests to appease the most militant of the Arabs? What would the world think if Israel and the United States submitted to such blackmail? And so the arguments went, until in despair Kissinger turned to Nixon for help. A letter from Nixon to Meir on May 4 warned her not to allow Israeli actions to jeopardize the favorable trends in the area. Otherwise the United States, out of friendship for Israel and a sense of responsibility, would have to reexamine the relationship between the two countries.

In Damascus the next day, Kissinger avoided precise discussion of the Israeli line of disengagement. Instead he emphasized to Asad the weakness of Prime Minister Meir's domestic position and the linkages between Israeli domestic politics and its foreign policy. He raised the issue of U.S. aid to help Syria with reconstruction. Asad remained adamant that the disengagement line would have to be west of the October 6 line but seemed to show flexibility on other issues, such as force limitations. The following day, however, he repeated to Kissinger his "nonapproval" of the idea of limited-force zones. Kissinger, for his part, then tried to encourage Egyptian, Algerian, and Saudi pressure on Asad to moderate his views.[52]

In the course of the next several days, Israel began to modify its proposal on the disengagement line.[53] Part of Quneitra would now be returned to Syria, but the western part of the city must remain under Israeli control. Kissinger told the Israelis that Asad would not accept such an arrangement. On May 7 Kissinger flew to Cyprus to brief Gromyko on the talks and found that the Soviets were prepared to remain neutral.[54]

Despite some progress in Israel on May 6 and 7, Kissinger was not optimistic. In Damascus on May 8 he disclosed some of Israel's concessions to Asad, but he withheld others so that he would have something to show on later trips. The tactic was risky, but Kissinger felt he had to avoid whetting Asad's already substantial appetite for Israeli concessions, while at the same time being able to show continued progress.[55] In any event, on May 8 Asad began to talk seriously about a line in the vicinity of that proposed by Israel.[56] Quneitra and the three surrounding hills now loomed as the main obstacle.

Kissinger continued to seek Egyptian, Algerian, and Saudi help. He kept the leaders well informed on the negotiations and asked for their support. At the same time he tried to persuade the Israelis to make more concessions, but to little avail. On May 9 he reported to President Nixon that he was organizing forces for what he expected to be his "climactic meeting" with President Asad on May 11.

Instead of the hoped-for breakthrough, Kissinger encountered a stalemate. Asad insisted on all of Quneitra as well as the three surrounding hills. Israel would simply not yield on the hills, the "Himalayas of General Gur," as Kissinger termed them. On May 13, however, he did get Israeli agreement to a Syrian civilian presence in all of Quneitra, along with two other minor concessions.[57] He decided on one last trip to Damascus on May 14; then he would return to Washington. In Damascus he found that Asad was not satisfied with the last Israeli proposal, insisting that the line must lie along the peak of the hills and that UN troops, not Israelis, must occupy the peaks. By now the bargaining concerned a few hundred meters, but neither side seemed prepared to yield.[58]

At this point President Nixon weighed in with Kissinger, urging him to continue to work for an agreement and promising him his full support. If Israel was intransigent, Nixon was prepared to go very far if necessary. On May 14 he asked for a list of all military and economic aid promised to Israel, as well as the total of tax-free private contributions to Israel.[59] He also asked for ideas on aid to Syria as a possible incentive.

This was what the Israelis had long feared—pressure on them and offers of aid to the Arabs. In this instance, however, Nixon did not cut aid to Israel. Instead the negotiations inched forward, as Kissinger shuttled back and forth. Encouraged by some members of the Israeli cabinet, Kissinger decided on May 15 to begin to introduce his own ideas in talks with Asad and the Israelis. As he had done in January once the gap had been narrowed, he would try to find a compromise that left each side's basic interests intact. Perhaps the Syrians would find his ideas easier to accept than Israel's.

On May 16 Kissinger succeeded in inducing the Israelis to pull back to the base of the hills. He immediately flew to Damascus to try out ideas of his own.[60] The next day he reported to Nixon that he was close to an agreement on a disengagement line. In Damascus on May 18, however, it seemed as if the remaining gap could not be bridged. Kissinger decided to leave, began drafting a departure statement, and had his luggage sent to the plane. At the last moment Asad dropped his insistence on controlling the hills west of Quneitra and urged Kissinger to keep trying for an agreement. Israel could keep the hills if Kissinger would guarantee that no heavy weapons capable of firing into Quneitra would be placed there. On May 19 Kissinger was able to obtain Israel's assent to Asad's request, and on May 20 he returned to Damascus with a map of the agreed line.

With agreement on the line of disengagement virtually assured, the problem arose of force limitations and the size of the restricted armaments zones.[61] In addition, Asad wanted Israel to give up all the positions on Mt. Hermon. Syria also wanted only a small UN force in the buffer zone, whereas Israel preferred at least 2,000 to 3,000 UN troops. After two more days of haggling over these issues, on May 22 Kissinger began to lose heart. Once again he drafted a departure statement and planned to leave the next day. Egypt, however, had sent General Gamasy to Syria, and by the time of Kissinger's next visit to Damascus, on May 23, Asad had changed his position to accept a large UN force and a wider buffer zone of ten kilometers and limited-force zones of fifteen kilometers. He was still insisting, nevertheless, on fairly sizable armaments in the limited zones, while accepting the concept developed on the Egyptian front of keeping surface-to-air missiles and heavy artillery out of range of the other side's lines. Kissinger returned on May 24 to Israel, where he faced demands that Asad commit himself to preventing terrorist attacks from his side of the lines. Israel also asked for a U.S. commitment that the UN force would not be withdrawn without the consent of both parties to the agreement. Israel also wanted reassurances on long-term military supplies. From this point on, Prime Minister Meir and Defense Minister Dayan were extremely helpful and flexible in working out the final details of an agreement.

On May 26 the drafting of the final documents began. To Kissinger's consternation, issues that he thought had been settled were now reopened by Asad. Once more it seemed as if the talks would collapse.[62] On May 27 Asad backed down and after ten hours of talks, Kissinger agreed to make one more trip to Israel to work out compromises on several more points. Then, on May 28, in four hours of private conversation, Asad gave Kissinger his oral commitment that he would not allow the Syrian side of the disengagement line to become a source of terrorist attacks against Israel. With that concession in hand, Kissinger flew to Israel, and on May 29 the announcement was made that Syria and Israel had reached agreement on the terms of a disengagement agreement. Two days later Syrian and Israeli military representatives signed the necessary documents in Geneva.[63]

The agreement consisted of a public document, a map, a protocol on the status of the UN forces, and several secret letters between the United States and the two parties detailing the understandings on force levels and other issues.[64] The force-limitation agreement specified a UN buffer zone paralleling the post-1967 line and including the city of Quneitra. In zones of ten kilometers east and west of the buffer zone, each party could station two brigades, with no more than 6,000 men, 75 tanks, and 36 short-range (122 mm) artillery pieces. In adjacent zones of ten kilometers, no artillery with a range of more than twenty kilometers, and no more than 162 artillery pieces, would be allowed. No surface-to-air missiles could be closer than twenty-five kilometers to the front lines. UN Disengagement Observer Forces (UNDOF) would have the right to inspect these zones, and U.S. aircraft would carry out reconnaissance flights as in the January Egyptian-Israeli accord. Agreement was reached on the exchange of prisoners, and both sides declared that disengagement was only a step toward a just and durable peace based on UN Resolution 338.

Nixon wrote to Asad on May 29 to confirm that Israel would observe the cease-fire on the hills around Quneitra, that no Israeli forces or weapons would be stationed on the eastern slopes of the hills, and that no weapons would be placed on the hills that would be capable of firing into Quneitra. Nixon also informed the Israelis that the last paragraph of the public agreement was to be interpreted to mean that guerrilla raids were contrary to the cease-fire and that the United States recognized Israel's right of self-defense in the event of violations. As usual, the Israelis also insisted on a memorandum of understanding dealing with such contingencies as a breakdown in the cease-fire at Syria's initiative and on the pacing of the negotiations. To the Syrians, the United States committed itself to work for the full implementation of UN Resolution 338.

With the signing of the agreement between Syria and Israel, together with all the side agreements conveyed through the United States, Kissinger and Nixon could point to another outstanding achievement in their Middle East diplomacy. By itself, the step was modest, but in light of the recent history of Syrian-Israeli relations it was substantial indeed. The lingering question, of course, was whether it was a step toward a more comprehensive peace agreement, or whether it would prove to be merely a pause before another round of fighting at a later date. Was Kissinger determined to continue his efforts, or, after spending one month of murderously difficult negotiations for limited results, would he conclude that no further progress was possible? Would "step-by-step" remain his preferred tactic, and if so, where would the next step be? All these questions would have to be dealt with in the near future, but first President Nixon wanted to reap the rewards of Kissinger's efforts by staging a whirlwind tour of the Middle East. The adulation of the Egyptian crowds might take his mind off Watergate.

NIXON TO THE MIDDLE EAST

President Nixon's trip to the Middle East was an odd affair.[65] Inevitably he was accompanied by an enormous retinue of aides, security men, and journalists. Every detail of the visit had been worked out by advance men. The local governments were nearly overwhelmed by the onslaught of American technicians, public-relations experts, TV crews, and assorted hangers-on.

Nixon himself was not in good health, his leg being inflamed and sore from a mild attack of phlebitis. Presumably his emotional state was less than serene as well. He reportedly spent his free time listening to the possibly incriminating Watergate tapes. The House Judiciary Committee was holding hearings on whether there was sufficient evidence to warrant his impeachment. Subpoenas for evidence had been issued, Nixon had refused to comply, and the Supreme Court would have to decide the matter.

Even Kissinger was under attack, not for his Middle East efforts, for which he had won overwhelming praise, but for his alleged role in ordering the wiretapping of members of his own staff in 1969. In Salzburg on June 11, the first stop of the presidential party, Kissinger had emotionally denied any wrongdoing and had threatened to resign if his name was not cleared. The one man who could instantly have cleared his name by assuming responsibility for the wiretapping, President Nixon, remained silent.

For the next several days Kissinger seemed to sulk in the background as Nixon received an incredibly enthusiastic reception in Cairo and Alexandria. Sadat went to great lengths to emphasize the new chapter in U.S.-Egyptian relations that he had helped to open. In public the two men were friendly, and the immense crowds almost succeeded in raising Nixon's flagging spirits. After all, it was the first official visit of an American president to Egypt, and Nixon liked firsts. Moreover, he could be proud of the results of his foreign policy. He saw himself as a man working for peace against adversaries at home and abroad, and as someone misunderstood by those who were seeking to bring him down. A touch of the martyr in Nixon showed through as he disobeyed his doctor's orders and needlessly tired himself to remain on display before the cheering Egyptian crowds.

In private Nixon was uncommunicative. Conversations were stilted and marked by frequent pauses.[66] He did, however, make promises of future American assistance. Egypt would be allowed to purchase a nuclear reactor for energy production,[67] and economic aid would continue; Nixon even turned over his personal helicopter to Sadat. In the diplomatic arena Nixon promised he would work for the restoration of the international frontier as Egypt's border in a final settlement, a position that had not been taken since the ill-fated Rogers Plan in 1969. The president also agreed that the Palestinians should be brought into the negotiations at an early date. Sadat suggested that the United States should secretly talk to the PLO leaders, and Nixon seemed receptive, if noncommittal. The talks concluded with the issuance of a joint statement of principles.

Nixon then flew to Saudi Arabia for two days of talks on June 14 and 15. Here the focus was primarily on strengthening bilateral relations and on oil. He next went on to Damascus, for a somewhat restrained reception and cordial talks with President Asad. Full diplomatic relations were restored on June 16. Nixon and Asad also discussed next steps in the peacemaking process. The president said that the Geneva conference should be reconvened in September. Then to an astonished and delighted Asad, he explained that the purpose of step-by-step diplomacy was to persuade the Israelis to pull back gradually on the Syrian front until they reached the edge of the Golan Heights, tumbled over, and returned to the old borders.[68] The imagery was fanciful, but the Syrians took it as a commitment to work for full Israeli withdrawal. As he left Damascus, Nixon drafted a long list of possible aid projects that might be offered to Syria. He feared that Asad might require substantial inducements to remain on good behavior.

The president was more at home on his next stop, Israel, than earlier. His counterpart, however, was no longer the worthy friend and adversary of former crises, Golda Meir, but rather Yitzhak Rabin, the new prime minister of Israel and something of an unknown quantity, despite his years in Washington as ambassador. The Israelis, who had not been informed in advance, were less than pleased with the American offer of nuclear reactors to Egypt, and to soothe them, Nixon made them the same offer. He also talked at some length about the importance of dealing quickly with King Hussein on the fate of the West Bank. Better Hussein now, he observed, than Arafat later.[69] When discussing terrorism with the Israelis, Nixon startled his hosts by leaping from his seat and declaring there was only one way to deal with terrorists. Then, Chicago-gangland style, he fired an imaginary submachine gun at the assembled cabinet members. Strange behavior, strange president. Best friend or dangerous enemy of Israel? It was hard to tell.

Nixon concluded his swing through the Middle East by visiting Jordan.[70] Determined to proceed with talks concerning disengagement on the Jordan-Israel front, Nixon invited Hussein to Washington in late July.

On June 19 the president returned to Washington. Three days later, the Judiciary Committee completed its hearings, which had been watched by a fascinated television audience while Nixon was winging his way through the Middle East. On June 24 the committee issued four more subpoenas to Nixon. The next day he left for Moscow. Affairs of state continued to provide him with some relief from Watergate, and he could be sure that the Soviet leaders would not take seriously the charges against him of obstructing justice and misusing the office.

THE FINAL DAYS

Back in Washington, Nixon agreed on the last day of the fiscal year to waive Israel's repayment of $500 million in credit for arms, a bit more carrot in anticipation of negotiations between Jordan and Israel. Throughout July Nixon and Kissinger kept up the pressure for an agreement.[71] Sadat was prepared to reverse his previous stand and endorse King Hussein as the spokesman for the Palestinians living in the Hashemite Kingdom of Jordan.[72] The Israeli cabinet, which had been toying with a formula providing for Israel to talk with the PLO if the PLO ended acts of terrorism and accepted Israel's existence, quickly reversed itself and went back to the position that Jordan was the spokesman for the

Palestinians.[73] On July 21, however, the cabinet rejected the concept of disengagement along the Jordan River, and in talks with Foreign Minister Yigal Allon the next week Kissinger was unable to persuade the Israelis to change their position.[74]

American involvement in the search for an agreement between Jordan and Israel was temporarily deflected by another Middle East crisis, this one in Cyprus. For several weeks Kissinger and his top aides were engaged in trying to prevent Greece and Turkey, two NATO allies, from going to war. The Arab-Israeli conflict, for the first time in months, was eclipsed by a crisis elsewhere in the world.[75]

But the gravest crisis, in certain respects, was in Washington. On July 24 the Supreme Court unanimously ruled that Nixon must turn over the records of sixty-four subpoenaed tapes. Three days later the House Judiciary Committee began voting the first of three articles of impeachment. Nixon seemed committed to fighting to the last moment to save his presidency and his reputation, but on August 5 the final bit of evidence that alienated even his most ardent supporters was made public. In a taped conversation on June 23, 1972, shortly after the Watergate break-in, Nixon was clearly heard ordering that the CIA be used to prevent the FBI investigation into the case. Two days later the president reluctantly reached the conclusion that he would have to resign, a decision he announced at 9:00 p.m. on August 8. At noon on August 9, Richard Nixon ceased to be president. His successor, Gerald Ford, was sworn into office as the country's first nonelected president. He quickly assured a troubled nation that Secretary of State Henry Kissinger would remain in the cabinet to conduct the foreign policy of the country. It would be some time before Middle East affairs would become the new president's strong suit. And Kissinger himself would have other preoccupations in the weeks ahead. Step-by-step diplomacy seemed to have reached an end, at least for the moment.

CONCLUSIONS

It is impossible to know with certainty whether American policy toward the Middle East after October 1973 would have been substantially different without the deleterious effects of the Watergate scandal. On the whole, the answer seems to be no. The policy that grew out of the October crisis had little to do with Watergate. It was aimed at ending the multiple pressures generated by the war and bringing the United States to a position of influence over the peacemaking process between

Israel and its Arab neighbors. The level of commitment and the amount of energy expended in pursuit of this policy could not have been greater. Nor does it appear as if the pace of diplomacy could have been quickened, or that more substantial agreements might have been reached. After all, the Israelis, Egyptians, and Syrians were operating under severe constraints. Even the modest disengagement agreements strained their political systems almost to the breaking point.

Kissinger has been criticized for specific decisions that he took during the negotiations, such as discouraging the Israelis and Egyptians from reaching agreement at Kilometer 101 in November. He has been accused of exerting too much pressure on Israel, of being less than straightforward in his dealings with the parties, and of being more of a tactician than a strategist. Yet his critics have rarely presented a viable alternative to his gradualist, step-by-step diplomacy, and few would argue that more could have been achieved in the first seven months after the October war.

Serious doubts do arise, however, about whether Kissinger conceived of his diplomacy as a step toward a comprehensive political settlement or whether, pessimist that he often was accused of being, he saw his efforts as aimed at buying time and reducing pressures on the United States and Israel. To the Arabs Kissinger consistently stressed the former goal, while reassuring the Israelis with the latter.

If step-by-step diplomacy as carried out by Kissinger is to be judged on its own merits, it rates high as a tactic but fails to convey any sense of long-term purpose. To gain or lose a few kilometers of Sinai or Golan was surely not worth repeated crises of confidence with Israel and substantial offers of aid to all parties. Kissinger's justification for his efforts was that without the disengagement agreements there would be another war, accompanied by another oil embargo and by a resurgence of Soviet influence in the Arab world. To prevent these upheavals was ample justification for his endless travels and his deep involvement in the disengagement negotiations.

Kissinger knew what he wanted to avoid better than he knew what positive goals he might be able to achieve. The October war was his immediate point of reference. The simple lesson from that crisis was that the status quo in the Middle East was volatile and dangerous, and could disintegrate, with serious consequences for American global and regional interests. Consequently the status quo had to be stabilized through a combination of diplomacy and arms shipments. A political process must begin that would offer the Arabs an alternative to war, but it must be carried on at a pace the Israelis could accept. This was the extent of Nixon's and Kissinger's initial conceptualization. There was no overall American peace plan—that had been tried in 1969 and had failed.

Without a convincing picture, however, of where step-by-step diplomacy was heading, would the parties to the negotiations ever be able to address the core issues of peace, security, and the Palestinians? And would the United States indefinitely be able to remain uncommitted to outcomes? The answer was unmistakably no, and by mid-1974 Nixon found himself making private commitments to Sadat, Asad, Rabin, and Hussein on where American diplomacy was heading.

With strong presidential leadership, step-by-step diplomacy might have turned into a search for a broader settlement, including Jordan and the Palestinians. Instead the United States was involved in an unprecedented crisis of authority, and Nixon's successor was unlikely to convey a clear sense of purpose in foreign policy. Step-by-step diplomacy therefore remained a tactic for buying more time, a tactic cut off from a larger political concept of peace in the Middle East. Unable to move beyond step-by-step diplomacy, yet fearing the loss of momentum if no results were achieved, Kissinger was obliged to continue the search for partial solutions, either on the Jordanian or the Egyptian front, whichever seemed more feasible. The chance for a more ambitious policy was lost when Nixon was forced to resign, and considerable time would have to pass before a strong American initiative in the Middle East would be resumed.[76]

PART THREE

The Ford Presidency

CHAPTER NINE

Beyond Disengagement?
Ford and Kissinger, 1975

Gerald Ford was an unlikely president. He had not sought the office. As a long-time member of the House of Representatives, his political ambition had been to become Speaker of the House—until Richard Nixon selected him as vice-president in October 1973. Less than a year later, in early August 1974, the final act of the Watergate scandal brought Ford to the White House.

There is a strong presumption in American politics that it does matter who occupies the Oval Office. Immense sums are spent on presidential election campaigns. And in no other area is presidential discretion thought to be so great as in foreign policy, or at least so it seemed in the pre-Vietnam, pre-Watergate era.

This president, however, was different from his predecessors. He had not been elected. His initial popularity stemmed from his apparent honesty and openness, not from confidence in his ability or leadership, and even that popularity began to wane after he pardoned Richard Nixon. Foreign policy was obviously not his field of expertise, and it seemed likely that he would defer to his prestigious secretary of state and national security affairs adviser, Henry Kissinger. But could Kissinger be as effective as he had been in the past without a strong president to back his initiatives? Although Kissinger may have harbored misgivings about Nixon, he had admired Nixon's decisiveness and his willingness to take risks. Would Ford have the same attributes?

Little was known of Ford's views on foreign policy generally. As a congressman he had supported a strong defense and had backed Nixon in his Southeast Asian policy. He was known to be a good friend of Israel, but otherwise his ideas on the Middle East were uncertain. It would probably be some time before a distinctive Ford foreign policy would take shape. For the moment, Kissinger would remain in charge.[1]

Kissinger had adopted step-by-step diplomacy as the means to deal with the problems created by the October 1973 war and to establish the United States as the key diplomatic broker between Israel and the Arabs.

Despite some reservations, Egypt, Syria, and Israel had all gone along with Kissinger's approach, and he had even been able to enlist the support, or tacit agreement, of Saudi Arabia, Algeria, and Jordan. By mid-1974 two disengagement agreements stood as testimony to the success of Kissinger's efforts. But the issues between Israel and its Arab neighbors went well beyond the disengagement of military forces, and subsequent diplomatic moves would have to address many more complex political issues than those considered in the first round of step-by-step diplomacy.

Kissinger may well have had his doubts about the wisdom of continuing to seek political agreements on each Arab front separately. But what were the alternatives? A global negotiation at Geneva was sure to fail unless carefully prepared in advance. The Israelis were wary of Geneva, and Kissinger himself was opposed to bringing the Soviet Union back into the peacemaking moves. A U.S.-Soviet imposed settlement would require both a higher degree of superpower agreement than existed and a strong American president. A suspension of U.S. diplomacy was a possibility, but it ran the risk of weakening the "moderate" Arab coalition Kissinger had been trying to encourage.

By a process of elimination Kissinger came back to step-by-step diplomacy, with all of its obvious limitations, as the best means to keep the peace process alive. But where to begin? The answer, never fully thought through, was the Jordan-Israel front. The unstated belief was that it was worth trying to bring Jordan into the diplomacy as a way of undercutting the more radical PLO. Kissinger would also continue to press for a second step between Egypt and Israel.[2]

A JORDANIAN-ISRAELI SETTLEMENT?

Negotiations on the Jordanian-Israeli front presented Kissinger with unprecedented problems. "Disengagement" was hardly an appropriate concept here, since there had been no military engagement between the two countries in the October war. Rather than separate military forces along cease-fire lines, Kissinger would have to deal with sensitive political issues such as sovereignty and the status of the Palestinians. Despite the tacit cooperation that existed on some levels between Jordan and Israel, the prospects for reaching agreement were unusually dim, largely because of domestic Israeli politics and inter-Arab pressures on King Hussein. Israel was now led by an untried and untested leader, Prime Minister Yitzhak Rabin. On foreign-policy matters he was obliged to work closely with his popular defense minister, Shimon Peres, and his foreign minister,

Yigal Allon. Unfortunately for Rabin these two key figures in his cabinet did not often see eye to eye. The only consensus Rabin was able to develop regarding the West Bank was essentially negative: he would call elections before agreeing to anything affecting the former Jordanian territory.

The pressures on Hussein were equally confining, but less focused. His own sense of responsibility, and his understandable fear of being accused of selling out to the Israelis, led him to insist on negotiating terms that he could defend before other Arabs and before the Palestinians. Despite Hussein's own "moderate" inclinations, and his genuine acceptance of Israel's right to exist, he was not in a position to capitulate to Israeli demands. He needed to prove to his people and to the Arab world that he, like Presidents Asad and Sadat, could recover Arab territory held by Israel. Above all, he could not accede to the Israeli position of administering the populated areas of the West Bank while Israel retained military control of the area.

Kissinger recognized the danger that negotiations might fail on the Jordan-Israel front. If they did, the momentum he had hoped to develop through step-by-step diplomacy might be dissipated, precious time might be lost, and Kissinger's own reputation might suffer. An alternative strategy did exist; namely, to concentrate on another quick step on the Egyptian-Israeli front and then to move on to more comprehensive negotiations at Geneva during 1975. Kissinger wavered, but finally opted for a half-hearted attempt at a Jordanian-Israeli agreement.

Within days of becoming president, Ford was conferring with Middle East diplomats and leaders, while Kissinger tried to bring him up to date on the intricacies of the Arab-Israeli negotiations. First to arrive for talks with Ford was Egyptian Foreign Minister Fahmy.[3] A few days later King Hussein met with Ford, Kissinger, and Secretary of Defense James Schlesinger. The king was told that the United States would accord priority to the search for a Jordanian-Israeli agreement, while also exploring possibilities for another step in Sinai. Next Syrian Foreign Minister Abd al-Halim Khaddam arrived to see Kissinger, on August 22. Not to be outdone, Prime Minister Rabin came to Washington on September 10 for discussions with the new president. Rabin made it clear he favored another interim step with Egypt, not one with Jordan.

The upshot of all these preliminary consultations was another Kissinger trip to the Middle East. Israel was still reluctant to pull back from the Jordan River, and Hussein would accept nothing else.[4] The alternative of Israeli withdrawal from the town of Jericho, and perhaps even from the important Nablus area, had been suggested, but neither side was enthusiastic. Kissinger therefore began his travels with little chance of success. In talks with Sadat he tried to press for Egyptian support of Jordan at the forthcoming Arab summit conference in Rabat. That support had slipped somewhat during September, and the dynamics of inter-Arab politics might well produce a ringing endorsement of the PLO, to the exclusion of Jordan, which Kissinger wanted to prevent. As bait he discussed with Sadat the outlines of another agreement between Egypt and Israel. Sadat's position was firm: in a second step he must recover the Mitla and Giddi passes and the oil field at Abu Rudeis. Nothing less would justify the risks for Egypt of entering into a second agreement with Israel.

In Amman Kissinger and Hussein reviewed the bleak prospects for an agreement and discussed the possibility that at Rabat the PLO would be endorsed as the sole negotiator for the West Bank and as the only spokesman for the Palestinians. If that happened, the king would withdraw from the negotiations entirely. Many Jordanians would be delighted to wash their hands of the whole Palestinian problem. It would be far better to concentrate on developing the East Bank and on building ties to Syria and Saudi Arabia than to run the risk of isolation and violent opposition that might result if the king signed an unpopular agreement with Israel. For the time being Hussein and Kissinger agreed to await the outcome of the Arab summit in Rabat. With support from Sadat, Kissinger felt sure that Hussein would emerge with a mandate to negotiate for the West Bank.

To Kissinger's considerable annoyance and dismay, the Arab heads of state who assembled in Rabat during the last week of October did not behave as he anticipated. On October 28 the conference unanimously endorsed the PLO as the sole legitimate representative of the Palestinian people. Hussein had no more right in the eyes of the Arab world to negotiate for the West Bank than any other Arab leader. Faced with such an overwhelming consensus, even Hussein had accepted the final resolution. Sadat had tried to bring about a more ambiguous outcome but had failed. Saudi Arabia, ostensibly a moderate Arab state, and Syria had been among the most vocal champions of the PLO.

The Rabat summit, followed shortly by the appearance of PLO Executive Committee Chairman Yasir Arafat at the United Nations on November 13, suddenly propelled the Palestinians to the front and center of the Arab-Israeli conflict. Kissinger was unprepared for this turn of events. He had hoped to put off the Palestinian issue until later, while trying to strengthen King Hussein at the expense of the PLO. He had expected Egypt, Saudi Arabia, and perhaps even Syria to recognize the practical necessity of keeping Jordan in the negotiations. Now his carefully constructed policy had been derailed. American public opinion, which had strongly supported his efforts until then, began to express skepticism of step-by-step diplomacy, as well as firm opposition to pressure on Israel to deal with the PLO. Some felt that Rabat symbolized the failure of Kissinger's diplomacy, that Egypt and Syria were now preparing to back Arafat in his demands for dismantling the Zionist state, and that the proper response of American policy was to throw all its weight behind Israel, while invoking any sanctions available against the Arabs.[5]

In fact, the Rabat action was much less decisive than it appeared at the time, but it did cause problems for Kissinger. To salvage his policy and his reputation, he needed another success. Because it could not be on the Jordan front, it would have to be in Sinai. Egypt, however, was not the strong leader of the Arab world that it had been under Nasser—the Rabat meeting had shown that to be true—and would have to move carefully in any next step. At the same time Israel was hardly in the mood to make concessions, nor did the new government seem to have any clear diplomatic strategy. Golda Meir may have been tough and difficult to deal with, but at least she was in control of the government. It was less clear that Rabin could guide the divided country through a complex set of negotiations, particularly with his defense minister, Shimon Peres, eager to take his place if he should falter. To reach any agreement would definitely take time. Meanwhile other Middle East issues demanded attention.

OIL PRICES AS AN ISSUE

Issues have a curious way of coming and going in American politics, and that is especially true of complex problems such as the energy crisis. Few people understand the economics and politics of oil and energy, or the nature of the international petroleum market.

The Arab oil embargo was at least a concrete act that could be isolated from other issues and dealt with accordingly. It had a clear beginning and end. Yet the crisis did not seem to go away when the embargo was lifted in March 1974. In fact, it seemed as if the embargo per se had not really had much impact on the U.S. economy. But then what about the price of oil?

Oil prices became a major issue in the latter part of 1974, when the price of Persian Gulf oil reached almost $10 a barrel. At that price the United States would be spending approximately $20 billion a year on petroleum imports. Even if the United States could afford such a drain on its economy, Europe and Japan might not be able to handle the cost. The sheer magnitude of the financial transactions between oil importers and exporters might overwhelm the international financial system.

New terms like *petrodollars* and *recycling* began to appear. The rush to sell goods to Saudi Arabia, Iran, Iraq, and other oil-rich countries was on. Despite pious calls for cooperation among oil consumers and between consumers and producers, the reality was one of fierce competition. How long could that situation go on?

Kissinger began to worry about the international economic repercussions of the high price of oil sometime in the fall of 1974. The continued sluggishness of the Western economies, combined with high rates of inflation and unemployment, were apparently linked to oil prices. American public opinion tended to blame the Arabs for these economic ills, failing to note that other OPEC members, such as Iran and Venezuela, were more militant on prices than Saudi Arabia was. The net effect of this shift in mood was to make it even more difficult for Kissinger and Ford to pursue a diplomatic strategy aimed at promoting an Arab-Israeli settlement. After all, why do favors for the Arabs when they were threatening to bring down the economies of the Western democracies by their irresponsible behavior?

Kissinger made several efforts to try to persuade the Saudis and the Iranians to take the lead in lowering oil prices. At the same time the United States worked out an agreement with the OECD (Organization for Economic Cooperation and Development) countries of Europe and Japan for the sharing of oil in an emergency.[6] In addition, a producer-consumer dialogue was begun. Behind these efforts was the realization that in the event of another war between Israel and the Arabs, another embargo might occur, followed by oil-price increases. No one was quite sure, but it seemed plausible that progress toward a settlement of the Arab-Israeli conflict would remove the incentive for Arab oil producers to manipulate supplies and prices as a means of pressuring the United States.[7] Meanwhile the public concern over oil prices and possible embargoes was weakening the support for Kissinger's diplomacy, and an alternative strategy of counterpressure against the Arabs, including the use of force, began to receive a hearing.[8] A number of rather lurid pictures of impending financial chaos were painted. If OPEC did not collapse, the economies of the industrialized west were bound to do so. Neither, of course, happened, but throughout the next phase of Kissinger's diplomacy, petroleum and its financial ramifications were very much part of public and official preoccupation. Only gradually did the intense concern over the issue wane, as prices stabilized at a high level, adjustments were painfully made, and economic recovery began in the latter part of 1975.[9] By 1976 the issue had all but disappeared as a topic of public debate.

A SECOND EGYPTIAN-ISRAELI STEP

Kissinger's technique for arranging limited agreements between Israel and the Arabs was by now well developed. It began by eliciting proposals from each side, getting preliminary reactions, identifying obstacles, and then starting the diplomatic process that would eventually bridge the substantive gaps. This process would include a heavy dose of reason and persuasion, as Kissinger would explain the dire international consequences of failure to reach an agreement; it also involved marshaling forces that might influence the parties, such as other Arab countries or the U.S. Congress. Then Kissinger would commit his own prestige to bringing about an agreement, shuttling back and forth between the two sides. At this last stage Kissinger was likely to involve the president if additional pressure on Israel or commitments on future aid were needed.

Even before the Rabat meeting, Kissinger had obtained a fairly good idea of the Egyptian and Israeli objectives in a second step. Egypt wanted Israel to withdraw beyond the strategically important Mitla and Giddi passes and to relinquish control over the Abu Rudeis and Ras Sudr oil fields, which were providing Israel with about 50 percent of its total oil needs. Sadat wanted this step to be treated as another military disengagement, with only minimal political overtones. He felt he could not afford to be seen in the Arab world as having withdrawn from the conflict with Israel.

Israel's objectives in a second agreement with Egypt were quite different. Israel hoped to split Egypt from Syria and thus reduce the prospects of a combined Arab offensive such as had occurred in October 1973. To do so would require that Egypt make substantial political concessions as the price of further Israeli withdrawals. Israel would demand that Egypt renounce the state of belligerency, that the new agreement be of long duration, and that Israeli withdrawal would not include the passes or the oil fields.

During November and December 1974 Kissinger was able to clarify each side's position. He was convinced that Sadat would settle for nothing less than Mitla, Giddi, and the oil fields and that he would not formally renounce the state of belligerency. He so informed the Israelis, urging them to concentrate instead on the "functional equivalents" of nonbelligerency, such as the end of the economic boycott.

As Egypt and Israel began to show readiness for a second agreement, two potentially dangerous sources of opposition appeared. The Syrians were well aware that Israel was trying to isolate Egypt, which would then leave Syria alone to confront the militarily superior Israeli forces. Asad was therefore opposed to a second step on the Egyptian front. To underscore his attitude, Asad ordered his armed forces on high alert in mid-November, just on the eve of the renewal of the mandate of the UN forces. The crisis subsided, but not before Asad had made his point.

The second source of opposition to Kissinger's strategy was the Soviet Union. By now the Soviets saw clearly that one of Kissinger's primary goals was to weaken Soviet influence in the Middle East, especially in Egypt. President Ford and General Secretary Brezhnev met in Vladivostok on November 23–24, 1974, primarily to discuss a second strategic-arms agreement but also to consider the Middle East. The two sides remained far apart, the Soviets insisting on reconvening the Geneva conference and Ford favoring a continuation of step-by-step diplomacy, at the request, of course, of Egypt and Israel.[10] On the whole, U.S.-Soviet relations were cooling, as would become clear on January 14, 1975, when the Soviet Union rejected the offer of most-favored-nation trading status on terms that would have required a liberalization of emigration for Soviet Jews.

Meanwhile, despite Syrian and Soviet opposition, Kissinger pressed forward, his task complicated by the curious unfolding of the Israeli negotiating position. On December 3, 1974, in an interview with the newspaper *Haaretz*, Prime Minister Rabin openly stated that Israel's goal was to separate Egypt from Syria and delay negotiations until after the U.S. elections in 1976. Because of the oil crisis, Rabin said, there would be seven years during which Israel would be subjected to heavy pressures for concessions, but by the early 1980s alternatives to petroleum would have been found, thus weakening the power of the Arab world. Rabin added that it was unrealistic to expect Egypt to offer nonbelligerency at this stage of the negotiations.[11]

A few days after the Rabin interview, Foreign Minister Allon arrived in Washington for talks with Kissinger. For several hours on December 9 they discussed a ten-point proposal Allon had brought with him.[12] The points included an end to the state of belligerency, the demilitarization of evacuated territory, an end to economic and propaganda warfare by Egypt against Israel, a duration of twelve years for the agreement, and a number of other demands similar to those written into the January disengagement accord. In return for these demands, Israel would withdraw thirty to fifty kilometers, but would remain in control of the passes and oil fields.

Kissinger and Ford were unimpressed by Israel's offer. Allon hinted that it was only a bargaining position and might be changed. For example, the duration of the agreement could be five years instead of twelve. Kissinger's main problem with the Israeli proposal, however, was the demand for nonbelligerency, which Rabin himself had termed unrealistic, and the refusal to cede on the passes and oil fields. The Israeli points were nonetheless transmitted to Sadat, and Sadat's expected rejection was duly received. Kissinger then asked the Israelis to make a new proposal.

As frequently happens in Arab-Israeli affairs, external events impinge on the local parties in unanticipated ways. In late December an important development took place in Soviet-Egyptian relations. After a short visit to Moscow by Egypt's foreign minister and its chief of staff, it was announced on December 30 that the expected visit by Brezhnev to Cairo had been canceled. Kissinger had been planning to await the results of the Brezhnev visit before pressing ahead with his own strategy. Now it seemed as if Egyptian-Soviet relations were indeed very poor; more than ever, Sadat needed to demonstrate that his turning to the United States had not been foolish. Without Soviet arms he would not easily be able to make war, but with American support he might recover his territory anyway and get on with the urgent task of developing the Egyptian economy.

When Allon arrived in the United States for another round of discussions with Kissinger, he acknowledged that the cancellation of the Brezhnev visit had created a new situation, but during his talks with Ford and Kissinger on January 15–16, 1975, he had nothing new to offer except an invitation to Kissinger to return to the area. Kissinger repeated his warning to Allon that an agreement could not be reached on the basis of the Israeli proposal.[13] He would nonetheless make another trip to see if the gap could be narrowed. After an exploratory round of talks in

February, he would return in March to complete the negotiations, but Israel would have to drop the demand for nonbelligerency and be more forthcoming over territory.

Before Kissinger's departure Sadat publicly endorsed his efforts, adding that the United States now held virtually all the trump cards.[14] These words were precisely what Kissinger wanted to hear from Sadat. From the Syrians and the Soviets, however, he was continuing to encounter resistance to his efforts. As Sadat seemed to move forward toward another agreement, Syria began to band together with Jordan and the Palestinians in opposing him, with growing support from the Soviet Union.[15]

Even though Syria and the Soviet Union were aligning against Sadat, Israel at least seemed to be softening somewhat in its demands. On February 7 Rabin gave an interview to John Lindsay, former mayor of New York, in which he stated that "in exchange for an Egyptian commitment not to go to war, not to depend on threats of use of force, and an effort to reach true peace, the Egyptians could get even the passes and the oil fields."[16] Kissinger was appalled at Rabin's carelessness in revealing Israel's position in such a forum—he would no doubt have preferred to appear responsible for achieving such an Israeli concession—but at least the chance for an agreement now seemed brighter. On this somewhat optimistic note, Kissinger left for the Middle East on February 9.

Kissinger's February trip was admittedly exploratory. He did not expect to reach agreement, but he did hope that Egypt and Israel would each recognize the constraints the other was operating under and modify some elements of their proposals. Instead he found little new. The Israelis seemed to ease up a bit on the issue of nonbelligerency, and Sadat indicated a willingness to end some hostile actions against Israel, but a substantial gap remained. Nor did Kissinger succeed in persuading the Syrians to drop their opposition to a second step in Sinai.[17] The only positive note of the trip came from Kissinger's talks with the shah of Iran in Zurich on February 18, when the shah said he would be prepared to provide Israel with oil if it gave up Abu Rudeis and Ras Sudr.

For the next several weeks Kissinger continued to urge the parties to moderate their positions, for he wanted an agreement, and soon. But he did not want to embark on a third "shuttle" until he was virtually certain of success. Assuming that the parties now understood the minimum terms required for a successful negotiation, Kissinger left for the Middle East once again, arriving in Egypt on March 8.

Kissinger's task was complicated by a number of domestic and international developments. Both he and Ford were experiencing a decline in their popularity. Congress was becoming more assertive in its demands to guide foreign policy. Indochina was progressively coming under communist domination. A leftist coup in Portugal had created a potentially dangerous situation in the western Mediterranean. U.S.-Turkish relations were at a low point because of a congressional ban on arms to Turkey. Only on the Egyptian-Israeli front was there the chance of another Kissinger spectacular. The Israelis seemed apprehensive that Kissinger was a bit too anxious for success. They, after all, would be asked to make the major concessions, and that was more than Rabin's weak government was anxious to do.

Kissinger did succeed in obtaining new Egyptian proposals during the March shuttle. Sadat was prepared to say the following: the conflict with Israel would not be solved by military means; Egypt would not resort to force; it would observe the cease-fire and would prevent all military and paramilitary forces from operating against Israel from Egyptian territory; a new agreement would remain in effect until superseded by another agreement; hostile propaganda against Israel in Egyptian-controlled media would be reduced; and the economic boycott would be selectively eased.[18]

Israel's position, as first conveyed informally by Rabin to Kissinger on the evening of March 9, consisted of seven points entitled "Proposal on Main Elements of Agreement between Israel and Egypt." Israel sought a separate agreement with Egypt that would not depend on agreements with other Arab parties. The agreement must be a step toward peace in some practical aspects, such as the free passage of Israeli cargoes through the Suez Canal, the end of the economic boycott, and the free movement of persons between Egypt and Israel. Egypt must agree to the end of the use of force through a "renunciation of belligerency clearly and in its appropriate legal wording." A real buffer zone must be created between the military forces of both sides. Some solution must be found for the "dilemma of vagueness" about the duration of the agreement. An understanding must be reached on the relationship between an interim agreement in Sinai and what might happen later at Geneva. Finally, Israel would agree to discuss the question of the line of withdrawal only after Egypt had responded to the first six points.[19]

Kissinger was dismayed that Israel was still holding out for nonbelligerency. Sadat was prepared to meet some of Israel's demands but insisted on knowing whether Israel would remain in the passes. He also flatly refused to agree to nonbelligerency, though he would consider a formula based on the "nonuse of force." After several days of shuttling, Kissinger managed to persuade the Israelis to accept the nonuse-of-force formulation, but Rabin and his negotiating team were adamant that Israel would not withdraw from the passes for anything less than nonbelligerency. At best they might consider pulling back to a line halfway through the passes, but at no point in the negotiations did the Israelis provide Kissinger with a map showing a line they would accept. Complicating the bargaining further was Israel's insistence on maintaining control over an electronic intelligence station at Umm Khisheiba at the western end of the Giddi pass. Sadat would not agree to Israel's keeping the station, even if it was formally placed in the UN zone. Consequently the negotiations deadlocked on the issues of nonbelligerency and its functional equivalents, on the extent of Israeli withdrawal in the passes and the oil fields, and on the status of the Umm Khisheiba facility.

After ten days of shuttling between Egypt and Israel, with side trips to Syria, Jordan, and Saudi Arabia, Kissinger was still not able to get the Israelis out of the passes. Israel agreed to cede the oil fields but refused to give Egypt control over a road connecting the fields to the Egyptian zone. On Friday, March 21, Kissinger arrived in Israel with Sadat's final word: Israel could not keep the intelligence station, and the mandate of the UN forces would be renewed only for a second year. Without further Egyptian concessions the Israelis would not budge. Even a tough letter from President Ford, which reached Israel on March 21, was unable to change the situation.[20] It may, in fact, have stiffened Israel's will to resist. In any event, the cabinet met Friday night and rejected virtually all Sadat's demands. Kissinger conveyed Israel's rejection to Egypt and awaited Sadat's reply. Meanwhile he spent the day of March 22 touring the historic site of Masada, where, nearly two thousand years earlier, Jews had taken their own lives rather than surrender to the Romans. The symbolism of Masada hung over the talks later that evening when Kissinger met with Rabin and other top Israeli officials. Kissinger was deeply concerned. According to the notes of his remarks, he stated:

The Arab leaders who banked on the United States will be discredited. . . . Step-by-step has been throttled, first for Jordan, then for Egypt. We're losing control. We'll now see the Arabs working on a united front. There will be more emphasis on the Palestinians, and there will be a linkage between moves in the Sinai and on Golan. The Soviets will step back onto the stage. The United States is losing control over events. . . . Our past strategy was worked out carefully, and now we don't know what to do. There will be pressures to drive a wedge between Israel and the United States, not because we want that but because it will be the dynamics of the situation. Let's not kid ourselves. We've failed. . . .

An agreement would have enabled the United States to remain in control of the diplomatic process. Compared to that, the location of the line eight kilometers one way or the other frankly does not seem very important. And you got all the military elements of nonbelligerency. You got the 'nonuse of force.' . . .

This is a real tragedy. . . . We've attempted to reconcile our support for you with our other interests in the Middle East, so that you wouldn't have to make your decisions all at once. . . . Our strategy was to save you from dealing with all those pressures all at once. . . . If we wanted the 1967 borders, we could do it with all of world opinion and considerable domestic opinion behind us. The strategy was designed to protect you from this. We've avoided drawing up an overall plan for a global settlement. . . . I see pressure building up to force you back to the 1967 borders—compared to that, ten kilometers is trivial. I'm not angry at you, and I'm not asking you to change your position. It's tragic to see people dooming themselves to a course of unbelievable peril.[21]

This was vintage Kissinger. He could have made virtually the same remarks at any point from October 1973 on. The emphasis on U.S. control of the diplomacy, on breaking issues into manageable parts, and on avoiding an overall peace plan were all basic elements of the strategy developed in the midst of the October war. Now that strategy seemed to have failed. The next day Kissinger left Israel, having announced that his negotiating effort was being suspended.[22] After Kissinger returned to Washington on March 24, President Ford ominously announced that there would now be a reassessment of U.S. policy toward the Middle East.[23]

REASSESSMENT

Kissinger's disappointment with the Israelis for thwarting his efforts to arrange a second agreement in Sinai was genuine. He felt the Israeli leadership was shortsighted, incompetent, and weak. In his view Israel had no foreign policy, only a domestic political system that produced deadlock and stalemate. A David Ben-Gurion or a Golda Meir might be able to lead Israel, but not the Rabin-Peres-Allon triumvirate, in which each man pulled in a different direction. In his less guarded moments Kissinger suggested that the Israelis were trying to bring him down. Reassessment, however justified, became in part an instrument for Kissinger to vent his exasperation with Israel.

President Ford, whatever his sentimental attachment to Israel might have been in the past, was also irritated at Israel, and publicly blamed

Rabin for his lack of flexibility.[24] He lent his weight to a serious reassessment of policy during which new military and economic agreements with Israel were suspended. Like each of his predecessors, Ford found that his sympathies for Israel and his perception of American global and regional interests did not always mesh. When the two seemed to come into conflict, Ford was as capable as Nixon of putting pressure on Israel for concessions. The test, however, would be whether pressure could produce the desired results—and whether Israeli counterpressure might not raise the cost of the effort.

Israel, after all, was not without influential friends and supporters in the United States, nor did it lack effective spokespersons who could defend it before the American public against the charge of inflexibility. If the administration insisted on withholding needed aid, Israel could appeal to Congress to support its requests. The Israeli case did seem plausible: in return for making important economic and territorial concessions, Israel was merely asking that Egypt renounce belligerency. Why was that unreasonable or inflexible? Should Israel risk its security for anything less?

Kissinger's case against Israel was less convincing to many Americans. He claimed that the Israeli leaders had misled him into undertaking the shuttle when they knew that nonbelligerency could not be achieved, and yet they continued to insist on it. Israel had refused to make the minimal territorial concessions in the passes and around the oil fields. Kissinger argued that an agreement was necessary to preserve the delicate balances he had brought into being after the October 1973 war. On occasion, he implied that the alternative to an agrement might be war and another Arab oil embargo.

During the nearly three months of reassessment that followed the collapse of the Egyptian-Israeli talks on March 22, American foreign policy witnessed the final denouement of the Southeast Asia conflict and the beginning of a tragic civil war in Lebanon. In both cases the United States seemed powerless to act constructively. The Cambodian capital of Phnom Penh fell to communist forces on April 17. Shortly thereafter, on April 29, Saigon also came under communist control. So much for the peace with honor in Indochina that Nixon and Kissinger had proudly proclaimed in January 1973. Events in the Middle East, too, did not hold out the hope of peace. On March 25 one of the mainstays of American policy in the area, King Faisal of Saudi Arabia, was assassinated. A period of uncertainty began. Was Saudi Arabia on the verge of revolution?

Would the new rulers continue the same foreign policy of friendship for the United States and support for Sadat? It would be some time before anyone would know. Meanwhile the always tense situation in Lebanon was about to explode. On April 13 right-wing Christian gunmen had opened fire on a busload of Palestinians, killing twenty-two of them. Not long afterward a vicious cycle of reprisals and counterreprisals was under way.

Against this disquieting background Kissinger carried out the promised policy reassessment. On April 1 he met with a group of prominent men from the foreign-policy establishment—Dean Rusk, McGeorge Bundy, George Ball, Douglas Dillon, Cyrus Vance, George Shultz, Robert McNamara, David Bruce, Peter Peterson, John McCloy, William Scranton, and Averell Harriman. Some of the group, such as Ball, had been openly critical of Kissinger's step-by-step policy and Israel. Ball favored a more comprehensive agreement in which the United States and the Soviet Union would work out the guidelines for a settlement, which would then be negotiated by all the parties at Geneva. He had criticized Kissinger for ignoring the Soviets and trying to divide the Arabs. He did not shy away from the notion of an imposed settlement.[25] Others at the meeting also favored a return to the Geneva conference and a major effort to work out an American peace plan.

Over the next several weeks Kissinger heard essentially the same recommendations from his closest aides, from eminent academics, and from American ambassadors to the key Middle East countries.[26] The time for step-by-step diplomacy was past. A more ambitious strategy was needed. The Palestinians could no longer be ignored. The Soviets would have to be brought into the negotiations. It all sounded reasonable in the abstract, but Kissinger was haunted by the fear that this approach, too, would fail. No one could detail the steps that would be required to ensure success. And it would be costly in domestic political terms, since it would surely require heavy and sustained pressure on Israel. Ford and Kissinger were not at all certain they wanted to take on that battle unless the results were sure to warrant the effort.

By the third week of April reassessment had produced three basic options for the president. The first, supported by many in and outside the government, was a return to Geneva with a detailed American peace plan. The United States would call for Israeli withdrawal, while offering strong guarantees of Israel's security. The Soviets would be invited to cooperate. A second option would aim for a virtually complete settlement, especially on the Egyptian-Israeli front, but would fall short of calling for full withdrawal and final peace. The third option was to resume step-by-step diplomacy where it had left off in March.[27] Ford referred publicly to these three options in a general way on April 21.[28]

For several weeks it seemed as if a new American approach to peace in the Middle East might emerge, but gradually the realization set in that nothing of the sort could be expected. Kissinger's consultations with Allon, King Hussein, and the Soviets had not given him any reason to be optimistic about a new policy. American public support for a global initiative was not strong, and Congress was beginning to respond to arguments that Kissinger was exerting too much pressure on Israel. On May 21 seventy-six senators sent a letter to President Ford, urging him to be "responsive to Israel's economic and military needs." This was a clear sign that continued pressure on Israel would be politically counterproductive. Ford and Kissinger realized that the only viable strategy, in light of these realities, was to resume step-by-step diplomacy.[29] Ford himself would participate in talks with Sadat and Rabin to explore the prospects for an agreement. Sadat helped to improve the atmosphere by unexpectedly announcing that the Suez Canal would be reopened on June 5 and that the mandate of the United Nations Emergency Force would be extended. The Egyptian president still seemed to want to reach an agreement.

On June 1–2 President Ford and Sadat met for the first time, in Salzburg. The two men got on well together, feeling relaxed in each other's company and finding it easy to talk. Sadat appealed for a public statement from Ford that Israel should withdraw to the 1967 lines, but Ford demurred, reportedly repeating instead Nixon's private commitment of the previous year to work for that goal.[30] Ford then sounded out Sadat on his willingness to try again for a limited agreement in Sinai. Sadat was favorably disposed, but his terms were still those of the previous spring: Israel must leave the passes and the oil fields and must not demand nonbelligerency. Sadat was still opposed to the idea of the Israelis' keeping the intelligence-gathering facility at Umm Khisheiba, but he did say he might accept an American presence there.[31] The idea of an American military contingent in the buffer zone had been raised earlier in the spring, but Kissinger had been unenthusiastic. The more modest concept of an American civilian presence, however, soon began to emerge as the solution to one of the problems in the negotiations.[32]

SINAI II

By the time Prime Minister Rabin reached Washington for talks with President Ford and Secretary Kissinger on June 11–12, the decision to continue with step-by-step diplomacy had basically been made. The alternative of Geneva, of a U.S.-Soviet imposed settlement, or of a withdrawal from the peacemaking effort had all been rejected. Ford and Kissinger felt the situation in the Middle East required continued diplomatic progress; as had been shown early in 1974, that could best be done through U.S. mediation. If progress toward a settlement was not made during the next few months, the United States might not be able to launch a new initiative until 1977. After all, 1976 was an American election year, and Middle East politics could hardly hope to compete for attention with a presidential campaign.

Ford, now very much involved in the conduct of Arab-Israeli diplomacy, asked Rabin to be more forthcoming in the negotiations and pressed for a new Israeli line of withdrawal to the eastern ends of the passes. Rabin was anxious to end the painful and costly confrontation with the United States. His refusal of Kissinger's demands in March had greatly contributed to his prestige within Israel. Now he might be able to negotiate with more confidence. A new line therefore was drawn to demonstrate Israel's good will, and this was seen as a modest step in the right direction. Ford reciprocated by promising that after the next interim agreement between Egypt and Israel, "the overall settlement can be pursued in a systematic and deliberate way and does not require the U.S. to put forward an overall proposal of its own in such circumstances. Should the U.S. desire in the future to put forward proposals of its own, it will make every effort to coordinate with Israel its proposals with a view to refraining from putting forth proposals that Israel would consider unsatisfactory."[33]

Despite these assurances from Ford, Rabin was unable to win cabinet authorization to make further concessions. A week later he was obliged to return to Israel's previous offer of withdrawal halfway through the passes.[34] Once again Ford and Kissinger were angry at Rabin for his apparent inflexibility and his awkwardness.

During the next six weeks Kissinger remained in Washington while Israeli and Egyptian positions were refined and transmitted through him to the other side. Israel's ambassador in Washington, Simcha Dinitz, was his channel to the Israeli government, and the American ambassador to Egypt, Hermann F. Eilts, shuttled back and forth between Cairo and Washington with messages and clarifications.

Sometime in the last half of June the Israeli leaders apparently decided it would be impossible to obtain the desired political concessions from Sadat and undesirable to resist the United States indefinitely. If Egypt would not make peace, then at least Israel could bargain with the United States on issues involving Israeli security. If the Americans wanted an agreement so badly, they could pay for it. Israel would agree to withdraw to the eastern slopes of the passes but would maintain control over the high ground above the passes. At the urging of Defense Minister Peres, Israel also sought to make the buffer zone between the two sides into a genuine barrier to military surprise attack by stationing American civilians there to monitor early-warning stations. The Americans could also serve as a cover for continued Israeli use of the intelligence facility. If Sadat objected, the Americans could offer to build a comparable facility for him as well.

Sadat was also prepared to be somewhat more forthcoming. He would agree to three annual renewals of the mandate of the UN forces and to the continued Israeli use of the intelligence facility, provided he was given one facing the Israeli lines. He accepted the idea of easing the boycott of some companies dealing with Israel and promised to tone down anti-Israeli propaganda. And finally, he would be willing to have most of the terms of the agreement published.

It remained for the United States and Israel to work out their own understanding of the American commitments necessary to gain Israel's consent to a new agreement. Early in July Dinitz met with Kissinger in the Virgin Islands to present the full package of Israeli proposals and requests.[35] In addition to a promise of about $2 billion in aid, the United States agreed to drop the idea of an interim step on the Jordan-Israel front and to accept that only "cosmetic" changes could be expected on the Golan Heights in another step. Israel also wanted a clear commitment that the United States would prevent Soviet military intervention in the Middle East.[36]

During the next several weeks further discussion of these and other points took place.[37] By the time Kissinger left for Israel on August 20, an agreement was within reach. Only the exact location of the Israeli line, the levels of U.S. aid, and the technical aspects of the American civilian presence in the passes remained to be negotiated.

Kissinger was received in Israel with unprecedented hostility, mainly from the right-wing opposition parties, and demonstrators accosted him at each stop. Nevertheless, his discussions with the leadership progressed. This time Rabin wanted an agreement. Kissinger continued to harbor misgivings about the American presence in Sinai, which by now was an essential ingredient of the Israeli package, but he was prepared to go along with the idea. Sadat was willing to accept this condition, but some quibbling still went on over the exact location of the line.[38]

By August 25 Kissinger was working with the Israelis on the language of a draft agreement. Gradually Israel began to soften its position on the line of withdrawal, finally agreeing to give Kissinger a map for Sadat's consideration late in the second week of talks. Squabbling over withdrawal in the Giddi pass continued, as well as over the oil fields. Only at the very last minute did Israel agree to complete withdrawal from Giddi. Very detailed discussions on force limits and on the American presence were also required. Then, in a nonstop session in Jerusalem lasting from 9:30 p.m. August 31 to 6:00 a.m. the following day, the United States and Israel worked out the fine points of their bilateral military relationship, assurances on Israel's supply of oil, and an understanding on the need for consultations in the event of Soviet military intervention in the Middle East. Israel was disappointed with the weak language on Soviet intervention but otherwise could point to a very impressive list of American commitments. Later that afternoon both Egypt and Israel initialed the text of the agreement. It was formally signed in Geneva on September 4, 1975.

Unlike the January 1974 accord, Sinai II was greeted with a sigh of relief, but with little real enthusiasm by the parties to the negotiations. Within both Israel and the Arab world, many were violently opposed to the agreement, although for entirely different reasons.

The agreement itself was modeled in part on the previous disengagement pacts.[39] The two parties committed themselves to resolve the conflict between them by peaceful means and not to resort to the threat or the use of force against each other. The UN force would continue its function, and the lines for each side's military deployments were designated on a map. Egypt agreed to allow nonmilitary cargoes destined for or coming from Israel to pass through the Suez Canal, which had been reopened to traffic the previous June. The agreement would remain in force until superseded by a new agreement.

Attached to the agreement was a detailed annex dealing with military deployments and aerial surveillance. At Sadat's insistence the forces allowed in the limited zone under the agreement were slightly larger than those permitted in January 1974: up to 8,000 men in eight battalions, with 75 tanks and 72 short-range artillery pieces. Neither party, however, was permitted to locate any weapons in areas from which they could reach each other's lines.

The arrangements for U.S. manning and supervision of the early-warning systems in the buffer zones were also spelled out in detail. Israel and Egypt would be allowed to have up to 250 technical and administrative personnel at their respective surveillance stations. U.S. civilians would operate three other smaller watch stations and would establish three unmanned sensor fields as well. Israel's willingness to implement the terms of the agreement was contingent on U.S. congressional approval of the U.S. role in Sinai. The United States also signed five secret agreements, four with Israel and one with Egypt. A sixteen-point U.S.-Israeli memorandum of understanding dealt with military assistance, oil supply, economic aid, and several political points. The United States and Israel agreed that the next step with Egypt should be a final peace agreement. The same should be true on the Jordan front. The United States also agreed to consult promptly with Israel in the event of any threat to Israel from a "world power," namely, the Soviet Union. In an addendum on arms the United States gave a vague commitment to provide a "positive response" to Israeli requests for F-16 aircraft and the Pershing missile with a conventional warhead.[40] In effect, the freeze on new arms agreements, which had begun the previous April, was ended.

A special memo dealing with Geneva was signed, which spelled out the policy of the United States with respect to the Palestinians: no recognition of and no negotiation with the PLO until it recognizes Israel's right to exist and accepts UN Resolutions 242 and 338.[41] The United States would also carefully coordinate its strategy at Geneva with Israel and agree to keep the negotiations on a bilateral basis. In addition, Ford wrote a letter to Rabin stating: "The U.S. has not developed a final position on the borders [between Israel and Syria]. Should it do so it will give great weight to Israel's position that any peace agreement with Syria must be predicated on Israel remaining on the Golan Heights. My view in this regard was stated in our conversation of September 13, 1974."[42]

As for Egypt, the United States merely committed itself to try to bring about further negotiations between Syria and Israel, to provide assistance for the Egyptian early-warning system in the buffer zone, and to consult with Egypt on any Israeli violations of the agreement.

REACTIONS TO SINAI II

In his more optimistic moments Kissinger had justified step-by-step diplomacy as a process by which parties to a negotiation would gain confidence, become committed to achieving results, and be carried along by the momentum of peacemaking to resolve issues that had previously seemed intractable. But Sinai II came closer to confirming his more somber vision of the Arab-Israeli conflict. The issues were so complex, the emotions so deeply involved, that peace between the two sides was unattainable in this generation. Although some agreements might be reached, they would be modest and imperfect at best. The diplomat aspiring to mediate between Israel and the Arabs would have to be content with small achievements. These, at least, were better than nothing. The stabilization of the region, the reduction of the chances of war, and the end of the oil embargo were far preferable to renewed hostilities and superpower confrontation. Egypt, in any case, seemed firmly committed to a moderate course.

Kissinger had not consciously sought to provoke dissension among the Arabs. On the contrary, he was deeply concerned that Saudi Arabia continue to back Sadat's policies. He also recognized that Syria played a vital role in inter-Arab politics, and he genuinely wanted to draw Syria toward a moderate settlement with Israel.[43] The objective situation, however, thwarted his efforts. Golan was not Sinai, and a second step there would be difficult to manage unless Israel was prepared to give up the settlements beyond the post-1967 cease-fire lines. Israel had just demonstrated a remarkable capacity to hold out against American pressures and to exact a high price for eventual compliance. Was it worth the effort for a few kilometers on Golan? Sadat had very much wanted a second agreement, whereas Asad, by contrast, was lukewarm to the idea. He did not entirely reject the concept of a second step, but he made it clear that he was not prepared to pay much of a price for it. Instead Asad began to attack Sadat for having forsaken the struggle against Israel and to press for international recognition of the PLO. Inter-Arab politics had a dynamic of its own that was unleashed by Sinai II. Short of abandoning step-by-step diplomacy, it is not clear what Kissinger could have done to keep Egypt and Syria from drifting apart.

Kissinger's most serious effort to demonstrate his continuing willingness to work for a comprehensive peace agreement came before Syria's renewal of the UN disengagement observation force in late November 1975. On November 10, 1975, the UN General Assembly had passed a resolution defining Zionism as "a form of racism or racial discrimination." The United States had voted against the resolution, and the U.S. ambassador to the UN, Daniel Patrick Moynihan, had stated that "the United States . . . does not acknowledge, it will not abide by, it will never acquiesce in this infamous act." American public reaction had been strongly supportive of Moynihan's tough words. Many expressed their contempt for those nations who had presumably succumbed to Arab oil blackmail. In this atmosphere it was particularly remarkable that on November 12 the deputy assistant secretary of state for Near Eastern affairs, Harold H. Saunders, appeared before a House of Representatives subcommittee to make a policy statement on the Palestinians.

The Saunders document, as it came to be called, infuriated the Israelis and encouraged the Arabs. It spoke of the Palestinian dimension of the Arab-Israeli conflict as being, in many ways, the "heart of that conflict." Saunders went on to state that "the legitimate interests of the Palestinian Arabs must be taken into account in the negotiation of an Arab-Israeli peace." It was a question of how, not whether.[44] Although there was little new in the statement, its timing was significant. It was meant to symbolize a continuing willingness on the part of the administration to work for a peace settlement. Kissinger had gone over the draft carefully, had checked the wording, and had reportedly cleared it with President Ford. When confronted with Israel's hostile reaction, however, he dismissed the Saunders statement as an academic exercise. Nonetheless, the United States seemed to take a somewhat more flexible position than in the past when the issue of PLO participation in the UN debate scheduled for January 1976 came up. Briefly, Arab hopes were raised, but they were to be disappointed. Behind the symbolic shift in American policy there was no real substance.

Public opposition to dealing with the PLO was only one aspect of a broader disenchantment with Kissinger's foreign policy. Détente, once the hallmark of the Nixon-Kissinger policy, was increasingly being attacked, not only by such inveterate cold warriors as Henry Jackson but also by former defense secretary James Schlesinger and by Moynihan, once he had ceased to be the UN ambassador.[45] Furthermore, the Nobel-prize–winning Russian author who had been forced into exile by the Soviet government, Alexander Solzhenitsyn, was drawing considerable attention by his gloomy warnings about the dangers of détente with the Soviet Union. All these opponents of détente proved to be ardent supporters of Israel: Israel was anti-Soviet; Israel was in the forefront of defending the human rights of Soviet Jews; Israel was democratic. American pressure on Israel for the sake of détente or Arab oil was especially to be deplored, in the eyes of these critics.

Congress, for its part, was not very pleased with Sinai II as an example of Kissinger's diplomatic prowess. At a minimum, U.S. aid to the Middle East in fiscal year 1976 would exceed $3 billion, $2.25 billion of which would go to Israel, thereby cutting deeply into aid funds available for the rest of the world.[46] Moreover, Congress initially balked at the idea of sending American civilians to monitor the buffer zone between Egypt and Israel. The Vietnam analogy was raised, although it was not sufficiently compelling to cause Congress to reject the idea. Then, too, even the most ardent supporters of Israel were dismayed to find Pershing missiles among the military items requested by Israel. It seemed doubtful that Congress would authorize the sale of Pershings to Israel, and in December 1975 Israel withdrew its request, at least for the time being.

As the election year 1976 began, it became apparent that President Ford would be preoccupied with domestic politics. His position within his own party was precarious, and it was not certain that he would even be nominated at the Republican convention in August. Ronald Reagan, former governor of California, was mounting a strong challenge, with the support of the most conservative elements in the party. Kissinger and his foreign policy were emerging as a campaign issue for the Reagan Republicans as well as for the Democrats. And although the Middle East was not initially one of the issues in the campaign, the criticisms aimed at Ford and Kissinger did drive them to a tougher stance toward the Soviet Union, as symbolized by American policy in Angola, and precluded an ambitious new initiative in the Arab-Israeli arena.

Despite these election-year pressures, however, President Ford persevered in the attempt to improve U.S.-Egyptian relations. In October 1975 Sadat had been the first Egyptian president to pay an official visit to the United States. During that visit Sadat had appealed for American economic and even military assistance. A complex debate between Congress and the administration ensued, with Ford reducing requested aid for Israel in fiscal year 1977 from $2.25 billion to $1.8 billion and simultaneously urging Congress to consider the approval of a limited sale of six C-130 transport planes to Egypt.

Congress not only favored higher levels of aid to Israel but also felt that Israel should receive a supplemental grant to cover the "transitional quarter" from July 1976 to October 1, 1976, the beginning of the new fiscal year. In one of the rare instances of public disagreement between Ford and Kissinger, Ford opposed on budgetary grounds additional aid to Israel for the transitional quarter, whereas Kissinger said the administration would not mind if Congress chose to vote an additional $500 million.

The consideration of arms for Egypt took a new turn in mid-March 1976, when President Sadat announced the abrogation of the fifteen-year treaty of friendship and cooperation with the Soviet Union. Against the background of the news that Israel, according to CIA analysts, possessed from ten to twenty operational atomic weapons,[47] opposition to the sale to Egypt faded, although Congress preferred that it be handled purely as a commercial transaction. Eventually Egypt got the planes, worth about $50 million, and Israel received the supplementary aid, worth many times more.

Ford's willingness to take a hard line on aid to Israel and to oppose in the United Nations the Israeli policy on settlements in the occupied territories lasted through the first part of the election campaign. By the fall, however, when Governor Jimmy Carter of Georgia, the Democratic candidate, was enjoying a huge lead in the polls, the president began to play up his credentials as a strong supporter of Israel. In the last month of the campaign the Middle East became a topic of occasional debate, wherein Carter and Ford tried to outdo each other as the better friend of Israel, and Carter in particular hinted at very severe action against any future Arab oil embargo.

Carter's narrow victory over Ford on November 2, 1976, settled the issue of who would be the next president, but neither the Israelis nor the Arabs had any clear idea of what the next president's policies would be. Both expected new initiatives, and both were apprehensive.

THE LEBANON CRISIS

Throughout the early part of 1976, as the Americans turned their attention inward, inter-Arab relations continued to deteriorate in the absence of progress toward a settlement. Egypt was trying to emerge from the isolation produced by Sinai II, but only Saudi Arabia offered support. Syria and Jordan were moving together, and the Palestinians were still denouncing Sadat as a traitor to the cause.

In January 1976 the ongoing crisis in Lebanon grew more acute as hundreds of casualties were registered every day. Conspiratorial interpretations of the events in Lebanon abounded, producing a particularly suspicious and mistrustful mood in the Arab world. The only party that seemed to be profiting from the Lebanon crisis, in the eyes of many Arabs, was Israel. Some would also add the United States and Egypt. Lebanon was deflecting attention from Sinai II and was ensuring that combined Arab pressure could not be brought to bear on Israel or the United States. In addition, the right-wing Christian groups in Lebanon, armed and supported by the West and even Israel, were inexplicably pressing their attacks against the Lebanese left, and the Palestinians in particular. Some saw these attacks as part of a master plan, orchestrated in Washington, to destroy the PLO. Then Egypt, Syria, and Jordan could make peace with Israel under U.S. auspices.

Syria's objective in Lebanon appeared to be to bring the fighting to an early end. Initially Syria allowed several battalions of the Palestine Liberation Army to enter Lebanon. The tide of the battle seemed to turn in ensuing months, to the point where the left, headed by Kamal Jumblatt, spoke of an impending military victory over the right. This possibility concerned the United States, because a leftist Lebanon might allow Palestinian guerrilla attacks against Israel, which could eventually lead to war. Syria, and perhaps even Egypt, would be drawn in. During this period, then, the United States played a very active role in urging restraint on Israel and Syria.[48] Above all, the United States feared that large-scale Syrian intervention on the side of the Palestinians would provoke an Israeli military reaction, thus threatening to upset the fragile stability of the agreements so laboriously negotiated by Kissinger.

The warnings to Syria may have struck home. Asad was perfectly aware that a leftist- or Palestinian-dominated Lebanon would cause him problems. It might invite Israeli attacks, drawing Syria into premature military action against Israel. Or it might align itself with Syria's bitter rival, Iraq. What Asad most wanted was a Lebanon responsive to Syria's leadership, but as the fighting went on it became clear that the left and Palestinians were not about to take orders from Damascus. The American assessment of Syria's interests in Lebanon began to change, and by May the United States, with the encouragement of Jordan's King Hussein, was saying that a limited Syrian military intervention in Lebanon might help to stabilize the situation and restore security. Inasmuch as the United States, and presumably Israel as well, no longer opposed a Syrian move, Asad ordered his armed forces into Syria on a large scale in early June to protect the embattled Christians and rightists against the left and the Palestinians.

Soon most of Lebanon was under Syrian control, but the fighting raged on, especially in Beirut. Syria's intervention in Lebanon was roundly condemned by other Arab states, especially Egypt, which joined forces with Iraq, Libya, and the PLO to thwart the Syrian moves. New conspiracy theories began to emerge, linking Syria's action to Kissinger's diabolical policies: Syria would crush the PLO and would be rewarded by the return of the Golan Heights. Jordan would recover the West Bank. A Pax Americana would then descend over the area. Radical forces and Soviet influence would be banished. Saudi oil money would finance the flow of American technology.

The only flaw in the theories was that they bore little resemblance to reality. American officials, rather than having a grand policy for dealing with the Lebanon crisis or the Palestinians, were confused and perplexed by the internecine war in Lebanon. Kissinger dealt with the crisis chiefly as an extension of the Arab-Israeli conflict; hence the warnings to both Israel and Syria not to intervene during the spring of 1976. The conflict had a logic of its own, however, as did Syrian policy, once the commitment to Lebanon was made early in 1976. Asad was not playing the American or Israeli game in Lebanon, whatever the superficial appearances. Kissinger and Ford, quite simply, had no game in mind, other than to prevent a full-scale Arab-Israeli war. Apart from urging the evacuation of Americans in Lebanon, the United States did little.[49]

The fighting in Lebanon continued into the fall, and the Christians consolidated their control over a small coastal strip between Beirut and Tripoli. For all intents and purposes this became an autonomous region with its own government and armed forces. Even the newly elected president, Elias Sarkis, had little sway over the Christians. Syria helped them by removing the Palestinians from the mountainous areas to the east of the Christian-held areas, gradually and methodically pushing them toward their stronghold around the port of Sidon. The Palestinians, with help from the Iraqis, Libyans, and Egyptians, fought against great odds but could not withstand the Syrian offensive.

At the moment of impending Syrian victory, Saudi Arabia flexed its diplomatic and financial muscles, summoning President Asad and Sadat, along with PLO Chairman Arafat, to Riyadh in late October 1976 for an urgent conference to end the bloodshed in Lebanon. Asad conducted himself with considerable sophistication, seeking a reconciliation with Sadat in return for Egypt's endorsement of Syria's predominant role in Lebanon. Within hours the course of events in the Arab world reversed direction. A hastily convened Arab summit meeting in Cairo a few days later ratified the agreements reached in Riyadh, the key element of which was the creation of an Arab peacekeeping force, consisting mainly of Syrians, which would restore law and order in Lebanon. The PLO, reading the new Arab consensus correctly, concluded that it had no alternative but to acquiesce. By November most of Lebanon was under effective Syrian control, and the eighteen-month-long civil war seemed to be at least at a temporary end. Only in southern Lebanon, where Syrian troops were constrained by Israeli threats, was the situation still explosive, but even there neither Syria nor Israel seemed to be anxious for a confrontation.

The Arab coalition, which had fallen apart over Sinai II, now seemed to be resurrecting itself. With Saudi encouragement, Egypt and Syria were back on speaking terms, Jordan maintained good relations with Syria, and the PLO, chastened by its severe setbacks in Lebanon, gave off signals that some interpreted as a willingness to pursue more moderate policies in the future. Perhaps not coincidentally, the Arabs seemed to be putting their own house at least partly in order to be better able to confront the new American president with a coherent position. The divisions that had so crippled them throughout the American election year were apparently forgotten, although in other times and in other circumstances they would almost certainly come to the surface again. For the moment, however, the renewed sense of Arab solidarity could be a valuable asset in a new round of diplomacy, just as it could raise the risks of war if diplomacy failed.

THE KISSINGER LEGACY

Henry Kissinger's impact on American foreign policy will be debated endlessly. Of the accomplishments credited to him, few were not also in part the product of circumstances or the actions of others. But Kissinger will undoubtedly be regarded as one of the most powerful and most successful of American statesmen in the post–World War II era. How he managed to achieve such prominence is a story in its own right, revealing

Kissinger's remarkable talents as a bureaucratic maneuverer and politician. His more enduring legacy, however, will be his policies and the concepts behind them.

After several false starts Kissinger finally developed a coherent approach to the Arab-Israeli conflict after the October 1973 war. He started from the premise that the United States need not choose between a pro-Arab or pro-Israeli policy. In fact, it was the American special relationship to Israel that compelled the Arabs to deal with Washington instead of Moscow when it came to diplomacy. Consequently, if an alternative to war could be offered to the Arabs, their interests, quite apart from their sentiments, would lead them to deal with the United States. A credible diplomatic process was therefore essential to the weakening of Soviet influence in the Middle East. This view, once stated, seems unexceptional, perhaps obvious; even so, it was often ignored, on occasion by Kissinger himself.

Kissinger's second contribution to American diplomacy in the Middle East was the development of specific negotiating techniques designed to produce limited agreements between Arabs and Israelis. If Kissinger's grand strategy often seemed fairly conventional, his tactical skills as a negotiator and mediator were unsurpassed. Here his originality, his sense of timing, his intelligence, and even his personality served him especially well.

Kissinger demonstrated that, in practice, successful negotiations require an ability to break issues into manageable pieces that can then be imaginatively recombined into viable agreements. Mastery of detail is essential to success, as is a sense of context and nuance. A sustained, high-level effort, fully supported by the president, is the only American approach to negotiations likely to produce results. Kissinger showed that such an effort could succeed, as well as how difficult it could be.

Finally, Kissinger translated into practice his belief that power and diplomacy must always go hand in hand. The United States can never rely solely on force or on negotiations in the Middle East. The test of statesmanship is to find the critical balance of the two. Arms supplies to the Israelis or the Arabs must be viewed as part of the diplomatic process, not as a technical military issue. Whatever troubles Kissinger may have had in practice with this principle, he clearly saw that political considerations outweighed narrowly military ones in decisions of this sort.

Kissinger's successors no doubt pondered the value of these views and reflected on both the strength and the limits of the Kissinger approach.

Kissinger was unable to decide how to deal with the Soviets in the Middle East. He wavered between exaggerating their role and then minimizing it. Similarly, his views on a comprehensive approach to negotiations seemed to fluctuate between a recognition that some kind of framework was essential and a belief that each step could and should be taken in isolation from the others. Behind this ambiguity seems to have been a doubt whether peace between Arabs and Israelis could really be established in his lifetime. At times he acted as if he believed it could be, whereas on other occasions he seemed to be prepared to settle for a stable status quo.

Lastly, Kissinger had a blind spot toward the Palestinian issue. He knew that at some point the problem would have to be confronted. He even appeared to be tempted by the idea of dealing directly with the PLO leadership. But he geared much of his diplomacy to trying to circumvent this crucial issue, to putting off the moment of truth, and to weakening the appeal of the Palestinian movement, all the while hoping that some alternative would appear. Perhaps with time, with better luck, and with a strong president behind him, Kissinger would have helped find acceptable solutions to all these unanswered problems. But Ford's defeat brought Kissinger's public career to an end and left to the Carter administration the unenviable task of shaping an American policy toward the Arab-Israeli conflict.

PART FOUR

The Carter Presidency

PART FOUR

CHAPTER TEN

Ambition and Realism: Carter and Camp David, 1977–78

Jimmy Carter came to the presidency with remarkably little experience in foreign affairs. He had served one term as governor of Georgia, and had earned a reputation for his strong commitment to civil rights. But as far as the Middle East was concerned, he had no known record apart from a few comments made during the campaign that offered little guide to what his policies might be.

If Carter's specific views on Arab-Israeli issues were difficult to anticipate, he had displayed certain habits of mind that might be revealing of his basic approach. Trained as an engineer, Carter seemed to believe complex problems could best be tackled by careful study, detailed planning, and comprehensive designs. To say the least, he was a problem solver more than a grand strategist.

Carter also seemed to have an optimistic streak that led him to believe problems could be resolved if leaders would simply reason together and listen to the aspirations of their people. Here he may have been consciously influenced by his experience with the civil rights movement and by his personal beliefs as a born-again Christian. None of these attributes ensured that Carter would take a strong interest in the Arab-Israeli conflict, but they did suggest that he would not be deterred from doing so by the difficulty or complexity of the issue. He might even sense a challenge in tackling a problem that had for so long defied solution.

Much would depend on his foreign-policy team, and there the evidence suggested that he would rely on mainstream figures from the Democratic party establishment. For secretary of state he selected Cyrus R. Vance, a seasoned negotiator, international lawyer, and the deputy secretary of defense during the 1967 Arab-Israeli war. Vance's views on Middle East issues were not widely known, but his would be a voice for continuity, negotiations, and steady, quiet diplomacy.

As national security adviser, Carter selected the Polish-born academic Zbigniew Brzezinski. Unlike Vance, Brzezinski had left traces, primarily in the form of numerous articles and books, mostly on Soviet-related topics but a few on the Middle East as well. Brzezinski was an activist who believed in competing for influence with the Soviets, and who saw the Arab-Israeli conflict as a source of instability and radicalism in a sensitive geostrategic region. He had publicly endorsed the idea of a Palestinian state in the West Bank and Gaza and was one of the signatories of the controversial Brookings Report.[1] Brzezinski, who clearly hoped to achieve the stature of his predecessor and academic rival, Henry Kissinger, seemed determined to put the Arab-Israeli conflict near the top of the new administration's agenda.

While other players in the policy game moved in and out of the inner circle, Carter, Vance, and Brzezinski were the key decisionmakers. On defense matters Secretary of Defense Harold Brown carried great weight and exhibited a sharp intellect, but he was not particularly forceful in pushing his views on most policy issues outside his immediate area of responsibility. Vice President Walter Mondale had close ties to the Jewish community, and he was particularly attuned to any step that would produce a negative reaction there or in Congress. From time to time he would intervene strongly in internal deliberations, but he did not have an important role in policy formulation. Nor did the "Georgia mafia" of Hamilton Jordan, Stuart Eizenstat, Jody Powell, and Robert Lipshutz have much influence, although Jordan, who eventually became chief of staff, was a shrewd tactician and had unimpeded access to Carter. He and Mondale were attentive to the domestic fallout from Carter's Middle East policy, but they were not architects as much as they were damage controllers.[2]

THE INITIAL ASSESSMENT

Within days of reaching Washington, President Carter's foreign policy team was beginning to discuss how and whether to launch a new Middle East peace initiative. Both Secretary Vance and National Security Adviser Zbigniew Brzezinski were on record with the president as favoring a strong U.S. role in Middle East peace negotiations. Their assessment, and that of most Middle East specialists at the State Department, was that early 1977 was a good moment for the United States to exercise leadership in a new round of negotiations. The key Arab states seemed to be ready for serious talks, and a degree of consensus appeared to have been forged through Saudi mediation in the fall of 1976. The conflict in Lebanon had subsided, and the oil situation had begun to stabilize. Egypt's president, Anwar Sadat, who enjoyed great prestige in Washington, was urging the new administration to take advantage of this moment of moderation in the Arab world, a message seconded by the Saudis.

Israel also seemed to expect the United States to return to the diplomatic arena after the enforced absence of the election year. The cabinet of Prime Minister Yitzhak Rabin was to face elections in the spring, and was on the defensive to an unprecedented degree. But Washington officials felt that preliminary talks could be conducted before Israelis went to the polls, and even if they were not, that any new government would be built around the Labor alignment that had ruled Israel since its birth. And Labor was a known element, likely to adopt a tough stance in negotiations but ultimately prepared to bargain and to coordinate policies with Washington. Three disengagement agreements had been hammered out with Labor governments, and American negotiators had come to respect the skills of leaders like Golda Meir, Yitzhak Rabin, Moshe Dayan, and Shimon Peres.

If political realities in the Arab world and in Israel were seen as conducive to a new round of diplomacy, the shadow of the October 1973 war served as a constant reminder of the dangers of a collapse in the peace process. Barely three years had passed since that round of hostilities, and the memories of the near-confrontation between the United States and the Soviet Union, the nuclear alert, and the oil crisis were still very much in mind. Rarely mentioned but also present was the recognition that full-scale war in the Middle East could some day involve the use of nuclear weapons. This possibility made the region exceptionally dangerous and added a strong impulse to peacemaking efforts.

Having made this initial assessment, the Carter administration spent little time on whether to accord the Arab-Israeli conflict high priority. Most of the early discussion centered on means. It was widely believed that Henry Kissinger's technique of shuttle diplomacy to achieve limited agreements had run its course with Sinai II. The United States had paid a high price for a partial Israeli withdrawal that had not opened the way for any further such agreements. Neither Syria nor Jordan was prepared to follow Sadat's lead, and even Sadat was insisting that the next step should move toward an overall settlement. And the Israelis were also disinclined to be edged back from their strategically solid positions in Sinai for less than a peace agreement and direct negotiations with Egypt.

At a meeting on February 4, 1977, the Policy Review Committee of the National Security Council agreed to recommend to the president that the Middle East should be dealt with as a matter of urgent priority and

that Secretary Vance should go to the area immediately to begin
discussions on procedures and substance. The president's key advisers
felt the United States should promote an agreement on broad principles
and then seek their staged implementation. From the Arab side the
administration should seek a clear definition of peace, and from the
Israelis it should try to get an understanding that security could be
achieved without significant territorial adjustments in the 1967 lines. At
this stage in the internal discussions, there was no sense of urgency about
going to Geneva for a formal conference, and the emphasis was on pre-
Geneva talks to prepare for more formal negotiations at a later date. It
was also agreed at the meeting that the Soviets should be kept informed
of the progress of U.S. conversations with the parties but should not be
involved in the negotiations at this stage.[3]

The president approved of these suggestions and noted that his own
meetings with Middle East leaders over the coming few months could
help lay some of the substantive groundwork before direct talks among
the parties began. Already in these discussions among the president and
his advisers, however, one could detect a nuance of difference between
those who were more inclined to see Geneva as a desirable goal in itself,
who felt cooperation with the Soviets was to some degree inevitable, and
those who were more skeptical of both Geneva and Moscow. Interestingly,
no one raised the argument that early U.S. initiatives might prove to be
destabilizing in Israel, or might raise Arab expectations to unrealistic
levels.

In mid-February Vance was already in the Middle East sounding out
each of the leaders on how he saw the situation, while making it clear
that the United States also had some ideas of its own. Rabin, Sadat, King
Hussein of Jordan, and Saudi Crown Prince Fahd were all invited to
come to Washington to meet the new president, and the idea of a meeting
between Carter and President Asad of Syria was also raised.

A formal meeting of the National Security Council was held after
Vance's return on February 23. He reported that all the parties with
whom he had consulted professed to be ready for a peace agreement.
They all agreed to go to a Geneva conference in September and to discuss
substance prior to those talks. All concurred that the three main issues
on the agenda were the nature of peace, withdrawal, and the Palestinian
question. The most difficult procedural issue was how to include representatives of the Palestinians in the negotiations. Vance seemed to believe
that the Arabs might form a single delegation at Geneva, which could

include members of the PLO. He had told the Arab leaders it was up to them to produce an acceptable position on this question before Geneva. Sadat had urged the United States to include the PLO, but had also raised the possibility of representing them through some other means, such as a representative of the Arab League.[4]

In talks with Israeli leaders during his first trip, Secretary Vance had been told that no Israeli government would agree to talk to the PLO so long as it remained committed to the destruction of Israel. Vance had asked Foreign Minister Yigal Allon if it would make any difference if the PLO were to accept UN Resolution 242 and Israel's right to exist as a state. He replied that a PLO which accepted Israel's existence would no longer be the PLO, and Israel's attitude would be different.[5] This answer encouraged the United States to look into the possibility that the PLO might change its formal position on 242. The Egyptians and Saudis both promised to use their influence, and the Egyptians went so far as to say that they would urge the PLO to change its covenant, which called for Israel's destruction.

The next phase of the U.S. strategy included a highly public use of presidential power to try to break the logjam on several substantive issues. Carter and his advisers had little patience with some of the conventional wisdom on how the American role should be played. He had little sympathy for the Arab refusal to make peace with Israel, or to even use the word *peace*; and he strongly believed Israel would in some way have to come to terms with the Palestinians, and probably with the PLO, names he used almost interchangeably in his early months in office. And though he was very sympathetic to Israel's security concerns, he did not feel that territorial aggrandizement was the key to that security.

Carter was willing, even anxious, to speak out in public on all these issues, and to discuss them in private. One of his criticisms of the Kissinger style had been the emphasis on secrecy, which kept the American public in the dark about major foreign problems. Carter's inclination was to talk openly about the foreign-policy initiatives he was considering. At times this openness jangled the nerves of more traditional diplomats, and of foreign leaders, but Carter often seemed to be trying to do so deliberately. He appeared to feel he had a limited period in which to make his mark on Middle East policy and that controversial issues should be tackled early in the administration. This viewpoint led to a profusion of comprehensive plans to settle all sorts of problems, including the Middle East. On occasion, the president spoke with an awareness of the political cycle, the need to stake out strong positions during the early honeymoon phase of the administration, knowing perhaps that he would be obliged to settle for less in the end, but also hoping for a breakthrough here or there.

On March 7–8, 1977, Carter met with Prime Minister Rabin at the White House for very serious substantive discussions. The personal chemistry between the two was not particularly good, but the record of the talks shows that both leaders conducted thoughtful explorations of what might come out of the forthcoming negotiations. In retrospect, these talks stand out as one of the best substantive discussions Carter had with any Middle East leader. Shortly after the talks, however, a misunderstanding arose. Rabin publicly claimed that Carter had supported the Israeli idea of "defensible borders." Carter did not want to leave the false impression that he had offered Rabin a blank check, so the White House issued a clarification. This episode left the false impression that a crisis had broken out in U.S.-Israeli relations, a notion that may have contributed to Labor's defeat at the polls two months later.[6]

Almost immediately after meeting with Rabin, and in part to counter some of the Israeli leaks about what had been discussed, Carter publicly spelled out the three basic principles, as he saw them, of a comprehensive Middle East peace. These entailed the need for concrete manifestations of peace and normal relations, such as trade and the exchange of diplomats; the need for security arrangements for all parties, but without prejudice to the establishments of recognized borders along the 1967 lines; and the need for a solution to the Palestinian problem, which had a political as well as a humanitarian dimension. A few days later, on March 16, in Clinton, Massachusetts, Carter reiterated these points, using for the first time the formulation of a "Palestinian homeland."[7] Needless to say, the Israelis were stunned and apprehensive, and the Arabs were generally encouraged.

Although the Palestinian homeland became the focus of much of the public debate, Carter's two central assumptions, which deserved careful scrutiny, were his belief that a peace settlement must evolve from prior agreement on basic principles—the comprehensive framework—rather than through piecemeal bargaining over discrete issues, and his conviction that Israel could achieve security (as well as peace and recognition) within the geographic confines of 1967, with only minor adjustments. This latter point was based on the belief that no Arab leader would ever agree to recognize Israel unless most of the territory captured in 1967 was returned, and that ultimately Israel's security would be as much a function of the quality of political relationships with its neighbors as of its military might. The final judgment lying behind Carter's public statements was that Egypt, the Arab country most willing to make peace with Israel, would not do so unless some broader peace process was under way. Sadat himself was the most insistent in arguing this point.

Over the next three months Carter met with Sadat, Hussein, Fahd, and Asad. In each meeting the substantive trinity of peace, borders-security, and the Palestinian question was discussed in some depth, along with procedural questions on how to get the Palestinians represented in the upcoming negotiations. The most encouraging sign during this phase was Sadat's willingness to accept the idea that peace would entail normal relations with Israel, including the exchange of diplomats and full recognition.[8] But also, the Israeli government, while insisting that it would never accept an independent Palestinian state on the West Bank, was prepared to discuss withdrawal and was open to the idea that security would not necessarily require significant border changes beyond the 1967 lines. In addition, Rabin, Allon, and Peres all talked of the need to solve the Palestinian problem if there was to be peace in the region. And the Arab leaders were confidently predicting that the PLO would consider softening its position on the recognition of Israel.

By midyear, then, the Carter administration was well launched with its peace initiative, and the results were fairly encouraging. It is fair to say, however, that the president often felt frustrated with the seeming intractability of the issues, with the complexity of the problem, with the domestic political sensitivities aroused by his public comments, and by the sheer amount of time required to move the process forward.

Then, on June 21, 1977, the unexpected happened. Menachem Begin, whose Likud bloc had won the Knesset elections the previous month, became prime minister of Israel. Begin was an unknown figure in Washington. Insofar as administration officials knew his views, they were aware that he opposed Labor's approach to "territorial compromise" with Jordan as a means of dealing with the West Bank and the Palestinian question. Begin was known to favor an expansion of Israeli settlements, and one of his first acts that irritated the Carter administration was his visit to Elon Moreh, where he announced he would support many more such settlements. These two issues—Begin's unwillingness to accept the principle of withdrawal from the West Bank under any circumstances, and his commitment to settlements—became the main sources of conflict between the United States and Israel over the next two years.[9]

POLICY REAPPRAISAL

Somewhat surprisingly, Carter's first meeting with Begin was much more cordial than the one with Rabin. Carter apparently believed Begin would become more rigid if pressured, and some of his advisers were convinced that Begin would respond best to a respectful, polite initial encounter. The personal chemistry between the two men was hardly warm, but the talks were conducted in a friendly manner.

Although Begin came prepared with procedural proposals for negotiations with the Arabs, he showed no sign of wanting to discuss substance with the United States. This, in fact, was one of the initial differences between Begin and Rabin: Begin argued that the United States should not be involved in the substance of Arab-Israeli talks but should limit its role to getting the parties together. He obviously feared that the U.S. stand on many issues would be closer to the Arab position, and therefore he wanted as little substantive role for Washington as possible. Previous Israeli governments had, by contrast, insisted on close consultation with the Americans as a way of preventing unilateral moves that might undercut Israel's bargaining position. Begin seemed to be saying that Israel did not feel the need to consult, and at the same time asked that the United States refrain from putting forward any ideas of its own on substance.

Unfortunately for Begin, the United States was already rather far down the road of trying to devise draft principles that should be agreed on before a Geneva conference. In discussions held within the administration early in July, five principles had been agreed on, and during Begin's visit these were discussed. The first point set the goal of comprehensive peace; the second reiterated the relevance of UN Resolutions 242 and 338 as the bases of negotiations; the third defined the goal of peace as involving normal relations, not just an end of belligerency; the fourth dealt with the question of borders and withdrawal in stages; and the fifth point concerned the Palestinians and their rights, including means "to permit self-determination by the Palestinians in deciding on their future status."

Vance, and then Carter, reviewed these points with Begin on July 19–20 and found, not surprisingly, that Begin entirely rejected the fifth point on the Palestinians, and was insistent that on point four the United

States should not say in public or private that it favored withdrawal to the 1967 lines with only minor modifications. During an evening session alone with Begin, Carter agreed not to mention the 1967 lines with minor modifications in public, and in return he asked Begin to show restraint on settlements. This compromise was part of an effort to calm the heated atmosphere prior to Geneva, but it also reflected a slight shift toward accepting the idea that little real progress could now be made until the parties began to talk to one another. Procedural issues began to assume greater importance, and prior agreement on key principles before Geneva came to be seen as unlikely, given the enormous gap between Begin and even the most moderate Arab leaders.[10]

Secretary Vance, who began to focus on the question of how the PLO might be represented at Geneva, found himself leaning increasingly toward the idea of a single Arab delegation that would include Palestinians. Israel had made it clear it would not deal directly with the PLO as a separate delegation but would not object to Palestinians within the Jordanian delegation. Jordan, however, had no intention of representing the Palestinians and preferred the Syrian idea of a common Arab negotiating front, primarily as a way of preventing unilateral moves by Sadat. Egypt favored a PLO delegation but had shown a willingness to consider other formulations as well. During much of July, August, and September this issue was a major topic of discussion, and some progress seemed possible.

Meanwhile Vance had been toying with ideas on how to deal with the West Bank in a somewhat different context than in the other occupied territories. He was intrigued first by the idea of a referendum among the inhabitants of the West Bank to get their views into the negotiating process. Later he fastened on the idea of a "trusteeship" for the area for a transitional period, and several studies were done to assess the practicality of this notion.

In early August 1977 Vance left on a very important trip to the Middle East. With him he took a revised set of the five principles to discuss with leaders in Egypt, Israel, Syria, Jordan, Saudi Arabia, and Lebanon. He also had with him four possible ways for the Palestinians to be included in the Geneva negotiations, and he was prepared to try out his new idea of a trusteeship as well.

During Vance's talks in Egypt, Sadat showed considerable anxiety about the shift toward procedural discussions and away from the idea of prior agreement on principles before Geneva. In his view Geneva should be used for signing a pre-agreed document, little more. Sadat had little patience with the idea of negotiating with Israel, preferring that the United States present a plan, to which all the parties could react. To encourage this line of thought, Sadat presented a highly secret document to Vance in Alexandria.[11] It was the draft of a peace treaty that Sadat said he would be prepared to sign, but he did not want any of the other parties to know it existed. Instead he urged Vance to ask the Israelis to put forward a draft treaty of their own; then Vance could unveil the Egyptian draft, which would lead to an eventual U.S. compromise proposal. In a tactic that he was to use repeatedly, Sadat took the Egyptian draft and wrote in the margins in his own handwriting the further concessions he would be prepared to make. These notations were intended, presumably, to convince Vance that Sadat would be flexible on most substantive points, though not on "land and sovereignty," as the Egyptian president repeatedly said.[12]

During the talks with the Egyptians, Vance was also encouraged to believe the PLO was about to change its position on UN Resolution 242. To add an incentive, Vance recommended that President Carter publicly repeat that the United States would be willing to enter into high-level talks with the PLO if the PLO accepted 242, even with a statement of reservation. Carter did so a few days later from Plains, Georgia, while Vance was in Saudi Arabia, all of which ensured that Vance's arrival in Israel was less than warm.[13] At a dinner in the secretary's honor Begin gave a long, and in the view of most of the Americans present, very offensive speech, implying that anyone thinking of talking to the PLO should be compared with those who had sought to appease Hitler before World War II. Begin's reputation for verbal excess and extremism gained considerable credibility during Vance's trip, and little remained of what Begin wistfully later called the good feelings of July 1977. The Israelis did agree, however, to provide the United States with a draft peace treaty, and arrangements were made for further meetings between Vance and the various foreign ministers in New York in conjunction with the UN General Assembly.

September 1977 proved to be an eventful month in the evolution of Carter's Middle East strategy. American efforts were concentrated on four parallel, potentially even conflicting, goals. First was the attempt to get each of the parties to provide a written draft of a peace treaty. Israel complied, with a lengthy and legalistic document that left the delicate question of the border and the status of settlements in Sinai obscure.

Jordan and even Syria eventually submitted a list of principles that should govern any peace agreement. Although the drafts per se were far from what was needed, they did provide Vance with some building blocks from which to fashion an American compromise proposal, and they had the positive effect of getting the parties to think of committing themselves to concrete positions on paper.

The second strand of policy, largely working through the Syrians, but also pursued in other channels, was an attempt to find a solution to the question of how the Palestinians would be represented in upcoming negotiations at Geneva. Agreement was reached on how the PLO might express its reservation to UN Resolution 242, but the conditions demanded by the PLO for an overt acceptance of 242 were beyond what Washington was prepared to promise.[14] Nonetheless, by early October Sadat had informed Carter that the PLO would agree to be represented in a unified Arab delegation by a Palestinian who was not a PLO official. Since everyone had by then accepted the idea of a unified Arab delegation that would include Palestinians, this issue seemed to be nearly resolved.[15]

The third focus of U.S. efforts was to try to develop some understanding among the negotiating parties about the procedures of the Geneva talks. Sadat was still insistent that Geneva must be "well prepared" in advance; otherwise it could bog down and turn into a hopeless stalemate. He remained wedded to the Kissinger model of highly secret talks at the level of head of government, which would then be finalized and legitimized in a public forum like Geneva. If the actual negotiating was to be done in a semipublic forum like Geneva, he seemed to fear that the other Arabs would try to restrict his freedom to maneuver, and that the United States would be subject to the ever-present pro-Israeli pressures generated by American public opinion and Congress. Israel tended to share this suspicion of Geneva, and Foreign Minister Moshe Dayan warned that a unified Arab delegation was a formula for stalemate. Syria, and to a lesser extent Jordan, favored a single delegation as a way of preventing the much-feared separate Egyptian-Israeli agreement they had come to expect after Sinai II.

The American compromise proposal, largely crafted by Vance, was to get everyone to accept the idea of a unified Arab delegation. The main purpose, in his mind, was to bring the Palestinians into the peace process by that means. After a formalistic opening of the Geneva conference at which the Arab side would appear to be a single delegation, talks would break up into subcommittees, which would essentially be bilateral, except for the discussion of the West Bank and Gaza, in which Egypt and Jordan would join the Palestinians. The American side, mistakenly, did not realize the Syrians would object to being left out of the talks on the Palestinian issue. The main problem seemed to be to get Israel to agree that the Palestinians could be at the talks in their own right, not just as members of the Jordanian or Egyptian delegations.

The fourth, and probably least carefully thought out, part of the U.S. strategy was aimed at the Soviet Union. As Geneva became more of a real concept, rather than just a symbolic umbrella for a whole series of contacts and talks, the United States had to address the question of the role to be played by the other cochairman. A number of procedures had already been worked out in December 1973, when the Geneva conference had convened in plenary session for the first and last time. To the extent possible, it was useful to adhere to those precedents. But the Soviets were clearly seeking more of a role, and in mid-September they presented a draft of a joint statement to Secretary Vance. For a Soviet document it was remarkably balanced. It did not include calls for a Palestinian state or participation by the PLO. It paid due regard to the need for security and normal peaceful relations among the states of the area. Most of the language was from UN Resolution 242. Practically the only formulation the United States had not itself used was a reference to Palestinian rights, which went a step beyond the standard American reference to Palestinian interests.

The task of trying to work out an agreed text was turned over to Ambassador Alfred L. Atherton, Jr., who was advising Vance on Arab-Israeli peacemaking, and a Soviet diplomat, Mikhail Sytenko. With little effort, these two professionals produced a generally acceptable text. The question that was hardly discussed was how and when to issue this joint statement so as to advance the other efforts that were under way. At the time it was thought that a strong statement by the Soviets in conjunction with the Americans might put some pressure on Syria and the PLO to cease their haggling over procedural matters and to agree to enter negotiations on the basis of a joint invitation from the superpowers. Little thought was given to Israel's reaction, or to the need to prepare public opinion in the United States. The Israelis were shown a draft in late September, and Dayan's initial reaction was restrained.

Among the potentially controversial elements in the draft were an explicit call for reconvening the Geneva conference by the end of the year; the fact that the Soviet Union would be cochairman; the lack of explicit reference to UN Resolution 242; and a formulation the United States had not previously used referring to Palestinian *rights*. Largely because of these references the Israelis were uncomfortable with the document. But the Carter administration had not picked up any warning signals from Dayan. Thus, when the U.S.-Soviet communiqué was issued on October 1, 1977, few on the American side anticipated the storm of adverse reaction from Israel and Israel's supporters in the United States.[16] (See appendix D for the text.)

While American efforts were aimed in these various directions, Egypt and Israel were embarking on a round of secret diplomacy. At Sadat's initiative a meeting was held between Dayan and an aide to Sadat, Hassan Touhamy, in Morocco in mid-September.[17] Similar contacts had been held over the years, including that month, between Israeli and Arab leaders, so even when the United States learned of this meeting after the fact, it was not viewed as a vote of no confidence in the ongoing U.S. strategy. In retrospect, one can see that Sadat was beginning to hedge his bets for fear that Geneva would become a straitjacket for his free-wheeling style of diplomacy. It is fair to say that the American side consistently underestimated the degree of distrust between Sadat and Asad, and also tended to take Sadat at his word when he repeatedly said he could never afford to make a separate peace with Israel.

Not surprisingly, with so many initiatives under way during September, something was bound to come unstuck. The proximate cause of the explosion was the U.S.-Soviet communiqué and the firestorm of negative American and Israeli reaction it provoked. Much of the pent-up anxiety and frustration with Carter's Middle East policy now spilled over, finding willing allies in the neoconservative, pro-Israeli, anti-Soviet circles. What was in fact a political error, showing considerable amateurishness, was portrayed as a move of vast significance that would reestablish the Soviets as a major power in the Middle East. To read the text of the communiqué several years later is to wonder what all the fuss was about. The words themselves are innocuous, and even Begin used the phrase "Palestinian rights" at Camp David. Nonetheless, the political reality of early October 1977 was that Carter was under great pressure from the friends of Israel, and the Israelis played on his discomfort with extraordinary skill.

Many analysts believe Sadat went to Jerusalem in November 1977 to escape the dead end of a U.S.-Soviet sponsored Geneva conference. They often emphasize his desire to keep the Soviets out of the diplomatic arena. But the available evidence, including Sadat's own account, does not support this widely held belief.[18] When first informed of the U.S.-Soviet joint communiqué, Sadat termed it a "brilliant maneuver," since he, like some U.S. officials, thought it would soften up the Syrians.[19] In any case, he had ensured against Geneva becoming an Arab-Soviet trap by opening his own direct channel to the Israelis, and from that contact he seemed to be assured that whenever he was ready to sign a separate peace with Israel he would recover most of Sinai. In early October Sadat was still testing to see how much more he could get with U.S. help. It was not the U.S.-Soviet communiqué that disillusioned him; it was Carter's apparent inability to stand up to Israeli pressure, coupled with evidence that Carter was tired of spending so much time on an apparently intractable problem, that seems to have convinced Sadat to strike out on his own.

If this interpretation is correct, then the crucial step along the way was the meeting between Carter and Dayan in New York on October 4, 1977.[20] Dayan began by asking if Israel was expected to accept the U.S.-Soviet communiqué as the price of going to Geneva. He termed the agreement totally unacceptable to Israel but said Israel would still go to Geneva on the basis of 242. Carter said Israel did not have to accept the communiqué. Then Dayan upped the ante by asking Carter to reaffirm publicly all past U.S. commitments to Israel as a way of calming the crisis atmosphere set off in Israel by the communiqué. He said that if Carter did not do so, Israel might feel obliged to publish these agreements. He also asked for a statement that the United States would not use pressure on Israel to accept a Palestinian state. When Carter said he did not intend to use pressure but did not want to make any such statement, Dayan said he would therefore be obliged to say that he had asked and Carter had refused. Having issued these barely veiled threats, Dayan proceeded to deal in a businesslike way with Secretary Vance on the question of Palestinian representation, going further toward the U.S. position than Begin had probably authorized, and thus winning back for himself the reputation of being the most pragmatic and reasonable of the members of the Israeli cabinet.[21] After a formula for including Palestinians at Geneva was worked out fairly smoothly, Carter returned to the discussion.

Dayan made a strong pitch for American support for a separate Egyptian-Israeli agreement. In Dayan's words, "the future is with Egypt. If you take one wheel off a car, it won't drive. If Egypt is out of the conflict, there will be no more war." The discussion then turned to politics, and Dayan said he could help Carter quiet the fears of American

Jews if Dayan could announce an agreement on Geneva between the United States and Israel. "But if we say we have to deal with the PLO or a Palestinian state, and this is bad for Israel, then there will be screaming here and in Israel. We need an agreed formula so I can say there is agreement, not confrontation, to Israel and American Jews." Secretary Vance was clearly very nervous about the image of a joint U.S.-Israeli position and suggested that both parties should state their own positions separately. Dayan objected, saying that something should be announced at the end of the meeting, or it would be very bad. President Carter then agreed that the two sides should try to issue a common statement dealing with Geneva and explaining that the U.S.-Soviet communiqué was not a precondition for Israel's participation at Geneva. After several more hours of drafting, Dayan and Vance appeared in the early morning hours of October 5 to reveal the U.S.-Israeli "working paper," as it became known.[22] To the Arabs, including the Egyptians, this document appeared to be a major retreat from the U.S.-Soviet communiqué, as well as evidence of the considerable power Israel could wield because of its strong base of support in Congress and U.S. public opinion.

In brief, the whole episode left Carter exhausted and somewhat cautious, the Israelis both distrustful and aware of their power, and the Arabs confused and alarmed at the spectacle of the United States appearing to retreat under pressure on the eve of the Geneva conference. In retrospect, it is easy to see the significant role played by the careless handling of the U.S.-Soviet communiqué. Most of the American officials involved subsequently acknowledged that they should have been more attentive to the negative political fallout from such a joint move with the Soviets. The simple truth is that not much thought was given to the matter because so many other important developments were occurring in the Middle East arena by late September.

The next step along the way in Sadat's decision to go to Jerusalem came later in October. By then the procedural tangles of forming a unified Arab delegation had produced a near deadlock between Syria and Egypt. Progress in resolving the impasse was glacial, and Carter seemed to feel that time was running out. He repeatedly said that he and Secretary Vance had other pressing matters to attend to and could not spend all their time on the Middle East, especially when the problems were among the Arab parties themselves. In this spirit, one Friday morning toward the end of October, Carter decided to send a very personal appeal to

Sadat in the form of a handwritten note to be delivered directly to the Egyptian president. In it he reminded Sadat of their mutual pledge in April to do all they could for peace. Carter came close to saying that he had little more to offer, and that the time had come for a bold move from Sadat. No specifics were mentioned, but the point was clear: if further progress was to be made, Sadat would have to take the initiative.[23]

Within a week the response came, first in the form of a handwritten note from Sadat, and more formally and with more details as a cable from Cairo. Sadat's idea was to convene a super-Geneva conference in east Jerusalem, to be attended by the heads of state of all the permanent members of the Security Council, as well as by the leaders of Egypt, Syria, Jordan, Israel, and the PLO. It all seemed a bit grand and implausible, and Carter's response was cool.[24] By his own account Sadat began to think of a solo venture to Jerusalem to break the deadlock. But this time he did not bother to tell President Carter. Thus, on November 9, when Sadat publicly revealed his intention to go to Israel, Washington was caught by surprise, just as it had been by Begin's election. And once again the United States was obliged to adjust its strategy because of events in the Middle East that had proved to be beyond its control.

AFTER JERUSALEM

The initial reaction to Sadat's trip to Jerusalem in official Washington was one of admiration for the personal courage required, and some puzzlement over what Sadat had in mind for an encore. He had often said that 99 percent of the cards were in American hands, but now he seemed to be ready to play his own cards without much help from Carter. No one in Washington proposed that the United States should try to thwart his moves, but there was some concern that negative Arab reactions, coupled with Begin's essential rigidity on the Palestinian issue, would cause the initiative to fall far short of the psychological breakthrough that Sadat sought. Consequently, sooner rather than later the problem would end up back in the American lap. In any case, Sadat's move would not be helped by its appearing to have been made in the United States. These considerations, coupled perhaps with some envy on the part of the politically minded members of the administration for a media-catching move they would have liked to have thought of themselves, led to a fairly reserved public posture, which was strongly criticized at the time by the friends of Israel.[25]

It took some weeks for American officials to correctly assess Sadat's reasons for going to Jerusalem. The depth of animosity between Egypt and Syria had not been recognized, but Sadat's contemptuous comments toward Asad and other Arab leaders after his trip to Israel suggested that he was determined to go it alone for the time being. When asked whether the United States could do anything helpful in Damascus to temper opposition to his moves, Sadat replied that the United States could inform Asad that Egypt was the center of the Arab world.[26]

By early December the internal consensus in the administration was that Sadat's initiative should be supported strongly but that the United States should continue to use its influence to try to get as broad agreement as possible. The administration still felt that Sadat would, in the end, not make a separate peace with Israel and that at least some measure of agreement on the Palestinian question would have to serve as a cover for any Egyptian-Israeli deal. Syria would henceforth be ignored for most practical purposes, as would the PLO, but American policy would continue to focus on some form of West Bank–Gaza accord. During the second week of December, Secretary Vance went to the Middle East to consult with the various governments and to begin the process of redefining American strategy.

Just after Vance's return from the area, Begin invited himself to Washington to see President Carter. Vance had seen the prime minister only a few days before, and Begin had not put forward any new ideas, but now he said he had important proposals to discuss with the president before going to a scheduled meeting with Sadat in Ismailia on Christmas day. Some in Washington were suspicious that Begin's purpose was to try to elicit an American endorsement of his ideas before they were shown to Sadat.

Carter's talks with Begin on December 16–17 confirmed the American suspicion. Begin practically pleaded with the president to say that his proposals were a fair basis for negotiation. In fact, Carter did tell him his Sinai proposal looked promising, adding the caveat that there might be points in it that he did not fully understand yet. (This comment became a source of discord later when the Israelis claimed that Carter had approved of the Sinai proposal, knowing it included a provision that Israeli settlements would not be removed.)

If Begin's Sinai proposal was genuinely seen in positive terms, the same could not be said for his "home rule" proposal for "Judea, Samaria and the Gaza District."[27] In lengthy discussions with Begin, the president, the vice-president, Vance, and Brzezinski all tried to encourage Begin to modify his plan. Several points stood out. The home rule proposal was intended as a permanent arrangement, not as a transition to the return of the territory to Arab political control once a peace agreement had been reached. The plan also contained the type of detail that would be bound to irritate Sadat, and Begin was urged to present a simpler set of principles, perhaps only orally. But Begin seemed to be proud of his creation and rather arrogantly told the American side that he did not need their advice on how to negotiate with Sadat. Begin was so eager to win U.S. endorsement, however, that he did imply he would make some improvements in the plan after consulting with his cabinet. With that, he promptly went public with a statement that came very close to saying the president had approved of his plan, which required a clarification from the American side to the effect that the plan was a positive step in the direction of negotiations.

Some in the administration saw merit in Begin's proposal, in part because they thought he could be tricked into turning it into a proposal for only a transitional period.[28] They saw as positive elements Begin's willingness to leave Israel's claim to sovereignty over the West Bank and Gaza in abeyance for five years; his acceptance of the idea that a special administrative regime would go into effect in all the territory of the West Bank and Gaza; and his suggestions about equality of rights and obligations for Arabs and Israelis. (Some of the most attractive points were dropped a few days later from the proposal that was actually presented to Sadat, which left the American negotiators feeling that Begin had used the meeting with Carter just as they had expected and that their entreaties for greater moderation and flexibility had fallen on deaf ears.)[29]

Indicative of the gap between the Egyptian and Israeli positions was the difference in Begin's and Sadat's accounts of their meeting in Ismailia. According to the Israeli version, Sadat was on the verge of accepting the Israeli proposals and issuing a common declaration of principles, but was persuaded not to do so by his hard-line advisers from the Foreign Ministry. Sadat's account, by contrast, said that Begin had not grasped the importance of his Jerusalem visit and that the Israelis were trying to haggle and tread on sovereignty. He was quite caustic in his remarks, suggesting there was little point in going on with direct negotiations.

Carter and Vance, who had anticipated that further U.S. help would be needed to keep the negotiations alive, believed a continuing negotiating process was essential if the United States was to use its influence. Consequently a meeting of the so-called political committee was arranged in January at the level of foreign ministers. For Egypt this meant that Muhammad Ibrahim Kamel, Sadat's new foreign minister, would make his first visit to Jerusalem, something he obviously did not welcome. In fact, the talks seemed to proceed fairly well on the technical level, with the objective of drafting a declaration of principles. (By now the United States was pushing the Aswan formula calling for "the right of the Palestinians to participate in the determination of their own future.") For reasons still not entirely clear, but perhaps reflecting Kamel's anger at a toast delivered by Begin at a dinner the first night, Sadat suddenly called his delegation home. Vance, who had seen many negotiations go through such moments, termed it "a bump in the road" and returned to Washington to help forge a new approach in light of events that once again seemed to have taken a somewhat alarming turn.

U.S.-EGYPTIAN COORDINATION

Discussions within the American negotiating team in January led to a strategy of trying to change two key elements in Begin's position: to achieve a freeze on the construction of new settlements in the occupied territories, an issue of special concern after Begin blatantly allowed new settlements to be started in Sinai within days of his talks in Ismailia with Sadat; and to convince Begin to return to the previous Israeli formula for the West Bank and Gaza by offering to withdraw, at least partially, as the quid pro quo for peace and recognition. This latter point was put in terms of Begin's unwillingness to accept the fact that the withdrawal provision of UN Resolution 242 applied to the West Bank and Gaza. The Labor party in formally accepting 242 in mid-1970 had interpreted the resolution as requiring "peace for withdrawal" on all fronts, and because of this Begin had left the national unity government that existed at the time.[30]

The Americans thought that the two issues of settlements and withdrawal were intrinsically important if there was to be any chance of a negotiated peace, and that on these issues Begin was vulnerable at home and in the American Jewish community. They therefore decided to mount a campaign of public pressure against Begin on these two points, and to that end they prepared a very comprehensive "white paper," which showed conclusively that Begin did not accept 242 in the same terms as previous Israeli governments had. The document was never released, but it was used for judicious leaking to the press. On settlements, the administration in public and private tried to get a settlements freeze, and indeed the record of 1978 shows very few new settlements being established that year, even though Begin never formally agreed to a freeze until the Camp David talks.

The Carter administration felt it was on sure ground on the two issues of settlements and withdrawal, provided the United States remained clearly committed to Israel's security and supported the Israeli idea that peace should entail normal relations. But Carter felt that Sadat should help the campaign to pressure Israel and worried that Sadat's decision to pull out of the political talks in Jerusalem would weaken the case against Begin. Consequently Carter decided to invite the Egyptian president to Washington in February for a serious review of strategy.

One idea discussed before Sadat's arrival was to try to work out with the Egyptians a series of coordinated moves that would maximize the pressure on Begin. The risk of appearing to collude with the Egyptians was obvious, but Sadat's reputation for making sudden and sometimes unhelpful moves was very much on the Americans' minds. It was also thought that Sadat would be delighted at the prospect of playing a somewhat Machiavellian game aimed at Begin.

A second American effort in early 1978 was to redraft Begin's autonomy proposal into a number of general principles that might be agreed upon between Egypt and Israel as a formula for a transitional period of three to five years. By the time of Sadat's arrival at Camp David in the first week of February 1978, a nine-point document had been developed.[31]

Sadat and Carter spent the weekend at Camp David alone. The weather was cold and there was snow on the ground. Sadat was not in good health and clearly disliked the setting, so far from his normal winter refuge of Aswan. By the time the sessions with advisers began, Sadat had convinced Carter that his initiative had nearly reached an end and that he saw no point in going on. Sadat, it must be remembered, was a consummate actor, and some of his posture was no doubt theater, but some was also real. After a lengthy exposé by Carter of all the problems, during which Sadat looked despondent, the president asked his pipe-smoking guest if he had any comment to make. Sadat puffed on his pipe, looked grave, and finally said he had only one question to ask: would there be an American proposal? The answer from Carter was yes, and much of the rest of the day was spent developing an agreed strategy that would culminate in a U.S. proposal.

The Americans insisted that Sadat must first return to the negotiating table and reiterate his commitment to the peace process. Then Begin would be invited to Washington, and Carter would privately press hard on the issues of settlements and Resolution 242, issues that the Egyptians would also stress. The United States would also present the nine-point plan as a basis for a possible joint declaration. Part of the strategy also meant getting a formal Egyptian counterproposal to Begin's home rule plan before an American proposal would be put forward. Sadat was urged to make his initial proposal fairly tough, even at the risk of creating a crisis in the negotiations, so that the United States could be in a position of arguing with both Israel and Egypt over aspects of their proposals. To be in that position would help protect Carter's flank at home, since one-sided pressure on Israel could not easily be sustained. The key point in this strategy was that Sadat would, at the appropriate point in the crisis, moderate his position and accept American compromise proposals, making it possible for U.S. pressure then to turn on Israel. The strategy was complex, a bit devious, and only partly internalized by the American and Egyptian officials who were supposed to carry it out. But Sadat loved it. His long-sought goal of forging a joint U.S.-Egyptian strategy seemed to be at hand.[32]

What happened to the Sadat-Carter accord of February 1978? First, the agreed-upon calendar, which envisaged an American proposal by midyear, was thrown off by the decision to seek congressional approval for the sale of advanced aircraft to Saudi Arabia, Egypt, and Israel. The F-15s for Saudi Arabia proved to be very controversial, and the administration had to spend large amounts of time and political capital to get the sale through. This issue arose right at the moment that the first stage of the joint U.S.-Egyptian strategy should have been taking shape. Second, Sadat was a bit shaky in carrying out his side of the bargain. He tended to ignore the themes of 242 and Israeli settlements in his public statements, making it appear that Carter was being more pro-Arab than Sadat himself. In addition, when he finally did send the United States a proposal, it was very general and did not really serve as a counter to Begin's autonomy plan. Third, Vance decided to ask the Israelis to clarify their views on what would happen at the end of the five-year period of autonomy, and the Israelis took a long time to answer. When they did so, they basically confirmed what was already known of Begin's annexationist intentions.

By midsummer neither Carter nor Vance seemed to feel that the more manipulative aspects of the strategy discussed with Sadat could be made to work, although both remained wedded to the idea that a U.S. proposal should be developed. But no one seemed to relish the idea of a showdown with Begin, except perhaps for Brzezinski, who felt Begin was manipulating the United States and needed to be reminded that Washington was capable of pursuing its national interests in a vigorous way and would not always succumb to domestic pressures.

While the American side was edging away from a joint U.S.-Egyptian strategy by mid-1978, Sadat seemed to be operating on the assumption that the general outline of what had been discussed at Camp David was still valid. Thus he periodically adopted extreme positions in public, threatened to call off talks with Israel, talked ominously of October 1978 as the expiration date of the Sinai II agreement (not true), and generally seemed to be trying to engineer an Egyptian-Israeli crisis into which Carter could step with a compromise proposal. Though prepared to go along with the stage setting insisted upon by the Americans, such as the Leeds Castle talks at the level of foreign minister in July, Sadat was clearly getting impatient for the showdown with Begin.

Through the spring and summer of 1978 little substantive progress was made in an endless series of contacts with Egyptian and Israeli leaders. Carter was impatient with the slow pace of diplomacy and seemed to feel a desire to get more directly into the act. During much of July a highly secret planning group began to develop a U.S. proposal under Vance's supervision, and the president followed the progress with interest. On July 20 he discussed with his advisers an idea he had been toying with for some time—a summit meeting at Camp David with both Begin and Sadat.[33] Carter seemed to view a summit as the only way to force decisions to a head, and he doubtless counted on his own role as mediator to bridge the still very large gaps. His view of a summit was psychological and political: once the leaders were committed, they could not afford to fail, and he counted on the special atmosphere of Camp David, away from the press and the burdens of everyday governing, to help produce a positive result. The rest of the foreign-policy team was somewhat more wary of the summit idea, tending to focus on the need for very careful substantive preparations. In early August Vance went to the Middle East to invite Begin and Sadat to Camp David in early September. Both accepted readily, and no doubt Sadat saw this event as the much-awaited moment of truth when he and Carter would corner Begin.

THE CAMP DAVID SUMMIT

Carter, Sadat, and Begin, along with their top advisers, isolated themselves at the president's mountaintop retreat, Camp David, from September 5 to September 17. Little information reached the outside world of these deliberations at the time, so many were surprised at the news on the last day that agreement had been reached on two frameworks for negotiations. The first dealt with the principles of an Egyptian-Israeli agreement; the second, more complex and less precise, consisted of a formula for an interim period of self-government for Palestinians living in the West Bank and Gaza. The outcome was not quite what anyone had expected at the beginning of the historic summit.

Carter prepared himself meticulously for the talks. His briefing book contained an analytical paper entitled "The Pivotal Issue," which focused on the question of "linkage" between agreements on Sinai and on the West Bank.[34] The point was made that Begin would seek to ensure that any agreement he might reach with Sadat concerning Egyptian-Israeli relations should in no way be dependent on resolving the Palestinian question. Sadat, by contrast, would want some relationship between the two so as to protect himself from the charge that he had abandoned the Palestinians and had accepted a separate peace with Israel. The problem for Carter would be to see if an agreement could be reached at the summit that would make it possible to use the incentive of reaching peace with Egypt to moderate Begin's position on the Palestinian question, without at the same time making Egyptian-Israeli relations entirely subject to whether a solution could be found to the most difficult part of the Arab-Israeli conflict.

The American delegation had identified several specific issues that were likely to be obstacles to a successful agreement at Camp David. First was Begin's unwillingness to accept that the principle of withdrawal from occupied territory, as called for in Resolution 242, should apply to the West Bank and Gaza at the end of a transitional period. Second was the problem of Israeli settlements in Sinai and in the West Bank. Third was the question of how to associate Jordan and the Palestinians with subsequent rounds of negotiations.

The American team felt it was pointless at Camp David to try to resolve the questions of the border between Israel and a Palestinian-Jordanian entity.[35] Not only would Begin be at his most intransigent, but also the Arab parties most directly concerned would not be present. Similarly the Americans felt the question of sovereignty over the West Bank and Gaza, as well as the status of Jerusalem, should be deferred. Instead they thought that Egypt and Israel could make some headway on outlining a transitional regime for the West Bank, building on Dayan's idea of dismantling the military occupation and replacing it with an elected Palestinian body with broad responsibility for day-to-day affairs, perhaps including control over state lands (which would have effectively foreclosed the possibility of extensive new Israeli settlement activity during the transitional period).

No one on the American side anticipated insurmountable problems in reaching a general agreement on principles regarding Sinai. Israel was expected to leave the settlements and the airfields, provided firm security arrangements could be worked out. Sadat was taken seriously when he said that he could not bargain over land or sovereignty, but that everything else could be negotiated.

These assessments led the American team to think in terms of seeking agreement between Begin and Sadat on general principles regarding both Sinai and the West Bank and Gaza. Begin would have to cede on the applicability of 242 to the West Bank and Gaza in any final settlement, and to a freeze on settlement activity, in return for which he could expect Sadat to be forthcoming on Israeli security requirements in Sinai and the West Bank, and to accept a very loose linkage between negotiations on the two fronts. In Vance's view an agreement of this sort would serve to guide the efforts of the foreign ministers as they sought to translate the principles agreed upon by the political leaders into a concrete document leading to an Egyptian-Israeli peace treaty and to a formula for Palestinian self-government for a transitional period.

President Carter's initial reaction to the advice of his team was that it should have aimed higher.[36] Rather than just seek agreement on principles concerning an overall settlement, he wanted to work out the details of an Egyptian-Israeli peace treaty, including specific security arrangements. At Camp David this became his special project, and the first draft of the Egyptian-Israeli accord was done in his hand.[37] Carter, it is fair to say, was less concerned with the so-called linkage problem than were other members of the American team, and he was also more optimistic about the chances of reaching a satisfactory agreement through direct talks with Begin and Sadat.

Those who were somewhat more pessimistic about the prospects of bridging the very large gaps between the two parties were also more inclined to see the Camp David talks as part of an ongoing process. From this perspective, even if the talks fell short of full agreement, negotiations would continue, with the issues, it was hoped, more narrowly focused than before. This somewhat apolitical view stood in sharp contrast to the position taken by the president's domestic affairs advisers, who felt Carter needed to leave Camp David with an apparent success.

Carter's views proved to be partly correct and partly wrong. He was right in sensing that the best avenue for real progress lay in getting a detailed understanding between Begin and Sadat on Sinai and on the basic elements of an Egyptian-Israeli peace treaty. Begin skillfully withheld his final concessions on removal from Sinai of Israeli settlements and return of three airfields to Egypt until the very end, but from the outset it was clear that an agreement was possible. Carter was wrong, however, in believing that the talks could be concluded quickly and that the three leaders could work well together to solve problems. After only two sessions with both Begin and Sadat in the same room, the president realized it would be better to keep them apart.[38]

Sadat arrived at Camp David ready for a fight with Begin. To ensure that it would happen, he presented to Carter and Begin an Egyptian draft of a fairly tough agreement. Begin reacted sharply, and the Israelis began to write a counterdraft. At the same time, however, Sadat privately told Carter that he was prepared to be flexible on most points, except for land and sovereignty, but that Carter should put forward proposals for both delegations to react to.[39] On the Israeli side, Attorney General Aharon Barak had also reached the conclusion that the time had come for the United States to put forward proposals of its own, and that Begin and Sadat should be kept apart. Thus, by the first weekend, the American team began to polish the first of many negotiating drafts.

Over the next ten days a pattern developed whereby the U.S. delegation, and often just the president and Secretary Vance, would meet separately with the Israeli and Egyptian leaders. They would work from nonbinding written drafts, each time trying to elicit concrete reactions to proposals. These would then be discussed within the American team, and a new draft would be produced, often only marginally different than the previous one. By this means the main issues of disagreement surfaced quickly.

On Sinai there were essentially two problems: settlements and airfields. Both were resolved satisfactorily toward the end of the talks, with Begin reserving his position on settlements by saying the issue would have to be put to a vote of the Knesset. Predictably, the final status of the West Bank and Gaza and the question of linkage were the main stumbling blocks. In addition, the Egyptians insisted on including language from Resolution 242 on the nonacquisition of territory by war. The Israelis refused, even though the language was found in 242, which Begin professed to accept. The not-very-elegant solution was to append the full text of 242 to the Camp David Accords, but not to single out that phrase in the text. For Begin this was a minor victory, typical of his tenacious concern for words and principles, and also indicative of Sadat's comparative indifference to precise language.

Two central issues seemed likely to prevent agreement as the days wore on. First was the bedeviling question of what would happen on the West Bank and Gaza after a five-year transitional period. The Egyptians, supported by the Americans, wanted to make it clear that a final agreement would be negotiated during the transitional period which would resolve the questions of borders, sovereignty, security, and recognition according to the same principles of 242 that would govern agreements on other fronts, such as Sinai. In other words, the "peace for withdrawal" formula would remain intact even if the details might be worked out somewhat differently and over a longer period. Begin would have none of it, but instead of fighting the issue head on, he preferred to focus on other matters until the very last days of the negotiations.

Begin, more than any of the other negotiators, seemed to have a feel for the strategic use of time, taking the negotiations to the brink of collapse over secondary issues to avoid being pressed on key problems. Sadat, by contrast, simply refused to negotiate at all over those matters of deepest concern to him—Egyptian land and sovereignty—while leaving to his aides the unhappy task of trying to stand up to Begin on the Palestinian issue. Carter, who often grew impatient with Sadat's subordinates, frequently went directly to Sadat to get them overruled, something that did not recommend itself on the Israeli side, since there it was Dayan, Defense Minister Ezer Weizman, and Barak who showed flexibility, while Begin was the hard-liner (a much stronger negotiating position to be in, as the results showed).[40] Begin's position was also strengthened by his willingness to accept a failure in the talks. Both Sadat and Carter were more committed to a positive outcome, and Begin could therefore credibly use the threat of walking out, as he did, to extract some concessions.

The second difficult issue was the question of settlements: the American and Egyptian teams wanted to get a freeze on them during the negotiations over Palestinian self-government. Again, Begin deferred the discussion of this issue until near the end of the talks.

September 16, a Saturday, proved to be the crucial day for addressing the hard issues involving the West Bank and Gaza.[41] Up until that time all of the American drafts contained language on the applicability of 242, including the principle of withdrawal, to the final negotiation on the West Bank and Gaza. And a paragraph calling for a freeze on settlements had always been included. That morning Dayan and Barak met with Vance. The Israelis explained why Begin would never accept the language on 242 and withdrawal. Barak added that he felt a solution could be found, but only if they were all prepared to continue negotiating for another week or so. Prophetically, he said that if agreement had to be reached that day, all they could hope to do was to paper over some very major problems that would come back to haunt them.

Apart from Barak and a few others, however, no one had the stomach for another week in the claustrophobic environment of Camp David. As a result, in the course of the day on Saturday, the American draft was fundamentally changed. The elements of 242, including withdrawal, which had previously been spelled out, were deleted. The language was changed to make it clear that the negotiations, but not necessarily the results of the negotiations, would be based on the principles of 242. And the negotiations about the West Bank and Gaza were artfully obfuscated by creating two tracks, one involving peace-treaty negotiations between Israel and Jordan, and the other involving talks between Israel and representatives of the Palestinians about the West Bank and Gaza.

Israel had no objection to saying that 242 should be the basis for negotiations with Jordan. In Begin's view Jordan had no right to the West Bank, and saying that did not imply a commitment to the "peace for withdrawal" formula. In the Israeli view, 242 did not apply to the talks on the final status of the West Bank and Gaza. A careful reader of paragraph 1(c) of the "Framework for Peace in the Middle East" signed on September 17, 1978, will see language about "two separate but related committees," and "the negotiations shall be based on all the provisions and principles of UN Security Council Resolution 242." It may take a lawyer to explain how, but Begin successfully protected his position of principle that 242 did not apply to the negotiations over the West Bank's future; the Americans accepted the ambiguity; and Sadat may well have wondered what all the verbal gymnastics were about. In any case, Begin won this round as well.

Later on Saturday evening Carter and Vance thought they had finally won a round with Begin. At a late-night session Carter insisted that Begin agree to a freeze on settlement activity in the West Bank and Gaza for the duration of the negotiations over autonomy. Carter agreed to delete the paragraph in the draft text and to substitute a letter from Begin to him, and he dropped his insistence that existing settlements should not be thickened. But he clearly thought a commitment had been made not to construct new settlements during the autonomy talks. Vance also understood Begin to have made such a promise, although he was concerned about Begin's hesitation to accept an open-ended commitment to a freeze.[42]

In any event, the issue should have been settled on Sunday morning, when Begin sent a draft letter on the topic to Carter. By this time Sadat had already been informed that Begin had agreed to a freeze on settlements. But the actual letter did not conform to Carter's understanding, and, without speaking directly to Begin, Carter sent it back. Begin had promised to freeze settlements for three months, a time period he had mentioned the previous evening. Now, however, Begin was linking the freeze to the duration of the Egyptian-Israeli negotiations, not to the autonomy talks, which was an entirely inappropriate and unprecedented step. Alarm bells should have gone off, but so many other issues were on the agenda that day, especially a diversionary argument over Jerusalem which erupted in the afternoon, that both Carter and Vance continued to act as if there had merely been a misunderstanding that would be cleared up as soon as Begin sent back a new draft.

The final version of the letter did not arrive until after the Camp David Accords had been signed, and in it Begin held stubbornly to his position that the freeze would last only through the three-month period of the Egyptian-Israeli talks. Another round went to Begin, and on a position of considerable importance to the skeptical Arab audience that was waiting to see what, if anything, would be offered to the Palestinians as a result of the Egyptian-Israeli separate peace apparently in the making. Carter never got over the feeling that Begin had misled him, and this episode caused deep mutual distrust between the two leaders.

Late in the afternoon of September 17 Sadat and Carter met for the last time to discuss the agreement that was nearing completion. Sadat was reserved, and his mood was not one of pleasure at a job well done. The American team also realized that many problems lay ahead, but in the end it had made the political decision to get the best agreement then available, while hoping that the next stage of talks would fill in some of the gaps and clarify areas of ambiguity. And it is also true that the key players on the American side tended to think the Camp David Accords would eventually win Saudi and Jordanian support. To a large extent this was wishful thinking, and in part it reflected a tendency to take the Saudis too literally when they mumbled positive generalities to visiting Americans.

CONCLUSIONS

During the lengthy talks that preceded Camp David and at Camp David itself, U.S. policy constantly had to adjust to two realities: events in the Middle East cannot be easily controlled or influenced, so developments there frequently caught the Americans by surprise and obliged them to revise their strategies; and domestic American political realities intrude with particular force on the decisionmaking process regarding the Middle East. A president must simultaneously adjust his plans to the unpredictable twists and turns of Middle East politics and keep an eye on his domestic political base. What seems possible and desirable in the first year of a president's term is likely to be seen as hopelessly ambitious by the third year.

The result of these Middle East and domestic pressures is to move American policy away from grand designs with strong ideological content toward a less controversial, and less ambitious, middle ground that can win bipartisan public support as well as acceptance by Arabs and Israelis. To do so, of course, is not always possible, as much as it might be politically desirable, so American policy toward the Middle East rarely manages to satisfy everyone that has an interest in shaping it. Presidents seem to tire of all the controversy generated by Middle East problems, and the intractability of the issues is a source of much frustration.

The Camp David Accords amply demonstrate the limits of what in fact can be achieved, even with a massive commitment of effort. But they are also a reminder that diplomacy can produce results, if the will, the energy, and the creativity are there. The historical verdict on Camp David cannot be fully rendered, although with each passing year it seems to be more widely accepted as part of the new reality of the Middle East. By any standard, however, this remarkable adventure in summit diplomacy achieved more than most of its detractors have been willing to acknowledge, and less than its most ardent proponents have claimed.

CHAPTER ELEVEN

Descent from the Summit:
To Link or Not to Link?

The two agreements reached at Camp David marked an important watershed in the peace negotiations, but much remained to be done before peace would actually be achieved. Many of the blanks in the Camp David Accords had to be filled in, and many of the ambiguities had to be resolved one way or another. Along the way there would be pauses, detours, some backtracking, and many dead ends. Egypt and Israel would finally reach their goal of a formal peace treaty, but the broader objective of finding a peaceful resolution to the Palestinian question remained elusive.

The phase of detailed drafting was now to begin, a seemingly technical task, but in fact a complex process during which major political battles were still fought and attempts to revise the basic framework of negotiations were still made. Although the technicians were sitting at the table drafting documents, the political leaders were still deeply involved.

Menachem Begin, Anwar Sadat, and Jimmy Carter each devised strategies for this phase of negotiations, but the special circumstances of the summit could not be recreated. Isolating the leaders from the press and their own public opinion had no doubt been a prime factor in reaching the two framework agreements. Now, however, each leader would have to return to the real world in which domestic constituencies would have their say.

As each of the Camp David participants felt compelled to justify what he had done at the summit, the gap separating them began to widen again. By the time of the self-imposed target of three months for negotiating the peace treaty between Egypt and Israel, the talks had come to a halt.

POST-SUMMIT STRATEGIES

Carter left Camp David with a feeling of real satisfaction. The reaction in Congress, the press, and the public at large to the news of an agreement between Begin and Sadat was overwhelmingly positive. Carter received much of the credit, and his political fortunes seemed to improve significantly as a result.

To sustain this political boost, however, Carter needed to make sure that the Camp David frameworks did not remain dead letters. Time was of the essence in reaching a formal peace treaty. Among other considerations, midterm congressional elections were scheduled for early November, and it would probably help Democratic candidates, and therefore Carter, if a peace treaty could be signed by then.

Although Carter was no doubt pleased by the domestic American reaction, he was worried by the early signs of disenchantment in the Arab world. He had implied to Sadat that he would make a serious effort to win support from Jordan and Saudi Arabia, and in his more careless moments he had said that anything he and Sadat agreed to would have to be accepted by King Hussein and the Saudis. But Hussein was wary of the accords reached at Camp David and refused to meet with Sadat on the Egyptian president's return trip to Cairo.

Carter's clear priority after Camp David was to conclude the treaty negotiations as quickly as possible, literally within days. As usual, the president tended to see the remaining issues as technical and therefore susceptible to rapid resolution. The deeper political problems faced by both Begin and Sadat were harder for him to fathom. Carter found it difficult to accept the fact that neither shared his own sense of urgency.

Not only did Begin not share Carter's feeling that time was of the essence, but he also wanted to slow down the pace of negotiations for fear that too much pressure would otherwise be put on Israel. Whenever Carter showed himself too eager for quick results, Begin seemed to dig in his heels to resist demands for Israeli concessions. He was particularly recalcitrant about the settlements in the West Bank and Gaza. As hard as Carter might press to resolve this issue, Begin simply said no to the idea of a prolonged freeze on new settlements. And that was that.

If Begin was attentive to the rhythms of American politics, and surely he was, he must have realized it would be increasingly difficult for Carter to play a strong role in the negotiations as 1979 unfolded. At some point the preelection atmosphere would take hold, and Carter would have to turn to shoring up his political position. He would not then want to engage in confrontations with Israel. Begin was well aware that Carter tended to side with Sadat on the Palestinian question and that the negotiations over the West Bank and Gaza would be extremely difficult.

It would be far better, then, not to begin talks on autonomy until sometime well into 1979, when Carter would have other preoccupations.

In many ways Sadat was in a weaker position than Begin, which inevitably influenced the outcome of the negotiations. If the talks now broke down, Israel would stay put in Sinai. Sadat would have nothing to show for his "historic initiative." And his hope for American economic, military, and technological assistance would fade if the peace negotiations collapsed because of his actions. Carter had already warned him of that at Camp David. Sadat worried less about time than Carter, but he too must have understood that Carter's role would have to change as the election year of 1980 approached.[1] Sadat also knew, however, that any show by him of impatience or eagerness to conclude the negotiations would be used by Begin to try to extract further concessions.

From the perspectives of Carter, Sadat, and Begin, the post-summit phase of negotiations was bound to be difficult. The unique circumstances of the thirteen days at Camp David had facilitated reaching agreement, but now most of the pressures were working in the opposite direction. It was not a propitious atmosphere in which to resume the talks.

PREPARING FOR THE NEXT ROUND

Carter was not content to sit and wait for the results of the Knesset vote on the Camp David Accords, scheduled for two weeks later. There was one item of unfinished business. On Monday, September 18, 1978, Begin had sent Carter the promised letter on the settlements in the West Bank and Gaza. The text was identical to the one Carter had rejected the previous day. Referring to his notes of the Saturday night conversation, Carter wrote down what he thought had been agreed to and had Assistant Secretary of State Harold Saunders deliver his version to the Israelis, along with the original of Begin's letter, which Carter refused to accept.

For several days American and Israel officials tried, without success, to find language that might resolve the difference. Sadat did not help matters when he said to the press on September 19 that he understood there would be a freeze for three months and that Israel had also agreed not to expand settlements during this period.[2]

Carter continued to look for ways to push Begin into agreeing to a freeze on settlements for the duration of the negotiations on self-government for the Palestinians. At one point Carter decided that until he had received the letter he sought on settlements, he would not send a letter to Begin promising to help build two airfields in the Negev. On

September 22 he signed a letter to Begin spelling out once more what he thought had been agreed on, pointedly noting that he had so informed Sadat on September 17. But the letter was never sent. A few days later, however, he dispatched an oral message to Begin, repeating his view on what had been agreed on and warning that "the settlements could become a serious obstacle to peace. Construction of new settlements during the negotiations could have a most serious consequence for the successful fulfillment of the agreement."

When Begin met with the American ambassador to Israel, Samuel W. Lewis, on September 27, 1978, he provided the text of Attorney General Barak's notes from the meeting on the night of September 16. According to Begin, the notes proved that he had not agreed to the freeze Carter had requested. He had agreed only to consider it. He went on to say he would never agree to give Arabs a veto over where Israelis could settle. In his view Jews had as much right to settle in Hebron as in Tel Aviv. That was precisely the crux of the disagreement.

Neither Carter nor Begin would budge, but soon Carter turned to other matters. To the many bystanders who were waiting to see the outcome of this dispute, round one seemed to go to Begin—not an encouraging sign for Sadat or King Hussein.

While Carter was trying to untangle the controversy over settlements, Secretary of State Cyrus Vance was traveling in the Middle East. His goal was to try to win Jordanian and Saudi support for the Camp David Accords. What he found instead was deep skepticism, coated only with a formal politeness that some Americans interpreted as an expression of hope that the next round of negotiations would succeed.[3]

Carter and Vance both felt that some of Begin's public interpretations of the Camp David Accords were making it difficult for King Hussein and the Saudis not to reject them.[4] The Americans were also frustrated by Sadat's seeming unwillingness to communicate with either the Jordanians or the Saudis.[5]

Despite all these problems, Carter remained somewhat optimistic that Jordan would join the negotiations.[6] Vance was more skeptical, especially after his visits to Amman and Riyadh. King Hussein had raised many questions, and Vance knew it would be difficult to overcome his doubts. In an attempt to do so, however, Vance did agree to give the king written answers to questions he might have about the accords.

Meanwhile through intelligence channels the PLO was making queries to Washington about the meaning of the agreements. Arafat was skeptical, but he showed a serious interest in finding out if there might be more to Camp David than met the eye. Although the Americans had no reason for optimism, they could see that an Arab consensus had not yet formed. If the Arabs took Begin's interpretations, or Sadat's contemptuous expressions, as the final words on the matter, the case would be closed. But the Americans hoped they might succeed in giving a more open-ended interpretation to the framework dealing with the Palestinians and thus prevent a strongly negative Arab reaction. They therefore decided to use the questions from King Hussein as the means for offering a liberal American interpretation of Camp David.

Not everyone in the administration was pleased with the idea of responding in writing to King Hussein. Vice President Mondale, for example, thought it was undignified for the United States to submit to this sort of interrogation. But Vance had given the king his word, and Carter decided to provide written answers. As soon as the fourteen questions arrived on September 29, the bureaucracy began to churn out answers. Most of them consisted of repeating well-known American positions, but in some cases they involved interpretations of Camp David. For example, the United States went on record as favoring the inclusion of the Palestinians in East Jerusalem in the election for the self-governing authority. And in an early draft the Americans had taken the position that sovereignty in the West Bank and Gaza resided with the people who lived there. When Mondale saw the draft, he strongly opposed such a formulation, and it was removed from the final version signed by Carter.[7] (See appendix F for the text.)

While the Americans were working to convince other Arabs to be open minded about Camp David, the Israeli Knesset met on September 27, 1978, to vote on the Camp David Accords, including the provision for withdrawing settlements from Sinai. After lengthy arguments, the vote was 84 in favor and 19 opposed, with 17 abstentions.

Carter phoned Begin the next day to congratulate him on the outcome of the Knesset debate. He also mentioned his hope that the "difference of opinion" between them over settlements in the West Bank and Gaza would soon be resolved. Begin said he had already sent the president a letter on the topic. Carter repeated that he was determined to solve this problem and that he and Begin should try to minimize their differences. He added that he would like to see a Sinai agreement within days. Begin said it should be possible if everyone agreed to use the standard form of a peace treaty and just fill in the blanks with appropriate details.

Carter then called Sadat, and the two agreed that negotiations on the peace treaty could begin in mid-October. With these conversations Carter seems to have given up the idea of trying to force Begin to change his position on West Bank and Gaza settlements. By continuing to dwell on that topic, Carter would risk the Sinai agreement he so badly wanted. He would also be reminding the other Arabs of one of the flaws in the Camp David framework. Instead, he apparently decided to end the public debate over the issue. For three months, in any case, there would be no more Israeli settlements, and during that period Carter hoped that a solution might be found. So that same day, September 28, he authorized Secretary of Defense Harold Brown to sign a letter to Israeli Defense Minister Ezer Weizman promising American support in building two airfields in the Negev.

On September 29, 1978, Secretary Vance spoke before the UN General Assembly. He had urged Carter to allow him to say something on the Palestinian question that might change the negative atmosphere growing in the Arab world. Carter agreed, and Vance included the following phrase in his text: "As the President said, our historic position on settlements in occupied territory has remained constant. As he further said, no peace agreement will be either just or secure if it does not resolve the problem of the Palestinians in the broadest sense. We believe that the Palestinian people must be assured that they and their descendants can live with dignity and freedom and have the opportunity for economic fulfillment and for political expression. The Camp David Accords state that the negotiated solution must recognize the legitimate rights of the Palestinian people."[8]

THE BLAIR HOUSE TALKS

To prepare for the next phase of negotiations, the American team had drawn up a draft of an Egyptian-Israeli peace treaty. Vance wanted to use the same procedure that had proved successful at Camp David. Each side would be asked to comment on the American draft, but changes in the text would be made only by the American side after consulting with the others. The device of a "single negotiating text" was one of the methodological devices the Americans had found useful, and both the Egyptians and Israelis had come to accept it.

Carter reviewed the draft treaty on October 9. His only comment was that Israel should withdraw fully from Sinai in two, not three, years. The draft treaty was a fairly simple document. It formally ended the state of war and established a relationship of peace. Israel would withdraw to the international border according to details to be worked out by the parties. On the completion of an interim phase of withdrawal, diplomatic relations would be established. The border between the two countries was defined as the former international boundary between Egypt and mandated Palestine. Article 3 of the treaty called for normal peaceful relations, the details of which were to be spelled out in an annex. Article 4 called for security arrangements in Sinai and along the border. Article 5 dealt with freedom of navigation. And article 6 spelled out the relation between this treaty and other international obligations of the parties.

From the beginning the Americans realized that several issues would be contentious. For Israel, there was the question of the timing of withdrawal. Israel's fear was that Egypt might get most or all of its territory back before entering into any form of peaceful relations with Israel. For the Israeli public, all the concessions would then seem to be coming from the Israel side. Israel therefore insisted that Egypt should establish diplomatic relations before final withdrawal and that some aspects of normal relations should begin at an early date. For Egypt, this timing posed a problem. Sadat wanted to withhold the exchange of ambassadors until Israel had at least carried out the provisions of the Camp David Accords that called for elections for the Palestinians in the West Bank and Gaza to establish their own self-governing authority. This was the famous issue of linkage, which here boiled down to when Egypt would send its ambassador to Israel. Since that was a matter of great importance to Begin, it acquired significance for Sadat as well. A test of wills quickly developed over the issue.

A second issue of likely contention was the so-called priority of obligations. Israel wanted the treaty to contain a clear statement that it superseded other Egyptian commitments, such as Egypt's many mutual defense pacts with Arab countries. Sadat found it intolerable to say in public that commitments to Israel counted for more than commitments to Arab states. For example, if Israel carried out aggression against an Arab state allied to Egypt, Sadat did not feel it would be a violation of the treaty if he went to the aid of that state. In reality, of course, whatever was written on paper would not guarantee what would happen in some future conflict, but these were issues of high symbolic importance for each party, and each was trying to make its position clear to the United States in the event of future disputes. Much more was to be heard about

.

the priority of obligations. Vance, the experienced international lawyer, realized from the outset that this issue would be a sticking point.

Perhaps most difficult was the question of how the two parties would express their continuing determination to work for a solution to the Palestinian question after they had signed the treaty. Begin wanted only a vague commitment to negotiate, whereas Sadat insisted on deadlines and specific commitments that would demonstrate that Egypt had not concluded a "separate peace." Here again was the linkage issue in its pure form.

Besides these difficult conceptual problems, there were also some complicated details. Israel wanted to retain access to Sinai oil, and wanted some form of guarantee from the United States if Egypt later refused to supply the oil. Some of the specific issues involving security arrangements in Sinai might also prove difficult, even though the military men on both sides had a good record of finding concrete compromise solutions.

This phase of the negotiations differed from Camp David not only in content but also in format and personnel. On the American side, Carter was less involved. He felt he had spent too much time on the Middle East and that he now had to turn his attention to other issues. Normalization of relations with China and the conclusion of SALT II with the Soviet Union were high on his foreign-policy agenda. Vance was designated as the principal negotiator on the American side, though he too had other responsibilities. He hoped to delegate much of the day-to-day work to Alfred Atherton, the U.S. ambassador for the peace talks.

The Egyptian team was also somewhat different. In the past Carter had relied heavily on his ability to deal directly with Sadat over the heads of the Egyptian delegation. Now that the time had come to put words to paper in a peace treaty, the Egyptian lawyers would have their chance again to push Sadat toward harder positions. Muhammad Ibrahim Kamel had resigned, and then without much explanation Sadat had also replaced Minister of Defense Abd al-Ghany Gamasy. The new minister of foreign affairs and head of the Egyptian delegation was Kamal Hassan Ali, who was assisted in the negotiations by Boutros Boutros Ghali and Usama al-Baz, both veterans of Camp David. Sadat also soon named a new prime minister, Mustafa Khalil, who had played no previous part in the negotiations.

The Israeli participants were more familiar, most of them having been at Camp David. Foreign Minister Dayan and Defense Minister Weizman led the negotiating team to Washington, accompanied by Attorney General Barak and Meir Rosenne, a legal adviser to the foreign minister. Begin refused to delegate much authority to the team, however, and the Israeli cabinet as a whole wanted to be kept abreast of most of the details of the talks. As a result, the comparative moderation of the negotiating team meant little.

The delegations arrived in Washington in the second week of October, and the first sessions were scheduled for October 12. Carter met with both the Israelis and Egyptians before the formal resumption of the talks in order to urge both sides to move toward agreement quickly. In his talks with the Egyptians on October 11, Carter said the negotiations in Washington should be used to deal with the problems of Sinai and the West Bank and Gaza. He urged the Egyptians not to give up on the Jordanians and Palestinians. At the same time, he said, the issues involving the West Bank and Gaza should not be allowed to impede progress toward an Egyptian-Israeli peace treaty.

In the meeting with Carter, Boutros Ghali took the floor for the Egyptians to make the case for linkage, or the "correlation" between the two agreements, as he was fond of calling it. After Egypt and Israel reached agreement, he asked, what pressure would there be on Israel to do anything about the West Bank and Gaza? If Egypt received some advantages in Sinai, the Palestinians must also have something. Otherwise Egypt would be isolated in the Arab world. This could jeopardize the approximately $2 billion that Egypt was receiving from Saudi Arabia. Al-Baz interjected the thought that the opposition to Camp David had already peaked in the Arab world and that within a few months King Hussein would be ready to join the talks. Carter concluded by repeating that he was committed to finding a solution to the West Bank and Gaza but that he did not want to risk the treaty between Egypt and Israel because of problems with Jordan or the Palestinians.

OPENING BIDS

For several days after these initial meetings the talks dragged on without any breakthroughs. The technicians were able to make some headway on the annexes, but the problems at the political level remained. Carter began to show signs of impatience. He was thinking of flying to the Middle East in late October, and even hoped, unrealistically, to be able to preside over the signing of the Egyptian-Israeli peace treaty at that time. An Arab summit was being talked about for early November, and Carter wanted to pin down the treaty before it convened. He also had his eye on the congressional elections.[9]

To speed up the talks, Carter decided to meet both delegations on October 17. Dayan complained about three issues: the language on priority of obligations in the treaty; the linkage between the treaty talks and the West Bank–Gaza issues; and Egypt's reluctance to speed up normalization. Then, in a shrewd gesture seemingly calculated to win Carter's support, Dayan announced that Israel was prepared to accelerate withdrawal to the interim line in Sinai. (The Camp David Accords called on Israel to pull back its forces from about two-thirds of Sinai within nine months of signing a peace treaty.) The town of Al-Arish, which had great symbolic value to Sadat, could be returned within two months instead of the nine envisaged in the framework agreement. Carter was pleased and saw the offer as a welcome sign of Israeli flexibility. In return, Carter agreed to talk to the Egyptians about moving quickly on normalization; he undertook to resolve a technical problem involving the location of the interim line; and he agreed to consider helping to finance the withdrawal of the Israeli military from Sinai, but not the cost of removing the settlers.

A few hours later Carter met with the Egyptian delegation. Kamal Hassan Ali informed the president that agreement had been reached on the delineation of limited-force zones in Sinai. Boutros Ghali then argued the case for some correlation between the treaty negotiations and the Palestinian question. In particular, he put forward the idea of establishing diplomatic relations in stages that would somehow be related to progress on the West Bank and Gaza. First would come the formal recognition of Israel, then a chargé d'affaires would be sent to Tel Aviv, and only later would ambassadors be exchanged. Carter was unhappy with this proposal and reminded the Egyptians that Sadat had orally agreed at Camp David that ambassadors would be exchanged at the time of the interim withdrawal. He then gave the Egyptians copies of his answers to King Hussein's questions and said they should help deal with the problem of linkage.

Carter also informed the Egyptians that the Israelis were prepared to accelerate withdrawal to Al-Arish. Now, he said, the Egyptians seemed to be backsliding on the timing of sending their ambassador to Tel Aviv. He argued that Egypt should reciprocate Israel's constructive attitude on

withdrawal by agreeing to an early exchange of ambassadors. Carter
ended the talks by asking the Egyptians to tell President Sadat of his
desire to visit the Middle East, before November 1 if possible.

Carter was now back in the middle of the negotiations. On October
20 he held a sometimes acrimonious meeting with the Israeli delegation.
He charged that Israel was ignoring the fact that the Egyptian-Israeli
framework was part of a broader commitment to work for a settlement
on the West Bank and Gaza as well. Barak asked if Carter thought the
treaty should be made contingent on whether an agreement could be
reached on the West Bank. Carter said that was not his intention. After
all, the West Bank formula might fail because of the actions or inactions
of third parties, in particular the Jordanians or Palestinians. But, Carter
asked, what if Israel was the party responsible for the failure of the West
Bank framework? Did Israel think that in those circumstances the treaty
would be unaffected? Barak answered that the treaty must be legally
independent of whatever happened on the West Bank and Gaza, even
though some degree of political linkage might exist. Carter then told the
Israelis that he was sure he could get Sadat to agree to an exchange of
ambassadors within one month of the interim withdrawal. Dayan asked
if the United States could write a letter guaranteeing that the treaty
would be carried out.

On the same day that Carter was having his difficult talk with the
Israelis, Assistant Secretary Saunders was in Jerusalem meeting with
Prime Minister Begin. He had previously been to Amman to deliver
Carter's answers to Hussein. He had also stopped in Riyadh and was
planning to meet with West Bank Palestinians.

First Saunders reported to Begin on Hussein's attitude, which was not
entirely negative. The king had told Saunders that he was not ready to
make a decision on entering negotiations until after the Baghdad summit
in early November, but that he would encourage Palestinians in the West
Bank to cooperate with the Camp David process. The Saudis had said
they would adopt a neutral attitude.

Begin complained that the Americans seemed to have great understanding for the political problems of Arab leaders, but none for his own. He
had been bitterly attacked by some of his oldest friends in the Irgun.
The Americans should appreciate the concessions he had already made
for peace. Then he told Saunders to convey to Carter his "deep sadness."
There had been no prior consultation with Israel over the answers to

King Hussein. Begin proceeded to launch into a point-by-point criticism of the answers, emphasizing what he considered to be all the deviations from Camp David that they contained. He attacked the United States for repeating its own position on Jerusalem, and for other statements of American positions that differed from his own. These positions, all well known to the Arabs, would, in Begin's view, harden their negotiating stance and lead them to expect American pressure on Israel. Although Carter's signature was on the answers to Hussein, Begin and his colleagues preferred to speak of the "Saunders document," and for several weeks Saunders was the target of a harsh campaign in the Israeli press.

Despite these contretemps with the Israelis in Washington and in Jerusalem, agreement *ad referendum* was reached on the text of the treaty. Each delegation had to refer back to its own capital for final approval, but the basic elements of the treaty were seemingly all in place. The Egyptians, however, had proposed during the talks that a parallel letter be signed by Sadat and Begin dealing with the West Bank and Gaza. The letter should coincide with the treaty and would commit the two parties to conclude the negotiations on the West Bank and Gaza by a fixed date, with elections to be held within three months after the treaty was signed.

Egypt also mentioned in the negotiations its special responsibility for Gaza, a reminder of Sadat's interest in the "Gaza-first" option whereby self-government would first be established in Gaza and only later in the West Bank, after King Hussein joined the negotiations. Al-Baz referred to this as a ploy to scare King Hussein and the Palestinians, in essence telling them that if they did not get into the negotiations soon they would be left out. He argued strongly that Israel should take a number of unilateral steps in Gaza before the withdrawal to the interim line in Sinai was completed.

Carter wrote to Sadat on October 22, spelling out the terms of the treaty as negotiated in Washington. He asked that Sadat accept the text in its current form, and that in addition he agree to a letter committing Egypt to send an ambassador to Israel within one month of the interim withdrawal. Carter repeated that he had asked the Israelis to withdraw more rapidly to the interim line than was called for at Camp David. Carter concluded the letter by saying he would like to visit the Middle East for the treaty signing, which he hoped could be at a very early date. A similar letter was sent to Begin. Carter noted that he did not yet have

Sadat's approval to send an ambassador to Israel within one month of the interim withdrawal, but he hoped that Sadat would have a positive attitude.

Sadat's reply came on October 24. He was willing to accommodate Carter on several points, including the exchange of ambassadors, provided some changes could be made in the text of the treaty. Egypt could not agree to permanent force limits in Sinai. Up to twenty-five years would be acceptable. (Carter noted, "Not a problem.") Second, article 6 of the treaty, the priority of obligations issue, made it seem as if Egypt's commitments to Israel were greater than those to the Arab League.[10] The language of the treaty should not downgrade Egypt's obligations under previous agreements. (Carter noted, "A problem.") Third, the treaty must clearly say that Egypt has sovereignty over Sinai. (Carter wrote, "Okay.")

A letter from Begin arrived the same day. In it the Israeli prime minister complained at length about the answers provided to King Hussein. The full transcript of Begin's talk with Saunders was appended to the letter. Then Begin reviewed the dispute over settlements in the West Bank and Gaza, noting that he had told the president there were plans to add several hundred families to the settlements in Judea and Samaria even during the three-month moratorium.

Meanwhile Dayan and Weizman were in Israel seeking to win cabinet approval for the draft treaty. They ran into considerable criticism, but nonetheless Begin pressed for cabinet support of the existing draft and won a sizable majority on October 26. For reasons of his own, and perhaps as a reward to some of the hard-line cabinet members, Begin accompanied the announcement of the cabinet's decision on the treaty with a decision to "thicken" settlements in the West Bank.

Carter was furious. He perfunctorily congratulated Begin on the cabinet vote and then commented on the decision to thicken settlements: "At a time when we are trying to organize the negotiations dealing with the West Bank and Gaza, no step by the Israeli government could be more damaging." In his own handwriting Carter added, "I have to tell you with gravest concern and regret that taking this step at this time will have the most serious consequences for our relationship."

In light of these developments, it was somewhat ironic that the Nobel peace prize was awarded the next day to both Begin and Sadat. Some of Carter's aides were bitter that the president was not included, but for the moment the more important problem was that peace itself seemed to be slipping away. Reports had even reached Washington that Sadat was about to withdraw his delegation and break off the talks. Carter contacted him and convinced him not to take any rash action, but the mood at the White House was gloomy. At a minimum, Carter would not be able to make his hoped-for trip to the Middle East before the end of the month.

During the last days of October the American team became increasingly aware that the Israelis were insisting on a very narrow definition of self-government for the Palestinians in the West Bank and Gaza. Dayan, in an unusually frank session with Vance on October 30, conveyed the most recent Israeli cabinet decisions on the treaty, and then went on to talk about the West Bank problem. Israel, he said, was prepared to talk to Egypt only about the "modalities" for holding elections. It would be a mistake to get into the question of the "powers and responsibilities" of the elected self-governing authority. To do so would open a Pandora's box. The Egyptians would inevitably argue that state lands should be under the control of the self-governing authority; Israel would reject that. Far better to limit the talks to holding elections; then Israel could work out with the Palestinians the powers of the body to which they had been elected.

The next day Dayan made many of these same points before the Egyptian delegation. He presented a strong case for limiting the discussions between Egypt and Israel to the question of how to organize the elections in the West Bank and Gaza. Otherwise the talks would drag on indefinitely. Al-Baz, speaking for the Egyptians, disagreed. The Palestinians had to know, he argued, what they were voting for. Unless the powers and responsibilities were defined in advance, the elections would be seen as a fraud. It would not be easier to grapple with this problem later. Dayan, who knew his prime minister well, said he would refer this issue to Begin if the Egyptians insisted. But he could tell them now that if Israel did consent to discuss powers and responsibilities, the negotiators would spend years trying to reach agreement.

When Carter read the accounts of these meetings, he was outraged. He saw them as further evidence of Israeli backsliding from the commitments made at Camp David. Vice President Mondale, Secretary Vance, National Security Adviser Brzezinski, and Hamilton Jordan, Carter's chief of staff, were called to the White House on November 1 for a strategy session. They decided to slow down the pace of the negotiations, to review Israel's commitments under the Camp David Accords, and to develop a series of steps to bring pressure on Begin to live up to those commitments. Responses to Israeli requests for arms could be delayed, and several other steps could be taken.

The next day Vance flew to New York for a brief meeting with Begin, who happened to be in town on his way to Canada. Dayan had earlier made it clear that Begin and the cabinet had ultimate authority and that he could do little more to resolve the disputes on remaining issues. Now, Begin found most of the treaty text acceptable but had problems with the side letter dealing with the West Bank and Gaza. Dayan and Weizman had said it should be possible to mention a target date for the holding of elections, but they did not want that date to coincide precisely with the interim withdrawal in Sinai. That would give the appearance of too much linkage. Begin, however, now said that Israel was adamantly opposed to the idea of any target date for elections. He argued that if for some reason beyond the control of Egypt and Israel the elections could not be held, that would call into question everything else, including the peace treaty. By contrast, Begin, always the legalist, found no problem in agreeing to the Egyptian request that powers and responsibilities of the self-governing authority be defined in advance of elections. On both these crucial issues, Begin ignored Dayan's advice. This was the first concrete evidence that Dayan's authority in this phase of the negotiations was much less than it had been in the preceding year.

Then Begin turned to bilateral issues. Israel would need $3.37 billion from the United States to help finance the withdrawal from Sinai, including the removal of the settlers. This aid should take the form of a loan at low interest rates. The cabinet would never approve the treaty, he said, unless the question of aid was solved first. Vance was noncommittal, refusing to give up one of the few elements of leverage the United States possessed.

As tensions rose in the U.S.-Israeli relationship, largely over the perception that Begin was diluting his already modest commitments concerning the Palestinians, pressure was mounting on Egypt to adopt a tougher position in support of Palestinian rights. The Arabs had held a summit meeting in Baghdad, and on November 5 they announced their conclusions. They criticized the Camp David Accords, and they decided that the headquarters of the Arab League was to be moved from Cairo if Egypt and Israel reached a peace treaty. The conference participants sent a small delegation to Cairo to meet with Sadat to dissuade him from continuing with the peace negotiations, but the Egyptian president refused to meet it. Instead, he publicly referred to the summit participants as "cowards and dwarfs." He would not pay any attention, he said, to "the hissing of snakes."

Still, within days the Egyptian position seemed to harden.[11] Sadat sent a message to Carter on November 8 saying there must be unequivocal agreement on what was to take place on the West Bank and Gaza. Otherwise he would be accused of making a separate deal with the Israelis and abandoning the Palestinians. Sadat was not prepared to open himself to such accusations from the other Arabs.

The time had come for the Americans to pause and assess the situation. A memorandum was prepared for Carter reviewing what Begin had been saying since Camp David about the West Bank and Gaza. On at least eight points Begin seemed to have deviated from what Carter felt was the agreed interpretation of the Camp David Accords. He noted on the memo: "To Cy and Zbig—Any aid-loan program if agreed must be predicated on Israeli compliance with Camp David agreements. J. C."

Carter met with his senior aides to review the negotiations on November 8. He was in a bad mood. Brzezinski was arguing for a tough line with Begin. He urged Carter to consider reducing aid to Israel by a certain amount for each new settlement that Begin authorized. "We do not intend to subsidize illegal settlements and we will so inform Congress." No decisions on aid should be made until Begin accepted a target date for elections.

Carter decided Vance should not go to the Middle East again as had been proposed. It was pointless for him to spend full time on a nonproductive effort. Carter had concluded that Israel wanted a separate treaty with Egypt, while keeping the West Bank and Gaza permanently. The creation of new settlements, he thought, was deliberately done to prevent Jordan and the Palestinians from joining the negotiations.[12] Carter and Vance now felt they must try to pin down the agenda for the West Bank and Gaza, even if that meant delaying the signing of an Egyptian-Israeli treaty. As usual, their sympathies were more with Sadat than with Begin.

Over the next few days the American side worked to complete the text of the treaty and all its annexes, as well as a letter on the West Bank and Gaza. Carter reviewed the entire package, and it was ready to present to the Israelis and Egyptians on November 11. In a late session at the State Department that same evening, Vance and Dayan tried to resolve some remaining issues in anticipation of a meeting between Vance and Begin in New York the next day. Dayan informed Vance that the Israeli cabinet was adamant in not agreeing to accelerate withdrawal to the interim line. He personally was inclined to accept a target date for elections in the West Bank and Gaza, but the date should not correspond to the interim withdrawal. As for the text of the treaty, Dayan seemed to be satisfied.[13]

Begin, however, was not in a conciliatory frame of mind. He refused to accept the idea of a target date, telling Vance on November 12 that Dayan had no authority to imply otherwise. He repeated his refusal to consider accelerated withdrawal. And as if he should be rewarded for his intransigence, he demanded that the aid for the withdrawal from Sinai take the form of a grant, not a loan. He had made a mistake, he said, when he earlier requested a loan and had promised that every penny of it would be repaid.

SADAT LOSES PATIENCE

Meanwhile Carter telephoned Sadat in Cairo to urge him to accept the same package. Sadat was more agitated than usual. He argued at great length that the Baghdad rejectionists should not get the upper hand. He must show that he had got something for the Palestinians, at least in Gaza, before Israel completed the interim withdrawal. He would even be willing to have the withdrawal delayed by a few months if that would allow the elections for Palestinian self-government to be held at the same time as the return of most of Sinai. Somewhat awkwardly, Sadat said he would not agree to the first phase of withdrawal without at least the beginning of self-government in Gaza. Carter made it clear he did not favor treating Gaza differently from the West Bank. Elections should be held in both areas by the end of 1979, he said.

Sadat repeated that the first phase of withdrawal should coincide with the day the Palestinians started their self-government in the West Bank and Gaza, or at least in Gaza. He accused Begin of trying to delay everything until the start of the American elections. Carter responded by urging Sadat to stop attacking Hussein and the Saudis. Sadat replied that he was punishing them for what they had done at the Baghdad summit. Give me Gaza, he pleaded. Carter was skeptical, but he agreed to try to come up with a new formulation.

Carter then called Begin in New York, pointing out that the prospects of agreement were now quite remote. Begin responded by saying that Israel had broken no promise in refusing to accelerate the withdrawal. Weizman should never have agreed to such an idea. In any case, Egypt had no right to use the Israeli decision as a pretext to refuse to send an ambassador to Israel, as Boutros Ghali had implied. Carter reassured him that Sadat would stand by his agreement to send an ambassador within one month of the interim withdrawal.

The next day Hermann F. Eilts, the U.S. ambassador to Egypt, met with Sadat and found him in an angry mood. Sadat said he and Carter were no longer speaking the same language. Egypt would not agree to peace with Israel without having reached an agreement at the same time on the West Bank and Gaza. Even if the interim withdrawal had to be delayed until November 1979, he said, that could be done if by then the Palestinians had their self-government, at least in Gaza. Sadat also said he could not accept article 6 of the draft treaty, since that made it seem as if his obligations to Israel took precedence over his obligations to his Arab allies. The only solution, he said, was for a confrontation between Carter and Begin to take place. He was planning to send his vice-president, Husni Mubarak, to see Carter the next day to discuss such a strategy.

Meanwhile a Saudi emissary arrived in Washington to meet with U.S. officials. He explained the position that the Saudis had taken in Baghdad, arguing that it would give the Saudis more influence with the radicals in the future. If only Egypt did not make a separate peace, and if there was some form of linkage, then Saudi Arabia could help defend the Camp David Accords in front of the other Arabs. But there must be some mention of ultimate Israeli withdrawal from Arab occupied territories and some mention of Jerusalem.

Several days later, on November 21, Begin telephoned Carter to say that the Israeli cabinet had voted to accept the text of the treaty and its annexes. Carter was pleased, but asked about the letter on the West Bank and Gaza. Begin replied that the cabinet had rejected the idea of setting a target date at the end of 1979 for elections in the West Bank and Gaza. And he added that there were also other problems. First, Israel wanted to resolve the question of a grant from the United States to help cover the costs of withdrawal from Sinai. Second, Israel needed assurances on oil, especially in light of the turmoil in Iran, the country from which Israel normally received its oil.

Carter tried to explain Sadat's position on the need for the interim withdrawal to coincide with the onset of self-government. Then Carter suggested that Israel might agree to delay the interim withdrawal until elections were held in the West Bank and Gaza, without setting a date for either event. Begin was surprised by this suggestion and said he would have to think about it.

Carter spoke by phone with Sadat the next day to inform him of the Israeli position. Sadat was still angry at Begin. Although he said little to Carter at the time, he was also annoyed at Carter's suggestion that the interim withdrawal might be delayed until elections were held for Palestinian self-government. Without some deadline, that could mean no withdrawal would take place at all. Sadat had suggested there might be a brief delay in withdrawal to make it coincide with the elections, but he was not ready to accept the possibility of no withdrawal at all.

Sadat remained in a foul mood for the next week. On November 28 he met with Senate Majority Leader Robert Byrd of West Virginia. Ambassador Eilts, who attended the meeting, reported that in more than 250 meetings with Sadat he had never seen the Egyptian president so emotional or upset. Two days later Eilts was handed a letter from Sadat to Carter strongly criticizing Begin for wanting only a separate peace. The talks had reached a crossroads. An Egyptian presence in Gaza was now essential. Article 6 of the treaty on priority of obligations was impossible to accept, and article 4 needed to be revised so that it did not imply permanent limits on Egyptian forces in Sinai. When Israel reneged on accelerated withdrawal, Sadat said, this upset the equation on an early exchange of ambassadors. He could no longer agree to send an ambassador to Israel one month after the interim withdrawal. Sadat also provided the Americans with the text of a sixteen-page letter he was sending to Begin.

Eilts tried to account for Sadat's temper. Egypt, he said, was feeling isolated in the Arab world. Sadat totally distrusted Begin and resented the narrow Israeli interpretation of the Camp David Accords. The debate over settlements had angered Sadat as well. The United States did not show much understanding of his problems with the other Arabs. And, Eilts concluded, Sadat was annoyed that the United States seemed to consider him the line of least resistance whenever the Israelis took a hard stand.

More constructive was Sadat's decision to send his prime minister, Mustafa Khalil, to Washington to consult with Carter. Khalil made a good impression on the Americans as a man of reason and as an able spokesman for the Egyptian side. In a meeting with Carter on December 1, Khalil pressed hard on the importance of simultaneity of Israeli withdrawal to the interim line and the establishment of the self-governing authority. He also wanted to revise article 6 of the treaty. Carter objected to the idea of revising the treaty but did suggest that interpretive notes could be appended to it.

Several days later, on December 4, Carter met with his Middle East team to review the details of the proposals Khalil had brought with him. Carter and Vance were both eager to know what Sadat's bottom line was. Would he insist on a fixed date for elections in the West Bank and Gaza? Carter favored a less precise formulation of a target date. On article 6, Carter thought Sadat might settle for some cosmetic change of words. But Carter was convinced that Sadat would insist on some explicit relationship between the implementation of the Sinai agreement and the establishment of self-government in the West Bank and Gaza. Brzezinski noted that the Camp David Accords were ambiguous on this issue of linkage, but Carter responded that Sadat was correct that some degree of linkage was implied by the agreements.[14]

Vance made it clear he did not want to make another trip to the Middle East. He suggested that Ambassador Atherton might go. Carter said there was no point in having anyone other than Vance or Mondale talk to Begin and Sadat. In a somber mood Carter said that if the negotiations failed, he wanted it to be clear that Sadat was not to blame. He wanted to be on Sadat's side. The Israelis would have nowhere else to go in any event.

Hamilton Jordan added the thought that at this point only success in the negotiations could help Carter politically. Once the treaty was signed, Carter would be in a stronger position to deal with the West Bank and Gaza issues. Carter seemed to be willing to take some political risks. He told Vance to press Israel hard, even if that ended up costing him the election and Jewish support.[15]

VANCE TO THE MIDDLE EAST

Vance set off for Cairo on December 9, 1978, with two clear objectives and one new proposal. First, he wanted to complete negotiations on the text of the treaty. Second, he wanted to make sure that the letter on the West Bank and Gaza would mention a target date of the end of 1979 for the establishment of self-government, or at least for the conclusion of the negotiations before the holding of elections.

Vance's new idea was one that originated with Carter in response to his belief that Sadat would be adamant about some form of linkage. The Camp David Accords had specified that diplomatic relations would be established after the interim withdrawal in Sinai, but there was no mention in writing about when ambassadors should be exchanged. Carter had earlier convinced Sadat that the exchange should be made right away, but after the Israelis dropped the idea of an accelerated withdrawal, the Egyptian position had become less certain.

Carter now felt it would be justified for Sadat to say that he would establish diplomatic relations after the interim withdrawal, but that the actual exchange of ambassadors would not take place until the self-governing authority in the West Bank and Gaza had been established. Sadat was likely to see considerable merit in this form of linkage, and Begin would inevitably react with horror.

Vance met privately with Sadat on December 10 and reviewed the new position on the timing of the exchange of ambassadors. As predicted, Sadat was pleased. In return, he showed some flexibility in accepting a target date instead of a fixed date for setting up the self-governing authority. He also agreed that article 6 could remain essentially unchanged, provided an interpretive note could be added making clear that this treaty did not prevail over other treaties to which Egypt was a party. In the side letter Sadat also wanted to mention the possibility that the self-governing authority might start first in Gaza, and he also inserted a provision for Egyptian liaison officers to be stationed in Gaza because of Egypt's former administrative role there.

Sadat readily informed Vance that a basis for agreement now existed but that he expected Begin to react negatively. Cheerfully, he said Vance should be ready for a big confrontation that might last for several months.

Over the next forty-eight hours the Americans hammered out a new package of documents. The treaty text was essentially unchanged, along with the annexes. Several interpretive notes were drafted. The side letter on the West Bank and Gaza was redone to reflect several of Sadat's demands. The United States agreed to draft a legal opinion of its own on the meaning of article 6, to the effect that nothing would prevent Egypt from honoring its commitments under other treaties in the event of armed attack against one of its allies. Most important, Sadat was now asked to write a letter to Carter committing himself to the exchange of ambassadors after the establishment of the Palestinian self-governing authority, at least in Gaza.

Vance and Sadat met again on December 12 to go over the entire package. At 7:45 p.m. Sadat said he was willing to accept everything in it, despite some remaining complaints by Khalil and al-Baz. But he stressed to Vance that this was as far as he could go. He pleaded with

Vance not to come back to him to ask for more concessions. In his words, there was no further room for compromise. He wanted the United States at his side in this final round. Vance said he would do his best.

As he set off for Israel Vance was aware that the three-month deadline for completing the negotiations was approaching. If at all possible, he wanted to have a package agreed on by December 17. He knew there would be some tough bargaining in Israel, but he had Carter's clear instructions to press the Israelis hard.

Vance began his meeting with Begin and his colleagues by reviewing the recent evolution of the Egyptian position. He explained that he had convinced Sadat to drop demands for changing the treaty and for a fixed date for establishing self-government. There would, however, have to be some interpretive notes to articles 4 and 6. Vance also mentioned the idea of a target date and the possibility of reaching agreement first on Gaza. Then he explained Sadat's new position on not exchanging ambassadors until after the self-governing authority was established.

Begin, always suspicious of U.S.-Egyptian collusion, looked tense during this presentation. When Vance was done, Begin did little to hide his anger. He accused Sadat of deviating from Camp David, especially on his promise to exchange ambassadors after the interim withdrawal. He rejected the idea that Egypt should have any special role in Gaza, and he maintained that Israel would never accept a target date for setting up the self-governing authority. Nor did he like the idea of interpretive notes. These seemed to dilute the strength of the peace treaty and might open loopholes for Egypt not to live up to its obligations.

Begin then went on at length to review all the concessions he had made and all the risks Israel was required to take. The United States, he said, was unfairly siding with Egypt, when it should instead be supporting Israel.

Vance eventually managed to defuse the Israeli concern over the minor issue of an interpretive note to article 4 of the treaty. Dayan even showed some interest in the idea of proceeding with autonomy in Gaza first. He also privately told Vance that there might be a way for Israel to accept the delay in the exchange of ambassadors, but that this point should not be spelled out in a letter. Any delay in exchanging ambassadors should be left vague until after the treaty was signed, and then Sadat could say whatever he wanted. On this suggestion, however, Dayan was clearly not speaking for Begin.

Vance was obliged to leave the Middle East somewhat ahead of schedule. The decision had been made to announce the normalization of relations with China, and Carter wanted him to be in Washington for the occasion. Vance had time to make only a quick stop in Cairo before he left. There he informed Sadat of Begin's angry reaction. Sadat smiled and expressed his pleasure. Vance said he had told Begin in private that the United States supported the Egyptian position.

While flying back to Washington, Vance received word that the Israeli cabinet had met and had issued the following statement: "The Government of Israel rejects the attitude and the interpretation of the U.S. government with regard to the Egyptian proposals." For once, Vance was genuinely angry. His inclination was to let the negotiations remain temporarily in limbo. An impasse had been reached, and nothing more could be done for the moment.

IMPASSE

As 1978 came to an end, the prospects for peace anywhere in the Middle East looked dim. Not only were the Egyptian-Israeli talks at an impasse, but also Iran was in turmoil. The shah's regime was on the verge of collapse, and no one in Washington seemed to know what to do about it.[16]

For the next several months American thinking about the Camp David negotiations was colored by what was happening in Iran. The strategic balance of power in the region was changing, and the positions of the negotiating parties were hardening. Israel seemed to be reacting by becoming even more insistent that the peace treaty with Egypt be independent of any commitments involving the Palestinians. Furthermore, access to Egyptian oil assumed special importance as Iranian production, hitherto Israel's main source of supply, dried up. And the spectacle of a pro-American regime in a Muslim country being swept aside by religious extremists did little to increase Israeli confidence in the long-term value of Sadat's promises.

As usual, the United States was pulled in several directions. The Iranian revolution made it increasingly important to conclude the peace negotiations between Begin and Sadat successfully. Not only was a peace treaty desirable for strategic reasons; Carter also needed a political success to offset the enormous failure in Iran. At the same time Carter sympathized with the Egyptian argument that Egypt should not be isolated from the rest of the region because of peace with Israel. If possible, Carter still wanted Sadat to be able to defend his dealings with Israel before the moderate Arab regimes. Egypt's potential role as a stabilizing force in the Arab world seemed essential now that Iran had become a new source of unrest in the region.

In brief, the American role in this last phase of the peace negotiations was heavily influenced both by Iran and by the domestic political clock. Iran provided a strategic rationale for pressing for a quick conclusion of the Camp David process; the political calendar told Carter that he would soon have to turn his attention to other matters, namely reelection. Either he needed a quick and dramatic success, or he would have to back away from further involvement in the negotiations and hope that the electorate would not accuse him of losing the chance for peace between Israel and the largest Arab country. Carter had invested so heavily in the peace process by this time that he was determined to make one last stab at agreement.

CHAPTER TWELVE

Going for Broke:
Treaty Yes, Autonomy No

When Secretary Vance left the Middle East on December 15, 1978, the talks seemed deadlocked, and Vance was frustrated. He authorized his staff to prepare a "white paper" explaining what had happened in the talks since Camp David. The obvious purpose was to answer the Israeli charge that Washington was being unfair. A draft was in fact produced on December 17 that tended to place the blame for the recent crisis on Prime Minister Begin. Some thought was given to making the document public, but in the end more cautious counsel was taken.

After returning to Washington, Vance spent the weekend at Camp David with Carter to discuss the foreign policy agenda for 1979. The president felt things were falling apart in the Middle East. Dealing with that region had also become his heaviest political burden. And it was incredibly time-consuming. But the stakes were too high to let the negotiations drop. Carter decided to "continue to move aggressively on it and not postpone the difficult discussions, even though they were costly to us in domestic politics."[1]

By mid-January the Americans were thinking of several ways of reviving the talks. Prime Minister Khalil and Foreign Minister Dayan could be invited to Washington; another summit could be arranged; a new U.S. proposal could be put forward. Most felt it would be best to resolve the minor issues before engaging the president and Vance once again. They therefore decided to send Ambassador Atherton and the State Department's legal adviser, Herbert Hansell, to the Middle East to work on articles 4 and 6 and any necessary legal interpretations. March was frequently mentioned as the time by which an agreement should be reached on the entire treaty.

On January 23, 1979, Brzezinski sent a memorandum to the president spelling out his concerns on the Arab-Israeli issue. "Events may make it difficult for us to pursue such a strategy, but I am firmly convinced for the good of the Democratic Party we must avoid a situation where we continue agitating the most neuralgic problem with the American Jewish community (the West Bank, the Palestinians, the PLO) without a breakthrough to a solution. I do not believe that in the approaching election year we will be able to convince the Israelis that we have significant leverage over them, particularly on those issues. . . . We have little time left."[2]

On February 6 Carter wrote to Begin and Sadat asking them to agree to a meeting in Washington involving Dayan, Khalil, and Vance. The talks would begin on February 21 and be held at Camp David. Vance had recommended this course of action in a memorandum to the president on February 1. There he suggested that Carter should ultimately persuade Sadat to drop the linkage of the exchange of ambassadors to the establishment of the self-governing authority in return for stronger commitments from Begin to do something on the Palestinian question. He also proposed some slight revisions of articles 4 and 6 and the text of a new letter on the West Bank and Gaza.

CAMP DAVID II

In preparation for the talks at Camp David, the Middle East team undertook one of its periodic assessments. It seemed clear that at some point Carter would have to deal directly with Begin and Sadat. Arabs and Israelis were both concerned that the United States had lost its way. The only conceivable success on the horizon for Carter in foreign policy was an Egyptian-Israeli peace treaty. Both Egypt and Israel knew the United States needed a success after Iran, and Israel had concluded that Carter would not fight hard for the West Bank.

On February 19, 1979, shortly after Secretary of Defense Brown returned from his Middle East foray, Carter assembled his Middle East team, along with Brown, Ambassador Eilts, and Ambassador Lewis. Brown gave his assessment, which boiled down to two points: everyone he had talked to was nervous about Iran, and Begin and Sadat were prepared to keep working for a peace treaty.

Carter realized he would probably have to meet again with the Egyptian and Israeli leaders. As he cast around for new ideas, he argued that Sadat should not try to speak for the West Bank. The president even speculated in front of his Middle East advisers that Sadat really "did not give a damn about the West Bank." He was more concerned with Gaza. If he would drop his interest in the West Bank, he could have his separate treaty with Israel, get something in Gaza, and embarrass Hussein.

Carter stated clearly that he did not want a public confrontation with

Israel. This was a time for progress on the overall negotiation, with details to be resolved later. Carter acknowledged that he had to take some of the blame for urging Sadat to link the exchange of ambassadors to the establishment of self-government, but Sadat would now have to drop that demand for linkage. Carter also said two mistakes had been made at Camp David. Too much emphasis had been placed on the timing of the exchange of ambassadors, and Sadat should not have agreed to negotiate in place of King Hussein if Jordan refused to join the talks.

The Saudi role was raised by Eilts, who said Sadat still wanted Saudi support but would be ready to go ahead even without it. Somewhat cavalierly, Carter said the Saudis would have nowhere else to go after the treaty was signed. "They have to work with the United States and Egypt."

The second round of talks at Camp David began on February 21. Vance, Dayan, and Khalil were the principal participants, and each was accompanied by several aides. Khalil continued to insist that Egypt could not afford to be isolated, especially with the turmoil in Iran. Any treaty must be defensible before reasonable Arab opinion. On specifics, Khalil showed some interest in holding elections only in Gaza, and he implied that the exchange of ambassadors need not necessarily be tied to West Bank and Gaza developments.

Dayan had little room for negotiating, and he repeatedly said Vance would have to deal directly with Begin on the outstanding issues. He did, however, imply that Israel might be able to make some unilateral gestures toward the Palestinians, a point the Egyptians had pressed hard.

Talks at this level seemed to hold little promise of further progress. Khalil had authority to negotiate, but Dayan did not. So Carter invited Begin to join the talks. On February 27 the Israeli cabinet rejected Dayan's recommendation that the prime minister attend, saying Begin would not participate in a summit with Khalil. Only Sadat would do. Carter was irritated but decided to ask Begin to come to Washington just to meet with him. Things now seemed to be working toward a climax.

CARTER AND BEGIN IN WASHINGTON

To prepare for his meeting with Begin, on February 28, 1979, Carter called together his top advisers—Mondale, Vance, Brzezinski, and Hamilton Jordan. Brzezinski bluntly stated that Israel seemed to want a separate peace and wanted Carter not to be reelected. Jordan agreed. Mondale drew the conclusion that Carter should therefore not confront Begin and should stand back and let things take their natural course.[3]

Begin arrived in Washington without Dayan or Defense Minister Weizman in his delegation. These comparatively moderate voices seemed to have lost Begin's confidence. Carter and Vance noted their absence with regret.

The first session between Carter and Begin took place on Friday, March 2, 1979. Begin opened with a strong argument that the United States should help Israel because only Israel stood in the path of a Soviet takeover of the whole Middle East. He maintained that Israel could help prevent a communist takeover in Saudi Arabia, and even went so far as to offer the United States an airbase in Sinai that he had already promised to return to Egypt. None of these remarks had much effect on Carter.

Next Begin turned to the outstanding issues in the negotiations. He said the talks were in a deep crisis. The American interpretations to article 6 on the priority of obligations were tantamount to making peace between Egypt and Israel contingent on the achievement of a comprehensive peace in the region. Such linkage would allow Egypt to use any pretext to tear up the treaty. Begin added that he was sure that some future Egyptian leader would recommend doing so. No interpretive notes would be acceptable. The text of the treaty must stand unchanged, whether Sadat liked it or not.

Begin then raised his objections to the side letter dealing with the West Bank and Gaza. It contained deviations from Camp David. There was no reason to separate Gaza from the West Bank, as Sadat now wanted to do, though if Egypt was prepared to drop all interest in the West Bank, Israel might consider discussing Gaza alone with Egypt. But Gaza would not then be a precedent for what might later be done on the West Bank.

Begin also introduced his own deviation from Camp David by claiming that Israel was under no obligation to discuss the West Bank unless Jordan joined the negotiations. Carter reminded him that Sadat had signed a letter, which was part of the Camp David Accords, saying that Egypt would assume the Jordanian role if Hussein did not step forward. Begin replied that the letters did not have the same value as the text of the agreement, a point Carter quickly rejected.

Next on the list of Begin's objections was the idea of setting a target date for elections to the self-governing authority. If for some reason the date was not met, Israel might be accused of violating the treaty with

Egypt, and Egypt might then break some of its commitments. Israel could not accept such linkage between the treaty and the future of the West Bank and Gaza.

Finally, Begin turned to the question of oil. Since signing the Camp David Accords, he said, Israel had lost access to Iranian oil. More than ever, Israel needed a firm guarantee from both Egypt and the United States that its oil supply would be met. If Egypt refused, Israel would not evacuate the oil fields in Sinai.

Carter was very discouraged by this meeting. There seemed to be no openings. Still, Vance was prepared to continue the talks over lunch at the State Department.

Brzezinski had made the argument to Begin that Sadat could not be pressed to renounce his commitments to Arab countries as the price of peace with Israel. That was going too far. Vance picked up on this point at lunch and told Begin that Sadat needed to be able to say the Egyptian-Israeli treaty "did not prevail over" other treaties. Begin said he did not object to that language, provided it was clear that if Egypt's treaty with Israel conflicted with its other treaty obligations, the treaty with Israel would be honored. In brief, Begin signaled a willingness to allow interpretive notes on article 6, so long as the priority of obligations went to the Egyptian-Israeli treaty. This essentially meant that Begin would say that the treaty was not meant to prevail over others, but that in practice it must do so. As Vance later wrote: "Of such are diplomatic compromises made; six months of negotiations to reach agreement with Begin on two contradictory statements in the same interpretation."[4]

Vance and his team took some time on Saturday to develop new language on article 6 and on the target date for elections in the West Bank and Gaza. The most significant alteration was tying the target date to the conclusion of the negotiations between Egypt and Israel rather than to the actual holding of elections. Meanwhile Carter had another session with his top advisers, in which he raised the possibility of going to the Middle East to bring the negotiations to a dramatic conclusion. Hamilton Jordan in particular favored it. As Carter was later to say, "My proposal was an act of desperation."[5] Later in the evening Carter had another unproductive private meeting with Begin.

A final session between the two leaders was scheduled for Sunday morning, March 4. They met against a backdrop provided by a message from Sadat, who said he was planning to come to Washington to denounce Begin for his intransigence. Carter had already begun to think the best way to proceed was for him to go to the Middle East, and he hardly welcomed the telegenic Sadat stealing the show in Washington with ringing denunciations of Israel. So an effort was made to resolve some of the issues and therefore to justify a trip by the president to the region.

Somewhat surprisingly, Begin was in a rather conciliatory mood on Sunday morning. Vance reviewed the new formulations on article 6, and after a brief discussion among the Israeli delegation in Hebrew, Begin made a minor suggestion for a change in wording and agreed to seek cabinet approval, provided the United States formally withdrew its previous legal opinion on article 6. Similarly, Begin said the new American proposal on setting a target date for concluding the negotiations on autonomy was serious and would be considered by the cabinet. After all, he commented, Egypt and Israel could assume responsibility for the timing of the negotiations, but the actual holding of elections for the Palestinian government could be blocked by "third parties." That was why he had opposed a target date for elections but could accept one for concluding the negotiations. This was a lawyer's point, but it gave Begin a pretext for changing his position without appearing to back down on a matter of principle.

The problem of oil supplies remained, along with the timing of the exchange of ambassadors, but Carter implied that he would deal directly with Sadat on both issues to find a satisfactory solution. To his surprise Carter found that the United States and Israel were now in agreement on most issues. The reason, it seemed, was not so much that Begin had been won over by Carter's argument but rather that the new American formulations went just far enough to overcome Israeli suspicions. Begin must have also realized that the moment had come to clinch the bilateral deal with Sadat.

As soon as the meeting was over, Carter sent a message to Sadat informing him that some progress had been made in the talks and that he did not want Sadat to say anything further in public, and especially not to commit himself to coming to Washington. In fact, said the president, he was considering a trip to the Middle East himself in the next few days.

The following day, March 5, 1979, the Israeli cabinet approved all the new American proposals. Carter now felt that success was at hand. A trip by him to the Middle East would produce a peace treaty and a much needed political boost.

Carter immediately decided to send Brzezinski to Cairo to see Sadat.

He wanted Brzezinski to have a broad strategic review with the Egyptian president, to inform him of the new proposals and ask for his support of them, and to tell Sadat "very privately that the President's domestic political situation was becoming more difficult and that Begin might even wish to see the President defeated."[6]

Brzezinski met with Sadat on March 6 and delivered the president's messages. Sadat made it clear that the new formulations would pose no problem for him. He was, however, reluctant to go back to the idea of sending an ambassador to Israel after the interim withdrawal.

Sadat then told Brzezinski of his most important "secret weapon"—a proposal that Carter would be allowed to convey to Begin for building a pipeline from the Sinai oil fields directly to Israel. Sadat denounced the Israelis as idiots for ignoring his proposal on Gaza, but nonetheless said he would do everything possible to make Carter's visit a big success. The treaty should be signed while Carter was in the Middle East. If all went well, Sadat would even invite Begin to Cairo for the signing. Carter was very pleased by this prospect.

Sadat then turned his anger on the Saudis, describing them as a scarecrow and a U.S. protectorate to which the Americans attached too much importance. The Saudis, he said, were indecisive and incapable of action. Sadat treated King Hussein in similar fashion, asserting that the United States should dismiss him altogether. Somewhat surprisingly, he urged the Americans to improve their relations with Iraq.

CARTER TO THE MIDDLE EAST

By the time Carter arrived in Cairo on March 7, 1979, he had every reason to believe his trip would be crowned with success. Sadat had essentially said Carter would have carte blanche to negotiate the final text of the treaty with Israel.[7]

Carter spent much of his time in Egypt celebrating the close ties between Egypt and the United States. Sadat put on an impressive show, including a train ride to Alexandria, which exposed the American president to larger and friendlier crowds than he was used to seeing at home.

Just before leaving for Israel, Carter and Secretary Vance met with Sadat and his top advisers at the Maamoura rest house near Alexandria. Carter pledged to get the best possible agreement for Egypt while in Israel and spoke as if he had Sadat's proxy in hand. Once the treaty was a reality, the United States and Egypt could plan for a "massive" government-to-government relationship in the military and economic fields. Carter also expressed the hope that the American private sector would invest in Egypt after the peace treaty was signed. In addition, Carter promised to use his maximum influence to get Jordan and Saudi Arabia to back the fait accompli of the treaty.[8]

While Carter and Sadat were congratulating each other on the achievement of peace, the Egyptian foreign ministry officials were showing anxiety. They still wanted Carter to persuade the Israelis to make some unilateral gestures to the Palestinians, and they hoped that Israel would agree to some form of special status for Egypt in Gaza. They also wanted a few minor changes in the treaty, including the replacement of a word in the notes to article 6 that they did not like. Carter and Vance promised to do their best.

Carter arrived in Israel after sundown on Saturday, March 10, 1979. He immediately drove to Jerusalem for a private dinner with Begin. To Carter's surprise, Begin made it clear that there was no chance of concluding the negotiations and signing the peace treaty while Carter was in the Middle East. The president was angry and suspected Begin of wanting him to fail. Begin was standing on procedure, arguing that the Knesset must have a chance to debate the agreement before it could be signed. Carter reminded Begin that this had not been necessary at Camp David, but Begin would not be rushed.

After all, for Begin a peace treaty with Egypt was an extraordinarily important achievement. He would not be stampeded into signing just because Carter had decided to put his prestige on the line by traveling to the Middle East. And even if Begin might agree to the text of the treaty, the Knesset did have to have its say, much as the Senate would in the United States.

Carter had little sympathy for Begin in the best of times. It was a bad start for what proved to be a difficult few days. The upbeat mood of Cairo had suddenly been replaced in Jerusalem by mutual suspicions and recriminations. And in that atmosphere, once again it seemed as if the chance for peace might be lost.

On Sunday, March 11, Carter and Begin met with their full delegations. Carter began by sketching his preferred scenario. Negotiations on the treaty text should be concluded within the next day or so; Sadat would fly to Jerusalem to sign; then Begin, Sadat, and Carter would all travel to Cairo together for a second signing ceremony.

Begin immediately poured cold water on the president's idea. The cabinet, he explained, would have to debate the matter fully, and then the Knesset would have to vote before any signature could be put on so solemn a document as a peace treaty. All this would take at least two weeks. Then Begin asked to hear the new Egyptian proposals.

Sadat and his advisers had not liked the wording of the proposed notes to article 6. The notes had been included to meet Sadat's desire to portray the Egyptian-Israeli treaty as part of the comprehensive peace mentioned in the Camp David Accords. To this end, the notes had said that article 6 of the treaty did not contravene the framework for peace agreed on at Camp David and that the treaty was not to be seen as prevailing over any other treaties to which the parties were bound. But to meet Israeli concerns, the notes went on to say these provisions did "not derogate from" the language of article 6, which in essence said that the provisions of the Egyptian-Israeli treaty would be respected without regard to actions of other parties even if a conflict arose with other obligations.

The Egyptians were bothered by the word "derogate." Carter therefore suggested that Israel accept the substitution of the following phrase: "The foregoing [the notes to article 6] is not to be construed as inconsistent with the provisions of article 6." From the Americans' standpoint, there was no substantive difference. The point was that the notes to article 6 should not be seen as changing the meaning of the treaty.

Carter also said Egypt was insisting on having liaison officers in Gaza to help prepare for self-government there. Vance then passed around the new texts of the notes to article 6 and the letter on the West Bank and Gaza.

Begin frostily replied that the United States and Israel had already agreed on the language of the notes when he was recently in Washington. Sadat had the right to object, but Begin would not budge. He rejected the new language and expected Carter to stand by the text that had been worked out in Washington. The two phrases "does not derogate from" and "is not inconsistent with" were worlds apart, he said. Article 6 was the heart of the treaty. Without it the treaty would be a sham document. Israel would not knowingly sign a sham document. At one point he said that if the words "is not inconsistent with" were used instead of "does not derogate from," it would mean that Egypt would start a war while it had a peace treaty with Israel.

Carter denied that Egypt was looking for a pretext to attack Israel. Begin then pulled out a sheaf of newspaper articles and began to read extracts from the Egyptian press that he saw as threatening to Israel.

Carter asked him what the point of such a display was. Begin referred to the terrible atmosphere in which the peace talks were being conducted and asked that the American ambassador in Cairo raise with Sadat the question of anti-Israeli articles in the Egyptian press.

Carter then asked if Begin had any counterproposals to make. Begin said no. He would stand by what had been agreed on in Washington. Begin went on to make a lengthy critique of the new note to article 6, paragraph 2. He had agreed in Washington to say in a note to the article that it should not be construed as contravening the framework for peace in the Middle East agreed to at Camp David. Sadat had wanted to add that Camp David had called for a "comprehensive peace," as in fact it did. Begin argued that by adding these two words, "comprehensive peace," Sadat was seeking a pretext to violate the treaty with Israel by making it contingent on other Arab states also making peace with Israel. Syria, he said, would then be able to render the treaty null and void by refusing to negotiate.

Toward noon Begin turned his impressive critical powers to the new letter concerning the West Bank and Gaza. He strongly objected to the possibility of implementing autonomy in Gaza first. Nor would he accept Egyptian liaison officers there. Then, for what must have been the tenth time, he objected to the term West Bank, giving a lesson to the president on the geographic and historical inappropriateness of the term and the importance of using the words Judea and Samaria. Only if Sadat were to renounce entirely his interest in those two areas, said Begin, would he agree to discuss Gaza alone with Egypt.

Other members of the cabinet joined the discussions, and for a while it seemed as if no headway would ever be made. Ariel Sharon intervened with his standard lecture on "Jordan is Palestine" and called the Hashemites the only foreigners in Jordan. He promised Carter that within twenty years one million Jews would be living in the West Bank and Gaza. No line would ever separate Israel from these areas.

After a break for lunch, the talks resumed at 3:00 p.m. Carter tried to regain Begin's confidence by promising an American guarantee of Israel's oil supply. He also said he was sure he could persuade Sadat to exchange ambassadors after the interim withdrawal if Israel would expedite the withdrawal, as originally agreed the previous November. He also said the United States would sign a memorandum of understanding with Israel on steps to be taken if Egypt violated the treaty.

Turning to bilateral U.S.-Israeli relations, Carter maintained that the two countries were equal partners. He added that what the United States did for Israel was more than balanced by what Israel did for the United States, a point that Begin had long been pressing on American audiences and that Carter did not really believe. Israel, he said, was a tremendous strategic asset to the United States, especially if it was at peace with Egypt, the other major regional friend of the United States. With these sweeteners, Carter urged the Israelis to try to find words to resolve the dispute over article 6, which eventually was done.

During a late afternoon session Begin told Carter that the Israeli cabinet would meet that evening to make its formal decisions on the matters under discussion. Then Vance could go to Cairo, and Carter could return home. In about two weeks, if all was proceeding smoothly, the Israelis might be ready to sign the treaty.

Carter responded by saying that Vance would not go to Cairo. The Egyptian position was already known to the Americans. They could conclude the negotiations right now. Begin replied that he was very tired and that the meeting should now be adjourned. Once again, the Americans felt Begin was deliberately trying to keep Carter from enjoying the fruits of his high-stakes trip to the Middle East.

Just before the meeting broke up, Carter again pleaded with Begin to try to reach agreement in the next day or so. Begin replied that the sky would not fall if agreement was not reached.

The next morning Carter and Begin and their advisers met again at 10:20 a.m. The cabinet had been in session all night, breaking up at 5:30 a.m. The Israelis looked exhausted. Carter began by making a strong case for the strategic benefits to Israel of peace with Egypt. He argued that the U.S.-Israeli relationship would grow even stronger and the United States could be even more forthcoming on aid if the peace treaty was concluded. Egypt and Israel could work together to prevent the kind of radicalism seen in Iran from spreading to the rest of the region. If the opportunity for peace was now lost, it would be hard to recover.

The Israeli cabinet had essentially confirmed the new wording of the notes to article 6, and Carter was satisfied. But the cabinet had adamantly refused to consider giving Egypt any special status in Gaza. Carter argued that its refusal would be hard for Egypt to accept. He pleaded with Begin to reconsider, but Begin refused.

The meeting broke up at 11:20 a.m. Begin and Carter left to prepare for their addresses to the Knesset. That event turned out to be somewhat less than edifying. In his remarks Carter rather undiplomatically implied that the Israeli public wanted peace more than its leaders did. During Begin's speech opposition members interrupted so frequently that it was hard to follow what was being said. Begin's old ally Geulah Cohen was ordered off the floor of the Knesset when she refused to observe parliamentary decorum. Begin seemed to enjoy the battle, but the Americans were less happy. Still, Begin had shown that he was not the most extreme hard-liner among the Israelis.

Carter went from the Knesset to a lunch with the members of the Foreign Affairs and Security Committee. During the lunch Carter revealed that he essentially had carte blanche from Sadat to conclude an agreement. Begin doubtless suspected this anyway, but now he must have become certain that Carter could be persuaded to cede on his insistence that Egypt be given a special role in Gaza.

Vance was scheduled to have one more session with the Israeli delegation on Monday afternoon, March 12. Carter hoped that the remaining problems on Gaza, on oil, and on the timing of withdrawal from Sinai and the exchange of ambassadors could all be settled.

Begin opened the meeting by saying that the cabinet had been in session for two hours and had decided to reconfirm its position on all issues. There would be no further changes from the Israeli side. Israel needed, he said, a clear-cut Egyptian promise to sell 2.5 million tons of oil to Israel each year. Begin did say he would agree to consider an Egyptian proposal to start the autonomy talks in Gaza, but this issue could not be included in the side letter. Nor could any mention be made of Egyptian liaison officers. Even on article 6 Begin insisted that the words "comprehensive peace" be removed from one of the notes, arguing that otherwise the treaty would appear to depend on the action of other Arab parties in making peace with Israel.

Begin did suggest that some expedited withdrawal to the interim line might be possible, but only if Sadat agreed to send an ambassador to Israel shortly thereafter. From this point on, the discussion quickly deteriorated. Begin accused the Americans of always showing an understanding of Sadat's concerns but never of his. Sharon harshly interjected that the Egyptians would never be allowed into Gaza in any form. They would only try to stir up the local population. Even the usually moderate Dayan and Deputy Prime Minister Yigal Yadin seemed to think Carter should not support the Egyptian claim to a special role in Gaza.

Vance tried to salvage the situation by urging that both the Gaza and oil issues be dropped from the agreement. Neither had been included in the Camp David Accords, and both could be dealt with later. Begin said oil was a matter of life and death and could not be left out of the agreement. Nor would Israel agree now to put in writing its willingness to accelerate withdrawal to the interim line.

To the surprise of the Americans, Begin then said that the talks were over and a joint communiqué should be issued announcing that some progress had been made, but that some questions still needed to be resolved. A text to this effect, obviously prepared well in advance, was passed over to Vance for his agreement.

Carter was immediately informed of the outcome of the talks. He decided there was no point for him to stay in Israel any longer. Begin clearly did not want an agreement at this time. The president ordered his plane to be prepared to return directly to Washington. But the hour was late, and to get all the presidential party and its luggage assembled in time would be difficult. Reluctantly Carter agreed to spend the night in Jerusalem, but he was a bitterly disappointed man.

FINALE

When the Americans reconvened at the King David Hotel, the mood was gloomy. No one saw much point in trying to come up with new formulations on the outstanding issues. Most of the Americans drifted off to have dinner together. No working sessions were planned.

Toward 9:00 p.m. one of Dayan's associates called Vance to suggest that the secretary should invite Dayan over for an informal talk. Dayan, it turned out, had been caucusing with members of the cabinet who were unhappy with the way the negotiations seemed to be ending. Dayan had got Begin's permission to see Vance. Weizman was apparently threatening to resign if the peace treaty was jeopardized by Begin's obstinacy.

Dayan made several suggestions and confirmed that most of the cabinet would accept the U.S. proposals on guaranteeing Israel's supply of oil and for accelerated Israeli withdrawal to an interim line in Sinai. In return for those concessions, Dayan suggested that the side letter should omit reference to Gaza as a special case and to a role for Egyptian liaison officers there. He urged Carter to meet again with Begin the next morning to put these proposals forward as new American suggestions. Meanwhile Dayan would try to prepare the way with Begin. Vance agreed to try, and for several hours the American team worked on a new set of proposals.

While Vance and Dayan were working to prevent a collapse of the talks, Carter's press secretary, Jody Powell, was briefing the press on the situation as it stood at 9:00 p.m. He painted a bleak picture, and this was the basis for the pessimistic accounts that most Americans read in their papers on Tuesday, March 13.[9]

By the time the American press accounts were being digested, the situation had already changed. Carter met with Begin alone on Tuesday morning; they were then joined by Dayan and Vance. Begin, as usual, held back from making a complete commitment to the new proposals. If Egypt accepted them, and if Sadat agreed to an early exchange of ambassadors, Begin would recommend the new proposals to the Knesset. Carter knew that was tantamount to having Begin's agreement. Pressing his luck a bit, he asked Begin if Israel would agree to undertake some unilateral gestures to improve the atmosphere for the Palestinians in the West Bank and Gaza. This issue was of great importance to the Egyptians. Begin said he would sympathetically consider this request. Carter finally knew he had an agreement in hand.

Carter then flew directly to Cairo, where he met with Sadat at the airport. Sadat's aides still had some objections, but Sadat was in no mood to quibble.[10] He had promised the president a success, and he was prepared to say that agreement had now been reached on all issues. At 5:00 p.m. Carter said that full agreement had been reached, and he placed a call to Begin from the airport to tell him so. Begin agreed to go to the cabinet the next day for final approval, but the outcome was no longer in doubt.

Carter and Sadat then walked out on the tarmac to tell the awaiting press corps that a peace agreement had been concluded. After so many ups and downs, and after the previous evening's pessimistic briefing, many of the journalists were amazed—and somewhat irritated that their previous day's stories would look bad.

On the plane back to Washington Carter's political aides were ecstatic. At long last Carter could point to a major foreign policy achievement that would be genuinely welcomed by most Americans. The foreign-policy advisers were a bit less jubilant, thinking as always of the many problems that lay ahead. Most of all, they were exhausted and grateful that the talks were over, at least for the moment. When they arrived at Andrews Air Force Base later that evening, a large crowd was waiting to congratulate Carter and Vance. It had been quite a day, starting in Jerusalem and ending in Washington.

SIGNING THE PEACE TREATY

The comprehensive Middle East peace that Carter had originally hoped for was still far off, but the largest of the building blocks in that design, the Egyptian-Israeli peace, was nearly a reality. Carter was ambivalent about whether the peace treaty would by itself bring stability to the Middle East, or whether it would set in motion an inevitable process that would widen the circle of peace around Israel. He certainly did not believe it could make matters worse than they already were.

Before the treaty signing, a few remaining issues had to be resolved. Ezer Weizman visited Washington to work out the new phases of withdrawal and to appeal successfully for additional military assistance.[11] Other bilateral U.S.-Israeli questions remained to be answered. In particular, how would the United States guarantee Israel's supply of oil if Egyptian oil was not available to meet Israel's requirements? And what would the United States promise to do if Egypt violated the treaty? What provision should be made for the contingency that UN peacekeeping forces would not be available for the Sinai after Israeli withdrawal? On all these points the United States had to find solutions. In some instances the final wording was not worked out until the actual day the peace treaty was signed.

But the problems of the draftsmen and mapmakers would not stand in the way of the signing ceremony on March 26, 1979. Carter was joined by Begin and Sadat on the north lawn of the White House. A large audience was invited to attend. Many political debts were paid that day. Egyptians and Israelis mingled freely and expressed hopes that peace might be at hand. Across the street in Lafayette Park some Palestinians and their supporters held a small demonstration against the treaty, a reminder that the next phase of negotiations would encounter opposition. But the day was one of optimism and good feeling, and it was crowned that evening by a magnificent banquet on the south lawn of the White House.

The formal Egyptian-Israeli agreement consisted of a thick file of documents that few people would ever read in their entirety. (See appendix G for the key documents.) Besides the text of the treaty, there were three annexes dealing with security arrangements, maps, and normal relations between the parties. Seven interpretive notes were attached to the basic documents. Sadat and Begin also signed a letter to Carter concerning negotiations on the West Bank and Gaza issues. Carter added in his own handwriting an explanatory note to the letter saying, "I have been informed that the expression 'West Bank' is understood by the Government of Israel to mean 'Judea and Samaria.'"

Sadat signed another letter to Carter promising that a resident ambassador would be sent to Israel within one month of the interim withdrawal. Carter conveyed this information to Begin in a letter, and Begin acknowledged its receipt. Carter also wrote to both Sadat and Begin to spell out what the United States would do to help monitor the security arrangements in Sinai and how the United States would use its best efforts to organize a multinational peacekeeping force if UN troops were unavailable.

On the day of the signing of the peace treaty, Vance and Dayan also put their signatures to a memorandum of agreement. Most of the commitments made in this document were hedged with qualifications, but it put the weight of the United States behind Israel in the event that Egypt violated the treaty. Promises made as part of previous memorandums of understanding were reaffirmed. An agreement on oil supply was signed at the same time.[12]

As for military aid to Israel, Secretary Brown wrote to Weizman committing the United States to $3 billion to help construct new airfields in the Negev. Of that amount, $800 million would be in the form of grants. The United States also informed Israel that it was prepared to act positively on a number of weapons systems that had been requested earlier. (During the negotiations Carter had deliberately held off making major decisions on arms so that he would have some remaining leverage over both Israel and Egypt.)

Brown wrote a similar letter to the Egyptian minister of defense, promising $1.5 billion in aid over the next three years. A list of military equipment that Egypt would be allowed to purchase was appended to this letter. Inevitably, a few loose ends were handled by memoranda for the record written by the legal adviser or other participants in the negotiations. None of the memos changed the basic outline of what had been agreed upon. They largely involved putting the United States on record with an interpretation of some ambiguous point in the treaty or in the annexes, or recording some informal understanding that had been reached after the text of the treaty had been completed.

At the last minute Carter was also required to write a secret letter to Begin affirming what Begin and Sadat had orally agreed upon on

March 26 concerning oil supplies. Carter also wrote to Egyptian Prime Minister Khalil to inform him of the results of his discussions with Begin about unilateral gestures toward Palestinians in the West Bank and Gaza.

Khalil, who had not known of the U.S.-Israeli memorandum of agreement until the last moment, wrote two letters to Vance spelling out sixteen reasons why Egypt rejected it. The day after the peace treaty was signed, Khalil also wrote to Carter protesting that Carter had not done enough to commit Begin to take positive actions in the West Bank and Gaza. But these were faint notes that attracted little attention, and Carter had long ago learned that Sadat would not make an issue out of such matters.[13]

ASSESSING THE TREATY NEGOTIATIONS

Complex diplomatic initiatives rarely work out quite the way their authors anticipate. Midcourse corrections are part of the normal negotiating process. For American presidents in particular, the intrusion of domestic political considerations is also part of the game. In light of these realities, one cannot judge results by the standard of initial designs or theoretical abstractions.

Instead one must look at the Egyptian-Israeli peace treaty in its political context. What more might have been achieved, given the very real constraints operating on all the parties? Could positive aspects of the agreement have been enhanced? Could the negative ones have been minimized? Why was Carter unable to make headway on the West Bank and Gaza? Why did he seem to care less about those areas than he did about Sinai?

First, Egypt and Israel were talking to each other and were ready to make decisions. The other Arabs were either opposed to the process or were sitting on the sidelines to see what would be offered them. Carter felt more of an obligation to Sadat because Sadat had taken risks for peace.

Second, the chance for a successful negotiation between Egypt and Israel was much greater than between Israel and any of the other Arab parties. Two disengagement agreements had already been signed in 1974 and 1975. Direct talks between the parties had shown that the distance between them on bilateral issues was not large. Carter's involvement could plausibly help bridge the remaining gap.

Third, Egypt was the most powerful Arab country. Peace between Egypt and Israel would not make war impossible in the Middle East, but it would dramatically change its nature. The danger of U.S.-Soviet confrontation would be reduced as well. On these grounds even a separate peace had immense strategic value for the United States.

Finally, one must frankly admit, the American political system makes it difficult for a president to tackle a problem like that of the Palestinians. Presidential authority in foreign affairs is theoretically extensive, but in practice it is circumscribed by political realities. And the Palestinian question has proved to be so controversial that most presidents have been reluctant to get deeply involved in it. Sadat, who was genuinely popular with the American public, was, in Carter's view, worth a fight with Begin. But the Palestinians had no domestic constituency, and when Sadat seemed less concerned about their fate than about Sinai, Carter found it impossible to be more demanding than the leader of the largest Arab country.

Among the participants, Carter had come to the negotiations with the least knowledge of the issues and with the greatest capacity to evolve in his understanding. The Middle East was important in his view, but he did not have fixed ideas on exactly how the problems should be solved. The engineer in him seemed to want the grand design of a comprehensive peace; left to his own devices, he might have remained wedded to that appealing notion. But he could not build the edifice alone, and so he began to concentrate on the part that was most feasible.

The idealist in Carter also played a role. The president deeply believed that men of goodwill could resolve problems by talking to one another. At Camp David he initially thought he would need only to get Sadat and Begin together and help them to overcome their mutual dislike. The agreement itself would then be worked out by the two leaders in a spirit of compromise and accommodation. The depth of their distrust, even hatred, was hard for him to understand. Begin's fixation on Judea and Samaria was especially hard for him to grasp. Finally, it was Carter who was forced to reexamine his assumptions and change his approach in the face of Begin's intransigence and Sadat's apparent willingness to settle for a bilateral deal.

The politician in Carter was slow to make his entry into the negotiations. For most of the first year domestic politics rarely seemed to concern the president as he tackled the Middle East problem. He was sometimes reckless in his disregard for public opinion, and he probably would have done better to have engaged in less controversy with Israel in public in the first months of his term. In retrospect, his behavior gained him little on the Arab side and may have helped marginally in Begin's rise to power. As time wore on, Carter, and especially his advisers, came to believe he was paying a heavy price for his involvement in the Arab-Israeli imbroglio. They also saw the Egyptian-Israeli peace treaty as one of the few potential successes that could boost the president's prestige at home and abroad.[14] By early 1979 politics had come to the fore in the decisions leading to the final push for peace. Soon after the peace treaty was signed, Carter turned over the next phase of Middle East diplomacy to a special negotiator, Robert Strauss, fully expecting him to help cover the president's political flanks as the campaign for reelection got under way.

THE AUTONOMY TALKS

The negotiations concerning the West Bank and Gaza were bound to be complicated. First of all, the Palestinians (and Jordanians) were adamant that they would not participate in the talks, so Egypt had to play the part of uninvited stand-in for them. Second, Egypt and Israel could not agree what they were negotiating about. Sadat was not very concerned with details or language, but he and his colleagues saw the negotiations as preparing the way, in stages, for the Palestinians to govern themselves, with limits on their control over foreign and defense policy only. Not surprisingly, the Egyptians fastened on those parts of Camp David that spoke of an elected "self-governing authority"; an interim period that should serve as a transition to a final agreement based on UN resolution 242; the withdrawal of Israeli forces to designated locations; and the "powers and responsibilities" of the elected Palestinian authority.

Begin, who felt that he had originated the idea of Palestinian "autonomy"—he did not like the term "self-governing authority"—had a very different notion of what the negotiations were all about. While he had agreed to postpone an Israeli claim to sovereignty during an interim period, he had not agreed to abandon such a claim. Indeed, when asked what would come after five years of Palestinian autonomy, Begin had a simple answer. Israel would at that point assert its claim to sovereignty; if the Arabs agreed, that would settle the matter. If they did not agree, autonomy would continue indefinitely. And during this prolonged period of autonomy, Israeli settlements would continue to be built in "Judea and Samaria"; East Jerusalem was not to be part of the autonomy plan at all; land and water resources would not automatically come under the control of the self-governing authority, since autonomy applied only to persons, in Begin's view, not to territory.

Insofar as Carter and Vance had developed their thinking on Palestinian issues, they tended to agree more with the Egyptian interpretation of Palestinian self-government as a transitional stage. Carter was on record as supporting the right of Palestinians from East Jerusalem to participate in elections for the self-governing authority; his views on the importance of a freeze on settlement activity were well known; and his interpretation of 242 was that Israel was obliged to withdraw, at the end of the transitional period, from most, if not all, of the West Bank and Gaza as the quid pro quo for Palestinian recognition of Israel's right to live in peace within secure and recognized boundaries. For some of the Americans involved in the negotiations, the fact that autonomy would apply to the entire West Bank and Gaza would provide the Palestinians with a sort of presumptive territorial claim when the time came to settle the "final status" of the territories. This was a point also made by some of Begin's right-wing critics, who saw in the autonomy idea the germ of a Palestinian state.

Whatever Carter's views on these matters might be, he was not inclined to engage his time and efforts in this next round of negotiations. Vice President Mondale and Hamilton Jordan had long urged Carter to find a more "political" negotiator, and Robert Strauss, fresh from his success as special trade negotiator, seemed to fit the bill. The fact that he knew little about the Middle East was not seen as a major problem.

Strauss's tenure as special negotiator was brief and uneventful. At one point he thought the problem of Jerusalem should be tackled head on, presumably on the theory that if the toughest problem could be solved first, all else would fall into place. But by fall 1979, with Carter's reelection prospects in question, Strauss left to head the reelection effort.

If Carter needed any reminding that the Palestinian issue was political dynamite at home he had only to reflect on the fate of his UN ambassador, Andrew Young. In August discussions were taking place about the possibility of amending UN Resolution 242 to make it more palatable to the Palestinians. Needless to say, the Israelis were intensely suspicious of any such move.

In his capacity as head of the Security Council, Young met with the PLO representative to see if a formula could be found that would bring the PLO to accept UN Resolution 242. Neither Carter nor Vance was informed of the meeting. Young personally appealed to the Israeli UN ambassador to keep the meeting quiet, but that was not to be. Vance was furious that Young had told the Israeli ambassador about the meeting before informing Washington and insisted to Carter that Young be replaced, which he was by his deputy, Donald McHenry.

The Andrew Young affair may have angered Israel's supporters, but it was the Iranian seizure of American hostages at the U.S. embassy in Tehran on November 4, 1979, that accelerated Carter's political decline. Unable to win their release by diplomacy and hesitant to use force, the president soon found himself trapped in the White House with the unresolved hostage problem confronting him day in and day out. Every night on the evening news the countdown went on—"This is day xxx of the hostages' captivity in Iran." As he struggled to cope with this most debilitating of foreign-policy crises, Carter had little time for Palestinian autonomy.

To replace Strauss, Carter selected another lawyer-negotiator with good credentials in the Jewish community, Sol Linowitz. With the experience of negotiating the Panama Canal treaty to his credit, Linowitz was a skilled professional, but he lacked familiarity with the complex details of the Arab-Israeli peace process. He also found himself dealing with an Israeli cabinet minus Moshe Dayan, who broke with Begin precisely over the latter's restrictive view of autonomy.[15] Similarly on the Egyptian side, the negotiators, except for Mustafa Khalil, showed little flexibility, correctly arguing that they had no mandate from the Palestinians to decide on details. At most, they were prepared to develop broad principles for the transitional period, setting in motion a process that would lead to some form of Palestinian self-determination, a far cry from Begin's vision of perpetual autonomy.

Not surprisingly, little progress was made on the toughest issues, although Linowitz had some success in resolving many of the more technical ones.[16] In the spring of 1980, while Linowitz was struggling to find common ground between Egypt and Israel on Palestinian autonomy, Carter's fortunes hit a new low with the abortive mission to rescue the hostages in Tehran. Vance, who had recommended against the operation, resigned and was replaced as secretary of state by Edmund Muskie, a senator from Maine.

Toward the end of the Carter administration, Linowitz reached the point where he felt that substantial progress had been made. But no agreement had been reached on such sensitive issues as whether East Jerusalem Palestinians could participate in the elections to the self-governing authority or as whether there would be a freeze on constructing new settlements, and only a hint had been given that some degree of shared authority over future development of water and land resources might be possible. In brief, on issues of vital importance to the Palestinians, the negotiations had not produced much. And without the direct participation of the Palestinians in the negotiations, Egypt would be reluctant to go much further in dealings with Israel. Thus for much of the next ten years, until finally the Palestinians joined the peace talks as full participants in 1991, the part of Camp David that dealt with the future of the West Bank and Gaza remained essentially a dead letter.

Carter's overwhelming defeat in November 1980 rendered hypothetical the notion that a reelected Carter might have turned his considerable abilities to completing the process started at Camp David. Instead, on January 20, 1981, a few minutes before the hostages were finally released from their captivity in Tehran, Carter turned over the office of the president to Ronald Reagan, like him a former governor and an outsider to the world of Washington. But in most other ways Reagan was to be a very different kind of president.

CONCLUSIONS

Jimmy Carter was unique among American presidents in the depth of his concern to find a peaceful resolution of the conflict between Israel and its Arab neighbors. More than any other foreign-policy issue, the Middle East occupied his time and energies.

At the beginning of his administration he knew little about the intricacies of the problem. But he felt the challenge of tackling an issue that had eluded solutions in the past. And he no doubt felt that American interests would be well served if peace could be brought to the Middle East.

As time went on Carter came to know many of the leaders in the Middle East, and he turned his extraordinary capacity for mastering detail to the negotiations between Egypt and Israel. He pored over maps of Sinai to identify lines for the interim withdrawal. He personally drafted the first version of the Egyptian-Israeli framework agreement at Camp David. And twice he put his political reputation on the line by engaging in summit negotiations that could easily have failed.

In the end Carter was able to preside over the signing of the Egyptian-Israeli peace treaty, perhaps the most noteworthy foreign-policy achievement of his administration. Yet he gained little in domestic political terms for these efforts, and some would argue that he even weakened his political base.

It does nothing to diminish Carter's achievement in the Middle East to acknowledge that he built on firm foundations laid by Presidents Richard Nixon and Gerald Ford, and especially by the remarkable diplomatic efforts of Henry Kissinger in brokering three Arab-Israeli agreements during 1974–75. Carter was also ably served by his secretary of state, Cyrus Vance, who deserves much of the credit for patiently shaping the Camp David Accords and the text of the peace treaty.

Carter's initiatives would have come to naught had the leaders of Egypt and Israel been unwilling to accept American mediation and to make peace between their two countries. At no point did Carter forcefully impose American views on either side, though often he was able to change the positions of either Prime Minister Begin or President Sadat, especially Sadat. American leadership was certainly a necessary condition for the success of the negotiations, but it was not sufficient. The parties to the conflict had to be ready for agreement.

Throughout the Egyptian-Israeli peace negotiations, Sadat maintained he needed to demonstrate that he had achieved something for the Palestinians. He repeatedly said he was not prepared for a "separate peace." What he wanted from Begin was a simple statement that Israel was willing to return Arab territory captured in the 1967 war in exchange for peace, recognition, and security from the Arabs. Also, he hoped for some form of commitment from Israel to Palestinian rights, including the right of self-determination. This commitment, of course, Begin would not give.

In retrospect, it is clear that Sadat and Carter both overestimated the role that Egypt could play in laying the groundwork for a negotiated settlement of the Palestinian issue. Both misread the attitudes of King Hussein and the Palestinian leaders. Both misjudged the part that the Saudis might be willing to take in the negotiations. Neither took Syria sufficiently into account.

Even with these errors it might have been possible to carry out the provisions of the Camp David Accords if the idea of self-government for the Palestinians in the West Bank and Gaza could have been given real content. For example, if Carter had succeeded in getting Begin's agreement to a freeze on settlement activity, if the self-governing authority had been given control over land and water resources, if genuinely free elections, including the right to vote for Palestinians living in East Jerusalem, had been promised, and if the military occupation authority had been abolished, then it might have been possible to attract Palestinians into the negotiating process.

But none of these measures proved feasible while Begin was prime minister, and thus the concept of autonomy was devalued in the eyes of those who were most crucial in determining its viability. When Begin refused to budge on these matters, neither Sadat nor Carter could find a way to persuade him to change his mind. It remained to be seen if Ronald Reagan would choose to pick up where Carter had left off, or whether he had other ideas in mind. In light of the deterioration in U.S.-Soviet relations after the Soviet invasion of Afghanistan late in 1979, it seemed likely that Reagan would accord much more attention to East-West issues than to Arab-Israeli peace talks.

Carter had been slow to recognize the depth of Begin's attachment to the West Bank and Gaza. He had also been slow to understand the linkage issue.[17] Once Egypt and Israel were at peace, Begin had few remaining incentives to deal constructively with the Palestinian question. Sadat did feel strongly about the need for linkage, and for many months he had tried to establish some explicit connection between what would happen in bilateral Egyptian-Israeli relations and the Palestinian negotiations. But when put under pressure by Carter, in the face of Begin's intransigence, and when confronted with hostility from other Arab leaders, Sadat resigned himself to accepting the separate agreement that he had hoped to avoid when he first set off for Jerusalem in November 1977.

PART FIVE

The Reagan Presidency

CHAPTER THIRTEEN

Cold War Revival: Who's in Charge?

The election of Ronald Reagan as president in November 1980 was a watershed event in American politics. Rarely had a campaign pitted two such different candidates as Reagan and Jimmy Carter against each other. Reagan, a two-term governor of California and a moderately successful movie actor, came from the conservative wing of the Republican party. He propounded two main themes: the federal government is too big and inefficient, and communism is an evil that should be fought relentlessly. Increases in defense spending were central to his foreign-policy program.

Apart from these broad principles, it was hard to know what Reagan would bring to the presidency, especially in the field of international affairs. But he certainly implied that he would break with Carter's approach to the world. No more embracing of Brezhnev, appeasing of dictators, courting of leftists, pressuring of friends. Reagan even seemed prepared to reverse course on relations with China, speaking admiringly of Taiwan in contrast to "Red China."

Even if Reagan had not come to the presidency as a determined anticommunist, recent events would have ensured that U.S.-Soviet relations would be strained. The invasion of Afghanistan late in 1979 by the Soviets was one worrisome sign that they were embarking on a more aggressive foreign policy, with implications for the Gulf region in particular. In addition, war between Iran and Iraq had broken out in September 1980, and many in Washington feared that the Soviets would try to exploit the conflict to advance into the sensitive Gulf region. With these concerns in mind, Reagan and his entourage were not inclined to press hard for movement in the Arab-Israeli peace process. In any event, Reagan's sympathies were with Israel, and Israel was in no hurry to move.

Reagan's familiarity with Hollywood seems to have introduced him, if only superficially, to personalities close to Israel. But his views on the Middle East were otherwise virtually unknown, except for a ghost-written opinion piece that had appeared during the campaign. There Reagan had displayed a strong commitment to Israel as the only reliable friend of the United States in the Middle East, because of both its democratic values and its military prowess. The contest in the Middle East was described almost exclusively in cold war terms, with scant mention of the peace process.

The only reference to the Palestinians in the article came in a warning against the creation of a radical Palestinian state on Israel's borders. The words "Camp David," "peace process," and "negotiations" were nowhere to be found. The idea of Israel and Egypt as partners in peace was missing, replaced by a description of Israel as a formidable strategic asset. Egypt, it was noted, might also be prepared to "take a front-line position in defense of Western security interests," but this possibility was clearly viewed as a "secondary" link that could not "substitute for a strong Israel in the ever-turbulent Middle East."[1]

On the surface, then, Reagan seemed likely to shift American policy in the region away from the Camp David approach toward a more muscular competition with Moscow for influence. Israel would be regarded as a strategic partner. Engaging in peace talks would be accorded lower priority than bolstering American influence in the Gulf region. American arms sales to some Arab countries, such as Jordan, might be reduced, while arms might continue to flow to Saudi Arabia. In view of campaign promises, it seemed possible that Reagan would also order the American embassy in Israel to move from Tel Aviv to Jerusalem, a highly symbolic act. In short, the Reagan agenda appeared likely to reflect the neoconservative, pro-Israeli views that were widespread among his advisers and senior officials.[2]

But Reagan was not only a pro-Israeli, anticommunist ideologue.[3] He was also remarkably uninterested in the kind of detail that fascinated his predecessor. He would seemingly be content with setting the broad lines of policy, leaving to his associates the fine points of interpretation and implementation.[4]

To say the least, Reagan evinced little interest in the nuances of Middle East policy.[5] Perhaps more than any other president, Reagan was very dependent on his staff—and on his wife, who was a keen judge of people and was fiercely determined that her husband should be protected from criticism. To get to the president, it was thought, one had to pierce the wall created by Nancy Reagan and the troika of his closest advisers—Edwin Meese, Michael Deaver, and James A. Baker III. Even a powerful cabinet member like Secretary of State Alexander M. Haig, Jr., felt frustrated in his efforts to deal with Reagan. The national security adviser, Richard Allen, was relegated to the White House basement and sent his memos to the president through the notoriously inefficient Meese. Among this group, only Secretary of Defense Caspar W. Weinberger seemed to have the kind of personal relationship with the president that allowed him regular direct access.

These three men, Haig, Weinberger, and Allen, who occupied the key foreign-policy positions in the Reagan administration, would presumably have considerable influence on how Reagan tackled Middle East issues. Haig had served in the military, as Kissinger's deputy at the White House, and as Nixon's chief of staff. He could be expected to be strongly pro-Israeli, somewhat skeptical of the peace process, and deeply suspicious of Soviet intentions in the region. On the face of it, his views and Reagan's did not seem to differ much.

Weinberger's foreign-policy views were less predictable. His prior government service had involved economic issues, and his business experience had been with Bechtel, a large construction company with extensive experience in the Middle East, including Saudi Arabia. Weinberger had spent time in Saudi Arabia and was presumably aware of Arab views. Sharing the president's conservative, anticommunist perspective, he might be counted on to boost the Saudis as a force for stability and moderation in the region.[6]

Assuming that Haig and Weinberger did indeed tilt in different directions on Middle East issues, it was anybody's guess how Reagan might decide concrete cases in the event of divided counsel. And his national security adviser seemed too weak to be an effective referee between such powerful figures as Haig and Weinberger. Similarly, Reagan's ambassador to the United Nations, Jeane Kirkpatrick, was unlikely to wield the kind of influence that comes with proximity to the president. Nonetheless, as one of the few intellectuals in the Reagan entourage, and as a committed neoconservative, her voice would be heard on occasion.[7]

Less visible, but quite important, was William J. Casey, Reagan's director of Central Intelligence. Casey had a background in intelligence from World War II, had written books on how to make money, and, by all accounts, had a penchant for covert action and an omnivorous appetite for facts and information. Rare among Reaganites, he read books. His was not, however, a reflective intelligence. He was a man of action. He had little use for abstract theorizing.[8] Given this background, one might expect that Casey would see in Israel a model ally—muscular, action oriented, anti-Soviet, and with a highly reputed intelligence service.

UNVARNISHED REAGANISM: THE FIRST YEAR

At one point during his campaign for the presidency, Reagan was quoted as saying, "Let's not delude ourselves. The Soviet Union underlies all the unrest that is going on. If they weren't engaged in this game of dominoes, there wouldn't be any hot spots in the world."[9] Such a perspective, if really an accurate reflection of Reagan's thinking, would have profound implications for his dealing with problems of the Middle East.

As president, Reagan's contribution to shaping American Middle East policy consisted primarily of injecting this theme of the Soviet instigation of regional unrest into the thinking of his subordinates. Secretary Haig, while much more attuned to nuances than the president, shared Reagan's view that the Middle East should be viewed primarily through the prism of the U.S.-Soviet rivalry.[10] Surrounding him at the State Department, and clustered at the White House and the Defense Department, was a group of like-minded newcomers with very little experience in making foreign policy. It was easy to hear top officials arguing that the most serious problem in the Middle East was the presence of twenty-plus Soviet divisions on Iran's northern border.

Early in the Reagan administration Haig began to speak of the need to try to forge a "consensus of strategic concerns" among the pro-Western regimes in the Middle East. If that meant anything at all—and the phrase was never explained clearly—it presumably meant trying to focus the attention of "our friends" in the region on the Soviet threat, while simultaneously attempting to push parochial local conflicts to the back burner. An early test case arose in the form of a decision to sell a sophisticated radar plane, called airborne warning and control system aircraft (AWACS), to Saudi Arabia.

In normal circumstances one would expect the Israelis to put up quite a fight, arguing that the presence of AWACS in Saudi Arabia could threaten their security. But if Israel and Saudi Arabia were both parts of the U.S.-sponsored strategic consensus, and if both saw the Soviet Union as the primary threat to their security, then the Israelis might be persuaded to allow the sale to go forward in the interests of strengthening the common front against the Soviets and their clients. But there was no such luck. Israel and its supporters in the United States decided to make it an all-out fight. In the end they lost. The AWACS were sold, but only after Reagan had put his prestige on the line and had gone some distance toward meeting Israeli concerns.[11] After the AWACS battle one heard far less talk of strategic consensus, and Haig himself repeatedly said the concept had never been correctly understood.

The AWACS debate was not the only sign that the pro-Israeli Reagan administration would nonetheless have disagreements with Israel. In mid-1981, on the eve of the Israeli national elections, Prime Minister Begin ordered the bombing of the Iraqi nuclear reactor on the outskirts of Baghdad. Although many in official Washington were no doubt impressed by Israel's technical prowess, and were quietly cheering Begin's bold action, open endorsement of this form of "nonproliferation" policy toward Iraq, a member state of the International Atomic Energy Agency (IAEA), would be hard to explain. So, for a moment, the United States rapped Israel's knuckles symbolically by holding up the delivery of F-16 aircraft.

In the midst of these unanticipated challenges the Reagan administration had taken comfort in the fact that Egypt under Anwar Sadat's rule seemed to be stable and friendly. But that assumption was dramatically challenged on October 6, 1981, when Sadat was gunned down by Islamic extremists. Among the charges they made against him was his orientation toward the West and his peace agreement with Israel. Sadat's successor, Husni Mubarak, was well known to the Americans, but no one could be sure if Egypt would remain stable. At worst, the peace with Israel, and therefore the final phases of Israeli withdrawal from Sinai, could be called into question, to say nothing of the Palestinian autonomy talks.

In these troubled circumstances another crisis erupted in December 1981, when Israel decided to extend Israeli law to the Golan Heights, a step just short of annexation. The Reagan administration had just signed an anti-Soviet strategic cooperation agreement with Israel at the end of November, but the agreement was suspended on December 18 as a sign of Washington's disapproval of Israel's action on Golan.[12]

In light of these developments, one might have begun to wonder wherein lay the substance of the vaunted strategic relationship with Israel. The answer was soon to be provided, at least from the Israeli perspective, by Begin's assertive defense minister, Ariel Sharon. And Lebanon was to be the testing ground.

CRISIS IN LEBANON

In the world of pure Reaganism, chronic problems such as those in Lebanon were either not worth much attention or were symptoms of Soviet mischiefmaking. No wonder White House aides had little patience for arcane discussions of the internal political dynamics of Lebanon. Who, they seemed to be saying, could keep track of all the sects and their leaders with unpronounceable names?

But Lebanon had a way of forcing itself onto the American agenda because of Israeli concerns. In early 1981 Israeli-PLO clashes had intensified across Israel's northern border. Syria had been drawn into the fray. The veteran diplomat Philip C. Habib was then called on by Reagan to try to calm things down. The United States thus found itself negotiating a cease-fire between the two archenemies, and after mid-1981 the Lebanese-Israeli border was quiet, although no one was confident that the calm could last for long.

Israeli leaders, and especially Sharon, had grander plans in Lebanon. For years the Israelis had been secretly cultivating the tough leader of one of the Christian Lebanese militias, Bashir Gemayel. With presidential elections in Lebanon slated for the second half of 1982, Israelis saw a chance to help bring their man to power. Sharon and his colleagues were also determined to crush the PLO's military presence in southern Lebanon. In some of the most dramatic scenarios, Israel might also try to drive Syrian forces out of Lebanon, inflicting a heavy blow on the leading client of the Soviet Union in the process.[13]

These possibilities were risky enough to require careful planning and an attempt at coordination with the United States. On visits to Washington, D.C., in early 1982, Israeli officials outlined their ambitious plan for Lebanon in great detail. Some State Department officials were appalled and were afraid that Sharon would get the impression from Haig's nonobjection that the United States was encouraging, or at least acquiescing, in his plan. What Haig did say, repeatedly, was that the United States would understand such a military move only in response to an "internationally recognized provocation," whatever that might mean.[14] To some, that sounded like an invitation to find a pretext to go to war. Some Israelis have claimed that Haig's statements were indeed interpreted as a "green light."[15]

During the early part of 1982 one of the key concerns in Washington was that the Egyptian-Israeli peace treaty be implemented smoothly.

This was by no means a foregone conclusion. Sadat's assassination had raised questions in Israeli minds about the durability of commitments given by Sadat. Some analysts thought Begin might be looking for a pretext to postpone the last phase of Israeli withdrawal from Sinai, particularly since such a move would put off the politically painful moment of dismantling Israeli settlements around Al-Arish and forcing the 15,000 Israelis living there to leave their homes. No one in Washington wanted a flareup in Lebanon to dampen the prospects for full implementation of the Egyptian-Israeli peace. So for several months considerable diplomatic effort went into containing the potential for conflict in Lebanon and facilitating the final withdrawal of Israeli troops from Sinai. Except for a small disputed area named Taba, all Israeli forces were removed from Sinai on April 25. When the United Nations proved unwilling to provide a peacekeeping force for Sinai, the United States took the lead in creating a multinational force, including U.S. troops. Both Egypt and Israel were satisfied with the arrangement, and it worked smoothly in ensuing years. Without much fanfare American diplomats successfully contributed to keeping Egyptian-Israeli relations on track.

As part of this effort Haig had even traveled to the region twice in January 1982 to try to breathe life into the stalled autonomy talks. But here Mubarak was showing great caution, and those efforts soon petered out. Thus, as tensions rose on the Lebanese-Israeli front, the peace between Egypt and Israel was cool, at best, and a broader negotiating process was not in sight.

Soon rumors of an Israeli move against the PLO and Syria in Lebanon were being heard regularly. By May 1982 those Americans most in the know seemed to accept the inevitability, if not desirability, of such a move.[16] All that was needed was a pretext. That came on June 3, 1982, in the form of an assassination attempt against the Israeli ambassador in London. Almost immediately it was clear that this exploit had been ordered by the notorious renegade terrorist, Abu Nidal. Whether it constituted the "internationally recognized provocation" that Haig had spoken of or not, Israel did not wait to find out. Israel struck at PLO ammunition dumps in Beirut, and the PLO retaliated by shelling towns inside Israel. Six Israeli divisions then crossed into Lebanon on June 6—"Operation Peace for Galilee"—and it was immediately clear that more that a small retaliatory raid was under way.[17]

When the Israeli invasion began, Reagan was traveling in Europe. His relations with Haig were already somewhat strained, and others in

Reagan's entourage seemed to be looking for a pretext to ease out the prickly secretary of state. Tactical differences over how to deal with Israel during the Lebanon crisis quickly emerged. One faction formed around Haig, who felt that Israel, whatever the original justification for Israel's intervention in Lebanon, should not be stopped short of destroying the PLO. Somewhat uncharacteristically, Jeane Kirkpatrick sided with Haig, normally her bitterest rival.[18] Opposed to Israel's grand design were Vice President George Bush, who was in charge of crisis management in the White House, and his close ally, Chief of Staff James Baker.[19] William Clark, who had replaced Allen as national security adviser early in 1982, also favored reining Israel in, as did Secretary of Defense Weinberger.

As the early days of the crisis passed, Sharon seemed intent on cutting off the Syrian forces and leaving them no option but a humiliating withdrawal. In this scenario President Asad might even be toppled. At a minimum, Lebanon would be out from under the Syrian thumb. This is what the Phalangist allies of Israel were most eager to see coming out of the Israeli invasion. By contrast, a defeat of the PLO that left Syria still in Lebanon was of lesser interest to the Phalange.

Sharon seems not to have counted on strong intervention from Reagan. That was a mistake. Reagan, for all his passivity, could be aroused by his advisers. When scenes of violence were brought to his attention, he would sometimes react quite emotionally. Thus, on June 9, Reagan wrote one of the harshest notes ever delivered to an Israeli prime minister:

I am extremely concerned by the latest reports of additional advances of Israel into central Lebanon and the escalation of violence between Israel and Syria. Your forces moved significantly beyond the objectives that you have described to me. The tactical advantages may be apparent, but a much more important need is to avoid a wider war with Syrian involvement, and possibly with that of the Soviets as well.

Today I received a letter from President Brezhnev which voices grave concern that a very serious situation has been created that entails the possibility of wider acts of hostility. Of course, I did not accept most of the points in his letter, but the danger of further escalation does exist.

It is now clear that escalation of Syrian-Israeli violence has occurred. I now call on you to accept a ceasefire as of 6:00 a.m. on Thursday June 10, 1982. I implore you to recommend to your government the acceptance of my proposal.

Menachem, a refusal by Israel to accept a ceasefire will aggravate further the serious threat to world peace and will create extreme tension in our relations.[20]

It is hard to believe that Reagan personally took the initiative to send such a message. More likely his aides made the case that Israel should be forced to stop, and Reagan went along.

By all accounts Haig was furious that his advice to let the Israelis finish the job was not being taken. On a whole series of issues, Reagan seemed to be ignoring his views. As early as June 14 Haig had hinted that he might resign unless Reagan gave him a clear vote of confidence. Finally, on June 25 Reagan met with Haig to accept a letter of resignation that had not been written.[21] But Haig hung on as acting secretary of state for some time, trying to steer the course of U.S. diplomacy from his retreat at the Greenbrier resort in West Virginia. Reagan, who had no stomach for confrontations, finally asked his designated secretary of state, George P. Shultz, to call Haig on July 5 and tell him to stop acting as if he were still in charge.[22]

This bizarre episode demonstrated clearly that Reagan was not only very susceptible to the influence of his advisers but was also reluctant to exercise much discipline over them. He apparently found personal confrontations unpleasant and tried hard to avoid them. With Haig's departure the Israelis feared that they had lost one of their best friends.

George Shultz, who had been Weinberger's boss at Bechtel, was viewed by Israelis with suspicion. A former secretary of both labor and the treasury, Shultz had been on Reagan's short list for secretary of state at the outset of the administration, but Richard Nixon had argued effectively on Haig's behalf.[23] During his initial confirmation hearings before the Senate in July, Shultz showed himself to be a careful, well-informed person, who seemed attentive to the nuances of the Middle East regional setting. He addressed the Palestinian issue in a forthright manner, thus confirming for some his pro-Arab reputation.[24]

As secretary of state, Shultz immediately turned his attention to the long-neglected peace process. In his view the Israeli invasion of Lebanon would destroy the chance for peace unless the United States took a new initiative. He was also worried about the impact of the invasion on the still-fragile Egyptian-Israeli relationship. Thus on July 17 he quietly convened a working group of senior officials to start planning for a "fresh start" on Arab-Israeli peacemaking.[25]

While supporting a resumption of peace diplomacy, Shultz did not look favorably on Yasir Arafat and the PLO. In his view Arafat should get no reward for leaving Beirut. But the moment the fighting in Lebanon was over and the PLO was on its way to a new location, Shultz was determined to have a peace initiative in place, and the initiative would not be postponed until the problems of Lebanon were resolved. Also, it would bear the imprint of the president, thereby giving it more authority. Reagan's willingness to go along with this approach was growing as he witnessed the Israeli shelling of Beirut. On July 30 Shultz showed Reagan a draft of the new peace initiative. Later that afternoon, National Security Adviser Clark called Shultz to say, "The president's friendship for Israel is slipping. Enough is enough."[26]

During much of August 1982 the United States, once again with the energetic assistance of Philip Habib, tried to bring the fighting in Lebanon to an end and to arrange for the evacuation of PLO fighters from Beirut.[27] An American military contingent was even sent to Lebanon as part of an international force to help oversee the PLO departure. Habib not only helped to end the bloodshed but also successfully pressed for the election of Bashir Gemayel as Lebanon's next president. To secure the PLO's departure from Lebanon, he also made explicit written commitments to the PLO that assurances had been obtained from the Israelis about the safety of Palestinian civilians left behind after the PLO's departure.[28]

THE REAGAN PLAN

By late August 1982 the Reagan administration seemed to be on the verge of success in the midst of the Lebanese agony, with a pro-Western president about to be inaugurated in Beirut, the Syrians badly battered in the Bekaa valley of eastern Lebanon, and the PLO driven from the country. (The Soviets, meanwhile, had shown themselves unable to do much to help their clients and suffered a loss of political prestige at a crucial moment in the revived cold war atmosphere of the early 1980s.)

Already on August 13 Shultz had won the president's approval of his "fresh start" initiative. Shultz felt Reagan was finally getting involved in Middle East policymaking. The following day he even arranged to have senior officials "role play" the likely reactions of Begin, Mubarak, and King Hussein to the new initiative. Watching the president's awakened interest, Meese observed that Reagan had been ready for this moment a year earlier, but Haig had kept him away from Middle East issues.[29]

With the PLO on its way out of Beirut, and the United States in a position of apparent diplomatic strength, Shultz urged the president to seize the moment to outline the new plan for a diplomatic settlement of the Israeli-Palestinian conflict. Shultz anticipated that the Israelis, in particular, would react negatively, but he nonetheless felt the United

States could help to shape the postwar agenda. On September 1, 1982, Reagan gave his first and only major speech on the Arab-Israeli conflict (see appendix H).

The core of the initiative was still Camp David, but with important substantive additions. Whereas Camp David had been vague on the so-called final status of the West Bank and Gaza after a transitional period, Reagan said the United States would oppose both Israeli annexation and an independent Palestinian state. The U.S. preference, he said, was for some form of association between the West Bank, Gaza, and Jordan. Lest any doubt remain, Reagan said the United States believed that the withdrawal provision of UN Resolution 242 should apply to the West Bank and Gaza, a position completely at odds with Begin and the Likud party's policy.

Within days the United States spelled out its views in greater detail. During the transitional period, for example, the United States would support a freeze on Israeli settlements. Palestinians should have real authority over land and resources; and Palestinians living in East Jerusalem should be allowed to vote in elections for a self-governing authority. As for the "final status" negotiations, the United States went on record as favoring the view that the extent of Israeli withdrawal from occupied territories should be influenced by the extent and nature of the peace and security arrangements offered in return. These were not positions likely to win approval from Begin. They did not. Begin reacted angrily to the Reagan Plan, as it inevitably was dubbed.[30]

The Reagan initiative clearly shifted the spotlight from Egypt to Jordan and the Palestinians. Syria was left out in the cold. Begin rejected the proposal immediately because it called for eventual Israeli relinquishment of most of the occupied territories as the price for peace. The Arab response was, on the whole, less categorical. Questions were asked, some positive noises were heard, and it was widely rumored that King Hussein (and Arafat as well) had been briefed in advance on the initiative and had indicated general approval.[31]

Shortly after the Reagan initiative the Arab states held a summit meeting in Fez, Morocco, and adopted a Saudi proposal that came to be known as the Fez plan. Though different in content from the Reagan proposal, the Fez plan at least gave the United States and the Arabs something to talk about.

The Reagan administration's decision to launch an initiative on the Palestinian issue, albeit with a strong Jordanian tilt, was predicated on the belief that the problems of Lebanon were on their way toward solution. Even before the war in Lebanon, some in the bureaucracy had been making the case for a revived peace effort. Sharon had told the Americans he would solve the Palestinian issue his way—by moving tanks into Lebanon. Once the PLO was crushed, the Palestinians in the West Bank would become pragmatic and ready to deal with existing realities.

The shortcomings of Sharon's vision became abundantly clear within weeks of the Reagan initiative. The comforting belief that Lebanon's travails were nearly over was literally and figuratively blown away with the assassination by pro-Syrian elements of Bashir Gemayel on September 14, 1982. General Sharon, who had discussed with Gemayel a plan for "cleansing" Lebanon of Palestinians, now saw a danger that Israel's long-term investment would be lost with Bashir's death. He pressed the leadership of the Lebanese Forces (a Christian militia) and the Phalange party to respect the deals he had arranged with Bashir and to prepare for "immediate action." In the circumstances Israel had great leverage over the Phalange, including the ability to withhold or grant support for the candidacy of Bashir's brother, Amin, as president.[32]

Some of the details of what happened next are not entirely clear, but the broad outline is known. Units of the Lebanese Forces militia under the command of Eli Hobeika moved into two Palestinian refugee camps, Sabra and Shatila, on the southern outskirts of Beirut. There, under the eyes of their Israeli allies, they systematically murdered as many as eight hundred Palestinian civilians. This massacre led to a strong reaction everywhere, including in Israel. Five months later Sharon and several other officers were censured for their role in not preventing the massacres and were removed from their posts.[33]

The American response to the Sabra and Shatila massacres was to put Lebanon and its ills back at the top of the agenda. American military forces, which had been withdrawn after the departure of the PLO, were returned to the Beirut area to protect the refugee camps and to provide visible backing for the embattled Lebanese government. To negotiate an Israeli-Lebanese agreement that would lead to the withdrawal of both Israeli and Syrian forces became a priority of U.S. diplomacy, to be pursued in parallel, or even before, the Reagan Plan for the West Bank and Gaza.[34] Shultz's hope that Arab-Israeli peace talks could avoid becoming hostage to Lebanon's ills was increasingly in doubt.

COURTING KING HUSSEIN

King Hussein, the object of the Reagan initiative in its first phase, began to watch how the Americans handled the Lebanese imbroglio as a test of how serious they were likely to be in dealing with the Palestinian issue. He, like many Arabs, felt that unless the Americans could get the Israelis out of Lebanon, there would be little chance of dislodging them from the West Bank. President Reagan further undermined the chances of success for his initiative by saying publicly that nothing could be done on the Palestinian question until agreement was reached on Lebanon.[35] For those who had opposed the Reagan initiative from the outset—and that included Begin, Asad, and the Soviets—this statement was an invitation to make things in Lebanon as difficult as possible, to ensure that "another Camp David," as the Syrians labeled the Reagan initiative, would not succeed.

King Hussein visited Washington in December 1982 for talks with President Reagan. In an effort to persuade the king to support the Reagan initiative, the president wrote two letters to him spelling out promises and commitments, including a supply of arms, if Hussein would agree to enter negotiations. Reagan also promised that he would convince Israel to freeze settlement activity in the West Bank once negotiations with Jordan began and that the transitional period might be shortened to less than five years.

By all accounts, Hussein was tempted, but he felt the need for Palestinian support. On occasion, however, the king left the impression that he would proceed without Arafat if the latter proved to be intransigent. Shultz, who was primarily in charge of the negotiations, was never quite sure what to make of King Hussein's comments. But he felt that the State Department "Arabists" tended to be too optimistic in their assessments.[36]

Talks between Jordan and the PLO took place over the next several months. Finally, in April 1983 the king concluded that there was no basis for developing a joint negotiating position with the PLO. The Jordanians blamed pro-Soviet hard-liners in Arafat's entourage for this inability to reach an agreement. Jordan, too, came under direct Soviet pressure not to go along.[37] On April 10, 1983, the king called Reagan to tell him that his talks with Arafat had failed. He was not prepared to move on his own. The same day he officially announced that Jordan could not accept the Reagan initiative, stating, "We in Jordan, having refused from the beginning to negotiate on behalf of the Palestinians, will neither act separately nor in lieu of anybody in Middle East peace negotiations." [38] For the moment, the Reagan Plan seemed dead.

LEBANESE-ISRAELI PEACE?

For much of the remainder of 1983, Arab-Israeli peacemaking became, from the American perspective, synonymous with trying to forge a viable Lebanese-Israeli agreement as a step toward the withdrawal of both Israeli and Syrian forces from Lebanon. Secretary Shultz, who had shown reluctance to engage directly in the shuttle-style travels of his predecessors, went to the Middle East to put the final touches on the Lebanese-Israeli accord. In part he did so to respond to the expressed concerns of Egyptian President Mubarak. Shultz was skeptical about Syria's role and tried to enlist Saudi support to pressure Damascus. He also ran into problems with the Israelis, who were unwilling to abandon their ally, Major Saad Haddad, in southern Lebanon. Despite all the obstacles, however, Shultz's shuttle seemed to pay off. On May 17, 1983, Lebanon and Israel signed an agreement that was just short of a peace treaty.

But the agreement was stillborn. Israeli withdrawal was made dependent on Syrian withdrawal, and Asad (who commanded a sizable constituency inside Lebanon) would not tolerate such a condition. Already the United States and Syria seemed to be on a collision course. In April the American embassy had been bombed with devastating effectiveness. [39] Americans traced the bombing to Lebanese allies of Iran, perhaps with some Syrian involvement as well. During the summer, fighting resumed in Beirut, and Arafat defiantly returned to the northern Lebanese city of Tripoli. Syria, by now fully rearmed by the Soviets, became increasingly assertive in Lebanon, including against the PLO.

As the violence mounted, the Israelis began to disengage from the Shouf mountains overlooking Beirut, leaving the American contingent near the airport exposed to hostile attacks. Before long the U.S. Marines found themselves, in their lightly defended positions, drawn into inter-Lebanese battles. The peacekeeping mission was gradually being eroded, and the United States was becoming a cobelligerent on the side of the Lebanese Christian forces. On October 23, at a time of mounting tension between the United States and Syria, a truck loaded with explosives drove into the compound of the American contingent of the multinational peacekeeping force. The effect was devastating. Two hundred forty-one

American servicemen were killed.[40] Simultaneously, French and Israeli units were attacked by suicide truck bombs.

Within days of the attack on the American troops in Beirut, President Reagan signed National Security Decision Directive 111, thereby reviving the strategic cooperation agreement that had been suspended in December 1981.[41] According to some accounts, Under Secretary of State Lawrence S. Eagleburger had concluded earlier in the year that close cooperation with Israel was essential for American policy in Lebanon to succeed. In reaching this conclusion, he was influenced by the decision taken by the new Israeli defense minister, Moshe Arens, to withdraw Israeli troops from central Lebanon, an action of great strategic importance that had been undertaken without coordination with Washington. Eagleburger seemed to hope that by restoring the strategic cooperation agreement, the Reagan administration would be better able to influence Israeli decisions that impinged on American interests. By November 1983, Joint Political-Military Group meetings had been agreed upon to develop areas of strategic cooperation.

Adding urgency to the rebuilding of U.S.-Israeli ties was the emergence of new leadership in Israel. To the surprise of many, on September 15, 1983, Menachem Begin, suffering from the recent death of his wife and seemingly depressed over the outcome of the war in Lebanon, announced his resignation and entered a period of seclusion that continued until his death in 1992. His replacement was Yitzhak Shamir, whose early political career had been with the Stern Group (Lehi), which had won him a reputation for extremism and violence. Relegated to the margins of Israeli political life in the early years after independence, Shamir spent some years in the Israeli intelligence service, Mossad, returning to politics in the 1970s as a member of Begin's party. At the time of the Camp David Accords he served as speaker of the Knesset; after Dayan resigned as foreign minister in October 1979, Begin hesitated before offering the post to Shamir, but eventually did so in March 1980.[42]

Now, with Begin's departure from the scene, Shamir won the Likud's endorsement to take his place. Instead of Begin and Sharon the Americans now found themselves dealing with Shamir and Arens, a change that some felt would be for the better.

Whatever the prospect for improved relations with Israel might have been, the situation in Lebanon offered little hope for Reagan and Shultz. After the October bombings, American policy became more overtly aimed at punishing Syria. On December 4, 1983, two American planes were shot down by the Syrians, with one pilot killed and one captured.[43]

By early 1984, when the politics of reelection were uppermost in the minds of some of the president's advisers, Reagan made a decision, over the opposition of Shultz, that the Marines should be "redeployed offshore." Critics termed the decision "cut and run." Whichever words one chose, the facts were the same. Reagan, who had pinned American prestige on a stable settlement in Lebanon, was removing the most tangible sign of that commitment.[44] Henceforth Lebanon would be left primarily to the squabbles of its internal factions and its two powerful neighbors.

A MISSED OPPORTUNITY?

Election years rarely witness serious initiatives for Arab-Israeli peace by American presidents. Their priorities lie elsewhere. Controversy, an inevitable corollary of any serious U.S. initiative in the region, is shunned. Pleas from Arab regimes for arms and diplomatic support are put off until after the elections.[45]

The year 1984 did not, however, prove to be entirely wasted. Early in 1984 Egypt was readmitted to the Islamic Conference, a sign that it was no longer isolated because of its peace agreement with Israel. A month later Mubarak and King Hussein made a joint appearance in Washington with President Reagan, which was symbolically important, even if Egypt's overt support for the PLO caused some ill feeling in American circles. In Israel, midyear elections produced a near standoff between Labor and Likud, resulting in a unity coalition of both parties and a rotating premiership. For the first two years Shimon Peres would be in the top job. Beginning in October 1986 Yitzhak Shamir would serve out the remaining two years of the term as prime minister. Throughout, Yitzhak Rabin would serve as minister of defense. As unusual as such an arrangement might seem, it did mean that the second Reagan administration would be dealing with Israelis in power who did not automatically exclude the key elements of Resolution 242 and its practical interpretation as spelled out by Reagan in September 1982. Indeed, it soon became clear that Peres and King Hussein were eager to explore areas for cooperation and were looking to Washington for help against the common adversaries of the Reagan Plan—the Likud, Syria, and the PLO.

This combination of regional developments, plus Reagan's extraordinary electoral victory over Walter Mondale in November 1984, seemed to set the stage for a new round of American involvement in the peace process. Rarely had conditions been better for trying to press forward with some version of an Israeli-Jordanian deal, provided that enough Palestinian support could be found to give the exercise an aura of legitimacy in Arab eyes.

During the fall of 1984 the new assistant secretary of state for Near Eastern affairs, Richard Murphy, had spent six weeks in the region probing for possible openings on the peace front. King Hussein gave the impression of being ready to proceed, perhaps without the PLO, and for the first time he did not insist on knowing the outcome of negotiations before joining the process. If that became a solid Jordanian position, it could radically change the prospects for peace, especially with a Labor-led coalition in power in Israel. Shultz began to be more hopeful about the long-stalled peace diplomacy.[46]

Arab leaders had often expressed the hope that they could deal with a reelected Republican president. This nostalgic view stemmed largely from the perception of the second Eisenhower term, and especially Dwight D. Eisenhower's tough treatment of the Israelis during and after the Suez crisis of 1956. Now, in 1985, the Arabs were again dealing with a popular, reelected Republican. So, one by one, Arab leaders trekked to Washington in the first half of 1985. First came King Fahd of Saudi Arabia, followed a month later by Egyptian President Husni Mubarak. Most important, King Hussein arrived in Washington at the end of May.

Much of Egyptian and Jordanian policy at the time was aimed at evoking a positive American response to a joint Jordanian-PLO position that had been formalized in a carefully worded statement signed on February 11, 1985.[47] In many ways the Jordanian-PLO position could be construed as a new attempt to respond belatedly to the 1982 Reagan initiative. Both parties announced that their common goal was the creation of a Jordanian-Palestinian confederation, to be established once Israel had fully withdrawn from occupied territory. They pledged to negotiate as a joint delegation within the framework of an international conference.

Shultz was wary of the idea of an international conference. As envisaged by the Arabs, such a conference could become a lopsided means of pressuring Israel for concessions. Even Peres would not accept such an arrangement, and his Likud partners were much more hostile to the idea. At most, Shultz would consider a symbolic conference to open the way to direct negotiations. Until Jordan made clear that the PLO would remain in the shadows and the international conference would not become a barrier to direct negotiations, Shultz would show little interest in the new Jordanian-PLO accord.[48]

Although the February 11, 1985, agreement raised more questions than it answered in the minds of the Reagan administration, the Jordanian attempt at clarification was reassuring. During their visit to Washington in May, Jordanian officials stated that the concept of confederation was really much closer to "federation," with responsibility for foreign affairs and defense clearly understood by both parties to be vested in Amman. The Jordanians, moreover, played down the importance of the international conference, stressing instead the need for U.S. contact with a group of Jordanians and Palestinians. They also made it clear that they thought the PLO could be brought to the point of accepting Resolution 242, perhaps in return for some form of American recognition of Palestinian self-determination within the framework of a confederation with Jordan.[49]

However tempted some American officials may have been to press forward with an initiative in these seemingly propitious circumstances, there were three offsetting considerations. In the first place, President Reagan was on record saying, in March 1985, that the United States did not want to participate in Arab-Israeli peace negotiations, despite the Camp David commitment for the United States to be a "full partner" in subsequent phases of the peace talks.[50] Reagan and Shultz repeatedly said that the problem was not for the United States to talk to the parties but to get the parties to talk to each other. Direct negotiations became something of a slogan, especially among key senators and representatives. The administration could not ignore these sentiments. Indeed, Hussein was told there was no chance for congressional approval of an arms package for Jordan unless he committed himself to direct negotiations with Israel.

A second problem in bringing the United States into a more active role in support of King Hussein's approach was reportedly Secretary Shultz's sense of disillusionment with most of the Arab leaders he had dealt with during 1982–83. He seemed to think that they wasted the opportunity provided by the Reagan plan and that their words could not always be counted on. The PLO, in particular, was not a fit partner for peace talks, in his view, although he did believe that Palestinians from the West Bank and Gaza would have to be included in a Jordanian delegation. But the idea of having Assistant Secretary Murphy meet with a joint Jordanian-Palestinian delegation proved to be controversial. As King Hussein saw it, such a meeting would set the stage for the PLO to accept UN Resolution 242; there would then be further contacts between the United States and a Jordanian-PLO delegation; next there would be an international conference; and only at that point would there be negotiations with Israel. Shultz, in contrast, insisted that any American meeting with a Jordanian-Palestinian delegation should be followed immediately by contacts with the Israelis.[51]

A third inhibition on American policy came from a concern for the political standing of Prime Minister Peres. During his first year in office he had become popular. The withdrawal of Israeli forces from Lebanon had been welcomed by a war-weary populace. Efforts to curb raging inflation were progressing, though with considerable pain. His management of the economy was turning out well for Peres. Quiet diplomacy with Jordan seemed to be laying the groundwork for a kind of condominium over the West Bank and Gaza at the expense of the PLO. Some American officials wanted to help Peres position himself for a showdown with the Likud. This desire led them to advise against anything that could be viewed as causing a strain in U.S.-Israeli relations, such as American dealings with the PLO or American support for Palestinian self-determination.

A practical test of American policy emerged during the summer. The Jordanians wanted to proceed with the idea of an American exploratory meeting with a joint Jordanian-PLO delegation. On July 19 King Hussein had met secretly with Peres in London to discuss his strategy. He had gone over a long list of possible Palestinian participants who might be part of a joint Jordanian-Palestinian delegation. Shultz was informed of the meeting by the Israelis on August 5. Peres was not enthusiastic about a preliminary U.S.-Jordanian-Palestinian meeting but would not oppose it strongly so long as no PLO members participated.

On August 9 Shultz informed Reagan of the state of play. Reagan was firm in his opposition to American officials meeting with anyone even vaguely connected to the PLO. Meanwhile, Foreign Minister Shamir sent a message to the White House expressing his adamant opposition to the idea of the Americans meeting with any Palestinians. Shultz pressed Reagan for a decision, and finally was given authority to allow Murphy to meet with a joint Jordanian-Palestinian delegation only if that led immediately to direct negotiations with Israel.[52]

The Jordanian response was noncommittal. Essentially the Jordanians said that an initial meeting should take place, and then next steps could be considered. As the Jordanians were quick to point out, their reply was almost a verbatim repetition of a long-standing American response to the Arabs' question of what would happen once negotiations with Israel began.

To try to organize a preliminary meeting between the United States and a joint Jordanian-Palestinian delegation, the Jordanians forwarded a list of seven names of possible Palestinian members of the delegation, from which the Americans were expected to select four. The Israelis had said they had no objection to two of the seven names but were quick to label the others as PLO. The Americans objected to at least three of the names, but, more important, they kept asking for assurances that any preliminary talks would be accompanied by a clear Jordanian-Palestinian commitment to direct negotiations with Israel.[53] Jordan, eager not to offend Syria, was not prepared to abandon the idea of an international conference in favor of U.S.-sponsored direct bilateral negotiations.

Despite these difficulties, for a moment in the summer of 1985 the United States seemed about to take the plunge. Assistant Secretary Murphy was sent to the Middle East, and members of a joint Jordanian-Palestinian team were assembled in Amman to meet him; but at the last moment he was told not to proceed with the meeting. Reagan's conditions could not be met, and Shultz therefore had to scrap the idea of a meeting. According to Shultz, Reagan had been immovable on the points of excluding the PLO and insisting on direct negotiations. But it is far from clear how hard anyone tried to persuade Reagan, and in any event Shultz was beginning to detect signs that the situation in the region was moving away from the possibility of productive peace talks.[54]

King Hussein made a final effort to persuade the Americans in the fall. He had been told that there was no chance of winning congressional support for a big new arms package for Jordan—something Reagan had promised the king in writing in December 1982—unless Jordan committed itself to direct negotiations. At his speech to the UN General Assembly, the king did make such a commitment, saying, "We are ready to negotiate with Israel under suitable, acceptable supervision, directly and as soon as possible, in accordance with Security Council Resolutions 242 and 338."[55] One month later the U.S. Senate rebuffed the king's request on arms, stipulating that no major sale could be concluded until "direct and meaningful" negotiations with Israel had begun. In the face of continuing congressional hostility to the sale, the administration finally withdrew the nearly $2 billion arms package for Jordan, on February 3, 1986.

October proved to be a disastrous month for Jordanian-PLO relations, as well as for Hussein's initiative. The month began with a spectacular Israeli bombing attack on Arafat's headquarters in Tunis, ostensibly in retaliation for a PLO attack on several Israelis in Cyprus a few days earlier. On October 5 King Hussein and Prime Minister Peres met secretly in London to develop a plan for joint rule in the West Bank.[56]

While Arafat was being abandoned by King Hussein, he was also being challenged by radicals from within his own organization. On October 7 a minor faction of the PLO—the Palestine Liberation Front of Abul Abbas—had the idea to hijack an Italian cruise ship, the *Achille Lauro*. Before the incident was over, one elderly American, confined to his wheelchair, had been murdered and thrown overboard. (The Syrians, eager to discredit the PLO, recovered the body on their coast and dutifully returned it to the American government, thus providing conclusive proof that the victim had been shot.[57]) At about the same time Jordan and the PLO failed to reach agreement on terms that would have allowed for a meeting of a joint Jordanian-PLO delegation with the British foreign secretary.

President Asad must have watched all these events with great satisfaction. He had opposed the February 11, 1985, agreement from the outset. He had labeled the U.S. efforts to arrange direct talks under its own auspices as tantamount to another Camp David, and now he found the Jordanian-PLO alliance coming apart. So Asad, working closely with the Jordanian prime minister, Zaid al-Rifai, encouraged the development of a working alliance with Jordan. The king was obliged to acknowledge past Jordanian misdeeds in allowing anti-Syrian terrorist groups to operate from his territory. Thus the stage was set for a Syrian-Jordanian rapprochement and a break between Jordan and the PLO, which was not long in coming.[58] On February 19, 1986, the king spelled out in graphic detail the reasons for the breakdown of coordination with the PLO.[59] The February 11, 1985, accord had lasted barely one year.

In retrospect, it seems clear that the Americans had never been enthusiastic about dealing with a joint Jordanian-PLO delegation. As one Jordanian minister put it early in the discussions in Washington, Jordan tried to stress that the PLO was relatively weak and therefore could be pressured to make concessions. The American reply, he said, was that if the PLO was weak, it should be excluded entirely from the diplomatic process.[60] Finally, when King Hussein began to conclude that the PLO was a liability in his dealings with Israel, Syria, and Washington, and that it was recreating a substantial presence in Jordan, he moved to sever the tie. In retrospect, Shultz concluded that neither Hussein nor Peres was politically strong enough to deliver the concessions needed to make the peace process work, even though their own thinking was not far apart.[61]

American involvement with the Arab-Israeli conflict can never be entirely isolated from other developments in the Middle East. In complex ways, events in Lebanon, Libya, and Iran all came to be entwined with Arab-Israeli diplomacy. If there was a connecting thread among these geographically remote locations, it was terrorism. By the mid-1980s the Reagan administration had become obsessed with the battle against terrorism, especially of the state-sponsored variety. And the three states topping the list of suspects were Syria, Iran, and Libya. All were actively involved in Lebanon, some with Lebanese groups and some with militant Shiites.

Already in 1984 Americans were falling victim to terrorist attacks. Malcolm Kerr, the president of the American University of Beirut and a leading specialist on Middle East affairs, was gunned down in cold blood in January 1984. Two months later the head of the CIA station in Lebanon, William Buckley, was kidnapped. In succeeding months, on into 1985, 1986, and 1987, fourteen more Americans were kidnapped from the streets of Beirut and held hostage. And terrorist attacks on airlines and airports claimed more lives.

Given the tough rhetoric of the Reagan administration against terrorism, the United States might have been expected to lash out at the states thought to be sponsoring such attacks. But only once did that happen, when Libya was held responsible for the bombing in Berlin that took two American lives. On April 14, 1986, American planes bombed Tripoli, nearly killing President Muammar Qaddafi in the process.

Curiously, Iran was treated quite differently from Libya, even though its involvement with the hostage takers in Lebanon was beyond doubt. During the spring of 1985, just as the joint Jordanian-PLO strategy was getting off the ground, some officials in Washington were beginning to debate the merits of trying to improve relations with Iran.[62] The rationale at the outset was presented in anti-Soviet terms. Iran was a large, important country that had not chosen sides in the cold war rivalry. After Ayatollah Khomeini left the scene, some argued, there would be a struggle for power, with pro-Soviet elements having a chance to gain the upper hand. The United States should therefore find some way to establish contacts with Iranians who were not pro-Soviet.[63]

On July 3, 1985, David Kimche, the director general of the Israeli Foreign Ministry, met at the White House with Robert McFarlane, Reagan's most recent national security adviser.[64] Israel had maintained some useful contacts in Iran after the revolution, and Kimche now offered to put these at the disposal of the United States in pursuit of the policy of improving relations with Iran. He told the Americans that at some point the Iranians, who were locked into a costly war with Iraq, would almost certainly ask for arms.[65] Within days of this conversation President Reagan was briefed on the Kimche conversation and reportedly gave general approval to the policy of cultivating "moderate" elements in Iran. During August Israel made a large shipment of American-made antitank missiles to Iran, and several weeks later an American hostage was released in Beirut. The "arms for hostages" exchange had begun.

Throughout most of 1986 the United States became more and more involved with Iran. Over the opposition of both his secretary of state and secretary of defense (who rarely agreed on much at all), and without their knowledge, Reagan signed an intelligence finding on January 17 that authorized the sale of American arms to Iran. Israel was to serve as the conduit. The moment of high drama—and even strange humor—came in May when McFarlane, accompanied by his National Security Council staff aides Oliver North and Howard Teicher, as well as Peres's adviser on terrorist affairs, Amiram Nir, traveled secretly to Tehran. As a symbol of their desire for a new relationship with the "moderates" in Iran, they took with them a chocolate cake with a small gold key on top of it—direct from a Tel Aviv bakery!

McFarlane soon learned that his Iranian counterparts were interested only in getting more arms and had no desire to discuss broad strategic issues or to deliver more hostages as a sign of their good intentions. He returned to Washington empty handed, although his energetic assistant, Oliver North, continued to press forward with the policy, developing in the process an innovative way of financing another of the president's pet projects, aid to the Nicaraguan Contras, which Congress had prohibited.

Finally, after the release of two more American hostages in Beirut, and the taking of an additional three, the news of McFarlane's secret visit to Tehran the previous May was published, and on November 25, 1986, the White House was obliged to confirm that arms had been sent to Iran, with the proceeds illegally diverted to the Contras. A political scandal of unprecedented proportions ensued, leading eventually to indictments against McFarlane; his successor as national security adviser, John Poindexter; and Oliver North. Reagan, who professed ignorance about the diversion of funds to the Contras, was weakened by the affair.

How, if at all, did the Iran-Contra affair affect American policy toward the Arab-Israeli conflict? First, just as the Jordanian-Palestinian initiative was getting off the ground in 1985, the attention of the White House was turning to the sensitive issue of the opening to Iran, and Israel was to play a key part in the strategy. This was no time to press the Israelis to be particularly forthcoming toward the Jordanians or Palestinians. In fact, the Israelis were in an excellent position to embarrass the Reagan administration if they ever had reason to do so.

Second, as the flow of arms from Israel to Iran got under way in 1985, Arab governments began to take notice and assumed a degree of American complicity. Simultaneously, the United States was openly tilting toward Iraq in the Iran-Iraq war. How could the two strands of policy be reconciled? At a time when American credibility was important for the possible success of the peace process, Egypt and Jordan seem to have developed doubts about the reliability of the United States.

Third, the initiative toward Iran caused deep divisions in the upper echelons of the American government, which Reagan was unwilling or unable to resolve. Divided counsels on the Middle East undermined a coherent policy toward the peace process. In the end, however, the Iran-Contra affair cannot be credited with causing the failure to exploit a possible opening in the peace process in 1985–86. But it did contribute to the erosion of American credibility at a crucial moment, weakening the president and perhaps leading to his further disengagement from foreign-policy issues as he approached the end of his second term.

CHAPTER FOURTEEN

Return to Realism: Shultz Tries Again

From the moment he became secretary of state in 1982, George Shultz had been the dominant architect of the Reagan administration's approach to the Arab-Israeli peace process. But on related matters in the Middle East, such as Lebanon and the Iran-Iraq war, he was not able to get his way so easily. Secretary of Defense Weinberger had persuaded the president to withdraw American troops from Lebanon early in 1984, a move that Shultz had opposed, and Casey, McFarlane, Poindexter, and North had been able to conduct the covert "arms-for-hostages" operation in 1985 and 1986, which both Shultz and Weinberger had objected to.

The Iran-Contra scandal clearly strengthened Shultz's hand in dealing with the White House. After firing Poindexter and North, Reagan could hardly afford to lose his respected secretary of state as well. The new national security adviser, Frank Carlucci, who took over in January 1987, was an experienced team player. He brought a degree of professionalism to the National Security Council that had been sorely lacking in previous years.

One sign of the new coherence in top-level policy circles came with the decision to support Kuwait's request early in 1987 to provide protection for its tankers from Iranian air attacks. For several years the United States had been tilting toward Iraq, and considerable concern had developed late in 1986 that Iran might be able to mount a major ground offensive in southern Iraq that would bring Iranian troops to the borders of Kuwait and Saudi Arabia. Shultz and Weinberger saw in the Kuwaiti request for "reflagging" of eleven of their tankers a chance to erase the stain of Iran-Contra and to signal to the Iranians that a threat to the oil-rich states of the Arabian peninsula would be of direct concern to the United States.

Besides wanting to restrain Iran, the United States was hoping to rebuild its damaged credibility with a number of Arab states. The fact that Kuwait had also requested, and received, Soviet help was another reason for a swift American response. By mid-July 1987 the United States was routinely escorting Kuwaiti tankers to the northern end of the Gulf and, equally surprising, was hard at work with the Soviet Union on a UN Security Council resolution calling for a cease-fire in the seven-year-old war. Resolution 598 was passed the same day that the first U.S-escorted Kuwaiti convoy sailed through the Gulf.[1]

On the whole, the reflagging operation was remarkably successful. At modest cost, and with relatively few risks, the United States helped to create conditions in which Iran finally felt compelled to accept a cease-fire—or in the words of Ayatollah Khomeini, "to drink poison"—thus ending the Middle East's costliest war to date. American prestige in the Arab world, which had sunk to a low point after the Iran-Contra revelations, was at least partially restored. Adding to the improved atmosphere in U.S.-Arab relations was an appreciation, especially in Jordan, that the United States had gradually been adjusting its position on the question of convening an Arab-Israeli peace conference.

REDISCOVERING THE INTERNATIONAL CONFERENCE

In early 1986, after the break between Jordan and the Palestine Liberation Organization, King Hussein had placed renewed emphasis on the idea of an international conference. He had always maintained that he needed either the PLO or Syria to provide cover for his talks with Israel. If the PLO was now out of the picture, it was all the more important that Syria be given an incentive to go along with any diplomatic efforts. Hence the need for an international conference of some sort. Inevitably, that would mean some degree of Soviet participation as well, an issue the Reaganites were still unenthusiastic about. American hostility to the idea of an international conference was partly rooted in the notion that such an arrangement would bring the Soviet Union back into the Middle East, from which it had supposedly been absent since Kissinger's maneuvering of 1973–74.[2]

In late 1985 Shimon Peres, still in the role of prime minister, had begun to speak positively about some type of international forum or sponsorship of direct Arab-Israeli negotiations. His expressed conditions for a conference were that it not be empowered to impose solutions and that the Soviet Union should restore diplomatic relations with Israel before the conference.

About the same time as the modification in the Israeli position, Shultz also began to hint that the administration's previous opposition to the idea of an international conference was weakening. As early as September

23, 1985, Shultz had tried out some ideas on King Hussein, who at that moment was not much interested. But Shultz was clearly edging toward the idea of some type of international "event" to accommodate Arab concerns. He was also beginning to think about how the idea of sovereignty could be reconceptualized to accommodate the complexities of the relations binding Israel, the Palestinians, and Jordan. Various forms of mixed and overlapping sovereignty seemed to him the key to overcoming the impasse over Israeli withdrawal from occupied territories.[3]

Without much fanfare, the international conference reappeared on the Arab-Israeli diplomatic scene as a potentially live issue. Quiet diplomacy then took over, with professional American diplomats trying to develop a basis of agreement between Israel and Jordan.

During much of 1986 Jordanian-Israeli contacts increased. King Hussein met with Defense Minister Yitzhak Rabin near Strasbourg in April.[4] Subsequently Jordan closed down PLO offices in Amman, and Jordan and Israel both encouraged the development of "Village Leagues" as alternative sources of leadership to that of the PLO-oriented nationalist leadership in the West Bank. Branches of the Cairo-Amman bank were opened in the West Bank, and a pro-Jordanian newspaper was set up in Jerusalem. The United States threw its support behind so-called quality-of-life measures, presumably on the theory that improved living standards would produce Palestinian political moderation.[5]

On the political front, however, the international conference remained of importance to Jordan, if only to help legitimize the de facto arrangements that were under way with Israel. In October 1986, as part of the rotation agreement between Labor and Likud, Yitzhak Shamir became prime minister. Peres took over as foreign minister, and Rabin stayed on as defense minister. Shamir had been kept informed of the contacts with Jordan but was unlikely to share Peres's enthusiasm for dealing with the king. Peres, however, was determined to press ahead, and by the spring of 1987 was within sight of an important breakthrough.

Jordan had firmed up its ties with Syria, to the point that an emissary of King Hussein met with Shultz on April 7, 1987, to say that Syria was prepared to attend an international conference of the sort Jordan had been proposing. Shultz was skeptical, but he realized that the Soviets might now be ready to help.[6]

Meanwhile King Hussein and Israeli Foreign Minister Peres met secretly in London to work out the principles for convening an international conference. Agreement was reached on April 11, 1987. Jordan and Israel both supported the idea that a conference would not have plenary powers. It could not impose its views or veto the results of bilateral negotiations that would take place under the umbrella of the conference. Both countries agreed there would be a ceremonial opening with representatives of the permanent members of the UN Security Council and those regional parties to the conflict that had accepted Resolution 242. One sticky issue, the question of what would happen in the event of a deadlock in the bilateral negotiations, the so-called referral issue, was finessed for the moment.[7]

On the day that Peres and Hussein reached agreement, an aide to Peres met with Shultz to plead with him to make the new document the core of an American initiative. Only in that way might Shamir be persuaded to accept it. Shultz refused to play this kind of game and insisted that Peres present his own agreement to Shamir before the United States would take any position on it. On April 20 Peres told Shultz that Shamir had been briefed, and two days later Shamir told Shultz that he totally rejected the London document.[8]

Shamir's rejection of the idea of a nonbinding international conference was rooted in his determination never to cede an inch of the historic Land of Israel—in practice, this meant no Israeli withdrawal from the West Bank. Moreover, the fact that Peres had negotiated the agreement behind Shamir's back ensured it of a frosty reception. Shultz was simply not prepared to take sides in this internal dispute, and a visit by Moshe Arens on Shamir's behalf on April 24 seems to have convinced Shultz not to embrace the London document. Still, he felt that Shamir had made a mistake, and he was encouraged to see that Hussein's idea of a conference was approaching his own.[9]

As a coda to this phase of diplomacy, a final effort was made, this time in collaboration with Shamir, to find some form of international sponsorship for Israeli-Jordanian talks. In mid-June Shamir had hinted to Shultz that he might consider some type of international meeting to endorse direct negotiations with Jordan. Shultz sent his aide, Charles Hill, to Israel in late July to explore this idea further. On August 6 an emissary from Shamir came to see Shultz to inform him that Shamir had met with Hussein. Shamir was still opposed to an international conference, but he would not object if the permanent members of the UN Security Council met to endorse direct Arab-Israeli negotiations. Shamir reported that his meeting with Hussein had gone well. Shortly thereafter, however,

Shultz heard from Hussein about the same meeting. Hussein characterized Shamir as "hopeless."[10]

In September Peres suggested to Hill the idea that Mikhail Gorbachev and Ronald Reagan, as part of their upcoming summit meeting, might invite Shamir and King Hussein to meet with them. Shultz was well disposed toward the idea, and Reagan was briefed on it on September 11. The president did not immediately agree, and Shultz sensed he was growing weary of the Middle East. Finally, on September 23 Reagan gave the green light.[11]

Shultz flew to the Middle East in October 1987 while en route to Moscow to put the finishing touches on arrangements for a U.S.-Soviet summit meeting in Washington before the end of the year. While in Jerusalem he persuaded Shamir to agree in principle to the idea of an American-Soviet invitation to come to Washington at the time of the summit, along with King Hussein, to receive a joint U.S.-Soviet blessing for direct negotiations.

The next day, October 19, Shultz presented the idea to King Hussein in London. The United States had made little advance preparation with Jordan, in contrast to its numerous exchanges during the fall with the Israelis. The king, who was about to host an Arab summit in Amman, was politically unable even to hint at an interest in an idea that would be ridiculed by the other Arabs. He also had no reason to think the Soviets would agree to the idea, and the Syrians, who were only mentioned as an afterthought as possible participants in the adventure, would certainly say no. So the king found himself put in the position of saying no to the Americans, a fact that was duly leaked to a pro-Israeli columnist a few months later.[12]

In normal times Hussein's hesitation would have been the last word on the peace process for the Reagan administration. With both American and Israeli elections slated for November 1988, Washington had little appetite for continuing to grapple with the seemingly intractable Arab-Israeli conflict. When the Arab summit was held in Amman in early November, it even seemed as if the Arabs had turned their backs on the Palestinian question. The Gulf, it appeared, was a much greater worry, and Arafat found himself the odd man out among the assembled Arab potentates. Even the acceptance of Egypt back into the fold, which most members of the Arab League endorsed, seemed driven more by Gulf concerns than by a desire to coordinate the diplomacy of Arab-Israeli peacemaking with Cairo.

THE INTIFADA AND THE SHULTZ INITIATIVE

During Israel's twenty-year domination of the West Bank and Gaza, there had never been trouble-free times. But the costs of the occupation had not been judged excessive by Israeli governments, and a semblance of normal life existed on most days for the growing numbers of Israeli settlers, and for the Palestinians, some 100,000 of whom had jobs in the Israeli economy as of 1988. Then on December 9, 1987, an unusually nasty series of incidents took place in Gaza, sparking large-scale Palestinian protests. Within days West Bank Palestinians joined the "uprising," or *intifada*,[13] as it was to be called, and even Israeli Arabs showed support. It soon became clear that something qualitatively new was happening. The previously quiescent Palestinians of the West Bank and Gaza were coming of political age, and with a vengeance.[14]

Though caught by surprise by the timing of the uprising and by how quickly it spread, the PLO had long been cultivating support in the occupied territories, and pro-PLO networks existed and were backed by the generally pro-PLO sentiment of the population. Before long, coordination between the Unified National Leadership of the Uprising, as the internal leadership referred to itself, and the PLO seemed to be far reaching.[15]

By January 1988 the Israelis were acknowledging that they had an unprecedented situation on their hands. Defense Minister Rabin took a strong law-and-order approach, publicly sanctioning a policy of beatings and breaking of bones as part of an attempt to frighten the young Palestinians who threw rocks and Molotov cocktails at heavily armed soldiers. Within days images of savage Israeli beatings of Palestinian youngsters were a part of the American evening television news. Public reaction was strong. Even from within the normally pro-Israeli American Jewish community there was an outpouring of criticism and concern.

Several developments then took place that convinced Secretary of State Shultz to reengage his prestige in trying to get Arab-Israeli peace talks started.[16] First, in a six and one-half page letter to Shultz dated January 17, 1988, Shamir hinted that the Israeli position on "autonomy" for the Palestinians might be softening. Second, American Jewish leaders, as well as some Israeli politicians, began to urge Shultz to become more actively involved. Third, President Husni Mubarak of Egypt came to Washington to make a forceful and convincing plea that American leadership was urgently needed to ward off a radicalization of the entire region.

Shultz approached the challenge methodically. He did not make a flamboyant speech, nor did he hold out great hopes of a breakthrough. But he did begin to explore ideas with all the parties, this time including Syria, the Soviets, and some individual Palestinians, as well as with Jordan and the Israelis. At the end of his second trip to the region in as many months, on March 4, 1988, Shultz formalized his initiative in a proposal he described as a "blend of ideas" designed to repackage and streamline the Camp David Accords.[17] (See appendix I.)

The Shultz initiative, as it was immediately labeled, was certainly the most important U.S. involvement in Arab-Israeli peacemaking since Reagan's peace initiative in September 1982. In essence, Shultz outlined the conventional goal of a comprehensive peace to be achieved through direct bilateral negotiations based on Resolutions 242 and 338. But Shultz added a new element with what he called the "interlock" between the negotiations on the transitional period for the West Bank and Gaza and the negotiations on "final status." Shultz had long felt that the time scale envisioned in Camp David should be compressed, and his initiative explicitly ensured that it would be.

The Palestinian issue, according to Shultz, should be addressed in negotiations between an Israeli delegation and a Jordanian-Palestinian delegation. Six months would be set aside for negotiating transitional arrangements. In the seventh month negotiations on the final status of the West Bank and Gaza would start—regardless of the outcome of the first phase of negotiations. A target date of one year for negotiating the final status of the territories was mentioned. Assuming that agreement could be reached on transitional arrangements, a transitional period would begin at an early date and would continue for three years. The United States, Shultz said, would participate in both sets of negotiations and would put forward a draft agreement on transitional arrangements for the consideration of the parties.

Preceding the bilateral negotiations between Israel and a Jordanian-Palestinian delegation, there would be an international conference. The secretary general of the United Nations would invite the regional parties and the permanent members of the Security Council.[18] All participants in the conference would have to accept Resolutions 242 and 338. Although the negotiating parties, by agreement, might report to the conference from time to time, the conference would have no power to impose its views or to veto the results of the negotiations.

Shultz also said that Palestinians should be represented in a combined Jordanian-Palestinian delegation. That delegation would deal with the Palestinian issue in its entirety, and those negotiations would be independent of any other negotiation.

In the months that followed his initiative, Shultz doggedly tried to wear down the opponents of his initiative in both Israel and the Arab world. His biggest problem was Prime Minister Shamir, who blasted the idea of an international conference—which Shultz saw as a marginal part of his initiative—in no uncertain terms. Shamir also rejected the "interlock" concept, claiming it was contrary to Camp David. As Shamir correctly noted, the Camp David Accords had made the "final status" talks dependent on prior success in reaching agreement on transitional arrangements. Under Shultz's proposal the talks on final status would begin whether or not agreement had been reached on an interim period, thus providing little incentive for the Palestinians to negotiate seriously on the initial transitional stage. The prospects for success in resolving the final-status issues were not bright, since, as Shamir said publicly, the exchange of territory for peace was foreign to him.[19]

Israeli criticism of the Shultz initiative was well publicized, even though Peres publicly welcomed the American effort. On the Arab side, King Hussein went to great lengths not to be put in the position of saying no to Shultz. He asked questions, sought clarifications, played hard to get, referred publicly to the importance of including the PLO in the game, and generally tried to keep his shrinking options open.

The Palestinian response was more categorical. Though pleased to see the United States responding to the uprising, the Palestinian leaders were unhappy with the second-class treatment they were given in the Shultz plan. They saw themselves as being assigned, at best, to the role of junior partner to Jordan.

The Soviet Union was also unenthusiastic about a central feature of the Shultz plan, the international conference. Whereas Shamir professed fears that the conference would become authoritative and would work to undermine the Israeli position, the Soviet concern was just the opposite. The international conference, as envisaged by the Americans, appeared to the Soviets to be only symbolic. The Soviets wanted a real role in the negotiating process, not just an opportunity to legitimize a made-in-America initiative that would ultimately leave them on the sidelines.

Syria, likewise, was cool to the Shultz proposal. Only Mubarak, whose country was already at peace with Israel, openly endorsed the new American plan.[20]

In the face of these obstacles the Shultz plan never had much chance of complete success. Nonetheless, it had wide support in American public opinion. There was little criticism of any features of the proposal, except for some sour words from Henry Kissinger about the whole idea of an international conference. Shultz and his colleagues were no doubt hopeful that they would get a lucky break and that a negotiating process might be started on their watch. But they also spoke of other purposes behind the initiative. Most important, they wanted to influence Israeli public opinion. With the prospect of peace negotiations with their Arab neighbors, the Israeli public, it was hoped, would vote in the scheduled fall 1988 elections for a leadership committed to compromise positions. That possibility might, of course, prove to be wishful thinking; much would depend on Shultz's producing an acceptable Arab partner for peace talks. Still, the American intention was to help shape the political debate in Israel so that the elections would become a referendum, of sorts, on peace.

The Shultz plan depended crucially on cooperation with King Hussein. During four trips to the Middle East in the first half of 1988, Shultz had tried to persuade Hussein, and had even reached out, without much success, to Palestinians in the West Bank. On July 31, however, the foundations of the Shultz initiative collapsed, when King Hussein, in an official statement, relinquished all Jordanian legal and administrative ties to the West Bank, stating bluntly that henceforth the PLO would be responsible for the Palestinians living there.[21]

A U.S.-PLO DIALOGUE?

With Jordan at least temporarily out of the picture, one might have thought the United States would lose interest in pursuing Arab-Israeli peace initiatives. Especially in an election year, attention was bound to be focused elsewhere. But each day the news from Israel brought more images of violence and radicalization of the Palestinians, particularly among the youth, as well as signs of increasing Islamic militancy. No one in Washington was comfortable with the worsening situation between Israel and the Palestinians. But what could be done, especially prior to both Israeli and American elections?

The idea of establishing direct contacts between Washington and the

PLO had frequently been explored in previous years. Insofar as there was episodic interest in the idea among American officials, the goal was to moderate the PLO position on peace with Israel and open the way for direct participation by legitimate Palestinian representatives in negotiations.[22] At least grudgingly, most American policymakers accepted the fact that the PLO was the most widely supported spokesman for the Palestinians. Only King Hussein was ever seen as a possible alternative. So, in one way or another, most administrations had tried to develop some contacts with the PLO.

As early as 1974 Kissinger had authorized meetings between the PLO and Vernon Walters, then with the CIA. In Beirut, intelligence operatives had maintained contacts for purposes of exchanging information on security. On occasion, diplomatic messages were exchanged in these channels. But after Kissinger's 1975 pledge that the United States would not recognize or negotiate with the PLO unless the PLO acknowledged Israel's right to exist and accepted Resolution 242, official contacts had been rare. The pledge had not stopped intermediaries from exchanging messages, sometimes with authorization and sometimes on their own.[23] But no ongoing, high-level, openly acknowledged relationship had ever existed between the United States and the PLO.

Few would have expected the pro-Israeli Reagan or the equally pro-Israeli Shultz to alter this policy. And these two men would probably argue that, in fact, they did not. Yet it was on their watch, in the waning days of the Reagan presidency, that the United State finally agreed to begin an official dialogue with the PLO.

According to the standard version of what happened, the PLO, in danger of being marginalized as the *intifada* gained momentum, and under pressure from both the Arab states and the Soviets, finally met the well-known American conditions, and therefore the dialogue began.[24] That is only part of the story.

As early as April 1988 a small group of American Jewish leaders began to explore the possibility with the Swedish government of meeting with the PLO to formulate a well-developed statement of the PLO's commitment to a peace settlement with Israel.[25] The Swedish foreign minister, Sten Andersson, had been a good friend of Israel during his career, but had been appalled by what he had seen during a visit to Israel and the occupied territories. Thus he set about trying to build bridges between Palestinians and Israelis, but soon settled on the idea of starting with a meeting between PLO leaders and prominent American Jews.

He informed George Shultz of his intentions. Hearing no objections, Andersson quietly went forward with his plans.

By his own account Shultz was not much interested in this exercise in private diplomacy, apparently paying little attention to it until later in the year.[26] He did, however, hold Andersson in high regard and took him seriously as a professional diplomat who could be trusted. This recognition proved to be important in the last phases of establishing the dialogue.

Meanwhile another track of private diplomacy opened up, to explore formulations the PLO and the United States might agree upon, initially in private, that would meet the political needs of both sides for beginning talks. The impetus for this initiative came from a Palestinian-American, Mohamed Rabie, shortly after King Hussein announced his decision to break legal ties to the West Bank.[27] Rabie was convinced that the PLO would now be ready to accept the American conditions if it could be assured in advance that an official dialogue would ensue, along with some expression of American support for the idea of Palestinian self-determination.[28]

By mid-August this initiative had been reviewed with the State Department. Draft statements that the PLO might make, and a corresponding American reply, had been reviewed.[29] The American attitude toward the initiative, to be conveyed to the PLO, was spelled out as follows:

—There has been no change in what it will take for the United States to agree to deal with the PLO.

—The United States and the PLO have come close to agreement in the past, only to see the chance slip away. If a serious effort is to be made now, there must be clarity on both sides. Ambiguity would be counterproductive, especially on the eve of Israeli elections.

—If the PLO made the kind of statement the United States required, talks could begin right away. For political reasons certain things may be easier to do after the U.S. elections, but there is no need to wait.

—Any conditional clause accompanying a statement of acceptance of Resolution 242 will not be accepted by the United States. Whatever conditions the PLO wishes to state should be done in a separate paragraph. The United States needs a "clean" acceptance of 242.

—The proposed U.S. statement seems fairly close to what the United States might be willing to say, but it will have to be reviewed personally by Secretary Shultz at the appropriate time.

—This initiative is worthwhile "if the PLO is serious." A very small group will be in charge of the initiative on the American side and will be available at all times. No other channel is pursuing this course.[30]

Shortly thereafter Rabie left for Tunis, where he presented the documents and the idea of the initiative to Arafat and other top PLO leaders. After lengthy talks he returned to Washington in early September with PLO approval of a slightly revised formulation, conditional on the United States making a statement that would approximate the sample that had been discussed with, but not yet approved by, Washington.[31] This information was immediately passed to State and was received with interest. Shultz felt he could help the next administration by starting the dialogue, but he was not prepared to endorse Palestinian self-determination, which he saw as a code word for a Palestinian state, as the necessary price.

For the Reagan administration the issue now arose of whether to tip its hand on what it would say in exchange for the PLO's acceptance of 242, its recognition of Israel's right to exist, and its renunciation of terrorism. Over the ensuing weeks news came from Tunis of impatience to hear the official American position. In mid-September the Soviets were informed by the PLO of the initiative, which they reportedly supported.

On September 16 Shultz made a major speech to a pro-Israeli group at the Wye Plantation in Maryland. He explained why the United States would not endorse the idea of Palestinian self-determination if it were seen as meaning an automatic right to statehood. He did add, however, that in negotiations the Palestinians were "free to argue for independence." But negotiations were the key thing.[32]

As frustrations began to mount on both sides, Shultz authorized that an oral message be conveyed to Rabie for Arafat on September 23, 1988. It stated: "We welcomed the receipt of the initiative, which we recognize as a serious effort. This issue has been given careful consideration and will continue to be seriously discussed. We expect to provide our reaction in six weeks or so." In brief, the American response to the proposed PLO statement would be sent after the Israeli and American elections.[33] But already one could detect that the Reagan administration was not passively awaiting PLO compliance. It was signaling a positive attitude and was reiterating that talks would in fact begin as soon as the well-known conditions were met. Previously, the stated policy was that talks could not take place unless the PLO accepted the American conditions, but even PLO acceptance of those conditions would not necessarily result in an official dialogue. Now it was explicitly stated that talks would follow immediately on the PLO's acceptance of the American terms.

In an effort to avoid having this initiative wither in the intervening weeks, the PLO provided a glimpse of its plans. On October 19 the PLO conveyed the position that it intended to take at the upcoming meeting of the Palestine National Congress (PNC). It would accept the principle of a two-state solution to the conflict, anchoring its acceptance in UN Resolution 181 of 1947, which had called for the partition of Palestine into two states and had been rejected by the Arabs at the time. In addition, the PLO would accept 242 and 338 as the basis for an international conference, along with the recognition of the rights of the Palestinian people, including their right to self-determination. The PLO would also condemn terrorism. After adopting these positions officially, the PLO would make the statement the United States wanted, and then the United States should respond.

On the basis of this information, several problems could be foreseen. The PLO still seemed to be insisting on American acceptance of Palestinian self-determination as the price for accepting 242. While condemning terrorism, the PLO was not willing to renounce it. Also, Israel's right to exist was not explicitly mentioned.

Shortly after receiving this message, the administration was told by the Jordanians that Arafat was no longer insisting on recognition of the Palestinian right to self-determination. If Israeli withdrawal could be achieved, and with the Jordanian legal claim to the territories annulled, the Palestinians would become the ruling authority in any territory vacated by Israel. While logical, the Jordanian position was not automatically credited as an accurate reflection of the PLO position.

With the Palestine National Congress scheduled to meet in November, Arafat conveyed some uneasiness about the reliability of the channel being used to communicate between Washington and Tunis.[34] More to the point, most likely, he was disappointed by what he was hearing. Shultz was not willing to tip his hand until after the PNC had met.

As that meeting approached, results of the Israeli and American elections came in. The Israeli elections again produced a standoff between the Likud and Labor parties, which in due course led to a Likud-led coalition with Labor, but this time without a rotation of the premiership and with Moshe Arens as foreign minister instead of the more dovish Shimon Peres, who moved over to the finance ministry. Rabin stayed on as defense minster, so Labor continued to hold influential posts in the cabinet. But foreign-policy decisions would henceforth be solidly under Shamir's control.

The American elections were more conclusive than those in Israel just a few days earlier. Vice President George Bush defeated Governor Michael Dukakis of Massachusetts in a landslide. A narrow window was now open during which a U.S.-PLO agreement might still be reached before the Reagan administration left office. Bush was especially eager that this be done before he was sworn in, but he did not play an important role in the decisions concerning the PLO.

When Arafat convened the PNC from November 12 to 15, he succeeded in pushing through his political program and in declaring the existence of a Palestinian state with himself as president.[35] The state was presumably to be established alongside Israel in the West Bank and Gaza. The PLO appeared to be accepting 242, but not unconditionally. And some of the language in the political document continued to express old slogans. Shultz was unimpressed.

Meanwhile the Swedish initiative was beginning to bear fruit. An initial meeting of PLO representatives and American Jewish leaders had been held in late November, and agreement had been reached on a general political statement. It took the form of an agreed interpretation of the recent PNC resolutions. The culmination of this effort was to be a public meeting of the American Jewish leaders with Arafat in Stockholm during which the new statement would be released. Before the meeting Andersson contacted Shultz to ask if he could convey anything of importance to Arafat. Shultz, who had just turned down Arafat's request for a visa to come to the United Nations on grounds that the PLO was a terrorist group, decided nonetheless to respond to Andersson.[36]

GETTING THE WORDS RIGHT

In a letter dated December 3, 1988, Shultz conveyed the long-awaited American position, along with a text of exactly what Arafat would have to say to meet the American conditions. In his letter Shultz made it clear he would not bargain further over the language. He also noted that the PLO could add other points to the basic statement, but that these should not condition or contradict its acceptance of the U.S. conditions. Finally, Shultz added that nothing in his letter should imply that the United States was prepared to recognize an independent Palestinian state. (See appendix J.)

The proposed PLO statement conveyed to Arafat by Andersson on December 7 read as follows:

As its contribution to the search for a just and lasting peace in the Middle East, the Executive Committee of the Palestine Liberation Organization wishes to issue the following official statement:

1. That it is prepared to negotiate with Israel a comprehensive peace settlement of the Arab-Israeli conflict on the basis of United Nations resolutions 242 and 338.

2. That it undertakes to live in peace with Israel and its other neighbors and to respect their right to exist in peace within secure and internationally recognized borders, as will the democratic Palestinian state which it seeks to establish in the West Bank and the Gaza Strip.

3. That it condemns individual, group and state terrorism in all its forms, and will not resort to it.

4. That it is prepared for a moratorium on all forms of violence, on a mutual basis, once negotiations begin.[37]

In return, Shultz promised, the United States would announce that it was prepared to begin substantive discussions with the PLO. The United States would recognize that the representatives of the Palestinians would have the right in the course of negotiations to raise all subjects of interest to them. Then, Shultz said, an American official would answer a planted question about whether the Palestinians could table their position on statehood, to which the answer would be "Yes, the Palestinians, as far as we are concerned, have the right to pursue an independent state through negotiations." This response was as close as Shultz would go to saying that Palestinians had a right to self-determination. In response to a PLO request, Shultz also agreed to answer a question on the international conference as follows: "The U.S. has long made its support for direct negotiations clear, but we remain prepared to consider any suggestion that may lead to direct negotiations toward a comprehensive peace. The initiative proposed by Secretary Shultz in the beginning of the year called for an international conference to begin direct negotiations. Any conference of this type must be organized so that it does not become an alternative to direct negotiations."

Arafat responded in two ways to Shultz's message. He told Andersson that he personally agreed to the language proposed by Shultz, and he even put his signature to the proposed text.[38] (See appendix J for Arafat's response.) But he added that he would have to seek agreement from the other members of the PLO Executive Committee. Then, in public, Arafat issued the statement that had been worked out between his representatives and the American Jewish leaders on November 21. Its operational language came close to meeting Shultz's concerns, but not quite. Instead of unconditionally accepting UN Resolutions 242 and 338 as the basis for negotiations with Israel, Arafat added the right of the Palestinians to self-determination as another basis for the conference, implying that this condition would have to be accepted in advance by the other participants, something that neither the United States nor Israel was prepared to do. Furthermore, though Arafat did "reject and condemn" terrorism in all its forms, he did not renounce it or pledge not to engage in it in the future. These may have seemed like verbal squabbles to some, but to Shultz they mattered. Perhaps most positive and significant, Arafat did state openly that the PLO "accepted the existence of Israel as a state in the region," a formulation he had not used before.

The next step in the process of trying to get Arafat to utter the magic words came during his appearance before a special session of the United Nations held in Geneva on December 13, 1988. Arafat had encountered some opposition within the PLO Executive Committee to the idea of using the precise language that Shultz had provided to Andersson. Nayif Hawatmeh was particularly hostile to the idea. Thus Arafat sent word to the Swedes that he would use the Shultz formulation in his speech, but it would be scattered throughout the text.[39] This message was apparently not clearly conveyed to the Americans, who were expecting to hear the exact words they had agreed upon.

As Arafat worked his way through his long and rambling speech, he made the point about "rejecting" and "condemning" terrorism in all its forms, but he did not "renounce" it.[40] Toward the end of the speech, Arafat addressed the issues of 242 and Israel's right to exist. The wording was complicated in Arabic but is probably best translated as follows:

The PLO will work to achieve a comprehensive peaceful settlement among the parties to the Arab-Israeli conflict, including the Palestinian state, Israel and other neighboring states, within the framework of the international conference for peace in the Middle East, in order to achieve equality and a balance of interests, especially the right of our people to liberation and national independence, and respect for everyone's right to exist, to peace and to security, according to Resolutions 242 and 338.

Some State Department officials listening to the speech felt that though Arafat had come close to doing so, he had not specifically mentioned negotiations with Israel or Israel's right to exist, nor had he renounced terrorism. Shultz and his influential assistant, Charles Hill, reacted negatively.[41] They had expected verbatim compliance and felt the speech was another sign that Arafat could not be trusted. The Swedes acknowledged that the speech did not meet the American conditions, but they felt it had almost done so. All Shultz would agree to was that Arafat could try one more time.

During the day on December 14 many people weighed in with Arafat—the president of Egypt, the Saudis, the Swedes, individual Americans—to try to persuade him to utter the exact words that Shultz was insisting on. Finally, in the company of several rich Palestinian businessmen who were in telephone contact with the State Department to check on acceptable wording, Arafat agreed to hold a press conference, where he finally said, in English (see appendix K for the full text):

Yesterday . . . I also made a reference to our acceptance of resolutions 242 and 338 as the basis for negotiations with Israel within the framework of the international conference. . . . In my speech also yesterday, it was clear that we mean . . . the right of all parties concerned in the Middle East conflict to exist in peace and security and, as I have mentioned, including the state of Palestine, Israel and other neighbors according to the resolution 242 and 338.

As for terrorism, I renounced it yesterday in no uncertain terms, and yet, I repeat for the record that we totally and absolutely renounce all forms of terrorism, including individual, group, and state terrorism.

Shultz finally agreed that Arafat had met the American conditions and so informed Colin Powell, the national security adviser, who then sought the president's approval to announce that the U.S-PLO discussions could begin at the level of the American ambassador in Tunisia. Reagan reportedly gave his consent quite easily. On December 14 the United States finally lifted the ban on dealing with the PLO. (See appendix K.) At least the incoming Bush administration would not have to wrestle with the problem of opening a dialogue. It, however, would face the equally daunting task of giving substance to the talks and relating them to the broader peace process.

ASSESSING THE REAGAN ERA

Reagan remained a popular figure throughout most of his presidency. He was widely credited with restoring American self-confidence after the gloom of the Carter years. More tangibly, he presided over the last phase of the cold war. By the time he left office, the world seemed a safer place as the two great nuclear powers began to reduce their bloated arsenals of weapons of mass destruction. On the economic front, many Americans were better off as the 1980s came to an end, but many at the lower rungs of the economic ladder were poorer than ever. By most measures the gap between rich and poor had grown significantly. And then there was the deficit. For all of Reagan's talk about the virtues of a balanced budget, never once did he submit one, nor did Congress come close to passing one. As a result, interest on the national debt had become the second largest item in the budget by 1989.

For most Americans these were the bread-and-butter issues that counted as they thought about the 1980s. But they were also aware that Reagan had blundered badly with his "arms for hostages" initiative in 1985–86. Some might even remember the horrifying scenes of Beirut being bombed, the Sabra and Shatila massacres, and the explosions in Beirut in 1983 that took the lives of more than three hundred Americans, more than died in any other Middle East situation under any American administration. Reagan and his top officials, however, never seemed to be blamed for such disasters, which led to the accusation that this was a "Teflon presidency."

Few broad overviews of the Reagan presidency take note of his Arab-Israeli diplomacy. No such monument as Camp David sticks in collective memory when Reagan's Middle East policy is evoked. Some would even say that there was no policy toward Arab-Israeli peace during the Reagan period. But that is manifestly untrue. Reagan, with Shultz as his mentor, gave one of the most carefully crafted speeches ever on American policy toward the Arab-Israeli conflict. A decade later it still set the parameters of American policy by both embracing and extending the Camp David Accords. At the time it enjoyed broad bipartisan support. Even the American Israel Public Affairs Committee (AIPAC) felt compelled to praise the speech, despite Begin's ferocious rejection of it. But if Reagan was unexcelled as a speechmaker, he and his aides failed to devise a strategy for translating words into practical diplomatic steps. In their defense, it can be said that even a brilliant strategist might have found it difficult to move the Likud governments of Begin and Shamir from their entrenched positions.

Still, in both 1983 and 1985, and especially the latter, Reagan and Shultz might have inched the peace process forward had they shown more drive and determination. Nothing like Kissinger's intense shuttle diplomacy, or Carter's summitry, was tried until early 1988, by which point time was running out. So the Reagan period produced little in the way of tangible progress toward Arab-Israeli peace, although several helpful additions to the Camp David framework were put forward by Shultz. On balance, Israel and its neighbors were no closer to agreement in 1988 than they had been in 1980.

Perhaps the most one can say is that things had not deteriorated beyond repair. Egypt and Israel were still at peace, even though the temperature of the relationship was tepid. The Palestinians were engaged in a sustained rebellion against the Israeli occupation, which convinced Jordan's King Hussein to pull back from the exposed position he had adopted in 1987. The long-pursued Jordan option was dead. But the Palestinians were signaling a willingness to accept explicitly Israel's existence as a state in the region, provided they could establish their own ministate alongside it in the West Bank and Gaza. This position, long discussed by Palestinians in private, finally came into the open in 1988 and, through a tortuous diplomatic effort cautiously encouraged by Shultz, led to the opening of a U.S.-PLO dialogue, one of the greatest surprises of the Reagan era.

The prospects for Arab-Israeli peace, however, did not advance during the 1980s under Reagan, and in one dimension the objective situation became more difficult. At the time of the signing of the Camp David Accords, about 10,000 Israeli settlers lived in the West Bank and Gaza (in addition to another 100,000 or so in the Greater Jerusalem area). Before Reagan, all American presidents had maintained that Israeli settlement activities in the occupied territories were not only illegal under the terms of the Fourth Geneva Convention but were obstacles to peace. Reagan, apparently influenced by the legal arguments of Eugene Rostow, professor of international law at Yale and a prominent spokesman for neoconservative, pro-Israeli views, switched position on settlements.[42] Henceforth American policy was that Israeli settlements in the occupied territories were not illegal, although they were still viewed as obstacles to peace.

Reagan's change of policy on settlements was not the reason that the number of Israeli settlers in the occupied territories grew to nearly 100,000 by 1992. But the permissive American attitude certainly encouraged the determined settlement policy of Shamir and Sharon. Some even concluded in the early 1980s that settlement activity had gone so far that a negotiated Israeli-Palestinian agreement was no longer possible.[43] Even those who resisted this conclusion acknowledged the difficulty of dealing with the large number of Israeli settlers living beyond the "green line." Reagan personally never seemed to worry much about this issue, because he was essentially uninvolved with the details of trying to advance the peace process. But his successor was to inherit the settlements issue as a major complication both in U.S.-Israeli relations and in the revived peace process of the 1990s.

It is hard not to conclude that Reagan's disengaged style as president, his lack of curiosity, and his passivity on issues related to the Middle East were impediments to creative U.S. peace diplomacy.[44] He was unwilling or unable to discipline his quarreling subordinates (Lebanon); he tolerated actions taken in his name that seemed to undercut his ostensible policies (Iran-Contra); he had no sense of strategy for dealing with Arabs and Israelis, except to make the Israelis feel secure and the Arabs almost desperate. Fortunately, during his watch the Soviet Union began to unravel, so his weaknesses and oversimplifications did not prove to be disastrous. And in his way he did lend his prestige to steps that his successor might build on.

When a president is passive and uninvolved, how much can his secretary of state hope to achieve? Shultz clearly dominated diplomatic moves toward the Arab-Israeli conflict throughout his tenure. During the last two years he was in charge of all aspects of foreign policy and was heading a team of considerable ability. Bureaucratic bickering came to an end. On some Middle East issues, such as the reflagging of Kuwaiti tankers, a policy of nuance was carried out successfully. But on Arab-Israeli matters Shultz seemed to hesitate when opportunities opened up, as in 1985. He stuck doggedly to his belief that King Hussein could be drawn into peace talks, and reassessed the situation only when his policy had clearly failed. His own formulation on an international conference was so convoluted that it failed to win support from either Arabs or Israelis, although some of the points survived in a different form under President Bush and his secretary of state, James Baker.

How much of Shultz's hesitation came from a realization that he could not count on much help from the president he served? How much came from a conviction that the Arabs needed to face up convincingly to the reality of Israel before the United States could help them? How much stemmed from a genuine admiration for the tough, pro-American Israelis with whom he dealt? How much can be attributed to domestic politics and the role of the pro-Israeli lobby? Shultz has not been communicative about his own motives, and those who worked most closely with him often found him enigmatic. But it seems fair to conclude that he admired the Israelis and was reluctant to pressure them; he became frustrated with the Arab leaders with whom he dealt and was skeptical about the wisdom of running after them unless they developed a strong commitment of their own to peace with Israel; and he shared Reagan's distrust of Soviet motives, although less so by the end of his tenure.

For both Reagan and Shultz—and they were the two key figures who counted on Arab-Israeli issues—policies emerged more often as reactions to events in the Middle East region than as part of a grand design. The Reagan initiative of 1982 was sparked by the Israeli invasion of Lebanon; the ill-conceived May 17, 1983, agreement between Israel and Lebanon was largely sponsored at Israel's behest; and the Israelis helped to plant the idea of the opening to Iran, which was then twisted and distorted by too zealous, insufficiently supervised Reaganites into an "arms for hostages" scheme and a slick means for avoiding the congressional ban on aid to the Contras in Nicaragua.

In much the same vein, the Shultz initiative of 1988 was a reaction to the *intifada*. Without the eruption of violence in the occupied territories, Shultz would probably not have devised his plan. And the opening to the PLO was a grudging reaction to King Hussein's announced relinquishment of responsibility for the West Bank.

When Reagan had strong convictions, as on how to deal with the Soviet Union, some elements of strategy became visible in the unfolding policies. But when Reagan was indifferent or uncertain, and when his advisers disagreed or were hesitant to act, policy became derivative or reactive. Not surprisingly, the record of promoting Arab-Israeli accommodation was unimpressive.

Even in the realm of U.S.-Israeli relations the legacy of the Reagan era is uncertain. Aid continued to flow at unprecedentedly high levels; Congress was unusually sympathetic to Israel; potential quarrels, such as the Pollard spying affair[45] were treated as aberrations; revelations about Israel's nuclear capabilities were ignored;[46] and the entire relationship was given a strategic rationale that had previously been missing, or had at least been less central.[47]

Many Israelis were delighted with the result. They basked in the glow of being treated as a "non-NATO ally"; American aid to the Israeli defense industry was welcomed; intelligence cooperation reached new heights. But without a vigorous peace process, the United States and Israel risked losing one of the solid links of the past. After all, the major steps in forging close U.S.-Israeli ties had come in the context of moves toward peace. Over time, would the American public and future administrations continue to provide generous support to an Israel that was not making moves toward peace with its neighbors? If the blame for the lack of peace was clearly on the Arab side, the answer might still be yes. But what if the perception was less clear? What if Israel was seen as more of an obstacle to peace than the Arabs were?[48] What if Israel's occupation of the West Bank and Gaza was seen as unjustified by a younger generation of Americans who no longer felt such close ties to Israel and who had no memory of how the conflict had come about?

President Reagan and the Likud party seemed to feel that a strong strategic alliance against the Soviet Union and its regional allies would provide enough support for U.S.-Israeli relations even without an active peace process. But what if the cold war ended and the Soviet Union was no longer a threat to the region? What then would bind the United States and Israel if not the more conventional shared values and common purposes? Could the pro-Israeli lobby alone keep the relationship intact if its strategic and moral premises were called into question? These matters never seemed to be considered during the Reagan period, and yet within a very short time U.S.-Israeli relations entered a very difficult period. Some would place the blame on Reagan's and Shultz's successors. Others would point to the overvaluation of the strategic relationship with Israel and the underinvestment in peacemaking during the Reagan era.

PART SIX

The Bush Presidency

CHAPTER FIFTEEN

Getting to the Table: Bush and Baker, 1989–92

Rarely, if ever, has a president assumed office with a more impressive foreign affairs résumé than George Bush. Before coming to the White House in January 1989, he had been director of Central Intelligence, head of the American diplomatic mission to China, and ambassador to the United Nations, and had spent eight years as vice-president under Ronald Reagan, with special responsibility for crisis management for the National Security Council. In addition, Bush was from a political family, had served with distinction as a pilot in World War II, was a graduate of Yale, had been elected to Congress, was a successful businessman in the Texas oil patch, and had been national chairman of the Republican party.

While Bush's credentials were impressive, they gave little clue to his own deeply held views on foreign affairs. He had not been in positions where he had primary responsibility for making and articulating policy. Except for his long stint as vice-president, during which he kept any views that differed from Reagan's closely guarded, he had not, in fact, held most of his jobs for long. During his unsuccessful bid for the presidency in 1980, he had presented himself as a moderately conservative Republican but had not spelled out his views on foreign policy. For a man of wide experience, he had left few traces.

Unlike Reagan, Bush was not a skilled communicator, at least not on television. He seemed to prefer informal meetings and off-the-cuff dealings with the press to set-piece speeches. Early on it became clear he would be a hands-on president when it came to foreign policy. He, after all, knew dozens of foreign leaders; he was reasonably conversant with most major foreign-policy issues; he had an appetite for dealing with the details and personalities involved in world affairs; he was inclined to pick up the telephone at a moment's notice and talk to leaders around the world.

Bush was clearly an internationalist who saw a continuing role for American leadership as the world entered the ambiguities of the post–cold war era. Initially his internationalism was tinged with a skeptical view of the Soviet Union and its leader, Mikhail Gorbachev. Bush's hard-line stance was rather surprising in light of Reagan's own mellowing toward Gorbachev in 1987–88.

One might have concluded from Bush's background that he would use the unique powers of the presidency to conduct a foreign policy that was active in pursuit of American interests, internationalist in tone, practical in execution, and essentially aimed at upholding the status quo. Nothing in Bush's past suggested that he had a radical vision for transforming international politics. He was, in fact, often criticized for not having "the vision thing." His aides described his style as "principled pragmatism." Others saw in Bush's views a familiar state-centered, balance-of-power approach to world affairs.

With respect to the Middle East, Bush had left few hints during his career of how he felt about the Arab-Israeli conflict. It was commonly known that he had urged Reagan to take a tough line against the Israeli invasion of Lebanon in 1982. As vice-president he had gone to Saudi Arabia in the mid-1980s to urge the Saudis not to let the price of oil drop too low. He was on good terms with the Saudi ambassador to Washington, Prince Bandar ibn Sultan. And it was rumored that he did not share Reagan's emotional attachment to Israel. But none of these observations added up to much with respect to policy toward the Arab-Israeli conflict.

As secretary of state, Bush selected a close friend and political ally, James A. Baker III, formerly Reagan's chief of staff and treasury secretary, as well as the manager of Bush's successful bid for the presidency in 1988. Baker, though never running for office himself, was a quintessential politician. His strengths were alleged to be found in "deal making." If politics was the art of the possible, then Baker was a supreme politician. And he would doubtless approach diplomacy in much the same way. His lack of experience in foreign affairs counted for little compared with the excellent rapport, sometimes tinged with friendly rivalry, that he had with the president.[1] Besides, he was a quick study. Bush and Baker seemed likely to form a team that might not include many other players. Both men prized secrecy and played their cards close to the vest.

Baker had a reputation among Republicans as a "moderate." Whether this label was deserved or not, Baker was clearly not cut from neoconservative cloth. Like Bush, he was likely to be problem-oriented, tactical in his approach, and suspicious of grand theory and strategy—a manager more than a conceptualizer. Rumor had it that Baker harbored ambitions of one day becoming president, which might mean he would seek to use his time as secretary of state to preside over a series of international successes, while avoiding anything that seemed destined for failure or aroused too much controversy.

Like the president, Baker had given few hints of his views on Arab-Israeli issues. An article on Baker, published in February 1989, portrayed him as a man of great self-control and manipulative skills. His favorite pastime, it seemed, was turkey shooting, which, in Baker's words, consists of "getting them where you want them, on your terms. Then *you* control the situation, not them. *You* have the options. Pull the trigger or don't. It doesn't matter once you've got them where you want them. The important thing is knowing that it's in your hands, that you can do whatever you determine is in your interest to do."[2]

Asked in an interview shortly before his confirmation as secretary of state what leverage the United States had in the Middle East, Baker replied:

The U.S. is and can be the most influential player. But it is important that we not permit the perception to develop that we can deliver peace, that we can deliver Israeli concessions. If there is going to be lasting peace, it will be the result of direct negotiations between the parties, not something mandated or delivered by anybody from the outside, including the U.S. We must do whatever we can to enhance the prospect of the parties negotiating the problem out among themselves. It is not the role of the U.S. to pressure Israel. At the same time, it is in Israel's interest to resolve the issue. Both sides have got to find a way to give something.[3]

Most new administrations take their bearings in foreign policy from the experiences of their immediate predecessors. In the case of Bush and Baker, they had been members of an administration whose record on Arab-Israeli peacemaking was hardly distinguished. It had produced plans and initiatives but few concrete achievements. It was a fair guess that Baker, in particular, would avoid launching new substantive plans, preferring to explore procedural openings and biding his time until the parties to the conflict showed a willingness to move. Part of this cautious stance was a matter of tactics; part was no doubt politics; and part was due to competing priorities, especially in the rapidly changing arena of East-West relations.[4]

WORKING ASSUMPTIONS

If Bush and Baker shared certain ways of looking at foreign policy, including the Middle East, they certainly did not seem to have a fully developed rationale for their low-key approach to Arab-Israeli peacemaking. That was provided by a small group of like-minded aides at the State Department and the National Security Council. Most important was Dennis Ross, head of Baker's Policy Planning Staff, a specialist on U.S.-Soviet relations with a strong interest in the Middle East. Ross had worked at the Pentagon, and at the NSC under Reagan, and had then joined the Bush campaign in 1988 as a foreign-policy adviser. During the summer of 1988, just before joining the campaign, he had played an important part in developing the logic of how a new administration should tackle the Arab-Israeli conflict.

As a member of the grandly labeled "Presidential Study Group" that produced an influential pamphlet entitled *Building for Peace*, Ross associated himself with an incrementalist approach to Arab-Israeli peacemaking. From this perspective the United States should be wary of substantive plans, international conferences, and highly visible initiatives. Instead the new administration should start from the realization that the Arab-Israeli conflict was not "ripe" for resolution. The differences between the parties were too great. A premature move to negotiations would doubtless fail. So, small steps to change the political environment should receive attention. The parties should be encouraged to engage in a prenegotiation phase of confidence-building measures. And the Soviets should be left on the sidelines until they had demonstrated by their actions a willingness and an ability to play a constructive role in peacemaking by putting pressure on the Arabs and reassuring the Israelis.[5]

Another important contributor to *Building for Peace* was Richard Haass, author of a book called *Conflicts Unending*, which promoted the tautological thesis of "ripeness" as the key to negotiations.[6] (A conflict is "ripe for resolution" if it can be solved.) Haass became the head of the Middle East office on the National Security Council staff. If taken literally, his views would call for a low-profile American approach to the region. In his analysis of the Arab-Israeli conflict, the United States could err by being too active in trying to promote a settlement. That, he argued, could make a difficult situation even worse. Until the parties to the conflict were ready to negotiate, the United States should concentrate on small steps to improve the environment.[7]

This "gardening" metaphor for Middle East policy seemed founded on a belief that previous bouts of American activism had been counterproductive. They had raised Arab expectations about American pressures on Israel, caused the Israelis to adopt a defensive stance to ward off such pressures, and had made Washington the centerpiece of all diplomatic moves, instead of placing emphasis on the parties' need to deal directly with one another. Like an attentive gardener, the United States might help the ripening process by watering the plants and weeding and fertilizing, but that was pretty much the proper extent of Washington's involvement until the fruit was ripe and ready to harvest.

Critics of the "ripening" approach thought the fruit might well rot before it ever got harvested. Time did not seem to matter to the gardeners. They appeared to believe that by concentrating on procedural issues first, the hard substantive issues could be dealt with more easily at a later date. Ripening seemed to be a natural process, not something that could be advanced or impeded by political action. But what if the parties to the conflict were not uniformly hostile to the idea of a settlement, had mixed feelings, or were evenly divided? In such circumstances, should the United States sit back and wait until things were clarified, or should it try to accelerate the ripening process by deliberate interventions of its own? These questions were all unanswerable in theory. Time would tell whether they received answers in practice.

Implicit in this approach was an anti-Carter, anti-Kissinger perspective. No comprehensive plans, no high-level shuttle diplomacy were warranted in this phase of the conflict. To many Israelis this was long-awaited music; for the Arabs, this approach led to intense suspicions.[8] It was not long before these initial assumptions were put to the test.[9]

On the surface the views articulated by Bush's Middle East team seemed to indicate strong support for Israel. But there was a catch. If and when the Palestinians or Syrians ever agreed to negotiate seriously with Israel, the United States might press Israel hard to reciprocate. At the outset of the administration, however, the assumption seemed to be that it was up to the Arab parties to move further. Prime Minister Yitzhak Shamir was viewed as a tough leader who could not be expected to make any concessions to the Arabs as a down payment for negotiations. Only if negotiations were under way was there a chance of moving Shamir off dead center.

No one in the Bush administration seemed sure whether Shamir's hard-line policy toward the Arabs was primarily a tactical ploy or an accurate reflection of his deepest beliefs. On balance, the judgment seemed to be that Shamir could be moved, but only slowly and carefully.

In any event, the administration's first initiative was built on the assumption that Shamir was interested in peace and could best be dealt with by pursuing ideas that bore his prior stamp of approval.

The paradox of the Bush presidency was that this initial agenda was probably more consonant with Israeli views than that of any previous president. And yet this same administration was soon widely viewed as the most hostile ever to Israel. The change, insofar as it was real, did not reflect a change of sentiment on the part of the top decisionmakers and their advisers.

THE TEAM

All along, Bush, Baker, and Brent Scowcroft, the national security adviser, were thought to be less emotionally involved with Israel than either Reagan or George Shultz had been. But no one in 1989 would have accused them of being anti-Israeli. And apart from Bush and Baker, the top echelons of the administration were filled with figures friendly to Israel, including the secretary of defense, Richard Cheney; the deputy secretary of state, Lawrence Eagleburger; and the entire Middle East team of Ross, Haass, Daniel Kurtzer and Aaron Miller. Several members of the team could speak Hebrew quite well. But no one who knew them felt that their sympathies were with the Likud party or Shamir. Rather, the Labor party, and especially Yitzhak Rabin, the Israeli defense minister, seemed more to their liking.

During most of 1989, as the new administration was developing its approach to the Middle East, other international issues demanded much attention. Relations with the Soviet Union and Gorbachev were of particular importance, and only toward the end of 1989 were Baker and Soviet Foreign Minister Eduard Shevardnadze beginning to develop an especially close bond. Meanwhile relations with China quickly soured after the Tiananmen crackdown in June 1989. Shortly thereafter the amazing sequence of events that resulted in the collapse of all the communist regimes of eastern Europe began, culminating in the dramatic execution of the Romanian dictator Nicolai Ceauşescu in the last days of 1989. With so many significant international developments taking place in 1989, it was a wonder that the administration had time left over for the Arab-Israeli conflict. Not surprisingly, caution was the watchword of the new "confidence-building" approach to Middle East peacemaking.

Early in 1989 Shamir and Rabin were told that the Bush administration would be interested in hearing new ideas on how to revive the peace process. Rabin, in particular, saw this as an invitation to Israel to set the agenda for the next round of diplomacy. By the time Shamir arrived in Washington in early April for his first meeting with President Bush, the Israeli cabinet had adopted a four-point proposal. Its centerpiece was a call for elections in the West Bank and Gaza to select non-PLO Palestinians with whom Israel would then negotiate, according to the Camp David formula, an interim agreement on self-government.[10] Implicit in this approach was that no international conference on the Middle East would take place, a point on which Likud and Labor differed and on which the Bush administration seemed to side with Shamir, at least for the moment. Washington's initial response to these ideas was sympathetic.

On May 22, 1989, Baker spoke at the annual AIPAC convention in Washington, D.C. Baker's remarks were predictably friendly toward Israel at the outset, noting the shared commitment to democratic values and the strong strategic partnership. Baker welcomed the Shamir initiative as "an important and positive start down the road toward constructing workable negotiations." He endorsed the idea of a prenegotiations phase of talks. Only when Baker turned to the missing element in the Shamir plan, the fate of the occupied territories, did he hit a discordant note. Interpreting UN Resolution 242 as requiring the exchange of land for peace, Baker referred to "territorial withdrawal" as a probable outcome of negotiations. Then, in a pointed reference to Shamir's ideology, Baker said: "For Israel, now is the time to lay aside, once and for all, the unrealistic vision of a greater Israel. Israeli interests in the West Bank and Gaza—security and otherwise—can be accommodated in a settlement based on Resolution 242. Forswear annexation. Stop settlement activity. Allow schools to reopen. Reach out to the Palestinians as neighbors who deserve political rights." The fact that Baker immediately enunciated a comparable list of requirements for the Palestinians did nothing to warm the chilly atmosphere that descended over the pro-Israeli crowd, which only a few years earlier had heard George Shultz, from the same platform, lead the chant "Hell no, PLO."[11]

Baker's speech, besides raising Israeli worries, marked a subtle shift toward a more active effort by the Bush administration to redesign the Shamir initiative into something that might be acceptable to the Palestinians. Doing so without losing Israeli support would be difficult, to say the least. Over the next several months Baker became increasingly involved in Arab-Israeli diplomacy, probing through his diplomatic contacts for any opening.

As of mid-1989 the operational goal of American policy was to persuade the PLO to allow negotiations with Israel to begin with Palestinians who were not from within the ranks of the PLO leadership per se. The reason was simple: Shamir, it was believed, would never agree to negotiate with the PLO.[12] At the same time it would be difficult for Washington to convince the PLO to stay entirely on the sidelines. After all, the PLO's claim to be the "sole, legitimate representative of the Palestinian people" was part of the bedrock of its position. Still, by the summer of 1989 the PLO was showing signs of flexibility on this score. The PLO could stay in the shadows on two conditions: if it could select any Palestinian delegation, and if at least one delegation member was from outside the West Bank and Gaza. The PLO also felt strongly that Palestinians residing in East Jerusalem could not be excluded from the list of eligible representatives, a point on which the United States had previously expressed its agreement.

Just as the United States was trying to win PLO acceptance of Shamir's election proposal as a starting point, strains began to develop in the bilateral U.S.-PLO talks that were being conducted in Tunis. First, a leak to the press revealed that the American ambassador had been meeting with Abu Iyad, a man associated in the minds of many Americans and Israelis with terrorism, but also one who had been instrumental in bringing about the shift of PLO policy toward greater pragmatism.[13] Shortly thereafter the Fatah Congress adopted a tough line. The Palestinians thought a U.S.-PLO meeting on August 14 had involved an American ultimatum that no Palestinians from outside the occupied territories could be included in a Palestinian delegation. That was not, in fact, a correct perception of American policy, but it contributed to a growing lack of mutual confidence.

As the U.S.-PLO dialogue faded during the summer, Egypt and Sweden stepped in to try to improve the prospects for getting the PLO to go along with Baker's approach. Because President Mubarak could deal directly with the PLO leader Yasir Arafat, officials in Washington soon found this was a more effective channel than the formal U.S.-PLO dialogue, from which Arafat was excluded. Egypt then became instrumental in crystallizing the PLO position. Mubarak, for example, spelled out, on behalf of the PLO, ten points that should govern elections in the West Bank and Gaza. Baker then responded, initially through diplomatic channels, to see if common ground could be found.[14]

By late in 1989 the Egyptians had indicated that Arafat had accepted

Baker's five points.[15] The most important of these points was the notion that the Palestinians could bring to the negotiations any position related to the peace process. The precise makeup of the list of Palestinians negotiators had not been settled, but a procedure had been agreed upon that would give Israel a virtual veto, but without calling it that. In short, the United States and Egypt would produce a list of Palestinians, after consultations with the PLO, that satisfied criteria laid down by the Israelis. Israel, in turn, would not ask too many questions about the origin of the list, provided the names were acceptable. No one knew for sure if Palestinians from East Jerusalem would be acceptable to Shamir, or whether someone from outside the territories might be included. But Baker was exploring all sorts of possibilities, including Palestinians with one residence in Jerusalem and one elsewhere; Palestinians who had recently been deported by Israel, but had normally been residents of the West Bank; and so on.

ISRAELI REACTIONS

Early in 1990 Baker seemed to feel he had Egyptian and Palestinian support for his basic approach. Now he turned up the heat on Shamir to accept what Baker kept insisting was Shamir's own plan. To start the process, Baker suggested that he meet with the Israeli and Egyptian foreign ministers in Cairo. The prime minister, by now, must have had his own reservations about taking this first step onto the slippery slope, but he also had ample domestic political reasons for balking. His right-wing allies, for example, were planning to bolt the coalition if Shamir accepted the American plan; Labor was threatening to withdraw from the national unity government if he did not.

In the midst of this political acrimony the Americans became alarmed at reports of large numbers of new immigrants from the Soviet Union going to the occupied territories to live. Shamir had minimized the issue, but in so doing he had made no mention of the large number of new immigrants moving into neighborhoods of East Jerusalem. President Bush, who felt strongly that settlements were an obstacle to peace, was fully briefed, with maps, on the location of new settlers, and he apparently believed Shamir had deliberately lied to him.

Meanwhile a powerful Likud voice, that of Benjamin Begin, son of the redoubtable Menachem, came out publicly against the Baker plan. The Likud establishment then met and recommended that Shamir not accept the plan. Just after that recommendation, word came from

Washington that Bush had spoken critically of Israeli settlements in the West Bank and East Jerusalem.[16] This was no slip of the tongue. American policy had long considered East Jerusalem to be part of the occupied territories,[17] but no previous president had singled East Jerusalem out for special comment when discussing settlements. The Israeli reaction was harsh. Shamir, who almost certainly had already decided to reject the Baker plan, now had a pretext for doing so, claiming that the United States had revealed its lack of objectivity as a potential mediator. With Shamir's blunt "no," the first phase of the Bush administration's peacemaking effort was put on hold.

For a few weeks Israeli internal politics was so uncertain that it seemed possible that Labor party leader Shimon Peres might be able to form a narrow coalition without the Likud. Had that occurred, there would have been widespread satisfaction in the Bush administration. But try as he might, Peres could not lure the religious parties away from Shamir, and when the dust had settled in May 1990, Shamir was still prime minister, but this time at the head of a very right-wing cabinet from which Labor was excluded.

CHALLENGES

While the Israelis were absorbed in their internal crisis, the Arab world seemed similarly disoriented. But there the proximate cause was the end of the cold war and the loss of Soviet patronage. Iraqi president Saddam Hussein chose the occasion of a meeting in Amman, Jordan, in late February 1990 to reflect on how the end of the cold war might lead to a Pax Americana-Hebraica in the Middle East.[18] For a leader who was receiving economic and political support from the United States, and who had been quietly assisted in his eight-year-long struggle against Iran, such comments might have been considered reckless. King Hussein, among others, thought the Iraqi leader was going too far in attacking Washington, but anti-American sentiment was on the rise in the Arab world, fueled, perhaps, by a sense of vulnerability in a one-superpower world, and reflecting as well the growing appeal of Islamic radicalism with its anti-Western, anti-Israeli overtones. Whatever the cause of these sentiments, Saddam seemed to be gambling on finding a positive Arab response to his increasingly strident attacks on the United States and Israel.[19]

With the peace process in limbo and anti-American sentiment being fanned from Baghdad, it was perhaps inevitable that the U.S.-PLO relationship would unravel. How it happened revealed the fragile under-pinnings of the dialogue on both sides. First came an unusually bloody incident in Israel, where a deranged soldier shot and killed seven Palestinians at Rishon le Zion. Subsequent riots resulted in more Palestinian dead. The PLO, with strong international backing, launched an appeal in the United Nations to take some action to prevent further violence against Palestinians in the occupied territories. Arafat was keen to come to New York to address a session of the UN. Bush and Baker did not share his enthusiasm, and a compromise deal seems to have been worked out. A special session of the UN would be held in Geneva, Arafat would be allowed to make his appeal, and the United States would support a resolution calling on the secretary general to send an envoy to the territories.

Just as the vote was about to be held on the resolution in Geneva, a Palestinian commando unit landed on the beach outside Tel Aviv. The Israelis managed to intercept and neutralize the group, which consisted of members of Abul Abbas' Palestine Liberation Front (the same group that had been responsible for the *Achille Lauro* affair), before any civilians were hurt, but it clearly seemed to be an intended terrorist action, at least as defined by Israelis and Americans.[20] As such, this event seemed to constitute a breach of the PLO pledge to renounce terrorism. In Israel and in the United States a cry went out for the United States to break off the dialogue with the PLO.

Under considerable political pressure at home, Bush authorized his representative at the UN to veto the resolution on conditions in the occupied territories, a step that infuriated Arafat and many other Palestinians. But Bush was reluctant to take the next step of ending the dialogue. Instead he insisted that the PLO condemn the commando raid and discipline those responsible for it. In particular, the United States wanted action taken against Abul Abbas, who was still a member of the PLO executive committee, although his membership was apparently frozen, which meant that he did not participate in decisionmaking.

Arafat seemed to be in no mood to meet the American conditions. Instead he began to spend increasing amounts of time in Baghdad, and reports were even received that he was thinking of moving his political headquarters there from Tunis. In mid-June, Arafat's deputy, Salah Khalaf (Abu Iyad), expressed his concern that Arafat was coming under Saddam's influence. The Abul Abbas raid, he maintained, had been an Iraqi operation. Its goal was to put an end to the PLO's policy of moderation and to its links with both Washington and Cairo. Saddam had something in mind, said Abu Iyad, something big. And he was maneuvering to get the PLO into his corner. This could only be bad, he thought, for the Palestinians. He was eager to find some way to prevent a break with Washington.[21] But it was too late. On June 20 Bush announced, more in sorrow than in anger, the suspension of the U.S.-PLO dialogue.

The summer of 1990 found American Middle East policy seemingly adrift. No one could see much future for the peace process, with an Israeli government bent on settling the occupied territories as rapidly as possible and a Palestinian movement drifting toward an alignment with an increasingly militant Iraq. And no one seemed to know what Saddam Hussein had in mind. He was making demands on the Gulf states for money and threatening Israel with chemical weapons if he was ever attacked, and by late July he began to move troops toward the Kuwaiti border to back up his demands for money. Within the region the prevailing interpretation was that Saddam was out to blackmail the Kuwaitis and Saudis by displaying his power. Egyptians, Jordanians, and Gulf leaders all advised Washington not to provoke Saddam by overreacting to his bullying. Instead talks would be held in Saudi Arabia, a deal would be struck, and Saddam would back off. But he did not. On August 2 his troops poured into Kuwait, occupying the country in a matter of hours and then annexing it, thus changing for years to come the politics of the region.

THE GULF CRISIS: AMERICA GOES TO WAR

This is not the place to analyze Saddam Hussein's motives for invading Kuwait. Nor is George Bush's response the center of this study.[22] Suffice it to say that Saddam must have calculated that Bush would not react militarily. In reaching such a conclusion, he may well have hoped that the force of Arab opinion would run so strongly against Western intervention that no Arab regime would dare collude with Washington to force Iraq to back down. This was a misreading of the Saudis and Egyptians in particular, both of whom agreed to cooperate with a massive deployment of Western, mostly American, forces in the region. And it was a misreading of George Bush, who had been raised on the lessons of Munich and did not need much coaching to conclude that American interests would suffer if Saddam Hussein got away with his bid for power.

If Saddam controlled Iraqi and Kuwaiti oil supplies directly, and if he kept troops on the Saudi border, he would in fact dominate the Gulf's vast reserves of oil and would become a one-man OPEC, able to manipulate the supply of oil to achieve whatever price he wanted. With his enormous oil revenues, he would also be able to accelerate his buildup of arms, including nuclear, chemical, and biological weapons. Before long the stage would be set for another war in the Middle East, this one involving Israel and Iraq, both possibly armed with nuclear weapons. Added to these tangible concerns were the matters of American leadership in the post–cold war world, of resistance to aggression, and of domestic political pressures on Bush to act.

While Bush methodically prepared for a war that America and its allies could not lose, Saddam tried to link his occupation of Kuwait to the Israeli occupation of Arab territories (and the Syrian occupation of Lebanon). Before asking Iraq to withdraw from territory that was rightfully Iraqi, Saddam implied, Israel and Syria should withdraw their forces. This stance was designed to win support from many in the Arab world who were inclined to see no particular difference among the three occupations and who held no special brief for the overly rich Kuwaitis in any case. Palestinians were particularly prone to grasp at Saddam's effort to link these issues, sensing the possibility that a powerful Arab savior, an echo of the great Nasser, might save them at a time when no one else seemed able to do so. Thus in Jordan and in the occupied territories, an outpouring of support for Saddam could be registered, if only briefly.

None of that support made much difference to Bush and his top aides in Washington. They were determined to oust Saddam from Kuwait, to destroy his war-making capability, to remove his weapons of mass destruction, and to do so with minimal casualties, quickly, and under the guise of UN legitimacy. On January 16, 1991, the American-led coalition launched massive air strikes against Iraq. Almost immediately it was clear the Iraqi fighting force was doomed. Saddam tried to drag Israel into the war by firing SCUD missiles at Tel Aviv. If the Israelis came into the war, Saddam believed, the Saudis, Egyptians, and Syrians would switch sides. But under considerable American pressure, Israel did not retaliate; the Arab allies in the coalition held firm; and Saddam's forces beat a hasty retreat from Kuwait at the end of February. Throughout, the Soviet Union did nothing to protect the Iraqi regime. In fact, the Soviets voted in the UN with the United States, in a graphic display of post–cold war cooperation.

What would the American-led victory, Saddam's defeat, Israeli restraint, and Palestinian support for Saddam mean for the stagnant peace
process? Bush had refused to accept Saddam's effort to link the occupation
of Kuwait with the Israeli occupation of the West Bank, but in a gesture
toward the Arabs he had hinted on October 1, 1990, that when he had
settled accounts with Saddam, he would turn his attention back toward
Arab-Israeli peacemaking.[23] In March 1991 many wondered if Bush's
comment had been more than idle rhetoric. Within weeks evidence began
to accumulate that Bush and Baker saw an opportunity coming out of
the Gulf crisis to relaunch the peace process. Indeed, Baker began to
resemble a former secretary of state, Henry Kissinger, who had rushed
to the region in the aftermath of another war, in 1973. Between March
and October 1991 Baker made eight trips to the region, spending endless
hours huddled with Syria's Hafiz al-Asad and Israel's Yitzhak Shamir.
As Kissinger had done, he also touched base in Saudi Arabia and other
Arab countries. But his most interesting innovation was that he began to
talk with Palestinians from within the occupied territories who were
known to have close ties to the PLO. Faisal Husseini and Hanan Ashrawi
became his interlocutors of choice on the Palestinian side. It proved to
be an important procedural shift, opening the way for Palestinian
participation in the peace process despite some residual ill-feeling on both
sides about the Gulf War.

ROAD TO MADRID

During the war against Iraq the Middle East team at the State Department
began to think the outcome of the war might create conditions in which
Arab-Israeli peace negotiations would prove possible. The reasoning went
as follows. The defeat of Iraq would convince even the most die-hard
Arab militants that a military solution to the Arab-Israeli conflict was
impossible. The fact that the Soviet Union had cooperated with the
United States during the crisis would further demonstrate that the old
cold war rules of the game were being rewritten, and that the United
States, more than ever, occupied the key diplomatic position. Palestinians
and Jordanians, who had allowed their emotions to draw them to Saddam's
side, would now realize that they had lost support among Arab regimes
and that time was working against their interests. Out of weakness,
therefore, the Palestinians might be expected to respond positively to any
serious diplomatic overture.

American officials also hoped that patterns of cooperation forged during the Gulf War might carry over into the postwar diplomacy. On the Arab side, this would mean that Egypt, Syria, and Saudi Arabia might be expected to work in tandem to support the peace process, something that had not happened since 1974. Indeed, one of the main debates within the Bush administration was over the role to be accorded Syria in the postwar era. In public many opinion leaders were warning of the danger of embracing Hafiz al-Asad, as if he were nothing more than a somewhat shrewder version of Saddam Hussein. Asad's past record on Arab-Israeli peace provided little comfort to those who thought he might be more flexible in this round. But the weight of consensus was that Asad should be put to the test. If he agreed to negotiate with Israel, the Palestinians would almost certainly follow suit. And if Israel saw the chance of talking directly with Syria, that might provide a positive incentive to join the process. By contrast, Shamir seemed to believe nothing good could come of talking just with the Palestinians.

Shamir remained something of an enigma for the Americans. On the one hand, he had surprised many by showing great self-control during the Iraqi SCUD attacks on Israel. At the American request, he sat tight, resisting the advice of some of his own military to strike back at Iraq. On the other hand, nothing in Shamir's personality gave reason to think that the issues on which the peace process had foundered a year earlier could now be easily swept away. Still, a judgment was made that objectively Israel was more secure than it had ever been. Furthermore, the fact that the United States had rushed Patriot missiles to help defend against the SCUDs, followed by infusions of aid to offset war-related losses, would presumably create conditions in which Shamir would be reluctant to say no to George Bush.

Finally, the Middle East team realized that the American-led victory in the Gulf would inevitably enhance the leadership potential of President Bush, at least for the near term. Bush was enjoying unprecedented popularity at home. No one would seriously question his judgment in turning from the Gulf victory to Arab-Israeli peacemaking.

One lingering question remained. What national interest would the United States now serve by tackling the congealed Arab-Israeli conflict? In the Gulf, Americans could be persuaded that the combination of oil and potential Iraqi nuclear capabilities justified the expenditure of lives and money to defeat Saddam. But why should the United States, especially in the post–cold war era, take another run at the impossibly complex dispute between Israel and its Arab neighbors? Was there really any chance of success? Was the stalemate so threatening to American interests? Only a few years earlier any answer to these questions would have noted the possibility of Soviet gains and of threats to oil supplies as reasons to tackle the Arab-Israeli conflict. But the Soviet threat was now gone, and oil supplies bore no obvious relationship to the course of the Arab-Israeli dispute, at least not in 1991.

If some old answers were no longer credible, others were. For example, it had long been assumed that the Egyptian-Israeli peace would be strengthened if the peace process could be revived. In the absence of further movement in the peace process, the cool relations between Egypt and Israel might collapse altogether, at great cost to the prospects for regional stability. That remained a valid concern. Another concern was that a prolonged stalemate in the Arab-Israeli arena would result in a radicalization of opinion in both Israel and among the Palestinians. In the worst of circumstances, the conflict would be defined increasingly in religious terms, Jews against Muslims, and destroy the prospects for any settlement.

Some within the administration were also worried about the effect of a prolonged stalemate on U.S.-Israeli relations. Would the American public continue to support large outlays of aid to Israel now that the "strategic asset" argument carried so little weight? What would the effect on American opinion be of more years of TV images of heavily armed Israelis shooting at Palestinian stone throwers? Without a peace settlement Israel would look more and more like a colonial state ruling over a restless people with its own national aspirations. No one believed Israel would offer the Palestinians equal rights within the Israeli political system, since that would radically dilute the Jewishness of the state. The only alternatives to a peace settlement with territorial withdrawal would then be prolonged second-class status for the Palestinians or their expulsion from the occupied territories. Neither option seemed compatible with strong U.S.-Israeli relations. Unless the two countries could again be seen as cooperating in pursuit of peace, some felt Israel ran the risk of a sudden loss of American public support.

The clinching argument for the Middle East team, however, seems to have been more related to the prospect of a future war in the region. Without a peace settlement, some feared, another war between Israel and some coalition of Arab states was still possible. The danger of such a war had been hinted at in the recent conflict with Iraq. Surface-to-surface missiles may not have been very effective in 1991, but who could be sure that accuracies would not be improved within the decade? And what about nonconventional weapons? This time Iraq had refrained from using its chemical weapons, and it did not yet possess nuclear weapons. But would the same apply to an Arab-Israeli war fought later in the decade? No one could be sure, but it seemed prudent to try to avoid another test of arms if at all possible.

With these arguments at hand, and with a legacy of past commitments in mind, the Bush administration moved quickly to explore the new terrain in the Arab-Israeli arena. From previous experience one could presume that there would be no grand design; that the emphasis would be on procedures for getting the parties to the negotiating table; and that big, new commitments of aid would not be part of the diplomacy. The main cost to the United States was likely to be the time and energy of the secretary of state and his top aides.

On March 6, 1991, Bush addressed a joint session of Congress, saying: "We must do all that we can to close the gap between Israel and the Arab states and between Israelis and Palestinians. . . . A comprehensive peace must be grounded in United Nations Security Council Resolutions 242 and 338 and the principle of territory for peace. This principle must be elaborated to provide for Israel's security and recognition, and at the same time for legitimate Palestinian political rights. Anything else would fail the twin tests of fairness and security. The time has come to put an end to Arab-Israeli conflict." (See appendix L.)

Within days of the president's speech Baker was on his way to the Middle East for what proved to be the first of eight such trips in 1991. He stopped in Saudi Arabia, moved on to Israel, where he also met with Palestinians, and then went to Damascus. Shortly thereafter Mubarak and Asad issued a call for an international peace conference on the Arab-Israeli conflict, and Shamir responded by saying that Israel might agree to a regional conference under U.S.-Soviet sponsorship.

From this first round of talks it seemed as if an effort was under way to bring Syria into the process. The price for doing so would be some form of international conference. To win Israeli support, any such conference would have to be stripped of coercive authority, providing little more than a venue for the parties to negotiate directly. Israel would resist any UN role as well. Nor was Israel enthusiastic about European participation. All these latter points would be matters for endless hours of argumentation with Asad, but none seemed insoluble. Baker's strategy seemed to be to win Asad's agreement first, on the assumption that Israel would not then want to say no.

Baker made two more trips to the region in April, without visible results. In contrast to previous forays into Arab-Israeli diplomacy, however, this time Baker did not let his frustrations show, and he did not repeatedly threaten to drop the whole matter if the parties refused to cooperate. Both he and the president gave the impression of steady determination to get the answers they wanted.

During May 1991 a potentially difficult issue surfaced. The Israeli ambassador in Washington announced that Israel would be requesting $10 billion in American loan guarantees over the next five years to help with the absorption of new immigrants from the Soviet Union.[24] At a time when Israel was building new settlements at breakneck speed in the West Bank (and around Jerusalem), this demand raised a question in Washington of how to respond. The previous U.S.-Israeli agreement on $400 million in loan guarantees for housing had left a bitter aftertaste in Washington, since the Israelis immediately rejected the notion that these funds could not be spent beyond the green line in East Jerusalem.[25] Neither Bush nor Baker wanted to be in a position of subsidizing Israeli settlements, which they genuinely believed to be an obstacle to any future agreement between Israel and the Palestinians. Needless to say, in his many meetings with Palestinian leaders Baker was told that negotiations could not succeed unless Israeli settlements were stopped. Appearing before a House Foreign Affairs subcommittee on May 22, Baker labeled Israeli settlement activity a major obstacle to peace. Bush echoed this view the following day.[26]

During the summer Baker tried to strengthen the architecture of prospective peace talks, avoiding substance but developing a structure that had substantive implications. On May 29 the administration launched a proposal on regional arms control. This, it seemed, was designed to appeal to the Israelis by drawing several Arab states, such as Saudi Arabia, into discussions on limiting arms in the region. But the most difficult issue for Baker was to work out an acceptable formula for Palestinian representation in the peace talks. No one had ever succeeded at this task. Shamir was adamant in his refusal to deal directly with the PLO, and even a veiled role for Arafat was more than he seemed willing to accept. By contrast, most Palestinians seemed to feel that only the PLO could validate the idea of negotiating with Israel, just as in 1988 only the PLO could have legitimized the idea that Israel had a right to exist as a state within a part of the former Palestine mandate.

Conceptually, a solution to this problem was not too hard to imagine, but it would require considerable political skill to find the right balance. The starting point in the quest seemed to be the point where Baker had left off in the spring of 1990. Then the PLO had already agreed that no one from the organization would be present in the negotiations with Israel. The idea had been explored that a list of names would be drawn up by the PLO but would be put forward by Egypt. Now, in 1991, the idea of the PLO forwarding a list through Palestinians within the occupied territories gained favor. But who would be on the list? Shamir made his views clear. No one from East Jerusalem; no one from outside the occupied territories; and no one involved in terrorist actions.

A year earlier Baker had supported the Palestinians in their desire to have someone from Jerusalem and from outside the territories, but now he would not do so. The PLO had lost ground because of the Gulf War. It would have to settle for less. So a formula was devised for a joint Jordanian-Palestinian delegation, with all the Palestinians coming from the occupied territories. At the same time they would all be selected by the PLO, whose role would only barely be disguised.

On the American side, some felt that the decline of the PLO would be a desirable development in itself, not just because Shamir objected to its inclusion in the talks. The idea was widespread in Washington that the Palestinians inside the territories were more moderate, more realistic, than those on the outside. The latter, it was believed, would always feel the need to defend the rights of the exiled Palestinians, including their right to return to their original homes, an issue on which the Israelis were immovable. Although this view had some merit, it missed the point that the so-called moderates in the West Bank and Gaza had very little mass following. Insofar as they could claim to speak for the Palestinians, it was because they were seen as representing the PLO. The grass-roots leaders, by contrast, were often more radical than the PLO, sometimes on the left, sometimes as part of the growing Islamic movement. So to get the moderate Palestinians into the game, and to give them political cover, the PLO was still necessary.

Early in June Bush sent letters to Shamir, Asad, King Hussein, King Fahd of Saudi Arabia, and Mubarak spelling out his ideas for convening a peace conference in the fall. The first positive reply came on July 14—from Damascus. Within days Baker was in Syria for talks with

Asad, then on to Jordan, where King Hussein agreed to the conference idea. Hussein also publicly endorsed an idea that Mubarak had suggested: the Arabs would drop the secondary boycott of Israel once Israel agreed to stop settlements in the occupied territories.

Now Baker turned to trying to win Shamir's agreement. As an inducement Baker told Shamir that the United States would continue to honor the terms of the letter sent by President Ford to Prime Minister Rabin on September 1, 1975. That letter had promised to "give great weight to Israel's position that any peace agreement with Syria must be predicated on Israel remaining on the Golan Heights."[27] Some suspected that Baker had probably made a commitment to Asad along the lines that the United States did not recognize Israel's annexation of the Golan and felt that the terms of UN Resolution 242 should be applied there. Both American promises were tenable, although one could forsee a possible contradiction somewhere down the road. But diplomats eager to make deals are often drawn to such parallel assurances. The question is not why they are given; rather, one wonders why they are so highly valued.

Lest anyone have any doubt about his views on substance, Shamir joined the debate on July 24, 1991, stating: "I don't believe in territorial compromise. Our country is very tiny. The territory is connected to our entire life—to our security, water, economy. I believe with my entire soul that we are forever connected to this entire homeland. Peace and security go together. Security, territory and homeland are one entity."[28] In short, Shamir would not go into negotiations with any prior commitment to withdrawal. A few days later, on August 1, Shamir announced his conditional acceptance of the American proposal for a peace conference in October. All that remained was to get a list of Palestinian negotiators with whom Israel would agree to meet.

What could the Palestinians hope for from the negotiations if the PLO was to be excluded and Shamir seemed unwilling to budge on withdrawal? Perhaps the Americans could at least try to stop the Israeli settlements, or at least refuse to subsidize them. Palestinian hopes may have been raised earlier in the year when Bush had postponed the decision on the Israeli request for a $10 billion loan guarantee. For the Palestinian establishment this issue was a crucial indicator of whether Bush could be a credible intermediary. If the United States was actively subsidizing new Israeli settlements, possibly on a massive scale, Palestinians would question whether American-brokered negotiations could yield them any of their rights. By contrast, if Bush could hold the line, perhaps he could be trusted.

During August an attempted coup against Gorbachev set the stage for dramatic change in the Soviet Union. Whatever slight chance there might have been for the Soviets to play an effective role as cochairman in the peace talks came to an end. Gorbachev's own position was irretrievably weakened, and the Soviet Union began to break apart. By year's end the Communist party had been banned, Gorbachev was out of power, and each of the constituent parts of the former Soviet Union was on its way toward independence. Boris Yeltsin was the new ruler of Russia. For the Palestinians and Syrians these dramatic events were further reminders that they now stood on their own, with no major power behind them.

But Bush was gaining credibility in Arab eyes, just as the Soviets were dropping off the map. On September 6, 1991, Bush asked Congress for a 120-day delay before considering the Israeli loan request. After encountering congressional resistance, Bush went public on September 12. He spoke out forcefully against Israeli settlements and against the Israeli lobby. Within days polls showed that a large majority of the American public supported the president in his stand on the Israeli aid request.[29] By contrast, many American Jews were deeply offended by what they saw as Bush's questioning of their right to lobby on behalf of issues they believed in.

During the next few weeks Baker made additional trips to the Middle East. One could sense the beginning of the endgame. Letters of assurances were being demanded and offered.[30] (See appendix M for the text of the letter to the Palestinians.) Symbolic gestures, such as Bush's call for the repeal of the UN resolution on Zionism as a form of racism, were freely made.

Finally, on October 18 Baker was given a list of the prospective Palestinian negotiating team. On October 20 the Israeli cabinet voted to go to the conference. On October 22 Faisal Husseini announced the names of the Palestinian negotiating team, along with those, including himself, who would form an advisory group. One member of the Jordanian part of the joint team was a Palestinian from outside the territories with close family ties to Jerusalem. So the Palestinians could finally say that they had chosen a representative negotiating team, while the Israelis could say that they were not dealing with the PLO and had not recognized East Jerusalem as having the same status as the rest of the occupied territories.

THE MADRID CONFERENCE

On October 30, under the joint chairmanship of Bush and Gorbachev, the Middle East peace conference opened in Madrid (See appendix N for the text of the U.S.-Soviet invitation.) Israel, Syria, Lebanon, and a joint Jordanian-Palestinian delegation were all in attendance; so was a representative of the UN secretary general and a representative of the European Community, but far from center stage. Of greater symbolic importance was the presence of Prince Bandar ibn Sultan, the Saudi ambassador to Washington, dressed in traditional garb.

The formal speeches were unlikely to be long remembered, with the possible exception of the unusually eloquent Palestinian speech.[31] (See appendix O for Bush's speech.) But no one could ignore the symbolic—and therefore political—importance of the parties' sitting together at the negotiating table. And for the first time in recent history, the Palestinians were present speaking on their own behalf. To prove that the formal ceremonies were not the end of the road, all the parties were even persuaded to engage in a few days of face-to-face talks. The fact that no substantive progress had been made was hardly surprising. The important point was that a commitment to an ongoing negotiating process seemed to exist.

After the procedural breakthrough of getting all the parties to the negotiating table, what did Bush and Baker have in mind? They had not even hinted at any new substantive ideas, although by getting the Palestinians to the table as an almost independent party, the administration had done what no other had done before. And Bush had strongly hinted that any increase in aid to Israel would be accompanied by some conditions to slow down the pace of settlements. Otherwise Washington seemed determined to play the part of convener, but not yet that of mediator. The parties would repeatedly be brought to the negotiating table—first in Washington in December 1991, once in January, in March, and again in April 1992, to be followed by more meetings in Rome. But despite appeals from the Arabs for more substantive American involvement, Bush and Baker held back.

The reason for their reticence was not hard to discern. The Americans had always been worried about raising Arab expectations that Israeli concessions would simply be delivered by Washington. This was not going to happen. The Arab parties would have to develop positions of their own and negotiate seriously before the United States would seek to bridge differences with proposals of its own.[32] In addition, on many of the points in dispute, the Americans had no strong views of how the issues should be resolved. What they wanted was a workable agreement. Whatever the parties could agree upon would easily pass muster in Washington. At most, the administration had views of workable compromises, but it was not eager to tip its hand prematurely. So it envisaged a prolonged phase of bilateral negotiations.

Complementing the bilateral talks would be the multilateral meetings on arms control, economic development, water, refugees, and the environment. No one expected any immediate results from these talks, but some useful ideas might be explored at the expert level which would then be available to feed into the political talks at appropriate moments. In a gesture to the Russians the first round of the multilateral talks took place in Moscow on January 28, 1992. Syria did not attend, but that did not prevent some other Arab parties from participating. In the follow-on talks Israel chose not to participate in the meetings on refugees and economics because of the presence of Palestinians from outside the territories, but the meetings proceeded in any event. No party's absence from a single session, it seemed, could now torpedo the negotiating process.

If the Israelis had reason to feel gratified that the United States was not intervening in the substance of the negotiations, they had less reason for joy on the matter of the postponed loan guarantees. The 120-day deadline came and went without a decision. By mid-January 1992 congressional leaders were exploring possible compromises. In one version, Israel would receive the first year of loan guarantees, some $2 billion, but any funds spent on settlements in the occupied territories would be deducted from future amounts. A well-informed *New York Times* columnist wrote on January 17, 1992, that Shamir would be wrong to think Bush would settle for such a compromise. One way or another, Bush wanted Shamir to agree to stop settlements.[33] A few days later Shamir said there was no chance that Israel would agree to a freeze.

Domestic political realities were clearly beginning to play a role in both Washington and Jerusalem. Israeli elections were now scheduled for June 1992, as a result of the defection of small right-wing parties from Shamir's coalition. Shamir was unlikely to make concessions on settlements in the best of times, but certainly not on the eve of elections.

Normally one would expect an American president going into a reelection campaign to avoid a showdown with Congress and Israel. But foreign aid was unpopular. Bush would not lose many votes by saying no to Shamir. And it already seemed obvious that Bush would not win many votes from the American Jewish community, which increasingly saw both the president and Baker as hostile to Israel. Still, Bush did not want to alienate Israelis across the political spectrum. Instead he decided to attach conditions to the loan guarantees that he knew Shamir, but not all Israelis, would find difficult to accept. Apparently Bush hoped that Shamir's unwillingness to accept the American conditions would lead Israelis to debate the wisdom of pursuing an unrestrained policy of settling the territories. Many of the new immigrants, in particular, might blame Shamir for missing the opportunity to secure assistance that would benefit them.

Few who knew Bush and Baker believed they were indifferent to the outcome of the Israeli elections. Shamir had been a difficult leader for them to deal with. His policy on settlements and his refusal to countenance withdrawal were genuine concerns as the administration tried to foresee the future of the peace process. And Labor, after a hard-fought internal campaign, was united behind Yitzhak Rabin, a man who just might be regarded by Israelis as combining the right dose of realism and toughness to see them through the next phase of the negotiating process. To grant the loans to Shamir without conditions might well ensure Shamir's victory at the polls. That Bush and Baker did not want to do.

On February 24, 1992, shortly after Rabin's victory within the Labor party, Baker laid out the conditions for granting the $10 billion in loan guarantees.[34] Efforts by Congress to find a compromise were rejected by Bush on March 17. For the moment, the issue of loan guarantees seemed dead.[35] And until after Israeli and American elections, the negotiating process would probably be on hold as well.[36]

THE ISRAELI ELECTIONS

Israelis went to the polls on June 23 and delivered a stunning defeat to the Likud party that had ruled, almost without interruption, since 1977. Only 25 percent of the electorate cast ballots for the Likud, yielding thirty-two Knesset seats, down from forty in the 1988 elections. The defeat for Shamir was so great that he announced his intention to step down as party leader. Moshe Arens, sometimes thought to be the heir apparent, decided to retire from politics, criticizing Shamir's views on Greater Israel as he left.[37]

If the Likud was the clear loser, Rabin and his Labor party were the winners. With nearly 35 percent of the popular vote, and forty-four

Knesset seats, Rabin was in a position to forge a narrow coalition without any of the right-wing parties. Although he spent some time exploring the possibilities of creating a broad coalition, on July 13 he presented a cabinet to the Knesset that represented a coalition of Labor, the left-wing Meretz bloc, and the Shas religious party. Together these three parties held sixty-two seats, and the coalition could probably count on five Arab Knesset members as well in a future vote of confidence.

Rabin moved quickly to assert his authority. He kept the Defense portfolio for himself. As foreign minister, he named Shimon Peres, his long-time rival. But he made it clear that he, not Peres, would oversee the peace process. As head of the Israeli team negotiating with the Syrians, he named a respected Tel Aviv University academic specialist on Syria, Itamar Rabinovitch. No such change was made at the head of the Israeli team dealing with Jordan and the Palestinians.

Within days of Rabin's investiture Baker arrived in Israel to push for a resumption of peace negotiations and to prepare the way for a Rabin visit to the United States. Shortly thereafter, in a trip that symbolized the new era, Rabin traveled to Egypt for a cordial meeting with President Mubarak. Two days later Rabin announced that more than 6,000 housing units planned for the West Bank would be canceled, and subsidies on the remainder would be reduced. (Some 10,000 units well on the way to completion would be finished, so a "freeze" on settlement activity was still not in sight.)

Rabin also injected into his rhetoric a sense of urgency about finding a negotiated settlement, especially with the Palestinians. But before long he was also expressing optimism that progress could be made on the Syrian front as well.[38] Meanwhile Shamir confirmed the worst suspicions of many when he allegedly said that if he had been reelected, he would have strung out the negotiating process for at least another ten years.[39]

The changes in Israel were warmly welcomed by Bush and Baker. By playing the issue of the loan guarantees as they had, they had contributed in some degree to Shamir's defeat. Not surprisingly, then, Bush received Rabin on August 10 in Maine with a degree of warmth that had been noticeably missing from his encounters with Shamir. Although details remained to be worked out, Bush was able to tell Rabin that he would now support the loan guarantees to Israel. On October 5 both houses of Congress voted for a foreign aid appropriations bill that contained the $10 billion in loan guarantees, with Israel covering the reserve costs of some $400 million. The president retained the authority to deduct from these funds amounts that Israel might spend on settlements beyond completion of the 10,000 units already under way. On the whole, Israelis had every reason to be very pleased with the outcome of this year-long struggle over aid.

BUSH'S DECLINING FORTUNES

Throughout the early part of 1992 Bush had pressed ahead with his foreign-policy agenda, including the Middle East, as if 1992 were not an election year. After all, he faced no serious opposition for his party's nomination. His support in the polls in mid-1991, after the Gulf War victory, had been at all-time highs, and the Democratic field of candidates did not look very impressive. The cloud on the horizon was the weak state of the economy and signs of growing disenchantment with Bush's leadership.

During the primaries Bush faced a surprisingly sharp challenge from Patrick Buchanan, a conservative columnist who was able to win about one-third of the votes in the early Republican primaries. Unlike Bush, he was essentially an isolationist, a protectionist on trade issues, an opponent of foreign aid, and a sometime critic of Israel. The net effect of his challenge was probably to push Bush more to the right on domestic political issues—so-called family values.

On the Democratic side, it was clear by late spring the Governor Bill Clinton of Arkansas would be the candidate after the July party convention. Clinton had a fairly good record of governing a small, poor state, but his views on foreign policy were almost unknown. As the campaign gained momentum Clinton launched some criticism at Bush for being too tough on Israel and for attaching conditions to the loan guarantees. But Rabin's election and the renewed warmth of U.S.-Israeli relations during the summer removed the loans as a major campaign issue. Indeed, most foreign-policy issues were ignored by both parties in favor of debates over domestic priorities or questions of character. Clinton spent more time attacking Bush's role in the Iran-Contra affair and in supporting Saddam Hussein before the invasion of Kuwait than on any contemporary issue of foreign policy.

The Democratic Convention in New York proved to be surprisingly harmonious. Clinton chose as his running mate Senator Albert Gore, Jr., of Tennessee. These young Democratic candidates presented themselves as the agents of change. Initial public opinion polls showed them with a commanding lead over President Bush.

Normally the Republican Convention, which nominated Bush easily, should have given the president a significant boost in the polls. But his campaign seemed disorganized and lacking focus. Rumors began to spread that the president would call on his friend and adviser, James Baker, to take charge. On August 13 the announcement was made that Baker would become chief of staff as of August 23. As he took his farewell from the State Department, Baker seemed to be speaking with a heavy heart. He had clearly relished the role of statesman and was unhappy about leaving the Arab-Israeli peace process, in particular, at a sensitive moment.

The sixth round of peace talks convened in Washington the day after Baker and his entire top team left for the White House. Middle East policy would now be technically in the hands of Acting Secretary Lawrence Eagleburger, assisted by Assistant Secretary Edward Djerejian. Few expected much of a push from the American side as negotiations resumed on August 24.[40]

During most of September and October Bush was fully occupied with running for reelection. Despite his absence and Baker's from the negotiating process, some modest gains were made on the Syrian-Israeli front. Asad spoke publicly of the need for a "peace of the brave," consciously echoing the words of former French president Charles de Gaulle.[41] Asad's foreign minister then spoke of "total peace for total withdrawal," which for the first time indicated that Syria might go beyond merely ending the state of belligerency with Israel. By the seventh round of negotiations in late October, the Israelis had reciprocated by using the word "withdrawal" in a formal document referring to the Golan front. And Israel was working with a Syrian draft paper to try to develop a statement of joint principles to guide the negotiations. All this was fairly encouraging, but both Asad and Rabin seemed frustrated that the United States was not helping to close the deal. Also, the Palestinians, who were seeing no comparable progress in their own negotiations with Israel, were getting nervous about the possibility of Syria concluding a separate peace.

Some observers believed the conditions in the fall of 1992 were such that a major commitment of time and energy by the Bush administration might have produced significant results. But precisely because of election-year imperatives, the United States was in no position to play the role of mediator, full partner, or deal maker that it had in the past.

Finally, on November 3, 1992, the long election campaign came to an end. Despite his foreign-policy achievements, his experience, and the doubts he had raised about his opponent's character, Bush was solidly defeated in his bid for reelection. The popular vote divided 43 percent for Clinton, 38 percent for Bush, and 19 percent for independent candidate Ross Perot, resulting in a one-sided victory for the Democratic candidate in the electoral college. Once again domestic politics intruded on the conduct of American policy in the Middle East, forcing a hiatus of several months before American leadership in the peace process might once again be expected.

Unfortunately, events in the Middle East rarely conform to the needs of the American electoral calendar. During the lame-duck period from the election on November 4, 1992, to January 20, 1993, when Bill Clinton was inaugurated as president, the tensions between Israelis and Palestinians mounted rapidly. During December alone, Palestinians killed more Israelis, and Israelis killed more Palestinians, than in much of the previous year. Rabin, under domestic pressures, struck back with an unprecedented decision to deport more than 400 suspected Islamic activists to Lebanon. In another unprecedented move, Lebanon, finally governed by a cabinet with considerable popular support, refused to allow the Palestinians into Lebanon. Thus, in difficult conditions, the Palestinians remained in a sort of no-man's-land in southern Lebanon.

Coming on the last days of the eighth round of peace talks in Washington, this action cast a pall over the negotiations. Palestinian spokesmen asserted that talks would not be resumed until the deportees were returned to their homes. Rabin refused to budge. Bush could do nothing, thus ensuring that the Clinton administration would inherit a stalled peace process in need of resuscitation rather than the ongoing, institutionalized one that had continued through most of 1992.

CONCLUSIONS

Bush and Baker had come to power with an interest in the Arab-Israeli conflict, but with a determination to avoid some of the mistakes of their predecessors. They would offer no big plans, no special negotiators, no heightened expectations. The administration would probe cautiously to see if the parties were ready to move. If not, it would hold back. It would wait for the conflict to ripen.

Events in the Middle East prove to be powerful teachers. Theories do not hold up well in the face of swiftly moving realities. So it is not surprising that the administration found itself drawn into an increasingly assertive role in late 1989 and early 1990, trying to break the impasse with a proposal for Israeli-Palestinian talks on holding elections in the West Bank and Gaza. This effort failed, and failure is also part of the learning process.

The Bush administration's greatest foreign-policy error, its misreading of Saddam Hussein before his invasion of Kuwait, also set the stage for one of its greatest triumphs—the mobilization of a broad international coalition to defeat Iraq and restore Kuwait's independence. This success, in turn, opened the way for a revived and improved effort to bring Arabs and Israelis to the peace table. Bush and Baker hit on an effective division of roles. Baker was the negotiator, the deal maker, the master of details. Bush held back, but he made the hard decisions on loan guarantees and lent his constant support to his secretary of state. With considerable effort, and at some cost to Bush's domestic position, the administration attained its initial goal. Despite his defeat in November 1992, Bush was successful in winning bipartisan support for his success in bringing Arabs and Israelis to the negotiating table.[42] Clinton promised to pursue the same policy.

Bush and Baker were widely credited with realizing that the end of the cold war and the defeat of Saddam Hussein created a new opportunity for Arab-Israeli peace diplomacy. Not everyone at the time thought a major American initiative was warranted, or could succeed.[43] Baker's persistence in working out the procedures for the Madrid conference also won high marks, as did his tactical skills as a negotiator. When he left to become chief of staff in August 1992, many believed his absence would be felt. And, in fact, little further progress was made over the ensuing several months.

Bush and Baker were not as widely credited for their handling of the loan guarantee issue. Democrats tended to criticize Bush for one-sided pressure against Israel. Yet to link the provision of aid to a curtailment of settlement activity may well have been one of Bush's most important decisions. Without it, Shamir might well have been reelected, which would have cast serious doubt on the chances for the peace process. Bush's critics, most of whom were happy to see Shamir replaced by Rabin, did not seem to notice the contradiction in their own stance.

Where Bush and Baker may fairly be criticized was in their initial caution. Throughout much of 1989 they acted as if the Soviet Union still represented a serious competitor in the Middle East. They also took the comfortable path of trying to work with Shamir on structuring the peace negotiations, seeming to believe he could be cajoled toward more moderate positions. Given the short time available to any president to tackle foreign-policy issues, the loss of most of 1989 on misguided Arab-Israeli initiatives is regrettable. By the time Bush and Baker were back on track, they were already well into their third year, leaving little time to bring their efforts to fruition.

Ultimately, no president can conduct a successful foreign policy, least of all on complex matters such as Arab-Israeli negotiations, without a strong domestic base. By allowing his domestic support to fade from the historic highs of spring 1991 to the abysmal lows of late 1992, Bush ensured that he would not be able to provide the leadership necessary to move beyond the first phase of the Madrid peace talks. Fortunately, the foundations that he and Baker constructed were robust enough to survive the absence of strong American leadership, at least for a while. Because support for the negotiations was fairly strong—in the region, internationally, and in the United States—Clinton did not have to face the challenge of forging a new policy toward the Arab-Israeli conflict. Instead he could work with the structure left to him by Bush and Baker. His challenge would be to add substance to the process, to move toward concrete agreements, and to use time and circumstances to make major steps toward Arab-Israeli peace.

PART SEVEN

Conclusions

CHAPTER SIXTEEN

Challenges Facing the Clinton Administration

With alarming regularity over the past thirty years, American presidents have found themselves dealing with Middle East crises for which they were poorly prepared. Many, but not all, of these crises have been related to the Arab-Israeli conflict. The June 1967 war, the war of attrition in 1969–70, the Jordan crisis of September 1970, the October 1973 war, the Iranian revolution in 1978–79, the Iran-Iraq war from 1980 to 1988, the Israeli invasion of Lebanon in 1982–83, the early years of the Palestinian *intifada* in 1987–88, the Iraqi invasion of Kuwait in 1990, and the subsequent war against Saddam Hussein in 1991 were enormous challenges for American foreign policy. Each evoked serious debate in Washington over the proper course of action. Each seemed to threaten some important American interest in the region. Each, to some extent, caught Washington by surprise.

The administration of Bill Clinton is in the enviable position of dealing with an ongoing Arab-Israeli peace negotiation. Since October 1991 the parties to the conflict have been in broad agreement on procedures for peace talks. What has been needed, besides direct negotiations, has been an effective mediator who can steer the negotiating teams toward realistic agreements, engage with political decisionmakers to extract command decisions, and offer both reassurance and pressure when necessary. James Baker showed what could be accomplished by such mediation in organizing the Madrid conference, but during much of the 1992 election year he and President Bush were unable to move the negotiations forward. For Clinton this means there will be less need for policy innovation than in the past and more need for effective follow-through.

THE BALANCE SHEET

The American record of managing Arab-Israeli crises and their aftermaths is mixed. On the whole, the United States has done best when it has tried hardest. From 1968 onward, successive administrations have tried to lay the foundations for peace between Israel and Egypt. In 1979 the

415

two countries signed a peace treaty, which they have observed ever since. As its contribution to this historic achievement, the United States, under six presidents, has invested important resources—time, energy, imagination, money, military equipment—to establish a framework for peace, to get the parties involved in a negotiating process, to clinch the formal deal, and to continue to bolster the normalization of relations well after the signing of the peace treaty between the two countries.

Peace between Israel and Egypt did not come cheaply, nor was the path smooth. Several wars were fought before serious negotiations began in 1974. The bilateral peace between Israel and its most powerful Arab neighbor left many other issues unresolved. It also probably exacerbated the problems of Lebanon and initially made the Israeli-Palestinian relationship even more intractable than it had been. But the Israeli-Egyptian peace also changed the strategic picture of the region, provided something of a model for negotiations on other fronts, bolstered American influence, and ultimately helped to persuade other Arabs that diplomacy offered a better course for redressing grievances than military threats.

For the United States the economic cost of Israeli-Egyptian peace has been substantial. Since the peace treaty was signed, Congress has allocated more than $5 billion a year to the two countries. In special circumstances, additional sums have been offered. Of this total, more than half has gone for the purchase of American military equipment. Since 1985 almost all aid has been on a grant basis. In 1990 Congress even took the unusual step of agreeing to write off nearly $7 billion of Egypt's military debt from earlier years. And Congress has shown a willingness to support up to $10 billion in loan guarantees to Israel to assist with housing and immigrant absorption. Suffice it to say that no other countries in the Middle East, or anywhere else for that matter, even come close to receiving such openhanded assistance.

Apart from the important achievement of peace between Israel and Egypt, the American record is less impressive. The most promising step has been the agreement in 1991 among almost all the parties to the Arab-Israeli conflict to a formula for negotiations. Even optimists assume that the negotiations will be long and difficult, but at least procedural hurdles have been successfully overcome. Substantive agreements, however, are not yet in sight. Still, the Madrid conference and its aftermath deserve to be considered a partial success.

On the other side of the ledger are the failures and fiascoes of American Middle East policy. Some have entered the popular jargon of politics—"Irangate," for the misguided attempt to trade arms for hostages in the mid-1980s, and more recently "Iraqgate," for the policy of trying to accommodate Saddam Hussein before his invasion of Kuwait in August 1990. No simple phrase encapsulates the multiple disasters of American policy in Lebanon during the early 1980s, but the bombs that blew up the American embassy in Beirut and the Marine barracks in 1983 left graphic and tragic reminders that American failures in the Middle East can come with a heavy price in American lives. More Americans were killed in Lebanon in 1983 than in the massive war against Iraq in 1991. If one adds the prolonged agony of American hostages held in Iran and in Lebanon to the costs of failed policies, the tally is even higher.

PROTECTING NATIONAL INTERESTS

Still, for all the shortcomings of American policy in the Middle East generally, and toward the Arab-Israeli conflict in particular, American interests in the Middle East have fared surprisingly well. The great fear of Soviet dominance in the region never materialized, nor did the possibility of direct military confrontation between the two nuclear superpowers. Despite images of a "Middle East tinderbox," the region did not play the part of the Balkans earlier in the century in igniting a global conflagration. Regional conflicts, on the whole, remained confined to the region. Nuclear weapons, though present, remained in the background. Terrorism, though a persistent threat, never succeeded in changing the course of events in fundamental ways. Revolution, though often talked about, took place only in Iran. Elsewhere the state system has proved to be remarkably resilient, despite its seeming artificiality.

With respect to oil, American interests have not gone unscathed, but part of the blame must be assigned to shortsighted policies on the home front. Disruptions of oil supplies in the Middle East were bound to have some impact on price, but the exaggerated effect of the 1973–74 and 1978–79 cutbacks was in part due to flawed domestic policies and the failure to purchase adequate insurance in the form of a strategic petroleum reserve. During the 1980s and early 1990s interruptions of oil supplies from the Middle East also occurred in conjunction with Gulf crises, but better policies were in place and the impact was less. Yet, whatever the reason, the United States and the rest of the world paid an extraordinarily high price in the 1970s and early 1980s as a result of Middle East oil-supply disruptions. The recessions of the 1970s and early 1980s were directly related to the higher costs of energy.

Finally, as regards the third main American interest, Israel's security has greatly increased in the post-1967 era. By the early 1990s Israel was more secure than at any previous time in its history. More Arabs were reconciled to the idea of a Jewish state in at least a part of historic Palestine than ever before. Many Arab states were on speaking terms with Israel for the first time. And new immigrants from the former Soviet Union held out the promise of a renewal of social and economic vitality into the next century. Economic and social problems existed, but the survival of the state seemed more assured than one could have imagined thirty years earlier.

Despite this relatively positive overview of how American interests have fared in the Middle East since 1967, one should not conclude that all is well. The region remains volatile; most regimes have little mass support; opposition movements that reject the present order are widespread and are often intensely anti-American. Economic development is stalled, except in the oil sheikhdoms, and population growth puts an almost unmanageable burden on weak governments.

The Arab-Israeli conflict still generates strong passions, and the achievements of the past could be lost if, for example, the regime in Egypt changed suddenly, if radical Islamic movements gained ground, or if Israeli extremists tried to achieve their goals by force. The region is still overarmed; weapons of mass destruction are already in the arsenals of many states in the region, along with surface-to-surface missiles. Although the danger of superpower confrontation is now gone, the risk of war is still present, and in such a war American interests could still be threatened. To reconcile the American commitment to a secure Israel with the long-term need for Middle East oil, the Clinton administration will no doubt continue to see the peace process as an important part of its broader regional policy.

INGREDIENTS OF SUCCESS

To deal effectively with these challenges in the Middle East in years to come, the Clinton administration would do well to learn from the past record of success and failure. For policies to produce desirable results—such as in the drafting of UN Resolution 242 in 1967, the 1974–75 disengagement talks, the Camp David and peace treaty negotiations in 1978–79, and the diplomacy leading to the Madrid conference in 1991—certain conditions must be met.

There must be a realistic appraisal of the regional situation. To influence governments in the Middle East, politicians in Washington must be keenly aware of what is taking place there. Sustained dialogue with the parties to the conflict is the best way to develop the necessary sensitivity to the real political constraints. Dealing with the Middle East parties through intermediaries does not work well. Wishful thinking, ideological blinders, and indifference are the enemies of success in trying to take the measure of the parties to the Arab-Israeli conflict. As with medicine, correct diagnosis is the key to effective prescription.

The president and his top advisers must be involved and must work in harmony. Unless the prestige and power of the White House are clearly behind American policy initiatives, leaders in the Middle East will not take them seriously. This is one reason that special envoys from Washington rarely succeed. Bureaucratic rivalries and presidential disengagement will also weaken the credibility of any U.S. policy. When policies have succeeded, Nixon and Kissinger, Carter and Vance, Bush and Baker were seen to be working closely together. Failures are associated with the Kissinger-Rogers rivalry, the Brzezinski-Vance disagreement over Iran in 1978, and the long-running Shultz-Weinberger arguments over policy toward Lebanon and arms to Arab countries. In these latter cases presidents who were ambivalent or uninterested allowed those quarrels to undermine their policies. Had they cared enough, however, each president had the power to end these feuds. One of the few unquestioned powers of a president is to fire any top adviser who does not meet his standards. Bureaucratic rivalries are commonplace, but presidents do not have to put up with them indefinitely.

The domestic basis of support for American policy in the region must be constantly developed. Presidents must work with Congress and must explain their purposes to the American public, especially if the costs of the policy are likely to be substantial. Presidents who are unskillful in managing the domestic politics of foreign policy will undermine their own purposes. The ability to mobilize support seems to be very much tied to context: Lyndon Johnson had broad backing for his Middle East policy in 1967, while he was losing support for his Vietnam policy; Richard Nixon won praise for his foreign policy, while losing his base over Watergate; Jimmy Carter succeeded in his Arab-Israeli diplomacy, while simultaneously losing ground over Iran and the hostage crisis; Ronald Reagan was universally praised for his September 1, 1982, speech on the Middle East, and universally criticized for the Iran-Contra fiasco; George Bush won domestic laurels in the war against Iraq, only to see his standing in the polls drop within a matter of months. The lesson must surely be that high-level attention to the home front is a constant preoccupation. No president can assume that Congress and public opinion will back him for long. At the same time policy toward the Arab-Israeli conflict cannot simply reflect the pro-Israeli tone of domestic politics without losing credibility with the Arab parties to the conflict. The president should seek a domestically sustainable policy of evenhandedness, even if it will always be somewhat precarious unless the peace process is moving forward.

Success as a mediator requires a feeling both for process—the procedures for bringing the parties to the negotiations—and for substance. Issues rarely arise that are devoid of substantive implications. The questions of who comes to the negotiating table, the structure of the agenda, and the symbols associated with the peace process are all likely to convey powerful substantive messages to the parties in the Middle East. The United States cannot advance the search for peace between Israel and the Arabs by simply playing the role of mailman; nor can it design a blueprint and impose it on reluctant parties. In between these extremes lies the proper role for the United States—catalyst, energizer, friend, nag, technician, architect. Some of each of these roles has been necessary whenever the United States has succeeded in bridging the gaps between Arabs and Israelis. Carrots and sticks must both be used, sometimes together, to influence reluctant parties. Public acrimony is usually counterproductive, although a display of presidential temper is sometimes useful to underscore serious intent. Threats to abandon the peace process are effective only with the weakest parties, and often lack credibility in any case.

There must be a substantial investment in quiet diplomacy, in "prenegotiation" exploration of the terrain, before deals can be cut. Formal settings, conferences, and direct negotiations are important for symbolic purposes, but most progress is made in secret talks with the top leadership in the region. Presidential letters, memoranda of understandings, and private commitments will all be part of the process of nudging parties toward agreement. Leaks of sensitive information and offhand remarks can complicate delicate negotiations. Tight discipline is needed. Words have consequences. Not everything can be discussed in public, although excessive secrecy can also backfire. Each participant in the negotiating process need not be told exactly the same thing, but any deliberate deception will prove counterproductive. One should assume that much of what one says will eventually be leaked by someone. All the more reason to avoid duplicity.

Pressure sometimes succeeds, but it must be skillfully exerted. Part of the conventional wisdom about U.S.-Israeli relations is that pressure on Israeli governments is bound to backfire. But the record suggests a much more complex reality. True, pressures do not always produce desired results and may sometimes stiffen resistance. Pressure on Israel can also produce domestic controversy and adverse congressional reactions. But at one time or another, each president has tried to persuade Israel to take some action by implying that refusal would be costly. In a surprising number of instances, such efforts at influence have succeeded, often with an added sweetener of rewards for compliance. The same has been true of dealings with Arab parties. To succeed in influencing parties to the Arab-Israeli conflict, the United States must ask for feasible concessions, while wielding both carrots and sticks as incentives.

Timing is crucial for successful negotiations. The American political calendar does not allow much time for launching initiatives and seeing them through to completion. Also, the parties in the region may not be ready to move when the politicians in Washington are. One reason crises are so often followed by initiatives is that crises tend to convince all parties to agree that something new must be tried. Those who argue for a passive stance, in the belief that time will work in favor of accommodation, have the burden of evidence against them. The deliberate policy of doing nothing in the period 1970–73 led to a major war; the stalemate of the 1980s led to the *intifada* and may have helped create the atmosphere in the Arab world that led Saddam Hussein to believe he could get away with his invasion of Kuwait. To say that each of these crises was followed by peace initiatives is hardly a recommendation for deliberately provoking crises. Policy that reacts only to crises is extremely dangerous. Carter demonstrated in 1977 that it was not necessary to wait for an explosion before taking an initiative. Too often, however, initiatives have come only in the aftermath of wars or violence. Clinton will have the opportunity to tackle the Arab-Israeli conflict without the prod of an imminent crisis, but rather at a moment of some expectancy that positive results can be achieved through negotiations. Only Carter among recent presidents inherited such a propitious moment.

CHANGING OF THE GUARD

These guidelines may seem noncontroversial, but translating them into practice proves to be extremely difficult. One reason is the relatively rapid turnover in top positions in the U.S. government. Little experience is accumulated. Continuity is rare. Even the record of past commitments is often hard to discover after a new administration takes over.

Since 1967 seven presidents have occupied the Oval Office. Only Reagan managed to complete two full terms. These seven presidents appointed ten secretaries of state, nine directors of central intelligence, eleven secretaries of defense, and twelve national security advisers. During this same period nine different assistant secretaries for Near Eastern and South Asian Affairs have served, as have nine directors of the Middle East office of the National Security Council. On average, then, the top personnel in charge of Middle East policy changes about every three or four years. Ambassadors to key Middle East countries are rotated with about the same frequency.

The turnover in high places in Washington contrasts starkly with the amazing continuity sometimes found in the Middle East. Yitzhak Rabin was chief of staff in Israel during the 1967 war, ambassador to Washington during the Jordan crisis, prime minister during the second disengagement negotiations, defense minister during the *intifada*, and again prime minister in 1992. As a result, he is likely to know more about the history of American involvement in Arab-Israeli diplomacy than most American diplomats. Similarly, Syria's Hafiz al-Asad has ruled without interruption as president since 1970 and was already defense minister in 1967. He also knows intimately the dossier of recent peace diplomacy, most of which he has opposed and often helped to undermine. King Hussein has been acquainted with every American president since Eisenhower and often seems to despair that every few years he must invest all over again in winning the trust of a new team in Washington. Even the indomitable Yasir Arafat has managed to stay on top of the PLO since 1969. He has outlasted most American peace initiatives.

INITIAL PREDISPOSITIONS

If Americans cannot compete with Middle Easterners in the length of their tenure, the depth of their direct knowledge of the issues, and their study of history, where can they get their bearings? This book places emphasis on two main sources: the predispositions that policymakers bring with them to office, and the views that they acquire on the job. Because of the short tenure in high positions, American policymaking reflects an almost continual process of bringing in new people and educating them in the realities of the Middle East (and the ways of Washington concerning the Middle East). Formal positions on substantive issues change relatively little, but policies, representing tactical judgments, change quite often.

Predispositions relevant to Arab-Israeli diplomacy come in many forms, but for analytical purposes they can be grouped into three clusters. Do the president and his team tend to see Arab-Israeli issues in their regional context or in a broader global context? Are they inclined to attach a high priority to Arab-Israeli issues, or would they prefer to leave these issues on the back burner? Are their sympathies primarily with Israel, or are they relatively evenhanded in their views? These predispositions may be related to other views that have to do with the state of U.S.-Soviet relations (for earlier presidents), the possibility of finding a solution to age-old disputes, and the place of domestic politics in the management of Arab-Israeli diplomacy. But context, salience, and sympathies are a good starting point for characterizing the views of the presidential team that deals with Arab-Israeli issues.

Nixon and Reagan were clearly globalists in their approach to the Middle East. The contest with Moscow was never far from their thoughts. Carter was much more of a regionalist. Bush, Johnson, and Ford were somewhere in between. Clinton is likely to see the region in regional terms, but against the backdrop of global changes in the world economy and the process of democratization.

For Johnson and Reagan the Middle East was rarely a top priority, except in moments of crisis. Nixon tended to see the Middle East as explosive but was persuaded by Kissinger not to be too eager to push for a settlement. After the October 1973 war Nixon, Ford, and Carter were all prepared to deal with the Arab-Israeli issue as a matter of top priority, as was Bush after the war against Iraq. Clinton is unlikely to treat the Arab-Israeli issue as his top priority, but it will not be far from the most important cluster of issues on his foreign-policy agenda.

Johnson and Reagan were no doubt the most pro-Israeli presidents. Nixon, Ford, Carter, and Bush seemed more evenhanded. Among secretaries of state, Henry Kissinger, Alexander Haig, and George Shultz were strong supporters of Israel as an important ally, whereas Dean Rusk, William Rogers, Cyrus Vance, and James Baker took a more evenhanded stance.

If these characterizations of initial predispositions are fairly accurate, they nonetheless cannot convey a full sense of the views of these key decisionmakers. Over time, nuances are added, more information is absorbed, personal relations develop, commitments are made, and lessons are drawn that modify these initial views. Shultz, for example, began his tenure as secretary of state with a reputation for being evenhanded, but later he was seen by the Israelis as their closest friend. And yet it was also Shultz who, in the last weeks of his reign, opened the dialogue with the PLO.

The easiest of these predispositions to change is the sense of priority one brings to the analysis of the Arab-Israeli situation. When tensions rise, or violence erupts, it is quite easy for presidents and secretaries of state to turn their attention to the Arab-Israeli conflict. Nixon and Kissinger immediately changed their assessment of the priority due to the Arab-Israeli dispute when war broke out on October 6, 1973. Alternatively, if the costs of activism seem too great, a president can try to disengage from Arab-Israeli diplomacy, as Carter did in mid-1979.

It seems to be somewhat harder for leaders to shift from a globalist to a regionalist perspective, or vice versa. Such views tend to be fairly well established as part of an overall approach to foreign policy. And yet Kissinger, the quintessential globalist, found himself avidly absorbing information about Middle East politics once he decided to engage in sustained negotiations with the parties to the conflict. Similarly, Bush was initially fairly hard line in dealing with the Soviet Union in the Middle East, but suddenly the Soviet Union collapsed and Bush and Baker found a regionalist perspective quite congenial. Only Carter moved somewhat in the opposite direction. After the Iranian revolution and the Soviet invasion of Afghanistan in 1979, and in the midst of his own reelection campaign, Carter adopted a tough anti-Soviet line. He termed Israel a strategic asset in the struggle to contain Soviet influence, said that he opposed a Palestinian state because it would be an outpost of Soviet influence, and generally adopted a position that was closer to that of Ronald Reagan than to his own earlier stance.

Sympathies seem to change least of all. Pro-Israeli officials do not stop sympathizing with Israel, but they may come to appreciate the need to cultivate relations with Arab leaders as well. This seems to have been true of Reagan, who never wavered in his support for Israel, but who also sold AWACS aircraft to Saudi Arabia, tilted toward Iraq, and authorized the opening of a dialogue with the PLO. Nixon, who seemed to have little emotional affinity for the Jewish state, nonetheless adopted policies, in large measure because of his global outlook, that were very pro-Israeli. Bush, who developed a reputation for being anti-Israeli, endorsed an Israeli proposal for Palestinian elections; crushed Iraq, Israel's principal Arab foe; sidelined the PLO from the official negotiations; continued economic and military support for Israel at all-time levels despite the end of the cold war; and found no trouble in patching up quarrels with Israel once Shamir had been replaced as prime minister by Rabin.

In short, no president and no secretary of state has remained narrowly bound by initial sympathies. All have come to realize that effective mediation requires an ability to deal with leaders on both sides of the conflict, whatever one's personal preferences might be. Thus, although such preferences resist the kind of change that other views may undergo, they also seem least important in the setting of policy. It will long be debated by serious Israelis, for example, whether the ostensibly pro-Israeli Kissinger and Reagan did more for Israel's long-term security than Carter and Bush did.

ON-THE-JOB TRAINING

In learning how to deal with the Middle East, American officials must assess past performance and draw lessons about what has worked and what has failed. On the whole, Americans agree on the successful cases: the adoption of UN Resolution 242; the Egyptian and Syrian disengagement agreements; Camp David and the Egyptian-Israeli peace treaty; and the Madrid conference and its aftermath. The problem with these successes is that they cannot easily be replicated. The lessons to be learned tend to be general ones, not specifically related to the context of existing problems. And by their nature, successes change the environment, leaving new problems in their wake.

Failures are another matter. They leave strong impressions about what not to do. Once a tactic is judged to have failed in one context, it will be hard to argue that it should be tried again in another. In the annals of Arab-Israeli diplomacy it is widely believed that the Rogers Plan of 1969 was a mistake; that the U.S.-Soviet joint communiqué of October 1, 1977, calling for a resumption of the Geneva conference was an error; that the May 17, 1983, agreement between Lebanon and Israel was fatally flawed; and that the deployment of U.S. forces to Lebanon in 1982 should never be repeated. No one has made a career in Washington in recent years by trying to argue that the Rogers Plan had some positive elements that eventually led to the Egyptian-Israeli peace treaty, or that it failed because it was undercut from within the Nixon administration as much as for any other reason. Few have questioned that the October 1, 1977, communiqué was misguided, and for years the standard rebuff to anyone suggesting that the Soviet Union should be involved in Middle East diplomacy was the example of the fate of that effort.

Other Middle East cases are harder to judge. Was the Jordan crisis a success or failure? Some of both, one could contend. King Hussein was strengthened; allies of the Soviet Union were checked; the crisis was contained. But the lessons drawn were the source of subsequent problems. Complacency set in; confidence grew in Israeli military prowess as the key to stability; and Arab frustrations were ignored. The "success" in handling the Jordan crisis led, in part, to the "failure" to anticipate the October 1973 war. But that "failure" in turn set the stage for the "success" of the disengagement talks. In brief, lessons of history are invariably drawn, but involve highly subjective judgments. Still, they serve as powerful guidelines in intrabureaucratic discussions.

Accumulated experience with Middle East diplomacy does not suggest a single correct method for pursuing the peace process. Each president has had a somewhat distinctive style. Johnson limited himself to spelling out the general principles for a peace settlement, while insisting that Israel should be allowed to hold captured Arab lands as bargaining leverage to achieve peace. The logic of that approach has rarely been questioned by his successors. Nixon, influenced by Kissinger, initially opted for a policy of confronting the Soviets in the region before tackling the Arab-Israeli conflict. Then, after the 1973 war, Nixon and Kissinger developed the technique of step-by-step shuttle diplomacy. Carter began with a comprehensive design but was obliged to scale back to a more modest, through still impressive, goal of peace on one front. Reagan and Haig preached a doctrine of strategic consensus, which had few regional supporters; then in 1982 Reagan gave a speech that spelled out as clearly as has ever been done what the United States would support in an Arab-Israeli settlement. The speech was not connected to a strategy, and the Reagan years saw little real progress in peacemaking, but the vision spelled out in that speech has informed policymaking ever since. Finally, Bush and Baker, after one false start, perfected the art of the deal, bringing all the parties to accept the architecture of a negotiating process. On the whole, this is an impressive record, to which Clinton will almost certainly be tempted to add his own contribution.

SUBSTANTIVE BUILDING BLOCKS

Over time presidents and their advisers have spoken less about the substance of an Arab-Israeli agreement and more about process. This "procedural bias" stems from a belief that big plans do not work, that they are too controversial, that they become targets of opposition rather than frameworks for agreement. Yet many of the most impressive monuments of American peacemaking in the Middle East are precisely sketches of both the content of peace and the process for achieving it. UN Resolution 242, which is still seen as a foundation for any Arab-Israeli peace, is essentially a statement of the main substantive trade-off that will have to be negotiated: the withdrawal of Israeli forces from territory occupied in 1967 in return for recognition, peace, and security arrangements for Israel. If 242 had flaws, they were primarily the total disregard of the Palestinians (a substantive issue that was dealt with through procedural arrangements in later years) and the feeble mechanism designed to promote peace (a UN-designated envoy without any powers). Besides providing the basis for the Egyptian-Israeli peace, UN Resolution 242 and its "land for peace" trade-off will almost certainly be at the core of a future Syrian-Israeli agreement.

The Camp David Accords went further than Resolution 242 in addressing the Palestinian issue. Their chief innovation was to call for an interim agreement between Israel and the Palestinians based on the concept of self-government or autonomy. The reason for this approach was that neither Israelis nor Palestinians seemed able to agree on more than such an interim step. The architects of Camp David also hoped that the experience of the "transitional" period would make the issues of a final settlement more tractable. Although Camp David is not explicitly the agreed basis for the negotiations between Israel and the Palestinians, the central idea of a two-stage negotiation, starting with interim self-government for the Palestinians, has been accepted by all the parties to the Madrid conference.

Reagan's substantive legacy was his elaboration on the missing part of Camp David—namely, what lay beyond the transitional period. Without going into great detail, Reagan said that the United States would not support Israeli annexation of the West Bank and Gaza or a fully independent Palestinian state. Instead the United States would favor some form of association between the occupied territories and Jordan. In one way or another, that is likely to be the outline of any future Israeli-Palestinian-Jordanian peace agreement.

The main substantive contribution of the Bush administration did not come in the form of plans or speeches. In the course of organizing the Madrid conference, Bush and Baker began to deal with the Palestinians as a full partner in the negotiations. This ostensibly procedural step had substantive implications, although these remain to be elaborated in the course of negotiations. Bush also returned to the emphasis on freezing Israeli settlement activity during the negotiating process. Carter had tried and failed to win this point. Bush, wielding the big stick of $10 billion in loan guarantees, was taken more seriously. Indeed, one of Bush's major contributions to the peace process was the boost he gave to the unseating of the ideologically rigid Yitzhak Shamir and his replacement by the more pragmatic Yitzhak Rabin. For the first time since 1977, Israel was governed by a cabinet committed to UN Resolution 242 in its original meaning—the exchange of land for peace, in conditions of security and mutual recognition, on all fronts of the conflict. Even Bill Clinton noted that Rabin's election was the most important contribution to the peace process in the year following the Madrid conference, although he gave George Bush no credit for pushing Shamir to the sidelines.[1]

FUTURE PROSPECTS

By 1992 the United States had succeeded in launching a new round of negotiations, more promising in architectural design and in scope than any before. The general framework for negotiations could be distilled from previous positions—mainly 242 and Camp David—but the road map to peace was sketchy at best.

Almost certainly, the United States will be called on to help elaborate the contents of future peace agreements if the negotiations are to succeed. Nothing in the historical record suggests that the parties will reach agreement if left alone in direct negotiations.

In many ways the American role in the future should be easier to play than in the past. The Soviet Union as a rival and potential spoiler is no more. The globalist bias that often adversely affected American policy in the Middle East has lost its rationale. With it has gone the notion that Israel is a strategic ally of such importance that it must be supported at all costs.[2] Public backing for Israel remains high, but the White House is under little pressure to offer Israel a blank check. Public opinion, if not Congress, is more prone than ever to support an evenhanded stance toward the Arab-Israeli conflict. Such an atmosphere provides a degree of tactical flexibility for a president seeking to find common ground between Arabs and Israelis.

Perhaps most encouraging for the peace process is the evidence that many Israelis and many Arabs are tired of the conflict and are finally ready for a historic compromise. Without such sentiment in the region, the United States can do little to promote peace. The Israeli elections in 1992 brought to power a government committed to swift movement in the negotiations, in contrast to the go-slow approach of the Shamir government.

The record of the peace process since 1967 shows that progress is not incremental or continuous. More frequently, long periods of stalemate have been succeeded by bursts of activity that have produced substantial changes in the nature of the Arab-Israeli conflict. Then the parties seem to need some time to absorb the results, to ready themselves for another major move, to build support on the domestic front.

One can credibly argue that the 1980s represented an unusually long lull in the peace process and that the stage is set in the early 1990s for significant breakthroughs. One possibility would be moves toward a Syrian-Israeli treaty, based on full peace and recognition for Israel, extensive security arrangements to reduce the chance of surprise attack, and Israeli recognition of Syrian sovereignty on the Golan Heights. All these principles could be implemented over a period of years.

On the Israeli-Palestinian front the prospects for an overall agreement are less promising. But some form of interim agreement, which would allow Palestinians extensive authority to govern themselves in the West Bank and Gaza, while Israel retained control over security, seems feasible. Eventually the very complex problem of Israeli settlements and the status of East Jerusalem will have to be confronted, but they may be finessed in the interim stage by common consent. And if progress is made on the Syrian and Palestinian negotiating fronts, the Lebanese and Jordanians will not be far behind.

For the peace process to move ahead in these uniquely hopeful circumstances, American leadership will be needed. That prospect is somewhat challenged by a revival of isolationist sentiment in the United States. This attitude affects Middle East policy less than other foreign-policy issue areas, but it places a limit on any initiative that is likely to require substantial resources. As a result, the United States, while still playing the key mediating role, will have to find partners who can help underwrite steps toward peace, toward regional development, and toward arms control.

As the peace process moves along, the United States will also be confronting other, related challenges in the Middle East. How should the next president deal with assertive Islamic movements? What is the place for democracy in this part of the world? Can economic development be accelerated, as in east Asia, as a complement to peacemaking and democratization? Can arms control make headway in a region where conflicts are so endemic? And can anything be done to prevent the proliferation of weapons of mass destruction in the region? All these new concerns will demand attention alongside the traditional peace process agenda. And even that agenda will have to address in creative ways the problems of regional security, confederal arrangements, the linkage between interim steps and subsequent stages of negotiations, and the future of Jerusalem, issues that have been ignored for too long.

Time is of the essence, not so much because peace must be achieved suddenly or not at all. Rather, the process is likely to take time, which means that political leaders in the region must be able to show results early and often if they are to retain the necessary support. This is especially true in Israel, where opinion is still deeply divided, and among the Palestinians, where public sentiment plays a larger part than in most Arab regimes. A prolonged stalemate in the peace process will frustrate moderates on both sides of the conflict, lead to public disinterest in the United States, and will set the stage for future crises in a radicalized Middle East whose oil resources will be increasingly important for the industrialized West.

Thus the peace process, with an increasing emphasis on the substantive elements of future peace agreements, is likely to be a priority for President Clinton and his foreign-policy team. The record suggests that Clinton's own predispositions will matter in the shaping of policy toward the Arab-Israeli conflict, even though by now there is a fairly strong consensus on the peace process and its rationale. Still, in those moments when judgment is called for, when crises clarify choices, and when trade-offs must be made, the person occupying the Oval Office makes a difference.

If presidents play their parts well, they can help advance the peace process. If they falter, they risk jeopardizing American interests. For better or worse, they will not be allowed to ignore the region for long. Their understanding of the basic issues of the Arab-Israeli conflict and their ability to learn from experience will be the keys to whether presidents become statesmen. If they do, they stand a good chance of contributing to the long-sought goal of Arab-Israeli peace.

PART EIGHT

Appendixes

APPENDIX A

United Nations Resolutions 242 and 338

UN SECURITY COUNCIL RESOLUTION 242,
NOVEMBER 22, 1967

The Security Council,

Expressing its continuing concern with the grave situation in the Middle East,

Emphasizing the inadmissibility of the acquisition of territory by war and the need to work for a just and lasting peace in which every State in the area can live in security,

Emphasizing further that all Member States in their acceptance of the Charter of the United Nations have undertaken a commitment to act in accordance with Article 2 of the Charter,

1. *Affirms* that the fulfillment of Charter principles requires the establishment of a just and lasting peace in the Middle East which should include the application of both the following principles:

(i) Withdrawal of Israeli armed forces from territories occupied in the recent conflict;

(ii) Termination of all claims or states of belligerency and respect for and acknowledgement of the sovereignty, territorial integrity and political independence of every State in the area and their right to live in peace within secure and recognized boundaries free from threats or acts of force;

2. *Affirms further* the necessity

(a) For guaranteeing freedom of navigation through international waterways in the area;

(b) For achieving a just settlement of the refugee problem;

(c) For guaranteeing the territorial inviolability and political independence of every State in the area, through measures including the establishment of demilitarized zones;

3. *Requests* the Secretary-General to designate a Special Representative to proceed to the Middle East to establish and maintain contacts with the

States concerned in order to promote agreement and assist efforts to achieve a peaceful and accepted settlement in accordance with the provisions and principles of this resolution;

4. *Requests* the Secretary-General to report to the Security Council on the progress of the efforts of the Special Representative as soon as possible.

UN SECURITY COUNCIL RESOLUTION 338,
OCTOBER 22, 1973

The Security Council

1. *Calls upon* all parties to the present fighting to cease all firing and terminate all military activity immediately, no later than 12 hours after the moment of the adoption of this decision, in the positions they now occupy;

2. *Calls upon* the parties concerned to start immediately after the cease-fire the implementation of Security Council Resolution 242 (1967) in all of its parts;

3. *Decides* that, immediately and concurrently with the cease-fire, negotiations start between the parties concerned under appropriate auspices aimed at establishing a just and durable peace in the Middle East.

APPENDIX B

Joint U.S.-USSR Working Paper, Fundamental Principles (The Rogers Plan), October 28, 1969

Israel and the UAR,

In consideration of their obligations under the Charter of the United Nations,

Confirming their obligations under Security Council Resolution 242 of November 22, 1967 and expressing their readiness to implement it in good faith in all of its provisions,

Recognizing the inadmissibility of the acquisition of territory by means of war,

Recognizing also the need to establish a just and lasting peace in the Middle East under the terms of which each State in this area can live in security,

Agree that their representatives under the auspices of Ambassador Jarring will follow the procedures the parties utilized at Rhodes in 1949 to work out without delay, starting on the basis of the following provisions, a final and reciprocally binding accord on ways of implementing Security Council Resolution 242 of November 22, 1967 to establish a just and lasting peace.

Point 1

The parties, in reaching a final accord (contained in a final document or documents) on a package settlement on the basis of these Fundamental Principles, would determine a timetable and procedures for withdrawal of Israeli armed forces from UAR territory occupied during the conflict of 1967 to boundaries to be delineated in accordance with Point 3 as well as an agreed plan for interrelated fulfillment of all other provisions of Security Council Resolution 242.

Point 2

The state of war and belligerency between Israel and the UAR would be terminated and a formal state of peace would be established between them, and both parties would refrain from acts inconsistent with the state of peace and the cessation of the state of war.

In particular:

1. No aggressive action by the armed and other forces—land, sea, or air—of either party would be undertaken or threatened against the people or the armed forces of the other.

2. Both parties would undertake to do all in their power to ensure that acts of hostility and belligerency whether by government agencies, personnel, or private persons or organizations will not originate from and are not committed from within their respective territory.

3. Both parties would refrain from intervening directly or indirectly in each other's domestic affairs for any political, economic, or other reasons.

4. Both parties would confirm that in their relations with each other, they will be guided by the principles contained in Article 2, paragraphs 3 and 4 of the UN Charter.

Point 3

The parties would agree on the location of the secure and recognized boundary between them, which would be shown on a map or maps approved by the parties which would become part of the final accord. In the context of peace, including the *inter alia* agreement between the parties on the establishment of demilitarized zones, on practical security arrangements in the Sharm al-Shaykh area for guaranteeing freedom of navigation through the Strait of Tiran, and on practical security arrangements and final disposition of Gaza, the former international boundary between Egypt and the mandated territory of Palestine would become the secure and recognized boundary between Israel and the UAR.

Point 4

For the purpose of ensuring the territorial inviolability of the parties and guaranteeing the security of the recognized boundary, the parties, following the procedures set forth in the last preambular paragraph of this document, would work out an agreement on:

(a) Zones to be demilitarized and procedures of ensuring their demilitarization;

(b) Practical security arrangements in the Sharm al-Shaykh area to assure freedom of navigation through the Strait of Tiran; and

(c) Practical security arrangements for and final disposition of Gaza.

Point 5

The parties would agree and the Security Council would reaffirm:

(a) That the Strait of Tiran is an international waterway; and

(b) That the principle of free navigation for vessels of all countries, including, Israel, applies to the Strait of Tiran and the Gulf of Aqaba.

Point 6

The UAR would affirm that, in its exercise of sovereignty over the Suez Canal, the ships of all nations, including Israel, will have the right of freedom of navigation without discrimination or interference.

Point 7

The parties would agree to abide by the terms of a just settlement of the refugee problem as agreed upon in the final accord between Jordan and Israel, and to participate as Ambassador Jarring may deem desirable in working out the terms of said settlement.

Point 8

The UAR and Israel would mutually agree to respect and acknowledge each other's sovereignty, territorial integrity, inviolability and political independence and each other's right to live in peace within secure and recognized borders free from threats or acts of force.

Point 9

The final accord would be recorded in a document which is to be signed by the parties and immediately deposited with the UN. After the parties have deposited such a document, the Secretary General of the UN would be requested by the parties immediately to inform the Security Council and all UN Member States to that effect.

In the implementation of the final accord, it would be understood by the parties that their respective obligations would be reciprocal and interdependent. The final accord would provide that a material breach of that accord by one of the parties shall entitle the other to invoke the breach as a ground for suspending its performance in whole or in part until the breach shall be cured. From the moment of deposit, the document would become binding on the parties and irrevocable, and implementation and observance by the parties of the provisions of the accord would begin.

Point 10

Both parties would agree that the final accord, including the map or maps delineating the final boundaries, would be submitted to the Security Council for its endorsement.

* * *

It would be understood that the accord between the UAR and Israel would be paralleled by an accord between Jordan and Israel, which would include agreement on a just solution of the refugee problem. Implementation of both accords would begin only after agreement had been achieved on the entire package.

It would also be understood that France, the United Kingdom, the United States and the Union of Soviet Socialist Republics would submit and support an appropriate Security Council resolution and pledge that they would concert their future efforts to help the parties abide by all of the provisions of the final accord or accords.

APPENDIX C

*Letter from President Ford to Prime Minister Rabin,
September 1, 1975*

SECRET

His Excellency
Yitzhak Rabin
Prime Minister of Israel

Dear Mr. Prime Minister:
I wish to inform you that the U.S. recognizes that the Israeli-Egyptian
Interim Agreement entailing withdrawal from vital areas in the Sinai
constitutes an act of great significance on Israel's part in the pursuit of
final peace and imposes additional heavy military and economic burdens
on Israel.

I want to assure you that the U.S. will make every effort to be
fully responsive within the limits of its resources and Congressional
authorization and appropriation on an ongoing and long-term basis to
Israel's military equipment and other defense requirements as well as to
Israel's economic aid needs, all of this based on the requests submitted
by Israel, joint studies and previous U.S. Presidential undertakings.

Further to those undertakings, it is my resolve to continue to maintain
Israel's defensive strength through the supply of advanced types of
equipment, such as the F-16 aircraft. The United States Government
agrees to an early meeting to undertake a joint study of high technology
and sophisticated items, including the Pershing ground-to-ground missiles
with conventional warheads, with the view to giving a positive response.
The U.S. Administration will submit annually for approval by the U.S.
Congress a request for military and economic assistance in order to help
meet Israel's economic and military needs. Realizing as I do the importance
of the Interim Agreement to the Middle Eastern situation as a whole, the
U.S. will make every possible effort to assist in the establishment of

The text comes from Michael Widlanski, ed., *Can Israel Survive a Palestinian State?*
(Jerusalem: Institute for Advanced Strategic Political Studies, 1990), pp. 120–21.

conditions in which the Agreement will be observed without being subjected to pressures or deadlines.

In the spirit of the special relationship existing between the United States and Israel and in light of the determination of both sides to avoid a situation in which the U.S. and Israel would pursue divergent courses in peace negotiations, the U.S. will take the position that these are negotiations between the parties. As I indicated to you in our conversation on 12 June 1975, the situation in the aftermath of the Israeli-Egyptian Interim Agreement will be one in which the overall settlement can be pursued in a systematic and deliberate way and does not require the U.S. to put forward an overall proposal of its own in such circumstances. Should the U.S. desire in the future to put forward proposals of its own, it will make every effort to coordinate with Israel its proposals with a view to refraining from putting forth proposals that Israel would consider unsatisfactory.

The U.S. will support the position that an overall settlement with Syria in the framework of a peace agreement must assure Israel's security from attack from the Golan Heights. The U.S. further supports the position that a just and lasting peace, which remains our objective, must be acceptable to both sides. The U.S. has not developed a final position on the borders. Should it do so it will give great weight to Israel's position that any peace agreement with Syria must be predicated on Israel remaining on the Golan Heights. My view in this regard was stated in our conversation of September 13, 1974.

Sincerely,

Gerald R. Ford

APPENDIX D

Joint Communiqué by the Governments of the United States and the Union of Soviet Socialist Republics, October 1, 1977

Having exchanged views regarding the unsafe situation which remains in the Middle East, U.S. Secretary of State Cyrus Vance and Member of the Politbureau of the Central Committee of the CPSU, Minister for Foreign Affairs of the U.S.S.R. A. A. Gromyko have the following statement to make on behalf of their countries, which are cochairmen of the Geneva Peace Conference on the Middle East:

1. Both governments are convinced that vital interests of the peoples of this area, as well as the interests of strengthening peace and international security in general, urgently dictate the necessity of achieving, as soon as possible, a just and lasting settlement of the Arab-Israeli conflict. This settlement should be comprehensive, incorporating all parties concerned and all questions.

The United States and the Soviet Union believe that, within the framework of a comprehensive settlement of the Middle East problem, all specific questions of the settlement should be resolved, including such key issues as withdrawal of Israeli Armed Forces from territories occupied in the 1967 conflict; the resolution of the Palestinian question, including insuring the legitimate rights of the Palestinian people; termination of the state of war and establishment of normal peaceful relations on the basis of mutual recognition of the principles of sovereignty, territorial integrity, and political independence.

The two governments believe that, in addition to such measures for insuring the security of the borders between Israel and the neighboring Arab states as the establishment of demilitarized zones and the agreed stationing in them of U.N. troops or observers, international guarantees of such borders as well as of the observance of the terms of the settlement can also be established should the contracting parties so desire. The

The text comes from "U.S., U.S.S.R. Issue Statement on the Middle East," *Department of State Bulletin*, vol. 77 (November 7, 1977), pp. 639–40. The statement was issued in New York City.

United States and the Soviet Union are ready to participate in these guarantees, subject to their constitutional processes.

2. The United States and the Soviet Union believe that the only right and effective way for achieving a fundamental solution to all aspects of the Middle East problem in its entirety is negotiations within the framework of the Geneva peace conference, specially convened for these purposes, with participation in its work of the representatives of all the parties involved in the conflict including those of the Palestinian people, and legal and contractual formalization of the decisions reached at the conference.

In their capacity as cochairmen of the Geneva conference, the United States and the U.S.S.R. affirm their intention, through joint efforts and in their contacts with the parties concerned, to facilitate in every way the resumption of the work of the conference not later than December 1977. The cochairmen note that there still exist several questions of a procedural and organizational nature which remain to be agreed upon by the participants to the conference.

3. Guided by the goal of achieving a just political settlement in the Middle East and of eliminating the explosive situation in this area of the world, the United States and the U.S.S.R. appeal to all the parties in the conflict to understand the necessity for careful consideration of each other's legitimate rights and interests and to demonstrate mutual readiness to act accordingly.

APPENDIX E

The Camp David Accords, September 17, 1978

A FRAMEWORK FOR PEACE IN THE MIDDLE EAST
AGREED AT CAMP DAVID

Muhammad Anwar al-Sadat, President of the Arab Republic of Egypt, and Menachem Begin, Prime Minister of Israel, met with Jimmy Carter, President of the United States of America, at Camp David from September 5 to September 17, 1978, and have agreed on the following framework for peace in the Middle East. They invite other parties to the Arab-Israeli conflict to adhere to it.

Preamble

The search for peace in the Middle East must be guided by the following:

—The agreed basis for a peaceful settlement of the conflict between Israel and its neighbors is United Nations Security Council Resolution 242, in all its parts.

—After four wars during thirty years, despite intensive human efforts, the Middle East, which is the cradle of civilization and the birthplace of three great religions, does not yet enjoy the blessings of peace. The people of the Middle East yearn for peace so that the vast human and natural resources of the region can be turned to the pursuits of peace and so that this area can become a model for coexistence and cooperation among nations.

—The historic initiative of President Sadat in visiting Jerusalem and the reception accorded to him by the Parliament, government and people of Israel, and the reciprocal visit of Prime Minister Begin to Ismailia, the peace proposals made by both leaders, as well as the warm reception of these missions by the peoples of both countries, have created an unprecedented opportunity for peace which must not be lost if this generation and future generations are to be spared the tragedies of war.

—The provisions of the Charter of the United Nations and the other accepted norms of international law and legitimacy now provide accepted standards for the conduct of relations among all states.

—To achieve a relationship of peace, in the spirit of Article 2 of the United Nations Charter, future negotiations between Israel and any neighbor prepared to negotiate peace and security with it, are necessary for the purpose of carrying out all the provisions and principles of Resolutions 242 and 338.

—Peace requires respect for the sovereignty, territorial integrity and political independence of every state in the area and their right to live in peace within secure and recognized boundaries free from threats or acts of force. Progress toward that goal can accelerate movement toward a new era of reconciliation in the Middle East marked by cooperation in promoting economic development, in maintaining stability, and in assuring security.

—Security is enhanced by a relationship of peace and by cooperation between nations which enjoy normal relations. In addition, under the terms of peace treaties, the parties can, on the basis of reciprocity, agree to special security arrangements such as demilitarized zones, limited armaments areas, early warning stations, the presence of international forces, liaison, agreed measures for monitoring, and other arrangements that they agree are useful.

Framework

Taking these factors into account, the parties are determined to reach a just, comprehensive, and durable settlement of the Middle East conflict through the conclusion of peace treaties based on Security Council Resolutions 242 and 338 in all their parts. Their purpose is to achieve peace and good neighborly relations. They recognize that, for peace to endure, it must involve all those who have been most deeply affected by the conflict. They therefore agree that this framework as appropriate is intended by them to constitute a basis for peace not only between Egypt and Israel, but also between Israel and each of its neighbors which is prepared to negotiate peace with Israel on this basis. With that objective in mind, they have agreed to proceed as follows:

A. West Bank and Gaza

1. Egypt, Israel, Jordan and the representatives of the Palestinian people should participate in negotiations on the resolution of the Palestinian problem in all its aspects. To achieve that objective, negotiations relating to the West Bank and Gaza should proceed in three stages:

(a) Egypt and Israel agree that, in order to ensure a peaceful and orderly transfer of authority, and taking into account the security concerns of all the parties, there should be transitional arrangements for the West Bank and Gaza for a period not exceeding five years. In order to provide full autonomy to the inhabitants, under these arrangements the Israeli military government and its civilian administration will be withdrawn as soon as a self-governing authority has been freely elected by the inhabitants of these areas to replace the existing military government. To negotiate the details of a transitional arrangement, the Government of Jordan will be invited to join the negotiations on the basis of this framework. These new arrangements should give due consideration both to the principle of self-government by the inhabitants of these territories and to the legitimate security concerns of the parties involved.

(b) Egypt, Israel, and Jordan will agree on the modalities for establishing the elected self-governing authority in the West Bank and Gaza. The delegations of Egypt and Jordan may include Palestinians from the West Bank and Gaza or other Palestinians as mutually agreed. The parties will negotiate an agreement which will define the powers and responsibilities of the self-governing authority to be exercised in the West Bank and Gaza. A withdrawal of Israeli armed forces will take place and there will be a redeployment of the remaining Israeli forces into specified security locations. The agreement will also include arrangements for assuring internal and external security and public order. A strong local police force will be established, which may include Jordanian citizens. In addition, Israeli and Jordanian forces will participate in joint patrols and in the manning of control posts to assure the security of the borders.

(c) When the self-governing authority (administrative council) in the West Bank and Gaza is established and inaugurated, the transitional period of five years will begin. As soon as possible, but not later than the third year after the beginning of the transitional period, negotiations will take place to determine the final status of the West Bank and Gaza and its relationship with its neighbors, and to conclude a peace treaty between Israel and Jordan by the end of the transitional period. These negotiations will be conducted among Egypt, Israel, Jordan, and the elected representatives of the inhabitants of the West Bank and Gaza. Two separate but related committees will be convened, one committee, consisting of representatives of the four parties which will negotiate and agree on the final status of the West Bank and Gaza, and its relationship with its neighbors, and the second committee, consisting of representatives

of Israel and representatives of Jordan to be joined by the elected
representatives of the inhabitants of the West Bank and Gaza, to negotiate
the peace treaty between Israel and Jordan, taking into account the
agreement reached on the final status of the West Bank and Gaza. The
negotiations shall be based on all the provisions and principles of UN
Security Council Resolution 242. The negotiations will resolve, among
other matters, the location of the boundaries and the nature of the security
arrangements. The solution from the negotiations must also recognize the
legitimate rights of the Palestinian people and their just requirements. In
this way, the Palestinians will participate in the determination of their
own future through:

(1) The negotiations among Egypt, Israel, Jordan and the representatives of the inhabitants of the West Bank and Gaza to agree on the final
status of the West Bank and Gaza and other outstanding issues by the
end of the transitional period.

(2) Submitting their agreement to a vote by the elected representatives
of the inhabitants of the West Bank and Gaza.

(3) Providing for the elected representatives of the inhabitants of
the West Bank and Gaza to decide how they shall govern themselves
consistent with the provisions of their agreement.

(4) Participating as stated above in the work of the committee
negotiating the peace treaty between Israel and Jordan.

2. All necessary measures will be taken and provisions made to assure
the security of Israel and its neighbors during the transitional period and
beyond. To assist in providing such security, a strong local police force
will be constituted by the self-governing authority. It will be composed
of inhabitants of the West Bank and Gaza. The police will maintain
continuing liaison on internal security matters with the designated Israeli,
Jordanian, and Egyptian officers.

3. During the transitional period, representatives of Egypt, Israel,
Jordan, and the self-governing authority will constitute a continuing
committee to decide by agreement on the modalities of admission of
persons displaced from the West Bank and Gaza in 1967, together with
necessary measures to prevent disruption and disorder. Other matters of
common concern may also be dealt with by this committee.

4. Egypt and Israel will work with each other and with other interested
parties to establish agreed procedures for a prompt, just and permanent
implementation of the resolution of the refugee problem.

B. *Egypt-Israel*

1. Egypt and Israel undertake not to resort to the threat or the use of force to settle disputes. Any disputes shall be settled by peaceful means in accordance with the provisions of Article 33 of the Charter of the United Nations.

2. In order to achieve peace between them, the parties agree to negotiate in good faith with a goal of concluding within three months from the signing of this Framework a peace treaty between them, while inviting the other parties to the conflict to proceed simultaneously to negotiate and conclude similar peace treaties with a view to achieving a comprehensive peace in the area. The Framework for the Conclusion of a Peace Treaty Between Egypt and Israel will govern the peace negotiations between them. The parties will agree on the modalities and the timetable for the implementation of their obligations under the treaty.

C. *Associated Principles*

1. Egypt and Israel state that the principles and provisions described below should apply to peace treaties between Israel and each of its neighbors—Egypt, Jordan, Syria and Lebanon.

2. Signatories shall establish among themselves relationships normal to states at peace with one another. To this end, they should undertake to abide by all the provisions of the Charter of the United Nations. Steps to be taken in this respect include:

(a) full recognition;

(b) abolishing economic boycotts;

(c) guaranteeing that under their jurisdiction the citizens of the other parties shall enjoy the protection of the due process of law.

3. Signatories should explore possibilities for economic development in the context of final peace treaties, with the objective of contributing to the atmosphere of peace, cooperation and friendship which is their common goal.

4. Claims Commissions may be established for the mutual settlement of all financial claims.

5. The United States shall be invited to participate in the talks on matters related to the modalities of the implementation of the agreements and working out the timetable for the carrying out of the obligations of the parties.

6. The United Nations Security Council shall be requested to endorse

the peace treaties and ensure that their provisions shall not be violated. The permanent members of the Security Council shall be requested to underwrite the peace treaties and ensure respect for their provisions. They shall also be requested to conform their policies and actions with the undertakings contained in this Framework.

For the Government of the Arab Republic of Egypt:

A. Sadat

For the Government of Israel:

M. Begin

Witnessed by:

Jimmy Carter,
President of the
United States of America

FRAMEWORK FOR THE CONCLUSION OF A PEACE TREATY BETWEEN EGYPT AND ISRAEL

In order to achieve peace between them, Israel and Egypt agree to negotiate in good faith with a goal of concluding within three months of the signing of this framework a peace treaty between them.

It is agreed that:

The site of the negotiations will be under a United Nations flag at a location or locations to be mutually agreed.

All of the principles of UN Resolution 242 will apply in this resolution of the dispute between Israel and Egypt.

Unless otherwise mutually agreed, terms of the peace treaty will be implemented between two and three years after the peace treaty is signed.

The following matters are agreed between the parties:

(a) the full exercise of Egyptian sovereignty up to the internationally recognized border between Egypt and mandated Palestine;

(b) the withdrawal of Israeli armed forces from the Sinai;

(c) the use of airfields left by the Israelis near El Arish, Rafah, Ras en Naqb, and Sharm el Sheikh for civilian purposes only, including possible commercial use by all nations;

(d) the right of free passage by ships of Israel through the Gulf of Suez and the Suez Canal on the basis of the Constantinople Convention of 1888 applying to all nations; the Strait of Tiran and the Gulf of Aqaba are international waterways to be open to all nations for unimpeded and nonsuspendable freedom of navigation and overflight;

(e) the construction of a highway between the Sinai and Jordan near Elat with guaranteed free and peaceful passage by Egypt and Jordan; and

(f) the stationing of military forces listed below.

Stationing of Forces

A. No more than one division (mechanized or infantry) of Egyptian armed forces will be stationed within an area lying approximately 50 kilometers (km) east of the Gulf of Suez and the Suez Canal.

B. Only United Nations forces and civil police equipped with light weapons to perform normal police functions will be stationed within an area lying west of the international border and the Gulf of Aqaba, varying in width from 20 km to 40 km.

C. In the area within 3 km east of the international border there will be Israeli limited military forces not to exceed four infantry battalions and United Nations observers.

D. Border patrol units, not to exceed three battalions, will supplement the civil police in maintaining order in the area not included above.

The exact demarcation of the above areas will be as decided during the peace negotiations.

Early warning stations may exist to insure compliance with the terms of the agreement.

United Nations forces will be stationed: (a) in part of the area in the Sinai lying within about 20 km of the Mediterranean Sea and adjacent to the international border, and (b) in the Sharm el Sheikh area to ensure freedom of passage through the Strait of Tiran; and these forces will not be removed unless such removal is approved by the Security Council of the United Nations with a unanimous vote of the five permanent members.

After a peace treaty is signed, and after the interim withdrawal is complete, normal relations will be established between Egypt and Israel, including: full recognition, including diplomatic, economic and cultural relations; termination of economic boycotts and barriers to the free movement of goods and people; and mutual protection of citizens by the due process of law.

Interim Withdrawal

Between three months and nine months after the signing of the peace treaty, all Israeli forces will withdraw east of a line extending from a point east of El Arish to Ras Muhammad, the exact location of this line to be determined by mutual agreement.

For the Government of the Arab Republic of Egypt:

A. Sadat

For the Government of Israel:

M. Begin

Witnessed by:

Jimmy Carter
President of the United States of America

LETTER FROM ISRAELI PRIME MINISTER MENACHEM BEGIN TO PRESIDENT JIMMY CARTER, SEPTEMBER 17, 1978

Dear Mr. President:

I have the honor to inform you that during two weeks after my return home I will submit a motion before Israel's Parliament (the Knesset) to decide on the following question:

If during the negotiations to conclude a peace treaty between Israel and Egypt all outstanding issues are agreed upon, "are you in favor of the removal of the Israeli settlers from the northern and southern Sinai areas or are you in favor of keeping the aforementioned settlers in those areas?"

The vote, Mr. President, on this issue will be completely free from the usual Parliamentary Party discipline to the effect that although the coalition is being now supported by 70 members out of 120, every member of the Knesset, as I believe, both on the Government and the Opposition benches will be enabled to vote in accordance with his own conscience.

Sincerely yours,

Menachem Begin

LETTER FROM PRESIDENT JIMMY CARTER TO EGYPTIAN PRESIDENT ANWAR EL-SADAT, SEPTEMBER 22, 1978

Dear Mr. President:

I transmit herewith a copy of a letter to me from Prime Minister Begin setting forth how he proposes to present the issue of the Sinai settlements to the Knesset for the latter's decision. In this connection, I understand from your letter that Knesset approval to withdraw all Israeli settlers from Sinai according to a timetable within the period specified for the implementation of the peace treaty is a prerequisite to any negotiations on a peace treaty between Egypt and Israel.

Sincerely,

Jimmy Carter

Enclosure:
Letter from Prime Minister Begin

LETTER FROM EGYPTIAN PRESIDENT ANWAR EL-SADAT
TO PRESIDENT JIMMY CARTER, SEPTEMBER 17, 1978

Dear Mr. President:
In connection with the "Framework for a Settlement in Sinai" to be signed tonight, I would like to reaffirm the position of the Arab Republic of Egypt with respect to the settlements:

1. All Israeli settlers must be withdrawn from Sinai according to a timetable within the period specified for the implementation of the peace treaty.

2. Agreement by the Israeli Government and its constitutional institutions to this basic principle is therefore a prerequisite to starting peace negotiations for concluding a peace treaty.

3. If Israel fails to meet this commitment, the "Framework" shall be void and invalid.

Sincerely,

Mohamed Anwar El Sadat

LETTER FROM PRESIDENT JIMMY CARTER TO ISRAELI
PRIME MINISTER MENACHEM BEGIN, SEPTEMBER 22, 1978

Dear Mr. Prime Minister:
I have received your letter of September 17, 1978, describing how you intend to place the question of the future of Israeli settlements in Sinai before the Knesset for its decision. Enclosed is a copy of President Sadat's letter to me on this subject.

Sincerely,

Jimmy Carter

Enclosure:
Letter from President Sadat

LETTER FROM EGYPTIAN PRESIDENT ANWAR EL-SADAT
TO PRESIDENT JIMMY CARTER, SEPTEMBER 17, 1978

Dear Mr. President:

I am writing you to reaffirm the position of the Arab Republic of Egypt with respect to Jerusalem:

1. Arab Jerusalem is an integral part of the West Bank. Legal and historical Arab rights in the City must be respected and restored.

2. Arab Jerusalem should be under Arab sovereignty.

3. The Palestinian inhabitants of Arab Jerusalem are entitled to exercise their legitimate national rights, being part of the Palestinian People in the West Bank.

4. Relevant Security Council Resolutions, particularly Resolutions 242 and 267, must be applied with regard to Jerusalem. All the measures taken by Israel to alter the status of the City are null and void and should be rescinded.

5. All peoples must have free access to the City and enjoy the free exercise of worship and the right to visit and transit to the holy places without distinction or discrimination.

6. The holy places of each faith may be placed under the administration and control of their representatives.

7. Essential functions in the City should be undivided and a joint municipal council composed of an equal number of Arab and Israeli members can supervise the carrying out of these functions. In this way, the City shall be undivided.

Sincerely,

Mohamed Anwar El Sadat

LETTER FROM ISRAELI PRIME MINISTER MENACHEM BEGIN
TO PRESIDENT JIMMY CARTER, SEPTEMBER 17, 1978

Dear Mr. President:

I have the honor to inform you, Mr. President, that on 28 June 1967—Israel's Parliament (The Knesset) promulgated and adopted a law to the effect: "the Government is empowered by a decree to apply the law, the jurisdiction and administration of the State to any part of Eretz Israel (land of Israel-Palestine), as stated in that decree."

On the basis of this law, the Government of Israel decreed in July

1967 that Jerusalem is one city indivisible, the Capital of the State of Israel.

Sincerely,

Menachem Begin

LETTER FROM PRESIDENT JIMMY CARTER TO EGYPTIAN PRESIDENT ANWAR EL-SADAT, SEPTEMBER 22, 1978

Dear Mr. President:

I have received your letter of September 17, 1978, setting forth the Egyptian position on Jerusalem. I am transmitting a copy of that letter to Prime Minister Begin for his information.

The position of the United States on Jerusalem remains as stated by Ambassador Goldberg in the United Nations General Assembly on July 14, 1967, and subsequently by Ambassador Yost in the United Nations Security Council on July 1, 1969.

Sincerely,

Jimmy Carter

LETTER FROM EGYPTIAN PRESIDENT ANWAR EL-SADAT TO PRESIDENT JIMMY CARTER, SEPTEMBER 17, 1978

Dear Mr. President:

In connection with the "Framework for Peace in the Middle East," I am writing you this letter to inform you of the position of the Arab Republic of Egypt, with respect to the implementation of the comprehensive settlement.

To ensure the implementation of the provisions related to the West Bank and Gaza and in order to safeguard the legitimate rights of the Palestinian people, Egypt will be prepared to assume the Arab role emanating from those provisions, following consultations with Jordan and the representatives of the Palestinian people.

Sincerely,

Mohamed Anwar El Sadat

LETTER FROM PRESIDENT JIMMY CARTER TO ISRAELI PRIME MINISTER MENACHEM BEGIN, SEPTEMBER 22, 1978

Dear Mr. Prime Minister:

I hereby acknowledge that you have informed me as follows:

A) In each paragraph of the Agreed Framework Document the

expressions "Palestinians" or "Palestinian People" are being and will be construed and understood by you as "Palestinian Arabs."

B) In each paragraph in which the expression "West Bank" appears, it is being, and will be, understood by the Government of Israel as Judea and Samaria.

Sincerely,

Jimmy Carter

LETTER FROM SECRETARY OF DEFENSE HAROLD BROWN TO ISRAELI DEFENSE MINISTER EZER WEIZMAN, ACCOMPANYING THE DOCUMENTS AGREED TO AT CAMP DAVID, RELEASED SEPTEMBER 29, 1978

September 28, 1978

Dear Mr. Minister:

The U.S. understands that, in connection with carrying out the agreements reached at Camp David, Israel intends to build two military airbases at appropriate sites in the Negev to replace the airbases at Eitam and Etzion which will be evacuated by Israel in accordance with the peace treaty to be concluded between Egypt and Israel. We also understand the special urgency and priority which Israel attaches to preparing the new bases in light of its conviction that it cannot safely leave the Sinai airbases until the new ones are operational.

I suggest that our two governments consult on the scope and costs of the two new airbases as well as on related forms of assistance which the United States might appropriately provide in light of the special problems which may be presented by carrying out such a project on an urgent basis. The President is prepared to seek the necessary Congressional approvals for such assistance as may be agreed upon by the U.S. side as a result of such consultations.

Harold Brown

APPENDIX F

Carter's Answers to King Hussein, October 1978

1. Does the United States intend to be a full partner in negotiations regarding the West Bank and Gaza and the Palestinian question in general? At what stage of the negotiations will the United States participate and in what role?

Yes, the United States will be a full partner in all the Arab-Israeli peace negotiations, leading to the achievement of a just, lasting and comprehensive Middle East peace.

The United States will use its full influence to see that the negotiations are brought to a successful conclusion.

President Carter will continue to take an active personal part in the negotiations.

2. What does the Framework agreement mean in its paragraph (A)1, where it refers to "the representatives of the Palestinian people?"

No comprehensive definition is attempted. In some cases, the representatives of the inhabitants of the West Bank and Gaza are specified. In one case, it is clear that "other Palestinians as mutually agreed" refers to representatives from outside the West Bank and Gaza and need not be citizens of Egypt or Jordan. Palestinians who are citizens of Egypt or Jordan may, of course, be members of the negotiating teams representing those countries. In other cases, the self-governing authority itself is mentioned.

The United States interprets the phrase "the representatives of the Palestinian people" not in terms of any single group or organization as representing the Palestinian people, but as encompassing those elected or chosen for participation in negotiations. It is expected that they will accept the purposes of the negotiations as defined in United Nations Security Council Resolution 242, and in the framework of a settlement will be prepared to live in peace and good neighbourly relations with Israel.

The text comes from a typed copy made available by the government of Jordan. The only point missing from this version is President Carter's signature at the bottom of the last page.

3. *Why has the duration of five years been chosen for the transition period in the West Bank and Gaza?*

The idea of a five-year transitional period for the West Bank and Gaza was an American suggestion which was first put to the parties in the summer of 1977. The key point is the concept of a transitional period—not the precise duration of five years which has been suggested and agreed.

We believe a transitional process of several years—at the outset of which the Israeli military government and its civilian administration will be withdrawn and a self-governing authority established for the West Bank and Gaza inhabitants—can demonstrate that the practical problems arising from a transition to peace can be satisfactorily resolved. We see the transitional period as essential to build confidence, gain momentum and bring about the changes in attitude that can assure a final settlement which realizes the legitimate rights of the Palestinian people while assuring the security of Israel and of the other parties.

4(A). *What is the geographical definition of the "West Bank" and of Gaza in the view of the United States Government? Is Arab Jerusalem and its surrounding Arab areas incorporated into Israel after June 1967 included in the definition of the "West Bank"?*

In the view of the United States the term "West Bank and Gaza" describes all of the area west of the Jordan River under Jordanian administration prior to the 1967 war and all of the area east of the western border of the British Mandate of Palestine which, prior to the 1967 war, was under Egyptian control and is known as the Gaza Strip.

With respect to negotiations envisaged in the Framework agreement, we believe a distinction must be made between Jerusalem and the rest of the West Bank because of the City's special status and circumstances. We would envisage, therefore, a negotiated solution for the final status of Jerusalem that could be different in character in some respects from that of the rest of the West Bank.

The final status of Jerusalem should not be prejudged by the unilateral actions undertaken in Jerusalem since the 1967 war. The full United States position on Jerusalem remains as stated by Ambassador Goldberg in his address to the United Nations General Assembly on 14 July 1967, and by Ambassador Yost to the Security Council on 1 July 1969.

4(B). *At the end of the five years of transitional arrangements, what would be the status of the West Bank and of Gaza from the point of view of sovereignty?*

The final status of the West Bank and Gaza, including the question of sovereignty, should be determined on the basis of Security Council Resolution 242 in all its parts in negotiations among Jordan, Egypt, Israel and the elected representatives of the inhabitants of the West Bank and Gaza, which should begin not later than the third year after the beginning of the transitional period. Under the terms of the Framework agreement, the outcome of those negotiations—including determining the issue of sovereignty—shall be submitted to a vote by the elected representatives of the inhabitants of the West Bank and Gaza for ratification or rejection.

Since the negotiation of the peace treaty between Israel and Jordan and the negotiations on the final status of the West Bank and Gaza are interrelated, the Framework provides that representatives of the inhabitants of the West Bank and Gaza should participate in both these negotiations.

Thus Palestinians will participate in each negotiation to resolve the final status of the West Bank and Gaza.

4(C). *What is the United States' position regarding these questions?*
The view of the United States on the geographical definition of the term "West Bank and Gaza" is stated in paragraph 4(A) above. The United States' position regarding the question of sovereignty in the West Bank and Gaza is expressed in paragraph 4(B) above.

4(D). *Will any Israeli forces remain in any part of the West Bank and of Gaza after the transitional period of five years? If so, by what right and with what justification?*
Security arrangements after the five-year interim period in the West Bank and Gaza, including the question of the possible retention of Israeli security personnel and the duration of any such presence, must be dealt with in the negotiations on the final status of the West Bank and Gaza that are to begin no later than the third year after the beginning of the transitional period.

4(E). *What is the United States' position regarding these questions?*
The United States believes that the agreement on the final status of the West Bank and Gaza must meet the legitimate aspirations of the Palestinian people and provide for Israel's security needs. The United States would not oppose, if agreed to by the parties, the stationing in the West Bank and Gaza of limited numbers of Israeli security personnel in specifically designated areas, and with a defined role, as one element in providing for the security of Israel.

5. *During the transitional period of self-government in the West Bank and Gaza, under what higher supervisory authority would the self-governing authority operate? Would it be a United Nations or a similar neutral international supervisory authority? What source would finance the budgetary needs of the self-governing authority? What would be the extent of its powers? What would constitute the limitations on its powers?*

The Framework provides that the parties, i.e., Egypt, Israel and Jordan, with Palestinians in the Egyptian and Jordanian delegations, "will negotiate an agreement which will define the powers and responsibilities of the self-governing authority to be exercised in the West Bank and Gaza." Thus the self-governing authority in the transitional period is established by an international agreement among the three parties. The agreement will define the powers of the self-governing authority and provide full autonomy for the inhabitants. Nothing in the Framework excludes the parties from deciding, should they so agree, to give a supervisory or other role to a United Nations or similar neutral international authority or to decide that there should be no supervisory authority. In addition, during the transitional period, representatives of Egypt, Israel, Jordan and the self-governing authority will constitute a continuing committee which may deal with matters of common concern. Methods of financing of the self-governing authority were not discussed at Camp David and remain to be set out in the agreement among the parties.

6(A). *Where the document refers to the self-governing authority which is to be constituted in the West Bank–Gaza area, does the jurisdiction of this authority extend to the part of Jerusalem which had been part of the West Bank when it fell under occupation as well as other annexed area around it, both in terms of territory and people?*

As stated above, the issue of the status of Jerusalem was not resolved at Camp David and must be dealt with in subsequent negotiations. The questions of how the Arab inhabitants of East Jerusalem relate to the self-governing authority remains to be determined in the negotiations on the transitional arrangements.

6(B). *What is the United States' position on this question?*

In those negotiations the United States will support proposals that would permit Arab inhabitants of East Jerusalem who are not Israeli citizens to participate in the elections to constitute the self-governing authority and in the work of the self-governing authority itself. It is probably not realistic to expect that the full scope of the self-governing authority can be extended to East Jerusalem during the transitional period. Such an outcome would not, however, prejudge the final status of Jerusalem, which must be resolved in the negotiations that are to begin no later than the third year after the beginning of the transitional period.

7(A). *At the end of the five-year transitional period, what would be the status of occupied Arab Jerusalem?*
The status of the West Bank and Gaza, and their relationship with their neighbors, as well as peace between Israel and Jordan, will be determined in the negotiations referred to in paragraph A.I.(c) of the Framework. The United States believes that the status of that portion of Jerusalem which Israel occupied in 1967 should be resolved in those negotiations.* The Framework envisages that these negotiations will involve Egypt, Israel, Jordan and the elected representatives of the inhabitants of the West Bank and Gaza.

7(B). *What is the United States' position on this matter?*
The position of the United States on Jerusalem is stated in Paragraph 4(A) above. The final status of Jerusalem should not be prejudged by the unilateral actions undertaken in Jerusalem since the 1967 war. Whatever solution is agreed upon should preserve Jerusalem as a physically undivided city. It should provide for free access to the Jewish, Muslim, and Christian holy places without distinction or discrimination for the free exercise of worship. It should assure the basic rights of all the City's residents. The holy places of each faith should be under the full authority of their representatives.

8(A). *What would happen to the Israeli settlements in the occupied areas during and after the transitional period? What would happen to the properties acquired and construction made there and what would their status be?*
The Framework does not deal with the status of Israeli settlements in the occupied areas, nor with the properties acquired or construction made there. The powers and responsibilities of the self-governing authority, which will exercise full autonomy on the West Bank and Gaza during the transitional period, will be defined in an agreement to be negotiated between Egypt, Israel, Jordan and, as provided in the Framework, Palestinians from the West Bank and Gaza or other Palestinians as mutually agreed to be on Egyptian and Jordanian national delegations.

*Provisions regarding Jerusalem could be included in the agreements that emerge from either or both of these negotiations. (This note appears in the original text.)

The question of the Israeli settlements in the West Bank and Gaza, and their relationship with the self-governing authority during the transitional period, will have to be dealt with in the course of those negotiations. The Framework also provides for a continuing committee, including representatives of Egypt, Israel, Jordan, and the self-governing authority, which may deal with outstanding matters of common concern during the transitional period.

The question of the Israeli settlements and their status after the transitional period would be a matter for discussion during the negotiations regarding the final status of the West Bank and Gaza referred to in paragraph A.1.(c).

8(B). *What will be Israel's obligation, during the coming period until the end of the transitional period, regarding the policy of settlement?*
It is the position of the United States that Israel should refrain from creating new settlements on the West Bank while negotiations are under way on the establishment of the self-governing authority. These negotiations will determine the question of existing settlements as well as any new settlement activity during the transitional period.

8(C). *What is the United States' position regarding both of the above questions?*
The United States' position is that settlements established during a military occupation are in violation of the Fourth Geneva Convention on the Protection of Persons in Time of War. However, in a relationship of peace, the parties to the peace should define the mutual rights of inhabitants to do business, to work, to live, and to carry on other transactions in each other's territory.

9(A). *Will the Israeli citizens who reside at present in the settlements be eligible for participation in the establishment of the self-governing authority and its subsequent activities?*
Israeli citizens residing in settlements on the West Bank and Gaza could participate in the establishment of the self-governing authority only as members of the Israeli negotiating delegation; there is no provision for their separate participation. Their participation, if any, in the self-governing authority must be determined in the negotiations for the transitional regime.

9(B). *What will be the status of the Israeli citizens residing in the West Bank and Gaza during the transitional period and will there be any, and if so what would their status be after the end of the transitional period?*

The negotiations under paragraph A.1.(b) defining the powers and responsibilities of the authority will deal with the status of Israeli settlements on the West Bank and Gaza and, accordingly, with the status of Israeli citizens residing in them. Whatever number that might remain beyond the transitional period, and their status, would presumably be agreed in the negotiations concerning the final status of the West Bank and Gaza envisaged under paragraph A.1.(c).

10(A). *At the end of the five-year transitional period, will the inhabitants of the West Bank and Gaza exercise in freedom the right of self-determination in order to decide their political future?*
The Framework provides for the elected representatives of the inhabitants of the West Bank and Gaza to participate fully in the negotiations that will determine the final status of the West Bank and Gaza and, in addition, for their elected representatives to ratify or reject the agreement reached in those negotiations. The Framework further provides that the solution from the negotiations must also recognize the legitimate rights of the Palestinian people and their just requirements. The wide acceptability of the results of this process is in the interest of all parties and is directly related to its being carried out "in freedom." In this respect, at the time the process described above is taking place, a strong local police force will exist and will be responsible to the self-governing authority to ensure that there is no interference in the political process that ensures these rights.

10(B). *What is the United States' position on this question?*
   The United States supports the right of the Palestinians to participate in the determination of their own future, and believes that the Framework provides for such participation in all the important steps in determining the future of the West Bank and Gaza. The United States believes that paragraph A.1.(c) (2) does not preclude the holding of an election by the inhabitants of the West Bank and Gaza, after the conclusion of an agreement on the final status of the West Bank and Gaza, for the express purpose of electing representatives to whom that agreement will be submitted for a vote.

11(A). *What solution does the Framework Agreement envisage for the problem of the Palestinians living outside the occupied areas as refugees and for the restoration of their rights?*
Paragraph A.4. of the Framework provides that Egypt and Israel will work together with other interested parties to agree on a resolution of the

refugee problem. Implementation of the procedures agreed upon is to be prompt, just and permanent.

Paragraph A.3. of the Framework provides for a continuing committee to decide on arrangements for the admission to the West Bank and Gaza of persons displaced from those areas in 1967.

In addition, as the political institutions of self-government take shape on the West Bank and Gaza through negotiations among the parties the relationship between those institutions and the Palestinians living outside the area would be addressed.

11(B). *What does the United States regard as the basis for the solution of this question? How does it define these rights?*
The United States believes that a resolution of the refugee problem should reflect applicable United Nations Resolutions. Any program for implementation must provide those refugees living outside the West Bank and Gaza a choice and opportunity in settling themselves permanently in the context of present-day realities and circumstances.

12. *What does the Framework Agreement envisage for the future of the rest of the occupied Arab territories? What is the United States Government's position on this question?*
The Framework states that it is intended to constitute a basis for peace between Israel and each of its other neighbors. It further states that the objective is a just, comprehensive, and durable peace and that each negotiation must carry out all the provisions and principles of United Nations Security Council Resolutions 242 and 338. Paragraph C.1. specifically states that the principles of the Framework should apply to treaties between Israel and Jordan, Syria, and Lebanon in addition to Egypt. Concerning the West Bank in particular, paragraph A.1.(c) requires negotiations based on all the provisions and principles of Resolution 242 which will resolve, among other matters, the location of boundaries. The United States continues to advocate a comprehensive peace involving all of Israel's neighbors. As regards the possibility of negotiations for a peaceful settlement between Israel and Syria, the United States will support the application of all the principles and provisions of Resolution 242 to such a settlement.

13. *In the definition of the security requirements in the area, does the United States Government endorse the principle of reciprocity on these requirements or does the United States Government regard these requirements to be one sided only?*

The United States fully endorses the principle of reciprocity as applied to security requirements in the context of Middle East peace negotiations. The preamble of the Framework specifically refers to reciprocity as the basis on which the parties can agree to special security arrangements. The Framework also refers to the security concerns "of all parties" and to the security of "Israel and its neighbors."

14. *As Security Council Resolution 242 is stated to be the basis of any negotiations for the settlement of the West Bank–Gaza and other aspects of the conflict, what would the United States Government do in the event of conflicting interpretations between the negotiating parties particularly in view of the United States Government's previous interpretations of Security Council Resolution 242 and commitments based thereon which were the basis of acceptance by Jordan of the said Resolution?*

The United States will, first, adhere to its own consistent interpretation of Resolution 242, and in particular to its interpretation that the withdrawal provision of that resolution applies on all fronts. In the event of conflicting interpretations among the negotiating parties, the United States will seek, as it did during the intensive negotiations at Camp David, to bring about a consensus among the parties and will make known its own interpretations as required to bring about resolution of the conflict. The interpretations of the United States remain those it has held since 1967.

APPENDIX G

Egyptian-Israeli Peace Treaty, March 26, 1979

TREATY OF PEACE BETWEEN THE ARAB REPUBLIC OF EGYPT AND THE STATE OF ISRAEL

The Government of the Arab Republic of Egypt and the Government of the State of Israel;

Preamble

Convinced of the urgent necessity of the establishment of a just, comprehensive and lasting peace in the Middle East in accordance with Security Council Resolutions 242 and 338;

Reaffirming their adherence to the "Framework for Peace in the Middle East Agreed at Camp David," dated September 17, 1978;

Noting that the aforementioned Framework as appropriate is intended to constitute a basis for peace not only between Egypt and Israel but also between Israel and each of its other Arab neighbors which is prepared to negotiate peace with it on this basis;

Desiring to bring to an end the state of war between them and to establish a peace in which every state in the area can live in security;

Convinced that the conclusion of a Treaty of Peace between Egypt and Israel is an important step in the search for comprehensive peace in the area and for the attainment of the settlement of the Arab-Israeli conflict in all its aspects;

Inviting the other Arab parties to this dispute to join the peace process with Israel guided by and based on the principles of the aforementioned Framework;

Desiring as well to develop friendly relations and cooperation between themselves in accordance with the United Nations Charter and the principles of international law governing international relations in times of peace;

Agree to the following provisions in the free exercise of their sovereigny, in order to implement the "Framework for the Conclusion of a Peace Treaty Between Egypt and Israel":

Article I

1. The state of war between the Parties will be terminated and peace will be established between them upon the exchange of instruments of ratification of this Treaty.

2. Israel will withdraw all its armed forces and civilians from the Sinai behind the international boundary between Egypt and mandated Palestine, as provided in the annexed protocol (Annex I), and Egypt will resume the exercise of its full sovereignty over the Sinai.

3. Upon completion of the interim withdrawal provided for in Annex I, the Parties will establish normal and friendly relations, in accordance with Article III(3).

Article II

The permanent boundary between Egypt and Israel is the recognized international boundary between Egypt and the former mandated territory of Palestine, as shown on the map at Annex II, without prejudice to the issue of the status of the Gaza Strip. The Parties recognize this boundary as inviolable. Each will respect the territorial integrity of the other, including their territorial waters and airspace.

Article III

1. The Parties will apply between them the provisions of the Charter of the United Nations and the principles of international law governing relations among states in times of peace. In particular:

a. They recognize and will respect each other's sovereignty, territorial integrity and political independence;

b. They recognize and will respect each other's right to live in peace within their secure and recognized boundaries;

c. They will refrain from the threat or use of force, directly or indirectly, against each other and will settle all disputes between them by peaceful means.

2. Each Party undertakes to ensure that acts or threats of belligerency, hostility, or violence do not originate from and are not committed from within its territory, or by any forces subject to its control or by any other forces stationed on its territory, against the population, citizens or property of the other Party. Each Party also undertakes to refrain from organizing,

instigating, inciting, assisting or participating in acts or threats of belligerency, hostility, subversion or violence against the other Party, anywhere, and undertakes to ensure that perpetrators of such acts are brought to justice.

3. The Parties agree that the normal relationship established between them will include full recognition, diplomatic, economic and cultural relations, termination of economic boycotts and discriminatory barriers to the free movement of people and goods, and will guarantee the mutual enjoyment by citizens of the due process of law. The process by which they undertake to achieve such a relationship parallel to the implementation of other provisions of this Treaty is set out in the annexed protocol (Annex III).

Article IV

1. In order to provide maximum security for both Parties on the basis of reciprocity, agreed security arrangements will be established including limited force zones in Egyptian and Israeli territory, and United Nations forces and observers, described in detail as to nature and timing in Annex I, and other security arrangements the Parties may agree upon.

2. The Parties agree to the stationing of United Nations personnel in areas described in Annex I. The Parties agree not to request withdrawal of the United Nations personnel and that these personnel will not be removed unless such removal is approved by the Security Council of the United Nations, with the affirmative vote of the five Permanent Members, unless the Parties otherwise agree.

3. A Joint Commission will be established to facilitate the implementation of the Treaty, as provided for in Annex I.

4. The security arrangements provided for in paragraphs 1 and 2 of this Article may at the request of either party be reviewed and amended by mutual agreement of the Parties.

Article V

1. Ships of Israel, and cargoes destined for or coming from Israel, shall enjoy the right of free passage through the Suez Canal and its approaches through the Gulf of Suez and the Mediterranean Sea on the basis of the Constantinople Convention of 1888, applying to all nations. Israeli nationals, vessels and cargoes, as well as persons, vessels and cargoes destined for or coming from Israel, shall be accorded non-discriminatory treatment in all matters connected with usage of the canal.

2. The Parties consider the Strait of Tiran and the Gulf of Aqaba to be international waterways open to all nations for unimpeded and non-suspendable freedom of navigation and overflight. The Parties will respect each other's right to navigation and overflight for access to either country through the Strait of Tiran and the Gulf of Aqaba.

Article VI

1. This Treaty does not affect and shall not be interpreted as affecting in any way the rights and obligations of the Parties under the Charter of the United Nations.

2. The Parties undertake to fulfill in good faith their obligations under this Treaty, without regard to action or inaction of any other party and independently of any instrument external to this Treaty.

3. They further undertake to take all the necessary measures for the application in their relations of the provisions of the multilateral conventions to which they are parties, including the submission of appropriate notification to the Secretary General of the United Nations and other depositaries of such conventions.

4. The Parties undertake not to enter into any obligations in conflict with this Treaty.

5. Subject to Article 103 of the United Nations Charter, in the event of a conflict between the obligations of the Parties under the present Treaty and any of their other obligations, the obligations under this Treaty will be binding and implemented.

Article VII

1. Disputes arising out of the application or interpretation of this Treaty shall be resolved by negotiations.

2. Any such disputes which cannot be settled by negotiations shall be resolved by conciliation or submitted to arbitration.

Article VIII

The Parties agree to establish a claims commission for the mutual settlement of all financial claims.

Article IX

1. This Treaty shall enter into force upon exchange of instruments of ratification.

2. This Treaty supersedes the Agreement between Egypt and Israel of September, 1975.

3. All protocols, annexes, and maps attached to this Treaty shall be regarded as an integral part hereof.

4. The Treaty shall be communicated to the Secretary General of the United Nations for registration in accordance with the provisions of Article 102 of the Charter of the United Nations.

Done at Washington, D.C. this 26th day of March, 1979, in triplicate in the English, Arabic, and Hebrew languages, each text being equally authentic. In case of any divergence of interpretation, the English text shall prevail.

For the Government of the Arab Republic of Egypt:

A. Sadat

For the Government of Israel:

M. Begin

Witnessed by:

Jimmy Carter
President of the
United States of America

AGREED MINUTES TO ARTICLES I, IV, V AND VI AND ANNEXES I AND III OF TREATY OF PEACE

Article I

Egypt's resumption of the exercise of full sovereignty over the Sinai provided for in paragraph 2 of Article I shall occur with regard to each area upon Israel's withdrawal from that area.

Article IV

It is agreed between the parties that the review provided for in Article IV(4) will be undertaken when requested by either party, commencing within three months of such a request, but that any amendment can be made only with the mutual agreement of both parties.

Article V

The second sentence of paragraph 2 of Article V shall not be construed as limiting the first sentence of that paragraph. The foregoing is not to be construed as contravening the second sentence of paragraph 2 of Article V, which reads as follows:

"The Parties will respect each other's right to navigation and overflight for access to either country through the Strait of Tiran and the Gulf of Aqaba."

Article VI(2)

The provisions of Article VI shall not be construed in contradiction to the provisions of the framework for peace in the Middle East agreed at Camp David. The foregoing is not to be construed as contravening the provisions of Article VI(2) of the Treaty, which reads as follows:

"The Parties undertake to fulfill in good faith their obligations under this Treaty, without regard to action or inaction of any other Party and independently of any instrument external to this Treaty."

Article VI(5)

It is agreed by the Parties that there is no assertion that this Treaty prevails over other Treaties or agreements or that other Treaties or agreements prevail over this Treaty. The foregoing is not to be construed as contravening the provisions of Article VI(5) of the Treaty, which reads as follows:

"Subject to Article 103 of the United Nations Charter, in the event of a conflict between the obligations of the Parties under the present Treaty and any of their other obligations, the obligations under this Treaty will be binding and implemented."

Annex I

Article VI, Paragraph 8, of Annex I provides as follows:

"The Parties shall agree on the nations from which the United Nations force and observers will be drawn. They will be drawn from nations other than those which are permanent members of the United Nations Security Council."

The Parties have agreed as follows:

"With respect to the provisions of paragraph 8, Article VI, of Annex I, if no agreement is reached between the Parties, they will accept or support a U.S. proposal concerning the composition of the United Nations force and observers."

Annex III

The Treaty of Peace and Annex III thereto provide for establishing normal economic relations between the Parties. In accordance therewith, it is agreed that such relations will include normal commercial sales of oil by Egypt to Israel, and that Israel shall be fully entitled to make bids for Egyptian-origin oil not needed for Egyptian domestic oil consumption, and Egypt and its oil concessionaires will entertain bids made by Israel, on the same basis and terms as apply to other bidders for such oil.

For the Government of Israel:

M. Begin

For the Government of the Arab Republic of Egypt:

A. Sadat

Witnessed by:

Jimmy Carter
President of the
United States of America

LETTER FROM ISRAELI PRIME MINISTER MENACHEM BEGIN AND EGYPTIAN PRESIDENT ANWAR EL-SADAT TO PRESIDENT JIMMY CARTER, MARCH 26, 1979

Dear Mr. President:

This letter confirms that Egypt and Israel have agreed as follows:

The Governments of Egypt and Israel recall that they concluded at Camp David and signed at the White House on September 17, 1978, the annexed documents entitled "A Framework for Peace in the Middle East Agreed at Camp David" and "Framework for the conclusion of a Peace Treaty between Egypt and Israel."

For the purpose of achieving a comprehensive peace settlement in accordance with the above-mentioned Frameworks, Egypt and Israel will proceed with the implementation of those provisions relating to the West Bank and the Gaza Strip. They have agreed to start negotiations within a month after the exchange of the instruments of ratification of the Peace Treaty. In accordance with the "Framework for Peace in the Middle East," the Hashemite Kingdom of Jordan is invited to join the negotiations. The Delegations of Egypt and Jordan may include Palestinians from the West Bank and Gaza Strip or other Palestinians as mutually agreed. The purpose of the negotiation shall be to agree, prior to the elections, on the modalities for establishing the elected self-governing authority (administrative council), define its powers and responsibilities, and agree upon other related issues. In the event Jordan decides not to take part in the negotiations, the negotiations will be held by Egypt and Israel.

The two Governments agree to negotiate continuously and in good faith to conclude these negotiations at the earliest possible date. They also agree that the objective of the negotiations is the establishment of the self-governing authority in the West Bank and Gaza in order to provide full autonomy to the inhabitants.

Egypt and Israel set for themselves the goal of completing the negotiations within one year so that elections will be held as expeditiously as possible after agreement has been reached between the parties. The self-governing authority referred to in the "Framework for Peace in the Middle East" will be established and inaugurated within one month after it has been elected, at which time the transitional period of five years will begin. The Israeli military government and its civilian administration will be withdrawn, to be replaced by the self-governing authority, as specified in the "Framework for Peace in the Middle East." A withdrawal of Israeli armed forces will then take place and there will be a redeployment of the remaining Israeli forces into specified security locations.

This letter also confirms our understanding that the United States Government will participate fully in all stages of negotiations.

Sincerely yours,

For the Government of Israel:

M. Begin
Menachem Begin

For the Government of the Arab Republic of Egypt:

A. Sadat
Mohamed Anwar El-Sadat

Note: President Carter, upon receipt of the Joint Letter to him from President Sadat and Prime Minister Begin, has added to the American and Israeli copies the notation:

"I have been informed that the expression 'West Bank' is understood by the Government of Israel to mean 'Judea and Samaria'."

This notation is in accordance with similar procedures established at Camp David.*

*Explanatory note with the original documents.

LETTER FROM PRESIDENT ANWAR EL-SADAT
TO PRESIDENT JIMMY CARTER, MARCH 26, 1979

Dear Mr. President:

In response to your request, I can confirm that, within one month after the completion of Israel's withdrawal to the interim line as provided for in the Treaty of Peace between Egypt and Israel, Egypt will send a resident ambassador to Israel and will receive a resident Israeli ambassador in Egypt.

Sincerely,

A. Sadat
Mohamed Anwar El-Sadat

LETTER FROM PRESIDENT JIMMY CARTER TO ISRAELI
PRIME MINISTER MENACHEM BEGIN, MARCH 26, 1979

Dear Mr. Prime Minister:

I have received a letter from President Sadat that, within one month after Israel completes its withdrawal to the interim line in Sinai, as provided for in the Treaty of Peace between Egypt and Israel, Egypt will send a resident ambassador to Israel and will receive in Egypt a resident Israeli ambassador.

I would be grateful if you will confirm that this procedure will be agreeable to the Government of Israel.

Sincerely,

Jimmy Carter
Jimmy Carter

LETTER FROM ISRAELI PRIME MINISTER MENACHEM BEGIN
TO PRESIDENT JIMMY CARTER, MARCH 26, 1979

Dear Mr. President:

I am pleased to be able to confirm that the Government of Israel is agreeable to the procedure set out in your letter of March 26, 1979 in which you state:

"I have received a letter from President Sadat that, within one month after Israel completes its withdrawal to the interim line in Sinai, as provided for in the Treaty of Peace between Egypt and Israel, Egypt will send a resident ambassador to Israel and will receive in Egypt a resident Israeli ambassador."

Sincerely,

M. Begin
Menachem Begin

LETTERS FROM PRESIDENT JIMMY CARTER TO EGYPTIAN
PRESIDENT ANWAR EL-SADAT AND ISRAELI PRIME
MINISTER MENACHEM BEGIN, MARCH 26, 1979[*]

Dear Mr. President: [*Prime Minister*]:

I wish to confirm to you that subject to United States Constitutional processes:

In the event of an actual or threatened violation of the Treaty of Peace between Egypt and Israel, the United States will, on request of one or both of the Parties, consult with the Parties with respect thereto and will take such other action as it may deem appropriate and helpful to achieve compliance with the Treaty.

The United States will conduct aerial monitoring as requested by the Parties pursuant to Annex I of the Treaty.

The United States believes the Treaty provision for permanent stationing of United Nations personnel in the designated limited force zone can and should be implemented by the United Nations Security Council. The United States will exert its utmost efforts to obtain the requisite action by the Security Council. If the Security Council fails to establish and maintain the arrangements called for in the Treaty, the President will be prepared to take those steps necessary to ensure the establishment and maintenance of an acceptable alternative multinational force.

Sincerely,

Jimmy Carter
Jimmy Carter

[*]Separate but identical letters were sent to President Sadat and Prime Minister Begin.

APPENDIX H

President Ronald Reagan's Speech and Talking Points, September 1, 1982

TEXT OF PRESIDENT REAGAN'S SPEECH,
TELEVISED FROM THE OVAL OFFICE

My fellow Americans, today has been a day that should make us proud. It marked the end of the successful evacuation of the P.L.O. from Beirut, Lebanon. This peaceful step could never have been taken without the good offices of the United States and, especially, the truly heroic work of a great American diplomat, Ambassador Philip Habib. Thanks to his efforts, I'm happy to announce that the U.S. Marine contingent helping to supervise the evacuation has accomplished its mission. Our young men should be out of Lebanon within two weeks. They, too, have served the cause of peace with distinction and we can all be very proud of them.

But the situation in Lebanon is only part of the overall problem of conflict in the Middle East. So, over the past two weeks, while events in Beirut dominated the front page, America was engaged in a quiet, behind-the-scenes effort to lay the groundwork for a broader peace in the region. For once, there were no premature leaks as U.S. diplomatic missions traveled to Mideast capitals and I met here at home with a wide range of experts to map out an American peace initiative for the long-suffering peoples of the Middle East, Arab and Israeli alike.

It seemed to me that, with the agreement in Lebanon, we had an opportunity for a more far-reaching peace effort in the region and I was determined to seize that moment. In the words of the scripture, the time had come to "follow after the things which make for peace."

Tonight, I want to report to you on the steps we've taken and the prospects they can open up for a just and lasting peace in the Middle East.

The text of the speech comes from the *New York Times*, September 2, 1982. The talking points accompanied a letter sent by President Reagan to Prime Minister Menachem Begin of Israel. The same points were presented to Arab governments. See *New York Times*, September 9, 1982.

America has long been committed to bringing peace to this troubled region. For more than a generation, successive U.S. administrations have endeavored to develop a fair and workable process that could lead to a true and lasting Arab-Israeli peace. Our involvement in the search for Mideast peace is not a matter of preference, it is a moral imperative. The strategic importance of the region to the United States is well known.

But our policy is motivated by more than strategic interests. We also have an irreversible commitment to the survival and territorial integrity of friendly states. Nor can we ignore the fact that the well-being of much of the world's economy is tied to stability in the strife-torn Middle East. Finally, our traditional humanitarian concerns dictate a continuing effort to peacefully resolve conflicts.

When our Administration assumed office in January 1981, I decided that the general framework for our Middle East policy should follow the broad guidelines laid down by my predecessors.

There were two basic issues we had to address. First, there was the strategic threat to the region posed by the Soviet Union and its surrogates, best demonstrated by the brutal war in Afghanistan; and, second, the peace process between Israel and its Arab neighbors. With regard to the Soviet threat, we have strengthened our efforts to develop with our friends and allies a joint policy to deter the Soviets and their surrogates from further expansion in the region, and, if necessary, to defend against it. With respect to the Arab-Israeli conflict, we've embraced the Camp David framework as the only way to proceed. We have also recognized, however, that solving the Arab-Israeli conflict, in and of itself, cannot assure peace throughout a region as vast and troubled as the Middle East.

Our first objective under the Camp David process was to insure the successful fulfillment of the Egyptian-Israeli peace treaty. This was achieved with the peaceful return of the Sinai to Egypt in April 1982. To accomplish this, we worked hard with our Egyptian and Israeli friends, and eventually with other friendly countries, to create the multinational force which now operates in the Sinai.

Throughout this period of difficult and time-consuming negotiations, we never lost sight of the next step of Camp David, autonomy talks to pave the way for permitting the Palestinian people to exercise their legitimate rights. However, owing to the tragic assassination of President Sadat and other crises in the area, it was not until January 1982 that we were ale to make a major effort to renew these talks. Secretary of State Haig and Ambassador Fairbanks made three visits to Israel and Egypt early this year to pursue the autonomy talks. Considerable progress was made in developing the basic outline of an American approach which was to be presented to Egypt and Israel after April.

The successful completion of Israel's withdrawal from Sinai and the courage shown on this occasion by Prime Minister Begin and President Mubarak in living up to their agreements convinced me the time had come for a new American policy to try to bridge the remaining differences between Egypt and Israel on the autonomy process. So, in May, I called for specific measures and a timetable for consultations with the Governments of Egypt and Israel on the next steps in the peace process. However, before this effort could be launched, the conflict in Lebanon pre-empted our efforts. The autonomy talks were basically put on hold while we sought to untangle the parties in Lebanon and still the guns of war.

The Lebanon war, tragic as it was, has left us with a new opportunity for Middle East peace. We must seize it now and bring peace to this troubled area so vital to world stability while there is still time. It was with this strong conviction that over a month ago, before the present negotiations in Beirut had been completed, I directed Secretary of State Shultz to again review our policy and to consult a wide range of outstanding Americans on the best ways to strengthen chances for peace in the Middle East.

We have consulted with many of the officials who were historically involved in the process, with members of the Congress, and with individuals from the private sector, and I have held extensive consultations with my own advisers on the principles that I will outline to you tonight.

The evacuation of the PLO from Beirut is now complete. And we can now help the Lebanese to rebuild their war-torn country. We owe it to ourselves, and to posterity, to move quickly to build upon this achievement. A stable and revived Lebanon is essential to all our hopes for peace in the region. The people of Lebanon deserve the best efforts of the international community to turn the nightmares of the past several years into a new dawn of hope.

But the opportunities for peace in the Middle East do not begin and end in Lebanon. As we help Lebanon rebuild, we must also move to resolve the root causes of conflict between Arabs and Israelis.

The war in Lebanon has demonstrated many things, but two consequences are key to the peace process:

First, the military losses of the P.L.O. have not diminished the yearning of the Palestinian people for a just solution of their claims; and second, while Israel's military successes in Lebanon have demonstrated that its armed forces are second to none in the region, they alone cannot bring just and lasting peace to Israel and her neighbors.

The question now is how to reconcile Israel's legitimate security concerns with the legitimate rights of the Palestinians. And that answer can only come at the negotiating table. Each party must recognize that the outcome must be acceptable to all and that true peace will require compromises by all.

So, tonight I'm calling for a fresh start. This is the moment for all those directly concerned to get involved—or lend their support—to a workable basis for peace. The Camp David agreement remains the foundation of our policy. Its language provides all parties with the leeway they need for successful negotiations.

I call on Israel to make clear that the security for which she yearns can only be achieved through genuine peace, a peace requiring magnanimity, vision and courage.

I call on the Palestinian people to recognize that their own political aspirations are inextricably bound to recognition of Israel's right to a secure future.

And I call on the Arab states to accept the reality of Israel, and the reality that peace and justice are to be gained only through hard, fair, direct negotiation.

In making these calls upon others, I recognize that the United States has a special responsibility. No other nation is in a position to deal with the key parties to the conflict on the basis of trust and reliability.

The time has come for a new realism on the part of all the peoples of the Middle East. The State of Israel is an accomplished fact; it deserves unchallenged legitimacy within the community of nations. But Israel's legitimacy has thus far been recognized by too few countries, and has been denied by every Arab state except Egypt. Israel exists. It has a right to exist in peace, behind secure and defensible borders, and it has a right to demand of its neighbors that they recognize those facts.

I have personally followed and supported Israel's heroic struggle for survival ever since the founding of the state of Israel 34 years ago. In the pre-1967 borders, Israel was barely 10 miles wide at its narrowest point. The bulk of Israel's population lived within artillery range of hostile Arab armies. I am not about to ask Israel to live that way again.

The war in Lebanon has demonstrated another reality in the region.

The departure of the Palestinians from Beirut dramatizes more than ever the homelessness of the Palestinian people. Palestinians feel strongly that their cause is more than a question of refugees. I agree. The Camp David agreement recognized that fact when it spoke of the legitimate rights of the Palestinian people and their just requirements. For peace to endure, it must involve all those who have been most deeply affected by the conflict. Only through broader participation in the peace process, most immediately by Jordan and by the Palestinians, will Israel be able to rest confident in the knowledge that its security and integrity will be respected by its neighbors. Only through the process of negotiation can all the nations of the Middle East achieve a secure peace.

These then are our general goals. What are the specific new American positions, and why are we taking them?

In the Camp David talks thus far, both Israel and Egypt have felt free to express openly their views as to what the outcome should be. Understandably, their views have differed on many points.

The United States has thus far sought to play the role of mediator. We have avoided public comment on the key issues. We have always recognized, and continue to recognize, that only the voluntary agreement of those parties most directly involved in the conflict can provide an enduring solution. But it has become evident to me that some clearer sense of America's position on the key issues is necessary to encourage wider support for the peace process.

First, as outlined in the Camp David accords, there must be a period of time during which the Palestinian inhabitants of the West Bank and Gaza will have full autonomy over their own affairs. Due consideration must be given to the principle of self-government by the inhabitants of the territories and to the legitimate security concerns of the parties involved.

The purpose of the five-year period of transition which would begin after free elections for a self-governing Palestinian authority is to prove to the Palestinians that they can run their own affairs, and that such Palestinian autonomy poses no threat to Israel's security.

The United States will not support the use of any additional land for the purpose of settlements during the transitional period. Indeed, the immediate adoption of a settlement freeze by Israel, more than any other action, could create the confidence needed for wider participation in these talks. Further settlement activity is in no way necessary for the security of Israel and only diminishes the confidence of the Arabs that a final outcome can be freely and fairly negotiated.

I want to make the American position well understood: The purpose of this transition period is the peaceful and orderly transfer of authority from Israel to the Palestinian inhabitants of the West Bank and Gaza. At the same time, such a transfer must not interfere with Israel's security requirements.

Beyond the transition period, as we look to the future of the West Bank and Gaza, it is clear to me that peace cannot be achieved by the formation of an independent Palestinian state in those territories. Nor is it achievable on the basis of Israeli sovereignty or permanent control over the West Bank and Gaza.

So the United States will not support the establishment of an independent Palestinian state in the West Bank and Gaza, and we will not support annexation or permanent control by Israel.

There is, however, another way to peace. The final status of these lands must, of course, be reached through the give-and-take of negotiations. But it is the firm view of the United States that self-government by the Palestinians of the West Bank and Gaza in association with Jordan offers the best chance for a durable, just and lasting peace.

We base our approach squarely on the principle that the Arab-Israeli conflict should be resolved through negotiations involving an exchange of territory for peace. This exchange is enshrined in United Nations Security Council Resolution 242 which is, in turn, incorporated in all its parts in the Camp David agreements. U.N. Resolution 242 remains wholly valid as the foundation stone of America's Middle East peace effort.

It is the United States' position that—in return for peace—the withdrawal provision of Resolution 242 applies to all fronts, including the West Bank and Gaza.

When the border is negotiated between Jordan and Israel, our view on the extent to which Israel should be asked to give up territory will be heavily affected by the extent of true peace and normalization and the security arrangements offered in return.

Finally, we remain convinced that Jerusalem must remain undivided, but its final status should be decided through negotiations.

In the course of the negotiations to come, the United States will support positions that seem to us fair and reasonable compromises, and likely to promote a sound agreement. We will also put forward our own detailed proposals when we believe they can be helpful. And, make no mistake, the United States will oppose any proposal—from any party and at any point in the negotiating process—that threatens the security of Israel. America's commitment to the security of Israel is ironclad and, I might add, so is mine.

During the past few days, our Ambassadors in Israel, Egypt, Jordan and Saudi Arabia have presented to their host governments the proposals in full detail that I have outlined here today.

Now I am convinced that these proposals can bring justice, bring security and bring durability to an Arab-Israeli peace.

The United States will stand by these principles with total dedication. They are fully consistent with Israel's security requirements and the aspirations of the Palestinians. We will work hard to broaden participation at the peace table as envisaged by the Camp David accords. And I fervently hope that the Palestinians and Jordan, with the support of their Arab colleagues, will accept this opportunity.

Tragic turmoil in the Middle East runs back to the dawn of history. In our modern day, conflict after conflict has taken its brutal toll there. In an age of nuclear challenge and economic interdependence, such conflicts are a threat to all the people of the world, not just the Middle East itself. It's time for us all, in the Middle East and around the world, to call a halt to conflict, hatred and prejudice; it's time for us all to launch a common effort for reconstruction, peace and progress.

It has often been said—and regrettably too often been true—that the story of the search for peace and justice in the Middle East is a tragedy of opportunities missed.

In the aftermath of the settlement in Lebanon we now face an opportunity for a broader peace. This time we must not let it slip from our grasp. We must look beyond the difficulties and obstacles of the present and move with fairness and resolve toward a brighter future. We owe it to ourselves, and to posterity, to do no less. For if we miss this chance to make a fresh start, we may look back on this moment from some later vantage point and realize how much that failure cost us all.

These, then, are the principles upon which American policy toward the Arab-Israeli conflict will be based. I have made a personal commitment to see that they endure and, God willing, that they will come to be seen by all reasonable, compassionate people as fair, achievable, and in the interests of all who wish to see peace in the Middle East.

Tonight, on the eve of what can be a dawning of new hope for the people of the troubled Middle East—and for all the world's people who dream of a just and peaceful future—I ask you, my fellow Americans, for your support and your prayers in this great undertaking.

TEXT OF TALKING POINTS SENT TO PRIME MINISTER BEGIN BY PRESIDENT REAGAN

General Principles

A. We will maintain our commitment to Camp David.

B. We will maintain our commitment to the conditions we require for recognition of and negotiation with the P.L.O.

C. We can offer guarantees on the position we will adopt in negotiations. We will not be able, however, to guarantee in advance the results of these negotiations.

Transitional Measures

A. Our position is that the objective of the transitional period is the peaceful and orderly transfer of authority from Israel to the Palestinian inhabitants.

B. We will support:

The decision of full autonomy as giving the Palestinian inhabitants real authority over themselves, the land and its resources, subject to fair safeguards on water.

Economic, commercial, social and cultural ties between the West Bank, Gaza and Jordan.

Participation by the Palestinian inhabitants of East Jerusalem in the election of the West Bank–Gaza authority.

Real settlement freeze.

Progressive Palestinian responsibility for internal security based on capability and performance.

C. We will oppose:

Dismantlement of the existing settlements.

Provisions which represent a legitimate threat to Israel's security, reasonably defined.

Isolation of the West Bank and Gaza from Israel.

Measures which accord either the Palestinians or the Israelis generally recognized sovereign rights with the exception of external security, which must remain in Israel's hands during the transitional period.

Final Status Issues

   A. U.N.S.C. Resolution 242

   It is our position that Resolution 242 applies to the West Bank and Gaza and requires Israeli withdrawal in return for peace. Negotiations must determine the borders. The U.S. position in these negotiations on the extent of the withdrawal will be significantly influenced by the extent and nature of the peace and security arrangements offered in return.

   B. Israeli Sovereignty

   It is our belief that the Palestinian problem cannot be resolved [through] Israeli sovereignty or control over the West Bank and Gaza. Accordingly, we will not support such a solution.

   C. Palestinian State

   The preference we will pursue in the final status negotiation is association of the West Bank and Gaza with Jordan. We will not support the formation of a Palestinian state in those negotiations. There is no foundation of political support in Israel or the United States for such a solution. The outcome, however, must be determined by negotiations.

   D. Self-Determination

   In the Middle East context the term self-determination has been identified exclusively with the formation of a Palestinian state. We will not support this definition of self-determination. We believe that the Palestinians must take the leading role in determining their own future and fully support the provision in Camp David providing for the elected representatives of the inhabitants of the West Bank and Gaza to decide how they shall govern themselves consistent with the provision of their agreement in the final status negotiations.

   E. Jerusalem

   We will fully support the position that the status of Jerusalem must be determined through negotiations.

   F. Settlements

   The status of Israeli settlements must be determined in the course of the final status negotiations. We will not support their continuation as extraterritorial outposts.

Additional Talking Points

   1. Approach to Hussein

   The President has approached Hussein to determine the extent to which he may be interested in participating.

   King Hussein has received the same U.S. positions as you.

Hussein considers our proposals serious and gives them serious attention.

Hussein understands that Camp David is the only base that we will accept for negotiations.

We are also discussing these proposals with the Saudis.

2. Public Commitment

Whatever the support from these or other Arab States, this is what the President has concluded must be done.

The President is convinced his positions are fair and balanced and fully protective of Israel's security. Beyond that they offer the practical opportunity of eventually achieving the peace treaties Israel must have with its neighbors.

He will be making a speech announcing these positions, probably within a week.

3. Next Procedural Steps

Should the response to the President's proposal be positive, the U.S. would take immediate steps to relaunch the autonomy negotiations with the broadest possible participation as envisaged under the Camp David agreements.

We also contemplate an early visit by Secretary Shultz in the area.

Should there not be positive response, the President, as he has said in his letter to you, will nonetheless stand by his position with proper dedication.

APPENDIX I

The Shultz Initiative, March 4, 1988

I set forth below the statement of understanding which I am convinced is necessary to achieve the prompt opening of negotiations on a comprehensive peace. This statement of understandings emerges from discussions held with you and other regional leaders. I look forward to the letter of reply of the Government of Israel in confirmation of this statement.

The agreed objective is a comprehensive peace providing for the security of all the states in the region and for the legitimate rights of the Palestinian people.

Negotiations will start on an early date certain between Israel and each of its neighbors which is willing to do so. These negotiations could begin May 1, 1988. Each of these negotiations will be based on the United Nations Security Council Resolutions 242 and 338, in all their parts. The parties to each bilateral negotiation will determine the procedure and agenda at their negotiation. All participants in the negotiations must state their willingness to negotiate with one another.

As concerns negotiations between the Israeli delegation and the Jordanian-Palestinian delegation, negotiations will begin on arrangements for a transitional period, with the objective of completing them within six months. Seven months after transitional negotiations begin, final status negotiations will begin, with the objective of completing them within one year. These negotiations will be based on all the provisions and principles of United Nations Security Council Resolution 242. Finally status talks will start before the transitional period begins. The transitional period will begin three months after the conclusion of the transitional agreement and will last for three years. The United States will participate in both negotiations and will promote their rapid conclusion. In particular, the

Text of the letter that Secretary of State George P. Shultz wrote to Prime Minister Yitzhak Shamir of Israel outlining the American peace proposal. A similar letter was sent to King Hussein of Jordan. See *New York Times*, March 10, 1988.

United States will submit a draft agreement for the parties' consideration at the outset of the negotiations on transitional arrangements.

Two weeks before the opening of negotiations, an international conference will be held. The Secretary General of United Nations will be asked to issue invitations to the parties involved in the Arab-Israeli conflict and the five permanent members of the United Nations Council. All participants in the conference must accept United Nations Security Council Resolutions 242 and 338, and renounce violence and terrorism. The parties to each bilateral negotiation may refer reports on the status of their negotiations to the conference, in a manner to be agreed. The conference will not be able to impose solutions or veto agreements reached.

Palestinian representation will be within the Jordanian-Palestinian delegation. The Palestinian issue will be addressed in the negotiations between the Jordanian-Palestinian and Israeli delegations. Negotiations between the Israeli delegation and the Jordanian-Palestinian delegation will proceed independently of any other negotiations.

This statement of understandings in an integral whole. The United States understands that your acceptance is dependent on the implementation of each element in good faith.

> Sincerely yours,
> *George P. Shultz*

APPENDIX J

*Letter from Secretary of State George P. Shultz
to Swedish Foreign Minister Sten Andersson,
December 3, 1988*

Note: Shultz's letter was accompanied by two attachments. One was the text of a statement that the PLO should make to meet the known American conditions. The copy provided here contains the PLO handwritten changes that were agreed on after Swedish mediation. Arafat signed the revised version, reproduced here, and gave it to Andersson with a note saying that it had his approval and that "we will work to have it issued officially after being presented to the Executive Committee."

The second attachment consisted of a statement that the United States would be prepared to make in response to the proposed PLO statement. The original of that statement is not available, but a translation from the Arabic, as noted by the PLO, is provided.

THE SECRETARY OF STATE

WASHINGTON

December 3, 1988

Dear Sten:

I received through Ambassador Wachtmeister your message concerning the meeting in Stockholm next Tuesday. I greatly appreciate the constructive approach which you are taking toward this issue.

The attached papers constitute my reply to the question you raised in your message. I want to make three points in this regard:

-- First, we will not engage in any effort to make this the start of a negotiation over language; in other words, we will not accept counter-drafts.

-- Second, I am aware that the PLO may wish to add, following the statement that we have proposed, certain positions to which they feel committed and from which they would claim their basic statement is derived. We would have no objection to their doing so, provided those positions neither condition nor contradict their acceptance of our conditions.

-- Third, nothing here may be taken to imply an acceptance or recognition by the United States of an independent Palestinian state.

You may share this letter with your visitor if you believe it would he useful.

Sincerely yours,

George P. Shultz

Attachments:
    As stated above.

His Excellency
    Sten Andersson,
            Minister of Foreign Affairs of Sweden,
                Stockholm.

PROPOSED PLO STATEMENT

assuming the role of the provisional government of the state of Palestine

As its contribution to the search for a just and lasting peace in the Middle East, the Executive Committee of the Palestine Liberation Organization wishes to issue the following official statement:

1. That it is prepared to negotiate with Israel a comprehensive peace settlement of the Arab-Israeli conflict on the basis of United Nations resolutions 242 and 338.

within the framework of the international conference

2. That it undertakes to live in peace with Israel and its xx other neighbors and to respect their right to exist in peace within secure and internationally recognized borders, as will the democratic Palestinian state which it seeks to establish in
X the West Bank and the Gaza Strip. *the palestinian occupied territories in 1967*

3. That it condemns individual, group and state terrorism in all its forms, and will not resort to it.

X 4. That it is prepared for a moratorium on all forms of violence, on a mutual basis, once negotiations begin.

(American draft of proposed PLO statement, provided by Secretary of State George Shultz to Swedish Foreign Minister Sten Anderson, with hand-written changes from Palestinian side. December 6, 1988)

PROPOSED AMERICAN STATEMENT

The P.L.O. today issued a statement in which it accepted U.N. Security Council Resolution 242 and 338 and recognized Israel's right to exist and renounced the use of force. As a result, the United States is prepared to begin substantive discussions with representatives of the P.L.O. The United States believes that the negotiations to reach a peaceful settlement of the Arab-Israeli conflict must be based on resolutions 242 and 338 and calls on all parties to renew their efforts in the search for peace without delay. The United States recognizes that the representatives of the Palestinian people have the right to raise in negotiation all subjects of interest to them.

Questions to be answered by Secretary Shultz:*

Q. Does your statement mean that the Palestinians can put on the negotiating table their position on a Palestinian state?

A. Yes, the Palestinians, as far as we are concerned, have the right to pursue their desire to establish an independent state through negotiations. It is through the process of negotiation and direct exchange between the concerned parties that a lasting result can be achieved.

(After Swedish mediation, the U.S. agreed to another question and answer)

Q. Do you agree that negotiations should take place within the framework of an international conference?

A. The United States has long made its support for direct negotiations clear, but we remain prepared to consider any suggestion that may lead to direct negotiations toward a comprehensive peace. The initiative suggested by Secretary Shultz in the beginning of the year called for an international conference to begin direct negotiations. Any conference of this type must be properly organized so that it does not become an alternative to direct negotiations.

---

*The PLO notes indicate that Secretary Shultz was to provide these answers personally, but this was denied by the American side. In reality, it was the American ambassador to the UN who provided these clarifications.

As its contribution to the search for a just and lasting peace
in the Middle East, the Executive Committee of the Palestine
Liberation Organization, assuming the role of the Provisional
Government of the State of Palestine wishes to issue the following
official statement:

1. That it is prepared to negotiate with Israel within the framework
of the International Conference a comprehensive peace settlement
of the Arab-Israeli conflict on the basis of U.N. resolutions
242 and 338.

2. That it undertakes to live in peace with Israel and other
neighbours and to respect their right to exist in peace within
secure and internationally recognized borders, as will the
democratic Palestinian State which it seeks to establish in the
Palestinian occupied territories since 1967.

3. That it condemns individual, group and State terrorism in all
its forms, and will not resort to it.

Y. Arafat

7 / 12 / 88

APPENDIX K

Statements by Yasir Arafat and George Shultz, December 14, 1988

STATEMENT BY YASIR ARAFAT, GENEVA

Let me highlight my views before you. Our desire for peace is a strategy and not an interim tactic. We are bent to peace come what may.

Our statehood provides salvation to the Palestinians and peace to both Palestinians and Israelis. Self-determination means survival for the Palestinians.

And our survival does not destroy the survival of the Israelis as their rulers claim.

Yesterday in my speech, I made a reference to the United Nations resolution 181 [on the partition of Palestine] as the basis for Palestinian independence. I also made a reference to our acceptance of resolutions 242 and 338 as the basis for negotiations with Israel within the framework of an international conference. These three resolutions were endorsed at our Palestinian National Council session in Algiers.

In my speech also yesterday it was clear that we mean our peoples' right to freedom and national independence according to resolution 181 and the right of all parties concerned in the Middle East conflict to exist in peace and security and, as I have mentioned, including the state of Palestine and Israel and other neighbors according to the resolution 242 and 338.

As for terrorism, I renounced it yesterday in no uncertain terms, and yet I repeat for the record that we totally and absolutely renounce all forms of terrorism, including individual, group and state terrorism. Between Geneva and Algiers, we have made our position crystal clear.

Any more talk such as the Palestinians should give more—you remember the slogan, the Palestinians should give it more—or it is not enough, or the Palestinians are engaging in propaganda games and public relations exercise will be damaging and counterproductive.

The text for both statements comes from the *Washington Post*, December 15, 1988.

Enough is enough. Enough is enough. Enough is enough. All remaining matters should be discussed around the table and within the international conference.

Let it be absolutely clear that neither Arafat nor any [one else] for that matter can stop the intifada, the uprising. The intifada will come to an end only and only when practical and tangible steps have been taken toward the achievement of our national aims and the establishment of our independent Palestinian state.

In this context, I expect the EEC [European Economic Community] to play a more effective role in promoting peace in our region. They have political responsibility, they have moral responsibility and they can deal with it.

Finally, I declare before you and I ask you to kindly quote me on that: We want peace. We want peace. We are committed to peace. We want to live in our Palestinian state and let live.

STATEMENT BY GEORGE SHULTZ, WASHINGTON, D.C.

The Palestine Liberation Organization today issued a statement in which it accepted U.N. Security Council Resolutions 242 and 338, recognized Israel's right to exist in peace and security and renounced terrorism. As a result, the United States is prepared for a substantive dialogue with PLO representatives.

I am designating our ambassador to Tunisia as the only authorized channel for that dialogue. The objective of the United States remains, as always, a comprehensive peace in the Middle East.

In that light, I view this development as one more step toward the beginning of direct negotiations between the parties, which alone can lead to such a peace.

Nothing here may be taken to imply an acceptance or recognition by the United States of an independent Palestinian state. The position of the United States is that the status of the West Bank and Gaza cannot be determined by unilateral acts of either side, but only through a process of negotiations. The United States does not recognize the declaration of an independent Palestinian state.

It is also important to emphasize that the United States' commitment to the security of Israel remains unflinching.

APPENDIX L

Excerpts from Speech by President George Bush, March 6, 1991

. . . Our commitment to peace in the Middle East does not end with the liberation of Kuwait. So tonight, let me outline four key challenges to be met.

First, we must work together to create shared security arrangements in the region. Our friends and allies in the Middle East recognize that they will bear the bulk of the responsibility for regional security. But we want them to know that just as we stood with them to repel aggression, so now America stands ready to work with them to secure the peace.

This does not mean stationing U.S. ground forces on the Arabian Peninsula, but it does mean American participation in joint exercises involving both air and ground forces. It means maintaining a capable U.S. naval presence in the region, just as we have for over 40 years. Let it be clear: Our vital national interests depend on a stable and secure gulf.

Second, we must act to control the proliferation of weapons of mass destruction and the missiles used to deliver them. It would be tragic if the nations of the Middle East and Persian Gulf were now, in the wake of war, to embark on a new arms race. Iraq requires special vigilance. Until Iraq convinces the world of its peaceful intentions—that its leaders will not use new revenues to rearm and rebuild its menacing war machine—Iraq must not have access to the instruments of war.

And third, we must work to create new opportunities for peace and stability in the Middle East. On the night I announced Operation Desert Storm, I expressed my hope that out of the horrors of war might come new momentum for peace. We've learned in the modern age, geography cannot guarantee security and security does not come from military power alone.

All of us know the depth of bitterness that has made the dispute between Israel and its neighbors so painful and intractable. Yet, in the

The text comes from the *Washington Post*, March 7, 1991.

conflict just concluded, Israel and many of the Arab states have for the first time found themselves confronting the same aggressor. By now, it should be plain to all parties that peacemaking in the Middle East requires compromise. At the same time, peace brings real benefits to everyone. We must do all that we can to close the gap between Israel and the Arab states and between Israelis and Palestinians. The tactics of terror lead nowhere. There can be no substitute for diplomacy.

A comprehensive peace must be grounded in United Nations Security Council Resolutions 242 and 338 and the principle of territory for peace. This principle must be elaborated to provide for Israel's security and recognition, and at the same time for legitimate Palestinian political rights. Anything else would fail the twin tests of fairness and security. The time has come to put an end to Arab-Israeli conflict.

The war with Iraq is over. The quest for solutions to the problems in Lebanon, in the Arab-Israeli dispute, and in the gulf must go forward with new vigor and determination. And I guarantee you: No one will work harder for a stable peace in the region than we will.

Fourth, we must foster economic development for the sake of peace and progress. The Persian Gulf and Middle East form a region rich in natural resources with a wealth of untapped human potential. Resources once squandered on military might must be redirected to more peaceful ends. We are already addressing the immediate economic consequences of Iraq's aggression. Now, the challenge is to reach higher to foster economic freedom and prosperity for all the people of the region.

By meeting these four challenges we can build a framework for peace. . . .

APPENDIX M

James Baker's Letter of Assurance to the Palestinians, October 18, 1991

The Palestinian decision to attend a peace conference to launch direct negotiations with Israel represents an important step in the search for a comprehensive, just and lasting peace in the region. The United States has long believed that Palestinian participation is critical to the success of our efforts.

In the context of the process on which we are embarking, we want to respond to your request for certain assurances related to this process. These assurances constitute U.S. understandings and intentions concerning the conference and ensuing negotiations.

These assurances are consistent with United States policy and do not undermine or contradict United Nations Security Council resolutions 242 and 338. Moreover, there will be no assurances provided to one party that are not known to all the others. By this we can foster a sense of confidence and minimize chances for misunderstandings.

As President Bush stated in his March 6, 1991 address to Congress, the United States continues to believe firmly that a comprehensive peace must be grounded in United Nations Security Council Resolutions 242 and 338 and the principle of territory for peace. Such an outcome must also provide for security and recognition for all states in the region, including Israel, and for legitimate political rights of the Palestinian people. Anything else, the President noted, would fail the twin tests of fairness and security.

The process we are trying to create offers Palestinians a way to achieve these objectives. The United States believes that there should be an end to the Israeli occupation which can occur only through genuine and meaningful negotiations. The United States also believes that this process should create a new relationship of mutuality where Palestinians and Israelis can respect one another's security, identity, and political rights. We believe Palestinians should gain control over political, economic and other decisions that affect their lives and fate.

Direct bilateral negotiations will begin four days after the opening of the conference; those parties who wish to attend multilateral negotiations will convene two weeks after the opening of the conference to organize those negotiations. In this regard, the United States will support Palestinian involvement in any bilateral or multilateral negotiations on refugees and in all multilateral negotiations. The conference and the negotiations that follow will be based on UN Security Council Resolutions 242 and 338.

The process will proceed along two tracks through direct negotiations between Israel and Arab states and Israel and Palestinians. The United States is determined to achieve a comprehensive settlement of the Arab-Israeli conflict and will do its utmost to ensure that the process moves forward along both tracks toward this end.

In pursuit of a comprehensive settlement, all the negotiations would proceed as quickly as possible toward agreement. For its part, the United States will work for serious negotiations and will also seek to avoid prolongation and stalling by any party.

The conference will be co-sponsored by the United States and the Soviet Union. The European Community will be a participant in the conference alongside the United States and the Soviet Union and be represented by its Presidency. The conference can reconvene only with the consent of all the parties.

With regard to the role of the United Nations, the UN Secretary General will send a representative to the conference as an observer. The co-sponsors will keep the Secretary General apprised of the progress of the negotiations. Agreements reached between the parties will be registered with the UN Secretariat and reported to the Security Council, and the parties will seek the Council's endorsement of such agreements. Since it is in the interest of all parties for this process to succeed, while this process is actively ongoing, the United States will not support a competing or parallel process in the United Nations Security Council.

The United States does not seek to determine who speaks for Palestinians in this process. We are seeking to launch a political negotiating process that directly involves Palestinians and offers a pathway for achieving the legitimate political rights of the Palestinian people and for participation in the determination of their future. We believe that a joint Jordanian-Palestinian delegation offers the most promising pathway toward this end.

Only Palestinians can choose their delegation members, which are not subject to veto from anyone. The United States understands that members of the delegation will be Palestinians from the territories who agree to negotiations on two tracks, in phases, and who are willing to live in peace with Israel. No party can be forced to sit with anyone it does not want to sit with.

Palestinians will be free to announce their component of the joint delegation and to make a statement during the opening of the conference. They may also raise any issue pertaining to the substance of the negotiations during the negotiations.

The United States understands how much importance Palestinians attach to the question of east Jerusalem. Thus, we want to assure you that nothing Palestinians do in choosing their delegation members in this phase of the process will affect their claim to east Jerusalem, or be prejudicial or precedential to the outcome of negotiations. It remains the firm position of the United States that Jerusalem must never again be a divided city and that its final status should be decided by negotiations. Thus, we do not recognize Israel's annexation of east Jerusalem or the extension of its municipal boundaries, and we encourage all sides to avoid unilateral acts that would exacerbate local tensions or make negotiations more difficult or preempt their final outcome. It is also the United States position that a Palestinian resident in Jordan with ties to a prominent Jerusalem family would be eligible to join the Jordanian side of the delegation.

Furthermore, it is also the United States position that Palestinians of east Jerusalem should be able to participate by voting in the elections for an interim self-governing authority. The United States further believes that Palestinians from east Jerusalem and Palestinians outside the occupied territories who meet the three criteria should be able to participate in the negotiations on final status. And, the United States supports the right of Palestinians to bring any issue, including east Jerusalem, to the table.

Because the issues at stake are so complex and the emotions so deep, the United States has long maintained that a transitional period is required to break down the walls of suspicion and mistrust and lay the basis for sustainable negotiations on the final status of the occupied territories. The purpose of negotiations on transitional arrangements is to effect the peaceful and orderly transfer of authority from Israel to Palestinians. Palestinians need to achieve rapid control over political, economic, and other decisions that affect their lives and to adjust to a new situation in which Palestinians exercise authority in the West Bank and Gaza. For its part, the United States will strive from the outset and encourage all parties to adopt steps that can create an environment of confidence and mutual trust, including respect for human rights.

As you are aware with respect to negotiations between Israel and Palestinians, negotiations will be conducted in phases, beginning with talks on interim self-government arrangements. These talks will be conducted with the objective of reaching agreement within one year. Once agreed, the interim self-government arrangements will last for a period of five years. Beginning the third year of the period of interim self-government arrangements, negotiations will take place on permanent status. It is the aim of the United States that permanent status negotiations will be concluded by the end of the transitional period.

It has long been our position that only direct negotiations based on U.N. Security Council Resolutions 242 and 338 can produce a real peace. No one can dictate the outcome in advance. The United States understands that Palestinians must be free, in opening statements at the conference and in the negotiations that follow, to raise any issue of importance to them. Thus, Palestinians are free to argue for whatever outcome they believe best meets their requirements. The United States will accept any outcome agreed by the parties. In this regard and consistent with longstanding US policies, confederation is not excluded as a possible outcome of negotiations on final status.

The United States has long believed that no party should take unilateral actions that seek to predetermine issues that can only be resolved through negotiations. In this regard the United States has opposed and will continue to oppose settlement activity in the territories occupied in 1967, which remains an obstacle to peace.

The United States will act as an honest broker in trying to resolve the Arab-Israeli conflict. It is our intention, together with the Soviet Union, to play the role of a driving force in this process to help the parties move forward toward a comprehensive peace. Any party will have access to the co-sponsors at any time. The United States is prepared to participate in all stages of the negotiations, with the consent of the parties to each negotiation.

These are the assurances that the United States is providing concerning the implementation of the initiative we have discussed. We are persuaded that we have a real opportunity to accomplish something very important in the peace process. And we are prepared to work hard together with you in the period ahead to build on the progress we have made. There will be difficult challenges for all parties. But with Palestinians' continued commitment and creativity, we have a real chance of moving to a peace conference and to negotiations and then on toward the broader peace that we all seek.

APPENDIX N

U.S.-Soviet Invitation to the Mideast Peace Conference in Madrid, October 18, 1991

After extensive consultations with Arab states, Israel and the Palestinians, the United States and the Soviet Union believe that an historic opportunity exists to advance the prospects for genuine peace throughout the region. The United States and the Soviet Union are prepared to assist the parties to achieve a just, lasting and comprehensive peace settlement, through direct negotiations along two tracks, between Israel and the Arab states, and between Israel and the Palestinians, based on United Nations Security Council Resolutions 242 and 338. The objective of this process is real peace.

Toward that end, the president of the U.S. and the president of the USSR invite you to a peace conference, which their countries will co-sponsor, followed immediately by direct negotiations. The conference will be convened in Madrid on 30 October 1991.

President Bush and President Gorbachev request your acceptance of this invitation no later than 6 p.m. Washington time, 23 October 1991, in order to ensure proper organization and preparation of the conference.

Direct bilateral negotiations will begin four days after the opening of the conference. Those parties who wish to attend multilateral negotiations will convene two weeks after the opening of the conference to organize those negotiations. The co-sponsors believe that those negotiations should focus on region-wide issues such as arms control and regional security, water, refugee issues, environment, economic development, and other subjects of mutual interest.

The co-sponsors will chair the conference which will be held at ministerial level. Governments to be invited include Israel, Syria, Lebanon and Jordan. Palestinians will be invited and attend as part of a joint Jordanian-Palestinian delegation. Egypt will be invited to the conference

This is the complete text of the invitation to the Madrid peace conference held on October 30, 1991, obtained by the *Jerusalem Post*. The invitation was jointly issued by the United States and the Soviet Union to Israel, Syria, Jordan, Lebanon, and the Palestinians.

as a participant. The European Community will be a participant in the conference, alongside the United States and the Soviet Union and will be represented by its presidency. The Gulf Cooperation Council will be invited to send its secretary-general to the conference as an observer, and GCC member states will be invited to participate in organizing the negotiations on multilateral issues. The United Nations will be invited to send an observer, representing the secretary-general.

The conference will have no power to impose solutions on the parties or veto agreements reached by them. It will have no authority to make decisions for the parties and no ability to vote on issues or results. The conference can reconvene only with the consent of all the parties.

With respects to negotiations between Israel and Palestinians who are part of the joint Jordanian-Palestinian delegation, negotiations will be conducted in phases, beginning with talks on interim self-government arrangements. These talks will be conducted with the objective of reaching agreement within one year. Once agreed the interim self-government arrangements will last for a period of five years. Beginning the third year of the period of interim self-government arrangements, negotiations will take place on permanent status. These permanent status negotiations, and the negotiations between Israel and the Arab states, will take place on the basis of Resolutions 242 and 338.

It is understood that the co-sponsors are committed to making this process succeed. It is their intention to convene the conference and negotiations with those parties who agree to attend.

The co-sponsors believe that this process offers the promise of ending decades of confrontation and conflict and the hope of a lasting peace. Thus, the co-sponsors hope that the parties will approach these negotiations in a spirit of good will and mutual respect. In this way, the peace process can begin to break down the mutual suspicions and mistrust that perpetuate the conflict and allow the parties to begin to resolve their differences. Indeed, only through such a process can real peace and reconciliation among the Arab states, Israel and the Palestinians be achieved. And only through this process can the peoples of the Middle East attain the peace and security they richly deserve.

APPENDIX O

Excerpts from President George Bush's Address to the Mideast Peace Conference, Madrid, Spain, October 30, 1991

Peace will only come as the result of direct negotiations, compromises, give-and-take. Peace cannot be imposed from outside by the United States or anyone else. While we will continue to do everything possible to help the parties overcome obstacles, peace must come from within.

We come here to Madrid as realists. We don't expect peace to be negotiated in a day, or a week, or a month, or even a year. It will take time. Indeed, it should take time—time for parties so long at war to learn to talk to one another, to listen to one another. Time to heal old wounds and build trust. In this quest, time need not be the enemy of progress.

What we envision is a process of direct negotiations proceeding along two tracks, one between Israel and the Arab states, the other between Israel and the Palestinians. Negotiations are to be conducted on the basis of U.N. Security Council Resolutions 242 and 338.

The real work will not happen here in the plenary sessions, but in direct bilateral negotiations. This conference cannot impose a settlement on the participants or veto agreements. And just as important, the conference can only be reconvened with the consent of every participant. Progress is in the hands of the parties who must live with the consequences.

Soon after the bilateral talks commence, parties will convene as well to organize multilateral negotiations. These will focus on issues that cross national boundaries and are common to the region: arms control, water, refugee concerns, economic development. Progress in these fora is not intended as a substitute for what must be decided in the bilateral talks. To the contrary, progress in the multilateral issues can help create an atmosphere in which longstanding bilateral disputes can more easily be settled.

For Israel and the Palestinians, a framework already exists for diplomacy. Negotiations will be conducted in phases, beginning with talks on interim self-government arrangements. We aim to reach arrangement

Text comes from the *New York Times*, October 31, 1991

within one year. And once agreed, interim self-government arrangements will last for five years. Beginning with the third year, negotiations will commence on permanent status.

No one can say with any precision what the end result will be. In our view, something must be developed, something acceptable to Israel, the Palestinians and Jordan, that gives the Palestinian people meaningful control over their own lives and fate and provides for the acceptance and security of Israel.

We can all appreciate that both Israelis and Palestinians are worried about compromise, worried about compromising even the smallest point for fear it becomes a precedent for what really matters. But no one should avoid compromise on interim arrangements for a simple reason: nothing agreed to now will prejudice permanent status negotiations. To the contrary, these subsequent negotiations will be determined on their own merits.

Peace cannot depend upon promises alone. Real peace—lasting peace—must be based upon security for all states and peoples, including Israel. For too long, the Israeli people have lived in fear, surrounded by an unaccepting Arab world. Now is the ideal moment for the Arab world to demonstrate that attitudes have changed, that the Arab world is willing to live in peace with Israel and make allowances for Israel's reasonable security needs.

We know that peace must also be based on fairness. In the absence of fairness, there will be no legitimacy, no stability. This applies above all to the Palestinian people, many of whom have known turmoil and frustration above all else. Israel now has an opportunity to demonstrate that it is willing to enter into a new relationship with its Palestinian neighbors: one predicated upon mutual respect and cooperation.

Throughout the Middle East, we seek a stable and enduring settlement. We've not defined what this means. Indeed, I make these points with no map showing where the final borders are to be drawn. Nevertheless, we believe that territorial compromise is essential to peace. Boundaries should reflect the quality of both security and political arrangements. The United States is prepared to accept whatever the parties themselves find acceptable. What we seek, as I said on March 6, is a solution that meets the twin tests of fairness and security.

Notes

CHAPTER ONE

1. The formative works on bureaucratic politics are Graham Allison, *Essence of Decision: Explaining the Cuban Missile Crisis* (Little, Brown, 1971); and Morton Halperin, *Bureaucratic Politics and Foreign Policy* (Brookings, 1974). For an excellent critique, see Robert Art, "Bureaucratic Politics and American Foreign Policy: A Critique," *Policy Sciences*, vol. 4 (1973), pp. 467–90.

2. See Mitchell Geoffrey Bard, *The Water's Edge and Beyond: Defining the Limits to Domestic Influence on United States Middle East Policy* (New Brunswick, N.J.: Transaction Publishers, 1991).

3. See William B. Quandt, *Camp David: Peacemaking and Politics* (Brookings, 1986), pp. 6–29.

4. For a more detailed discussion of these three approaches, see William B. Quandt, *Decade of Decisions: American Policy toward the Arab-Israeli Conflict, 1967–1976* (University of California Press, 1977), pp. 3–28.

5. See Daniel Yergin, *The Prize: The Epic Quest for Oil, Money and Power* (Simon and Schuster, 1991).

6. See Raymond A. Bauer and Kenneth J. Gergen, eds., *The Study of Policy Formulation* (Free Press, 1968), p. 15.

7. Charles E. Lindblom, "The Science of 'Muddling Through,'" *Public Administration Review*, vol. 19 (Spring 1959), pp. 79–88.

8. John Steinbruner, *The Cybernetic Theory of Decision: New Dimensions of Political Analysis* (Princeton University Press, 1974), pp. 109–24.

9. Ernest May, *"Lessons" of the Past: The Use and Misuse of History in American Foreign Policy* (Oxford University Press, 1973).

10. Merle Miller, *Plain Speaking: An Oral Biography of Harry S. Truman* (Berkley Publishing, 1973).

11. Lynn E. Davis, *The Cold War Begins: Soviet-American Conflict over Eastern Europe* (Princeton University Press, 1974).

12. Alexander L. George, "The Case for Multiple Advocacy in Making Foreign Policy," *American Political Science Review*, vol. 66 (September 1972), pp. 751–85; and Irving L. Janis, *Victims of Groupthink: A Psychological Study of Foreign Policy Decisions and Fiascoes* (Houghton Mifflin, 1972).

CHAPTER TWO

1. Abba Eban, *An Autobiography* (Random House, 1977), pp. 354–55, gives an account of Johnson's early concern with Israel. Among Johnson's close friends

who were strong supporters of Israel were Arthur Krim, president of United Artists and chairman of the Democratic National Party Finance Committee, and his wife Mathilde; Abraham Feinberg, president of the American Bank and Trust of New York; Abraham Fortas, Supreme Court Justice; and Arthur Goldberg, ambassador to the United Nations. See Donald Neff, *Warriors for Jerusalem: The Six Days That Changed the Middle East* (Simon and Schuster, 1984), pp. 80–85, 156–58.

2. The report prepared in the fall of 1966 by Ambassador Julius Holmes contained this theme.

3. Lyndon Baines Johnson Library, oral history project, Lucius Battle interviewed by Paige Mulhollan, November 14, 1968, p. 36; and author's conversation with Battle. David Nes, who was in charge of the embassy in Cairo between Battle's departure and the arrival of Richard Nolte, wrote to a colleague in the State Department on May 11, 1967, stating: "We seem to have driven Nasser to a degree of irrationality bordering on madness, fed, of course, by the frustrations and fears generated by his failures domestic and foreign. Our debate here revolves around where he will strike next—Libya, Lebanon? . . . In brief, we now face all the dangers inevitably flowing from having pushed Nasser into a financial and food corner and from endeavoring to thwart him within his first two 'concentric circles.' Now we have the showdown I referred to last October." David Nes to Rodger Davies, May 11, 1967, secret (declassified November 14, 1984).

4. See Michael Brecher, *Decisions in Israel's Foreign Policy* (Yale University Press, 1975), pp. 359–61, for a review of these threats. The best documented, and the one that was carried by UPI and showed up in the *New York Times* on May 13, consisted of a background briefing on May 12, 1967, by the Israeli head of military intelligence, Aharon Yariv. John Cooley, *Green March, Black September: The Story of the Palestinian Arabs* (London: Frank Cass, 1973), p. 160, quotes from a tape of the briefing: "I could say we must use force in order to have the Egyptians convince the Syrians that it doesn't pay [to let the Palestinians carry out attacks across Syria's borders]. . . . I think that the only sure and safe answer to the problem is a military operation of great size and strength." Some analysts have mistakenly assumed that it was Chief of Staff Yitzhak Rabin who made the "threat" against Syria. See *Middle East Record, 1967*, vol. 3 (Jerusalem: Israel Universities Press, 1971), p. 187.

5. Although Israeli threats to take action against Syria were not very precise in this period, it does appear that some retaliatory action was contemplated. Michael Brecher, *Decisions in Crisis: Israel, 1967 and 1973* (University of California Press, 1980), p. 36, states that on May 7, 1967, "Israel's Cabinet decided that if Syria did not heed her public warnings and if all other noncoercive methods of persuasion failed, Israel would launch a limited retaliation raid." For the Egyptian reaction, see Mohamed Heikal [in Arabic, Muhammad Hassanayn Haykal], *1967: Al-Infijar* (Cairo: Markaz al-Ahram, 1990), pp. 445–56.

6. Heikal, *1967: Al-Infijar*, pp. 371–72, greatly exaggerates when he implies that Johnson was obsessed with Nasser and engaged in a conspiracy to bring him down.

7. Stephen Green, *Taking Sides: America's Secret Relations with a Militant Israel* (William Morrow, 1984), pp. 204–11.

8. On this incident, which in the words of Yitzhak Rabin caught Israel "with its pants down," see Avner Yaniv, *Deterrence without the Bomb: The Politics of Israeli Strategy* (Lexington, Mass.: Lexington Books, 1987), pp. 84–85.

9. Some, including Egypt's then–foreign minister, Mahmoud Riad, have maintained that Egypt only asked that UNEF be withdrawn from the border area, not Sharm al-Shaykh. That may have been the intention behind the initial requests, but Egyptian commanders in the field made it clear that the UNEF contingent at Sharm al-Shaykh should also leave. Riad's own letter to U Thant on May 18 requested the removal of UNEF from the territory of the UAR. See Mahmoud Riad, *The Struggle for Peace in the Middle East* (Quartet Books, 1981), p. 18; and "Report of the Secretary-General on the Withdrawal of the United Nations Emergency Force, June 26, 1967," reprinted in John Norton Moore, ed., *The Arab-Israeli Conflict*, vol. 3: *Documents* (Princeton University Press, 1974), p. 756. U Thant has been criticized for acceding too hastily to the Egyptian request, for not referring the question to the General Assembly, in short, for not calling Nasser's bluff. See, for example, Nadav Safran, *Israel: The Embattled Ally* (Harvard University Press, 1978), 394–95. Heikal, *1967: Al-Infijar*, pp. 457–74, argues that Nasser did initially favor only a partial withdrawal of UNEF, while Abd al-Hakim Amr ['Āmir], the head of the armed forces, wanted UNEF to leave completely. There are many indications from Egyptian sources that the Nasser-Amr rivalry was a serious problem throughout this whole period. For a good overview of the relevant facts, see Richard B. Parker, "The June 1967 War: Some Mysteries Explored," *Middle East Journal*, vol. 46 (Spring 1992), pp. 184–96.

10. Lyndon Baines Johnson, *The Vantage Point: Perspectives of the Presidency, 1963–1969* (Rinehart, Holt and Winston, 1971), p. 290; and M. Gilboa, *Six Years, Six Days* (in Hebrew) (Tel Aviv: Am Oved, 1968), p. 144.

11. Harold Saunders, a staff member of the National Security Council (NSC) at this time, was responsible for compiling the White House documents on the 1967 crisis for the Johnson Library. In a reflective cover memorandum entitled "The Middle East Crisis: Preface," December 20, 1968, top secret (declassified October 14, 1983), Saunders notes that "we 'decided' at the outset of the crisis to try to restrain Israel from trying to settle its own problems militarily. . . . The alternative was to let the Israelis do as they had so often done before—respond militarily on their own. This alternative was rejected, almost out of hand. . . . I had the impression that President Johnson himself, though he wanted to avoid war, was profoundly skeptical that we would succeed in rallying practical international support for keeping the Straits open. If we failed, our last hope was to negotiate with Nasser's Vice President. If that didn't work, we would be left to open the Straits in direct confrontation with the whole Arab world."

12. Gilboa, *Six Years, Six Days*, p. 145; and *Middle East Record, 1967*, vol. 3, pp. 194, 196.

13. The text of the February 11, 1957, aide memoire can be found in Moore, *Arab-Israeli Conflict*, vol. 3: *Documents*, pp. 638–39. On February 24, 1957, Eban

sought a clarification from Dulles to the effect that Israel could invoke the right to self-defense under article 51 of the UN Charter if its ships were attacked. Dulles agreed with Eban's position. The public manifestation of this "assent" was somewhat vague. Golda Meir spoke at the UN on March 1 and stated that Israel would exercise its inherent right of self-defense if armed force was used to interfere with Israeli shipping in the Strait of Tiran. Henry Cabot Lodge, the American ambassador to the United Nations, took note of this declaration and said that it did not seem "unreasonable." Eban was unhappy with this formulation, and therefore Eisenhower wrote to Ben Gurion on March 2, 1957, saying that Israel would "have no cause to regret" its withdrawal from Sinai and that the expressed Israeli views were "reasonable." All the relevant texts can be found in Nina J. Noring, ed., *Foreign Relations of the United States, 1955–1957: Arab-Israeli Dispute, 1957* (Government Printing Office, 1990), pp. 254–348.

14. Michael Brecher, *Decisions in Israel's Foreign Policy*, p. 375, quoting Ambassador Avraham Harman to Assistant Secretary Battle.

15. Gilboa, *Six Years, Six Days*, p. 123, quoting Rostow to Harman, May 20. Michael Bar-Zohar, *Embassies in Crisis: Diplomats and Demagogues behind the Six-Day War* (Prentice-Hall, 1970), p. 56, confirms this.

16. Gilboa, *Six Years, Six Days*, p. 145; Brecher, *Decisions in Israel's Foreign Policy*, p. 375; Bar-Zohar, *Embassies in Crisis*, p. 68. The full text of the Johnson letter is in Department of State telegram 198955, May 21, 1967, secret (declassified May 24, 1990).

17. In mid-October 1969 Abba Eban submitted an article to the *New York Times Magazine* that was prepared for publication but was withdrawn at the last moment. A copy of the galley proofs are in the author's possession and they differ in significant ways from Eban's later account in his autobiography. His words concerning the May 21 letter in the draft were: "Nothing could have been less promising than these early reports. Indeed, it was their lack of virile purpose and Johnsonian authenticity which had swayed my decision to go to Washington. This was not Johnson language; a frightened bureaucrat bleated from every line. Nothing except the signature seemed to have anything to do with the firm and candid personality which Israel had respected throughout all of his vicissitudes—and ours—at home and in the world."

18. The original draft of the letter, with Johnson's own corrections and additions, is available from the Johnson Library (declassified May 8, 1981.) See also Mohamed Heikal, *The Cairo Documents: The Inside Story of Nasser and His Relationship with World Leaders, Rebels, and Statesmen* (Doubleday, 1973), p. 243. Nolte delivered the letter, plus a more substantive "note verbale," which warned of war by miscalculation, to the Egyptian foreign minister, Mahmoud Riad. Three areas of concern were emphasized: continuing guerrilla activities against Israel from Syrian territory, withdrawal of UNEF, and troop buildups. The note went on to say, "We are convinced that any interference whatever with these international rights [of free and innocent passage in the strait for ships of all nations] could have the gravest international consequences." For the "note verbale," see Department of State telegram 199710, May 22, 1967, confidential (declassified January 4, 1990).

19. Rusk added a message to the Israelis suggesting that UNEF be transferred to the Israeli side of the border.

20. Johnson, *Vantage Point*, pp. 290–91.

21. Johnson did take one step on May 22 that had continuing importance during the crisis: he ordered the Sixth Fleet, with two aircraft carriers, the *Saratoga* and the *America*, to the eastern Mediterranean.

22. Brecher, *Decisions in Israel's Foreign Policy*, p. 378.

23. "President's Decisions Israeli Aid Package 23 May 1967," top secret (declassified May 9, 1983). A subsequent decision was made to approve the sale of gas masks. See *The Department of State during the Administration of President Lyndon B. Johnson, November 1963–January 1969*, vol. 1: *Administrative History*, pt. 4, chap. 4, section H-1, secret (declassified September 16, 1983), pp. 20, 33. According to the same source (p. 45), Eugene Rostow believed the United States had pulled the Israelis back from preemptive strikes on May 23. The United States had also asked Israel not to test the closure of the strait by sending its flagships through. Therefore, Rostow felt, an enormous responsibility fell on the United States.

24. "The United States Calls for Restraint in the Near East: Statement by President Johnson," *Department of State Bulletin*, vol. 56 (June 12, 1967), p. 870.

25. Brecher, *Decisions in Israel's Foreign Policy*, p. 381, refers to Evron's cable on why the United States was planning to take its case to the United Nations.

26. Johnson, *Vantage Point*, pp. 291–92.

27. Ibid., p. 291; and Eugene V. Rostow, *Peace in the Balance: The Future of American Foreign Policy* (Simon and Schuster, 1972), pp. 259–60. The Israeli ambassador had already called on Eisenhower on May 24, presumably to remind the former president of the commitments that had been made in 1957 concerning the strait.

28. "Record of National Security Council Meeting held on May 24, 1967 at 12 noon—Discussion of Middle East Crisis," top secret (declassified October 14, 1983). On September 10, 1992, additional portions of this document were declassified. The intriguing points are that CIA Director Helms categorically asserted that there were no nuclear weapons in the area, while General Earle Wheeler, chairman of the Joint Chiefs, was "more skeptical." Later in the discussion the president returned to the question of "what we would do after relying on Israeli forces. General Wheeler noted that a long war would hurt the Israeli economy. At that point we would have to decide whether we were going to send in forces and confront Nasser directly." The next section of the transcript is still classified.

29. Johnson, *Vantage Point*, p. 292; Gilboa, *Six Years, Six Days*, p. 143; and Bar-Zohar, *Embassies in Crisis*, p. 98.

30. Bar-Zohar, *Embassies in Crisis*, p. 123; Gilboa, *Six Years, Six Days*, pp. 145–46; and interview with Eugene Rostow, February 17, 1969.

31. Bar-Zohar, *Embassies in Crisis*, p. 125.

32. During the NSC meeting on May 24, Wheeler said that "it would be harder to open the Gulf of Aqaba than we had at first thought. Because of the two Egyptian submarines in the Red Sea, we would need a ASW [artisubmarine

warfare] unit, the nearest of which is now in Singapore—two weeks away." Shortly thereafter "a brief discussion of possible presence of unconventional weapons followed." "Record of National Security Council Meeting held on May 24, 1967 at 12 noon—Discussion of Middle East Crisis," p. 3, top secret (declassified October 14, 1983).

33. These messages were sent at the instigation of the chief of staff, Yitzhak Rabin, who was eager to force an American decision. Either Johnson would have to commit himself to concrete action or Israel would be free to act on its own. See Yitzhak Rabin, *The Rabin Memoirs* (Little, Brown, 1979), pp. 86–89; Gideon Rafael, *Destination Peace: Three Decades of Israeli Foreign Policy. A Personal Memoir* (Stein and Day, 1981), pp. 144–45; Eban, *Autobiography*, pp. 348–49; and Steven L. Spiegel, *The Other Arab Israeli Conflict: Making America's Middle East Policy from Truman to Reagan* (University of Chicago Press, 1985), p. 450, note 95, for a slightly different version.

34. Brecher, *Decisions in Israel's Foreign Policy*, p. 386; and, with more detail, Brecher, *Decisions in Crisis*, pp. 130–32; Bar-Zohar, *Embassies in Crisis*, p. 109; and Moshe Dayan, *Moshe Dayan: Story of My Life* (William Morrow, 1976), p. 329.

35. Brecher, *Decisions in Israel's Foreign Policy*, pp. 386–87; and Bar-Zohar, *Embassies in Crisis*, pp. 112–13. Eugene Rostow called in Egyptian Ambassador Kemal and warned that Egypt must not attack Israel. The Soviets were also asked to use their influence to restrain Nasser, which they reportedly did. Heikal, *Cairo Documents*, p. 244; Gilboa, *Six Years, Six Days*, pp. 145–46; Brecher, *Decisions in Israel's Foreign Policy*, p. 387; and Bar-Zohar, *Embassies in Crisis*, pp. 111–12.

36. While Eban was making his pitch at the State Department, the CIA had received an alarmist report presented by an Israeli intelligence official to the CIA station chief in Tel Aviv. It warned of a Soviet takeover of the region if Nasser was not forced to back down. Interview with Richard Helms, June 8, 1992.

37. Brecher, *Decisions in Israel's Foreign Policy*, pp. 387–88. Harman saw Eugene Rostow and Joseph Sisco.

38. Bar-Zohar, *Embassies in Crisis*, p. 114–15. We now know that the Egyptian military, in particular Abd al-Hakim Amr, had issued orders for the Egyptian air force to carry out air strikes on the morning of May 27. The Israelis must have gotten wind of this. According to Egyptian sources, Nasser countermanded the order on May 26. See Muhammad Fawzi, *Harb al-Thalatha Sanawat, 1967–70: Mudhakirat al-Fariq Awal Muhammad Fawzi* (The Three-Year War, 1967–70: Memoirs of General Muhammad Fawzi) (Cairo: Dar al-Mustaqbal al-Arabi, 1984), p. 123; and Abd al-Muhsin Kamil Murtaji, *Al-Fariq Murtaji Yarwa al-Haqa'iq* (General Murtaji Narrates the Facts) (Beirut: Al-Watan al-Arabi, 1976), pp. 79–81. Also, Heikal, *1967: Al-Infijar*, pp. 573–75.

39. See Tom Wicker, *JFK and LBJ: The Influence of Personality upon Politics* (William Morrow, 1968), pp. 195–99.

40. Eban, *Autobiography*, pp. 349–51; Brecher, *Decisions in Israel's Foreign Policy*, pp. 389–90; and Bar-Zohar, *Embassies in Crisis*, p. 115.

41. The previous evening, May 25, 1967, Johnson had met with Helms and Wheeler to discuss a recent Israeli intelligence assessment that was viewed as alarmist. The president had asked for the Israeli assessment to be "scrubbed

down." On May 26 a joint CIA-DIA (Defense Intelligence Agency) assessment was ready. It concluded that Israel would gain air superiority in Sinai within twenty-four hours if Israel took the initiative, and within two to three days if Egypt struck first. The assessment went on to conclude that the Egyptian defense lines would be breached within several days. Interview with Richard Helms, June 5, 1992.

42. Gilboa, *Six Years, Six Days*, pp. 146–47; and Brecher, *Decisions in Israel's Foreign Policy*, p. 390. Bar-Zohar, *Embassies in Crisis*, p. 117, claims that McNamara expressed his opposition to the multilateral naval fleet at this meeting.

43. The Johnson Library files for the 1967 crisis contain a complete review of the commitments made in 1957. Presumably this document, dated February 26, 1957 (declassified October 19, 1982), was provided by the Israelis and summarizes the understandings reached with Dulles. This must be one of the documents reviewed by policymakers, who appear not to have been fully aware of the extent of the American commitment, especially the acknowledgment that Israel had the right to use force to reopen the Strait of Tiran if it was ever closed by force.

44. "Memorandum for the President: Your Conversation with the Israeli Foreign Minister," May 26, 1967, secret (declassified and sanitized, August 30, 1982).

45. McNamara did not oppose the president's policy, however.

46. See Rusk's handwritten draft using these words, Johnson Library (declassified June 27, 1983). This key sentence was used frequently in later communications, sometimes in slightly different forms. The Israelis spent considerable time trying to figure out if the message constituted a subtle form of encouragement to act on their own. To Rusk, it seems, it did not. Rusk's handwritten draft was edited by Johnson, who added the phrase "We cannot imagine that it will make this decision" right after the "go alone" sentence. This became the aide-memoire handed to Eban during the meeting that evening. See marked-up draft of the aide-memoire, Johnson Library, May 26, 1967, secret (declassified September 21, 1983).

47. The view was expressed that no overt act of aggression had yet occurred. Until Egypt resorted to the use of armed force, according to this argument, the U.S. commitment to Israel would not be activated.

48. The above summary is from rough notes of the meeting taken by Harold Saunders, May 26, 1967. See also Neff, *Warriors for Jerusalem*, pp. 142–43, especially for the text of Walt Rostow's memo for the president in preparation for this meeting. Rostow stated, among other things, that Eban would want to know "what can you offer right now better than a pre-emptive [Israeli] strike."

49. Jonathan Trumbull Howe, *Multicrises: Sea Power and Global Politics in the Missile Age* (MIT Press, 1971), pp. 362–67. Howe interviewed an unnamed White House source (John Roche), who stated that Johnson was stalling Eban because he had just been shown the memo of the Dulles-Eban talks of 1957 and wanted to check its authenticity.

50. Evron recalled Johnson as having said that without congressional approval for any action taken, Johnson would be "just a six-foot-four-inch friend of Israel."

He went on to say that "Israel is not a satellite of the United States. Nor is the United States a satellite of Israel." In retrospect, Evron felt that this was Johnson's way of saying that Israel was on its own. The message was less clear, he believed, when Johnson spoke to Eban, relying on the State Department briefing papers, shortly after this meeting. Interview with Ephraim Evron, June 4, 1992.

51. Brecher, *Decisions in Israel's Foreign Policy*, pp. 390–91, provides the full text of Evron's official account of his meeting with Johnson.

52. "Memorandum of Conversation, May 26, 1967," secret/nodis (drafted by Joseph Sisco, sanitized and declassified September 21, 1983). See also Brecher, *Decision in Israel's Foreign Policy*, p. 392. Johnson, *Vantage Point*, p. 293, says he told Eban the United States would use "any and all means" to open the strait. The official transcript reports on pp. 7–8 that Eban, choosing his words carefully, said, "I would not be wrong if I told the Prime Minister that your disposition is to make every possible effort to assure that the Strait and the Gulf will remain open to free and innocent passage? The President responded, yes." Earlier in the conversation, however, Johnson did say that the United States would pursue "any and all means" to reopen the strait. The difference between these two formulations—"every possible effort" and "any and all means"—became a source of controversy between the two governments a few days later.

53. Interview with Eugene Rostow, February 17, 1969; and Howe, *Multicrisis*, pp. 362–67. Howe quotes White House aide John Roche to the effect that Johnson said after his meeting with Eban: "[Israel is] going to hit them." Roche's account can be found in his oral history interview with the Johnson Library, July 16, 1970, tape 2, p. 68. Just after the meeting with Eban, Johnson took a call from Ambassador Goldberg in New York. This conversation must have led Goldberg to ask for an urgent meeting of his own with Eban, who was transiting New York on his way back to Tel Aviv. The two met at the Waldorf Astoria. Goldberg, speaking authoritatively, underscored the point the president had made about the necessity for congressional support for any U.S. action. Goldberg offered his personal opinion that this meant that the United States could do nothing militarily to help Israel. Rafael, *Destination Peace*, p. 145, provides part of this story. In addition, see the oral history interview with Arthur Goldberg, LBJ Library, March 23, 1983, p. 22. In the same interview Goldberg claims that Johnson had asked him to take charge of the crisis because Rusk had disqualified himself by making anti-Israel remarks earlier in his career (p. 16).

54. Brecher, *Decisions in Israel's Foreign Policy*, pp. 398, provides the text of this message: "The Soviets stated that if Israel starts military action, the Soviet Union will extend help to the attacked States. . . . As your friend, I repeat even more strongly what I said yesterday to Mr. Eban: Israel just must not take pre-emptive military action and thereby make itself responsible for the initiation of hostilities." Johnson then requested a two-to three-week delay before Israel would resort to force to open the strait. The original draft of the message had said "It is essential that Israel not. . . ." From his Texas ranch, Johnson strengthened this to read "Israel just must not. . . ." He also suggested including the following language: "Without exception our Congressional leaders have made it clear that

preemptive actions would find no support here." Memorandum from Jim Jones to Walt Rostow, May 27, 1967 (declassified and sanitized, September 21, 1983).

55. Brecher, *Decisions in Israel's Foreign Policy*, p. 400. Brecher, *Decisions in Crisis*, p. 146, claims that this message had a significant impact on Eshkol's thinking and probably kept the cabinet from deciding on war that day.

56. Interview with Daniel P. Levitt, law clerk for Justice Fortas in 1967, on August 8, 1991. Levitt indicated that he believed but could not confirm that Johnson had asked Fortas to play the role of "informal intermediary" with Israel.

57. See Laura Kalman, *Abe Fortas: A Biography* (Yale University Press, 1990), p. 301; and, from the same source (Levitt), Robert Shogan, *A Question of Judgment: The Fortas Case and the Struggle for the Supreme Court* (Bobbs-Merrill, 1972), p. 139.

58. On Robert Kennedy's position, see Dean Rusk, *As I Saw It* (Norton, 1990), p. 385: "Bobby Kennedy, then a Senator from New York, told McNamara and me, 'I don't know what you fellows in Washington think about the attitude of my Jewish friends in New York, but they don't want any part of this [U.S.-led multilateral fleet].' "

59. National Archives, presidential diaries, April 1, 1967, to June 30, 1967 (microfilm, part II, reel 9), especially May 27–31, 1967.

60. Interview with Walt Rostow, October 16, 1991; and Walt Rostow, *The Diffusion of Power: An Essay in Recent History* (Macmillan, 1972), pp. 417–19.

61. On May 30, 1967, Rusk and McNamara prepared a joint memorandum for the president that recommended a number of steps to "test" Egyptian intentions regarding the blockade. For example, consideration was given to a plan for sending an Israeli-owned ship into the Gulf of Aqaba. "If that passed without interference, we might attempt passage with a more 'strategic' cargo (e.g., oil). Within this period, such tests would involve no armed escort and no counteraction in the event passage was refused. The purpose would be to clarify the limits of UAR policy and to build a public case for support of free passage" (p.4). A stronger military option was also being considered. In both cases, consultation with Congress would be essential. "While it is true that many Congressional doves may be in the process of conversion to hawks, the problem of 'Tonkin Gulfitis' remains serious" (p.6). The memo concluded with the note that military contingency planning with the United Kingdom would be under way by the end of the week of June 5. LBJ Library, "Memorandum for the President," secret, May 30, 1967 (partially declassified September 27, 1991).

62. Johnson, *Vantage Point*, p. 294; Bar-Zohar, *Embassies in Crisis*, pp. 159–60; and Brecher, *Decisions in Israel's Foreign Policy*, pp. 338, 413. The full text of Eshkol's message, which Walt Rostow characterized as "somber" in a covering note to Johnson, has never been published. According to one source, Eshkol did refer to "the intelligence cooperation which you have authorized." Brecher, who has seen the letter, quotes the following sentences from it: "One of the difficulties that I face is that I must call on my people to meet sacrifices and dangers without being able fully to reveal certain compensatory factors such as the United States commitment and the full scope of your determination on the matter of the Straits of Tiran" (p. 338). Eshkol also referred to the need to stand up to Nasser soon,

noting the effect he was having on Jordan. "President Nasser's rising prestige has already had serious effects in Jordan. . . . The time is ripe for confronting Nasser with a more intense and effective policy of resistance" (p. 413). This latter point impressed Rostow, and probably the president as well. Reacting to this same Eshkol message, Harold Saunders wrote to Walt Rostow on May 31 and urged him to consider a "quite different alternative," presumably to that of the multilateral fleet. In a recently declassified portion of the message, Saunders notes that the British and Canadians "are wobbling" and the "Eshkol's message suggests that we may be up against this choice sooner rather than later." "Memorandum for WWR," secret (declassified, October 14, 1992).

63. Brecher, *Decisions in Israel's Foreign Policy*, p. 414; Gilboa, *Six Years, Six Days*, p. 197; and Bar-Zohar, *Embassies in Crisis*, p. 160. According to Rabin, *Rabin Memoirs*, p. 95, the report of this conversation between Rostow and Evron had a significant effect on Eshkol, who interpreted it as meaning that he could not count on Johnson to take firm action.

64. Transmittal of "Yost's first Report" from Walt Rostow to the president, received LBJ Communications Center in Texas, May 30, 1967, at 2:17 p.m., secret (declassified June 27, 1983).

65. Heikal, *Cairo Documents*, p. 245; Brecher, *Decisions in Israel's Foreign Policy*, p. 420; and Bar-Zohar, *Embassies in Crisis*, p. 168. Anderson's report of his talk with Nasser reached Washington on June 2. See Department of State telegram, Lisbon 1517, June 2, 1967, top secret (declassified September 3, 1982). Nasser told Anderson that Egypt would not attack, but expected the Israelis to strike. Nasser said that "he was confident of the outcome of a conflict between Arabs and Israelis."

66. Bar-Zohar, *Embassies in Crisis*, pp. 160–61.

67. Interview with Evron, November 5, 1991.

68. Bar-Zohar, *Embassies in Crisis*, p. 157, states that on May 30, after Jordan threw in its lot with Egypt, Walt Rostow expressed the opinion that he no longer saw a political solution.

69. Brecher, *Decisions in Israel's Foreign Policy*, p. 417. See also Ian Black and Benny Morris, *Israel's Secret Wars: A History of Israel's Intelligence Services* (Grove Weidenfeld, 1991), p. 537, referring to an interview with Amit, who claims he went to Washington "to tell [the Americans] that we were going to war, and to hear their reaction."

70. Letter to William B. Quandt from Abba Eban, July 26, 1990. Eban, *Autobiography*, pp. 384–85, gives a more extensive account of this message but without any mention of Evron or Fortas by name. According to Eban, an American close to Johnson (Fortas) reportedly said, "If Israel had acted alone without exhausting political efforts it would have made a catastrophic error. It would then have been almost impossible for the United States to help Israel and the ensuing relationship would have been tense. The war might be long and costly for Israel if it broke out. If Israel had fired the first shot before the United Nations discussion she would have negated any possibility of the United States helping her. Israelis should not criticize Eshkol and Eban; they should realize that their restraint and well-considered procedures would have a decisive influence

when the United States came to consider the measure of its involvement." Fortas reportedly understood that "time was running out and that it was a matter of days or even hours." But Fortas believed that "if the measures being taken by the United States prove ineffective, the United States would now back Israel." Abba Eban, *Personal Witness: Israel through My Eyes* (Putnam's, 1993), p. 405, repeats this account, this time naming Fortas.

Johnson and Fortas spoke at 8:43 p.m. on May 28, according to the president's daily calendar. Johnson tried again to call Fortas on May 31, but Fortas was in Puerto Rico. See also Shimon Peres, *David's Sling* (Random House, 1970), p. 236, where he writes: "As the month of May approached its end, it became clear that there was no longer any prospect of a maritime operation through the Straits. Even in certain circles in Washington the view was heard that the only one able to find a way out of the impasse was Israel herself. This view reached the ears of Jerusalem."

71. Brecher, *Decisions in Israel's Foreign Policy*, p. 417, indicates that Eban had also seen Amit's report, with its judgment that "there is a growing chance for American political backing if we act on our own." Eitan Haber, *Today War Will Break Out: The Reminiscences of Brigadier General Israel Lior* (Jerusalem: Edanim/ Yediot Aharonot, 1987) (in Hebrew), p. 213, notes that on June 1 Eban concluded that there was no longer any need to wait for U.S. action. His change of mind was seen by some as providing a green light for military action. According to Haber, Yariv had already reached the conclusion that the United States was not serious about the maritime fleet and that therefore Israel was free to act on its own (pp. 205–06).

72. Johnson, *Vantage Point*, p. 294, without naming Evron, reveals part of this incident. The rest is based on interviews with participants.

73. By contrast, the American embassy in Cairo strongly felt that the Egyptians would react militarily to any attempt to reopen the strait. See cable on May 26, 1967 (Cairo 8007, secret), May 28, 1967 (Cairo 8093, secret), and June 3, 1967 (Cairo 8432, secret), all declassified on January 4, 1990.

74. Interview with Evron, December 30, 1974. Notes of this meeting were made by Harold Saunders, who was present, and have been consulted as well.

75. Evron was busy on June 3. Early in the morning, he presented a long list of Israel's military needs to McNamara, who implied that the arms could never get to Israel in time, since the war would be quickly over. Evron read this as a hint that the United States was confident that Israel would win and that there was no need to wait for American action. Later in the day Evron saw Rusk, who, during a very cordial meeting, gave him Johnson's letter to Eshkol. That same evening he dined with Walt Rostow, who talked at some length about what should be done in the region after the war was over. In his view, these three senior American officials, all aware of his and Amit's messages, had several chances that day to warn Israel not to take military action, but instead they talked as if war was a foregone conclusion. Interview with Evron, November 5, 1991.

76. According to Evron, this was the closest Johnson came to responding to the messages from him and Amit that time was running out and Israel might have to act soon. By acknowledging these signals, he thought Johnson was saying

to Israel that "the red light has turned to amber." Interview with Evron, October 22, 1991.

77. Interview with Richard Helms, June 8, 1992. Amit told Helms that Israel needed nothing from the United States except the supply of arms already agreed upon, diplomatic support, and holding the Soviets at bay if necessary. Amit interpreted his and Ambassador Harman's recall to Jerusalem on June 1 as an indication that the decision for war was imminent. In Amit's view, Nasser was not planning a ground attack, but Israel could not afford to wait for his next move. The economic costs were too great, and the political pressures on Eshkol were intense. In addition, there was the possibility of an Egyptian air strike, perhaps at the Dimona nuclear reactor. According to Shlomo Aronson, *The Politics and Strategy of Nuclear Weapons in the Middle East: Opacity, Theory, and Reality, 1960–1991. An Israeli Perspective* (State University of New York Press, 1992), p. 109, an Egyptian aircraft had overflown Dimona on May 17, 1967, on a reconnaissance flight. Aronson makes an elaborate argument that Nasser's primary objective in the crisis that led to the June 1967 war was to put Egypt in a position to strike at Dimona before Israel acquired nuclear-tipped surface-to-surface missiles. Eshkol was reportedly preoccupied with the possible threat to Dimona. See Haber, *Today War Will Break Out*, p. 161.

78. Letter from President Johnson to Prime Minister Eshkol. Available with cover memorandum, June 3, 1967, from the Johnson Library, secret (declassified April 5, 1982), with the intriguing note from Walt Rostow that "It may be urgent that we put this letter on record soon." See also Brecher, *Decisions in Israel's Foreign Policy*, p. 420. Bar-Zohar, *Embassies in Crisis*, p. 175, also printed part of this text. Dayan, *Moshe Dayan*, pp. 345–46, states that a letter from Johnson was read to the ministerial defense committee meeting on June 4 at which the decision for war was made.

79. Department of State telegram 297977, June 3, 1967, p. 3, secret (declassified January 9, 1990).

80. Levitt to Quandt, August 8, 1991; and Kalman, *Abe Fortas*, p. 301.

81. Nasser had sent Johnson a letter on June 2, which reached the president the following day, that agreed to the visit of Muhieddin, but was, in the words of Walt Rostow, otherwise "quite uncompromising." See Rostow memo to Johnson, June 3, 1967, with text of Nasser letter, secret (declassified August 27, 1982), Johnson Library. Anderson's discouraging report of his talk with Nasser also reached the president at about this time.

82. Gilboa, *Six Years, Six Days*, p. 199. A participant in the meeting noted that Amit reported that the United States would bless whatever Israel did if it succeeded in getting rid of Nasser. See also Andrew Cockburn and Leslie Cockburn, *Dangerous Liaison: The Inside Story of the U.S.-Israeli Covert Relationship* (HarperCollins Publishers, 1991), pp. 145–46, quoting from Eshkol's cabinet secretary. For the original source, see Haber, *Today War Will Break Out*, pp. 216–18. Amit's own version is that he said something to the effect that the United States would not mourn if Israel struck at Egypt (interview, June 4, 1992). Amit also told the cabinet members that the "Red Sea Regatta" should not be taken seriously. During the subsequent June 4 cabinet meeting, when the

decision to go to war was officially taken, Eshkol said that Johnson had now softened his stand and would give Israel political support. See Brecher, *Decisions in Crisis*, p. 167.

83. Outgoing telegram, Department of State, Circular to Arab Capitals, Eyes Only for Ambassador from Secretary, June 3, 1967, 7:17 p.m., secret (declassified January 4, 1990). "You should not assume that the United States can order Israel not to fight for what it considers to be its most vital interests. We have used the utmost restraint and, thus far, have been able to hold Israel back. But the 'Holy War' psychology of the Arab world is matched by an apocalyptic psychology within Israel. Israel may make a decision that it must resort to force to protect its vital interests. In dealing with the issues involved, therefore, we must keep in mind the necessity for finding a solution with which Israel can be restrained. . . . It will do no good to ask Israel to accept the present status quo in the Strait because Israel will fight and we could not restrain her. We cannot throw up our hands and say that, in that event, let them fight while we try to remain neutral."

84. Merle Miller, *Lyndon: An Oral Biography* (Putnam's, 1980), p. 480. The formal Israeli cabinet decision to go to war was taken at the end of a seven-hour meeting on June 4, which ended about mid-afternoon Israeli time. If this anecdote is true, Feinberg must have based his report to Johnson on the prior decision in principle to go to war on June 5 taken by the Israeli "inner cabinet," first on June 2 and again on June 3. Evron termed the Feinberg story "bunk" in an interview on October 22, 1991. No one in the United States, he said, knew at that point when exactly the war would begin.

CHAPTER THREE

1. On the second day of the war, Arthur Goldberg forwarded to the White House a message from Israeli Prime Minister Eshkol, conveyed to him through the chief justice of Israel: "Eshkol 'hopes you understand' the action taken by Israel; that it resulted from a judgment that their security situation had so deteriorated that their national existence was imperiled. Eshkol strongly hopes that we will take no action that would limit Israeli action in achieving freedom of passage through the Gulf of Aqaba. They understand your difficulties in achieving this result; and are prepared to handle the matter themselves." See memo from Rostow to Johnson, June 6, 1967, 11:00 a.m., secret (declassified August 23, 1982).

2. Memorandum for the record, National Security Council Meeting, June 7, 1967, secret (declassified August 27, 1982). "The president said 'he was not sure we were out of our troubles.' He could not visualize the USSR saying it had miscalculated, and then walking away. Our objective should be to 'develop as few heroes and as few heels as we can.' It is important for everybody to know we are not for aggression. We are sorry this has taken place. We are in as good a position as we could be given the complexities of the situation. We thought we had a commitment from those governments, but it went up in smoke very quickly. The President said that by the time we get through with all the festering problems we are going to wish the war had not happened."

3. "Memorandum for the Record: Walt Rostow's Recollections of June 5, 1967," November 17, 1968, top secret (declassified October 23, 1984), p. 3: "I might just say parenthetically that President Johnson has never believed that this war was ever anything else than a mistake by the Israelis. A brilliant quick victory he never regarded as an occasion for elation or satisfaction. He so told the Israeli representatives on a number of occasions. However, at the time, I should say that, war having been initiated against our advice, there was a certain relief that things were going well for the Israelis. . . . It did look as though we would not be put in a position of having to make a choice of engaging ourselves or seeing Israel thrown into the sea or defeated. That would have been a most painful moment and, of course, with the Soviet presence in the Middle East, a moment of great general danger."

4. Interview with McGeorge Bundy, December 11, 1968.

5. Clark Clifford was called in to help determine how the war had begun. He quickly concluded that the Israelis had preempted. In the words of Walt Rostow: "his view was that the Israelis had jumped off on minimum provocation in a very purposeful effort to deal with air power and then go after the UAR armies which of course had assembled in the Sinai. It was his judgment at the time as I recall that it was a straight Israeli decision to deal with the crisis by initiating war, although we were all conscious of the provocations at the Straits of Tiran and mobilization in the Sinai." "Memorandum for the Record: Walt Rostow's Recollections of June 5, 1967," p. 3.

6. Jonathan Trumbull Howe, *Multicrises: Sea Power and Global Politics in the Missile Age* (MIT Press, 1971), p. 70.

7. Ibid., p. 90 (interview with Rusk).

8. Ibid., pp. 91, 93, where Rusk states that an immediate cease-fire, favored by the United States, would have left Israel only fifty miles inside Sinai.

9. Johnson was informed on June 7, 1967, of the views of a high-ranking Israeli official who had informed his American counterpart that "the Syrians will get their blow as we deal with each country in turn." The same official raised the question of what the United States had in mind for Nasser when the war was over. This was taken as more than a veiled hint that Israel would like to consider joint action to remove Nasser from power.

10. Clark Clifford, a member of the President's Foreign Intelligence Advisory Board, was asked to determine who was responsible for the *Liberty* attack. According to the notes of the NSC Special Committee meeting on June 9, 1967, Clifford reported that it was "inconceivable that it was an accident." A marginal note says that "President agreed 100%" (declassified August 12, 1985). For more on the *Liberty* affair, see James M. Ennes, Jr., *Assault on the Liberty: The True Story of the Israeli Attack on an American Intelligence Ship* (Random House, 1979); James Bamford, *The Puzzle Palace: A Report on America's Most Secret Agency* (Houghton Mifflin, 1982), pp. 217–29; Hirsch Goodman and Ze'ev Schiff, "The Attack on the *Liberty*," *Atlantic Monthly*, September 1984, pp. 78–84; and letters to the editor, *Atlantic Monthly*, December 1984, pp. 7–8. Many American officials believed at the time of the Liberty attack that Israel had acted deliberately. In later years some participants in the crisis claimed that intelligence information

showed that the Israeli pilots knew they were attacking a ship flying the American flag. Several motives have been suggested by those who believe the attack was deliberate. The one most frequently cited is that Israel was planning its assault on the Golan Heights and did not want the United States to have evidence that Israel was deliberately breaking the UN cease-fire.

11. Lyndon Baines Johnson, *The Vantage Point: Perspective of the Presidency, 1963–1969* (Holt, Rinehart and Winston, 1971), pp. 301–02.

12. See "Memorandum for the Record: Hot Line Meeting June 10, 1967," top secret, October 22, 1968 (partially declassified February 22, 1982, and February 2, 1993).

13. Dean Rusk, *As I Saw It* (Norton, 1990), pp. 386–87.

14. Mohamed Heikal, *1967: Al-Infijar* (Cairo: Markaz al-Ahram, 1990), p. 371–75, 439, 651; and Mahmoud Riad, *The Struggle for Peace in the Middle East* (Quartet Books, 1981) p. 37. Once the war was under way, some Israelis apparently reached the conclusion that the United States wanted Israel to "finish with Nasser once and for all." See Eitan Haber, *Today War Will Break Out: The Reminiscences of Brigadier General Israel Lior* (Jerusalem: Edanim/Yediot Aharonot, 1987) (in Hebrew), p. 238, quoting the views of Yosef Tekoah of the Israeli Foreign Ministry.

15. Stephen Green, *Taking Sides: America's Secret Relations with a Militant Israel* (William Morrow, 1984) pp. 204–11; and Green, *Living by the Sword: America and Israel in the Middle East, 1968–87* (Brattleboro, Vt.: Amana Books, 1988), p. 235.

16. An equally unproven account of Johnson giving the Israelis some encouragement to go to war comes from Wilbur Crane Eveland, a disgruntled former CIA agent. In *Ropes of Sand: America's Failure in the Middle East* (Norton, 1980), p. 324, he states that Johnson asked James Angleton, a mysterious figure at CIA who was in charge of both counterintelligence and Israeli affairs, to "inform Evron that the U.S. would prefer Israeli efforts to lessen the tension but would not intervene to stop an attack on Egypt. This American position stipulated that there must be no Israeli military action against Jordan, Syria, or Lebanon." Angleton was strongly pro-Israeli and may well have played some role in the crisis, especially during the visit of Meir Amit, but once again the evidence is simply not there and Evron completely denies the story.

17. The CIA received a report of undetermined reliability in June 1967 from a "medium level Soviet official" who stated that "the USSR had wanted to create another trouble spot for the United States in addition to that already existing in Vietnam. The Soviet aim was to create a situation in which the US would become seriously involved, economically, politically, and possibly even militarily and in which the US would suffer serious political reverses as a result of its siding against the Arabs. This grand design, which envisaged a long war in the Middle East, misfired because the Arabs failed completely and the Israeli blitzkrieg was so decisive." To this end, the USSR "had encouraged the Arabs in their hostile attitude toward Israel" (sanitized and declassified, February 28, 1984).

18. See Sydney D. Bailey, *Four Arab-Israeli Wars and the Peace Process* (St. Martin's, 1990), p. 211, based on letters to the author from Rusk. Rusk said: "It would be a serious distortion of anything said by President Johnson to Abba

Eban to suppose that the President gave Israel a 'blank cheque' or that Israel had a right to believe that Israel would have United States support whatever they decided to do." Also, see Rusk's highly informative and revealing "backgrounder" to the press on June 9, 1967, 5:05 p.m., available from the Johnson Library. According to the notes of an NSC Special Committee meeting on June 14, 1967 (declassified August 12, 1985), Rusk spoke about self-determination for the West Bank. "Israel's keeping territory would create a revanchisme for the rest of the 20th c." Rusk, *As I Saw It*, p. 385, did acknowledge that the Israelis were well informed about thinking in Washington: "One thing the Israelis have is good intelligence. If any other country ever penetrated the American government the way they did, we would probably break relations with them."

19. In drawing their conclusions about Johnson's views in this crucial period, the Israelis had several sources to draw on: Harman and Evron were in frequent contact with Fortas, who was a trusted intermediary with Johnson; Evron saw Walt Rostow in this crucial period to explore a scenario of Israel's striking to open the strait; Amit came to Washington to check with intelligence and defense officials; and a number of other friends of Israel, especially the Krims, were intimately familiar with the president's thinking in these crucial days from spending many hours each day with him. In addition, Arthur Goldberg was in regular telephone contact with the president and saw it as his responsibility to offset Rusk's alleged biases. In brief, the Israelis enjoyed access to Johnson and his inner circle that virtually no other government could count on. And they correctly concluded that Johnson would not blame them if they went to war. All of the Israeli accounts make it clear that this was a crucial consideration for Eshkol and Eban, if not for some of the generals. Before deciding on war, they wanted to be sure there would be no repeat of Suez.

20. As early as June 6, 1967, Walt Rostow had noted to the president that a simple cease-fire that left Israel in control of territory would mean that "we could use the *de facto* situation on the ground to try to negotiate not a return to armistice lines but a definitive peace in the Middle East" (declassified March 3, 1982). The following day, in a handwritten memo to the president, Walt Rostow wrote that "Bill Moyers reports via Fineberg [sic] from Eban: 1. When USSR asks withdrawal from cease-fire lines, Eban will say: NO DRAW-BACK WITHOUT DEFINI-TIVE PEACE. . . . 3. Fineberg says this is route for the President totally to *retrieve* position after 'neutrality' and all that." Rostow was referring to a statement made on the first day of the war by the State Department spokesman that the United States was "neutral in thought, word and deed." This had set off a fire storm in the pro-Israeli community, which read it as a statement of indifference.

21. Evron conveyed this point to Walt Rostow on June 5.

22. By chance, the Israeli cabinet decided that same day that it would be prepared to pull back to the international border with Egypt and Syria in return for peace and demilitarization. This decision was conveyed by Rabin to Rusk on June 22, 1967. See Yitzhak Rabin, *The Rabin Memoirs* (Little, Brown, 1975), p. 135. The West Bank would be subject to negotiations, but Israel would not commit itself to full withdrawal, and East Jerusalem had already been annexed within the expanded municipal borders of Greater Jerusalem.

23. For an excellent summary of the diplomacy of this period at the UN, see David A. Korn, *Stalemate: The War of Attrition and Great Power Diplomacy in the Middle East, 1967–1970* (Boulder, Colo.: Westview Press, 1992), pp. 31–45.

24. Ibid., pp. 84–86.

25. The text of the "agreed minute" was transmitted to the Department of State in telegram 1278, October 9, 1967, from USUN New York (secret/exdis). Reference can be found in Nina J. Noring and Walter B. Smith, "The Withdrawal Clause in UN Security Council Resolution 242 of 1967: Its Legislative History and the Attitudes of the United States and Israel since 1967," February 4, 1978 (secret), p. 5.

26. Rusk, *As I Saw It*, p. 389, said that "we never contemplated any significant grant of territory to Israel as a result of the June 1967 war." See also Donald Neff, "The Differing Interpretations of Resolution 242," *Middle East International*, September 13, 1991, pp. 16–17, which draws on classified documents from the time, including Ambassador Goldberg's commitment to King Hussein that was conveyed on November 3, 1967. To obtain Jordan's acceptance of the resolution, Goldberg gave assurances to the Jordanians that the United States would work for the return of the West Bank to Jordanian authority. When George Ball, who became U.S. ambassador to the UN in June 1968, visited the Middle East in mid-July, he was authorized by the Israelis to convey to King Hussein that they were prepared to return the West Bank, with minor modifications, to his authority in return for peace.

27. On October 24, 1967, the State Department announced that forty-eight A-4 Skyhawk jets, agreed on in February 1966, would be delivered to Israel. This came one day after the Egyptian sinking of the Israeli naval ship *Elath*. Eventually the Johnson administration agreed to sell one hundred A-4s to Israel.

28. Israeli Prime Minister Eshkol stated in *Davar*, January 24, 1969, that Johnson had effectively given him a veto over whether the United States should sell tanks to Jordan.

29. Johnson reportedly delayed announcing his tentative decision on the F-4s in the hope of interesting the Soviets in an arms-limitation agreement for the Middle East. The Soviet position was consistent and negative: before a political settlement, there could be no agreement to limit arms to the area. Just before leaving office in January 1969, Johnson finally authorized the sale of the F-4s. See Korn, *Stalemate*, p. 66, for the differing American and Israeli versions of what Johnson promised.

30. The announcement came after unsuccessful talks earlier in October between Rusk and Gromyko on limiting arms to the Middle East. The atmosphere created by the Soviet invasion of Czechoslovakia in August had made agreement in such talks unlikely. In addition, on October 8 Israeli Foreign Minister Eban presented a nine-point "peace plan" to the UN. Eban, consistent with American preferences, subsequently downplayed the need for direct negotiations and endorsed Resolution 242 as a useful set of principles "which can help the parties and guide them in their search for a solution."

31. Riad, *Struggle for Peace*, pp. 90–92; and Rabin, *Rabin Memoirs*, p. 140.

32. For evidence of Fortas's strong pro-Israeli sentiments, see Laura Kalman, *Abe Fortas: A Biography* (Yale University Press, 1990), p. 302.

33. See Joseph A. Califano, Jr., *The Triumph and Tragedy of Lyndon Johnson: The White House Years* (Simon and Schuster, 1991), pp. 204–05. Johnson's pro-Israeli sentiment did not keep him from exploding when he thought his efforts on behalf of the Jewish state were not appreciated by Israel's friends. Many American Jews had been angry at a State Department statement on June 5 that defined the U.S. position as "neutral in thought, word and deed." Johnson came under immense pressure to distance himself from that statement, and some of his advisers urged him to address a pro-Israel mass rally in front of the White House on June 7. Unless he did, said some, it could turn anti-Johnson. Spotting one such aide in the hallway outside the Oval Office, Johnson shouted at him: "You Zionist dupe! You and [Ben] Wattenberg are Zionist dupes in the White House! Why can't you see I'm doing all I can for Israel. That's what you should be telling people when they ask for a message from the President for their rally."

34. According to a high-ranking intelligence official, Angleton and the CIA chief of station in Amman tried, on the second or third day of the war, to warn the political leaders in Washington that something should be done immediately to bring about an Israeli-Jordanian understanding on Jerusalem. Otherwise, they feared, this would become an insoluble problem. Their advice was ignored.

35. The United States was not heavily dependent in 1967 on Arab oil. Walter Levy, acting as adviser to the State Department, correctly predicted that an Arab oil embargo would not be very effective.

36. Some new faces were added to the circle of Johnson's advisers once war broke out, in particular, McGeorge Bundy, who was named chairman of the Executive Committee of the National Security Council to deal with the Middle East on June 6, 1967.

CHAPTER FOUR

1. LBJ Library, June 5, 1967 (declassified December 22, 1982).

2. Richard M. Nixon, *RN: The Memoirs of Richard Nixon* (Grosset and Dunlap, 1978), p. 435. Nixon received about 17 percent of the Jewish vote in the 1968 election, compared with about 80 percent for Hubert Humphrey.

3. See I. M. Destler, *Presidents, Bureaucrats and Foreign Policy: The Politics of Organizational Reform* (Princeton University Press, 1972), pp. 121–27, for a description of the NSC under Nixon.

4. Initially this was called the Interdepartmental Group (IG).

5. Kissinger's staff consisted of several close personal assistants as well as specialists in certain geographic and functional areas. Those who participated in Middle East policy included his deputy, Alexander Haig, two special assistants, Peter Rodman and Winston Lord, and his senior Middle East specialist, Harold H. Saunders, who had been on the NSC staff since the Kennedy administration.

6. Nixon, *RN*, p. 477. Nixon expressed concern that Kissinger would have difficulty working with Arabs because of his Jewish background. Henry Kissinger, *White House Years* (Little, Brown, 1979), p. 348, said that Nixon "suspected that my Jewish origin might cause me to lean too much toward Israel."

7. Kissinger, *White House Years*, p. 348. Nixon "calculated that almost any active policy would fail; in addition, it would almost certainly incur the wrath of Israel's supporters. So he found it useful to get the White House as much out of the direct line of fire as possible."

8. Two other office directors were influential in the shaping of Middle East policy during this period: Richard Parker, in charge of Egyptian affairs, and Talcott Seelye, office director for Arab Republic Affairs (ARA), which covered Jordan, Lebanon, Syria, and Iraq. Deputy Assistant Secretary Rodger Davies was also involved in most of the policy deliberations during this period.

9. Before being named to his White House post, Kissinger had spelled out a middle-of-the-road strategy for negotiations and the disengagement of American troops from Vietnam. In an article published in January 1969, he expressed a concern that was to haunt the Nixon administration throughout its first term: "what is involved now is confidence in American promises. However fashionable it is to ridicule the terms 'credibility' and 'prestige,' they are not empty phrases; other nations can gear their actions to ours only if they can count on our steadiness." "The Viet Nam Negotiations," *Foreign Affairs*, vol. 47 (January 1969), pp. 211–34.

10. Richard M. Nixon, "Asia after Viet Nam," *Foreign Affairs*, vol. 46 (October 1967), pp. 111–25.

11. Kissinger, *White House Years*, pp. 562–64, provides his clearest assessment of the differences between his own views on the Middle East and those of Nixon. Most significantly, Nixon believed that the Soviets were strengthening their position in the region in the aftermath of the June 1967 war; Kissinger felt that their position would be undermined as long as Israel was kept strong and the Soviets' inability to satisfy Arab demands was repeatedly demonstrated.

12. Kissinger, *White House Years*, p. 347.

13. The "Nixon Doctrine" was outlined by the president on July 25, 1969, during a news conference on Guam. The first practical manifestation of the policy, "Vietnamization," was announced by Nixon in a speech delivered November 3, 1969.

14. See Nixon, *RN*, p. 343, for the "powder keg" analogy.

15. Middle East oil was, of course, an important concern, but U.S. dependence on Arab oil was still virtually nil in 1969–70; prices were comparatively low, and alternative sources seemed available. The main worry was continued supply of oil to Europe and Japan and, to a lesser degree, the repatriation of profits of American oil companies and their favorable contribution to the U.S. balance of payments.

16. It was feared that excessive pressure on Israel, such as withholding conventional arms, might accelerate Israel's search for a nuclear option. Indifference, on the other hand, might also encourage the Israelis to go ahead with their program.

17. The administration's opposition to an imposed settlement was twofold: it probably would not last for long, because the parties would have little sense of commitment to its terms and outside powers would tire of trying to enforce it; and it would be unfavorably received in this country.

18. Kissinger, *White House Years*, pp. 349–52. "I . . . doubted the advisability of American pressure for a general settlement until we could see more clearly what concessions the Arabs would make and until those who would benefit from it would be America's friends, not Soviet clients. . . . I thought the prerequisite of effective Middle East diplomacy was to reduce the Soviet influence so that progress could not be ascribed to its pressures and moderate governments gained some maneuvering room."

19. Nixon, news conference on January 27, 1969, *Department of State Bulletin*, vol. 60 (February 17, 1969), pp. 142–43.

20. This account was obtained in interviews with participants in the first NSC policy review of the Middle East. Kissinger's reaction to these State Department initiatives is found in *White House Years*, pp. 352–53. For background on the State Department proposals, including evidence that the Soviet position began to show signs of flexibility in mid-1969, see David A. Korn, *Stalemate: The War of Attrition and Great Power Diplomacy in the Middle East, 1967–1979* (Boulder, Colo.: Westview Press, 1992), pp. 150–56.

21. Prime Minister Eshkol died on February 26. Golda Meir was sworn in as head of government on March 17.

22. Hedrick Smith, "Big Four May Meet on Mideast Soon," *New York Times*, March 26, 1969, p. 11.

23. See Yaacov Bar-Siman-Tov, *The Israeli-Egyptian War of Attrition, 1969–1970: A Case Study of a Limited War* (Columbia University Press, 1980); and Korn, *Stalemate*, pp. 165–88.

24. See Kissinger, *White House Years*, p. 362–63. According to Kissinger, King Hussein was prepared to agree to fairly substantial rectifications in the borders of the West Bank if he could gain Gaza.

25. Ibid., pp. 360–62.

26. The American position in April on the terms of a settlement had been summarized in nine points and given to Ambassador Jarring. These were expanded upon subsequently, but in essence they covered the major issues:

—Agreement on the full package was necessary before implementation of any part.

—The parties must engage in more direct contact at later stages of the talks.

—There must be a contractually binding peace with international participation.

—Security considerations on both sides must be taken into account and final boundaries must not reflect the weight of conquest.

—Special arrangements would be required in Gaza.

—There should be a Jordanian economic, civil, and religious role in a unified city of Jerusalem.

—The refugee problem should be settled through negotiation, with controls and conditions, to take place over a long period, or through compensation and resettlement.

—There should be free navigation in the Suez Canal and the Gulf of Aqaba.

—Special security arrangements would be necessary at Sharm al-Shaykh.

Kissinger expressed strong reservations on these points, but managed to get

Nixon only to authorize some cosmetic alterations (*White House Years*, pp. 364–65). The main concession to Kissinger was that Sisco would not present all these points at one time to the Soviets, but rather in stages. It was also agreed that the American position would be that Israeli withdrawal to the 1967 Egyptian-Israeli border was "not necessarily excluded." See Korn, *Stalemate*, pp. 155–56.

27. This was revealed by Secretary Rogers in a news conference on June 5, 1969. "Excerpts from Transcript of News Conference by Secretary of State Rogers," *New York Times*, June 6, 1969, p. 8.

28. By now the U.S. position on several issues was more explicit:

—All territories evacuated by Israel should be demilitarized.

—The status of Gaza should be settled by negotiations including Israel, Egypt, and Jordan.

—The parties to a peace agreement would be responsible for preventing acts of force by military or paramilitary forces on their territory (for example, Egypt and Jordan would have to control the fedayeen).

—The state of war would end on the date the accord went into effect.

—The international frontier between Egypt and Israel would "not necessarily be excluded" as the final peace border.

See the summary of the U.S. and Soviet proposals provided in "U.S. and Soviet Plans on Mideast Show Some Accord but Many Differences," *New York Times*, October 19, 1969, p. 16.

29. Between July 31 and August 25 the Soviets commented on Sisco's July 15 proposals in talks held in Moscow with Ambassador Beam. No new Soviet position was forthcoming, however.

30. Israel made the formal request for the one hundred A-4s and twenty-five F-4s on September 15, 1969.

31. Kissinger, *White House Years*, pp. 368–69.

32. Ibid., pp. 370–71; Golda Meir, *My Life: The Autobiography of Golda Meir* (London: Futura, 1976), pp. 326–30; and Yitzhak Rabin, *The Rabin Memoirs* (Little, Brown, 1979), pp. 150–57. Meir mentions a request for eighty Skyhawks, but the number was, in fact, one hundred.

33. Rabin, *Rabin Memoirs*, pp. 156–57; Abba Eban, *An Autobiography* (Random House, 1977), pp. 464–65; and Gideon Rafael, *Destination Peace: Three Decades of Israeli Foreign Policy. A Personal Memoir* (Stein and Day, 1981), pp. 210–11.

34. Kissinger, *White House Years*, p. 372. Nixon's own account differs. "I knew that the Rogers Plan could never be implemented, but I believed that it was important to let the Arab world know that the United States did not automatically dismiss its case regarding the occupied territories or rule out a compromise settlement of the conflicting claims. With the Rogers Plan on the record, I thought it would be easier for the Arab leaders to propose reopening relations with the United States without coming under attack from the hawks and pro-Soviet elements in their own countries." Nixon, *RN*, p. 479.

35. Mahmoud Riad, *The Struggle for Peace in the Middle East* (Quartet Books, 1981), pp. 110–11.

36. The December 9, 1969, speech by Rogers contained most of the points

in the October 28 document. He described United States policy as "balanced," emphasizing friendly ties to both Arabs and Israelis. He referred to three principal elements of a prospective peace agreement:

—binding commitments by the parties to peace, including the obligation to prevent hostile acts originating from their respective territories.

—Rhodes-style negotiations to work out details of an agreement. Issues to be negotiated between Egypt and Israel would include safeguards in the area of Sharm al-Shaykh, the establishment of demilitarized zones, and final arrangements in Gaza.

—in the context of peace and agreements on security, Israeli forces would be required to withdraw to the international border between Egypt and Israel.

The full text of the speech can be found in "Text of Speech by Secretary Rogers on U.S. Policy in Middle East," *New York Times*, December 10, 1969, p. 8. See also Korn, *Stalemate*, pp. 158–61.

37. Nixon had authorized the presentation of the proposals for an Israeli-Jordanian agreement on December 17, but, according to Kissinger, *White House Years*, p. 376, at the same time he conveyed private assurance to Golda Meir via Leonard Garment "that we would go no further and that we would not press our proposal."

38. Points 1, 2, 4, 5, 7, 8, 9, and 10 of the October 28 document were essentially repeated in the December 18 proposal.

39. A summary of the text of the December 18 document appears in *Arab Report and Record*, December 16–31, 1969.

40. *Arab Report and Record*, December 16–31, 1969, p. 549.

41. The Soviet note was published in *New York Times*, January 13, 1970. According to Egypt's foreign minister, once Israel had rejected the proposals, there was little reason for Egypt to accept, "for it would mean further concessions within the framework of a settlement which we were doubtful the US could get Israel to accept." Riad, *Struggle for Peace*, p. 114. Moscow's rejection of the Rogers Plan came after extensive consultations with Egyptian officials in Moscow, including Vice President Anwar Sadat, Minister of War Fawzi, and Foreign Minister Riad. According to Riad, the Soviets were worried by the escalating fighting along the Suez Canal but saw no contradiction between providing arms to Egypt to liberate the Sinai and pursuing a political settlement. In fact, Leonid Brezhnev reportedly made far-reaching promises during these meetings, offering sixty Soviet pilots and SAM-3 missile batteries with their crews. Riad, *Struggle for Peace*, p. 113.

42. Korn, *Stalemate*, pp. 174–92.

43. Dayan was quoted in Raymond H. Anderson, "Israeli Jets Raid Suburbs of Cairo; Shoppers Watch," *New York Times*, January 29, 1970, p. 1, as saying that one of the purposes of the bombing raids against Egypt was to bring home to the Egyptian people the truth about the war. "We are saying, 'Now look here. Your leaders are not doing you any good.' " The same theme is picked up in comments by Prime Minister Meir, *Le Monde*, January 18–19, 1970.

44. A debate exists over what was actually decided during Sadat's visit to Moscow in December and what Nasser accomplished by his visit the following

month. See Mohamed Heikal, *The Road to Ramadan* (Quadrangle Books, 1975), pp. 83–90. See also Uri Ra'anan, "The USSR and the Middle East: Some Reflections on the Soviet Decision-Making Process," *ORBIS*, vol. 17 (Fall 1973), pp. 946–77, for the case in favor of the decision to send Soviet forces being made before Nasser's visit. Whatever the facts, most officials in Washington seemed to believe that Israel's deep penetration bombing was the cause of the stepped-up Soviet role in the fighting. They were, therefore, hesitant to support the Israeli request for more F-4s during the spring, despite the Soviet buildup. See Korn, *Stalemate*, pp. 189–97.

45. The full text of the Soviet note appears in "Nixon-Kosygin Letters," *Arab Report and Record*, March 1–15, 1970, p. 167.

46. Kissinger, *White House Years*, pp. 560–61.

47. "Nixon-Kosygin Letters," p. 168.

48. *U.S. Foreign Policy for the 1970s: A New Strategy for Peace*, A Report to the Congress by Richard Nixon, February 18, 1970 (Government Printing Office, 1970), pp. 80–81.

49. The chairman of the Joint Chiefs took the position that the one hundred A-4s should be sold but not the F-4s.

50. See Robert H. Trice, Jr., "Domestic Political Interests and American Policy in the Middle East: Pro-Israel, Pro-Arab and Corporate Non-governmental Actors and the Making of American Foreign Policy, 1966–1971," Ph.D. dissertation, University of Wisconsin, 1974, pp. 274 ff.

51. Tad Szulc, "Rogers and Dobrynin Confer for 70 Minutes on Mideast," *New York Times*, March 26, 1970, p. 3. In addition, there was a lull in the fighting along the canal in early March, which was interpreted in some quarters as the result of Soviet pressure on Nasser. Raymond H. Anderson, "Suez Lull Linked to Moves by the Big Four," *New York Times*, March 12, 1970, p. 5.

52. Rabin, *Rabin Memoirs*, pp. 169–72; and Kissinger, *White House Years*, pp. 568–70.

53. Also, Nasser had warned in mid-February that the United States would lose its economic interests in the Arab world within two years if it agreed to sell additional Phantom jets to Israel. James Reston, "Excerpts from Interview with President Gamal Abdel Nasser of the U.A.R.," *New York Times*, February 15, 1970, p. 18.

54. The record of Sisco's April 12, 1970, meeting with Nasser shows the Egyptian leader in a very bitter frame of mind. According to Sisco's report, Nasser said that he had "no confidence in the USG. US is strong and UAR sees its only security in Soviet Union, on whom it must depend completely. Nasser said he therefore prefers have dialogue through Soviets than directly with US." Despite the harsh words, Nasser, as usual, was cordial to Sisco and said that he wanted to keep the door open. He said that he was prepared to make peace with Israel but only if all Arab demands were met. See Sisco's cable reporting on the April 12, 1970, meeting, Department of State telegram, Cairo 803, April 13, 1970, secret/nodis (declassified April 3, 1990).

55. Nasser's "final" appeal, repeated in a letter to President Nixon the following day, stated: "The USA, in taking one more step on the path of securing military

superiority for Israel will impose on the Arab nation an irrevocable course from which we must draw the necessary conclusion. This will affect the relations of the USA and the Arab nation for decades, and, maybe, for hundreds of years. . . . We will not close the door finally on the USA, in spite of the offences against us, in spite of the bombs, the napalm and the Phantoms. . . . I say to President Nixon that there is a forthcoming decisive moment in Arab-American relations. There will be either rupture forever, or there will be another serious and defined beginning. The forthcoming developments will not only affect Arab-American relations alone, but will have wider and more far-reaching effects." Part of the text appears in "Nasser Appeals to Nixon on U.S. Arab Relations," *Arab Report and Record*, May 1–15, 1970, p. 276.

56. This point was repeated in a letter from President Nixon to Prime Minister Meir dated June 20, 1970, just after the second Rogers initiative had been launched. See Eban, *Autobiography*, p. 466.

57. Meir did not believe that Israel had ever accepted UN Resolution 242, although Israel's ambassador at the UN had publicly done so in 1968. Rafael, *Destination Peace*, p. 215.

58. During the second week of June a minicrisis erupted in Jordan as the Popular Front for the Liberation of Palestine, led by George Habash, seized hostages, including Americans, in two Amman hotels. On June 12 President Nixon ordered the 82d Airborne Division on alert.

59. See text of Rogers's letter to Egyptian Foreign Minister Riad, dated June 19, 1970, *New York Times*, July 23, 1970, p. 2; and "U.S. Initiative toward Peace in the Middle East," *Department of State Bulletin*, vol. 63 (August 10, 1970), pp. 178–79.

60. See Michael Brecher, *Decisions in Israel's Foreign Policy* (Yale University Press, 1975), chap. 8, for details of the Israeli response.

61. Marvin Kalb and Bernard Kalb, *Kissinger* (Little, Brown, 1974), p. 193.

62. "A Conversation with the President," Interview by John Chancellor and Howard K. Smith, July 1, 1970, *Department of State Bulletin*, vol. 63 (July 27, 1970), pp. 112–13.

63. This decision was made in response to a letter from Prime Minister Meir dated July 2, 1970, in which she appealed for help in dealing with the threat posed by the SAMs that were being moved closer to the canal. The ECM equipment was first used by the Israeli air force on July 18.

64. All the jets under the December 1968 contract had been delivered by the end of August 1970. According to Tad Szulc, "U.S. Mideast Plan Urges Both Sides to 'Start Talking,' " *New York Times*, June 26, 1970, p. 1, the Israelis were reassured that they would be allowed to purchase additional aircraft if the cease-fire proposal of June 19 were to fail or to break down.

65. Heikal, *Road to Ramadan*, pp. 93–95.

66. Egypt orally accepted the U.S. proposal "unconditionally." The subsequent formal written reply was somewhat more guarded.

67. Inasmuch as Jordan and Israel were formally respecting the cease-fire, one might ask why Jordan was included in the second Rogers initiative. The answer seems to be that the United States wanted to ensure that both Egypt and Jordan

would be committed to controlling the fedayeen, who were expected to oppose any political settlement based on the Rogers plan. In accepting the Rogers proposal of June 19, King Hussein clearly understood that he would be held responsible for preventing all acts of force from his territory. He informed his cabinet before his acceptance that this might mean further military clashes with the fedayeen.

68. Michael Brecher, *Decisions in Israel's Foreign Policy* (Yale University Press, 1975), pp. 493–94; and Ariyeh Tsimaqi, "The Message That Tipped the Balance," *Yedi'ot Aharonot*, July 31, 1970, p. 4. The letter reached Israel July 24.

69. Brecher, *Decisions in Israel's Foreign Policy*, p. 495. In addition, President Nixon stated at a news conference on July 30 that the United States was committed to "maintaining the balance of power in the Mideast. Seventy-one Senators have endorsed that proposition in a letter to me which I received today." Nixon further reassured Israel that it would face no risk of a military buildup during the cease-fire because there would be a military standstill during that period. Text of the interview in "President Nixon's News Conference of July 30," *Department of State Bulletin*, vol. 63 (August 17, 1970), pp. 185–87. A letter signed by seventy-three senators had been sent to Secretary Rogers on June 1, 1970, urging the sale of one hundred A-4s and F-4s. The text of that letter and the signatures appear in *Congressional Quarterly Weekly Report*, vol. 28 (June 5, 1970), p. 1475.

70. See Prime Minister Meir's speech to the Knesset, August 4, 1970, printed in *Jerusalem Post*, August 5, 1970, p. 3.

71. See the text of the cease-fire agreement in *Arab Report and Record*, August 1–15, 1970, p. 457; and the Egyptian, Jordanian, and Israeli replies to Rogers's proposal of June 19, ibid., pp. 458–60.

72. For example, in his news conference on July 20, 1970, Nixon emphasized the importance of the peace initiative then under way, stating, "That is why we have not announced any sale of planes or delivery of planes to Israel at this time because we want to give that peace initiative every chance to succeed." *New York Times*, July 21, 1970, p. 16.

73. See William Safire, *Before the Fall: An Inside View of the Pre-Watergate White House* (Doubleday, 1975), p. 394.

CHAPTER FIVE

1. Yitzhak Rabin, *The Rabin Memoirs* (Little, Brown, 1979), p. 182, states that the United States asked Israel for permission to fly U-2 flights along the canal. "But inexplicably, the IDF military attaché in Washington received an order from a senior personage in Israel's defense establishment to notify the Americans that Israel objected to aerial photographs being taken just before the cease-fire went into effect! This bizarre cable contained an even more incomprehensible hint: if American planes attempted to take photographs of the battle zone, Israel would intercept them." See also Gideon Rafael, *Destination Peace: Three Decades of Israeli Foreign Policy* (Stein and Day, 1981), p. 230, on Dayan's apparent disinterest in the verification issue and his assumption that "in any case, he expected the Egyptians to move their missiles into the prohibited zone." Also, David A. Korn,

Stalemate: The War of Attrition and Great Power Diplomacy in the Middle East, 1967–1979 (Boulder, Colo.: Westview Press, 1992), pp. 264–68.

2. On August 12, 1970, the Department of State termed Israeli evidence of Egyptian violations "inconclusive." Several days later, on August 19, Ambassador Walworth Barbour urged the Israelis to end the public discussion of cease-fire violations and to name a representative to the Jarring talks.

3. Henry Kissinger, *The White House Years* (Little, Brown, 1979), pp. 582–85, notes that Soviet Ambassador Dobrynin had informed Rogers that the Soviets agreed to a standstill cease-fire; but while the United States and Israel spelled out what was meant by "standstill," Egypt was not informed of this understanding until one day after the cease-fire, and the Soviets were never formally made a party to the agreement.

4. According to "U.S. Affirms Report of Israeli Breaches," *New York Times*, September 17 1970, p. 19, Israel had also technically violated the standstill provision of the cease-fire by reinforcing near the canal. See also Korn, *Stalemate*, p. 269.

5. In early September 1970 U.S. intelligence sources detected what appeared to be preparations for a Soviet submarine base in Cienfuegos, Cuba. Secretary Rogers tended to dismiss the report as unimportant, but Kissinger treated it very seriously, alluding to it in a briefing in Chicago on September 16, just on the eve of the acute phase of the Jordan crisis. The story became public in Robert M. Smith, "U.S. Warns Soviets Not to Build Base for Subs in Cuba," *New York Times*, September 26, 1970, p. 1. It seems clear that the Cienfuegos incident accentuated Nixon's and Kissinger's distrust of Soviet intentions during this period. See Marvin Kalb and Bernard Kalb, *Kissinger* (Little, Brown, 1974), pp. 209–12.

6. According to Kissinger, *White House Years*, pp. 589–90, his relationship with Rogers was by now very poor. Nixon, when faced with such controversy, usually procrastinated, but the pace of events was soon to make that option untenable.

7. A fourth hijack attempt, led by Leila Khaled of the PFLP, against an El Al plane in London failed.

8. See William B. Quandt and others, *The Politics of Palestinian Nationalism* (University of California Press, 1973), pp. 124–28.

9. The PLO temporarily suspended the PFLP from the Central Committee because of the unauthorized hijackings, but welcomed it back once the fighting broke out on September 16.

10. Kissinger, *White House Years*, p. 597.

11. Ibid., pp. 602–06; and Seymour M. Hersh, *The Price of Power: Kissinger in the Nixon White House* (Summit Books, 1983), p. 235.

12. Kissinger, *White House Years*, p. 606.

13. Elmo R. Zumwalt, Jr., *On Watch: A Memoir* (Quadrangle, 1976), pp. 295–96, provides a brief account of a WSAG meeting on September 10 at which David Packard, deputy secretary of defense, argued against any form of ground involvement in the crisis by American troops.

14. Kalb and Kalb, *Kissinger*, p. 197; Henry Brandon, *The Retreat of American*

Power: The Inside Story of How Nixon and Kissinger Changed American Foreign Policy for Years to Come (Doubleday, 1973), p. 133; Frank Van der Linden, *Nixon's Quest for Peace* (Robert B. Luce, 1972), p. 77; and Kissinger, *White House Years*, pp. 610–12.

15. *Chicago Sun-Times*, September 17, 1970; and Hedrick Smith, "Nixon Hints He May Act If Outsiders Join the Fight," *New York Times*, September 19, 1970, p. 1.

16. Brandon, *Retreat of American Power*, p. 134.

17. Terence Smith, "Washington Reported Weighing $500-Million in Aid for Israelis," *New York Times*, September 18, 1970, p. 1.

18. Kissinger, *White House Years*, p. 618. The Syrians went to considerable lengths to make their intervention appear to consist of units of the Palestine Liberation Army. Tanks were hastily painted with PLA symbols.

19. The most damaging evidence of Soviet complicity in the intervention came from reports that Soviet military advisers had accompanied Syrian tank units as far as the Jordanian border.

20. Kalb and Kalb, *Kissinger*, pp. 200–01; and Kissinger, *White House Years*, p. 619.

21. See Kissinger, *White House Years*, p. 619, for a partial text of the note.

22. Hedrick Smith, "Rogers Calls for End of 'Invasion'—Note Sent to Moscow," *New York Times*, September 21, 1970, p. 1; and Kalb and Kalb, *Kissinger*, p. 202. Rogers's personal views were less hawkish. He reputedly favored a joint U.S.-Soviet effort to end the fighting but was rebuffed by Nixon and Kissinger.

23. Communications in Amman between the American embassy and the royal palace were extremely difficult. Radio and walkie-talkie were used, and the fedayeen often eavesdropped on sensitive conversations.

24. Kissinger, *White House Years*, p. 620.

25. Van der Linden, *Nixon's Quest for Peace*, pp. 81–82; and Kissinger, *White House Years*, p. 621.

26. Kissinger, *White House Years*, p. 622.

27. Ibid., p. 623. Rabin, *Rabin Memoirs*, p. 187, gives a somewhat different version. Rabin claims that Kissinger conveyed the king's request for Israeli air strikes and asked for an immediate Israeli reply. Rabin then asked what the U.S. was recommending, and Kissinger said he would have to call back. An hour later, according to Rabin, Kissinger called, saying, "The request is approved and supported by the United States government." "Do *you* advise Israel to do it?" Rabin asked. "Yes, subject to your own considerations," replied Kissinger."

28. Kissinger, *White House Years*, p. 623. See also Kalb and Kalb, *Kissinger*, pp. 202–07; and Benjamin Welles, "U.S.-Israeli Military Action on Jordan Was Envisioned," *New York Times*, October 8, 1970, p. 1.

29. Kissinger, *White House Years*, p. 625.

30. The United States had no independent aerial intelligence-collection capabilities to follow the course of the battle. It had to rely on Israeli reconnaissance flights and Israeli and Jordanian accounts of what was happening on the ground.

31. Kissinger, *White House Years*, p. 626. Kissinger asserts that he was not

entirely happy with this decision, since it might have been impossible to contact King Hussein to determine his views if the situation deteriorated sharply.

32. Israel asked for clarification of the U.S. position on seven points. This was given orally. But Adam Garfinkle seems to be correct when he challenges the conventional wisdom, as in Kalb and Kalb, *Kissinger*, p. 206, who claim that an agreement was actually reached. See Adam H. Garfinkle, "U.S. Decision Making in the Jordan Crisis: Correcting the Record," *Political Science Quarterly*, vol. 100 (Spring 1985), pp. 117–38. According to Garfinkle, "Thus, while Nixon did surely endorse Israeli air strikes into Jordan, he never 'authorized' an Israeli ground attack of any kind—even though he would have done so had it not been for Kissinger's intercession on the morning of the 21st. Nor did Nixon ever pledge in unequivocal terms that the United States would protect the Israeli rear flank against possible Soviet or Egyptian intervention, as is universally claimed in the scholarly literature" (p. 131). See also Alan Dowty, *Middle East Crisis: U.S. Decision-Making in 1958, 1970, and 1973* (University of California Press, 1984), p. 172. As Dowty notes, no "operationalization" of the American commitment took place beyond some routine Defense Department procedures (p. 173).

33. The Syrian air force, commanded by General Hafiz al-Asad, did not intervene, nor did the Iraqi troops in Jordan, confronted as they were by a full division of the Jordanian army.

34. Kalb and Kalb, *Kissinger*, p. 204, misinterpret the meaning of this message.

35. Alone among analysts of the Jordan crisis, Alexander Haig maintains that Israeli air strikes did, in fact, occur and were instrumental in turning the tide of battle. Haig initially states that Israel "may" have destroyed some Syrian tanks, but two paragraphs later states: "The Israeli air strikes, together with strong American diplomacy backed by credible military maneuvers suggesting that overwhelming United States air, sea, and ground power would be committed to the conflict if necessary, preserved King Hussein's regime, and, with it, the frazzled peace in the region." Alexander M. Haig, Jr., with Charles McCarry, *Inner Circles: How America Changed the World. A Memoir* (Warner Books, 1992), p. 251. Interviews with Joseph Sisco, Alfred L. Atherton, Harold H. Saunders, Richard Helms, and information from Israeli general Aharon Yariv, all confirm that no Israeli air strikes took place.

Nixon's own recollection of the Jordan crisis is reflected in the following anecdote. Talking to Kissinger by phone during the October 1973 war, Nixon said about the Jordan crisis: "We really—with no cards at all . . . played a hell of a game." Walter Isaacson, *Kissinger: A Biography* (Simon and Schuster, 1992), p. 517.

36. Elmo R. Zumwalt, Jr., *On Watch: A Memoir* (Quadrangle, 1976), p. 299, provides a copy of a memorandum that went to the president at this time detailing American military capabilities for action in the eastern Mediterranean.

37. Kissinger, *White House Years*, pp. 628–29; and Brandon, *Retreat of American Power*, p. 137. Kissinger decided to attend the Egyptian reception in part to improve his image with the Arabs.

38. According to Kissinger, *White House Years*, p. 631, on September 25 Israel was formally notified that "all aspects of the exchanges between us with regard

to this Syrian invasion of Jordan are no longer applicable. . . . If a new situation arises, there will have to be a fresh exchange."

39. Dowty, *Middle East Crisis*, pp. 138, 142–43, provides ample evidence that Laird, partly because of public reaction to the Cambodian crisis earlier in the year, was unenthusiastic about U.S. military intervention in the Jordan crisis.

40. The British had announced in 1968 that they would remove their military presence east of Suez by the end of 1971. This led to considerable planning within the bureaucracy on how to fill the ensuing vacuum.

41. Speech by President Podgorny, September 23, 1970. See Mohamed Heikal, *The Road to Ramadan* (Quadrangle Books, 1975), pp. 98–100, for evidence that the Soviets urged "utmost restraint" on Egypt during the Jordan crisis.

42. Rabin, *Rabin Memoirs*, p. 188. As Adam Garfinkle, "U.S. Decision Making," comments, the Hebrew version of Rabin's memoirs says the United States considered Israel's request for an umbrella commitment "with difficulty" (p. 131, note 37). Joseph Sisco, in an interview on October 18, 1991, recalled that there was no written commitment that he was aware of. The issue had been left hanging. There was ambiguity about the nature of any American commitment. In any event, diplomatic contacts with the Soviets seemed to be working, and the Soviets were showing considerable caution in the face of very blunt American pressures.

CHAPTER SIX

1. See Henry Kissinger, *The White House Years* (Little, Brown, 1979), p. 1285. "What finally got me involved in the execution of Middle East diplomacy was that Nixon did not believe he could risk recurrent crises in the Middle East in an election year. He therefore asked me to step in, if only to keep things quiet."

2. On October 12, 1970, Kissinger and Sisco gave a background briefing to the press on the post-Jordan-crisis situation in the Middle East. Sisco addressed the question of the Palestinians in the following terms: "more and more the Palestinians are thinking in terms of a given entity, wherever that may be. . . . So that if I were to look ahead over the next five years, assuming that we can stabilize this area, it would be on the basis of the Arabs having adopted a live and let live attitude, that is, willing to live alongside of Israel; Israel's meeting at least part of the Arab demands insofar as the occupied territories are concerned; and, lastly, giving expression to the Palestinian movement and very likely in the form of some entity."

3. The administration sought an understanding on the conditions under which Israel might use the new weapons.

4. William Beecher, "U.S. Officials Say Israelis Will Get 180 Modern Tanks," *New York Times*, October 24, 1970, p. 1. The supplemental defense appropriation, including $500 million in credits for Israel, was signed by Nixon on January 11, 1971.

5. Senator J. William Fulbright, chairman of the Senate Foreign Relations Committee, and not known as a particularly close friend of Israel, publicly endorsed the idea of a U.S.-Israeli security treaty as part of a settlement involving full Israeli withdrawal.

6. Hedrick Smith, "Mrs. Meir Sends a Note to Nixon," *New York Times*, December 2, 1970, p. 6.

7. Peter Grose, "Israel Still Asks Pledges by U.S.," *New York Times*, December 7, 1970, p. 11; and Hedrick Smith, "A Firm U.S. Stand on Mideast Likely," *New York Times*, December 8, 1970, p. 17.

8. Terence Smith, "U.S. Says It Would Join a Mideast Peace Force," *New York Times*, December 15, 1970, p. 3.

9. Meir speech to the Knesset, as cited in Lawrence L. Whetten, *The Canal War: Four-Power Conflict in the Middle East* (MIT Press, 1974), p. 142; and Tad Szulc, "U.S. Officials Say a Series of Commitments Won Israelis Return to Mideast Peace Talks at the U.N.," *New York Times*, January 1, 1971, p. 8. Shlomo Aronson, *The Politics and Strategy of Nuclear Weapons in the Middle East: Opacity, Theory, and Reality, 1960–1991. An Israeli Perspective* (State University of New York Press, 1992), p. 146, may have these understandings in mind when he refers to a 1971 agreement on "secure boundaries" that included American recognition of Israel's nuclear potential. But Aronson has only an interview with former Ambassador Simcha Dinitz to rely on, and no other account mentions anything about nuclear weapons.

10. The idea of a mutual thinning out of forces along the canal had first been officially raised in Washington on September 19, 1970, by Israeli Ambassador Rabin and General Aharon Yariv.

11. Little was known in Washington about Sadat when he became president. The biography prepared by the CIA was less than flattering. It prominently mentioned that Sadat had gone to the cinema on the night of the Egyptian revolution in 1952, implying that this was typical of his political style. Sadat openly discusses the incident in *Revolt on the Nile* (John Day, 1957).

12. *Arab Report and Record*, January 16–31, 1971, p. 75.

13. "Cairo Sees No Progress," *New York Times*, February 2, 1971, p. 2.

14. The text of Sadat's February 4, 1971, speech can be found in *New Middle East*, March 1971, pp. 32–35.

15. For Jarring's memorandum, along with the Egyptian and Israeli replies, see *Arab Report and Record*, March 1–15, 1971, pp. 158–59. The United States had strongly urged Israel not to include the sentence on refusing to withdraw to the pre-June 5, 1967, lines.

16. Meir's February 9, 1971, speech is reproduced in *New Middle East*, March 1971, pp. 35–39.

17. In an interview with *Newsweek* on February 15, Sadat spelled out in more detail his concept of an interim agreement. If Israel was prepared to withdraw to a line running from Al-Arish to Ras Muhammad, nearly two-thirds of the way across Sinai, he would reopen the canal within six months, extend the cease-fire, and allow international forces to remain at Sharm al-Shaykh to ensure freedom of navigation. Sadat's concept of a partial agreement was very far removed from Dayan's initial idea, but it could be assumed that this opening definition of the line of Israeli withdrawal might be softened with time. See Arnaud de Borchgrave, "A Talk with Sadat on Peace Terms," *Newsweek*, February 22, 1971, pp. 40–41. Sadat seemed to realize that Israel would not agree to his terms, but thought

perhaps he could enlist the United States on his side. Over the next several weeks he repeatedly queried Washington on its attitude to his February initiative and encouraged Nixon to take an active diplomatic role in the search for a settlement.

18. *U.S. Foreign Policy for the 1970's: Building for Peace*, A Report to the Congress by Richard Nixon, February 25, 1971 (Government Printing Office, 1971), pp. 129–30.

19. *Al-Ahram* editor Mohamed Heikal soon began a series of articles on the need to "neutralize" the United States.

20. Hedrick Smith, "Israel Denounces Plans of Jarring and U.S. on Sinai," *New York Times*, March 11, 1971, p. 1.

21. Meir interview in *The Times* (London), March 13, 1971, p. 1. Meir's comments set off a lively debate within Israel. The right-wing Gahal party accused her of being too conciliatory.

22. Raymond H. Anderson, "Egypt Proposes Truce If Israelis Pledge Pull-back," *New York Times*, April 2, 1971, p. 1.

23. William Beecher, "U.S. Selling Israel 12 More F-14 Jets; Weighs New Bid," *New York Times*, April 20, 1971, p. 1.

24. Arnaud de Borchgrave, "Sadat: 'We Are Now Back to Square One,' " *Newsweek*, December 13, 1971, pp. 43–47.

25. Whetten, *Canal War*, pp. 182–83; Peter Grose, "Israeli Cabinet Briefed on Rogers Talks," *New York Times*, May 10, 1971, p. 3; and Meir speech of June 9, 1971, reported in "Israel Asks U.S. for New Arms Deal," *New York Times*, June 10, 1971, p. 9.

26. Sadat claimed subsequently in his interview in de Borchgrave's, "Sadat: 'We Are Now Back to Square One,' " that Sisco had illustratively sketched lines on a map of Sinai indicating the depth of Israeli withdrawal. Sadat suggested that UN peacekeeping forces should be stationed between the Egyptian and Israeli line.

27. These ministers included Sami Sharaf, in charge of presidential security; Sharawi Guma, minister of interior; and General Mohammed Fawzi, minister of defense.

28. For Kissinger's critique of the effort to revive the Jarring talks, see Kissinger, *White House Years*, pp. 1278–80. He termed the effort "activity for its own sake amid self-generated deadlines that could be met only by papering over irreconcilable differences that, in turn, made a blowup all the more inevitable. . . . My aim was to produce a stalemate until Moscow urged compromise or until, even better, some moderate Arab regime decided that the route to progress was through Washington."

29. See Mahmoud Riad, *The Struggle for Peace in the Middle East* (Quartet Books, 1981), pp. 203–04, for his negative view of the idea of an interim settlement and of the Bergus memorandum.

30. Kissinger, *White House Years*, pp. 1283–84, expresses his dismay at the Bergus operation. He concludes that Sadat must have thought the United States was incompetent or deceitful. Sadat later complained on many occasions that he had accepted 90 percent of the American proposal in the Bergus paper and that the United States had then ignored his reply. There seems to be little doubt that

Sadat viewed the paper as an official statement of U.S. policy. See Mohamed Heikal, *The Road to Ramadan* (Quadrangle Books, 1975), p. 146.

31. Sisco tried to persuade the Israelis to accept a two-stage agreement, with only a token Egyptian force crossing the canal. "Sisco Is Reported to Suggest a 2-Phased Israeli Withdrawal," *New York Times*, August 9, 1971, p. 2.

32. Rogers seems to have first termed 1971 the "year of decision" in the Middle East. See "Secretary Rogers' News Conference of December 23," *Department of State Bulletin*, vol. 64 (January 11, 1971), p. 43.

33. Kissinger, *White House Years*, p. 1285, dates his operational control over Middle East policy from this point. He notes that Rabin approached him in October 1971 to urge that he get personally involved in the interim accord negotiations: "He told me confidentially that Israel might be more flexible in its terms if I were involved and it had Presidential assurances that the demands would not be open-ended" (p. 1287). Kissinger was simultaneously being asked by an Egyptian emissary to meet with Heikal.

34. Henry Tanner, "U.S. Assures Israel on Sinai Memo," *New York Times*, June 30, 1971, p. 3.

35. Kissinger, *White House Years*, pp. 1280–89.

36. See Heikal, *Road to Ramadan*, pp. 140, 152–55. Kissinger, *White House Years*, p. 1276, dates the beginning of the back-channel contacts with Sadat to the spring of 1972.

37. De Borchgrave, "Sadat: 'We Are Now Back to Square One.'"

38. William Beecher, "U.S. Said to Plan to Help Israelis Make Own Arms," *New York Times*, January 14, 1972, p. 1.

39. Paul Erdman, "The True Story of a Spy Coup: How Israel Got Blueprints for France's Hottest Fighter Plane," *New York*, August 30, 1976, pp. 35–45.

40. Yitzhak Rabin, *The Rabin Memoirs* (Little, Brown, 1979), p. 209, gives an account of Meir's positions, which, he states, were confirmed a few days later by the president. But on p. 211, Rabin maintains that he never heard the president express agreement to shelving the Rogers Plan or to Israeli demands for border changes in Sinai.

41. Kissinger, *White House Years*, p. 1289. See also Rabin, *Rabin Memoirs*, pp. 206–09. The Israelis apparently understood from these exchanges that the Rogers Plan was a dead letter.

42. Peter Grose, "Israelis Approve Talks with Egypt on Opening Canal," *New York Times*, February 3, 1972, p. 1. According to Ambassador Rabin, in *Maariv*, December 1, 1972, the memorandum of understanding also acknowledged that Israel would not be expected to make a commitment on full withdrawal as part of an interim agreement.

43. *U.S. Foreign Policy for the 1970's: The Emerging Structure of Peace*, A Report to the Congress by Richard Nixon on February 9, 1972 (GPO, 1972), p. 133, which quotes Nixon's media briefing of June 18, 1971.

44. Ibid.

45. Tad Szulc, "Behind the Vietnam Cease-Fire Agreement," *Foreign Policy*, no. 15 (Summer 1974), pp. 34–41.

46. See Kissinger, *White House Years*, p. 1494, for the text of the agreement. Elsewhere Kissinger minimizes the importance of these principles, saying that he conducted a "delaying tactic" in his talks with Gromyko (pp. 1247–48). My impression is that Kissinger took the exercise somewhat more seriously, and almost certainly Nixon did. And though written in general terms, the principles did not simply parrot UN resolutions, as Kissinger implies.

47. "Basic Principles of Relations between the United States of America and the Union of Soviet Socialist Republics," May 29, 1972.

48. The texts of both the basic principles and the joint communiqué are found in *United States Foreign Policy, 1972: A Report of the Secretary of State* (April 1973), pp. 598–603.

49. Heikal, *Road to Ramadan*, pp. 183–84; and "Arab Aide's Talk with Nixon Called Factor in Sadat's Decision," *New York Times*, July 24, 1972, p. 2.

50. Uri Ra'anan, "The USSR and the Middle East: Some Reflections on the Soviet Decision-Making Process," *ORBIS*, vol. 17 (Fall 1973), pp. 946–77, has called into question whether Sadat took the initiative in asking the advisers to leave. Ra'anan raises some intriguing points but seems to underestimate Sadat's anger at the Soviets. See also David Kimche, *The Last Option: After Nasser, Arafat and Saddam Hussein. The Quest for Peace in the Middle East* (Scribner's, 1991), pp. 22–24, for another argument that Sadat and the Soviets colluded on the withdrawal of Soviet advisers as a step in Egypt's plan to go to war.

51. Nixon interview with Garnett D. Horner of the *Washington Star*, November 5, 1972; and "Statements from Pre-Election Interview with Nixon Outlining 2d-Term Plans," *New York Times*, November 10, 1972, p. 20.

52. Heikal, *Road to Ramadan*, pp. 200–02; and Henry Kissinger, *Years of Upheaval* (Little, Brown, 1982), p. 213.

53. Heikal, *Road to Ramadan*, pp. 202–03. The estate belonged to the chairman of the board of Pepsi-Cola, Donald Kendall, who was an ardent Nixon supporter and a proponent of improved U.S.-Egyptian relations.

54. Kissinger, *Years of Upheaval*, pp. 214–15.

55. Ibid., p. 222; and Rabin, *Rabin Memoirs*, pp. 215–18.

56. The premature story appeared in Marilyn Berger, "Nixon Assures Mrs. Meir of Aid," *Washington Post*, March 2, 1973, p. A21. A more complete story on Nixon's decision appeared in William Beecher, "Israelis Will Buy More Jets in U.S.; Total Is Put at 48," *New York Times*, March 14, 1973, p. 1.

57. Arafat and other top Fatah officials have always denied any direct involvement in the assassinations.

58. Kissinger, *Years of Upheaval*, p. 225. On March 26, 1973, Sadat had formed a "war cabinet" with himself as prime minister. Three days later he told Arnaud de Borchgrave of *Newsweek* that war was imminent. De Borchgrave rushed the text of the interview to Kissinger before its publication on April 9, 1973.

59. *U.S. Foreign Policy for the 1970's: Shaping a Durable Peace*, A Report to the Congress by Richard Nixon, May 3, 1973 (GPO, 1973), p. 138.

60. After returning from Moscow, Kissinger consulted with Israeli officials on Israel's reaction to the May 1972 principles. He was told that Israel was

opposed to the idea altogether, but that if such principles were announced they should call for negotiations and should only speak of Israeli withdrawal to secure and recognized borders.

61. Kissinger, *Years of Upheaval*, pp. 226–27. Kissinger concludes that Sadat had already made his decision for war in the summer of 1972 and that the meetings with Hafiz Ismail were essentially a diversionary tactic. According to a well-informed Israeli source, Kissinger had reason to believe that Egypt had decided on war. According to Moshe Zak, King Hussein had told him of the Egyptian-Syrian plan for war, and Kissinger had told the Israelis. On May 21, 1973, Dayan informed the general staff: "The IDF must prepare, by the end of the summer, for Egypt and Syria launching war against Israel, without Jordan." See *Jerusalem Post*, September 22, 1991, p. 5.

62. Richard Nixon, *RN: The Memoirs of Richard Nixon* (Grosset and Dunlap, 1978), pp. 884–86.

63. "U.S.-U.S.S.R. Joint Communiqué, June 25, 1973," *Department of State Bulletin*, vol. 69 (July 23, 1973), p. 132.

64. Kissinger was concerned by signs of Faisal's growing involvement in the Arab-Israeli conflict. He feared that Saudi activism would ultimately bring down the monarchy, which might then be replaced by a Qaddafi-like regime. Each time King Faisal made some reference to the use of oil as a weapon against the West, however, one of his aides would hasten to inform U.S. officials that such remarks were meant only for domestic Arab consumption.

65. Edward R. F. Sheehan, *The Arabs, Israelis, and Kissinger* (Reader's Digest Press, 1976), pp. 27–28.

66. See Kissinger, *Years of Upheaval*, pp. 202–03, 211–12, for a comparison of Kissinger's and Nixon's views. According to Kissinger, Nixon "deep down wanted . . . to impose a comprehensive settlement sometime during his term in office" (p. 202). For a detailed account of how Nixon saw the Arab-Israeli conflict in the early 1990s, which tends to confirm the view that he favored a comprehensive settlement, see Richard M. Nixon, *Seize the Moment: America's Challenge in a One-Superpower World* (Simon and Schuster, 1992), pp. 217–30.

67. By contrast, Nixon seemed eager to press forward on Middle East peace, warning on one occasion in early 1973 that "this thing is getting ready to blow." See Kissinger, *Years of Upheaval*, p. 211.

CHAPTER SEVEN

1. Roberta Wohlstetter, *Pearl Harbor: Warning and Decision* (Stanford University Press, 1962), provides a classic study of the misinterpretation of evidence indicating an impending surprise attack. See Alan Dowty, *Middle East Crisis: U.S. Decision-Making in 1958, 1970, and 1973* (University of California Press, 1984), pp. 207–13, for the reasons behind the American intelligence failure; and Michael Brecher, *Decisions in Crisis: Israel, 1967 and 1973* (University of California Press, 1980), pp. 174–91, on the "conception" that kept the Israeli decisionmakers from correctly interpreting Arab actions. Kissinger's reasons for the surprise can be found in *Years of Upheaval* (Little, Brown, 1982), pp. 459–67, along with the intriguing

piece of information that King Hussein, in May, had warned that Syrian and Egyptian military preparations were "too realistic to be considered maneuvers" (p. 461).

2. In an interview with Arnaud de Borchgrave, "The Battle Is Now Inevitable," *Newsweek*, April 9, 1973, pp. 44–49.

3. See excerpts of the report of the House Select Committee on Intelligence, chaired by Representative Otis Pike, as reprinted in "The Mid-East War: The System Breaks Down," *Village Voice*, February 16, 1976, pp. 78–79. (Hereafter Pike Committee report.) The full report can be found in *U.S. Intelligence Agencies and Activities: The Performance of the Intelligence Community*, Hearings before the Select Committee on Intelligence, September 11, 12, 18, 25, 30, October 7, 30, 31, 1975, 94 Cong. 1 sess. (Government Printing Office, 1975). See also the account written by the director of the Intelligence and Research Bureau of the State Department, Ray S. Cline, "Policy without Intelligence," *Foreign Policy*, no. 17 (Winter 1974–75), pp. 121–35.

4. On September 10 Sadat, Asad, and Hussein met in Cairo. Syria and Jordan agreed to restore diplomatic relations. Jordan, without being told of specific war plans, committed itself to preventing Israeli troops from attacking Syria through northern Jordan in the event of future hostilities.

5. After the air battles on September 13, Arab newspapers, especially in Beirut, carried stories about Syria's dissatisfaction with Soviet military equipment and the Soviet advisers.

6. The Watch Committee, whose task it is to evaluate intelligence for signs of impending hostilities, reached the same conclusion. See Pike Committee report.

7. Conor Cruise O'Brien, *The Siege: The Saga of Israel and Zionism* (Simon and Schuster, 1986), pp. 512–17, argues at length that Kissinger, perhaps implicitly or indirectly, encouraged Sadat to go to war. His evidence is meager, but he does rely heavily on Mohamed Heikal, *Autumn of Fury: The Assassination of Sadat* (Random House, 1983), pp. 49–50. Heikal argues that information reached Egypt through Saudi intelligence channels that Kissinger favored a "heating up" of the situation before he would be prepared to tackle it. This was supposedly confirmed in the meetings between Hafiz Ismail and Kissinger. I do not believe that Kissinger wanted Egypt to go to war. He did, on occasion, talk about the circumstances that would convince him to tackle the Arab-Israeli conflict. Those circumstances included a deterioration of the situation that would threaten American interests or an opening that would make a diplomatic effort productive. And Nixon had, of course, written an entire book, *Six Crises* (Doubleday, 1962), with the subtheme that crises could provide opportunities for solving problems. Although it may be true that Sadat calculated, correctly, that a resort to war would unblock the frozen diplomatic landscape, I do not believe that either Nixon or Kissinger deliberately encouraged Sadat to go to war.

8. Some analysts at the CIA reportedly played down evidence of Egyptian and Syrian preparations for hostilities, fearing that any such conclusions might be communicated to the Israelis and serve as a reason for a preemptive attack.

9. Richard M. Nixon, *RN: The Memoirs of Richard Nixon* (Grosset and Dunlap, 1978), pp. 920–21. "I was disappointed by our own intelligence shortcomings,

and I was stunned by the failure of Israeli intelligence. They were among the best in the world, and they, too, had been caught off guard."

10. Matti Golan, *The Secret Conversations of Henry Kissinger: Step-by-Step Diplomacy in the Middle East* (Quadrangle Books, 1976), pp. 37–39, contains a detailed account of the Israeli message. Kissinger, *Years of Upheaval*, pp. 465–66, discusses this message, which Kissinger says he did not see until the following morning.

11. Interview with high-ranking Israeli intelligence official, December 1975.

12. Israel received confirmation that the Arabs planned to attack at about 4:00 a.m. Israeli time, October 6. It was expected that hostilities would begin about 6:00 p.m. See Chaim Herzog, *The War of Atonement, October 1973* (Little, Brown, 1975), pp. 52–54.

13. This meeting was chaired by Kissinger's deputy, General Brent Scowcroft, and was attended by Defense Secretary James Schlesinger, Chairman of the Joint Chiefs of Staff Admiral Thomas Moorer, Deputy Secretary of State Kenneth Rush, CIA Director William Colby, Deputy Assistant Secretary of State for the Near East Alfred Atherton, Deputy Assistant Secretary of Defense for International Security Affairs James Noyes, and several staff members. As a member of the National Security Council staff during this period, I attended most of the WSAG meetings. The accounts of these sessions included here are based on memory, interviews with participants, and brief notes on the main substantive topics discussed at each meeting. Kissinger's memoirs, *Years of Upheaval*, also discuss these meetings in some detail. The full record is, of course, still classified, and the sources I have been able to use are in no way definitive. I have tried to concentrate on recording the themes that recurred in the discussions, on the major concepts that participants relied upon in reaching judgments, and on the mood that existed on each day of the crisis. Decisions were not usually made at WSAG meetings. Their real value lay in keeping top-level decisionmakers on the same wavelength. There was very little controversy or argument during any of the meetings.

14. See the same version in the Watch Committee report, October 6, 9:00 a.m., printed in *Village Voice*, February 16, 1976, p. 78, note 305. "We can find no hard evidence of a major, coordinated Egyptian/Syrian offensive across the Canal and in the Golan Heights area. Rather, the weight of evidence indicates an action-reaction situation where a series of responses by each side to preconceived threats created an increasingly dangerous potential for confrontation."

15. Kissinger made a point of this in his discussion with Mohamed Heikal, November 7, 1973, as translated from *Al-Anwar*, November 16, 1973, in "Interviews: Kissinger Meets Haikal," *Journal of Palestine Studies*, vol. 3 (Winter 1974), p. 213.

16. The president's phone logs do not show any conversations with Kissinger on October 6, and Kissinger makes no such reference in his memoirs. But Kissinger was adept at invoking Nixon's authority in front of other members of the administration. He presumably was in touch with Haig, but Haig himself did not talk to Nixon after noon on that day. See President Richard Nixon's daily diary, October 6, 1973.

17. Granting the Soviets most-favored nation (MFN) trading status was a key issue in the fall of 1973. Senator Henry Jackson had introduced an amendment that would withhold MFN treatment for the Soviet Union unless Soviet Jews were allowed to emigrate freely. Nixon and Kissinger opposed the amendment, arguing that quiet diplomacy would be more effective and that the Soviets would not accept such interference in their internal affairs. Ultimately the Soviets refused MFN tied to free emigration.

18. Golan, *Secret Conversations of Kissinger*, p. 64; and Marvin Kalb and Bernard Kalb, *Kissinger* (Little, Brown, 1974), pp. 462–63.

19. Kissinger subsequently told Egyptian officials that he was very impressed when they began to send messages through the back channel shortly after the war began. Interview with high-level Egyptian diplomat, April 1976. Nixon and Kissinger attached considerable importance to the possibility of improving U.S.-Arab relations after the war was over. See Kissinger, *Years of Upheaval*, pp. 481–82. Until receiving this back-channel message, says Kissinger, "I had not taken Sadat seriously."

20. Golan, *Secret Conversations of Kissinger*, p. 45.

21. Membership at WSAG meetings varied, but the following members were usually present: Kissinger, Schlesinger, Moorer, Colby, Scowcroft, Rush, Sisco, Clements, and several staff assistants. When oil was discussed, Deputy Secretary William Simon, former governor John Love of Colorado, and Charles di Bona might participate.

22. Kissinger apparently was aware that the Soviets, six hours after the war had begun, had suggested to Sadat that he accept a simple cease-fire at an early date. The Soviets had repeated the request on October 7. See William B. Quandt, "Soviet Policy in the October Middle East War," *International Affairs*, vol. 53 (July 1977), pp. 377–89, and vol. 53 (Ocober 1977), pp. 587–603; and Sadat's own account in *Al-Hawadith*, March 19, 1975, and *Al-Jumhurriyah*, October 24, 1975. See also, Mohamed Heikal, *The Road to Ramadan* (Quadrangle Books, 1975), pp. 209, 212–15.

23. Libya had recently decreed that American oil-company personnel were not free to leave the country without government permission. The erratic behavior of President Muammar Qaddafi led some U.S. officials to fear that he would order attacks against American interests and citizens. Instead, Libya cooperated in allowing Americans leaving Egypt to transit Libya, for which Qaddafi received a message of thanks.

24. The U.S. position favoring a cease-fire based on the status quo ante was opposed by a number of American ambassadors in Arab countries. Kissinger replied that if the United States called for a vote on any cease-fire resolution that was not linked to a full Israeli withdrawal, the resolution would be defeated; then a vote would be called on a cease-fire tied to withdrawal, which the United States would have to veto. This, in his view, would hurt U.S.-Arab relations worse than Scali's tentative call for a cease-fire based on the post-1967 lines. Above all, Kissinger wanted to avoid a vote in the Security Council until he could be sure of its desirable outcome. This required U.S.-Soviet agreement; Soviet agreement seemed to require Arab acquiescence.

25. Kalb and Kalb, *Kissinger*, p. 466. See also Edward N. Luttwak and Walter Laqueur, "Kissinger and the Yom Kippur War," *Commentary*, vol. 58 (September 1974), p. 36. Kissinger, in *Years of Upheaval*, p. 485, writes, "When I had bad news for Dinitz, I was not above ascribing it to bureaucratic stalemates or unfortunate decisions by superiors."

26. Kissinger arrived at 5:55 p.m. and was already well briefed on the course of the day's fighting.

27. Henry A. Kissinger, "The Nature of the National Dialogue," address delivered to the Pacem in Terris III Conference, Washington, D.C., October 8, 1973, printed in *Department of State Bulletin*, vol. 69 (October 29, 1973), pp. 525–31. In the speech, Kissinger, who discussed détente at some length, said (p. 528):

> "Coexistence, to us continues to have a very precise meaning:
> —We will oppose the attempt by any country to achieve a position of predominance either globally or regionally.
> —We will react if relaxation of tensions is used as a cover to exacerbate conflicts in international trouble spots.
> The Soviet Union cannot disregard these principles in any area of the world without imperiling its entire relationship with the United States. . . . Our policy with regard to détente is clear: We shall resist aggressive foreign policies. Détente cannot survive irresponsibility in any area, including the Middle East.

28. Kissinger, *Years of Upheaval*, pp. 491–93; and Kalb and Kalb, *Kissinger*, pp. 466–67.

29. Some have concluded from Kissinger's use of the word *blackmail* that Dinitz must have raised the specter of Israel resorting to nuclear weapons if its requests were not met. See especially Seymour M. Hersh, *The Samson Option: Israel's Nuclear Arsenal and American Foreign Policy* (Random House, 1991), pp. 228–30. I doubt that any explicit threat was made, but there was an element of nuclear blackmail intrinsic in the military situation. It was widely believed that the Israelis possessed nuclear arms and the means to deliver them, including surface-to-surface missiles. If Israel was on the verge of a military defeat, one could hardly rule out the use of such weapons. In addition, at some point early in the crisis, American intelligence did pick up signals that the Jericho missiles had been place on alert. Taken together, these facts would have led any American official to conclude that there was some relationship between Israel's likely reliance on nuclear threats and American resupply decisions. For Meir's confirmation that she was thinking of flying to Washington, see Golda Meir, *My Life: The Autobiography of Golda Meir* (London: Futura, 1976), p. 362.

30. See Kissinger, *Years of Upheaval*, pp. 495–96, including the content of his message to Dinitz informing him of the president's decision on resupply. At this point there was still no talk of an American airlift, unless an emergency need for tanks arose. Kissinger told Dinitz that everything on Israel's list except laser bombs was approved and that all losses in planes and tanks would be made up. According to Dowty, *Middle East Crisis*, p. 238, Kissinger mentioned to Dinitz

that the United States intended to keep a low profile and that charters might be used by Israel to carry supplies.

31. Insight Team of the London Sunday Times, *Yom Kippur War* (Doubleday, 1974), p. 279. Kissinger, *Years of Upheaval*, p. 499, says that he spoke to Dinitz around mid-day on October 10, who conveyed Meir's thanks for Nixon's decision on resupply. Kissinger urged Israel to push back to the prewar lines "as quickly as possible, or beyond them on at least one front. We could not stall a cease-fire proposal forever."

32. Mohamed Heikal, *The Road to Ramadan* (Quadrangle Books, 1975), pp. 223–24; and Kissinger, *Years of Upheaval*, pp. 499–500.

33. Kissinger, *Years of Upheaval*, p. 498.

34. Quandt, "Soviet Policy in the October Middle East 1973 War" (both parts), summarizes available data on the Soviet delivery of military equipment by air and sea during the war.

35. Kalb and Kalb, *Kissinger*, pp. 468–70; and Golan, *Secret Converstions of Kissinger*, p. 65. Kissinger, *Years of Upheaval*, p. 501, states that Scowcroft told Dinitz of the Soviet proposal for both major powers to abstain in the UN on a cease-fire vote and urged the Israelis to speed up their military efforts over the coming forty-eight hours. Kissinger also argues strongly that the delay in arranging for charter flights was not intended to be a form of pressure on Israel to get it to accept the cease-fire. I am not entirely convinced. Whatever Kissinger's intentions, the Israelis did feel under pressure to finish military operations quickly and without benefit of an all-out American airlift.

36. Richard M. Nixon, remarks at a Medal of Science presentation ceremony, October 10, 1973, *Weekly Compilation of Presidential Documents*, vol. 9 (October 15, 1973), pp. 1236–37. Nixon's views on the cease-fire-in-place idea are not known. He did favor a stalemate on the battlefield (Nixon, *RN*, p. 927), and he spoke to Kissinger often about the need to impose a settlement in concert with the Soviets. So Nixon would not have necessarily been averse to pressuring the Israelis, but there is no specific evidence that he tried to delay the resupply effort during this period as a deliberate form of pressure.

37. Insight Team, *Yom Kippur War*, p. 279. This has been confirmed by a highly placed Israeli source.

38. Nixon, *RN*, pp. 926–27.

39. Kissinger, *Years of Upheaval*, p. 509. The Israelis were told that a vote in the United Nations would not be scheduled before late afternoon October 13.

40. Brecher, *Decisions in Crisis*, p. 214. The decision was made on October 12 in the afternoon, Israeli time. Earlier in the day, the inner cabinet had decided to postpone a decision on an attempted crossing of the canal. Ibid., p. 173.

41. "Secretary Kissinger's News Conference of October 12," *Department of State Bulletin*, vol. 69 (October 29, 1973), pp. 532–41.

42. Kissinger, *Years of Upheaval*, pp. 512–13, describes in detail his meeting with Dinitz at 11:20 p.m., October 12. Kissinger was surprised that Israel had not launched its offensive. Dinitz attributed this to a shortage of supplies. By 1:00 p.m., with no guidance from Nixon (the presidential logs show no calls from

either Kissinger or Haig in this time period), Kissinger decided on some initial steps to speed the delivery of arms. Kalb and Kalb, *Kissinger*, p. 474; Golan, *Secret Conversations of Kissinger*, pp. 53, 61, 66–67; and Insight Team, *Yom Kippur War*, pp. 279–80. According to Defense Secretary Schlesinger, "Kissinger called me Friday night. . . . He indicated Israel was running short. To say the least, he was a little bit concerned." Interview with James Schlesinger, *Jewish Telegraphic Agency Daily Bulletin*, July 1, 1974, p. 4. In his October 26, 1973, news conference, Schlesinger stated that on October 13 "there were some who believed that the existence of the state of Israel was seriously compromised." At least one author, Nadav Safran, *Israel: The Embattled Ally* (Harvard University Press, 1978), p. 483, assumes that Kissinger was motivated by a fear that Israel might resort to nuclear weapons.

43. Kissinger, *Years of Upheaval*, pp. 516–19. See also Kissinger's talk with Heikal on November 7, 1973, "Interview: Kissinger Meets Haikal," pp. 210–15. There he refers to his proposal for a cease-fire in place, conveyed to the Soviets and the Egyptians on October 10, and the subsequent Egyptian refusal, communicated through the Soviets and the British. He describes the Israelis as furious, "but eventually they yielded" to his proposal. See also Insight Team, *Yom Kippur War*, pp. 280–82, where it is reported that the British ambassador met with Sadat a second time at 4:00 p.m., October 13, at which time Sadat gave his final word refusing the U.S. proposal. *Washington Post*, October 14, 1973, p. A1, also mentions the link between the arms-supply decision and Israel's acceptance of a cease-fire. In a press conference on October 26, 1973, Schlesinger stated: "The United States delayed, deliberately delayed, the start of its resupply operation, hoping that a cease-fire would be implemented quickly." "Secretary of Defense Schlesinger's News Conference of October 26," *Department of State Bulletin*, vol. 69 (November 19, 1973), p. 624.

44. See Walter Isaacson, *Kissinger: A Biography* (Simon and Schuster, 1992), p. 521, quoting from the transcript of a Kissinger-Haig telephone conversation early on October 13. Haig said, "He's [Schlesinger] ready to move MAC [Military Assistance Command] aircraft in there immediately. I think that would be foolish." "That would be disaster, Al," Kissinger replied. "How can he fuck everything up for a week—he can't now recoup it the day the diplomacy is supposed to start." This exchange tends to confirm the view that Kissinger did see a link between the airlift and the possibility of an early cease-fire.

45. Kissinger, *Years of Upheaval*, pp. 514, 515. At 12:30 p.m. on October 13 Kissinger was able to tell Dinitz that giant C-5As would fly directly to Israel until the charter issue was sorted out. Fourteen F-4s would also soon be on their way. See also Edward N. Luttwak and Walter Laqueur, "Kissinger and the Yom Kippur War," *Commentary*, vol. 58 (September 1974), p. 37; and Isaacson, *Kissinger*, p. 522.

46. The only other SR-71 flight took place on October 25. See Pike Committee report, p. 78.

47. It is extremely difficult to ascertain the degree to which the U.S. airlift affected Israeli strategy. From interviews with top Israeli officials, I have concluded that the impact of the airlift on strategic decisions was minimal on the Syrian

front and only slightly more significant on the Egyptian front. The crossing of the canal had been seriously recommended by Bar Lev on October 12. (See Herzog, *War of Atonement*, pp. 202–07.) After the Israeli victory in Sinai on October 14, it would have been ordered even without the assurance of U.S. resupplies. However, the crossing might not have been exploited so aggressively if arms had not been on their way. Some items, such as TOW and Maverick missiles, were being used to good effect in the last few days of the fighting and may have raised the prospect of a full defeat of the Third Army Corps. Ironically, the U.S. resupply put Israel in a position to do something that Kissinger was determined to prevent.

48. Faisal and Sadat were sent messages explaining the airlift in those terms before it became publicly known. Kissinger later used the same argument with Heikal; see "Interviews: Kissinger Meets Haikal." The Soviets were also informed in advance of the airlift and were told that the United States would stop if they ended their resupply to the Arabs.

49. From October 14 until the October 25 cease-fire, the U.S. resupply effort delivered approximately 11,000 tons of equipment, forty F-4 Phantoms, thirty-six A-4 Skyhawks, and twelve C-130 transports. Included were only four tanks on the early C-5 flight, and fewer than twenty were sent during the entire airlift. From October 26 until the airlift ended on November 15 another 11,000 tons of equipment were delivered. In all, 147 sorties were flown by C-5s, with 10,800 tons aboard, and 421 sorties by C-141s with 11,500 tons. During the same period, El AL aircraft carried about 11,000 tons of military supplies to Israel in more than 200 sorties. By November 15, the first ships were beginning to reach Israel with resupplies, and the airlift became superfluous. *Aviation Week and Space Technology*, vol. 99 (December 10, 1973), pp. 16–19, contains information on the airlift.

50. Heikal, *Road to Ramadan*, p. 224.

51. Golan, *Secret Conversations of Kissinger*, p. 67.

52. Impromptu comments by Nixon on October 15 at a Medal of Honor ceremony caused some consternation in Arab diplomatic circles. U.S. policy, he stated, is "like the policy that we followed in 1958 when Lebanon was involved, it is like the policy we followed in 1970 when Jordan was involved. The policy of the United States in the Mideast, very simply stated, is this: We stand for the right of every nation in the Mideast to maintain its independence and security. We want this fighting to end. We want the fighting to end on a basis where we can build a listing peace." *Weekly Compilation of Presidential Documents*, vol. 9 (October 22, 1973), p. 1251. The president's reference to Lebanon and Jordan raised the specter of U.S. military intervention. Nixon was presumably simply mentioning the two other Middle East crises in which he had been personally involved.

53. Heikal, *Road to Ramadan*, pp. 232–34, gives a somewhat distorted version of these talks but covers most of the main points.

54. Golan, *Secret Conversations of Kissinger*, p. 70.

55. Ibid., p. 72.

56. Kosygin left Cairo at 2:55 a.m., Washington time, on October 19.

57. Kissinger, *Years of Upheaval*, p. 542.

58. Golan, *Secret Conversations of Kissinger*, p. 75.

59. Kalb and Kalb, *Kissinger*, pp. 481, 483; and Ze'ev Schiff, *October Earthquake: Yom Kippur, 1973* (Tel Aviv: University Publishing Projects, 1974), p. 264.

60. He was accompanied by Joseph Sisco, Alfred Atherton, William Hyland, Winston Lord, and Peter Rodman. Helmut Sonnenfeldt joined the party during a refueling stop in Copenhagen. Ambassador Dobrynin also flew to Moscow aboard the secretary's aircraft.

61. Kissinger, *Years of Upheaval*, pp. 546–48.

62. See Theodore White, *Breach of Faith: The Fall of Richard Nixon* (Atheneum, 1975), pp. 328–42.

63. Nixon did send Kissinger additional instructions to seek agreement with the Soviet Union on a strategy to impose a comprehensive peace in the Middle East. Kissinger ignored the instructions. See Kissinger, *Years of Upheaval*, pp. 550–52.

64. In a side agreement both parties agreed that "appropriate auspices" meant that "the negotiations between the parties concerned will take place with the active participation of the United States and the Soviet Union at the beginning and thereafter in the course of negotiations when key issues of a settlement are dealt with." Ibid., p. 559.

65. Insight Team, *Yom Kippur War*, p. 380. At no time during the crisis did Nixon speak on the phone with any of the leaders in the Middle East.

66. Upon learning that Kissinger was stopping in Israel, Sadat invited him to come to Egypt as well. Kissinger declined, but expressed hope that he would be able to visit Cairo soon. Heikal, *Road to Ramadan*, pp. 248–49.

67. Golan, *Secret Conversations of Kissinger*, pp. 84–87, states that Kissinger hinted that Israel would not be held to strict observance of the cease-fire. Kissinger, *Years of Upheaval*, p. 569, says that he told the Israelis that a few hours' "slippage" in the cease-fire deadline while he was flying home would not be a problem. Joseph Sisco, testifying before the Committee on Foreign Affairs of the House of Representatives, December 3, 1973, stated, "The Israelis were anxious for a ceasefire at the time [October 22] the ceasefire was concluded as were the Egyptians." *Emergency Security Assistance Act of 1973*, Hearings before the Committee of Foreign Affairs of the House of Representatives, 93 Cong. 1 sess. (GPO, 1973), p. 56. See also Walter Laqueur, *Confrontation* (Quadrangle, 1974), p. 194; and *Maariv*, October 26, 1973.

68. During a stopover in London Kissinger called the Soviets, urging them to press the Syrians to call off an offensive planned for the following day.

69. Kalb and Kalb, *Kissinger*, p. 486.

70. Heikal, *Road to Ramadan*, pp. 251–52, prints the text of two of Nixon's letters to Sadat on October 24. In addition, Nixon wrote Sadat on October 23 to make it clear that the United States had only committed itself to engage in a process designed to make possible a political settlement but had not guaranteed any specific outcome of that process.

71. Kalb and Kalb, *Kissinger*, p. 488.

72. Ibid., p. 489.

73. See Kissinger, *Years of Upheaval*, pp. 575–83.

74. Nixon, *RN*, p. 938.

75. An enhanced alert status of seven Soviet airborne divisions was first noted on October 11; the alert status was altered on October 23. See "Secretary of Defense Schlesinger's News Conference of October 26," pp. 617–26.

76. One other consideration that may have contributed to the decision to call a global alert was the arrival during the evening of October 24 of an intelligence report that a suspicious Soviet ship had given off neutron emissions as it transitted the Bosphorous on October 22 on its way to Alexandria. Some thought this might indicate that the Soviets were introducing nuclear warheads into Egypt. Kissinger, *Years of Upheaval*, p. 584, mentions some "ominous signs," probably referring to this report. See also "Secretary Schlesinger's News Conference of October 26"; Raymond L. Garthoff, *Détente and Confrontation: American-Soviet Relations from Nixon to Reagan* (Brookings, 1985), p. 378; and Dowty, *Middle East Crisis*, p. 275.

77. Dayan was subsequently quoted as saying that Kissinger threatened to send U.S. forces to resupply the Third Army Corps. Other Israelis, including Eban, have contended that Kissinger stated that the Soviets might try to resupply the Egyptian forces. The latter seems more plausible, perhaps with the addition of an implied threat not to help the Israelis if they found themselves in confrontation with the Soviets over the fate of the Third Army Corps. This issue is discussed by Theodore Draper, "The United States and Israel: Tilt in the Middle East," *Commentary*, vol. 59 (April 1975), pp. 29–45, and the exchange of letters in *Commentary*, vol. 60 (September 1975), pp. 18–24. Moshe Dayan, *Moshe Dayan: Story of My Life* (William Morrow, 1976), p. 544, says the Americans "more or less" gave Israel an ultimatum to allow supplies through to the Third Army Corps but does not go into details.

78. See Richard Ned Lebow and Janice Gross Stein, "We All Lost the Cold War," draft, April 1992, chap. 12, p. 21. (To be published by Princeton University Press in 1994.)

79. According to ibid., chap. 12, Kissinger refused to comment when asked in an interview if, as was commonly believed, Nixon was unable to participate in the meeting because he had drunk too much that evening.

80. Kissinger, *Years of Upheaval*, p. 593. This meeting was the first that Nixon learned of the measures taken overnight.

81. See "Secretary Kissinger's News Conference of October 25," *Department of State Bulletin*, vol. 69 (November 12, 1973), pp. 585–94, for the complete text. The following day, October 26, Nixon held a press conference in which he discussed the alert: "We obtained information which led us to believe that the Soviet Union was planning to send a very substantial force into the Mideast, a military force. . . . When I received that information, I ordered, shortly after midnight on Thursday morning, an alert for all American forces around the world. This was a precautionary alert. The purpose of that was to indicate to the Soviet Union that we could not accept any unilateral move on their part to move military forces into the Mideast. . . . The outlook for a permanent peace is the best that it has been in twenty years. . . . Without détente, we might have

had a major conflict in the Middle East. With détente, we avoided it." "The President's News Conference of October 26, 1973," *Weekly Compilation of Presidential Documents*, vol. 9 (October 29, 1973), pp. 1287–94.

82. The debate over Kissinger's role in the October war has spawned a remarkably partisan body of writing. Kalb and Kalb, *Kissinger*, are favorable to Kissinger and erroneously portray Schlesinger as the obstacle to the airlift to Israel. Tad Szulc, "Is He Indispensable? Answers to the Kissinger Riddle" *New York*, July 1, 1974, pp. 33–39, points the finger at Kissinger instead. Luttwak and Laqueur, "Kissinger and the Yom Kippur War," try to set the record straight, but overlook the importance of the cease-fire effort of October 10–13. Gil Carl AlRoy, *The Kissinger Experience: American Policy in the Middle East* (Horizon Press, 1975), is a bitterly anti-Kissinger polemic. Golan, *Secret Conversations of Kissinger*, is better informed, but equally hostile to Kissinger. Edward R. F. Sheehan, *The Arabs, Israelis, and Kissinger: A Secret History of American Diplomacy in the Middle East* (Reader's Digest Press, 1976), is sympathetic to him. Very few writers have been able to discern Nixon's role in the formulation of U.S. policy during the war or to distinguish between those aspects of policy designed to preserve détente and those aimed at promoting a new relationship with Egypt.

83. The president's daily diary provides a detailed log of all meetings and telephone calls. For the seventeen days of the crisis that Kissinger was in Washington, he spent on average thirty-four minutes each day in private or very restricted meetings with Nixon. (This excludes cabinet meetings and briefings of congressional leaders where Kissinger was present.) In addition, they spoke by telephone about two times each day, each call averaging some six minutes. Altogether, Kissinger was in direct touch with the president for about three-quarters of an hour a day, or nearly an hour each day if the larger meetings are also counted. As chief of staff, Haig probably spent more time with Nixon, but much of that must have involved the Watergate mess.

CHAPTER EIGHT

1. Nixon was more inclined than Kissinger to consider a forceful American role in imposing a settlement in the region and was not reluctant to talk of pressuring Israel. But he was neither able nor determined to follow through on these sentiments.

2. He expressed this concern to Mohamed Heikal in Cairo on November 7, as reported by Heikal in a lengthy account of his talk with Kissinger in *Al-Anwar*, November 16, 1973, translated in "Interviews: Kissinger Meets Haikal," *Journal of Palestine Studies*, vol. 3 (Winter 1974), pp. 210–15.

3. See "Interviews: Kissinger Meets Haikal," pp. 211–12. Kissinger reportedly told Heikal that he had not dealt with the Middle East crisis before October 1973 because of his fear of failure. Not enough elements of the situation were under his control to ensure success.

4. Ibid., p. 214. "The USSR can give you arms, but the United States can give you a just solution which will give you back your territories, especially as

you [the Arabs] have been able to really change the situation in the Middle East. . . . Politics in our age is not a question of emotions; it is the facts of power."

5. Edward R. F. Sheehan, *The Arabs, Israelis, and Kissinger: A Secret History of American Diplomacy in the Middle East* (Reader's Digest Press, 1976), p. 51, refers to a coherent Arab policy based on a "quasi-alliance" between Washington and Cairo and on the promotion of American technology as a means of increasing American influence in the Arab world.

6. See William B. Quandt, "Soviet Policy in the October Middle East War," *International Affairs*, vol. 53 (July 1977), pp. 377–89, and vol. 53 (October 1977), pp. 587–603.

7. Nixon and Kissinger may also have been irritated by Moscow's unwillingness to live up to the commitment it undertook on October 20–21 to work for the immediate release of Israeli prisoners held in Egypt and Syria.

8. William B. Quandt, "Domestic Influences on U.S. Foreign Policy in the Middle East: The View from Washington," in Willard A. Beling, ed., *The Middle East: Quest for an American Policy* (State University of New York Press, 1973), pp. 263–85.

9. See Kissinger, *Years of Upheaval*, pp. 615–16.

10. William B. Quandt, "Kissinger and the Arab-Israeli Disengagement Negotiations," *Journal of International Affairs*, vol. 29 (Spring 1975), pp. 33–48.

11. In his first meeting with Kissinger, Fahmy agreed that the Third Army Corps would be resupplied only with nonmilitary items if Israel agreed to pull back to the October 22 lines. Fahmy at the time was acting foreign minister. He was named foreign minister on October 31.

12. Kissinger, *Years of Upheaval*, pp. 616–17. Kissinger did promise that Israel would not launch a military offensive from its position on the west bank of the Suez Canal. He also agreed to send a high-level representative to Cairo at an early date.

13. Ibid., pp. 619–24.

14. Kissinger met again with Prime Minister Meir on November 3. The following day the prime minister was reportedly called by Nixon's chief of staff, Alexander Haig, and by Nelson Rockefeller, who both conveyed Nixon's displeasure at her attitude. Matti Golan, *The Secret Conversations of Henry Kissinger: Step-by-Step Diplomacy in the Middle East* (Quadrangle Books, 1976), p. 111.

15. Kissinger had seen the Syrian representative to the United Nations on November 2, but there was still no channel for continuing contacts between Washington and Damascus.

16. Kissinger, *Years of Upheaval*, pp. 636–41. See also Sheehan, *Arabs, Israelis*, pp. 48–51.

17. An experienced career diplomat, Hermann Eilts, was named as American ambassador to Egypt, and American-educated Ashraf Ghorbal became Egypt's ambassador to the United States.

18. The text of the agreement can be found in Kissinger, *Years of Upheaval*, p. 641.

19. Ibid., p. 664, states, "Had I understood the mechanism of oil pricing

better, I would have realized that Saudi production cutbacks were more dangerous than the embargo since they critically affected world supply and therefore provided the precondition for the impoverishing price rise."

20. Sheehan, *Arabs, Israelis*, pp. 70–73, contains a partial transcript of the Kissinger-Faisal meeting. See also Kissinger, *Years of Upheaval*, pp. 659–66.

21. Several days later, in Peking, Kissinger spoke of Israeli "withdrawals" as part of a settlement, in a deliberate effort to signal his good intentions to the Saudis. The Israelis were not particularly pleased; they worried about Kissinger's mention of U.S. guarantees, fearing that external guarantees would become a substitute for Arab concessions. See "Secretary Kissinger's News Conference of November 12, 1973," *Department of State Bulletin*, vol. 69 (December 10, 1973), p. 713.

22. Moshe Dayan, *Moshe Dayan: Story of My Life* (William Morrow, 1976), p. 556, refers to Yariv's November 22 proposals.

23. Golan, *Secret Conversations of Kissinger*, pp. 120–21. He states that Kissinger did not use direct pressure but made his preferences known to the Israelis. See also Kissinger, *Years of Upheaval*, p. 752.

24. Kissinger, *Years of Upheaval*, p. 634, quotes Nixon as saying to the cabinet that "it might be necessary to apply pressure on Israel to avert a serious oil shortage."

25. Dayan, *Moshe Dayan*, p. 548, states that he opposed the kilometer 101 talks because he felt the United States should be involved in the negotiation.

26. Nixon wrote to Sadat on December 1, proposing that Egypt attend a conference in Geneva on December 18.

27. Sadat's reply to Nixon's invitation, dated December 8, confirmed Egypt's willingness to go to Geneva but did not mention Syria.

28. Kissinger's speech before the Pilgrims of Great Britain on December 12 discussed the October war and the energy crisis. It contained the revealing admission that "it is fair to state . . . that the United States did not do all that it might have done before the war to promote a permanent settlement in the Middle East." *Department of State Bulletin*, vol. 69 (December 31, 1973), p. 780.

29. Kissinger spent four hours with Sadat on December 13 and five hours on December 14. They discussed what they might do if Israel refused to attend the Geneva conference. Sadat also promised to work for the lifting of the oil embargo in early January.

30. Kissinger, *Years of Upheaval*, p. 759, quotes from the letter.

31. Nixon's tone in these letters was reflected in remarks he reportedly made to a group of seventeen governors on December 13. "The only way we're going to solve the crisis is to end the oil embargo, and the only way we're going to end the embargo is to get the Israelis to act reasonable. I hate to use the word blackmail, but we've got to do some things to get them to behave." Thomas O'Toole and Lou Cannon, "Jobs, Oil Put Ahead of Environment, Israel," *Washington Post*, December 22, 1973, p. A1.

32. These promises were codified in a memorandum of understanding. See David Landau, "Kissinger Obtains Jerusalem's Consent to Attend Geneva Parley," *Jerusalem Post*, December 18, 1973, p. 1.

33. Kissinger, *Years of Upheaval*, pp. 777–86. Sheehan, *Arabs, Israelis*, pp. 95–97, includes transcripts of portions of these talks.

34. Asad did agree to the opening of an American-manned interests section in Damascus. Thomas Scotes was sent to head the mission.

35. Marvin Kalb and Bernard Kalb, *Kissinger* (Little, Brown, 1974), pp. 526–27. Kissinger also told Golda Meir that Sadat was moving toward moderate views and that by talking of disengagement, Israel could put off negotiations on final borders.

36. Kissinger, *Years of Upheaval*, pp. 1249–50, reproduces the text of a memorandum that he sent to Nixon on December 19, 1973, summing up the positions of the parties on the eve of the conference.

37. Ibid., pp. 821–29; and Kalb and Kalb, *Kissinger*, pp. 534–35.

38. Kalb and Kalb, *Kissinger*, p. 539.

39. The text and map appear in "The Agreement: New Deployment of Forces along the Suez Canal," *Jerusalem Post*, January 20, 1974, p. 1, and in Kissinger, *Years of Upheaval*, p. 839 (map) and p. 1250.

40. The memorandum of understanding is described in general terms in Bernard Gwertzman, "Congressmen Get Mideast Briefing," *New York Times*, January 22, 1974, p. 1.

41. Kissinger, *Years of Upheaval*, p. 1251, provides the text. The stipulation concerning six batteries of short-range artillery later became a source of controversy. In the Israeli army, a battery consisted of six guns; in the Egyptian army, it contained twelve. The first reconnaissance flights after the implementation of the disengagement agreement found seventy-two artillery pieces on the Egyptian side and thirty-six on the Israeli. After angry Israeli complaints in late March, Sadat agreed to reduce his forces to the Israeli level of thirty-six guns.

42. Ze'ev Schiff, "After Accord Signed on Friday, Separation of Forces Begins Next Sunday, Will End in 40 Days," *Jerusalem Post*, January 20, 1974, p. 1, contains a generally accurate account of the secret provisions of the agreement. See also "Secretary Kissinger's News Conference of January 22, 1974," *Department of State Bulletin*, vol. 70 (February 11, 1974), p. 137.

43. "Secretary Kissinger's News Conference of January 3, 1974," *Department of State Bulletin*, vol. 70 (January 28, 1974), p. 78. On January 6, 1974, Defense Secretary Schlesinger raised for the first time the possible use of force if the oil embargo should continue indefinitely.

44. For details of the Jordanian proposals, see Bernard Gwertzman, "U.S. Laying Groundwork for Syrian-Israeli Talks," *New York Times*, February 10, 1974, p. 1, and Terence Smith, "Hussein Said to Urge an Israeli Pullback to Western Edge of the Jordan Valley," *New York Times*, February 15, 1974, p. 3.

45. Golan, *Secret Conversations of Kissinger*, p. 182.

46. These messages, which seemed to imply that Nixon wanted the embargo lifted for domestic political reasons, later proved an embarrassment to him. When the Saudis failed to live up to their promises to lift the embargo, Kissinger hinted that he might be obliged to release the texts of the commitments undertaken by Faisal. The Saudis responded by suggesting that they, too, might have some

embarrassing messages to release. The issue was quickly dropped. See Kissinger, *Years of Upheaval*, p. 947: "In the tenth month of his [Nixon's] torment he was still in thrall to the idea that a dramatic lifting of the embargo under his personal leadership was the cure-all for his Watergate agonies."

47. Bernard Gwertzman, "Israel and Syria to Confer in U.S.," *New York Times*, March 3, 1974, p. 1. There were sixty-five names on the list, more than some observers had expected.

48. During his visit to Washington on March 12, King Hussein had requested $130 million in budget support, in addition to other sums for military assistance. The administration at the time was considering $100 million, which was about twice the amount provided the previous year. The formal aid request for the Middle East for fiscal year 1975 was sent to Congress on April 24 and contained an uncommitted $100 million, presumably to be used as aid for Syria if diplomatic relations were resumed.

49. Dayan's visit had nearly been called off by the Israelis in protest over what they viewed as Egypt's violations of the terms of the disengagement agreement. The dispute over the violations is mentioned in "Arabs Assess Talks Progress," *Washington Post*, March 26, 1974, p. A13.

50. Joseph Alsop, "American Arms Sales to Egypt?" *Washington Post*, April 26, 1974, p. A31.

51. Nixon had met with Boumedienne at the White House on April 11 and had given a small private dinner for him in the evening. The talks had gone well, although Boumedienne pressed Nixon hard on the Syrian-Israeli disengagement and the Palestinians.

52. Kissinger sent Saunders to Saudi Arabia and Algeria to brief Faisal and Boumedienne on the talks and to ask for their support.

53. Kissinger, *Years of Upheaval*, pp. 1052–1110, gives a detailed account of the Damascus-Jerusalem shuttle. Sheehan, *Arabs, Israelis*, pp. 94–106, covers this period, including texts of some of the conversations between Kissinger and Meir. See also Golan, *Secret Conversations of Kissinger*, p. 194.

54. *Pravda*, May 20, 1974, did, however, warn Asad not to settle for half-measures.

55. Sadat fully endorsed this approach to Asad.

56. Golan, *Secret Conversations of Kissinger*, p. 196; and Bernard Gwertzman, "Syria-Israel Gain Seen by Kissinger," *New York Times*, May 9, 1974, p. 1.

57. Nixon had sent Meir a letter on May 10 expressing his concern that an agreement be reached.

58. The Americans had anticipated difficult negotiating around Quneitra and had come armed with large aerial photographs of the area. The photographs were actually used for drawing the final lines instead of maps because of their extraordinarily accurate detail.

59. Kissinger, *Years of Upheaval*, p. 1078, recounts Nixon's orders to cut off all aid to Israel. In the context of the Palestinian terrorist attack on Israelis at Ma'alot that occurred on May 15, Kissinger felt such action would be particularly inappropriate and he opposed it.

60. After four hours with Prime Minister Meir and eight with President Asad,

Kissinger reported to Nixon that May 16 had been his toughest day yet. The previous day Israel had been traumatized by the Ma'alot massacre, which had resulted in the deaths of numerous schoolchildren. This contributed to the defiant mood in Israel concerning concessions to Syria and added to the difficulty of Kissinger's task.

61. "Two Issues Said to Delay Troop-Separation Accord," *New York Times,* May 23, 1974, p. 1.

62. Sheehan, *Arabs, Israelis,* p. 126.

63. As late as June 2, Syria was still trying to make changes in the disengagement line. Israel refused.

64. For the text of the agreement, see *Arab Report and Record,* May 16–31, 1974, p. 215.

65. Kissinger, *Years of Upheaval,* pp. 1123–43; and Richard M. Nixon, *RN: The Memoirs of Richard Nixon* (Grosset and Dunlap, 1978), pp. 1007–18.

66. Sheehan, *Arabs, Israelis,* p. 132.

67. Nixon had never quite overcome his belief in the Eisenhower-Strauss plan of bringing peace to the Middle East by making the deserts bloom through the provision of fresh water produced by nuclear-powered desalting plants. Like many bad ideas, this one was difficult to kill, and the offer of nuclear power plants to Egypt and Israel was a variant of it.

68. Kissinger, *Years of Upheaval,* p. 1134.

69. Golan, *Secret Conversations of Kissinger,* pp. 214–17.

70. Kissinger did not accompany Nixon to Jordan. He flew instead to Canada for a NATO meeting.

71. Golan, *Secret Conversations of Kissinger,* pp. 220–21, claims that arms shipments were delayed as a form of pressure on Israel.

72. Egyptian-Jordanian Joint Communiqué, July 19, 1974, in Foreign Broadcast Information Service, *Daily Report: Middle East and North Africa,* July 19, 1974, p. D1.

73. Information Minister Aharon Yariv stated in July 1974, "Negotiations with the PLO would be possible should the PLO . . . declare its readiness to enter into negotiations while acknowledging the existence of the Jewish state in Israel and calling off all hostile acts against it." "Israel for the First Time, Gives Basis of Talks with Palestinians," *New York Times,* July 13, 1974, p. 1.

74. Golan, *Secret Conversations of Kissinger,* pp. 220–22.

75. During July 1974, however, Secretary of the Treasury Simon did travel to Egypt, Israel, and Saudi Arabia to discuss economic cooperation. He had little to offer but learned that the Egyptians were developing a very large appetite for American aid and technology and that the Israelis were contemplating a five-year military modernization program that would cost $4 billion a year, of which at least $1.5 billion was earmarked as American grant aid. Peace in the Middle East would not come cheaply.

76. Kissinger, *Years of Upheaval,* p. 1247, note 1, recognizes this criticism but argues that in the immediate aftermath of the October 1973 war nothing more than a step-by-step approach could have worked. I agree for that period, but I think more might have been done to build on the second disengagement agreement

if presidential authority had not been so badly undermined. In brief, American influence might have made a difference, but it was not available from mid-1974 on.

CHAPTER NINE

1. Ford shared Kissinger's suspicion of the Soviet Union. See Gerald R. Ford, *A Time to Heal: The Autobiography of Gerald R. Ford* (Harper and Row, 1979), p. 183: "Even before I became President, Kissinger had achieved significant success in easing the Soviets out of the Middle East. I thought they didn't want a bona fide settlement there and that their only aim was to promote instability, so I wanted to keep them out."

2. See Cecilia Albin and Harold H. Saunders, "Sinai II: The Politics of International Mediation," FPI Case Study 17, Johns Hopkins University, School of Advanced International Sudies, Washington, 1991, for the best detailed account of these negotiations. The authors point out that Ford himself was inclined to concentrate on the Egyptian-Israeli front, in part because it seemed more feasible in political terms (pp. 37–38).

3. Fahmy told Ford that Egypt was prepared to go ahead with another partial agreement with Israel before an Israeli-Jordanian agreement was reached. He also expressed the opinion that simultaneous negotiations on these two fronts was impossible. Ibid., pp. 29–30.

4. Ibid., p. 30, indicates that King Hussein made an important concession by accepting the idea that Israeli forces could remain behind in designated locations along the Jordan River after a disengagement agreement. This is referred to as the "leopard spots" concept.

5. See, for example, William Safire, "Arab Council of War," *New York Times*, October 31, 1974, p. 41. A more thoughtful analysis can be found in Richard H. Ullman, "After Rabat: Middle East Risks and American Roles," *Foreign Affairs*, vol. 53 (January 1975), pp. 284–96.

6. In November 1974 the International Energy Agency was established under OECD auspices. It agreed upon a program to build up oil stocks, to plan for reducing demand in the event of oil-supply interruptions, and to share oil if any member of the group was subjected to a selective embargo. By agreeing to these terms, the United States in theory became as vulnerable to an embargo as Europe or Japan.

7. For a discussion of the link between the Arab-Israeli conflict and the energy crisis, see William B. Quandt, "U.S. Energy Policy and the Arab-Israeli Conflict," in Naiem A. Sherbiny and Mark A. Tessler, eds., *Arab Oil: Impact on the Arab Countries and Global Implications* (Praeger, 1976), pp. 279–94. In a major address on energy at the University of Chicago on November 14, 1976, Kissinger maintained that the price of oil would come down only when the objective situation changed. In other words market forces, not political favors, would be the means of reducing prices.

8. Kissinger was pressed by an aggressive interviewer to state that the use of force against oil producers could not be excluded in the event of actual "strangula-

tion" of the Western economies. "Kissinger on Oil, Food, and Trade," *Business Week*, January 13, 1975, pp. 66–76. Detailed discussions of the circumstances in which force might appropriately be used appeared in Robert Tucker, "Oil: The Issue of American Intervention," *Commentary*, vol. 59 (January 1975), pp. 21–31; and Miles Ignotus [presumably Edward Luttwak], "Seizing Arab Oil," *Harper's*, March 1975, pp. 45–62.

9. An article by Hollis Chenery, vice-president of the World Bank, marked an important turning point in the debate over oil prices. See "Restructuring the World Economy," *Foreign Affairs*, vol. 53 (January 1975), pp. 242–63.

10. The joint communiqué issued on November 24, 1974, said that the search for peace in the Middle East should be based on UN Resolution 338, "taking into account the legitimate interests of all the peoples of the area, including the Palestinian people, and respect for the right to independent existence of all States in the area." *Department of State Bulletin*, vol. 71 (December 23, 1974), p. 880.

11. Matti Golan, *The Secret Conversations of Henry Kissinger: Step-by-Step Diplomacy in the Middle East* (Quadrangle Books, 1976), p. 229.

12. Ibid., pp. 229–30; and *Haaretz*, December 17, 1974.

13. Ford also weighed in with advice to the Israelis to be more flexible. See Ford, *Time to Heal*, pp. 245–46, for his view that Israel was sufficiently strong to be able to make concessions.

14. *Le Monde*, January 21, 1975.

15. On February 3, 1975, Syria and the Soviet Union issued a joint communiqué calling for the reconvening of the Geneva conference.

16. Golan, *Secret Conversations of Kissinger*, p. 232.

17. Asad's position on a second step in the Golan Height remained ambiguous. He did not appear particularly anxious for such an agreement, but neither did he preclude it.

18. Wolf I. Blitzer, "Kissinger Reveals Sadat's Twelve 'Concessions,' " *Jerusalem Post*, May 12, 1975, p. 1. According to Albin and Saunders, "Sinai II," p. 58, Sadat also gave Kissinger a fallback position to use as needed. This became a standard Sadat tactic in later negotiations.

19. Edward R. F. Sheehan, *The Arabs, Israelis, and Kissinger: A Secret History of American Diplomacy in the Middle East* (Reader's Digest Press, 1976), p. 156. See also Albin and Saunders, "Sinai II," pp. 56–58 for a summary of these points.

20. See Golan, *Secret Conversations of Kissinger*, pp. 236–38, although he incorrectly gives the date of the letter as March 19. Yitzhak Rabin, *The Rabin Memoirs* (Little, Brown, 1979), p. 256, provides a partial text of the letter, in which Ford threatens "reassessment" of U.S. policy, including relations with Israel. Ford, *Time to Heal*, p. 247, said that he was "mad as hell" at the Israelis over their negotiating tactics.

21. Sheehan, *Arabs, Israelis*, pp. 160–62, contains parts of the transcripts of these talks. It should be noted that the transcripts are not verbatim records but reconstructions of the conversations in dialogue form based on notes taken during the sessions by one of Kissinger's aides. A slightly different version of Kissinger's soliloquy can be found in Albin and Saunders, "Sinai II," pp. 69–70.

22. Before his departure Kissinger called on Golda Meir. Although she

publicly supported Rabin, she privately implied to Kissinger that Rabin had mishandled the negotiations and that she would have known how to get the cabinet and the Knesset to support an agreement.

23. Ford met with Max Fisher on March 27, 1975, to express his irritation with Israeli policy. Fisher was a wealthy Detroit businessman, a Republican, and a leader in the American Jewish community. He often served as an informal channel of communication between the United States and Israel. See Ford, *Time to Heal*, pp. 247, 286.

24. Ford interview with the Hearst newspaper chain, March 27, 1975. See Bernard Gwertzman, "Ford Says Israel Lacked Flexibility in Negotiations," *New York Times*, March 28, 1975, p. 1.

25. George Ball, "How to Avert a Middle East War," *Atlantic Monthly*, January 1975, pp. 6–11.

26. During this period Stanley Hoffmann brilliantly argued the case that it was in Israel's own interest to come up with a comprehensive peace initiative. The major flaw in his argument was that such a policy would require a strong Israeli government backed by a broad public consensus. That apparently was lacking. See "A New Policy for Israel," *Foreign Affairs*, vol. 53 (April 1975), pp. 405–31.

27. Sheehan, *Arabs, Israelis*, p. 166; and Albin and Saunders, "Sinai II," p. 79.

28. He also referred to U.S. policy as "evenhanded."

29. Ford, *Time to Heal*, p. 287, says that he publicly welcomed the letter from the senators, but "in truth it really bugged me. The Senators claimed the letter was 'spontaneous,' but there was no doubt in my mind that it was inspired by Israel. We had given vast amounts of military and economic assistance to Israel over the years and we had never asked for anything in return."

30. Sheehan, *Arabs, Israelis*, pp. 176–77.

31. Golan, *Secret Conversations of Kissinger*, p. 59; and Ford, *Time to Heal*, pp. 290–91.

32. Ford, *Time to Heal*, p. 291, says that he also offered Sadat significant amounts of economic assistance ($800 million) and C-130 transports. Offensive military equipment was ruled out because of Israel's strong objections.

33. Ford letter to Rabin, September 1, 1975, referring to their meeting of June 12, 1975. Reproduced in Michael Widlanski, ed., *Can Israel Survive a Palestinian State?* (Jerusalem: Institute for Advanced Strategic and Political Studies, 1990), pp. 120–21. According to Albin and Saunders, "Sinai II," p. 92, Ford told Rabin that he was inclined to put forward a U.S. plan.

34. Golan, *Secret Conversations of Kissinger*, p. 245; and Terence Smith, "Israel Offers Compromise to Egyptian Sinai Accords," *New York Times*, June 25, 1975, p. 1. Rabin, *Rabin Memoirs*, p. 267, states that the proposed map was approved by the Israeli negotiating team and conveyed to Egypt, where it was rejected.

35. Golan, *Secret Conversations of Kissinger*, p. 248, although he mistakenly gives the date of this meeting as early August. Bernard Gwertzman, "Kissinger Visited by Israeli Envoy for Secret Talks," *New York Times*, July 4, 1975, p. 1.

36. Albin and Saunders, "Sinai II," p. 86, note that Israel was very intent on

getting more military assistance to fund its ten-year modernization program called Matmon-B.

37. Rabin and Ford met in Bonn on July 12, after which the Israeli cabinet authorized a new negotiating position. See *Arab Report and Record*, July 1–15, 1975, p. 401; Terence Smith, "U.S. Is Considering Proposal That It Man Posts in Sinai," *New York Times*, July 13, 1975, p. 1; and Kathleen Teltsch, "Kissinger Warns Majority in UN on U.S. Support," *New York Times*, July 15, 1975, p. 1. Egypt's reply was forthcoming on July 21, but was rejected by Israel on July 27. Israel then presented an "absolutely final" position to Kissinger, who transmitted it to Sadat via Eilts on July 31. The Egyptian response reached Kissinger in Belgrade on August 3, and by August 7 Dinitz had responded with the Israeli position. During the next few days, further exchanges took place, and by mid-August United States and Israeli officials had completed work on a draft agreement. Ford then instructed Kissinger to undertake another trip to the Middle East to pin down the details of an agreement.

38. Sheehan, *Arabs, Israelis*, p. 184.

39. The text of the agreement can be found in *Department of State Bulletin*, vol. 73 (September 22, 1975), pp. 466–70. The secret part of the agreement was published in "U.S. Documents Accompanying the Sinai Accord," *New York Times*, September 17, 1975, p. 4, and "U.S.-Israeli Pact on Geneva," *New York Times*, September 18, 1975, p. 16. The map was also released by the Department of State.

40. Kissinger had kept Sadat informed of most of the commitments he was making to Israel but did not mention the Pershing missile. This irritated the Egyptians and raised doubts about other secret agreements that Kissinger might not have mentioned.

41. According to Albin and Saunders, "Sinai II," p. 100, the Israelis had sought much stronger language. The American negotiating team at the time interpreted this commitment as leaving room for contacts with the PLO.

42. This letter remained secret until published in Widlanski, ed., *Can Israel Survive?* pp. 120–21.

43. On September 29, 1975, Kissinger spoke to the Arab representatives at the United Nations. He said that the United States was prepared to work for a Syrian-Israeli second step, if that was wanted; that the United States would consider ways of working for an overall settlement; and that he would begin to refine his thinking on how the legitimate interests of the Palestinian people could be met. "Furthering Peace in the Middle East," Toast by Secretary Kissinger, *Department of State Bulletin*, vol. 73 (October 20, 1975), pp. 581–84.

44. The Saunders statement can be found in "Department Gives Position on Palestinian Issue," *Department of State Bulletin*, vol. 73 (December 1, 1975), pp. 797–800.

45. Schlesinger was dismissed by Ford on November 2, 1975, to be replaced by Donald Rumsfeld; CIA Director Colby was replaced by George Bush; and Kissinger was relieved of his position as national security affairs adviser, to be replaced by Brent Scowcroft. Moynihan resigned on February 2, 1976.

46. Even without Sinai II, of course, the level of aid for Israel and Egypt would have been substantial. The marginal cost of Sinai II should be measured as several hundreds of million dollars, not several billion. For an account of the congressional debate on Sinai II, see Bernard Gwertzman, "Senate Unit Asks Word from Ford," *New York Times*, October 1, 1975, p. 14. The House and Senate voted in favor of United States technicians in Sinai by large majorities, on October 8 and 9, respectively. Ford, *Time to Heal*, pp. 308–09, provides his rationale for increased aid to Israel: "If we provided the hardware, we could convince Israelis that they were secure. Then they might be willing to accept some risks in the search for peace."

47. Bernard Gwertzman, "Israel Indicates a Cool Reaction to Egypt's Ideas," *New York Times*, March 15, 1975, p. 1.

48. In late March the State Department repeatedly warned Syria against military intervention in Lebanon. On March 31 the former ambassador to Jordan, L. Dean Brown, was sent to Lebanon to try to promote a political settlement. Shortly thereafter a modest number of Syrian troops did enter Lebanon. The United States and Israel both augmented their military capabilities in precautionary measures. Throughout April, while Syria was working to achieve agreement that Elias Sarkis should replace President Suleiman Frangieh, riots broke out on the West Bank after the victory on April 12 of Palestinian nationalists in the municipal elections. Despite the increase of tensions, however, both the United States and Israel began to perceive the Syrian role in Lebanon as potentially stabilizing. Sarkis was elected as Lebanon's new president on May 8 but was not scheduled to take office until September. As fighting continued, Syria increased its military involvement in Lebanon in late May and early June. On June 5 Syria and Egypt withdrew their diplomatic representatives in each other's capitals.

49. A new ambassador, Frank Meloy, took over from Brown in late April. Subsequently, Brown criticized Kissinger for having discouraged Syria from sending troops into Lebanon. "We reined in the Syrians too much, in order to please the Israelis. It resulted in a lot more killing." *Arab Report and Record*, May 16–31, 1976, p. 321. Meloy was kidnapped and assassinated, presumably by dissident Palestinians, on June 16, 1976. He was replaced by an experienced Arabist, Talcott Seelye, but in short order the American diplomatic community in Beirut was reduced to a token force and Seelye returned to Washington. Two evacuations by sea were successfully carried out on June 20 and July 27, 1976, with the cooperation of the PLO. Throughout this period, discreet contacts between the United States and the PLO were undertaken in the interests of arranging for local security.

CHAPTER TEN

1. *Toward Peace in the Middle East*, Report of a Study Group (Brookings, 1975). This report was subsequently credited with steering the Carter administration toward a comprehensive approach to an Arab-Israeli peace agreement, with the Geneva Conference as the centerpiece of the strategy. It is true that Vance and Carter both read the report and many of its suggestions were incorporated into

policy, but it would be an exaggeration to say that the report served as a blueprint for the policies of the first year.

2. The rest of the Middle East team consisted of Alfred L. Atherton, Jr., the assistant secretary of state for Near Eastern and South Asian affairs and later ambassador-at-large for the peace talks; Harold H. Saunders, the director of intelligence and research at State, and later the assistant secretary for Near Eastern affairs; and me as staff member of the National Security Council. All of us had been involved with Kissinger's shuttle diplomacy and were personally well acquainted, which helped to reduce the normal State-NSC frictions and ensured a large measure of continuity with past negotiating efforts. Two other people came to play important roles as the negotiating process got under way: Hermann F. Eilts, ambassador to Cairo and an experienced Middle East hand; and Samuel W. Lewis, ambassador to Israel, who had considerable experience with the United Nations and proved to be a very popular and influential envoy to Israel.

3. For more detail, see William B. Quandt, *Camp David: Peacemaking and Politics*, (Brookings, 1986), pp. 38–40.

4. Ibid., pp. 41–43.

5. Cyrus Vance, *Hard Choices: Critical Years in America's Foreign Policy* (Simon and Schuster, 1983), p. 171.

6. See Yitzhak Rabin, *The Rabin Memoirs* (Little, Brown, 1979), pp. 292–99, for his version of the meeting. See also Jimmy Carter, *Keeping Faith: Memoirs of a President* (Bantam Books), 1982, p. 280; Zbigniew Brzezinski, *Power and Principle: Memoirs of the National Security Adviser, 1977–1981* (Farrar, Strauss, Giroux, 1983), pp. 90–91; and Vance, *Hard Choices*, p. 173.

7. "Clinton, Massachusetts: Remarks and a Question-and-Answer Session at the Clinton Town Meeting, March 16, 1977," *Public Papers of the President: Carter, 1977*, vol. 1 (Government Printing Office, 1977), p. 387.

8. Quandt, *Camp David*, p. 51.

9. See Carter, *Keeping Faith*, pp. 284–88, for his reaction to Begin.

10. See Quandt, *Camp David*, pp. 77–82; Moshe Dayan, *Breakthrough: A Personal Account of the Egypt-Israel Peace Negotiations* (Knopf, 1981), pp. 19–20; and Carter, *Keeping Faith*, p. 290.

11. Ismail Fahmy, *Negotiating for Peace in the Middle East* (Johns Hopkins University Press, 1983), pp. 216–19.

12. Quandt, *Camp David*, p. 90.

13. Ibid., p. 91.

14. Ibid., pp. 101–03.

15. Fahmy, *Negotiating for Peace*, p. 252.

16. Quandt, *Camp David*, pp. 122–23.

17. Dayan, *Breakthrough*, pp. 38–54.

18. For a review of the evidence, see Martin Indyk, *"To the Ends of the Earth": Sadat's Jerusalem Initiative* (Harvard University, Center for Middle Eastern Studies, 1984), pp. 41–43; and Quandt, *Camp David*, pp. 123–25.

19. See the letter written by Ambassador Hermann Eilts, "The Syrians Have Been Their Own Worst Enemies," *New York Times*, January 12, 1982, p. A14.

20. Quandt, *Camp David*, pp. 125–31.

21. Dayan, *Breakthrough*, p. 71.

22. Ibid., pp. 70–71.

23. Quandt, *Camp David*, pp. 139–41.

24. Fahmy, *Negotiating for Peace*, pp. 262–63.

25. See Steven L. Spiegel, *The Other Arab-Israeli Conflict: Making America's Middle East Policy, from Truman to Reagan* (University of Chicago Press, 1985), pp. 341–44.

26. Quandt, *Camp David*, p. 152.

27. Ibid., p. 156; and Vance, *Hard Choices*, p. 199.

28. Brzezinski, *Power and Principle*, pp. 115–20.

29. See Quandt, *Camp David*, p. 158; Carter, *Keeping Faith*, p. 300; and Dayan, *Breakthrough*, pp. 359–61, for the revised text of the Self-Rule proposal.

30. On August 5, 1970, Begin explained before the Knesset why he was resigning from the cabinet: "As far as we are concerned, what do the words 'withdrawal from territories administered since 1967 by Israel' mean other than giving up Judea and Samaria. Not all the territories; but by all opinion, most of them."

31. Quandt, *Camp David*, pp. 171–72.

32. Ibid., pp. 173–76.

33. Ibid., p. 201.

34. Ibid., pp. 212–14.

35. Ibid., pp. 216–17.

36. Ibid., p. 218.

37. Ibid., appendix F, p. 369.

38. Ibid., pp. 222–25.

39. Ibid., p. 222.

40. See Shibley Telhami, *Power and Leadership in International Bargaining: The Path to the Camp David Accords* (Columbia University Press, 1990), pp. 162–67.

41. Quandt, *Camp David*, pp. 242–47.

42. Ibid., pp. 247–51.

CHAPTER ELEVEN

1. On Sadat's political position at this time, see William B. Quandt, *Camp David: Peacemaking and Politics* (Brookings, 1986), p. 262.

2. "President As-Sadat Addresses U.S. News Media," Foreign Broadcast Information Service (FBIS), *Daily Report: Middle East and Africa*, September 20, 1978, pp. D1–D4. Israelis have frequently quoted Sadat's remark to prove that Begin was correct in his interpretation of what was agreed on. But Sadat was not present when the issue was discussed between Carter and Begin. When Sadat spoke on September 19, he had already been told that Begin had agreed only to a three-month freeze. Sadat is also wrong in saying that Israel had agreed not to expand settlements. That language had been dropped at Israeli insistence. According to Sadat's aides, the Egyptian president chose to play down the issue of settlements in the West Bank so as not to put pressure on Carter. He assumed that Carter would find a solution in due course.

3. On September 19, 1978, the Saudi News Agency released an official Saudi cabinet statement critical of the Camp David Accords because they did not call for full Israeli withdrawal and did not provide for Palestinian self-determination. Nonetheless, the cabinet statement went on to say that it did not dispute Egypt's right to recover Sinai. See FBIS, *Daily Report: Middle East and Africa*, September 20, 1978, p. C3.

4. See Jimmy Carter, *Keeping Faith: Memoirs of a President* (Bantam Books, 1982), p. 405, in which he notes that Begin seemed to want to keep both the peace with Egypt and the West Bank; and Cyrus Vance, *Hard Choices: Critical Years in America's Foreign Policy* (Simon and Schuster, 1983), p. 229. Begin had made some particularly hard-line public comments on the day after signing the Camp David Accords. Carter was so angry that he took Begin aside during their joint appearance before the U.S. Congress and told him, in Sadat's presence, that his remarks could cause serious problems. Interview with President Jimmy Carter, Plains, Georgia, May 22, 1985.

5. Sadat had the impression from Carter that the United States would deliver Saudi support for Camp David. See Hermann Frederick Eilts, "Improve the Framework," *Foreign Policy*, no. 41 (Winter 1980–81), p. 9.

6. Zbigniew Brzezinski, *Power and Principle: Memoirs of the National Security Adviser, 1977–1981* (Farrar, Straus and Giroux, 1983), p. 274.

7. Vance, *Hard Choices*, pp. 230–31, summarizes the answers to Hussein's questions, but mistakenly includes the point that sovereignty resides with the people in the West Bank and Gaza.

8. Vance speech in "United Nations: 33d General Assembly Convenes, Statement at the Opening Session of the U.N. General Assembly on September 29, 1978," *Department of State Bulletin*, vol. 78 (November 1978), p. 49.

9. Brzezinski, *Power and Principle*, p. 276, says that Carter had hoped to have the treaty signed by election day.

10. According to Ambassador Eilts, Sadat was irritated with the way his negotiating team in Washington had handled the language of article 6 of the treaty. This was one of the reasons he brought Mustafa Khalil more directly into the negotiations from that point on. Interview with Hermann Eilts on November 30, 1984.

11. According to Kamal Hassan Ali, after the Baghdad summit Sadat was very sensitive to the priority-of-obligations issue. This slowed up the negotiations on the Egyptian side. Interview in Cairo, February 4, 1985.

12. Carter, *Keeping Faith*, p. 409; Brzezinski, *Power and Principle*, pp. 276–77; and Vance, *Hard Choices*, p. 238.

13. The text of the November 11, 1978, draft of the treaty was leaked to the press by the Egyptians and Israelis. It is available in Meron Medzini, ed., *Israel's Foreign Relations: Selected Documents, 1977–1979*, vol. 5 (Jerusalem: Ministry of Foreign Affairs, 1981), pp. 577–81.

14. Ezer Weizman, *The Battle for Peace* (Bantam Books, 1981), p. 375, essentially agreed with Carter and Sadat when he wrote that it was naive to believe there was no link at all between the two agreements. After all, they were signed together.

15. Brzezinski, *Power and Principle*, pp. 277–78.

16. See Gary Sick, *All Fall Down: America's Tragic Encounter with Iran* (Random House, 1985), pp. 130–40.

CHAPTER TWELVE

1. Jimmy Carter, *Keeping Faith: Memoirs of a President* (Bantam Books, 1982), p. 412.

2. Memorandum from Brzezinski to Carter, January 23, 1979.

3. See Zbigniew Brzezinski, *Power and Principle: Memoirs of the National Security Adviser, 1977–1981* (Farrar, Straus and Giroux, 1983), p. 279. Brzezinski thought that Iran made it impossible for Carter to stand aside. "To let the Camp David Accords slip away would be to turn a triumph into disaster, with unforeseeable consequences for the Middle East as a whole." Carter by this time had also concluded that all that could be attained was a separate peace, followed by prolonged negotiations on the West Bank and Gaza. Carter, *Keeping Faith*, p. 413. In a memorandum to Carter written on February 28, 1979, Brzezinski had said that Begin believed he could afford a failure and Carter could not. "He believes that election year realities will increasingly weaken our hand in the negotiations." It was also clear that the United States would have to be very forthcoming on aid to get Israel to budge on the remaining issues of the treaty. Bilateral issues were now as important as Egyptian-Israeli differences.

4. Cyrus Vance, *Hard Choices: Critical Years in America's Foreign Policy* (Simon and Schuster, 1983), p. 244. The language quoted by Vance is the text as it was finally agreed on, but at this stage the Americans had proposed language to which the Egyptians later took exception.

5. Carter, *Keeping Faith*, p. 416.

6. Brzezinski, *Power and Principle*, p. 282. Carter, in an interview on May 22, 1985, did not recall having sent any such message to Sadat. Brzezinski, in an interview on June 3, 1985, recalled in some detail his conversation with Carter. Because Brzezinski was carrying a "political" message to Sadat from Carter, Vance did not object to his going to Cairo.

7. Carter had called Sadat on March 5 to tell him of Brzezinski's visit, and Sadat had promised him that the president's trip would be a great success. Carter felt he had a guarantee from Sadat that the negotiations would not fail because of any U.S.-Egyptian differences. As Carter later wrote. "Once more, I wanted Begin to have his way with particular phrases and depended on Sadat to be flexible on language and to take the long view concerning the effect of the agreement." Carter, *Keeping Faith*, p. 417.

8. While in Cairo, Carter had a strained meeting with his ambassador to Saudi Arabia, John C. West. He told West in no uncertain terms that he was disappointed with the Saudis and instructed him to be blunt in telling Crown Prince Fahd that he expected Saudi support in the future.

9. Jody Powell, *The Other Side of the Story* (William Morrow, 1984), pp. 93–97.

10. When Khalil asked Carter to try to change the text of the agreement in several places, the president replied: "For the last 18 months, I, the president of

the most powerful nation on earth, have acted the postman. I am not a proud man—I have done the best I could—but I cannot go back to try to change the language."

11. Ezer Weizman, *The Battle for Peace* (Bantam Books, 1981), p. 381; and Leon H. Charney, *Special Counsel* (New York: Philosophical Library, 1984), pp. 147–54.

12. See Moshe Dayan, *Breakthrough: A Personal Account of the Egypt-Israel Peace Negotiations* (Knopf, 1981), pp. 356–58, for the texts of these two memoranda.

13. These letters from Khalil can be found in *White Paper on Treaty of Peace between Egypt and Israel* (Cairo: Ministry of Foreign Affairs, 1979), pp. 155–77.

14. Ironically, according to public opinion polls, Carter gained very little as a result of the peace treaty. See Powell, *Other Side of the Story*, p. 102.

15. Dayan, *Breakthrough*, pp. 303–04.

16. For a solid account, including the texts of the Israeli and Egyptian proposals, see Harvey Sicherman, *Palestinian Self-Government (Autonomy): Its Past and Its Future* (Washington: Washington Institute for Near East Policy, 1991), pp. 21–34, and appendixes 6 and 7. Sicherman also includes the text of Linowitz's report to the president on the autonomy talks, dated January 14, 1981 (appendix 7). Linowitz provides an additional perspective in "The Prospects for the Camp David Peace Process," *SAIS Review*, no. 2 (Summer 1981), pp. 93–100. In a news conference on September 6, 1989, Linowitz claimed that "some 80% of the areas of responsibility to be conveyed to the self-governing authority" had been agreed upon. See "Ambassador Sol M. Linowitz's Press Conference: Middle East Peace Negotiations," *Department of State Bulletin*, vol. 80 (December 1980), p. 51.

17. Carter later showed that he understood the linkage issue quite well. In *The Blood of Abraham* (Houghton Mifflin, 1985), p. 45, he wrote: "From Begin's point of view, the peace agreement with Egypt was the significant act for Israel; the references to the West Bank and Palestinians were to be finessed. With the bilateral treaty, he removed Egypt's considerable strength from the military equation of the Middle East and thus gave the Israelis renewed freedom to pursue their goals of fortifying and settling the occupied territories and removing perceived threats by preemptive military strikes against some of their neighbors."

CHAPTER THIRTEEN

1. Ronald Reagan, "Recognizing the Israeli Asset," *Washington Post*, August 15, 1979, p. A25. The rhetorical flourishes and the line of argument suggest the influence of Joseph Churba, who became an adviser to Reagan during his 1980 campaign for the presidency. Churba may well have been the ghostwriter for this piece. See Joseph Churba, *The Politics of Defeat: America's Decline in the Middle East* (Cyrco Press, 1977), p. 97, in which the author speaks of "the conflict and tension endemic to the [Middle East] region. This condition is traceable largely to the sectarian and fragmented nature of Middle East society." Reagan's article says, "The Carter administration has yet to grasp that in this region conflict and tension are endemic, a condition traceable largely to the fragmented sectarian nature of Middle Eastern society." See also Ronald Reagan, *An American Life* (Simon and

Schuster, 1990), p. 410, on his reasons for supporting Israel. There he stresses "moral responsibility," not Israel's importance as a strategic asset.

2. Reagan won an unusually large proportion of Jewish American votes, some 39 percent, in the 1980 election. See Steven L. Spiegel, *The Other Arab-Israeli Conflict: Making America's Middle East Policy from Truman to Reagan* (University of Chicago Press, 1985), p. 397. Normally, Democratic presidential candidates can count on winning about 80 percent of the Jewish vote.

3. According to Lou Cannon, *President Reagan: The Role of a Lifetime* (Simon and Schuster, 1991), pp. 288–91, Reagan was also fascinated by the Biblical story of Armageddon, and attached special importance to the founding of the Jewish state in 1948 as a portent that Armageddon was approaching.

4. Ibid., p. 35, where Cannon states: "He could act decisively when presented with clear options, but he rarely initiated a meeting, a phone call, a proposal or an idea. He thought his staff would tell him anything he ought to know and invested most of his energy and interest in the public performances of the presidency. . . . He thought of himself as a man of principle, and he was difficult to push on the issues that mattered most to him. As president, he was at once the most malleable and least movable of men."

5. See Raymond Tanter, *Who's at the Helm? Lessons of Lebanon* (Boulder, Colo.: Westview Press, 1990), a book written by a member of the National Security Council staff. Reagan is hardly mentioned as a participant in the policy process.

6. Weinberger's views on the Middle East are best spelled out in "Defense Chief Weinberger on Peace Prospects Now," *U.S. News & World Report*, September 27, 1982, pp. 26–28. Among other points, Weinberger said, "We need several friends in the Mideast—not Israel alone, but clearly our relationship with Israel should be maintained."

7. Jeane Kirkpatrick, formerly a Democrat, attracted considerable attention in conservative circles with her article "Dictatorship and Double Standards," *Commentary*, vol. 68 (November 1979), pp. 34–45.

8. See Bob Woodward, *Veil: The Secret Wars of the CIA, 1981–1987* (Simon and Schuster, 1987), pp. 35–49, 71–88.

9. From an interview cited in Karen Elliott House, "Reagan's World," *Wall Street Journal*, June 3, 1980, p. 1.

10. On Haig's views generally, see Alexander M. Haig, Jr., *Caveat: Realism, Reagan and Foreign Policy* (Macmillan, 1984), especially pp. 20–33.

11. See Spiegel, *Other Arab-Israeli Conflict*, pp. 407–11; and Reagan, *American Life*, pp. 412, 415–16, on the AWACs fight and his anger at Begin for lobbying on Capitol Hill against the president's policy after having promised not to do so.

12. Helena Cobban, *The Superpowers and the Syrian-Israeli Conflict: Beyond Crisis Management?* (Praeger, 1991), pp. 83–84; for the text of the memorandum of understanding, see Nimrod Novik, *Encounter with Reality: Reagan and the Middle East (The First Term)* (Boulder, Colo.: Westview Press for the Jaffee Center for Strategic Studies, 1985), pp. 86–88.

13. See Ze'ev Schiff and Ehud Ya'ari, *Israel's Lebanon War* (Simon and Schuster, 1984); Itamar Rabinovich, *The War for Lebanon, 1970–1983* (Cornell University

Press, 1984); and Yair Evron, *War and Intervention in Lebanon: The Israeli-Syrian Deterrence Dialogue* (Johns Hopkins University Press, 1987).

14. Haig, *Caveat*, pp. 332–35.

15. Schiff and Ya'ari, *Israel's Lebanon War*, pp. 62–77. See also David Kimche, *The Last Option: After Nasser, Arafat and Saddam Hussein. The Quest for Peace in the Middle East* (Scribner's, 1991), p. 145: "Israel's political leaders, especially Prime Minister Begin and Defence Minister Sharon, had become convinced, during those spring months of 1982, that the Reagan administration was not averse to an operation in which the PLO, and perhaps even the Soviet-aligned Syrians, would be taught a lesson." Kimche states bluntly, on his own considerable authority, that there was no strong resistance to Sharon's plans in Washington. He quotes both Haig and Reagan as being understanding of Israel's objectives. "When Begin sent an oral message to Reagan in May 1982 warning that it might become 'imperative and inevitable' to remove this PLO threat, Haig's reaction was that the United States would probably not be able to stop Israel from attacking. And when Sharon met Haig in Washington later that month, Haig was reported to have told him: 'We understand your aims. We can't tell you not to defend your interests.' "

16. Just a week before the Israeli invasion, on May 26, 1982, Haig gave a major speech on the Middle East in which he focused on the Iran-Iraq conflict, the autonomy negotiations, and the explosive situation in Lebanon.

17. See Cobban, *Superpowers*, pp. 35–40.

18. Allan Gerson, *The Kirkpatrick Mission: Diplomacy without Apology. America at the United Nations, 1981–1985* (Free Press, 1991), pp. 138–55.

19. Ibid., p. 134.

20. Translated from the Hebrew version of the letter from Reagan to Begin, June 9, 1982, as published by Arye Naor, *Cabinet at War* (in Hebrew) (Tel Aviv: Lahav, 1986), p. 76. American officials have confirmed the essential accuracy of this version but add that Brezhnev's message was not particularly menacing. They imply that Reagan deliberately exaggerated the danger of escalation to make an impression on Begin.

21. Alexander M. Haig, Jr., *Inner Circles: How America Changed the World. A Memoir* (Warner Books, 1992), p. 547.

22. Cannon, *President Reagan*, pp. 202–04; and Haig, *Inner Circles*, pp. 547–48. Haig claims that he was on the verge of achieving agreement on PLO withdrawal from Lebanon in early July and that this effort fell apart when he was suddenly dismissed.

23. Cannon, *President Reagan*, pp. 202–05.

24. Bernard Gwertzman, "Shultz Declares Palestinian Needs Must Be Resolved," *New York Times*, July 14, 1982, p. A1.

25. George Shultz, *Turmoil and Triumph: My Years as Secreary of State* (Scribner's, 1993), pp. 85–86. The working group consisted of Robert McFarlane, Lawrence Eagleburger, Nicholas Veliotes, Robert Ames, Paul Wolfowitz, Charles Hill, William Kirby, and Alan Kreczko.

26. Ibid., p. 87.

27. Reagan, *American Life*, pp. 425–29; and Michael Deaver, *Behind the Scenes: In Which the Author Talks about Ronald and Nancy Reagan . . . and Himself* (William Morrow, 1987), pp. 165–66. Deaver takes credit for persuading Reagan, against the advice of the NSC staff, to call Begin to tell him to stop the bombing of Beirut. When Begin agreed, Reagan reportedly turned to Deaver and said, "I didn't know I had that kind of power." Also see Gerson, *Kirkpatrick Mission*, pp. 164–69, on the UN diplomacy in this period, especially the delaying tactics on the French-Egyptian proposal, which called for mutual Israeli-PLO recognition.

28. See Rashid Khalidi, *Under Siege: P.L.O. Decisionmaking during the 1982 War* (Columbia University Press, 1986), p. 177.

29. Shultz, *Turmoil and Triumph*, p. 92.

30. See Kimche, *Last Option*, p. 157, where he quotes Begin speaking to his Israeli colleagues on September 1: "We have been betrayed by the Americans, the biggest betrayal since the state was established. They have stabbed us in the back. We now have a completely different fight on our hands."

31. Veliotes had made a secret trip to Amman to brief King Hussein on August 20. Arafat was also given an advance briefing on the speech while still in Beirut. Begin was briefed by Ambassador Lewis only on August 31. Shultz, *Turmoil and Triumph*, p. 92, discloses the Veliotes mission and describes Shultz's rationale for going ahead in the face of probable Israeli opposition.

32. According to notes, made available to the author, of Sharon's meeting with Pierre Gemayal in Bikfaya on September 16, 1982, Sharon referred to his discussions with Bashir and again called for "the necessity of immediate action to prevent establishment of new facts by the present government in its final days, and the danger that hostile elements would try and modify political processes desirable to us." Some of the relevant background to this meeting is covered by Schiff and Ya'ari, *Israel's Lebanon War*, pp. 246–58.

33. For the results of the official Israeli inquiry, see *The Beirut Massacre: The Complete Kahan Commission Report* (Princeton, N.J.: Karz-Cohl, 1983).

34. See Geoffrey Kemp, "Lessons of Lebanon: A Guideline for Future U.S. Policy," *Middle East Insight*, vol. 6 (Summer 1988), pp. 57–68, on debates over the role of the multinational force from September 1982 until the withdrawal of the American contingent in February 1984.

35. See William B. Quandt, "Reagan's Lebanon Policy: Trial and Error," *Middle East Journal*, vol. 38 (Spring 1984), pp. 241–42.

36. Shultz, *Turmoil and Triumph*, p. 440.

37. The best account of the background to the king's decision can be found in two Pulitzer-prize-winning articles by Karen Elliott House: "Hussein's Decision: King Had U.S. Pledges on Peace Talks but Met a Maze of Arab Foes," *Wall Street Journal*, April 14, 1983, p.1, and "Hussein's Decision: Fears for His Kingdom, Sense of History Drove Monarch to Seek Talks," *Wall Street Journal*, April 15, 1983, p.1. According to the king, General Secretary Yuri V. Andropov had taken him aside in early December 1982 during a visit to Moscow to warn, "I shall oppose the Reagan plan, and we will use all our resources to oppose it. With due respect, all the weight will be on your shoulders, and they aren't broad enough to bear it."

38. Text of "Jordan's Statement on Its Refusal to Join the Reagan Peace Initiative," *New York Times*, April 11, 1983, p. A12.

39. Among the victims of the bombing was Robert Ames, one of the top CIA officials with responsibility for the Middle East, and one of the core group of officials who had worked closely with Secretary Shultz at the inception of the Reagan initiative.

40. For an inquiry into the reasons for the vulnerability of the U.S. Marine compound, see *Report of the DOD Commission on Beirut International Airport Terrorist Act, October 23, 1983* (Department of Defense, 1983). Before the bombing of the Marine compound, the Israelis had begun to withdraw from the Shouf area, a step on the way toward the new Israeli policy of consolidating a security presence in southern Lebanon only.

41. Cobban, *Superpowers*, pp. 87–88.

42. On Shamir, see Avishai Margalit, "The Violent Life of Yitzhak Shamir," *New York Review of Books*, May 14, 1992, pp. 18–24.

43. See John K. Cooley, *Payback: America's Long War in the Middle East* (Brassey's, 1991), pp. 94–97.

44. Kemp, "Lessons of Lebanon," p. 67. Kemp concludes that only a strong president can put a stop to squabbling between powerful cabinet members such as Shultz and Weinberger. In his words, "In the case of Lebanon the President never once ordered the Secretary of Defense to play a more assertive role in supporting U.S. policy in Lebanon. Indeed, at the height of the debate within the White House over whether or not the marines should be redeployed to ships in February 1984, Reagan's own viewpoint was difficult to discern. The decision in favor of withdrawal was made by a simple majority within the inner circle of advisors."

45. See William B. Quandt, *Camp David: Peacemaking and Politics* (Brookings, 1986), pp. 25–27.

46. Shultz, *Turmoil and Triumph*, p. 440.

47. See Quandt, ed., *Middle East*, p. 473, for the text of the February 11 agreement. Both Jordanian and Palestinian sources say that some amendments were later made to the basic text. The authorized English translation of the first principle called for "total withdrawal from the territories occupied in 1967 for comprehensive peace." The Arabic text simply said "land in exchange for peace."

48. Shultz, *Turmoil and Triumph*, p. 445.

49. On Israeli-Jordanian contacts during this period, see Adam Garfinkle, *Israel and Jordan in the Shadow of War: Functional Ties and Futile Diplomacy in a Small Place* (St. Martin's Press, 1992), pp. 109–20.

50. Text of "President's News Conference on Foreign and Domestic Issues," *New York Times*, March 22, 1985, p. A12.

51. Shultz, *Turmoil and Triumph*, p. 446.

52. Ibid., pp. 453–54.

53. Garfinkle, *Israel and Jordan*, p. 120, provides four of the names: Hanna Siniora (Jerusalem-based editor of *Al-Fajr*), Fayez Abu Rahme (a lawyer from Gaza), Sheik Abd al-Hamid Sayah (the speaker of the Palestine National Council), and Nabil Sha'ath (a political adviser to Arafat and prominent member of the

Palestine National Council). In addition, the list mentioned Khalid al-Hassan (prominent in Fatah and occasional emissary to Washington), Hatem Husseini (former PLO representative in Washington), and Salah Ta'amari (Fatah activist who had been imprisoned by Israel and had the distinction of being married to a former wife of King Hussein). Jerusalem Domestic Service, July 19, 1985, in Foreign Broadcast Information Service (FBIS), *Daily Report: Middle East and Africa*, p. 11. Neither the Americans nor the Israelis had any objections to Siniora and Abu Rahmeh. Nabil Sha'ath presented the most complicated case. For the PLO, his inclusion was essential. For Israel, it was out of the question. The Americans vacillated.

54. Shultz, *Turmoil and Triumph*, p. 454.

55. See the text of the September 27, 1985, speech in Amman Domestic Service, FBIS, *Daily Report: Middle East and Africa*, September 30, 1985, p. F3.

56. Garfinkle, *Israel and Jordan*, pp. 122–23.

57. In the denouement of the *Achille Lauro* affair, U.S.-Egyptian relations were strained as American F-14s intercepted an Egyptian airliner carrying the hijackers to Tunis, where the PLO would have allegedly put them on trial. The Egyptian plane was forced to land at a NATO base in Sicily, which caused a great outpouring of anger in Cairo and self-congratulations and boasting in the United States. On the *Achille Lauro* affair and its aftermath, see David C. Martin and John Walcott, *Best Laid Plans: The Inside Story of America's War against Terrorism* (Harper and Row, 1988), pp. 235–57; and Woodward, *Veil*, pp. 414–16.

58. Garfinkle, *Israel and Jordan*, p. 124, credits King Hussein with initiating the move toward Syria as a means of preventing Arafat from winning Syrian support while Jordan pursued its new strategy with Israel. Peres had reportedly accepted the idea of an international conference in order to give the king something to use with Syria.

59. The full text is found in Amman Television Service, February 19, 1986, FBIS, *Daily Report: Middle East and North Africa*, February 20, 1986, pp. F1–F16. According to American sources that were closely involved in the diplomacy of early 1986, a last-ditch effort was made to find a formula whereby the PLO would accept Resolution 242 unambiguously as the basis for negotiations with Israel and then would spell out its additional demands. King Hussein told the Americans that the PLO needed a quid pro quo for such a step, and the United States therefore made some concessions on how the PLO would be invited to, and represented at, an international conference. The PLO was still not prepared to accept Resolution 242. Arafat insisted that the United States endorse the Palestinian right of self-determination and open direct channels of communication to the PLO instead of negotiating through the Jordanians. The Jordanians had told the PLO that the United States would not budge on the issue of self-determination and urged the PLO to accept 242 anyway. The final meeting between Hussein and Arafat ended acrimoniously. The Jordanians and Americans concluded that the PLO was neither serious nor trustworthy. This conclusion had a significant impact on subsequent diplomatic moves. Hussein's public account does not cover all of these points, but the tone and substance of his remarks give credence to this interpretation.

60. Garfinkle, *Israel and Jordan*, p. 121, states that Jordan wanted to co-opt a weak Arafat, and Israel, much like the United States, wanted to eliminate him.

61. Shultz, *Turmoil and Triumph*, pp. 461–62.

62. According to Kemp, "Lessons of Lebanon," p. 67, the Shultz-Weinberger deadlock over Lebanon had convinced some Reaganites, especially Casey and NSC staffer Oliver North, that a capability should be developed to carry out covert actions "outside the system."

63. Many sources provide the basic chronology of what came to be known as the Iran-Contra affair. See especially *The Tower Commission Report: The Full Text of the President's Special Review Board* (Random House, 1987). Woodward, *Veil*, pp. 413–501, provides insider detail, as does Martin and Walcott, *Best Laid Plans*, pp. 227–34, 323–61. See also Kimche, *Last Option*, pp. 208–20, for his own and Israel's role in the opening to Iran.

64. McFarlane served as national security adviser from October 1982 until the end of 1985. After his retirement he remained involved with the arms for hostages affair, and when he made his infamous trip to Tehran in May 1986, he no longer held an official position in the government. By then, the national security adviser was the intensely secretive John Poindexter. See Martin and Walcott, *Best Laid Plans*, p. 331.

65. Kimche, *Last Option*, pp. 211–13.

CHAPTER FOURTEEN

1. See Thomas L. McNaugher, "Walking Tightropes in the Gulf," in Efraim Karsh, ed., *The Iran-Iraq War: Impact and Implications* (St. Martin's Press, 1989), pp. 171–99.

2. For additional reasons to be skeptical of an international conference, see Peter W. Rodman, "Middle East Diplomacy after the Gulf War," *Foreign Affairs*, vol. 70 (Spring 1991), pp. 10–18.

3. George Shultz, *Turmoil and Triumph: My Years as Secretary of State* (Scribner's, 1993), pp. 454–57, and chap. 44.

4. Adam Garfinkle, *Israel and Jordan in the Shadow of War: Functional Ties and Futile Diplomacy in a Small Place* (St. Martin's Press, 1992), pp. 128–29.

5. For more information on the efforts to create a sort of Israeli-Jordanian condominium, see Yossi Melman and Dan Raviv, *Behind the Uprising: Israelis, Jordanians, and Palestinians* (Greenwood Press, 1989), pp. 187–200.

6. Shultz, *Turmoil and Triumph*, chap. 44.

7. For the text of the London Document, see William B. Quandt, ed., *The Middle East: Ten Years after Camp David* (Brookings, 1988), pp. 475–76.

8. Shultz, *Turmoil and Triumph*, chap. 44.

9. Ibid.

10. Ibid.

11. Ibid.

12. See William Safire, "The Little King," *New York Times*, January 13, 1988, p. A23.

13. The word *intifada* in Arabic means "shaking off," as in shaking off the occupation.

14. Two seasoned Israeli journalists give their account of the early phase of the *intifada* in Ze'ev Schiff and Ehud Ya'ari, *Intifada: The Palestinian Uprising. Israel's Third Front* (Simon and Schuster, 1989).

15. See Helena Cobban, "The PLO and the Intifada," *Middle East Journal*, vol. 44 (Spring 1990), pp. 207–33.

16. By this time Shultz was fully in charge of the foreign policy of the United States. Weinberger had left in November 1987, to be replaced by Frank Carlucci. General Colin Powell then took over the job as national security adviser, Reagan's sixth in seven years. Also, Casey had died in January 1987.

17. Shultz, *Turmoil and Triumph*, chap. 47.

18. The use of the word "parties" instead of "states" suggested that the Palestine Liberation Organization might be invited to the conference.

19. Shamir's statement prompted Senators Rudy Boschwitz, Carl Levin, and twenty-eight other senators, including many friends of Israel, to write a letter to Shultz, dated March 3, 1988, expressing their concern about the Israeli position. Shamir's reply was published in "Text of Letter from Shamir on Criticism from Senators," *New York Times*, March 10, 1988, p. A10.

20. Shultz, *Turmoil and Triumph*, chap. 47, states, "I was frustrated by Shamir's inflexibility and by the fact that divided government, as had existed in Israel since late 1984, meant that no one could be held responsible and accountable." His comments on King Hussein were that he was "candid and gloomy: he again gave me nothing but wanted me to 'persevere.' " Asad put Shultz through an "exercise in agony," concluding by saying, "I can give you nothing but 'continue.' "

21. See the text of the king's speech of July 31, 1988, in Foreign Broadcast Information Service, *Daily Report: Middle East and North Africa*, August 1, 1988, pp. 39–41.

22. At the Algiers Arab Summit meeting in Algiers in June 1988, the PLO had circulated a document entitled "PLO View: Prospects of a Palestinian-Israeli Settlement." Bassam Abu Sharif, a close adviser of Arafat's, soon claimed authorship. Most American officials who took note of the document were encouraged by its content and tone but were unsure whether it truly represented a new, more moderate tendency within the PLO. For the text, see Quandt, ed., *Middle East*, pp. 490–93.

23. John Mroz, from the International Peace Academy in New York, had many talks with Arafat in 1981–82 that were conveyed to the State Department. According to Harvey Sicherman, *Palestinian Self-Government (Autonomy): Its Past and Its Future* (Washington: Washington Institute for Near East Policy, 1991), p. 37, Haig never used the channel for any official messages.

24. Congress in August 1985 added one more condition of its own. No American official could negotiate with the PLO unless the PLO met the conditions laid down in 1975—acceptance of UN Resolutions 242 and 338 and Israel's right to exist—and renounced the use of terrorism. Public Law 99-83, section 1302, August 8, 1985.

25. Among the Jewish personalities involved were Rita Hauser, a New York attorney; Stanley Sheinbaum, an economist and publisher from Los Angeles; Menachem Rosensaft, a Holocaust survivor who later regretted his participation;

Drora Kass, from the American branch of the Israeli International Center for Peace in the Middle East; and A. L. Udovitch, professor of Middle Eastern history at Princeton University, who joined the group just before the Stockholm meeting.

26. Shultz interview with Swedish reporter Susanne Palme, March 30, 1992 (made available to the author).

27. Mohamed Rabie is an economist by training and the author of a number of books, including *The New World Order: A Perspective on the Post–Cold War Era* (Vantage Press, 1992).

28. Rabie approached me on August 2, 1988, with his idea. As far as I knew then or know now, it was his own proposal, not one initiated by the PLO in Tunis. At this initial meeting we agreed to try to develop language that would meet the requirements of both sides. Rabie assumed that I had contacts in the State Department, and he assured me that he could communicate easily with the PLO leadership. Over the next several months he dealt exclusively with the PLO leadership, especially Abu Mazin, and I dealt with a handful of people in the State Department and NSC who were aware of this initiative. Rabie and I would then convey to each other whatever we had learned of importance to the success of the initiative. The main result of this effort, I believe, was to establish that both sides were interested in beginning a dialogue before the end of the Reagan administration and in demonstrating that mutually acceptable language would not be too difficult to develop. See Mohamed Rabie, "The U.S.-PLO Dialogue: The Swedish Connection," *Journal of Palestine Studies*, vol. 21 (Summer 1992), pp. 54–66.

29. The proposed text of what the PLO might say, as conveyed to the State Department on August 12, was as follows:

As its contribution to the search for a just and lasting peace in the Middle East, the Executive Committee of the Palestine Liberation Organization has met and decided to issue the following official statement:

1. That it is prepared to negotiate a comprehensive peace settlement of the Arab-Israeli conflict on the basis of United Nations resolutions 242 and 338.

2. That it considers the convening of an international conference under the auspices of the United Nations as an appropriate framework for negotiating a political settlement and ultimately achieving peace in the Middle East.

3. That it seeks to establish a democratic Palestinian state in the West Bank and Gaza strip and to live in peace with its neighbors and respect their right to live in peace.

4. That it condemns terrorism in all its forms and is prepared for a moratorium on all forms of violence, on a mutual basis, once negotiations under the auspices of an international conference begin.

These points are derived from the PLO's commitment to the following principles: all the states in the region—including Israel and a Palestinians state—are entitled to live in peace within secure and internationally recognized borders; that all peoples in the region—including the Israelis and the Palestinians—must enjoy the right of self-determination; and that no state should violate the rights of others, acquire land by force, or determine its future by coercion.

Israel's acceptance of these same principle is a precondition for meaningful negotiations to begin.

After talking at length with Rabie, the PLO made a few minor changes, most important of which was the addition of the idea that "all parties to the conflict, including the PLO, should participate in the international conference on an equal basis."

30. I conveyed these points, on behalf of the State Department, to Mohamed Rabie on August 13, 1988. I was told that they had been cleared by Shultz's office, which meant, at a minimum, Shultz's aide, Charles Hill, had cleared on them and that Shultz was informed. I did not at any point deal directly with Shultz or Hill, although my interlocutors regularly did. See Shultz, *Turmoil and Triumph*, chap. 47, for his account of these developments.

31. The PLO wanted the United States to say:

The U.S. Government welcomes the new PLO initiative and wishes to make the following statement:

1. The United States considers the PLO statement as a commitment to seek a political settlement of the Arab-Israeli conflict through peaceful means.

2. Recognizing the right of all peoples to self-determination as called for in the charter of the U.N., the United States believes that the Palestinian people have the right to self-determination, and should be enabled to do so through negotiations leading to a comprehensive peace settlement.

3. The United States believes that U.N. resolutions 242 and 338 embody the basic principle upon which a political settlement to the Arab-Israeli conflict can be established.

4. The United States considers the PLO's endorsement of U.N. resolutions 242 and 338, its condemnation of terrorism, its commitment to a political settlement through peaceful means as having removed the obstacles which in the past prevented the United States from having official contacts with the PLO.

Consequently, the U.S. government is prepared to meet with designated representatives of the PLO, the legitimate representatives of the Palestinian people, as soon as the Executive Committee names its representatives. Finally, the United States calls upon all parties to seize the opportunity to renew the search for peace without delay.

32. Shultz had been disappointed by Arafat's speech in Strasbourg on September 13. The PLO had signaled that this speech would not contain the new PLO position, but Shultz was still critical. For the text of Shultz's remarks, see "The First George P. Shultz Lecture on Middle East Diplomacy," Washington Institute for Near East Policy, September 16, 1988.

33. About this time consultations took place between the United States and the Soviet Union, and the Soviets made it clear that they were supporting the initiative. Shultz, *Turmoil and Triumph*, chap. 47, implies that he did not authorize the sending of a message to the PLO, but in fact one was sent.

34. Shultz, *Turmoil and Triumph*, chap. 47, notes that the PLO was able to communicate with him through the CIA. Arafat used this channel on occasion to clarify points but not for ongoing negotiations.

35. For an English translation of the resolutions of the Nineteenth PNC, see *Journal of Palestine Studies*, vol. 18 (Winter 1989), pp. 213–23.

36. In his interview with Susanne Palme, on March 30, 1992, Shultz said: "[The Swedish ambassador] came to me [on December 2] and asked: Sten Andersson wants to know what the PLO could say that would cause us to be willing to have a dialogue with them and what kind of response we would make if they made these statements. And so I produced a statement and an answer and [the Swedish ambassador] came to my home and got it and I told him this is strictly for Sten Andersson. I have nothing to do with the American Jews that are there, I don't want them to see it, the dialogue between them and the Palestinians is something you are running, it's something totally separate from this. . . . Sten was a person I trusted and had confidence in and so I thought if he is going to talk to Arafat and if he seems to think this is a serious possibility we will get him a statement. And we had learned some things about some PLO sensibilities from the Quandt [and Rabie] interchange. So that helped I think a little bit in the phraseology of what we said." See Shultz, *Turmoil and Triumph*, chap. 47, for more on these developments, especially his reasoning in denying a visa for Arafat to come to the United Nations.

37. This document was quite close to the draft that Rabie had brought back from Tunis in September with PLO approval, with the addition of several key words referring to not engaging in terrorism in the future. For reasons that are not clear, the PLO objected to the fourth point on the moratorium on violence—after having accepted it the previous September—and Shultz accepted this deletion. A few other word changes were also agreed upon through the Swedes, including the addition to point one that negotiations should take place "within the framework of an international conference."

38. This led American officials to believe, for a brief moment on December 7, that the breakthrough had been achieved.

39. A PLO internal account of this incident reads as follows: "Many voices were raised warning of the outcome of embarking on this step. And here too Hawatmeh played a disruptive role. He tried to contact Kuwait and others to incite our brothers to refuse it. He did the same thing within his organization; he began to dispatch letters and messengers. All of that led Abu Ammar (Arafat) to work to distance himself from the step, and for that reason he took another look at his speech to remove most of the commentary that it contained and that complied with the proposed text from the Americans. Abu Ammar feared for national unity and imagined that the DFLP [Hawatmeh's group] and the PFLP [of George Habbash] might leave the PLO which might influence the *intifada*, just as it would affect the total credibility of the PLO which desired an acceptable democratic appearance." From an internal PLO document in Arabic, p. 195.

40. In Arabic, he used the verbs *abaa* and *rafada* (condemn and reject), not *nabadha* (renounce, abandon, or forsake). Shultz felt that rejecting or condemning terrorism did not involve admitting that one had been engaged in it. In one form

or another, he wanted the PLO to say that it would stop doing something that it had been doing previously.

41. Shultz, *Turmoil and Triumph*, chap. 47, revealingly notes that he told Reagan that Arafat, in his speech, was saying in one place "'Unc, unc, unc,' and in another he was saying, 'cle, cle, cle,', but nowhere will he yet bring himself to say, 'Uncle.' "

42. See Eugene Rostow, "Palestinian Self-Determination: Possible Futures for the Unallocated Territories of the Palestine Mandate," *Yale Law Studies in World Public Order*, vol. 5 (1979), p. 147. Rostow has made the same point about the legality of Israeli settlements in a number of other publications. This theme was picked up and popularized by George Will in his syndicated column in the early 1980s.

43. Meron Benvenisti wrote in 1983 that the clock had struck midnight. For an example of his thinking, see his essay "Demographic, Economic, Legal, Social and Political Developments in the West Bank," in *The 1987 Report: The West Bank Data Base Project* (Boulder, Colo.: Westview Press, 1987), pp. 67–80. See also Meron Benvenisti, *Conflicts and Contradictions* (Villard Books, 1986), pp. 169–82.

44. Reagan's memoirs, *An American Life* (Simon and Schuster, 1990), give many examples of his lack of care with details in discussing the Middle East. For example, Reagan says that UN Resolution 242 called on Israel "to withdraw from all the territories it had claimed after the 1967 war, including the West Bank" (p. 414); he casually interprets his September 1, 1982, initiative as supporting the right of Palestinians to "self-determination and self-government" (p. 430); and he states that Israeli settlements, which he had said were not illegal, were "in continued violation of UN Security Council Resolution 242" (p. 441). All three statements are inaccurate.

45. See Wolf Blitzer, *Territory of Lies: The Exclusive Story of Jonathan Jay Pollard. The American Who Spied on His Country for Israel and How He Was Betrayed* (Harper and Row, 1989).

46. The first account of the information provided by Mordechai Vanunu appeared in Peter Hounam and others, "Revealed: The Secrets of Israel's Nuclear Arsenal," *Sunday Times* (London), October 5, 1986, p. 1. See also Seymour M. Hersh, *The Samson Option: Israel's Nuclear Arsenal and American Foreign Policy* (Random House, 1991), pp. 307–12.

47. See Karen L. Puschel, *US-Israeli Strategic Cooperation in the Post–Cold War Era: An American Perspective* (Boulder, Colo.: Westview Press, 1992), chaps. 2–4.

48. For the first time, in November 1991, poll results showed that more Americans blamed Israel than the Arabs for the lack of progress in making peace. See Gerald F. Seib, "On Day One of Mideast Talks, Calm Prevails amid Ceremony," *Wall Street Journal*, October 31, 1991, p. A18.

CHAPTER FIFTEEN

1. On the Bush-Baker relationship, see Marjorie Williams, "His Master's Voice," *Vanity Fair*, October 1992; and John Newhouse, "Shunning the Losers," *New Yorker*, October 26, 1992, pp. 40–52.

2. Some Israelis saw this article on Baker as an early sign of his hostility to Israel. Early in the stream-of-conscious musings, Baker is quoted as wondering if it will ever be possible to get peace in the Middle East. Then, right after the comment on turkey-shooting tactics, he mentions Israel and notes that Israel is internally divided. "But creating something productive when Israel is divided internally is going to be real tough. Who knows?" See Michael Kramer, "Playing for the Edge," *Time*, February 13, 1989, p. 44. For an Israeli interpretation of how this shows Baker's hostility toward Israel, see Dore Gold, "US and Israel Enter New Era," *Jerusalem Post*, February 28, 1992, p. 9A.

3. Kramer, "Playing for the Edge," p. 30.

4. Bush's other key foreign policy appointments, Secretary of Defense Richard Cheney and National Security Adviser Brent Scowcroft, were not known to have strong views on the Middle East and seemed most likely to wield influence on U.S.-Soviet relations and arms control issues.

5. Washington Institute's Presidential Study Group, *Building for Peace: An American Strategy for the Middle East* (Washington: Washington Institute for Near East Policy, 1988).

6. Richard Haass, *Conflicts Unending: The United States and Regional Disputes* (Yale University Press, 1990), pp. 30–56.

7. Haass's views did apparently evolve somewhat. On September 13, 1991, he said that "one of the things we've learned, and it has affected a lot of my thinking, is that even when you try to think small and avoid some of the most sensitive, final status issues, a kind of step-by-step approach, you find that people see precedents everywhere." See "The Impact of Global Developments on U.S. Policy in the Middle East," *From War to Peace in the Middle East?* Sixth Annual Policy Conference (Washington: Washington Institute for Near East Policy, 1991), p. 10.

8. Arab suspicions were also heightened by the fact that the four top advisers to Bush and Baker on the Middle East were all Jewish—Dennis Ross, Richard Haass, Aaron Miller on the Policy Planning staff, and Daniel Kurtzer in the Near East Bureau. Somewhat ironically, the presence of Jews in such prominent positions did not seem to reassure some Israelis, especially Likud supporters, who soon were speaking crudely of "Baker's Jew boys" as responsible for the strains in U.S.-Israeli relations. See Margaret G. Warner, "Whose Side Are You On?" *Newsweek*, June 1, 1992, p. 57.

9. One significant development had taken place after the publication of the Presidential Study Group's *Building for Peace*. That was the onset of the U.S.-PLO dialogue. Those who had contributed to the report had taken a very skeptical attitude toward the PLO, indicating that the prospects were much better for finding a Palestinian negotiating partner for Israel from within the West Bank and Gaza, where objective circumstances imposed a kind of realism and pragmatism. But in December 1988 Shultz, with the support of both Bush and Baker, had agreed to the opening of a U.S.-PLO dialogue. From the outset Bush and Baker made it clear that they wanted the dialogue to continue, albeit with discretion. In addition, Bush and Baker rejected the proposal of the report that a special negotiator for the Middle East should be named.

10. The other three points of the Israeli proposal, which received less attention because they were less original, emphasized the need for negotiations with Arab states to conclude peace treaties, the importance of settling the refugee problem, and the necessity for the Camp David partners to renew their commitment to the agreements and to peace. For the text of the initial plan, see *Jerusalem Post*, April 14, 1989, p. 8. On May 15, 1989, *Jerusalem Post*, p. 2, published an expanded twenty-point version of the government's peace plan. This latter document is sometimes referred to as the May 14, 1989, initiative.

11. Address by Secretary Baker, "Principles and Pragmatism: American Policy toward the Arab-Israeli Conflict," *Department of State Bulletin*, vol. 89 (July 1989), p. 24. One of the members of the Baker Middle East team called the speech "reality therapy." Another said that "slight tension with Israel is the price we pay for having credibility with the Arab side."

12. Shamir may not have been prepared to negotiate with the PLO, but he did apparently establish contact in early 1989. According to Salah Khalaf (Abu Iyad), in an interview with the author in February 1989, Shamir had sent a message to him via an Arab leader. Shamir wanted to know if Abu Iyad continued to believe that a Palestinian state in the West Bank would simply be a stage on the way to the elimination of Israel. Shamir followed up by sending one of his political allies to Morocco to engage in lengthy discussions with Abu Iyad. Subsequent meetings were envisaged but never took place.

13. See, for example, Salah Khalaf (Abu Iyad), "Lowering the Sword," *Foreign Policy*, no. 78 (Spring 1990), pp. 91–112. Somewhat earlier Abu Iyad had videotaped a statement to Israelis that indicated a shift in his views toward acceptance of a two-state settlement. The tape was shown in Israel and produced extensive commentary, especially in the peace camp.

14. Baker also tried to enlist the help of the Iraqi government. On November 9, 1989, he sent a message to the Iraqi foreign minister informing him that the administration had decided to act favorably on grain credits for Iraq. Baker went on to say: "We are at a critical point in our diplomacy. The Government of Egypt is working closely with Palestinians to respond positively to our five-point framework, enabling us to get an Israeli-Palestinian dialogue launched. It would be useful if you could weigh in with them and urge them to give a positive response to Egypt's suggestions." Elaine Sciolino, "Baker Telling Iraqis of Loan Aid, Asks Help on Palestinian Talks," *New York Times*, October 26, 1992, p. A6.

15. For the text of Baker's five points, see Thomas L. Friedman, "Advance Reported on Mideast Talks," *New York Times*, December 7, 1989, p. A11.

16. See David Makovsky, *Jerusalem Post* (International Edition), March 24, 1990, p. 2.

17. In a letter attached to the Camp David Accords, Jimmy Carter had reiterated (albeit obliquely) the official policy that the United States considered East Jerusalem to be occupied territory to which the fourth Geneva Convention should apply. See William B. Quandt, *Camp David: Peacemaking and Politics* (Brookings, 1986), p. 386.

18. For the text of Saddam Hussein's speech, see Foreign Broadcast Information Service (FBIS), *Daily Report: Near East and South Asia*, February 27, 1990, pp. 1–5.

19. See Saddam's speech in which he said Iraq possessed binary chemical weapons and threatened their use against Israel if Israel were to attack Iraq. FBIS, *Daily Report: Near East and South Asia*, April 3, 1990, pp. 32–35.

20. Some Palestinians and their supporters argued that the intended target was military, that no one was hurt, and that the action had not been authorized by Arafat. Therefore, it should not be seen as a violation of the PLO's pledge not to engage in terrorism. Such arguments fell on deaf ears in Washington, partly because at about the same time an Israeli had been killed in a bomb explosion that intelligence sources traced directly to Fatah.

21. Author's interview with Abu Iyad, June 15, 1990.

22. For a generally convincing account, see, Bob Woodward, *The Commanders* (Simon and Schuster, 1991).

23. See Bush's speech before the UN General Assembly, reprinted in *New York Times*, October 2, 1990, p. A12, where he says that "in the aftermath of Iraq's unconditional departure from Kuwait, I truly believe there may be opportunities for Iraq and Kuwait to settle their differences permanently, for the states of the gulf themselves to build new arrangements for stability and for all the states and the peoples of the region to settle the conflicts that divide the Arabs from Israel."

24. The actual budgetary impact of granting the loan guarantees was difficult to assess. A small percentage of the total value of the loan—an amount to be determined on the basis of risk assessment—would have to be appropriated and set aside in a reserve fund. This amount could run from $50 to $800 million. Assuming that Israel repaid all the loans on time, there would be no further costs to the taxpayer. But if Israel defaulted, the costs would, of course, be substantial at a later date.

25. Baker and Israeli Foreign Minister Levy concluded agreement on a $400 million housing loan guarantee, after lengthy discussions, in October 1990. Within days, however, it became clear that Israel did not accept the American condition that no funds should be used in East Jerusalem. See "Israel Retracts Pledges to U.S. on East Jerusalem Housing," *New York Times*, October 19, 1990, p. A16. In the spring of 1992 a National Security Council staff member, Richard Haass, was quoted as saying that Israel had not given the administration a satisfactory reply about how it had spent the $400 million in loan guarantees. See *Haaretz*, April 15, 1992, p. A1, as reported in FBIS, *Daily Report: Near East and South Asia*, April 16, 1992, p. 36. See also David Makousky and Allison Kaplan, "What Went Wrong with the U.S. Aliya Loan Guarantees," *Jerusalem Post*, March 20, 1992, p. 5A, for further evidence that the Israeli government deliberately withheld cooperation in providing information on how the $400 million loan was being used.

26. Thomas L. Friedman, "Baker Cites Israel for Settlements," *New York Times*, May 23, 1991, p. A5. Thomas L. Friedman, "Bush Backs Baker View of Mideast Peace Barriers," *New York Times*, May 24, 1991, p. A3. According to one source, Shamir gave Baker a commitment in February 1991 not to build beyond a "baseline" rate of settlement growth in the West Bank. See *Report on Israeli Settlement in the Occupied Territories*, vol. 2 (Washington, July 1992), p. 1,

quoting a report from the Jewish Telegraphic Agency giving Baker's comments to a delegation of leaders from the American Jewish Congress on May 10, 1992.

27. See Martin Indyk, "Israel's Grand Bargain," *New York Times*, July 24, 1991, p. A21. The text of Ford's letter can be found in appendix C.

28. Linda Gradstein, "Shamir Bars Losing Territory," *Washington Post*, July 25, 1991 p. A27.

29. See "Excerpts from President Bush's News Session on Israeli Loan Guarantees," *New York Times*, September 13, 1991, p. A10. Thomas Dine of AIPAC later called September 12 a "day of infamy."

30. For the text of the U.S. "letter of understanding" given to the Israelis, see *Yedi'ot Aharonot*, September 17, 1991, p. 17, as reported in FBIS, *Daily Report: Near East and South Asia*, September 17, 1991, p. 28. For the Palestinian reply to Baker, see *Al-Dustur* (Amman), October 26, 1991, p. 26, as reported in FBIS, *Daily Report: Near East and South Asia*, October 28, 1991, p. 1.

31. For excerpts from the speeches, see "3 Speeches: The Area Is a 'Dangerous Battleground,'" *New York Times*, November 1, 1991, p. A10. A Wall Street Journal/ABC poll showed that 37 percent of Americans identified Israel as the main obstacle to peace, while 35 percent so labeled the Arabs. See Gerald F. Seib, "On Day One of Mideast Talks, Calm Prevails amid Ceremony," *Wall Street Journal*, October 31, 1991, p. A8.

32. The Palestinians put forward an initial proposal for an interim self-governing authority on January 14, 1992, and then developed a more elaborate version on March 3, 1992.

33. Leslie H. Gelb, "Bush's Ultimatum to Shamir," *New York Times*, January 17, 1992, p. A29.

34. Thomas L. Friedman, "U.S. Details Terms Israel Must Meet for Deal on Loans," *New York Times*, February 25, 1992, p. A1.

35. Thomas L. Friedman, "Bush Rejects Israel Loan Guarantees," *New York Times*, March 18, 1992, p. A11. At the same time, Baker met with Arens on March 17, 1992, to discuss reports of military technology transfers from Israel to China. A General Accounting Office report, *Report of Audit: Department of State Defense Trade Controls*, on the same topic was released in March 1992 by Sherman M. Funk, inspector general, Department of State. Some saw a mounting campaign by Bush and Baker against Israel, but the administration soon pulled back, perhaps fearing that the Israeli electorate would rally around Shamir if too much pressure was applied. For a detailed analysis of U.S.-Israeli relations in early 1992, see Leon T. Hadar, "The Last Days of Likud: The American-Israeli Big Chill," *Journal of Palestine Studies*, vol. 21 (Summer 1992), pp. 80–94.

36. Talks were held in Washington in April 1992 without results, but it was now commonplace for a PLO-related person to be in the background, coordinating with Tunis. In May 1992 multilateral talks were held: on environmental issues in Tokyo, on arms control in Washington, on economic issues in Brussels, on water in Vienna, and on refugees in Ottawa.

37. See Clyde Haberman, "Arens Faults Prime Minister's 'Greater Israel' Concept," *New York Times*, June 29, 1992, p. A3.

38. Indicative of Rabin's new tone were remarks that he made on September

3, 1992: "We should back away from illusions and seek compromises in order to reach peace or, at least, make practical moves to promote it. We should drop the illusions of the religion of Greater Israel and remember that we must take care of the Israeli people, society, culture, and economy. We should remember that a nation's strength is not measured by the territories it holds but by its faith and its ability to cultivate its social, economic, and security systems." FBIS, *Daily Report: Near East and South Asia*, September 3, 1992, p. 26. Also indicative of a new tone from Rabin was his view of Israel's importance to the United States. Rather than emphasizing the "strategic asset" argument, Rabin stressed the "peace partner" role. "The more the U.S. can say it is bringing peace to the area—assisted by Israel acting in its own interests—the more Israel will serve the mutual interest in creating stability and leaving less room for the extremists." Leslie H. Gelb, "America in Israel," *New York Times*, June 15, 1992, p. A19.

39. See Clyde Haberman, "Shamir Is Said to Admit Plan to Stall Talks 'for 10 Years,' " *New York Times*, June 27, 1992, p. A1. Subsequently, Shamir claimed that he had been misinterpreted. But even his clarifications indicated that he envisaged the "interim" agreement as lasting an indefinite time, during which Israel would continue to build settlements.

40. Bush and Baker had indicated that they would remain deeply involved in the negotiations, despite Baker's change of title. But according to Eagleburger, Baker played little role in foreign policy after going to the White House. See Don Oberdorfer, "Baker-less State Department Not in Idle, Officials Say," *Washington Post*, October 16, 1992, p. A23.

41. Asad, speaking to a delegation from the Golan Heights, reported on Syrian Radio, September 9, 1992, in FBIS, *Daily Report: Near East and South Asia*, September 9, 1992, p. 41.

42. Newhouse, "Shunning the Losers," pp. 50–51, in an otherwise quite critical article on Bush's foreign policy. Michael Kramer, "Bush's Reward for Courage," *Time*, August 3, 1992, p. 44, also gave Bush and Baker "considerable credit" for their handling of the loan guarantees and the negotiations more generally.

43. Kissinger expressed the view that the United States should not spend so much effort trying to organize negotiations that were destined to fail. Later he softened his views somewhat. See Henry Kissinger, "Land for Time in the Middle East," *Washington Post*, June 2, 1991, p. D7, and "If Not Peace, at Least Progress," *Washington Post*, October 31. 1991, p. A21. See also the harsh judgment of neoconservative thinker Irving Kristol, " 'Peace Process' That Heads Nowhere," *Wall Street Journal*, June 18, 1992, p. A16.

CHAPTER SIXTEEN

1. Trude B. Feldman, "On the First Anniversary of the Peace Talks in Madrid Bill Clinton Pledges to Maintain the Momentum," *Middle East Insight*, vol. 9 (November–December 1992), pp. 10–15.

2. Karen L. Puschel, *US-Israeli Strategic Cooperation in the Post–Cold War Era: An American Perspective* (Boulder, Colo.: Westview Press, 1992), pp. 153–54,

correctly concludes that "peace is the watershed issue that will determine whether strategic cooperation is significantly expanded in terms of aid and commitments. Certainly, when there has been demonstrable progress on the peace front, U.S. aid has followed in its wake. . . . In the absence of peace, particularly should Israel be perceived as an obstacle, it is hard to envision a US decision to significantly expand U.S.-Israeli strategic cooperation."

Selected Bibliography

Albin, Cecilia, and Harold H. Saunders. "Sinai II: The Politics of International Mediation." FPI Case Study 17. Johns Hopkins University, School of Advanced International Studies, Foreign Policy Institute, Washington, D.C., 1991.

Bailey, Sydney Dawson. *Four Arab-Israeli Wars and the Peace Process*. New York: St. Martin's Press, 1990.

Bard, Mitchell Geoffrey. *The Water's Edge and Beyond: Defining the Limits to Domestic Influence on United States Middle East Policy*. New Brunswick, N.J.: Transaction Publishers, 1991.

Bar-Siman-Tov, Yaacov. *The Israeli-Egyptian War of Attrition, 1969–1970: A Case Study of a Limited War*. New York: Columbia University Press, 1980.

Bar-Zohar, Michael. *Embassies in Crisis: Diplomats and Demagogues behind the Six-Day War*. Englewood Cliffs, N.J.: Prentice-Hall, 1970.

Beling, Willard A., ed. *The Middle East: Quest for an American Policy*. Albany: State University of New York Press, 1973.

Black, Ian, and Benny Morris. *Israel's Secret Wars: A History of Israel's Intelligence Services*. New York: Grove Weidenfeld, 1991.

Blitzer, Wolf. *Territory of Lies: The Exclusive Story of Jonathan Jay Pollard. The American Who Spied on His Country for Israel and How He Was Betrayed*. New York: Harper and Row, 1989.

Brandon, Henry. *The Retreat of American Power: The Inside Story of How Nixon and Kissinger Changed American Foreign Policy for Years to Come*. New York: Doubleday and Co., 1973.

Brecher, Michael. *Decisions in Crisis: Israel, 1967 and 1973*. Berkeley: University of California Press, 1980

——. *Decisions in Israel's Foreign Policy*. New Haven: Yale University Press, 1975.

Brzezinski, Zbigniew. *Power and Principle: Memoirs of the National Security Adviser, 1977–1981*. New York: Farrar, Straus and Giroux, 1983.

Cannon, Lou. *President Reagan: The Role of a Lifetime*. New York: Simon and Schuster, 1991.

Carter, Jimmy. *The Blood of Abraham*. Boston: Houghton Mifflin Co., 1985.

——. *Keeping Faith: Memoirs of a President*. New York: Bantam Books, 1982.

Cobban, Helena. "The P.L.O. and the Intifada." *Middle East Journal*, vol. 44 (Spring 1990), pp. 207–33.

——. *The Superpowers and the Syrian-Israeli Conflict: Beyond Crisis Management?* New York: Praeger, 1991.

Cockburn, Andrew, and Leslie Cockburn. *Dangerous Liaison: The Inside Story of the U.S.-Israeli Covert Relationship*. New York: HarperCollins Publishers, 1991.

Cooley, John K. *Payback: America's Long War in the Middle East*. New York: Brassey's, 1991.

Dayan, Moshe. *Breakthrough: A Personal Account of the Egypt-Israel Peace Negotiations*. New York: Alfred A. Knopf, 1981.

———. *Moshe Dayan: Story of My Life*. New York: William Morrow and Co., 1976.

Dowty, Alan. *Middle East Crisis: U.S. Decision-Making in 1958, 1970, and 1973*. Berkeley: University of California Press, 1984.

Eban, Abba. *An Autobiography*. New York: Random House, 1977.

———. *Personal Witness: Israel through My Eyes*. New York: G. P. Putnam's Sons, 1993.

Eilts, Hermann Frederick. "Improve the Framework." *Foreign Policy*, no. 41 (Winter 1980–81), pp. 3–20.

Ennes, James M., Jr. *Assault on the Liberty: The True Story of the Israeli Attack on an American Intelligence Ship*. New York: Random House, 1979.

Fahmy, Ismail. *Negotiating for Peace in the Middle East*. Baltimore: Johns Hopkins University Press, 1983.

Ford, Gerald R. *A Time to Heal: The Autobiography of Gerald R. Ford*. New York: Harper and Row, 1979.

Friedman, Thomas L. *From Beirut to Jerusalem*. New York: Farrar, Straus and Giroux, 1989.

Garfinkle, Adam. *Israel and Jordan in the Shadow of War: Functional Ties and Futile Diplomacy in a Small Place*. New York: St. Martin's Press, 1992.

———. "U.S. Decision Making in the Jordan Crisis: Correcting the Record." *Political Science Quarterly*, vol. 100 (Spring 1985), pp. 117–38.

Garthoff, Raymond L. *Détente and Confrontation: American-Soviet Relations from Nixon to Reagan*. Washington, D.C.: Brookings Institution, 1985.

Gerson, Allan. *The Kirkpatrick Mission: Diplomacy without Apology. America at the United Nations, 1981–1985*. New York: Free Press, 1991.

Golan, Matti. *The Secret Conversations of Henry Kissinger: Step-by-Step Diplomacy in the Middle East*. New York: Quadrangle Books, 1976.

Goodman, Hirsch, and Ze'ev Schiff. "The Attack on the Liberty." *Atlantic Monthly*, September 1984, pp. 78–84.

Green, Stephen. *Living by the Sword: America and Israel in the Middle East, 1968–87*. Brattleboro, Vt.: Amana Books, 1988.

———. *Taking Sides: America's Secret Relations with a Militant Israel*. New York: William Morrow and Co., 1984.

Haass, Richard. *Conflicts Unending: The United States and Regional Disputes*. New Haven: Yale University Press, 1990.

Haig, Alexander M., Jr. *Caveat: Realism, Reagan and Foreign Policy*. New York: Macmillan, 1984.

Haig, Alexander M., Jr., with Charles McCarry. *Inner Circles: How America Changed the World. A Memoir*. New York: Warner Books, 1992.

Heikal, Mohamed. *Autumn of Fury: The Assassination of Sadat*. New York: Random House, 1983.

——. *The Cairo Documents: The Inside Story of Nasser and His Relationship with World Leaders, Rebels, and Statesmen*. New York: Doubleday and Co., 1973.

——. *1967: Al-Infijar*. Cairo: Markaz al-Ahram, 1990.

——. *The Road to Ramadan*. New York: Quadrangle Books, 1975.

Hersh, Seymour M. *The Price of Power: Kissinger in the Nixon White House*. New York: Summit Books, 1983.

——. *The Samson Option: Israel's Nuclear Arsenal and American Foreign Policy*. New York: Random House, 1991.

Indyk, Martin. *"To the Ends of the Earth": Sadat's Jerusalem Initiative*. Cambridge, Mass.: Harvard University, Center for Middle Eastern Studies, 1984.

Insight Team of the London Sunday Times. *The Yom Kippur War*. New York: Doubleday and Co., 1974.

Isaacson, Walter. *Kissinger: A Biography*. New York: Simon and Schuster, 1992.

Johnson, Lyndon Baines. *The Vantage Point: Perspectives of the Presidency, 1963–1969*. New York: Holt, Rinehart and Winston, 1971.

Kalb, Marvin, and Bernard Kalb. *Kissinger*. Boston: Little, Brown and Co., 1974.

Kalman, Laura. *Abe Fortas: A Biography*. New Haven: Yale University Press, 1990.

Kemp, Geoffrey. "Lessons of Lebanon: A Guideline for Future U.S. Policy." *Middle East Insight*, vol. 6 (Summer 1988), pp. 57–68.

Kimche, David. *The Last Option: After Nasser, Arafat and Saddam Hussein. The Quest for Peace in the Middle East*. New York: Charles Scribner's Sons, 1991.

Kissinger, Henry. *White House Years*. Boston: Little, Brown and Co., 1979.

——. *Years of Upheaval*. Boston: Little, Brown and Co., 1982.

Korn, David A. *Stalemate: The War of Attrition and Great Power Diplomacy in the Middle East, 1967–1970*. Boulder, Colo.: Westview Press, 1992.

Lebow, Richard Ned, and Janice Gross Stein. "We All Lost the Cold War." [To be published by Princeton University Press in 1994.]

Linowitz, Sol. "The Prospects for the Camp David Peace Process." *SAIS Review*, no. 2 (Summer 1981), pp. 93–100.

Luttwak, Edward N., and Walter Laqueur. "Kissinger and the Yom Kippur War." *Commentary*, vol. 58 (September 1974), pp. 33–40.

Martin, David C., and John Walcott. *Best Laid Plans: The Inside Story of America's War against Terrorism*. New York: Harper and Row, 1988.

Meir, Golda. *My Life: The Autobiography of Golda Meir*. London: Futura, 1976.

Melman, Yossi, and Dan Raviv. *Behind the Uprising: Israelis, Jordanians, and Palestinians*. New York: Greenwood Press, 1989.

Miller, Merle. *Lyndon: An Oral Biography*. New York: G. P. Putnam's Sons, 1980.

——. *Plain Speaking: An Oral Biography of Harry S. Truman*. New York: Berkley Publishing Corporation, 1973.

Neff, Donald. *Warriors against Israel*. Brattleboro, Vt.: Amana Books, 1988.

——. *Warriors for Jerusalem: The Six Days That Changed the Middle East*. New York: Linden Press/ Simon and Schuster, 1984.

Nixon, Richard M. *RN: The Memoirs of Richard Nixon*. New York: Grosset and Dunlap, 1978.

———. *Seize the Moment: America's Challenge in a One-Superpower World*. New York: Simon and Schuster, 1992.

Novik, Nimrod. *Encounter with Reality: Reagan and the Middle East (The First Term)*. Boulder, Colo.: Westview Press for the Jaffee Center for Strategic Studies, 1985.

O'Brien, Conor Cruise. *The Siege: The Saga of Israel and Zionism*. New York: Simon and Schuster, 1986.

Parker, Richard B. "The June 1967 War: Some Mysteries Explored." *Middle East Journal*, vol. 46 (Spring 1992), pp. 177–97.

Powell, Jody. *The Other Side of the Story*. New York: William Morrow and Co., 1984.

Puschel, Karen L. *U.S.-Israeli Strategic Cooperation in the Post-Cold War Era: An American Perspective*. Boulder, Colo.: Westview Press, 1992.

Quandt, William B. *Camp David: Peacemaking and Politics*. Wahington, D.C.: The Brookings Institution, 1986.

———. *Decade of Decisions: American Policy toward the Arab-Israeli Conflict, 1967–1976*. Berkeley: University of California Press, 1977.

———. "Kissinger and the Arab-Israeli Disengagement Negotiations." *Journal of International Affairs*, vol. 29 (Spring 1975), pp. 33–48.

———. "Reagan's Lebanon Policy: Trial and Error." *Middle East Journal*, vol. 38 (Spring 1984), pp. 237–54.

Rabie, Mohamed. "The U.S.-PLO Dialogue: The Swedish Connection." *Journal of Palestine Studies*, vol. 21 (Summer 1992), pp. 54–66.

Rabin, Yitzhak. *The Rabin Memoirs*. Boston: Little, Brown and Co., 1979.

Rafael, Gideon. *Destination Peace: Three Decades of Israeli Foreign Policy. A Personal Memoir*. New York: Stein and Day, 1981.

Reagan, Ronald. *An American Life*. New York: Simon and Schuster, 1990.

Riad, Mahmoud. *The Struggle for Peace in the Middle East*. New York: Quartet Books, 1981.

Rostow, Eugene V. *Peace in the Balance: The Future of American Foreign Policy*. New York: Simon and Schuster, 1972.

Rostow, Walt. *The Diffusion of Power: An Essay in Recent History*. New York: Macmillan Co., 1972.

Rusk, Dean. *As I Saw It*. New York: W. W. Norton and Co., 1990.

Safran, Nadav. *Israel: The Embattled Ally*. Cambridge, Mass.: Belknap Press of Harvard University Press, 1978.

Schiff, Ze'ev, and Ehud Ya'ari. *Intifada: The Palestinian Uprising. Israel's Third Front*. New York: Simon and Schuster, 1989.

———. *Israel's Lebanon War*. New York: Simon and Schuster, 1984.

Sheehan, Edward R. F. *The Arabs, Israelis, and Kissinger: A Secret History of American Diplomacy in the Middle East*. New York: Reader's Digest Press, 1976.

Shultz, George. *Turmoil and Triumph: My Years as Secretary of State*. New York: Charles Scribner's Sons, 1993.

Sicherman, Harvey. *Palestinian Self-Government(Autonomy): Its Past and Its Future.* Washington, D.C.: Washington Institute for Near East Policy, 1991.

Sick, Gary. *All Fall Down: America's Tragic Encounter with Iran.* New York: Random House, 1985.

Spiegel, Steven L. *The Other Arab-Israeli Conflict: Making America's Middle East Policy from Truman to Reagan.* Chicago: University of Chicago Press, 1985.

Tanter, Raymond. *Who's at the Helm? Lessons of Lebanon.* Boulder, Colo.: Westview Press, 1990.

Telhami, Shibley. *Power and Leadership in International Bargaining: The Path to the Camp David Accords.* New York: Columbia University Press, 1990.

Vance, Cyrus. *Hard Choices: Critical Years in America's Foreign Policy.* New York: Simon and Schuster, 1983.

Wallach, Janet, and John Wallach. *Arafat: In the Eyes of the Beholder.* New York: Carol Publishing Group, 1990.

Washington Institute's Presidential Study Group. *Building for Peace: An American Strategy for the Middle East.* Washington, D.C.: Washington Institute for Near East Policy, 1988.

Weizman, Ezer. *The Battle for Peace.* New York: Bantam Books, 1981.

Whetten, Lawrence L. *The Canal War: Four-Power Conflict in the Middle East.* Cambridge, Mass.: MIT Press, 1974.

Woodward, Bob. *The Commanders.* New York: Simon and Schuster, 1991.

———. *Veil: The Secret Wars of the CIA, 1981–1987.* New York: Simon and Schuster, 1987.

Yergin, Daniel. *The Prize: The Epic Quest for Oil, Money and Power.* New York: Simon and Schuster, 1991.

Index